THE RED WHEEL

A Narrative

in Discrete Periods of Time

Aleksandr Solzhenitsyn

NOVEMBER 1916

THE RED WHEEL / KNOT II

Translated by H. T. Willetts

Farrar, Straus and Giroux

New York

Farrar, Straus and Giroux
19 Union Square West, New York 10003

World copyright © 1984 by Aleksandr Solzhenitsyn
Translation copyright © 1999 by H. T. Willetts
All rights reserved
Printed in the United States of America
First published in 1993 by Voyennoye izdatelstvo, Moscow, as Krasnoe koleso. Uzel II:
Oktyabr shestnadtsatogo
First published in the United States in 1999 by Farrar, Straus and Giroux
First Farrar, Straus and Giroux paperback edition, 2000

Library of Congress Cataloging-in-Publication Data
Solzhenitsyn, Aleksandr Isaevich, 1918–
[Oktiabr' shestnadtsatogo. English]
November 1916 / Aleksandr Solzhenitsyn ; translated by H.T.
Willetts.
    p.   cm. — (Red wheel ; knot 2)
    Includes index.
    ISBN 0-374-52703-2 (pbk.)
    1. Russia—History—Nicholas II, 1894–1917—Fiction.
I. Willetts, H.T.   II. Title.   III. Series: Solzhenitsyn, Aleksandr
Isaevich, 1918– Krasnoe koleso.   English ; knot 2.
PG3488.0403913   1998
891.73'44—dc21   98-14263

Publisher's Note

November 1916 is the Second Knot in Aleksandr Solzhenitsyn's *The Red Wheel*, the author's epic of the roots and outbreak of the Russian Revolution. (The Third and Fourth Knots will deal with March and April of 1917.) These volumes can be read independently as well as consecutively. Thus, readers whose first encounter with *The Red Wheel* is *November 1916* will comprehend and appreciate it without recourse to its predecessor. They may be interested to know that the First Knot, *August 1914* (published in English in 1971 and revised and much expanded in 1989), deals largely with the Battles of Tannenberg and Masurian Lakes, in East Prussia, at the outbreak of World War I. Disastrous defeats of the Russians by the Germans under Hindenburg and Ludendorff, they were as much a mark of Russian ineptitude as of German military skill, culminating in the suicide of General Samsonov, commander of the Second Corps.

A number of fictional characters from the First Knot are in the Second Knot, and their continuing roles are clear. The main protagonist is Colonel Georgi Vorotyntsev, a man far more interested in surveying the fighting front at first hand than in courting higher-ups on the General Staff.

The dates have been changed, according to the author's wishes, to the Western (Gregorian) calendar, setting them twelve to thirteen days ahead of the old (Julian) system used in pre-revolutionary Russia.

Author's Note

The recent history of our country is so little known, or taught in such a distorted fashion, that I have felt compelled, for the sake of my younger compatriots, to include more historical matter in this Second Knot than might be expected in a work of literature. But in presenting the stenographic records of meetings and the texts of speeches and letters, I was reluctant to burden my book and the reader with the verbosity, indeed the empty verbiage, the redundancies, the irrelevancies, and the wishy-washiness so often characteristic of these utterances. I have therefore sometimes taken the liberty of condensing a whole text, or particular sentences in a text, to heighten the effect, without, however, the slightest distortion of meaning. The passages cited are always authentic, though not always verbatim. Art demands distillation of actuality.

For the fragmentary chapter "From the Notebooks of Fyodor Kovynev," I have used compressed excerpts from the published stories of F. Kryukov, and his private archive—his own unpublished letters and diaries, and letters from his onetime pupil at Orel, Zinaida Rumnitskaya.

Andozerskaya is, among other things, a vehicle for the views on monarchy of Professor Ivan Aleksandrovich Ilin.

Historical personages are introduced almost invariably under their own names and with accurate biographical data. This is true also of real but comparatively obscure characters of the period, such as the legendary leader of the Tambov peasant rising (1919–21), G. N. Pluzhnikov, and even the district clerk at Kamenka, Semyon Panyushkin (still alive when I visited the place), the secretaries of the Workers' Group, Gutovsky and Pumpyansky, G. K. Komarov (member of the Workers' Group at the Obukhov factory), the Shingarev and Smyslovsky families (shown in the apartments they actually occupied at the time), the inventors Kisnemsky, Podolsky, and Yampolsky, and others. The treatment of historical characters in synoptic and narrative chapters is strictly factual. For A. I. Guchkov, in addition to all the sources in the public domain, I have used his unpublished correspondence and family records.

For my treatment of three characters—the writer Fyodor Dmitrievich Kryukov, the engineer Pyotr Akimovich Palchinsky, and General Aleksandr Andreevich Svechin (the first perished in the Civil War, the other two were executed by the Bolsheviks)—the material I was able to collect did not suffice for subsequent Knots, so that, without taking excessive liberties, I needed greater freedom of conjecture as to their behavior and their whereabouts at particular times. To give myself the necessary latitude I have changed the surnames of the first two and the given name of the third. Most of the details given about them are nonetheless historically accurate. (For all of them, as for K. A. Gvozdev and A. G. Shlyapnikov, I also made use of private memoirs preserved in the U.S.S.R.) Without altering his name I have made slight changes in the circumstances of General Aleksandr Dmitrievich Nechvolodov.

The interval between 27 October and 17 November 1916 contains relatively few events of historical importance (the disorders on the Vyborg side on 30 October, the proceedings of the State Duma from 14 November, including Milyukov's famous speech, and a few other episodes). But the author has chosen to deal with this period in the last prerevolutionary Knot because it encapsulates the stagnant and oppressive atmosphere of the months immediately preceding the Revolution. The author was for a long time undecided whether or not to interpolate between *August 1914* and *November 1916* an intermediate Knot on the course of the war, *August 1915*, which would have been rich in events. He finally decided against it, but fragments of the abandoned Knot are included in the present Knot II—namely, Chapter 19, a panoramic survey of 1915, and other flashbacks to the first two years of the war, as well as Chapter 7, a retrospective survey of the whole previous history of the Kadet movement.

The author began working continuously on *November 1916* in March 1971. The structure of the work quickly became clear, but the collection of material was a lengthy task, and because of harassment by the Soviet authorities in 1971, that work went slowly. However, in the course of 1971–73 the whole of the first draft, and several chapters of the second, were finished (at Ilinskoye, Rozhdestvo-Na-Istya, and Firsanovka). But at this stage, in accordance with the original plan, the work included only two of the eventual seven Lenin chapters.

To collect material on the Kamenka rural district, and on other places in Tambov province, the author visited the area incognito on various occasions in the summers of 1965 and 1972, and subsequently supplemented his information from published sources. He originally reconstructed the battle at Skrobotovo from manuscripts in the Moscow Historical Museum, then drew on émigré sources to fill out his account. He has made use of the publications of the Workers' Group attached to the War Industry Committee and of specialist literature on the artillery used in 1914–17. The passages on the Grenadier Brigade draw on holdings of the Central Archive of the History of War in Moscow (military and administrative documentation, muster rolls, horse counts). The author also visited, in 1966, the brigade's position at the Uzmoshye estate.

The author's banishment to the West interrupted work on *The Red Wheel* for almost the whole of 1974. But Zurich provided rich materials and direct observations that made possible a fuller treatment of the Lenin theme. All the Lenin chapters, including those intended for Knot III, were finalized in March 1975, and published in the autumn of that year in a separate volume entitled *Lenin in Zurich* (Paris, YMCA Press, 1975). The author originally intended to include the chapter on Shlyapnikov, completed in the U.S.S.R., but in the event the volume covered only political activity abroad.

In 1975–79 materials from émigré publications, Russian collections abroad, and the memoirs of participants in various events sent to the author enabled him to make a considerable number of additions and corrections to *November 1916*, and in late 1979 and 1980 several chapters were again reworked. Additional chapters were written on the imperial family (Chapters 64, 69, and 72 were not part of the original plan).

The final version of the Knot was completed while the work was being set up in Vermont in 1982–83.

A full bibliography will follow Knot III.

Contents

CONTENTS

CONTENTS

CONTENTS

CONTENTS

CONTENTS

CONTENTS

CONTENTS

CONTENTS

CONTENTS

CONTENTS

CONTENTS

CONTENTS

CONTENTS

CONTENTS

ACT ONE

REVOLUTION

Only the ax can deliver us, and nothing other than the ax . . . Russia summons us to the ax.

From a letter to Aleksander Harzen's newspaper, The Bell, *1860*

KNOT II

NOVEMBER 1916

(27 October–17 November)

Birds don't like some forests. There were fewer birds in skimpy, stunted Dryagovets than in Golubovshchina, three versts* to the rear. Crows, ravens, kites flocked there to batten on the leavings of war (mice and rats poured in too), but song thrushes flew by and the white storks, guardians of happiness, had left their posts on the high roofs. The peasants, though, said that it was always the same even before the war: birds didn't like Dryagovets, but did like Golubovshchina. An old coach road from Catherine's time ran through the soggy patch between the two woods. There, war or no war, the lapwings kept up their plaintive cry, and no other sound was heard.

Golubovshchina was parkland, not dense forest: thick-trunked trees stood as if on parade; there was clean, sweet grass over the whole expanse. Even now, after a year close to the front line, it was populated by throngs of birds. And in May there was such cuckooing and gurgling and chirring and twittering and hooting and trilling that Sanya, a native of the southern steppes, felt weak at the knees, longing to sink onto the silky grass, and his chest swelled to take in not just air but the singing of birds.

The ammunition belts tugging at his shoulders, and his bulky revolver, seemed all the heavier.

All these birds, you might think, could have easily flown away from the whine of shells, the smoke of explosions, the waves of gas, gone another ten versts or so to the rear. But no! Heedless of man's black and noisy war, although they were sometimes among its victims, many birds went on living in the places that were theirs of old, obedient only to the imperative within them, their own strict meridian.

Golubovshchina belonged to a Polish landowner, but had been leased to a simple villager, whereas Dryagovets was a peasant wood. What exactly its name meant Sanya never discovered, but the very sound of it told you that here was something inferior, contemptible. And so it was, a sickly, scrawny wood that gladdened no one's heart and was now, through no wish of their own, peopled from end to end by grenadiers—the rear services and reserves of the infantry, in among the limbers, horses, and dugouts of the artillery. Just behind Dryagovets stood the guns of the 1st Division, Grenadier Brigade.

No dugout could have been roofed with the thin trunks of Dryagovets, and there would have been no wood left long ago but for a timely order to fell no more trees either there or in delectable Golu-

---

*Verst: An old Russian measure, roughly two-thirds of a mile. [*Trans.*]

bovshchina. Stout beams were brought on flatcars from the Russian heartland to serve as fortification, and put on wheels so that peasants, for three rubles a load, could haul them a few steps at a time in the dead of night, with German rockets overhead, right up to the front line. (The peasants had left villages farther forward, but were still living and seeding their fields at Staiki and Yushkevichi. The Germans shelled the open fields, but did not aim at the peasants working them.)

Sanya had spent the past year, almost the whole of his war, in these surroundings, the few square versts within his field of vision. His battery had been standing to the rear of Dryagovets since the previous September, and Sanya had always taken the same path to what used to be their observation post: first through Dryagovets, which was teeming with soldiers, then, in full view of the enemy, along the old highroad, where troops broke formation and vehicles passed one at a time; from the still undamaged wooden cross with a wire mesh shielding the figure of the Saviour, he bore left and walked a verst and a half, humiliatingly doubled up, along a communication trench, bumping into people coming the other way, and stumbling over earthfalls until he came to the infantry trenches, narrow slits in the marshy ground. Taking this path from day to day, squelching through the mud in spring and autumn, sometimes over your boots in trench water, you might wonder, if you did not already know, how anyone could have let it come to this: retreat to the worst possible positions and allow the Germans to cross the Szara, occupy the Torczyc Heights, and convert the manor house on the hill at Michalowo into a fortress.

But Sanya had seen something of last August in the Grenadier Brigade and remembered the last stage of that terrible retreat: flattened by raking artillery fire, or sometimes by poison gas, they had huddled all day in sketchy trenches, under pounding bombardments, with no shells of their own, and retreated by night, never catching sight of the enemy infantry, which had no need to do anything. With no shells, and having to count every rifle bullet, they had rolled and staggered back beyond Baranowicze to Stolpce and might have gone on to Minsk, when suddenly they discovered that the Germans were no longer pinching their behinds. They turned and stood, stood fast. Then, from month to month, watched and fired upon by the enemy, the whole Grenadier Corps laboriously and with great losses, crawled back, again "advanced to the closest proximity," tediously digging their way forward to occupy two and a half versts of wilderness abandoned by the Germans as useless.

It is hard to see how anyone could come to love these versts of humiliation, sweat, and death. But strangely, during the year he had spent there, the place had become as poignantly dear to Sasha as his homeland and he had come to know every bush, every hummock, every field path there as well as those around his native Sablya. Nearby, Sasha discovered, was Mickiewicz's true homeland—to the right, toward

Lake Koldyczew—and it would have been strange if the poet had not loved the scene of his childhood games and youthful dreams. But are not the places where you spend your turbulent years closest of all to your heart? They stand out against the whole world's expanses as though caught by lightning; they witness not your unthinking and un-heeding birth, but the deeds you do surprised by manhood, and, per-haps—today? tomorrow?—your death. As you tramp about your business through the rustling grass, you may be walking past the cross that will say you are dead, past your future grave.

It amazed him to think of all that he had lived through, of how much he had changed, in a year. Walking from the observation post to the battery, worn out and deep in thought, he had paid no attention to the shell hideously whistling overhead until he saw on the fringe of Dryagovets a black column three times higher than the forest, and topping it a bright red cap of belching flames, and higher still a flight of thick sticks. Before all this collapsed, and in spite of the incredible din, he had made the connections: an eight-inch shell had fallen on the battery's ammunition dump, the sticks were splintered seven-inch beams, and the blasts were Russian shells exploding vertically. You might think (but at the time you would not be thinking) that it was against nature for any living creature to rush to its death. It was not Sanya's duty to be with the battery at that moment, and no one would have been surprised or blamed him if he had arrived ten minutes late, but without stopping to think he rushed to the gun site as fast as his legs could carry him. Beams were still falling in a cloud of soil (two of them stuck upright as though pile-driven into the ground) and an ammunition box full of shrapnel burst into flames. There was no of-ficer to be seen, and only a handful of gunners, a junior bombardier, and a few soldiers from the ranks who had taken cover at the moment of the explosion. Sanya shouted at them to follow him and raced to-ward the shell box. Smoke was pouring from its shattered sides (the powder in the broken shell cases was burning). They all rushed with him to prevent the explosion, expecting to be hit by it, and also ex-pecting at any moment to be hit by another shell capable of scooping out a crater thirty-five feet in diameter and nine feet deep. But the next one didn't arrive, and in the meantime they had hacked off the burning casing with axes and hurriedly thrown out the shells (their wrapping already red-hot) before even one could go off. The work was done in such tearing haste that Sanya didn't have time to feel fright-ened. It was only when they had finished and were mopping their brows that he felt his legs trembling and refusing to support him.

He had still not got over his surprise at himself and the men who had helped him when they received a St. George's Cross each, and the Awards Council bestowed an Officer's Cross on Second Lieutenant Lazhenitsyn.

Then, and at many other times, Sanya's life might have ended in his twenty-fifth year, in the lush and pleasant locality between Vlasy and Melikhovichi with their clumps of tall poplars. And though the front might move elsewhere, and however often the scene of danger and of short-lived soldierly joys might change, this place in which they had spent a whole anxious year would always be remembered as his lost homeland.

There was another enigma: a boundary line which had never existed before, and which would later be obliterated, plowed under, surviving only in the memory of old men, now separated the two intruding armies, and so divided and alienated from each other two pieces of a continuous and long-cultivated tract of land. Everything should have been just the same on the other side of the line—and everything seemed entirely different. It should have been another cozy piece of the homeland, embellished with a scattering of farmhouses and peasant huts, with the same eighteenth-century coach road sparsely lined with birches and disappearing over a rise and beyond the river, the same windmills, poplars, and derelict stork's nests—but instead it was a parcel of alien land under alien rule.

That spring, when the Rostov Grenadier Regiment had dug in close to the Torczyc Heights, they had made a successful sally before dawn, taken the German trenches by surprise, and might have crossed the Szara if there had been any backup. Sanya happened to be on duty at the observation post in the Rostov Regiment's forward trench, and went with the attack. He could not have given them artillery support—the use of shells was prohibited and the operation had developed suddenly at the regimental level—but Sanya ran across those 1,500 yards of land scanned day in and day out, studied stone by stone, surmounted the two-crested hill, and gasped: it really was another world over there. Not barren, broken land with nary a bush, but, from immediately beyond the German trenches, a green slope down to the river, flourishing oaks, pollarded willows, luxuriant shrubbery along a stream, and a soft morning river mist caressing these lovely creations. No sooner had the machine guns and rifles fallen silent than a nightingale, nearby but invisible, came to life and began pouring its heart out, uninhibitedly, with all the expected grace notes and trills and dying falls. . . . He too would not be driven by the war from his accustomed place!

This steep green bank beyond the Torczyc Heights, this mist, this unexpected nightingale seemed to Sanya a paradise on earth. What strength and what love had gone into its creation. How strange to think that at either end the Torczyc slope and Golubovshchina rang still with their eternal song while in the shadow zone between them where the twenty-foot crucifix had survived without a scratch, a thousand men had in a fit of madness burrowed into the ground to blaze away at each other with the whole arsenal of twentieth-century technology.

This sprint before dawn with pounding heart to where neither orders nor a sense of duty had sent him, but his own overmastering urge to feel for the first time in his life what it was to attack, seemed to have given him wings, he felt light-headed and half conscious as though after a night of happiness and love. There was a charge and a victory, but it was a lighthearted affair, without casualties. For that half hour Sanya was disembodied and unafraid of raking lead, he had no ears for the bullets that began to whistle toward them from beyond the Szara.

Something else, however, had stolen into Second Lieutenant Lazhenitsyn's mind. In spite of his sleepwalking weightlessness, and rapt as he was by the nightingale's song, he used that brief lull to cast an eye over the German trenches: they were clean, dry, deep enough to stand up in, lined and solidly floored with planks, they had sentry boxes for the winter, the dugouts were shored up with beams, impenetrable by Russian field artillery, and some of them were even fortified with concrete. And although it had always been easy to deduce that the Russian positions must be wide open to scrutiny from this point, it was only when he had looked for himself through the observation slits in the concrete that the second lieutenant realized with a shock how awkwardly placed, how exposed, how defenseless the Russian forces were—almost as though they were waging the war according to the other side's rules.

He also took from a nail in a bunker a magnificent pair of Zeiss field glasses with sixteen-power magnification. Many months later, he would look out from the old, low-lying position at those even more inaccessible Torczyc Heights, now fortified with five barbed-wire fences, and at the tops of the oaks beyond them, and find it hard to believe that he had been there, but for the splendid, heavy field glasses always hanging on his chest or at his eyes and often borrowed by his comrades or senior officers, because they had only Russian army issue with no more than eight-power magnification.

They were like the Firebird's feather plucked by the sleeping prince as an enduring proof of what he had seen in his dreams.

[2]

Lieutenant Colonel Boyer had assigned Second Lieutenant Lazhenitsyn out of turn to No. 3 Battery's lateral observation post near the village of Dubrowna at 10 a.m. on 27 October, so that he could take part in the battery commander's target practice.

This was a breach of training procedure. Whatever his three platoon commanders were like they should have been given equal training opportunities and each have taken his turn with the guns. But under the curse of having to fight with an army thinned out beyond recognition, in which real, regular officers had been replaced by nondescripts, and NCOs with long service by half-trained common soldiers, the lieutenant colonel could afford not to worry too much about using the commander of No. 3 Platoon, who was better trained and more conscientious than the others, though, like them, no soldier at heart. The commander of No. 1 Platoon, Chernega, promoted from sergeant major to ensign, was as brave a fighter as anyone could wish, but was lacking in knowledge and skill, not always quick to react, and not easily geared into a strictly disciplined system. Ensign Ustimovich, a forty-five-year-old schoolteacher recalled from the reserve, was burdened with family and other cares, was, moreover, an infantryman assigned to the battery only because of the dearth of artillery officers, and though, to his own discomfort and that of his battery commander, he was nominally in charge of No. 2 Platoon, never looked like he had the makings of a gunner and even seemed incapable of adjusting to military discipline.

There had been two days of unrelievedly dull weather: no rain, but never a glimmer of sunshine. From early morning this had been another day of unbroken cloud, but it was dry, not too cold, and an occasional brightness promised clearer weather. The barometer, however, was falling, and made raincoats advisable.

No. 3 Battery's forward observation post, in the infantry trenches facing the Torczyc Heights, commanded a narrow view deep into the enemy position, and so for major bombardments Boyer always manned a lateral post, on high ground partly captured from the Germans. The field of view from there was both broad and deep, but because the post was too far to one side, the firing drill became complicated: the observer did not see what the gunners saw, spacing measurements involved angular measurements and this called for quick calculation and adjustment. It was useless putting Ustimovich there, and Chernega would have been no less confused.

The last hundred yards or so, branching off from the Pernov Regiment's communication trench, was the battery's own thoroughfare; it was nearly six feet deep, so that the tall lieutenant colonel would not have to stoop very much. The observation post itself was covered with three layers of beams lashed together with wire, so that medium-caliber gunfire would not part them.

The lieutenant colonel took another look, saw that the yellowish light in the sky was growing and the field of view would be good, crouched down and held his cap as he lifted the canvas curtain at the entrance, and dived into the trench, followed by his orderly. Inside, the trench had been made still deeper for the lieutenant colonel's benefit, and Second Lieutenant Lazhenitsyn, a shorter figure with a tentative beard half covering his chin, was standing on a beam at an observation slit, making entries in a notebook on a plywood board propped against the breastwork in front of him. When the commander appeared, he stepped down from the beam and saluted.

There were many breaches of army discipline to be seen, and the commander's eye, though not yet used to the half-darkness, had been quick to notice the two telephone operators squatting on stumps with their instruments on the bare ground beside them, their rifles propped against the wall, one with its muzzle so placed that loose soil was likely to dribble into it, and the three gas masks on nails driven into the board facing. The second lieutenant did not call the men to attention, and his salute was less neat and snappy than it should have been, though better than a year ago. Nor did he report what was presently going on at the observation post. But the simplifications introduced by the war into the military code had gone too far for there to be any hope of bringing them back within bounds. And Lieutenant Colonel Boyer, who was doomed to be painfully aware till the day he died of any departure from regulations even on the part of casually encountered civilians, reacted only to those that were meant to be provocative.

Lazhenitsyn did not know himself why he did not report. He had something ready to say, but he suddenly felt that it would be embarrassingly theatrical in the presence of three soldiers and in the confined space of the shelter. Besides, he was a little afraid of the lieutenant colonel, although he had never heard him raise his voice. Chernega always behaved correctly and with presence of mind even when he was at fault. Lazhenitsyn somehow always felt guilty even when he had done nothing wrong. The lieutenant colonel's eyebrows barely twitched above his pince-nez. The look in his eyes was invariably one-quarter contemptuous and half dissatisfied. The upturned tips of his mustache were so perfectly symmetrical that a smile would have immediately disturbed their balance. The long neck in the stiff collar of his tunic gave his head no freedom of movement, and defied those he addressed to feel at ease with him. At that moment his whole demeanor seemed to say, "Whatever you are doing here cannot possibly be serious."

But the lieutenant colonel said not a word, quickly returned Sanya's salute with a neat unhurried lift of hand to temple, picked up his notes, and began reading in silence.

These notes (conscientiously begun an hour before the appointed time, as the lieutenant colonel noted with no outward sign of approval) were the usual routine record of every move and every change at the enemy camp, with exaggerated significance given to trivial happenings:

0905   Enemy continuing earthworks apparently commenced
          overnight at dormer No. 5.

0912 Enemy one-and-a-half-inch gun discharged five shells
at No. 8 trench.

Lazhenitsyn kept up with the lieutenant colonel's reading from line to
line.

0927 Russian howitzer at . . . discharged three rounds . . .
at . . .

0941 Enemy discharged eighteen heavy mortars at northern
outskirts of Dubrowina. No damage caused.

The lieutenant colonel had seen this last attack as he approached, and
from down below he had even thought that the enemy was aiming
accurately at the Russian observation post—one hit by such a heavy
mortar from close by could tear the shelter wide open. But the second
lieutenant had naturally not made a major event out of a near miss.
It was plainly stated in standing orders that officers in artillery units
must ensure the most efficient observation possible without consideration for their own safety. Enemy artillery fire was scrupulously
logged by every battery at two observation posts and from every gun
site, and their returns were then tabulated by the duty officer: type of
gun, caliber, target, number of rounds fired, and, most boring of all,
the pattern of the craters formed—in other words, where shells had
fallen in relation to Russian weapons, dumps, limbers, and dugouts.
The lieutenant colonel knew that all his platoon commanders found
these meticulous notes, measurements, and diagrams tiresome, that
Chernega concocted it all out of his head without measuring anything,
that Ustimovich grumbled and groaned, and that Lazhenitsyn did what
was ordered, much as he detested it. The lieutenant colonel saw to it
that no one ever read in his face how much he disapproved of these
reports, but refrained from inquiring too closely whether all the craters
had really been measured. Nothing in army procedures must be
laughed at: once you start knocking out the props you don't know on
whom the whole edifice will fall. The daily records were then summarized in a general divisional report, and delivered to Brigade HQ.
Before long they filled several fat volumes. Brigade and Corps HQs
searched for cupboards to store them in, then open shelves, then sheds,
no longer even thinking of using them to analyze the intentions and
tactics of enemy artillery. But there could be no question of relaxing
the rules, and Lieutenant Colonel Boyer coldly and sternly examined
the platoon commanders' reports.

0955 A blindaged structure apparently intended for long-
term use is being erected near the Orthodox burial
ground.

Here Lazhenitsyn in a diffident murmur invited the commander to
take a look through the Zeiss binoculars or the stereotelescope.

It had to be done cautiously, since the Germans sometimes posted
snipers with optic sights who could smash a stereotelescope to smith-

ereens. The German front line had been drawn nearby on the same rise in the ground.

The whole terrain, now brightly lit, was visible through the observation slit. A brilliant sun had broken through to the rear of the Russian position and lit up the yellowish-brown crests of the trees by the Orthodox graveyard, the thatched roofs of the village beyond it, the white Catholic church in hilly Stolowicze, and even, far away to the right, the steep slope over Lake Koldyczew.

Boyer placed his pince-nez on the breastwork and accepted Lazhenitsyn's superior field glasses. Quite right—the platoon commander's deductions made sense. Construction had only just begun, and not much fresh earth had been thrown up as yet, but what was planned was obviously of major importance. Here was another target to be added to the day's program. The new construction must be brought under fire before it was finished.

The orders Lieutenant Colonel Boyer had been given for the day were to breach the enemy's barbed-wire defenses in several places where they faced the Ekaterinoslav Regiment, and mislead him into thinking that an attack was imminent. All that was really intended was to observe the other side's system of mobilization for defense.

If there was one thing the Russian three-inch guns did well, it was clearing away barbed-wire barriers. Defensive works of solid timber, let alone those of concrete, they could not destroy. Their range was too short for them to paralyze the enemy's rear. For fear of grazing shots, they could not create a curtain of fire ahead of attacking Russian infantry. Once the naval guns had been withdrawn from Golubovshchina, the only guns with real destructive power in the whole sector, for several versts to right and left, belonged to the mortar battalion attached to the grenadiers, and even these were only four-inch as against the German eight-inch guns.

"How many shells do you need for placement?"

"Four."

When he was at work Lazhenitsyn was always slow and deliberate, never rushed things. That boded well.

"Three. You mustn't lose the advantage of surprise. How long before you open up with the whole battery?"

There was no encouragement in Boyer's voice or in his look. His manner indicated that these tyros were more likely than not to be wrong—how could they be expected to answer correctly? Lazhenitsyn was therefore cautious.

"Three minutes," he said.

"Two, no more. You've got to stun them. Get all the orders worked out and pass them to the battery in advance. The first shells will be in the breech beforehand and all we have to do is to correct for range and angle."

Lazhenitsyn was surprised.

"Am I doing all the firing?"

"Yes. How many shells do you need?"

Again the reply was slow and cautious.

"Forty."

"We've got to do a thorough clearing job. Take sixty."

Shells were coming up from the rear these days with the words "Bang away regardless" on the boxes. It wasn't like 1915.

Moreover, the lieutenant colonel had patiently trained his whole battery, dealing with each gunlayer individually, to "shoot into the fire." There was nothing about this in standing regulations. Boyer had picked it up in courses from one or two generals, who had not succeeded in converting the War Ministry, but had acquired followers in the batteries. Instead of platoon commanders standing by their guns and directing the firing from right to left—"Number two! Number three! Number four!"—which was the general practice in the Russian artillery, each gunlayer stood holding the string, with one eye on the gunlayer to his right. The battery fired in unison and all the platoon commanders were freed for more useful work.

Lazhenitsyn immersed himself in calculations, resting the duty observer's notebook on a smooth part of the board to jot them down. There was no great hurry, but he might well have been a little quicker. His judgment was not at all bad, but there was too much of the civilian in his habit of checking and rechecking his reasoning over and over again. All the same, Boyer was hopeful that the lad would get the knack of it in time. He believed that an enthusiasm for war was a natural masculine characteristic and that it could be awakened and developed in any man.

The second lieutenant ordered the duty telephone operator, a Tartar with a receiver dangling at his ear from a cord tucked under his cap, to ring up Blagodarev, the bombardier on No. 1 gun, and spoke to him squatting by the instrument. Then he spoke to the other platoons. Then Boyer got on the infantry telephone and obtained the regimental commander's permission to begin the bombardment.

Lazhenitsyn was excited, and anxious not to make a mistake. Responsibility for this unexpectedly heavy bombardment rested entirely on him, though the battery commander hovered like an examiner, eyeing him skeptically. But the lieutenant colonel did not countermand a single order once it was issued. Lazhenitsyn's calculations determined and drove the pace. Three spacing shots to a strike, not forgetting to switch one gun onto the new structure by the graveyard. What a thrilling moment it was when your own small voice, which nonetheless has in it something of the metal of those gun barrels, cries, "Raking shot! Fire!" and is magnified a thousand times in that great roar, when the weakness of your arms and their short reach is superseded by the far-ranging sweep and thump of shells and, surprised to find yourself a hurler of thunderbolts, you have only to look through your field glasses to see the shaggy gray sheaf rear up as each round explodes, the twisted scraps of barbed wire, the fragments of mangled birch stakes mingle with the dust and smoke—the whole ingenious fabric which so many men had taken so many nights to contrive blown sky high by you in the space of three minutes. When shells are spent as freely as they were that day, you feel a strength far beyond the limits of any individual man, and feel . . . proud?

Surely not. Pride? Well, the lieutenant colonel said, "Not bad," in a voice gratifyingly free of censure. What a pity that it was only a maneuver and that no one would advance through those breaches.

On his chest under his greatcoat was a medal—the order of St. Stanislav, third class, but with swords—in whose modest story the battery commander had also played a part. More inspiring still was a St. George's Cross for bravery during a fire at a battery position. The light touch of this brand-new medal on his chest seemed to concentrate and reorient all his ideas on man's aims and his duty.

It not only commemorated the past but implied an obligation for the future.

The day's work had been well done. The rules of artillery fire had been intelligently applied. It had cost sixty shells but they must have killed and wounded quite a few people in the German trenches that day.

Yet somehow it made no impression.

Two shells overshot their mark and landed on the Orthodox graveyard, raising black clouds there. And violating graves.

When he had duly noted the number of shells fired, their objectives, and the results, Lazhenitsyn was ready for his next job. This was going to be even more interesting. The lieutenant colonel intended to try out the new thirty-six-second fuses of which he had so far received only a small consignment. The brigade had been fighting for two years with twenty-two-second fuses, and the range of a shrapnel shell was five versts. In terrain like this, where it was impossible to find cover for guns closer than Dryagovets, their shrapnel fire was concentrated entirely on the forward edge of the German defenses. Thirty-six-second fuses would extend the range two versts deeper into enemy territory.

The new data were worked out on a two-verst map spread out on the breastwork. The second lieutenant gave his orders and watched intently the distant puffs of white smoke which were shrapnel bursts. There was a mathematical beauty, and nothing at all sinister, about this exercise. They compared their impressions of its results.

Not that this bombardment did much to disturb the peace of the enemy's fighting day. Occasional single rounds, with no attempt to concentrate them on any definite target, were just a routine disturbance of the air over the front. It would have taken a clever observer to realize that shells were exploding so deep in German territory not because the Russians had changed their position but because they had acquired new fuses.

One shrapnel burst caught a cart and bowled it over, horses and all. Another time they landed their shells as close as they could to the church at Stwolowicze, where the Germans undoubtedly had an observation post.

Sharing his work equally with the lieutenant colonel was something for Sanya to be proud of. They stood resting their elbows on the boarded patch of breastwork which had become home away from home to them, busy with their diagrams, calculations, and conjectures, not like commander and subordinate but almost like friends, except that the peculiarly icy politeness of the lieutenant colonel's voice, as always, forbade intimacy. Nonetheless, to have been singled out from the other officers, to be able to show his ready grasp and his proficiency, boosted Sanya's morale.

The shrapnel bursts were whiter, more brilliant, and more beautiful every time. It was only toward the end that the lieutenant colonel and the second lieutenant realized why: during their three or four hours at work the weather had changed—there were no more gleams of subdued sunlight, clouds were blotting out the sky and getting darker. The distant steep slope down to Lake Koldyczew was hidden in mist.

Lieutenant Colonel Boyer had done all that he meant to do and was ready to move on. Sanya decided that this was a good time to approach him once more about Bombardier Blagodarev's promised leave. This although the lieutenant colonel had trained his subordinates not to raise the same question twice: a single yes or no must be the end of it. Still, the way Sanya felt that day, he thought it worth trying.

They had meant to send Blagodarev on leave a month earlier, but it was rumored that an imperial decree had canceled leave for soldiers in the ranks, and permits were held up in consequence. Then came an order from General Evert, commander of their Army Group—no leave to be given to soldiers as of 14 October. Like all orders from high up, this one seemed absurd to those in the depths. If there had been any signs of major shifts on the front, preparations either by the Russians or by the Germans to take the offensive . . . but there was no hint of it, and it was not something that could happen without warning. They would most probably be staying put throughout the winter, not advancing at all, and there would be no serious fighting. If there had been a shortage of men, and no one to replace those on leave, it would be understandable, but although the corps was short of many things, numbers was not one of them. Men could perfectly well have gone off for a time to their families and farms, and there were some who had distinguished themselves. But no! The Army Group commander, who had never been near the place, and of whom nothing was known except his German name—and that only to the officers—had from afar and on high smashed the dearest hopes of tens of thousands. It would have been different if they had lined the men up and told them clearly and frankly, so that everybody could hear and understand. But once again—they didn't. The order was treated as a military secret. Battery commanders read it, and signed an undertaking not to divulge it. Platoon commanders then had the embarrassing task of refusing uncomprehending soldiers their promised and eagerly awaited leave.

Sanya, of course, invoked none of the broader arguments, knowing that the lieutenant colonel would not listen to doubts about the wisdom of Evert's orders. He spoke only of Blagodarev, who always took adversity so lightly, and instruction so readily. Most impressively, he had knowingly put himself in danger to drag shells away from that fire, but his commendation had got lost in the bureaucratic maze, and Blagodarev had received his medal only recently, later than the others. He was entitled to leave twice over—ordinary leave and special leave—but now all leave had been suspended.

Diving after the lieutenant colonel under the canvas curtain between the dugout and the communication trench, no longer within hearing of the telephone operators, Sanya spoke up.

"Please, sir, Colonel, dare I mention once again . . . It's Blagodarev. It's very upsetting, I feel ashamed. If we do this sort of thing, the army will go to pieces. After his George medal got mislaid for so long . . . Couldn't we do something—just for him?"

It was lighter than in the dugout, but here too the gloom had gathered. The lieutenant colonel was still without his pince-nez, and the peak of his cap was pulled down so far over his brow that his mustache would have needed only a slight additional twist to reach it. He was symmetrical, solid, rock hard. All at once he seemed to have decided to make the second lieutenant his accomplice.

"Let me tell you confidentially," he said, lowering his voice, "that Major General Belkovich has recently moved out, and is to be replaced by Colonel Smyslovsky. He might release the man, on his own responsibility. I could, perhaps"—he paused to think for a moment—"approach him. Or I'll send for you at a convenient moment."

Sanya was as pleased as if he himself was being given leave.

"Thank you, thank you, you've saved the day, Colonel, sir!"

The unsmiling lieutenant colonel's unbending manner made it clear that army regulations made no provision for thank-yous.

They set out with the lieutenant colonel's orderly on the long journey through the communication trenches.

They had made a pretty good job of it. It was really work for a senior officer, a regular—but someone with crossed cannons on his epaulets, and a poor gunner, could shame and disgrace them all by winging shells heaven knows where. In fact, Boyer supervised all operations in person. Suppose he was put out of action tomorrow—who would direct the main bombardments in the hours that followed? The lieutenant colonel was preparing Lazhenitsyn for just that, without telling him anything. The battery was short of the signals officer and the reconnaissance officer who should, according to regulations, have been on its roster. Noncommissioned officers deputized for them. There was moreover a shortage of experienced bombardiers throughout the Grenadier Brigade—too many of them had been crammed into other units, even infantry units, in the period of administrative chaos at the beginning of the war, and killed off.

In the present sector, near Kroszyn, the Germans had only one division, and that merely a Landwehr division, second class, facing the Grenadier Corps, but the grenadiers still did not feel that they had the upper hand and could pound the enemy. They were, of course, held in check not by the Landwehr troops but by the technical superiority of the Germans in so many respects—their heavy artillery, their abundant supply of shells, their ability to correct aim and range by means of aerial reconnaissance, and a succession of novelties which struck awe into Russian soldiers: bomb throwers, mortars, armored cars, gas attacks, and most recently trench mortars and flame throwers. Then just the other day the 22nd Landwehr Regiment, which had been stationed on that very spot, left of Dubrowna, had been sighted—in Romania, although its disappearance from its previous station had passed unnoticed by the grenadiers. The enemy was making it obvious what he thought of them. To face a Russian Grenadier Corps and the Polish Rifle Brigade he had left only a thinly stretched Landwehr division, minus one regiment. Boyer had taken this as a personal insult.

But trench warfare had reached such an impasse that neither side could exploit local superiority. In whole Army sectors there was deadlock and paralysis. All military decisions had become so complicated, and were referred to such remote heights, that nothing smaller than an Army Group could bestir itself. All that was left was raids and maneuvers.

A raid had been attempted three days earlier to their left, in the 2nd Grenadier Division's sector. Gas was discharged in the direction of the enemy after midnight, on the calculation that a sufficiently steady wind was blowing from east of Kroszyn, and the Germans would all be gassed while they slept in their trenches. But when the gas had dispersed, and a battalion of the Samogitian Regiment advanced toward the German wire, they were suddenly illuminated by searchlights, caught in a hurricane of shots, and forced to retreat in disorder, losing fifty-five grenadiers and two officers.

It was indeed a long time since the Grenadier Corps, which had fought at Borodino and taken part in the capture of Paris, had done anything to add to the glory it had earned in its hundred-year history. By now the reputation of the corps did not stand very high, and few could have explained what distinction, or what special feature of its past, the soldiers' yellow epaulets, the yellow flashes on officers' epaulets, and the grenade with a flame on their buttons were intended to represent. The corps had not distinguished itself in the Turkish war and had played no part in Manchuria. The Rostov Regiment had even sided with the insurgents in 1905, whereas the 1st Artillery Brigade had opened fire on them. The corps had been stationed in Moscow for many years, and so its officers included not only the best graduates of the military schools but also useless drones with influential connections. In addition to this the corps gave interim appointments to Guards and General Staff officers who were not in the Grenadier Division long enough to take root even if they had wished to. There were, moreover, sudden disruptive changes in the style of leadership: at times it was unpardonably easygoing, at others inordinately harsh, as under Mrozovsky, a man whose inability to distinguish between authority and tyranny sapped the self-confidence of his regular officers and made them dread their commander more than defeat in battle.

The corps was involved in heavy fighting in 1914 and 1915. Only one of its engagements had ended in victory (that at Ternawka), and some of its defeats (those at Goraje and on the Vistula, for instance) were costly. If particular regiments won victories of their own it was usually when attached to other units and under different command. The commander of the 1st Grenadier Division, Postovsky, had no victories to his credit at all. Mrozovsky, as corps commander, squandered his men in disastrous engagements, mishandled the distribution of equipment and horses at regimental and battery level, and was then promoted and transferred to command the Moscow Military District. The Most August will of the Supreme Commander of the Russian army was exempt from criticism—even when, as Mrozovsky's replacement, Kuropatkin was retrieved from ignominious oblivion, now seventy years old, but tireless in his efforts to vindicate his honor as a commander in the field. What he was really good at was making the rounds of the men's dugouts, peering into their cooking pots, arranging bath days and mail deliveries, and all this improved the well-being of the corps. But Kuropatkin again pushed the grenadiers into futile offensives without working out the routes carefully, sending them with no cover into lethal fire, after which he too was promoted, and transferred to command the Northern Army Group. In two years of war the Grenadier Corps had spent a total of five days in reserve, and had now been stationed for more than a year in the marshy lowlands, carrying out endless trenching operations, handing over each sector once dug to the unit nearest to them, then digging and digging night after night to get within striking distance of the enemy.

In those two years Boyer and his like, grenadiers through and through, had been denied an officer's chief joy—pride in his unit. They were given no occasion to hear their old colors flapping in the breeze and all they could do was keep up a bold front and try through daily drudgery to drag all these surrogate officers and soldiers into the musty shade of the nineteenth century.

Meanwhile proud Pecherzewski had relieved the taciturn Zanigatdinov at the observation post, and was testing the telephone lines in a strong Polish accent. The relief observer, an ensign, had not yet arrived. And although the second lieutenant was not duty-bound to wait for him, etiquette demanded that he stay behind a little after the battery commander's departure. He went over again to the observation slot and stood looking through it, making occasional notes.

1510   No. 2 machine-gun nest more active than the others. Fired at any sign of movement in No. 3 Battalion.

1536   Heavy mine bombardment of No. 1 Battalion's trenches from Torczyc Heights. Perhaps forty mines.

The day had been a good one. Sanya had worked well and distinguished himself in his commander's eyes, and his fresh hope for Blagodarev added to his satisfaction. Good.

Good. Along the breastwork he scribbled with a long, jagged splinter that had flown through the observation slit when shells were bursting nearby that morning.

Good as far as it went, but he was a little uneasy. He had distinguished himself, but he was not altogether happy about it. Because he was quicker on the uptake than the others he would be singled out all the time. For *this*.

Who would endure such a war, a war of millions against millions, if they had to be killed one at a time and face to face? Sanya himself had never fired a revolver at a fellow man, and never would. But the careful calculations of angles and distances, the protractors, made it all seem so remote. And innocent.

Observation was becoming more and more difficult, visibility was decreasing rapidly. The poplars lining the road to Stwolowicze could no longer be seen. And even the graveyard nearby was wreathed in a damp mist.

His good mood had evaporated. Why had he let himself be carried away? Why had he felt so excited? An autumn wind seemed to blow through him, leaving him cold and empty.

In such gloomy weather the flash of cannon is easier to pinpoint, and it is more dangerous to fire yourself: the flicker of flame at the cannon's mouth can be seen and gives away its position.

Like old sodden leaves, his feelings were swept away, and he was left hollow. Standing by the slit, he was now observing himself, as he had been earlier that day. He did not recognize himself.

Visibility became poorer and poorer. Firing and movement died down. The damp early evening mist subdued both sides.

Sanya felt lonely, and guilty. Blameless, yet guilty. He couldn't have explained it to anyone.

Then it began spitting with rain. A light rain, but persistent. The dugout was damper and chillier than ever. One day very soon the third winter of the war would begin, and even an officer could hardly help feeling depressed.

With his field glasses around his neck, tucked under his greatcoat, and the hood of his cape pulled down hard over his cap, the second lieutenant too made his way back to the battery. By now it was slippery in the clayey trench, and he could not help rubbing against its sweating walls with his gas-mask case on one side and the bulky holster of his unnecessary revolver on the other.

He felt the measured tapping of raindrops on the canvas over his head.

The light was fading fast and he could walk to Dryagovets out in the open. Sanya took a big jump and hung from the edge of the trench, dirtying himself against its clay walls, then hauled himself out onto the grass, and strode boldly off to get to his warm bunker, dry out, and eat something hot as soon as possible. It was a relief not to be humiliatingly churning up mud in a hole but walking as befits a human being.

He had dreamt of devoting his life to literature or philosophy, but there was no knowing whether it would ever happen. He had plenty of free time for verse, but had given up writing, couldn't do it. His contribution to the general course of events was days of gunnery such as this, smashing down barbed-wire entanglements, knocking out machine guns, cutting down distant figures as they scurried from place to place. And of course writing and drawing with his own hand any number of reports and diagrams.

It was the same with his soldiers—Blagodarev, Zanigatdinov, Zhgar, Khomuyovnikov—whether they handled weapons, ammunition, and horses well, whether or not they observed regulations to the letter, each of them might have a long life ahead of him, each had a place that he loved, and a wife whom he loved or did not love, each had more than one child, each had land to till or a trade to follow, and calculations and plans that went with it, horses of their own, with no War Ministry tag on their tails, hunting, fishing, fruit growing, not the greatness of Russia, these were the things that mattered in their lives, not enmity toward Wilhelm, the things they told each other about, more or less articulately, in the bunkers at night, and told their officer too if he spoke to them kindly. In their native villages or provincial towns, there were people who knew them by their works, but this knowledge did not go beyond the immediate district. The real essence of their lives would never be communicated to anyone—how could it possibly affect the general movement of mankind? If Ulezko, Kho-muyovnikov, or Pecherzewski could influence the fate of his country, or of Europe as a whole, it would be by cleaning gun barrels, by speed in loading and firing, by briskness with the shovel, by alacrity in splicing telephone cable.

But if the movement of mankind is not made up of the real lives of ordinary people, where does this leave ordinary people? What becomes of mankind?

* * *

*IT'S WITH WORRYING AND GRIEVING
I KNOW I'M STILL LIVING.*

* * *

[3]

The three platoon commanders shared a bunker. Built in warm, dry weather, it never got damp. It was quite deep, so that once through the door there was no need to stoop. It was roofed with ten-inch pine beams laid crisscross. The walls were lined with lath and the floor was boarded. The battery tinsmith had knocked together a stove with a merrily roaring draft and a great appetite for wood. When the stove was lit the bunker was warmer and cozier than any living room. Shelves had been fitted between the props, and nails and tacks driven in for the hanging of trench coats, swords, revolvers, pouches, caps, and towels, not to mention the guitar on which Sanya and Chernega strummed, each in his own fashion. The little window looked out on the bottom of the trench, but light sometimes got through in the middle of the day. On the smooth-planed trestle table there was room for eating and for the officers' paperwork, although they got in each other's way. Not one of the three had an officer's camp bed. When the bunker was dug, a long, high earth platform ("the merchant's bed," they called it) had been left for Ustimovich, and there were two lath bunks one above the other—not because there was no room for three beds at ground level, but because Chernega liked sitting and sleeping up aloft, over the stove or on a top bunk.

Although he was six years older than Sanya, and far more heavily built, he swung himself up in two easy movements and jumped down with a thud. It was difficult now to imagine the bunker without Chernega grinning down from his perch. The light up there was too poor for reading, but Chernega had no appetite for that.

Sanya, drenched to the skin, came into the bunker bending his head. Tsyzh, the orderly, had been looking out for his second lieutenant, and had dashed off to his own bunker to warm up some food.

Terenti was lying up above as usual, counting the beams in the ceiling. He rolled over onto his side to watch the new arrival take off his heavy wet clothes and hang them up.

"Whew—is it coming down that hard?"

Sanya hadn't noticed that the rain had been getting heavier all the time as he walked along. The stove was not lit, but it was warm in the bunker.

It was impossible to look at Chernega's spherical head, with its chubby cheeks and its tiny ears, without smiling.

"Turned in already? A bit early, isn't it?"

"You know what they say: a dog with no tail sits wondering where to put it."

"Where are you taking yours?"

"In this rain? And in the dark?"

"You can still see a little way, but in half an hour you'd fall in a hole."

Lying on his side, neither dressed nor undressed, in his shirtsleeves and barefoot, but with his breeches on and suspenders over his shoulders, Chernega said, "I don't know. Buzz off to Gusti's, maybe. Or maybe not."

Chernega could just as easily dress again or finish undressing. Sanya would like it better if he stayed—Ustimovich was on duty, and he somehow didn't want to be left alone. But his advice was what he thought would be best for his friend. "Take off while it's still light."

"What about coming back?" Chernega rounded his lips like a bugler and blew like a bugler into his mouthpiece.

Sanya, relieved of greatcoat and belt, with his tunic, wet about the shoulders, outside his trousers, St. George Cross showing, tugged off his wet boots, put on slippers made from cut-down felt boots—they took turns wearing them around the dugout, off duty, except that they didn't fit Ustimovich—and started pacing the rough floor. At least with such weather, God willing, they should have a quiet evening and a quiet night. It could be quieter and cozier in the bunker than it sometimes was at home.

He suddenly remembered: "What were those bangs? A six-incher maybe? Was it close?"

"Dead on No. 2 Battery!" Chernega made a disparaging noise.

"I heard firing just as I was leaving Dubrowina—ten rounds right over Dryagovets. Sounded at first as if they were answering us, but then it didn't seem like that somehow. But they were aiming at something close."

Chernega nodded. "Yes, No. 2 Battery. They buckled the shield of one gun and knocked a wheel off. Wounded three men. But the horses were some way off, they were all right."

"Who saw it?"

"I went over myself."

"I thought you were here at home?"

"Well, it was quite near, so I popped over."

Catch Chernega staying put when it was only half a verst away and he could pop over and take a look! His stoutness didn't stop him from running and jumping. He was all muscle, not fat.

"D'you know a man named Cheverdin over there, gunlayer? Lanky fellow with a straggly beard. From Tagil."

"Yes, I think so."

"Got one in the belly. They're afraid to move him. Never get him there alive."

Right. Here I am, getting dry, making myself comfortable, belt off, slippers on. And just up the road a soldier lies dying. Better get used to it. If he lands a six-incher on us in the night our roof beams won't be of much use.

Here's Tsyzh, doesn't waste much time, looks after me like an uncle, here he comes with some soup, smells good—so let's have it!

"Just smelling it is a feast! Good old Tsyzh!"

And a soft crust of bread. And a raw onion on the side.

"Good old Tsyzh!"

Sanya sat at the table and was soon spooning his soup.

Tsyzh was getting on in years and had five grandsons, but was always brisk and busy. He was mess orderly for all three platoon commanders. This had been Sanya's idea. If they each had an orderly they'd be in the way. One man could wait on them all, and the other two could be up in the line.

But the smell was stronger up above than down below, and Chernega, rolling over on his side, took a deep breath through his wide nostrils.

"Tsyzh! Any soup left?"

"Sorry, sir." Tsyzh, unshaven, couldn't have been sorrier if he himself had been left without. "I've drained the last drop."

Chernega flopped back on his pillow. Sanya had never seen anything more beautiful than that soup, but he called out to Chernega, "You can have some of mine. Come and get it."

"I couldn't," Chernega said to the ceiling. "You've been freezing all day."

"No, come on, it's all right!"

"There is some buckwheat left over, sir. I could bring you some of that, with some fat."

"So don't tease—let's have it!" Chernega ordered.

Tsyzh lurched out of the bunker in a hurry.

Chernega drummed on his belly. "I had dinner two hours ago, and now you've gone and . . . No doubt there's a chicken waiting for me at Gusti's. Should I go or not?"

There were villages near the front which had not been evacuated.

They were used to the war by now and went on living a normal life. Apart from their regular sources of income the peasants could fetch and carry for the army, the carpenters among them reinforced communication trenches, teenage boys and girls dug second-line trenches and they were all paid, and fed from army cookhouses. Peasants who got their call-up papers were sometimes put in nearby units—including Sanya's battery. Many peasant huts had soldiers for lodgers, who sometimes worked in their landlords' fields, and gave their landladies linen to wash, or else as a present: the army was rich, and would always issue a replacement. Some bold spirits, like Chernega, surreptitiously reinforced and further extended this extended family, by taking mistresses in the villages and visiting them regularly.

Chernega swung his Turkish-trousered legs over the side of the bunk and wiggled his bare, knobbly toes interrogatively. "Shall I go, or shall I not? She stays cheerful for a couple of days. Any longer and she gets miserable."

"You don't, though. You seem to manage."

When Chernega was sitting on his bunk, his head with its snug covering of silky hair touched the sloping ceiling. He couldn't put his cap on, let alone throw up his arms. So he flung them out, as though drawing to its full extent a wide accordion, and his well-covered body quivered under his shirt.

"There's no comparison, Sanya, my boy. Steer clear of things you know nothing about. D'you really think it's the same for women as it is for us? What makes them cheerful or glum, d'you think? It all depends on whether they've had it or not."

Chernega was hanging over him, Chernega was strong as an ox, Chernega's laugh was so self-assured—it would have taken more than Sanya to argue with Chernega. He and his fellow students had thought of these things so much less crudely, but in the army, in their tight unrelievedly masculine milieu, they all, without exception, talked like that in their evening conversations. Or at any rate nobody said anything different out loud. Sanya was dismayed, he resented the insult to women, but he couldn't argue, he was dumb. What experience did he have?

He did make a feeble protest. "Come on, Terenti, there's more to it than that."

"And I'm telling you that's all there is to it," Terenti said, loudly striking one palm against the other. "There's never any other reason. She can look so worn out she can't drag her feet along, you give her a bit of a tickle and there you are. Sometimes you think something's eating her, you think maybe she's grieving about something. But you throw her on the bed, she has a bit of rough-and-tumble, a bit of a rest, and all of a sudden she's merry and bright and running to the stove to bake pies."

Chernega guffawed. "What a child you are, Sanya. But you're still young. You'll learn yet!"

So many times he'd teased Sanya about it. But that crude way of looking at things clashed with Sanya's whole attitude toward life and toward human beings. It couldn't be like that! It couldn't possibly be like that!

Tsyzh arrived with the buckwheat: a bowl for the second lieutenant with a leftover piece of meat, and a bowl for the ensign with no meat, but so thick that the handle of a wooden spoon stood upright in it.

"Give it to me!" Chernega seized the bowl from above. He rammed the wide wooden spoon repeatedly into his mouth.

His forehead was almost touching the roof beams. "Not ba-ad, not bad at all," he said. "At Gusti's I'd have had milk in it, though."

He polished off the buckwheat with enjoyment, and looked hard at the wet footprints and smears of clay Tsyzh had left on the floor.

"Is it that slushy outside? No, I won't go. I'm not that stupid."

He tossed the bowl to Tsyzh and swung his legs back onto the bed.

"What makes the soldier happy? Eating his fill and taking a nap."

He rolled over onto his back and stared at the beams, musing aloud. "How d'you think Rasputin got where he is? What else could have made her listen to him? She would have shipped him off to Siberia long ago. No—he's all a man should be. Slacken the rein on a woman she'll kick up her heels."

It all seemed so simple to Chernega. No good contradicting him. Most of their conversations were like that. Sanya wouldn't even begin to argue.

But they were good friends.

Sanya had finished his buckwheat and was sitting at the empty table absentmindedly popping the last few bread crumbs into his mouth.

"Mm, yes," he said. "These Grishkas are unlucky for Russia. A Grishka is sure to turn up when things are going badly. First it was Grishka Otrepev, now it's . . ."

Chernega flared up.

"What's Grishka got to do with it? D'you think Grishka started this war of theirs? They were in a hurry to get to the bog—and they ended up shitting themselves."

All very well, but what about Serbia? What about Belgium? And how do you account for those stories and photographs of German atrocities, of Germans cutting off the ears and noses of Russian prisoners? (Though nothing of the sort had ever happened in their sector.) Although Chernega's strength, his quickness and his jollity made army life easier for him than for others, he took a much gloomier view of the war than Sanya: he saw it as a universal, lingering plague, with no possible sense or purpose.

Sanya rose from the table.

"Not going to bed, are you?" Terenti asked, suddenly remembering. "Wait a minute, dear fellow, there's still work to be done!"

"What work?"

"The orders are over there." He nodded at Ustimovich's bed. Sanya had in fact seen the pile of papers, and ignored it.

"Everybody else has read them, you're the last. Get going and sign your name. The baron looked in and was going to take them, but I kept them till morning, for you."

"The baron" was Baron Rokossovsky, the senior officer in No. 2 Battery. Chernega was particularly fond of the word "baron" for some reason. He had always disliked barons, counts, and princes, and used foul language about them, but he had a strange, proud feeling, now that he was an officer, that he had become almost the baron's equal, almost a member of the same club. He never called him by his name, or "captain," but always "baron." The regular officers pulled rank, put on airs, made invidious comparisons—the Mikhailovsky officers' school is older than the Konstantinovsky—but look at me, from a training depot in the sticks, cheek by jowl with a baron and eat your hearts out!

Sanya went over to Ustimovich's roomy bed and grabbed with both hands the untidy heap of white, buff, and pink files, folders, and documents loosely clipped or pinned together, all covered with contributions from a multitude of clerks, handwritten, or typed with black or violet ribbons. It was incredible how much conscientious effort had gone into compiling all this! And how much of it there was to read! To go through it all systematically and in detail would take half the night for sure. This was what made trench warfare much the same as life behind the lines. For some reason, when the front was dangerously shifting, when columns of flame rose to the sky, nobody bothered to write and issue these endless orders and directives: battles could rage and roll without them. But as soon as the fighting slowed down, as soon as it got easier and there was some hope of a breather, a rest, the flood of orders was in full spate again, and growing steadily with every month of immobility. Officers in the line were expected to do a great deal of writing—but those higher up were no slouches! For fear that they might not have documentary justification for their actions, should it be needed, the armies at the front were slow to destroy or hand in old files, and lugged around great heaps of papers wherever they went.

No alternative, though. Must look through it all and try to keep some of it in mind, or tomorrow may be your day to make a mistake.

There were Western Army Group orders, 2nd Army orders, Grenadier Corps orders—only their own battalion orders were, thank God, not given in writing, although they too had a typewriter, which was kept busy logging operations.

Sanya transferred all this paper to the clean end of the table, moved the oil lamp nearer, and started from the top of the pile without sorting it. Directives on expenditure came first. To Brigade Paymaster, Titular Counselor so-and-so . . . deductions from officers' pay for officers' library . . . for medals . . . to the fund for families of soldiers killed or wounded . . . to the Mikhailovsky School fund . . . from the officers' loan capital . . . from the brigade club collection . . . money for the purchase of devotional literature for the divisional mullah . . . the below-mentioned clerks have permission to take the examination for promotion to . . .

Even skimming it, however cursorily and reluctantly, would take at least two hours. And it was the last thing he wanted to be doing.

Medical Orderly so-and-so is ordered to proceed to Nesvizh to pick up medical supplies . . . to Minsk to buy kerosene . . . Bombardier so-and-so to obtain horseshoes . . . Junior Bombardier so-and-so of No. 5 Battery has entered into lawful wedlock with a peasant girl . . . to be entered in his service book . . . make Ensign so-and-so a grant equivalent to four months' pay to buy a horse and carriage . . .

"Why are you reading to yourself? Read it out loud!"

"What for?"

"I didn't read it very carefully, and I wouldn't mind hearing it again."

"Terenti, it'll take too long."

"So where are you hurrying off to?"

"It's you who have to be off."

"Ah, but I may not go at all. Read away!"

Terenti made himself comfortable, lying on his side, with his bullet head on the pillow, looking down at Sanya as though he was expecting an adventure story or a love story.

"Come on, read!"

Sanya couldn't refuse. He read whatever his eyes could see, whatever his stumbling tongue could articulate, skipping quite a bit.

"Increment for George medal . . . for greasing boots, twenty-four grams per soldier per month . . . in accordance with Order No . . . from the Minister of War . . . the below-mentioned are admitted to the examination for the rank of ensign."

"All very well," Chernega grumbled. "But it's better being a sergeant major. You've got more authority." (Sanya skimmed through two orders silently while he was saying it.) "Still, ensigns are the backbone of the army . . . But why have you stopped?"

"Officers' shoes available from the Corps Quartermaster's supply depot in Minsk at sixteen rubles twenty-five kopecks a pair."

"Phew! What a racket! Better buy some, though, mine are more or less worn out."

"After . . . soldiers will be issued with padded breeches, jerkins, donkey jackets, sheepskin coats, and flannelette puttees . . . On the supply of basic rations, hot meals, tea, tobacco, and soap . . . In view of the decline in butter production in the empire, as of 14 October this year fifty percent of dairy butter will be replaced by vegetable oil . . . as of 28 October lower ranks will be issued with only twelve zolotniks of sugar, and a money equivalent will be paid in lieu of the other six . . ."

"Hmm . . . In '14 they came up with a pound of meat a day, you could eat till you burst, and we got a quarter of fatback as well . . . you could live like a king, and have some for the dog. You'd be glad of that fatback now to give a bit of a taste to your gruel."

Tsyzh, who was bringing in the copper kettle, with steam still billowing from the spout, heard this. "Never mind, s', it's a sin to complain. We still get half a pound of meat. And a pound of fatback a week."

Tsyzh made a barely perceptible distinction between real officers, who began at second lieutenant, and ensigns, calling the former "sir" and ensigns "s'." But he wrapped his tongue around it so nimbly you'd never catch him on it.

Tsyzh poured some of the strong tea, just boiled up and fragrant again, into the second lieutenant's earthenware mug. He brewed twice a day, so the tea was always aromatic.

The gentlemen officers' sugar was in a sugar bowl.

"Will there be anything else, sir?" he asked as he cleared the plates away and wiped the table.

"Yes, a jug of honey," Chernega trumpeted.

Tsyzh, with a sprinkling of gray in his hair and a white cloth over his arm like a tavern waiter, smiled. "Sorry, sir, the bees have flown away. No honey till next year."

His sense of humor was another of his strong points. War likes a joke. He knew that the gentlemen officers always had worries and problems. He probably had some of his own, but serving officers' meals was not just something that had to be done, he made it fun. Almost as though they were visiting him and the little woman at home.

But being waited on by someone old enough to be his father was a constant embarrassment to Sanya. He couldn't get used to it. Glancing at the stove—everything was neatly arranged there too—the second lieutenant smiled and said, "No, we don't need anything else, go to bed now. Just find Blagodarev and tell him to come and see me in, say, half an hour."

Now that the table was wiped clean he spread his papers out and went on reading. A sheaf of instructions on the treatment of scurvy. Scurvy had taken hold of the brigade in the middle of the summer: there was sufficient bread, cereals, meat, and fish, but no green vegetables or new potatoes; you couldn't buy them in neighboring villages and importing them from anywhere in the empire was prohibited by order of the Supreme Commander. The sudden outbreak of scurvy was the result not only of poor diet but of continual night duty—and lack of rest all through the spring and summer. Many of the men were sick and too weak for duty, but the authorities took a long time authorizing and arranging their removal to the sanatoria operated by the Union of Zemstvos, where complete rest and green vegetables awaited them, or allowing units to procure potatoes, cabbages, and beets by their own efforts, even from inside the empire. But now that the scurvy was no more, belated orders repeated over and over again how, and how often a day, dugouts should be aired (fit extra windows, install plank beds, and stop soldiers from sleeping on the ground or make them put branches under their mats) and who should be released from duty for rest and when . . .

"Come on, read it out loud." Chernega wouldn't give up.

"I thought you were asleep. Want some tea?"

"No, not without honey."

"Halters, bridles, horsecloths, currycombs, brushes, nose bags, gas masks for horses . . . The horse Charlatan, on the roster since 1909, is redesignated for the use of officers, and the mare Shelkunya is redesignated for use in the line by other ranks."

"Shelkunya, let's see, that's the baldish bay with a tuft on her right forefoot. She's still a good one. Changing her, eh—wonder if he's found a better one."

Chernega knew every single horse in his own battalion by sight, and many of those in other battalions too. There followed a long list of horses transferred from one category to another—officers' horses privately owned, army horses, saddle horses for the artillery, draft horses for the artillery, cart horses—Shorokh, Shved, Shut, Shatobrian, Shanghai, Shchedry—with a full description of sizes, coloring, bald patches, flashes and other markings, all of it signed by the brigade commander, who might or might not have read it, and Sanya would have left out everything concerning other batteries and battalions, but Chernega had come to life, dangling and flicking his plump, stubby hand like a rider's crop, urging him on, approving or scolding.

"As if the remount depots stick to the rules about grading nowadays! They send any horse anywhere, as long as the number's right. While we're in one place it doesn't matter, but suppose we have to get started tomorrow. Every horse should be right for its job!"

Sanya also liked horses and knew a bit about them, but wasn't as passionate as Chernega: listening to it all for the second time around, he expressed his agreement or disagreement with what was said about every horse, always with an eye for neglect or dishonesty on somebody's part.

"On examination . . . some horses have sharp lugs on both rear shoes, which causes them to hitch . . ."

"Bastards! Ought to be shod like that themselves!"

"The below-mentioned horses belonging to officers are registered for a fodder allowance . . . the below-mentioned are returned to their original status . . . from the brigade's racing capital in the Moscow Merchant Bank . . ."

Sanya went through all the horses to please Chernega and only then spotted it: "Are you playing tricks on me or what? Did you put the most important orders on the bottom?"

"Must be Ustimovich. Threw 'em down as he read 'em. So the first batch went to the bottom."

"So you should have done the opposite!"

"Don't blame me. He read them to me, like you're doing."

Sanya felt peeved. A quiet evening, he could have made good use of it, and here he was blathering away, reading all this drivel. But Chernega wouldn't let him read to himself.

"Out loud, Sanya, my boy," he begged. "Out loud!"

Chernega was crafty all right, listening to it twice instead of reading it once. "I don't understand anything out of books, I only understand what I hear for myself."

Next came the operational orders. Every regiment was to have a specially trained officer as "gas commandant."

The battalion already had one. Ustimovich. Let him read it.

". . . all batteries to record transfer of defensive fire from their own to adjacent sectors . . . to corps commanders . . ."

"Not us, thank God!" Chernega said with a loud yawn.

"Choose which of your positions . . . present on tracing paper . . . step up trenching operations in October."

The whining of the order machine reverberated hollowly in his head.

"Increase the wire net to three or four strands, each greater in width . . . raise parapets to the proper height, and camouflage them . . . corps and battalion reserves to detail one-quarter of their complement daily for this work . . ."

"Never any rest! Get over the scurvy without it! Left hand never knows what the right hand's doing! Poland's famous for muddling through, but Russia's even worse . . ."

Five German three-inch shells exploded not far away. The glass in the window jangled, the lamp dipped, and a few dribbles of earth fell through the ceiling.

Next came a number of orders about communications . . . In spite of the ban some people are still using the open telegraph line . . . placing one-way signal lines underground in the vicinity of the enemy is forbidden.

There had been a lot of bother about eavesdropping in recent months. It was a constant surprise to find that the Germans knew the disposition and duty periods of Russian units at the lowest level. Tests were made with an amplifier, and it turned out that telephone messages were easily intercepted. So now:

Army HQs to work out code words and phrases and present some

to the Western Army Group HQ so that a single code can be devised
. . . How silly, why a single code? . . . Western Army Group. Today, on
the name day of our Sovereign leader, the Heir Apparent, the armies
of the Western Army Group tender their most loyal congratulations
and offer up their fervent prayers . . . in reply His Majesty was pleased
to favor me with the following telegram . . . to be read, by order, in all
companies, squadrons, Cossack hundreds, batteries, and detachments
. . . C in C, Western Army Group, Infantry General Evert . . . From the
same, noting that there are still instances of the appointment of Jews
as clerks and in quartermasters' supply depots, and also as cattle drovers, which is absolutely impermissible . . . You are ordered to remove
them from these posts immediately and make no further appointments
of the sort . . .

"Remove the Hymies!" Chernega said approvingly, lashing the air
with his hand. "They cling to the safe jobs like flies around a stove.
You won't find them sticking their necks out!"

Sanya stopped reading and raised his clear eyes.

"After all, Terenti, these are fellows with some education. Some of
them are students—Barukh, in my platoon, is a university graduate.
Every third one could be an officer, not just a clerk."

"An officer? Are you crazy?" Chernega rolled over to the very edge
of the bunk; his chest was on the last rod, he might come crashing
down on the floor at any minute . . .

"Just think where officers like that would lead us! *They'd* know what
orders to give us!"

"Depends which ones. Some of them are said to have the George
medal."

"Said to! Somebody saw some somewhere, sometime. Think about
it—why the hell should they fight for Russia?"

Terenti found Sanya's obtuseness laughable. Any fool could see it,
why couldn't he?

"Let one of them in and tomorrow there'll be ten! They'll walk all
over us. You haven't learned it all yet, you haven't lived with them.
Equal rights, they call it. Only we don't skin each other alive, and they
do skin us. Equal rights would soon mean 'we're more equal than you.'
Put officer tabs on your Beinarovich tomorrow, and the day after tomorrow you'll want to desert."

Beinarovich? Hmm. Beinarovich, with the hot, black, angry eyes.
Maybe Chernega had a point there. But Barukh? Barukh was well educated, polite, reserved. Sanya always felt uneasy with Barukh's ironic
gaze upon him: how can I give him orders, what tone of voice should
I use to him, when he's taken his degree and I haven't?

"Whose country is it—ours or theirs?" Chernega swung his dangling
hand like a flail. "I bet there aren't any out on the steppes where you
come from. Try living in Kharkov province, then I'll listen to you."

Peaceable as he was, Sanya didn't give way easily. He took his time and answered with a friendly smile, but stuck to his guns. "Well, if it isn't their country, why do we make them join the army? It's unfair. If you're right, we shouldn't call them up at all."

"So let's not call them up!" Chernega conceded. "We won't lose much if we don't. But they live among us! If we don't call them up, maybe we shouldn't take anybody except Russkies and Ukes. It used to be like that. Sarts weren't called up, Caucasians weren't . . . Finns still aren't. D'you know how many of our kind have been killed? In East Prussia alone?"

Terenti fidgeted on the very edge of his little upper space, as though poised to swoop. Sanya had room to stand up and walk around, but he sat quietly, leaning on the table, with his elbow on all those orders, and his fingers spread over his forehead, touching his corn-colored hair.

"Look," he said reflectively. "What it comes down to is aggravated distrust of each other. The state refuses to regard Jews as real citizens, suspecting that they don't see themselves that way. And the Jews don't genuinely want to defend this country, suspecting that they won't earn any thanks for it anyway. How do we get out of it? Who's going to make the first move?"

"Damn it, maybe you're one yourself." Chernega guffawed, rolling onto his back and playing his invisible accordion. "Why should you worry who takes the first step? It doesn't matter if nobody does. The order's clear enough. Kick the Jews out of their staff jobs. Why are they sitting pretty in staff jobs everywhere? Is that fair? Isn't that an insult? I'm telling you, you don't know anything, you haven't lived with them, so you just don't know. A very special people they are, they all stick together, and they worm their way in everywhere. Don't forget they're the ones who crucified Christ."

Sanya removed his hand from his head and spoke sternly to the man up above. "Terenti, that's not a joking matter. Don't talk wildly. D'you think we wouldn't have crucified him? If he'd come from Suzdal instead of Nazareth, and come to us first, d'you think we Russians wouldn't have crucified him?"

At rare moments, confronted with his younger friend's deep seriousness, the older man quieted down. He answered back, with only the slightest tinge of humor in his voice. "We would? Ne-ever."

It wasn't today's problem. Why tear each other's hair out?

But for Sanya it was today's problem, and mild as he was, once he got his teeth into something, beating him over the head wouldn't make him let go.

"Any people would have rejected and betrayed him! Understand? Any one of them! That was the intention. Nobody could have taken it in: he came and said straight out that he was from God, that he was the son of God, and had brought us God's will! Who could endure that? Who would not beat him? Who would not crucify him? People were killed for much less. No human being can endure a revelation directly from God. He must flounder and fumble his way to thinking that it is the product of his own experience."

[4]

There was a knock.

"May I come in, sir?"

The voice was subdued, deliberately kept low. But recognizable even through the door.

"Come in, Blagodarev, come in!"

Bowing his head, and his shoulders too, burly Blagodarev entered, and closed the door carefully so that it would not bang. Only then did he straighten up and raise his hand to his cap, with something less than military precision, but not unnecessarily flouting the rules.

"Reporting as ordered, sir."

He had five or ten paces to step from dugout to dugout, without his greatcoat, and there were spots of rain on his well-worn, yellow-rimmed bombardier's shoulder boards. He might have been in bed already, but he had not arrived improperly dressed. His belt was neatly buckled, and he was wearing a gunner's cap and a bombardier's white leather sword knot. He was neither sulky nor jolly: he had been sent for, and there he was, awaiting orders. Late at night—but war was war.

The second lieutenant was excruciatingly aware of what he had left unsaid to Chernega, and it blocked all other thoughts until it faded. Because of that, he spoke absently, his mind elsewhere.

"Ah, Arseni . . . right." Then, realizing that it looked bad, he corrected himself. "Take a seat! Sit down!" He pointed at a place near the table.

Blagodarev realized that it wasn't going to be fun. "Sit down" was as much as to say this won't be quick, no glad tidings as you step through the door. He took off his cap. (He'd let his hair grow a bit, hoping to go home.)

He hadn't been banking on good news, but had come along hopefully. Could this be it? Though his whole army experience told him that once the brass turned the key they weren't going to unlock the door. He had, just before reporting, been sitting by the kerosene stove in his dugout with a folded sheet of paper spread out on a plywood board, finishing a letter, and writing in what little space was left on one side that he evidently would not be coming as soon as they had promised. There was no room, though, to let yourself go on that scrap of paper. It was folded so you could gum it together, the front was a greenish brown, with fearsome horsemen galloping over it, sabers drawn, frighten you to death if you ran up against them, thank God they weren't galloping around anymore, but it would give them the shakes when they saw it back home. The stamp wouldn't stick—must have been around the batteries. On the back of the letter form, pigeons were flying with letters in their beaks. There was no room to write anything. If you had good eyes you could make out, in tiny print, the words "passed by the military censorship." If you opened it out, there were two pages inside. But the left-hand side was taken up by a ready-made message in beautiful dark blue lettering, such as not even the cleverest clerk could write:

> Dearly beloved parents!
>
> I hasten to notify you in the first lines of my letter that I am by God's mercy alive and well, and I wish you the same from the bottom of my heart. I further inform you that I am happy with my life in the army and that I have good officers. So do not grieve for me or worry.

And that was all. Add any greetings you wanted to send, sign your name, and there was your letter. To be fair, there was a very little space for a very few words, and you could . . . Could what? You could say I order my dear wife Katerina to obey her father-in-law and mother-in-law, and to look after the little ones, and to await me hopefully. But although there was room enough the rules did not allow him to write directly to the most important person, Katya. Nobody wrote about the things closest to his heart—he'd be ashamed to. Silly, loving words weren't allowed in letters, let alone the secret ones you whispered in somebody's ear—the letter had to be read out loud for whatever relatives and neighbors came to hear it. It would be awkward complaining that you weren't being allowed the leave you'd earned, that you were sick and fed up with it, and that if the war heated up again in the spring there'd be no chance of going at all. Tsyzh had darted in at that moment.

"Senka! The second lieutenant wants you for something. In half an hour. I don't think he's going to chew you out."

Senka felt weak. Could this be it? Maybe things had changed? The second lieutenant wouldn't be sending for him on such a dark night for some military reason, and wouldn't have said "in half an hour" if that was it.

The nights were cold now, and Katya would be sleeping in the big hut with the others, and getting up to see to the child. Suddenly he had a vision of her sleeping like a child herself in the cold hallway, in late autumn, with her half-sheepskin coat pulled up over her head—when she was hidden under it you wouldn't find her. One step and you were with her.

What if there was somebody else there? Wouldn't he take that one step? What was to stop some wily womanizer from sitting around, lying around, biding his time?

No. No. No.

But he shouldn't have allowed himself to hope. "Sit down," the second lieutenant had said, "I want to talk to you."

The second lieutenant smiled nicely, and tried to soothe his ruffled feelings. "It's like this, Arseni. Don't give up hope. I spoke to the lieutenant colonel today. We may be able to do something for you."

Do something! Do something for you! Heavens above! I haven't misheard, have I? Just let me go, kind sirs, and when I come back I'll fight like two big guns!

Arseni's rubbery lips widened in a grin.

The second lieutenant, glad to share his happiness but fearful of promising too much, explained.

"It's not for sure, you know. But I'm hopeful. I'm telling you this so you won't be too downhearted. But don't tell anyone for the time being, don't get them excited. As a general rule, leave is still not allowed."

All those months, when his citation was missing, Arseni had never grumbled, never looked reproachful, never let his face cloud over for any length of time, and had tactfully tried to conceal his sense of grievance from the second lieutenant. So now he uttered no special words of thanks, but he could not bring his lips back to their proper place, and his hands, palm upward on his knees, were weak in every finger.

He was not wearing his two George Crosses—they were on his greatcoat. But how proud he would be, going home to his village with two Georges! Home! Straight from the front!

The holiday mood is infectious, and those granting leave can catch it. The second lieutenant, separated from village life by university and a broader understanding of so many things, felt like the boy he was, two years younger than Blagodarev.

But he was "senior" even to Tsyzh. The second lieutenant had been credited with the wisdom to judge whether a soldier was good or bad, whether he should be promoted to a higher position on the gun crew, or to the rank of bombardier, or transferred to reconnaissance or map reading. But there was no question of taking Blagodarev off the gun. He could assemble and dismantle the lock, and set and read the sights, panoramic sights included, so quickly, he knew the structure of a shell, and the action of fuses—without such assistants in his platoon an officer's life was not worth living. Now that the level of soldierly proficiency had fallen so low, where would you find such a grenadier?

Chernega, dangling his bare feet, bawled down at them.

"What's he want leave for? Let him get a bit of service in! He's been for one walk already."

Not his own platoon commander—but any one of them could spoil things. When nobody was getting leave. Arseni stared at Chernega and spoke softly—he was an officer, if a barefooted one.

"That's where I got my first one."

"And what was your first one for?" Chernega asked sternly. "Sitting around at HQ somewhere, I'll bet."

"How would I get one there?" Blagodarev knew that Chernega was ribbing him, but didn't dare adopt the same derisive tone. The other man couldn't affect his leave—or could he? Could he find some way?

"Those Georges of yours, they dish 'em out right and left at HQs. In fact, it's your George made me think you must have been at HQ. You say you were going around with some colonel all that time. Where was that, then?"

"You know as well as I do," Arseni said with a smile. It was the very devil having to say "you" instead of "thou" to an officer promoted from sergeant major. Why "you"? There was only one of him. People said "thou" to God himself.

"I don't know anything about it!" Chernega shouted.

"In Prussia."

"You mean you were in the encirclement?"

"Yes, we were surrounded." Arseni showed him how with his arms.

"Lies, all lies!" Chernega gabbled, swinging his legs and turning his cheese of a head to look approvingly at Blagodarev. "Listen, Sanya my boy, let me have him in my platoon. No need at all for him to go on leave. I'll find him a woman right here, a Pole! A beauty! And I'll let him leave the lines without asking any lieutenant colonel. But he keeps telling these lies. Why? I ask you. If you were there, encircled with Samsonov, how was it I didn't see you? Where were you making for?"

Blagodarev was getting bolder. "Well, I didn't see you either," he said with a grin. "We covered a lot of ground, but we didn't see you. Were you really there, or weren't you?"

He screwed up his eyes.

"Is that the way to talk to me!" Chernega shouted. "I'll have you in the guardhouse in no time!"

He jumped down onto the floor, landing as surefootedly as a cat. He thrust his bare feet into the pair of old galoshes that served them all in turn when they went out in the night, but fitted only Ustimovich.

He laid a plump, heavy hand on Blagodarev's shoulders.

"Come on, then, do what I say. We'll go and see the women together."

Blagodarev answered, still squinting, no longer feeling awkward, and without rising. "And when do I get to see my children?"

"Pooh, what a question! We'll make some new ones, and you can forget the old ones. How many have you got?"

"Two."

"What are they?"

"A son and a daughter."

"Why did you settle for a girl? And there I was thinking you were a hero. Some good you going on leave! How old is she?"

"Nine months."

"What did you call her?"

"Apraksiya."

"All right, you can go, only make a son this time. We're going to need all the sons we can get, I can tell you!"

He put his cape on over his shirt, put nothing on his head, and shuffled out in the sloppy galoshes to relieve himself.

Chernega had found out with his pushy questions things what Blagodarev's platoon commander did not know about him. Chernega was a rogue if ever there was one, but he always managed to notice everything there was to notice in a horse, and to learn all there was to learn about a man. Whereas Sanya spent much of his time thinking, and there were times when he needed to be alone to think. So he missed things. Like the most important part of Blagodarev's life, which had been there to be seen all along, but which had nothing to do with his adroitness as a gunner and could not influence the course of world history.

"And what's your village called?"

"Kamenka. The estate's Khvoshchovo."

"Big village?"

"About four hundred households. More than a thousand male souls."

"Who's the squire?"

"Davydov, Yuri Vasilich. But he's in Tambov, in a top job."

"What top job?"

The skin on Blagodarev's forehead moved reflectively.

"Zemstvo or something. Anyway, they've sold out to us . . . Or leased it . . . There are three brothers, they've gone their different ways."

"Where to?"

Holding his cap upside down on his knee, and basking in all this goodwill, Arseni told his story with a slight smile.

"Vasil Vasilich and the deacon's son got the peasants together in the bushes and tried to turn them against the Tsar. Well, the peasants reported them to the police inspector. Vasil Vasilich and his wife caught on in time and took off for Rzhaksa. They waited for the third bell, then nipped onto the train. Then, in Tambov, the story goes, Yuri Vasilich came down to the station with passports all ready for them. So they got clean away. To France. So they say."

"When was this, then?"

"When I was still little." A twitch of the brow and the wrinkle disappeared. He looked more cheerful. It was beginning to look as if he would get his leave.

"Before the riots."

Damp air swung in through the door with Chernega. He snorted, and shook his big wet head like a dog.

"What's that? Riots? Ignorant clods! When was this rioting?"

"Ten years ago. There wasn't really much rioting in our village, in Kamenka. But they started fires in Aleksandrovka and in Panovy Kusty. They plundered the house of Anokhin the merchant and the Solovovs'. Our Vasili Vasilich always used to say rob the rest of all they've got, I'll hand mine over and welcome! But Mokhov, the headman, called a village meeting and said, 'Men! Maybe we ought to hold off. You can choke yourself on other people's property.' So our people decided: yes, they'd hold back. It was the same in Volkhonshchina, the next village."

Chernega slipped off the galoshes and stood barefoot on the floor.

"No, I'm not going sweethearting. If she gets more sleep she'll be up to milk the cows earlier. Sanya, why don't you give the stove more of a draft."

"It's warm enough."

"You just pop outside and see. Still, I won't freeze up top."

Fat-chested, fat around the middle, fat-legged, he did not so much climb—with one foot on an angular projection, he flung himself, almost sprang aloft, and flopped so heavily onto his bed that the rods gave, bent inward, then straightened themselves again. A solid piece of work, that bunk.

"And how did it end?" he asked from above.

"The Cossacks were there pretty quick, sorting it all out with their whips. They reported to the general that the Kamenka estate had not been touched. What? he says. You mean it? So give those smart fellows twenty-five rubles for vodka. They rolled out the barrel, and all the village helped drink it. While in Fyodorovo the peasants were flogged to a man. It was winter, and they were flogged out in the snow. Then the general took the Cossacks off to Tugolukovo. And gave the folks there a good hiding too."

"Tugolukovo? Riots there as well?" Chernega called out merrily, as though greeting his platoon.

"Ah, there's a place where the people really love freedom. They have fistfights every Sunday. Not a man leaves the field without a shiner."

"Right, then," said Chernega appreciatively. "Go home to your woman." He punched his pillow into shape.

He turned on his side, with his back to the dugout, and pulled the blanket over himself.

The second lieutenant was worrying. "That's fine, but if you go, who can we put in your place?"

They thought about it. Could so-and-so manage?

"Get him ready to take over from you. And you be ready. As soon as we get permission you're to be out of here in half an hour. So if they change their minds and cancel it you'll be away."

"Sir! You can slip me that bit of paper when I'm fast asleep and I'll have my puttees on and be away in five minutes! I'll keep clear of all the command posts and go straight to the station."

He left, ducking through the door.

Chernega was already breathing heavily.

Sanya again felt a shiver of apprehension.

It often happened to him. He could be talking, or in the middle of some business, and something would grate on his heart—he would hardly notice it at the time but everything would cloud over, fade from view, and things that had seemed worthwhile suddenly meant nothing. The only thing to do was to seek solitude and try to retrieve without interference what exactly it was that had grated. And how to put it right. There were times when by thought, patience, promise to amend, and hard work equilibrium was restored.

Now, as he sat at the table with his head in his hands, one thought came into his mind: Cheverdin. Cheverdin, in No. 2 Battery, to whom Sanya had never done any harm.

If it had been in his own battery, and in reply to his own fire, it would have been understandable. As it was, there was no rational connection.

No, that wasn't the way to look at it. The Landwehr officer who shouted his order into the telephone would never know about someone named Cheverdin. Sanya himself must have buried a few on the other side that day. This, from the point of view of the Russian high command, was highly desirable; without it, all military activity would lose its sense, and instead of hypocritically wearing a soldier's uniform a man should take it off and report to a punitive battalion. Still, Sanya would not have been so full of doubt but for Cheverdin. The thought wouldn't go away: would the man die or wouldn't he?

The empty dugout was getting colder all the time, but Sanya sat, with his eyes buried in his hands, trying to pull together the tatters of his lacerated soul, trying to heal his wounds.

It had been what was called a good day's fighting. He had rarely fired so much or so accurately, and the lieutenant colonel had unambiguously praised him. Then he, an officer—the last thing he had ever thought he would be—from whom confident orders were expected, had suddenly felt lost, overwound once too often, oblivious of himself and what he should be doing. The splendid life he had planned for himself was out of gear, useless, worse than useless, harmful. To live to be fifty, turning like a blade in somebody's mincer, would be a worse fate than being killed at twenty-five.

Neither his fellow officers nor the battery commander, nor, if he had gone home, his father and brothers, could have made it any easier for him.

Throwing his cape over his shoulders, and slipshod in the shared galoshes, Sanya went up and out.

It was a moonless night, and rain was falling. The murk was impenetrable. If you took a step at all, it was by half remembering, half feeling your way. He could not make out the surroundings he had known so well for a year past, could not even see, against the sky, the tops of familiar trees, scorched or skewed or splintered.

The front line wasn't sending up flares.

Nor firing. And there was no wind. Just a soothing, natural downpour lashing branches, leaves, and the ground. It made the silence still deeper.

The whole world was completely invisible. No Stwolowicze, and no Yushkevichi, with its white churches. No Poland. No Russia. No Germany. Under the invisible cloud-wrapped, dark depths of the sky—nothing, just one man.

Yet in the little dugout something had been missing. And here the gap was filled. Ordinary, simple, unshaming human activity. Openhearted, meditative communion with the darkness, with the rain, with all nature. Your whole body welcoming the world about you.

Sanya just stood there. Getting used to the darkness. Letting the rain fall on him. Letting it pepper his cape.

He took a couple of steps on the slippery ground. A few gleams of light from deep-set dugout windows met his eye.

A flare soared up. A dark red one. The Germans. Because the opposing trenches were so close they often put up flares at night. The Russians didn't. They were being economical.

The flare soared upward, opened out in a claret-colored light (somehow the nastiest of reds), and carved out a sinister red segment in God's invisible but unchanging heaven. The segment moved across the sky, spreading its light over the Russian lines and three versts beyond, and revealing trees, shattered, mangled, but still standing.

The flare faltered, shuddered, fell. And was extinguished.

But the redness and the silhouettes of trees lingered on the retina. Sanya remained standing there, his face upturned to the steady rain. He was almost at peace.

A man walking in a forest can be heard a long way off. Squelching footsteps. Twigs snapping as the walker brushed against bushes.

Somebody was coming. But was slow in coming.

One man. Nearer now.

"Who goes there?" Sanya asked, not like a sentry challenging—there was one standing a little way off by a cannon—but firmly. ("Let's have no nonsense!")

"Friend. Father Severyan," a familiar voice said.

"Father Severyan?" Sanya was delighted. "This is a surprise. And a very pleasant one. This is Lazhenitsyn. Hello."

"Hello, Lazhenitsyn," the brigade chaplain said cordially.

"Have you lost your way?"

"I think I have."

"Come over here. Move toward my voice."

Splashing and squelching, the chaplain came up close.

"Where are you going so late, Father Severyan?"

"I'm trying to get back to HQ."

"But where are you going right now? You'll tumble into a ditch. Or land in a puddle up to your knee. Why don't you spend the night with us."

"I have to take a service tomorrow morning."

"Once it's light everything will be fine. But right now one of the sentries could easily take a shot at you. There's a spare place in our dugout."

"Is it really spare?" An unmilitary voice, this. None of the inflections we've all acquired. A weary voice too.

"Yes, really. Ustimovich is on duty. Give me your hand."

It was a cold, wet hand.

"All right, let's go. Have you come far?"

"From No. 2 Battery."

"Ah, ye-es." Sanya remembered. He hadn't made the connection . . . "They've had casualties?"

The priest caught his foot on something. "One man has died."

"Not Cheverdin?"

"Did you know him?"

[5]

Father Severyan had on a round cloth cap and a shapeless gray over-coat—both of a sort never worn in civilian life, but generally adopted by priests on active service—and knee boots. He was carrying a cane and a small grip containing the requisites of his office, which went everywhere with him.

Seeing the broad back and the bullet head of the sleeper on the upper bunk, he lowered his voice. "Is it all right? We might wake him up."

"Chernega? He won't wake up if a shell falls on the dugout."

The priest protested once again that he could easily get home. But when he saw that Sanya's urgings were not mere politeness, he took his cap off—it was soaked through—and his thick, wavy, black hair fell into place. His beard was just as thick, but clipped short.

He had his cap off, but before he surrendered it looked around the walls, the upper part of the dugout, in the corners. As is often the case in officers' dugouts, there were so many things hanging up he could not immediately find what he was looking for. Then he saw it: a little crucifix, the sort that would fit into the pocket of a tunic, hanging in a dark place on a corner post.

It was Sanya who had hung it there. He had found it lying on the ground in Poland during the retreat. Otherwise there might not have been one. That would have been rather embarrassing.

The priest crossed himself before the Catholic crucifix, then turned to Sanya and handed over his overcoat too. It was wet through and clung to his cassock. It cost Sanya an effort to pull it off.

"Oh dear, your cassock's wet too. Why don't you get in bed right away. I expect your legs are wet as well. I'll start the stove up, and it'll dry out in no time."

"Won't it be a nuisance?"

"Why should it be? We sleep twelve hours at a stretch in winter—just in case. That's your bed shelf—the one-and-a-halfer."

Father Severyan stopped standing on ceremony and admitted that he would like to lie down right away. It was obvious that he was not just tired but dejected and near the end of his tether.

The big pectoral cross on a metal chain weighed heavily on his strengthless hands as he laid it carefully on the table. He also took the little leather bag containing the elements of the host from around his neck. Sanya opened out the overcoat and cassock and hung them on pegs knocked into the lath wall.

Against his very white undershirt Father Severyan's black beard and hair looked still blacker, and his black eyes still deeper.

He lay down immediately, with his head high on the pillows, and half covered himself. But he did not close his eyes.

Sanya happily started lighting the stove. Thanks to Tsyzh it was not much trouble: he had left ready separate heaps of kindling, thin sticks, thicker sticks, dry wood, damper wood. And there was a stool for the stoker near the stove placed so that the flap would be on a level with his chest. The poker was in its place. And the ash from the last time the stove was lit had been raked out and carried away, so that there need be no dust. All that was necessary was to take a few pine splinters, set fire to them, place them so that the fire would travel upward along their rough surface, then carefully lean dry sticks against them, one after another. There was a crackling noise. The wood was catching.

In his present mood Sanya could not have had a more welcome guest.

Only the guest's mind was not on Sanya. His folded hands lay motionless on the blanket. His lips were slack: his eyes were not moving.

But even his silent presence had made a change. Somehow the ache was eased. The emptiness was less painful.

The wood crackled. Rain falling on the earth above cannot be heard through the roof of a dugout, even one with a window.

There was no gunfire.

Without rising from the stool Sanya removed the lid from the pail, ladled water into the burnished copper kettle, using a tin mug, moved aside the ring on top of the stove with the poker, and put the kettle over the open fire.

He put in more wood. The fire took hold boldly, cheeringly. The light through the stove door was brighter now than that from the kerosene lamp. A merry, youthful light. Chernega up above gave a sudden loud snore. Had he woken up? Should they invite him to join them? No, he just wrestled his chunky body onto the other side, and went on snoring just as resoundingly now that there was heat in the dugout as he had before.

The stove was well alight now, and beginning to roar.

Father Severyan gave a deep sigh. Another. And another. Finding relief in his sighs.

Sanya kept his eyes to himself, but he felt the priest's oblique gaze resting on him.

Yes, a gap had been filled. Solitude weakens a man. All it takes to brace him is another living soul at his side.

Father Severyan had been in the brigade less than a year. Though they had seen each other occasionally and exchanged a few words, they didn't really know each other. But Sanya was attracted by the priest's liveliness, his tirelessness, his dogged determination—he even insisted on learning to ride a horse—his eagerness to fit in with the brigade.

The priest sighed again, this time a sigh not of weariness but of suffering.

"It's hard," he said. "Trying to give the last rites to someone who doesn't need you. When the dying man answers, 'What last words of comfort can you give me when you yourself are without grace?' "

Sensing that to look around would be an intrusion, Sanya kept his eyes on the stove. It was hard, all right, the priestly office in an age of unbelief; forcing yourself on someone who perhaps didn't want to know you, to hear his confession and remit his sins. Trying to find appropriate words without lowering the dignity of the rite. And if you were rebuffed you would have to return to the charge, begin your exhortations all over again, as earnestly as before.

"Cheverdin was an Old Believer."

"Ah, so that was it." That explained a lot. He immediately saw Cheverdin in his mind's eye, a tall man with a dark red beard, and understood the look of complete self-sufficiency in his eyes: he was one of those peasants who knew. Sanya could easily imagine how those eyes would repulse the priest.

"He refused to confess or take communion. Said I was in his way . . ."

As bad as that.

What, though, was a priest to do? Give up? He had no right to. Compromise? A priest must always be superior to other people or where would he find strength?

The priest continued in a desolate voice. "To Muslims we send a mullah. But to our own Old Believers, the most Russian of Russians, we send nobody, they must do without. The popovtsy do have one priest—one for the whole Western Army Group. We lay claim to their bodies, through the recruiting officer, to defend Russia. When it comes to that we take them to our bosom. But their souls we treat differently."

Scarlet light flickered from the half-closed door of the stove. Sanya stared into the leaping flames and could not take his eyes away. If they refuse communion—burn them: that was Sofia's decree. If they take communion under protest—burn them afterward. Lower jaws were wrenched open and the "true" host stuffed down throats. For fear of weakening, of accepting the sacrilegious element, they had sometimes set fire to themselves. We shoved what had been our own church books into the fire with them—how could they help thinking that we were servants of Antichrist? How can we wriggle out of this situation? Who can mend it with words?

Sanya glanced at the priest. His eyes were shut. Even his strength had its limits. It was lucky that he had stumbled into a bed for the night.

Sanya put more wood on, and leaned back from the stove.

When he had lived in Moscow he had visited the Old Believers' cathedral. Crossing the road to get to the church, you were struck by the prosperous and important look of the heavily bearded men, by the stern brows of the women, and by the seriousness of the adolescents. They looked as they would have three centuries ago, their staidness belonged to an earlier age, but with it went an openheartedness, a welcoming warmth. On Whitsunday the cathedral was a sea of white, as though it was full of angels: the women stood apart, and all together, wearing identical smooth white dresses with an unusual silvery sheen. The iconostasis had no incrustations, no rizas, no scrollwork, it was all of a piece, austere and brown, you were meant only to pray and humble yourself before your Saviour's brilliant eye. As for the singing, you couldn't say that it was as beautiful as in a reformed Orthodox church—but when the bearded men in kaftans boomed, it touched you to the quick. Two immense chandeliers, one with lamps, the other with candles, hung from the vaulted ceiling, and suddenly an enormously tall ladder moved from one side of the crowd as though to besiege a fortress, and a church servant in a black cassock climbed heavenward carrying a candle. Up in the heights he crossed himself and began lighting candles one by one, hovering almost horizontally over some of them, stretching upward to reach others with difficulty.

Then slowly, slowly, he set the cumbersome chandelier turning. When the service ended he would climb up again and snuff the candles one after another. No instantaneous blaze of electric lighting for them. But throughout the cathedral three thousand people would cross themselves or bow to the ground at one and the same moment. Making you feel that "we are transient—they will not pass away."

The stove was purring, glowing cherry red, filling the dugout with a cozy warmth. What more could they ask for than that space shut off by beams and laths? The wet clothes along the walls were beginning to dry out. The guest had no need to pull the blanket over his chest and his shoulders. The black growth framing his head stood out against his very white undershirt. Lying on his back, he looked like a sick man, if not a dying man, himself.

"I've been among them," Sanya said. "Talked to them."

Imagine how they felt: what they saw yawning before them was not an abyss, not a bottomless pit, but a narrow, crooked, dark crack in the ground with heaps of corpses down below and an unclimbable broken cliff above. Their faith had been their whole life—and suddenly the faith was changed. At one time the sign of the cross with three fingers was anathema, now only the three-fingered sign was correct and the two-fingered anathema. Wasn't it a matter of simple addition: the millennium plus 666, the number of Antichrist, gives 1667—and the Council that anathematized them met in the 1667th summer from Christ's birth. Then the Orthodox Tsar, Alexis the Meek, bribed the Mohammedan Sultan to reinstate the deposed and nomad patriarchs, and so made doubly sure that one group of Orthodox Christians would trample others underfoot. And did he who with Mordvin savagery laid hands on the icons in the Kremlin cathedral and smashed them—did he yet remain Patriarch of Russia? The indifferent and the mercenary could endure it all without pain—reverse the curse tomorrow if you like. But those whose hearts ached for truth—they would not consent, they sought refuge in the forest, they were marked for destruction. It was not just promiscuous slaughter—the blow was aimed at the best of the people. And as if this were not enough—Peter's crushing weight fell upon them. It is not hard to understand them: "Cut off our heads, but don't touch our beards!"

"They believe what they were taught to believe when Russia was first baptized—how then can they be called schismatics? Suddenly they are told the beliefs held by your grandfathers and your fathers and you yourselves till now are incorrect. We shall change them."

The priest raised his eyelids. He said, using as little voice as he could, "Nobody tried to change the faith. They changed the rite. That is subject to change. Stubbornness in matters of detail is obscurantist."

The second lieutenant, though not very sure of himself, said, "Yes, but reformist tinkering with details is small-minded. There is much virtue in rigidity. In our age, when so much is changing, so much being turned upside down, stubbornness seems to me a precious quality."

Surely, spelling the name of Jesus ("Iisus") with one *i* ("Isus"), saying two "Alleluias" instead of three, and walking around the lectern from the "wrong" side did not threaten Orthodoxy with collapse. Was it for this that so much of what was best, strongest, and most vital in Russia had been driven into the fire, into the underground, or into exile? While informers were paid with the proceeds from the sale of confiscated estates and shops? A closer eye should have been kept on earlier translators and copyists and if, even so, a few errors crept in—well, let them.

The quiet second lieutenant, with his light brown hair dangling over his brow, was as agitated as if it had all happened that very day, and in their brigade.

"My God, how could we trample the finest of our race into the ground? How could we ourselves pray and be at peace with God after we had torn down their chapels? And cut out their tongues and cut off their ears! And we refuse to this day to acknowledge our guilt! Don't you think, Father Severyan, that until we ask forgiveness of the Old Believers and are reunited with them Russia can expect nothing good?"

He was as deeply troubled as though destruction was imminent, wafting through the night like a wave of choking, greenish gas.

"My own belief is that there was no schism. Maybe there will be no reunion in our lifetime, but in my heart it is as if all were united. If they will let me approach without cursing me, I will enter their church with the same feelings as I enter my own. What sort of Christians are we if we are divided against one another? Where Christians are divided, no one is a Christian. It makes no sense."

They heard the rumble of several explosions at a distance, but so heavy that the shock waves reached them through the ground. Further confirmation that it was too late, that Christians were already tearing each other to pieces.

Raised up on his pillows (Ustimovich had a stack of them), the priest turned his head and looked sadly at Sanya.

"Is there any country in which religion has not broken down? It has in all of them, in one way or another. In the last four centuries especially, mankind has moved steadily away from God. Every nation in its own way—but the trend is the same everywhere. For centuries past, the infernal power has writhed like an insidious fog over Christendom. That is why Christians are divided against one another."

At that point the kettle started singing, and steam billowed from it. Tsyzh's brew was ready. The teapot had been washed out. Everything was at hand. The mug was earthenware—not too hot to drink from. And there was cherry essence from the brigade shop.

"No, no, don't get up whatever you do, Father Severyan. I'll bring it to you!"

The priest, half reclining on his side, took the tea from a stool moved up to his bedside and began sipping. His strength seemed to return to him almost with the first gulp.

"Yes, I've let things get me down a bit today."

Sanya had moved his own stool closer to the priest's bed, he could have reached out and touched him. He spoke down at him.

"In a general way, Father Severyan, I think that the laws of individual lives and those of large foundations are similar. An individual cannot escape paying for a grave sin, sometimes in his own lifetime, and still less can a society, or a people—they will pay in time. Everything that has happened to the church since . . . from Peter to Rasputin . . . Maybe it's a punishment for our treatment of the Old Believers?"

"So what are we to do now? Exterminate ourselves? The Church did not end with Nikon."

"But the Church cannot base itself on injustice." Sanya finished in a whisper, as though keeping it secret from the sleeping Chernega, or perhaps even from the man he was talking to.

The priest answered with great assurance: "Christ's Church cannot be sinful. The hierarchy can make mistakes, yes." He sounded so sure of it, as though it was a lesson learned by heart.

"Now that's an expression I simply can't understand. Is the Church as such never to blame for anything? Protestants and Catholics butcher each other, we butcher the Old Believers—and you say the Church is without sin? And we, each and every one of us, who have lived and died in the past three centuries, are we not the Russian Church? I say we are. Why can't we repent and admit that we have committed a crime?"

Many such tangential thoughts had occurred to Sanya in his short life, while he was arguing or reading. They did not all meet at a single point but left a crooked triangular island on which the Church, undermined, barely stood.

And when the state later on relaxed its persecution of the Old Believers, the Church itself grew harsher and badgered the state—to make it harsh again.

"And where did the Church end up? Where it is now—the state's captive. But the Church is the hardest of prisoners to understand. It has declared all earthly ties transitory. Why then allow itself to be bound hand and foot?"

The priest peered at him closely. "Is all this your own idea, or . . . ?"

Sanya nodded. "Yes, or . . . I did actually start thinking like this in the upper classes at high school. But we have a lot of different sects in the North Caucasus, and I visited several of them and learned a great deal. All sorts of theories and rival interpretations. I used to go to the Dukhobors in particular. And I read Tolstoy a lot. I got most of it from him."

"Yes, of course." The priest smiled as he saw the connection. "Tolstoy, that's obvious. But what were your own family? Were they Dukhobors, or Old Believers? What are you?"

Sanya smiled shyly, apologetically. He made a helpless gesture. He didn't know himself.

"No, I couldn't just sit over the bread and salt like the Dukhobors. And I'm no Tolstoyan. Not now. I don't accept that Christ's teaching is a recipe for a happy life on this earth. Why should anybody think that? Or that love is dictated by reason. What sort of love? I wonder."

Sanya found it difficult to go fast when he was trying to work out a problem, in contrast to expressing firm and deeply felt views. His words came slowly and hesitantly, irritating impatient students and martinet officers. He spoke like that because, however long a thought had been in gestation, at the moment of utterance it would still not be fully mature, and might prove false after all. Uttering a thought was his way of verifying it.

"Besides . . . Tolstoy is much too sweeping in his rejection of everything that . . . The faith of ordinary people, of my parents say, of our village, of everybody who . . . Icons, candles, incense, the blessing of the water, communion bread . . . He rejects them all, he leaves us nothing . . . Or take the singing that rises up to the dome . . . and the incense smoke up there is streaked with rays of sunlight . . . Those little candles—people put them there with a full heart, and with their thoughts on heaven. For my part I love all this, and have since I was a child. Or take Rogozhskoye—that service, would he be so nonsensical as to say that it's all a show, something we've arbitrarily tacked on to Christianity? . . . That's piffle. But what I felt most keenly of all is what he says about the cross. Tolstoy tells us not to regard representations of the cross as sacred, not to bow down to it, not to put it on graves, not to wear it. Such insensitivity! I can't go along with that. You know the saying—a grave uncensed is just a black hole. And it's even truer of a grave without a cross. No cross? Where there's no cross I get no feeling of Christianity."

He listened carefully to his own ringing phrases, checking for false notes.

"I tried following Tolstoy's advice at one time, and forbade myself to make the sign of the cross. But I can't help it, my hand moves automatically. If I didn't cross myself while I was praying, the prayer would seem incomplete. Or when death comes flying, whistling through the air—my hand makes the sign of the cross involuntarily. What could be more natural when it might be the last thing you do on this earth? . . . I have this feeling that I didn't have to learn to cross myself, that it was there inside me before I was born."

Father Severyan beamed affectionately. If only one in twenty Russian students responded to the aura of the Church ritual as something above rational analysis, the faith was not yet lost in Russia!

"Did it ever occur to you that Tolstoy was not a Christian at all?"

"Not at all?" Sasha was stumped. His jaw dropped.

"Just read his books. *War and Peace*, say. He takes on 1812, an epic year in the life of a devout people, and who ever says a prayer in the hour of need? Princess Maria—but who else? Can you believe that those four volumes were written by a Christian? He found plenty of room for Freemasonry—but for Orthodoxy? None at all. I know that he did not leave the Orthodox Church in later life—but then he was never in it. Churchgoing was not part of his childhood training. He was a regular product of our freethinking gentry class. And he was not single-minded and humble enough to adopt the faith of the peasants."

Sanya held his brow with five fingers, as though palpating it.

"I never thought of it like that." He sounded surprised. "What makes you say so? Isn't his interpretation true to the gospels? By now, haven't we utterly forsaken the gospels? We recite the commandments without hearing them. But everybody heard them when he spoke. Strip away all the incrustations on Christ's teaching, he told us. He was right. How can we commit acts of violence and still call ourselves Christians? We are told not to take oaths—but we do. Our excuse, in effect, is that Christ's commandments cannot apply to ordinary human life. But Tolstoy says no, they can be applied. How can you say, then, that his is not a pure version of Christianity?"

Father Severyan had recovered from his despondency, the life had returned to his face, and now that he was feeling better he answered readily, as though this solitary lieutenant was precisely the audience he had long been awaiting.

"How sadly our conception of the faith must have declined for Tolstoy to look like an outstanding Christian! He pulls out a verse of the gospels here and a verse there and displays them on his hawker's tray ... The arguments that earn him such enormous popularity are those of a schoolboy. The fact is that his criticism of the Church was grist for the mill of our educated public. True, the teaching he offers society is useless—society could not exist on that basis. But the liberal public didn't care about his teaching, his spiritual quest, it had no use for religion, reformed or unreformed. No, Tolstoy appealed to its political passions! See how the great writer trounces state and church! Fan the flames! Educated society never read any of the philosophers who replied to Tolstoy."

"We-ell, I don't know." Sanya was dazed. "How can it be the pure doctrine of the gospels, and not Christianity?"

"Why, Tolstoy discarded two-thirds of the gospels! Simplify the gospels! Reject all that is unclear! He simply creates a new religion. His 'closer to Christ' means 'bypass the evangelists.' It's as much as to say:

since I'm to be your fellow believer, I'll start by reforming this two-thousand-year-old faith! He imagines that he is a discoverer, but he's just going down the slope with society and dragging others with him. He reproduces the most primitive variety of Protestantism. We'll take the ethical element from religion, why not—even the intelligentsia agrees with that. But morality can be implanted in a race even by blood feud. Morality is a set of schoolboy rules, the underside of God's far-sighted dispensation."

It was evidently not the first time Father Severyan had found himself discussing these matters, and he was obviously no ordinary priest.

"Tolstoy was moved by pride. He was unwilling to humble himself and adopt the common faith. The wings of pride carry us over seven icy abysses. But there is something just as important as developing our own individualities, and that is standing among the lowly and the ignorant, rubbing shoulders with them, pressing our fingers, the fingers of the elect, to the same stone floor on which others have just walked in street-stained shoes—yes, and pressing our wise foreheads to it. Waiting our turn to take communion from a spoon touched by the lips of others, some healthy, some perhaps sick, some clean, some perhaps not. One of the greatest spiritual accomplishments is knowing how to humble yourself. To remind yourself that for all your gifts and for all your prowess you are only God's servant, no whit superior to others. No ethical system is a substitute for this accomplishment—the practice of humility."

"That we must humble ourselves—I agree completely."

"But Tolstoy is forever seeking God, whereas God, you might say, is really in his way. What Tolstoy wants to do is save people without any help at all from God. When he took up preaching, something seemed to happen to him: all the things in this world that elude reason, the things that govern our lives and give us strength, things that he knew when he was writing novels—he seemed suddenly to lose his feel for them. How wretchedly earthbound is his exposition of the Sermon on the Mount! It's as though he has completely lost his intuition. Here is a great artist—and he does not touch on the immense universal design, or God's intense concern for each and every one of us! Worse—he rejected it all as irrational. Our own immortality, our participation in the divine essence—he rejected it all."

Father Severyan had raised himself from his pillow in his animation and his eagerness to pursue the argument. His eyes were bright and steady. He had dragged himself to this dugout on reluctant legs and with a faltering heart, and even here he was doomed to get no rest.

"There must have been times when he was appalled to find himself so helpless and insignificant. To feel himself so weak, so impotent, so much in the dark. When there is no strength left for independent action—with what strength is left we try to pray. We want only to pray, to take in the strength that flows in abundance from the Almighty. And if we succeed in it, it is as though our hearts are flooded with light, and our powers return. And we realize the meaning of the words 'preserve and pardon us with thy grace!' Do you know that state of mind?"

Sanya, on his stool, nodded. "That was my state of mind when I met you today. In fact, I was hoping to meet someone . . . I didn't know it was you . . . I do often feel that I lack the strength even to think about things."

There was a loud burst of machine-gun fire. The noise came from the outer trenches, but in the cold and rainy night they heard it very clearly. Somewhere down there a couple of dozen large rounds flew over to burrow into the ground, riddle planks, lodge in beams, and perhaps wound somebody, although these stupid shots in the night were meant mainly just to scare.

How had he come to be wearing epaulets and giving orders: "No. 2 gun, volley-fire!"

"Why did you never come and see me?"

"I told you about it. At confession once. But I don't think you understood me."

[6]

"At confession? When was that?"

"In Lent. You'd only just joined us."

"Ah, that's probably the reason. I've got a poor memory for faces and I see new ones all the time."

The second lieutenant wasn't finding it any easier now. It was like making his confession all over again.

"I complained to you . . . that I found fighting difficult. I told you I'd joined up without waiting to be drafted. I could have finished my university course. But I volunteered. Which means that I voluntarily took all the sins and murders committed here upon myself."

"Yes, yes, yes!" Father Severyan had remembered. "Of course! It was the only confession of that sort I heard from an officer, and I wouldn't have missed it for anything. We'd have gone on from there if it hadn't been in my first few days. Absolutely everybody was coming to confess—it was Passion week. But why didn't you come again?"

"I had no way of knowing that it had made any impression. I thought maybe others talk like that and you were a bit bored with it all. Or maybe there was no answer. The main thing was that you gave me absolution for my sin and my doubts—but I hadn't absolved myself. It all came back to plague me again. Should I have gone back to you? A second and a third time? To repeat what I'd already said, in the very same words—as if I was rejecting the absolution you'd given me? And even if you didn't reproach me, what could you do? Only repeat: 'I, an unworthy priest, by the authority given to me by God . . .' And I would be answering back, as you covered my head with your robe: 'No, don't forgive me, it won't help!' In confession there's no avoiding it: you have to pardon me in the end." He looked at the priest quizzically. "Couldn't you not forgive me? If I'm to bear the very same burden tomorrow, because you can't relieve me of it, don't forgive me! Send me away unrelieved. That would be more honest. How can I ever relieve myself of it while the war goes on? I can't. The fact that I can't see the people I'm killing doesn't change matters. I wonder what the final score will be. And how I shall justify myself? The only way out is for me to get killed. I don't see any other."

Father Severyan followed closely the movements of Sanya's mind and his eager interest showed in his mobile young features.

"Well, you know, in the ancient Church warriors returning from a campaign were not immediately absolved. They were made to do penance first. But there is another way out: change your ideas."

"I've tried. Tried to see things simply. Like all the others, like Chernega, for instance. He fights—and is cheerful about it. I tried to do the same. For several months. It didn't work. You bombard the enemy and get no answer. It's Cheverdin who gets the answer."

The priest wasn't at all put out by the second lieutenant. His keen gaze searched the features of his slow-spoken companion.

How unusual it was to meet such a person among the officers of this brigade (most of them regulars, following their vocation formally, shamefacedly or laughingly)—and a student at that. Such people were even more unusual among students. Back home in Ryazan, Father Severyan's activities were conducted in a murky atmosphere of ridicule and contempt created by the whole educated stratum of society— contempt not just for him but for the whole Orthodox Church. Repulsed by their contempt, he, who came from the same sort of family and the same cultured milieu, was driven back toward the ignorant and uneducated petty bourgeois who still thickheadedly saw some sense in lighting candles and going to church instead of reading newspapers and attending theaters and lectures. Father Severyan did not blush for his calling and his costume, and would have been content to remain with the educated stratum to which he belonged, but he was forced out of it. He had had to come all the way from the Ryazan diocese to the front line to hear a student talk like this.

But Sanya went on bitterly. "Besides, the way I look at it, Father Severyan, since we're in the same brigade and your job is to contribute to the success of Russian arms, there's little comfort you can give to me. You are too involved in it all, and—forgive me for saying so—

may be sinning yourself. You distribute amulets, and make sure every last man has one around his neck. You carry the cross along the trenches before an attack, and sprinkle the men with holy water. Or you take an icon around the dugouts for tomorrow's corpses to kiss. Priests have been known, when there are no officers left, to jump at the chance of relaying their regimental commander's battle orders. But the most dreadful thing of all is when a service is held in the field, and the candles are placed on pyramids of four rifles leaning together."

Father Severyan did not lower his head. Father Severyan did not avert his eyes. He listened attentively to the second lieutenant's re-proaches, even urging him on with expressive movements of his eye-brows, asking for and welcoming more of the same.

"I realize that you did not come here of your own free will, that you were sent."

"You're mistaken. It was my idea."

"Yours?"

"Well, what about you? Priests aren't drafted. Either they volunteer or their diocese sends them to fill an official quota. But a diocese will keep back those it thinks best, and send the dross to the army in the field: the weak ones, those who have been convicted of offenses, po-litical undesirables. Though I myself might well have been included in the last category because of my reformist ideas. But I didn't wait for that, I volunteered. I actually thought that this was the more natural place for me to be in time of war."

"For most men, yes." The second lieutenant still wasn't convinced.

"For a priest too," the priest insisted with the stubbornness he had shown in learning to ride. "Life as it is must be our field of action."

It was strange to hear a priest speak like that. Something along the lines of "Love those who hate you" is what you would have expected. The second lieutenant smiled and murmured, "The overturned cart."

"What?"

"I think the same, just the same. But you . . . Your position is a special one, a delicate one. Can a priest voluntarily go to war?"

Father Severyan propped himself up higher, on his elbow. His eyes blazed.

"Isaaki . . ."

"Filippovich."

"Isaaki Filippovich!" All that he had not managed to say at confes-sion came tumbling out in one breath. "At no time has the world been without war. Not in seven or ten or twenty thousand years. Neither the wisest of leaders, nor the noblest of kings, nor yet the Church— none of them has been able to stop it. And don't succumb to the facile belief that wars will be stopped by hotheaded socialists. Or that rational and just wars can be sorted out from the rest. There will always be thousands of thousands to whom even such a war will be senseless and unjustified. Quite simply, no state can live without war, that is one of the state's essential functions." Father Severyan's enunciation was very precise. "War is the price we pay for living in a state. Before you can abolish war you will have to abolish all states. But that is unthinkable until the propensity to violence and evil is rooted out of human beings. The state was created to protect us from violence."

The second lieutenant seemed to have risen slightly from his seat without leaving it and his face shone brighter although the stove was no longer red-hot and the lamp was burning with an even flame. Father Severyan kept his mind fixed on the same thought, resisting any temptation to digress.

"In ordinary life thousands of bad impulses, from a thousand foci of evil, move chaotically, randomly, against the vulnerable. The state is called upon to check these impulses—but it generates others of its own, still more powerful, and this time one-directional. At times it throws them all in a single direction—and that is war. So then, the dilemma of peace versus war is a superficial dilemma for superficial minds. 'We only have to stop making war and we shall have peace.' No! The Christian prayer says "peace on earth and goodwill among men." That is when true peace will arrive: when there is goodwill among men. Otherwise even without war men will go on strangling, poisoning, starving, stabbing, and burning each other, trampling each other underfoot and spitting in each other's faces."

Meanwhile, carefree Chernega, who knew nothing of such problems, was snoring up above—the only sound to be heard anywhere on the Russo-German front.

The stove was no longer crackling. The coals were glowing noiselessly.

Father Severyan's ready answer flowed effortlessly.

"War is not the vilest form of evil, not the most evil of evils. An unjust trial, for instance, that scalds the outraged heart, is viler. Or murder for gain, when the solitary murderer fully understands the implications of what he means to do and all that the victim will suffer at the moment of the crime. Or the ordeal at the hands of a torturer. When you can neither cry out nor fight back nor attempt to defend yourself. Or treachery on the part of someone you trusted. Or mistreatment of widows or orphans. All these things are spiritually dirtier and more terrible than war."

Lazhenitsyn rubbed his brow. One of his ears, that nearer to the stove, was burning. He rubbed his brow, feeling somewhat easier, but still examining the priest's words fastidiously. He could never answer quickly, or in monosyllables.

"Not the vilest form of evil? But the most wholesale form. The victims of individual murders, or individual miscarriages of justice, are individuals . . ."

"Multiplied by thousands! There are just as many of them. Only they are not assembled in one place in one short period of time, like those killed in war. Think of the great tyrants—Ivan the Terrible, Biron, Peter. Or—yes—the reprisals against the Old Believers. No need for war there—they were effectively suppressed without it. Over the years, and counting all countries, the sum of suffering is no less without war than with it. It may even be greater."

Lazhenitsyn was livening up. Brightening. And the priest spoke with even greater ease, beginning to look his own age, thirty-five or thirty-six, again.

"The real dilemma is the choice between peace and evil. War is only a special case of evil, concentrated in time and space. Whoever rejects war without first rejecting the state is a hypocrite. And whoever fails to see that there is something more primitive and more dangerous than war—and that is the universal evil instilled into men's hearts— sees only the surface. Mankind's true dilemma is the choice between peace in the heart and evil in the heart. The evil of worldliness. And the way to overcome this worldliness is not by antiwar demonstrations, processions along the streets with signs bearing slogans. We have been granted not just one generation, not just an age, not just an epoch, to overcome it, but the whole of history from Adam to the Second Coming. And throughout history our combined forces have failed to overcome it. You could rightly reproach neither the student nor the priest who voluntarily joined the fighting army—they naturally went where so many others were suffering—but those who do not struggle against evil."

But did Sanya mean to reproach anyone? Himself, yes—but no one else. He was thinking it over, easier in his mind but still uncertain, afraid to step too hastily on this new and crucial terrain.

An idea so wide-ranging would need lengthy consideration. But he would risk one obvious objection: "Does any of this make murder in battle more forgivable than murder with malice aforethought? Or murder by a torturer, or a tyrant. It's just that here we have a ritual, it's made to look like a matter of routine—'everybody else is doing it, I can't be the odd man out'—and this ritual deludes us. Gives us a false reassurance."

"Yes, but if you think about it, a ritual has to have some sort of basis in reality. Nobody has yet made a ritual of killing the defenseless. In fact, torturers sometimes go mad. There is no folklore about torture chambers, about unjust courts, about the general disharmony. But about war—there's no end of it! War divides, yes—but it also creates comradely union, it calls on us to sacrifice ourselves—and how readily men answer the call! When you go to war, you risk being killed yourself. Say what you like, war is not the greatest of evils."

Sanya was thinking.

Father Severyan gave him time to reply. He expected objections, but heard none.

If you knew Sanya you would know that it was difficult to change his mind, that he would never hastily adopt new beliefs and was slow to part with old ones. But when he did yield to an argument he seemed pleased rather than resentful. He was thinking it through carefully, so as not to make a mistake. There was a pause for reflection in every sentence.

"What you say . . . comes as a surprise to me. I hadn't thought enough about it. It's a great relief. But everybody should be told about these things. Nobody knows about them."

He opened the stove and stirred the fire. In the warm light of the glowing coals he was silent. The priest's arguments had hit home with him.

Chance, the quiet time of night, and like-mindedness had united them. There was probably no one else in the whole brigade for either of them to talk to.

"Yes, they need to be told."

Sanya again: "As it is, malicious people say that the Church sanctifies war. Anyway . . . forcing religion on young soldiers in barracks simply kills it." He stirred the fire and stared into the embers. "Anyway . . . Mankind has lapsed from Christianity as water trickles through the fingers. There was a time when Christians, by their sacrifices, their martyrdoms, their incomparable faith, did indeed command the spirit of humanity. But, with their quarrels, their wars, and their complacency, they lost it all. And it is doubtful whether any power could restore it to them."

"If you believe in Christ," the priest said, remote in the darkening depths, "you don't need to count his present-day followers. Maybe there are only two of us Christians left in the whole world. 'Fear not, my little flock, for I have conquered the world!' He has given us the freedom to go astray—and left us with the freedom to find our way home."

Sanya poked the fire.

"Ah, Father Severyan," he answered quietly, "there's no shortage of reassuring quotations, but things are pretty bad all the same." Sanya raked the coals into one last little heap. There was still a faint glow.

"And why, in this situation, when all the world is the loser, does every denomination insist on its unique and exclusive rightness? The Orthodox, the Catholics, and all the other Christians. They all say they're the only ones, they're superior. This can only accelerate the general decline."

Should one rage against the apostates, the doubters, the seekers who refused to find? Should one not rather marvel at the way in which the idea of God is awakened even in those whom the Good News has not reached? For thousands of years the earth teems with mean and trivial creatures—then suddenly, like a blinding light, comes the realization. Hearken, fellow men! All this did not come into being of itself! It was not created by our own miserable efforts! There must be someone up there above us! . . .

Sanya stared fixedly into the dying embers.

How could anyone suppose that the Lord would withhold the true faith from all the remote races? That throughout the whole history of the planet Earth only one small people in one small place would be allowed to see the light, then the neighbors apprised of it—and no one else? So that the yellow and black continents and all the islands would be left to perish? They had prophets of their own—were they not from the same, the one God? Were those peoples doomed to eternal darkness simply because they did not acquire from us our superior faith? Can a Christian really believe that?

"The one way for a religion to prove itself superior is to approach other religions without arrogance."

"Yes, but no creed can command belief without the assurance that it is absolute truth." There was a hint of steel in Father Severyan's voice. "The exclusiveness of my creed does not demean the beliefs of others."

"I . . . er . . . I don't know . . ."

In fact, any sect, once it has broken away, starts insisting that it has a monopoly of truth. Exclusiveness and intolerance have marked all the movements in world history. The one way in which Christianity could have surpassed them was to forswear exclusiveness and grow into a tolerant and receptive creed. To accept that we have not cornered all the truth in the world. Let us curse no one for his imperfection.

It was getting dark in the dugout.

God's truth was like "Mother Truth" in the folktale. Seven brothers rode out to look at her, viewed her from seven sides and seven angles, and when they returned each of them had a different tale to tell: one said that she was a mountain, one that she was a forest, one that she was a populous town . . . And, for telling untruths, they slashed each other with swords of tempered steel, and with their dying breaths bade their sons slash away at each other, to the death. They had all seen one and the same Truth, but had not looked carefully.

It was getting darker.

Outside, a loud, menacing noise warned of trouble to come.

It was . . . what do they call it? . . . that explosion . . . oh yes; an artillery shell.

[7]

(ORIGINS OF THE KADETS)

As two crazed horses harnessed together, but driverless, one pulling to the right, the other to the left, are bound to smash the cart, overturn it, drag it down a slope and perish with it, so did state and society, once mutual distrust, animosity, hatred had rooted and burgeoned in them, bolt and draw Russia toward the abyss. And there seemed to be no one with the reckless bravery to seize the reins and halt them.

Who now can say where and how it began? Who started it? Anyone who tries to halt the unbroken stream of history, take one cross section and say, "This is it! This is where it all begins!" will be proven wrong.

This irreconcilable hostility between the state power and society—did it really begin with the "reactionary" reign of Aleksandr III? Perhaps it would be truer to say with the assassination of Aleksandr II? Ah, but that was the seventh attempt—Karakozov's being the first—on his life.

We cannot possibly date the beginning of this hostility later than the Decembrist conspiracy. But was it not the same dissension that doomed Paul? Some people like tracing the rift to the time when Peter first made us substitute German attire for our Russian dress—and there is a lot to be said for their view. But why not go still further back, to the Church Councils of the seventeenth century? It is enough for our purpose to stop at Aleksandr II.

Why, at the first stirring of that program of gradual reform which was to be more comprehensive than the most farsighted could have prophesied (reforms forced upon him, our countrymen call them, as though there were actually any useful reforms that were not enforced by life itself), were they in such a hurry? "Young Russia," with its cry of "We can't wait for reforms," Chernyshevsky, the oracle of the age, summoning Russia to the ax, Karakozov with his flash in the pan? Why this coincidence, why did these people, so energetic, so sure of themselves, so ruthless, enter the Russian social arena in the very year that the serfs were set free? Who and what made them so sure that slow processes cannot change history, made them wreck gradual reform in their hurry to liberate by means of explosives?

To what was Karakozov's bullet the answer? Surely not to the liberation of the peasants, however late in the day it was?

Two years after Karakozov, the Bakunin-Nechaev alliance was sealed and there would be no more intermissions: the People's Will Party was crystallizing among Nechaev's followers.

Dostoevsky was the only one to ask them at the time why they were in such a hurry. Was it to frustrate at the outset Aleksandr's move toward a constitution? On the day of his assassination he approved the creation of reform commissions with zemstvo participation, and the terrorists had literally only a few days left to abort a Russian constitution.

In 1878, Ivan Petrunkevich tried in the Kiev discussions to persuade the revolutionaries not (of course) to renounce terror but to suspend the use of it: wait a while, stop shooting for a bit, and let us, in the zemstvos, openly and loudly call for reform. The answer came from St. Petersburg—Zasulich's shot at Trepov. Within a year the People's Will Party had matured, and in somebody's head the wording of a future ultimatum was already taking shape:

> Regicide is very popular in Russia. It is greeted with joy and sympathy.

The social atmosphere was becoming overheated, and no one dared cross the bombers any longer.

Without patient small print we cannot reach an understanding about the period of history stolen from us. We invite only selfless readers, in the first place our fellow countrymen, to follow us so far into the past. This quite voluminous and by now rather cold material may seem only tenuously connected with what is promised in the title *November 1916*, and it will be wearisome to any readers except those to whom the tense nineteenth century of Russian history is still alive and who can draw from it lessons for today.

FROM PREVIOUS KNOTS

November 1904

July 1906

What were they counting on? How could they expect to earn concessions from a monarch by killing his predecessor? The new ruler would have to be a spineless creature. No normal person can forgive the murder of a father. In fact, Aleksandr III did not sign a single important enactment in the thirteen years of his reign without remembering: my father gave them freedom, gave them reforms, and they killed him, so his path was the wrong one. It was tit for tat. In return for the bombers Russian society got the reactionary 1880s, got thrown back to the time before Sevastopol. Only then, by way of an answer, was the Okhrana established. (Not that it amounted to much by our standards!)

The group now planning the assassination of Aleksandr III (for 13 March 1887) explained its program as follows.

> Aleksandr **Ulyanov:** At the present time the Russian intelligentsia can defend its right to think only by terrorist means. Terror was created by the nineteenth century as the only form of defense to which a minority, strong only in its spiritual strength and the consciousness that it is right, can resort. I have given much thought to the objection that Russian society shows no sympathy for terror, and is indeed hostile to it. But that is a misconception.

And he was shown to be right ten to fifteen years later, when Russian society greeted an outbreak of terrorism as the coming of spring.

> **Osipanov:** Our hope is that if we apply terror systematically the government will give way. We hope by the use of terror to awaken an interest in domestic politics among the masses. The people are forming combat groups of their own to fight this or that body of oppressors, and gradually all of them will merge in a general uprising. Once it comes, we shall try as far as possible to limit the number of casualties and the violence.

Tit for tat. The Ulyanov-Osipanov group was formed in response to the breaking up of a meeting in memory of Dobrolyubov. (You can, if you like, go back to Dobrolyubov himself. He too breathed this poisonous hatred into the air about him.)

There was no lull in the expression of hatred with weapons for half a century afterward. And hapless Russian liberalism, caught between two fires, raced frantically from one to another, prostrating itself, dropping its spectacles, raising its head again, throwing up its hands, urging moderation, and generally making itself a laughingstock. Let us note, however, that liberalism was not an honest broker, it was not impartial, it did not react in the same way to shots and menaces from each of the two sides. It was not in fact really liberal. Educated Russian society, which had long ago ceased to forgive the regime for anything, joyfully applauded left-wing terrorists and demanded an amnesty for all of them without exception. Through the 1890s and the early decades of this century the rhetoric directed at the government by liberals grew more and more wrathful, but it was thought impermissible to reason with the revolutionary young, when they knocked their lecturers down and prohibited academic activity.

Just as the Coriolis effect is constant over the whole of this earth's surface, and the flow of rivers is deflected in such a way that it is always the right bank that is eroded and crumbles, while the floodwater goes leftward, so do all the forms of democratic liberalism on earth strike always to the right and caress the left. Their sympathies always with the left, their feet are capable of shuffling only leftward, their heads bob busily as they listen to leftist arguments—but they feel disgraced if they take a step to or listen to a word from the right.

Kadet liberalism (and liberalism the world over), if both of its eyes and both of its ears had developed evenly, if it had been capable of following a firm line of its own, would have escaped its inglorious defeat and its wretched fate (and might not have been labeled "rotten liberalism" by the left).

Nothing is more difficult than drawing a middle line for social development. The loud mouth, the big fist, the bomb, the prison bars are of no help to you, as they are to those at the two extremes. Following the middle line demands the utmost self-control, the most inflexible courage, the most patient calculation, the most precise knowledge.

* * *

The zemstvo, if you give the word its broadest meaning, is a social union of the whole population of a given district. More narrowly, it is a social union only of those who are connected with the land, those who own it or work it, and excludes town dwellers. In the Zemstvo Act of 1864, which was thought of at the time as a first step, the word was interpreted in the narrowest possible way, to mean local self-government for the most part by landlords.

Zemstvo work, however, was voluntary. The gentry did not enroll in large numbers, the self-interested saw nothing there for themselves, and so only those who were obsessed with social problems and a longing for justice went in for it.

Whether it was for this reason, or because, as the most eminent of zemstvo activists, Dmitri Nikolaevich Shipov, reminds us, common endeavor to achieve the common good, and not the championship of group or class interests, was traditional in Russia, the zemstvo ideal was something higher than the usual municipal concept: it was a matter not merely of local self-government but of furthering the demands of social justice, and gradually weakening the social injustices which had taken shape in the course of history. Members of the Zemstvo Union contributed to local funds in proportion to their income, but spent the money on the less well-off classes.

The zemstvo as originally established did not strike roots among the lower stratum of the population. There was no rural district zemstvo to become a genuine organ of peasant self-government. Nor did the institution extend outward to the non-Russian periphery or upward beyond the provincial level. The provinces had no legal right to form interprovincial or All-Russian associations. Growth in all these directions was, however, implicit in the reform of Aleksandr II, and given a period of patient, nonrevolutionary development, we might by the end of the nineteenth century have had, with the monarchy intact, a self-governing society, ethical in complexion, and free of party politics.

Alas, Aleksandr III, who thought he saw the seeds of revolution in any independent social activity, put the brake on most of his ill-thanked father's initiatives, and checked and distorted the development of the zemstvos: he made bureaucratic supervision more stringent and reduced the scope of their activity. Instead of gradually equalizing the rights of different social classes within the zemstvos, he aggravated class distinctions: enlarging the rights of the gentry, the educated section of which had turned away from the aristocracy, and leaving the peasantry, which alone could have been the natural prop of the monarchy, in its degraded situation, and even subject to corporal punishment. Even in those circumstances, the zemstvos remained faithful to the ideas of the Great Reforms—collaboration between progressive society and the traditional state power. Beset by constant suspicions of disloyalty, the zemstvos became ever quicker to take offense, and more and more adroit in evading, circumventing, and cunningly surmounting obstacles put in their way by the government. But society's hopes of gaining the understanding and cooperation of authority were not yet dead and cold, and the moment Nikolai II came to the throne many zemstvos turned hopefully toward him in their first loyal addresses. Zemstvo activists assumed that the young Tsar, unaware as he was of the mood of society, and unacquainted with the needs of the population, would eagerly accept their proposals and their memoranda.

Several such moments, when there was some chance of ending the mindless strife between the regime and society, of bringing them together in creative collaboration, twinkle like warm orange lights along Russia's path over a century. But for it to happen each side would have had to restrain itself and try to trust the other. The regime would have had to think: "Maybe there is some good in what society wants. Maybe there are things we don't know about our country." And society would have needed to think: "Perhaps the regime is not entirely bad. The people are used to it, it is firm in its actions, it stands above party, perhaps it is not its country's enemy, but is in some ways a blessing."

But no, in the life of states, even more than in private life, the rule is that voluntary concessions and self-limitation are ridiculed as naïve and stupid.

Nikolai II's celebrated reply was:

> Some people in zemstvo assemblies have let themselves be carried away by senseless dreams of participation by zemstvo representatives in matters of internal administration. I shall defend the principles of autocracy as firmly and unswervingly as did my late and unforgettable parent.

Any sort of association between zemstvo men from different provinces was considered illegal, so much so that Goremykin, appointed Minister of the Interior just before the coronation, forbade the chairmen of provincial zemstvo boards to discuss the pooling for a single charitable purpose of funds which would otherwise be wasted on presentations (the traditional "bread and salt," with silver tray and saltcellar) from all the zemstvos. As a great privilege the zemstvos were given permission to hold consultations in private apartments, provided that not a single word about these gatherings got into the press. (No small concession, however, by the standards of the 1970s.)

Sipyagin, as Minister of the Interior, tightened the screws of bureaucratic administration, for the good of his sovereign and of his country, and was killed by terrorists in April 1902. The intelligent martinet Pleve followed the same policy for two more years, until he too was killed, to swelling applause from the public. The Machiavellian Witte wound his serpentine way in and around them. Too shrewd a minister for that country, he understood everything, but would not take risks, or sides. He drafted a memorandum to the Tsar arguing that the zemstvo system was incompatible with autocracy: its theme seemed to be that the autocracy must not be undermined, but its hidden message was that autocracy must hold back self-government no longer. He was, however, thinking a hundred moves ahead: others could work it out for themselves, he wasn't going to put it in so many words.

The Russian regime entered the new century, the twentieth, with the same fixed and paralyzing idea—to halt the evolution of the country. As a result, it lost the respect of society, and aroused its indignation by absurd administrative procedures and the unreproved high-handedness of thickheaded local authorities. Measures to broaden the zemstvos' power were halted. The student disturbances of 1899 and 1901 set the regime and society at loggerheads: in the turbulent protests of the young, the liberals admired themselves as they might have been, though they had not stood their ground in their own day. Society chose to see the murder of the Minister of Education by a student (1901) as a symbol of justice, and the forcible enlistment of rebellious students in the army as a symbol of tyranny. Events of 1902 further exacerbated the discord between the regime and society: with the turbulent students now out on the streets, the energetic Pleve took advantage of Witte's deviousness to deprive the zemstvos even of their right to deal with the most basic local matters—he refused to let representatives of zemstvo assemblies take part in the "conferences on the needs of agriculture." His object was to keep out the zemstvo "third element"—the paid specialists employed by zemstvo boards, among whom many revolutionaries had indeed found employment—or, as Pleve called them,

> the cohorts of sansculottes and doctrinaires, second-rate bureaucrats whose style of work was perfected during their leisure periods in jail.

Nevertheless, it was natural for the zemstvos to feel wounded and alarmed: if they were excluded from discussion of essentially agricultural matters, would the zemstvos continue to exist at all? In May 1902, a gathering of leading zemstvo men took place in Shipov's apartment on Sobachya Square in Moscow—a private (and illegal) interprovincial conference. The resolutions adopted were very moderate and sensible: one to the effect that they would not boycott the government's provincial consultations but would find ways to connect them with the activities of the zemstvos themselves, and so mitigate the crude and clumsy behavior of the government. But the resolution pointed out that to solve the particular problems of agriculture, it was necessary to

> raise the personal status of the Russian peasant, equalize his rights with those of people of other classes, protect him with the correct type of court, abolish corporal punishment, and expand education. And also to make eligibility for membership in zemstvo assemblies independent of social class.

An immense backlog of work to be done blocked Russia's path into the new century. The long-suffering zemstvos did not insidiously seek to blow up the obstruction, but reached out workmanlike hands to dismantle it. Intelligent people concerned to change their country for the better know that a gradual approach is essential.

> **Shipov:** If you hope to succeed, you cannot refuse to take into account the views of those whom you are addressing. Before any reform can be carried out, not only must society at large realize the need for it but the state leadership must be reconciled to it.

Such were the views and the actions of the zemstvo men, but they still failed to persuade the regime. On Pleve's insistence, those who took part in the unauthorized conference at Sobachya Square were rebuked by the Tsar and warned that they might be forbidden to take part in any public activity. Needless to say, their request to be represented in preliminary discussions of draft legislation affecting local government (before it was submitted to the Tsar) was rejected. An Imperial Manifesto dated February 1903 promised to suppress

> unrest fostered in part by persons with designs inimical to our system of government, and partly by persons infatuated with ideas alien to the Russian way of life.

This was all that autocracy could promise: no accommodation! no hearing for its subjects, however well-intentioned! It alone, with no need for any popular assembly, helped only by its retinue of bureaucrats concerned above all to protect each other's privileges on every rung of the ladder, could determine Russia's real needs.

But the zemstvo, as it lost hope for the regime's goodwill, defended its own social philosophy all the more stubbornly. The interprovincial Zemstvo Union, though illegal, was gradually becoming a reality. Personal contacts made it easy for provinces and districts to adopt similar resolutions and petitions, and to make a similar show of intransigence, to the growing annoyance of the government.

Imperceptibly at first, and with no abrupt transition—as always at the headwaters of history—the zemstvo milieu changed its nature, it split into two unequal parts, a diffuse majority and a tiny minority. As time went on, the majority associated more and more with non-zemstvo elements in the municipal administrations, in the judicial system (in particular the barristers), and among the professional intelligentsia, joining with them in the broad grouping of "constitutionalists," and later, in July 1903, in the fascinating games of what was called the League of Liberation. If their activity was prohibited—it would have to be carried on illegally. And if all the revolutionaries could successfully organize in conspiratorial parties, why shouldn't liberals start a party of the same kind? But since they did not have to manufacture and store bombs, there was no need for them to abandon their normal way of life—no need to hide behind false names, to leave their comfortable homes, to go into exile, to endure the rigors of party discipline. Everybody who sympathized with the militant League was ipso facto a member of it, and no heavier demands were made on anyone. So that the whole of educated "society" was automatically part of the League, no formal admission being required. It cost the government no effort to discover the membership of the League, because everybody was a member. The League was illegal, yet virtually without concealment, known to everybody, and hardly to be considered criminal. Whatever they felt like saying that could not be said in Russian conditions was published abroad, and their journal, *Osvobozhdenie (Liberation)*, was freely distributed in Russia.

The non-zemstvo men were au courant with all Western socialist doctrines, trends, and resolutions, they read everything, knew everything, discussed everything, could very confidently criticize Russia and compare it with other countries. The one thing they lacked was the practical experience of government which would tell them what to do and how to build if it was suddenly their turn tomorrow (not that they showed any great eagerness for it). The zemstvo men proper were the only ones in Russia, apart from the Tsar's bureaucrats, who possessed long (though in their cases purely local) experience in administration and a penchant for it, the only ones who knew the Russian land and the broad Russian population and understood their needs. But it was the non-zemstvo men who, being nimbler and more sophisticated, acquired greater influence and set the course.

The League began with a three-word program: "Down with Autocracy!" That should unite everybody! They supposed that the whole mass of the illiterate common people was longing for political freedom. All we have to do is overthrow the monarchy—and then a magical, omniscient Constituent Assembly, composed of supermen, would give precise expression to the people's will and work out all the details. The reigning monarch must at once, before the Constituent Assembly met, be removed from all influence on the life of the state. The existing system was required not to restructure or improve itself, but simply to disappear. The Liberationists—that is to say, the majority of the Russian intelligentsia, its fine liberal flower—wanted no reconciliation with the regime. Their tactic was to seize every convenient opportunity to aggravate the conflict. They did not even try to discover whether anything in Russia's present and her existing institutions could be reformed and find a place in the future: it must all be lopped off and completely replaced. Their thoughts, and their theoretical studies, were on Constitution with a capital C; once introduced it would solve all Russia's problems.

A year went by, and it was seen that "Down with Autocracy" was a program with no appeal to either peasants or workers. So they worked out a broader program, hoping to attract those two groups with specific promises on matters affecting them, while the nation as a whole, which was assumed to be tormented with frustrated longing to participate in politics, was offered an assortment of intoxicating freedoms that would make this possible. They assembled under thirty headings all that was needed to construct a life on the best Western models. (Against which no reasonable argument can be found until you have experienced them in your own country and for yourself.)

"Down with Autocracy" was a principle that seemed to unite all those who wanted to join in. Russian radicalism (which went on calling itself liberalism) made common cause with all the revolutionary movements, and so could not condemn terrorism: indeed it censured those who censured terror. Russian radicalism adopted the principle that terror was justified if it was directed against the common enemy. All political disturbances, strikes, and the sacking of gentry estates were considered justified. Indeed, revolution itself was acceptable if it was needed to sweep away autocracy. It was, in any case, a lesser evil than autocracy.

The editor of *Liberation*, the prolific Pyotr Struve, had by then flirted with everything in sight, helped to found the RSDRP (and written its manifesto), discussed plans for *Iskra* with Lenin and Martov in Pskov, fallen out and in again with Plekhanov more than once—and now there he was printing in the organ of the free liberals his view that

> it is not too late for Russian liberalism to become the ally of social democracy.

Ah, but it was too late! The Second Congress of the RSDRP repulsed the liberal-Liberationists, leaving them deeply distressed and hurt. In October 1904, neither the Bolsheviks nor the Mensheviks went to Paris for the first (and last) conference of opposition parties, at which Milyukov, Struve, and Prince Dolgorukov, in accordance with the principle of solidarity with the revolutionary tendencies, sat in conclave with the SRs, Azef, and the defeatists, who were buying weapons with Japanese money and sending them to Petersburg to start an uprising, taking advantage of the war. (All means were good in the struggle with autocracy, so even if the money was known to be Japanese, why not take it?)

The imperial government was still in existence, but in the eyes of the Liberationists it might have ceased to exist. What they did not for a moment envisage was that between the regime and the population at large there were not only cruel differences but also a cruel bond: they were rowers in the same boat, and if it went to the bottom, they would all go with it. What the Liberation movement could not imagine and refused to imagine was the attainment of its ends by smooth evolutionary means.

But that was precisely the path to follow, the path which the zemstvo minority sought to follow. A fragile minority, but led by Shipov, who was chairman of the Moscow Provincial Board, and in effect the acknowledged leader of the as yet unfounded All-Russian Zemstvo. Other members included the two remarkable Princes Trubetskoy, and three future presidents of the State Duma.

Shipov's philosophy of life and his social program can be summarized as follows:

The purpose of life is not to assert our own will but to seek understanding of the principle that rules the world. Nevertheless, although the inner development of the person has priority over social development (there can be no genuine progress until the hearts and minds of the majority are changed), the systematic improvement of the forms of social life is also a necessary condition. These two processes should not be seen as in opposition one to the other, and no Christian has the right to be indifferent to the social order. Now, rationalism shows an exaggerated concern for man's material needs and neglects his spiritual essence. That alone made possible the emergence of a doctrine asserting that every social system is the natural result of a historical process, and so obviously does not depend on the good or ill will of particular persons, or the delusions and errors of whole generations, and that the main stimulus in social and private life is self-interest. The whole modern Western parliamentary system, with its political parties, their constant strife, their vote-chasing, and the constitutions which regulate the contest between them, stems from the assertion of private and sectional interests above all else. This whole system, in which legal forms are set above ethics, is beyond the pale of Christianity and Christian culture. The slogans of the people's sovereignty and the people's rights muddy the waters of human life. They incite people to involve themselves in the struggle to defend their rights, sometimes completely forgetting about the spiritual side of life.

On the other hand, it is wrong to attribute to Christianity the view that all power is of divine origin and that it must be humbly accepted in its existing form. State power is of terrestrial origin and bears the imprint of human wills, mistakes, and failures. State power exists everywhere, because human nature is weak, and man cannot do without an ordered form of life, without coercion. But the state power itself has its share of human weakness, and a large share, since power corrupts, and corrupts more thoroughly than ever when the ruler is spiritually weak. Power is fatally flawed. It can never rid itself of its inherent faults entirely, but only more or less. A Christian must therefore actively endeavor to improve the holders of power and the state system.

But the general good cannot be realized through the struggle of interests and classes. Rights and freedoms can only be assured by the moral solidarity of all. Importunate struggle for political rights, so Shipov believed, was alien to the spirit of the Russian people, and he was against involving them in the dangerous excitements of political struggle. The Russian idea from of old had been not to fight against authority but to work in unison with it, to order men's lives according to God's will. The Tsars of ancient Russia, who made no division between themselves and the people, were of the same mind.

"Autocracy" meant independence from other rulers, and certainly not arbitrary rule. Earlier monarchs sought not to impose their own will but to express the collective conscience of the people—and it was still not too late to revive the spirit of that older order. Shipov affirms that when the Assembly of the Land used to meet, there was never strife between it and the Tsar, and that there is no known instance of the Tsar acting contrary to the consensus: if he had parted company with the Assembly the Tsar would only have weakened his own authority. For a state in which rulers and ruled must above all aim at justice in their relations, instead of pursuing their own ends, Shipov believes that monarchy is the best form of government because a hereditary monarch stands above the clash of sectional interests. But the monarch must feel that there is something more important than his authority—the implantation on earth of God's justice. He must regard ruling as service to the people, and make sure at all times that his decisions accord with the collective conscience of the people as expressed through a popular representation. Such a system is superior to any constitutional system, because it envisages not strife between the Sovereign and society, not brawling between parties, but cooperation in the quest of the good. The zemstvo established by Aleksandr II, which embodied in itself a moral idea, was to be the institution to resurrect the Assemblies of the Land in a new form, to establish a "state plus zemstvo" system. And all this could be achieved by patient persuasion and in a spirit of mutual love.

It was, alas, a very difficult undertaking, for at the turn of the century those who held power in Russia had lost faith in themselves. And on the other hand,

> the supreme power cannot be expected to trust a society like this, devoid of moral force and incapable of cooperating with it. A negative attitude, both toward the faith of their fathers and toward the history, way of life, and outlook of their people, is predominant in educated society. The liberal course is as extreme and as false as that of the government. It is nonetheless possible to seek to eliminate and succeed in eliminating the distrust between the state and society, and to establish a lively reciprocity between them. The authorities must stop thinking that all spontaneous activity on the part of society undermines autocracy. The public must here and now begin to manage matters of local concern independently, and not be subject to bureaucratic arbitrariness and caprice. Measures proposed by government agencies should be open to public criticism before they are confirmed by the Sovereign.

And that was all he asked, to start with! Was it really so very much, Your Imperial Majesty? Shipov was not proposing a constitution, he was not calling for armed struggle, only for moral solidarity with the people. Surely the zemstvo men would have done no worse for their own localities than bureaucrats with no knowledge of the land issuing instructions from Petersburg.

Such were Shipov's thoughts and actions during his four terms of office in the zemstvo. Early in 1904 he was elected for a fifth term of three years. Such was his prestige, not only in the Moscow zemstvo but with the zemstvo movement throughout Russia, that in spite of the growing dissension and the schism in which it resulted, his opponents voted for him and invariably wanted him and no one else as chairman. (His spiritual purity, his considerate gentleness, his reasonableness, and his firmness charm even the modern reader of his unhurried pages.) Shipov tried to deal with Minister Pleve in the same spirit of receptive, loving kindness, and was first deceived by him, then subjected to harassment, the inspection of his correspondence, and subsequently nonconfirmation of his fifth term. Pleve called him pretender to leadership of an "All-Russian zemstvo" and said that his "activity in trying to widen the competence of the zemstvos and uniting them is politically damaging." In the spring of 1904, Shipov had no choice but to give up zemstvo work and withdraw to his estate at Volokolamsk. Then, on 28 July, Pleve was killed by a terrorist.

> This news had a depressing effect on me. It was always intellectually and emotionally inconceivable to me that anyone aspiring to reshape the frame-

work of our lives on principles of good and of higher truth could take the path of murder.

Struve, though, had prophesied long ago that

the life of the Minister of the Interior is ensured only insofar as there are technical difficulties in putting him to death.

With the murder of the intransigent Pleve, the hopes of the liberals flared up like a crimson solar eruption. There was rejoicing all over Russia, it was springtime in politics. But the Japanese war was still on—a war begun for no clear reason, alien, distant, and ignominious, so distant and so ignominious that the humiliations it caused had passed all bounds, that people began to welcome further humiliation, indeed longed for defeat, so that the bankrupt autocracy would have to make concessions at home. Those months saw the birth of the word "regime" (which in Russian has penal associations) instead of "state system," and in a theater in the capital the audience yelled at a ballerina, the mistress of the Navy Minister, Grand Duke Aleksei Aleksandrovich, "Out, out! You're wearing our battleships around your neck!" *Liberation*, addressing the military, said:

What we need from you is not senseless bravery in Manchuria but political courage in Russia; turn against your true enemy, he is in Petersburg and Moscow, it is autocracy.

Society no longer had any fear of authority (and we can see now that there was nothing for them to be afraid of). Speeches against the government were made at street meetings, and terrorists were thought of as "doing the people's work."

The government immediately lost heart, sagged, gave way, as though it had depended entirely on Pleve and had no self-propelled program (as indeed it had not), but looked only at the balance of forces: if you're holding your own, increase the pressure; if your hand is weakening, smile and give in. The revolutionaries, though, hissed that the liberal bastards would reap the benefit of revolutionary sweat and smother revolution with reform again.

A chance of agreement, like a warm point of light, flashed once more on Russia's path. In the summer of 1904, Prince Svyatopolk-Mirsky was appointed Minister of the Interior. He had little relevant experience and was not a strong character, but he declared sincerely in his very first speech in September that

the success of the government's labors depends on goodwill toward and trust in social institutions and in the population. Without mutual trust we cannot expect lasting success in reorganizing the state.

But that was exactly the program of Shipov and his minority! The minister's concession was seized on by the whole zemstvo majority. He was inundated with telegrams, and preparations for the long-planned general congress of prominent zemstvo men (mandated only by themselves) were immediately set in motion. Svyatopolk-Mirsky's pliability prompted the zemstvo men to ask for more than they had previously wanted: legal guarantees instead of promises from the new minister. The organizing committee of the Zemstvo Congress consisted entirely of constitutionalists, almost all of them members of the League of Liberation, and they voted against Shipov, a minority of one (in spite of which they asked him to continue acting as chairman), to withdraw the previously proposed diffident questions about the shortcomings of zemstvo institutions, the condition of the countryside, and educational policy, and instead to call for discussion of "the general condition of the state." The trusting Svyatopolk-Mirsky, on previous representation from Shipov, had asked the Tsar to permit a congress devoted to local questions, but now the congress was beginning to resemble the long-dreamt-of Constituent Assembly, and society fell silent in tense expectancy. The Tsar meanwhile was busy with military parades, and when Svyatopolk-Mirsky reported that he had made a mistake and was the innocent victim of deception, it was too late: a hundred zemstvo men were already converging on Petersburg. At the last moment they were reluctantly granted the status of a "private conference." They met on 6–9 November, in private apartments, changing and keeping secret their addresses, in spite of which the police politely stood guard over their gatherings and delivered telegrams from all ends of the country, even from political exiles. (Milyukov, back from the conference of defeatists in Paris, haunted the corridors with the program of the League of Liberation.)

Shipov did not decline to take the chairmanship. He hoped to have a pacific influence on a conference which started with the conviction that

> if proper foundations are not laid Russia will inevitably move toward revolution.

The abnormality of the present administrative system . . . society is excluded from participation . . . centralization . . . there are no guarantees to protect the rights of each and all . . . freedom of conscience, religion, speech, the press, association, assembly . . . inviolability of the home . . . independence of the judiciary . . . liability of officials to criminal prosecution . . . equalization of classes and national groups . . . Nothing in this list of demands from the program of the League provoked disagreement in the Zemstvo Congress. It was nonetheless split. Should it specify that the national assembly must have powers to legislate, to confirm the budgets, and to scrutinize the actions of the government (the majority view)? Or should it call only for an assembly that would participate in legislation, for which purpose the State Council would become a State-Zemstvo Council, and its bureaucratic membership would be replaced by persons chosen in pyramidal elections, beginning at rural district and ending at provincial level (the view of the minority)?

Shipov's arguments sound particularly interesting in our day, when we have all accepted the view of his opponents and regard direct and secret elections on an equal franchise as the acme of freedom and justice. Shipov points out:

> The national representation must express not merely the will of the majority of voters, formed fortuitously during the elections, but the real direction of the national spirit and the mind of society, so that the state, by basing itself on this, can acquire moral authority. To this end, the most mature forces of the nation, who would see their activity as a moral duty to put the country's life in order, and not as a mere display of popular sovereignty, should be brought into the representative body. In direct elections on a universal franchise the personalities of the candidates remain virtually unknown to the electors, who vote for party programs which they are not really able to understand, so that they actually vote for crude party slogans which appeal to selfish instincts and interests. It can only do harm if the whole population

is drawn into the political struggle. The assumption of the modern constitutional state that every citizen is capable of forming an opinion on all the matters which come before the national representation is in fact false. No, in order to deal with complex matters of state the members of the national representation must possess practical experience and a sound philosophy of life. The less enlightened a man is, intellectually and spiritually, the readier he is to resolve, confidently and lightheartedly, life's most complicated problems. The more highly developed a man is, intellectually and spiritually, the more cautious and circumspect he is in arranging his own private life and that of the community. The less experience of life and of matters of state a man has, the more susceptible he is to extremist political and social enthusiasms; the more knowledge and experience a man has, the more clearly he realizes the impracticability of extremist doctrines. Moreover, the national representation must bring to state affairs a knowledge of those local needs which require imminent attention in the country. The best school for all this is preliminary participation in local—zemstvo or municipal—self-government.

So, instead of direct elections on a universal franchise, modeled on the Western parliamentary system, Shipov proposed three-stage general elections unrelated to class, in which the electors would choose capable people well known to them. Rural districts would elect county zemstvo assemblies, counties would elect provincial assemblies, and provinces the All-Russian assembly. At each stage, special provision would be made for big towns, and the assembly would have the right to co-opt up to one-fifth of its total membership,

> so that very useful public figures not elected for fortuitous reasons—a greater number of worthy candidates than of places to be filled, unfavorable personal circumstances, etc.—would not be left out.

And at all stages the principle of proportionality would be observed, so that nowhere would the representatives of minorities be excluded or denied a hearing.

Next, ministers would be appointed by the Tsar, but from among the members of the representative assembly. The State-Zemstvo Council could address questions to them, but they would be responsible only to the Tsar. This meant, the majority retorted, that absolute monarchy would be preserved, and that the national representation would have only a consultative voice. Shipov's answer was:

> Yes, from a legalistic point of view—that is, if you think that the purpose of a national representative body is to limit the power of the Tsar. But if you bear in mind the close unity between them, if the monarch and the national representation bear the same burden of moral duty—how can the monarch fail to reckon with them? That being so, whether the national representation has a deciding or a consultative voice is a superfluous question.

Alas, there was no monarch of that sort in Russia in 1904, nor would her clamorous educated public have permitted the election of such representatives.

The reality is that the split within the Zemstvo Congress went deeper than the forms of election or the rights of the national representation, deeper than practical and organizational questions, right down to the roots of the two opposing philosophies.

Shipov was trying to show the majority that making rights and guarantees the basis of reform meant destroying, frittering away the religious and moral idea which was still intact in the mind of the people. In return, his opponents in the majority called him a Slavophile, although he did not recognize either the divine origin of absolutism or the superiority of Orthodoxy to other forms of Christianity—but it had become the custom half a century earlier (and remained so half a century later) to call anyone who chooses to deviate from direct imitation of Western models, anyone who assumes that Russia's path (or that of any other continent) might be peculiar to itself—a reactionary, a Slavophïle.

 When this schism took place in Vladimir Nabokov's apartment, those present did not fully realize its importance, but thought of it as a disagreement on one point out of a dozen. It was in fact a schism between zemstvo-constitutionalists and zemstvo men proper, between—if we want to use bad language—zemstvo-Bolsheviks and zemstvo-Mensheviks (one of history's little jokes seldom remembered by our historians). It differed, however, from the schism in the RSDRP, which had taken place two years earlier, in one respect: the majority in this case insisted on including the minority view in the final resolution side by side with its own. And also in that the majority (in effect the Kadet Party, though it did not yet think of itself in that way) wanted peaceful reform, wanted evolution.

Svyatopolk-Mirsky was given a memorandum about these desirable reforms.

> The present war has exposed the sores of our bureaucratic system even more thoroughly than the Crimean War . . . The old order is condemned in the judgment of man and of God . . . As at the time of the Emancipation, the government must take the lead, and not trail behind society.

There was, then, this one warm, inviting glimmer of hope. The congress had exceeded its mandate and its limits, but it almost seemed as though there was a second chance (the first was lost long ago) of concord between the public and the state. Svyatopolk-Mirsky, risking dismissal, confronted the Tsar with the need to initiate reforms, sincerely intending to follow through with them. And the Tsar seemed not to object. He was simply undecided. His usual distrustfulness and reticence prevented him from agreeing straight off.

In the meantime the zemstvo majority, flushed with success, raced around Russia talking of victory. They had now merged with the enraptured League of Liberation and, acting on its instructions from abroad, and taking advantage of Svyatopolk-Mirsky's relaxation of restrictions on the press and public meetings (a concession which they had ridiculed), set their "banquet campaign" rolling all over Russia. In every important town there were large, noisy gatherings of anybody and everybody who could pay for his portion of snow-white tablecloth, perfume, and champagne, egging each other on with ever bolder toasts, listening now to a gray-headed professor on the behests of Voltaire, now to a pockmarked land surveyor on the program of the Social Democrats, and instead of hailing as the triumphant achievement of the General Zemstvo Congress what it was in fact offering, crying, "Down with Autocracy," joyously filling their lungs to shout, "Long live the Constituent Assembly," as though the whole country was already cowering in the ruins and the urgent need was to establish a government of whatever sort.

What a festival for the daring liberals! What joy to stand before a long white table, just a little drunk, speak against authority with nothing to fear, and propose a toast to the valiant revolutionaries who had brought such freedom to Russia!

From the throne it looked as if this was what the zemstvo men really wanted, as if they were only pretending to want agreement. Give way to this clamor now, and all would be lost. (And that was no more than the truth.)

So, on 25 December, Nikolai II canceled the clause about a national representation, whether consultative, legislative, or of whatever kind. The rest of the Zemstvo Congress's program was, in essentials, accepted, but this was no longer good enough for the educated public, particularly as large gatherings were condemned and discussion of matters of state was forbidden. Svyatopolk-Mirsky thereupon resigned.

The point of light had become red-hot, exploded, and left darkness behind it.

Events gathered speed. On 22 January 1905 a workers demonstration was fired on in Petersburg. On 18 February the governor-general of Moscow, Grand Duke Sergei Aleksandrovich, was assassinated. And immediately the Russian monarch's ideas and his language changed. Whereas on 25 December

> zemstvos and municipal institutions and associations are under obligation not to concern themselves with matters which they are not empowered by law to discuss,

suddenly, in a decree of 3 March:

> In Our tireless concern for the improvement of the state services . . . We have recognized that it would be good to make it easier for Our loyal subjects to be heard by Us. The Council of Ministers will discuss views and proposals submitted by private persons and by institutions.

What incurred punishment on 25 December 1904 was gratefully received on 3 March 1905. Preparations for the establishment of a State Duma were set in motion. The force which recognized only force was retreating.

The League of Liberation, which was "more fully" representative of Russia than the retrograde zemstvo men, poured in through the opening—and swept the great gates away! The League had no discipline, no organization, but its ideas were immediately taken up by a sympathetic intelligentsia—and that was its great strength. Its instructions initiated the creation of unions in Russia—to begin with, only for the "intellectual" professions (i.e., lawyers, writers, actors, academics, teachers), not to defend their professional interests but to put forward identical hackneyed proposals for universal franchise, a Constituent Assembly, and a constitution. The fashion spread to any and every group which could find a name for itself—there was a veterinary union, a peasants' union, an equal rights for Jews union. They all submitted the very same proposals, and soon merged in a Union of Unions, which embodied "the will of the people" (Milyukov). What else? (Unless it was what Trotsky called it: "the zemstvo bridle, thrown by the Liberationists over the democratic intelligentsia"?) The main object was to overheat the social atmosphere! In the League of Liberation itself, zemstvo members had long ceased to be equal partners with non-zemstvo members: flooded with ever greater numbers of left-wing intellectuals, it bulged even farther to the left. In April 1905 another conference of zemstvos was held—still under Liberationist influence, with banquets and resolutions "superb in its radicalism, establishing a new political record" (Milyukov).

Shipov's slow-moving group left the conference, swept off the highroad of history.

An amazing time, a delicious time had arrived for the thinkers among the Russian intelligentsia! An informal circle consisting of gray-headed jurists such as Muromtsev and Kovalevsky, together with certain learned youngsters, was in session while the big guns boomed at Tsushima, working out the future Russian constitution (and giving preference to direct elections, so that deputies would not be so close to local realities, would feel less of an obligation to their electors, and would be not rustics but detached persons of high culture). Contributions for the future party of the intelligentsia were already being collected from rich ladies and munificent businessmen. In the best town houses the rich and free, dressed to the nines, listened with bated breath to the bold words of the latest fashionable lecturers, among them the semi-legendary, ever so revolutionary Milyukov, whose academic career had been cut short ten years earlier by his prophecy of a Russian constitution. Since then he had suffered cruel persecution. For a lecture to students purporting to show that terrorism was inevitable, his residence rights were restricted: he could come into Petersburg for the day, but lived out at Udelnaya. He was banished to distant Ryazan. But most of the time he traveled abroad, lecturing in England and America on Russia's inveterate vices and pseudonymously storming in the journal *Liberation*. He saw and read a great deal of things foreign, had contacts with socialists (and even with Lenin), and (in history the right man always turns up in the right place at the right age) behold the forty-year-old Milyukov descending on Russia before the new party is founded, to become its leader, as guest lecturer in Moscow putting forward the seductive idea of reconciling constitutionalism with revolution, liberals with revolutionaries, and if Guchkov, his friend from university days, accuses him of bookishness, rootlessness, remoteness from Russian reality, Milyukov can note with justification that

the general feeling was, of course, on my side.

Invoke revolution, welcome its approach, hurry it on with all the powers of the intelligentsia—this situation, this simulation of revolution (it is not here yet, but behave as though it has already begun and has set us free!) was more and more to the liking of progressive Russian society. The Union of Unions, in congress sometimes as often as twice a month, called on its members throughout the country not to ask for freedom but to take it—get to work, make excuses for demonstrations, for political struggle, organize conferences, rallies, street meetings. Milyukov found himself in the chair at one such congress, and

the hope that we would be heard has been taken from us. All means are legitimate against the present government! We appeal to all among our people capable of responding to a brutal blow—strive with all your strength for the immediate removal of the usurping robber gang and put the Constituent Assembly in their place.

The shrewd Milyukov knew what he was doing when he penned the words "robber gang": they helped him to repair and reinforce his reputation with the left when people had begun to accuse him of trying to make peace with the right—a stigma it was impossible to live with at such a time. It was the words "robber gang," he believed, that drew the boundary between him and Guchkov, between bold Kadetism and collaborationist Octobrism. Milyukov was becoming more and more convinced that making today's history was more laudable, more interesting, and no whit more difficult than studying that of the past.

The simulacrum of revolution was looking more and more like the real thing. At the beginning of July another conference of zemstvos and towns, this time minus Shipov's minority, gathered in the huge palace of the Dolgorukov princes on Znamensky Lane, Moscow. The police arrived to break up the unauthorized congress, but were turned away, because those assembled were only "carrying out the Tsar's wish," expressed on 3 March,

> to make it easier for Our loyal subjects to be heard by Us.

They resolved to

> enter into the closest association with the popular masses in order to discuss the impending political reform with the people.

What they had in mind was simply one more fait accompli—a Constituent Assembly. These constitutionalists planned to exploit the agrarian and labor problems in particular to inflame the passions of the masses. Socialists of all hues were busy among the masses in those same weeks trying to "unleash" revolution, and SR terror squads were murdering village constables, police officers, and even governors, in country places and in provincial capitals, while the increasingly politicized masses responded by striking, and setting fire to manor houses in what Gertsenshtein laughingly called the "rural illuminations." Everything then was moving in the direction of a Constituent Assembly. Some constitutionalists, however, those who had a nice and not at all burdensome bit of property, of modest or even immodest dimensions, showed signs of fear and backsliding, and Pavel Nikolaevich Milyukov, unshakable in his principles, had to rebuke them sharply:

> If members of our group are so squeamish about physical methods of struggle, I am afraid that our plans for a party will prove barren. No doubt you all rejoice in your hearts at certain acts of physical violence which everyone expected in advance, and the historical significance of which is enormous.

The gathering, duly shamed, adopted the necessary resolutions and disseminated them throughout Russia.

Just half a year earlier a stubborn government had refused to satisfy the smallest demands—and now even big concessions could not blunt society's appetite. In July the Tsar held a secret conference of his senior retainers to draft a scheme for a Duma. (Also admitted to this conference was Klyuchevsky. Milyukov coyly tells us that

> they revealed all their confidential plans to Klyuchevsky, and Vasili Osipovich, with something of his characteristic craftiness

relayed them nightly to his former pupil, in a Petersburg hotel.) On 19 August another manifesto was promulgated, this time on the establishment of a consultative Duma. If it had appeared in Svyatopolk-Mirsky's time, it might have sufficed. But now the government was showing weakness, not strength. Moving toward reform, not because it had any fixed good intentions, but under threat, the government showed, in every word it said, every step it took, that it did not understand the situation in the country and the mood of society, and had no remedy for them. All the moderate elements calmed down and drew back, but the enraged kept up their mass meetings and flooded the pages of the press. The proposed Duma was rejected not only by the Bolsheviks, even Milyukov's group wavered (for some reason keeping a wary eye on Trotsky), but the whole lot of them were put in the Kresty prison for a month, the government acting ridiculously, as always, governing as badly as it could, and letting them out a month later without once interrogating them, just giving them a halo. Russia's rulers had entered the circle of hopelessness in which God takes away reason. In that same fraught August the government gave way and granted autonomy to higher educational institutions—which only meant creating islands of revolution inaccessible to the police: the students raged unchecked in mass meetings, and all sorts of people flocked in to listen and use bad language. Who now needed a consultative Duma? The General Zemstvo Congress in September decided not to boycott it (it was they, after all, who would be elected to it), but to blow it up from inside. After the withdrawal of Shipov's minority, a newly formed group around Guchkov argued unavailingly with the intellectual theorists of the League of Liberation. The League itself was awash with Social Democrats, and even hid, in private apartments, members of the Soviet of Workers' Deputies wanted by the police.

And so the Constitutional Democratic Party took shape—the Kadet Party, as people soon began calling them with the sort of familiar abbreviation usual among revolutionaries. (The Kadets accepted this nickname. It came to be confused with the term for trainees in military schools, innocently at first, maliciously later on, and when the young men in question found themselves defending those same intellectuals as they fled from the same revolution, the whole bunch of them were doomed and all "Kadets" together.) True, the new party quickly realized that the combination of the letters "K" and "D" meant very little to the ordinary Russian, and they casually changed their name to Party of People's Freedom: it had a fine ring, and sought to identify them with the people at large. But the new banner would flutter in vain: all tongues trotted out the extra word "Kadets." Still, the substitution was not just a gimmick: the Kadet leaders genuinely believed that the whole huge nation expressed itself through their minds and mouths, after letting slip in speeches the claim to be spokesmen for the people's aspirations, which they knew so well.

The founding congress of the party met in Moscow. (In Milyukov's comic juxtaposition: "Russia's first capital is the birthplace of Kadetism.") The general strike was on the way, and the railwaymen's strike was spreading, so that three-quarters of the delegates could not in fact get there. Illegal, underground parties had existed for many years in Russia (and had come to the surface in the heat wave of 1905), but this was the first party that was legal from birth. Its program showed the leftward dislocation of the neck obligatory for radicals the world over: its slogans, and its coloring, often expressed not the considered view of the party but the need to preserve nourishing ties with the left. The newly ascendant leader, Milyukov, proudly emphasized that they were the youngest of European liberals, and that their program was

> farther left than any of those put forward by comparable political groups in Western Europe.

Sharply dissociating himself from all to the right, on the grounds that they were moved by class interests, Milyukov, with the unanimous agreement of the congress, appealed to the potential allies on the left. Indeed, the new party was itself so far to the left that

> the founding congress declares its complete solidarity with the political strike movement. Members of the KD Party have decisively abandoned all thought

of seeking to attain their aims through negotiation with representatives of the government.

Before the congress ended, a member of the staff of the "professors' newspaper," *Russkie Vedomosti*, dashed in, faint with delight and flourishing a still-wet galley containing the Manifesto of 30 October.

What joy! What a victory! But should they believe it? Or shouldn't they? Was it a trick? A delaying tactic? Had the enemy lost heart? The delegates flocked to a banquet on Bolshaya Dmitrovka Street, heaved Milyukov onto a table in the gaming room, and called for a speech. He had already sized up the situation and now proclaimed:

Nothing has changed! The war goes on!

Russia must be led further down the road which had brought her to the Manifesto:

. . . by combining liberal tactics with the threat of revolution. We fully understand and recognize the supreme right of the Revolution.

It became fashionable to quote a line from Virgil: *Flectere si nequeo superos, Acheronta movebo.* (If I cannot bend the Olympians, I will call up the river of Hell.)

And why not, if revolution was an ally you could use against the government, to frighten it out of its wits? How could you do otherwise if in those first days of the constitution a placard calling for armed uprising hung in the Conservatoire and money was collected from individuals beneath it? If talks on the relative merits of the Browning and the Mauser were given openly? When you had been beating your heads in vain against an unyielding, mindlessly obtuse bureaucracy for so many years, how could you resist the urge to soar on the red wings of revolution in the heat of debate? If stony-faced idiots would not be taught, how could you muster up patience for endless wearisome persuasion? How could you resist the urge to whack them on the skull with a big stick?

As soon as the Manifesto appeared, Witte invited the Kadets to join the cabinet he was in the process of forming. A road had opened for the party, so recently founded, to enter the government, to join responsibly in seeking and patiently erecting a new state structure. What more could they dream of? Was not this what they had striven for—a chance to take over power and show how to rule? But the Kadets were as nervous as they were loud and they made it clear right at the start that they were not prepared to move on from speeches about the demolition of government to the actual work of governing. How much more respectable, how much less constricting to be a critical opposition! (We shall see many of them behaving in just the same way twelve years later: helplessly rejecting power at a moment of acute political crisis.) Their delegation to Witte, headed by the young ideologist and orator Kokoshkin, adopted a provocative tone right from the start. Demanding the creation not of an effective government but of a Constituent Assembly, and an amnesty for terrorists, he would have left the existing government no authority, and indeed no raison d'être. What, otherwise, would have been said to the left of them! If the Kadets had cooperated even minimally with Witte, how could they claim to differ from the right?

Alas, they still did not succeed in pleasing the left. No sooner was the Kadet Party founded than the Moscow Liberationists started leaving it, and those in Petersburg, who had not gotten to the congress in time, did not join, either then or later. The League of Liberation slewed leftward, almost following in the wake of the Soviet of

Workers' Deputies. The Social Democrats saw in even the most negative negotiations with Witte

> a shameful step, a deal between the bourgeoisie and the government at the people's expense,

and ambition to latch on to ministerial posts.

D. N. **Shipov,** on the contrary, explained the behavior of the Kadets as follows:

> This party united in its ranks the best intellects of the country, the flower of the intelligentsia. But the political struggle was for them an end in itself. They were unwilling to wait until the nation's life was put in order, as different areas of it were discussed by trained and knowledgeable experts; they wanted to involve the whole people, even the unenlightened, in the hottest political struggle as quickly as possible. They called impatiently for elections on a universal franchise in an atmosphere as turbulent as it could be. They refused to understand that the rule of law, the problems of government, and indeed the idea of the state are foreign to the mass of the people, in spite of which they hastened to incite and aggravate discontent, to awaken egoistic interests among the people, to inflame its baser instincts, while ignoring its religious feelings.
>
> The Kadets were indifferent, if not hostile, to religion. Their own irreligion made it difficult for them to understand the real spirit of the people. This was why, while sincerely striving to better the lives of the masses, they tended to corrupt the soul of the people by encouraging manifestations of spite and hatred—directed, to begin with, at the property-owning classes, but subsequently at the intelligentsia as well.

While **Guchkov** tells us:

> I have never concealed my absolutely negative attitude toward the KD Party. That party, in my belief, played a fatal role in the infancy of political freedom in Russia. I was present at its conception and at its birth, and gave a timely word of warning. The Kadets smartly hitched themselves to the wagon of the Russian revolution, taking it for the triumphal chariot which would carry them to the summit of power, not realizing that it was a rickety cart which would finally get bogged down in mud and blood.

The First Duma was opened on 10 May 1906, which proved to be not a day of national reconciliation but the occasion for a new flare-up of hatred. The Kadets arrived flourishing their hats in unison—soldier-politicians! A Duma elected under Witte's "experimental" electoral law (and consisting partly of people to whom legality in any form was alien) made no attempt at self-restraint whatsoever, and demanded nothing less than everything at once, not half everything or a quarter of everything. Defying the constitution, the First Duma let itself be tempted to act as if all by itself it represented both the people's will and the will of the government, as though it was a new form of autocracy. Kokoshkin, indeed, argued that the Duma was not obliged to carry out instructions from anyone in the country.

It took another thirty years for V. Maklakov—not a typical Kadet, but the cleverest of them—to recall with the hindsight of an émigré that

> in 1906 there was no revolution. Our convalescence was beginning. The mon-

archy had given up its most important privilege—autocratic power. It had renounced another of the fundamentals—the "caste" system, which had been such a heavy yoke for Russia to bear. What had been the liberal program now appeared in the government's program: the gradual transfer of land to the peasants, the development of local self-government everywhere, legality, the independence of the courts, education. Society, personified by the Duma, was given the possibility of verifying the implementation of this program, obstructing reactionary deviations, and even initiating reforms. Why then, from the very first day, even before the first session, did it declare war on the government instead of attempting to collaborate? Instead of taking on the thankless but honorable role of trying to moderate the unreasonable impatience of society, the Duma had exacerbated it. It did not wish to hear about reform step by step. Radical amendment of the still untried constitution, the establishment of total popular government, simultaneous mass expropriation of private lands, the formation of a government consisting of members of the Duma and subordinate to it—these were its *first* demands. Giving in to them would have meant bringing the revolution forward by eleven years.

True, the Mensheviks hesitantly, and the other left-wingers with no misgivings at all, boycotted the First Duma, urging and inciting revolution to return. So that the Kadets, to their own surprise, with no cover to their left, proved to be very left themselves. The only ones with an unblushing mastery of European electoral tactics, they snatched more than a third of the seats and became the largest group in the Duma—but were still disinclined to consider anything as disgracefully moderate as normal legislative activity. Victory in the elections clouded their vision. It seemed to promise that they could just as easily overthrow the government. They rejected caution, and refused to spend four years on what a determined onslaught could achieve in as many weeks. So when Milyukov at the Kadets' pre-Duma congress showed for the first time the braking power of his hooves, and tried to divert the party away from its thrilling revolutionary course and toward the drabness of parliamentarianism, he was rebuffed by his fellow Kadets. Ignore the government! Ignore the laws promulgated since 30 October! Ignore the State Council! Carry out your program by means of ultimatum! If the government will not resign—appeal to the people! Die for freedom!

> The eloquent **Rodichev**: The Duma cannot be dissolved! Whoever clashes with the people will crash into the abyss!
>
> **Kizewetter:** If the Duma is dissolved it will be the government's last act, after which it will cease to exist.

In the same vein the handsome gray-headed president of the First Duma, Muromtsev, already practicing to become the first President of Russia, refused to meet or talk to ministers, and even ordered people not to refer to them as the government. Maklakov sums up Muromtsev as follows:

> The type that needs a parliament. He needs resolutions by a collective in order to formulate his beliefs. He will defend his own opinion furiously until a decision is taken, then will obey without demur. Such people can demand in speeches what they know to be impossible, and create an illusion, indeed

themselves believe, that reactionaries have prevented them from bestowing a necessary boon on the country. They take no personal responsibility: their estimate of themselves depends on what they read in the papers.

In its first address to the monarch this neurasthenic Duma spoke to the Supreme Power as though delivering an ultimatum, and the Supreme Power replied in a didactic tone, as if to a subordinate institution. Friends to the left—the serried ranks of the Caucasian Social Democrats—egged the Kadets on, and the Duma demanded an amnesty for terrorists and regicides, while itself refusing to pass moral judgment on terrorism. This was so much a part of the Kadet mentality that the patriarch of the party, I. Petrunkevich, with whose efforts at peacemaking this chapter began, exclaimed:

Condemn terror? Never! That would mean moral ruin for the party!

Nonetheless, it was still seriously suggested that this First Duma and its Kadet majority should be entrusted with the task of forming a government and allowed to lead Russia. There were secret discussions at court, ministers bustled around from meeting to meeting, and Milyukov—who "ran the Duma from the buffet and the press gallery," because he was not a deputy—conferred with them. Milyukov was eagerly expecting to become Prime Minister, but the discussions came to nothing, because the Kadets refused to retract their demand for a general expropriation of land. As the dissolution of the Duma became more and more obviously imminent, the Supreme Power's candidate to replace Goremykin as Prime Minister and dissolve it was . . . Shipov.

Only . . . The opponent of the constitution, and of political parties generally, told the Tsar that the dissolution of the Duma now that it was in being, aggressive though it was, seemed to him unjust and even criminal. Since 30 October he had accepted the constitution, by command from the Highest, as had all Russian subjects. He now felt obliged to be loyal to it, and expected no less from the Sovereign himself. In his opinion, the Duma would be much less militant if the government further developed the principles of the Manifesto instead of departing from them. The Fundamental Laws, dividing power among the Sovereign, the Duma, and the State Council, had already been promulgated and the speech from the throne included a declaration that the day of the opening of the Duma would be the day of moral renewal for the Russian land. By the same token, Shipov could not undertake to lead a coalition government, as proposed, but thought that a government headed by the Kadets would be very much in accordance with the spirit of the times. It would forcibly deliver them from elements opposed to the state, and irresponsible opposition, and make them a party loyal to the state. They might then dissolve the Duma themselves, to rid themselves of their left wing. When the Tsar asked Shipov to suggest a possible head for such a government, he answered that Milyukov had to be regarded as the most influential, talented, and erudite of the Kadets, but that he was deficient in religious feeling, or, in other words, in any sense of moral duty to the Highest Principle and to other people, so that if he became Prime Minister his policy would hardly help to raise the spiritual level of the population. Apart from that he was too "autocratic" and would be too domineering with his colleagues. Shipov recommended Muromtsev.

But in the grip of a left-spinning whirlwind, and with their heads twisted leftward, how could the Kadets take on the burden of government? Stolypin, the Minister of the Interior, was sure that they could not, that they would end by derailing the state. A man of action, he could not see the point of such an experiment, of seeing where they take us, so that when we all break our necks, we shall be so much the wiser.

Under Shipov's influence, the Tsar seemed inclined to create a Kadet cabinet, but was so minded for no more than a week. Meanwhile the terrorists were still at work. And the Kadets took fright and censured Milyukov, who was still concealing his secret discussions with ministers from the party. They were even more restive when Milyukov tried to put the brake on such neoparliamentary methods as an appeal to the people on the agrarian question (the Kadets, as always, eager to inflame peasant feelings). The appeal spoke of converting state, appanage, treasury, monastery, and church lands to peasant use and of forcibly expropriating those in private ownership!

Prime Minister Goremykin, a moderate and sluggish sixty-six-year-old with a complacency acquired in a long bureaucratic career, was incapable of anxiety, believing that history always repeats itself and that no one man is strong enough to change its course. He had seen throughout that any attempt to work with that Duma would be a failure, but had carried on, imperturbably, things being as they were, and while the Tsar wished it. Now, however, the Duma had overstepped the mark, and Goremykin saw that the Tsar would like to dismiss the Duma but lacked the resolve: he was haunted by dreadful visions of 1905 and the thought that its horrors could repeat themselves in even more virulent form. The old man resolved upon the greatest exertion of his life: he went to the Tsar with a family icon, prayed with him for God's aid, and asked for an order to dismiss the Duma, to retire and to transfer the reins from his tired hands to the firm hands of the young and strong-minded Stolypin. He duly received the order, went home, arranged for the dissolution, then declared himself not at home to anybody, and forbade the servants to call him or come looking for him no matter who wanted him. In fact, the Tsar had second thoughts about his desperate decision within a matter of hours, and would have called on Goremykin to reconsider—but Goremykin was nowhere to be found.

Stolypin calmed down a Duma agitated by rumors. (Will they dismiss us? If they do, let's remain in our seats as the Roman senate did! Let's appeal to the country! The whole country will rise in our defense! No, they'll never dare!) And then on Sunday, 22 July, he stationed soldiers near the Tauride Palace, hung a big lock on the door and a royal proclamation on the walls:

> Those elected by the people, instead of constructive, legislative work . . .

What were the Kadets to do next? Where did they stand with revolutionary Russia? From Sunday morning on, there was a rush to assemble the deputies, and while this was going on a fresh appeal was being drafted on a dusty piano top in a locked apartment. Vinaver claimed to find in Milyukov's proposed version

> no elemental force of indignation, whereas this cry of outrage should resound like a thunderclap.

The appeal was finalized by Vinaver and Kokoshkin, but some of Milyukov's exhortations survived: don't pay your taxes! (direct taxation, however, accounted for an insignificant part of revenue), don't provide the state with conscripts! (but the call-up was not due until November).

They had planned, in anticipation of dissolution, to go to Vyborg, on free Finnish territory. Circumspect peasant deputies, to whom Milyukov's whole appeal was addressed, did not, alas, go, not one of them. About a third of the Duma went, the fieriest of them (of those, thirty subsequently stole away). That same Sunday evening a session was held in the Belvedere Hotel, with the splendid Muromtsev inevitably in the chair. Some Trudoviks (legal SRs) and some Social Democrats ("reserving their position on armed insurrection") also attended.

There were speeches by Kokoshkin, the everlasting Petrunkevich, Frenkel, Gertsenshtein, Iollos, and the Trudovik leaders Bramson and Aladin, all of them ablaze with indignation, not one of them able to suggest a counterstroke that would be fatal to the government. The resulting manifesto was not one for which the people, alas, was likely to shed its blood.

Should they declare themselves a Constituent Assembly? Take on the functions of a government? Consider themselves a full Duma and remain in session?

> **Zhordania** (Social Democrat): Although only one-third of the Duma are here, it is they and they only who are the rightful . . .
>
> **Ramishvili** (Social Democrat): Just a little while ago we were sure that we should not return home without land and freedom. But [scornfully] you are not prepared to take decisive measures.
>
> (The Trudoviks): The people's cause is in the hands of the people itself. The army, weapons in hand, must defend freedom. The government is no longer a government. Obeying the authorities is criminal!

But what should they do? Once again they were left with nonpayment of taxes and rejection of military service. (They were unwilling to recognize that these were blows not against the government but against the state as a whole.)

> General strike?
>
> Armed uprising?
>
> We cannot call for an armed uprising. It would be the end of constitutionalism in Russia.
>
> Vinaver (Kadet): We must go back to Petersburg and let them arrest us there—that will be a useful symbol and an incitement to social struggle.

Morale was sagging.

> Gredeskul (Kadet): After all, we are not calling for anything terrible—only passive resistance, which is entirely constitutional. There is one other measure: to call on the people to abstain from vodka.

(A good laugh for anyone who knows Russian ways.)

No, morale was sagging. Before dissolution they had looked strong—to themselves and to their opponents. Now they felt bankrupt. Differences of opinion hardened. The manifesto was discussed, article by article. There might perhaps have been no Vyborg appeal if the governor had not appeared in the hotel and said, "Gentlemen, you must close your meeting immediately. Vyborg, as you know, is a garrison town, and martial law may be declared at any minute."

Yes, yes, yes! We mustn't abuse the hospitality of our Finnish friends. Oh well, we must submit to force majeure . . .

The President and Prime Minister manqué of Russia hastily donned his overcoat and left the platform.

Muromtsev: Many of those who signed the Vyborg appeal were not at all in agreement with it.

There was no time for further debate. They adopted the whole package on a single vote.

TO THE PEOPLE FROM THE PEOPLE'S REPRESENTATIVES:

CITIZENS OF ALL RUSSIA!
STAND FIRM IN DEFENSE
OF YOUR TRAMPLED RIGHTS!
NO POWER CAN HOLD OUT
AGAINST
THE UNITED AND UNBENDING WILL
OF THE PEOPLE.

The Vyborg appeal seduced nobody and frightened nobody. Indeed, the authorities were reassured by its feebleness: they at least had been expecting revolution.

So ended the first test of the newly founded People's Freedom Party: with the forfeiture of the first Russian parliament, in which the Kadets had so cheaply won and so cheaply let slip their majority.

*   *   *

IF YOU AND I ARE BOTH GENTS NOW—
WHO'LL BE LEFT TO FOLLOW THE PLOW?

*   *   *

[8]

That summer, at a patriotic concert in the old Morozov house, now a hospital for officers, Alina was presented with a breathtaking bouquet of roses. She had never, whatever the occasion, been given one like it. It was no courtesy bouquet, but one she could barely get both arms around. The sort of bouquet a woman may be given once in a lifetime.

The nurse who brought it to her was hidden behind it, and afterward there was no one to ask. At that moment Alina could only look at the hundreds and hundreds of pink, white, and yellow petals, could only gratefully raise her eyes to the hall where people were still applauding and where the person who sent the flowers must be sitting, could only look down again at the bouquet, burying her face in it, breathing in, drinking in its fragrance.

There was no note. Perhaps it had fallen out? Alina naturally expected him to approach her, behind the scenes, on the staircase, or surely in the vestibule, as first she and then the bouquet were handed into the cab. How would she feel? Who would it be? She waited, wondering what she could possibly say.

He did not come. No sign of him.

She was still waiting the next day. And for several days after. But no one declared himself. No visitors. No note. No name heard.

An enigma. No doubt it would always be.

Perhaps that made it all the more beautiful? A sort of "garnet bracelet."*

There had to be one moment in which life was at its most beautiful.

But could whoever it was have written to her? Using her new privilege as an artist, she gave her concerts under the name of Siyalskaya, but for other purposes was known by her husband's ponderous surname—ten years now, and she still couldn't get used to it. On her passport her first name too was different: Apollinaria, unpronounceable from the concert platform (though anyone with imagination would have recognized it as a feminine version of Apollo).

She gave another concert at the same hospital, hoping to provoke a miraculous coincidence. But there was no repetition.

Who was he, this mysterious admirer? Most probably a wounded officer. Perhaps that had been his last evening before he left for active service? Or could it be one of the hospital doctors? Hardly. Or a visitor from Moscow, who had happened upon the concert and, smitten with admiration the moment she touched the keys, at once sent out for a bouquet?

She hoped he would appear, but was nervous in anticipation. She would be hopelessly embarrassed. From her youth onward Alina had been outwardly skittish, excitable, impulsive, but in reality she was incorrigibly shy. She always avoided talking about the facts of life with other girls or her mother, saying boastfully, "I know! I know!" and because of her constraint she knew nothing when all the others did. Her ignorance was a secret she shared with no one. Alina sparkled, laughed, flirted, but might as well have been behind plate glass. This hidden shyness would always be part of her character.

Meeting her admirer would lead nowhere.

She would never dare to follow it up.

It was more beautiful this way . . . An enormous bouquet, too big to hold, a symbol of the brilliant life, full of emotions just as enormous, for which, Alina saw now, she had been born, with that talent of hers, if only she had developed it and not let herself sink from sight in marriage, in the dismal humdrum existence of an officer's wife. Of her friends at the Borisoglebsk high school, one was the wife of a French diplomat and now lived abroad, another was forever traveling with her

---

*Reference to a story by Aleksandr Kuprin in which a lover destined to remain unknown sends a garnet bracelet to his beloved.

very rich husband, and a third, married to a senior civil servant, moved in the best Petersburg society. Alina had always been enthusiastically applauded at school or other local concerts, and had often thought of continuing her musical education at the Conservatoire. But then there was that concert in Tambov, when the thirty-year-old staff captain, after one hearing, had laid siege to her and rushed her into marriage.

Georgi did not much resemble the ideal man whose image Alina had carried in her heart since her school days: there was nothing of Pechorin in him, none of that cruel and lofty contempt for the world and for women which makes the Pechorins irresistible. What he did have was a frank and simple delight in her—and that, of course, was as it should be in a knight. She did not at first recognize in him the husband of her choice. She hesitated. But then she came to believe in him, and would go on believing in him through the years, captivated by his own belief in his destiny: he would go to the Academy, his mind teemed with plans, his comrades jokingly called him "the future Chief of the General Staff."

She put her faith in him—and surrendered her life to him unconditionally. They married and moved to Petersburg—but by the back door, not to a Petersburg of leisure and ease and social occasions, in which she could cultivate and expand her talents. Sacrifices had to be made for the sake of his future—and sacrifices are a woman's lot. They lived frugally enough, and still his modest stipend made further economies necessary. But Alina got used to this lifestyle. It became second nature to deny rather than indulge herself. She even came to enjoy it and applied her natural ingenuity to it. Condemned to childlessness after their early disappointment, they treated each other with sensitive affection, showed each other consideration in small things—if Georgi could be said to have eyes for anything except his military duties. He was passionately absorbed in his work, the way he closed his study door meant keep out, don't distract me. He encouraged her to play the piano more, but what he heard through the wall was not an artistic creation but a featureless flow of background music to his studies. Alina reconciled herself even to this slight. She played to help him think. She came to like their life together, their daily routine, just as it was—confident that she was helping her husband up the steep climb to success.

It didn't work out that way. Graduating from the Academy with a first-class diploma, and teaching there for a time, led to nothing. His military circle was broken up and his colleagues scattered around backwoods garrisons of soul-destroying dreariness. There were even deadlier holes than Vyatka. Hopes of a brighter future collapsed and were snuffed out. They were gripped by an oppressive feeling that this was the end of everything. It was like drowning in a marsh. And then, of course, Alina sometimes imagined that rough housework had robbed her fingers of their suppleness forever, and that she would never appear on any good platform. But she was willing to endure even this gloomy prospect: she steeled herself for what might be years of stagnation. To have fallen so low was hard for her, but it was no easier for her husband, and his misfortunes grieved her more than him.

Still, before the year was out there was a change for the better. Promotion, this time to Moscow, came his way. But no sooner had they moved and settled in than war broke out.

In wartime, the lot of all soldiers' wives is the same—or is it? What matters to all of them is "Will he come back alive?" But if we are talking about regular soldiers, something else is just as important: his position in the army. The whole object of a military career is promotion. And Georgi, after his brief elevation to the General Staff, had come to grief and been sent down to his regiment. Even this disaster could have been handled in more ways than one. The natural thing to do was not to reconcile yourself to demotion, to humiliation, but to try to put things right. Alina offered her husband all her emotional support. Alas! It gradually became clear that he was in the grip of some sort of psychological illness. It was not just that he reconciled himself to his fallen state and felt himself that he did not deserve to rise, not just that there were no more soaring hopes, no more crowding plans, but that other feelings, normal human feelings, seemed one by one to shrivel up, even the simple desire to take a month's leave, to which he was entitled, and to rest. Such sentiments as "the home front, and all I hear about it, is more and more unpleasant to me," "the home front disgusts me," surfaced in letter after letter. The grim summer of defeat and withdrawal had ended, and a whole year had gone by, giving Georgi the right to take leave, but he wrote to say definitely that he would not come home, and inviting her to spend a couple of weeks with him in Bukovina, almost at the front, in rented accommodations. It was a bizarre whim, quite impossible to explain to anyone in Moscow, nor indeed could she make sense of it herself. Every officer looked forward to his leave, and indeed looked for any official excuse to get away. But a wife who knows her duty must also know what sacrifices can be asked of her. So although this was not just any month, but that of Alina's thirtieth birthday, she went—almost into the front line, a shaking experience for a woman. But the whole visit was depressing.

She found her husband in an even worse state than his letters had led her to expect. True, he had never yet been hospitalized, although he had been bandaged up at times. But he was more dispirited, more apathetic than she had ever seen him. For the first few days he spent most of the time recumbent, saying nothing, just sighing heavily, without realizing that he was doing it. Alina felt frightened. She had lost her husband! This was not Georgi! Then, as the days went by, he recovered from his paralysis and started conversing. If that was the word. This was no husband-and-wife conversation. He could talk about nothing except his dead soldiers, Russian losses, the hopeless muddle, and his sickness over it all, and whatever she said in return he either didn't hear or answered absentmindedly. With his fanatical officer's code he had never in his life paid much attention to ordinary human stories. He could not have explained his present state very well himself, but Alina studied him with a woman's eye more closely than ever before and reached a conclusion. It was not their separation that had made strangers of them, it was Georgi's reaction to the war. He had let his spirit get weighed down with chunks of iron and was drowning with them. He had dedicated his whole life to war—and found that he could not bear it. The war with Japan he had borne very well, but not this one. His strength had unexpectedly failed him. His fire had gone out. Horrified, she watched him slowly sinking, and was powerless to help. He saw himself how low he had fallen, and had no wish to pick himself up. Worse, he was dragging her down with him into the morass of hopelessness. To drown together? No! She must save him, distract him, amuse him, enliven him with refreshing comments on Moscow life. This would have been easily done at home, in Moscow: a whole month there and he would have been himself again. But he had refused to come. As it was, their only diversion was dreary walks through small-town streets up into the foothills. So Alina's visit to her husband, which should have been a holiday, brought her grief instead. He had no thought for her. It was Vyatka all over again—the same degrading backwoods existence. And Georgi had changed so much in the last few years that it was as if they were having to get to know each other all over again, disagreeing and even quarreling at times. The visit ended, and he was still very far from being his former self. And it was clear now that the great future to which she had so joyfully looked forward with him was not to be. He had not just suffered a career setback at GHQ, he had proved unequal to his task. His dreams and his plans had come to nothing. His protests had failed. She was desperately sorry for him.

For him—and for herself. He was still part of her life—yet it was as though he was lost to her.

He, on the other hand, was not sensitive enough to enter into his wife's feelings, to realize what he was doing to her, what it was like for her. Many months later, going over their whole ten years together, Alina found an explanation. Before his military interests had out-weighed all else, absorbed him completely, he could be tender and affectionate, though he was entirely wrapped up in his own concerns. Now that this premature aging of the emotions, this atrophy of all vital impulses had come upon him, the little island reserved for his personal life had suffered most of all. Lying beside his wife, he had thawed out a little, but seemed to have had no deep-felt need for her to be there.

To be united with him, Alina had sacrificed what might perhaps have been a brilliant life, she had never failed in her duty, she had found ways of brightening their cramped existence, had even endured the backwoods of Vyatka, but it never occurred to him to show that he appreciated how much she had sacrificed. It was not his fault. He was just not very sensitive.

Their parting was miserable. Those two weeks had not brought them closer—on the contrary. They had less in common than ever before. Alina vowed never to spend his leave with him in that way again. Let Georgi come to Moscow.

It was lucky that they had set up house in Moscow before the war. Moscow had liberated Alina, given her scope to exercise her powers, helped her to try her own wings and find them stronger than she had realized in the previous Cinderella role. She had been her husband's prisoner for eight years, forgetful of her own unrealized possibilities. They could not be hidden forever. A sensitive and complex personality always has ungratified interests. The war brought an upsurge of public eagerness to help Russian eagles to victory, and in it Alina had found her own airstream. Not immediately. She had begun, like everybody else, by rolling bandages and counting soldiers' underwear. But then they had the idea of organizing "patriotic concerts," to raise money for the wounded and disabled, help the families of enlisted men, and send parcels to the defenders of their native land. Alina had known hardly anyone in her first years in Moscow, but now she made new acquaintances quickly. Till then her husband had monopolized the right to be energetic, and she had rarely applied the word to herself. But now it was Alina's energy that became a byword among the other women active in the same cause. Her enterprise, her tirelessness, her eloquent appeals to those who had power in the Union of Towns made her a conspicuous figure. She got through to Chelnokov on two occasions. She succeeded in obtaining certain essential permits from the Military District Command, and won the astonished gratitude of hospital boards. She and her husband had lived in Petersburg for six years, but only now in Moscow, in the midst of all this brisk and rewarding activity, did she feel a metropolitan buoyancy. She was one of the first to succeed in getting permission to form volunteer groups to give "flying concerts" for the army in the field. Wherever she went her piano playing won grateful applause from an audience innocent of Conservatoire snobbery, and Alina flourished in this bracing atmosphere. It was shown, and proved beyond doubt, that she was a person in her own right, not just an appendage to her husband. (Georgi, saying goodbye in Bukovina, had told her to live her life to the full, and give all the concerts she could.)

There were about a dozen people in her concert party. There was a fat-faced funny man who did comic Ukrainian songs. A mustachioed quartermaster lieutenant colonel who sang baritone. A violinist of Mephistophelian appearance. A young lawyer's clerk who performed monologues. Two ladies who sang and one who danced. (All of these were regularly accompanied by the fair-headed fellow with the strong jaw who used to play the piano at the Union cinema.) And every member of the group had his or her own circle of friends, which further broadened Alina's Moscow acquaintance.

She became especially friendly with Susanna Iosifovna Korzner, the most amiable thirty-five-year-old wife of a well-known Moscow lawyer. Susanna performed monologues and recited verse, and Alina volunteered to accompany her recital to the music of "Çakya Muni," "The White Veil," and other pieces. This necessitated joint rehearsals at home, and in the case of Sholem Aleichem's stories, and excerpts from "The Gadfly," consultation with the authorities to make sure that they fitted into the approved framework of patriotic concerts. Alina readily undertook these démarches, and carried them out successfully. This brought her and Susanna Iosifovna still closer together, and they began calling on each other. Susanna had no pretensions, did not care whether she was applauded, didn't envy the success of other performers, and was not too proud to sit down and turn the pages for Alina.

"You wouldn't think it took much learning, would you?" Alina said laughingly. "But I never could teach my husband to follow the music well enough to turn the pages. There are some primitive souls who just won't respond to the arts. I could be playing away in the next room, and if I asked him afterward what I'd just played, he would never know the answer, not if I played the same thing twenty times over! A man of wood . . ."

Susanna Iosifovna was always such a marvelous listener—to music, with her shoulders tensed as she listened, or, with her olive green and red-brown eyes open wide, absorbing anything you told her, however ordinary—that Alina slipped more and more easily into the habit of confiding in her: it was no good locking everything up inside herself and brooding silently.

"Heavens above, Susanna Iosifovna, I've made so many sacrifices for him, conscientiously humbled myself for so many years, to help him in life's battle. But I could always believe then that I would be rewarded someday and we would start living like other people! But no— he's throwing his own life, and mine with it, into some gaping black hole. Imagine him refusing to come home on leave! I ask you, what normal officer would ever do that?

"But that's not the worst of it. He was always inclined to be a dry stick, but during the war he's grown cold and apathetic, given up completely—and he's only forty! His life is a failure. Even when the war ends he'll never be his old self again."

She told the story of their marriage—how she had refused him at first, and how he had captured her by his passionate admiration of her. He had expressed his feelings so vividly, especially in letters, and she showed Susanna Georgi's old letters and her old album from her girl-hood in Borisoglebsk, and Susanna bore witness to the presentation of the unforgettable bouquet. The album so often pored over in solitude, of course, meant little to an outsider—every entry was more than just that, it was a whole remembered event, a meeting of soul with soul, a moment of enchantment, a speaking look, none of which paper could preserve, and in any case what was written down was always less than what was felt. That whimsical "To Diana," for instance, was more than an epigram, it faithfully caught something of the original, her profile, her arm, and so something of her character. Ah, how different Alina's life might have been.

The friends shared their efforts to economize, in the manner newly fashionable among women in the capital: altering old frocks instead of buying new ones, not visiting restaurants, dismissing superfluous ser-vants (Alina, though, had only a part-time maid, whereas Susanna had a cook and a chambermaid too, not to mention her husband's chauf-feur in the daytime). Moscow had always been more sober than Pe-tersburg where dress was concerned, and was now more austere than ever. Ostentation in dress had become indecent. Even Shchukin's daughter went to the theater, drawn by those fabulous horses capari-soned with blue netting (there was, however, a move to do without horses), modestly dressed and without diamonds. The expensively dressed refugees from Warsaw and the nouveaux riches were the only eyesores. They cared for nothing and no one, but this was a stratum which did not belong to the enlightened middle class, and the sources of their wealth were dubious. For someone of restricted means like Alina, it was all the more imperative to show restraint in her dress, even on the concert platform, and more often than not to deny herself even a new hat, like the fashionable broad-brimmed sort with the slant-ing feather that seemed to carry you along like a wing.

People gave up lavish receptions, but lively dinner parties went on—where else could you talk? Alina was flattered to be invited to the Korzners' for the evening. There were always ten, or sometimes twenty, dining, all of them quite prominent people, mostly from legal circles: Levashkevich, who was Korzner's associate as legal adviser to the Azov-Don Bank, Krestovnikov . . . The famous Gruzenberg sometimes looked in, as did Mandelstam, the leader of the "left-wing Kadets," and the brilliant Tyrkova—member of the Kadets' Central Committee, and Duma correspondent—occasionally put in a brief appearance. On one occasion the illustrious Maklakov turned up. Alina was not present, and much regretted missing him.

The Korzners rented an eleven-room apartment on Ilinka Street, in the business quarter. Besides Korzner's office there was a reception room for his personal assistant, a general reception room, a drawing room, a bedroom paneled with light maple, a big dining room paneled with dark oak, furnished in the modern style, with a massive table to seat twelve, or, opened out, twenty-four, a snack cart to wheel around, and a table for the samovar at the far end of the room: often, one samovar was not enough and a second was brought in. There was a room for the English governess, who had not yet moved on, and two rooms for the servants. The apartment was, truth to tell, rather dark, and the dining room got very little daylight, but with its heavy hangings it was very cozy in the evening.

Both her husband and her eighteen-year-old son, a law student, were at home with her, and Susanna's family life was scarcely affected by the war. They lived a life of ease and plenty. Her husband was a success in his profession, they had their own car, their own country villa, a reserved box at the Bolshoi Theater. Susanna confessed her superstitious anxiety: "You know the legend of Polycrates's ring? When things are going too well you must make a sacrifice to fate, conciliate it so that it will not get angry with you."

Discussion of their welfare work for the troops, and even their artistic interests, was silenced by the conversation at the Korzners' table. Here political passion ran high. Many of the guests played a central role in the main events in Moscow, they arrived flushed from a session of the Moscow City Duma, or one of its sections, or the Moscow branch of the Kadet Party, or some other committee—there were so many of them now—and reported the latest news fresh and hot, before it was known anywhere else.

They, like the whole of progressive society in Moscow and throughout Russia, wanted, expected, and demanded victories, although they had met with so many disappointments. At the Korzners' they analyzed the situation and looked for reasons. For defeat in the field. For the unprecedented rise in the prices of foodstuffs (so steep in recent weeks that even the fairly well-off urban middle class was beginning to feel it). The growers, with their intransigent greed, were to blame, they were making their pile, and the government refused to curb them, the peasants were skinning the towns alive, carting home money by the sackful, putting it under the mattress. And the cause of all causes was the paralytic inefficiency of the government and its blind and pigheaded refusal to cede power to the trusted representatives of the intelligentsia.

Then they would give rein to their anger at the tragicomic restrictions on the press, or with the British democrats and French socialists who, in their enthusiastic loyalty to the alliance with the Tsar, were driving nails into the coffin of liberty in Russia. They indulged in witticisms, especially about the venality of officials and the embezzlement of government funds: "I didn't see the notice 'I receive from three to five' in time and, like an idiot, gave him ten!" Or: "How to interpret the language of secretaries and junior officials: 'not enough to act upon,' 'have to give my superiors a bit more to go on,' 'it takes time' ('it's take time')."

Practical plans were also discussed. For instance, how to develop the nongovernmental organizations for aiding the war effort and the victims of war, so that they could play a part in political campaigns. Not one of the "copies" circulating in Moscow bypassed the Korzners' apartment: whether it was Kerensky's letter to Rodzyanko saying that the "nest of traitors" was in the Foreign Ministry, not among the Social Democratic deputies, or a speech in the Duma's Budget Commission which did not find its way into the press, or the spicy pages about Rasputin in the book by Iliodor. In the space of a few years a whole library of such material had accumulated—from Alix's old letter to Rasputin, which Guchkov had once circulated, to a recent letter written by the same Guchkov to General Alekseev. It may even have been from this apartment that the "copies" began their journey. The Korzners had a typewriter, so they would not have to copy things by hand.

Those who had seen something of Milyukov during his last visit that October passed on the interesting conclusions he had reached about Moscow. According to Pavel Nikolaevich, the city had got over the trivial cares and petty illusions with which Petrograd was still largely preoccupied. Moscow was now Russia's leading city, the advance post of free thought! If the elections to the Fifth Duma, due next year, took place, the Kadets might find themselves too far to the right for it. It was now difficult to believe that not so long ago Moscow was a bulwark of the monarchy, and as recently as last year people had dissociated the guilty Sukhomlinov from the innocent Tsar. But no reasonable person could still be a monarchist. Ministerial leapfrog had done more to enlighten minds than decades of revolutionary propaganda. Moscow had been the first to see the light, and realize that the whole imperial family was guilty, and that the Tsar was no cleaner than his Alix, whether you were talking about Rasputin, or the Stürmer-Protopopov affair, or negotiations for a separate peace with the Germans. In Moscow circles the language now was that of implacable revolutionaries, spoken before 1905 only among the émigrés in Switzerland!

Igelson, however, sounded an alarmist note: "The Black Bloc has a lot of power nowadays, gentlemen! It's like a storm cloud hanging over us, and its efforts to bring about an ignominious peace are horrifying. I can give you the facts to prove it."

Which made it all the more obvious! They all agreed, it was clear now to everybody, present or not, that the men in power in Russia were absolutely hopeless! We were faced with an obtuse government, impervious to the language of logic.

David Korzner had a favorite gesture and a favorite formula for such occasions. "The fist!" he said, holding out his own at the full extent of his short arm, not really a very menacing fist, rather small, its smooth skin taut over the knuckles of four fingers, with a sprinkling of little black hairs on the back of his hand, protruding from a starched cuff. The fist was not menacing in itself, but the voice was, and the expression on his face, and the implicit meaning. "The fist—the only thing they understand, the only language in which we can and must and will address them!"

He had once found himself uttering these words impromptu at a conference of left-wingers. They had gone down well, and Korzner now loved repeating them and drilling them into his listeners.

"There's no other language! *They* will understand nothing else! All these negotiations between pale pink liberals and the government only lead society into a blind alley. The fist! One good punch on the nose! And they will give way!"

[9]

It amused David that his Susanna had signed up with the Black Hundreds concert party. The ear, of course, still had difficulty in distinguishing the "patriot" from the "Black Hundreder." They always used to mean the same thing.

And their concert party really was not irresistibly attractive, you would need some very good reason to go on tour with it. It was enough to look at that piano player with the stone jaw—an obvious scoundrel, the very image of a Jew beater. These concerts, arranged by the Union of Towns, were obviously his way of evading military service. And that went for the singer of Ukrainian folk songs too. The supply officer was an insufferable martinet, the soprano with shoulders like bolsters was an earsplitting vulgarian, the vaudeville dancer was just what you'd expect . . . that left Alina Vladimirovna, who was the most decent member of the troupe, and socially altogether acceptable. Besides, the troupe's bookings depended entirely on her and her inexhaustible enthusiasm and determination. Some small-town humorist had remarked in her schoolgirl album—quite correctly—that there was something of the goddess Diana, that proud toss of the head, the swift upswing of the arm, the imperious wave of the hand, all well suited to her present role. But Susanna gently warned her not to dress too brightly and to avoid excessive show when she appeared onstage.

They spent a great deal of time together, traveling to concerts, rehearsing, sharing problems, and the more Susanna shunned the rest of the troupe, the closer she became to Alina. She was cheerful and

good-natured, never put out by awkward moments, indeed always helpful at such times. People were won over by her straightforwardness and
lack of guile. She took a childish pleasure in applause, and made no
attempt to hide it: her gray eyes shone, and she would remind people
of her triumphs long afterward. But her candid nature made occasional
emotional effusions unavoidable.

There are as many special relationships as there are people, or married couples: life is lavish with combinations. Alina and her husband,
for instance, were a childless but uncomplaining couple, bonded by
ten years together. There seemed to be no hint of a rift, but from
Alina's ingenuous account, insofar as you could see into the depths of
other people's lives, it would seem that their union was perhaps less
than perfect. Alina insisted on reading his letters aloud—and they were
not the letters of a battle-hardened colonel, but more like skillful exercises in the amorous epistolary game by a young schoolboy with his
head in the clouds, and full of the set phrases of chivalrous devotion
to womanhood, but with no imprint of the Alina of flesh and blood.
This was especially true of the letters written in their early years together, overemotional, elaborately poetical effusions that jarred on the
ear and aroused a sneaking suspicion of pastiche.

"You'll introduce him to me one of these days, won't you?" Susanna
said noncommittally.

Alina could be a little tiresome, but never really exasperating. People
liked her. One of the likable things about her was that though she was
not overburdened with education she felt too much of an affinity with
educated people to be potentially hostile in contentious matters. True,
in a different social circle, under different influences, she might just
as readily accept the opposite viewpoint. But—and this always makes
itself felt—the urge to contradict was not in her nature. If, for instance,
an argument flared up in the troupe about the pogrom against the
Moscow Germans in May last year, Susanna could be sure that Alina
would stand by without contradicting her.

They had all had a good view of those painful scenes in Moscow.
The first stone through the plate-glass window of a German shop had
sealed its fate. Everything in the shop was ruthlessly flung outside—
boxes of millinery, lengths of velvet, worsted, and linen, underclothes
and outer garments, guitars, toys, kitchen stoves, sewing machines. A
Zimmermann piano crashed onto the pavement from the second story
and hammers completed its destruction. There was a blizzard of feathers from mattresses and pillows of German manufacture. Shops that
were locked and shuttered were set ablaze. Some German establishment was set alight and nearby Russian property caught fire. Lathes
were smashed, machinery was wrenched out of shape and trampled in
the roadway. Warehouses, workshops, and Keller's pharmaceutical factory were torched. Nobody knows how much property was destroyed.

Braun's rubber factory, Stritter's distillery, and Ding's confectionery went up in flames. Fires blazed in Kitaigorod, on Sheremetiev, in Middle and Upper City Rows, on Ilinka, Varvarka, Nikolskaya, on Kuznetsky Most, on Lubyanka Square, on Myasnitskaya, Maroseika, Petrovka, and Sretenka streets, Tverskoy Boulevard, and in Cherkassky Lane. Enormous clouds of smoke, like those from a forest fire, enveloped Moscow, the smell of burning was everywhere, fire engines, motorized and horse-drawn, and ambulances hurtled to and fro. The air was troubled with fumes, shots, wild cries, cheering, curses, the crash of vandalized property, sobs, laughter, the shrilling of whistles and honking of horns, the clatter of hooves, tram bells, and on top of it all groups of noisy demonstrators carrying patriotic portraits. When the liquor stores were fired the drunkenness that had been in abeyance for a year returned, and men lay around on the streets, overcome by drink. Outside Tilmans's office innumerable bills, memoranda, invoices, and letters blew around all over Myasnitskaya Street—treasure lost to the bookkeepers, and useless to anyone else. In all, the damage was said to be as much as 40 million. Schröder, the factory owner, and his family—wife and two daughters—were badly beaten, then drowned, naked, in a ditch.

"The people expressed its feelings!" This from the thickheaded oaf of a piano player, arms defiantly akimbo. It was hard to imagine him meekly crouched over his instrument in the darkened cinema. "It was an explosion of wounded national pride, because the government had failed to deliver us from German domination earlier, at the beginning of the war. It was revenge for the gas! The Germans had used poison gas."

So they had—but at the front and against troops. But were these the culprits, and was this the place to take revenge? And was revenge the right word anyway? There was more looting than wrecking. Bundle after bundle of goods was carried off, with no one trying to stop it, and transported by tram from the city center to Sokolniki. Any town can produce an ugly mob, of course. There were many workers among the looters—the uptown districts all joined in sacking the center. Still—of the two persons seen tossing frippery out of a top-floor window on Myasnitskaya Street—one was a student and the other a pupil in a Modern School. Wolf's bookshop on Kuznetsky Most was looted by students—male and female! In Zamoskvorechie an officer (not himself the looter) was seen poking about with his sword in a pile of looted goods and taking his pick. On Tverskoy Boulevard, fine ladies wearing hats sorted through silk dress lengths! Students of the university and the Commercial Institute were spotted among the looters.

The mustachioed quartermaster: "If there'd been that many Russian shopkeepers in Berlin d'you think they wouldn't have been attacked? They would—and much sooner!"

The startling thing was not the behavior of the mob, but that of the respectable, civilized public who went to watch and refused to interfere.

Susanna had drawn her own conclusion from what she had seen: "The terrible thing is that it was no isolated incident, no freak event! You can see the essential character of Russian history coming to the surface. The itchy hand is typically Russian. Russians are no good at defending their interests systematically, they put up with everything, slavishly submit—then suddenly there's a pogrom. The pogrom last May is a reminder of many things in the past and a portent of still worse to come. We have a savage elemental force below us. It may erupt at any moment and scald us all with white-hot lava!"

"Oh, come on, Susanna Iosifovna," the lawyer's clerk protested. "That's not how it was! It wasn't elemental and spontaneous! It was all planned in advance!"

Planned in advance! Why had the newspapers been so eager to publicize German atrocities? If some philanthropic group or other helped wounded German soldiers—this was called "criminal charity." Lists of those expelled from the city were published. Governor-General Yusupov had pronounced himself, in his princely way, "on the side of the working people!" Action groups of some sort met in teahouses on the eve of the pogrom. Some people were given money, and leaflets with the names and addresses of German firms were passed around.

The quartermaster would have none of it. "There was no advance plan. A rumor went around that the Germans had poisoned thirty people, some said three hundred, at the Prokhorov plant. And at the Zeidel factory it was the manager's own fault. He drew a revolver on the crowd, and that started it!"

"Never mind that, the main question is where were the police? Why was it that right through the first day they didn't simply refrain from firing on the crowd, they didn't even use their whips, they just tried to talk them into dispersing? Sometimes they just kept out of sight— why? It was only on the second day, after the night fires . . . But by then things had gone too far in some places, people had started tearing up pictures of the Empress."

Still, Moscow was not Kishinev! There was a public collection and meals were provided for firemen who fell asleep on the street. The City Duma held an emergency meeting and the stenographic report was circulated. And its own volunteer militia was sent out on the streets.

All the same: "If there's no subterranean lava, volcanoes don't erupt—plan away, bore all the holes you like, you still won't make them. The cry now is 'Bash the Germans for using gas!' But 'Germans' is just a temporary excuse because, after a series of accidents, Russia is at war with them."

Notices were displayed in prominent places: "This shop was damaged by mistake: the firm and all its employees are Russian." People with other foreign names suffered more than the Germans. Paradoxically, there were signs saying, "Do not touch! This firm is Jewish!" Russia's allies would find Jew bashing unforgivable nowadays. But, in their mind's eye, those who attacked the Germans saw themselves attacking Jews! Wait just a bit, when the time comes we'll settle accounts with you! The whole war could end in an epidemic of pogroms! Many people are thinking of closing down their businesses right now—the next wave of pogroms might hit them! This conversation among the members of the concert party touched a raw nerve in Susanna, and when she and Alina were getting ready for bed in their poky hotel room, she still had something to add.

"One winter when I was a little girl my mother took me to buy toys. I was well fed and warmly dressed. Right in front of the shop a little boy with no winter clothes held out his bare hand and said, 'Please give me something, miss.' His shivering made me shiver in my fur coat. Suddenly I didn't want any toys, and I said, 'Give him the money, Mama!' So try to imagine, and don't ever forget that the Jews feel out in the cold, that they are forever shivering, that they feel helpless and hopeless in this country. Our situation is humiliating. All roads are closed to us! We are denied the right to reside in respectable civilized towns. My brother wasn't allowed to study in Kiev—he had to go all the way to Irkutsk! Then the Jewish community sent him on to Switzerland, he got a doctorate in philosophy at Bern, came back to Russia, and—guess what? Now he's a dentist! That's the sort of career open to us. Equality of rights—that's all we dream of! It's been my passion from my earliest days."

Alina was sincerely sympathetic. "Equal rights? Of course! Certainly you should have equal rights!"

"If you'd ever seen a pogrom when you were only a child—the crowd pouring down the street with banners and a calvary—how d'you think you'd feel for the rest of your life every time you saw a religious procession or so much as a crucifix? Or went past a church? You'd naturally feel hatred. Don't misunderstand me, I'm not prejudiced, I'm not one of those who feel that the Jews are a superior people. I revere German music. I adore French painting. And Russian literature is my spiritual home. Whereas singing Jewish songs and doing Jewish dances I don't like one little bit. But I've never bent the knee, and I never will. I'll never consent to be a second-rate person, accept that Jewish feeling of being a defenseless chicken."

She realized that she had put back on and fastened the bracelet and brooch previously taken off for the night.

"And everything is twisted into an attack on us. They raided the stockbrokers' quarter on Ilinka and found seventy Jews without residence permits—so the rumor goes around that the brokers are Jews to a man. If there's no small change, the Jews are to blame. If there are food shortages and prices are high, it's because the Jews are hoarding. Now there are these unfair charges against Rubinstein and the sugar refiners. Suppose some people are individually guilty—they should be brought to trial individually, without any of this poisonous talk about the Jews always being to blame for everything. Whatever happens to the Russian state the Jews have to take the rap."

She was carried away by a passion more powerful than any she expressed on the stage.

"Of course, we were always downtrodden, and it's always easier to deflect the people's wrath onto us, away from the real culprits. And of course the Jew-baiting atmosphere of so many years is bound to have its consequences. The Beilis case isn't over and done with yet—the wounds it left are still too fresh. You can see the idea clearly enough: use the Jewish question to split society, which is united in rejecting the government. Now they're fostering anti-Semitism in the army as well so as to turn the discontent of the troops in the same direction. They've shamelessly whipped up this spy mania—even searching synagogues for concealed wireless telegraphs! They've evacuated people from Kurland, Kovno, and Grodno provinces like bailiffs evicting defaulters, the old, the weak, the sick—you hear terrible stories. Put yourself in their place, Alina Vladimirovna, just think what evacuation means: torn from your hearth, with just a day or two's warning, deprived of the possessions that make life livable, hustled off to some place on the Volga, or even a Siberian village. Where can you find a home? What are you to eat? How will your children grow up? They let the traitor Sukhomlinov out on the town—and the Jews are bogged down in rural exile. Worse still—refugees are put to forced labor, a new form of serfdom is being introduced, people are no longer their own masters."

When she thought of the position of the Jews it was not just the cruel cuts, the heavy knocks, the sharp blows to the body that hurt her, but the lightest finger laid on a single hair—she would start in anticipation before it was touched.

"This spy mania is particularly painful to me because it is connected with the most insulting of all the humiliations we have to bear—the accusation that Jews are cowards. That brother of mine, Lazar, of whom I am very proud, formed a Jewish Self-Defense Group with some other youngsters in Kiev in 1905, got a big thrill out of going on night duty with a revolver, and discovered for the first time what a marvelous feeling it is not to be afraid, to know that if you die—you'll die fighting!"

Susanna, in her nightdress now, and about to put the light out, could see no lurking mockery in Alina's clear eyes, and so grew still more confiding.

"Our history tells us that our men could be lions. In public life everybody can see it's the same even today. In the army the opportunity doesn't arise—but when it does they'll show what they're made of."

And as she was blowing out the lamp: "Not only doesn't it depress me, I'm proud and happy to be a Jewess! Of the same stock as those talented, spiritually strong and—brave people. Yes, brave! Good night."

It was her only reason for traveling around with that excruciating troupe, to ridiculous concerts that took her away from her family, with wearisome journeys and uncomfortable overnight stops, to recite things her silent semi-literate audience did not always understand—her determination to repay honestly her debt to the war and to the army, and to refute arguments against the Jews. Each according to his powers.

[1 0]

(A GLANCE AT THE NEWSPAPERS)

"ROMANIAN SOLDIERS! I have summoned you to carry your banners beyond our frontiers. The nation will **glorify** you throughout the ages!"

Now that Romania has made its move, the road to the Balkans lies open. Nor can the end of treacherous Bulgaria, now hemmed in on all sides, be long delayed . . .

"The left flank of the Russian army is now completely secure against surprises from any quarter," Lieutenant General Brusilov told a correspondent. The spirit of the Romanian army is magnificent. General Brusilov is confident that Austria will not be able to hold out for very long, and the war may end in August 1917.

HORRIFYING DISCOVERY in the garden of the German Embassy in Bucharest: explosive substances, bacillus cultures . . .

Poor potato harvest in Germany, no bread or meat for a long time. Ringed by an implacable blockade . . .

There are reports that peasants, because of some totally incomprehensible fear for the future, are not bringing grain to the market but burying it . . . The peasants must be encouraged to sell their grain. (*Rech*)

FIXED GRAIN PRICES AND THE PEASANTS' INTERESTS: The psychology of the village today: peasants are endeavoring to save their grain, on which their whole existence depends, for a rainy day. Only organized intervention can ensure observance of the law on fixed prices.

... telegram from the Ministry of Agriculture. A fixed price for flour is to be established. We have been waiting for this telegram like manna from heaven. It has untied our hands ... The establishment of uniform fixed prices makes a flour shortage unthinkable ... The rural population must accept this measure with civic courage ...

... the grain crisis can be rendered less acute—by lowering fixed prices and introducing large-scale requisitioning of cereals. (Russkie Vedomosti)

Letter to the Editor ... At the present time, when prices are continually rising, there can be no thought of leaving life to the mercy of the iron law of supply and demand ... *Emergency measures to regulate supply, and not the abolition of compulsory tariffs and fixed prices* ...

... sugar prices up ... granulated sugar 20 kopecks a pound ...

SAVE THE HARVEST! Teams of schoolchildren ... Voluntary pilgrimage of schoolboys and students to the fields ... **moral rebirth of Russian youth** ...

(Photographs) "Our soldiers are always cheerful" (two shown with broad smiles). "One who will enjoy the fruits of our victory" (shows a Russian soldier holding a *Turkish child*).

... Russian prisoners harnessed to the plow ten in line ... prisoners made to pull carts to gather potatoes and kale ... forced to manufacture poison gas ...

How powerfully Germans dominated Russian life. Why were we so inordinately indulgent? For fifty years Russian scholars and Russian artists looked at the world through German eyes, and our decadents still seem unable to come to their senses: although the performance of German works is forbidden (as in Italy and France), various concert artists are gradually raising their heads and showing their spiritual bankruptcy, apparently unable to do without **Beethoven** and **Wagner**. The public must boycott such concerts. (*Novoye Vremya*)

LECTURE ON "THE SOUL OF WOMAN" ... Weininger's negative answer ... Woman as portrayed by Maupassant and Chekhov ... in the works of Shakespeare ... Tolstoy's view ... The emancipated woman ...

AT THE CAPITAL'S CINEMAS

LOVE'S ACCORD, THE MORPHINE GIRL, THE GOLDEN DREAM

FOR SALE: a white lacquered **DRESSING TABLE**.

SENSATIONAL PRESENT: War games for children and adults, Pestalozzi Institute.

BEAUTY AIDS OF THE ANCIENT HELLENES. Wax and marble soaps.

WOODEN-SOLED FOOTWEAR, cheap and comfortable. From **Zemgor** workshops.

LOVER OF ANTIQUES PAYS GOOD PRICES for porcelain, pictures, bronzes, furniture.

Situation sought as **SECOND PARLOR MAID**.

H.M. THE EMPEROR INVESTED with British Order of the Bath, Military Division, First Class, for services to the war effort.

. . . until our army and the armies of our allies meet in a fraternal embrace beneath the walls of Berlin . . .

The Russian and Romanian forces have drawn back a little . . .

From a British journal . . . "Invincibility of our eastern ally . . . traditional Russian tactics . . . retreat in order to strike more effectively . . .

British *"Tommies"* have christened their new armored car with the monosyllabic appellation "tank," which means "cistern." These are box-shaped landgoing ships. The "cistern" was fathered by Winston Churchill . . .

According to the Reuters agency, morale in Germany is now as low as could be . . . The end of Austria-Hungary is at hand . . . **men of 50 to 60 called to the colors** . . .

. . . the reporter saw with his own eyes a German soldier with no butter spreading axle grease on his bread . . . Germany's position in the third year of war . . .

From the army in the field . . . Clubs used by the Germans to finish off soldiers overcome by poison gas. Many such clubs studded with blunt nails have been picked up in German trenches occupied by our forces . . .

FIXED PRICES. The atmosphere is extremely tense . . . rural population in Melitopol province has no faith in fixed prices . . . buyers leave empty-handed . . .

EKATERINOSLAV . . . Grain market unprecedentedly quiet. Now that new fixed prices have been confirmed, growers prefer to hold back their grain. Mills are ceasing production because of the grain shortage.

BREAD AND FLOUR are not in short supply in Rostov! The alleged shortage has been created by the inhabitants themselves, who have greatly increased their purchases. Bakers claim that people are taking much more bread than they need . . . Must be limited to one pood of flour per person.

. . . Some people ask whether requisitioning would really be so easy. Could we take grain away from landowners and peasants at a price which they consider too low? Would this not cause unrest among a section of the Russian people? However that may be, we probably cannot avoid requisitioning. In a country where elementary honesty and spirit do not exist threats are necessary. (*Rech*)

In provinces where export of vegetables is not prohibited they vanish completely. Middlemen go around the villages buying up everything they can lay their hands on— butter, eggs, mushrooms, wool—and carrying it off into the unknown . . .

TIFLIS. Forty wagonloads of concealed grain have come to light here. Some of it has rotted.

PROFITEERING by the Nobel and "Mazut" companies.

PROFITEERING IN GALOSHES

1914 **TO THE APATHETIC, OUR COMMISERATION—TO THOSE AGAINST US, OUR RESPECTS—TO COMRADES-IN-ARMS, OUR GREETINGS** . . . our task goes far beyond the framework of contemporary events . . . must free ourselves from foreign tutelage of any kind . . . safeguard Russian independence and the nation's energies . . .

PATRIOTISM AND HEALTH RESORTS . . . Chaos at Simferopol station. Hordes of people begging for a lift besiege the lucky few who manage to get an automobile or a carriage . . .

UNCOUTH GENIUS. In *The Barber of Seville*, Karakash sang something incorrectly and "Maestro" Chaliapin demonstratively beat time with his foot, then yelled at the top of his once-heroic voice, "If you can't sing, why don't you forget about it!" Karakash walked off into the wings, pursued by unprintable abuse from the mouth of the genius.

POTATO CHEESE is almost the equal of Swiss cheese in flavor and nutritional value . . .

THE RUSSIAN COMPANY "MACHINE GUN."

Our specialty: **MOURNING FOR LADIES,** bespoke or ready-made.

Wet nurse, countrywoman, seeks position.

BLOODSTOCK FOR SALE

FOR SALE: **SABLE CLOAK**

PLEASE HELP! For the attention of kind people! Land surveyor's wife asks kind and compassionate people for material assistance . . . in extremely difficult situation, two daughters, deserted by husband . . . all belongings pawned . . .

AT IMPERIAL HQ. On the name day of the Heir to the Throne, the Most Reverend Metropolitan Pitirim celebrated divine service . . . His Imperial Majesty was presented with a benedictory letter from the Most Holy Synod together with an icon of the All-Merciful Saviour.

AUSTRIAN PRIME MINISTER STÜRGKH SHOT by newspaper editor Friedrich Adler . . .

Russian and Romanian troops have pulled back a little in the Dobrudja . . .

In our time millions of people have got used to living with the thought of death. They die without a word of reproach, fully conscious of the enormous significance of their death . . . "We shall be no more, but our children will know the joy of the free and beautiful life without sorrow which will come to our tear-drenched earth . . ."

SCURVY IN THE GERMAN ARMY

CLASS ENMITY IN GERMANY

Germany slanders Russia . . .

STATEMENT BY RODZYANKO . . . In view of the discussion in the press as to whether M. V. Rodzyanko should accept a ministerial post, the president of the State Duma asks us to inform the public that no such proposal has ever been made to him.

IN THE BUDGET COMMISSION OF THE STATE DUMA. A plan for the reorganization of food distribution was submitted by the Minister of Agriculture . . . Broadest participation of sections of the public and of senior plenipotentiaries and their assistants . . . The Ministry of the Interior has also completed work on a plan for a new law on food supplies. Responsibility for supervising food supplies throughout the empire will rest with the Minister of the Interior, provincial governors, and city prefects.

Tambov. The governor is threatening to requisition grain. In the name of patriotism, the governor calls on traders and producers to report to the plenipotentiary immediately any stocks of salable grain in their possession.

Novocherkassk. Full authority in supply matters is vested in the plenipotentiaries and various consultative bodies and committees, but when disaster strikes, the population turns to the ataman.

GROWERS MOBILIZE. Landowners in Saratov province are preparing to protest against the fixed prices set for cereals.

(MISCELLANEOUS) Women are not turning out to work. Money is so plentiful in the countryside that people do not want to work anymore. (Rech)

The supply of butter to Petrograd is not at all reliable. By contrast, there is a butter surplus in the Baltic provinces, **but the export ban makes it impossible to deliver it to Petrograd.**

The Tula sugar refinery has no raw material, while beets are rotting in Ryazan and Tambov provinces because of the export ban.

KOSTROMA. There is a fuel crisis in this forest kingdom.

POLICE RAID IN ODESSA on the biggest nest of black marketeers in the center of the city . . . ended with the arrest of several dozen black marketeers, brokers and middlemen.

In Vladikavkaz, Nikolai and Vladimir Zapalov were sentenced by the governor-general to three months' imprisonment, without the option of a fine, for receiving 700 pairs of stolen shoes.

In refutation of incorrect reports about the kerosene trade which have found their way into the press, the **BOARD OF DIRECTORS OF NOBEL BROS. & CO.** considers it necessary to publish this statement . . . Stocks of kerosene are not being concealed anywhere, by anyone.

PATRIOTIC AND PROFITABLE. Buy **WAR BONDS** at 5½% per annum. This is the easiest of your duties to your country, and after the war your savings will enable you to begin a new life.

. . . woman wanted to steer barge . . . woman pump hand.

General meeting of SOCIETY FOR PROTECTION OF THE JEWISH POPULATION . . . Sanatoria in the Crimea.

FROM THE COMMITTEE FOR STRUGGLE AGAINST GERMAN DOMINATION . . . Liquidation of German landholdings in southern Russia proceeds at full speed.

GRAND GYPSY CONCERT

KATYUSHA SOROKINA . . . With the gracious participation of Tamara Platonovna Karsavina of the Imperial Ballet.

LARGE REWARD offered for assistance in renting **GENTLEMAN'S APARTMENT**.

BEAUTIFUL BIRCH-PANELED BEDROOM SUITE for sale . . .

LUXURIOUS PERSIAN AND SMYRNA CARPETS . . .

HOME SHOE REPAIRS—anyone can learn.

Fully trained laundress . . .

A HIGH-HANDED ACTION. The German and Austrian manifesto on the creation of the kingdom of Poland . . . without asking the Poles whether they want the German yoke . . . usual revolting behavior of the German government . . . on the Russian side the only reason why steps have not yet been taken to reorganize the kingdom of Poland is that it is impossible to carry out such a reorganization at the height of the war.

. . . *Daily Telegraph:* "We are gradually beginning to understand the Russian spirit . . . The unwavering loyalty for which we are so grateful . . . Everything which idealistic visionaries vaguely dreamt of . . . the endurance, kindliness, and chivalry of the Slavs have begun to stand out against the general background of suffering and misery . . ."

. . . Friedrich Adler, son of the Social Democratic Party leader Viktor Adler, married to a Russian student, favorite pupil of the illustrious Mach. **A passionate Social Democrat** . . . Indicated that the reason for his action was the ban on a socialist gathering. (*Rech*)

. . . It is indeed embarrassing to recall that the universal conviction in our country was that military operations would be over quickly, in four to five months. Continuation of the war for more than a year was thought to be out of the question, if only because the German population would die of starvation. But the twenty-eighth month of the war shows that . . . We have not only experienced an acute shortage of military supplies, we are confronted with the astounding fact that the food supply, in an empire which before the war fed more than one Western state, is totally disorganized.

IN THE BUDGET COMMISSION OF THE STATE DUMA. Speech by Protopopov, Minister of the Interior . . . "We must not let the noble slogan 'everything for victory' turn into 'nothing for the home front' . . . When I was in England . . . We are late in . . . Private initiative must be allowed to thrive, because that is where the genius and the resilience of our nation shows itself . . . Introduction of ration cards would bring all trade to a halt . . ."

WHERE RUSSIAN GRAIN GOES . . . At a well-attended conference of plenipotentiaries for procurement of cereals in Kharkov . . . While Russian cities cannot obtain a single sack of grain huge quantities are exported to Finland unhindered . . . (*Novoye Vremya*)

NOVOCHERKASSK. Duty on potatoes no higher than 75 kopecks per pood . . .

. . . An acquaintance of ours from Taganrog has just got home from Moscow . . . "Compared with Moscow, or even Kharkov, Rostov is an earthly paradise, *it is ashamed of its prosperity* . . ."

PROCEEDINGS OF THE STATE DUMA . . . "On measures to prevent the consumption by the population of meat and meat products from adult cattle, calves, sheep and lambs, pigs and piglets . . ."

CONCEALMENT OF STOCKS. At the kvass brewery on the Polyustrovskaya Embankment . . . at the Zhigalov Brothers warehouse 33 barrels . . .

ODESSA. The Shapiro, Rauchberger, and Spoliansky factories, which are known to have made use of defense materials for private profiteering purposes, are still under investigation. The police have discovered buried documents and ledgers. (*Russkie Vedomosti*)

NOBEL BROS. AND KEROSENE . . . Why do they try to deny it? In many towns, to say nothing of the villages, there is no kerosene and prices are exorbitant. Oil profits are such that the company's shares are priced at six times their face value.

. . . the present war is a PEOPLE'S WAR and the war loan must become the PEOPLE'S CAUSE . . .

SOCIETY FOR COMBATING LUXURY AND EXTRAVAGANCE . . . We appeal to Russian women in the hope that not one of them will take part in this indecent competition—a fancy-dress ball with prizes for extravagance in costumes and jewelry.

NURSES! ANSWER THE CALL!

. . . Last days of the *ARTIFICIAL LIMBS* exhibition. Hay making with an artificial left arm . . . The Cossack with artificial legs. A nose made of soft material . . . An electromagnetic hand operated by means of a plug.

ROAD CASUALTIES. CARELESS DRIVING... Car No.... knocked down a cabby on the Palace Embankment... On Kamennostrovsky, Car No.... ran over a seven-year-old boy... Car No.... drove into a gas lamppost... Car No.... broke the pole of an electric tram and disappeared...

ATTENTION! No more need for sugar! Save your health and your money! Drink RUSSIAN BERRY AND FRUIT TEA.

LADIES with a liking for fancy underwear and chic matinee coats—hurry up and buy from your traveling salesman.

DIVORCE—quick and cheap. No.... **Nevsky Prospect.**

Renaissance. Amazing **DARK OAK SUITE,** foreign leather upholstery.

... maid of all work

MOTORCYCLE WANTED

... by the sacred and sovereign will of God's Anointed, our fervently adored Emperor, who...

... our evacuation of Constantsa... Grain elevators and oil storage tanks fired.

... The Greek government has accepted all of the French admiral's conditions...

BULGARIAN ATROCITIES... A nation of fratricidal Cains.

VICTORY MUST BE OURS!

The Times indicates that the main reason why Germany has announced the creation of a kingdom of Poland is its **need for Polish troops.**

The main obstacles to the activity of parliamentary institutions has come from none other than Stürgkh. The uncompromising reactionary character of his recent activities emerges clearly from press reports. He has antagonized the broadest circles of society. This makes Adler's motives for shooting him sufficiently clear. (*Rech*)

London. Public meeting opposes premature peace.

NEW LAW ON PENALTIES FOR SPECULATION. Long awaited by the population... promulgated at long last... for demanding exorbitant prices for foodstuffs... for concealing stocks or suspending trade without valid reasons... 8 to 16 months' imprisonment.

THE BANKS AND THE GRAIN TRADE... Conference of bankers to discuss their part in provisioning...

The Moscow press is perturbed by rumors that preliminary censorship of Moscow newspapers is to be introduced... everybody understands the need for military censorship, but civilian censorship is another matter. What political secrets does the government need to conceal from its own people? If we have censorship, "oral newspapers" will appear, and it is very doubtful whether they will be to the government's liking. We journalists belong at present to the "naturalistic" school, but with censorship we shall become "symbolists." (*Utro Russii*)

IMPORT OF LUXURY GOODS FORBIDDEN

. . . Measures to combat consumption of varnishes and polishes by drinkers.

YELLOW LABOR. In many Russian towns Chinese are seen more and more frequently.

WHICH OF US DOES NOT WISH TO HELP OUR BRAVE WARRIORS? MAKE HASTE TO BUY 5½% WAR BONDS. Every 100-ruble bond is three rounds of shrapnel at the enemy.

ODESSA. WOMEN RIOT. In connection with the zemstvo's inventorying of produce, rumors that "serfdom is coming back" spread through the villages . . . A crowd of about 100 women . . .

A GANG OF SWINDLERS. A special panel of the Petrograd Superior Court examined the case of a gang of swindlers operating throughout Russia . . . The head of the whole concern is Tsereteli, a personage of some note. He obtained something like 100,000 rubles by means of a fraudulent telegram . . . gave 4,000 rubles to charity and was universally respected as a result . . . "I have lived and given life to others."

EXHIBITION OF ARTIFICIAL LIMBS. Feeling of amazement at such hugely ingenious inventiveness . . . The life of each prosthesis is two to three years, and a new one costs **100 to 150 rubles.** The disabled person will quite shortly have to make do with a wooden leg, and special attention ought to be given to this primitive device . . .

I shut my mind to care and questions,
In my hammock gently sway,
Half-seeing on the sand beneath me
Cigarette ash dead and gray.

Storms there have been, storms there will be.
I hear the garden softly sing
And in the blue and white above me
Like a swallow I take wing.

V. Bryuson

WHAT TO EAT INSTEAD OF MEAT. Instructions on the preparation of tasty, filling, and cheap dishes.

TEETH PURCHASES. Old false teeth and even broken dentures at highest prices. I pay 50 kopecks a tooth . . . I also purchase scrap gold and silver and various medals.

ALL THINGS IN THIS LIFE CHANGE! Except the unique S.E.R. cigarettes, which were, are, and always will be of unchanging high quality.

R A C I N G today.

YOUNGISH PARISIENNE seeks post as lady's companion.

LUXURIOUS WHITE BEDROOM SUITE. Paris workmanship.

REFUGE FOR PREGNANT WOMEN, MATERNITY HOME. Confidential midwife.

CULTURED CHILDREN'S NURSE sought.

Wanted: *SWISS GOAT*.

RETURN OF H.I.M. THE EMPEROR. His Imperial Majesty the Emperor, together with the Heir Apparent, the Grand Duke Aleksei Nikolaevich, arrived at Tsarskoye Selo from the army in the field on 1 November.

FRENCH BREAKTHROUGH AT VERDUN!

. . . the Russian and Romanian troops have drawn back slightly . . .

. . . Russia will be approaching the zenith of its might next year. 99 percent of Russians demand the continuation of the war to final victory. The outcome of the war will be decided next summer.

LATEST INTERVIEW WITH GENERAL BRUSILOV. "We have already won the war," the valiant Russian general told a British reporter. "It's just a question of time. The Romanian army's setbacks have no real significance."

The Times: "At present we are all for Russia. Let us hope that these warm feelings will not be replaced by indifference."

> The organ of the German Social Democrats declares that the main sufferer from this act was not the murdered man, who left no family. One tragic figure is the "old man on the throne," Franz Josef, who has already lost in the same circumstances a brother, a son, a wife, and a nephew. But still more tragic is the fate of the assassin's father, Viktor Adler, and the sympathy of the proletariat must now be addressed to him. It was he who once led the Austrian socialist movement out of its terrorist phase, to plant it on granite foundations of Marxist doctrine— and now anarchy has struck him a dreadful blow. (*Rech*, 2 November)

THE BAVARIAN PRINCE LEOPOLD
NAMED KING OF POLAND.

Male population of Serbia deported by Austrians.

. . . it must be admitted that Germany, thanks to timely and careful measures of strict regulation and economy, has not so far suffered any real shortage of foodstuffs . . .

Holders of white chits ordered to reregister in Petrograd . . .

PLENTY OF MEAT IN PETROGRAD...

The Supreme Council of the Union of the Russian People thinks that Russia is under no threat of revolution at the present time: these are all fabrications . . .

All solar and terrestrial magnetic phenomena have now reached their maximum . . . The northern lights will frequently be observable in Petrograd during the coming winter.

"I DON'T CARE WHO KILLS GERMANS"—**JACK LONDON** . . . Sad news of the writer's death . . . And so the words quoted above sound like his last dying wish . . .

. . . *on the premises of the Petrograd Military Hotel (formerly the Astoria), a tea party:* "*PETROGRAD—FOR THE DEFENDERS OF THE MOTHERLAND . . .*"

NURSES! ANSWER THE CALL!

CAUCASIAN RESORTS . . . Great influx of visitors . . . Meat 30 kopecks per pound, chickens a ruble each . . .

I PAY FULL PRICE for diamonds, pearls, gold . . . Fistul, Jeweler.

YOUR PERSONAL FUTURE instantly and infallibly revealed by my magic cards.

CULTURED YOUNG LADY *offers massage, general or local* . . .

RUSSIAN COACHMAN, able to drive troika . . .

[1 1]

This year Alina had firmly resolved not to visit her husband at the front: she wouldn't humiliate herself again by seeming to beg for the treat to which she was entitled. If he wanted to, he would come without being asked, as other officers did.

And so that November she faced the prospect of a birthday without her husband. She tried to think up some original way of celebrating it, to make it memorable. Whom should she invite? (Just suppose whoever had given her the bouquet of roses should arrive from out of the blue! How would she feel about that?)

But it cost Alina something of an effort to think about it all: she had little money to spare, and it was doubtful whether she could get up her courage for anything too eccentric. She began to think that the best thing might be simply to visit her mother in Borisoglebsk and see a few of her girlhood friends.

Then suddenly, on Friday, 27 October—a telegram! And he was already in Kiev! And would be in Moscow that Saturday! How mar-

velous! Darling Georgi! I'll soon blow the cobwebs away! The last time
you were in Moscow was when you were dropped by GHQ—and that
was only for three days.

As luck would have it—just two weeks to her birthday. So he wasn't
a completely hopeless case after all.

What a relief! No need to exert herself thinking up something extravagant. No need for ingenuity. Just relax at home, easier that way.
Life is always easier if you let it take its own course.

Friday was, as it happened, one of the cleaning woman's days. The
two of them busied themselves cooking and prettifying the apartment—and rehanging the tulle curtains, washing the lace table mats,
beating carpets. Georgi had forgotten all about home comforts, so she
would lovingly remind him with every little detail, with every little
cushion on the couch . . .

Ever since 1914, when they had made their lucky escape from Vyatka
to Moscow, they had lived in a pleasant, recently built house opposite
the Commercial Training School on Ostozhenka between the two
Ushakov Lanes. There was a clean and handsome staircase, the steps
were of marble, there were brown parquet floors on the landings,
quaint ear-shaped doorbells ("please tweak"). There were no back
stairs, but a chute made it unnecessary to carry rubbish out the front
way. There was central heating, and in a difficult autumn, like this
one, when firewood was dear, there was no need to worry about fuel,
such worries could be left to the priest who had built the house on
the grounds of his church (the Church of the Dormition) and still
managed it. They had grown so used to it, and so fond of it—their
marvelous little three-room apartment on the third floor looking out
on Ostozhenka and the churchyard. From the side windows there was
a still better view of the street, all the way to HQ Moscow Military
District, to which Georgi had been transferred in 1914. (He had remained in contact with many officers, and could still have arranged to
be posted back from his regiment, but he turned a deaf ear to friendly
hints.)

Alina was busy late into the evening arranging and rearranging her
husband's prized possessions, trying to remember how it was most
convenient for him to reach his desk or look around from it. What
holds a family together is a home, in which every little thing must be
a good one of its kind, in its proper place, just right for its purpose,
meant to make life easier. And if anybody knew instinctively the only
possible place to put things, and just where to hang photographs on
the walls, it was Alina. In his two years of roughing it at the front
Georgi had lost contact with the things that make a home, but it would
surely come back to him! After the discomforts of army life he would
value them all the more.

Looking back, she could see that insensitivity had always been

Georgi's trouble—there was nothing new in it. He had no real gift for love, for responding to anyone else's (and especially a woman's) changeable emotions, to the particularities of people's life stories. It was a pity for him, poor silly fellow: his emotional underendowment harmed him more than anyone. Well, that was what a wife was meant to do: keep watch on her husband's thoughts and feelings and try to correct his congenital faults. And apathetic as he now was, he would surely liven up and take more interest once he was at home.

As she tidied up, Alina wondered how best to spend the two weeks of his visit. It was a marvelous time of year, the best for music, a concert by Rachmaninoff and Ziloti was advertised for the end of the month, Koussevitzky's orchestra would be at Nazlobin's theater from Monday, and tomorrow would see the first of six meetings of the Russian Musical Society, this one devoted to French music, the whole of musical Moscow would be there—but that was one they would have to miss. It was essential for Alina to attend such concerts—to develop her artistry, breathe the musical atmosphere. But how much more vivid the experience would be if she went not with women friends but arm in arm with her soldier husband, an imposing colonel (a general by now but for his own pigheadedness), and strolled about the foyer in the intervals introducing him to one after another of her new Moscow circle.

Not knowing when he would arrive, she had been ready for him all day. At last the sweet little doorbell gurgled, Alina opened the door wide and let those great paws seize her, embrace her, squeeze her (stronger than ever?), and even lift her off her feet, felt that beard rasp her face (I'll trim it for you, it's grown too much!).

"You're safe! You're safe!" She clung around his neck. Her husband was safe, to confound all his enemies—drat them!

He was wearing a fur hat instead of his forage cap. It suited him very well. His skin was more deeply tanned and rougher than ever. His eyes were as quick as always (he was coming to life already). His uniform was brown, not of the usual gray-green cloth. Quite handsome! But why? Was that a new form of camouflage? Still, it had a certain elegance. What am I wearing today? Have you noticed at all, or are you a block of stone? Which day of ours does it remind you of?

They walked about the room with their arms around each other. She tried to point out some of her bright ideas, but he had no eyes for them yet. Give me another squeeze. That's right.

She watched to see whether certain objects which their life together had made dear would raise a smile as they used to. Everything was just where it had been—or moved to a better place. She led him around the apartment, searching his face for signs of relief after the hardships of the front, or amazement that when whole countries had been trampled and churned up, here everything was still in place.

There was a glimmer of some such feeling, but a faint one. Haven't you noticed how tidy it all is, stupid?

"Remember what that table mat's called?"

It was cobweb lace, adorning a circular occasional table made of dark wood.

"The little spider!"

He did remember!

"And that chest of drawers?"

He smiled. "Tubby."

He remembered that their gramophone was called Grum. They had given names of their own to many of the familiar and cherished possessions which made life easier. It all helped to make home a magical place.

Alina persisted, using the baby talk they also indulged in.

"Nice little housikins? Whose little hands did it all, then?" She screwed up her eyes and held both hands out to be kissed.

He slipped off his ammunition belts, but it gave him no relief, and he sank onto the sofa as though his own body was too heavy for him.

He heaved a sigh.

"Lord, oh Lord." She sighed in sympathy. She felt in her own body the iron heaviness in him. "How hard it all is for you!" She pressed against him and ruffled his hair. "It is hard, isn't it? Very hard."

"Yes, yes, yes." He sighed again, heavily, hopelessly.

"What? Things in general?"

"Yes. Things in general."

"But what in particular?"

He sat motionless, and sighed again. "Hell . . . we'll never make up for what we're losing."

"You mean all the men killed?"

"Killed, wounded, done for . . . sickened by it all . . . Everything . . . Nothing will ever make up for it . . . Never."

"Lord, oh Lord. How tired you are. How terribly tired." She stroked his head.

"Tired, yes. I'm tired all right, but . . ."

"You should have come home on leave last year. You've tortured yourself all your life. You're your own worst enemy! You ought to think of yourself sometimes! You need to come up for air!"

She rang the little Chinese bell. Did he remember the bell? Its tuneful tinkle used to call him from his work to meals. This was where he was going to be really pleased! You can't learn someone else's tastes in a year, but she knew his of old—that was what being married meant.

In their Petersburg years, they had rented rooms with board, so they could do without servants. In that hole Vyatka, officers' wives, for lack of anything better to do, did their own cooking. Alina tried her hand at it, and as always when she made a serious effort, the results were excellent. Georgi greatly enjoyed her cuisine, never failed to notice and to praise whatever she made, so that she didn't mind exerting herself. Housewifery proved to be a world of its own and a complicated one, demanding an ability to learn, taste, and methodical habits, but these were among Alina's wealth of talents, and were fruitfully applied. During the war many people in Moscow too had started managing without help in the kitchen, some of her Moscow acquaintances among them— which made it all the easier for Alina.

But these last few months the food situation had become very much worse. Several items were unobtainable. Georgi made fun of her: as bad as when a supply train is cut off in the mountains and there's nothing to eat for three days? No, not like that, but anything in short supply was sold at an inflated price, twice or three times more than usual. Even the wretched Dolgachev, in Princess Lvova's basement across the road, kept things out of sight and made you beg. The recently established cooperative shop for officers helped to some extent. There were queues everywhere. He must have seen them on his way there.

"Do I stand in line? Not likely. I would have no time left for living. I have to sit at the piano for five hours a day. I can see you don't remember anything . . ."

Of course he remembered.

Well, she did queue sometimes for meat. And French rolls first thing in the morning. There was no sugar to be had at all. They'd introduced ration coupons for sugar the week before. Still, we've got some of Mama's jam from Borisoglebsk . . . Expensive sweets and honey you could get anywhere. All at twice the price.

"Do you really have any idea what life is like here? You get your rations, everything's taken care of for you. But here . . . the refugees make it worse, they've descended on us in droves, and some of them are rich. And they get a living allowance on top of it all. And how much d'you think servants are paid now? You have to give them a raise almost every month."

His face clouded over. "So how do you . . . ?"

"It's hard, of course. Things are bad. Mama helps. Who else is there?"

Alina's mother, as the widow of a senior civil servant, had a large pension for life. Alina herself had been in receipt of a sizable pension because of her father, but, as the law stipulated, only till she married. He knew she was no spendthrift, but living on an officer's pay had always been a bit of a struggle. Being assigned to GHQ had meant an improvement in status but no extra money.

Alina knew, though, that he didn't play cards, didn't drink, didn't go to restaurants. He had always detested the average Russian gentleman's profligacy, and was a work fanatic.

"I have to save myself, dear. You do see, don't you? For the future. And for you."

Of course, of course. He looked confused, miserable, downcast. No, he wasn't beyond hope. When he was living in a warm family atmosphere again, he would be as sensitive as ever.

In fact, he was perking up already. In a day or two he would thaw out and be himself again.

Their hands, with identical wedding rings, moved about the little table, transferring food from serving dish to plate.

"Is it nice?" Alina smiled, sure that it was. "After what you get in the trenches?"

He liked it, loved it. His head swayed toward her.

"Behave yourself! Be patient!" She coquettishly wriggled away from him. "Oh, look, you've got some gray hairs! Better pull them out, who wants a gray-headed husband?"

She was joking. The husband she had was the one she wanted. She must be a loyal wife and work hard to polish the rough diamond as best she could.

Happily fussing over him, Alina failed for the first time ever to notice that uneasy, hangdog look: it meant not that Georgi was sorry for something he had done but that he was afraid to tell her something. But when she started making plans, talking about concerts they simply must go to next week—(Meichik, Frei)—she saw that things weren't so simple, that something was wrong, that the load on his mind was getting heavier all the time.

At last, with embarrassment and painfully slowly, he came out with it. He simply couldn't help it. This was not leave; rather, he had been sent on urgent business to the War Ministry. Strictly speaking, he should have gone straight to Petersburg via Mogilev, not via Moscow.

Alina was deeply hurt. "Why didn't you tell me?" she wailed. "You treat me like dirt."

Over her sparkling dinner service, over all the things she had gone to such trouble to prepare, she shed tears of mortification. It was so cruel, so humiliating.

"You should have gone straight there! And told me nothing about it! Then I wouldn't have gotten all excited. It would have been kinder that way."

She was right, absolutely right, and there was nothing he could say in reply. He hovered uneasily behind her.

"All the things you said in your letters! That you were miserable not hearing from me! That it would be more than you could bear if we didn't see each other this year. That when we met you wouldn't be able to say a word, you'd just kiss me and kiss me . . ."

It was a peculiarity of his. If he made someone happy, he had to do something to spoil it, had to cast a cloud. If he went to a concert he would grumble about the waste of time all evening. At the theater he would refuse to go to the buffet during the intermission, pretending that it would clash with the mood of the play. He had bought her a camera once, but when he wouldn't look at her photographs, she lost interest in mounting them, getting them enlarged, classifying and showing them off, although they were quite splendid. Why was he so unfeeling?

Wait, though: "What about my birthday? D'you mean you won't be here for that?"

Yes, yes, he would—his face told her so as he came from behind her. How many days would he be in Petersburg? Still looking guilty and apprehensive—er, four days, say . . . All right then, my birthday's twelve days away, so that's not too bad. But was he absolutely sure?

They finished eating her delicious lunch. The usual ritual after a meal was a kiss on the cheek. But this time Alina felt entitled to a kiss on the lips.

After lunch Georgi came into the kitchen while she was washing the dishes, perhaps intending to say something, but she had put the light on—it was a dull day—and, cold fish or not, he noticed the translucency of her ear—her ears were indeed one of Alina's best features, shapely, delicate, shell-like, like two exquisite treasures plucked from the ocean—and, standing behind her, kissed it. Then her neck. Then drew her out of the kitchen, not even giving her time to dry her hands properly.

Whatever the clock said, the light was fading fast as they lay there. Alina felt happy and at peace. Suddenly she wanted to tell him things. When you talk about your experiences to someone you love you relive them, live them more fully than before, make them more meaningful. And so much had happened in the last few months. They'd once given a concert in the Botkin house, for instance. And a charity concert at the Huntsman's Club—the acoustics were a bit strange. Chelnokov, the mayor of Moscow, no less, had kissed Alina's hand.

"And one lieutenant colonel told me the next day, 'Do you know, after hearing you play Chopin's ballade I couldn't sleep all night.'"

But Georgi wasn't at all thrilled. He lay there smoking (he'd taken it up again after his dismissal from GHQ and made no effort to stop), taking care not to miss the ashtray and drop ash on the bedside table. He listened without interrupting, but showed no interest. After all the time they'd been apart. He didn't even respond to her most cherished dream—that, though belatedly and in a roundabout way, this hectic concert giving would help her to make up for missing the Conservatoire.

He was still lost in a fog! He really had grown dull, cooped up in a trench for all those years. Why shouldn't she aspire to the heights of art? Nothing in this world was higher than that. Was his masculine pride perhaps hurt by the blossoming of her talent when he himself had dried up and gone to seed?

"Aren't you pleased by my success? Are you jealous or something? Would you rather I spent all my time within four walls?"

He assured her that he was pleased, very pleased—by the bouquets and all the rest of it.

She was eager to hear what he had to say. But he wasn't going to talk. And Alina suddenly realized that this was their one and only evening together! How best to spend it? They must make up their minds quickly. "Why don't we just stay in?" Georgi said hopefully.

"It's your own fault! You should have got yourself sent to the Moscow Military District. It's too late to get tickets for anything. But we can invite ourselves out." (And I can show him off to Susanna.) "Will you wear all your medals?" No, that was only on ceremonial occasions. Just the George and the Vladimir. Pity.

Alina's mind raced. How could she let people know? Where could they all get together? She dressed carefully. Lucky they now had a wall telephone out on the landing. No need to go to the pharmacy.

She went out, made several calls, and came back.

"We're meeting at Muma's. She'll sing, and I'll accompany."

Georgi looked sour. Go all that way just to hear you accompany? It would be better if you just stayed at home and played, I like your music best when you play by yourself.

Alina protested. "You think accompanying is demeaning? You're a freak! You don't know the first thing! There's nothing a pianist enjoys more than accompanying. Have you any idea what ensemble playing means? Have you ever asked yourself how I could bear our long separations if it wasn't for music?"

He looked as though he would like to merge with the wallpaper.

"You no sooner come home than you're away again, and I'm left all alone. I'm spiritually starved. My friends are my world—the atmosphere I breathe and in which I blossom. When you go away, all I have left is what those people think of me. Won't you let me feel just for a little while that I'm not a grass widow to them? Help them remember that I have a husband somewhere?" She saw that he was upset. "I will play too, of course! And you can tell us about the front— everybody needs to know about it, not just me!"

So the party was at Muma's. She was a good friend of Alina's, and had a contralto voice and a splendid Becker grand. The guests were whoever could be assembled in a hurry, including even Muma's neighbors. Never mind, the main object was to show Georgi off to Susanna.

The musical part of the proceedings went off very well. Muma sang an aria from *Samson and Delilah* superbly. Alina played a few charming Chopin mazurkas and Liszt's headlong "Rome-Naples-Florence" étude. There was also an "artistic whistler." Everybody enjoyed the program and applauded warmly. By suppertime Alina was in high spirits. She drank a glass of wine and needed no persuasion to take a second.

Then, as always happened when an officer on active service appeared in company, everyone was eager to hear what Colonel Vorotyntsev could tell them. But the mean creature had no stories for them, not one single episode, although he was a good raconteur. (Wouldn't make an effort for his poor little wife's sake!) It was amazing how they all took to him in spite of this, and Alina felt proud. They saw his medal ribbons, his sunburnt and weather-beaten features, the dormant—perhaps excessive—willfulness: he looked at first disapproving, and seemed to be restraining himself from taking command and giving everyone present a dressing-down. But later he relaxed. Everybody was asking Alina how they could arrange another occasion and hear what he had to say.

Alina was interested to see what impression Georgi would make on Susanna. They moved away from the company to sit on a distant sofa. Alina walked past, quite close, eavesdropping. Might have known! Georgi on his, Susanna on her own hobbyhorse.

"Is it honest," Susanna was asking, "to shift the blame for your own defeats, retreats, and general obtuseness onto Jewish spies?"

"I absolutely agree with you. It's dishonest."

"But if they can mount such a campaign against the Jews while the war is on, what's it going to be like when we win? And how can Jews be expected to want us to win?"

"Again, I agree. If Jews are denied any of the rights Russians enjoy, they can't be expected to love Russia unreservedly. And it's not insulting them to suppose that many Jews have more sympathy with Germany, where they enjoy equal rights."

Susanna had nonetheless taken a close look at him, and said to Alina later that evening, "Oh no, he doesn't look emotionally stunted to me! So keep a close watch on him. When you're in company, notice how he looks at women, and how they look at him."

"Really, now!" Alina said, laughing. "Thanks for the warning, but that's one thing I don't have to worry about. Women are outside his field of vision. And always were. No other woman will ever take my place. In fact, it would make me proud, Susanna Iosifovna, if he was capable of strong emotions. But all that went into making the Russian Schlieffen manqué."

On the way home she wondered whether to go with him to Petrograd right then. She was quite capable of impulsive decisions, indeed there was nothing she liked better than abrupt changes of plan. What did he think? Well, you know, it's difficult getting tickets. I barely managed to book a seat in the international class. Anyway, she was taking part in a concert in two days' time, and it would be a pity to miss it. I know! Stay on for two days and you can hear me at full volume in a good concert hall, not just in a living room, and after that we can go to Petrograd together. What do you say?

[1 2]

When he was sent away from GHQ in August 1914 to command a front-line regiment, Vorotyntsev had left nothing of himself behind, had transferred his whole existence to this new locale. He knew as well as anyone that his busybodying in high places at the time of the Samsonov disaster had been futile, that he deserved to be sent down and harnessed to the immediate task. He merged into his regiment, rooted himself in it, more deeply than duty demanded. Since taking over he had never once gone on leave, neither this year nor the year before. A wall of resentment shut him off from the privileged and the free, and indeed from civilian life generally, and he would not permit himself to abandon his regiment for as much as a week. He had dedicated his life to military service—well, now he was stuck with it to the end of his days. When Nikolai Nikolaevich, Yanushkevich, and Danilov were replaced, Vorotyntsev could have made some attempt to start up the ladder again. He didn't do it. Out of pride. The horror of repeated setbacks in the field overshadowed such trivialities as Colonel Vorotyntsev's wrecked career. He had not lost his strategic insight and often found himself unable to believe, from all that he could see, that operations into which their division, their corps, their army were drawn had any higher significance. At the regimental level it was obvious that scrambling over the Carpathians, and without shells, was a major absurdity. But he would not allow himself to get too hot under the collar. With his regiment he was just where he should be, and that was enough. He was no longer eager to distinguish himself, to adorn himself with medals, to go up in the world again: he had spent a little time up there, and it had lost its attraction. He shrank into his new shell, decided to consider himself doomed, and at times was genuinely, recklessly indifferent to death. But he was only wounded twice, superficially. With the months of prudent trench squatting came a calm consciousness of having done his duty to the best of his ability. And the more sordid and offensive stories about the rear filtered in—through men returning from leave— stories about what civilians were driven to and how they had gotten used to war as their normal element—the more the home front disgusted him, the cleaner he felt in the atmosphere of the trenches, with men pure of heart around him, men ready to die from one hour to the next. Once no more than front-line soldiers, they were reborn, a new breed of men. They? Who, exactly? The regular officers, reservist NCOs, case-hardened ensigns, yes. But the men in the ranks, the mainstream, had been channeled in under duress, they were held in under duress, and why they should be there to get wounded and to die was more than he could easily have said. Vorotyntsev had been roughing it with them, grinning and bearing it, burying man after man after man for the past twenty-four months, and he could not help looking at the war from inside the common soldiers' doomed but uncomplaining hide.

Strange, perhaps, for a regular officer to start questioning the utility of war.

Vorotyntsev had with due deliberation dedicated his life to the army, so that for him war was the supreme form of activity. All that was best in him was geared to waging war. From his earliest days his one wish was to serve in the army, his only dream was to help improve it—to what end, if not to make war? The soldiers' task was simply to implement a declaration of war. It had never occurred to him before that an officer might entirely disapprove of a war waged by his motherland. He had fought all through the Japanese war and never once thought that. Some of the generals had aroused his indignation, and so had the sarcastic, indeed the downright treasonable attitude of educated society, and that was all. He himself believed that he thoroughly understood the war: Russia was hacking herself a window onto the Pacific, and if two historic powers in the course of their growth came into close contact on tightly drawn frontiers, a trial of strength to determine the dividing line was inevitable. It was the same with all living things on earth. (Later, he realized that moderation would have given Russia a way out, but greedy mouths were watering for what belonged to others.)

Nor had Vorotyntsev felt the slightest misgiving at the beginning of this war, or during the hectic maneuverings in its first phase. A youthful joy in anticipation of battle gripped him. Just once—in the forest slaughterhouse in East Prussia—a strange thought had strayed briefly into his mind: what are we doing in this war?

But two years dragged by, month after weary month, every one an endless tale of Russian soldiers destroyed in his own regiment, his own sector and those adjoining it, and it was more and more painfully, blindingly borne in on Vorotyntsev that this particular war was all wrong. They had blundered into it—on the wrong foot. And were waging it self-destructively. Russia was not in danger of defeat in the field, but he could not see her winning.

Vorotyntsev felt all those blood-soaked bandages cutting into his own flesh, telling him that "we cannot go on fighting this war!"

Which, he asked himself, did he love most: did he really put the soldiers' trade before his fatherland? He was a soldier, yes, and owed a duty to war—but for Russia's sake, not for the sake of war.

And so, Vorotyntsev, who had dedicated himself to war, began feeling out of place in it.

What idle pens called from time to time the Great War or the Patriotic War, or the European War no longer seemed to have been unpreventable.

And he knew now that no war should be fought unless it was unpreventable. Why did we fight the Japanese war? Why did we encroach on the Chinese? Come to that, why the Turkish war? Or the Central Asian campaign? The Crimean war, yes—it had to be fought, and should have been fought properly. So we couldn't wait to give in.

Vorotyntsev would not have been able to fight at all if he had raised barriers between himself and his men. He had always disliked "officers only" activities—billiards playing, "a bit of a dance . . ." He had never held either a billiards cue or a pack of cards. He had no time for fast-living officers.

For centuries, with no thought for anything but ourselves, we denied our serfs all rights, neglected the moral and cultural education of our people, left that for the revolutionaries to take care of. But this war has brought us a measure of unity with the common people such as I have never known in my life. Unless, perhaps, as a child in Kostroma, with the boys at Zastruzhe. It has brought this unselfconscious oneness: we are "we"—all of us—sitting here in holes in the ground, and the others, those shifting and slithering around and shooting at us, are all "they," and what we have to do is stop them.

An officer's duty, first and foremost, was to look after his men, keep them out of trouble. A common soldier knows nothing about war, he trusts his superior to look after him. And the better we look after him, the more surely we shall win: he shows his gratitude by fighting better, and all is right with the regiment. Vorotyntsev had no equal when it came to keeping his subordinates alive.

But when soldiers look up to us as though we were their fathers, what does it feel like to be deceiving them, leading them down the wrong road?

The guilt feelings which had tormented the Russian intelligentsia for a whole century had found a voice—and what it said was: "We cannot justify this war to our people." That we are equally in danger makes us no less guilty.

After living for those two years cheek by jowl with his men, much closer to them in and out of action than a regimental commander is expected to be, Vorotyntsev could not help realizing that the peasants were not enthusiastic about this war and could see nothing in it except futile deaths and waste of working time. The minds of the people were unprepared for this war, unripe for it. It had burst upon their lives like a natural disaster. Hardly one in a hundred soldiers felt any hostility toward Austrians or Germans, they were only angry, rightly angry, about the poison gas. (After the first gas attacks, against Russians with no defense, enemy soldiers who surrendered were bayoneted—something that had never happened before.) Apart from that, nobody had any grievance, any hard feelings against the enemy, nobody clearly saw the object of all those wounds and deaths, nobody knew what Russia had to fear so much from the Germans.

Vorotyntsev himself could not see that Germany had the muscle and the weight to conquer Russia.

But if the soldier's heart is not in this war, and we are incapable of inspiring him, how long and to what limits and with what conscience can we continue urging him on to his death, urging him into head-on attacks, over exposed marshes and wooded cliffs?

They will stand anything, of course. But have I the right to stand it for them?

For all those soldiers' lives, what have we given in return? Surely we can't call Constantinople compensation for all the men killed? And Constantinople is the most we shall get.

These thoughts were not mutinous. Vorotyntsev was not the first to have them. Aleksandr III had told Bismarck, long ago, that he would not give a single Russian soldier for the whole of the Balkans.

And he was right!

This war has exceeded all limits, gone beyond the dimensions of war as previously understood. It has become a calamity for the whole nation—not a natural calamity, but one caused by those in charge of it, by us.

And there lies the danger: that the people will not forgive us for this war, as it has not forgiven us for serfdom. Though it nurses its grudge secretly.

It also makes a big difference which land you are called on to die for. For the aching beauty of Belorussia, for the song-filled Ukraine, for the humble plains of central Russia I'm ready to die at any time— and so are my men. If the Germans had advanced deep into Russia, it would be a different war, and we would all feel differently about it. But fight for the Carpathians? Fight for Romanian mud, for a foreign quagmire that means nothing to us?

Vorotyntsev felt that, day in and day out, he was committing a crime, burying Russian soldiers in this place.

The whole war, the greatest war ever known, made no sense for any other country either. It had happened because Europe had grown too fat. But he was tied to Russia, and his heart ached for her first. We don't need this war. And the end is only dimly discernible in the distance. The Germans may be still worse off—they are caught in a mousetrap. But, more to the point, the war has so often gone beyond what seemed to be the limits of destructiveness that the victor will have little more cause to rejoice than the vanquished.

The people never spoke of "victory" or "defeat": "making peace" was their usual expression. As long as it came to an end, win, lose, or draw was a matter of indifference to them.

Vorotyntsev, after two years in the ground at the front, after dispatching more than one full complement of his regiment to death or disablement, after listening to the soldiers in their dugouts, had reached in his heart the same conclusion: to save Russia, to save our roots, our race, our seed, so that it will not perish, will not disappear from the face of the earth—we must "make peace," make peace at any cost, no Constantinople as a reward, and such an outcome now would even be preferable to victory in a year or two's time.

He had dozed off once in a dugout where nobody knew him, and woke to hear the soldiers talking.

"It's time for a change at the top. What is our little father the Tsar thinking of? It's time they were all thrown out."

They! They were a clearly defined concept in the soldier's mind. And the terrible thing was that they were not imaginary but really existed—that bloated, torpid, somnolent, exalted ruling stratum. They contrived to float comfortably somewhere above the war, oblivious of their fearsome responsibility.

They had been presented with the army reform program after the Japanese war, and thrown it out. They had been given Stolypin, a man capable of great exertions and great deeds, and they had rejected him, brought him down, given him to the assassin. (If everything was still in Stolypin's firm hands, either this war would never have happened or it would have been fought differently.) It had been in their power not to fight the war with enfeebled incompetents in command, but to let fresh air blow through the ranks of the generals. The German army, long before the war, had fearlessly observed the "blue envelope" procedure at New Year's: the enforced retirement of any senior officer judged inefficient. Whereas Russia had no inefficient senior officers! And all the most irredeemably obtuse, irresponsible, complacent, and utterly selfish of them latched on to the Supreme Commander, his misdirected favors and his ill-considered kindnesses.

But inevitably your thoughts always moved upward from "them." Him. What did he feel about all these casualties? He had been given even bigger opportunities: not to meddle at all in Europe's insane brouhaha, not to dive headfirst into this war, but to let Russia remain an immovable mass looming over the war-torn continent! Instead, he had plunged millions of gasping Ivans into the war.

If he believed in that bogus muzhik, he should feel all the more responsible for the genuine one, the half-saint!

Then this business of taking over the supreme command, knowing that he himself controlled nothing, leaving the ministers in Petrograd at sixes and sevens, helplessly plying between GHQ and Tsarskoye Selo or, worse still, dashing from one parade to another? Could anything be more exasperating than these military reviews in wartime? Vorotyntsev felt ashamed for the Tsar, as though he himself had dreamt up these reviews, dragging fighting men away from their rest behind the lines, herding several regiments together, even hauling grimy and exhausted soldiers out of the trenches, hastily washing them, and brushing them down, drilling them through the night—all just to goose-step them past the eyes of the All-Highest, hear them call out the standard replies to orders, and have a few photographs taken—and every time He would be wearing a different regimental uniform (never, needless to say, ordinary service dress). He would ride around the ranks and say a few words that touched no one. His addresses to the army contained no eloquent phrases, lacked the ring of authority, they were what he might say on any regimental anniversary. The newspapers invariably said that "interminable, thunderous cheers accompanied the beloved monarch as he left." But at the front a superstitious belief had grown up that the Tsar's incursions brought bad luck.

Vorotyntsev himself had seen the Emperor that spring reviewing troops at Kamenets-Podolski. True, it was impossible not to feel a thrill of anticipation, while he was still unseen, but imminent, your heart pounded, you were conscious of his symbolic greatness, you felt the approach of all Russia concentrated in one man! You could not help expecting something extraordinary! But when what appeared was a rather short colonel, with a mild unmilitary manner, and obviously ill at ease, your enthusiasm flagged at once, and you were conscious, in your heart and in your eyes, only of intense curiosity. The unfortunate ranks drew themselves up, threw back their heads, shouted "Hurrah!"—and the Tsar's face merely looked tired (from previous reviews?), apathetic, lifeless, and even rather sullen.

Vorotyntsev fastened his eyes on him, asking himself whether this monarch had given himself heart and soul to Russia, as was his duty. There were so many parades in his life! When did he find time to think about the state? And what were his feelings when he signed yet another order calling up category 2 militia? Did he ever reflect that he was ruining the countryside? Or wonder whether they would be any good as soldiers? Or how many months it would take to make them so?

Vorotyntsev dearly wished that he could love the Tsar. But he could not even force himself to respect the cult. He suffered, because the Tsar was what he was. In those fateful years—to have a Tsar with so little power over his country, mentally so limited, and so weak-willed. So inarticulate. And so inactive. Did he have any inkling of all this himself?

On top of it all he was Supreme Commander of an army twelve million strong. There was no way out of the mess. All you could do was wait for the war to end, or for the next reign. (But why should that little boy be any better when he grew up?)

Then again, what worse punishment could have been inflicted on the Tsar than the present string of useless ministers? One after another they were replaced. Everyone saw how sorry a procession it was, and not even the most zealous subject had a word to offer in excuse. At every army headquarters the uselessness of the government and the squalor of the court were quite openly discussed, so, indeed, was the Tsar himself—pityingly, and contemptuously.

Discontent was focused above all on the Tsaritsa. She was vilified uninhibitedly and unmercifully. Officers accused her of encouraging "Rasputin's filthy goings-on" so openly that the men in the ranks heard. Vorotyntsev didn't believe for a minute that she slept with Rasputin or was engaged in treasonable activities. (Some insisted that she had helped the German submarine to locate the ship carrying Kitchener and that she regularly disclosed Russia's plans for offensives to the Germans.) He suspected that this was an example of ordinary human readiness to make farfetched accusations against remote and enigmatic personages. People would always paw over and peddle the crudest and nastiest interpretation. But suppose just one-eighth of what was said was true! Rasputinism determining policy? Some witch doctor taking the helm and having a say in ministerial appointments? That matters of state should be decided at the level of Rasputin was outrageous.

It could not all be absolutely false, suppose just one-eighth of it . . .

And then those photographs of the Empress—the stony face of the wicked witch who wasn't invited to the wedding . . .

As if the disease of war was not enough—must he catch the sickness raging on the home front? As if what they saw every day was not harrowing enough—rumors that things were worse and more distressing back there drifted in like clouds of poison gas. Vorotyntsev tried not to breathe in this choking stuff, but there was no protection against it, everybody who came from outside carried it, in the form of rumors and gossip—and anyway, it emanated almost unhindered from the pages of the press. Columns of print in authoritative newspapers were not just gossip, and they too hinted, or croaked in so many words, that the trouble was not the war but a bad government, hostile to its own country. You there, marooned at the front, don't know what to think: it's two years since you were in Russia, how can you possibly judge what's happening?

Still, the opinions of those same newspapers on what was happening at the front were usually wide of the mark, so maybe they were wrong about other things too. Vorotyntsev had nothing but contempt for newspapers.

But there was something else. Among all the dirty rumors the Empress was said to be secretly negotiating with the Germans for a separate peace!

The story was told with extreme disapproval, but it took Vorotyntsev's breath away: how clever of her, if it was true! It was probable enough: she, a Russian Empress of German blood, must feel more divided, more excruciatingly torn by this war than anyone. Looking at the possibilities, it was obvious from afar, and everybody agreed, that of the royal couple she was the stronger, the leader. Whatever she took it into her head to do—she would bend the Tsar to her will. So there might be grounds for hope?

Vorotyntsev studied the Empress's portrait with new feelings. No doubt about it—she was strong-willed, resolute, perhaps even intelligent. She knew exactly what she wanted. If only . . . how clever it would be of her! How clear-cut the problem was, and how clearly it could be seen from above: if there was no indication that total victory was imminent (and there was none! If there were it would make itself felt even where he was!), it was the duty of those with power in the state not to tax people's patience with new ordeals and further sacrifices.

Yes, in return for peace, here and now, Vorotyntsev would forgive his Emperor everything!

He grew more and more restless: he seethed, he was dizzy with a feeling that events could not simply be allowed to run on downhill to exhaustion and ruin. He could not simply endure it all and wait. The urge to act hammered in his breast. And the time had come to act—everything pointed to it: the incessant wrangling back home, the hopeless plunge deeper and deeper into the Romanian wilderness, the setbacks and the muddle of the two-month Romanian campaign, all those fresh graves in another land . . .

To act—but how, and where? The answer eluded him. Only one thing was clear—that action could not mean leading his regiment over wooded mountains, deeper and deeper into Transylvania.

He was so far ahead in his thinking that he could see nobody around who would share his thoughts. They all grumbled about the home front, and some of them about the government, but with whom could he, as one officer to another, share his belief that the war itself was intolerable and unnecessary?

No, if he was to act it would obviously have to be somewhere in the rear. In one of the capitals, perhaps. With whom, though? And how? What did an officer know about civilian life?

Nothing. We're all ignoramuses.

But surely an energetic man would find allies, and channels through which to act? There would certainly be such people there, in the rear.

In any case, idle moping was useless. That was Russia's curse—from top to bottom: indecision.

Svechin had written to him once, inviting him to drop in at GHQ when he had an opportunity. Perhaps he should take soundings there?

So that autumn Vorotyntsev had ceased to feel the fatalistic indifference to all around him that had been with him for two years of war, and a dizzying anxiety bored into him. He vaguely discerned some new application for his not altogether exhausted powers. For two years now he had turned his back on the home front in disgust, but now he needed it and would consider going there. Before long he was ready to go even though the situation at the front was rather unsettled. Just to size up the situation. See one or two people. If there was nothing for him to do, he could at least learn something. See how his state of mind compared with that of thinking people in the capitals. He was obviously very much out of touch. He could have no influence stuck where he was. In his muddy hole beyond Kimpolung, Vorotyntsev felt like a compressed spring unable to release its tension.

Then, one day, he happened to be at Corps HQ and was shown Guchkov's letter to General Alekseev. Quite openly, not in confidence, just between friends. It had obviously been written to be shown around—but was dated 28 August, and it was early October when Vorotyntsev read it. Ostensibly, the letter asked one specific question, about the failure to take delivery of half a million rifles from England (an obsolete question, since Russian factories were now turning out 100,000 rifles a month, and the army had enough and to spare), but, in Guchkov's usual manner, it was laced with bold generalities: "the regime is rotting where it stands," "the rotting rear is a menace to the front," "a conflagration, the dimensions of which cannot be foreseen," was at hand.

Maybe it's all true? Guchkov must surely know more than I do. But however much he knows about what goes on in Petersburg he can't know what a quagmire we're stuck in here. He can't know the whole story! He should be told! I must see him.

With Guchkov's letter the spring was released and Vorotyntsev was catapulted forward and upward, with all that had been accumulating within him finding no release. Almost within the hour, still on his way through the HQ hutment, he had made up his mind to go, look, learn. Maybe that was where he could be most useful. Petrograd was the obvious place to go. A unique moment was approaching—so Guchkov had hinted in his letter.

His shoulders and his back ached for action. He must give whatever strength he had left.

In those few hours at Corps HQ, he heard yet another rumor, from two officers of his acquaintance (separately): that there was a conspiracy to carry out a coup d'état in Petrograd—and that everybody knew about it!

What could it mean? What could the conspirators have in mind? And what chance had they when news of it had reached even his Corps HQ without the use of telephone or telegraph?

What sort of conspiracy was it if everybody knew about it? Or was it so overwhelmingly strong, so sure of success, that concealment was unnecessary?

That very evening he applied for leave. Three days later he handed over the regiment to his replacement. And sped off along his scorching vector.

*   *   *

*I'D MAKE PEACE WITH THE TURK,
BUT THE TSAR SAYS NO.*

*   *   *

[1 3]

Fired by its high design, the heart leaps instantly ahead, but the body is slow: first, the captured Austrian narrow-gauge line from Kimpolung, then the first little trains, with frequent changes, and no passengers except soldiers behaving as they had learned to do in the Transylvanian mountains, where they saw no civilians at all, let alone a real live woman. In the officers' carriages you heard the usual officers' conversation, and although they were all new faces, from many different regiments, with different tales to tell, they all dwelled on the same humdrum experiences—the lieutenant with the black rubber glove concealing a mutilated hand, the burly Caucasian cavalry officer with a sword in an enameled sheath, and the overexcited staff captain full of complaints against his superior—"that GHQ Jesuit."

Later, he slept as far as Vinnitsa. From Vinnitsa onward there were many civilians on the train, and every fellow passenger brought a fresh accretion of information, preparing him for the vastness of the rear, a more populous world after all than his own. He couldn't shut his ears to any of it, he felt that he must drink it all in—or what would be the point of his journey? More information than he could comfortably accommodate forced itself into his head and buzzed restlessly around.

Then there were the papers, bought at stations along the line, and read now as a duty, not just out of curiosity, and full for the most part of arguments about which ministry should be put in charge of the food supply. He couldn't make head or tail of it. At Kiev he was surprised to see such crowds at the station—crowds of lively people with apparently not a care in the world. And although he was speeding as though catapulted, propelled still by his obsession, Vorotyntsev could not help feeling a certain very pleasurable slackening of the tension.

He was vaguely aware of passing officers, saluting without really seeing them. He also tried not to notice sad and anxious faces, and had no eyes for women in mourning, but only for those who were wearing their best and gaily chattering. Suddenly, he longed for anything that reminded him of life before the war. There was nothing unnatural about it—but it was something he would never have expected to feel. A forgotten sensation, a pleasurable but somehow dishonorable one. It was as if he was getting younger from one half hour to the next. He did not slacken in his flight, but the nature of the flight was changing.

His destination was Petersburg, with no stops on the way, and he had intended to hurry there before his ardor cooled, and without letting his wife know, but suddenly, in this new frame of mind, he wavered: perhaps he should look in on her first? To make his decision easier, the Moscow train would leave six hours before the through train to Petersburg. He didn't feel like a tedious wait, and he told himself that Guchkov might well be in Moscow, as he often was.

Once persuaded, he was happy. He bought a ticket for Moscow and immediately sent a telegram to Alina, pleased for her and for himself.

In the station restaurant he found himself at the same table with a sailor from Sevastopol, and heard a staggering item of news that had not been reported in the newspapers. A week ago, just before dawn on 20 October, fire had broken out in the forward ammunition locker of the *Empress Maria*, causing a big explosion and a general conflagration. Admiral Kolchak had hastened to the rescue and personally supervised the flooding of the remaining lockers on the listing ship. It had worked, and there were no more explosions. The battleship had capsized and sunk, but neither the harbor approach nor the city was affected. Still, the pride of the Black Sea Fleet was no more, and two hundred men were dead and several hundred injured.

How could such a thing happen? Nobody knew. The culprits had not been found. It emerged, however, that workmen were, as often happened, brought in on the night before the explosion to carry out repairs, without a roll call, or inspection of their bundles, or supervision on board. Anybody could have wandered on and dropped anything he pleased through a ventilator into the hold.

What a way to fight a war!

The finest ship in the fleet!

Why have I let myself be distracted and diverted? I shouldn't be going via Moscow!

Vorotyntsev was half asleep and half awake. He had lost touch with civilian life, and there was something to startle him at every turn. Thoughts of the unknown people he was about to look up swarmed in his mind. Every new arrival had something fresh to say, and he felt compelled to listen.

Between Kiev and Bryansk one incorrigibly talkative passenger lengthily aired views which he seemed to think self-evident: the government was intolerable, Russia was ruled by the gigantic figure of a debauched bumpkin, and the country's one hope of salvation was the Unions of Zemstvos and Towns. The man turned out to be a grain and fodder buyer for the army, and talked about fixed prices, repositories, station warehouses, mills, milling standards, and deliveries to the towns and to the troops.

Soldiers and civilians had different concerns, different scales of importance. A soldier at the front was in constant contact with timeless things, and what seemed of prime importance to civilians was laughable to him.

The hours passed, the train went deeper and deeper into the rear, and Vorotyntsev, weary and distracted as he was, listened carefully, schooling himself.

His companion's knowledge was not limited to wheat. Some of the things he talked about Vorotyntsev might have surmised, except that you can't see far from a trench.

The "liquidation of German domination" act. What was the point of it? What would Russia gain by it? German landowners and settlers were being driven off the land, 600,000 desyatins* would remain unsown, model farms would go to rack and ruin, farms that used to manufacture their own threshers and seed drills.

The refugee problem. Why had they invented it anyway? To scare off the Germans? By displacing millions of people, to come pouring in like lost souls, blocking the railroads and the cities in the hinterland? Anyway, it had been obvious long ago that the war wouldn't be over in a month, so these people should have been resettled—the state had reserves of vacant land in various places, besides that taken from the Germans. The new farmers should have been given financial aid to settle in and start tilling the land. Should have been, but weren't. So these millions of people were without work, while labor was recruited from outside, and Chinese brought in to aggravate the congestion. It was no good—Vorotyntsev's head couldn't take it all in. How could he hope to make sense of it all in the few short days of his furlough? He could only marvel at the vastness of the administration's problems, the impossibility of solving them at a stroke, and the unlikelihood of any one person being able to grasp them.

From what he knew of Guchkov, he wouldn't be able to either.

I must find people who already know the answers.

As soon as the train reached stations under civilian control his eye was affronted by the occasional glimpse of a uniformed "zemstvo hussar." These officials of the Unions of Zemstvos and Towns had no connection with the army, and never turned up anywhere near the

*Desyatin: A unit of land area equal to 2.7 acres. [*Trans.*]

front, but they wore a smart uniform, almost like that of an officer, with embroidered epaulets, but narrow ones like those of an army doctor or a civil servant.

They of course held forth louder than anybody on the train. What they were surest of was the state of the Russian government, and the final disaster for which Russia was heading. There was no arguing with them—they were too well-informed—and Vorotyntsev was more and more alarmed. Had he woken up too late? Maybe all was lost, and his journey was pointless? Perhaps the situation in the rear was worse than that at the front?

Yet he heard the same fellow travelers deplore negotiations for a separate peace. (His heart beat faster. They didn't know what a raw nerve they had touched! Was someone really talking peace?)

One of these people, wearing the same sort of uniform, got on at Bryansk—a man of rather more than thirty with a blond mustache, a quiet, pleasant person. When he heard that the colonel had just come from Romania he fired questions at him. He had been there several times himself before the war on business for his firm. He was, it appeared, an engineer, Swiss by birth, and Gerber by name. He had been brought to Russia as a small child—his father was also an engineer—had grown up as a Russian and had traveled around the country a lot. When another zemstvo hussar said snootily, "You have Zemgor* and the War Industry Committee to thank for your shells, they supply most of them," Gerber calmly contradicted him.

"No, you're wrong. Most of them come from government factories."

"How do you know that?" the other man said heatedly. "I manage Zemgor's central garage in Moscow, and I know what its trucks carry."

They went out into the corridor for a smoke, and Gerber told him the extra bit he didn't want to mention in the other man's presence: not long ago a consignment of shells from a government factory had been brought to the station, and by the time they were loaded the next morning the crates had Zemgor stamps on them. A neat trick—and the troops at the front would be taken in.

They went on talking, and Gerber declared that the whole intelligentsia was in the grip of an epidemic, a contagious disease: it made them abuse the government and lose their sense of responsibility to state and people. They would stop at nothing to undermine the government.

"And how did you escape infection?"

"Probably because I'm not Russian," Gerber said with a smile, "so I can take a detached and impartial view. However bad a government is, changing it in the middle of a war would lead to anarchy."

These additional impressions from Gerber were more than Vorotyn-

*Zemgor: The Unions of Zemstvos and Towns. [*Trans.*]

tsev could take in. He dozed off after Sukhinichi, but slept badly. His worries and uncertainties, and not least his mixed feelings, at once pleasurable and anxious, about Moscow gave him no respite.

Coarsened by life at the front, he had not realized how powerfully it would affect him: to stroll around Moscow, his own city, and look across the river from rising ground at the jumble of buildings marked here and there with the blue and gold of cupolas.

To dispense with his batman, Vorotyntsev was traveling almost without luggage. In the glass-roofed Bryansk station he went straight to a telephone booth, called the operator, asked for the apartment of Guchkov's brother Nikolai Ivanovich, and was told that Aleksandr Ivanovich was at present in Petrograd and not expected in the next few days.

It was more obvious all the time that he should have gone straight from Kiev to Petrograd. Coming to Moscow was a mistake, he needn't have been so impatient. If only he hadn't sent that telegram to Alina, damn it, he could have gone straight from station to station, without risking distraction and loss of impetus: Georgi had burned his fingers so often in the past—impetuously making premature promises.

But when he thought of his wife he was conscience-stricken.

He had been the same all his life: family matters always took second place to his real concerns, there was never room for them.

He had sent the telegram because he liked making Alina happy. He could imagine how happy she would be, and all the little preparations which were so important to her; it would be more enjoyable for her that way than if he descended unexpectedly.

But although it would have been faster to go straight home, Vorotyntsev, who liked putting first things first, made for Nikolaevski station.

The No. 4 tram (from the Dorogomilov Gate to Sokolniki) went straight there, but when Vorotyntsev got into the street he saw something new to him: people clinging in clusters to the handrails on the steps of the tram's rear platform, losing hold, running to catch up, landing on other people's feet, clutching at other people's arms.

There were, however, plenty of unoccupied cabs outside the station, but what used to be a fifty-kopeck ride cost three rubles—take it or leave it. Now they were crossing the new Borodino Bridge, and to their right a big black cloud was drifting from the Sparrow Hills over an already overcast sky. The cabby pointed his whip at it. "Let's hope it doesn't mean snow. We've had one fall already. Froze over as well."

Yes, Moscow was having a cold October, while in Romania there was only slush. Vorotyntsev had had the foresight to wear his big fur hat but had not put on a fur-lined tunic under his greatcoat. It always made him too hot, and there was nothing he dreaded more than feeling as though he was in a steam bath.

So here I am—riding through Moscow as though in a fairy tale!

His mind was still occupied with Guchkov, but his eyes were fixed on his surroundings, staring with childlike enjoyment at the city of his birth.

It was as if he had never before appreciated its inimitable contours—boulevard after boulevard, building after building—but of course no observer from outside would ever see in the city what an old inhabitant knew to be there. The great houses, yes—but does he see the spacious grounds behind them? And then, in a lane hard by, the sort of tavern you would find in a run-down country town, a cheap bathhouse, life going on as it had two centuries ago, people drinking tea from samovars in weedy yards. And you didn't just know all these things—every corner, every tree, every paving stone as it passed before your stirred emotions and memories. How much that did not meet the eye was lodged in them! Yet people went by, trod it all underfoot noticing nothing.

He was carried away, as if this was what he had come for, to look his fill of Moscow. To come from another world, from absolute nothingness to your native place—what greater thrill can there be! And the memories that came to him were not of recent things, not of the months just before the war, but of days long gone, of childhood.

He could so easily have never returned to look at it all. One little lump of lead, half an ounce of iron, would have been enough.

But all those people. The city was not its old self. The jostling crowds, an unbroken stream, the tram drivers desperately ringing their bells and knocking on their windows to get pedestrians to move out of the way. And the trams themselves were packed. Well, there was a war on, and Moscow was overpopulated. Many of the passersby you could tell at a glance were not Muscovites. They were better dressed than most of the locals. Were they from Poland? The Baltic States? Languages other than Russian reached him from the pavement. And when he had telephoned from the station the young lady had answered "*zajęte*," and only when he had asked her to repeat it did he realize that she meant "*zanyato*." So there must be Polish girls working at the exchange. He remembered being told on the train about the refugees. There were many anxious faces. But there were many others on which the war had left no imprint at all.

What was this, though? People of different ages, mostly women, bunched together here and there, blocking the pavement, in a strange formation, each pair of eyes fixed on the back of someone's head. Like blind people waiting their turn for something, or soldiers standing with mess tins ready when the field kitchen arrives—but there it was always quick. Here in the city it was weird to see one person studying the back of another's head.

The cabby explained: "Standing in line."

Did Alina have to do this too?

Something else he'd never seen: women tram drivers, women conductors, women changing the points. Women in place of yardmen. He caught a glimpse of a girl wearing a messenger boy's red cap.

All of which went to show how right he was: Russia at war could not carry on like this.

The cabby complained that his horse was losing weight: you couldn't buy enough oats.

Another thing: streamers with red crosses hung on many buildings, as if one-quarter of Moscow was engaged in treating the wounded. Could there be so many military hospitals? The cabby explained that anybody could hang out a streamer if he took in just five wounded men in a single apartment. And were people taking them? Certainly they were.

Looked at one way, this showed magnanimity; looked at another, it showed poor organization. How could they scatter the wounded around in such a fashion? And there were so many men in bandages on the streets. Most of them apparently lightly wounded or making a good recovery. There were also a lot of disabled men on crutches.

What did victory matter to them now? Even victory plus Constantinople? Back there, he was aware only of men leaving. But here was where they were all gathering. And here they weighed much more heavily on his conscience. How could it go on like this?

Heavy trucks went by from time to time, overtaking carts and cabs. And some armored cars. There were also passenger cars, open-topped or covered.

The sheer size of Russia! Who could possibly take this great mass in hand, reform it, give its life a new direction, save it? Was there somewhere a handful of men, soldiers or civilians, capable of it?

It was his own Moscow, but strange to him. Something irremediable had happened. Was happening.

At the Nikolaevski station he found that train service was subject to interruption, so that he had done well to buy his ticket before all else. Some passenger trains had been canceled, to clear the line for freight trains. Passenger traffic between Moscow and Petrograd, he learned, had recently been canceled altogether for a whole week. Even first-class seats were not available for the following day, so he had to book international class.

The cabby was waiting to take him home, to Ostozhenka Street.

Vorotyntsev had tried so hard to decide for the best—had he gone wrong again? Now that he was traveling via Moscow, could he possibly spend only one night at home? Alina would be terribly upset, and he would be upset too, and scared. How could he tell her? Should he invent an official assignment? That was it—he wasn't on leave, it was a duty trip. To Petrograd. An urgent one. Anyway, his travel arrangements were made, his ticket was in his pocket, he knew the time of departure, his worries could take a back seat while he just looked at the city.

Alina was so near now—and Georgi's agitation grew. To think of it . . . in twenty minutes there she would be, his wife, his own devoted, dearly loved, delightful wife . . . why did she always seem to come last with him? Nothing in his life fitted in tidily.

Myasnitskaya Street brought them out onto Lubyanka Square, where trams still carrying large advertisements on the sloping sides of their roofs turned around with a metallic screech.

And there was Nikolskaya Street, always busy, always crowded, and the Slav Bazaar—all just as it had been, no visible sign of the war here.

Beyond that the quickest and clearest route for a cabby in a hurry lay through the Kremlin.

A true Muscovite always bares his head under the Spassky Gate. Vorotyntsev unhesitatingly raised his fur hat, with reverent pride.

Over the Square of the Tsars, over the Emperor's Square—best of all playgrounds when he was a boy. And the best route for a passenger wishing to indulge in tender memories of his younger days.

How easily childhood memories come back, to stir our emotions more deeply than any others. Their gentle touch makes us want to live all over again, live longer, live a fuller life, revisit all the places we have known before.

And yet there had been one period at the front when he had been completely resigned to death, and felt no regret at all.

Yes, Georgi had played here like other boys, but even in childhood the Kremlin squares had been more to him than convenient empty yards, even in childhood he had been obsessed with Russia's history, and felt a premonition that his own future life would be bound up with it. He was not indifferent to the fact that St. George, second-in-command of the heavenly host, was the city's patron saint. And little Georgi never forgot when he was playing ball there that this stone fastness in the middle of wood-built Moscow was not intended to be a playground, that real live Tartars had been repelled from its battlements, and that the Poles had gained entrance to it by treachery. That the Kremlin had lived through things unimaginable—and stood as an eternal stony reproof to all that Peter the Great stood for. And now as he passed over those deserted flagstones, with grass growing between them in places, before the smooth-chiseled stones of the cathedral churches, the upper galleries where royal ladies lived, the little cupolas, the little porch of the Church of the Annunciation, his heart stood still, so powerful was the atmosphere of history incarnate. But for the cabby, and a handful of passersby, on foot or in carriages, he would have stood under the darkening sky, taken off his hat, crossed himself, knelt, no, prostrated himself, becoming one with those stones and reaffirming his loyalty to them. Nothing had loosened the old secret bond between them, indeed the war had brought them still closer.

But to anyone watching, it would have looked like playacting. Of all the churches they had passed that day these were the first before which Georgi felt too embarrassed to cross himself. That habit, inculcated by his nurse, was a thing of the past—an embarrassingly old-fashioned gesture, so that what an old woman passing by could do in her simplicity was somehow incongruous in a staff officer. "For the faith" were the first words of the army's motto, the army was supposed to be Christian, to be based on Christianity, and officers were not only not forbidden to believe, they were supposed to take the lead and cross themselves on church parade—but it was always done with the hint of a smile, with a mocking air of educated superiority, and had become something to be ashamed of. And although regimental services were held and praying soldiers chanted on officers' orders, at every critical moment in the field soldiers crossed themselves spontaneously and officers either not at all or furtively.

From the Borovitsky Gate they bounced out onto the embankment, cut through the crush on the Great Stone Bridge, with the gilded dome of the Church of Christ the Redeemer already visible through the gloom ahead, rounded the corner of its terrace, then took a shortcut through Zachatiev's back lanes, and came out on the Ostozhenka directly opposite Petrov's, the famous watchmaker's shop—and yes, there he was, just where he should be, working behind his plate-glass window, pretending to have no idea why passersby paused to stare at him, startled by his incredible (and no doubt carefully cultivated) resemblance to Lev Tolstoy: it was as though the untamable old man had returned from the grave and was busy mastering yet another trade!

Vorotyntsev cheered up. If Petrov was in place all Ostozhenka Street must be in place. The same blue-and-white sign over Chichkin's dairy (but where did they get enough milk?). The same giant pretzel hanging over Chuev's bakery (were there any pretzels, though? There was no queue). And here's our tiny Church of the Assumption (Samsonov's day—he could never forget it), with an image on the wall before which elderly passersby crossed themselves. (But you won't—even here.) Gee-up! They rolled up to the front entrance quite stylishly.

Vorotyntsev's early years had not been spent on Ostozhenka Street, he had moved there only a few months before the war, but still—he was home! His heart beat faster at the thought that he was about to see Alina. He had felt annoyed with himself that morning for traveling via Moscow, but that feeling had subsided and instead he was racked with guilt: he had disturbed her unnecessarily and he had deceived her. Still, his feelings toward her were warmer than during their unhappy time together in Bukovina: his soul had woken up in the course of this journey.

He was hurrying to her, full of tenderness and affection—and compunction. He would upset her again. He had never been able to make her truly happy, and he could not now: it was not in his nature. He had always known that he was to blame. What sort of life did she have, had she ever had with him, and what was there for her to look forward to? Georgi should really have had the sort of wife who would not have been unhappy even in a campaign tent.

There was no elevator (they'd installed a telephone, though), but the stairs were not difficult for young legs. It was harder for the eyes to believe that so little had changed! (Perhaps the staircase was darker than it used to be.) A whole war had rolled by, whole divisions had perished, they had descended into the Hungarian plain, and retraced their steps, frozen stiff, and torn their fingernails in the Carpathians, somersaulted backward, surrendered Galicia, taken Bukovina, sidestepped into Transylvania—and after all that, here was the old familiar brightly polished, drooping door handle: "please turn."

He was alive! He was back!

My loving little wife! My gentle little wife! Let me sweep you off your feet and waltz around with you! I can't believe it—you're younger than ever! And you look a lot happier than when you came to see me last year. That proud toss of the head on the slender neck. As demure as a little girl. And so pretty! He felt good. His features relaxed. A sense of belonging suffused his whole being. That feeling of ease in familiar surroundings that comes only with the years. Here I am then, at home. That's good. It isn't where I meant to be, but once through the door . . . it smells so good. You look after it so marvelously, Alina, with your clever hands. He gazed into her dear gray eyes. He hadn't meant to show her how sorry he was for himself, but he couldn't help it. He gave a groan. It was only now, as he sank like a dead weight onto the sofa, that he realized how impossibly overburdened he was.

He started explaining, but it was no use. No good trying to tell anybody all at once. Least of all Alina.

You're a wonderful cook. What a tremendous spread! A meal like this, after living on the land.

Meat was easy enough to get on permitted days. But there was a rumor that it would be rationed. And money was losing its value. Apartments were more expensive all the time. Moscow now had a population of two million, because of the refugees.

From what I can see, things are worse here than at the front.

But all the time he was tortured by the thought that he must tell her. That tomorrow, and no later, he must be on his way to Petrograd. He hadn't the heart to do it, to make those trusting eyes cloud over. But he couldn't put it off for long. He was doing what was most important to him—and he felt guilty about it.

He began cautiously, telling her that he was not on leave but on an official mission. Gradually he confessed in full.

A storm followed. And her reproaches were all the more dismaying because she was in the right. His dash home was bound to seem crazy to her. And it would be hopeless trying to explain the real motive for his journey. She couldn't be asked to share his burden. Why should she? She reproached him with such bitterness: she loved him, she missed him, she pined for him! And what did she get in return? What sort of time had he given her in Bukovina? Was that his idea of "home leave"? (True enough, they had not got on very well on that occasion, he had felt so uncomfortable that it was a relief when she left.) And in two whole years he had not missed his wife enough to come home to her? (He could have come, of course.) You've lost all feeling. You're quite heartless! You're emotionally deficient! (Yes, that was true. Must be my age.)

But he'd be with her again on his way back! He'd be back soon! For her birthday, of course. That finally pacified her.

He listened to her stories of her new life as a concert artist, and was glad for her. A marvelous opportunity! With your exceptional ability! There's nothing you can't do. No, never mind about your admirer, I don't want to know about it.

Georgi really did like her playing, loved watching those nimble fingers. And—with no children—what else was there for her, except to develop her talents? He couldn't remember seeing her so animated. It was good that he had got her to Moscow before the war began. It was all he had been able to do for her. An officer's career didn't even give you security in old age. If he'd gone into engineering after leaving school he would have been earning a lot more.

Perhaps he should have tried long ago to make her the sort of partner to whom a man can reveal his plans without reserve. But was it necessary, indeed was it even possible to do that with a woman? What would be the point? Anyway, it would have cost a lot of effort. After his disgrace at GHQ she hadn't nagged as other wives might, but privately she had blamed him.

By now, he was doing his best not to yawn, looking away whenever she started talking about concert tours.

The peace and comfort of home, with a quiet domestic evening ahead. Peace and quiet, that was what he most wanted. After the din and the damp of shell-shocked trenches, expecting to be blown sky high at any minute, how good it would be to sit between the four safe walls that were home, looking through the drawers of his desk, leafing through old books, or just weighing them in his hand—those volumes of Soloviev, for instance, reminding him of his eternally unpaid debt to ancient Russian history—he had never found time to sort out all those old princes, and doubted whether he ever would.

But no, Alina had taken it into her head to go visiting. What a ridiculous business! I struggle home for one solitary evening and have to drag myself off to see people. Exhibit myself, meet new faces, force myself to make small talk. Look, Alina, my love, I'm not used to polite society nowadays, or company of any sort. I'll find it hard to refrain from coarse language. Please let me off!

She doesn't know herself that she is the good spirit of the domestic hearth, and so most attractive right here, at home. Still, on this of all days it would be heartless of me to refuse to do my social duty, if she's so set on it. At least the company of real live people will be better than pacing the foyer of some concert hall, which was what she originally wanted. Besides, I need to gather all the impressions I can.

Only when they were dressing for the evening did Alina notice his new sword hilt—that of a holder of the George medal. She was overjoyed—and she was hurt: Why didn't you tell me right away? Why did you never mention it in your letters? What an abnormal person you are!

It was Saturday, and when they were on their way to Muma's in a cab bells started ringing for the late service. It was so long since he had heard it that it took him by surprise. First and nearest, the Cathedral of Christ the Redeemer boomed out right behind them. Then almost immediately—from near and far, to the right and to the left, behind and ahead—all Moscow's matchless, incomparable, and inimitable bells. The bells filled the dark Moscow air with a clamorous glow, and his breast with the warmth of childhood remembered: he remembered so vividly his nurse taking him to church, always to the late service, with no prompting from his parents, and lifting him up to light a candle, let it drip and set it with his own hand.

Deep-voiced, booming, hollowly reverberating, meditatively slow—the chimes all fused together, and it was as though the Moscow evening sky was ringing—but no! Only to the inexperienced ear were these golden tones a confused clangor, anyone who knew them and listened carefully could distinguish the voices of the Kremlin, the clamor of Kitaigorod, Khamovniki's answering call, the distant tidings from the churches around Tver Street and the Sadovaya, and the breathless chimes of Zamoskvorechie, that great outcrop of provincial merchant Russia, which they were just entering. Anyone who knew them really well (not just like Vorotyntsev) could distinguish amid the blurred and confused noise not only distance and direction but even individual bells. The ringing had still not stopped when they entered the house.

The guests seemed an oddly assorted bunch: two elderly couples of modest social standing, a somewhat effeminate young man who whistled arias, a few unaccompanied ladies, and two unmarried girls.

Muma (Maria Andreevna) herself had no children and lived alone. She was handsome in the Russian, indeed in a specifically Zamoskvorechie way: somewhat overblown, white-faced, with hair like a raven's wing, and dressed in mauve. She was no mere amateur, she had studied singing, and sang in a deep contralto. Georgi enjoyed it greatly, and applauded. Applauded too Alina's dizzy runs and arpeggios. Applauded, finally, the whistler, who put over a few remarkable arias. Life is full of surprises.

Georgi felt that he was adrift without a compass, and incapable of surprise wherever the current carried him. He had not let himself be surprised by the present company, and was not surprised when after the concert the conversation turned to Rasputin. People here were much more preoccupied with Rasputin. At the front people scratched their heads and swore, here they smacked their lips over all sorts of real or invented tidbits.

No one could be appointed to any responsible position until he presented himself to Grishka. He was said to have his own fees: 25,000 rubles for ennoblement, 3,000 for a decoration. (Horrifying. Surely it couldn't be true.) The crowds calling on him at his Gorokhovaya Street apartment could be seen by any passerby, so now he was to have a house of his own in the suburbs. He was better guarded than the Tsar himself.

"And don't forget the bribery that goes on in connection with war supplies. Rubinstein's arrest."

"Don't forget that the Rubinstein case has been deliberately blown up to give it an anti-Semitic flavor."

"And why did Polivanov come a cropper? He'd still be War Minister if he hadn't had the nerve to take four army cars away from Grishka."

If that's what you think it shows how much you know. Maybe the rest of your information is worth just as little. But I can't be bothered to argue.

The ceiling was so high, so very much higher than a man needed, higher than in a dugout. Dry and warm—no damp in the air. Chairs so soft you could drown in them. A tender ham, fillets of sturgeon, and brawn on the table. And all they could do was grumble . . . "brought us to the brink of ruin, no bread anywhere in Russia, supposed to be the granary of Europe, rolls all sold out by eleven o'clock, nothing but corn bread or black bread."

"He kisses all the women, even when their husbands are looking."

"His theory is if you don't sin you'll have nothing to repent. You have to sin here below so that you will be pure up above. He sends a woman to church to take communion, and tells her to come to him that evening . . ."

"And if a woman won't have him he goes with her to pray."

The conversation was four-cornered: it went from Rasputin to Stürmer to Protopopov to famine in Russia and back again to Rasputin.

"They say he's got peculiar eyes that light up with a red glow. Magnetism."

"Talking about magnetism—here's something that's supposed to have happened not long ago. A woman telephoned Rasputin, and was seen by him in the morning. He took her into the bedroom and told her to undress. Embraced her. She shook him off. 'Don't want to?' he says. 'Why did you come, then? All right, come back at ten this evening.' The lady dines in a restaurant with her husband and a doctor friend. At ten o'clock, she suddenly becomes extremely agitated. 'I've got to go,' she says. The doctor had difficulty bringing her out of hypnosis and holding her back."

These stories were told indignantly, but you suspected that both the tellers and the listeners were less indignant than they might have been, that what they felt was not just disapproval but also curiosity and indeed a certain prurient enjoyment. Vorotyntsev got the impression that as soon as they heard the latest about Rasputin every one of these ladies bustled around town spreading it. The young ladies too were all ears.

"He likes apricot jam, and eats it from the jar with his fingers. Then he lets some deserving lady lick his fingers while the others look on and envy her."

"He has such power over women that they flaunt their shame instead of hiding it."

"They say he's allowed to bathe the young Grand Duchesses."

"Protopopov and Stürmer are both Rasputin's lackeys. They both report to him."

And off they went around the rectangle again. Protopopov was clinically insane. Stürmer was a German spy. Russia was starving. And Grishka . . .

Perhaps Vorotyntsev should have been angry with himself and his wife for this waste of an evening in such stupid company. But somehow or other he felt more relaxed, felt his inner tension slackening. Was he slowing down? It no longer galled him that he had so little time. There was time enough ahead of him. For the time being he was absorbing this so unreal Moscow reality. The unbelievably white tablecloth. The cut glass. The two dinner services—where a few mess tins would have sufficed. The body grows limp. If there was an alarm now he wouldn't be on his feet right away.

"You know the latest mot in Duma circles? We can understand power with a whip, but not power that's whipped itself."

They stole glances at Vorotyntsev to see how he was taking it so far, they hadn't let themselves go on the subject of the Tsar. For fear of shocking him? To spare an officer's monarchic sentiments?

Right now it left him unmoved. Guiltily, he felt that he was losing his initial impetus. It was enjoyable just sitting there, it was pleasant having women to look at. The gowns differed in color and design, and their wearers were just as different. Muma had her own ways, and Susanna hers.

What the ladies most wanted, it appeared, was to hear from him.

They had come together to listen to him, not to music—that they could do at any time. They looked expectant, and began questioning him directly.

Oh no. He couldn't do it. Sitting there was all right. But tell them about the war? No point. And did they really want to know? Presumably they skimmed the newspaper reports every day.

Somebody said that Guchkov had been arrested in Petrograd a few days earlier for his famous letter to Alekseev.

"No, no!" Vorotyntsev came out of his daze when he heard something that concerned him.

"It isn't true. I was talking to his brother only this morning."

Those rumors! Others came to mind: Guchkov dying, poisoned, Nikolai Nikolaevich likewise, the Tsar divorcing the Tsaritsa because of Rasputin.

Then some of them were moved to enthuse over Brusilov's offensive, echoing the fanfares in the press. Were they just humoring him? He had to cut it short.

"Brusilov's offensive? It didn't do much good. Took some of the pressure off the Italians, and the Allies at Verdun, that's all. But we ourselves didn't manage to take Lvov or Kovno or even Vladimir Volynsk. Although Brusilov's forces outnumbered the enemy."

Really? They were amazed. Was it true, though, that the Germans had burned ten thousand Russians to death with streams of fire?

Muscovites or not, they were ignorant savages. This was what the home front had made out of the rumors that flame throwers had been seen. They were full of martial spirit, though! All for continuing the war to victory!

And very, very eager to hear from him.

But Vorotyntsev begrudged them his knowledge of the true state of affairs at the front. How could he talk about it there to these people? What words could he find? . . . It's just a lot of holes in the ground. Fresh holes with a sprinkle of black earth over them. Old ones, buried under snowdrifts as soon as winter came. They stick a cross made of twigs on those they managed to fill in. From an unfilled hole you see what could be a poker sticking out, but it may once have been an arm. A bit of gray cloth torn from a Russian uniform hangs on the enemy's barbed wire for months, flapping in the wind . . .

None of this could be fitted into their neat picture.

He might make an effort to talk about it all—but not there.

He would not be ready to talk until he had all his wits about him. Here, among these people, he felt slightly shell-shocked—half seeing, half hearing, half understanding what was going on.

With Susanna Iosifovna, he talked for a while, coherently and sensibly, it seemed to him, but he couldn't be sure of recalling what they had said, and in what order. He remembered not so much her conversation as her way of sitting down and rising from her chair without using her hands, and the single string of pinkish pearls she wore over her black silk frock, with no other adornment or touch of color, also some sort of emanation from her eyes, or her whole face, turned eagerly toward her companion, or perhaps even from her shoulders, as they seconded her facial expressions. They were talking politics—but the way she narrowed and widened her eyes to show the depth of her understanding and sympathy, the wiry, coffee-black hair smoothly braided around her head, but still bouffant, and the little hairs, golden in contrast, on the faintly freckled skin above her wrist—these were for some reason his lasting memories of their conversation.

[1 4]

"All right, let's see who you'll be traveling with." Alina said briskly, carefully maneuvering her broad-brimmed hat through the narrow doorway as she preceded her husband into the carriage.

Vorotyntsev, eyes on the red carpet, followed, carrying a small suitcase. He had been feeling guilty all morning.

She stopped at the compartment they wanted, said good morning too loudly and cordially for comfort in an almost empty first-class carriage, and turned the curling edge of her hat brim toward her husband.

"You're in for a disappointment! Not a lady in sight!"

The fellow passenger who rose to pay his respects proved to be a man of medium height and modest appearance, not at all what you might expect in an international carriage. His suit was rather common, and his tie clumsily knotted.

Alina sat down and praised the carriage and its comforts, cheerful as could be, then suddenly in mid-sentence, between two inspections of the compartment, there was an abrupt change of mood—so like her, poor thing—and she could not keep up her lively chatter. Georgi, embarrassed by his wife's loudness just a moment ago, now felt sorry for her. Naturally, she was hurt: why shouldn't she be traveling with her husband after such a long separation? After all, she didn't know the reason for his journey. She had taken it hard at home, earlier on, but seeing with her own eyes how cozy the train was, thinking how they could have enjoyed it together, made it all the more hurtful that he was going alone.

Alina's head drooped on her long, slender neck, and she had no more jokes for her neighbor. Suddenly she rose to her feet and went off without saying goodbye!

Vorotyntsev followed, hanging his head. He felt acutely sorry for her. What had she done to deserve such a life? Did she really need such a husband? Could he really do anything to brighten her existence?

On the platform Alina made no complaints, but urged him to go back and get his suitcase so that they could travel together. He couldn't wait two days, till the concert? All right, they'd go tomorrow. But together. If he wouldn't, he was quite heartless.

Georgi was shocked out of the compassion that had been taking hold of him. This other extreme was equally impossible. As it was, he had lost twenty-four hours in Moscow. And if he did take his wife, what would he do with her? He'd be giving in all along the line.

In his automatic recoil he shook off in a flash the temptation to make things easier for her.

But there were still several minutes left. And those last minutes made him nervous. No avoiding the stroll back and forth, the length of the dark brown paneled carriage, peering from time to time at the big clock under the dim station roof, which stretched almost as far as the train.

He kept a steadying hand on the hilt of his sword, with its George medal knot, as he walked.

He lit a cigarette. But smoking was not enough to get you through those dragging minutes.

"Alina, my love . . . I've tried to explain . . . this isn't leave. It's official business."

She was bound to think it heartless, of course. But if on his travels he got involved in something really important she'd be out of place anyway.

Poor little bird. He put an arm around her and drew her close.

She was a child at heart, though, and, like a child, was capable of seeing reason if you talked to her gently. "Look, I'll be back before your birthday." "How long before?" "Well, before." "So can I invite guests?" "Go ahead." "And will you tell me all about it then?" "Yes."

That cheered her up a bit.

Especially with time so short, the sensible thing was to promise, make it up with her, and leave with an easy mind. It's always better to give in where you can, makes life easier.

Luckily, the train was leaving on schedule, giving Alina no time for another abrupt switch. Right on time—three resounding clangs from the station bell, a shrill blast on the chief conductor's whistle, an answering hoot from the engine, and Vorotyntsev, releasing his wife, apparently reconciled, from his final embrace, blew her a kiss over the conductor's shoulder as the train was already moving, heard her requests—something about gloves, and please write every day.

His fellow passenger had no one to see him off, no one to wave to him through the window. He had been busy writing in a notebook. He closed it, and gave Vorotyntsev a routine fellow passenger's smile.

His looks were not obviously those of an educated man. Rather a common face, with its high cheekbones. Very thick, close-cropped black hair, in tufts that refused to be combed in one direction. But he tried to mitigate his somewhat unpolished appearance by painstaking good manners.

Vorotyntsev unbuckled his sword, hung it up, and took off his greatcoat. After that he would have preferred to retire into himself and travel the whole way in silence. But he felt bound to say something.

It was the usual train conversation. When do we get in? There's no knowing, exactly, the timetable is all over the place. To be as much as an hour overdue surprises nobody nowadays. They blame it all on the war. And it's true enough that the railways have five masters. How d'you make that out? Just count them: there's the Ministry of Communications, the Quartermaster General, the Hospitals and Evacuation Service, the Unions of Zemstvos and Towns, and where the front-line areas cut across railway routes: whatever rolling stock, supplies, or freight the commands swallow up, don't bother asking for them back. The Directorate of Military Communications under the Supreme Commander is a state within a state.

In the first few minutes underway, with the whole journey ahead, you know that it's entirely up to you, but you aren't sure yet what to do with yourself. Lie down? Just sit? Read? Look through the window and think?

Outside, the dreary, smoky station approaches were still going by.

His fellow passenger talked away uninhibitedly, in the same vein. A million poods of fish in Uralsk, but no way of shipping it out. Frozen carcasses at one Siberian station, a thaw sets in, the meat starts spoiling, but can't be sold to the local people because it belongs to army supplies . . . so it all rots . . . Grass sprouted on a pile of grain at Kuzyomovka station last year, and still they wouldn't move it . . . You couldn't say Rostov was all that far from Baku, but there's no kerosene there . . . Neither the storage sheds nor the stations themselves are geared to big shipments . . . A lot of locomotives are old and unserviceable.

"Are you on the railroad yourself?"

"Well, no," his companion said with a smile. He had a charming smile and his unclouded features seemed to belie his alarming words. "But I can't help noticing things. I travel a lot and keep my eyes open. I enjoy doing that."

The coat and hat hanging by him were civilian dress. No badge, no official piping.

Whenever he left her hurt, he felt an aching pity, but there was nothing to be done about it. Anyway, that was only at first. It would stop troubling him after a while.

Then again, a lot of railwaymen have been called up, of course. Fuel for locomotives is in short supply. Some trains have had to be equipped as hospitals, others armored. The railway district administrations aren't allowed to pool their empty freight cars. From the first winter of the war you couldn't get a freight car without a bribe . . . Some people can go on begging till they're fit to burst, others get what they want with their first telegram . . . And when you do get one you have to keep paying at every single junction or you won't be hooked up . . . There's this swarm of pushers around—they stop at nothing to push their own loads through. Send them from the front to the rear, from north to south . . . you have to declare what you're loading, but they just lie. Or name a bogus consignee, to get around the ban.

In those two days in Moscow I've let my mind wander, slowed down. It's time to pull myself together, pick up speed. This is just what I'm going for. I need to know these things.

"Sometimes a freight train is put together by order and produce is rushed to the railhead. But when they get there it's just the other way around—agent won't let them load. Or else four hundred freight cars go out empty, sealed by the agent, and nobody has the right to load them en route, they mustn't be touched. Say there's an appeal for rusks for the army. Local government offices are overwhelmed with sackfuls of the stuff. But nobody picks it up, and the rats gnaw it. So the locals see how stupid those in charge are."

She had spoken self-confidently in this man's presence, pretending to be strong, but really out of weakness.

You can't keep up with all those instructions, nobody knows what can or what can't be done, or where to turn for advice. There are plenty of people everywhere giving orders, but there's no system. Some speak for the government, others for the social organizations. You'd think they were deliberately causing confusion. One circular contradicts another.

Never mind, she's changed a lot, and for the better. Found something to occupy her, won't be so reliant on her husband. That's how it should be.

There are plenipotentiary agents sitting on top of each other, everybody has to have his own on every line, and they all countermand each other's orders. There are army purchasing agents, and there are agents from the Special Conference on Food Supplies. They're at war with each other, everyone trying to show he's more important than the next man. Then again the big towns and the northern provinces have agents of their own to procure grain.

I saw some such person on the Kiev train. They seem to make a point of sitting next to me.

"You aren't by any chance a procurement agent yourself?"

"Oh dear, no." His fellow traveler smiled, but somewhat ruefully. As if he would have liked to be one, but had been unlucky. He loosened his tie and opened his high starched collar—he was obviously uncomfortable in them.

If you take a pood of grain from one agent to another you may be caught and jailed. No agent has any guarantee that another with powers still more plenary will not turn up to take his grain from him. Over the merely plenipotentiary there are superplenipotentiaries traveling around. And special plenipotentiaries. In special carriages. Dining on the best.

Rough terrain we're passing through. Steep drops, high hills. Good defensive position over there, for instance, along that ridge.

"Do you know where some idiots get their grain from? Say a mill or a malthouse has grain in stock. Right—they requisition it and leave the mill idle."

The roofs of crossing keepers' huts, and cabins near the tracks, had a damp gleam. Bare copses and withered grass were wet from a recent rain. It's going to rain again. Sky's gray, overcast. Warm and dry in this compartment, though. Mahogany, those panels. Walls lined with embossed leather. Coming straight from the front, I can really appreciate this.

"They set traps and lie in ambush at fairs and in markets, if for some reason or other they suddenly decide to requisition a particular commodity. You'd think they were deliberately trying to get the countryside out of the habit of feeding the towns."

Fields and meadows knee deep in mud, but here it's dry and peaceful. I couldn't spend every day in this carefree way and not be impatient for tomorrow—but coming from the front and due to return, just for this one day, it's great, really great! Cross legs, loll back against the seat—it's great!

Every governor is authorized to prohibit at his own discretion the export of any commodity from his province. It's as though Russia has broken up into appanage principalities again. The new frontiers have customhouses of their own. And smugglers of their own. Every province has its own official prices, and people naturally try to sell their goods in the dearest market. So you get profiteering.

There was nothing in the whole course of Russia's historical experience, or in her present, that Vorotyntsev was so ill equipped to understand as trade and industry—these official prices, for instance. Surely he should try to? Maybe if he didn't understand that, he'd understand nothing? But his traveling companion's worrying story unfolded so spontaneously, so readily, with such solicitude for his listener and for people in general, that it was not really worrying, was even soothing. Or perhaps the reason was rather his own unflagging confidence, always more powerful in him than any other feeling: though all was black today—in his career, the progress of the war, his personal life, or that of society—a healthy instinct told him, defying all gloomy arguments and misgivings, that if only he stood firm all would end well. This feeling greatly eased the burden of living.

His fellow passenger's name was Fyodor Dmitrievich. A pleasant, mild-mannered fellow. Lacking, however, in energy and self-assurance. Wouldn't make a good officer, would be negligent and slapdash, would give orders and go back on them, say one thing one minute and something different the next.

"This year's hay harvest is the best ever, especially in the north. But nobody ever looks north for hay. Nobody tries to estimate and coordinate stocks of hay over the whole country. The Quartermaster Department, Northern Army Group, arranged to procure hay in the neighborhood of Petrograd, and forbade anybody in that district to bring hay into the city. So although the Quartermaster Department didn't take all of the hay, the peasants couldn't go into the city and sell it. Hay has been left to rot on the very outskirts of Petrograd, while in the city itself there's no fodder for dairy cows. So now the city has no milk of its own."

His stories are a bit long-winded. Any other time I'd stop listening. But on a train journey it's bearable. What is hard is adjusting to all this, trying to make sense of it. Isn't there a single bright spot, damn it all, in this outrageous muddle?

"They'd never seen anything like last year's hay in Vologda province. Peasants were queueing up to cart it to the station at ten kopecks a pood. So what happens? The plenipotentiaries couldn't agree on storage, on freight cars, on loading arrangements, or on when and how to pay. That went on all winter. In March, when it was getting wet and the roads were no good, they started inviting the peasants to please bring it in for as much as half a ruble a pood. But not many got through, and the hay wasn't much good by then. So everybody was the loser—and Russia was loser number one."

He excused himself and removed his starched collar altogether. Obviously feeling more at home, he became even more relaxed in manner. He was about forty-five. Heavy bristling mustache. No beard at all.

"Or take Siberian butter. There was something in *Novoye Vremya* the other day. As soon as war broke out they stopped exporting it, and the price immediately slumped—from fourteen rubles a pood to eight. That's when the government should have bought it up and stockpiled it. Nothing of the sort happened. They bankrupted the dairymen and in no time lard was selling at twice the price of butter. So they've started rendering Siberian butter down for soap."

That touched a raw nerve in Vorotyntsev. Siberian butter—for soap? It was unbearable! Just like that July, when the harvest was in full swing, and they called up the reservists, then canceled the decree ten days later. How could anybody be so stupid? Who was in charge of the government? (Can that monarch of ours make an even bigger mess of the rear than of the front? Or does "society" share the blame? Has he bungled his duties as monarch even worse than those of Supreme Commander? And anyway, why does he stay on at GHQ, now that there are no military operations in progress? Why doesn't he sort things out in Petrograd?)

Fyodor Dmitrich's tone was that of one who knows better. Not a didactic tone, though, he seemed used to the idea that no one would attach any importance to what he said, that he would convert no one, including this phlegmatic officer. He spoke without urgency, in a relaxed manner, ready to stop at any minute.

"So what was their solution? To authorize butter exports again. So a million and a half poods have gone abroad to Holland and Denmark among other places. Denmark! As though they had no butter of their own. It goes to Germany, obviously."

Russian butter? To Germany? If only the train would speed up! He was in a hurry to meet people and start doing something. He wouldn't put up with this for a single week, a single day longer! Vorotyntsev had been in a great hurry to begin with—but now, with this touch of the whip along the way . . .

"But you read the papers yourself, so you know. They report all sorts of similar cases . . ."

Vorotyntsev laughed and came clean: "Well, you know . . . I don't go in much for newspapers."

"You can't really mean that!"

His companion sounded surprised, but the amusement in his green eyes showed that it was just as he had expected.

In different company Vorotyntsev might have been ashamed to make such a confession, but with this funny fellow, not at all. How had it happened, though? However busy he was in his years at the Academy he had still read them. Only at the front had he started noticing that the newspapers were somehow artificial, insincere, sometimes too prejudiced, and always somehow alien.

"What is there to read? The summaries and analyses of military operations, completely unsatisfactory. They're drafted either by ignoramuses in a tearing hurry or by exceedingly wily politicians, you'll never understand from them how an operation was carried out. You'll only learn how it really was from visiting officers or eyewitnesses."

Learn as fully and precisely as he, for instance, could talk about the doings of his own regiment and division.

"Ye-es, ye-es." His funny, naïve, talkative companion seemed to be in respectful agreement. "It's the same everywhere, in the rear too, in trade and industry too, you can only learn from somebody who's seen it for himself . . . But if you write the whole truth, as I'm telling it to you now, they slash it to bits, so people still can't find out."

"Ah, yes," Vorotyntsev went on, "but what does a newspaper set itself to do? Keep its readers fully informed, perhaps? No, to twist the reader's mind into its own particular way of thinking. Especially when it comes to the government, the Duma, or Zemgor—who's going to write about them impartially? All those *Vedomosti—Russkie Vedomosti, Birzhevye Vedomosti*—all those *Slovos* and *Bogatstvos* are too partisan. If you went by what you read in the papers you wouldn't be able to fight: everything is bad at the front and worse in the rear—and the top is utterly rotten."

His companion seemed less pleased to hear this than might have been expected, indeed quite upset. He cringed as though Vorotyntsev had struck him, and turned away to look out the window.

There was something comic about him, something rather catlike about his round whiskered face and his greenish eyes. And he looked so unsure of himself, somehow aggrieved, as though life had always sprung unwelcome surprises on him.

Vorotyntsev tried to cheer him up a bit. "There may be serious articles in some of the journals. But the illustrated press . . . well . . ."

He felt ashamed to say it, as though he had published the stuff himself. "Every time you open a magazine . . ." It would have been quite improper for an officer of the imperial army to finish the sentence. On every centerfold—those decorous family portraits, of its individual members, of the women by themselves, in nurse's uniforms (he had heard from an officer who had been a patient at Tsarskoye Selo that the Tsaritsa didn't do dressings very well), the heir to the throne separately, sometimes the whole family together. The Empress sends gifts of thousands of crosses and amulets, as though she couldn't trust the soldiers to bring their own from home. She sent icons to the forts at Ivangorod and Kovno—and they surrendered the day afterward. On every royal occasion—and there are a dozen of them in a year—there's a service in every regiment, and better not balk at it. None of these things matter greatly, not worth chewing over, but they all add up to . . .

An officer could say no more out loud, but a Russian talking to an intelligent fellow Russian didn't need to: "every centerfold" said it all. Who else could he mean?

Fyodor Dmitrich brightened up again and looked approving. Vorotyntsev too was pleased that they were not talking at cross-purposes, as students and cadets, or politically minded civilians and officers excluded from politics, and never daring to discuss affairs of state, had been for many years past. None of that hostility which had caused many officers to give up an army career. The war, for all the sufferings it has brought, has shown us that we are Russians first and foremost.

With no great effort they could have found still more in common by talking about Germans. The same jokes circulated at the front and in the rear. The Emperor, on parade, had "taken prisoner a whole retinue of German generals," or else "although surrounded on all sides by Germans he had not laid down his arms." They could have—but it would have been improper. Vorotyntsev himself was of two minds about the Germans in Russia's service. He knew dozens of them personally and they were all honest professional soldiers. All the same, that there were so very many of them was a flaw in the system, a radical miscalculation inherited from Peter the Great, perhaps best put this way: however honorably they served, they served only the throne and did not identify heart and soul with the real Russia. Because of that they were all in the wrong place. Peter the Great had imposed the German imperial system on Russia, and it had lasted ever since.

The man was comic all right, but also likable. He didn't put on airs. Didn't look crammed with knowledge, but as if he hadn't been given enough education and wanted more.

Vorotyntsev's cryptic allusion to the monarchy emboldened Fyodor Dmitrich to lean forward over the table and confide in him sadly. "But what about the Duma? The Duma doesn't know what it's doing either. The 'meatless days' law, for instance. Four days a week you can't kill cattle or serve meat, but the other three you can? It's a joke! Only half-baked city folk could think up such a thing: driving cattle into the abattoir and keeping them there for days on end losing weight. And what about Siberia? Meat's all they eat, and they've got so much they don't know where to put it. They'll stop the cattle drives from Mongolia next."

City folk? Of course, that was it. There was something quite uncitified about the man. A rustic with some education.

"At supply conferences they're all city folk who can't tell soft wheat from hard, or oats from barley for that matter, and as for growing them, and what it costs, they don't know the first thing. All city folk can do is set up 'committees on price inflation,' so they won't have to dig so deep into their pockets. And where's it got them? What sort of idiot will supply them at those prices?" His indignation almost choked him. "There's a proverb that says, 'Prices are fixed by God.' Prices are determined by psychological factors, and we can't keep track of them. You need a good head to tamper with prices. If exports come to a stop, shouldn't grain be more plentiful? And cheaper? Well, in this country it's dearer, and there isn't any. What do you make of that?"

Here we go again! You bring your own agony with you, and imagine that there can be nothing more excruciating than all those casualties, the depleted units, your weariness—and en route another terrible problem is rushing to meet you: where has our grain gone? This was the second time he'd been told all about it, his brain was scarcely able to process it all: pricing in general, and now these fixed prices.

"What concerns the towns most is: Why do the villages ask such a high price for what townsfolk eat? Well, the townsfolk have newspapers and lawyers, they set up citizens' councils and fix maximum market prices without consulting the peasants, what they call a 'tariff.' While the peasants, although they're three-quarters of Russia, are like so many dumb oxen—they have no newspapers, nowhere to get across their point of view."

What, then, was the solution?

Fyodor Dmitrievich assured him that fixed prices should be abolished, the sooner the better. And the government should . . . "No, forget the government. Not worth tiring your tongue with it. In Russia the government only exists to get everything wrong." (Precisely my view!) "We had one excellent Minister of Agriculture, Krivoshein. They fired him because he wasn't a toady, and put Naumov in his place—lightweight, didn't know a thing, so as soon as he started learning they fired him, without explanation, as usual. All through the summer months, and harvest time, the post remained unfilled."

"Can it really be true"—Fyodor Dmitrich didn't want to believe it, but his eyebrows climbed his forehead nevertheless—"can it really be true that there's a secret organization here working for Germany? You hear all sorts of rumors from ordinary people. First there's a direct line from Tsarskoye Selo to Berlin, and the Tsaritsa reports everything to the Germans. Then we're supposed to be making shells to fit German, not Russian, guns. Then the generals are all traitors and sell military secrets . . ."

Rumors of treason stole across the warring country and the restive army like a malodorous plague. The public thirsted for the blood of spies. There was a universal passion, shared by the military, for the punishment of traitors. Driven to desperation, the mob naturally explains muddle by treachery. But Russian factories producing shells for German guns . . . well . . . On commerce, and prices, this man's knowledge seemed unlimited, but his experience, like everyone else's, had its limits. Vorotyntsev drew the line at the story of the shells.

"Traitor generals would make things only too simple, Fyodor Dmitrich. Two or three of them would be found out sooner or later. But what if there are no traitors, just a hundred idiots, and no hope of firing them? Anyway, our shells are of a different caliber."

"Well, why haven't we got any for ourselves?"

"Didn't have, not haven't got. We have got them now. And take it from me, the reason we didn't have any wasn't treason, and wasn't really even stupidity."

It was the other man's turn to look astonished. "Eh? What was it, then?"

"It just happened. We never found ourselves short of military supplies in the war with Japan. And, basing ourselves on the rate of use then, we had stocks for six months of the present war, which wasn't bad. Should we have laid in more? How could we know when war would come? And what if it didn't come? It would take more than half a century to use up all those shells in training exercises. Besides, smokeless powder and time fuses can't be kept for long. And new types of shells and detonators appear over the years—so how can you lay in big stocks?"

Fyodor Dmitrich looked dazed. He couldn't take it in.

"You mean to say they didn't make a mistake with the shells?"

"There was a mistake all right. But it wasn't failing to build up stocks—it was not getting the factories ready to produce more. And not adjusting to the situation quickly enough after the first month of the war. It was obvious from the East Prussian campaign alone that you needed seven thousand, not one thousand, shells a year for a three-inch gun. Try getting it into their thick skulls. The French, mind you, went into the war with no howitzers at all. But nobody there accuses the government of treason. You can't allow for everything. Mistakes will be made. You need to readjust quickly."

"You mean even Sukhomlinov isn't guilty?"

"In my view, only of carelessness and stupidity. The arrest of the War Minister in wartime is, of course, a disgrace—and more of a disgrace for Russia than for him. The government's credit was damaged, not Sukhomlinov's. What they should have done was quietly retire him long before. But who raised the outcry about treason? The Duma did. They're so blinded by political passion they don't stop to think."

What people in railway carriages kept telling him would need careful sieving. Were things really so bad, or was this just a manner of speaking the public had adopted, seeing in every setback signs of malfeasance and the collapse of central government?

"So there isn't any espionage?"

"Of course there's espionage. The Germans aren't such misers as to begrudge the money for a few agents. Take the *Empress Maria*, for instance—the ship that blew up at Sevastopol." (Fyodor Dmitrich hadn't known.) "I can easily believe that a German agent blew her up." Only just commissioned, a new, first-class ship of the line! It makes your heart ache. What a blow!

Vorotyntsev's stories were meant at the end of the line for other hearers, he ought to be unbosoming himself to very important people and ridding himself of all the anxieties that were like hot coals in his breast—and obviously not to a comic character who happened to be in the same railway carriage. But the train beat out its inexorable rhythm, lapping, cradling, lulling his overeager mind, his important schemes, in its soothing rhythm. You can't jump off, you can't get there any quicker. From Moscow to Petrograd nowadays takes a long evening, and the night, and the morning hours before dawn, a wasted, blank day in your life, one you didn't need, a day you could have spent on anything you pleased, only it seemed there was nothing to spend it on. Outside, a sodden, darkening landscape—what little could be seen of it. Are train journeys anywhere as long as in Russia? Your ties with the past slacken, you feel as yet no ties with the future, the only real people for today are the attendant who offers to unfurl the heavy linen covers onto the velvet seat if you want to lie down early, and the comical fellow passenger with the big notebook—look away for a moment and he will be writing in it or taking it out into the corridor. Are you from Bryansk? You've mentioned the place twice. No, I've got a brother there, a forester. It appeared from another of his stories that he had been a schoolteacher. He was at the front occasionally, with a Duma group inspecting food supplies and medical facilities. Did you ever get as far as Romania? Well, heaven forbid you should. If you haven't been there you don't know what misery is.

Romania isn't Russia's ally—she's a misfortune and makes us a laughingstock. While she was neutral she protected us on one side, like a sandbag. Now the sand's all run out and our chests and ribs bear the brunt. France hitched us up with this other little ally. Our front on land is half as long again, an extra six hundred versts, the whole of the Balkan range, which was previously fenced off. And the Germans needed only three divisions to topple this whole great state and break through a week ago to the Black Sea. While we send small contingents to stiffen the Romanians, and come to grief. So Romania is swallowing up our troops and contributing nothing herself.

"You ought to see their army! A few artillery rounds will send a regiment running in all directions, and you won't reassemble it in three days. The Romanians could at least withdraw in good order, but it's every man for himself, trailing his rifle—it's a sight that has to be seen—like a lone deserter. They've got no machine guns, no shovels, no idea how to dig themselves in. If you hear rapid fire, don't be too sure that's what it is—it may mean that the Romanians have abandoned two-wheelers carrying cartridges and they're on fire. People say that when they saw the war coming the corn-mush eaters sold the Austrians a lot of food and military equipment, right down to telephone wire, at a good profit, reckoning all those things would be provided to them by their Russian allies. Mind you, I don't think myself that they ever had telephone wire, they don't know the first thing about field communications. Their artillery is the most antiquated in Europe. They slept through the Japanese war, and they're sleeping through the world war. They even contrive to point their batteries at each other's backs! Their officers are effeminate creatures who wear corsets and use face powder and lipstick. And they're such liars—as soon as they snap out of their panic they start bragging, or deliberately misrepresent the situation because they're ashamed to own up to the Russians. They retail malicious local gossip in official reports and change instructions almost hourly. They abandon positions without warning their Russian neighbors. They allow civilians into the front-line areas with their troops. No, I just can't tell you what it's like!"

Fyodor Dmitrievich's eyebrows shot up still higher. He opened his notebook and seized his pencil, but was too polite to make notes. His eyebrows shot up—but he was not completely lost for words.

"Yes, but, Georgi Mikhalich, that's Romania. Never mind about Romania, we don't have to live there. But here at home everything is stolen and for sale, that's the frightening thing. There's thieving at every station. At one time one pood of sugar to a freight car would be lost en route, now it's thirty. When we were retreating last year and cattle were being evacuated, the head drovers were whooping it up in cafés on public money, and getting away with it. Crooked speculators bred like flies, they would lose hundreds of thousands at cards in a single evening—where did they get the money from? I've heard it said food and supply depots were set on fire during the retreat to cover up the quartermasters' thieving."

"They set fire to them because they have to. Nobody wants to see fatback or sugar or canned goods go like that, of course. But what are we supposed to do? Leave them for the Germans?"

Hmm, well . . . But Fyodor Dmitrich knew of something worse still.

"The ruthless profiteering in the rear, that's the most terrible thing of all right now. If you've got something you can't sell openly because you're ashamed to name the price, you put it in storage and hang on to it—till the price is even higher. Inflation isn't the word for it—it's daylight robbery. Why this mad rush to make a fortune out of a national disaster? It's a psychological epidemic, this shameless rapacity. Seems to me it's the enemy within who's ruining us. Hordes of speculators have sprung from nowhere. They grab anything that looks like it might disappear and talk up the price. Say some dirty little third-rate merchant is supplying the army with rubbishy felt boots or mildewed flour. These characters grab all they can, then donate part of their profits to field clinics. They steal the boots off a cripple's feet with one hand and light a candle in church with the other. You wouldn't get away with it in Germany, that's for sure, that's a strict society, they've got courts-martial to deal with that sort of thing. I've heard that some general here wanted to hang a banker, a merchant, and a stationmaster on a flatcar, couple it to an express train, and take them around on exhibit."

Fyodor Dmitrich stared intently at his companion. His gaze was keen and searching.

There's nothing comic about him. Why did I think there was?

He went on, with something like horror in his voice. "Jewelers, furriers, and ladies' dressmakers are making fabulous sums—so somebody has money to burn, some people aren't taking the war too tragically. Just look at Petersburg by night—it's wallowing in luxury. Then there are all those pompous organizations—Northern-Help-the-Poor—Northern-God-Help-the-Poor, or Northern-Help-Yourself, some call it. They make a pile out of the refugees, hundreds of thousands pour in unaccounted for. Yes, that's the most frightening thing: the way everybody is feathering his own nest. The whole country seems to have lost its conscience. How do you explain that? How do you explain the shameless profiteering?"

Vorotyntsev felt a chill down his spine. This is indeed frightening! Worse than "the government is useless." Surely this general corruption is something new? This is the real calamity, this is what we have to struggle out of!

"And there's no firm hand in the country," Fyodor Dmitrich complained. "The villains go unpunished, and there's no strong effort to uphold the law. We need a lot of honest and experienced people in every locality. But they seem to have been wiped off the map. Where are they all? That's what everybody is asking: where are the people we need?"

Yes. Yes, indeed! Firm and honest government is what we need! A firm government, and above all not an inactive one. Oh, how sorely we need it—if we are to save the country.

"It's more noticeable from one month to the next, this year from summer to autumn, say. That's the general feeling now—talk to anybody, go wherever you like, everybody considers himself cheated, shortchanged, robbed. Some blame the peasants, some the towns, some the banks, some the refugees, some the workers, some the police, some the Duma, some our homegrown Germans, but absolutely everybody blames the government. Nobody would give you a bent kopeck for the government. And the idea has somehow gotten around that something bad and unavoidable is on the way—maybe the assassination of members of the government, maybe some sort of conspiracy . . ."

"Conspiracy?"

"There's a sort of despondent feeling of instability, of distrust. In fact, some people would love to see a few murders! And they use the foulest language about ministers and—I'm sorry to say—about the most august personages. Then there's that Rasputin: no ordinary peasant, people say, would put up with such obscene goings-on in his own house as the Emperor does. It's a disgrace. Things got off to a bad start at the beginning of the war and they've been going wrong ever since. Life used to seem so stable—you thought it would go on just the same for centuries. But something gives—and it all goes from bad to worse. Sometimes you see a melon lying in the garden. Its rind is unbroken, it looks firm, but pick it up and it falls to pieces, it can't stand the pressure of your hands."

Surely things can't be that bad! Surely not! People tend to exaggerate the dark side. The Duma and the newspapers always take that particular line—denigrating all things Russian. And this fellow too seems to have collected everything bad that others could tell him.

"Anyway, it's no worse than last year, during the retreat."

"Yes, but when we were afraid the Germans would invade, when we almost surrendered Minsk, the country was united, and the home front was sound. Now the army has weapons, and nobody expects the enemy to reach Petrograd and Moscow. But nobody thinks of getting to Berlin either, as they did in '14. The country is no longer united, either by enthusiasm or by fear. And the internal situation has become critical."

A persuasive fellow: and he doesn't really belabor his point, just trots out one example after another, obviously knows what he's talking about. No good trying to argue with him. Where's he been to get so smart? Says he traveled with a hospital train—but how much would he see there? Now he's talking about the Donetsk coalfield. There's nowhere he hasn't been.

"They all pour into the pits, to get a deferment and save their necks. Some of them have never worked there before, some don't even need a wage. They're all quite open about it—just hanging on till the war ends, hoping peace will come soon." He sighed in sympathy with them. "Yes, Georgi Mikhalich, a peace made of straw is better than an iron battle."

Well said! That's a good proverb. A true one.

But the spirit of contradiction rose up in him—he had to defend the army in the field. It isn't like that with us yet, thank God. It's cleaner, morale is healthier. Danger makes men equals, the proximity of death cleanses them. In the rear, farther away from danger, people weaken, rottenness and corruption are rife.

"Yes," Vorotyntsev said. "The peasants behave honorably and let themselves be netted by the army. But how many townspeople have evaded military service? The worst and quite legitimate deserters are in the Unions of Zemstvos and Towns. You don't happen to be one of them, do you?"

"Oh no," his fellow passenger said with a good-natured smile.

"They've invented for themselves epaulets with fantastic monograms to disguise the fact that they're fit to serve."

"They ought to be called up," his companion agreed, "and there's no reason why they should be paid such dizzy salaries. Some of them get two salaries, in fact, from their previous place of employment and from the Union."

There's no knowing what they might have got onto, but the conductor was walking down the corridor happily announcing Klin. "Hey, conductor, have you locked my door?" somebody called out from the other end of the corridor.

"You have to pull a bit harder, it's an international door," the conductor called back cheerfully.

Fyodor Dmitrich reached for his notebook and wrote that down. Wrote more than had been said. Making a note of something else, no doubt.

Get out and stretch our legs? They put their overcoats on.

At the carriage door Fyodor Dmitrich did not fail to question the conductor, and was told, "We only get thirty rubles, and we sometimes have to pay for repairs out of our own pocket. A pipe bursts, say, and you call in the maintenance man—and have to hand over your pet ten-ruble note."

Conductors still get by somehow, no doubt.

Fyodor Dmitrich made another note.

They went out into the damp and the cold. It was pleasant at first to cool down after sitting so long in the warm compartment.

A cripple limped along the platform, then came another. Begging from the better-off passengers.

Not so long ago they had been brave soldiers. And before that had lived ordinary peaceful lives, little knowing what fate had in store. Now they had withdrawn into crippledom, like men forgotten at the bottom of a well.

Ten times as many soldiers hung around on the platform and in the station yard—reservists, with slack belts, crumpled greatcoats, and epaulets awry, but at least they came to attention and saluted. They weren't patrolling the station, weren't on duty at all, they moved around in small bunches or singly. Out for a stroll perhaps? Train watching?

"You see them at every station, in every marketplace," Fyodor Dmitrich informed him. "They search hen coops, looking for eggs. They're idle and insolent."

Ought to look for the commandant, but haven't got time.

A black cloud hung low overhead and it began to rain again.

Back to the carriage.

They were no longer mere strangers. Some sort of fellow feeling had been established. So much so that Fyodor Dmitrich coyly suggested "a little glass of wine from the Don."

"Come on—it's prohibited. Where'd you get it?"

"They've been drinking moonshine all through the war down on the Don. The ban on wine up to twelve percent alcohol was lifted a few days back. It can be exported legally from wine-growing areas, to sell here or even ship abroad. This is some from home I'm taking for my Petersburg friends. Give them a sip of sunshine."

He put one foot on the stepladder, reached up to the luggage recess, and, using both hands, gently drew toward him a demijohn in a straw casing. There were big square gaps in the casing and the golden-dark liquid glowed alluringly through them.

Fyodor Dmitrich produced glasses, smiled at the wine too as he poured it in little splashes, smiling at it approvingly, and said in a slow voice, "At home in the village you don't always want it even for free, it's worth no more than water there. But in wartime, or in jail . . . You remember it then, oh, how you remember it . . ."

"You mean you've been in jail as well?"

"Just for a bit. Three months in the Kresty. I'm a Vyborger."

Vyborger? And I'd just decided this nomad who's been everywhere must come from the Don. But no, he's from Vyborg. Or maybe he's served in the Vyborg Regiment, the 85th?

Memory made all the connections, Usdau, the trenches, the bombardment, Arseni Blagodarev, the yellow toy lion—but somehow it didn't fit. He was obviously no soldier. Perhaps he meant Vyborg was his hometown?

"Vyborger?"

Fyodor Dmitrich was eyeing him keenly, quizzically, expecting some sort of sharp retort. He didn't get it.

"I signed the Vyborg appeal," he said with a modest, almost apologetic smile.

"Ah, I see! Yes, of course . . ." (Somewhat at a loss.)

Vyborg appeal? I seem to remember something of the sort. Appeal from whom and to whom? And why Vyborg? There was no end of those appeals. Is he a revolutionary or something? Doesn't look it. I've spent two hours with this ordinary, average-looking person, and heard nothing but riddles.

The train started moving, smoothly, without a jolt, gliding along, so that the glasses, full to the brim, didn't spill a drop.

Fyodor Dmitrich, a little hurt, was soon smiling again.

"A good driver. It's difficult, you know, getting a grip on a long train like that. There are no young engine drivers on passenger trains, especially on the Nikolai line."

"Why is that?"

"Takes a long time to work your way up. You start as a greaser, then you're a fireman, then a driver's mate, then you drive shunting engines, then freight trains. And after that there are different classes of passenger trains. Your health!"

"Likewise."

They sipped. Fyodor Dmitrich smacked his lips.

"An experienced driver who knows his sector well can perform miracles. At Yelets there's a ten-minute stop, no time at all for the passengers to eat at the station. But at one time a waiter would dash over to the locomotive and hand the driver a silver tray holding a shot glass of vodka and an open sandwich with caviar. 'Please accept this, Vasili Timofeich. Abdul Makhmudovich' (the refreshment rooms are all leased to Kazan Tartars) 'says don't be in too much of a hurry to leave.' 'Tell Abdul Makhmudovich it's all right.' Then he says to his mate, 'Go see the duty foreman, tell him the bearings need lubricating.' The train stands for twenty-five minutes . . . and three full dinners are served to the driver's cab too. Before they get to Gryazi, they've made up for lost time. Vasili Timofeich knows all the upgrades and inclines."

Vorotyntsev's glass was topped up before he could empty it.

All at once he felt sorry for the man. Seems somehow a loser, doomed to fail, yet not at all embittered. For all his omniscience and his facile judgments—he somehow lacks confidence. And he's quite incapable of keeping himself to himself, shutting himself off, holding his tongue. An independent person—yet somehow dependent on everybody and everything.

The train went on its way unhurriedly, the wheels beating out a steady, reassuring rhythm, persuading him, commanding him to look more closely at this passing acquaintance—if he was still no more than that.

"I'm sorry, I don't remember your Vyborg appeal. What was it about? And when?"

Fyodor Dmitrich looked aggrieved again. Sourish.

"When the First Duma was dissolved we all met at Vyborg and debated what to do . . . Then signed the appeal."

"Forgive me . . . but who are 'we'?"

"The members of the State Duma. Or some of them."

"So you are . . . what? A member of the Duma?" (Is he joking?)

"Ex-member. Of the First Duma." He smiled apologetically, readily admitting that he did not look the part.

Ah, the First. A long time ago.

"But you aren't now?"

Fyodor Dmitrich's embarrassment for the colonel made his good nature more obvious than ever.

"Well, you see . . . since then . . . we were deprived of political rights."

"So you're a politician?" There was a hint of mockery in Vorotyntsev's long stare.

"Not at all—anything but. It was just an accident."

"Forgive me—what is your surname?"

"Kovynev."

"No, I've never heard of you." That was awkward, wouldn't like to upset him, but still—haven't heard of him. "Where's your constituency?"

"On the Don. Ust-Medveditskaya electoral district."

"And what's your party?"

"How shall I put it? . . . I was a so-called Trudovik. And I was accused of helping to found the National Socialist Party. The charge was dropped, or I'd have gotten a year. In those days of freedom and high hopes, no political meeting could do without me. Afterward the ataman of the Don Cossacks banished me from the Don."

"So you were a Cossack?"

"And still am."

"Come on—what sort of Cossack are you now?"

"Well, I go home for the hay making and the harvest and to look after the orchard. My sisters aren't married and can't manage alone." He smiled to himself. "Cossacks! Do you know what it means to be a Cossack? Suppose they're all harvesting wheat on a July day. Suddenly Cossack couriers with red flags on their lances gallop through the villages and across the fields. That means war—report to the colors. That same day, before nightfall, by five o'clock everybody must be outside the local government office in uniform, and with all their equipment, on a horse fit for army service. So they abandon the harvest in mid-swath, abandon wife and children, and a few hours later there are four hundred fully equipped fighting men outside the local government office."

He radiated pride. Was he too ready to mount and ride?

"So where do you normally live now?"

"Petersburg."

"And what do you do—teach?"

Fyodor Dmitrich looked abashed, and his eyes shifted from the table to the wine and from there to his notebook.

"Not nowadays . . . nowadays I'm sort of . . . you might say an essayist . . . I write for the papers."

So that's what he is! One of the very people who write all those *Slovos* and *Bogatstvos*!

[15]

(FROM THE NOTEBOOKS OF FYODOR KOVYNEV)

*   *   *

"Sir, sir," Signei said timidly, edging toward the lieutenant colonel, "permission to ask. Is it true what they're all nattering about?" He lowered his voice confidentially. "That the 'Merican Tsar has sent a letter to Russia . . . Says he wants some Cossacks of his own . . . Says the Russian Tsar can't feed his Cossacks, so let them come to America, they won't go hungry with me."

"God only knows," the lieutenant colonel yelled, "what nonsense they'll dream up next! Where did you get that from?"

"Tongues will wag, your honor . . . It's mostly the women babbling."

"Troublemakers! Spit in their eyes! Your home is here—on the free steppes of the quiet Don."

Signei dolefully seconds him: "Where all our roots are."

"And you won't find a better place anywhere in the world!"

"Quite so, your honor."

*   *   *

A Cossack who had risen to officer rank came home from the army.

The best room was full of guests—the old men at the table, relatives and neighbors on benches, young men standing by the stove—and there was a sweating ruck of spectators looking in from the storeroom.

"Is that your own uniform, Gavril Makarich?"

"It's the one that goes with the rank of ensign."

"It's a very beautiful uniform."

"Only farming may come hard to you in that rank. While you've been in the army, you've probably forgotten what it's like working in a field."

"Well, of course, I wanted to stay on in the regiment, but my father wouldn't give his blessing. I wanted to come home as well, of course, to the things I was born among."

"And the food you'll get here is a bit plain. Plenty of noodle soup, mind you. Stuff yourself till you can crack a flea on your belly—that's how things are here."

A brainy neighbor with a beard asks if "things are quiet in Russia now."

"It's all right at present, the riots have been put down."

"From what the newspapers say it doesn't look much like it . . ."

"No, they've quieted down now. There used to be these strikes, for instance, but you never hear of them now."

An old man with a shaven skull and a George medal on his blue cloth smock says, "Gavrusha, can you kindly tell me why these riots happen? Why do those people turn so nasty?"

"Well, they're dissatisfied, of course."

"Is it land they want?"

"Some want land, others are feeling the pinch because things are so dear in the shops. But all in all you have to put it down to ignorance."

"Yes, but who's to blame, which side? Some loudmouths say its the authorities."

"Whatever the authorities are like, the rioters have to share the blame, grandpa: they must educate themselves."

The old man shakes his head. "I don't think that's the main thing. People lived before them without getting educated . . . and managed without rioting. Life was freer and easier. There weren't any orchards, but you could pick all the cherries you wanted in the woods, or apples, or pears, or sloes . . . and all the fish! Now all that's vanished. But everybody's educated now, everybody wears galoshes."

Karpo Tiun rises and speaks haltingly. "Get educated, you say, Gavril Makarich . . . But let me ask you . . . where is there free access? Claiming your rights costs money—where is it supposed to come from?"

The soldier's jaw sets firmly. "If you have anything in your head," he says, "you'll find a way in."

* * *

A bright March day. Ice on the Neva, dry and brittle, marbled with dark streaks. Happy agitation in my heart. On the embankment a slim, well-dressed woman in black, with black eyes and eyebrows, heavily made up, seems troubled by something. A singer perhaps. Our eyes meet, mine express compassion and fellow feeling.

* * *

6 April 1913. St. Petersburg. Last night, the eve of Ascension Day, we had a meeting of the editorial committee. Korolenko took his time going over the manuscript in great detail. He spoke to me about my story with such enthusiasm, his small but beautiful, gentle eyes sparkling affectionately. He has a beautiful face framed by a gray beard, and his head is a mass of dark gray curls. He has the face of a man used to hard physical work, fleshless but firm, and made handsome by an expression that speaks of strength, endurance, intellect, and prudence. My heart ached with admiration. His quiet, even, enchanting voice was at once extraordinarily sad and lively. When he got up from behind his desk I noticed that his boots were patched.

* * *

5 August. Riding to the station. Swarms of women wearing white head scarves. Carriages, bullock carts, rejoicing workers. Meadows as green as if it were spring! Fodder galore! A mass of green, ages since we saw the like. "When we took Turkey on—it was just like this." Grain rattling into harvesters' bins. The dear, nourishing prosperous smell of ripe wheat. For some reason it occurred to me that I shall never again see such a harvest, such wealth, such lushness.

* * *

The hair on old Cossack heads—dry feather grass.

* * *

Mustaches like shortened Turkish yataghans.

* * *

Wrote to Z. Told her that in the village nowadays young men ride around on bicycles, wearing bowler hats and transparent blouses, and play cards in the presence of grown-ups. The young ladies walk along the dusty street in tight frocks and French court shoes, stepping around pungent cowpats just left behind by the herd. Village life is changing. People want different things. She says the young simply want more, especially from love. The ability to give yourself and form firm attachments is getting rarer all the time.

*   *   *

Fine rain rustling in the leaves. The smell of dill. I'm sitting in a cabin, waiting, hoping some girl will come along. Nothing in my heart except desire—and fear of falling sick. Long birdcalls in the orchard.

*   *   *

An old Cossack with a beard joins the singing, one hand raised, fingers splayed, bending toward his neighbors and wagging his head as though telling them a story.

Another old man reminisces: "There was one ataman called von Ryaby"* (meaning von Grabbe or von Taube; an ataman like that was too much for Cossack tongues). "A fierce general he was, blew his top at the least little thing. Ripped one Cossack's nostril with a pencil for arguing."

*   *   *

In Pamfilich's orchard.

"Tell me, Pamfilich, which was better the old days or now?"

"It's better now, I reckon. Life's a bit brighter. Gramophones, nice clothes. We used to have nothing but homespun, like sackcloth."

"But what about the way young people swear?"

"Yes, we never had anything like that. Mother-swearing, do they call it? The Mother of God is our intercessor. I remember my grandfather saying, 'Our children have got it coming to them, and our grandchildren will really suffer.' "

*   *   *

A gray-blue steppe with hillocks and gullies. Stunted oaks along the gullies and the drying river Medveditsa. Squat shanties smelling of smoky dung fires. A peeling village church. I remember how I used to

---

*"Pockmarked" in Russian. [*Trans.*]

love running to vespers in the half-empty church in my bast clogs. And I loved even more the view from the belfry, when I was allowed up there.

✳   ✳   ✳

Cradled in the womb of a placid life.

✳   ✳   ✳

"Never get anywhere near the bottom of it."

✳   ✳   ✳

"My son has a medal for bravery. Pin it on, Grishka—where have you put it?"

The clumsy, pockmarked Cossack takes his silver medal on a scarlet ribbon from his pocket, affixes it to his chest, and says solemnly, "A St. Anna."

"For what exactly?" the matchmaker asks respectfully.

"I was on stable duty. The commanding officer came during the night, sees everything's in order, and I hadn't slept a wink all night. 'Well done!' he says. And puts my name in for a medal."

✳   ✳   ✳

Z. writes, after a performance of Gorky's *The Petty Bourgeois* at Tambov: "I was feeling very dejected, left the theater like a robot, walked down the middle of the street, and got stuck in the mud. There was a complete vacuum inside me, as though everything had been removed and nothing put in its place. The big question—what is there to live for?—remains unanswered. All the negative characters (as Gorky portrays them) find that life is dull, dead, uninteresting, while all his positive types do nothing but exclaim, 'It's good to be alive! Life is good!' but nobody makes any attempt to say why. Nil is a self-satisfied, overfed bull of a man, trampling and stifling all who cross his path— and he's Gorky's idea of the hero of the future? Can the heroism of the future reside in cruelty? Gorky echoes Nietzsche: 'Knock down whatever must fall.' If that means obsolete institutions, I understand, but surely not people? Why should we? Just because they were born before us? It's nasty, it's depressing, it's vile. If it hadn't been so late I'd have fled—anywhere, maybe to my aunt in the convent. And you, my dear, mean to 'expose our present conditions, Russian reality'? Is that it? If so I beg you not to, it's all false, just self-indulgence."

A little provincial girl, seen nothing of the world, but so bold in her judgments. Try telling the staff of *Russkoye Bogatstvo* that sort of thing.

*   *   *

A grimace of effort (on the face of a docker) that looked like a smile.

*   *   *

"If I start talking about my life it would fill a whole library. There's not as much water in the Volga as I've had troubles to put up with."
"What in particular"
"No end of them. I once had my new galoshes and a samovar I'd just soldered stolen on the same day."

*   *   *

"If something like an armful of a woman comes my way, all right . . . but all this stuff about the meaninglessness of life is not my specialty."

*   *   *

"You aren't a socialist, I hope. So why don't we have ourselves a drink?"

*   *   *

The sound of many voices calling back from a distance—like gravel pouring out of a bucket.

*   *   *

Ilyich on his son:
"First off, he's no good on his feet. His feet are useless, they sweat so much you can wring them out."
Agafon, a weedy little chap, four feet and a bit, says, "I found the wounded man the other day. Missing a leg but still laughing. We've got to squash those German sons of bitches good and proper."
"But what if they capture you and me, Agafon? The Germans are threatening to water their horses in the Don."
Agafon, holding his cigarette in the air at ear level, answers scornfully. "Whatever we're asked we'll do, but I could never respect a German."

"What if he flies over in an airplane and swipes us?"
"He can beat me black and blue. I won't give in."

* * *

Changes of heart can be quite unforeseeable. After being demoted so often Filip volunteered for the army. They sent him back as a lieutenant, and his son was put in the same regiment, with the rank of ensign. They were stuck on reconnaissance the first three weeks. The father was promoted to captain, and got a Vladimir, fourth class, an Anna, second class, and a George medal holder's sword knot. The son was promoted to lieutenant, also got a medal, and was killed in the offensive.

* * *

Cross meets cross: a second lieutenant with a George medal and a Red Cross nurse.

* * *

Letter from my brother Aleksandr: Peasant carriers have been mobilized for compulsory haulage of firewood to the arms factory. But it's all a muddle. They make the men drive forty versts with a single horse (some from neighboring districts as well), leaving two or three at home idle. If they used only the nearest they'd all be kept busy. Next, the boss tells the foresters to stop delivering wood to the Bryansk arsenal and to load it for the police chief.

* * *

Letter from my sister Masha: A Cossack with a farm out at Sebryakovo came in yesterday to get a parcel for his son in the army repacked. He says "my mother baked me a batch of cakes with butter and eggs and a touch of sour cream, and the boss at the post office asked what's sewn up in that parcel, come on, tell the truth. So I say a shirt, some underdrawers, some mittens, and my mother's popped a few dried crusts inside some stockings. No, he says, that's absolutely forbidden, you'll have to make it up again!"
It's a long way back to the farm, so he comes to me. While he's unstitching it I ask him news about his son. "Well, in his last letter he wrote that they've declared a campaign against the Germans. An enormous amount of blood is being shed, and untold numbers are dying. Lord, oh Lord, we've just one little son. My lad and his woman are quiet folk, they've got nobody, only one little child. Syomushka

comes home from the regular army, just has time to beget one child, and he's off again to the war . . . There you are, my love, I've unstitched it, but I'm thinking maybe I could slip some rusks, just a dozen say, into this coat lining? Would it get through, d'you think? His mother wanted to put a duck in, but his wife said no, rusks he can pop in his pocket and eat on the move as he goes along. And she guided little Vanya's hand and his little foot and made him write a few extra words: Strike the cruel German enemy with my hand, Daddy, and kick him with my foot, so they won't drink your blood, dear father, and make your one and only baby an orphan, and bring your own dear mother to the grave. Look, you can see her tears on the paper—she cried and cried."

While I'm sewing it up I ask what else the Cossacks are writing. "Mostly they write that they aren't allowed to write the whole truth about it, and there's no time! Those in the Carpathians write that they're hungry and cold, there's lots of meat but usually no bread, the horses under them are too weak to move. Those in Aleksandropol write that they're expecting the Turk to attack, and mending the fort. Working like chain gangs, they say, carrying sacks of sand on their own backs. 'But never mind, dear parents, it's safer here than where there's fighting. We'll rest up after the sand and bust our fists on Turkish snouts. It's time we got moving, we can't bow our heads to those hook-nosed devils.' Say what you like, my love, a lot of Russian strength has been buried in the ground. Sewn it up? Oh dear, the old woman will be scolding me about the rusks."

*　　*　　*

One peasant to another (from Pskov):
"You want just a medium swing of the scythe, but you snatch at it. You don't know a thing about scythes. You've disgraced the 'Skov province in the eyes of all Europe."
"Just give me a proper tool, then you can talk. Scythes like this are all right for shifting frozen shit, but not for mowing."
"It's the meadow I'm condoling with, not you. You'll hack it all up for nothing."

*　　*　　*

"You can tell a serious man by the way he knocks it back."

*　　*　　*

I went into the X-ray room at the Ksenia field hospital. A young Tartar was brought in. Very slim, a slip of a boy, breathing with difficulty, feverish eyes. "A remarkable case," said the doctor (something of an actor). "Legs paralyzed, but no wound. Shell-shocked apparently." They X-rayed him, found a bullet in his spine, and were even more astonished: there was no sign of an entry wound. They discussed it, thought it over. The Tartar's breathing was labored. A nurse came up. "I like little Tartar boys," she said, stroking his cheek and chin tenderly. "They're so nice. Do you want to go home?" There was a gleam of happiness in the boy's feverish, bloodshot eyes, he laughed soundlessly, openmouthed, forgetting his sufferings. The orderlies carried him out on a stretcher, but the radiant look did not leave his face.

The magical power of a woman's caress.

*　　*　　*

A fat voice—like the crackling of hot fat in a pan.

*　　*　　*

Letter from my brother: "According to *Russky Invalid*, we can expect the front to liven up a lot soon. If we could just once hit the Germans where it hurts. Will we manage it? Things are so tense I fear a catastrophe. I only hope there'll be no bread riots in Passion Week and at Easter. Everything's gone up 500 percent for the holiday. You can only marvel at the bare-faced greed of the trading class. Let's hope it doesn't end in total chaos on the home front. You can't find anybody to help in the house, you can't even get a little girl to mind a child at ten rubles a time, and she's right, ten rubles used to be real money, but what is it now? So you have to do your own job and look after the house. Spring is here, we've run out of meat, and we're down to porridge and milk—who would want to be a forester!"

*　　*　　*

Rumors going around the village about the pickings to be had on the battlefield have excited some imaginations. Old Ulyana, a polecat of a woman, shot off first, all the way to the Carpathians, to join her man. When she got back the women were around her like flies . . . She's a skinny, pockmarked creature, but with handsome black eyebrows.

She told them quite a tale. "Eh, my sweet ones, we never once slept soundly. We were on the watch all the time, like geese on a pond in autumn."

"Still, he must have picked up a bit of extra cash?"

The women waited with bated breath to hear how her Rodion had made out.

"Twenty-three rubles was all he had in the kitty."

"Come on—tell the truth and shame the devil!"

"As God's my judge!" Ulyana crossed herself, looking at the grocer's sign in lieu of an icon. "I was there three days, and all I came out with was a three-ruble note. They skinned me alive, so he took me off the till."

"Folks said you'd made a pile."

"Just talk, dearie. Some of them have made a bit, but mine blew it all gambling as fast as he raked it in. Then they had to move up the line and he says all I need now is the bay . . . no good you tagging on behind with a bag of rusks. Go home and say a few prayers for me."

"It was all over the village—Ulyana's gone to make her pile."

"Well, I did buy myself some cloth for a jacket, and that's all I got out of it."

*   *   *

Last year's rusty leaves, and the young grass pushing through them in the first days of its life: little green files, tiny oar blades, green-gold spearheads, the velvety grayness of spreading wormwood.

*   *   *

A drunken Cossack to his love for the occasion: "I love women more than any other cattle!"

*   *   *

Zinaida: "Easter week. People are passing my windows on their way back from the service. They're all carrying candles flickering in the light breeze, I can hear laughter, their faces are cheerful and animated. And I stand at the window with darkness in my soul, and cold and death at the bottom of it. I can't respond to their live emotion."

*   *   *

Letter from Aleksandr: "They've taken it into their heads to build a sawmill to produce railroad ties and firewood. Everything costs the earth, there are no workers—neither carpenters nor bricklayers. You can't get anything, for love or money. To military and Zemgor establishments prices are no object, they're the ones who inflate them. Yesterday I tried to hire laborers to dig a well for the factory. They wanted 500 rubles to take out six cubic sazhens.* Now the inspector is trying to speed up construction of a narrow-gauge line to the storehouse at

*Sazhen: A unit of length equal to 1.89 yards. [Trans.]

the mill. But there are no roads, and we have to bring in sand, ballast, and rails from thirty-five versts away, because they were ordered for Belye Berega, not our station. It's terribly heavy work, but it has to be done. And all this time the Germans have had the use of the enormous forests in our western provinces—while we're without railroad ties."

He also writes: "I've been given thirty-seven POWs. Now I've got my work cut out trying to feed them, find them clothes and shoes and work, and make it worth their while. I don't suppose Russian prisoners over there get looked after like this."

* * *

"I was a sergeant major, with a black mustache, a white body, and an easygoing nature. And she—there wasn't enough of her to spit on, she was no bigger than a thimble . . . And while I was still in the army, she presented me with a . . ."

* * *

Morning in the forest. Gnats buzzing quietly around my ear. At infrequent intervals a grasshopper chirrups. Cocks crow across the river. All is green, rustling. Not a thought in my head, just this yearning: if only some woman would come my way . . .

* * *

"The other day they brought a German officer in, wounded, and the women gathered around. One old woman says, 'I could scratch your eyes out, you ugly German pig! I've lost two sons because of you!' He can speak Russian, and says, 'I've got children of my own, old lady, and I didn't leave them because I wanted to.' And he burst out crying."

* * *

My brother writes: "The way our building work's going, it's like watching steam rise from wet shit. Orders come pouring in from all sides. They don't give you time to turn around. All the same, in spite of wartime difficulties, more work, two or three times more, has been done in the state forests than at ordinary times, and processing has expanded.

"I'm very pleased with the prisoners. I'll have them making hay for the work horses."

* * *

Zina: "We must move either toward or away from each other. I put no value on any other sort of relationship, and wouldn't want to keep it up . . ." Eternal loving enemies (man and woman).

*   *   *

Sweat stains on the back of a mower's dark blue shirt, like patches of black cloth.

*   *   *

Grass has to be cut nice and easy, like eating pancakes with warm cream.

*   *   *

A cabby: "My oldest son went to school for one winter, started reading well, but, being poor, I put him to sausage making with my brother-in-law. The brother-in-law works in a sausage shop. I gave him my little girl as well, to mind the children."

"Does he treat them well?"

"Not too bad, only they've stopped believing in God. It isn't just eating meat on fast days, they've stopped believing altogether. I talk about God to them, and they say, 'What I earn I've got, but God won't help me. There's nothing up there.' I say, 'What about nature, then?' 'There's no such thing as nature either!' 'Rubbish, nature does exist and somebody great must be in charge. If your father and mother hadn't given birth to you, how would you have come into the world?'

"I come out just about nightfall, have a nap on the box, and back to work again. Stable one horse and harness up another."

*   *   *

29 July 1916. On the embankment, at the pearly hour of a white night, a red sunset, warm, the Neva all silvery, soldiers, girls, men in jackets, men in Russian shirts, women with shawls over their shoulders. Snatches of conversation reach me.

A woman's voice: "My husband's in the army and my lover's in the army . . ." A masculine baritone: "Squeeze the rich, they've got spirits and cognac, and we have to drink rat poison at two rubles a time, only you can't even get that" . . . "They won't give our sort a job these days—women have taken over all along the shore. Women get three rubles a day unloading wood."

*　　*　　*

The "Litany of Grigori, New Horse Thief," is going the rounds:
"Rejoice, O profanation of the Church of Christ . . . Rejoice, defilement of the Synod . . . Rejoice, Grigori, great polluter . . ."

*　　*　　*

My brother: "Ordinary people are getting so out of hand . . . no sense of decency, no conscience. Everybody and everything is in a hopeless state of confusion. People rush around grabbing all they can and doing as little as possible. Even the prisoners of war have taken their cue from our folks and started slacking."

*　　*　　*

The contractor charges us two and a half rubles a day for a Chinese laborer, and pays him sixty kopecks. He's the only one who knows Chinese.

*　　*　　*

Zina makes no distinction between "great" and "small" deeds. Each person, she says, has a certain fund of moral strength and everyone who uses his strength to the full has performed a great deed. All such people are equals, although to the outside world their actions are incommensurate.
Can she be right?

*　　*　　*

Children's voices springing like sparks from dry kindling.

*　　*　　*

"Five kopecks for a cabbage like that?"
"I'm asking five but might settle for four."
"What about the official price list?"
The assessor pokes the cabbages contemptuously. His gaze is icy. The woman is silent.
A compassionate voice from the crowd speaks up for the woman: "Well, if we were people with book learning, sir . . . but we're steppe people, not readers and writers . . . We've heard there's this 'ficial price list, but what it amounts to we don't know . . . We're like blind people."

"It applies to all basic necessities. The fixed price for cabbage is forty kopecks a pood. What do you think the list is for?"

"Only we've never, ever, sold it by weight, but by the head. Where would I get a scale? I've made your good lady a present of one head as it is. Cabbage as pure as a teardrop."

A buzz of voices in the crowd: "If there's a list it must be for everything, your honor. But calico, say, you can't get near it . . ." "And what about matches? And kerosene?"

The peasant women got cheeky: "You water them all summer—and you'd soon know what a hundred hairpins cost! I'm not voting for your price list!"

*   *   *

The fixed-price list had made a discreet appearance in the village market. It was pasted up on a fence near the toilets and that was that. Those who needed to knew it by heart already.

The Cossack farmer couldn't understand why customers who used to haggle till they were blue in the face suddenly chose what they wanted without a word.

"Carp, maybe? Or have you got wild carp?"

"Yes, your worship. Here you are, must be around five pounds. Or maybe this one . . ."

"Weigh them!"

"You want both?"

"Weigh both of them!"

The Cossack weighs them on his scale, the purchaser puts them in his basket without asking the price, counts out seventy-four kopecks, and hands them to the Cossack without a word.

"Sir! What's this supposed to be?" the Cossack asks in amazement, holding on his upturned palm some of those scraps of grubby paper that pass for money nowadays.

"That's the fixed price, my dear fellow," the customer says, aiming his finger at the fence. "Take a look yourself, if you can read."

"Give me my fish back!" the Cossack yells, tossing the notes into the customer's basket. "You could get a bellyache eating it at the fixed price!"

"What if I shout for a policeman?"

"Shout all you like, but hand the fish over!"

Four hands latched on to the basket . . .

*   *   *

In Ust-Medveditskaya a box of matches costs as much as forty kopecks. All prices are rising steeply.

My brother: Bryansk was always expensive, but now the traders have kicked over the traces. Prices rise every day. Some goods go into hiding periodically and reappear at very much higher prices. What next? The blame for it all rests with the government, no doubt about that—it is waging a systematic struggle against Russian society on behalf of Germany. We can look forward to something still more shameful and disgraceful—the betrayal of our allies. Revolution is unavoidable. And will be very bloody. The whole thing is horrible . . .

        ✻   ✻   ✻

She was hopping on one foot in the moonlight. "I've missed you so!" But I hadn't come . . .

        ✻   ✻   ✻

The soaring cost of living isn't just a matter of high prices—it goes with a particular state of mind, a universal dread. If things are worse today than yesterday, what will they be like tomorrow? It's a peculiar feeling of despairing defenselessness that comes over you whenever you buy something in the market. Unmanageable prices throttle you. Invisible people, enormously rich already, are concealing goods somewhere nearby, behind that stone wall perhaps, and choking every last kopeck out of you! Outraged, you imagine that these profiteers, these sharks, are encouraged by the government and have the police in their pay. What other explanation can any ordinary person find for the government's failure to curb these highway robbers? It's impossible to believe that there's no food to be had in Russia, Russia always has plenty, so why is there none in the shops? Obviously they're concealing it to fleece the customer. This and nothing else is what people most resent about the government.

        ✻   ✻   ✻

25 October. Cavalry General Pokotilo has issued an order forbidding anyone to carry printed material, notebooks, or even private correspondence across the frontier. What are we coming to!

        ✻   ✻   ✻

Cabby: "We keep on asking for freedom but never think of our duties. There's this professor, a chemist, they're a family of eight, their only servant is an old woman who gets up at five and goes to bed at midnight, they think nothing of it. And they're the ones who're crying out for freedom."

As we pass the Church of St. Michael the Archangel: "The heavenly warrior. I read a book about him. Seems funny, those wars. Why would spirits need to fight? They did, though."

[1 6]

He had called himself an "essayist"—"writer" was how he really thought of himself, but he was too shy to say so. To the nonliterary ear, that of this colonel, say, who, it seemed, read neither newspapers nor magazines, and perhaps not even books, and who had never come across the name Fyodor Kovynev, "writer" would sound ludicrously pretentious. And anyway, Kovynev *was* an essayist. For nearly twenty years now, he had eagerly and indiscriminately devoured with his eyes and ears everything around him, beginning with and delighting above all in his native village, seizing on every oddity of speech and thought, and promptly consigning it in his minute, oblique handwriting to the latest of innumerable notebooks. His notebooks became, as it were, the receptacle of his spiritual life, so that if he had lost them he would have been robbed of his whole past and of any real reason for living. The content of these books did not, however, languish unused. Whenever Kovynev was not observing he felt compelled to process this material and make it available to others.

This was the pattern of his life. He took notes not for himself but so that others, and especially his Don Cossacks, could see and hear and learn it all. But he garnered so much that it threatened to burst the bulging leather covers of his notebooks, leaving him barely time enough to transfer material by the spadeful to manuscript pages, giving no thought to structure, adding explanations and fresh recollections . . . The result could only be called "essays" or "sketches."

What better and quicker way to relieve your soul of an importunate burden than by tirelessly taking notes, writing them up in sketches, and sending them to your editor? But when the pressure was eased, when after a while there were vacant hours to leaf through those sketches, you sighed and admitted to yourself that they were perhaps too long and too many. Arrange those rough notes more patiently, combine them differently, hunched over your desk in a sudden happy fit of inspiration, and you could see for yourself that what you had written had much more sparkle. It was something you could call a "story" or "novella."

It was like making sunflower oil; you had to crush the seeds, press them, drain them over and over again. Or like processing timber. What people need most is simple firewood, but once you've supplied them with that, and there's plenty of wood left and you know that, secretly, you're no mere woodcutter but a carpenter—then your calling is to bend patiently over the lathe, shaving and smoothing and grooving until the work you've put into it is worth more than the wood you started with. Then people will tear themselves away from the very warmest of stoves and come looking for your work.

But you have an inborn need to pour out your heart: in a green gully between plowed fields, buds burst on the bushes and their golden dust rises to the trilling of skylarks . . . or, at the funeral of a soldier, the whole ritual, at once mournful and stirring, the time-honored songs they sing—you want to convey the way they sing, and indeed to quote all the words, because no one who is not a Don Cossack knows them . . . and in your eagerness to find room for this scene from Cossack life, you forget what you had set out to say, so that your narrative overflows like the spring floods of the Don and the Medveditsa . . . and your editors complain about the number of pages.

Like all beginners, Kovynev had waited a long time for recognition. His fragments had floated almost unnoticed on the journalistic sea, and he was over thirty when his first volume of stories, *Cossack Themes*, appeared. Then Korolenko, no less, had singled him out as a specialist on the Don region, and the doors and covers of *Russkoye Bogatstvo* opened wide for him. Suddenly—for one sweet moment!—he had believed in himself! Had he, then, reached his peak? No, this was only the beginning. He was commissioned, and begged, and expected to produce . . . things somehow different, and more and more different, from what welled up in his heart. Editors and critics found his descriptions of flowering ravines and clouds floating over the Don very charming, but wanted him to speak up for justice and freedom. If Cossacks it must be, let him write about the abominable uses to which they were put by the oppressor—otherwise Cossackdom would look like a reactionary theme. Or else he could write on other subjects of importance to the editors, such as Stolypin's cruel experiment at the expense of the peasant—the breaking up of communal land into small farms. Or, for that matter, on anything in which love of freedom was vividly expressed.

What made them think that Fyodor Dmitrich needed to be prodded? That his own ideas were any different? He too felt strongly that the use of Cossacks for punitive purposes besmirched their honor. He had seen for himself, and could write about, unsuccessful small farmers on the steppes along the Volga. He himself had done three months in the Kresty jail—just the sort of thing the public liked to hear about! Well, he was free to write about anything at all, but no socially significant episode must escape his keen writer's eye, even if it was only the high-handedness of a railway policeman or the money-grabbing schemes of a greedy priest. Then again, after so many years as a high school teacher, what a brilliant light he could shed on that revolting character, the obtusely conformist monarchist pedagogue, who might well harbor an unclean passion for schoolgirls, and surreptitiously lend money at usurious rates of interest.

And indeed Kovynev, who had seen a great deal and surmised much more, wrote about it all in the manner expected of him and glided smoothly along the journalistic road, winning public recognition, though sometimes taken to task for depicting intellectuals as spiritually impotent, flimsy creatures. (Which was fair enough, because, as Fyodor Dmitrich ruefully admitted to himself, although he was one of them he had no great understanding of intellectuals.) And again and again, he indulged himself by returning to his tales of Cossack life.

The literary circles were complimentary, but sales were poor—book buyers did not seem to know his name. He would walk up to a counter and feel furious—there lay a volume by F. Kovynev, its cover discolored by sunlight and warped by heat. Obviously unsalable . . . and he would silently curse them all: "So, gentlemen, God damn you all to hell, you don't want to know the song in a Cossack heart."

Kovynev was known to Glazunovskaya, his native village—known as a "mocker." He was known to bookish people on the Don, who regarded him as their bard. But Russia as a whole, in all its immensity, did not want to know about Kovynev.

And who, of all people, could impress on you the extent of your failure with a special cruelty that you could not endure? Tell you that the leisurely lyricism of which you were so fond—all those buds and skylarks and old-world ditties—was a long-winded bore. That those repetitious descriptions of the Don steppe ruined the whole structure of the work, that the author's best phrases, those of which he was particularly proud—sorrow decked in the beauty of a quietly dying sunset, the heart like a bird with a wounded wing, and rapture flickering out like a tremulous spark—were not the high points of stylistic beauty but so much literary garbage—it was shameful to see it over Kovynev's name. Strangely, it was not Korolenko, nor any of his famous colleagues on *Russkoye Bogatstvo*, who would say this, no, but an impertinent little girl in Tambov. A former pupil of his, Zina Altanskaya, who owed whatever understanding of literature she had to him, had started saying such things in letters. (Schoolgirls! You can't say that only some Black Hundreder and village usurer of a schoolteacher cherishes an unclean passion for them. Can any normal teacher of the male sex remain indifferent to, refuse to discriminate between, those thirty girlish faces turned toward him in the top class? How can he help secretly feeling a special liking for one or another as he collects her exercise book or takes back the chalk from her whitened fingers—and wondering, "What if one of these days . . . ?")

But how could a girl with a limited provincial outlook, your very own pupil, show such grasp, such assured taste, and a level of critical understanding not inspired by your lessons? She could be so hurtful that you didn't want to open her letters, but after a while you would read them and find that the wretched girl's criticism stuck fast and couldn't be shaken off. Sometimes, for a joke, you relayed them to your brother, in return for his enthusiastic praise, and he was amazed:

"You show yourself no mercy! You really must be a genius if you can take that!"

One thing Fyodor Dmitrich was quite sure of—and Zina confirmed it: he had an extraordinary memory for everything that ever caught his ear. Conversational exchanges seemed to linger in his memory, undistorted, for years on end. And he could retrieve a slice of life from such depths that it had no need of psychological embellishment to fascinate. He knew very well that he had these abilities. He knew his real potential. In his fifteen years as a writer no one had yet divined it—but he knew. Something inside him, something secret, miraculously communicated to him when he was little more than an infant, had made him choose this path and plod along it. He had a strange, fearful presentiment of the heights to which he could rise and the soul-stirring books he could someday write. And sure enough, in the past few years his rough sketches had begun to mold themselves into something like a finished product. This main character, that episode, these completed chapters—are they right? Is that how they should be? There were no precise limits, everything was in flux, it would not set, it was not strictly speaking a novel, it would be more like a prose poem, perhaps with the simplest of titles—*The Quiet Don*, because the Don and the nourishing scents of his beloved patch of land pervaded the whole thing. Part One was, in fact, finished, but Fedya was too shy to offer it to the public. There was no knowing what the result might be. What if they complained in chorus that there was too much irrelevant description of Cossack life, too much landscape, and that freedom's cause seemed to be neglected?

The main obstacle was not the hostility or envy of others, but himself. Perhaps his taste really was insufficiently discriminating. Or perhaps his way of life was all wrong. Perhaps he should stop traipsing around Russia and haunting editorial offices, perhaps, like the colonel there, he should even stop reading newspapers. Cut himself off from talkative acquaintances, boon companions, extrovert friends, and inquisitive women.

Only . . . that way he might never write anything.

Meanwhile, I mustn't let my traveling companion slip through my fingers. As soon as he goes out into the corridor, I'll open my notebook on the table and quickly, furtively jot down his characteristics. It may never be needed, but it might find a place in the novel, you never know. And just in case—let's have something about his wife, with her wide hat and the brittle notes of command in her voice. Women like that were too hungry for power, and Fyodor was afraid of them. Let them start screaming, and there'd never be an end to it. Best to give in right away. Such women always insisted on traveling with their husbands. Strange that she'd let him go alone.

The colonel wore the aiguillettes of a General Staff officer. He was absorbed in his own thoughts, and had looked at Fedya to begin with as if through a fog. His face was framed by a vigorous, close-clipped, bristly, auburn beard. He seemed very sure of himself (once his wife had gone). He sat cross-legged, quite motionless, without the slightest change of position, at rest, but not slumped in his seat (his training? professional stiffness? trench cramps?). He seemed to have become one with the seat. No fidgeting of the hands, no rubbing of the knee, no stroking of the beard. Not so much as a pursing of the lips. But those slight turns of the head showed that his mind was busy, and the look in his eyes changed continually. When he was listening, they showed that he was taking in all that was said. When he spoke, another look showed that he was intent on making himself understood. You could tell from his eyes whether he was about to speak or remain silent.

The general line in contemporary literature, the general feeling among editors and intellectuals was one of hostility toward army officers, of contempt for them as boneheaded servitors of the regime, drilled in their benighted training schools to be arrogant, self-opinionated, and cruel. And Fedya himself did not like those of them who came from aristocratic families, officers at whose feet an effortless career in the Guards unrolled like a soft carpet. A Cossack by birth and at heart—but unhappily barred from military service by poor eyesight, and now too sluggish anyway, for lack of a horse to ride—Fedya could not help liking and understanding army life, and secretly envying those daring and dashing people for whom the army meant a life of constant exposure to battle. How ardently he would have embraced a Cossack career! He found little in common with writers, but officers he liked. He was glad to be traveling with one, and wanted to be accepted as an equal.

A bit disconcerting, of course, that he never reads our stuff. And he hadn't even heard of the Vyborg appeal. Imagine that!

What an occasion that had been, in the Hotel Belvedere at Vyborg. A gathering of rebel parliamentarians presided over by the president of the Duma, the superb Muromtsev, in person. In the corridors bewitching lady intellectuals hopped onto easy chairs, without removing their shoes, to scarify eminent jurists with their scorching arguments. The dissolution of the First Duma had looked like the great turning point in Russia's history, the end of the Liberation movement. Accept it without protest and no Duma would ever again be summoned! It would mean the end of the newborn parliament, of newborn freedom! The government had committed a crime against the state, and the people would not forgive its representatives if they did not answer blow with blow! After all those furious denunciatory speeches in the Duma how could they remain silent now? Not words but deeds (what deeds, though? *what* deeds?) must show the people the path of resistance— and it would follow! (And although Kovynev, as a sober inhabitant of an out-of-the-way rustic spot, knew very well that the people would be going nowhere, that this cry from the parliamentarians—don't give them soldiers! don't pay your taxes!—would come to nothing, would be obeyed by no one, he too acknowledged his overriding obligation to freedom, and signed together with other overheated deputies.) After which they returned from Finland burning to disseminate the appeal in millions of copies, and fearlessly expecting to be arrested to a man as soon as they reached Beloostrov! Not a finger was laid on any of them.

And in spite of it all the inert mass of the people did not stir. The rebellious deputies were brought to trial after long delay. No attempt was made to halt the long speeches of the defendants. Trivial sentences of three months' imprisonment were handed down, and they were disqualified from office in their own localities for ten years. And now, ten years later, a colonel on the General Staff didn't know what a Vyborger was.

How *could* the masses be moved? *Could* the masses ever be set in motion?

The First Duma! The deputies had entered the Tauride Palace not to collaborate with a moldering government, but to continue the majestic march of the revolution! People saw off deputies at railway stations with intransigent cries of "Land and Freedom!" And when the deputies traveled from the Winter Palace to the Tauride by river steamer the Petersburg crowd on the embankment cried "amnesty!" (for terrorists). Delegations of electors forced their way into the Catherine Hall, peasant petitioners arrived from far-off places, elegant women descended from the galleries to embrace delegates who had made daring speeches or twitter encouragement to those about to speak.

And now, ten years later?

As for Kovynev's own modest speech (lavishly praised in the lobbies at the time, and tailored for his audience: no one rose to make a speech unless it had a high anger content), it had left no mark on Russia's history. Yet, as you mounted the Duma platform, you had to imagine that your words would cause an upheaval and change everything. Why was it Cossacks who were forced to crush the revolutionary people? Cossackdom bore the yoke of a service that disgraced it! The oath of loyalty had been perverted: they had been hypnotically distracted while subjugation to authority was substituted for defense of the fatherland. It was a terrible code that demanded unquestioning obedience! (But could it be otherwise in an army?) Demobilize our regiments! Release us from the hangman's role! Our age-old Cossack freedom and the freedom for which the whole Russian people now strives are one and the same.

It was not the strength of the wine, nor its bouquet, as he poured it two-handed from the heavy bottle into the tumblers, but his consciousness that it came from home, from the Don, from Cherkassk, that made him warm to the colonel—who, anyway, seemed friendly enough, by no means obtuse, and capable of understanding things outside his experience, though at present very much preoccupied.

"Just try to put yourself in the position of a Cossack . . . semi-intellectual, let's call him—there aren't many of them—who's thumbed through Herzen and Chernyshevsky, then finds himself at an early age, and with no say in the matter, wearing a uniform jacket and wide breeches with side stripes, detached willy-nilly from the land and village life, enrolled for what?—to defend the throne against all enemies. There's a man like that from my part of the world, same age as me—Filipp Mironov, maybe you've heard of him? He's a lieutenant colonel now, second-in-command of the 32nd Don Regiment?"

"Er—no, I don't think so . . . Though the 32nd Don Regiment isn't so very far from us."

"You might have heard about him in the Japanese war. He served there with great distinction. And it's the same this time. Reconnaissance . . . surprise attacks . . . amazing river crossings . . . he goes looking for death. One minute he's blowing up a bridge behind German lines, the next he's rescuing a surrounded regiment with a single company. By now he has seven or eight medals, including a Vladimir. Well, in 1906 he was sent with a detachment to crush some rebellious peasants. So what does he do but parcel out the landowner's meadows to them! That's the way he operated! Then at the Ust-Medveditskaya district meeting about the same time . . ." [In their district meeting at Ust-Medveditskaya in those heady days of freedom, who do you think were the main orators? Fedya and Filya, who else?] "he urged category 2 Cossacks not to let themselves be drafted for police duty! And they didn't report! Later on Filipp too was a candidate for the Duma, the Second, but the prosecutor struck his name off. And he was under house arrest for eight months. But the revolution was petering out by then. And General Samsonov, the ataman appointed by the Tsar, pardoned him and sent him back into the service at the very time when he banished me from the district. But can you explain to me how a man can serve once he starts thinking? You can serve *either* the people *or* the Tsar, obey either your conscience or your oath—there's no avoiding the choice."

"Serving your country is the same as serving the people," Vorotyntsev retorted.

"Maybe so. Maybe not. A Cossack in Mironov's company got a letter telling him his wife had died, his mother was sick, and there was nobody to look after his two children. Mironov promised him a month's leave and let him go into town to send a telegram. But the Cossack was so fazed he met the regimental commander in town and didn't salute him. The commander ordered Filipp to punish the man. He stands him in full marching order for two hours, then goes to try to arrange his leave. The commander's answer? Punishment insufficient, leave denied. Well, you get rats like that wearing epaulets, don't you?"

"Alas, yes." The colonel agreed almost too readily. "Still, if we gave up saluting the army would go to the dogs."

There was a grinding of brakes, but for some reason the carriages did not budge. Then the locomotive backed slightly, and slowly moved out.

"Yes, but there was more punishment to come! Think of it—for the grave offense of failing to salute, twenty-five strokes of the birch before the whole company. That's the sort of hangmen we Cossacks are: we get thrashed ourselves, like little children. Mironov begged the commander to cancel the order. Very well, then, flog him before the whole *regiment*! I ask you, how can anyone serve with such people."

Such people? Meaning "with you"?

"The days when officers struck their men are over," the colonel said confidently. "Nowadays an officer would feel ashamed to do it. And birching is a rarity. It was introduced to make courts-martial unnecessary."

"Well, Mironov stood before the regiment and gave this order: 'So-and-so, ten paces forward, march! As your immediate superior officer I *forbid* you to lie across that bench of shame. About face, fall in!' "

The colonel's eyebrows twitched very slightly. Soldiers must salute officers, but *this* showed spirit.

"And what happened?"

"It was his third offense! He was obviously incorrigible. He was recalled to Novocherkassk, the same General Samsonov watched his adjutant strip the mutineer of his lieutenant's epaulets, and his service in the Don Army was over. That's how it is—you may be a hero, and famous and a medal winner, but once you begin thinking . . . How are we Cossacks supposed to think? Isn't it harder for us than for anyone else? But still people curse us . . ."

Kovynev mopped his brow. He squinted through the window. The light was fading, and he could hardly see a thing.

"And that's what vexes me. What a malicious joke history has played on us. It had to be the Cossacks. The Cossacks, who were the most intransigent enemies of servitude. They fled from it to the outermost edge of the land, in search of freedom. Only to return to Russia, reborn in their posterity, to deprive others of that freedom. Deprive the have-nots from whose ranks they themselves sprang. To gallop, whooping and whipping, into the thick of their own people. The Cossack soul has been corrupted. It is pitiful. They aren't evildoers—they just don't know what they're doing."

The colonel would not be drawn on the subject of servitude and freedom, but he wanted to know what became of Mironov in the end.

"He had to think what to do, and this was it. His father wasn't at all well fixed, he couldn't afford a horse for his son to take to the army, he used to carry water around Ust-Medveditskaya in a barrel. So now the cashiered lieutenant did the same. He pinned all his medals on his army greatcoat—without epaulets—and started taking water around in a barrel himself, a kopeck for a bucketful!"

A vignette for a fine artist in prose—thrown away, blurted out to a traveling companion. Life was so full of people, of happenings—what pen could keep up with them?

"Suddenly they felt ashamed of themselves. They made him a clerk in the agricultural office at Novocherkassk. Filipp was as uppity as ever: he submitted a scheme for redistribution of all Don Cossack lands . . . Once the seed of freedom is sown in a man there's no curing him."

Fedya himself was an example.

"He volunteered to fight in this war. And how gallantly he's fighting!"

The light outside was ebbing. The tantalizing glimpses of the changeable scene grew fainter, distracting the passengers less and less, concentrating their attention on each other more and more.

"So you're a Don Cossack born and bred?"

"In fact, my father was village headman."

"But you never served yourself?"

"I myself never served," Fyodor Dmitrich confessed, embarrassed as always, as though it was a disgrace. "Because of my eyesight. Nor my brother—he's lame. So we didn't have to find mounts either. I studied at St. Petersburg, in the Historical and Philological Faculty. I taught for ten years at the Orel high school and another four at Tambov."

"Tambov? I went there myself once." The colonel laughed. "To get married."

"Really?" Fyodor Dmitrich said hesitantly, "D'you know, I myself very nearly . . ." He heaved a sigh. "In the winter I'm in Petersburg, but I spend three or four months in the village every year. And the folks back there accept me, they come to me for advice as if I was a justice of the peace or a lawyer. Sometimes even use me as a doctor. Or I'm chairman of the village cooperative."

(Or you can laze around with the young Cossacks, the bachelor boys, by the wattle fence under the cherry trees. Never mind that you're fiftyish. In fact, that makes it all the better. They're your own kind, those boys, part of you, like the grass and the earth.)

"So I can tell what the village is thinking. And how the city sees things. When I'm living in the village I forget all about Petersburg. I feel that I'm a Don Cossack, and nothing more. And I judge everything in the world according to whether it will be good or bad for the Don alone. Then I go back to Petersburg, and in a matter of hours, after the first few editorial meetings, or in the Mining Institute, where I'm librarian and lodge with another man from the Don, I come to my senses, my field of vision expands to take in all Russia again, and it seems strange that three days back I couldn't see beyond the Don, and didn't want to know anything more. Looked at from Russia, the Don is its mischievous child. And looked at from the Don, the Don is not Russia."

"What do you mean, the Don isn't Russia?"

"You find that strange?"

As if the Don or any other river could take it into its head not to be Russian! Still, not just the Don, but that little wedge of land between the Don and the Medveditsa, miserable and infertile though it might be, was a place apart.

Other rivers could make no such claim. The Don could. It had its own songs, its own legends. The steppe even had a smell all its own. No, he had put it badly: he was not equally at home with the Don and with Petersburg.

"Nothing hurt me more than being deprived of the Don in 1907. Tambov isn't all that far away. But to me it was exile."

(Where people had a highly developed sense of belonging to a unified fatherland it would be different. But in our country . . .)

"When the first tremors came in 1905 and after—our blood was up. I've got a photograph of Filipp, the one I was talking about, with a caption: 'We will lay down our lives for the autonomy of the Don Cossacks.' "

No, this was too much for the colonel. He was tempted to laugh.

"We've nearly finished your wine, you know. Let's call it a day. You're going to Petersburg straight from the Don, and you won't have any left for your Cossack friends."

"No, not straight from the Don. I stopped somewhere on the way."

The clatter of the train wheels made him feel closer to this chance companion—a stranger yesterday, a stranger tomorrow, but today almost an in-law. This shuddering little house on wheels released him from all restraints, disciplinary and professional, all ties of party and family, isolated him even from the jolly conductor and from fellow passengers walking unseen past the thick frosted glass of the door. It left just the two of them, confidingly tête-à-tête.

I can tell him—or I can skip it. What can these details mean to a fellow passenger? But opening up is somehow pleasurable . . . I could confess that I left the Rostov train at Kozlov, checked my baggage, and took myself off, feeling twenty years younger, with pounding heart . . . to Tambov.

They sat there side by side, Vorotyntsev straining forward, looking toward Petersburg and tomorrow, Kovynev longing to slow things down, looking backward to yesterday and Tambov.

Tambov? It gave him pleasure even to say the word out loud, it was as sweet on his lips as *her* name. Naming the town was like naming her. Zina Altanskaya!

[1 7]

It was in Tambov that Kovynev had made the great transition—from the hopeless lot of a provincial high school teacher to a career as a writer on the staff of a metropolitan magazine. He had arrived in Tambov an outcast from the Don, he left for the capital an acknowledged success. And in Tambov, though it was long before he realized it, he had left behind . . . There had been so many of them over the years, schoolgirls in pelerines sitting at their desks, holding their hands out for corrected essays . . . It had been there in the back of his mind for years. But never, till then . . . And, unluckily, at the very last minute . . .

They had an interminable evening ahead of them. The gentle rocking of the train was soothing. Two men, no longer young, who had both seen a good deal of life, elbows resting on the solid little table . . . Why not tell him?

But where to begin?

"Yes, of course, I know a lot of people all over the place, I've loved all sorts, you know how it is."

You speak one way, you think another. There are things one man can't bring himself to say to another without making a joke of it, without disparagement. Loved all sorts!

"They're all long gone and forgotten. But for this one girl . . ." (His voice almost failed him at the word "girl.") "I've just been to see her, and a hundred versts didn't seem out of my way."

He gave a self-deprecating little laugh.

But inside was the red-hot agony from which the conversation so far had been merely a distraction. He had put it behind him once, and it should never have gone any further, but no, he had got off at Kozlov and caught the Tambov train . . .

These were things you shouldn't be telling anybody, let alone this colonel . . . and anyway you've forgotten it all a dozen times over, and only now remember . . . the pigtail brushing the exercise book, a scrap of paper inflated into a sort of bogey, a fancy bookmark left deliberately in her literature essay book, a sudden mysterious fit of giggles, the way she stared at you, all eyes, from the front row. The endearing thing was that all this was addressed not to the former Duma deputy nor to the future writer, at a time when the people of Tambov were not yet breathless with hope and dread that Fyodor Kovynev would "put them on paper"—no, it was meant for that rather seedy, forty-year-old high school teacher.

Then she left school and went away. They met again purely by chance. If either of them had come by a minute earlier or later nothing would have happened.

"Do you remember that pretty spot in Tambov—the long embankment over one arm of the Tsna? And a bit higher up there's a street with houses on one side only, little wooden houses. People sitting on every porch, and at wide-open windows. With samovars. Sipping tea and looking at the river. At the boats. And the meadows beyond. Well, we met in full view of all those tea drinkers, stopped to talk for two minutes. Couldn't stand there any longer—or the gossip would spread like wildfire. She was as tall as me, she'd put her hair up like a grown woman, but her face was still girlish, a little pudgy, not fined down, but unlined. Chin in the air, she asked me quite brazenly, 'Fyodor Dmitrich! Can I come and see you, at your place, today or tomorrow?'

Relationships between a male teacher and a female pupil are frequent, but can be quite innocent. There are boundaries to be drawn, things that "are done" and things that "are not done," your sense of duty. But your feeling for a girl pupil, or even a girl who was once your pupil, is a special one, unlike your feeling for anyone you meet as a mature woman. You are placed in a position of superiority to her right from the start—to this young creature, on the brink of womanhood, eager to please you. And the older the teacher is—getting on for forty in my case—the more flattering it is, and the harder it is for him to withhold himself. But then again, the older you are, the more hidebound you are, the less capable of making a move . . . You become so much the more timid and uninteresting. Suppose your objective description of yourself in a story goes like this: "The teacher was a rustic figure, quiet and self-effacing, with a wispy mustache and a sparse beard, eyes that blinked helplessly, a halting voice, a dull plebeian face, without a single striking feature." In actual fact it was not quite that bad. In fact at times . . . and as seen by a good-looking seventeen-year-old girl . . .

Still, to get involved in that way with a young girl, not knowing what might come of it, God help you! All those tricky maneuvers . . . all that ducking and weaving . . . why all that worry and trouble, when there are other teachers' wives, all sorts of encounters on your travels, and, back in the village, widows, or young women pining for their soldier husbands? Best leave Tambov quickly and for good . . . Anyway, aren't you just getting started on your big story? You can't fit in an affair, you don't need it. Besides, if a girl starts this way, what does it tell you about her character? What will she do next?

"Two minutes went by, and I was still lost for an answer. She raised her head still higher and walked off. Two days later there was a letter in the mail: 'I don't really know why I'm writing to you after what happened—I just want to make it clear that I do *not* love you, as you appear to have sometimes thought, and might have thought there on the embankment. But I do like you, as someone out of the ordinary, unlike almost anyone I have met.' (Who out of the ordinary could she have possibly met in Tambov? That's laughable!) 'If this letter becomes public property it won't matter in the least to me, but it would greatly upset my mother.' I read it . . . and was filled with regret. What a clumsy oaf I am! How could I let this pristine sweetness pass me by? I wrote back inviting her to visit me on a certain evening. And what d'you think the answer was? 'That day, when I invited myself to your place, I was in a foul mood, and there was nobody in Tambov I could talk to! But that's over now, thank you. Anyway, I thought there was a hint of frivolity in your invitation, you somehow seem to have misunderstood me.' So then I have to write and explain myself: really how can you, of course I didn't misunderstand you! . . . Well, two months later I left Tambov altogether to live permanently in Petersburg."

It was embarrassing to tell another man about it, but . . . there followed an endless correspondence with the wretched girl (the only one in Tambov he wrote to). He kept all her letters, and read them over and over again. In Tambov he couldn't spare her a single evening, but in Petersburg he had squandered many evenings answering her letters, although piles of notes were waiting to be written up. He felt awkward, telling the colonel these things.

But, surprisingly, the colonel understood. "A letter closes the gap between you, you make up for your separation by showing affection. A letter is always stronger and more effective than anything you say in the ordinary run of things. As words pass through the pen, it gives them an extra twist."

"I didn't write at first, she found my address herself. Says there's something in me she finds endearing, something that makes her feel close to me. She treasures just that, and wants no more. Whereas if our relationship went beyond certain limits, that would be lost."

And, of course, you can't help feeling flattered if your letters fill her with "a sort of reckless daring." Or if she writes, "The way I feel toward you right now—if I had wings or a balloon I would fly to your pillow and inspire 'golden slumbers.' But when we meet, I won't be so bold. In fact, I'm afraid of getting to know you better . . ." It was as though she stood beside him—by the table, by the arm of his chair, looking over at the letter. He could almost see her bending toward him, more vividly real than reality, her dress nipped in at the waist, the wrists, the throat—so alluring. But she never came. There were only letters.

The colonel held a cigarette between two fingers and went into the corridor for a smoke. (It seemed people couldn't steer clear of these love affairs. Whatever more important concerns they might have they got onto that subject sooner or later.)

Where did she get that easy style? Schoolgirls don't write like that. And her handwriting moved just as easily, winging its way into your heart—the provocative tone and the handwriting were somehow of a piece. Even the contours of the text were her own; a wide gap between sentences, a mere sigh between paragraphs, lines uneven, awkwardly terraced, as though normal punctuation, dashes and rows of dots, were not enough for her. The pattern varied—you could tell what mood she was in the moment you unsealed her envelope. Reading a letter of hers was like seeing her face to face. (Fyodor Dmitrich had taken careful note of all this, meaning to write about it.)

She never flattered, never praised him. She wrote not to admonish, not to wheedle, but proudly, unconstrainedly. A chit of a girl, twenty years his junior, looked deep into him, through his letters, his essays, his articles, and said what she thought with a bluntness he wasn't used to, and would have taken amiss if there was anyone else to hear, but it was just between the two of them, nobody else knew. "You adapt too readily to whatever company you find yourself in! You're too much in thrall to 'progressive' ideas and that is a handicap for an artist! The way you progressive journalists have puffed up Maria Spiridonova! Don't forget that I know her. She went to our school, and everybody knows she was expelled from the seventh grade because her teacher found a note from a lawyer that showed she'd been his mistress for some time. She went on traveling around the province with him and shot him dead in a private apartment in a fit of jealousy. So you progressive journalists invented the tale that she was a committed member of the SR Party, that she shot him because he had helped suppress the uprisings, that it was on a railway station, and that a squadron of Cossacks had raped her on the spot. There was no such squadron, no such rape, no such station even: she did her lover in sitting on his lap, and ended up a revolutionary icon. That's where your progressive journals get you, so just look out!"

Zinaida herself made no pretense of "serving" anyone or anything, she insisted that she had no "social" feelings, no "higher aspirations" in favor of progress—and if you don't like it, you can lump it! She ridiculed "red study groups" but was equally dismissive of her aunt, who was a nun. She was a rebel—against what, neither she nor anyone else knew, a rebel pure and simple. She concealed none of her negative characteristics—she wrote about herself as she was. But she didn't spare him either: "I'm sorry for you, you're always so wishy-washy, you never carry anything through to the end, you just moan about 'Russia' and 'the system,' but if you were suddenly confronted with complete freedom you wouldn't know how to organize your life. There's no knowing whether you'll ever write a proper book." At other times she was rapturous: "What a joy life must be when the young make your ideas their own!" Then the old refrain again: "There are times when I'm so sorry for you, you're something and nothing, passed over by life, I would like to smooth your furrowed brow and even kiss your black muzhik head. I love seeing your mousy handwriting on an envelope." "Mousy handwriting" was impertinent, offensive, but apt. He hadn't noticed it till then. It was humiliating to hear such pointed criticism from a slip of a girl, but he was hooked, and felt miserable when there was no letter.

The colonel was back. By now the compartment was in semi-darkness, they could hardly see each other's faces, but Vorotyntsev didn't suggest putting the lights on, and Fedya certainly didn't want them. A story like his needed the right atmosphere and it was much more comfortable in the twilit compartment.

"Of course, to keep such a correspondence going—you know how it is—you have to write in a way that says, 'I am not and never have been on such terms with any other woman, I'm amazed at myself, I just can't understand it.' All the same, when I invited her to visit me, she wouldn't. She would suddenly be overcome by doubt—was no other sort of relationship possible between beings of opposite sex? As though any 'other sort' was what she wanted. You try to explain to her: 'Look, Zina, my love, if there's nothing sensual behind it people aren't interested in each other.' To which she replies, 'I've rigorously reviewed my feelings for you this week and found nothing immodest in them. *That* wasn't the sort of love you used to tell us about in your lessons!' Yes, but lessons are—just lessons. In real life, you explain to her, everything that happens is the result of an instinctive impulse. We have to take what life offers. She snaps back, 'No! Not everything life offers! You have to be very choosy! Otherwise you won't notice the good things among all the rubbish that pours in! To accept whatever comes means you have no self-respect. Anyway, you don't really think that way, I don't believe it!' Hopeless trying to explain to her how different from them we are. Sometimes, just to heat things up, perhaps you come out with a whopper, drop hints about some woman met by the wayside. Right, my love, if you're so frank let's see if you can stand a bit of masculine frankness for a change. A man always tries to hide his other women, but I'll come clean. Does it repel you? And what do you think? She stood for it. Didn't stop writing."

Fyodor Dmitrich smiled, one man of the world to another. "You could drive yourself crazy trying to understand them, best not to trouble your head. You fix yourself up with two or three women in the village. 'Why quarrel? I hate your quarreling,' you tell them, 'there's love enough in my heart for the three of you, don't quarrel.' If a Cossack troubles his head over a woman's caprices he is done for! But if some woman's pining for you—don't let her get away."

The colonel swayed, shifting his seat in the half-darkness. Was he going to say something? No.

"Anyway, there's no love that lasts forever. Everything passes, all love is transient. And if you put yourself in a woman's hands she'll twist your whole life out of shape."

That's the way it goes. First you turn her down, then you're hankering after her—she's the one, I must have her now, nobody else will do!

Zina, my love! Don't let our "holiday of the heart" pass us by! Come to me! Come!

No! To be human is to be alone. When we meet we only touch elbows.

"She did come once, though. Thought of taking a dentistry course in Petersburg. We didn't just touch elbows. Just once I drew her very close to me . . . but no, she went away."

And you would always remember the way her long yellow scarf dangled over her breast.

She went away, but didn't stop writing. "You've known women since you weren't much more than fifteen, but you'll always be warming yourself at somebody else's flame, no 'holiday of the heart' for you . . . You're too circumspect, and your desires are actually too feeble. 'F' for 'Fyodor' and 'F' for 'footling.' I can hardly bring myself to gratify you by writing your name. You're one of those who like to go mushrooming but not to get their feet wet. Go and defend your fatherland, why don't you! And joy go with you!"

A fractious girl! Listening to her insults was all the more hurtful because there was truth in them. He should, indeed, be at the front. He regretted missing the Japanese war. As a writer, he should have been there. And as a Cossack—of course.

At last! At long last the glumly humorous black-haired conductor had reached them, with a half-gallon samovar on a tray, still purring, and a teapot on top of it. A crimson glow filtered through the vents around the samovar into the gathering darkness of the compartment.

Electric light from the corridor spilled over the conductor's shoulders. He asked anxiously whether their bulb was dead. No, we just don't want it on, Fyodor Dmitrich explained. The easygoing conductor left it at that.

He hadn't put sugar on the tray—sorry, there isn't any. But Fyodor Dmitrich climbed up top again, felt in his basket, and brought out a jar. His companion was astonished to find him so well supplied.

"It's easy to see you spend your whole life traveling! You're remarkably well equipped!"

"I like housekeeping, and I like doing things properly," Fyodor Dmitrich said complacently. "So what do you say, shall we do without light for a while?"

He didn't want to see his companion just now, it would only distract him. And that burning inside him . . . no, he didn't want more light.

In the subdued, warm crimson glow from the vents in the samovar everything on the table—glasses, spoons, fingers—was easily distinguishable. It was as if the little flames glowed with his own heat, and her spirit seemed to hover in the impenetrable darkness overhead.

Once more, the colonel was agreeable. He fumbled his contribution onto the table—the usual train traveler's share-and-share-alike. It's tastier between two. Mmm—this jam of yours! What big cherries! . . . Don cherries . . . cherries are our best thing, except maybe grapes. Oh, and melons.

Eating and drinking was a distraction, a delay. A good place to break off, forget the story?

But the little flames in the samovar were glowing crimson and its brass body was still singing its troubled tune.

No, there was no stopping now. Sometimes speaking aloud, sometimes running it over in his mind . . .

". . . a child . . ." (Was that out loud?)

"Ah, so after all that . . ."

"No, it was another man's child." Fyodor Dmitrich wondered anxiously how to explain. He didn't altogether understand it himself.

"You may find it surprising . . . but that was by no means the end of it. On the contrary, it was just the beginning . . ."

He couldn't see the look on the colonel's face. Was it the same tense, impatient expression he had worn when he came into the compartment? Or had he composed himself to listen?

It had been dragging on for six years, but when had the unretractable step been taken? And was it really impossible to extricate himself even now?

Head thrown back, just like that time on the embankment—only now a head that had sunk beneath the waves and resurfaced, a head armed now with knowledge, with common sense, and even with power—no longer childishly full-cheeked but with lines of suffering etched in her face, her whole being concentrated in the unspoken question: can I come to you today?

"We wrote to each other all through 1915, without ever meeting. And she let slip fewer and fewer words of sympathy and affection, more often than not she was poking fun at me. Then, suddenly, like a cry for help: 'If you too are sick at heart, share your feelings with me, if you're at ease spare me . . . Because my heart is full of trouble!' Then, in the next letter, she seemed to have forgotten all that, just talked about a book she'd read or a play she'd seen. But you know how it is, we don't read women's letters five times over, looking for coded messages between the lines. They turn our letters upside down, hold them up to the light . . . And what do we do? Pick out the tasty bits, squeeze the juice out of them—and pop the letter into a chest. We're differently constructed: things that are of the utmost importance to them we don't even notice. Where we see a tumbler running over they see a whole deluge. Run a skillful finger along her spine and it affects her more than . . . the dissolution of the Duma. Her character was a mess before, but now it's completely ruined. Anyway, with the war on, everybody is more independent."

It was the old story: a jilted girl isn't going to stay on her own forever.

It was just as you'd expect. She starts hanging around with a crowd from the Tambov powder factory. One of them is an engineer of some sort, "a pure Chekhov type," a shrinking violet, melancholy, a dreamer, in fact a complete washout. His wife (Zinaida speaking) is, of course, "extremely colorless," "a lifeless person." Zinaida begins by bawling him out for hinting at a flirtation. But after blowing hot and cold for a bit she gives in—and immediately sends the engineer off to tell his wife everything! Oh, yes—she wanted the other woman to know!

"Just like that? He had to tell his wife about it himself?" the colonel asked with some animation.

"Yes. He was to go to her himself and tell her."

"But why?"

Fyodor Dmitrievich didn't really understand it himself. "I suppose she thought, 'I can't be happy with a dishonest relationship!' The devil only knows how a girl's mind works. I'm telling you, you'll drive yourself crazy if you ever try to keep track of it."

"So what did the engineer do?"

"Went to his wife. And came clean."

The colonel tutted and hemmed. "And . . . ?"

"And they went on like that for a few months."

"Don't you think it makes a kind of sense? Being honest and open? Why does it always have to be the other way?"

A black world was speeding past their black windows, relieved only by the pale shuddering reflection of neighboring windows, and the occasional faint twinkle of village lights.

"Or . . . can you imagine taking a flying leap? All shackles cast off for one moment of flight! Up again? Or down? Either way, who could help being envious? What wouldn't we give for such an experience!"

Seen through the dark window the distant girl seemed to hover outside their compartment, speeding through dark space, borne along with the train. On feet? Wings? A broomstick?

"Or maybe it's like one squeezed lemon calling out to another. What a merry dance we had! But the juice squeezed out was as sour and as cloudy and as boring as lemon juice always is. So was it worth it, Fyodor Dmitrich?"

Was it Fyodor Dmitrich who drove you into his arms? I'm sorry for you all right, but Fyodor Dmitrich can't be bothered with you anymore. Just now Fyodor Dmitrich's one wish is to solve a riddle: why the lemons? Their affair had come to end. The wife might be colorless, she might be limp—but she reclaimed her husband. And the naughty little girl took a tumble—from a carousel in full career. And, picking herself up wiser and stronger, to whom did she turn? Toward . . . the platform on Tambov station.

Fyodor Dmitrich had forgotten to drink his tea. Bent over his glass, transfixed, he was thinking. As though here, with just the two of them, thinking might get him somewhere.

The charcoal in the samovar had stopped glowing and turned to ash. It was like sitting by an extinguished campfire.

"Then, suddenly, it was: Fyodor Dmitrich, my mother has died! And I couldn't even show myself at her funeral . . ." Why on earth not? Your mother! What could possibly stop you? . . . "And her letters were not coming from Tambov anymore, but from somewhere near Kirsanov. Why? I wondered. Another riddle. It took a few more letters for me to work it out. She hadn't been at her mother's deathbed because she was concealing her pregnancy. She had borne the child in hiding, down in the country."

All alone there, carrying her child, giving birth, feeding it, helpless, like a wounded bird . . . and there was only one person she could still speak to without shame—Fyodor was the one from whom she hid nothing, the one with whom she did not feel ashamed. Living in a hovel with a sagging ceiling, scarcely able to keep the stove going, cooking her own meals for the first time, and incompetently, she no longer tried to show off her well-turned phrases and clever thoughts, she no longer affected frivolous nonchalance, she gave up her crazy flights of fancy. Her milk had dried up! It sounds so beautiful—love without thought of marriage, selfless affection—but here was an exhausted mother with a feeble little mite and no milk for him. One wet nurse followed another. The future of Russia was immeasurably more important, she would agree, but when dear, soft little lips seek the source of life and you disappoint them, have nothing to give . . . The old high-and-mightiness, the insolent tone, the mockery were no more—she wrote asking in so many words for comfort: Fyodor Dmitrich, I have no past and no future, I have lived a senseless life, and my strength is exhausted . . . And I don't believe in God the Comforter.

And yet—she is unrepentant. Regrets nothing. Doesn't let the tittle-tattle in her distant hometown prey on her mind. Doesn't suffer from injured pride. It's just the numbing fear of loneliness.

Flesh cannot enter through the double window from the eddying darkness outside. But she flies in pursuit, after the train, at their own speed, never falling behind. And perhaps penetrates their compartment with a chilling draft.

Suddenly he had found himself writing back with a warmth he had never shown before, an affectionate candor new to their relationship. She had a child by another man, but he felt no jealousy. Zinaida's letters changed as the weeks went by—they grew more frequent and crossed his in the mail, so that they were no longer just answers to his own. She wrote freely and happily about her "little rascal," how she worried about him, how he made her laugh, how everybody used to despair of her and say such a featherheaded girl would never make a mother, and here she was seeing to diapers and pacifiers with a song on her lips. And when the toothless little mouth laughed, the uprush of happiness was quite painful.

Why (she wondered) did she feel such tenderness for Fyodor Dmitrich? Well, "in spite of your 'instinctual impulses' (remember?) I've always known that through your trivial amours you were really seeking a higher happiness."

Then an unexpected outburst: "I want to go to the Moscow Arts Theater!"

And one rainy August night, with a blustering wind banging the bucket against the wellhead, pitch-darkness outside, a dim oil lamp on the table ("we're economizing on kerosene")—"I know it's disgraceful, I know it's wicked in wartime, but I want bright lights, noise, color, music! . . . I read an advertisement in the *Tambov Gazette* for a concert by a Polish woman pianist, I'd heard her before, and I felt like rushing off to Tambov that very moment! It's twelve versts from Korovainovo here to the Inzhava branch line, and then you have to wait for a connection to Kirsanov . . . but I'm joking, of course, I'll never leave my little one."

"After that there was a foggy patch, she didn't seem able to work out what she felt. But, without putting it into words, she was asking me to come." Anyway, he'd already had the idea of visiting her down in the country, in spite of the Inzhava branch line and the twelve versts by horse and carriage from the station.

The colonel came to life: "Listen—why didn't you just marry her? Before she met the engineer or anybody else?"

"Georgi Mikhalich! . . . Come on! How could I?"

Did he really not see why?

He carefully slid the tray with the samovar toward the window. Then the glasses. And the jam jar.

"If you're a man in your forties? If you're already set in your opinions? If independence is the first principle of your existence?"

To be deprived all at once of leisure and freedom to move? To be eternally tied to her by some obligation? To be no longer yourself?

Both elbows resting firmly on the table. His head between his hands. Speaking into the unreadable quarter-light.

"Anyway, who knows how the marriage would have turned out? Can anybody ever fathom a woman's character before marriage? What if it went wrong? Besides, there were four of us—two brothers and two sisters—left orphaned. One sister was an invalid—she had what they call a wasting disease. The other one was never going to marry either. And it was up to me to give my younger brother a start in life. It was for their sake I spent fourteen years giving the same old lessons, listening to the same old answers, till it nearly choked me, but what way out was there? They were orphans, and I was responsible for them. The holding and the house were joint property, from our father. If I married anybody it would have to be a Cossack girl, what else? But how could I, as I now was, marry an uneducated Cossack girl now? I adopted young Petya, he goes to secondary school now, he'll make a splendid Cossack. When he gets a bit bigger, I'll have to rustle up a full set of Cossack gear for him—a warhorse, a pack, thirteen different items of equipment, not counting ammunition.

" 'I mean it! Please, please! Come and see me! Here, at the back of beyond, in this out-of-the-way corner of the Kirsanov district, which no writer has ever visited and no one will ever write about, a spot with nothing at all to boast about, but come all the same! Our river, the Mokraya Panda, runs through a ravine out in the steppe—a remarkable spot, you'll see. Do, do come, Fyodor Dmitrich, come right now, this September! I'm longing to see you!' "

As it happened, Fyodor could go. It fitted in with his plans. He promised.

By return mail came an agitated letter. "We've exchanged so many letters, but seen so little of each other! I'm so frightened!" He didn't go after all. He was detained in his village. It was autumn, there was work to be done in the orchard, and he stayed to help his sisters. Not that this necessarily prevented him altogether, he could have made an effort and found time. But . . . the same old foggy patch, the same old blind corner . . . There was always some hitch, some reason for second thoughts . . . He didn't go.

"I was looking forward so much to seeing you! I thought your coming would mean a whole new world for me! There was one evening of moonlight, such bright moonlight, with the river sparkling and the forest rustling, the village was asleep on the slopes down to the ravine, and there was I, so young, so friendless, with a new little life on my hands, yet so carefree, wandering around outside, telling myself, 'This could be the day he comes,' and hopping to make my guess good! I would have taken you into the forest, along a moonlit cutting, chattering and laughing, we would have sat on the grass. Why, oh, why didn't you come? . . . Anyway, you didn't, and the mood of the moment was over. I'll write to you with pleasure, but I'm no longer so eager to see you. Anyway, nothing good could come of our meeting."

Ah, but by now some force superior to his will or hers had intervened. Something was propelling them toward each other, and nothing could prevent it. Their meeting had been put off, but hasty telegrams followed: He could make it after all, not to the village, though, but to Tambov. She could come into town!

"But what about my son? I can't leave him! It would upset me to leave him! I've never left him for a moment! . . . All right! I'll be there! I'll come!"

She had warmed up so much, become so passionate, so ardent bearing a child—never mind that it was not yours—so unlike her former self, live or in photographs, that he scarcely recognized her! How stupid he would have been not to go!

But the engineer? She hadn't been unfaithful, that was the extraordinary thing. It was her way, however roundabout, to Fyodor.

So all their reservations, all the years of deliberate delay, were of no avail: they were thrown together just the same. And it was a fearful joy to hear her say, raising her head from the pillow, with a toss of her hair and her earrings, "No, you still don't love me nearly enough! You're going to love me a lot more!"

It could stifle a man! Fedya's one great success in life so far had been not getting tied down, not letting anybody hobble him. And here he was, carried away, rolling helplessly downhill, with nothing to clutch at, nothing to check his fall.

"Why did you never come straight out with it and order me to follow you? That's what caused it all."

The snag was that, with Tambov now so far away, she was still beside him, still there, indeed more powerfully present than ever! It was as though she had splashed over him some dark, hot liquid, drenched him in it, and the hurt was still burning relentlessly. Usually, when you turn your back on a woman you yawn and forget her, but this time . . . Which made it all the more dangerous to succumb. How had it happened? How could he, with his experience, his common sense, and at his age, have risked himself so recklessly? With her it was a very serious matter, she wanted to take possession of him body and soul, wanted every last bit of him.

No, I must think of something. And write to her. That could be my salvation. Tomorrow from Petersburg.

"It's such a hackneyed word," she explained, snuggling up to him. "Everybody uses it, for no good reason. But it does happen, love does happen, Fedenka, not very often, but . . ."

Something like this: yes, I fell for you, but the fact is . . . although I never told you . . . there's somebody else. That "somebody else" would erect a barrier between them. The only possible defense against a woman is another woman.

Defend myself—yes. But the thought of giving her up tears my breast with hot hooks. Presented with a girl like that when I'm pushing fifty—how can I give her up?

Fedya had been thinking aloud less and less, and by now his lips were moving soundlessly. Whether his companion was still listening, or dozing, he made no response. He might perhaps have given Fedya some helpful advice, but he did not react.

A man tumbling downhill has no time to think—bouncing helplessly, rebounding, bumping his head, now back, now front, he flings out his arms, clutching wildly, and if they meet a stone, a root, a blade of grass—grab it! You can't make out what it is, but grab it! Farther on there will be nothing, no fences no gentle slope, nothing will save you!

Vorotyntsev had in fact heard more of this story than he could have wished, more than he would ordinarily listen to. He had unwittingly let himself be diverted from his own anxious preoccupations, listened—and marveled.

Not at Fedya—he was just another example of a very common type, the man who gets in a muddle over such a simple matter as marriage. But what Vorotyntsev felt, listening to him, was not condescending pity, it was something like dread.

He was astonished by that woman. Hopping on one foot. God forbid that he should ever tangle with such a twisted creature, but did such things really happen? Did such a woman exist? A woman with a child by someone else—yet able to exercise such attraction? This consuming passion under a humdrum exterior—that was what amazed him.

And awakened his envy.

And a vague feeling that he had missed something.

✶
✶   ✶

About my shoulders you have draped the cloak of sadness,
In my belly put the cold stone of barrenness.

[1 8]

Vera Vorotyntseva was fourteen years younger than her only brother, and so they had not shared their childhood. Georgi had graduated from cadet school, and been assigned to a regiment while Vera was being tutored for high school. In the year of his wedding she hadn't yet taken off her schoolgirl's apron. When she moved to Petersburg, Georgi had already been pushed out of the Academy and sent to Vyatka.

Because they had not shared their childhood they remembered their mother and father differently, as they had appeared to two different pairs of childish eyes. In Georgi's childhood his parents were his friends, full of fun, with lots of hopes, with all of life ahead of them. In Vera's childhood they had seemed old, sad, and estranged from one another. The little girl had realized it very early, and it had saddened her more than anything, though the reason for it remained an enigma to her all her life. When she was old enough to look back and think things over she reflected that her own birth, that she herself, should have reinforced family ties—and so she did, but not for long. If Vera had been as old as Georgi, she would have looked more deeply and understood what he in his self-absorption would never even think of looking for: what had happened between Mama and Papa. There seemed to have been no explosion, no quarrel, no rupture, they had each of them gradually withdrawn into separate worlds of their own, becoming more and more self-centered. There were kisses, affectionate words, but there seemed to be something missing. They were probably very well aware of it themselves, but never put it into words. They needed each other less and less, the bonds between them slackened, each of them was alone with a bitter sense of being deserted. How had it all fallen apart? Was there really no way of mending things? The reasons remained hidden, reproaches remained unspoken, both were noble creatures, and both set hard in a hopeless fixity.

Their marriage had collapsed.

Zastruzhe too differed just as much in the memories of brother and sister. For him it was the scene of happy family invasions, always full of life, for her it was an eerie place, half deserted, with a melancholy, gray-headed father, who had given up his post in Moscow, sought solitude in a Zastruzhe as decrepit as himself, to indulge his misery to the full—and died there, snowbound and alone.

Vera and Georgi had not shared their childhood, but one thing, unique and unchanging, they had in common; their nurse Polya, the very same Pelagea Ivanovna who had always paid occasional visits to her native village, and had gone back there for good when Georgi was a big boy, but then Vera was born, and the nannying she had loved so much began all over again. Their experience of their nanny was so exactly similar, and gave brother and sister so much in common, that it was as though they had in fact grown up side by side. All sorts of little details came back to them simultaneously, and in identical form. Polya's village, Muratovo, standing on the banks of the Oka—although they had never seen it, they saw it all, from the copse over the steep riverbank down to the last blade of grass in the pasture, no less vividly than their own Zastruzhe. Nanny spinning fine flax—stretching it over the frame, combing the tow out, then spinning. Her younger brother, the horse thief, who was beaten up by Bashkirs, and her older brother, the barge master, he wasn't as famous as their uncle, but plying between the Moscow wharf and Nizhny he'd never run a barge train aground. A lot of men in their village, from their grandfathers' and great-grandfathers' time, had worked as bargemen along the Oka— that's what Muratovo was famous for—and nanny Polya herself in her young days, when her cheeks were red as apples, had traveled on her brother's barge from spring thaw to autumn, cooking for everybody, washing their clothes, and singing them songs. She had sung to Georgi too, and later on to Vera—religious songs on church holidays, sentimental or jolly songs on other days, the same songs with an interval of fourteen years. It was a remarkable form of kinship—she was not a blood relation, she had not suckled them, but she had reared them and they became her kin. This peasant woman's life story entered into the children's minds almost as though it was part of their own family history, indeed it was often more real and vivid than anything they heard from their parents. The village had known Polya as a modest, hardworking girl, and she could have made a good match, but every suitor wanted to take her to his home, no one could be drawn into her own poor home, to share it with her old mother and her nieces, the horse thief's children. Then her brother, the bargeman, brought her a good suitor, Ivan, from the river, not from Muratovo, they lived together for two happy years, a son was born and the only upsetting thing was that the priest christened him Arkhip, although Polya cried and cried, because it was a name she very much disliked. Whether because nanny had made so much of it, or because they themselves had, one apparently unimportant detail stood out in their memories, lodged there as long as they lived: how nanny Polya had taken her little Arkhip to the water meadow where his father was mowing, and the spring flood had left behind big puddles, with big fish in them as if caught in a trap, little Arkhip sat on a stone, staring and staring at the water. Whether or not she had felt some foreboding, sensed some menace, nanny pronounced the words "staring and staring at the water" in a special way that made the children's blood run cold.

Then Ivan was taken away to be a soldier, out of turn for some reason, though he'd been given a deferment. There was no war on, but she still cried when she saw him off—forever. He wrote for a year, said they'd even promised to make him a sergeant if he signed up to do extra time. Then his letters stopped, and notification came that, in nanny's words, "Ivan Tikhonov is not alive." There was no explanation, and Polya never learned anything more, just that he "was not alive."

That same autumn little Arkhip kept walking about in water, and one day he came home all wet, with his teeth chattering. Nanny Polya gave him hot milk and put him on the bench by the stove, but by morning his throat was so sore he couldn't speak. She had buried him. So she went on the last autumn steamer to Murom to look for a place with a family.

From their earliest years the children saw Nanny's face more often than Mama's. And the icon they remembered best was not over their own bed, but over Nanny's: St. Nicholas, a bent old man walking through a dense forest with a bundle over his shoulder. In the children's imagination all pilgrimages were like that. (Georgi wrote that he had recognized the Grünfliess Forest as the one in Nanny's icon.) There was also a china egg on a silk ribbon hanging next to the icon, and if you held it up to the light and looked through a little hole, you saw Christ in the Garden of Gethsemane. Nanny told the story of Judas and of Our Lord's Passion very clearly and begged Mama to let them go to church more often, and send them without fail to the all-night service on the eve of Good Friday (Papa and Mama never went to church themselves).

Nanny firmly believed that she would meet her litle Arkhip in the life to come. Nanny's beliefs were not just simple, they were almost comically naïve. She said prayers to time the boiling of eggs: for soft-boiled—two Our Fathers and three Hail Marys. One night in the nursery as she was saying bedtime prayers, she bowed down to the floor and her eyes strayed under Vera's bed. She interrupted herself: "Just look at that"—she sounded worried—"I haven't put your potty down here for the night!" And in the same breath went on with her prayers. Was such simple faith a sign of weakness or of strength? The older Nanny Polya got, the more sure she was that all the trivial events of life took place in the sight of God and the angels, and that there was no need to be ashamed of any of them. Georgi, always on the move, careering boylike about the world, parted company with most of his childish beliefs: traces remained at the deepest level of his soul, but up above all was eroded by the wind of action, of violent movement, and of battle. But Nanny's little world, her simplehearted scheme of things, lived on in his sister, was her natural element. She had, as it happened, read many more books than her brother, many controversial theories and ways of thinking had flowed into her mind, but none of them could harm Nanny's lesson of gentleness and kindness. It might have existed on a different plane.

Nanny became a member of the Vorotyntsev family, and was greatly offended if anyone called her a servant (although, unlike their town-bred maidservant, she called Mama and Papa "master" and "mistress," never by name and patronymic). When Vera was a bit older her mother would tell her in moments of anger that Polya was stupid. This upset Vera, who didn't see it that way. Patiently and sympathetically, she read out letters from Polya's village with long, long lists of greetings and good wishes, and wrote replies in the same vein dictated by Polya. Although Nanny lived away from her native village, she still lived in it. From what she earned, and from presents given to her (every Christmas and Easter, and on Georgi's and Vera's name days, she got a gold ruble from each of their parents), she bought presents and sent them home, although her nieces were the closest relatives of hers left there. She had arranged with the church to remember in its prayers some two or three dozen names. An educated woman could never have compiled such a list: she would have a much narrower conception of kinship and of Christian duty. When the children were old enough, Polya sometimes asked for leave to visit her village. She would make lengthy preparations, tying up bundle after bundle of presents, and take a hackney cab to the harbor, but instead of embarking on the steamer like everybody else she would spend several nights in the bargeman's shelter on the quay, making tea and cooking for the men just like in her young days. Until a barge from Muratov put in and she could sail with it.

Papa and Mama died, and Georgi was lost to her, a rolling stone, but Vera, still unmarried, stayed with Nanny. Before the war she and the old woman, toothless but still clear-voiced, bestirred themselves and moved all the old Vorotyntsev furniture to Petersburg, where Vera had found employment as a bibliographer at the Public Library. If there was anything that the Vorotyntsevs could still call home—and her brother acquiesced in calling them that, when his wife was not listening—it was the three third-floor rooms that Vera shared with Nanny on the corner of Italyanskaya and Karavannaya streets, near the Mikhailovsky manège. Some of its windows gave an oblique view of the Fontanka, others looked out on a square with a monument, and in summer if you leaned out over the windowsill and looked along the meandering Karavannaya, you could see the Anichkov Palace. Vera had taken this apartment simply because it was near the library, just a pleasant ten-minute walk away. You could go either around by the Fontanka, along the canal, and up the Nevsky Prospect or else along Karavannaya, but Vera usually went past the Nobles' Assembly Room, turned onto Ekaterinskaya, and in two more steps she was in the semi-darkness of the Public Library's vaulted rooms. Between the eternally hushed shelves, which muffled all footsteps, with her eternally hushed steps, a narrow figure in a narrow space, in a dress as gray or dark brown as the bindings, she withdrew into her corner (looking onto the Aleksandrinka) to sit at her desk for two hours at a time without so much as a shrug of the shoulders, without a single movement except those of her fingers turning over pages. Nobody needed to tell Vera—smooth, noiseless, economical movement was natural to her. In the same way, her handwriting (in what she wrote for herself, not just in what she wrote officially for the library) consisted of small, neat, legible letters, slanting no more than you bend your head when you write, economical, without a single superfluous stroke of the pen—more of her time was spent on writing than on talking. So Vera's life ran quietly on, morning and evening, and sometimes for weeks on end. She went backward and forward along the same few streets four or even six times a day, seeing nothing at all of the rest of Petersburg.

With Nanny to look after her, she hardly noticed how run-down Petersburg had become by that autumn. In the sections of the city she walked through there were no queues, and Vera, who scarcely glanced at or tasted what she was eating, would not have noticed what was missing except that Nanny never stopped groaning and telling her how awful things were: for as long as she could remember, in Muratovo or in Moscow, even during the other war and the troubles, you could always get whatever you wanted, walk up and buy it and off you go, so why all this standing in line staring at each other's backs for an hour or two at a time, in the rain maybe? And even then not being able to buy all you needed? You had to stand in line for white rolls, stand in line for milk—we're lucky we haven't got any children! (What's lucky about it? Life would be a lot brighter with children! But somehow they don't want my Vera, my angel.) Sugar had nearly vanished—smack your lips and pretend, or buy candy or honey, now they're on coupons, thank God. When the telegram came to say that Georgi was on his way, Nanny clapped her hands and wept and rejoiced, but above and before everything she beat her breast: Holy Mother of God, there's only a handful of wheaten flour, you can't buy any, and I must bake flat cakes, whatever happens! So make them with rye flour! What are you saying? He's had all the rye he can swallow in the trenches!

My brother! They hadn't seen each other since the war began. And he hadn't written very often. But even a few sentences on an army letter form kept alive what neither of them ever doubted and could never conceal: their simple awareness that neither time nor distance would ever make them strangers. Returning his feelings twofold, Vera never took offense, never waited for him to answer, but wrote a gossipy letter once or twice a month just as though she was talking to him. Not about Nanny or herself—there was never anything new there— but about Petersburg, the theaters, the controversies, its turbulent public life, and the many well-known personages who could not avoid the Public Library, or once inside a bibliographer named Vera Mik- hailovna. Vera was proud of her acquaintance with many of them, remembered their pronouncements, or scraps of conversation, and was quite willing to evaluate and quote them in letters to her brother. He had no other source, it was all useful and necessary, he wanted to know as much as possible, but to pick it up out of the air without wasting time or sitting down to study. There in the trenches, in hours of empty boredom, letters with a dash of Petersburg life in them were bound to be all the more interesting to him. That autumn, in anticipation of his trip, he had scribbled a note from Romania to say that if he came to Petersburg he would like to meet any public figure she thought might interest him.

She had arranged such a meeting. As she went to meet her brother at the Nikolaevski station, Vera did not expect a single minute of embarrassment after her lively letters to him. Their meeting would be as relaxed as if it had not become something out of the ordinary. Just as long as . . . as long as he was coming without his wife. The telegram left it unclear.

Vera had seen Alina only very occasionally, and they did not corre- spond except to exchange greetings once or twice a year. There was no quarrel between them (nor for that matter were they friends, though Georgi longed to bring them together, and refused to accept the idea of their being strangers), but Alina's presence now would strike a chill, create tension, spoil the whole encounter. Or rather, it would not be Alina but something about husband and wife together that would spoil it. In his presence Alina behaved better, was less abrupt and could hold her tongue. But in Alina's presence Georgi too was different, although he seemed unaware of it, seemed not to be looking over his shoulder at her, not on the alert for signals from her—but suddenly his laugh would be not quite so carefree, his talk less enthusiastic, everything he said would be more trivial than you expected from him.

Georgi could without embarrassment complain to his sister that he was hungry or in need of sleep or out of funds or despondent—but he never spoke frankly about things at home. In all other areas of life friends and loved ones can warn, advise, and help, and a man has no difficulty in asking them to do so. But in this taboo area advice is forbidden, warnings are unacceptable, attempts to explain a man to himself are tactless. In this sphere alone a man proudly condemns himself, and is condemned by all those around him, to make the best of his own poor vision and his own uncertain movements, like someone playing blindman's buff. And, however dearly loved a sister you are, though he might still playfully pull your ear or your hair, that is one subject on which your views are not sought or welcomed.

Vera was still at school when she heard of her brother's marriage. She was excited and happy about it, she could not wait to see Alina, to love her as an older sister—if my wonderful brother has chosen her she must be the nicest there ever was!

But their first few meetings put her off, left her feeling helpless. There was something missing, something not quite right, and she couldn't really say what it was.

Later on she had said to him that marriage was more final than a transfer from one regiment to another, perhaps even than an order on the battlefield—and he had laughed heartily.

To give up her one and only, her brilliant, clever, brave brother to someone so alien and artificial? Was it really a love match? Your own unblinking eye saw it all so clearly—but your brother's eyes saw nothing. But did Mama?

The little girl sensed that her mother did not like Alina either. But Mama would never venture to advise such a strong-willed son, even before he was thirty and a captain. Since he was a year old little Georgi had always known what he did and did not want, and no toy could ever distract him.

And anyway . . . there were such things as tact and good breeding. Mama could say nothing.

Masculine influence was completely lacking. Vera's father had never made his will felt in the home, and his advice always fell flat.

How could it happen? Why couldn't Georgi see for himself? He had looked at her more closely and longer and harder than anybody, and still he couldn't see.

Every union of two people has its secrets. You see the outside, and it is bad, but perhaps inside what there is between them may be very good. And if whatever it is lasts one, then three, then five or even ten years, it must be good, and it is not for you to judge.

What was the point of passing judgment anyway? They were lawfully wedded husband and wife.

"Is it on time? . . . Thank you."

She opened her umbrella, although it was not raining. There was rain in the air, but nothing falling. Typical Petersburg weather.

It was not for an unmarried girl to pass judgment on a marriage. But if you always had your eyes open, how could you help passing judgment? When people were genuinely happy it was obvious to every-body. Take the Shingarevs, for instance, they were happiness personi-fied, with no jarring notes, just perfect harmony. Their five children seemed not to be a burden but to have quintupled their happiness, given them greater strength. And because of his own five children Andrei Ivanovich's heart went out to all children, wherever he saw them or heard of them, with the generosity that characterized all his feelings.

And wasn't Mikhail Dmitrich just as easy to read? A man burning with a steady but melancholy light. His powers could never show them-selves fully, and the reason was clear to see: his marriage (or liaison) was like an iron net cast over him.

Cast by whom? By himself. A strong, healthy, natural man—and a half-crazed ether sniffer, with a child, a little girl, by another man. And yet he loved her? He loved her.

How could you judge, when you had never crossed the threshold yourself?

And once you crossed it, it would be too late.

But when you saw people like your brother or Mikhail Dmitrich you had to believe that the world was teeming with others like them. How could anyone commit his whole life simply hoping for the best? Once and for all? To an illusion?

The rain had held off. With folded umbrella, handbag over wrist, she walked along the platform.

"Hoping for the best" is the ultimate in pusillanimity. At least, to somebody whose feelings are as firmly under control as the letters in her handwriting.

She had been lucky, found the right niche in life: working in the best Russian library, for the best Russian readers—Duma deputies, journalists, writers, scholars, engineers. The best possible position for a woman—working quietly for those who lead.

But it is easier to keep your end up in a forest, in the desert, in a cave, anywhere at all, than in the midst of completely congenial people.

They ask your advice, thank you profusely, take catalogue cards from your hands, and a flicker of compassion in their eyes says that they are passing sentence on you. Perhaps, though, there is nothing in it, perhaps you only imagine that they are secretly calculating—twenty-four! twenty-five! twenty-six!—like so many muffled hammerblows in your breast! And there is no one you can tell with a stamp of the foot: It's my choice not to get married! Mind your own business!

Even with her brother this was a line not to be crossed: the subject was never mentioned out loud. Even with her brother. She could not grasp his hand and say help me, brother, tell me I'm right, strengthen my resolve! Don't others hold out under siege?

The train was coming. White steam stood out boldly against the grayness of the day. A whistle signaled its approach. The strong, pliant rails groaned happily in anticipation of the fearsome load they were to bear. However long you waited, however many guesses you made, you always ended half running to the carriage you wanted. A quick look at every window as it passes: Ah, there he is, there he is! In the corridor, hands raised and pressed against the plate glass. He's seen me! He's laughing! His beard looks longer and thicker. He's tanned and weather-beaten, that's no Petersburg complexion.

Is he alone? Looks like it. Good, good!

People were slow leaving the carriage. Baskets of some sort, and a big bottle in a wicker case, came out first.

None of that for my brother! Just a little case in his left hand, his right free to salute, he was as erect as always, his movements quick and light. They kissed. She slid down from his prickly beard, but was not released. An arm and a suitcase enwrapped her.

Let me look at you, brother! It's been three whole years, you know! Time and again you could have been killed or wounded. You weren't wounded, though, were you? You weren't telling a lie?

"Never seriously, honestly. A scratch or two, nothing important."

As quick as ever. But he seemed to have grown a sort of protective covering. Browned and case-hardened by the war.

"Will you always be like that?"

"Till I'm a general," he said, laughing. "Which means for quite a while." He stroked her hat, her temple, her cheek, her shoulder.

It was just as she had expected—from the moment he stepped off the train no awkwardness, no strangeness. It was as though they saw each other frequently. They walked arm in arm, close together.

"So how's Nanny? Still hasn't mastered the forty-two generations in Matthew, Chapter 1? Still looks at the book and recites from memory?"

"Yes, only she has to wear glasses now. She can answer the telephone herself as well. Or solemnly ask for the number her young mistress wants. She's baked you some flat cakes this morning. But what about you? And how are things in Moscow?" With an effort: "How's Alina?"

"I'm here for a few days."

"What's the golden hilt mean, Georgi? What's this inscription? 'For bravery'?"

"I got a George Cross."

Her brother was the same as ever. Good, we've dealt with Nanny, we've dealt with the flat cakes, we can't hang around all day, it's Monday, remember. Guchkov's letter to Alekseev—have you heard about it?

"Long ago! All Petersburg's reading it. Copies of things like that are circulated through our library. There's Chelnokov's letter to Rodzyanko and . . ."

"Through the library? Well, I never! Do they have any effect?"

"Indeed they do! People read them till they fall apart. There are whole manuscripts—about the food crisis, about the war . . . aperçus of all sorts . . . whichever institution they find their way into makes extra copies—typewritten, cyclostyled, hectographed. Some enthusiasts copy them by hand. Nobody gives a hoot for the censor nowadays."

He was astonished. He shook his head.

In the stir and bustle of the station, looking at his chastely pretty, radiant sister, whose gathered brown hat worn to one side reached his nose, he suddenly felt the joy of arrival! Freedom to move! To do what he wished with himself! There would be so much to see in those few days! But there was one thing he must make sure of now.

"Where is the telephone booth?"

He must make his decisions there, at the station, so that he could start off in the right direction.

He went into the booth and made his call.

"Can I speak to Aleksandr Ivanovich? . . . What about later today? Won't be here tomorrow either? . . . But he usually is here? Thank you."

He looked thoughtful.

"No, Vera dear, I won't be going home right now." He narrowed his gray eyes thoughtfully. "I've been saddled with a few jobs to do. At the General Staff. Anyway, you probably have to go back to work."

When didn't she? She'd had difficulty slipping away even for this.

"I'll be there for dinner. What time is that?"

"And what about this evening? Still following your own program? Or can you follow mine for once?"

"What do you have in mind?"

Eyeing her brother, she answered in her usual quiet, unassuming way. "You said you wanted to meet people. Well, I told Andrei Ivanovich Shingarev you were coming. And he said he'd like to see you. He's asked us over."

Georgi was surprised. "Shingarev?" he said doubtfully. "You mean the famous Kadet? The Duma deputy?"

The words tumbled out, driven by his impatient mind. His sister, in contrast, was calmly insistent. "Calling Shingarev a Kadet tells you nothing about him. He's the only one of his kind in Russia. Our miracle man. And the darling of Petersburg."

She laid a dark kid-gloved hand on the lapel of his greatcoat, so lightly that she seemed scarcely to touch it. "You'll find he isn't really a politician at all. He's a man modeled on all the finest people in Russian literature."

"Shingarev?" Her brother searched his memory. "Is he the one who opposed the military budget before the war?"

"Well, things are quite different now. In fact, he's now chairman of the Duma's Military Commission. And a member of the Special Defense Conference. He very much wants to keep up with what's happening at the front."

"Good . . . Shall we have a cup of coffee?"

They went into the buffet and sat down.

"You know that sort of passionate idealist? When he was still little more than a boy he began to have guilt feelings toward the common people. He took a brilliant degree in science and they wanted to keep him on in the Botany Department, but he left to look for the 'true meaning of life.' Then he took a degree in medicine, thinking that doctors would best be able to draw the people and the intelligentsia together. You know how uncompromising some intellectuals are: neither science nor art nor politics is worthwhile unless it serves the people."

A long downward stare questioned her. Uncompromising? Why should they compromise? And was an army officer's life any different?

"He practiced medicine without even a local government salary. He caught diphtheria from a child and nearly died. He collected statistics and wrote *The Dying Village*—a terrifying book. There were two printings in 1901, and people still ask for it. Shall I tell you what he is? He's the common people's champion. He isn't typical of any party in Russia, but there are a few people like him in all parties."

"Is that right?" Georgi gave a little laugh. "And there I was, thinking you wanted to convert me to the Kadet Party."

She laughed and looked down guiltily. Every hair was taut and in place on her sleek head.

"D'you know, even the nationalists thought so well of Shingarev that they withdrew their own candidate for the chairmanship of the Military Commission and made way for him. The simple fact is, you see, that he loves Russia and he loves people, and everybody, even in the Duma, feels that. Enemies of the Kadets call Milyukov 'Papa' and Shingarev 'Mama': the one has logic, the other feeling and sincerity, and he easily carries conviction when even Milyukov can't. He has this way with him . . . such a smile . . . He's so easily moved, even by a book, Dickens say . . . He says, 'I know it's silly to grieve over the sad parts in a book, but somehow . . .' "

Her brother nodded. "Ah, Dickens. You spent half your childhood crying into Dickens yourself." He looked at her, beaming.

He thought over what she had said, and seemed inclined to agree. "What does he want with me, though? How old is he, by the way?"

"I can tell you exactly. Forty-seven."

"Well, since he's older than me I'll go."

"To tell the truth, he knows about you. He knows you're out of favor, that you've suffered for the truth."

"Well, well. Did you tell him?"

"He knew about it anyway."

So all right, in Guchkov's absence seeing Shingarev will do very well. I'll be making a start on Petersburg anyhow. Must sniff more than one breeze. It will be all to the good.

"A tête-à-tête? Or is it a party?"

"A party on Monday? His motto is: Don't live better than the people. There are never any servants. There may be open sandwiches—black bread, not wheaten bread. And maybe potatoes."

"Will you come with me?"

"I'm invited."

"Vera, my dear, why are we sitting here? Let's go. I'll walk you to work. It's on my way, and you can tell me more. I want to know more about the Kadets."

On Znamenskaya Square his heart missed a beat. This too was part of him, not to be rejected. They turned onto the Nevsky. The straightness of it! The length of it! Even on a gloomy day under a slate-gray sky. Dim in the distance, the Admiralty spire was like a reward at the end of a long journey.

Looking far and straight into the distance, Vorotyntsev saw opening up before him a new field of action.

[19]

(SOCIETY, THE GOVERNMENT, AND THE TSAR IN 1915)

From the very first days of the war the Kadets found themselves in an unforeseen and complex situation. Within hours, not days, of general mobilization the mood of the people as a whole and even that of the educated classes showed the power of that very same "patriotism" which until then had served as a word of abuse, and which they had ceased to think of as a real phenomenon. It proved impossible from the start to oppose this war, as they had opposed the war with Japan. And it was suddenly impossible to go on reviling the government as they always had. It had suddenly become popular! All the Kadet leaders could produce was this exhortation:

Let internal dissensions be forgotten. Let the union of Tsar and people grow ever stronger!

No one should suppose that the Kadets had suddenly taken a liking to the Tsar. A shrewd long-term calculation was taking shape in their minds: By entering the war in alliance with Britain and France, the Russian Emperor had put himself in the hands of the great Western democracies, and victory when it came would be not that of the Tsar but of free Russian society. The Kadets quite quickly saw the uses of patriotism and even acquired a taste for it: not in the primitive, savage sense of love for Russia as the dwelling place of the Russian spirit, but in the sense of love for a state solidly welded together, standing firmly on its feet, a country worth living in and worth ruling over when they came into their inheritance.

Let us put aside our disagreements. Let us maintain Russia's position in the ranks of the world powers.

Milyukov, no genius, but a stubborn purveyor of his half-solutions, would be trotting out the same old stuff all through the war:

Constantinople, and a sufficient part of the adjacent littoral, the hinterland . . . The keys to the Bosphorus and the Dardanelles . . . Oleg's shield on the gates of the Imperial City. *These are dreams cherished by the Russian people* throughout its existence.

To which must be added:

The defense of culture and spiritual values against the barbaric onslaught of German militarism. This is a war to abolish all war.

Milyukov and Puryshkevich had shaken hands demonstratively in the Duma!

What sort of situation had the Kadets landed themselves in with this unqualified support of their fatherland's hated regime? Should they just hang on to the government's coattails? Unthinkable! They had never been used to any such role! So they had only one recourse—to *outdo* the government in patriotism and even in the actual struggle against German militarism. And even to squeeze the government out of many activities relevant to the war (though not, of course, the conduct of military operations) and in doing so seize as many key positions as possible.

They were helped in the scramble for control of organizations contributing to the war effort by the Union of Zemstvos and the newly formed Union of Towns (the two shortly merged under the name of Zemgor). In the atmosphere of crisis during the early days of the war they were permitted by the Tsar to help sick and wounded soldiers at the state's expense, and were bound by no formal restrictions in the expenditure of government money—no requirement to submit estimates or accounts, no limitations on numbers of staff or on salary scales—because their civic pride would not allow them to accept state supervision. There was nothing to stop them from paying their own staff three or four times the salary of state officials in the same grade. And since employment in the Unions also conferred exemption from military service, the number of those so employed grew rapidly and unchecked. The Unions further chose those areas of activity in which they could make the best showing and win most public approval, whereas the Treasury had the unprofitable task of covering all areas. The government, satisfied with this measure of support from educated society, did not venture to interfere.

Nor did this exhaust opportunities for the Kadets to undermine the government's prestige. They tried, for instance, with considerable success, to make a mockery of prohibition. At the beginning of the war, in an effort to create a healthier atmosphere, the Emperor had acted to prohibit the sale of vodka (controlled by a state monopoly) in Russia. This had earned the government the approval of the people as a whole. The Kadets then publicly suggested that the government should ban the sale of all alcoholic drinks, even wine with a low alcoholic content, by private traders. Their calculation was that if the government refused it would make the ban on vodka look hypocritical and show that it was out to increase its revenues by encouraging excessive consumption of other drinks. The government took the bait, and general prohibition was proclaimed. The result was an absurd situation, which became more and more obvious as the months went by: the sale of strong drink was simply driven underground, causing widespread resentment.

Whenever the Kadets were presented with opportunities to maneuver in this way, at the center or at the local level, they never failed to grasp them.

In spite of this, the enforced loyalty of the Kadets was for several months quite astonishing. True, it was made easier by the absence of a militant student or socialist movement in the country. Everyone was keeping quiet, with the sole exception of the Bolshevik group in the Duma. When they were tried in February 1915 (on quite trivial charges: drafting proclamations—"Sweep Tsarist autocracy from the face of the earth! Seize it by the throat and plant a knee on its chest!" and "We have no enemies beyond our own frontiers"—insisting that a German victory would be a blessing for Russia, using codes, forging passports, and planning armed uprisings), the Kadets refrained from paying their standing debt to the left and did not speak up for the accused deputies.

The normal rules of human intercourse gave them the right to expect some concessions from the regime in return for such a long spell of loyalty: extension of the Duma's powers, legislation for the benefit of the Jews, an amnesty for revolutionaries. But neither amnesty nor benevolent legislation was forthcoming. The regime did not reward the Kadets for their heroism.

Dissension, distrust, suspicion, and trickery had driven such a deep wedge between educated Russian society and the Russian government, and they were on such bad terms when they entered the war, that although both sides now desired victory each suspected the other of defeatism.

Duma circles, cut off from reality by a screen of communiqués announcing our brilliant victories in Galicia, took a long time to realize that the war was off to a bad start. Guchkov was the first to return from the army in the field, in the autumn of 1914, with exaggerated reports that everything was collapsing, that the war was "nearly lost already"—and the Kadets, eternal oppositionists, did not believe this hotheaded duelist who never stopped boasting of his military expertise. It was only in January 1915, through the Budget Commission of the Duma, that they began to learn a few things about the shortage of shells and the defects of the supply system generally. But even in closed sessions, blithe, self-intoxicated Sukhomlinov caroled, unabashed, that all was well with the army. By January 1915 the Kadets had decided in closed session to resume their conflict with the government. But in an open session of the Duma—a laughably short, three-day session, meant to show that the government had no need of that body—Milyukov kept up the line previously adopted: although the government was taking advantage of the truce with the opposition to strengthen its own hand in domestic policy, the Kadets would not join battle in public, so as not to undermine the morale of the army or feed the enemy's Schadenfreude.

This was no longer the Milyukov who used to invite students to commit terrorist acts—for one thing, he had since then been threatened with assassination himself, and nobody likes that—and who had sought to reconcile constitution with revolution: he had become slightly more statesmanlike, and very much more cautious. Besides, he was not eager to make a frontal assault on the regime while the students were so quiet and the socialists so timid. Why should the Kadets have to take the lead?

The February session was short, but the Duma had ceased to insist on long ones: the truce with the government went on and on, and the deputies no longer knew how to conduct themselves. In May, however, Rodzyanko, the president of the Duma, returned from the front and painted such a picture of the retreat in all its immensity—almost as far as the Western Bug—that silence was no longer possible: the government was plainly destroying Russia—and perhaps there was a conspiracy to do so? Deliberately to bring the country under the German jackboot, so as to crush progressive society? Two cities fell in quick succession: Peremyshl (the Tsar himself had attended the recent and rash celebrations of its capture) and the illustrious city of Lvov, also the recent scene of great celebrations. As though to mock its opponents, the government was headed by none other than the muttonchop-whiskered court sycophant Goremykin, now a feeble old man of seventy-five, but showing no intention of dying, an unsinkable dreadnought of a State Secretary. He had been Minister of the Interior before Stolypin, before Pleve, before Sipyagin—all in turn assassinated, while he, alternating in office with these doomed ministers, had never got in the way of a revolutionary bomb, although it was he who had dissolved the First Duma. Now here he was, in use again, like an old fur coat taken out of mothballs. The whole world was astounded to see this decrepit old man presiding over the government at such a dangerous time.

Contemporaries never know the inside story of government reshuffles. It was rumored that the post of Prime Minister had been offered more than once to Krivoshein, the Minister of Agriculture. There seemed to be very good grounds for such an appointment, and he had been in the cabinet for seven years, longer than any of them. But, for reasons unknown, he was not the one chosen.

It was actually Krivoshein's own decision not to accept the premiership, which was offered to him several times. He had long been intimately concerned with the problem of cabinet unanimity: he was the author of a perceptive memorandum to the Emperor in the summer of 1905, before the revolution was in full swing. It said that ministers in the Russian government did not act in agreement with each other: each of them was directly subordinate to the Tsar and for a short time after an audience with him would feel that he was expressing His Majesty's will and would take even less account of his colleagues. This recalled the state of Louis XVI's government when the States-General were convened. The Duma now being convened should find itself faced with a strong and unified authority, and opposition from within the government should not be allowed. The specter of revolutionary France made some impression on the

Emperor—he had a feel for history—and he thought of including something relevant in the Fundamental Laws of 1906, but faltered yet again and was dissuaded. No such clause was included, and the government drifted on without rigorous procedural rules. (Anyway, if the government was firmly united, would not the Autocrat be sidelined?)

Krivoshein was an outstanding figure among the servants of the Russian state. He did not belong to the highest level of society, and had no connections in high places, but owed his rise solely to his own talents and efforts. He had served so long that he could pass for a bureaucrat born and bred. He was indistinguishable from all the others in striving for advancement and suffered cruelly from setbacks. What made him different was his political sense and his eagerness to do great deeds. At the same time, he knew the limits beyond which he should not aspire: he lacked Stolypin's drive to make history, to become a great leader of men. And so, circumspect and subtle, he took care not to occupy the first place (which in any case attracts envy and hatred) but chose one close enough to it to assure him the advantages of real power. Characteristically, he sought to influence developments without taking full responsibility for them. He knew how fickle the Tsar was, and where there was no certainty of success he showed an extraordinary flair for anticipating changes of mood and fluctuations of authority, so that he could divine the right time to act. He was reputed to be a staunch conservative, he had good personal relations with bureaucrats, court circles, and anyone likely to become influential. He was even close to the royal couple—well liked by the Empress (because of their shared interest in peasant handicrafts) and the Tsar's trusted adviser (it was he who penned the solemn Imperial Manifesto declaring war on Germany). He who had once fought at the side of Stolypin, the bugbear of educated Russian society, became over the years more and more acceptable and congenial to society. He had direct links with the stiff-necked Moscow merchants through his wife, who belonged to the Morozov family, which also meant that he was financially secure for life. He had been ready for Stolypin, having headed the Resettlement Agency from 1896, and for his agrarian reform. (He had been actively concerned with those problems before Stolypin, but not strong-minded enough to commit himself to one side or the other in the great debate.) After Stolypin's death he had put many years of honest work into such causes as reform of the peasant commune, the improvement of agricultural methods and of land use, and resettlement, and had brought them within sight of victory. He made wide and confident use of volunteer helpers among the educated public, and relied greatly on the "third element" in the zemstvos, so earning the goodwill of educated society, especially by his laconic toast in Kiev in 1913:

> In such a huge state as Russia it is impossible to control all things from the center. It is essential to enlist the aid of local social forces and to place the necessary resources at their disposal. My belief is that our fatherland will only achieve prosperity if the division between "us" and "them," meaning government and society, ceases to exist, and people begin saying simply "we," meaning the government and society together.

He was seeking a way out of what was the basic conflict in late-nineteenth- and early-twentieth-century Russia, a way to break through the inherent misunderstanding between government and society. He tried to become the intermediary between them.

(*Rech*, however, saw his challenge as capitulation on the part of the government. And Prime Minister Kokovtsov reproved him for what he too saw as capitulation.) Furthermore, in his seven years as a minister Krivoshein had succeeded in remaining on excellent terms with the Duma, thanks to good personal relations with influential deputies, and had obtained credits for agriculture without once speaking in the Duma itself, which would have meant formulating his views and policies clearly and so displeasing either society or the monarch. Krivoshein had achieved the impossible, winning the confidence of both the Emperor and the State Duma.

The news of Stolypin's assassination had reached Krivoshein at his summer home in the Crimea. He was by then such a prominent member of the cabinet that he could expect to be offered the premiership. However reluctant he might be to accept it, refusal at that moment would be embarrassing—it would look as though he was afraid of the terrorists. And the Emperor was already on his way to the Crimea! Krivoshein hurriedly left to attend the funeral, and so miss him.

Nevertheless, the Emperor offered to crown his career with the premiership two years later, at Livadia. Krivoshein then refused explicitly, alleging that he had heart trouble and got overexcited when he had to make public speeches. He lacked the courage to cross the fateful borderline and take supreme power. But he had begun to feel uncomfortable in the cabinet under the austere Kokovtsov, especially because Kokovtsov, as Minister of Finance, was primarily interested not in the development of the country's productive forces but in amassing a reserve of idle gold, and so refused to give generous credits for the development of agriculture and for land reform. ("Such thrift is more ruinous than the most reckless prodigality," said Krivoshein.) He had to get Kokovtsov removed if development was to replace financial sclerosis. For those who resort to political intrigue the most dubious cards may have their uses. The right-winger Prince Meshchersky had fallen out of favor with the Tsar, but Krivoshein foresaw from the start that they would make up, because they had similar views on the nature of the imperial power. He subsidized the prince's journal—and sure enough, Meshchersky, back in favor, helped Krivoshein to change the government, replacing Kokovtsov as Finance Minister with the trusty Bark, and as Prime Minister with . . . with whom? Meshchersky urged Krivoshein to take the post himself. But he refused yet again, and suggested the aged Goremykin, with whom he had been on the best of terms ever since those distant days at the turn of the century when Minister Goremykin had done so much to advance an obscure civil servant named Krivoshein. Goremykin could now temporarily occupy the highest post without hindering Krivoshein in the exercise of real power within the cabinet, and should it be necessary, the old man would cheerfully surrender the office of Prime Minister. (Krivoshein explained to his intimates that after Stolypin no one would be given real power—the Emperor was so jealous and suspicious that whoever was Prime Minister would find himself with more responsibility than power. Kokovtsov, almost echoing Stolypin, said that "in Russia the Prime Minister has nobody to rely on. He is tolerated only until he begins to loom too large in the mind of the public, and to play the part of a real ruler.") This long and little-known story explains why the government of our mighty and by then flourishing Russia was headed by the timeserving old dodderer Goremykin at the beginning of the fateful year 1914.

Krivoshein was the real Prime Minister in that government, and he further strength-ened his position at the end of 1914 by bringing in a supporter of his, the liberal zemstvo activist Count Ignatiev, as Minister of Education. (The Tsar, who had an extraordinary memory for people and occasions, readily consented. He remembered that twenty-one years earlier Count Ignatiev, then an NCO in the Preobrazhensky Guards Regiment, had been an excellent song leader after exhausting maneuvers. Shortly afterward, Prince Shakhovskoy was appointed Minister of Trade and Industry, thanks to the Tsar's grateful memory of the way in which in the September of Sto-lypin's assassination he had organized that river trip along the barely navigable Desna from Kiev to Chernigov, and then in May 1913, in celebration of the dynasty's ter-centenary, that marvelous cruise along the Volga. He had also done an excellent job of improving the main roads in the Crimea, along which the Tsar was now driven at great speed.) Goremykin readily yielded the limelight to Krivoshein and gave him a free hand. On all important matters they were at one until the summer of 1915. Krivoshein's influence extended to foreign policy as well as to all other matters. (He and Sazonov had a good understanding.) He held the title of "His Majesty's Secretary of State," which gave him the right to issue verbal instructions in the name of the Emperor. There remained, however, within the cabinet a group of ministers who re-fused to submit to him and sometimes mounted intransigent rightist opposition: Su-khomlinov, Nikolai Maklakov, Shcheglovitov, and Sabler. Internal conflict reached a point at which, for the sake of unanimity within the government, it became necessary to get rid of those ministers. At cabinet meetings Krivoshein and Sazonov pretended that they could not see or hear Maklakov. The retreat of 1915 speeded up develop-ments.

In the first six months of the war Sukhomlinov's radiant optimism, and the peculiar system which gave the government no say in the administration of the armed forces, meant that ministers shared the general ignorance of shortcomings in the military supply system. It was not until February 1915, in the course of a private conversation at GHQ, that Shcheglovitov and Bark were told about the disastrous shortfall in the supply of shells. The spring retreat, coming on top of this, exacerbated public hostility. The cabinet majority began conspiring to remove the ministers detested by society, threatening to resign unless they got their way. The idea originated with Sazonov, and the whole Krivoshein circle, including Grigorovich, the Navy Minister, but excluding Goremykin, met secretly at his apartment. Mutiny had broken out within the govern-ment, but it seemed to be in a good cause; a war can be successfully waged only if government and society are at peace with one another.

Goremykin himself was not seen as an obstacle, and to ask for his removal as well would have been asking too much. Krivoshein saw clearly who the best candidates for office were and promptly presented a full list of replacements.

The Emperor was dismayed to find one group of ministers plotting behind the backs of another ("That sort of thing isn't done in the regiments"), but gave in: defeats in the field can make a stubborn man more reasonable. Stunned by the retreat from Peremyshl and Lvov, he did not want to quarrel either with his ministers or with society, and Krivoshein stood higher in his estimation than ever. So, dearly as the Emperor loved Nikolai Maklakov, he agreed to remove him from the Ministry of the Interior.

The removal of the War Minister called for greater exertions. Krivoshein journeyed to GHQ before the other ministers were summoned and worked hard to persuade Grand Duke Nikolai Nikolaevich that Sukhomlinov should be replaced by Polivanov. (Polivanov's candidature had been persistently urged by Guchkov, with whom Krivoshein was on friendly terms and had family connections.) A triumphally publicized photograph shows the Council of Ministers in session at GHQ in Baranowicze that June, all wearing white tunics—only Sabler and Shcheglovitov were absent, which made it easier to persuade the Emperor that they too should be dismissed. Goremykin did as Krivoshein wished, and was himself eager to create the united cabinet so urgently needed. The new Minister for Justice, however, Khvostov (the uncle), was Goremykin's not Krivoshein's candidate. The new Procurator of the Holy Synod was Samarin, chosen by Krivoshein because of his influence in Moscow. The announcement of these two changes was held up by the Emperor until the beginning of July.

The situation meanwhile was getting out of hand. The Kadets set out their grievances against the government at a conference in June. Military setbacks and poor organization on the home front were at the bottom of the list. Much more aggravating were government distrust of voluntary aid organizations, irritating monitoring of contacts between intellectuals and ordinary soldiers (was it true that pamphlets from the revolutionary years were taken away from the wounded?), the harsh treatment of the Uniates in Galicia, and the government's refusal to make concessions to the Jews and the Poles. And why had the Bolshevik deputies been tried and condemned, and why had the terrorist Burtsev, who had patriotically returned from abroad, not been honored for it but banished? The Kadets were more and more inclined to criticize the government in public. In their eyes its composition was the real trouble, and two dismissals only left them hungry for further changes, for the reconstitution of the government so that it would enjoy the confidence of society—let it be made up of bureaucrats so long as they were congenial ones. (This was the latest Kadet ploy. That phrase—"a government enjoying public confidence"—was camouflage for the "ministry answerable to parliament," which was impossible for the time being. It was easier to agitate for and obtain a government enjoying public confidence, which would then gradually turn into a "responsible" government.) The Kadets now intended to insist on the convocation of the Duma and a lengthy session.

Hotheads proposed convening the Duma summarily—that is to say, without seeking authorization. Milyukov sought to cool them down:

> At present the eyes of all Russia are on the battle front. If the Duma assembles in a spontaneous, revolutionary fashion, all Russsia will instantly turn to look in amazement at a spectacle which can rejoice only our enemies. And the "spontaneous" Duma itself will be dissolved without difficulty. The result will be a pale and wretched copy of the Vyborg appeal . . . Should we perhaps summon the masses to come out in support of us? The government is unaware of what is happening in the "depths of Russia," but observers like ourselves, intellectuals, see clearly that we are walking on the brink of a volcano. The present equilibrium is so precarious that a single jolt would suffice to create general instability and disarray. There would be another mob orgy . . . of the sort that nipped the splendid promise of the 1905 revolution in the bud. A strong regime, whether good or bad, is needed more now than

ever before . . . All we can do is open the government's eyes and reform the cabinet without exerting undue pressure.

Some said that the country's salvation lay in an amnesty for revolutionaries and a Kadet government, but the party's leaders—V. Maklakov, Shingarev, Rodichev—urged restraint, saying that the time for this had not come and that they must contribute to victory in the field, even if it meant forgetting their program in its pure form.

To those who lived through it the army's retreat from Warsaw almost beyond the Niemen was a military disaster without parallel. Some of the details were in the press, the rest was supplied by hearsay. And whom could the press and rumor blame, if not an incompetent and possibly traitorous government?

Meanwhile the Tsar was silent, lying low in Tsarskoye Selo as if the retreat had nothing to do with him and was happening on someone else's territory.

On whom else could hopes be placed, if not on the State Duma? The deputies assembled in Petersburg on their own initiative and demanded an extended session.

Meanwhile, the Union of Zemstvos and the Union of Towns had also started putting pressure on the government. It was increasingly obvious to them that the long-term objective must be not so much Russian victory in the field, which would not necessarily advance the cause of freedom, as the occupation of political positions from which to bring about future constitutional changes. At their congress in June they called for the convocation of the Duma, warning the government in uncompromising terms:

Those who know their jobs will be the country's masters.

The conviction that the government and the state apparatus as a whole did not know their jobs was assiduously propagated, and the Unions annexed more and more branches of the military supply system. While the regime, as though admitting the worst that was thought of it, surrendered without a murmur one field of activity after another—and this in a country at war—to self-appointed committees, making no attempt to bring them under single management. When the "social" organizations insisted that they were disinterested and had the talent, no one ventured to voice a doubt.

It was then, in that hot June and July of 1915, that the government, spoiled by ten months of silent support from the Duma, suddenly found itself exposed, an object of general reproach and vilification. The approaches to Riga had now begun to appear in communiqués, and machinery had not yet been evacuated from the five hundred or so factories of threatened Riga and Libau (Kurlov, newly promoted, was the man in charge). With the temperature rising so fast the dismissal of a few detested ministers did nothing to mollify a wrathful public. On 24 July the Unions, without official authorization, convened an All-Russian conference to discuss price increases. This was like splashing water onto a red-hot frying pan. Members of the general public assembling, unbidden, to discuss the rising cost of living (workers too were invited): could they possibly have made it hotter for the government?

Indeed, the helplessness, irresolution, and inactivity of the government were enough to make any detached observer despair, especially amidst the chaos left behind in front-line areas by the retreating army. It was impossible to concoct an explanation, and nobody offered one in public.

We still hardly recognize how much great happenings in the history of nations depend on insignificant people and events. In March 1914, Russia's Minister of War, the prattling court lackey Sukhomlinov (who was much more exercised by the antics of his beautiful young wife than by the defense of the empire), had suggested to the Emperor that he appoint as Chief of the General Staff a toady of his, the insidious professor of military administration and pseudo-soldier General Yanushkevich. As always, the Russian monarchy being what it was, extremely important appointments of this kind were decided lightheartedly, as a favor to a petitioner and without too much attention to the qualities needed in a particular post. The self-intoxicated nonentity Yanushkevich had more damage in store for Russia than three capital villains. There had been many sins of omission before, but in three months in office he failed not only to correct shortcomings but even to discover what needed correcting. Thus, July 1914 had found him without a plan for partial mobilization, and it was his advice and his performance above all that dragged the Tsar into general mobilization, leaving Russia no hope of avoiding a most ill-omened war. On that same fateful day, 29 July 1914, he had thrust under the nose of the Tsar (never an enthusiastic reader of dull papers and at that time exhausted by several days of crisis) a thick sheaf of "Rules for the Administration of the Army in the Field." The Tsar had signed without looking closely.

These regulations, very conveniently for the military and for Yanushkevich personally, since he expected to become Chief of Staff to the Supreme Commander, assigned full powers to the military not only in the theater of war but in all territories where the armed forces were deployed (Petersburg and even Archangel included!), leaving the Council of Ministers with no authority even in the capital itself, nor even the right to decide procedure for liaison with the Supreme Command, nor to take decisions for areas of deployment on matters of nationwide importance. The empire was divided into two detachable parts, one subordinate to GHQ, the other to the government. In this way, a single puffed-up nobody, free from all supervision, determined all that was done on the home front.

True, the regulations were drawn up on the assumption that the Emperor himself would be Supreme Commander, and would keep the peace between the two parts of the empire. But when he did not take command you had to go a long way around to annul an order from the military: any petition to the Tsar would be passed to Grand Duke Nikolai Nikolaevich, and at his HQ all power rested with Yanushkevich, who had given the government its orders in the first place. The problem did not become acute until we had to retreat in depth. But with the beginning of the 1915 retreat this relationship became altogether hopeless. The military administrators rolled back ahead of their armies, and began taking charge deep inside the country. There was no way of knowing whose orders to carry out. Any depot commandant, any ensign could give orders, and there was no one to take responsibility. Evacuation, planned on an ambitious scale, was carried out in a particularly chaotic fashion. Some organizations were given the order to move just a few hours before a town was surrendered. Nearly all of them were directed to areas of resettlement without the prior consent of the provincial authorities concerned. Trainloads of officials with their impedimenta, and evacuated military hospitals, arrived unexpectedly in places where there was neither accommodation nor food for them.

The government was losing control everywhere, but what further complicated and aggravated things was that it could not say so publicly, because that would weaken the position of the Supreme Power, the Emperor, and up to this point no complaint had been made to the Emperor in person. The ministers finally lost patience on 29 July, in the closed session that always followed the open one. (Yakhontov, the meticulous secretary, has left us substantial excerpts from the Council's proceedings.) Once they were alone, Polivanov, the War Minister, made an abrupt and theatrical declaration:

> I consider it my duty as a citizen and as a servant of the crown to state that the fatherland is in danger.

An apprehensive silence followed. No one had ever made such a sensational statement before the whole cabinet. (But a group of ministers which had held frequent meetings at Krivoshein's villa on Aptekarsky Island, was forewarned of Polivanov's intention.) The Minister of War was no military man, but during his month in office he had with difficulty learned something about the situation, not from the secretive GHQ but by indirect routes, and now hastened to report his findings. What might be the decisive phase of the war was approaching. The Germans had an inexhaustible supply of shells, and were forcing us to retreat with artillery fire alone, keeping their massive infantry in reserve, and suffering no great losses, while on our side casualties ran into the thousands. It was impossible to see how and with what we could check their offensive. Faith in our commanders had been undermined. Desertion and voluntary surrender were becoming more and more frequent. Men were injected into the front line unarmed, with orders to pick up the rifles of the dead.

> Polivanov: There is one circumstance fraught with grave consequences on which we can no longer remain silent: GHQ is in a state of growing confusion; it has no system, no plan of action, no bold maneuver in mind. At the same time, GHQ jealously preserves its prerogatives, and sees no need to consult those who should be its closest collaborators. The saddest thing of all is that the truth does not reach His Majesty. On the brink of the greatest events in Russian history the Russian Tsar ought to be hearing the opinion of all the responsible commanders and the whole Council of Ministers. The final hour is, perhaps, approaching, and heroic decisions are necessary. It is our duty to beseech His Majesty to convene at once an Extraordinary Council of War chaired by himself.

The ministers, some of them warned in advance, agreed unanimously to appeal to the Tsar, pointing out:

> The populace are at a loss to understand the apparent indifference of the Tsar and his government to the catastrophe which has befallen our armies at the front.

They were all in a state of high excitement, and the discussion grew confused. Ministers ought to be kept informed about what was going on, for heaven's sake! And ought to be given a hearing! Even in the capital the food supply and labor relations were more a matter for the commander of the 6th Army than for them:

> Krivoshein: No country can continue to exist with two governments. GHQ should either take over everything and relieve the Council of Ministers of responsibility, or it should respect the interests of the civil administration.

One feels acute unease for the future. The Germans are beating us at the front, and Russian ensigns are finishing the job at home.

Prince **Shcherbatov** (Minister of the Interior): Provincial governors are inundating me with telegrams about the intolerable situation in which the military authorities place them. The least little protest is met with abuse and threats.

Khvostov (Minister of Justice): Polish legions, Latvian battalions, and Armenian detachments are being established without authorization from the Council of Ministers. Later on they will be an embarrassment to our nationalities policy.

Rukhlov (Minister of Communications): We all work just as hard for Russia and are no less concerned for the salvation of our native country than are the military gentlemen. It is intolerable: all our plans and calculations can be arbitrarily thwarted by the lowliest rear-echelon warrior. The government machine is falling to pieces, there is chaos and discontent everywhere. We, the ministers of the crown, are given guidelines and binding instructions by GHQ.

At no time during the war had there been such a grim cabinet meeting. And all those present seem unanimously and unambiguously to have condemned GHQ. Except for the circumspect courtier Goremykin, who gave this warning:

Gentlemen, we should approach the problem of GHQ with particular caution. Annoyance with the Grand Duke is coming to the boil at Tsarskoye Selo. The Empress Aleksandra Fyodorovna, as you know, was never well disposed toward Nikolai Nikolaevich, and protested when in the early days of the war he was called to the post of Supreme Commander. She now considers that he alone is to blame for our misfortunes at the front. The flames are rising higher, and it is dangerous to pour oil on them. A report on the proceedings of today's Council of Ministers would be just that sort of fuel to the flame.

He proposed an adjournment to give time for thought, and won over the ministers.

A week went by, and not only was there no improvement but on 5 August Warsaw was surrendered. The whole country was stunned. Warsaw was not just another city, it was a capital city. Not so very long ago the best Siberian divisions, as yet untouched by war, had been paraded through its streets to show that we would never surrender Poland to the Germans, and enthusiastically cheered from sidewalks and windows, from balconies and roofs, by Polish men and women, who believed in Russia's promise of autonomy. And now—Warsaw surrendered? Could it be?

The secret session of the Council of Ministers on the following day was just as tense and jittery, the Duma had now been convened, and public indignation, whipped up by the press, was running higher all the time. In Krivoshein's circle exasperation with Goremykin, as well as with others, was growing. And the sharpest criticisms of GHQ were aimed at Yanushkevich personally.

Krivoshein: I can no longer remain silent, whatever the consequences for me personally may be! I cannot shout it aloud in the forum and at the crossroads, but I am bound to say it to you and to the Tsar.

The ministers agreed to a man that the Grand Duke should be disburdened of Yanushkevich. A final twist was given:

> **Sazonov** (Minister of Foreign Affairs): It is horrifying that the Grand Duke
> is the prisoner of such persons. Thanks to self-infatuated nonentities of his
> kind we have disgraced ourselves in the eyes of the whole world. It is not
> His Majesty's way to ignore public opinion. He is doing all he can to win it
> over.

The conciliatory Goremykin, however, repeated his warning:

> My earnest advice is to be extremely cautious when speaking on matters
> concerning GHQ and the Grand Duke in the hearing of the Emperor. An-
> noyance with the Grand Duke at Tsarskoye Selo is assuming a character
> which threatens to have dangerous consequences.

Whether they wanted to be at one with society, or were simply ignoring the Tsar's
irritation with him, the ministers directed more and more of their criticism away from
the Grand Duke and against Yanushkevich alone. Besides, the great height and military
bearing of the Grand Duke made him a favorite with the army and the public. He
was more and more lavishly praised as a national hero, his stern treatment of generals
and his love of the common soldier were becoming legendary, and his well-known
hatred of the Germans made a great impression.

("Society" had disliked him before 1914, but his undisguised disapproval of the
government had made him popular.) Now the dismay caused by the retreat, and the
recriminations after each defeat, somehow left him unscathed.

The Duma met on 1 August, the anniversary of the outbreak of war. In a dead,
perfunctory voice Goremykin read out a declaration drafted by Krivoshein:

> The government can take the path of great exertions and great sacrifices only
> with your full agreement, gentlemen of the Duma.

The Kadet leader's well-honed reply was:

> The Duma is moving from the stage of patriotic fervor to that of patriotic
> alarm. The government arrogantly considers itself able to manage merely
> with the help of its antiquated bureaucratic machine . . .

(If only it had the chance!)

> but the source of its errors lies in its abnormal relationship with the forces
> of society. The people wants to correct those errors itself and sees us as the
> first lawful agents of its will.

As always, Russian liberalism spoke directly in the name of the people, expressing
"the people's" mind and feelings, on the assumption that there was no divide, no rift
between "the people" and itself.

Voices and passions quickly rose so high in the Duma that its excited eloquence
had the government reeling, and especially its questions about chaos at the front—
but not about GHQ. Nothing of that sort occurred to any of the speakers, and all this
was addressed to the same old shabby, bumbling, tongue-tied government. Shcherbatov, Minister of the Interior, had to prevaricate, not daring to reveal that he was
denied access not just to power but to knowledge of what was going on. And so,
condemnatory speeches rained down on the government, and were disseminated
throughout the country and abroad, inviting the whole world to believe that Russia's
ministers were hopelessly incompetent. The Duma was by now demanding that those

responsible for the shortfall in supplies to the front should be investigated and brought to trial. (The Council of Ministers did in fact set up a commission to investigate Sukhomlinov, until recently one of its own.) But there was no one in sight with the authority to listen and decide whether or not to take action, instead of affecting deafness and paralysis like the government. Russians being what they are, it would have been better if the ministers had argued and gone on the offensive, met abuse with abuse, instead of cowering and dithering. It was nobody's duty to know, and nobody could guess, their secret difficulties. Those speeches in the Duma alarmed all sections of the population and obviously affected its attitude toward the regime.

No one perhaps was more inflamed with the spirit of rebellion than the industrialists, merchants, and bankers. They had held an Industrial Congress at the end of May, ostensibly to deal with practical matters but actually to castigate an ineffectual government. Konovalov reinforced Ryabushinsky's hysterical speech with his own indignation. This was the beginning of the entrepreneurs' drive to take the job of supplying the front out of the government's hands and into their own. "War Industry Committees" began to spring up everywhere. They were not always successful in demarcating their territory or the scope of their activities, but they were all excitedly eager for action. This movement was taken over by Guchkov, who had always had an eye to the main chance, and had been hurt by the loss of his Octobrist Party and his leading role in educated society. He was elected chairman of the Central War Industry Committee on 7 August and obtained government ratification of its charter on 17 August. (His kinsman and well-wisher Krivoshein helped him in this, rapidly channeling the proposal through Goremykin, and denying other ministers and, for that matter, industrialists and businessmen time to acquaint themselves with it and give it some thought. What is more, the martial Polivanov was in league with him. Guchkov was, exceptionally, invited to a cabinet meeting, snapping back at them as if he was in a den of robbers, and allowed no changes of substance: his committee desired only to serve its country disinterestedly, therefore nothing in the text could be rejected.) The newspapers reported the feverish activity of the War Industry Committees, in their endeavor to save a country which the government was doing its best to ruin. There was general confusion: members of the committees had free access to the War Ministry departments responsible for contracts and procurement. Nothing was kept secret from them, and now that the award of contracts was entirely in their hands they could induce manufacturers to compete for their favors, and reward themselves for their patriotic mediation with a commission on military orders worth millions paid from the public purse—a pretty crazy situation for a country at war. The Central War Industry Committee now took on the guise of an additional government, more concerned with the course of the war than was the Council of Ministers.

And where did the Council of Ministers stand in the midst of this furor? Above all, what was its attitude toward the Duma? Forgetting all serious work on legislative projects, that body was taking a loftier tone. Its ambition to seize power was more and more glaringly obvious. The regime was no longer under siege, it was the object of a frontal assault.

> **Goremykin:** Give the Duma a short run on condition it passes the draft law on category 2 militia, then dissolve it.

Krivoshein agreed completely. Stop them as soon as possible! When we convened it we were thinking of a short session, say until early August. Even mid-August is unacceptable. The Duma hinders us from introducing extraordinary measures under Article 87. We must explain to our well-wishers among the deputies, and to those who are at least capable of talking to the "hated bureaucracy," the impossibility in wartime conditions of making do with normal legislative procedures.

The call-up of category 2 militia was yet another tyrannical excess on the part of GHQ: without considering the nation's strength, or the needs of the economy, the Grand Duke had demanded millions more men under arms (or not even under arms, since there was a shortage of rifles). The government was understandably reluctant to mobilize the militia. But if it had to be done . . .

> **Shcherbatov:** It is absolutely essential to put the law on the militia through the State Duma. The results of the draft are poorer all the time. The police cannot cope with the mass of draft evaders. Men hide in the forests and in unharvested fields. Given the present mood of the people, I'm afraid that without the Duma's sanction we won't get a single man. Agitators are at work full blast, with enormous funds from some source or other at their disposal.
>
> **Grigorovich** (Navy Minister): We know what the source is—Germany.
>
> **Shcherbatov:** I am bound to point out that this agitation is taking on a more and more frankly defeatist character. Its direct effect is surrender en masse to the enemy.
>
> **Samarin** (Procurator of the Holy Synod): A host of gray greatcoats are running wild on the home front. Can't some more useful role be found for them in the battle zone?
>
> **Krivoshein:** My civilian eye is affronted by this multitude of loafers in gray greatcoats in our cities, our villages, along the railway lines, and over the whole face of Russia. Why strip the population of its last working hands when all we need to do is take hold of this horde of vagabonds and put them in the trenches? However, this comes under the heading of military matters outside the competence of the Council of Ministers.

Polivanov, whose exasperated sarcasm defied all restraints, informed them—eyes flashing, jaw jutting—that the situation at the front, with GHQ in control, was one of complete disarray in total defeat:

> I place my hopes on Russia's insurmountable expanses, on Russia's impassable mud, and on the mercy of St. Nicholas of Myra.
>
> **Kharitonov** (State Control): Meanwhile our triumphal progress through the Caucasus continues uninterrupted. What exactly are we shoving in there for—if you'll excuse the expression?
>
> **Polivanov:** Everybody knows that—to create a Greater Armenia. The gathering of the Armenian lands is the great ambition of Countess Vorontsova-Dashkova

(wife of the vice-regent of the Caucasus).

But perhaps the most destructive consequence of our defeat in the West was the flood tide of refugees. The waters had risen, and no governmental or public body could channel and control them.

Krivoshein: Of all the grievous consequences of the war this is the most unexpected, the most dangerous, and the most intractable. And the really awful thing about it is that it is not caused by real need or by a spontaneous popular impulse. It is deliberately contrived by our wise strategists to deter the enemy. Sickness, suffering, and poverty are spreading all over Russia, and the people's curses go with them. The hungry and the ragged are sowing panic everywhere. They advance in serried ranks, trampling the crops, ruining the meadows and forests, leaving what is virtually a desert behind them. Even the rear echelons of the army have been stripped of their last reserve of provisions. I imagine that the Germans contemplate the results with some satisfaction and are glad to be relieved of concern for the population. This second great migration of the peoples, organized by GHQ, will drag Russia to revolution and ruin.

In the war of 1812 compact armies maneuvered over limited areas and the number of refugees was not so huge. Now, copying the tactics of that war and applying them along an unbroken front, the generals were laying waste whole provinces, uprooting millions from their ancestral homes, never pausing to think how to deal with horses and cattle in the railway age. At least 120,000 freight cars were in use simply to provide living space for refugees.

The all-powerful Yanushkevich was nonetheless so inconspicuous in the shadow of the Grand Duke that he might still have stayed put had he not extended this measure of forcible resettlement in the inner provinces to all Jews, at the same time accusing them one and all of sympathizing with the enemy and of spying. Yanushkevich dreaded being blamed for the enormous retreat—and had the unfortunate idea of shifting the blame for military failures onto the Jews. And although his measures were all countersigned by the Grand Duke, the inner provinces unambiguously identified Yanushkevich as the culprit. In the outside world Russia as a whole was considered culpable. Outrage in the West was instantaneous. The allied governments stated emphatically that failure to make peace with the Jews would affect Russia adversely.

This question was discussed as a matter of great urgency in early August at several meetings of the Russian cabinet: everywhere in the West (and by domestic banks also) the credits Russia needed to carry on the war had been cut off, all the sources of funds without which Russia could not continue for a week had been closed. This was true above all of the United States, which had become warring Europe's banker.

Shcherbatov: Our efforts to make GHQ see reason are meeting with no success. All of us, individually and collectively, have spoken, written, pleaded, complained. But the all-powerful Yanushkevich does not feel bound by considerations of the interest of the state as a whole. Hundreds of thousands of Jews are moving eastward from the theater of war, and it is impossible to distribute this whole mass within the limits of the Pale of Settlement. Local governors report that everything is full over and above capacity, and that furthermore they cannot answer for the safety of the new settlers when passions are running high and soldiers returning from the front engage in anti-Semitic agitation. This makes it necessary for us to settle evacuated Jews outside the Pale, if only temporarily. The boundary is being overstepped already. The leaders of Russian Jewry are urgently demanding that it be put on a basis of law. In the heat of discussion I have been told to my face that revolutionary feeling is growing uncontrollably among the Jewish masses. People abroad are also beginning to lose patience, and their requests are beginning to sound almost like ultimata: "If you expect to be given money to carry on the war you should . . ." We must temporarily suspend the rules on the Pale of Settlement. We must do something to facilitate the rehabilitation of the Jewish people, who have been blackened by rumors of treason. And we must make haste, so as not to be left behind by events.

Krivoshein: The Minister of Finance, who is presently being torn limb from limb by the State Duma, asks for some action on the Jewish question of a demonstrative character. He was visited the other day by Kamenka, Baron Ginsburg, and Varshavsky, to inform him of the general indignation in their community. The gist of what they said was: "Give, and we will give in return." There is a knife at our throats, and no two ways about it. While they are still asking politely we can set conditions: If we make major changes to the Pale of Settlement, you can give us financial support and use your influence on all the newspapers and journals dependent on Jewish capital (which means almost the whole press) to change its revolutionary tone.

Sazonov: Our allies are also dependent on Jewish capital, and will answer our requests with instructions to make our peace with the Jews.

Shcherbatov: We're caught in a vicious circle. We're helpless, and without them we can't raise a kopeck.

Goremykin: The Jews may have residence rights only in cities. We must protect the rural areas.

Shcherbatov: And we have a convincing argument for doing so: the village is more and more inclined to pogroms. We have to protect the Jews from that, since the rural police is almost nonexistent.

Krivoshein: The Jews themselves understand that very well. They feel no attraction to the villages. Their interests are entirely bound up with the urban centers.

Sazonov: I know from a reliable source that even the omnipotent Leopold Rothschild does not venture outside the towns.

Rukhlov: All Russia is suffering the hardships of war, yet the Jews are the first to be given relief. It confirms the saying that if you have money everything is for sale. There is no doubt that the underlying reasons for our action will be generally recognized. Forget the Jewish bankers. What impression will it make on the army and the Russian people at large? Let's hope that there will not be an explosion of indignation, with bloody disasters for the Jews themselves. The way the question is put has taken me by surprise, and I find it difficult to answer with an easy conscience.

Samarin: I fully understand this feeling of spiritual protest. I too find it painful to agree to an action which will have tremendous consequences, and which Russians will have to pay for in the future. But such is the combination of circumstances that we have to make the sacrifice.

Polivanov: As the minister with responsibility for the Cossack territories, I am obliged to state that the right of unrestricted residence for the Jews can hardly be applicable even to the towns in those areas. An exception must be made for Cossack urban centers in the interest of the Jews themselves. Historically, Cossacks and Jews have never been able to live at peace with one another, and their encounters have always ended unhappily. Nor should we lose sight of the fact that it is mainly Cossack units that are carrying out General Yanushkevich's orders to save the Russian army from Jewish sedition.

The following day, 19 August, the ministers met again, and the secret session began with further discussion of the same subject. Goremykin reported that he had informed the Emperor of the ministers' views, and that His Majesty had approved in principle the abolition of residence restrictions on the Jews as far as towns were concerned. (Something he did not agree to in 1906, when Stolypin pressed him to do it. Necessity is a great persuader. In that retreat in the summer of 1915 Russia was reminded that with the three partitions of Poland she had bitten off more than she could chew.)

Krivoshein: The interests of the economy have long called for the involvement of as many entrepreneurs as possible. The transfer of Jewish businesses from the western border areas will stimulate the development of industry and bring new life to other localities. The Jews will shake the sleeping kingdom and give a healthy shock to Russian businessmen who have grown idle under a protectionist system. There are in fact quite a few Jews already in some of the oldest and most Russian towns—most of them, however, are rich Jews.

Rukhlov: My heart and mind protest against the fact that the first effect of our military setbacks is concessions to the Jews. There has been talk here of financial and military considerations which favor this gesture. But we have only to recall the role of the Jews in the events of 1905, and the percentage of persons of Jewish origin among those who carry on revolutionary propaganda or belong to underground organizations. I categorically refuse to add my signature. But I do not feel entitled to declare my disagreement openly and so shift the burden of such a crucial decision onto our Russian Tsar.

Shcherbatov: Sergei Vasilievich is, of course, profoundly correct when he points to the destructive influence of Jewry. But what else can we do, with the knife at our throats? When the money is in Jewish hands . . .

Bark: It is not we who have created this crisis, but those with whom we pleaded in vain to refrain from aggravating the Jewish problem with the aid of Cossack whips. Foreign markets are now closed to us, and we shall not get a single kopeck there. I have received broad hints that we shall not get out of these difficulties until we make demonstrative moves on the Jewish question. As Minister of Finance, I see no other way out. The days of Minin and Pozharsky have seemingly gone, never to return.

Krivoshein: I too usually identify the Russian revolutionary movement with the Jews, but shall nonetheless sign the act granting concessions. Let us make haste. We cannot wage war on Germany and on the Jews simultaneously. That is beyond the powers even of such a mighty country as Russia, although General Yanushkevich is of another opinion.

The discussion had come to an end, and they began considering procedure.

Goremykin: In present conditions we cannot set off a debate on the Jewish question in the Duma. It could take a dangerous turn and serve to exacerbate ethnic strife. There is no assurance that the bill would get through. And a lengthy legislative process would rob the measure of the required demonstrative effect and of its graciousness.

Kharitonov: Take my word for it, nobody will let out a squeak about proper legislative procedures and there will be no protests. Not only the Kadets and those further to the left but the Octobrists too will feel duty-bound to welcome the act. Interpellations and protests are out of the question.

Bark: The French Rothschilds sincerely desire to help the Allies defeat Germany. And Kitchener has said several times that one of the important conditions of success in this war is relaxation of restrictions on Jews in Russia. Our decision today will have an extremely favorable effect on our finances.

This, however, did not happen. Indeed, still in August, the Allies demanded that, for a start, one-quarter of Russia's gold reserves should be sent to England and America to guarantee payment for arms purchases.

Kharitonov: So our kind allies hold a knife to our throat and put the squeeze on us—give us your gold or you won't get a thing. God bless them, I'm sure, but that is no way for decent people to behave.

Krivoshein: Even Shingarev disapproves of the way London and Paris are acting. They are thrilled by the heroic efforts we are making to save the Allied fronts at the cost of Russian defeats and the millions of casualties Russia is suffering, but when it comes to money they squeeze us harder than any usurer. And America takes advantage of the situation to get fat on Europe's misfortunes.

Shakhovskoy: So we have been given an ultimatum by our allies?

Bark: Yes. If we refuse to send the gold abroad the Americans will demand payment in gold for every single rifle.

They then considered conditions to put before influential Jewish groups: that they should try to make the Jewish masses put an end to revolutionary agitation and should also help to change the attitudes of the press.

Meanwhile, another shock awaited the ministers at their 19 August session. Until that moment General Polivanov had taken little part in the exchange of views. He had sat sunk in gloom, and a habitual twitch of the head and one shoulder had become more pronounced. Then Goremykin asked him to report on the situation in the theater of war. (Sukhomlinov had never treated them to such reports, because he was never adequately briefed himself.) Polivanov readily obliged. His colleagues had previously observed that the gloomier and more hopeless his reports were (and he always exaggerated), the more complacent, not to say happier, he looked. He might have been reporting the destruction of the enemy. On this occasion too he drew a picture of total collapse.

We can expect an irremediable catastrophe at any minute. The army is no longer withdrawing, it is on the run. The least little rumor of the enemy's approach causes panic and the flight of whole regiments. Our salvation for the time being is the artillery. But we have hardly any shells. GHQ has lost its head completely, it gives contradictory orders, and swings from one extreme to the other. The whole organism of GHQ is rotten with the psychology of defeat. It sees no way out except by the ill-famed strategy of luring the enemy deep into the interior.

No way out! On any consideration the High Command had to be changed if Russia was to be saved! The whole Council of Ministers must beg the Emperor to reorganize GHQ!

Ah, but Polivanov had something even worse in store for his colleagues:

However awful what is going on at the front may be, Russia is threatened by something much more frightening. I will deliberately break my oath of military secrecy and my promise to remain silent for the time being. His Majesty informed me this morning of his decision to dismiss the Grand Duke and take over the Supreme Command himself.

This created a sensation among the ministers! They all started talking at once, across each other, so that it was impossible to make out what any single one was saying.

It is extraordinary. You might suppose that they were sick to death of the high-handed GHQ, of the mad-headed Grand Duke, of the intriguer Yanushkevich. You might suppose that once the Emperor assumed the Supreme Command the existing Rules for the Administration of the Army in the Field would finally come into their own, with no need to change anything. But no! Nothing could have come as such a shock to the ministers as this news.

Polivanov: Knowing how sensitive and how stubborn the Emperor is when he makes decisions of a personal nature, I tried in the most cautious way possible to dissuade him. In the present state of our forces we have no hope at all even of limited success, let alone of halting the victorious progress of the Germans. I did not feel that I had the right to disguise the possible consequences for the internal life of the country if troops commanded by the Tsar in person should fail to stop the enemy's advance. The impression it would make on the country if the Tsar personally had to order the evacuation of Petrograd or Moscow does not bear thinking about. His Majesty replied that he had weighed all the possibilities and that his decision was irrevocable.

Shcherbatov: It would have to be now, at the least favorable moment possible! When revolutionary feeling is on the increase. Letters passed to me by the military censors blame the Tsar himself for many things. Whereas in spite of all that is happening at the front the Grand Duke has not lost his popularity, and has the goodwill of the Duma because of his attitude toward the social organizations!

—meaning Zemgor. And there was the rub. What if the Tsar took it into his head to curb Zemgor? Society's reaction would be hostile. The people at large would be deeply disturbed by the removal of the Grand Duke. How could it be otherwise when there were photographs of him everywhere? And once he took over the Supreme Command, how would the Emperor be able to absent himself from the army to visit the capital? No Tsar had put himself at the head of the army since Peter the Great!

And if His Majesty leaves for the front I cannot vouch for the security of Tsarskoye Selo. There are hardly any soldiers there and police protection is inadequate. A handful of enterprising villains could put the garrison in a very difficult position. I find what the Emperor has said deeply disturbing.

Goremykin: I have to confirm what the War Minister has said. His Majesty forewarned me some days ago. Which is why I kept warning you to treat the subject of GHQ with caution.

Sazonov: How could you conceal this danger from your colleagues in the cabinet? The Emperor's decision is disastrous!

Goremykin: I did not think that I could possibly divulge something which the Emperor had ordered me to keep secret. I speak of it only because the War Minister found it possible to violate a pledge of secrecy and divulge it without His Majesty's permission. I am one of the old school and for me a command from the Highest is law. I have to tell you that nothing you can say will persuade the Emperor to refrain from taking the step he has in mind. Neither intrigue nor any other person's influence has had anything to do with the decision in question. It was prompted by his perception of his duty as Tsar. I too asked him to postpone his decision until circumstances were more favorable. But the Emperor, while understanding perfectly the risk involved, will not change his mind. All we can do is bow to the will of our Tsar and give him our help.

Sazonov: There are occasions when it is the duty of a loyal subject to stand up to the Tsar. We must also take account of the fact that the dismissal of the Grand Duke will make an extremely unfavorable impression on our allies, who have faith in him. Nor can one conceal the fact that people abroad have little faith in the Tsar's strength of character, and are afraid of the influences by which he is surrounded.

Krivoshein: It is entirely in keeping with the Tsar's spiritual makeup and his mystical understanding of his royal calling. But this is an absolutely inappropriate moment. And an act of the greatest historical importance is put before the government as a fait accompli. The fate of Russia and the whole world is in the balance. We must protest, plead, insist, beg, do anything to dissuade His Majesty from this irrevocable step! The fate of the dynasty, and of the throne itself, is at stake! It is a blow to the monarchic principle, on which the whole strength and future of Russia depends! Ever since Khodynka and the Japanese campaign the people have regarded the Emperor as ill-starred, as luckless. Whereas the Grand Duke's name is a slogan to which great hopes are attached. It takes especially strong nerves to endure all that is happening.

Shcherbatov: The Emperor's decision will be attributed to the influence of the notorious Rasputin. There is already gossip about it in the State Duma, and I'm afraid that a public scandal may be the result.

Kharitonov even tried to scare them with the thought that the Grand Duke, highly strung, sensitive, and vain as he was, might put up some resistance from GHQ. Polivanov made a despairing gesture: anything could happen. The others incredulously dismissed it.

Bark: His Majesty's decision will damage our credit. The Tsar taking command of the army will look like our last desperate throw.

Shakhovskoy: The whole Council of Ministers must ask for an audience and beg the Emperor to reconsider his decision.

They were all in a state of high excitement and only the superannuated Prime Minister, secure in his otherworldly wisdom, remained calm and detached. He had presided over that other government which a year ago had combined to dissuade the Tsar from assuming the Supreme Command.

Goremykin: I am against a collective démarche of that sort. You know the Emperor's character, and what sort of impression such demonstrations make on him. Things are hard enough for the Emperor as it is, without us worrying him with our protests. I have done all I can to restrain him. But his decision is unshakable. I call on you to bow to His Imperial Majesty's will, close ranks around him at this grave moment, and devote all your strength to our monarch.

But this revised and liberalized Council of Ministers was not likely to be impressed by a too solemn adjuration from its chairman: indeed, some of them did not pause to listen but went on eagerly discussing ways of talking the Tsar into changing his mind. Krivoshein looked at Goremykin sadly and wonderingly: the old man had been his candidate for the post, and for the past months he had done what was required, settled differences. This was the first time he had obstinately stuck to his guns and this was when Krivoshein regretted at last not taking the premiership himself. As things now were, the ministers, however little regard they had for their chairman, could not approach the Tsar collectively without him. They had to leave all pleas to the Tsar to Polivanov, who had been entrusted with the secret. They were all worked up, not to say exasperated: how could the Emperor make such a decision without consulting his government?

In fact, the Emperor had been preparing to make this decision for several months. He could never forgive himself for not taking command of the army in the field during the war with Japan. It was the Tsar's duty to be with his troops in the hour of danger. At the very beginning of the present war the Emperor had been determined to assume the Supreme Command, but had been talked out of it by a cabal of indignant ministers. While his uncle Nikolasha, once his squadron commander in the hussars, had become a very prominent figure in the Russian army and was a natural choice to command it for the time being. He was accordingly made Commander in Chief, although the Empress was, even then, against his appointment. The Emperor had regretted ever since not assuming his natural role. His many visits to the fronts and his regimental reviews were so many attempts to unite with the army, even if it meant bypassing GHQ. He loved his army, and his role in it, and was jealous of Nikolasha. Now that disaster loomed at the front, Nikolai believed more firmly than ever that it was his sacred, his mystical duty to take command and conquer or perish together with his troops. (Moreover, exchanging his present existence for that of a soldier would deliver him from interviews with ministers, malicious Petersburg gossip, and all the problems and preoccupations of the home front.)

The Empress had approved his decision long ago and encouraged him in it. She had in the first autumn of the war begun to suspect that Nikolasha wanted to make use of his position as Supreme Commander to usurp the throne. She found confirmation of this in Nikolai Nikolaevich's actions and demeanor. He did not report regularly to the Emperor on military matters. He summoned ministers to GHQ, bypassing the Emperor, to brief them and give instructions. The Emperor was frequently confronted with decisions taken at GHQ without prior consultation. Nikolai Nikolaevich took too great an interest in matters that concerned the state as a whole, rather than the armies in the field. (Underground postcards with pictures of Nikolai Nikolaevich captioned "Nikolai III" were an additional irritant.) We still have letters written by the Empress earnestly admonishing her absent husband. (In quoting them side by side with the public utterances of other persons we rely on the reader to make the necessary allowances. *They* too may have expressed themselves more harshly among friends.)

> He is trying to play your part. No one has the right to behave as he does in the eyes of God and of men. He will do some great harm which you will find it difficult to undo. He understands so little about domestic affairs and about our country, but he overawes the ministers with his loud voice and gesticulations. Everybody is indignant to see ministers reporting to him. They say that the Emperor has been stripped of power. Our Friend and I were both struck by the fact that Nikolasha adopts your style in telegrams replying to provincial governors. Then again, it is Nikolasha's fault and Witte's that the Duma exists at all. Nikolasha is not at all clever, he's stubborn, and he is led by others. His Montenegrin women egg him on. He has behaved improperly—toward your country, toward you, and toward your wife. And since he has gone against the Man sent by God his deeds cannot find favor with God and his opinions cannot be correct. A man who has himself betrayed the Man of God cannot find favor with God.

She goes on to recommend action as follows:

> To hell with GHQ! No good can come from that quarter. The soldiers need you, not GHQ. Don't look at things through Nikolasha's eyes, make him look through yours. In the midst of general collapse unshakable authority is needed. Remember that you are Emperor, and that no other dares take so much upon himself, you have been on the throne a long time and have more experience than others. May God send you more faith in your own wisdom, so that you will not listen to them, but only to our Friend and your own soul. Never forget who you are, and that it is your duty to remain an autocratic Emperor. A good loud voice and a stern look can sometimes do wonders. Be more resolute and surer of yourself. They must remember better who you are.

So then his decision to remove Nikolai Nikolaevich and assume the Supreme Command—simultaneously thwarting the plot being hatched (or rather gossiped about) at GHQ to relegate the Empress to a convent—had gradually ripened during the spring and summer of 1915.

In those months the Emperor yielded to public indignation and replaced a number of ministers. Some of these changes were made with the Empress's knowledge and consent. She considered all the dismissals justified. Thus, of Shcheglovitov, although he was very far to the right, she said:

> I don't like him in his present place. He ignores your orders and tears up petitions which he supposes to have come through our Friend.

She shared the Emperor's unhappiness over the retirement of Sukhomlinov. But she had not been able to keep an eye on all the new ministerial appointments. Some of them had been suggested to the Emperor, and accepted, while he was away at GHQ—and it soon turned out that his nominees were unsatisfactory.

> Forgive me, but I do not like your choice of War Minister. Is Polivanov the sort of man one can rely on? I would like to know all your reasons. Can he really have parted company with Guchkov? And isn't he an enemy of our Friend? That always brings misfortune.

While Shcherbatov, promoted for no known reason from the remount service (perhaps because his brother was Nikolasha's adjutant) was

> a coward and a weakling. He gives the press too much freedom. He too is probably hostile to our Friend, and so to us.

But Samarin, in the role of Procurator of the Holy Synod, got the worst treatment of all:

> His appointment reduces me to despair. He belongs to that nasty clique of sanctimonious humbugs, that gang of Muscovite bandits who have entangled us like a spider's web. The plots against our Friend will start all over again, and everything will go badly. I have been unhappy ever since I heard of this appointment. Nikolasha suggested him specially, knowing that he would try to harm Grigori. He is stupid and insolent, and has talked to me impertinently. I sensed his hostility. He won't be satisfied until he has got me, our Friend, and Anya into terrible trouble. At his first audience with you, tell him very firmly that you forbid any intrigue against our Friend and any talk against him. You are the head and the protector of the Church, and he tries to undermine you in the eyes of the Church, he is beginning to express doubts about your instructions. Samarin will fall into the pit he is digging for me. Russia does not share his opinions. We must send Samarin packing, the sooner the better. Anybody at all would be better than him . . . If you knew how many tears I have shed today, you would understand the enormous importance of this. It isn't female nonsense, it is the simple truth.

And then again, with the composition of the government so dangerously altered . . .

> Why must you join Nikolasha at GHQ and summon a meeting of your ministers there? They may take advantage of your soft heart and make you do things which you would not do if you were here. They're afraid of me, so they come to you when you're alone. They're afraid of me because they know my cause is just.

But all admonitions and hesitations seemed to be over, and at the very worst moment, with Russia's armies rolling back in retreat, the Emperor was assuming the burden of the Supreme Command. On 22 August he sent his trusty War Minister,

Polivanov (ignorant of his real feelings), to GHQ, to inform Nikolasha tactfully and confidentially of his decision and to settle the procedure for handing over command. The Grand Duke was offered the viceroyalty of the Caucasus in place of Vorontsov-Dashkov.

For the Grand Duke, resignation at a time of unrelieved failure was like an open confession of incompetence. But he accepted the blow, did not rebel, and indeed took it as an act of grace that he was not retired completely but sent to command the Caucasus: the one thing he earnestly begged for was that he should be allowed to take the precious Yanushkevich with him. Yanushkevich himself and the other top brass were desperately disappointed, and for a few weeks GHQ was more or less on strike, neglecting its work and the supervision of the retreating army.

After all this the Emperor said in answer to the Grand Duke that the change of command would not take place all that quickly, but would be a matter of weeks.

Meanwhile towns were surrendered one after another. German artillery salutes greeted the surrender of Kovno on 18 August (General Grigoriev, the commander of that fortress, had fled) and of Grodno and Brest-Litovsk on the 28th. Many people could not believe that such a reverse was not the result of treason. Excited workers at the Kolomna and some other factories accused their management of deferring to German interests and refusing to step up production. The unrest threatened to become violent. The workers were prepared to send a deputation, not to the government, which everybody had been told over and over again counted for nothing, but to the Duma or to GHQ. The ministers hastily asked Rodzyanko (who loved doing just that) not to receive these deputations.

> **Goremykin:** The president of the State Duma is in such a state of excitement that it is useless talking to him. The Minister of the Interior and the Minister of War must take all necessary steps to prevent ugly scenes. We know what peaceful deputations can lead to.

> **Shakhovskoy:** The atmosphere in factories is extremely tense. The workers are looking everywhere for treason, for treachery, for sabotage on behalf of the Germans, they're obsessed with the search for someone to blame for our failures in the field.

> **Shcherbatov:** Revolutionary agitators are taking advantage of the workers' feelings and aggravating the indignation of the masses about the shell shortage. That is the most fashionable question of all, in the Duma, in society at large, in the press. It provides fertile soil for disorders. It is very important to some people to bring the crowd out on the street by whatever means.

Over and over again they laboriously debated ways of blocking the Emperor's decision before it was made official.

> **Samarin:** I was in Moscow and could not attend the last meetings. God grant that I am mistaken, but I expect the change of Supreme Commander to have dire consequences. The removal of the Grand Duke and the assumption of command by the Emperor is not just a spark but a whole lighted torch thrown into a powder magazine. Revolutionary agitators are working tirelessly to undermine by all possible means the remnants of faith in Russia's

fundamental institutions. And then like a thunderclap comes the news that the one person on whom all hopes of victory are pinned is dismissed. At the very beginning of his reign the people formed the opinion that the Tsar is dogged by misfortune in all he undertakes. I am well acquainted with several parts of the country, and especially with Moscow, and I assure you that the news will be greeted as a major national disaster. We must implore the Emperor on our knees not to destroy his throne and Russia. Can the Tsar's closest servants not get him to listen to them? If not, how can they conduct the business of state?

Goremykin did not lose his nonchalant poise:

This discussion could take us to the point of no return.

But it came to the ministers' ears that the Emperor, on assuming the title of Supreme Commander, would establish his headquarters in Petrograd, so that it would be near at hand, and not really like GHQ at all, while General Ruzsky, who was apparently on the very best of terms with General Alekseev, would be in complete control at the front. This was at once felt to be an improvement. It had substantial advantages—Yanushkevich would be out of things, GHQ would be in close proximity to the government, and perhaps, even, the unification of civil and military authority might now be possible. Or would this proximity lead to still greater confusion?

Krivoshein, a masterly drafter of businesslike memoranda, suggested ways of making the change of command—if it was irrevocably decided—understandable to the people and easier for them to accept. They should ask the Emperor to express his sovereign will in the form of a "most gracious rescript" addressed to the Grand Duke, declaring that the Tsar would not wait for the hour of victory to share their danger with his troops, that he was ready to perish fighting the foe but not to fail in his duty. And saying how highly he esteemed the Grand Duke. Krivoshein was already at work drafting the statement. A rescript of that sort would smooth down many awkward corners, and the Grand Duke would not feel insulted by his displacement.

Sazonov undertook to lay this idea before the Tsar at his next audience. (Only Samarin persisted in arguing that what they needed was not a rescript, but to dissuade the Emperor.) The Emperor approved, and asked them to present a draft as soon as possible.

In the meantime rumors about the impending change of command filtered out and reached, among others, the effervescent Rodzyanko. As the "second personage in the state," and "super-arbiter," he dashed off to Tsarskoye Selo to try his hand at dissuasion. The Emperor received him, with ill grace, on 24 August, and remained immovable. Rodzyanko then rushed off to upbraid the ministers. He found them in session, called Krivoshein, the most influential of them and the best disposed to the politically minded public, out to the vestibule, and began abusing him for the government's failure to stand up to the Emperor. Krivoshein said evasively that he was merely Minister of Agriculture. Rodzyanko then called Goremykin out. But he was still more resistant: the government followed the dictates of its conscience and needed no advice from the outside. With a cry of "I am beginning to believe those who say Russia has no government," Rodzyanko made for the exit with an insane look on his face and without saying goodbye. So distraught was he that he forgot his cane, and when the doorman offered it to him, he jumped into his carriage yelling, "Damn the wretched stick!"

The next day Rodzyanko sent the Emperor a written statement, which was subsequently passed around and widely read.

> Sire! You are a symbol and a banner, and you cannot permit a shadow to fall on that sacred banner. You must remain outside and above the organs of government, which bears the primary responsibility for repulsing the enemy. Surely you will not voluntarily submit your sacrosanct person to the judgment of the people—that way lies the ruin of Russia. You are of a mind to replace the Supreme Commander, in whom the Russian people still has boundless trust. The people will find no other explanation for this step than the influence of the Germans around you. The people will begin to feel that the situation is hopeless and that chaos in the government of the country is imminent. The army will lose heart, and revolution and anarchy will inevitably flare up throughout the country, sweeping away everything in their path.

The muddleheaded fat man had begun quite effectively. The Emperor himself had anxiously wondered what would be left of the authority of the throne if the steady succession of retreats continued under his command. But Rodzyanko had then gone beyond the bounds of tact and, as only he could, defeated his own argument.

Rumors that the popular Supreme Commander was to be replaced spread ever wider: the Duma heard them, Zemgor heard them, then all Petrograd, all Moscow—and everybody, needless to say, was indignant.

The government rejoiced that the changeover was at least hanging fire. Maybe the Emperor would back down? Why couldn't he direct his urge to take control to the home front rather than to the battlefield? Meanwhile the retreat continued and the confidence of the masses in the Grand Duke was quickly declining. With a little further delay, perhaps the Emperor's assumption of command would be acceptable?

Samarin uncompromisingly insisted that the step planned by the Emperor put the dynasty and Russia in mortal danger. Polivanov's behavior, always devious, became more and more self-contradictory: he at one and the same time opposed the assumption of command by the Emperor, made damaging remarks about the Grand Duke, and tried to turn his colleagues against Goremykin. Krivoshein's arguments, expressed more and more fully as time went by, were as follows:

> The uncertainty that has been created cannot continue, if only because General Yanushkevich continues with it. His presence at GHQ is a greater danger than the German armies. Apart from that, the damage has largely been done: the Emperor's decision is no secret to anyone, it is talked about on almost every street. Further holdups may rob the Emperor's resolve of whatever is admirable in it. We must without delay ask the Emperor to summon a Council of War, with ministers taking part, to review our war plans. The best venue would be GHQ, and the Grand Duke's presence is absolutely essential. His Majesty has such an extraordinary talent for dealing with people, even those he knows to be no friends of his, that he will succeed in making it appear that he and the Grand Duke are on good terms. And if we

are fated to go through a change of command, *after* the Council of War it will appear to be the result of consultation with the government and the senior commanders. This will blunt its impact on the minds of the public. Everybody is saying at present that no action is apparently being taken in high places.

The Emperor agonized for weeks, day in and day out. He went to the Elagin Palace to see his mother, and her answer was: You are not equipped to play such a role, you will not be forgiven for it, do not lead Russia to destruction, and anyway the business of state requires your presence in Petrograd. Do not repeat the error of Paul I: he too, in the last year of his reign, began turning away all those who were devoted to him.

Loyal old Vorontsov-Dashkov also advised against it: At present you are head of state and sit in judgment—if you become head of the army, you may face judgment.

Many others used similar arguments to test and bend the will of the Emperor.

Only the voice of his royal spouse, the never silent voice he listened to more easily than to others, supported the line he had taken.

> Modesty is one of God's greatest gifts, but a supreme ruler must make his will felt more often. Be sure of yourself and act! Everybody takes advantage of your angelic goodness and patience. You are a little too hesitant in making up your mind, and vacillation is never good. You must show that you make your own decisions and have a will of your own. Be firm to the end, reassure me of that, or I shall be ill with anxiety. In Russia, there must be a master as long as the people are uneducated.

All these discordant voices evidently weakened the Emperor's resolve, and the change he had decided on was a long time coming. He had never in his life found it so hard to make up his mind. The most awful thing was that he did not know whom to believe, who was telling the truth. The Emperor remembered his nightmare experience with Witte in October 1905. He had made a mistake he couldn't undo, yielded when there was no need, and it horrified him. His ministers had badgered him in May—fire those four and things will immediately change for the better. So he had dismissed the four, his devoted and well-loved Nikolai Maklakov among them, but had he succeeded in appeasing the public? He would have been no further from pleasing them, from winning their goodwill, if he had refused to dismiss those ministers: the Duma was now declaring that it could not possibly work with the present government. And the new ministers had devised no new ways of governing. He had thought that the four ministers he was adding were not the least bit to the left—but the government as a whole had taken a sharp left turn and loyal old Goremykin could scarcely hold them in check. No, forced concessions never improved matters. To save Russia, to make sure that God would not desert her, perhaps a propitiatory sacrifice really was necessary. Well—the Emperor would be that sacrificial victim. If the retreat had to continue to the very end, he would take responsibility for the retreat. At the same time the Emperor could not forget his invariable bad luck. All the misfortunes he had ever feared had always fallen upon him, none of his undertakings had ever ended in success. He prayed alone in various churches, and went to the Cathedral of Our Lady of Kazan with the Empress. He tried to convince himself that he was not just influenced by his wife and by Grigori, but that when he stood before the great icon of the Saviour in the church at Tsarskoye Selo some inner voice urged him to stand fast in the decision he had taken. He had suffered all his life from timidity, and he had to overcome it!

Meanwhile, the whole world was chewing over the change of command—but the change was not happening. The Grand Duke's transfer could come to be seen as a disgrace, not a mark of royal favor. (Rasputin was telling people that it was he who was removing the Grand Duke.) Nikolai Nikolaevich irritably asked the Emperor to speed up his transfer to the Caucasus. Yanushkevich, deeply hurt, had already been removed, and replaced by General Alekseev.

> **Krivoshein:** I never expected such demeaning behavior from His Majesty. However painful his personal feelings are, he has no right to abandon the army to the whim of fate.

> **Samarin:** Rumors of secret influences have recently reappeared, and they are supposed to have played a decisive part in the business of the Supreme Command. I shall ask the Emperor openly about this, I have a right to do so. When His Majesty offered me the post of Procurator of the Holy Synod he told me to my face that all this tittle-tattle was fabricated by enemies of the throne. I will now remind him of our conversation and ask him to release me. I am willing to serve my rightful Tsar to the last drop of my blood, but not . . . We must put a stop to the dissemination of rumors which do more to undermine the monarchic principle than any revolutionary activity.

> **Goremykin:** I have said repeatedly that the Emperor's decision is irrevocable. Instead of fraying his nerves with our démarches our duty is to rally around our Tsar and help him.

> **Shakhovskoy:** I was against the change of command. But it is now too late to go back on it, because everybody knows of His Majesty's intention. A retraction would be interpreted as a sign of weakness and fear.

> **Krivoshein:** The Grand Duke is obviously finished. His popularity has declined not only among the troops but also among the civilian population, who are dismayed by the influx of refugees and the endless recruiting drives at a time when there is no one to harvest a splendid grain crop. History offers an example. When our retreat before Napoleon was beginning to look inordinately hasty and desperate, Arakcheev, Shishkov, and Levashev demanded that Aleksandr I withdraw from the army: if Barclay should be beaten, Russia would only grieve, but if the Emperor of All the Russias were beaten, Russia would not be able to endure it. Let General Alekseev play the part of Barclay, and let the Emperor rally his army in the rear.

In any case, the government was no longer sure that it would itself remain in Petrograd for long, and took the precaution of discussing secretly whether to start evacuating the treasures of the Hermitage, the royal palaces, and the Public Library via the inland waterways to Nizhny Novgorod. But they were afraid of causing a panic: as it was, people were withdrawing their savings from the banks in dangerously large amounts.

General Ivanov, however, was proposing evacuation to a depth of a hundred versts behind the Southwestern Front, and a few days later, without waiting to hear from anyone else, and without even asking the government, he began preparing to evacuate Kiev.

> **Shcherbatov:** The military have finally lost their heads and their common sense. Local life has been turned upside down. It would be better to die in the last battle than to sign Russia's death warrant.

> **Kharitonov:** People are crying out in agony on every side that they are being ruined for no reason and to no purpose. It would be good for the Emperor to take a look at what is going on in the name of evacuation. The whole thing must be taken out of the hands of hotheaded ensigns and put into those of experienced civilian administrators. It's infuriating, our helplessness in the face of our generals' valor in retreat.

> **Krivoshein:** My whole soul is revolted by the thought that the mother of Russian cities, Russia's ancient holy of holies, Kiev, is doomed to undergo the horrors of evacuation. In truth, extraordinary conditions have been created by the fencing off of part of Russia as a theater of war. We must implore His Majesty to summon a Council of War, an elementary measure which people were reluctant to consider thirteen months ago. History will not believe that Russia waged war and came to the brink of destruction blindfolded, that millions of people were sacrificed to the conceit of some and the criminality of others. A Council of War would work out a plan for the further conduct of the war and for a strictly orderly evacuation.

Food stocks were taken from the civilian population and paid for with coupons of some sort. Headquarters staffs retreated in a mad rush, not as if temporarily withdrawing, but as if they expected never to return: they laid whole districts waste, burned crops and buildings, slaughtered cattle, threatened landowners with violence. Acting on instructions from their generals, retreating troops took the curses of the population with them. Smolensk province and its neighbors groaned under the influx of refugees, the dearth of provisions, the unmanageable numbers of soldiers. Hospital trains and military transports blocked the railroads. That great strategist, "Black" Danilov, dismissed with Yanushkevich, gave a banquet on the train in one of the stations. And GHQ was already planning to redraw the boundaries of the theater of war—the theater of its own chaotic authority and the government's impotence—still deeper in the interior, along a line from Tver to Tula.

> **Shcherbatov:** We cannot let the central provinces be torn to pieces by a horde of behind-the-lines heroes. The abolition of normal authority plays into the hands of revolutionaries.

> **Krivoshein:** People are falling victim to a sort of mass psychosis, an eclipse of sense and reason.

The government was overpowered by extreme anxiety combined with a sense of its own helplessness. The ministers debated every problem eagerly, at length and inconclusively. They saw more and more clearly that nothing depended on the result of their deliberations. They lacked any means or mechanism for influencing events, they could only talk to people, issue warnings, and make suggestions. They showed no resolve, expressed no firm opinion, put up no resistance. Not only was a quarter of the country taken away from them and given to the generals to administer; they found no firm footing in the rest of it and felt as if they were suspended in midair. It would be natural for the government to look to the monarch for support—he had created it and it was subordinate to him—but he took practically no account of them and paid no attention to their opinions. The Unions of Zemstvos and Towns issued instructions throughout the country without consulting the government. The Duma and the social organizations acted more and more openly as though they were out to seize power, demonstratively ignoring the government. In its legislative capacity the Duma simply kept the brakes on, so that no serious law could get passed, especially if it was urgently needed.

> **Krivoshein:** Even the Convention refrained from associating with the mob. We, thank God, have no revolution as yet. But the time may be much closer than we expect. People refuse to understand the government's clemency and take advantage of it to engage in revolutionary agitation.

> **Kharitonov:** The Duma has broken loose from its chains and is biting people right and left. The Tsar has no confidence in his ministers. I dread to think what may happen.

The population was fed rumors about bribery in connection with military contracts, and stirred up by sensational leaflets with fictitious "news." In Moscow disorders were sparked by patriotic rejoicing when newspapers reported that we had seized the Dardanelles. In Ivanovo–Voznesensk the immediate cause of the trouble was the arrest of persons inciting the workers to strike.

> **Shcherbatov:** It was time to start shooting, but we couldn't be sure of the garrison. We could expect repercussions in other industrial areas. But the Minister of the Interior is powerless: home-front ensigns with despotic inclinations and little understanding of the matters entrusted to them rule the roost everywhere. I am just an ordinary citizen, even in the capital of the empire, and can act only insofar as it does not call into question the fantasies of the military authorities. We must take action, of course, but how, when we have no support from any quarter?

Metropolitan society, in the throes of patriotic alarm—"Everything for the war effort" was the cry—still did not give up its cabarets, its all-night drinking sessions. Nightclubs and restaurants reverberated with music and blazed with light.

> **Shcherbatov:** It's a practical matter, not just a matter of principle—this waste of electricity when factories are short of power.

> **Samarin:** All these boozy "victory celebrations" make the worst possible impression on the people. They blame the government for permitting debauchery in the capital. The Holy Synod has called on the people to fast and pray in response to the disasters that have befallen their motherland. An Orthodox government ought to close down places of entertainment in these days of penance.

As for the press, it was completely out of hand, to an extent which would not have been permitted in any republican country. (In France the press was under rigid official control and contributed to the war effort.)

> **Sazonov:** Our allies are horrified by the unbridled license that reigns in the Russian press.

Goremykin: Our newspapers have gone completely mad. Their whole effort is directed to shaking the authority of the government. This is not freedom of speech—I'm damned if I know what to call it. Even in 1905 they did not permit themselves such outrageous antics. His Majesty told us then that in time of revolution our reactions to the abuses of the press cannot be governed by the law alone, that we cannot permit anyone to inject poison into the people with impunity. The military censors cannot remain indifferent to newspapers which sow sedition in the country.

Krivoshein: Our press oversteps the bounds even of elementary decency. There is a mass of articles completely unacceptable in content and tone. Until now it was just the Moscow papers, but quite recently the Petrograd papers too seem to have kicked over the traces. Nothing but abusive language, incitement of the public against the authorities, the dissemination of sensational false reports. It's plain for all to see that they are trying to revolutionize the country—but nobody is willing to intervene. I thought we had a law on wartime censorship!

Shcherbatov: Prior censorship of civilian publications was abolished long ago, and my department has no means of preventing the promulgation of the blatant lies and inflammatory articles which fill our newspapers. The law gives us no right to institute civilian censorship.

Nor to impose a fine, nor to close a newspaper down. There was military censorship in the theater of military operations (which, however, included Petrograd) and that was all. It held back only things that might be of use to enemy intelligence, but the military censors were not required to inspect printed matter from a civilian viewpoint. Yanushkevich's instructions from GHQ prohibited only criticism of the imperial family; everything else was a legitimate target, military censorship did not intervene in civil matters. The press openly preached the need for a decisive assault on the government, intensifying public hostility to it. This aroused groundless hopes ("amnesty!"), and blame for their nonfulfillment fell upon the government.

Krivoshein: The propagation of revolutionary sentiments is more helpful to the enemy than all the other misdemeanors of the press. What recommendations can we make to the military censors—except to use their common sense and behave patriotically? Not one of us has ever been a censor, but everybody understands what is impermissible in the destructive work of the contemporary press.

Meanwhile the tone of the State Duma had become extremely aggressive. For instance:

Kerensky: The catastrophe which is upon us can be averted only by changing the executive immediately. To those now carrying the banner, with no right to do so, we must say, "Depart! You are destroying the country! We want to save it! Let us govern the country or it will perish!"

This had a brave ring in the Duma. But what the cabinet saw was:

Krivoshein: . . . something between the Convention and the Committee of Public Safety. Under cover of patriotic alarm they are trying to introduce a sort of second government. It's an insolent assault on the government and yet another excuse to shout about the frustration of self-sacrificing public initiatives. We cannot keep backing down—if we do, there will be no limit to their demands. The Duma is getting too big for its boots, it's practically converting itself into a Constituent Assembly and trying to create a Russian legislature that ignores the executive. It's some sort of psychosis, a disorder of the senses.

Kharitonov: This is the kind of absurdity into which partisan political ambitions can lead people. All these gentlemen should be made to sit for a while around the cabinet table and see what it's like hour after hour in the ministerial frying pan. Many of them would soon find their dreams of tempting portfolios fading.

But those dreams were very stubborn. And government in Russia seemed so nearly extinct that, on 26 August, Ryabushinsky, rudely as ever, blurted out in his *Morning Russia* a proposal to set up a new government, with Rodzyanko as Prime Minister, Guchkov as Minister of the Interior, Milyukov at Foreign Affairs, Shingarev at Finance, and V. Maklakov at Justice. Of the bureaucrats only the two most acceptable to the public were retained: Polivanov as Minister of War and Krivoshein as Minister of Agriculture.

Conscious of his special position as a bureaucrat not anathematized by the public, Krivoshein undertook to look for a way out. As the Duma session was extended into August, and its members grew louder and shriller, some form of collaboration had to be sought. (As a start he obtained a vice presidency of the Duma for the amenable Prince Volkonsky.) He had in mind the example of Stolypin, who had succeeded in avoiding conflict with the Duma and controlling it, with the support of a majority, without being responsible to it. In the Fourth Duma, however, there was no majority, merely a number of distinct factions. Krivoshein was the first to think of creating a majority by welding as many of the factions as possible into a single bloc on which the Prime Minister could openly rely, ignoring the Tsar's vacillations and his zigzag changes of mood. For there were only two paths the government could follow: it could show that governmental authority still existed in Russia by introducing an iron dictatorship (but the conditions for this did not exist, given the general indiscipline, nor was there anyone in sight who could assume dictatorial power), or else it could make concessions to the public and rule in agreement with it.

Members of the Duma adopted the idea. During that August so-called progressive personalities began meeting in the Duma lobbies and in private apartments, and the required majority began to take shape under the name of the Progressive Bloc, including Kadets, Octobrists, who were supposed to be quite incompatible with them, and Nationalists. Only the extreme right and the extreme left were excluded. Milyukov, with his usual foresight and industry, kept a brief record of those secret negotiations.

Shulgin (Nationalist): Since the Kadets have become semi-patriots, we patriots have become semi-Kadets. We start with the assumption that the government is quite useless. We must bring the pressure of a bloc three hundred strong to bear on it.

A. D. **Obolensky** (centrist): On the contrary, if we do not join in solidarity with the government the Germans will defeat us.

The Bloc was created, but seemed not altogether well disposed toward a moderate government. The metaphor in vogue with members of the Bloc was:

> We and the government are fellow travelers, seated alas in the same compartment, but refusing to make each other's acquaintance.

A clever comparison. But who, if anybody, was the engine driver?

> **Krupensky** (centrist): The legislative chambers have a harmful influence on the masses with their speechifying.

> Vl. **Gurko** (rightist): You could grant the country all kinds of freedoms and still be defeated in war. We need to organize for victory.

> D. Olsufiev: But we must prepare the country even for possible defeat, so that failure will not bring in its train an internal upheaval.

The thoroughgoing Milyukov suggested drawing up a program acceptable to all of them.

> **Efremov** (leader of the Progressists, formerly left Octobrists): What do you mean, program! What we want is not a program but a change of government!

Nonetheless they began discussing a program. It was complicated. Every natural demand—class equality, the introduction of rural district zemstvos in the East, cooperatives, the indefinite extension of prohibition in Russia—looked like a long-term peacetime objective. What were the immediate nonnegotiable issues which simply could not be postponed? All the ethnic problems and above all that of the Jews.

> **Obolensky:** The Jewish question is three times as important as the rest of the program. It is essential to our credit, to the standing of Russia. The Americans are making free access of American Jews to our country a condition.

> **Krupensky:** I am a born anti-Semite, but I have come to the conclusion that we must make concessions for the good of our motherland. The Jews are a great international force, and the support of our allies depends on them.

Second in importance was the question of the amnesty, which had been over two years in coming.

> **Obolensky:** Until the government grants an amnesty we can have no trust in it.

> **Milyukov:** And remember that we must demand an amnesty for all political prisoners, including terrorists.

> **Shingarev:** The program must be an ultimatum to the government, not just good advice.

All sorts of things were smuggled into the program—most important:

> Only a government of people enjoying the trust of the country can lead our fatherland to victory.

> **Olsufiev:** In fact, we are demanding parliamentary government.

> M. Kovalevsky: We will be the winners if it gets into the press that the Bloc wanted to create a government of national defense and the Duma was then sent packing.

A "government of trust" meant one trusted by the three hundred members of the Progressive Bloc, and hence by the people as a whole. But who were these persons? That old question. Can't you see that *we* are, the Duma orators, known to everybody. Only

V. **Maklakov:** People popular in the Duma will soon cease to shine in government.

Come, come! Surely we can't manage worse than the Tsar's obtuse bureaucrats!

Gurko: Yes, everything hinges on personalities, or rather on a single personality who can take full responsibility and choose others to suit himself. We must put the right man at the rudder.

Secretly many hearts beat faster: can I be the one?

To think how readily they had rejected Witte when he offered ministerial posts to the Kadets! How quick they had been to refuse power in 1905 . . . and since then no one had renewed the offer.

Then Milyukov proposed that they draw up a list of the most suitable candidates, provoking a horrified reaction.

Vl. **Bobrinsky:** Any discussion of names will get into the press. It will be used against us! And if we single out one man it will be so much the worse: the powers that be will destroy that candidate!

A leak occurred in one of Ryabushinsky's publications. A very unwelcome disclosure. Still and all . . . they had to name a Prime Minister.

Unexpectedly, they started mentioning Krivoshein! That's how timid Russians can be—even the most prominent of them! Timid enough to choose a bureaucrat, when there were progressive public figures on hand.

Milyukov: This changes the whole political purpose of our coalition.

They lacked courage—as they might lack air climbing a mountain. It was after all a frightening step to take—from coining slogans to naming names. To say, "We are your normal rulers, not they." Guchkov was nominated, and Milyukov said, "That doesn't suit us." Perhaps, though, it really was too soon to name a Prime Minister? Goremykin, the experienced, worldly-wise, in fact rather blasé courtier with the tired eyes, fluffy mustache, and long sideburns like two beards, took his surreptitious little trips from Petrograd to Tsarkoye Selo and back, but would not enter into negotiations with the bloc. He put a cynical interpretation on the statesmanlike preoccupations of the liberals: they couldn't wait to exchange their rented apartments for ministerial accommodations at public expense, ministerial salaries, and official cars.

Goremykin dawdled through his duties completely indifferent to the post he occupied. He made no move to reach an accommodation with the Duma, he was too old to fear terrorists and too experienced to fear a ministerial revolt, and whereas he might once have feared royal anger he now felt only pity for the Tsar.

Krivoshein himself, after refusing the premiership so often, in the assurance that he could always take over from the aged Goremykin, now found to his astonishment that he could not take over. Times had changed. Goremykin had stopped being amenable and docile and was stubborn beyond all reason in his loyalty to the Tsar, especially in this accursed matter of the Supreme Command. He was a millstone around the necks of the more liberal ministers, he ruined relations with the Duma, he must be removed right now!

True, in the eyes of the Emperor, Krivoshein had remained Goremykin's agreed-upon successor, but Goremykin showed no signs of retiring.

But if we look deeper we can see that every man has limits he cannot overstep.

Now, as in the past, Krivoshein could not have brought himself to assume prime ministerial responsibility. He was, and always had been, one of nature's number twos.

Nearly all the ministers, except Goremykin and old Khvostov, held frequent secret meetings to ply their intrigue, on the banks of the Bolshaya Nevka, in the Botanical Gardens on Aptekarsky Island, or at Krivoshein's villa, since the capital was so airless in summer. In these secret conferences the fate of the government was up for decision. Who should replace Goremykin? They settled on Polivanov. Polivanov was Guchkov's man, Krivoshein could get along with him, the Duma would welcome him (he flattered it in every public statement he made), and the Emperor himself ought to be pleased with the idea of promoting the War Minister to the premiership in time of war.

Krivoshein did in fact put the idea to the Emperor, who liked it, although he was not fond of Polivanov. Krivoshein then grew even bolder and proposed that Guchkov should join the government.

The Emperor's face clouded over and he immediately withdrew into himself. He regarded Guchkov as his inveterate personal enemy.

He immediately saw the whole proposal as a conspiracy (which indeed it was).

And by reflex reaction he turned against Krivoshein, for the first time in many years. The change of the Supreme Command had begun to look like a dormant, successfully bypassed question, but suddenly it was explosively touched off by the Moscow City Duma. On 31 August, that body adopted three resolutions: to send the Grand Duke an enthusiastic telegram, to call for a "government of trust," and to demand, though in respectful terms, that the Emperor receive its own representatives. This was not the business of any City Duma, but that of Moscow was regarded as the flag-bearer of Russian educated society, its preferred spokesman and its center.

On 1 September, the Council of Ministers, fearful and helpless, was in a whirl. They interrupted and contradicted each other without listening.

> **Shcherbatov:** The Moscow Duma's request for an audience with the Emperor is unacceptable in form and substance. Discussions with the Tsar cannot be conducted behind the backs of the government and the legislative institutions. Either we have a government or we do not. Other cities will fall in behind Moscow, and the Emperor will be overwhelmed with hundreds of petitions.

> **Goremykin:** The easiest thing is not to answer all these loudmouths and to pay no attention to them once they trespass on things which are none of their business. We must support our Sovereign Emperor in these difficult times and find the answer that will make his position easier. These so-called public figures are entering upon a line of activity on which they must be firmly resisted.

> **Kharitonov:** A matter fraught with consequences. We must not forget that the Muscovites speak under the flag of loyalist feelings. Their address to the Grand Duke is a warning—and one we cannot ignore.

> **Polivanov:** I cannot consent to oversimplified solutions of matters of the greatest political importance. After the Moscow resolution the change of Supreme Commander will have a demoralizing effect and will be interpreted as an act of defiance. What is so very revolutionary in their resolution? A

government relying on the confidence of the population—that's normal in any state.

Sazonov: What has happened in Moscow convinces me that the question of the Supreme Command must at all costs be postponed.

Samarin: The mood in Moscow is a quick and vivid confirmation of what I have been saying. A change of command threatens our motherland with the gravest consequences. Nor can the mayor of Moscow be denied a hearing—that would be a gratuitous affront to the senior capital. Indeed, his reception must be particularly gracious and welcoming; they must make a big fuss over him.

Just a few days ago they had all been reconciled to the change of Supreme Commander, and busy thinking up emollient phrases for the imperial rescript, but now the Moscow Duma had revived their old objections.

Krivoshein: That agrees with what I myself hear from Moscow: feelings there are running very high, and could create a situation in which we would be unable to continue the war. We must avoid exacerbating the public's irritation. The question confronting us is much broader and more crucial. Where will we be if the whole organized public begins to demand a government invested with the confidence of the country? This sort of situation cannot long continue. We must speak frankly about this to the Emperor, who is unaware of what is going on around him and does not realize the situation in which his government and the whole state machine find themselves. We must open our sovereign's eyes to the critical nature of the present moment. And tell him that he must either react forcefully and with confidence in his own might

(he mentioned this possibility for form's sake, nobody still believed in that possibility) or openly seek to win public confidence for the regime. The golden mean infuriates everybody. There must be either military dictatorship or reconciliation with society. Our cabinet does not measure up to public expectations, and must make way for another in which the country can have confidence.

(Though he himself certainly expected to survive in the new cabinet.)

The Emperor's decision to take over the Supreme Command, which is now universally known, is disastrous. It may have the gravest consequences for Russia and for the outcome of the war. And that is a risk for the dynasty. We must ask the Emperor to summon us all together so that we can implore him to give up his intention of replacing the Grand Duke and at the same time radically revise the character of his policy on the home front. I hesitated for a long time before finally coming to this conclusion but now every day is like a year. It isn't a question of revolution, but of the population's boundless fear for the future. The dismissal of the Grand Duke is unthinkable, but all the same a complete retraction would affect the authority of the monarch. A compromise is necessary: he should make the Grand Duke his aide. We must be firm with the Emperor, we must not just ask, we must demand. Let the Tsar cut off our heads, let him banish us to remote places (that, alas, he would not do), but if he rejects our representations we must announce that we are no longer able to serve him loyally.

Shakhovskoy: We are at a turning point on which the whole future depends. While the public's aspirations are still moderate it would be dangerous to reject them outright.

Polivanov: According to rumors reaching the War Ministry, soldiers in the trenches are saying that their last protector, the only one who keeps the generals and officers in check, may be taken from them.

Ignatiev (Minister of Education): There is a ferment among student youth, ostensibly caused by sympathy for the Grand Duke. The student body may mount demonstrations and protests . . .

Samarin: And what sort of impression will it make on worshippers when the Grand Duke, mentioned by name in prayers for the Supreme Commander for a year past, ceases to be named in the liturgy? This is another detail to which the Emperor's attention must be drawn. Surely the Council of Ministers is not so impotent that it cannot get the Emperor to accept a salutary compromise?

So a wall of bold ministers was formed, and Goremykin agreed not to obstruct their last attempt, although he himself believed the Emperor's decision to be immutable. He did, however, urge them to take great care not to speak of the Grand Duke's prestige as a military leader in conversation with the Emperor.

He asked for an audience immediately, and they were summoned to Tsarskoye Selo for the evening of 2 September. The Tsar was astonished. His cabinet as turbulent as the left wing of the Duma? Had the storm waves risen so high? On any other question he would have tolerated their opposition and listened to their advice. But how dare they intrude upon his deepest and most sacred feelings, his sense of duty to the country and of oneness with his people? His imperial vocation as the instrument of Divine Providence? Why were they invading a place where only a reverent hush and the Tsar's prayers should be heard? And anyway, what did they know of military matters? Which of them had ever served in a line regiment? Or even taken part in maneuvers? Could they appreciate how insolently Nikolasha had conducted himself—as though he was Russia's lord and master? He had exploited his post in such a way that he really might attempt to usurp supreme power. And why should the appointment of a Supreme Commander be a matter not for the Tsar but for the Moscow Duma, for a lot of lawyers and journalists? Or, for that matter, ministers? And wasn't it angry public criticism of GHQ that had first prompted the Tsar to think about the change? What remained of the monarchy? For a whole year the Tsar had looked inert and impassive and everybody was unhappy about it. Now he had finally decided to show what he was made of—and everybody was unhappier still.

To command his army was his most cherished dream. He was summoned to that destiny by an inner voice, by his duty as Anointed Sovereign, whether in victory or in defeat. His conscience could not deceive him!

Nor did the Empress's voice flag in support.

> They are too accustomed to your gentle, all-forgiving goodness. They must learn to tremble before your courage and your will. I know how dearly it costs you, but to be firm is your only salvation. Your reign will be glorious when you stand firm against the general wish. Pay less attention to the advice of others. When, oh, when will you finally bang the table and cry out that

they are acting wrongly. They are not afraid of you. You must frighten them, or everybody will ride roughshod over you. If your ministers feared you, everything would go better. It maddens me that the ministers quarrel among themselves—they're supposed to be a government. You are too gentle. Things cannot go on like this. All those who love you want you to be sterner. Please, please, my little boy, make them tremble before you!

For his part, he had made up his mind irrevocably, and all those weeks of vexatious delays were caused by his ministers with their vacillations and excuses. (And he did like the wording which would in the future appear at the foot of orders: "His Majesty's GHQ.") But now he had to face another collision with them—and the Emperor, conscious of his tendency to give way, was afraid that they would dissuade him. So before going out to see them he combed his hair with a magic comb, which, so Grigori assured him, would help to stiffen his resolve. He knew too that the Empress and Anya Vyrubova would stand outside the lighted room, on the balcony, to look at him, pray, and admire him.

The Tsar found that excruciating session an extraordinary strain. Great drops of sweat stood out on his brow, as he listened to their fervent urgings and objections, some coherent, some chaotic—and still he did not give in! He held his own! With a supreme effort, summoning up all his willpower, he retorted: Yes, yes, and yes! I am taking the Supreme Command and leaving for GHQ without delay, so that discussion of this question is closed.

In any case, now that the whole country knew, how could he possibly withdraw? How could he present Nikolasha with such a triumph? (He had written saying, "I forgive you"—meaning both Nikolasha and Yanushkevich—"your sins." Plots included.)

Since he had, uncharacteristically, not given in to the chorus of ministers, he forgave them too—forgave their impertinent opposition, because he had proved more certain of himself than they had. Having triumphed over them, he looked on them complacently. (Whereas, if he had given in, he would have found defeat so intolerable an hour later that he would have felt bound to dismiss them all, to rid himself of them.) He therefore kindly agreed to their other request: on 4 September, he would graciously and solemnly open the Special Conference on Defense, dealing with military supplies, fuel, and transport. The conference would now admit Duma deputies and other members of the public to work with ministers.

The cabinet, extremely perturbed by its failure, met again on 3 September at the Elagin Palace. Sazonov and Polivanov were provoked beyond endurance. The tone they now took was what you would expect from the Duma opposition rather than from members of the government. Krivoshein absented himself, preferring not to waste any more time there. The oppositionist ministers had met secretly on the eve of the Tsarskoye Selo session, and were to have met secretly again on 3 September, but now, in Goremykin's presence, with their minds on two things at once, they found themselves letting out some of their secrets. Still, this meeting too was supposed to be secret.

They saw that although they had spent the whole of the previous evening reasoning with the Emperor, nothing had been decided about the future course of internal policy. Was it to be dictatorship or concessions to the public? And what reply should they give to the Moscow Duma?

Goremykin proposed a message of gratitude for the loyal sentiments expressed. Others objected that this would sound ironical, seeing that the Moscow telegram was written in the blood of people suffering agonies of anxiety for their homeland. The best thing would be to carry out all the wishes of the Moscow Duma. (What? And reopen the question of the Grand Duke?)

> Shcherbatov: And what if hundreds of similar telegrams pour in from towns everywhere? We cannot declare them revolutionary. The answer to Moscow will determine the course of internal policy.

> Polivanov: Russia must be able to see in that reply what awaits her in the near future.

> Grigorovich: In such a critical situation we can't play hide-and-seek. We have been marking time for a whole month now.

The Emperor had declared the day before that he had confidence in the Grand Duke. But . . .

> Sazonov: What person could reconcile "confidence in the Grand Duke" with his relegation to the Caucasus. People will start saying that we have a Tsar who does not keep his word.

So no final decision had yet been taken about the Grand Duke either?

> Grigorovich: It is our duty to make one final attempt. We must make a written submission to His Imperial Majesty on the dangers to the dynasty, and urge him as loyal subjects not to take an irrevocable step, not to touch the Grand Duke!

> Goremykin: The Sovereign Emperor said quite definitely yesterday that he would leave for Mogilev in a matter of days and make known his will there. What submissions can we possibly make? It is unthinkable for the Council of Ministers to trouble the Tsar at this historic hour in his life, and to trouble an infinitely harassed man to no purpose.

> Sazonov: Our duty at this critical moment is to tell the Tsar frankly that in the circumstances which have arisen we are unable to govern the country, powerless to serve with a good conscience.

Goremykin had begun to realize that the ministers had reached an agreement behind his back:

> Putting it simply, you want to present the Tsar with an ultimatum?

> Sazonov: Only loyal entreaties are open to us. Let us not quarrel about words. It's not a question of ultimatums but of making one last attempt to point out the full extent of the risk to Russia, and warn him of the deadly danger.

> Shcherbatov: A government which has the confidence neither of the Emperor, nor of the army, nor of the cities, nor of the zemstvos, nor of the merchants, nor of the workers cannot exist for long. We have pleaded with him orally, let us try one last plea in writing. If the Emperor and the army and the people are not willing to respect our opinions it is our duty to go.

> Shakhovskoy: In drafting our submission we must avoid the slightest sug-

gestion of what might be thought of as a ministerial *strike*. The Emperor came out with that word yesterday.

Ignatiev: We must avert the reproach that we kept silent at a moment of the greatest danger to Russia.

Samarin: Russia's whole future is in question, and we are participants in a great tragedy. In the voice of the country at large we can hear a healthy and justified sentiment inspired by anxiety for the motherland.

Goremykin: This exaggerated belief in the Grand Duke, and all this shouting of his name, is nothing but a political assault on the Tsar. What they're after is limitation of the monarch's powers. Leftist politicians want to create difficulties for the monarchy, and are exploiting Russia's present misfortune to that end.

Sazonov: We categorically reject any such interpretation of society's initiatives. They are not the result of intrigue, they are an outcry in self-defense. We ourselves should add our voices to that cry.

Goremykin: I earnestly beg you all to inform the Emperor of my unfitness for my post and the need to replace me. I shall be grateful from the bottom of my heart for that service. I will bow low to the man who replaces me. But I shall not myself tender my resignation. I shall stand by the Tsar until he finds it necessary to dismiss me.

Not one of them had expected such outspoken obstinacy from that tediously circumspect old man. But there was nothing personal in the quarrel; it became more and more an argument about different conceptions of the monarchy in its hour of difficulty. Sazonov, who was more to blame for the origins of this war than anyone else present, said:

When the motherland is in danger a chivalrous attitude toward the monarch is admirable, but it can also do harm in an infinitely broader context. We want to warn the Tsar against a fatal step, while you would lead yourself and Russia to destruction. Our patriotic duty does not permit us to assist you. Find yourselves other collaborators. For our part, we must explain to the Tsar that only a conciliatory policy toward society can save the situation.

Goremykin: My conscience tells me that the Sovereign Emperor is God's Anointed. He personifies Russia. He is forty-seven years old, and has been responsible for Russia's fortunes for many a long day. When the will of such a man has been made manifest, loyal subjects must submit to it, whatever the consequences. It is too late for me, on the brink of the grave, to change my convictions. I cannot retreat from my own conception of service to the Tsar.

Shcherbatov: Both Samarin and I are former provincial marshals of the gentry. Nobody has ever yet regarded us as leftists. But neither of us can understand a juncture in the affairs of the state at which the monarch and his government have views radically at odds with those of all reasonable members of society. (There is no need to talk about revolutionary intrigues.) It is our duty to tell the Emperor that in order to save the state from the greatest disaster he must move either to the right or to the left. The situation does not allow him to sit on the fence.

The ministers talked of resolute action in one direction or another, but what they in fact resolved on was concessions.

Sazonov: The Emperor is not the Lord God. He can make mistakes.

Goremykin: Even if the Tsar should be mistaken, I cannot desert him at a moment of danger. I cannot ask to be released at a moment when all must close ranks around the throne and defend the Emperor. This whole matter of the Supreme Command has been deliberately blown out of proportion. For the Emperor to back down from his decision now would be fraught with much graver consequences.

Samarin: I too love my Tsar, I am deeply devoted to the monarchy and I have proved that by my whole career. But if the Tsar moves to harm Russia I cannot humbly follow along behind him.

Kharitonov: If the Tsar's will threatens Russia with serious upheavals we must refuse to carry out his will and resign. We serve not just the Tsar but Russia also.

Goremykin: In my way of looking at it those concepts are inseparable.

Kharitonov: Unlike you, we consider that subordination must be open-eyed. We cannot join in something which we see to be the beginning of our motherland's destruction.

Sazonov: It would be difficult, given the way people feel today, to prove that the will of Russia and that of the Tsar coincide. It's just the opposite.

Samarin: The Tsar of Russia needs servants with minds of their own, not people who slavishly carry out orders. The Tsar can send us to the gallows, but we are still obliged to tell him the truth. We should respond to society's spontaneous gesture with a show of goodwill.

Goremykin: No Russian can abandon his Tsar at the parting of the ways. That is what I think and I shall die in the same persuasion.

Only one member of the government, the Minister of Justice, supported the Prime Minister. Old Khvostov was

not convinced by an analysis of the situation according to which we are dealing with a disinterested patriotic movement. All sorts of dubious characters adopt its coloring and exploit it to achieve partisan objectives. The fiercest patriots and enthusiasts for oppositionist demands have appealed to the Moscow workers for support, but have been disappointed: the answer from the factories was that they would work on to final victory. Appeals of that kind are not a patriotic act but one punishable under the law. Demands for change in the state system are made not because such changes are necessary for victory, but because military setbacks have weakened the position of the regime, so that pressure can be put upon it, a knife held to its throat. In my view, a policy of concessions is always wrong, and in wartime is unthinkable. Nowhere in the world has such a policy led to anything good, it has always drawn the country down the slippery slope. The slogans emanating from Guchkov, the left-wing parties in the Duma, and Konovalov's Congress are intended to bring about a coup d'état. That would result in the destruction of the fatherland.

Sazonov: You have no faith even in the State Duma! And for their part

they have no faith in us. We, however, are of the opinion that the way out
lies in conciliation, in the creation of a cabinet which . . .

So then the debate returned over and over again to the main question. What mattered was not the Grand Duke, but a ministry in which the public could have confidence. The Duma did not want the existing government—and the ministers
themselves did not want to be where they were. They raged out of control, without
fully understanding what they were about.

> Goremykin: Concessions will get you nowhere. All parties favoring a coup
> exploit our military setbacks to intensify their pressure on the regime so as
> to limit the monarchic power.

That very evening there was a gathering in Sazonov's office, on Palace Square, by
the Pevchesky Bridge, of eight ministers. (It would have been ten, except that military
protocol made it impossible for the War Minister and Navy Minister to take part. Not
counting Frederiks, there were thirteen ministers in the cabinet.) The eight signed a
collective letter to the Emperor, giving notice of their resignation en masse because
of policy differences. It was, in effect, an ultimatum—something unprecedented in
the history of imperial Russia. (But they assumed that the Emperor could not part
with eight ministers at once.) The author of this move was Samarin, and he too drafted
the original text, which was then finalized by Krivoshein and Kharitonov and copied
out in his elegant handwriting by Bark. It was passed to the Emperor via an aide-de-
camp.

> Do not hold our bold and frank appeal against us. Yesterday we laid before
> you our unanimous request that Grand Duke Nikolai Nikolaevich should not
> be removed. But we fear that Your Majesty was not pleased to accede to our
> plea, which we venture to think was also that of all loyal Russia . . . It is
> becoming impossible for us to feel that our service can be of any use to you
> and to our motherland.

The following day, on 4 September, the official opening of the Special Conference
on Defense took place, following the procedure previously agreed on, and all the
ministers had to attend and dazzle with their decorations. The objective was the
official involvement of the legislative organs and the commercial and industrial class
in matters affecting the conduct of the war. The Emperor delivered a speech written
for him by Polivanov and Krivoshein, then graciously moved among the company.
(The Empress and the Crown Prince also appeared. The little boy, looking sickly even
in his soldier's tunic, was a depressing sight.) There were fears that the crazy Rodzyanko would produce one of his embarrassing homilies, but all went well. Both sides
glowed with satisfaction. The ministers watched the Emperor anxiously, surprised to
find that his manner toward them was unchanged. (It was just that he had not yet
received their ultimatum.)

The country was convulsed by what might be its death throes, but the ceremony
in the Winter Palace was peaceful, dignified, and cordial.

That same evening, the Tsar left for Mogilev, to take over from the Grand Duke,
abandoning his ministers to uncertainty about the fate of their ultimatum.

> I have today taken upon myself the command of all land and sea forces
> within the theater of military operations.

And that very day another important event was announced—the formation of the Progressive Bloc.

But the more resolute the ministers became in their dealings with the sovereign, the more dependent they were on a rapprochement with the Duma. They forgot all about Shakhovskoy's advice—to lay before the Duma a loaded bill which would cause dissension among the diverse parties in the Bloc. Instead, Krivoshein's group sought support for the government from the Bloc, and tried to reach an agreement on a joint plan of action. The Duma's slogans pierced the government's protective cover and lodged in the hearts of ministers seductive slogans like "union with society" (didn't the ministers consider themselves part of "society"?), "union with the people" . . . and they themselves, of course, might be invited to join such a government; they would no longer have to sit in conference with Goremykin's intransigent coonskin coat, but would lead Russia secure in the full powers bestowed by the people. The Bloc, however, did not represent the arithmetical average of the parties united in it, it moved further left, became more hostile to the government, and did not conceal the fact that it was interested above all in a change of personnel, not a program: removing Goremykin first of all, then squeezing out others. The leaders of the Bloc were in session with other progressive figures daily.

> **Chelnokov:** The conditions put forward by the Bloc must not take the form of an ultimatum. The Bloc too can make concessions. Society can still influence the government by means of a campaign of demonstrations.

> **Konovalov:** Negotiations with the government are futile. The lower orders are near to despair.

(As a factory owner I should know.)

> **Prince G. Lvov:** The government is driving society to despair. We must save it from anarchy.

(People had already noticed that the prince was in training for the premiership himself.)

> **Ryabushinsky:** No work can be done under the present government. At present they're holding their hands out to England for another loan. As soon as they get it, they'll dissolve the Duma.

> **Efremov:** If they dissolve the Duma, it must refuse to break up! It must appeal to the people!!

> **Milyukov:** They haven't a hope of dismissing the Duma.

Deputies just back from visits to the armed forces cried out, "Never! If they so much as touch the Duma, the whole army will hear alarm bells!"

While the rightists, who always went against the people, clamored in the Duma, "You've sat here long enough! There's work to be done on the land! And at the front!" With that they walked out of the session and dispersed without waiting for permission.

The government was already wondering what to do with the Duma. For all their differences the ministers were inclined to think that the most convenient thing would be to dismiss it, let it take a vacation.

> **Krivoshein:** For all practical purposes the Duma has exhausted its agenda, and the atmosphere there is becoming worrying. Speeches and resolutions may take on an openly revolutionary character. People get carried away by

their own verbosity, and there is no end to it. Sessions with no legislative business turn the Duma into a mass meeting on current questions.

Goremykin:In the West at present parliaments do not meet as a whole, only parliamentary commissions—but we have commissions at work too.

It would have been hopeless to try putting laws and measures made necessary by the war through the Duma, and while it was in session, under Article 87 they could not be introduced behind its back.

Shcherbatov: No, not all the bills have yet been dealt with. We need the Duma's sanction for a Special Conference on Refugees. The presence of elected representatives in it is essential, so as to relieve the government of sole responsibility for the horrors of the refugee problem, and let the State Duma share it.

Krivoshein: I think they'll let it through without delay. The need is only too obvious.

Kharitonov: The Duma has taught us not to be optimistic. It is governed by party considerations, not by what is in the general interest. If they find that dissolution is postponed only because of the refugees they will drag out discussion of the bill.

Goremykin: Whatever happens they'll shift all the responsibility onto the government. The Special Conference on Defense contains elected members, but we and we alone get blamed for supply failures.

Krivoshein: There must be a recess until 14 September. In the present situation we must bid our farewells to the Duma with due decorum—it must be done in agreement with the Presidium, not come like a bolt from the blue.

Kharitonov: Rodzyanko will be up on his hind legs claiming that Russia's salvation lies only in the Duma.

Goremykin: Once we talk to Rodzyanko that bigmouth will be shouting it out for all the world to hear.

Ignatiev: We can't discount the possibility that the Duma will refuse to obey and will remain in session.

Shcherbatov: Hardly. The great majority of them are cowards who tremble for their hides.

Squall followed squall in that horrible summer of 1915. Before they had recovered from their fears of an explosion of popular indignation at the change of command, they had to worry about an explosive reaction to the dissolution of the Duma. Goremykin had in hand decrees signed in advance by the Emperor (because he was leaving for GHQ) suspending the work of the legislative institutions, and it had been left to him to write in the date. But what date? And should he?

Khvostov: Mr. Milyukov, so I am told, openly boasts that he has all the strings in his hands, and that on the day when the Supreme Command is changed he has only to press a button to start disturbances throughout Russia.

Goremykin: I have too much faith in the Russian people to entertain the thought that it will respond to its Tsar with disturbances, especially in wartime. It is only in minds already unbalanced that the speeches of left-wing deputies and abuse of the printed word sow discord.

Shcherbatov: An intensive propaganda campaign is being carried out in garrisons and military hospitals in the rear.

Sazonov: The dissolution of the Duma will certainly entail disturbances among the workers. We cannot simply ignore the politically active elements of the public.

Grigorovich: Disturbances are unavoidable, the mood of the workers is very ugly. The Germans are carrying out an intensive propaganda campaign, and showering money on organizations hostile to the government. The situation at the Putilov plant is particularly critical: the workers are standing at their benches doing nothing and demanding a twenty percent raise in pay. I am very much afraid that interrupting the sessions of the Duma will have a damaging effect on the internal situation in Russia.

Polivanov: Preparations for defense depend entirely on the educated public and the workers. If both groups are reduced to despair . . .

Goremykin: It is a mistake to look for a connection between the dissolution of the Duma and the workers' movement. That will go on as before. I don't deny that dissolution will be exploited by agitators. But even if the Duma stays on, we have no surety. Whether we act with the Bloc or without it makes no difference to the workers' movement.

Krivoshein: If we are afraid of everything all will be lost. I repeat: we cannot continue down the middle of the road any longer.

In Krivoshein a predilection for strong government, for decisive action, struggled to prevail. He was prepared to take strong action. But perhaps . . . not quite prepared. So now, when Goremykin's days were numbered, when no candidate could reasonably be preferred to Krivoshein, when talks with the Duma on the Bloc's program were imminent, he felt impelled to leave the stage, not to tie his hands with negotiations or with the program, but to avoid the more important discussions and make contact with the core of the Moscow opposition. At that critical time he went to visit his merchant relatives and friends in Moscow.

Meanwhile, on 7 September the Progressive Bloc published its program and submitted it to the government. The situation was becoming more complicated all the time.

Sazonov: Would it pay us to dissolve the Duma without discussing the acceptability of this program with the majority? I'm sure we could reach an agreement, and then dissolve it. They would go off home in the knowledge that the government was ready to meet their justified requests. The Bloc is essentially moderate, and we should support it. If it collapses, another much further to the left will appear. It would be dangerous to provoke nonparliamentary forms of struggle. These are people who feel for their motherland— how can anybody call them a lawless rabble? The government cannot remain suspended in the void with nothing but the police to support it.

Was there ever such a terrible summer? Every question they touched doubled, trebled, multiplied endlessly, and truth was elusive.

Goremykin: In my view the government cannot think of talking to the Bloc. We can only deal with the legislative institutions as such, and not with a random association of their representatives. The Bloc has been formed to seize power. Its barely concealed aim is the limitation of the monarchy. It will in any case collapse, and its participants will soon be at sixes and sevens.

Shakhovskoy: The dissolution of the Duma and its prolongation are equally dangerous. My vote is for dissolution, but it must be done in a friendly way, we must discuss their program with representatives of the Bloc. In that way we shall offer a way out to the deputies themselves, who long for dissolution, because they realize the hopelessness of their position.

Shcherbatov: The whole country is exasperated by our differences with the Duma. But we must find a way of dissolving it that will not provoke an outcry. There is no denying it, the program of the Bloc is patently drafted as a basis for bargaining. The collapse of the Bloc would be of no advantage to the government, but would leave it face to face with leftist trends. We cannot allow the more reasonable part of the Duma to disperse feeling snubbed. Rodzyanko is more peeved than any of them, because the government doesn't take him seriously.

Sazonov: The majority in the Duma think dissolution is necessary and will not try to prevent suspension.

They arrived at the conclusion that some of the ministers should engage in talks, unofficial for the time being, with some of the leaders of the Bloc. Just to demonstrate that the government did not refuse even to recognize the forces of society.

Analysis of the Bloc's program led to a surprising conclusion: apart from demagogic spluttering about a "government enjoying the people's confidence" it was quite timid. Some of its demands were already being carried out, some were not of cardinal importance, and on others the Bloc did not particularly insist but was ready to compromise. They demanded a political amnesty, but it was easy to read between the lines— what they really wanted was a pardon for those who had joined in the Vyborg appeal, so that they could stand for election. The government had no objection to that.

Khvostov: Many political cases have been settled by a royal pardon, and quite a few such gentlemen are now at large.

But, privately, leading parliamentarians chided the government because it was forever releasing one political prisoner or another but was incapable of advertising the fact widely and making political capital of it—which would also be of advantage to Duma deputies.

Shcherbatov: We must arrange publicity whenever we do it. Pick a dozen or two of the best-loved liberators, turn them all loose on the world, and see that it is reported in all the papers.

It was the same with the cleanup of local government and the reform of administrative procedures—the government lacked advertising skills.

The Bloc's renewed insistence on the need for religious tolerance was largely decorative—tolerance was already becoming the rule.

Goremykin: But what would you have us do when people use religious immunity as a cloak for the attainment of political aims?

On the Polish question a great deal had already been done, and the Bloc had no very clearly defined additional measures to recommend. It cost nothing to grant certain privileges to the Ukrainian press (though not, of course, to the separatist papers nurtured by the Austrians). On the Jewish question the Bloc's program was itself full of tortuous evasions. It spoke of "moving toward repeal of legal disabilities"—but the Pale of Settlement had just been breached, and all the cities were open to Jews, who were not even asking to be allowed into rural areas, while restrictions on entry into higher educational institutions and the professions were being lifted all the time. Develop the Jewish press? Certainly. Let them spend money on organs of their own, and not on perverting the Russian papers. "Goodwill in policy toward Finland" caused no argument. How could the government possibly show more goodwill? Finland did not contribute to the financing of the war; speculation had driven the Finnish markka to dizzy heights against the ruble and at the expense of Russia proper. The Finnish population was exempt from the call-up and from compulsory services to the state. Persecution of workers' mutual aid societies? It didn't happen unless they served as a cover for underground activity.

> Sazonov: If we make it all look respectable and give them a loophole the Kadets will be the first to want an agreement. Milyukov is an out-and-out bourgeois and fears nothing so much as social revolution. In fact, most of the Kadets tremble for their capital.

> Samarin: The word "agreement" cannot properly be used with reference to such a motley crew, most of whom are moved by dastardly ambitions to seize power at all costs.

So then on 9 September four ministers met the leaders of the Bloc in Kharitonov's apartment for an exchange of information.

What the meeting showed was something that the ministers had foreseen: it was not the detailed points in the program that separated them from the Bloc (in any case, the Bloc was prepared to compromise on them), but the diffuse preamble:

> ... a government relying on the confidence of the people ... creation of a government of persons enjoying the confidence of the country ...

(The whole country—just like that.)

Who were those people? Where were they?

The leaders of the Bloc meant, of course, themselves: that was the whole purpose of the program—to hint at who would constitute the next government. The existing situation seemed to them a very convenient one for such an initiative. They had anticipated a chance to bargain with the government, but not apparently the dissolution of the Duma.

> Goremykin: There is no point in the government tagging along behind the Bloc. The present situation, external and internal, calls for action, otherwise everything will collapse. Whether the Duma disperses quietly or rowdily is a matter of indifference. But I am sure that it will pass without trouble, and that the fears expressed are exaggerated.

> Sazonov: There could be serious conflicts with grave consequences for the country.

> Goremykin: It doesn't matter, it's all nonsense. Nobody except the newspapers cares about the Duma, and everybody is sick of its babbling.

> Sazonov: I insist emphatically that my question *does matter*, and is not

nonsense. As long as I remain in the Council of Ministers I shall go on repeating that the attitude of the deputies does influence the psychology of the public.

  Polivanov and **Ignatiev:** What finally matters is the manner in which, and the conditions under which, the Duma is dissolved—whether it goes off smoothly or in a hostile atmosphere.

  Shcherbatov: Of late the Duma's stock in the country at large has fallen greatly. But the population now also has a fixed belief that the government is standing aside and is unwilling to act.

Goremykin conducted this cabinet meeting on 10 September believing, as before, that they were discussing only whether to dismiss the Duma, and if so the date and the formalities, yet he could still get no clear agreement from the ministers. At this juncture, Krivoshein, back from Moscow, and until then inscrutably silent, joined in. It was remembered that four days earlier, before his departure, he had been in favor of dissolving the Duma before 14 September, and asked only for a shared and uncompromising resolve on the part of the government. But since then he had taken his trip to oppositionist Moscow, where he had picked up different ideas and undergone some sort of change, although he tried to make it look as though he was saying what he had said before. His intervention now gave a new twist to the whole discussion.

  Krivoshein: Another question occurs to me. What sort of announcement can the government possibly make on the dissolution of the Duma? Whatever we say, whatever promises we make, however much we flirt with the Progressive Bloc—nobody will believe us for a minute. The requirements of the Duma and of the whole country come down to the same thing: not a particular program of action, but people to whom power can be entrusted.

They should, he went on, not choose a date for dissolution, but ask His Imperial Majesty what in principle was his attitude toward

  the government as at present constituted and toward the country's demand for an executive invested with the confidence of the public.

He was planting a bomb under that stale and ineffectual government. He spoke in the phraseology of the Bloc, like a representative of "society," not of the cabinet—so greatly had his Moscow trip boosted his self-assurance.

  Let the monarch decide what course he wishes internal policy to follow in the future—that of ignoring such requests

(they had been called demands a while before)

  or that of conciliation, in which case he should choose someone who enjoys the goodwill of the public and lay on him the responsibility of forming a government.

In other words, he was calling for the dismissal of Goremykin and had finally decided to make a bid for the premiership himself!

  The imperturbable Goremykin understood all this, but went on as though nothing had happened, trying to steer the government to a decision on the date of dissolution. Krivoshein, however, was unwilling to talk about dates at all, and a succession of ministers showed that they were either in league with him or of one mind with him. In short, the "ministerial strike" was not called off.

Sazonov: I entirely concur. This crystallizes what we've been hemming and hawing about for several days. We must bring it to His Majesty's attention.

Ignatiev: I support that.

Kharitonov: I agree completely.

Goremykin (reluctant to yield): So the question of dissolution is to be postponed until ministerial portfolios are redistributed? And until the monarch's prerogative to choose his own ministers is curtailed?

Krivoshein (following up his advantage): I'm prepared to let the dissolution and the changes of government take place simultaneously.

Yes, but seven days had now gone by since they had decided on collective resignation—and the Emperor was still silent. It was very doubtful whether the Emperor was leaving the ministers in place to show his favor. Now a unique opportunity had presented itself—to take control of the government, assisted by the dismissal of the Duma.

Shcherbatov: It is indeed time for us to stop sitting on the fence. Discontent in the country is growing with menacing rapidity. New people must be brought in. It is our duty to ask the Emperor to end the uncertainty. The whole country desires a change of government, and I side with it.

But the intransigent monarchist stuck to his guns.

Goremykin: So instead of making up our own minds we leave it to the Emperor?

Yes! said Shcherbatov and Shakhovskoy, while Krivoshein enlarged on the subject as follows:

We long-term servants of the Tsar take upon ourselves the unpleasant duty of dissolving the Duma, and at the same time declare to the Sovereign Emperor that the position in which the country finds itself demands a change of cabinet and policy.

Goremykin: But who are these new people? Representatives of groups in the Duma or government officials? Do you contemplate submitting names to the Emperor at the same time?

Krivoshein: I personally do not intend to make suggestions. Let the Tsar invite some particular person and leave it to him to select his collaborators.

(This had never been done in Russia before. The Emperor had always appointed all ministers himself.)

Goremykin: You mean deliver an ultimatum to the Tsar? That the Council of Ministers resigns and a new government is found that suits the requirements of the Progressive Bloc? Foisting on the Tsar persons uncongenial to him I consider an impossibility. My views are archaic, but it is too late for me to change them.

Samarin was a late arrival. And although a week earlier he had been mainly responsible for the idea of collective resignation, he now exhibited his independence.

I would have difficulty in putting my name to any reference to the wishes of the whole country, since no survey has been made and nobody knows what people are really hoping for. It cannot be assumed that the State Duma expresses the opinion of all Russia, for its uncompromising demands stem from party interests and calculations. If a change of government is our personal demand we have no right to shift the burden of choice onto the Tsar and so aggravate his difficult position. We must present His Majesty with the basis of a program and at the same time report that the Council of Ministers is not united and that we therefore appeal to him to form another government in place of ourselves. It will be our duty to indicate an acceptable person, for generalities about public confidence mean nothing and are merely a propaganda device. If the Emperor rejects our collective appeal, each of us will have to obey the dictates of his sense of duty as a loyal subject of his Tsar and servant of Russia.

The fog had thickened and Goremykin could no longer simply add the missing date to the draft decree dissolving the Duma. Now that the Emperor was no longer nearby he naturally went out to Tsarskoye Selo to seek reassurance and instructions from the Empress. Expressions of approval flowed first from her to her spouse in Mogilev.

By this act you have saved Russia and the throne. You have fulfilled your duty. Here begins the triumph of your reign. (Our Friend has said so!) I have never seen such firmness in you before. You have had to win a battle single-handed against them all. You have conducted yourself with the ministers like a real Tsar, and I am proud of you. Oh, my darling, do you now feel your own strength and wisdom, feel that you are master, and can refuse to let others dominate you? You have shown that you are the autocrat without whom Russia cannot exist. Now order Nikolasha not to dally on the way but to go south quickly. All sorts of bad elements congregate around him and try to use him as a banner.

She goes on to mention new causes of anxiety.

They [the Duma] cannot stomach your firmness—so carry on in the same vein! Now that you have asserted yourself it is easy to continue, show how energetic you can be, use your broom! The Duma has given you more trouble than joy. They ought now to be at work in the places they come from—but here they are, trying to interfere and to talk about things that do not concern them. Nothing but evil can come from them, they talk too much. The wretches try to play a big role, and to interfere in matters they should not venture to touch. Close the Duma quickly, before they get their interpellations in. (They don't dare mention our Friend.) It should have been closed down two weeks ago.

Things proved little better in the Council of Ministers.

If you give way to them just once they will become even worse. Several ministers ought to be turned out, and Goremykin left in place. He is a dear old man. One can talk to him quite frankly, it's simply a pleasure, he sees everything so clearly. And he is frank with our Friend. I long to see the ministers united. Goremykin and I are thinking about it. I try to keep up his energy. Oh, how they all need to feel an iron hand and iron will! So far yours has been a reign of gentleness, but now they must bow before your wisdom and your firmness. Forgive me, my angel, for pestering you so much. It's because others won't tell you anything that I express my opinion so frankly. I am so touched, dearest, that you want my help. I am always ready to do anything for you, but I have never liked interfering without being asked. May Almighty God help me to be a helper worthy of you. Tell the ministers to ask permission to present themselves to me singly and I will earnestly pray and make every effort to be really useful to you. I will hear what they have to say and pass it on to you. I have donned invisible immortal trousers, and long to show them to those cowards. We must give them all a shaking and show them how to think and act.

So it had taken only a few days for the Emperor's absence to be felt in the capital. Goremykin's visits to the Empress became known and were mentioned in the press. And Goremykin transported his old bones to Mogilev to receive the Emperor's decision on the Duma and report on the latest ministerial mutiny.

This old man, the laughingstock of Russia's educated society, still had all the courage and steadiness of vision which his ministers and the Duma leaders lacked in the prime of life. He saw with undimmed eyes that the ministers' hullabaloo was artificial, but that they were losing all self-control. He said as he left for GHQ:

It troubles me to have to upset the Emperor by telling him that the Council of Ministers is losing its nerve. My job is to divert attacks and discontent from the Tsar to myself. Let them blame and revile me—I am an old man and have not long to live. But as long as I am alive I shall fight for the inviolability of the monarchy. Russia's strength depends entirely on the monarchy. Without it we would be in such a mess that all would be lost. We must finish the war first, not preoccupy ourselves with reforms. When all around you see faith failing and spirits flagging you would a thousand times sooner go off to the trenches and perish there.

In Mogilev he told the Emperor about all the dissension in the government and offered his resignation as a solution. The Emperor's orders were that the Council of Ministers should stay as it was and the Duma should be sent on vacation immediately. The Emperor refused to call a Council of War with ministerial participation. He did, however, promise to talk to the ministers when the crisis at the front was over.

Goremykin got back from GHQ on 14 September. At the cabinet meeting on 15 September ministers were more edgy than ever before, and Sazonov was almost hysterical. Polivanov, if we can believe the secretary, raved uncontrollably and was fit to be tied. His treatment of Goremykin was quite improper. Krivoshein was sad and hopeless. (He had finally brought himself to act straightforwardly—and events had defeated his efforts.) The discussion jumped around erratically, lost itself, returned to where it had started . . .

Polivanov: Everybody expects the dissolution of the Duma to have serious consequences, including a general strike.

Goremykin: That's just scaremongering, nothing will happen.

Sazonov: It's said that some members of the Duma, together with the Congresses of the Unions of Zemstvos and Towns, mean to declare themselves a Constituent Assembly. Everything is in ferment, it's getting desperate, and in the middle of this dangerous situation comes the dissolution of the Duma. Where are they taking us, where are they taking Russia? It is clear to every Russian that the consequences will be terrible, that the very existence of the state is at stake. What has prompted His Majesty to give such a harsh order?

Goremykin: The definitively expressed will of the monarch is not a subject for discussion by the Council of Ministers.

But the situation was indeed dismaying. The recently initiated Special Conferences claimed the right to control the whole military supply system through the nongovernmental agencies, and even to send a representative of Zemgor, rather than a government agent, to make purchases with state funds in America.

Shcherbatov: The Unions of Zemstvos and Towns are a colossal mistake on the part of the government. It should not have allowed such organizations without a charter defining their competence. Their structure and membership are not regulated by law, or known to the government. They are really a rallying point for people evading service at the front, opposition elements, and gentlemen with a political past. These Unions have expanded their powers and their activities by usurpation.

Krivoshein: Prince Lvov has become de facto president of a sort of parallel government—he is the saviour of the situation, he supplies the army, feeds the hungry, heals the sick, organizes barbershops for soldiers—he's a sort of ubiquitous department store. But who are his intimates, his collaborators, his agents? That nobody knows. No one checks on his activities, although he is showered with hundreds of millions in state money.

Could these two dubious Unions be thinking of joining forces in a Constituent Assembly? They were, at this very time, loudly and threateningly, in congress in Moscow.

Shcherbatov: Moscow is in turmoil, everybody is exasperated, violently anti-government, looking for salvation only in radical changes. The cream of the opposition intelligentsia has gathered there and is demanding power.

And since these Congresses represented themselves as legitimate private institutions, the law could not even send government officials as observers. Their sessions should, therefore, have been closed to the public, but there was no way of ensuring this.

Goremykin: In Moscow emergency regulations are in force, so you can send the police to any meeting. If people let their tongues run away with them a meeting can be terminated. If it clearly presents a threat to public order. The duty of a government is to prevent ugly happenings, not to win prizes for scrupulousness.

Shcherbatov: But what would be your instructions for me as Minister of the Interior when I am not fully in control in Moscow because the military give all the orders? Disturbances may occur at any minute, and the authorities in Moscow have hardly any forces at their disposal—one reserve battalion, eight hundred strong, half of them on guard duty, a company of Cossacks, and two militia units on the outskirts. And none of these are reliable—using them against the crowd wouldn't be easy. In the surrounding countryside there are no troops at all. The city and district police both fall short of requirements. Then again, there are 30,000 hospitalized soldiers in

Moscow—an unruly mob, impossible to discipline, brawling in the streets, and fighting with the police to rescue anybody arrested. If there are disturbances this whole horde will side with the rioters.

How defenseless the Russian state was! It was there for them to see—but they could not understand.

Sazonov: And the Congress of the two Unions will take place just as the dissolution of the Duma sets the scene. I expect the worst.

Shcherbatov: It's said that in the event of dissolution some deputies intend to go to Moscow and organize a second Vyborg. If they hole up in private premises and draft a new appeal to the public what can the government do?

Krivoshein: And just remember who is now running GHQ, who is our Supreme Commander! It's terrible to think what the inevitable conclusions must be. It's a disastrous time. And you, Ivan Longinovich, what do you think you should do when members of the executive are convinced of the need for different measures and the whole machinery of government in your hands is opposed to you?

Goremykin: I shall do my duty to the Sovereign Emperor to the end, however much opposition and disapproval I encounter.

Sazonov: Tomorrow the streets will be running with blood! And Russia will plunge into the abyss!

Goremykin: Tomorrow the Duma will be dissolved, and no blood will flow anywhere.

Sazonov: I will have no part in a deed in which I see the beginning of my country's ruin.

Goremykin closed the session. Sazonov loudly called him insane (in French).

To speed up its victory the Progressive Bloc went over the heads of the virtually nonexistent government and addressed a memorandum directly to the Tsar, calling on him to set up a "government of trust" immediately and to define future policy precisely (and, needless to say, to the advantage of "society"). All this they thought perfectly possible in the existing situation. There was unrest among Moscow workers, and in Petrograd a strike at the Putilov plant brought out the metalworkers in sympathy. (The strikers were copiously subsidized throughout from some secret source.) The workers opposed the dissolution of the Duma and called for the return of the Bolshevik deputies from Siberia.

Meanwhile (although the front had now stabilized) the exodus from regions near the battle zones continued. People fled, with their livestock and all their possessions, "spontaneously" (with Cossack whips at their backs), threatening the inner provinces with impossible congestion. The reorganized GHQ confirmed that even Kiev must prepare for surrender, and a multitude of military authorities took uncoordinated and contradictory steps, spreading panic and confusion through the city. Polivanov sarcastically observed that "the need to abandon Kiev to the mercy of fate has now been confirmed by His Imperial Majesty the Supreme Commander."

Goremykin was uncertain what to do with the sacred relics in Kiev. The Emperor said that they should not be removed, the Germans would not touch them. But Samarin announced that the Holy Synod had already given its ruling and that removal had begun.

The decree suspending the work of the Duma was published on 16 September, with no sign of the threatened "shock to the whole army."

The ringleaders of the Bloc were kept informed of the cabinet's secrets by Polivanov and other ministers, and the executive body of the Bloc met in a private apartment the night before the decree was promulgated. They strove to come up with an answer to this fresh act of imperial impudence.

> **Efremov:** If we reconcile ourselves to dissolution all our words will have been wasted. We must start the fight by making all members of the Bloc withdraw from the Special Conferences.
>
> **V. Maklakov** (imperturbable and precise as ever): Participation in the Conferences is not a show of confidence in the government but work for Russia. Should the Unions also stop work—and let Russia perish? If the whole country went on strike the regime might give way, but that is not the kind of victory I would want. Our best reaction to dismissal is to say nothing.
>
> **Kovalevsky:** If we walk out of the Conferences, what complexion will that put on our patriotism? Our allies, and the neutrals, will say they're sacrificing the defense of their country to get even with old Goremykin.
>
> **A. Obolensky:** Some Englishman has said that Russians are more interested in the grand gesture than in getting results. At this moment of danger for our motherland it is important for us—don't you see—to be not just useful but morally correct. If the Germans beat us, and we try to put all the blame on the government, people will call us childish. No, we must not allow the dissolution of the Duma to set off a conflagration.
>
> **Milyukov:** Our first step must be to topple Goremykin. And that can be done by a policy of restraint.

Restraint! Yet again? Their program had been one of restraint—and had it been appreciated? Had they been invited to join the government? (The Empress's remark about the City Duma leaked, and was passed around: "Let those wretches stick to their sewers.")

The gulf between themselves and the regime was impassable.

How then should they respond? By refusing to disperse? By declaring themselves a Constituent Assembly?

The action shifted to Moscow, the center of exasperation with the government. Political circles in Moscow had thought of something: the creation of "coalition committees" to support the Bloc throughout the empire. They also tried to bring forward the Congresses of the Unions of Zemstvos and Towns, summoning extraordinary meetings for 20 September by telegram.

Meanwhile the Empress was keeping GHQ informed, and warned, at length, in daily letters.

> The leftists are furious, because everything is slipping out of their hands. Forbid the Congress in Moscow, it will be worse than the Duma. The Duma deputies also want to meet in Moscow—warn them that if they do the recall

of the Duma will be delayed. I'm losing patience with those windbags who want to meddle in everything. Firm action is necessary to prevent them from making mischief when they return. The press too must be taken firmly in hand—they are getting ready to launch a campaign against Anya, which means against me. They mean to write things about our Friend and Anya, simply in order to implicate me.

(The War Minister's deputy in charge of censorship got orders to bar all articles about Rasputin and Vyrubova.)

I'm sure that Guchkov is at the bottom of all this. We ought to get rid of him. But how? That's the question. We are at war—couldn't we find some excuse to lock him up? He aims to create anarchy, and he is hostile to our dynasty—it's sickening, the game he's playing, his speeches, his underhand activities . . . Can we really not have Guchkov hanged? . . . A serious railroad disaster, in which he was the only casualty, would be fitting, and well-deserved, divine punishment.

The Moscow workers (now feeling themselves in a strong position: they were no longer taken by the army, in fact some of those previously drafted were coming back, since labor was short everywhere) responded to the dissolution with a three-day strike, the most conspicuous effect of which was that the Moscow trams stopped running. As they hunted newly expensive cabs or trudged block after block on foot, Moscow politicos felt the full force of this physical argument. And they began to waver, to realize that any rebellion was a help to the enemy without.

The Kadets now regretted that the Bloc had not made greater concessions in its recent exchanges with the government, and that Milyukov and Efremov had not been more flexible. Nobody seriously believed that Prince Lvov could head a government. It would be quite sufficient for Krivoshein to replace Goremykin: he was capable of steering a course between the purely bureaucratic and the wishes of society. Now that agreement with the regime had become impossible the demands of the opposition were toned down.

How, though, should they conduct the Congresses of the Unions, and what should they say there? This was discussed the night before in Chelnokov's apartment, and as if to inflame the minds of those assembled, they were presented with a gloomy, indeed a spine-chilling exposé produced by supporters of *Russkie Vedomosti*, that most enlightened and "professorial" of Russian newspapers.

The story was that, as a counterweight to the Progressive, or as its enemies called it the "Yellow," Bloc, a Black Bloc had been secretly formed. Its members were Germanophiles, they had already driven all Russian patriots away from the steps of the throne, established an inert government, exiled Nikolai Nikolaevich, and taken the Emperor firmly in hand. Given his irresoluteness, they counted on preventing any decisive engagement and inducing him to *betray his allies!* (A black scheme if ever there was one! This made all the actions of the regime comprehensible!) The arguments put before the Black Bloc's royal prisoner were that a separate peace would strengthen the dynasty, whereas an Allied victory would mean the diminution or even extinguishment of the royal power; and that, under a separate peace, Russia would give up turbulent Poland, but would reinforce its Russianness by acquiring the Russian areas of Galica. An iron union of the Emperor of All the Russias and the Emperor of Germany would be a formidable hammer, capable of smashing the whole world. (Why have we been blind for so long to this treason?!) Of course, the Emperor could not take responsibility for such an inglorious about-face. But if a general strike broke out in Russia, if there were disturbances, if the people lost its organic ties with the army and the army lost faith in the people, a separate peace could legitimately be concluded, ostensibly for the salvation of Russia. Moreover, the whole blame could be put on revolutionary circles and the Duma opposition! This was why *the regime was trying to sow general discontent and sedition throughout the country!* The regime—no one else— was stirring up the depths and instigating rebellion. (These ravings were the origin of the insidious legend that would so fatally affect Russia's fortunes—the legend that the Russian monarchy was preparing to make a separate peace.)

What a strange twist of fate! The liberals were now the patriots, and only they could save Russia from an unpatriotic Tsarist regime!

But what exactly should they do? What should their tactics be? Why, they must do the very opposite of what the Black Bloc was doing: they must restrain Russia, prevent disturbances on the home front! (The workers must not strike, the trams must run.) When permission was given, the Duma would resume its deliberations pacifically, so that it would have a platform for public denunciations. And, little by little, it would create a "government of trust."

Strictly speaking, the Congresses should have been organizing help for the armies in the field. But learning that the motherland was on the brink of destruction, both of them, separately and jointly, began discussing "the current situation."

> **M. Fyodorov:** *This is no time to be discussing technicalities.* We are obviously on the eve of an armed uprising!

(Oh, how they had longed for its coming, in its mystic purple vestments!)

> The time is not far distant when bayonets will be turned away from the front and on Petrograd. It is our duty to save Russia!

> **Shingarev:** Every one of our wars ends in victory for society and the collapse of reaction. After 1812—the Decembrists! After Sevastopol—the liberation of the peasants! After the Japanese war—the victory of the Liberation movement! The decisive moment is at hand: for a bright future we must make one last great push, and we shall achieve what Russia's best people have always dreamt of!

(Shingarev's remarks in private were also reported by secret police informers.

> Frankly, the dissolution of the Duma has got us out of a serious difficulty. Everything having to do with the war had been settled, and the Duma would have had to go on to social questions. If they had been discussed the Bloc would have collapsed. As it is, we can make a show of unity.)

Astrov then "read out from an exercise book a lethal critique of all the government's measures."

> But we have reached a fateful divide, beyond which constitutionalist society cannot go. We cannot become revolutionaries.

> **Guchkov:** Like the Bloc, we all must unite and organize, not for revolution but simply to defend our motherland against anarchy and revolution. We

must make a last attempt to open the eyes of the Supreme Power to what is going on in Russia.

At both Congresses there was growing support for the idea of a deputation to inform the Emperor of the mood of Russian society at large (as they had in 1905). And if that did not help, "we know what we must do."

The lawyer Margulis, however, objected strongly to the idea of a deputation, considering it useless and humiliating to "society" and arguing that they knew the answer in advance.

> The time for petitions is over. The time has come to demand, not ask! And back up our demands with force!

The left wing of the Congress of Towns demanded an appeal not to the Tsar but directly to the people!

But it was a deputation to the Tsar that a majority at both Congresses elected, with instructions to open his eyes to the fact that the government was misleading him and had no wish to carry the war to a victorious conclusion. They voted for a respectful loyal address. Its diction was uneven and in parts very highfalutin.

> Your Imperial Majesty! Restore the majestic lineaments of spiritual wholeness to the life of the state! The form of government must correspond to the spirit of the people, grow out of it as a living plant grows out of the soil. We, like you, Sire, care nothing for our lives if the preservation of Russia is at stake. Her salvation is in your hands.

But there were also words of menace.

> The fact that the government is answerable to no one is an ominous obstacle . . . absence of any link between the government and the country . . . in place of the present government we need people who enjoy the confidence of society . . .

Meanwhile, a delegation of seventy workers came knocking at the door of the Congress of Towns: if the towns are having their say, the workers also wish to speak!

The Congress felt uneasy, with the streets demanding admittance. Chelnokov was insistent: no outsiders! Our rules are very strict! (And Chelnokov's reputation was destroyed on the spot by a resolution speedily drafted outside the hall, crying, "Shame on the liberal bourgeoisie!)" So strict were the rules that two of the most enthusiastic talkers, Duma deputies Kerensky and Chkheidze, who had arrived posthaste from Petrograd, were not admitted to the Congress. The excitable Kerensky aired his grievance to worker comrades in the corridors, confidingly clutching their lapels: they must not strike, but should set up an organization to plan for the future . . . and then the liberal cowardly bourgeoisie . . .

But what if (as it surely would be!) the Emperor's reply to the delegation was unfavorable? The left said, "All ways of negotiating with the government will then have been exhausted," and they must appeal to the streets! Or else (which might annoy even more?) summon another Congress to discuss price inflation! One Cossack delegate (also a leftist) said, "Cossacks are not what they were in 1905. The government can no longer rely on the Cossacks!"

In spite of all this the Congress of Zemstvos concluded its proceedings by rising and giving three cheers for the Tsar.

*   *   *

This seems to have been the first and last time in the two decades of his reign that Emperor Nikolai II sustained an effort of will for two weeks, and did not let himself be diverted from his chosen course.

One moment there was general upheaval, general uproar, auguring catastrophe, then suddenly things went very quiet. The state suffered no convulsions, Russia did not plunge into the abyss, rivers of blood did not run. What was more, the most terrifying retreat of the war suddenly came to an end. Only yesterday Kiev was to be evacuated, Riga was given up for lost, as was Dvinsk, there was anxiety for Pskov, and suddenly a halt was called. The tidal wave of refugees subsided. The civilian population calmed down. And at the front—yes—shells became a less rare sight. Russia had weathered the storm, and anyone who wished could give credit for this to the new Supreme Commander.

Perhaps the only place in which opposition was not hushed was the Council of Ministers. The Empress kept a watchful eye on them, kept Mogilev informed, and nagged away.

> It is more than Goremykin can stand, presiding over ministers who treat him abominably. I am afraid that the old man will not be able to go on with everybody against him. He earnestly begs to be released. Shcherbatov refused to send observers from the Ministry of the Interior to the September Congresses in Moscow. Polivanov shows Guchkov all War Ministry instructions and all army documents. Krivoshein also is too closely in contact with Guchkov, is two-faced and secretly hostile to Goremykin, looks to right and to left, is insufferably excitable, and carries on some sort of underground activity. As for Sazonov—he's the worst of all, shouts and shouts, alarms everybody else, and never turns up for cabinet meetings. (But where can we find someone to replace Sazonov?) After their meetings they go away and tell everybody what has been said. Such loathsome ministers—their opposition infuriates me! How I would love to flog almost every one of them, and send Shcherbatov and Samarin packing first of all. The cowardice of these ministers disgusts me. You must sort them out! Do come to Tsarskoe Selo if only for a day or two. Your visit will not be a holiday but a punitive expedition. You must now show them who you are and that you are sick of them. You have tried kindness and gentleness, now you must assert the will of a sovereign. Forbid Samarin to dismiss Suslik.* I lose my head completely with Samarin, and I do beg you to hurry back. Don't let anybody demean the Emperor or his wife. You have no right to turn a blind eye to this, this is the last battle for your victory. And as soon as Samarin gets out you must put your broom to work and clean out all the filth that has accumulated in the Synod. Get rid of them all, my love, and make it quick!

All the ministers were invited to come to Mogilev on 29 September. They were surprised and hurt to find that no one of any importance was there to meet them at the station, and they had to lunch in an ordinary station buffet. Then they were

---

*Bishop of Tobolsk. [*Trans.*]

conveyed to the governor's residence, where the Emperor, controlling himself with some difficulty, delivered a laconic and apparently relaxed reply to their collective statement. He expressed his extreme displeasure with the ministers who signed it: the views of the cabinet on the Tsar's assumption of the Supreme Command had been voiced before he had finally decided, and it was impossible to understand what grounds there could be for repeating them. The Emperor said over and over that the ministers ought now to be able to see how wrong they had been. Real Russia thought differently (and the Emperor had received many telegrams expressing delight with his decision). His explanation for the ministers' views was the "terribly nervous atmosphere in Petrograd." Here, in calmer surroundings, he looked at things differently.

He really could not understand their stubborn opposition to his autocratic will—which could only be an intuition of the working of Divine Providence.

An excruciating silence followed. The ministers could not avoid answering, but it was difficult for them to say anything. In the Emperor's short address could be seen the very opposite of what he meant to say: an acknowledgment of his defeat. He had withdrawn from the storm zone and was sustaining himself with specious telegrams. He had retreated from the center of power and conflict. How would that affect the fortunes of Russia? Did GHQ really depend on him? And could official Petrograd function without him?

But there was another way of looking at it: perhaps the ministers had exaggerated the importance of the surge of discontent in educated society. The tidal wave had passed and the ship of state continued on its way. Their collective letter was arm-twisting—an attempt to exploit the Emperor's weakness. Part of Krivoshein's reply was that they should not ignore public opinion at such a critical time, that society should be allowed to play a part in the war (it was playing far too big a part already), that the government must work together with the people (but where were the real people? Were those gathered at Morozov's house the people?), and he now sensed that through his own fault Russia's great chariot wheel was no longer rolling along in the old, invisible, but perhaps better groove. It had turned out that the Emperor's favor, the public's favor, and even the de facto premiership were not enough to make him Prime Minister. Things went their way regardless of him, and he was eased onto the sidelines with other unwanted advisers.

It was clear after the Tsar's reprimand that rebellious ministers would have to take retirement. Samarin and Shcherbatov were dismissed on 9 October. Krivoshein saw all the more clearly the absurdity and incoherence of all the playacting in August, on the part of "society" and on the part of the ministers, and quite rightly did not bank on a royal pardon. He realized that he should go voluntarily and not wait to be dismissed by the Tsar. (Nor indeed could he stay on in a reactionary government without disgracing himself in the eyes of "society.") So, at his very next audience, in October, he submitted his resignation. The Emperor looked relieved, almost happy: he need not himself dismiss his collaborator of many years. But in October it could have looked like a concerted ministerial walkout, another "strike," so he got Krivoshein to promise that he would keep his retirement secret for at least one month.

A month later his resignation was explained by ill health and accompanied by a eulogistic royal decree and the Order of Aleksandr Nevsky.

It remained to decide whether to receive the deputation from the Congresses of Towns and Zemstvos. The Empress wrote:

> Do not receive those wretches or it will look as if you are recognizing their existence. Don't allow them to influence you, it will be taken as a sign of fear if you give in to them. And they will raise their heads again.

The Unions were indeed intolerable. They meddled in things that did not concern them, brought chaos to a country at war, undermined the morale of the troops, and were now improperly intruding upon administrative matters. (But did not you yourself, Your Majesty, magnanimously authorize their establishment?) They carried no real weight—it was just that a very loud voice emanated from them. Their Congresses had heard innuendos (not understood by the Emperor) about a separate peace. And the unspoken thought behind all their fine words was: "Let's teach the monarch a lesson, limit him and force our own way to power." (In their innocence they imagined that power would be sweet.)

Then again, the memory of the audience he had given to a zemstvo delegation at Peterhof in 1905 still rankled. He had openheartedly trusted them, treated them graciously, and afterward they had whooped with malicious glee, ridiculed the whole occasion, openly admitting that it was just a maneuver.

Would it be the same again?

So then the Emperor let it be known through the Minister of the Interior that he could not receive a deputation to discuss matters outside the Unions' direct concern (help for the wounded).

Which was fair enough.

All the same, the Autocrat had to be persuaded to lend an ear, or half an ear, sometime, to something. You might imagine that somewhere in that vast land there were thinking people other than the Tsar's immediate entourage, that Russia as a whole had a greater variety of views than the Guards regiments and Tsarskoye Selo. These turbulent subjects were besieging the steps of the throne, calling not for its overthrow but for war to final victory. "Society" was asking for political concessions—but why should it not be assured of the Tsar's goodwill and granted a few kind words? He could meet them halfway and turn his bright gaze on them. Were they insincere about it all? Whether they were or not, it was part of the ruler's trade: you can't cut all bonds of trust with society—every last one. Even after the burning summer of 1915, the surrender of Warsaw, and the terrifying retreat, kind words might have gone far to mend matters. However you looked at it, the mortal dissension between the regime and society was a sickness, and while Russia suffered from it, it was impossible to march proudly on to final victory.

One who loved Russia must reconcile himself to it in all its variety. And the hope of reconciliation had not yet been exhausted.

But the Tsar lurked timidly behind several sealed oaken doors.

He who has long been strong rashly fails to notice weakness overtaking him, even weakness after weakness, even the last but one.

[20]

Shingarev lived on the Petersburg side, on Bolshaya Monetnaya Street. Hansom cabs had become very expensive, and it had taken Vorotyntsev just one day to adopt the household's frugal ways—it was foolish to waste money on cabbies, much better to contribute it to Nanny's housekeeping (the price of firewood had gone up four times, that of meat and butter five times). Vera laughingly told him about an important state attorney who was late for an appointment with a minister, couldn't find a cab anywhere, had to hire an empty coal sledge, and proceeded down the Fontanka standing upright with his briefcase under his arm. Brother and sister took the tram with a light heart.

Earlier Vorotyntsev had seen a bit of the Nevsky Prospect at night, and his heart had sunk. He was dismayed by the crowd of beautifully dressed and obviously leisured people, not on leave from the front, just people with nothing to do but amuse themselves. The crowded cafés, the theater bills, all advertising dubious "saucy farces," the coruscating lights of the cinemas (the film showing at the Palace on Mikhailovsky Square, right by Vera's house, was called *Forbidden Night*—how it must disgust her!), a sort of feverish glare everywhere, the frantic haste of smart carriages—is this what goes on while we are stuck in the darkness and damp of the trenches? There was too much jollification in the city. It was unpleasant. They were dancing on other men's graves.

This time they avoided the Nevsky, cut across Manezhnaya Square, past Nikolai Nikolaevich senior on his plinth, and waited near the Engineers' Castle for the red and blue lights of the No. 2 tram, which was no longer overcrowded at that hour. It carried them off as though intent on showing all that was most beautiful in Petersburg (except that the streets were not very well lit): across the Moika, looking back at the Mikhailovsky Palace, along Swan Boulevard, past the Parade Ground, over the Troitsky Bridge, with the best view of the capital to their left—the Winter Palace and the long façade of the Hermitage, the tip of Vasilevsky Island, especially at the moment when the bizarre and mighty Rostral Columns, dimly visible in the light from streetlamps, took the Stock Exchange neatly in their grip and immediately swung around to release it. It was light one moment, dark the next, but even in the dark a practiced eye could almost see remembered contours, and especially the unhealthy brown of the Petersburg palaces.

Vorotyntsev stared and stared, admiring sights he had grown unused to, but no true Muscovite can be overawed, made to feel small: our

Moscow has a soul, and this place does not. Our Moscow is always better.

Even the Petersburg trams are not like those in Moscow: back home strangers talk to each other on trams, here you talk only to your companion, quietly.

Cast a glance at the fortress over there. It always stands out against the sky unless it is pitch black—a black phantom, with the wall that is a warning to all future conspirators . . . Then the tram was gliding along the most modern, the glossiest avenue in the city, the Nevsky's triumphant rival. And it was time to get off. They had not far to walk, turning right from Kamennoostrovsky Prospect.

As they went Vera told her brother a little more about Shingarev, so that he would know what to expect, and he was all ears. Shingarev had, willy-nilly, become a financial expert. The Duma was full of Kadet professors, but not one of them was especially interested in finance, so Shingarev had taken it on. His jousts with Kokovtsov in budget debates were famous. Ill-wishers in his own party called him a dilettante, said he ought to know his limitations. "No," Georgi said approvingly, "there's nothing wrong with that."

He enjoyed listening to his sister's quiet, persuasive voice—no magpie chattering, she weighed every word. Since the moment he first saw her, slim and pretty, on the station platform, he had found it hard to believe that for so many years he had rarely thought of her, had hardly been aware that he had such a sister, so modest, so unassuming, but with such an understanding smile, so comfortable to be with. He had admired her on the tram, not just because she was his sister . . . her face, so animated, yet so demure . . . the only wife for a man with a life of labor and self-denial before him. Silently, tirelessly, inconspicuously, she would level mountains for the man of her choice. Why, little sister, are you not married? Georgi felt more and more grateful to his sister, more and more in love with her even, as the day went by.

Vera was telling him that Shingarev was also a councillor in the Petrograd Duma and the Usman zemstvo, and that he had toured half Russia giving public lectures with remarkable success.

"He can even get people to listen spellbound to statistics. It's not that his speeches are so highly polished, he sometimes expresses himself badly . . . it's his sincerity, his commitment!"

Meanwhile, with one hand under her weightless elbow, Georgi was steering her along Bolshaya Monetnaya, and the house numbers were getting higher and higher. Just a little further on the houses would become less imposing, and they would reach the outer limits of that respectable quarter and the fringe of the far from respectable Vyborg district.

"He's thoroughly Russian—only, like you, more energetic than Russians generally are, which is why I think you'll get on together. He's never so happy as when he has work to do, and nobody to hinder him."

"Listen, though—we aren't going to land in the middle of a Kadet get-together, are we?"

"You can never be altogether sure," Vera said with a little laugh.

"You said that on Mondays . . . ! So you've led me into a trap?"

"This is Petersburg! Life here means constantly calling on each other—to swap news and views, and nowadays what they call 'copies' . . . There has to be some substitute for civic freedoms. Besides, he's a very popular deputy, and even strangers are eager to see him."

At last—No. 22. The shiny tiles of its façade showed that it had been built recently. Into the hallway. No elevator, but the stairway was broader than usual, room and to spare for three abreast, and the steps were lit by wide triple windows.

"Fifth floor? That does surprise me. A man in his position, in the Duma and the party—why does he live as if he was hard up?"

Breathing easily, in spite of the steep climb, Vera explained. "Even an apartment like this costs half a deputy's stipend. They're paid quite modestly. And they all now contribute fifty rubles to the Duma hospital train. Besides—he's got five children. And he sends something to his three nephews. Anyway, he's frugal by nature, and he attaches no importance to comfort, he's indifferent to food—doesn't eat dessert at all. He's one of six children himself."

"You seem to have gotten to know each other well."

The ceilings, however, were just as high on the third and fourth floors. There were wrought-iron numbers on the doors of the apartments.

"People have offered him literary work through me, but he won't take just anything. Only things that are close to his heart. Even if they are unpaid. He earns a bit with his lectures. His family are hardworking and resourceful, they don't make any great demands on him. But he's now a sick man—and the doctors have tried to send him to a spa. He hasn't had a vacation in years, and goes for months on end without a rest."

Seen from afar, from a dugout, the major figures in the Duma were perched on some shining eminence, high above ordinary Russian citizens. But none of that squared with this modest Petersburg apartment and with all that Vera had told him. So that Vorotyntsev's curiosity grew as he climbed the stairs.

Kadet leaders, just like famous stage personalities, were portrayed on picture postcards. Vorotyntsev had seen Milyukov, Maklakov, Rodichev, and Nabokov in that format, but not, for some reason, Shingarev.

Andrei Ivanovich himself flung open the door—and that movement, and his whole person, told you at first glance, before you could distinguish details, that here was a man without affectation, with no wish to play a part.

"Hello, hello! Quite a climb, isn't it? Well, I'm a country bumpkin, and as such can't stand people walking about over my head."

He thrust out a large hand and took Vorotyntsev's in a firm grip.

"Still," said Vera laughingly, "you do live on Bolshaya Monetnaya*— as befits a shadow Finance Minister."

"You mean you still consider yourself a rustic?"

"Well, I've spent thirty years in towns but I still can't get used to town life."

First impressions might prove right or wrong, but Vorotyntsev felt more and more attracted to the man. And now, as he unbuttoned his holster in the hallway, he was delighted to meet with such an open-hearted welcome, with no standing on ceremony, no artificial politeness.

"Well, some of us live in holes in the ground, and there's always somebody tramping overhead."

Shingarev seized Vera's hands. "Marvelous! I'm so glad you've brought him."

The apartment went a long way back. Someone could be heard walking around and a little girl peeped out from one of the rooms, but Andrei Ivanovich's study was right there, first on the left. He opened the door with another vigorous push and invited Vera to join them.

"No, thank you, I'll just go along to Evfrosinya Maksimovna."

The room was narrow and made narrower by bookshelves on both sides and by several chairs, none of them, however, unoccupied—there were piles of newspapers, pamphlets, and documents on every one. The sagging sofa was not free either—it had a pile of its own. A desk drawn close to the single window at the end of the room was so cluttered and littered that only its owner could discern any principle of arrangement.

The owner himself, in his far from new second-best suit, was more unassuming even than his fifth-floor apartment. His manner said that to the chairman of the Duma's Military Commission any intelligent man fresh from the front was an important fund of firsthand information and advice. What with his work in the Duma, as a party leader, and as a lecturer, he couldn't often get away to visit the army in the field, and besides, he'd spent two months of the year trundling around Europe with a parliamentary delegation, doing his best to understand what was going on there. He'd rushed off to have a look at the Western Front—but what could an outsider on a flying visit hope to see? If you were a member of the Defense Conference or on Duma commissions you needed to gather, piece together, and condense other people's

*Great Mint Street. [*Trans.*]

experience if you were to have firm ground under your feet. He tried to see as many serving soldiers as he could. Up-to-date assessments were urgently needed.

So how soon could they start talking?

Well, an officer in the front line has only one dream—to be listened to. Back there, you're knocking your head against a wall, there's nobody to complain to.

His host sat him down on the ruptured sofa and pulled up a wicker chair for himself.

"So which army are you now serving in?"

"The 9th."

"Lechitsky's? I hear he's a good general."

Top marks. Knows what's what.

"One of the best."

"And you're out on the left flank?"

"That was a standing joke till last autumn. We were the 'extreme leftists,' to the left of all the socialists. We were covered on one side, but now we're exposed, thanks to the Romanians. And we've sprung a leak."

Question and answer, question and answer, all very businesslike, he understands, he remembers things. Yes, yes, Romania—that's all very worrisome, terribly hard to understand. Why did they surrender the Dobrudja? What was the Danubian Corps doing? What happened at Dorna-Vatra? (He could visualize it all without a map—good man.) Why are we retreating? Throughout the summer your 9th Army was advancing successfully. Is the fighting spirit still there?

Fighting spirit! So that was what interested him. Right, we'll get there in a minute via the Romanian sectors. He'll learn more than he's asking for.

But Shingarev pulled him up there. Pavel Nikolaevich had rung to say that he was on the Petersburg side and would be looking in within the hour.

"Pavel Nikolaevich? Sorry . . . that would be . . . ?"

"Milyukov. It would be a pity to waste an opportunity like this, he too very much needs to hear what you have to say! Mili Izmailovich will come along too—Minervin, that is. It will make more sense if all three of us listen together."

So the artful Vera had lured him into a Kadet get-together after all. Oh, well, Petersburg has gotten off to an amusing start. A marvelous start in fact.

But what to do in the meantime? In the meantime, since Shingarev was responsible for the delay, he was ready to answer questions and explain things himself. He was frank and straightforward, he concealed nothing, he was quite unlike a Duma leader. He had, it was true, the sort of haircut fashionable among prominent public persons, almost

but not quite a French crop. And streaks of gray were relentlessly annexing the dark hair on his head, his upper lip, and his chin. But in
the light shed on the wall through the opaque shade of the table lamp
a photograph showed a young man in a white blouse, worn outside his
trousers, holding a rabbit in his lap, a young man of the half-Gypsy
breed common along the old steppe frontier—and you were embarrassed to ask in case you were wrong, but couldn't stop yourself . . .

"Is that you?"

He probably could hardly believe it himself. Where now was that
wild shock of unruly black hair, those burning, darting eyes, that smile,
that eagerness to jump up, to run, to gallop, to act!

Twenty years back he had been a doctor, not an employee of the
zemstvo health service, nothing so grand, just a private practitioner
treating patients for five kopecks a visit. Yet he remembered with much
affection the bleak, poverty-stricken, ignorant countryside of which he
had measured every inch.

"You might be told the cow had to be sold because its color didn't
please the house sprite . . . Then if there was a cattle plague the women
would plow the fields around the village naked . . . Then there was
what some call 'folk medicine.' If a woman was having a difficult delivery they'd hang her upside down from the stove and a runner would
be sent to the church three versts away to ask the priests to open the
royal gates so as to ease the birth . . ."

Was he finding fault with the people? Not contemptuously, anyway.
Sadly, pityingly.

"In the Usman district, where my farm is now, they're a bit more
civilized, a bit cleaner and always were. But in Novozhivotinnoye,
where we did that statistical survey, I'm afraid that even today . . .
they're shackled to the earth like condemned men. They're landless,
horseless, poverty-stricken, their yards are unfenced, their huts are
slums, they get no part of their livelihood from the land, all from
seasonal work elsewhere, but all the same—the land is what matters!
They grub away in whatever bit of a plot is left."

"When were you there last?"

"It must be seventeen years. It's better everywhere now, incomparably better, the countryside is quite different, but I wasn't making it
up. In 1899 it was so bad that they didn't even have pickled cabbage
for the winter! Nothing to make cabbage soup with! Who had dared
bring the village to that? I ask you." His voice, deep and disarmingly
sincere, was suddenly tearful.

"Novozhivotinnoye is on the Don. There are rich deposits of limestone along the riverbank. The limestone belongs to nobody, it's God's,
as the saying goes, and it's been quarried for ages for building materials. So along comes one shrewd son of a bitch, a local peasant himself,
who doesn't give a damn for the popular belief that it's nobody's. And

officialdom gives him paternal assistance: he greases a few palms in Voronezh and is allowed to rent the quarries. Nobody dares take any limestone anymore—they all knuckle under. What else could they do? That's how the soul of our people decays and is lost to us. How can anybody reconcile himself to that for five minutes, and refuse to fight it?"

Without even seeing Shingarev's amiable face, just hearing the extraordinary timbre of his voice, it would be difficult not to like him. His voice seemed to come from the depths of his being, carrying with it all the warmth that was in him, lavishing it on his companion.

"Before that they used to quarry stone whenever they felt like it, take it to town, and sell it on their own account. But now they had to take whatever wage the leaseholder offered, thirty kopecks a day for the best workers. They burrowed into the ground down narrow shafts. It was damp and stuffy, they carried kerosene lamps and worked bent over double. Nobody bothered about props—they were in too much of a hurry to earn an extra kopeck—and the upper strata often caved in, especially in the spring. You'd be told every so often that one or another of them had been 'crushed by the hill.' One young man, his family's breadwinner, wasn't quick enough jumping out after his fellow worker, was hit in the back by a boulder, crippled, paralyzed in both legs, and worse than that the sphincter of his rectum gave out and he couldn't retain his feces. He lay there on straw in a poky little hut with never a murmur, and his parents and his wife were just as resigned to what was obviously God's will . . . The common Russian people, the meek, the martyred, the great Russian people . . ."

Vorotyntsev was chilled to the marrow. That bastard of a leaseholder, that crippled young man . . . A sound fellow, Shingarev . . . knows what needs to be done . . . Yes, he'll understand the soldiers' grievances just as well, and an officer need not be ashamed to tell him things he would ordinarily tell no one. We will understand each other! I'm in luck.

"You never cease to marvel at them. But you can't keep putting your hopes on them. They'll never change their lives by their own efforts. Only we can drag them out of the mire."

Whether it was that quarry. Diphtheria on a bed of dirty straw. Or the hardships heaped on men in the trenches over twenty-seven months of war.

"How can anyone devote so much as five minutes of his life to anything else? . . . I went among the people to heal. But frankly I might as well have left them unhealed. What's the good of slapping a poultice on someone who is hungry and illiterate? No—take the load off his back, let some light into his bowed head. Since my university days I have always been amazed by the gulf between the intelligentsia, with its impatient idealism, and the benighted and long-suffering people.

The gulf is too great a danger to our country. That way it must come to grief."

"The gulf is as wide as it ever was," Vorotyntsev warned, his mind on his own experience.

"Of course, that's just the trouble, that makes it worse, it means that our task is still what it was at the end of the last century—to exert all our strength and make haste to draw those above and those below closer together. The answer to all Russia's problems lies there. But we aren't being given much time. Once before, war broke out and was followed by revolution, then by reaction. Now we have war again and we have very little time left. Bring them closer, yes—but how? I used to think that it came more naturally to a doctor than to anybody else: he's accepted and made welcome in every peasant hut."

That was how it had all begun for Shingarev in his early days. His initial concern was with health and hygiene in a rural area, but to understand such matters you had to know about the budgets of peasant households and also about the zemstvo's budget. You began by organizing clinics, hot dinners in schools, day nurseries for working mothers at harvest time, then found yourself writing for publication, addressing public meetings, and at twenty-six a councillor in the Tambov provincial zemstvo, locked in a struggle with Prince Chelokaev, the leader of the Tambov conservatives.

But what could be done in the zemstvo if it was not allowed even to discuss things peaceably and its best draft proposals were returned with a reprimand? *They* themselves had given the public permission to think—and they themselves then vilified and ridiculed it for thinking. Conflict with the central authorities, with the government, became more and more obviously unavoidable.

Nobody should think that this was all in the past, it was the present reality, and this colonel must be made to see that clearly.

"In 1902 Witte summoned a congress of zemstvos—the first ever— to discuss 'the needs of agriculture.' Everybody was excited about it, the whole country responded. I myself made a speech at Voronezh on 'what the public treasury takes from the population and what it gives in return.' So who do you think arrived to snuff out sedition in our locality? The Vice-Minister of the Interior no less! He upbraided widely respected elderly people who had given their views not out of hot-headed obstreperousness but at Witte's request, ridiculed them, sneered at them, showing no consideration for age or social position. With the boorish insolence so characteristic of the autocratic Russian bureaucracy! I was too insignificant an insect to be challenged, they simply put me under police surveillance. But that was just what I found most painful and embarrassing—being left unscathed when all around me decent people were being destroyed. Not until they arrived in the night to search my place was my mind at ease and my conscience clear."

Vorotyntsev was getting impatient, he wanted to talk about his own main concerns, to speak out before anyone broke in on them. But he was reluctant to interrupt while the famous deputy was speaking so freely. Strange, he thought, that I've lived all these years in Russia, lived a very active life, yet never knew any of this, any more than I knew about the Vyborg appeal. And so he sat sunk in the old sofa listening, for some reason, to a detailed account of matters fifteen years out of date. With Shingarev looking down upon him from his wicker chair.

The apolitical doctor had, then, been sucked into the whirlpool of party politics. To begin with, he had joined the League of Liberation, which was so attractive to all intellectuals. Once parties with a separate identity appeared he found himself a Kadet . . . And anyway, when he was still a youngster, Fronya, also a student, engaged to Andrei Ivanovich, had taken part in a Christmas fortune-telling game. She wrote predictions on little slips, these were stuck onto the sides of a big basin, water was poured into the basin, and a little candle in a nutshell was floated on the water. Whichever slip it approached foretold your future. Shingarev's slip read: "Will be a deputy in the first Russian parliament." That was when Aleksandr III was still on the throne, and however hard he peered into the future nobody could imagine that a Russian parliament would ever be a reality. But it had come to pass, exactly as predicted. Shingarev was the first Kadet deputy elected to the First Duma from Voronezh. But the local committee of the Kadet Party didn't want him to go off to the capital, they kept him in Voronezh. And what was the result? The Vyborg appeal, a prison term, and disqualification from further political activity were the unavoidable lot of the first deputies—while Shingarev was elected to the Second Duma, and again to the Third. When he was not allowed to stand again in Voronezh, he was elected in Petersburg, where he was by then well known.

The point of this long story was that nothing can be achieved without a struggle against authority. If you thought about it—perhaps it really was so? Had not Vorotyntsev come along with some such idea in his head?

In the Second Duma no one had thought that the duty of the people's elected representatives was work, work, and yet more work. It was as though there was no Russia, no Russian people—just the ambitions of party politicians. The extreme left shouted, "We don't need this sort of Duma! To hell with it!" And a handful of rightists yelled back, "You don't deserve even a Duma of this sort! You've been too greedy." All the same, the day of its dissolution was an agonizing one.

"I foresaw that the government coup would pass almost unnoticed by the people."

(Was it really a government coup? It sounded strange. Vorotyntsev hadn't noticed or remembered anything of the kind.)

"But although I had fully expected it the silence of Petersburg and Moscow on 16 June was astonishing. The fact that something or other had happened to the Duma not only provoked no disturbances, it aroused not the slightest interest. The imperial manifesto was printed and posted on walls, but passersby didn't even pause to read it. Cabbies trotted briskly by, drays rumbled on their way. We thought of ourselves as 'the Duma of the people's aspirations,' but when we were dissolved nobody batted an eye."

(So maybe nothing terrible had happened?)

Shingarev moved over to sit beside him on the sofa, sinking into a second cavity. As he prepared to move on from reminiscence to the present, his searching gray eyes examined the other man closely. There was nothing of the big city about him, he was just an affable country doctor, concerned for his companion's health and ready to examine him and listen to his chest there and then.

Where had Vorotyntsev been at the time?

In June 1907? Right here in Petersburg. Taking my first-year exams at the Academy. To tell the truth, I didn't notice a thing.

Shingarev nodded. Quite so. The very ailment he had suspected.

"Still, in the Third Duma we were at one in wanting to work. Now, in the Fourth, everything has seized up, nothing gets done. All because of the obstinacy and stupidity of our rulers. Yet they have never had a more favorable time for rapprochement with the public than now, in the midst of this war! They didn't want it. Last year, after the retreat and the criminal surrender of the fortresses, our Military Commission submitted a very frank memorandum to the Tsar. And no answer was forthcoming. In spite of the fact that we're on the commission, and can discuss whatever we like—whereas in the Third Duma, Guchkov wouldn't have us on the Military Commission, he said the Kadets were 'not patriots.' "

This frankness deserved a frank reply.

"Nobody can say that about you personally, Andrei Ivanovich, but cast your eye over your party comrades—are they really patriots? I'd say Aleksandr Ivanovich was more or less right." He softened his boldness with a laugh.

"We are working for the good of the people—what does that make us?" Shingarev said heatedly.

Vorotyntsev stuck to his guns. "There's more than one way of doing that. You might think a strong Russia isn't necessary for the purpose, you might not mind if Russia collapses, if the result is freedom . . ."

"A strong Russia not necessary? We want just that—we want victory! We base all our calculations on the patriotism of the people—nothing else! That's our one salvation, this extraordinary gift of our people, the cure for all our maladies—and that after all the ill treatment the people have been made to endure!"

He had evidently sized up Vorotyntsev as a representative, though a peculiar one, of that same Russian people. Vorotyntsev sensed that some sort of decisive pronouncement was expected of him. But out of the corner of his eye he saw looming the rock that might at any moment divide them. So now *they* were patriots, greater patriots than he was? He didn't want to remind Shingarev that before the war he had held up the Duma's approval of budget allocations to the armed forces.

He wedged himself deeper into the ruptured sofa.

He longed to smoke but felt awkward about it. The air in the study was heavy with the smell of books, but there wasn't a whiff of tobacco.

Shingarev's view was that everything done for the war was the work not of the bureaucracy but of the "public." Russia should step up her war effort to the maximum by the end of the year and reach the zenith of her power early in 1917. But everything was going to pieces because of pigheaded obstruction on the part of the regime. The home front was shaky and might not hold up.

The home front again. Fixed prices, tariffs, compulsory procurement? The Defense Commission, the Budget Commission, hundreds of educated people with their statistical tables and economic reference books. And changing anything in Russia would mean more tables, more reference books, all those people would have to be consulted. And the sword hanging in the entrance hall, or two dozen such gimcrack swords, would be of no avail against that. Even at the Academy officers did not study civil law or administration.

Shingarev was piling it on ". . . a black period, a barren period. We produce no great statesmen. Prophets and great writers alike have abandoned Russia. But what I find hardest to understand is why no good generals come to the fore. This is the third year of a war without precedent, one such as Russia has never waged before, fourteen million men have borne arms at one time or another, so why have we no Suvorov? No Skobelev even?"

Generals . . . ?

"Do you mind if I smoke?"

Generals! Vorotyntsev never stopped thinking about them. (And of himself in the same context.) That none were produced was no accident. They were in fact produced—but somebody's stupidity made the upper rungs of the service ladder inaccessible to them. "There are now plenty of competent generals commanding divisions, corps, and even armies, compared with those around at the beginning of the war. Take Lechitsky, or Gurko, or Shcherbachev, or Kaledin, or Denikin, or Krymov . . . But higher up—the way is barred. It's the same as with you and the ministers."

Shingarev liked that. Restlessly twining and untwining his fingers, he began asking the sort of questions which should wrest the required answers from the colonel. He wanted to be told that the army's potential was still inexhaustible! That it had the strength to overcome all trials on the road to victory, and that its commanders would yet shine. Just rid us of this rotten government and victory is ours!

But the colonel he had chanced on could not and would not promise any of these things so passionately desired. Nor could he utter such words—half prayer, half promise—about the government and the Supreme Power, though he himself had no respect for them whatever.

Perhaps the complete mutual understanding they had hoped for was a mirage?

Vorotyntsev felt a growing desire to make a clean breast of it—but what an impossible position for an officer and a fighting soldier: to address a civilian audience like some sort of pacifist the moment he arrived from the front. It would be like a bass singer suddenly breaking into falsetto. These people are for the war and for victory—but am I? How easy it is for them to talk about "stepping up the war effort to its maximum"! Try stepping it up while you squirm in the trenches day after day!

People back here were very bellicose and victory-minded. But the more clearly Vorotyntsev saw what the nation really needed, the harder it proved to express it in educated language.

How can we win the war? Shingarev was waiting to be told. We've begrudged nothing, spared ourselves nothing. We dare not fail to atone for all the lives we've sacrificed—by winning the war. The shades of the dead would arise and ask, "For what did you destroy us?" Yes, the Kadets were ready to attack the government with whatever it took!

That was the very question that always hampered and challenged Vorotyntsev's present way of thinking. To what end have so many been sacrificed? What is our duty toward the dead? He was more keenly conscious of that duty than were those who might argue with him in Petersburg. The dead meant rows and rows of faces and names well known to him, or now half forgotten, often with the circumstances of their death, or burial, or dispatch to the rear gravely wounded. But though he never forgot a single one of them he was still more urgently aware of the groans of the living.

It was obvious what he should say—to Shingarev particularly, as chairman of the Duma's Military Commission. And someone who would never play a dirty trick. But it was difficult to get the words out. He began in a roundabout way. "Maybe the first thing to do is to reduce the army. Reduce it considerably. By as much as a third. We don't need an enormous army, we need an army of crack troops— almost entirely volunteers, to be used at decisive points. What we've rounded up isn't an army, it's a rabble. We're trying to make up with numbers for what we lack in expertise."

"Yes, yes," Shingarev said, unsurprised. "We've heard such opinions expressed occasionally. You share them, then? We can't allow ourselves to say it out loud in the Duma. There would be more hands to work the land, wouldn't there? Fewer mouths to feed, fewer supply trains?"

"The main thing is there'd be less of a scuffle in the trenches. One-third fewer wounded. We need to fight with skill not numbers. Do you know what our reserve units look like now? Battalions almost the size of divisions. Teeming hordes. Festering pockets of plague. The men loll around without weapons, with nothing to do. Just think—soldiers still in reserve units get the feeling that they are inescapably, and senselessly, doomed. When replacements reach their new regiment they know nothing, and have to be taught everything. The boneheads in the Defense Ministry and the government have one fixed idea: it's a big war, so rope in the greatest possible number of soldiers. Once those up top get something into their noodles what hope is there of changing their minds? Who can make them see reason?"

Up top? That was glaringly obvious to Shingarev. The Russian "top" casting its shadow over every sensible question, blocking every sensible way forward. Yes, indeed! So that even in Duma debates the deputies come up against a blank wall—and ours is not the sort of parliament to knock it down with a vote.

But Vorotyntsev knew it wasn't just up top . . . The man beside him, looking into his eyes, a sincere man for whom Russia was the breath of life . . . could he be made to think afresh? He was seeing difficulties already.

"Send workers back to the factories en masse? There'd be resentment in the army, petitions, recriminations—everybody would be saying, 'Why not me?' With the peasants it would be worse still. Those left behind would be demoralized. And what would the Allies say? Something very like demobilization in the middle of a war like this? They'd regard it as a betrayal. I talked to a lot of people in London and Paris this year and I simply can't imagine broaching any such subject. How could we prove to them that it is a practical necessity, that we are not conserving our strength at their expense? That we really haven't lost our determination to fight on to the last soldier and the last ruble?"

What? What's this I'm hearing? Can this be the same Shingarev?

"Andrei Ivanovich," he said vehemently. "What about the people in Novozhivotinnoye? Must they too fight to the last man? You . . . You have to realize that the infantry is at the end of its tether. The peasant cannot comprehend the need for all these sacrifices for the third year in succession. All he sees is that somebody, for some reason, is sacrificing him and that he must inevitably die or be left a cripple. You remember what you said about that leaseholder: that's how the soul of the people decays! That's just it—it is decaying!"

No! He didn't understand! The eyes were the same—eager, brilliant, sometimes moist, the look on his face was as cordial as ever, his voice just as disarmingly persuasive . . . No! He didn't understand! The young man crushed in the limestone quarry was not a casualty of patriotism . . . his fate had nothing to do with . . . the war, with victory, with the Allies, with Russia's historical destiny.

Vorotyntsev lost control of himself. "To hell with the Allies! Do you think they care about our losses? I wouldn't sacrifice even the last but one soldier for them."

Shingarev was astonished by the colonel's outburst. "But how could we make such an abrupt about-face? What would we have to do . . . and how?"

"Drastic actions would of course be necessary." Vorotyntsev spoke emphatically. He had no clear idea what those actions would be, and knew now that it was no good looking to his present companion for them.

Shingarev, however, shared the extraordinary readiness of all the Kadets to jump to conclusions, and saw Vorotyntsev's "drastic actions" in his own long-established perspective.

"You're right of course! Only drastic changes can save the country! Don't misunderstand me," he said apologetically, "I'm no leftist. I understand that a serious and responsible party, even in opposition, must support the government when it gets into an awkward situation. Otherwise the whole state would go to blazes . . . What worries my comrades is that if we cooperate with the government we may isolate ourselves from the left-wing groupings. And also that we might not do a good job of exposing the government, and that after the war, when it is brought to trial . . . will we live to see the day . . . ? We could be reproached for not . . . For my part I would cooperate with them to the full! I'd forgive them everything, I'd forgive the present regime everything, if I knew that their hearts too ache for the people. That they too, in their sleepless nights, think only of the people! But their hearts don't ache! They have no such thoughts even in broad daylight, sitting in uniform at their office desks. They don't understand, they don't feel that horrible events, heartrending events, are inexorably advancing on Russia."

Stinging tears clouded his eyes—the eyes of a good-natured bandit— and he had to close them.

"The government is in a state of collapse. The Tsar in command of the army—it's a catastrophe. We may be very close to the brink. Before long even the State Duma will not be able to keep the masses in check!"

Aha! This was the place for free speech! No one was so bold in the army.

Vorotyntsev held up a hand. "Andrei Ivanovich . . . surely you don't suppose . . . can anyone suppose . . . that there will be a revolution?"

Shingarev, dry-eyed now, looked hard at him.

"We, the Duma, exist for just that—to prevent revolution. We are the safety valve. A revolutionary explosion would relieve everybody of responsibility: they could say, 'If that hadn't happened to hinder us we would have . . . ' And what an enormous service revolution would do for Germany! We are the safety valve, and we reduce the pressure as much as we can. But what if the regime is impervious to all persuasion? Or what if treasonable thoughts are ripening within the government?"

"That's nonsense! Nothing like that is happening."

"What makes you so sure? What if Russia is being bundled along the road to defeat?" His hands fell resignedly into his lap. "Alas, this last year I've seen less and less hope of preventing it . . . It's probably no longer in our power."

The doorbell rang.

"That must be Pavel Nikolaevich!"

Shingarev raised a respectful, promissory finger. He rose with alacrity and went to the door.

Professor Milyukov next! They'll all be pitching into me! Have to think and answer back quickly.

Vorotyntsev hurriedly finished his second cigarette and quickly reviewed the major error in Shingarev's last words. Already half resigned himself to revolution? All the more reason to act, with a small compact force if necessary—to stop being timid, stop letting things slide, stop wasting time. That was something else they'd got wrong—why did they connect the government with defeat? Sapping the nation's spiritual strength was what it should be accused of. The great boulder had, after all, shifted and separated them. *They* want to "save the war." When what Russia needs is to free itself from the war.

Two bright female voices could be heard outside the door. Shingarev returned alone.

"No, it wasn't Pavel Nikolaevich. Two of our ladies, party members."

He lowered himself into his old hollow in the sofa, thought a minute, and returned to what he had been saying. His words were still doom-laden, but he now seemed almost to relish them.

"If revolution becomes a fatal necessity—what then? We can only try not to be too horrified. We can only try to believe in a miracle, believe that Russia will be reborn, even as a result of revolution. This bloody war, God willing, will bring complete freedom." He was not speaking only for himself, but for many others he could think of. "We shall yet see a great blossoming of social forces. We shall see enlightened, reasonable individuals, with respect for the freedom of a great people, in power. We must just not lose faith in Russia's future! We must believe in the spontaneously active forces in society. We must believe in the spiritual soundness of the people!"

At those last words his voice again sank and throbbed with emotion. For a moment he was unable to speak.

How muddled their minds were! Vorotyntsev could scarcely keep up with it: one minute—victory at all costs . . . the next—acceptance of defeat or even revolution, just so long as freedom followed.

Ah, but they contrived somehow to reconcile the two things.

"But then, after the revolution the army will acquire new strength, as happened in France. The officer corps will be reconstructed. Discipline will be reinforced. A new enthusiasm will spread through the ranks and the troops will . . ."

"You really think so?" In spite of himself there was a tinge of irony in Vorotyntsev's question.

"We all think so," Shingarev answered artlessly. "Could we have gone on for year after year without that faith?"

O blessed faith! If only you could surrender to it! But one regiment is one "people," another is another. And the same regiment is one people in the morning and another in the evening. And anyway, every regiment is just a faceless blur occupying so much space. Wars are won by volunteers, scouts, daredevils, the first into the attack. As surely as history is made by an elite minority.

He told Shingarev some of this, clumsily. And left him unconvinced.

But what about the young man crippled in the stone quarry?

Shingarev could not be diverted.

"Lately I've been reading a bit of French history, the late eighteenth century. D'you know what—the similarity is terrifying! You can't get away from the feeling that it's all happening now! That this is *our* debacle! That this is our own blind and brainless regime! That these are our lost battles! That those insidious rumors of treachery in high places are just like ours!"

"Andrei Ivanovich! Andrei Ivanovich!" Vorotyntsev felt bound to check him in full spate, seizing both his hands in a friendly grip. "Aren't we just asking for such analogies to be drawn? Shouldn't we be exerting ourselves to make them irrelevant? It's no good our repeating their history. How to avoid it—that's what we want to know! Spare us revolution, I beg you!"

"Well, since you ask," Shingarev said with a charming laugh. "But what do we get in return?"

Fair enough. When the state was stuck in a hopeless predicament what would any civilian expect from the military? "What are you waiting for? Why don't you help us?" Vorotyntsev was acutely, ashamedly, aware of this obligation. But how was he to help? Well, that was what he had come to find out.

"Of course," Shingarev said with a sigh, "a moderate coup d'état can be a splendid solution. But we Russians aren't very good at that sort of thing. Perhaps we're incapable of it. Guchkov says the regime has no props—one good push and . . . He's mistaken. It has many props. The state machine. The mental inertia of human beings. The self-interest of certain circles. The lack of courage in its subjects."

Were those words "lack of courage" a reproach? A hint? No, he was just thinking aloud. Anyway, courage was not enough—you had to have insight, you had to use your head, to learn, to understand. *You're all right, in the center of things here . . .* And once again Guchkov was cited. What a tight little world even sprawling Russia was!

"So all we can do is hope, Russian fashion, that something, somehow, sometime . . . If only the regime would come to its senses! That would be the simplest solution. It won't, though!" Shingarev clutched the graying but still thick hair on the top of his head. "It's astounding, this inability to understand the relentless march of history! To see that if you've got to give way in the end, it's best to do it in good time, while the going's good. No, they'll wait till they're smashed to smithereens before they give an inch. They just don't recognize that there's no avoiding the ladder of progress. Like it or not, we shall have to struggle up the same steps that the West has left behind it. But I grieve for the Russian people—we're paying too dearly for what others obtain cheaply. Do you know the legend of the Sibyl? It was quoted in the first issue of *Liberation*."

"*Liberation?*" Something else new. He didn't want to ask about it.

Another ring at the door.

"Pavel Nikolaevich!" Shingarev sprang up eagerly (all his movements were swift and purposeful) and went to open the door.

An elderly male voice was heard. Its owner was on first-name terms with Shingarev. "Has he come?"

"Not yet, but he's expected." And Vorotyntsev rose to greet another distinguished Kadet—a man with a tense, ironic, perhaps even mocking face, sharp eyes behind pince-nez, and a painstakingly elongated wedge of blond beard.

"Mili Izmailovich Minervin, a member of our Central Committee and of the Kadet group in the Duma. I was about to tell Georgi Mikhailovich the legend of the Sibyl. Will you? You do it better."

Of course he would! Without waiting to be asked twice, or inquiring why this unenlightened colonel wanted to know the legend of the Sibyl, he lowered himself onto the same old sofa, ignoring the hollow, and with no change of expression, voice, or manner he launched into a speech not just for this one-man audience but for a whole auditorium, calling upon all his histrionic and vocal skills, so that the dark red curtains of history's stage swayed mysteriously.

"She came to the Roman king Tarquin and offered to sell him the Book of the Fates. The king, however, thought the price too high and would not pay it. The Sibyl flung part of the book into the fire—and asked the same price for the rest. The king hesitated but still refused. Then the Sibyl threw another part of the book into the fire, and asked the same price for what was left. The Tsa-a-ar"—Minervin savored the word, shedding his historical disguise—"the Tsa-a-ar was shaken, consulted his augurs, and bought the remnants. And there you have it!!"

Gazing out at his public through the pince-nez attached by a long ribbon to his collar, Minervin espied some soldier or other in the front row, and explained the moral of the play to him. "It is dangerous to haggle with historical necessity; the longer you carry on, the more stubborn it becomes. Whoever refuses to read the Book of the Fates in the proper order will pay dearly for the last pages, for the denouement!!"

Stepping down from the stage, back again in Shingarev's study, he said, "We published that fourteen years ago. And what did our rulers think it meant? That they should give way to society and the Duma, and so avoid revolution? They've missed their chance year after year. Last year yet again. And even this year."

The telephone rang in the corridor and Shingarev hurried out.

"Pavel Nikolaevich," he said on his return. "Says he's held up."

* * *

SKIP, SKIP, SKIP, BUT MIND YOU DON'T TRIP.

* * *

Document No. 1

November 1916

TO THE PETERSBURG PROLETARIAT
Proletarians of all lands unite!

... this criminal war, brought about by the predators of international capital ... As soon as they have drained the vital juices from the peoples on the other side, the governing classes will say that their task is accomplished. The war brings unprecedented profits to the ruling class, giving them enormous returns on their capital.

The rule of the Tsarist robber gang complicates matters for Russia. The two-headed eagle hovers over the devil's dance of rampaging predators.

Only by declaring total *WAR ON WAR* ... HURRAH FOR *THAT* WAR! THE ENEMY OF EACH PEOPLE IS IN ITS OWN COUNTRY.

Long live the RSDRP!

Petersburg Committee of the RSDRP

[21]

In prim and proper army circles you could, especially if you never picked up a newspaper, afford to disapprove of the Kadets, or even despise them. But in their lively, quick-witted company you were bound to have mixed feelings: flattered by their welcome, you were also bewildered to find them so knowledgeable and well informed. Of the two Duma leaders one was impetuously outgoing, the other self-importantly sarcastic. There were two ladies, not, like most women, husbands' accessories, but party activists, presently engaged in collecting books, tobacco, underwear, toffees, and soap for the troops ("From Petrograd to the Defenders of the Motherland"), forever organizing something important, remarkable for their emancipated behavior, and the older lady (with the double-barreled name, Pukhnarevich something-or-other) also for her intelligence and her outspokenness. The younger of the two was rather pretty, and although nothing of importance tripped from her tongue her expression said that it was there, biding its time, waiting for an opening. The hostess was, by comparison, a simple housewife, made simpler by her large family, not like the consort of a parliamentary deputy. Another arrival was a young lecturer in economics, with black horn-rims, very guarded in utterance, very careful not to show his feelings. When he did speak, though, it was in a rich, compelling youthful bass which defied contradiction. This lecturer, rather than the two Kadet leaders, overawed Vorotyntsev: quite young, quite unknown, but so knowledgeable, so conspicuously clever. There must be so many like him in Petersburg society. An ocean of clever people. They knew so many things you didn't know. If the Russian state took a different turn tomorrow you would look to them for answers. They would have to point the way.

These were just the people he was interested in meeting. He had moved long enough in the company of soldiers.

The moment they left the study, and introductions were over, the lecturer informed them, quoting his sources in full, that the population of Petrograd was now a million and a quarter more than normal. He did not fail to add (undaunted even by Minervin's presence) that the urban population of Russia, thirty million before the war, or one-sixth of the empire, was now, as a result of mass migration, sixty million. This made the job of extracting foodstuffs from the peasants twice as hard as it used to be. They were money-grubbing profiteers, reluctant to put their grain on the market, and if this tendency wasn't nipped in the bud, it would be the beginning of social disintegration.

Some of the things he said were quite surprising, but the ladies present seemed to know the script, and spoke their own lines, declaring that the government, unlike the speakers, had anticipated nothing of all this. No amount of indignation sufficed for the government's absurd actions. Society, and the Duma, had given the motherland all they could, and society was not to blame if all those sacrifices had brought no results. The reason for the whole debacle was the tradition of ordering the people's lives without consulting the people themselves.

From that moment on, all Vorotyntsev heard told him that each of them knew in advance what the others would say, but that it was imperative for them to meet and hear all over again what they collectively knew. They were all overpoweringly certain that they were right, yet they needed these exchanges to reinforce their certainty. Only Vorotyntsev, who was ignorant of such matters, hung back, and couldn't get out a single word of any importance. He merely tried to follow. He nonetheless felt that he was being sucked into their shared certainty. Yes, oh yes! He was learning to see as they saw, and now he knew that he had long known some of these things beyond doubt.

He sought Vera's warm glances to reassure himself further. She had seemed well satisfied with the way the three men looked as they left the study, and glad that she had brought her brother along.

So this was what life in the capital was like! No need to invite guests specially, no fixed date or time (and this was Monday!), guests assembled anyway, as if they were all there on business—and suddenly it was a soiree after all, and everybody had to be fed. Not much of a party, though, with none of the ladies wearing evening gowns, but at most the sort of newish blouse favored by ladies of the opposition (a studied carelessness in dress carried over from student days as a sort of uniform). They all wore their hair slicked down, as far as possible diverting attention from their appearance. Vera's plain, straight brown dress was ostentatious in comparison.

Three girls, the oldest fourteen, also drifted in for supper, and were introduced. Shingarev's sons were not at home—the elder was in his last year in officers' school. (It crossed Vorotyntsev's mind that another little girl had died—Vera had warned him.)

Fathers often feel awkward with outsiders present, but Shingarev beamed whenever he looked at his children.

Vorotyntsev had never had a child. He knew that children were supposed to be life's greatest joy, that you were expected to admire them and ask them questions. But it was a tie he did not need himself.

No Pavel Nikolaevich just yet—might as well get to the table. As Vera had foretold, there was black bread, not white, fish in aspic, pickled mushrooms, boiled potatoes, and sauerkraut. But, to be fair, these people were as indifferent to what was put on their plates as to dress and the rickety furniture. They helped themselves without ceremony, but nothing seemed to find its way into their mouths. The talk was what mattered.

"They'll never learn!"

"They're hopeless!"

"You get nothing from an autocracy just for the asking!"

The older lady's elbow-length sleeves looked as though they were rolled up for work, or a fight. "Putting it bluntly," she said, "nothing worthwhile can be done until we get rid of this regime!"

The lecturer, eyebrows like devil's horns, elbows resting on his chest, and fingertips joined to form a triangle, said, "We can expect nothing as long as we have an autocratic system. Without a total change of government we can neither halt the Germans nor stem the wrath of the people."

Vorotyntsev heard all this without feeling insulted. He had heard the same old tune at home in his youth: the Decembrists had wanted what was best for the country, and only by continuing their glorious tradition could the country be saved. He found nothing reprehensible even in the undisguised wish of all present for a republic. Nobody talked or thought like that in military circles, but, from a broader view, the country could prosper under more than one form of government. Who could tell?

The girls ate heartily, without wasting words. They really were nice children. Vorotyntsev could imagine how happy they must all be in that large, harmonious, successful family.

Evfrosinya Maksimovna was not too busy to tell them which was the bought cabbage and which came from the school plot: the whole class had grown a splendid crop, supplied a military hospital, given all the girls some, and put some in brine for school use. Their pickled mushrooms they got from Grachevka—not just a wartime arrangement, they always had, every year. Grachevka? Yes, in the Usman rural district, his late father's farm, left to Andrei Ivanovich as the oldest of six children. The garden and the orchard we manage to cultivate with our own hands, we're there every year from spring to autumn, all of us except Andrei Ivanovich. The arable land and the meadows we can't manage ourselves, and renting them out would be immoral, so we allow the neighbors to use them.

Five children could be as much of a worry as a whole company of soldiers, to be sure.

Then it was back to those triply incomprehensible fixed prices. Shingarev, as it happened, was decidedly in favor of them. Vorotyntsev couldn't reconcile two things: Shingarev was the passionate champion of the village, but what he had learned on the train now told him that Shingarev was against the village.

There was no time to work it out and the topic slipped by without friction.

He did, without thinking, say something to the effect that firm prices needed a firm hand. He had nothing very special in mind, it was just an obvious association of ideas.

But his listeners were up in arms immediately.

"Firm hands aren't always clean hands!"

"Firm hands usually go with thick heads!"

Vorotyntsev was put out, and even blushed: was this a dig meant for him?

He was making the naïve newcomer's usual mistake—forgetting that he was more closely watched and more clearly seen by others than they were by him. Those present had of course heard a good deal about him in advance—most probably as a rebel against GHQ, *who had been unfairly treated because* . . .

"No," he said, answering somebody's question, "I didn't go to cadet school, I went to a modern high school."

They liked that.

"A modern-school boy? So you weren't meant for an army career? . . . Did you have any doubts about it?"

He could, and perhaps should, have humored them but he answered honestly. "No, I never had any doubts, I knew what I wanted from my childhood on. Father hoped I'd change my mind and persuaded me to put it off and go to modern school."

Shingarev meanwhile had glimpsed a still darker prospect in the wake of fixed prices. "If the war drags on, it will be too late to talk about voluntary initiatives and about private trade: I'm afraid we might have to say what proportion of his stocks each particular person *must* sell."

Minervin raised a forbidding finger toward his forbidding pince-nez, just as if he was speaking in the Duma, and seemed to shake his words out of it: "Ne-ver, ne-ver, ne-ver! Such a curtailment of freedom . . . !"

Shingarev, quite sure of himself, replied, "Be careful—even Protopopov uses the words 'freedom of trade.' Nowadays the Minister of the Interior makes solemn pronouncements on freedom of trade. But what he means is freedom for predators, and we are in fact in favor of regulation in the people's own interests. That's the paradox. What would become of Russia if in obedience to the principle of freedom we left the call-up to private initiative? It's the same with agriculture. War demands sacrifices. We ought to keep one eye on the enemy and take a leaf out of his book. The Germans tell a joke about us: which country has everything and yet has nothing? In Russia poor organization has turned abundance into shortage. In their country perfect organization means that in spite of shortages everybody has enough. Mobile kitchens distribute cheap meals throughout Germany. The state can take everything, but it can also give everything. When we recaptured the Pinsk Marshes this year we found them provided with the roads we hadn't gotten around to building in a hundred years."

Who wouldn't warm to him? And his voice could, when he wished, ring out imperiously. No wonder he was at the top of the political tree.

"If we want to win we must inevitably introduce organs of coercion, as all European countries have. War is nothing but coercion, and there's no getting around it, we shall be drawn into the sort of 'war socialism' that has taken over Germany. Grain, sugar, tea, kerosene, everything will have to be brought under central control if we're to get through the war. The Germans have conscription of labor from sixteen to sixty—and if we want to win we can't avoid it ourselves."

"Only"—Vorotyntsev couldn't help interrupting—"only, in Germany society and the government are allies, not enemies as they are here."

Nobody seemed to notice his demurrer. Shingarev had evidently bolted down a path of his own, at an angle to the party line. Pavel Nikolaevich had not arrived in time to scotch this heresy, but Mili Izmailovich had enough heavy artillery of his own.

"Am I to understand, Andrei Ivanovich, that you're taking the *government's* side?" A chill breeze passed around the table, causing the Kadet diners to reel back in horror.

"It's the government that contemplates regimenting labor, to prevent unwanted strikes. 'Workers, fall in at your benches!' " Minervin raised an expressively trembling hand, drip, drip, dripping his expressive phrases from the tip of a finger. "But our party cannot accept dictatorship as the price of victory. Serfdom all over again? Strip the people of the last vestige of freedom, for the sake of victory? Russia does not need victory at that price! We all, every one of us, have a burning desire for freedom, indeed we do! But victory as we understand it includes winning civic rights for the people!!!"

Vorotyntsev eagerly absorbed this argument, hearing all their voices, even the background chorus, at once. He was amazed by this combination of high culture and the decisiveness needed in those who govern.

The others, it seemed, were all on Minervin's side, but Shingarev was undeterred.

"No, they're on the right track, the only track. Labor conscription is an inevitable stage in the course of events. It's a universal requirement of modern war, compelling us to deviate from the ideal of freedom. Even if a government enjoying society's confidence is set up tomorrow, it will be forced to do the same thing!"

"You think so? Never!!" Minervin accompanied a sharp look through his pince-nez with a sharp little laugh. "And if you dare say such a thing from the Duma tribunal you'll become unpopular overnight!"

As though he was indeed on the rostrum and not in his own living room Andrei Ivanovich retorted, steppe dweller's eyes flashing, "I shall dare to say it just the same. I can't help it. Yes, fellow countrymen, the time has come to make sacrifices! Peasants, the state needs your bread! Fellow citizens, the state needs the labor of your hands! And if enlightened persons who truly love their people come to power, there will be such an upsurge of enthusiasm! The workers will stand at their benches without a murmur! Grain will flood in! The people will give its grain as it has given its children."

His voice failed. Overcome by emotion, he had to pause for breath.

They all raised their voices at once. The senior lady with the solid elbows gave her verdict without waiting to hear the balance of opinion.

"Well, of course, if we had a responsible government even dictatorship would be tolerable! As things are, the government is deliberately creating supply problems to get Russia out of the war."

The younger lady, with the slender, graceful arms (covered, however, to the wrist by the filmy fabric of her blouse), was not too shy to correct her. "We have been warned against the term 'responsible government.' It could expose us to attack by Black Hundreds agitators. We're supposed to say 'government trusted by the people.'" Her blouse was dark green, with mysterious flecks of brown. "Government by proxy, you might say."

It slipped out so glibly, almost as if such a government existed already, its membership generally known, man by man and post by post, a wonderfully heroic government into the bargain. Only Vorotyntsev, marooned in the trenches, had somehow failed to notice. Asking would have embarrassed him—even if they had left room for questions.

What was obvious was their certainty that such a government would be generally welcomed, popular, and salutary. To *that* sort of government, Vorotyntsev gathered, all things were permissible, whereas from the present government no gift was acceptable.

"The Progressive Bloc will assuredly lead Russia out of the impasse!"

"Educated society surely could not manage things worse than the thickheaded bureaucrats! Russia is governed by the thickest of the thick!"

"What is Russian society supposed to do with such a government? Educate the idiots? Impossible. Change their idiotic minds? Impossible. You live for decades completely at the mercy of idiots, and the moment you offer a helping hand they shush you: watch what you're doing, you'll have us all in the hole!"

"But how can we muzzle ourselves? We have no court of appeal."

"They have declared war on the whole people! As long ago as the 1860s!"

"A government of Asiatic despots, of bloodthirsty cannibals!"

"A policy of moderation toward it is as criminal as a policy of betrayal!"

"Milyukov imagines you can operate in starched cuffs, like Europeans!"

"There's a rule even doormen and yardmen know: start sweeping from the top of the steps!"

"The Kadet Party can save Russia—but only by abandoning its moderate stance to some extent, only in contact with the left."

"We should have lined up with the left, not the right, from the start!"

"Society will not be satisfied with just a change of ministers. What is wanted is a general amnesty! And the repeal of Jewish disabilities."

The whole discussion—with all of them, Vera included, taking part—sped dizzily into the distance, or fragmented, as the talk became more voluble and louder.

They were evidently only just beginning, but with every word they became more remote from the man who wanted only to determine how he himself should act for the best. The carousel was spinning at bewildering speed, there was no way of slowing it down, no way not to be dragged around with it.

Through the wordy deluge one note rang out clearly: those present understood the people's needs, had made them their own, and could infallibly satisfy them. Something the government could never do. Left helpless by their dizzying self-assurance, Vorotyntsev slumped silently in his chair.

"Our parliamentary methods are ineffectual against this insane regime!"

"No, gentlemen, no! Parliamentary means are the only ones! In *our* country might will never be recognized as right!"

"For two years now we've been longing for news of victories! And we get fobbed off with some ship sunk in the Gulf of Riga!"

"We in the Duma are partly to blame. We've always done our best not to kick up a fuss, we've been too careful not to damage the prestige of the army."

"Russia's old vice, Russia's vice through the ages—suffering in silence."

Shingarev too was a different man in this company. What is it that always forces us to adapt to the general tone? The whirl left Vorotyntsev dazed, like a ram staring at a new gate. He tried not to show even by his expression how much he disagreed.

"Never forget that the government is not honest with society!"

(No, and neither are you with the government. You say one thing and mean another.)

"No, no, with a Tsar like ours victory is impossible!"

"To go against the people and the Duma with the invader already deep inside the country is to play his game!"

"The international alignment favors a Russian victory as never before. Our ancient enemy England is with us, our recent enemy Japan is with us . . . !"

Ah, but what about our allies' idiotic Dardanelles operation? Vorotyntsev wondered. No good, though, trying to get a word in. They were all greater patriots than he was. They would settle for nothing short of total victory.

"If we're to save Russia from the Germans we need an immediate radical change of regime!"

"It's perfectly obvious *they* are deliberately aggravating the economic situation to give them an excuse for getting out of the war!"

A snag in the smooth surface of the carousel. Something wrong here!

Weren't you saying the very opposite before 1914—that they were deliberately inviting war, to get out of what was supposed to be a difficult economic situation?

He still hadn't the nerve to object, helpless against the compelling force of the carousel. He couldn't help noticing, though, that they argued in generalities. When it came to details they were much less knowledgeable than Fyodor Kovynev. Words at the ready, filling chests and mouths to overflowing, gushing out to stop the least little crack, though by now no one had anything novel or surprising to say.

"Russia is just one big lunatic asylum!"

"The new ministers haven't even bothered to move into their state apartments: they'll all be dismissed in a month anyway."

"The guards are planning a coup—everybody knows that! There will be a coup—take my word for it!"

Vorotyntsev was all ears. What was this coup everybody seemed to be babbling about?

"It's bound to come! Public discontent is greater now than it ever was in 1905!"

"Heavens above, they're going to let Sukhomlinov out of the Peter and Paul Fortress! What more do you need?"

"There's no dodging it! Revolutionary action must be planned now, to forestall a flare-up of popular discontent!"

Vorotyntsev found himself eyed more and more closely: this is right up his alley! If he really is a progressive officer, what has *he* to tell *us*?

Vorotyntsev had—or hadn't he?—catapulted himself there for that very purpose, to lend a hand. But he saw now that he was probably in the wrong place. He felt annoyed with himself for giving way so feebly, for his inability to resist or contradict at any point.

There were three kinds of jam on the table, all from Grachevka, all homemade. They had reached the tea stage, and the little girls were on their way out. They had sat in silence throughout the conversation. No doubt they were used to hearing such things day in and day out.

There was a ring at the door. Pavel Nikolaevich maybe? They all braced themselves, strained their ears. Shingarev jumped up smartly and went to the door. They listened eagerly. No—it was a woman's voice. Musical, measured, dignified.

"Strange." Minervin seemed surprised.

She didn't go away, she was obviously taking her coat off, but she and her host didn't join the company.

Vera, sitting next to her brother, whispered, "Professor Andozerskaya—the cleverest woman in Petersburg, so they say."

"Oh, yes?"

"You know how it is—both capitals like to claim fifty or so 'cleverest women' each. . . ."

"With all their prohibitions and restrictions and suspicions they drive people to the left . . ."

"They . . . they . . . are less afraid of Germany than of yielding to public opinion in their own country. As far as they are concerned, Zemgor and the War Industry Committees are subversive organizations—they see revolution everywhere! If they can suspect an independent and disinterested body like Zemgor . . ."

Vorotyntsev had held back as long as he could, but this touched a raw nerve in him. He had to distance himself. "Look, it's all very well, but you can't honestly call them disinterested."

The moment he said it, just that one little thing, they were all on their guard. They fell silent, as they had been speaking, in unison, and their silence was aimed at the colonel. The lecturer straightened his horn-rims, the older lady put on her tortoiseshells and became more forbidding, her quick, chunky elbows more menacing than ever. They were all waiting for an explanation.

He had started it—he had to go through with it. (Vera was looking at him anxiously.)

"At the front" (he wanted to get it across as precisely as possible) "you hear all sorts of different opinions about Zemgor. They do quite a bit, but it's strange, just to take one thing, that their medical effort is left to amateurs, who don't belong to any unit. They do quite a bit . . . but their staffs are too large, far too large. And every post is for some reason filled not by old men or discharged soldiers but by men liable to military service. Most of them young members of the intelligentsia. They employ deserters as medical orderlies . . ."

He knew already that he was up against a solid wall of disapproval.

The older lady was the first to react. "Just think of all the good they're doing," she burst out. "They're working for victory!"

Even before the protests began, before the tense, disapproving silence was broken, Vorotyntsev felt himself blushing. Talking in their presence was, he found, not at all easy. If you just listened they all prattled away merrily, but somehow, if you tried to say something yourself, however clear your thoughts were, you looked ridiculous.

"The train providing ablution facilities doesn't go as far as it might, and digging wells fifteen versts from the front line, or draining marshes, could wait for the end of the war . . . They aren't satisfying the army's real needs, but imaginary ones. They don't look after the wounded properly." But, under the pressure of their disapproval, he added, "I myself don't actually think . . ."

He had lied, prevaricated, betrayed his beliefs. Why couldn't he manage it? Say this is *my* opinion. This is what *I* think! Why was he so feeble? Why couldn't he put his thoughts into words? And the color in his cheeks—what a disgrace! Such a tense, unreceptive atmosphere. When he had attacked generals he had not been afraid. There *he* had been the revolutionary. *Here* he was afraid; his behavior was reactionary, and that was the most damning word of all.

He was tempted to tell them Zherber's story about the fictitious labels of origin on munition crates—but that would never do! He couldn't possibly say that here! Anyway, they wouldn't believe it and would be at his throat.

Minervin raised a portentous finger. "You're omitting the morale factor. Last year, during the 'great retreat,' at a time of national desperation, the forces of society burned with a sacred fire and breathed it into the ranks of our wavering army."

Vorotyntsev took this insult to the army personally and spoke more sharply than before. "They breathed nothing into us. And it would be better if instead of trying to, they . . ."

You've been longing for fifty years to "go to the people." So go to the people. The people are the infantry.

But he couldn't get it out. Instead he said, "The least they could do is to try not to create chaos. You can't operate three different military supply systems simultaneously."

He was wrong, quite wrong, they clamored. The colonel didn't understand, he'd swallowed government propaganda hook, line, and sinker. The fact was that the fatheaded government was gunning for Zemgor, accusing it of carrying on propaganda among the troops, and even of espionage, for which reason soldiers were forbidden to have anything to do with Zemgor personnel. Spies were planted in Zemgor tearooms, buffets, barbershops . . .

Those tearooms were in fact the main disseminators of malicious rumor and inciters of revolution. But Vorotyntsev made no comment.

"Bah—the government itself is a gang of filthy spies! Andrei Ivanovich will be back in a moment, and he'll tell you that they wouldn't even authorize the dispatch of doctors to cholera-stricken units in 1905—they were always arresting 'cholera personnel' on suspicion of encouraging peasants to loot gentry estates. They're less afraid of epidemics than of revolution!"

Vorotyntsev still didn't protest. How much did he remember of 1905 anyway? He had never thought about it properly. He gave ground, held his peace. Not because he felt he was wrong, but out of fear of saying something *reactionary*. Yes, divisions received such instructions—officers were to keep an eye on Zemgor activists, because they carried on subversive propaganda and were working for a revolution. Well, they *did* carry on propaganda. What was to stop them? They had ensconced themselves, made themselves at home, they felt safe, so what was to stop them from assaulting the soldier's mind? But why then should the government be forbidden to defend its army? The inviolability of the person was all very well, but what about the inviolability of the fatherland? And something of that sort went on in anticholera units too: in the heat of revolution wouldn't you expect conceited half-educated medical orderlies to fan the flames?

And still he couldn't bring himself to say it. He despised himself for it. Perhaps he should leave right away . . .

The company (so small but so dynamic, and already disappointed in this dubious colonel, but what could you expect from the conformist monarchists of the imperial army?), the company rode over him in full cry.

"They can't give us victories, so they fob us off with an insulting present instead—the right to graft the imperial standard onto the national flag!"

"Symbolizing the union of Tsar and people! Where's their sense of humor!"

"You can bet the rosy-cheeked cops won't be sent to the front."

"The lower orders are getting more and more exasperated. This crowd will never be forgiven by the people!"

Strange, really. So few of them, yet so quick to second one another. He wondered about Vera. She was with them so much, she must share these ideas. It was a contagious disease—there was no resisting it if you came too close.

"It's gotten to the point where schoolboys are tearing the royal arms off their caps."

"We've crossed some sort of fateful divide and are moving steadily toward the denouement!"

"Gorky's magazine is quite right. It's time to stop being afraid of what in police parlance is called 'disorder.'"

"The holders of power take fright very easily! They may *look* unassailably strong . . . In 1905 we saw how cowardly they really are!"

"In the long run *the worse things are, the better!* Even a catastrophe will get us somewhere! Anything's better than rotting away in this shameful fashion!"

"Meek acceptance, that's what's shameful! If serfdom has not rotted Russia to the core, things are about to happen!"

"Something *must* happen! It can't go on like this much longer!"

At which Minervin took the floor, raising an admonitory finger. Drip, drip, drip . . .

"Whoever clashes with the people will fall into the abyss!"

And his oratorical self-assurance, his whiter than white collar, his meticulously knotted tie, his unbroken record as a deputy, were no impediment, indeed they encouraged him in his belief that he was the summit, in the lead, at the cutting edge of that "people" which would clash with the government and hurl it into the abyss.

Ah, but if the people meant the infantry—here was Colonel Vorotyntsev, who had seen two full complements pass through his regiment, who in his free and easy way persisted in asking personal questions, even in the intervals between forward charges, who had learned and committed to his capacious memory six hundred, eight hundred, maybe a thousand faces, characters, life stories . . . Whereas Minervin—how many infantrymen had Minervin known? They rattled on about the government's culpability—but oh, how easy they found it to tongue-wag soldiers down the road to death. How simple everything looked from a Petersburg apartment!

A jolt. He was free. Free from the unbearable constraints, the bewitchment. He felt ready to insult them on their own ground. No more apologies. He had regained his freedom. He spoke loudly, challengingly addressing the whole gathering.

"You, gentlemen, keep repeating that Russia is ruled by the thickest of the thick, that its ministers are all idiots, that we desperately need better ones. But let's be frank about it: the last thing 'society' wants is good ministers in Russia. If good ministers came on the scene tomorrow 'society' would hate them even more than the bad ones!"

He no longer felt shy, no longer shrank. If he was flushed—it was with passion.

They were taken aback, but recovered quickly.

"Good ones? When did Russia ever have good ministers? Name them!"

That one had not sunk in on them. But, determined to get his own back for his humiliation, he refused to be diverted, and launched a frontal attack on "society's" opinions, unafraid of its jeers.

"No, I won't list the good ones, but there was one great one! We had one great Russian statesman, and which of you in educated Russian society noticed and acknowledged it? He was abused and reviled more than Goremykin or Stürmer. And he departed as he had come—unrecognized, unappreciated, indeed anathematized."

The ladies and gentlemen were nonplussed, but they had not yet lost all hope that this colonel was not a dyed-in-the-wool reactionary, that he was just muddleheaded. But whom did he have in mind? Surely not . . . ? He couldn't possibly mean . . . ?

"Yes, Stolypin!" With a sweep of his hand Vorotyntsev demolished their hopes and his own social reputation. His voice rang out a challenge.

"We were sent a man of integrity! A man incapable of compromise! A man sure that his cause was right! And that there was still plenty of sound sense in Russia, if you just listened! Above all, a man who knew how to act, how to break the logjam, instead of just babbling away. If he had a plan he acted on it! If he exerted his strength he got things moving! What he saw was the future, what he offered was the new. So—did you recognize him at the time? It was his boldness, his devotion to Russia, above all his wisdom that upset society. The 'Stolypin necktie' gibe stuck—people failed to see that there was a lot more to his premiership than the rope."

Witty, though—"Stolypin necktie." What was a necktie if not a symbol? Minervin adjusted his own, contemplated an annihilating tirade. Or should he try irony? Or just ignore it?

What could he say, though? It was as though a shell burst had dug an impassable hole between them. If this was the sort of colonel that got called a rebel, what could the rest of the officer corps, the non-rebels, be like? And if Stolypin was accepted as the epitome of Russia, could that country, which lacked a past anyway, be said to have a future? Did it deserve to be dragged out of the mire? Alas for Russian society! Unhappy the lot of progressive persons in that uncouth country!

So that was that, and they could have called it a day, gone their separate ways, never to meet again, except that they were not in a club, not in the street, but in Andrei Ivanovich's apartment, and some respectable solution had to be found. Except that after what had been said, even simple politenesses were hard to utter.

Vorotyntsev, however, felt relieved, though it worried him a little to see Vera looking pale and frightened.

The situation was saved by Andrei Ivanovich in person. He had apparently been in the room, standing behind Vorotyntsev, long enough to hear his speech. He now walked around the table, to the places vacated by the children, sat down without ceremony, letting one hand dangle over a chair back and pushing an empty cup away with the other. He was no longer the booming, the thunderous orator, calling on the people to make sacrifices, he was very quiet, very diffident . . . He looked uncertainly at Minervin, at the lecturer, at the ladies . . . Then spoke again in that deep throbbing voice that seemed to bring out all the bubbles of warmth clinging to the walls of his chest.

"Do you know . . . I had a remarkable encounter with Stolypin once in the Second Duma . . . I'd seen him many a time, of course, I'd heard him say 'You don't scare me,' and 'What you want are great upheavals,' and it all seemed plain enough, just another suppressor, a power maniac, a careerist—we never measured him by any other yardstick. I myself strongly condemned his agrarian reform bill in the Duma—said it was a bureaucratic ploy, that it would cause discord in every rural community, and in the family, that it threatened to destroy the ancient foundations . . . I was also the first in 1911 to sign the motion opposing Stolypin's policy on the western zemstvos. But I had to appeal to him on several occasions to show clemency to certain people—and he always did. A friend of mine, also a zemstvo doctor, had been banished by administrative order from Voronezh province for 'propaganda among the peasantry.' To be honest, he really had carried on propaganda, or putting it more simply, hadn't concealed his Liberationist ideas from his patients. But my pride wouldn't let me abandon a friend to rough justice—after all, I was a Duma deputy. So I up and wrote a letter to Stolypin."

Andrei Ivanovich told his story apologetically, and seemed surprised at himself. (Even now—eight years after the event. Meeting Stolypin at that time was tantamount to treason. He must have kept it quiet.)

"Well, he invited me to come and see him. I went. Gritting my teeth, full of hostility. We met in a small room in the ministerial suite, just the two of us. Not in the white glare of the Duma chamber, where every line in your face is etched deeper by the light from the chandeliers, and we ourselves and every sound we utter become so much more important, but in a little room, with a single desk. Stolypin was not a bit stiff, not on his dignity, not at all onstage, he was just tired, worn out, in fact. 'So you're a zemstvo doctor?' he said, 'I never knew!' He was smiling and he looked so kind, so gentle, I just couldn't resist him. He made such a good impression, in fact the best possible impression!"

His eyes moved around to Vorotyntsev, he gave him a good-natured grin, and went on, still sounding surprised.

"I felt that this way I could easily slip up, betray my principles, but I couldn't help giving him a friendly smile in return."

Not many people had such a becoming smile as Shingarev. When he smiled you wouldn't swap him for anybody.

"I couldn't keep a note of goodwill out of my voice. I answered frankly—yes, my friend did have Liberationist ideas, but he was by no means an extremist, he couldn't possibly call for any sort of upheaval."

A smile that melted himself and his listeners. How could anyone fail to respond?

"He gave his promise. And kept it. My friend was allowed to go home."

"Exceptions only prove the rule," Minervin reminded him curtly.

"Another time"—Shingarev was not to be put off—"I approached him about Pyanykh, an SR member of the Duma, tried for murder, to try to get the death sentence commuted to life imprisonment. He refused at first—Pyanykh had planted a bomb in a priest's house, and he didn't want to interfere with the court, but he arranged a reprieve just the same. And there was yet another occasion. Ten Voronezh peasants were condemned to death for murdering a landowner. I turned to him again: two of them had confessed, but they weren't all murderers, the others were innocent. He said, 'You don't realize what sort of people you're pleading for. If we don't keep murderers in check by terror they'll cut the throat of everybody who wears a frock coat, including you and me. If they should seize power you would be one of the first to be executed.' He got out a diagram and showed it to me. 'Look at this, it shows that while all that talk is going on in the Duma the number of murders, especially of constables, watchmen, and landowners, is mounting from day to day. Terrorist acts are on the increase—and I have to answer for it.' In spite of which he telegraphed orders to Voronezh to reopen the inquiry."

His guileless face promised all doubters a candid reply.

"Since then, I've sometimes been uneasily aware that even the very best parliaments can be too clumsy, too full of sound and fury. Take the British and French parliaments, as we saw them this spring. Our dream is to be like them. But when you consider it, we all get too embittered, we all say harsh things we don't really mean. There must surely be some better way . . . some more humane way of trying to persuade even our most savage opponents."

There might or might not be such a utopia somewhere, but Minervin merely wiped his pince-nez and let this pass.

Somehow, a film seemed to be forming over the ditch dug by Vorotyntsev's bombshell.

Another ring. The telephone this time. Shingarev hurried out, and the others listened hard. This time it was Pavel Nikolaevich!

But Shingarev came back looking embarrassed: he asks us not to wait for him any longer, he can't possibly come, something urgent has arisen. He hinted that it had to do with Protopopov.

With Protopopov, that traitor? Well, well. The whole company was on tenterhooks.

While the telephone call was going on, yet another voice, the musical female voice heard earlier, was addressing Minervin, quite forcefully, behind Vorotyntsev's back.

Not wanting to sit with his back to her, he looked around. A small, rather ordinary-looking woman in a dark gray English two-piece. She held her small head erect and motionless. Her dark hair was tousled, or untidily combed. And she was putting Minervin in his place.

Everybody here of course knew everybody else! No introductions were made. Vorotyntsev was the only new face.

He stood up abruptly, took a step, his spurs jingled as he clicked his heels and—although he had not kissed other hands in this room— bent over Professor Andozerskaya's hand. Just because he felt like it.

She raised her small hand and held it out to him. With a smile. Her eyes sparkled with frank approval.

She had heard the explosion!

*

*   *

Siberian regiments, famed in song and story,
bristling with bayonets, marching to glory.
Let the world know!

Over the bridges and Warsaw is ours!
Proud Polish beauties pelt us with flowers!
Let the world know!

[2 2]

A man who has long endured hardship and dangers, however accustomed he is to them, however firmly he shuts his mind to thoughts of a different lot, is gradually sapped without even realizing it by an instinctive urge to relax, a yearning for sympathetic attention and appreciation of his services. Even a little boy who spends the whole day scrambling about in trees and paddling in streams for crayfish looks for recognition and admiration at the family table in the evening. And the most dogged and tight-lipped of workers after a day, a week, a month of slog and frost expects at least one person, his wife, to show understanding and concern. A sense of physical and spiritual deprivation gnaws even more damagingly at the vitals of a soldier at the front, who cannot even be sure that his life will be prolonged from one day to the next.

Vorotyntsev, who was always tightly geared to the job in hand, had not realized until now how strong his yearning for these things had become. But the moment he stretched out on a bunk in an ordinary—to him utterly extraordinary!—civilian carriage on the Kiev–Moscow train, he had begun to feel an upsurge of this yearning. At home in Moscow, where it would have been most natural to appease his need, trivial distractions crept in, and there was no chance of sharing his most intimate feelings. In the train he had given Fyodor Kovynev a peep at the outermost edge of his thoughts. He had wondered, on the way to Petersburg, whether he would find people concerned enough, demanding enough, understanding enough for him to become the center of searching and grateful attention, to sit center stage and let himself talk and talk, suffering all over again the pain of his experience, yet delighted to feel his bones relieved of the ache long suffered in silence, to see military setbacks turned to good purpose, transformed by the ready understanding of this friendly company.

And then, in the fifth-floor apartment on Monetnaya Street, the very company he was hoping for seemed to have assembled, intent on hearing what he had to say, and on questioning him—but perhaps they asked questions only out of politeness, and there was indeed no real reason for them to listen, since party politics was their sole interest. As *he* listened to *them* the desire to pour out his most secret and saddest thoughts waned. These, after all, were people who before war came had ridiculed soldiers, and would not want to give them a hearing. While Vorotyntsev, in addition to his courses at the Academy, had been learning artillery tactics, and horsemanship, and acrobatics on horseback, these people had regarded the word "patriot" as a badge of shame. Somewhere, perhaps, on a different floor on a different street, those before whom he had hoped to lay the whole tangle of his anxieties were even now assembled. The trick was to find them.

But, of course, every private certainty is diminished by voicing it, telling it to others. Only between close friends, and sotto voce, can it be transmitted accurately.

So that Vorotyntsev would have done better to say nothing at all on this occasion. But, for one thing, it would have been impolite to deny them when they were all expecting something—and with Shingarev there, how could he possibly have done so? He and Shingarev had made a start and stopped short—but Shingarev was the one to whom he could open his heart. Shingarev's pensive reminiscence of Stolypin had been very moving. His guilelessly sensitive features, his unguarded gaze said that he was eager to learn. The sudden squabble about Stolypin had helped Vorotyntsev to pluck up his courage—he was in the mood now to challenge his company, not to ask their indulgence, but to fling in their faces the reality about matters on which, in their inordinate militancy, their thick-skinned unawareness, they passed judgment so lightly. Vera too had never been told properly, and he had no intention of telling her things individually. These thoughts, however, would not have taken shape so firmly but for the arrival of the little woman professor with the lace collar but with a masculine crease on her small forehead—and a steadily approving gaze for the colonel.

The lady professor, for no obvious reason, had prevailed, though they had not exchanged a word, and she had asked nothing. Her mere presence made Vorotyntsev feel at ease, at home, needed: here and now was where he should be telling his story. This was where he was most wanted!

Meanwhile they had all taken their places in readiness. Pavel Nikolaevich was no longer expected, but Minervin stayed on to hear the colonel.

Where should he start? What should he tell them about? Things which in his days in the trenches were of supreme importance, crying out for attention, might here, in this enlightened Kadet society, look trivial, evidence perhaps of an inability to take a broader view. Seen from here, the war was so long, so monotonous, and the ebb and flow of battle so kaleidoscopic, that it could only be envisaged in the most general outline. But if you generalized, made it more coherent and more detached, there would be nothing much left—they probably knew it all from the papers anyway.

The colonel, though, was fresh from the Romanian front. The only one still active—the others were at a standstill. So how were things there?

Romania? The Germans had struck there precisely because it was a new, open, undefended front. An army 300,000 strong—crumbling like rotted wood. The Romanian king couldn't wait to seize Transylvania, but was afraid of Bulgaria in his rear. He had stubbornly held out for an Allied attack from Salonika and a Russian strike across the Danube into Dobruja. What did the Allies care: just one more country to swell the rubble heap. (Careful, though, what you say about the Allies in this place!) But we ourselves—what were we thinking of? Everybody insisted that we needed a success on the main front—so we removed ourselves to a secondary one. Somebody had thought that this would put us in a stronger position, closer to the Bosphorus, but Mackensen had marched across that kingdom against our army on the Danube and turned us in the opposite direction, away from the Bosphorus. The Germans took over Romania's oil, took over its horses. The Romanian sector? I just can't tell you, it baffles the imagination! You can't call it an operetta—it's too bloody, we're ramming in one batch of reserve units after another to plug the gap. We would need to send in at least a quarter of a million men. But the railways could get nothing through, not even ordinary hospital trains—we're sending the wounded back in the freight cars that bring in our rations. Or on local trains, without lavatories and with broken windows. There is cholera in the Danube delta. Constantsa was surrendered just the other day.

But they didn't want him to talk spontaneously, just let it flow, whatever the drift of it, they wanted facts to confirm a conclusion known in advance, and nowhere better than in Petrograd: that the stupidity of the Supreme Power and the Supreme Commander was infinite, inexhaustible, and impenetrable, while the spirit of Russia's fighting men, officers and soldiers, was unwavering, glorious, and indestructible, so that liberal progressive society could rely on them in its calculations. Whether from Romania or Galicia, they wanted from him not vivid pictures with columns of black smoke rising from shell bursts, and horses supine with their hooves in the air, they wanted anecdotes in which against the bright background of the people's heroism the errors of the Supreme Command, and especially the ministers, would stand out like black blots, showing that it was they who were ruining everything, and that as long as the present regime existed victory was impossible.

For the army itself this was the most natural way of relieving bad feelings: who else was reviled in officers' bunkers if not those in the rear, GHQ, the staffs of army groups and armies, corps and division commanders! Vorotyntsev could give them as much of that as they could possibly want.

Take for a start the fact that Russia entered the war in 1914 without the ratio of artillery pieces to bayonets prescribed by Napoleon—five to every thousand. Then, in the first weeks of what was to be a short, three-month war, regiments were rushed to the front overmanned—four officers to a company, sergeant majors at platoon level, old reservist NCOs in the ranks beside privates—because no separate count of NCOs was kept in Russia's mobilization plan. That was how the War Ministry worked under Sukhomlinov. In those first few months so many NCOs were killed that for more than two years we had been scraping the barrel, sketchily training NCOs with little skill to command common soldiers and militiamen with none at all. Three-fifths of our regular officers had also been killed, another fifth disabled, and the remainder diluted with nongentry ensigns; with only five or six regular officers to a regiment left, how are we supposed to fight? Companies and battalions were commanded by lieutenants, or even ensigns.

And those new ensigns? A barely literate fellow, with or without having completed elementary school, becomes "Your Honor" after four months. Where one of them may realize that he is not yet up to it and try to educate himself another will get big ideas, throw his weight around, show the soldiers who is boss. Such ensigns "from the people" had not brought officers and soldiers closer together but helped to make them strangers.

Then again—what sort of reinforcements are we sent? The Moscow Military District, which Vorotyntsev knew well, was now commanded by the arrogant General Sandetsky, who had gotten into the idiotic habit of sending untrained soldiers to the front as quickly and in as great numbers as possible, soldiers who could neither shoot nor advance under cover. He was especially zealous in speeding the return of sick officers before they were cured. They were unfit to fight and often died of their diseases. He burst in on medical inspections and interfered with the doctors' work. One case would have found its way into the papers if the victim had not kept it quiet. An officer who could not straighten four fingers on his left hand as the result of a wound appeared before a medical board, which decided to discharge him from the army. Sandetsky was outraged. He ordered the officer to place his injured fingers on the table, and brought his own fist down on them with all his might. He broke all four fingers, and the officer lost consciousness.

A frisson ran through his audience. This was just the sort of thing they needed. Go on then, swallow the bait, that's just how it was, alas, and there's no getting away from it. They say that the Grand Duchess Elizaveta Fyodorovna tried to denounce Sandetsky, but she was not on good terms with her sister the Empress, and Sandetsky began poisoning the minds of people in Moscow against her, as a German. Sandetsky finally went elsewhere—but where to? To the Kazan Military District, so that he lost little and we were not the winners. The new general appointed to the Moscow District was Mrozovsky, who was less of a savage but just as stupid.

So many people in Russia are more concerned with their personal comfort than with doing their duty. The higher commands are grossly overstaffed—there's a plethora of correspondence, personal aides, liaison officers, superfluous carriages, too much leisure, eating and drinking and card playing—and the worst you can threaten a staff officer with is the trenches! Here is a little vignette for you. Attached to the Guards Corps, and living in a railway carriage, we find Grand Duke Pavel Aleksandrovich. It's a hot summer day. The roof of the carriage is covered with turf, and two soldiers are watering it. It's staff officers like these who plan halfhearted operations in which they send 50,000 men to their deaths—a matter too trivial to be recorded by history.

You want something bigger? East Prussia will do as well as anywhere. Do you think Samsonov's army is all we wrote off there? There have been a number of other catastrophes in Prussia since then. Rennenkampf, who was so slow to come to the help of the other man, shortly afterward had to move quickly to extricate himself from the same sort of trap by abandoning his artillery. (This, incidentally, was another occasion on which we had been in too much of a hurry to save the French, this time at Ypres.) After that, we invaded Prussia twice more, by the same unlucky roads, from the south and the east, with no change of tactics or of armament, crowding in yet again, still imagining that we could win by weight of numbers, pressing on to disaster for a second then a third time. That winter, the 10th Army was routed in Prussia, and we left behind the 20th Corps, Bulgakov's, not to mention some separate regiments. So that altogether we have barged into Prussia three times without proper preparation, simply to rescue the French. Ah, but! By way of punishment . . . (Those present all know it, they can put the words in your mouth.) Decorations were showered on senior generals. Kuropatkin was taken out of mothballs—sent to command first the Grenadier Corps, then an army, then an Army Group. The fossilized General Bezobrazov, a court favorite, is helping Brusilov to pulverize the Guards, but can't sink below the level of corps commander. Or take General Bebel, whose natural element is defeat. Or General Raukh: he disgraced himself and his cavalry division in Prussia, was given a whole cavalry corps as consolation, and when Lechitsky took it from him Raukh received a Guards corps by way of compensation from the Supreme Commander, and sent it into the Styrian marshes, where the Austrians did not even need to open fire, because the Russians were drowning anyway. Zhilinsky, as you know, had in the meantime become Russia's plenipotentiary at French GHQ. While Artamonov, who had destroyed Samsonov's army, emerged from the inquiry pure as pure, and Nikolai Nikolaevich bestowed on him an oscular congratulation. When they took Peremyshl no one was judged more suitable than Artamonov to preside over the celebrations. And he, after letting 20,000 prisoners slip through his fingers and surrendering the fortress to the enemy, sat back duly awaiting his next appointment.

Then there are all those people no one has ever heard of, pig-faced people, too big for their boots, with no real insight into the meaning of duty. People like General Gagarin, say, commander of the Trans-Amur Cavalry Brigade, who gets drunk and turns nasty with one of his regimental commanders: "You haven't got any machine guns? So send two cavalry squadrons to attack the Austrians and take their machine guns from them." Every such commander has thousands of subordinates, lays down their lives, and nothing is heard of it.

Without stopping to assess the results of the first six months of war—the irreparable loss of officers, NCOs, and regular soldiers, the squandering of shells, the shortage of rifles, the invariable superiority of the German artillery, in numbers and in caliber: we had almost exclusively three-inch guns—without taking any of this into account and drawing conclusions, to then make a dash in the following spring for the rocky passes of the Carpathians, to cross over into Hungary! Not even providing sufficient cover on the flanks of the attacking units, shedding rivers of blood.

The great Carpathian adventure! It was more galling than almost anything else. You couldn't bear to think about it. After taking Pere-myshl, without pausing to count their forces, they pressed on and on across the mountains, conquering crags with artillery fire, taking passes by storm . . . Such losses! So much blood! And all for nothing! The Hungarian lowlands were suddenly wide open—and at that very moment the order came to withdraw. And so precipitately, backing into those same steep slopes, wedging yourselves into gorges—so many losses again! A regiment might be written off in an hour . . . whole corps melted away . . . The ravines of the Carpathians were cemeteries for heroes.

What made orders from the remote summit so unbearable was that you didn't know, couldn't see with your own eyes, the necessity for them, but could only wonder why, oh, why did we get into this fix?

Mackensen's breakthrough at Gorlitsa made nonsense of our whole effort in the Carpathians. The Gorlitsa breakthrough set rolling the whole great 1915 retreat—Russians without shells, with bayonets or sometimes almost with clubs, fighting a rearguard action against a modern army. A divisional general thanks a battery commander for his excellent targeting and in the same breath threatens to demote him for wasting shells. They retreated by night, when the Germans were resting, and they retreated in broad daylight, in danger from time to time of encirclement, and with the German artillery mowing them down. (And then again don't forget we were surrendering fields of ripe corn, while columns of refugees struggled on alongside, people in rags, with looks of resignation on their faces, all their pathetic belongings on carts. If a horse fell, tears were shed over it, little burial mounds were raised over dead children.) When they exited from Galicia they hadn't a cartridge left, nothing to answer back with. Their reinforcements were taken prisoner the minute they disembarked from the troop trains. There were planes in the sky—but all were German. And as if all this was not enough, the Germans released their poison gas and exterminated us by the thousand—turning us into green, yellow, and gray corpses with goggling eyes and swollen bellies—nine thousand were gassed in one attack in the 2nd Army alone. We were simply not expecting it, we were completely unprepared, had no defense against it—unless you count a gauze bandage over the mouth or celluloid goggles. They all perished. And all we could belatedly think of was to set fire to the brushwood on the rim of the trenches so that the flames would cause the gas to blow over the trench.

The Russian army, marched out in so much more than fighting trim in 1914, by 1915 no longer existed. So much for the generalship of the Supreme Commanders. (His listeners would like that!) With our grateful allies complacently inactive, begrudging us even rifles. (Beg your pardon, mustn't say anything about the Allies here, they won't want to hear that. Such things are never mentioned.)

"How, then, do you explain . . . ?"

We began 1916 in just the same way—with thousands of surplus men on the rosters but unarmed. We gave such people trenching tools and hand grenades, and lo and behold, they were grenadiers!

"How, then, do you explain Brusilov's breakthrough?"

(We shall never hear the last of it!) That breakthrough, gentlemen, and more particularly the follow-up are not so glorious as all that. Two months of close combat with heavy losses ended with the capture of Lutsk and a few subsidiary townships. You can't call it an offensive if you just push ahead without annexing territory. There was no decisive result, so we withdrew quickly. Brusilov's successes are worth nothing, if you take into account all the men he lost in the ensuing months— probably more than a quarter of a million. What that breakthrough showed is that we still don't know how to attack, even now. And how many obscure and unheard-of offensives, without a distinctive name of their own, do you think there were? This March, for instance, as the thaw set in, on the banks of Lake Naroch?

No, gentlemen, Russia has nothing to boast about in what has so far been achieved in this war. Is this the way to wage war? These are not the successes you expect from such a giant exerting all its strength.

There was an embarrassed silence in the drawing room.

It's easy enough to tell these stories and to listen with malicious glee to tales of muddle and incompetence on high. But what about ourselves? Which of us is inclined to talk about the no less destructive muddle down below, about mistakes and failings in the middling and minor battles which fill most of our days? Local defeats are concealed from neighboring units and the High Command, in fact nobody ever hears of them. Those withdrawing try to conceal it, try to delude their neighbors. Reports speak of "trying to estimate losses," when in fact they are already known, but have to be concealed. Or you read "taken in battle," when there has been no battle (and "in my presence," meaning "give me a medal"). Or else they report taking places which have not been taken at all.

Or they may send several cases of grenades in time for a battle, but forget at HQ to send a case of percussion caps. So—no grenades.

Or else we launch an attack without knowing the enemy's positions—no aerial photographs, no drawings at ground level. Because attacks are sometimes intended not to bring about a real breakthrough, not to draw off enemy forces from another sector, but merely to figure in reports to HQ. Send in the Yelets Regiment—carpet the uplands with them!

A mortar battery and a regiment of field artillery suddenly received a consignment of shells after a long famine and furiously pounded a village in German hands. Telephone communication had broken down and there was some delay before orderlies from the infantry turned up asking, "Have you sons of bitches gone crazy? We went through that village during the night and are now fighting three versts west of it!"

Another time they might be firing not on a deserted village but on their own forward infantry or their own scouts.

Or a regiment might dig and dig and dig—only to find that it had entrenched itself in the rear of another regiment.

Hard work—digging for no good reason. Life at the front line consists much more of hard work and endurance than of fighting. Trenches are, after all, just open ditches. When it rains there's always water in them, and dugouts and bunkers are always damp. You're lucky if there's something to cover them with, but where there are no woods you have to sit around in unprotected positions or go ten versts on foot—I'm not exaggerating—to carry tree trunks on your backs, and carry them you will, if you want to go on living. Imagine what it's like discovering when you've fortified your position that it's "in the wrong place," because the command has made a mistake, or the situation has changed, and you have to move somewhere else, and tote all that timber on your back again. All engineering work has to be carried out by the infantry itself. A soldier has to do so much walking that no boots can stand up to it; they wear out so fast he looks like a tramp and has to make himself birch-bark clogs instead. There's never any rest. Men are sent back into divisional reserve—but their company still has to turn out every night to do sappers' work in the dark. So that there's never time to train soldiers who arrive untrained. And they do so much trudging around and so much donkey work that positional warfare is a holiday by comparison. But trenches make a good fixed target, and on the most ordinary of days we carry a few men out, cover them with their greatcoats, and bury them in the dark.

Or take the artillery harnessing ten horses to a shell box to haul it out of a rut. Or think of going over the top with mud by the bucketful stuck to your legs. And at the end of your run you suddenly find that the breaches in the wire are too narrow. So you're bunched up together and caught in cross fire.

Or you're up in the mountains, attacking waist deep in loose snow. The wounded simply drown.

The war is into its third year, and a variety of people, at various places in our fatherland, have gotten used to it, manage to thrive on it, pick up bits of information about what's going on, and discuss the victory to come—while this or that battalion, this or that regiment, has an hour or two to live. A detachment is thrown into the attack, head-on of course, always over an expanse of open ground, and you're lucky if you're sent running for less than a verst. Others are told to use a spare hour to advance, occupy an unreconnoitered sector, and only then attack. In that hour, advancing for the last time, you do not let yourself be distracted by unreal activities or irrelevant thoughts. You all march as one man to the place where four out of every five will lay down their lives, and each man's only hope is to be the fifth. Then you have to work out how long you must lie low to survive during our own artillery barrage—if any. How long will your wife remember you? Will your little children remember you at all? Yet your attack may be just a demonstration, just a sideshow. Three-quarters of a verst of open field under snow separates you from the enemy, you see the fringe of his forest like a black wall, and there, panting fit to burst, you find he has everything wrapped round and round with barbed wire, with nowhere to hide in front of it, your only hope is that there are hollows under the snow and you can flop into one of them and get out of sight. The scouts and grenade throwers crawl forward, and Division rings: why hasn't the battalion been thrown in? "We have to wait till they've . . ." "Your orders are not to wait!"

The guilty paralysis of the infantry officer who cannot help obeying orders. The paralysis of the prostrate infantryman—until his deathbed anguish explodes into the exhilarating desperation of the attack.

God forbid you should ever hear that "hurrah"—a pitiful wail from the inferno that is war, a cry not of triumph but of despair, wrung from them as they charge. Men fall like flies, the snow is pitted with them—which of them are dead, which waiting to die? The only survivors you're sure of are those plain to see beside you, the rest may all be dead. At Kolomea the Trans-Amur Infantry Division—a dozen long-service soldiers to a company, the rest all bearded militiamen—were hurled head-on at fortified positions, and mowed down to a man.

And then those forage caps with little crosses on them, those defenseless home guards, how many of them have we lost in battle? A man charging against the enemy has one consolation—he can choose his stopping places, he can find a false reassurance in his zigzag progress, hiding behind hillocks, stones, or even a tussock of withered grass. But a telephone operator sent to disentangle a line under fire is denied this means of self-deception: his line is his fate.

History can never record every incident. Sometimes there are no participants left. Those capable of understanding don't need to be told everything, or even very much, all they need to know about is, say, the village of Radzanovo, 190 feet above sea level, with a splendid view, fortified with barbed-wire fences, which at the time we lacked the ammunition to destroy. Besides, the approaches were marshy. But an infantry regiment was ordered to take it. The regimental commander judged it impossible to do so, and asked for the order to be canceled. Divisional HQ insisted. There was no way out. The following morning they attacked. They lost three hundred men, including irreplaceable officers. A day or two later you met dragoon officers whose regiments had been in that sector, had withdrawn and returned. They told us their story. They had come close to taking this wretched 190-foot mount, again without artillery, losing seven hundred men, infantry and cavalry, and had failed. We withdrew. After us a third regiment was deployed against Radzanovo—ordered to scale the same height.

Call it human sacrifice. When you have seen enough of it you lose all proper respect for wounds, for death, for corpses. A bloody cap on a lonely cross, or a trenching tool sticking up from a mass grave for infantrymen, is taken as a matter of course. You see a dead man lying on his side cradling his bloody head under his arm, as if he felt cold. You see people saying funeral prayers over a crumpled corpse without removing it from its stretcher. An even commoner sight is a cart with its side boards up, and half a dozen wounded men tossed and jolted on it, with whatever stumps they have preserved heavily bandaged and sticking up in the air, and their eyes, already aware of their irreparable mutilation, staring from the depths—just try to keep this sort of picture in mind, gentlemen. Not all of them will get treatment in time, before tetanus or gangrene sets in.

Or else a Cossack regiment is ordered to take an Austrian fortress, the approaches to which are girded with several barbed-wire barriers. But the whole regiment has only half a dozen pairs of wire cutters. (They can't manage to make enough of the things. The War Ministry hasn't done the arithmetic and is skeptical. So many soldiers have perished unnecessarily for lack of a pair of wire cutters!) What can you do? Use your swords. Without dismounting, remember. At night, remember. "Forward, boys, and the best of luck!"

It isn't all failure. Sometimes, even up to our waists in January rainwater, holding our rifles over our heads, we've attacked machine-gun posts and taken them! That's how we crossed the San.

Sometimes we take a position! We're victorious! We rejoice! Then suddenly an inexplicable order: "Withdraw to your previous position."

Why? Why did we take this one, then? Why didn't you think in time?

You carry this whole pyramid of bemedaled, overpromoted, ungainsayable generals on your head, like an Oriental woman carrying a pitcher of water. You may think, because you're a regimental commander, that you're free to make decisions of your own? Oh, no. You can scarcely move your head to right or left. The least little show of independence, fall back just a few hundred yards, and you're summoned to Corps HQ to make a statement on your "less than valiant conduct." Who can endure this feeling of constriction by absurd but unalterable orders? You see the mistake, the miscalculation, the malice, or the lack of consideration behind them, but you are shackled, your honor, your own pride, and military discipline all forbid you to protest. And on your last day, on the eve of your death, there is no one to tell how it really was.

Younger Guards officers have been known to get together and think up a way of protesting: Gentlemen! Let us make this hopeless attack with officers only, and not lead our soldiers into it!

Or take this one. The Rylsky Infantry Regiment couldn't hold out on the Strypa. It was stunned and sent reeling. It had to be saved—but with what? There was something—the Kargopol Dragoon Regiment. This was, as it happened, their holiday, the anniversary of the regiment's formation. Throughout the war no vodka had been brought anywhere near the front line; sobriety was strictly enforced even where men were stuck in subzero conditions. But the dragoons got hold of some, drank deep, and started singing. Toward sunset the division commander drives up. "We're rescuing the Rylsky regiment, boys!" And, knowing what the attack would be like: "The Kargopol Regiment must not die! Leave behind one officer and ten dragoons from every squadron to mount guard!" They drew lots. Embraced as they said farewell. But their heads were still muzzy, and their legs wobbly. Darkness fell. And over the plain deserted by the infantry, scored with trenches, pitted with foxholes and craters, tangled in barbed wire, where even in the daytime nobody would go without wire cutters, on foot let alone on horseback, they advanced at a trot in the dark and without a murmur. ("Best of luck, boys!") They fell into holes. Broke legs, broke ribs. Stumbled and were impaled on barbed wire. Galloping in the dark is always unnerving—more frightening for the horse than the man, not knowing what his next foot will fall on. The Germans were late spotting them. Rockets, searchlights. The Kargopol Regiment broke into a gallop! The searchlights chased gigantic spectral shadows over earth and sky, some tumbling head over heels, some looming ever nearer, even larger. The Germans couldn't stand it! They fled! Victory!

After a battle soldiers are so dazed they'll stand around in groups, in a village just taken and still burning, with Germans at the other end of the street, taking no precautions, ignoring their officer—if he wants them to lie low he will have to wrestle them to the ground one by one.

Worst of all, the idea has taken root, and is now generally accepted, that the more casualties there are, the better the battle and the greater the number of senior officers recommended for decorations. So that even when you could attack from the flank—no, charge head-on through the quagmire! The commander of the 49th Cossack Regiment exultantly reported to the ataman's HQ that "the company advanced on a fortified position over open ground, under fire, and in cavalry formation." One can only marvel at the heroism of this company, advancing according to orders to certain death, out of devotion to the throne!

With that sheeplike devotion we are recklessly shedding our blood, bleeding ourselves to death.

If contempt for death is the measure, there are many more authentic heroes than in all the magazine photographs together: "God-fearing warriors, crowned with blood and honor" (those whose relatives are quick to stake their claim). They greatly outnumber the George Crosses scattered to right and left. Two men, lightly wounded, lead a third with an abdominal wound, bent double, delirious, clutching his belly with both hands. The reserve unit in his path calls out ironical encouragement—"Hold on, don't drop it!" and he manages to answer, "I'll get it there—it's all mine, you know."

At the regimental level you have to grade commendations—often passing over genuine feats, which may not have resulted in victory—but then bravery in defeat is more striking. When a regiment has only three hundred bayonets left out of two thousand, and there is no relief in sight, and you are told that there will not be any for some days, but that the division commander is sure that the regiment will do its duty and that your positions must be held . . . while back at division HQ, and corps HQ, they strike out the recommendations you have made, to make room for the big brass and for the clerks.

Better to be wounded, to be killed even, in victorious battle than in some hugger-mugger. This summer one regiment was planning to use gas—three emissions of a hundred canisters, beginning at midnight—and then attack. But they dilly-dallied too long and released the first wave only at 3 a.m. The Germans detected it—rockets went up, trumpets and horns sounded the warning, iron sheets were hammered, beacons were lit. Our meteorological station then reported that the wind was becoming changeable, but the division commander ordered the release of the second wave. Men in the neighboring regiment, in a slightly forward position, were gassed. The wind became less favorable—but the third wave was ordered. This one traveled a little way, stopped, and was blown onto our own trenches. To make things worse—the canisters should have been placed in front of the trenches, with their pipes pointing toward the enemy, instead of which, contrary to instructions, the canisters were left in the trenches, with their pipes resting on the parapets. The Germans opened fire on our trenches, smashed the canisters, and panic-stricken men had to tug on gas masks in a hurry. Three hundred of them, officers and men, were buried in a common grave. The division commander's suspension was a poor consolation.

The casualty here was Shingarev. He had taken Vorotyntsev's story full in the chest, and was crawling back into the attack like those unfortunates who had advanced, without wire cutters, head-on against a hardened position. Slumped sideways, head in hand, elbow on table, he scanned the dark clods for a glimmer of hope.

Someone new appeared in the room. Someone with an anxious, wary face and nervous eyebrows. His eyes bored into the speaker.

Nor could Vorotyntsev be unaware that the iridescent gaze of Professor Andozerskaya was fixed unwaveringly upon him. Had she never seen a soldier before? Was he her first? She drank in all that he said. Looking him full in the face, never by so much as a pursing of the lips or a twitch of an eyebrow protesting against his most brutal and startling words. With her listening it was very easy to tell his story.

Vera was there too, silent, motionless, all eyes, dear, sweet Vera, even as a child a better listener than anybody.

But—morale? Was the fighting spirit of the army intact? Shingarev's burning eyes demanded an answer to the unspoken question. What strange passion had hoisted this country doctor to the parliamentary heights? If he could not believe in the divinely favored Russian people, in the men of Novozhivotinnoye now at the front—what was the point of all his efforts? Of the Duma itself? The former doctor could go on counting cartridges, fixing bread prices, delivering sizzling speeches on behalf of all Russia at the Sorbonne and at Oxford only for as long as he believed that the spirit of Novozhivotinnoye was intact and undimmed.

He asked the question. But was sure that he knew the answer himself.

Fighting spirit? When a regiment may number three hundred bayonets and a division eight hundred? When the sight of burnt-out villages and campfires stoked with village fences can no longer disturb even a peasant's heart? When the men look for excuses to avoid battle—escorting the wounded to the rear, for instance, or shooting their own fingers? And what of the inordinate number of prisoners? Are you not aware, gentlemen, that we have already surrendered more than two million men? The longer the war goes on, the readier our soldiers are to surrender. Glad just to be alive. They'll even work for the Germans—as wagoners or in bakeries and kitchens. This war is the first

in which orders have been given—by General Smirnov and his like—
to open fire on men attempting to surrender, shoot those who have
forgotten their oath, report capitulators so that their families' allowances will be stopped, and announce that at the end of the war all
who allow themselves to be taken captive will be put on trial. Of
course, none of this is actually being carried out . . . but it is still a fact
that such orders were previously unknown in the Russian army.

Now wait a minute! Let's be more precise! Minervin, deft Duma
duelist, peered sharply through his pince-nez. The will to win has
surely not been lost? The ordinary Russian soldier, the army as a whole,
still surely believes in victory? And what about you, Colonel?

Such irony!

When we are crouching in slimy trenches, mopping the clay up with
our greatcoats, or when we spend forty-eight hours in the open with
no sleep, in a frost so hard that the lubricant freezes in the machine
gun, and we have to warm it over the fire—we at the front share
one common grievance: that back in Russia *they* have forgotten us! In
such a protracted war, who would not hanker after some distraction,
after peacetime pleasures, restaurants, women in elegant dresses! They
send us "comforts"—tobacco pouches and candy—while they themselves . . .

But no! It seems they aren't indifferent to us after all! In fact they
look to us for victory! They ask: Where's your will to win? We ought
to throw ourselves into their arms and say we have wronged you!

But the human heart has its faults, and the resentment is not dis-
pelled, it lingers, it simply revolves on its own axis. Gentlemen liberals!
Gentlemen of educated Russian society! (This bit not out loud.) Can
I believe my ears? Have I perhaps misheard? Who was it who a mere
twelve years ago shouted, shrieked that a great power had no need of
war, that it was criminal to send our precious young men with their
social idealism to the slaughter? That the only problems were internal
ones, and that abroad it didn't matter if we retreated, if we lost, in
fact the sooner the better! Whose fault was it that we lost *that* war?
Whose nerve if not yours snapped so quickly, letting Russia down with
a bang? How could the country fight with the whole of educated society openly (and in the enemy's hearing) calling for defeat? And when
our hapless infantry, for the benefit of the world at large, were having
the novel tactics of twentieth-century warfare etched on their hides,
when they still marched in formation, and even in step, under artillery
fire, instead of hiding one man to a foxhole, why did you not inquire
then about our morale and our will to win?

Granted that arrogant underestimation of the untried Japanese, and
the vested interests of the useless Admiral Alekseev, played a part . . .
but Vorotyntsev, stuck in the present war, had changed his mind about
the last. After the Japanese war Germany was trying to set a "Russian

course" and we rejected her, preferring an unreliable friendship with Edward VII. But why, oh, why this trial of strength just because Germany is our neighbor to the west? Why do we need this war in particular, what can we possibly gain by it? Do you imagine you can escape retribution for the body blow you struck at our country then? *That* defeat, in a distant war, was bound to be followed by others nearer home. Of course, if you reckon on Russia ending with our generation you can permit yourself anything. Who, if not Stolypin, whom you so hate, dragged us out of the hole you had pushed us into? Gentlemen, gentlemen (these words were not spoken aloud), when did this great change take place, to make you all so belligerent? We "Young Turks" were abused as liberals, when we were in fact merely patriots. But it is too late, gentlemen, by the time these patriotic sentiments came over you, our army . . . our army . . . had ceased to . . . how can I put it?

Andrei Ivanovich, propped up awkwardly, head in hand, almost down to table level, said: Still, our soldiers aren't just victims driven to the slaughter? Our fellow countrymen in gray greatcoats do after all understand our war aims? The objectives of Russia and of universal freedom are not surely alien to the Russian soldier? The Dardanelles, now—that is not just a wild idea of Petersburg—they are necessary to the economy of the whole Russian South.

Vorotyntsev was embarrassed. Not for want of an answer, but simply to hear such a question from a statesman whom he had been admiring all evening.

You want it both ways. At the very top, you think: The worse things are, the better. But the army must have the will to fight and win, must set its heart on Constantinople.

Only, even before the war, we forbade the army to utter a single word on any political matter—for fear of upsetting the German and Austrian emperors. And what would you have it say today? That "the Germans are the age-old enemies of Slavdom"? I believe we're over the hump and into an age when such antitheses will cease to exist. Our soldiers' hearts are ahead of ours. Except for the gas attacks they bear the enemy no grudge. Besides, some of the "Austrians" speak the same sort of lingo as we do. Carry on to final victory, remain loyal to our allies—all that is easy enough to say back here. You know so much about the fatherland, gentlemen, but nobody has ever told the soldiers any of it. They have no such obsessive vision of "a country called Russia." They don't wake up and fall asleep thinking of it. The common soldier has no concept of victory like yours—only of making peace—let everybody stop shooting, nothing else matters. They can be youngsters or old reservists, all they want is to come safely out of battle, they no longer fight like the old regulars. An infantryman languishes at the front from one wound to the next, and will have nothing to remember, he was just there as a target. Instead of fighting spirit he has a sense of doom. In 1914 the infantry were self-confident and cheerful. Now they're resigned, apathetic, and smaller in build. That's why I say our army is no longer . . . no longer . . .

If a truehearted village doctor no longer has ears for the dread of men condemned to face frontal assault—not just one battalion for half an hour at a time, but all peasant Russia, week after week, month after month . . . cannot turn half an eye on all those Prussian, Polish, Galician, and Romanian fields strewn with the dead . . . Who will never rise again to complain and protest . . . There is no family in which prayers are not said for those who have gone, no village church in which memorial services are not held. They are long-suffering, of course—and we place our hopes on it. But maybe we should come to our senses sooner? Country doctors, parliamentarians, army officers— what excuse is there for any of us if we survive but leave the corpse of Novozhivotinnoye or Zastruzhe behind us? (Surely he can see this for himself?) If the fighting spirit of the army has already evaporated, if their bodies are worn out, how long can we go on trying the people's patience? If the soldiers are already murmuring among themselves, "Of course we'll defend ourselves, but when it comes to attacking, our legs don't seem to move." We mustn't wait for this to flare up openly!

Their condition is worse than fatigue: it's one of paralyzed bafflement. And that's how they die—baffled. For more than two years there has been no attempt to keep up morale by explaining anything, to inspire them, all they know is they have to die! Peasants believe firmly in some sort of higher justice. But during this war they've ceased to feel its existence: they are dying without knowing why. It isn't fear that keeps them going, but they have to force themselves. They would be equal to any sacrifice, but must see the necessity for it. Our people are so good-hearted, so docile, but we have abused their docility. They struggle and strain to carry out a duty they do not understand—but can this go on forever? You say that the people will not forgive this war: true, but it is not just the government they won't forgive, it is all of us!

For a professional soldier to utter such words in such militant company was almost unthinkable, incomprehensible: but people must be made to realize that all things, even Russia, have limits. There is a limit to expansion. It makes itself known in the strength of the expansionist will, in the depth of tillage and lushness of vegetation on every square yard of land enclosed. Expansion cannot continue indefinitely. Surely Russia did not need to expand further. She needed intensive cultivation within her existing borders. Awkward for a colonel in the regular army to say it in so many words, but was the war necessary for the survival of the state, and not just for its own sake?

What does it really mean to love your country? Those photographs of fallen "pious warriors," which you all scan working your way through five newspapers over your morning coffee—let them sink in, try to imagine that you are the channel they have run through to soak into the ground, leaving nothing but those brown spots behind. Tell yourselves that these are the very, very best, those incapable of shrinking and hiding. That it will take Russia more than two generations to make good these losses!

Try to feel what it's like to be wounded in the stomach. To get a bullet through your chest. To have your jaw dislocated. Your cheek torn out by a dumdum bullet. A corner of your skull sliced off.

If a man can feel none of this, what right has he to judge?

I managed to visit the plastic surgery exhibition on the Field of Mars today. Have you seen it? It's very near. Get down there, gentlemen, and you *will* feel something. There are no words for it in ordinary human language. Goya never drew anything like it. Faces so hacked up, so lacerated, so cruelly shattered—boneless faces, eyeless faces, no longer resembling anything human—and that's how they'll live the rest of their lives. Get down there, gentlemen.

An officer does better not to think about the wounded, of course. It weakens him. But say you go along to a dressing station to see a hero from your own unit, wounded a couple of hours ago. It's evening. In a dugout. There's a small kerosene lamp, high up on a shelf, scorching the air. Gloomy half-darkness. A few trestle beds along the walls, with a wounded man on each. And this medical post little wider than any ordinary dugout, this ill-lit airless coffin, is the last he sees of this earth, his last picture of this life. To see the wounded man's face you have to hold a candle near to it. In those two hours the brave young face has become unrecognizable: the eyes are enlarged, and there is such awareness in them, the mouth is sunken, the cheeks are yellow. He is wondering when the priest will come with the host.

Just think: a month ago (Nanny had told him) a Japanese prince came to Petrograd, the main streets were decked with Russian and Japanese flags and ordinary people were asking, "Why were we at war with them? Was it worth our while getting killed in the Japanese war?" Will they be greeting the Germans in the same way in a few years' time? (Meanwhile the Japanese despise us for not putting the lessons of that war to good use.)

I don't know—we might have been internally prepared for some other war, but not for this one. Now there's nothing we can do to mend things except cut it short. I don't know . . . maybe we could persuade the Allies to make peace. Or else . . . (must definitely not say this to anyone here present) . . . or else we could just leave the Entente and the Central Powers to sort it out between them, while Old Mother Russia cleans up, scrubs her floors, and lights her stove . . .

Does all this seem strange from me? Well, only a man who has himself been an active cog in that army for twenty years, and missed not a single day of the last war, or of this one, will dare say such things. A career officer is supposed to do everything he can to win any and every war for his fatherland, isn't he? But I'm not sure that I still am a professional soldier. One hundred and fifteen weeks, eight hundred days—after that the most inspired officer won't want to take his profession in such large doses . . . Or am I just too sensitive? The weariness, the monotony of all those deaths, the longing to be out of it, the insult of it all have gnawed at me, left me hollow inside, and I cannot go on living in this trade. Your knees give way, you need to sit. Your arms dangle helplessly. Your head droops . . .

Officers—what are they?

Aren't they part of the people? Yes, they are the mainspring and the will of our people. A gas attack has started, the soldiers already have their gas masks on, but somebody has to warn the line to the rear and Lieutenant Grushetsky from Tambov peels off his mask, telephones a warning, and is gassed. Or take Lieutenant Colonel Vevern, in command of a battery, he can't locate the enemy battery, so he goes through the German defenses alone, to see for himself, then come back and shell it. And what has to be done is done. You have limited vision from an artillery observation post, so Captain Shigorin rises to his full height to direct his battery's answering fire. Within a quarter of an hour he is struck on the temple by a shell fragment and killed. But what had to be done is done. It's the best of them who get killed. Happy the officer whose soldiers say, "You'll be all right with our man." Happy the officer whose soldiers follow him into the attack as one man. Even if his soldiers take to their heels he is still not the unhappiest of men, just as long as he can lug home a couple of machine guns single-handed.

Of every seven regular officers serving when war broke out there is now only one left. And the men despairingly sense that their new fledgling officers don't know their business and will be the death of them all.

If you'd known Lieutenant Skalon or Staff Captain Novogrebelsky (and stood over him, barely alive, face deathly pale, eyelashes still fluttering), or Lieutenant Colonel Chistoserdov, known them and lost them forever, you would realize that *the Russian army no longer exists.*

It has ceased to exist.

You needed only to see Captain Tarantsev, stark, staring mad, standing stiff as a post in a hail of bullets, five hundred yards from Radzanovo. People were shouting, "Captain Tarantsev! Get down! Get under cover!" and he shouts back, barely turning his head, "The company's gone! Nothing matters now!"

Are you still alive yourself when you surrender a village, watch it burning, and can see by the light of the flames Germans walking around and putting a final bullet into your wounded soldiers? When the personnel of a regiment changes completely four times in one year, so that the regimental commander never lays eyes on some of his men, just sends them into battle and carries away afterward whatever there is left to carry—is he still a regiment commander, or has he become merely a murderer?

What was it General Levachev used to tell us? An officer must be mercilessly strict only with himself. With fellow officers he must be gentler. And with other ranks gentler still.

Race with them over impassable leagues of empty country, rejoice with them in some sudden rise in the ground, cower with them against its lifesaving shoulder, with shells crashing around you, press your ear to the ground and hear the soldier's heart and your own heart flagging . . . And to that faltering rhythm you might tell them (tell whom? not the Kadets, not the right wing, not the government—tell whom?) that the best sort of victory now, the best way to preserve our honor is to save what is left of the Russian people. And there's nothing more to be said.

Never mind what names people give to such a peace: no Constantinople, no Poland, no Livonia would mean fewer anxieties. Just as long as we remain *ourselves*.

Whether you have yet reached this conclusion or not—the war has reached a stage at which to save Russia, to save ourselves, those who are left of us, before we are battered beyond all recognition, would itself be victory.

Even if it takes—some sort of revolution. (But that is not for your ears.)

*   *   *

I hereby inform you that I am happy with the army, and my officers are good ones. So don't you fret and don't you grieve for me.

(Soldier's letter form)

*
* *

We want no gold, orthodox Tsar, we want no silver.
Just let us go, orthodox Tsar, home to where we come from.
Home to our fathers, home to our mothers, home to
   Holy Russia.

[2 3]

As soon as a prolonged pause indicated that the speaker was disinclined to go on, the new listener with the nervously twitching eyebrows, bare chin, and pencil-line mustache was the first to break in before anyone else could comment or protest.

"Tell me, what are your views on the Ivanov antiaircraft mount? Have you seen it in action?"

In telling his agonizing story Vorotyntsev had taken a fateful step. The incrustation that had constricted body and mind seemed to have cracked and left a crevice through which he could escape. What he needed now was hours of unruffled stillness, without speaking or moving, just resting, perhaps just learning to sit casually in a chair as others did, and as he could not—he habitually sat so that he could spring up at the first alarm. Here was a blessed opportunity to let himself go and return to his long-lost and forgotten normal state. And for that what he very much needed was for the nice Professor Andozerskaya to go on sitting near him where he could see her, with those eyes that occasionally flashed green fire, enthusiastically approving. So that for the time being he did not want to take part in conversation. Here was the recognition so coveted after all his misfortunes. He had lugged his heavy burden to the right place at the right time, had shared it and was liberated. He had no wish now to answer any political rejoinder, any repetition of the need, as the Kadets saw it, for "speedy and decisive victory," or the impossibility of winning "with *this* Tsar" (or any other?). He had, he hoped, made it plain enough that what was needed was not to win the war but to get out of it quickly. Anyway, this company was capable only of repeating the same arguments: however often you told them that the army's war-weariness had passed all limits they still stuck to their old tune—that only the war held the country together, that without it discontent with the Tsar would have caused a general collapse. They were more deeply mired in the war than the Tsar himself.

Whatever else he had expected, it was not this question about the Ivanov mount. Vorotyntsev's neck tensed and he forced himself to raise his head. Was there lurking among these alien Petersburgers one of his own kind, camouflaged in a city suit? He couldn't have roused himself to answer any of the expected questions, but this . . . ?!

"It can be transferred from traveling position to operational with remarkable speed. If a column is on the move and enemy aircraft appear, the gun carriage is pulled over to one side and the piece is ready to fire in a matter of minutes. It's hard-wearing too. Better than the Radzivilovich model."

"What about its firing performance?"

"Well, none of them fire at the full angle of elevation. And the recoil dislodges the sights, so you have to replace them every time . . . which means that . . ."

This earnestly probing man with the anxious eyes, the rapid speech, the questioning mind racing ahead of the unavoidable polysyllables leaned toward Vorotyntsev, and Vorotyntsev toward him, until they were talking tête-à-tête across the room, and when drawings were needed the other man produced his notepad, his fountain pen, and offered them to the colonel.

Just as if all that had been said was of no importance to these two, as though Vorotyntsev was only pretending, and the rest of them could please themselves, because this was what really mattered. Things could hardly have been more awkward.

Andrei Ivanovich saved the situation, coming over to them with a friendly laugh—"Gentlemen, gentlemen!" (but unsmiling, his face as gray as that of a shell-shocked soldier surfacing from a fall of earth, his eyes unfocused, his voice uncertain of itself). "Gentlemen, before we go any further, let me introduce you . . . Pyotr Akimovich Obodovsky . . . A sort of soldier himself, you might say: not long ago he put down a miners' mutiny in the Lysva region with the resoluteness of a colonel, but without a drop of blood spilled, just by speechifying."

Obodovsky frowned, looked pained. What did all that matter? His hand was hot and dry.

"Russians being full of surprises, Pyotr Akimovich has more or less given up the mining industry and is interested only in artillery. He has set up a Subcommittee for Military-Technical Aid, under Guchkov's committee."

Everything was happening at once. How wonderfully well it had worked out! An engineer specializing in artillery was pretty much the same as an Academy-trained officer. And a collaborator of Guchkov? The second time he'd stumbled on that trail—on this first unplanned evening.

"Do you see Aleksandr Ivanovich often? Does he . . . ?"

They would have gone into a rapturous huddle over the notepad, although it was impolite to ignore the rest of the company, had not another of Vorotyntsev's eager listeners, the little professor in the stiff lace collar, brought them back into the company.

"Tell me, is the émigré Obodovsky, one of the Kropotkin circle, a relative of yours?"

The sound of her voice was happiness: it told Vorotyntsev that she was not preparing to leave, not turning her attention elsewhere. How he wished . . . how good it would be if she knew his whole history, how he had fallen from grace . . . She was the one he wanted to hear his story.

Obodovsky looked around abruptly, took a while to understand. "Who d'you say? Oh, yes. That's me."

And back to business. Vorotyntsev was drawn in again, willy-nilly— how could you refuse this engineer? But Andozerskaya, not to be put off, said, laughing at them, "Forgive me, my interest is merely theoretical . . ."

(How melodious her voice was. And how prettily the sinews in her neck moved.)

"How can you combine the beliefs of your first and second lives? Anarchism and artillery?"

Anarchism? Vorotyntsev had never seen a real-life anarchist. This engineer with the voracious need to know . . . ?

Obodovsky shied away, looking for cover. "Somebody pinned that label on me, and I'm stuck with it. When I was abroad I had the good fortune to become friendly with Pyotr Alekseevich. So people got it into their heads that I was an anarchist."

Minervin came to the rescue, forcefully, unanswerably. "The fragmentation of the Russian intelligentsia into parties is merely fortuitous. We all grew from the same root—from the need to serve the people, and we share the same view of the world. We all of us serve the cause as best we can—whether as anarchists or as gunners."

The answer had been given, and further insistence would be impertinent. But Andozerskaya, who was a head shorter than the chair back, was like a little girl invited to join in a grown-up conversation. She persisted. Her voice was light and quiet, but she had a commanding manner.

"Yes, but you had a revolutionary reason for emigrating?"

"People have made too much of it," Obodovsky said. "We had to run."

His wife finished his story for him—a smooth, quiet woman, also nearing forty, she explained to Andozerskaya and to anyone who would listen that "he was just half an hour ahead of the police. I went to the station to see him off, and when I got back the local policeman arrived to get an undertaking not to leave the district." Her dress was more than modest, it was frugal. She was plumpish and comfortable in her movements, to make up for her husband's lean restlessness. She had worn well, with her dark hair and her quiet Russian, rustic even, beauty—Tatyana Larina might have looked like that at forty. Obodovsky used the Public Library, but Vera had not seen his wife before.

Vera was very pleased. Proud of her brother. It had worked out even better than she had intended. Although in his impetuous way he had committed a few political indiscretions, his hair-raising story had made up for it. They had listened eagerly to every word. Vera had always thought her brother an outstandingly able man: if he had not risen to high position it was because of his own straightforwardness and the crookedness of the way to the top. He and Andrei Ivanovich had taken to each other. And look how readily he was now answering Obodovsky's questions. And he obviously had all Andozerskaya's attention.

This was more like business. Vorotyntsev answered readily. He hadn't known about the Subcommittee for Military-Technical Aid! Meeting Obodovsky could be invaluable. There was plenty of advice he should be given. He could be asked to give attention to things the army at the front couldn't get across however loud it shouted.

"Tell me. What about the trench gun? Will we be getting one? If so, when?"

"The first prototypes are at the front already. It's an excellent gun, a magnificent gun. We are going into mass production now at Obukhov's. I believe every regiment will have two of them by next spring. Incidentally, Andrei Ivanovich is also keeping a close eye on it."

Andrei Ivanovich came over and sat where he could talk to them.

He hadn't invited Obodovsky as a social gesture. What most of his guests had come for, the lecturer and the lady professor, was to return books or borrow others, which the ladies present wrapped up for them. That was Petersburg! Obodovsky he had invited to discuss business related to the Duma Defense Commission.

"Forgive me, Andrei Ivanovich, Dmitriev, the engineer, is in fact supposed to be ringing me tonight about the trench gun, and I took the liberty of giving him your number. Is that all right?"

"Of course, of course, Pyotr Aki . . ." The telephone rang at that moment. Vera blushed slightly. The call was for Andrei Ivanovich. As the receiver was passed to him, they heard the rather harsh tones of Pavel Nikolaevich no less. The room fell silent, straining to catch the drift.

Shingarev came back looking puzzled. Pavel Nikolaevich wanted him to go over at once, and bring Minervin, if he had not left yet.

Something had happened! *Something had happened!* Both leaders started getting ready, exchanging laconic remarks. The lecturer and the Kadet ladies were in a state of high excitement. The senior lady buttonholed Minervin to get what she could out of him.

"We'll take a cab," Minervin said.

Shingarev dismissed the idea. "A cab as far as Basseinaya costs three rubles now. We can get there on the tram."

Andrei Ivanovich, always the polite host, asked the company not to leave, they might be back quite soon.

The activists of the People's Freedom Party settled down to wait. This was interesting! Important! A rumor started by the older lady ran around the room: the traitor Protopopov had offered to meet the Duma leaders in private! They had to make a tactical decision. Should they meet him? Should they humiliate him by refusing? Should they put forward demands? Or just observe, just reconnoiter? Was he aiming to take over food supplies? Don't let him! Or maybe he had been given a secret mission to recruit additional members to the government? Obviously a trick!

Vorotyntsev was aware that Protopopov was the latest new face at the Ministry of the Interior. But whom was he betraying, and why, and why was a meeting with him so important?

Shingarev was saying goodbye to Obodovsky. But Obodovsky would have to stay on and wait for the telephone call from his engineer.

Andozerskaya? Shingarev didn't expect to see her when he got back. He shook hands and said goodbye.

Vorotyntsev reacted as if a piece had been torn out of his side. The party was breaking up. Andozerskaya would be leaving with the rest, and he hadn't even . . .

He found himself holding Shingarev's soft, warm hand. Looking at his honest untroubled brow, his friendly eyes. He hadn't gotten anywhere with Shingarev either. There could have been discoveries to make with him. But they would not be seeing each other again.

Should he himself, and could he, stay any longer?

Andozerskaya meanwhile sat still, showed no sign of leaving—and her gaze was going nowhere either.

"Do you use illuminated shrapnel?"

"You mean Bengal lights on parachutes? I've seen them. They're all right . . . But what we must try to do is reduce the use of shrapnel in favor of grenades."

"We're working on that. But don't expect more howitzer power. You'll have to make greater use of mountain artillery instead of howitzers."

Andozerskaya still didn't look the least bit bored. She sat beside them, a silent participant in their far from thrilling discussion, listening to both of them, looking attentively from one to the other, as though the specifications of the howitzer and official preferences for one weapon rather than another profoundly affected her. (Perhaps, though, academics were interested in everything?)

He was glad that she hadn't moved away and showed no signs of leaving, that she was sitting beside him, watching him. It meant, though, that he ought to put an end to all this artillery talk. But how, without being impolite?

Some sort of influence crossed the bridge of that warm gaze. And part of himself flowed back in return.

He had not, of course, been set free. Nothing that had happened affected his regiment, his corps, his whole Army Group in the slightest.

In three weeks he would be back wallowing in the same old mud, and death, which had spared him so long, would soon perhaps catch up with him. He had not been set free, but with this woman beside him his burden seemed lighter from one moment to the next. The dark picture he had painted seemed more and more remote.

So the artillery talk, with the greenish eyes sparkling, took on a delightful tinge. He had no wish at all to rise and interrupt it.

Obodovsky's wife, half hidden behind her husband, listening to their conversation, in which there was nothing to smile at, sat silently, dreamily content, almost smiling. Not wishing to be noticed, or even to speak.

Vera was there too, and the others were somewhere around. Whenever his dear, understanding little sister looked at him she was smiling—but was there a trace of anxiety there? Perhaps it was time to go? A bit awkward staying behind in his host's absence? He couldn't spare it much thought.

And anyway he hadn't the strength to rise.

His conversation with Obodovsky had covered all the main points and was flagging.

If only out of respect for Andozerskaya (snugly accoutred in her English two-piece and caught in the middle of their discussion) he must make an effort to change the subject.

"And how does the Allis-Chalmers tractor perform on those roads?"

Quick to spot this first sign that their conversation was wilting, Professor Andozerskaya broke in with the gentle firmness of a keel cleaving the water.

"Pyotr Akimovich, please don't think my questions impertinent but"—with an apologetic moue—"like you I have my own strictly defined special subject. We are, after all, more accustomed to seeing revolutionaries as destroyers, so a revolutionary who is also a creator is bound to attract attention. Please don't refuse to tell me: how do your present activities relate to the beliefs of your previous party?"

"Party?" Obodovsky turned sharply, with a slight frown under his bristling grayish hair, and looked at Andozerskaya with his faded pale blue eyes as though she had only just sat down there. This switch, not just of his active chin but of his thoughts through sector after sector after sector, pinned him as if by centrifugal force to the sloping back of his chair, and it took him some time to answer.

"As I said before, I have never been a member of any party. All political parties muzzle the individual."

Andozerskaya wanted it spelled out. "You mean because it implies coercion?"

"Exactly." Obodovsky, exhausted yet energetic, blinked. It was as though he had snatched a rest for half a blink and had no need for any more. His eyes looked less tired. "I'm a socialist by conviction, but an independent socialist. In 1905, I—remember Nusya?—if we wanted to insult somebody, we called him a Social Democrat; for us in Irkutsk, it was a term of abuse."

Room had been made for Nusya Obodovskaya and she slipped easily from her state of dreamy contentment into an explanation. "Some
of them were such ruffians, they behaved so high-handedly . . . They
brought their own tactics into disrepute. So although we ourselves
were ready at the time to fight at the barricades and die under rifle
fire . . ."

Nusya? On the barricades? This gentle, self-effacing person? It defied
imagination.

But, yes, it had almost come to that in Irkutsk. Intellectuals and
army officers paraded through the streets cheek by jowl, singing the
"Marseillaise" and "Dubinushka." The railwaymen were on strike,
the general public could not buy tickets, only soldiers could use the
trains: they were stronger than the strikers, and could take a recalci-
trant station apart in fifteen minutes. Obodovsky, stranded at a mine
beyond Lake Baikal, escaped in a freight car, talking politics to the
railwaymen and giving lectures on socialism throughout the journey.
Irkutsk was storm-tossed by rallies and political meetings. And Obodovsky with his practical good sense, his intelligence, and his stamina,
quickly and easily came to the fore. He, who had previously known
no way of life other than that of a miner, found himself propelled in
those mad weeks into one unfamiliar position after another—delegate, deputy, representative, elector, member of this, that, and the
other bureau, president of the local Engineers' Union, member of
some secretariat or other, and finally of the Irkutsk Executive Committee no less.

What could be more enjoyable than this state of relaxation? Of
being safe, with your duty done. Suddenly ceasing to feel like a shell
in flight. Just sitting there, not even asking questions. May I smoke?
Permission given. Light up. Pretending to listen to the Obodovskys.
Really just studying and being studied by Andozerskaya. No need to
catch her eye.

She, however, could manage that, and keep her eye on the target,
refusing to be distracted by Irkutsk reminiscences.

"But hating violence as you do, you must hate all forms of military
service."

"Of course," Obodovsky agreed. "Military service, and the army as
such! I've done a bit of soldiering myself. When you put on a uniform
your heart starts beating to a different rhythm. Stand at attention
whenever you see a general, salute every officer, don't absent yourself
without permission, any thinking to be done they'll do for you. You're
afraid of humiliation, of reprimand, you become so uptight that your
nerve snaps. My one salvation was that I dug up a regulation nobody
knew about—that on promotion to ensign you can resign the next day
if you feel like it. So I did just that!"

He laughed, with relief, although it was so long ago, before his emigration, before the revolution. He had spared his too sensitive nerves the ordeal of army life. Besides, he hated military service on principle as a form of coercion. But, also in Irkutsk, you couldn't if you were honest help admiring General Lastochkin.

... Two companies had remained loyal to him. The rest of the garrison had mutinied and moved in to attack these loyalists. A red-hot revolutionary mob of armed soldiers, officers and all! Lastochkin went out onto the porch without guards. "Shoot, then, I'm your man! Surrender? I can't! My oath and my honor won't let me!" And what did the garrison do? The garrison followed his example. The garrison cheered their commander and marched off in perfect order.

"Every inch a soldier!" Andozerskaya shook her head admiringly, visualizing Lastochkin, but sparing a glance for Vorotyntsev beside her.

He was feeling more at ease and happier all the time. Had he really been holding forth about the hopelessness of everything just half an hour ago?

Vera, apparently somewhat uneasy, kept coming close and moving away again. He refused to take the hint. She had, after all, talked him into coming ...

He was glued to the spot.

Olda Orestovna wanted to press her point, but Obodovsky was ahead of her.

"You're going to say that anyone who hates military service ought to be consistent and reject war?"

Professorial scholastic logic. Must be a boring lecturer. The contradiction she was trying to draw him into was transparent, childishly obvious, to Obodovsky.

"In principle I do reject war."

"Then how can you run the Military-Technical Aid Subcommittee?"

He laughed. Then suddenly, impulsively, with long-pent-up passion, he said, "It's true! The army—I hate it. But when everybody gets into a funk and runs away my sympathies are with garrison commander Lastochkin! I'm against violence, yes! Against all violence, all *initial violence*! I'm not a 'nonresister of evil'—I'm against it! If violence is used, how can you reply, except with force?" A nervous light flickered in his eyes. "Not to defend yourself is just spineless."

Good man! Vorotyntsev looked at him admiringly.

His wife took over, sailed in unhesitatingly: "No, sir and madam! He was never a defeatist! He was desperate to get into the Japanese war. When the *Petropavlovsk* was sunk he wore a black armband, said he wouldn't take it off till we won. Didn't you, Petya dear? The surrender of Port Arthur made him ill, he couldn't eat or drink." She touched her husband's hand compassionately. "But after Tsushima, and when the timber concessions came to light ... he still wanted peace, but not defeat . . . For this war he even bought a uniform, and was going to volunteer, but Guchkov dissuaded him."

Obodovsky wrinkled his brow and looked hard at the company. Where did they see a contradiction?

"Just because I love my country am I supposed to love its army? Do I have to be an enthusiast for violence in order to defend my country? I can't stand being beaten! That's natural enough, isn't it? And whoever beats Russia, beats me. And I'm not going to let myself be beaten, with or without her!"

But who was arguing?

Vorotyntsev? These protestations were not meant for him. Vorotyntsev sat quietly smoking, looking around, listening. Whatever needed to be said that nice clever woman would say it. Or Obodovsky would.

Andozerskaya? She had been arguing like an academic, but was now talking rather loosely. She was probably not used to giving way, probably always clung on, so she had to find some non sequitur. Half smiling, fluttering her eyelashes, she said, "So you must feel very strongly about the enemy?"

She looked at Vorotyntsev for support.

He was at a loss for words. Feel strongly?

Obodovsky nodded vigorously. "Yes. Hatred!"

Vorotyntsev had caught up. Hatred? He thought a moment. "Strange. All the time I've been fighting I've never felt any hatred for the Germans."

It was the engineer's turn to wrinkle his brow. How was this possible?

How indeed? Vorotyntsev himself didn't know. But it was true. True of the common soldier too.

"None, none at all, I remember that it was the same with the Japanese. Fighting meant defending Russia. Fighting was just like following a skilled trade. But hate them? . . . I suspect that among German officers . . . it's the same . . ."

Yes, but . . . Nusya Obodovskaya reminded him of the Russian wounded shot in the village occupied and burned by the Germans.

Yes, right. He was contradicting himself. Or was he? The heart in tatters. The heat of battle. Hatred? Yes! But for our own superiors, for those whose stupidity had caused us to surrender the village. The enemy . . . seen in the light of the flames . . . was like some elemental force—so many phantoms from hell . . . You can only hate live people, real people.

He realized that he must not waste this evening. He must say something special to Olda Orestovna. Leave some mark, like a cherished scar. But he hadn't found the right moment. He mustn't strike a false note. And how would she take it?

Vera joined them, and remained standing, behind the Obodovskys. The discussion petered out. Children's voices could be heard from the other room. The Kadet activists were also in the other room. There was a rattle of crockery in the kitchen. Peace, perfect peace. No shell bursts, no rifle fire, no booby traps, no mines.

His sister's eyes seemed troubled, newly observant. He looked away.

[2 4]

Now that she was nearly forty, and indeed by the time she was thirty, Nina Obodovskaya had learned not to expect admiration. She no longer needed to attract attention or to look for even the slightest bit of personal success. She had accepted long ago that her marriage was her fate and, having accepted it, never felt the slightest regret. She was welded to her husband's destiny, and that was good and as it should be. There was always work, the cause, and struggle. There was not the least little opening for anything else. When her husband had suggested today that they should take a little walk—not very far, wouldn't take long—from Syezhinskaya Street to Monetnaya, that part of the protracted visit that could be called socializing seemed to Nusya an extraordinary holiday.

Nina Aleksandrovna was born Bobrishcheva-Pushkina, and had been present as a girl at the young Tsar's coronation. She had cheered the Tsar's dazzling entry in procession into Moscow. She had stood, in a court dress with a train, bare shoulders, and a tall Russian headdress, at a levee in the great Kremlin Palace; and had first felt herself to be an adult at a ball given by the Moscow gentry in honor of the new Tsar. In those days she was an ardent student of the genealogy, antiquities, and traditions of her class (although, true to what we learn from Russian novels, she also distributed medicines, tea and sugar, and white bread to peasant homes, and was godmother to many peasant children). She was remarkably beautiful, worshipped a number of heartthrobs in rapid succession, and was, to begin with, not attracted to but rather annoyed by the implacable criticism of the seamstress's son who somehow turned up in their house, an ugly, supercilious, jumpy young man, a provincial student of mining engineering who gave lessons to support himself and had once fainted from hunger on the Nikolaevsky Bridge. Even when he shut himself up with a young lady in a dark cupboard to carry out some electrical experiment his principles would not allow him to touch her hand unnecessarily.

At seventeen you are so susceptible and so fickle that it is hard to know when you are really in love! But our decisions mature without us knowing, and Nina, making the choice which a girl can make only once, chose to share Pyotr Obodovsky's reckless and unrewarding lot; since then she had seen no more of society balls, or indeed of Petersburg, or for that matter of Russia, but, instead, dim cottage gatherings of mining engineers and managers, eager to outdo each other in the supply of meat pies and vodka, or frugal amateur concerts for émigrés, paid for from mutual aid funds.

Petya had firm convictions, formed in early youth; Nina had practically none, so she naturally started thinking as he did. He could not tolerate whatever was the conventional thing to do, and loathed high society, and especially Guards officers and jurists, if only because of the way they looked upon women. When he agreed to get married in church it was probably the only time in his life that he had waived his principles—simply because the ceremony was unavoidable. It was a torment for him to have to make his confession (still, a sympathetic progressive priest asked only two or three formal questions) and take communion. Nina herself, all of seventeen years old, refused communion, saying, "I don't believe that's the body and blood of Christ!" ("Nina love," her mother said reprovingly, "nobody believes nowadays, but they still take communion!") Nina didn't believe in the sacrament of marriage either, but the ceremony itself allured her, enchanted her, it was really like discovering a new life, the happiest day in a woman's life.

There the bridegroom's concessions to convention ended. He refused to pay the customary newlyweds' visits. He refused to join in such "romantic nonsense" as visiting the burial places of ancestors. He did not like his wife's sentimental reminiscences, did not like the stately home on the Volkhov and regarded the family estate itself as a crime, so that Nusya renounced her share of her inheritance. (Petya, however, even rebelled against working on the land with his hands, against all ties with the land, disliked farming as something in which incalculable forces might suddenly intrude—hail, drought, who knows what—and your expert calculations went for nothing.)

There were other, transient grievances in Nusya's young life in Petersburg. At twenty and even twenty-one she wanted—why not?—to dance a little. But she never had dance frocks or pumps, and the first time her parents gave her money for clothes her husband took it as a (nonreturnable) loan for a good cause. Nor did she have time for the concerts and lectures she had dreamt of: she was hard at work all day and in the evenings, multiplying and dividing for the mineralogists, entering the figures in a card file, often getting into a muddle and always bored, sitting at home all day as if in an office, with a relentlessly demanding husband. Relentlessly—but affectionately. And at the slightest sign of displeasure on her husband's face Nusya was ready to sacrifice anything. She grew accustomed to, happy with a life lived to please her husband. "Forgive me, Nusya my dear, for giving you such a hard time of it. It's only for a while. Someday things will get a bit easier and we'll go everywhere." But life went by, and that "someday" never came. Petya was never still for a moment. Even at a student ball he was in charge of collecting subscriptions to some fund or other, and on their first voyage to France he was too busy learning French to look at the sea—so how could he possibly have time left for his wife? One Christmas she escaped to a fancy-dress ball, but where was the girl she had once been? She was no longer good at party games, or quick-witted in conversation, and although she wore a charming Japanese costume she did not attract attention. She had looked forward to evenings spent discussing serious books with her husband, but even that was not to be. "You might at least educate me!" she implored: she felt very much in need of firm guidance. But her young husband retorted that he respected her too much as an individual to force his own views on her. "You must work it out for yourself."

What other views were there? How could she "work it out"? She simply accepted her husband's views anyway.

Obodovsky was invited to stay at the Mining Institute after he graduated, but he felt cramped there and refused. He was offered a post in the Donbass, which by then had all the urban amenities, but said no, because working there would be too comfortable. He was a born pioneer and felt the lure of the new. They went out to the Golovin mine in the wilds of Siberia, and as if that was not taxing enough, the "Socialist" mine started up shortly afterward at Cheremkhovo, where after working for one year every worker received gratis a share in the mine and its administration. This was an extraordinary scheme for 1904, and the socialist character of the enterprise was concealed from the government by disguising it as a joint-stock company. As they left for Siberia, Petya donated seven hundred of the one thousand rubles given him as a moving allowance to some social cause, without even asking his wife whether she needed anything. The one human character trait he never understood, and was repelled by, was stinginess. At the Golovin mine he sometimes went for months on end without salary while helping to pay the enterprise's debts, or else he was paid and used the money to settle with the workers. As for the Socialist mine—it was an abyss that simply swallowed money, while the coal proved to be of poor quality and no one would buy it. Petya had such hard going at the Socialist colliery that at thirty-two he was going gray, his heart missed beats, and he had attacks of "nerves" which sometimes reduced him to helpless sobbing.

Pyotr Obodovsky was so constructed that not only did he never evade responsibility, as Russians are so often inclined to do, but whenever he saw a duty (even when it was not directly his own) he rushed to perform it, plunge in and swim against the tide. He knew that he could master anything, organize anything more quickly and neatly and effectively than the next man. Other people were also quick to sense this, and joined in pushing him into the most difficult situations. At

any meeting or congress of engineers, any committee of experts, Obodovsky inevitably came forward with his projects and those projects
captivated all present, so that he was called a spellbinder, and wherever
he went was elected to bureaus, committees—and called on to implement his own proposals. Wherever he appeared—in the Irkutsk Social
Assembly (a club for intellectuals) or the Geographical Society—as
soon as the speeches were over he felt bound to rise, to contest and
amend what had been said, after which he could not escape election!

The well-off and enterprising world of engineers, lawyers, and merchants in Irkutsk appreciated Obodovsky and were ready to accept him
as one of their own, but he never felt at home with them, could not
fall in with their free and easy, pleasure-loving ways. They all spent
money freely, caroused, gambled recklessly; the wives of Irkutsk engineers had forty new frocks a year made for them and even ordered
Paris models—whereas in some years Nusya couldn't have a new dress
at all. The Obodovskys, forever paying back money borrowed by the
Socialist colliery, were so hard up that they often went hungry, and in
the Social Assembly, with engineers and lawyers noisily dining around
them, sat silently with anguished bellies, pretending to acquaintances
that they had just dined at home.

But Nusya had genuinely reconciled herself to their fate, got used
to it and even seemed to like it: to live as they did was like preserving
their youth indefinitely. "I don't want to get rich! I don't want a life
of habit!" She came to realize clearly that she and her husband would
never know financial ease, or peace of mind, or leisure, or amusements,
and she no longer coveted such things. The whole business of her life
was to be his wife. And if he was taking dynamite to Irkutsk for the
colliery, and declaring his freight so that proper precautions could be
observed was likely to take too long, they just carried it with them into
a passenger carriage. Nusya would sit on the lethal box, draping her
skirt over it to hide its fearful contents from the conductor's eye. And
ride over the bumps in this position.

But their tender affection for each other had never wavered from
their honeymoon on. Petya had been a virgin when he married, had
lived an immaculate life ever since, and had never known any other
woman. "I asked nothing from you that I couldn't offer myself." When
he went off to jail his confident parting words were: "You are my
wife—which is as much as to say that you are me!" They vowed that
whichever of them outlived the other would take the wedding ring
from the dead partner's finger, and thenceforward wear two of them.

It was Obodovsky's destiny to choose paths peculiar to himself, paths
that drained his strength and sometimes endangered his life. When in
1905 the revolution overtook Obodovsky in Irkutsk, his destiny confronted him with a knife-edge choice. To all appearances the day so
long desired and prayed for by all the most honorable martyrs of the

muted generations seemed to have dawned for Russia. Absolutely nobody could get on with his ordinary work or sit it out at home, everybody was helplessly swept along with the marching, shouting, voting,
when the ordinary bonds between particles of humanity snapped and
every single one felt, joyfully and fearfully, free to move independently
of matter as a whole, felt an imperative need to move, making no
attempt to imagine the shape of things afterward. Obodovsky, who
even before had never been at rest, was bound to spin, to whirl ten
times as fast! The shock waves in the world about him propelled him
inexorably to the forefront, to the summit. The difference between
him and innumerable other orators and deputies was that he did not
abandon his normal work.

Even after his arrest his characteristic of always becoming prominent
and of running not only his own life but the lives of all around him
never waned. He was elected headman in every communal cell, in the
New Isolation Prison, and again by fellow prisoners in transit to the
Aleksandrovskoye Central Jail. Since the prison regime was then so
lenient he could achieve a great deal, and spent whole days helping
his fellow prisoners to arrange their lives, obtain exemptions and amenities, and keep in contact with the outside world. Even in the Central
Jail he was called upon to make a plan of the prison so that the cost
of repairs could be estimated, and secretly made a copy, which was
afterward circulated among prisoners as an aid to escape.

So it was only to be expected that on his first visit to relatives in
Petersburg, Obodovsky immediately stumbled upon the summons issued by the League of Liberation to all progressives to attend an open-
air concert at Pavlovsk in order to protest against the war, and (this
was after the sinking of the Russian fleet at Tsushima) of course he
went along, taking Nusya with him. People wearing caps or head
scarves were not allowed in to listen to the band, only respectable
persons had gathered—and this made it all the more impressive when
this respectable audience interrupted the music by stamping its feet
and shouting, "Enough blood! Down with the war," Pyotr shouting
with them fit to burst. The musicians fled from the platform, and the
audience began barricading themselves behind piled-up benches, with
the police trying to disperse them. Once again, Obodovsky kept it up
longer than anybody, and when they were all running away into the
park he could not bear to run with them. White with anger, he took
Nusya's arm and led her, not away from the soldiers lined up there,
but, with slow triumphal steps, the length of the front rank. He walked
before the hateful ranks white in the face, biting his lip, his head
proudly high. The bugle had sounded, the officer had turned around
to order his men to fire in the air, but was flustered and worried that
the defenseless couple might be too near the volley. (Although Nusya
was afraid, she did not try to pull her husband along more quickly. If

he had made up his mind to it she was ready to die with him.) "You are taking a risk! Think of your lady! Go away as quickly as possible!" the officer begged. Petya answered sharply, as though the soldiers were under his command: "I shall go away when I see fit!" So husband and wife, slowly, and more slowly still, walked on to the gates. And there was no volley.

In emigration, in Paris, they lived in a seventh-story attic, poorer than the students around them, unable even to take a horse tram, saving the fare for food. And there a telegram from Siberia reached them, saying that one partner had defaulted and that repayment of a thousand rubles owed by the Socialist colliery had fallen due. Much as they loathed Nusya's mother's "estate" it was to her they had to turn.

Yes, being a revolutionary is easier if you come from the gentry, not from some other class.

Life in emigration—half starved, always hunting for work, anchorless, making puerile attempts to put on plays (Petya was a hopeless actor), joining in nonparty socials, fraternal labor exchanges, and mutual aid funds, living in a self-contained Russian colony in England without knowing a word of English—for Nusya this was the easiest and happiest time of her life.

The squabbles, the melancholia, the idle dreams of émigré existence were not for the Obodovskys. Petya had fled to Europe as a revolutionary and a wanted man, but once there he wished (with the approval of Kropotkin, whom he regarded not as a party leader but as one who could teach him how to live) to work as an engineer, yet not in the service of foreigners, but for Russia, while remaining abroad. Fortunately, he was sufficiently well known in Russian engineering circles, and was offered the right sort of work: surveying European ports and writing a monograph on them, organizing a floating exhibition of Russian goods and an industrial exhibition at Turin. He worked from 8 a.m. to 2 a.m., and when he had waited a whole year for his wages was told that "our credit is exhausted, and your services are no longer needed." His speeches on an industrial program for Russia were applauded, but for lack of funds nothing that he had written was published in his own country, and his words remained unheard and unheeded in Russia.

Obodovsky's anger with his fellow countrymen made him sick to his stomach, and as in his youth he was threatened by some sort of nervous collapse. His indignation with Russia was such that he thought of settling permanently in Argentina.

But, mysteriously, the work a man must do awaits him in the place where he was born, and nowhere else. Obodovsky's ancestry was Polish, but he recognized no connection with Poland and lived wholly for Russia.

So as soon as news came that he was no longer wanted by the law, the Obodovskys scraped together a few francs in small loans and sped home.

Yet although life in Russia was somewhat brighter, though the gloom seemed to be lifting and the cruel times unlikely to return, Nusya was somehow not at all eager to go back beneath the oppressive vaults of the fatherland. Where life would never again be as free of responsibilities as it had been in emigration.

Nusya had a presentiment—and others prophesied—that a terrible end awaited them both in their homeland.

*   *   *

EVEN THE DISTANT PINE WAVES TO ITS OWN COPSE.

*   *   *

[2 5]

Olda Andozerskaya hotly resented it when people seemed to connect her, because of her appearance or the company she kept, with the clan of old (or more or less old) maids, unmarried because they had failed to find a husband. She was unmarried at thirty-seven, but for quite a different reason. On principle. They had not been able to change their lives—she could have done so a hundred times, but had found no one worth doing it for. Intelligent people understood, but for the stupid majority the absence of a ring on her finger meant that she was a failure. She shied away from unattached women, avoided even sitting by them, let alone associating with them and courting comparison.

It was, though, the same with women in general. She had, in her lifetime, met a handful of interesting women, all old, but the great majority were so colorless, so far from being her equals, that they could not interest her or affect her in any way at all.

She knew Vera Vorotyntsev from the Public Library, but couldn't quite understand her function there. If you are master of your subject, you know what books the library has, which ones you need to take out, and surely need not entrust the search to someone called a "bibliographer." Though not in her first youth Vera was still (just) too young to have joined the accursed clan, but nothing else about her inclined Andozerskaya to show friendliness. And on this occasion, the young person would have done better to stop flitting anxiously around and keeping such a sharp eye on the colonel, as if she was his wife instead of his sister.

The colonel, of course, was married, but Andozerskaya's position excused her from paying such very close attention to the dividing line between married and single men, and allowed her not to attach exaggerated importance to such accidental matters as a marriage in the past.

Olda Orestovna had come on some little matter concerning a book, and should have left long ago. The evening had expired anyway. But the moment she had entered, when she had seen only the colonel's broad shoulders, but not yet his face, and heard only a few words from him, she was full of admiration. Then he turned around, and she saw his weather-beaten, sunburned face, fresh from the trenches, saw the white and gold of the George Cross and the crimson Order of St. Vladimir, heard him chiding the assembled Kadets, contradicting them in a way not usually heard in such company. At first Olda Orestovna was just slightly amused, then she was carried away by it, and felt the stirrings of an urge to join in and be a bit naughty herself. True, the company had broken up, but the colonel was still sitting there, and she was ready to exert herself just for him. Simply to show him how much alike they were.

Meanwhile, she kept up a conversation with the Obodovskys. This dialogue, though unexciting, was not without interest. It was more a matter of studying your interlocutor than of trying to convince him. The infinite variety, the endless shades of opinion, the inexhaustible permutations of a limited number of components never ceased to amuse and delight her. The variety, the uniqueness of people's beliefs was so obvious, from one moment to the next obliterating any dividing line between groups—only fanatics or knaves could insist that people were divisible into parties. People let themselves be divided into parties only because they had not thought enough, or didn't care enough, or were not mature enough. The characteristics, or principles, that united or divided people were clearly something more than their opinions.

This engineer—revolutionary and patriot—had exhibited yet another configuration of elements, peculiar but not contradictory. And he expressly rejected all political parties. Good for him.

Andozerskaya was also endowed with a greater than normal receptivity, which enabled her, while listening to whatever was said, and without relaxing her part in the conversation, to form and store up conclusions from what her eyes told her. So, without effort and for no special reason, Olda Orestovna drew her own conclusions from the mild serenity of the wife sitting beside her restless and vehement husband, from the affectionate way in which they touched each other and the affectionate words they exchanged, and felt that she could sum up the story of the Obodovskys' long, smooth, and unblemished married life, which had never been disrupted by an explosion of unreasoning passion or disturbed by subterranean fires. This semblance of fulfillment seemed to Olda Orestovna a deprivation. The impoverishment of those who believe too soon, with too little experience, that they have discovered and achieved everything. Men, absorbed in their work, can easily find in their wives a whole, unique, eternally serene, self-contained world, its boundaries drawn for as long as life lasts, and their wives may accept their uniqueness as mutual recognition that both have chosen aright. Perhaps they have.

With men like that an unmarried woman can talk only about politics.

No! Obodovsky wouldn't have it.

"That's just the trouble—the arrogance and conceit of the Germans, who must be taken down a peg, or else they'll squeeze us and throttle us. Have you ever lived in Germany? You ought to see for yourselves what sort of people they are! Ruthless! Just let them get their hands on Russia! And so boring . . ."

They had managed to involve Vorotyntsev in a battle of words again. What he wanted was just to sit there quietly, recover from the smoke and heat, begin to live again. And steal glances at the arrow-shaped amethyst brooch fastening the collar of her blouse.

Let them get their hands on Russia? That's what we don't want. But that isn't necessarily connected with hatred of the Germans. He was against letting them get their hands on a single inch of Russian soil. But (was this a respectable position for a colonel in the imperial army to take?) he meant, to begin with, truly *Russian* soil. And second, if you gave them nothing it followed that you shouldn't take anything. It was a simple matter of conscience.

Obodovsky leapt in, darting a glance at Andozerskaya. "Besides, we've got Siberia, and it's practically empty!"

"Exactly. So why this frantic fuss about Poland?"

They could have been enemies, but they had come one step closer and they fitted as snugly as two polished flagstones. They were agreed on the main thing: meddle less in the rest of the world, let them carry on as they please, and keep out of it.

Professor Andozerskaya's general theory found further confirmation in Vorotyntsev's freakish combination of idiosyncratic views. It is often like that when character, not logic, is the unifying factor.

There was a striking contrast between this officer's grim stories and his manner, in which there was no trace of despondency. Wedged into his chair he was like a great boulder, immovable but radiating power. An optimist in spite of everything.

(But she sensed, unconsciously, that the boulder, huge as it was, had not always been invulnerable. It was unchipped, but also unpolished.)

"But what makes you say that the Germans are so cruel?"

"This, for instance. I lived on the Rhine at one time near a school, and regularly every Saturday"—Obodovsky's twitching eyebrows arched in a grimace of pain, and there was a catch in his voice—"the names of all the children who'd been naughty at any time in the week were called out (at their age they'd probably forgotten and mended their ways since Monday!) and they were given the prescribed dose of the cane, conscientiously and relentlessly."

Vorotyntsev laughed aloud. "Is that all?"

"Well, those weekend floggings got on my nerves, made me sick! I couldn't bear to see it! We left the place!"

"By and large, I don't see anything wrong in corporal punishment for boys."

"What?!"

"Though not with that sort of calculated delay, not deliberately leaving it to Saturday. But Russian fashion, in hot blood. A parent or teacher is right to do it. Learning to take his punishment when young will stand a child in good stead later. When he grows up he'll face severer sanctions—the whole Penal Code, from his first day as an adult. So let him get used to the idea that there are limits to freedom of action, while he's still a child."

Nusya wanted to ask whether the colonel himself had been whipped as a child, and whether he had children of his own. She and Petya had none, but if they had . . .

"That way people will never grow up to be proud and free!" Obodovsky said indignantly.

Vorotyntsev, coarsened by the slimy trenches, said, "Well, humble obedience is more useful to society."

That made Andozerskaya laugh. Any gathering of Russian intellectuals—just go and ask those in the next room—would agree with Obodovsky and nobody would dare support the colonel's hopelessly benighted view.

But the diminutive professor had the temerity to side with him. "It's difficult to draw the line between protecting children and making idols of them. Idolized children despise their parents, and when they get a bit older they bully their countrymen. Tribes with an ancestor cult have endured for centuries. No tribe would survive long with a youth cult."

For all his soldierly boldness, his independence of mind, his resoluteness, Olda Orestovna detected in him an imperfect awareness of his own true nature, surprising in a man of forty. A rough diamond all right, and incapable of hiding it. I don't know why it is, my friend, but somehow . . .

Still, before you can decide how to bring up the young you must first define exactly what you intend to train them for. The engineer was in no doubt.

"Education is necessary above all to make the country strong and industrious."

"Yes, but it must not challenge the people's time-tested view of the world. When half-baked people with a grudge against the world go in for teaching, education damages young minds. And the more schools there are, the more people they corrupt."

Why "half-baked," if they know their business? What is this "time-tested worldview" that must not be challenged? A religious one? Obodovsky balked at that. "What if science itself challenges it?"

"Every nation has its own predispositions. And especially a preference for one form of social life rather than another."

Meaning? The form of government under which a people prefers to live? Was Russia supposed to be somehow different in this respect?

Obodovsky knew very well what form of government he wanted, and had his reasons ready. He wanted the broadest possible democratic, socialist republic, but with political parties denied any share of power. Every colliery, every university would be self-governing, making its decisions, wherever possible, independently of the central power. On the Swiss principle: the commune is more powerful than the canton, the canton more powerful than the President. Only this deserves the name "republic"—the concern of society as a whole not of just a few people. Only in this way can society really participate in and understand power. (He had himself tried to establish such a form of government at the Socialist colliery, though without success.) A remote supreme authority is always alien to people—always was, is now, always will be—and any number of parliamentary speechifiers can never compensate the people for their alienation from power. (This in spite of the fact that when many socialists boycotted the First Duma, Obodovsky had rushed from meeting to meeting speechifying: "If you're offered a weapon—take it!")

The colonel demurred, but halfheartedly. It seemed only too obvious that if you had a republic there was no need for such extremes of disorganization, with every company of soldiers administering itself and doing just what it liked. There'd have to be some sort of Doge's Council or Directoire. Self-government of the majority—wasn't it a contradiction in terms? They would flounder helplessly, maybe rush over a precipice, like the proverbial herd of swine. Only a strong, assured, self-reliant minority equipped to rule could make history.

Once again they were in agreement.

How is it that we share these extreme views? How is it that you and I, suddenly . . .

If Vorotyntsev was ever visited by secret thoughts about possible changes in the structure of government in Russia, they were the sort that called for action, not just discussion, even such discussion as this with the sensible engineer and the ever so clever lady.

Obodovsky rocked back in his chair. Brush the majority aside? Then for whose sake would we be doing it all? Yet this was only "in principle." Ideology aside, summing up in the simplest way his own experience, he had always shouldered twenty men's burdens, and it was he

himself with a few others—you could count them on your fingers—
who had always gotten things done. The majority did not really behave
as they were supposed to in theory: they had a fatal tendency to indecision, they shunned the risks taken by individuals, or rushed to
thwart them . . .

In educated Russian society, opinion is so slanted, leans so sharply
to one side, that by no means every view may be expressed. A whole
school of thought opposed to that particular slant is morally forbidden,
not merely in lectures but in private conversation. And the more "liberated" the company, the more heavily this tacit prohibition weighs
on it. Warned that "he's a rightist, you know"—"no! a rightist?"—
everyone recoils in horror. That man's entitlement to live, to express
opinions, is abruptly terminated. As though anyone could forgo the
use of his right hand, or buy only left-handed gloves. Only an innocent,
charging in recklessly before he has found his feet, would lay about
him as the colonel had today.

But it was because of him that Andozerskaya had plucked up her
courage. In her academic milieu she lived under the constant pressure
of this ban on thoughts unwelcome to "society." She had to choose
every word so carefully that she never dared speak her mind fully or
directly. Vorotyntsev's enviable freedom of expression had drawn her
out. And with the company trickling away the risk was small: nothing
could distract the eccentric engineer from his notebook, and his happy
wife was not one of those suspicious-minded progressive ladies always
spoiling for an argument. Flouting all the taboos, even the most inflexible (and foreseeing the colonel's jubilation), she looked at each of
them in turn through half-closed eyes and said laughingly, "You seem
to have plumped for a republic in a hurry, gentlemen! How lightly you
have rejected monarchy! Are you sure you aren't just slaves to fashion?
One person starts it, and the rest take up the parrot cry: the monarchy
is the main obstacle to progress. And this is the distinctive characteristic by which we recognize 'our side': abuse of monarchy in the past,
in the future, and at all times in the world's history."

Was she joking? Making fun of them? What wild nonsense was this?
A professor of general history, in the twentieth century, defending . . .
defending . . . not . . .

"Au-toc-racy?"

"That in particular. The slogan 'Down with autocracy' has blotted
out the whole sky, clouded all minds. Autocracy is blamed for everything in Russia. But, historically, the word 'autocrat' means simply a
ruler who does not pay tribute. A sovereign. It most certainly does not
mean one who does just what he likes. True, he has plenary powers
which he shares with no one, no other earthly authority limits him, he
cannot be brought before any earthly tribunal, but he must answer to
his own conscience and to God. And he must regard the limits im-

posed on his authority as sacrosanct, and observe them even more strictly than bounds drawn by a constitution."

Obodovsky could not believe his ears. An educated person defending, loud and clear, the barbarous, benighted institution called autocracy? Surely the time was past when a single word could be said in its defense? In defense not just of monarchy in the abstract but of the Russian autocratic police state? Perhaps even of that particular Tsar. The mere thought of that incompetent nonentity of a Tsar so sickened Obodovsky that when their floating industrial exhibition was anchored off Constantinople, and the personnel were invited to a party by the Russian ambassador, that ragged, half-starved émigré refused an opportunity to eat well for once so as not to have to drink the health of Nikolai II. "But unlimited power is directed by the greed of timeserving courtiers and sycophants, not by conscience before God!" the engineer exclaimed. "Once it has deprived the people of freedom, autocracy grows stupid, becomes deaf, and cannot will what is for the general good, but only what is bad. At best it can only be rendered helpless by its own might. The history of all ruling houses, everywhere, and not just our own, is criminal!"

When Andozerskaya wanted to expound something seriously she always struck a characteristic pose, arching her small hands before her, and stroking one with the other.

"Yes, many peoples have been quick to raise their hands against their monarchs. And some have suffered irreparable loss. In Russia, where there is only a thin veneer of social awareness, it will be a long, long time before anyone thinks up anything better than monarchy."

Obodovsky looked askance. Was she laughing at him? Trying to make a fool of him?

"But look, monarchy means above all stagnation. How can anybody want his country to stagnate?"

"A cautious approach to the new, a conservative sentiment, does not mean stagnation. A farsighted monarch carries out reforms—but only those for which the time is ripe. He does not go at it mindlessly, as some republican governments do, maneuvering so as not to lose power. And it is the monarch who has the authority to carry out lasting and far-reaching reforms."

"Are there any rational arguments in favor of monarchy in our age? Monarchy is a negation of equality. The negation of civic freedom!"

"Why should it be?" Andozerskaya countered, unperturbed. "Both freedom and equality can perfectly well flourish under a monarchy."

But she saw as yet no twitch of agreement on the colonel's weatherbeaten face. He was biding his time.

Wrinkling her small brow, summoning up all her strength (she wasn't going to give way now that she'd started it), she spoke not in her oracular, professorial manner, but laying her sentences before them one by one, with the practiced skill of a housewife setting out polished knives on a tablecloth.

"First, a firmly established line of succession saves a country from destructive rebellions. Second, with hereditary monarchy you don't get periodic electoral turmoil, and political strife in the country is reduced. Republican elections weaken a government's authority—they do not incline us to respect it: those who would govern have to truckle to us before the elections and work off their debt to us afterward. Whereas a monarch doesn't have to make election promises. That's number three. A monarch is able to strike an impartial balance. Monarchy is the spirit of national unity, whereas republics are inevitably torn by rivalries. That's four. The personal power and prosperity of the monarch coincide with those of the country as a whole, and he is simply compelled to defend the national interest if only to survive. That's five. For ethnically variegated multinational countries the monarch is the one binding force, the personification of unity. That's six."

She gave a little smile. The strong, broad-bladed table knives lay gleaming in parallel lines.

She looked triumphantly at the colonel, expecting that he would no longer withhold his strong support. That they would now speak with one voice.

But he remained silent, looking rather lost and uncertain of himself.

Surely you agree with what I have just said? Why this hesitation? Out of place, isn't it, in such a fine soldier, one of the few capable of command?

Have I got something wrong? . . . Do you find it somehow funny?

The roads you soldiers march along are not the only ones in life. There's many a byroad, on the verge of many an abyss.

Could a mountain cannon make its way along them? Or a packhorse?

No, no, of course not! How could you possibly think so?

"How can you possibly count on its capacity for self-criticism?" the engineer cried. The thought of having to go over all his arguments again left him exhausted.

"A monarch lives in a whirl of flattery. He is made to play the pitiful role of an idol. He lives in fear of subversion and conspiracy. What counselor can rely on logic to change the Tsar's mind?"

"To put your views across you have to change somebody's mind— if not the monarch's, that of your own party or those of a discordant public. Persuading a monarch is not the least bit more difficult and takes no longer than persuading the public. And would you deny that public opinion is often at the mercy of ignorance, passion, convenience, and vested interest? Don't people try to flatter public opinion, and succeed all too well? Sycophancy has still more dangerous consequences in free polities than in absolute monarchies . . ."

What made her so attractive? That toss of the head and the self-assured glance that went with it? The taut line of the sensitive neck? The subtly seductive, melodious voice?

If a packhorse couldn't . . . how could anyone use that byroad?

Nothing to it. Hold on to the folds of my dress. We'll get through!

"And bowing to a monarch doesn't go against the grain?" Obodovsky was trying to play on the most ordinary human feelings.

"You always have to subordinate yourself to somebody. If it's a faceless and uninspiring electoral majority, why is that pleasanter? The Tsar himself is subordinate to the monarchy, even more than you are, he is its first servant."

"But with a monarchy we are slaves! Do you like being a slave?"

Andozerskaya proudly held her head at an unservile angle.

"Monarchy does not make slaves of people; republics are more likely to depersonalize them. Whereas if you raise up an example of a man living only for the state, it ennobles the subject too."

The monarch as a purely theoretical example? That sort of argument could lead anywhere.

"But what force is there in any of these arguments if the accident of birth can overshadow them all? A man can be born a fool and reign for a quarter of a century. And no one can do anything about it!"

"The accident of birth is a vulnerable point, yes. But there are also lucky accidents. With a talented man at the head of a monarchy, what republic can compare? A monarch may be sublime. But a man elected by the majority will almost certainly be a mediocrity. And suppose the monarch is an unremarkable person. He is free at least from the temptations of wealth, power, and the honors list, he has no need to do stupid things to win promotion, he has complete freedom of judgment. Besides, efforts are made to correct accidents of birth: the future monarch is educated for his future role, conditioned to it from childhood on, and the best teachers are chosen for him." (A little girl in an armchair, hands raised, loosely folded, boldly defending herself.)

"And another corrective is his metaphysical . . ." (I've never said anything like that in a lecture. It was meant for you. Are you pleased? Do you agree?)

(Have I upset you? I didn't mean to . . . But there are some questions which cannot be . . .)

. . . Cannot be avoided—Nikolai I and Aleksandr III, for instance, came to the throne with no preparation for it at all . . . two strong examples. But not one of your arguments applies to the present Emperor, with his incomparable skill in surrounding himself with incompetents, and letting down honest people. Not one of your arguments really fits him. And when an accidental characteristic of the autocrat becomes an accidental characteristic of the Supreme Commander . . .

But although the colonel did not speak up in support of her he was unmistakably on her side, sitting beside her as though he had long ago enrolled in her guard.

". . . his metaphysical interpretation of his power as a duty to carry out a higher will. As the power of God's anointed."

"Anointed" was a word the engineer could not bear to hear, even used in jest.

"God's anointed! That moldy old formula! Will we never hear the last of it? What sort of maniacal self-hypnosis makes that most commonplace of men believe that he is God's anointed? How can any educated person today believe that God, whoever he may be, has really chosen and appointed Nikolai II to rule Russia?"

"That moldy old formula is very far from dead," Andozerskaya boldly insisted. There was no retreat now. "It expresses something real enough, that he is not chosen by human beings, and that he did not seek that post himself. As long as the succession is not forcibly interrupted—and we are discussing the pure form of hereditary monarchy—human will intervenes only in the choice of the first member of the dynasty. And you must admit that in Russia God took a hand in the accession of the first member of that dynasty."

Perhaps. But after that the chips began to fly. Struggles for the throne. Dethronements. Assassinations. (He kept this to himself. Not a subject for light conversation.)

"After which the dynastic tradition continues independent of human beings and of political struggle. As in Japan, where a single dynasty has ruled for more than two thousand years. It is like nature itself."

Vorotyntsev realized that Vera too was standing there. Not jealous and anxious, as before, but surprised at what she heard and eager for more.

"The essential point is that the anointed monarch is not free to renounce his position. He did not strive for power, but he cannot run away from it. He accepts it like a slave. It is his duty rather than his right."

A very attentive student, his sister. "Like a slave!"—that impressed her.

But her brother said not a word in Andozerskaya's support. He had already gone too far the other way, talking about a republic, a Doge's Council.

Obodovsky loved arguing if it was likely to lead to some practical conclusion—then the ground heaved under you and sent you running into action. But now that they had got onto "God's anointed" he'd had enough. He had his own scheme for an ultrademocratic republic pretty well worked out. It was time to leave anyway, but he had to wait for Dmitriev to ring. He stopped listening, leafed through his notebook, held it half open on the edge of the table, and started draw-ing.

Vorotyntsev leaned over toward Olda Orestovna, and spoke in a low voice. Anyone just out of earshot might have thought that he was whispering compliments.

"So what is the purpose of this unfortunate 'anointment'? To ensure Russia's inevitable doom?"

Vera moved away.

"That's something we can't know," Olda Orestovna answered, al-most whispering herself.

Answered, perhaps, with her eyes rather than her voice. Hazel eyes? Green eyes? Not at all professorial eyes.

"It will all be clear in time. After we've gone."

When hope is suddenly kindled—how to tell whether it deceives? (Whether she is . . . the one?)

Only the experienced heart . . .

Still she couldn't forgive him his "republicanism."

"What happens under republican governments?" she asked. "Mak-ing rational decisions becomes much more complicated. They have to struggle through thickets of human failings. Ambition burns much more fiercely in a republic: it must be appeased quickly. And then—the pyrotechnics of the electoral lie! You bank entirely on popularity—on pleasing. During an electoral campaign the future President is a petitioner, a crowd pleaser, a demagogue. No noble nature can prevail in such a contest. And the moment he's elected he's bound hand and foot by the trammels of distrust. A republic is based on bottomless distrust of the head of government, and even the ablest of men is reluctant to show his talent on the edge of an abyss. A republic cannot ensure consistent development in any particular direction. It is always changing course."

Obodovsky woke up. "In a republic the people recovers its reason and its will. And begins to live a full national life again."

Andozerskaya hit back. "People think you only have to call a country a republic and it will become happy at once. Why should anyone con-fuse the jolts and jars of politics with a rich national existence? Politics ought not to consume the whole of the people's spiritual strength, its attention, its time. Everybody from Rousseau to Robespierre tried to tell us that 'republic' and 'freedom' mean the same thing. But it is not so. And anyway, why should freedom be put before honor and dignity?"

Obodovsky flared up again. "Because the *law* protects the honor and dignity of everyone. The law which is above us all. But what good is law in a monarchy, when the monarch can flout it at will?"

Olda Orestovna shivered (one arm could easily encircle those slight shoulders) but persisted. "Is the law, then, incapable of error? Is it always drafted by farseeing minds? Are not laws often the product of chance? Or the triumph of one side's self-interest over another's? A settling of accounts? '*Dura lex, sed lex*' is a pre-Christian principle, and a pretty stupid one. Yes, the Lord's anointed, and he alone can flout the law. At the dictate of his heart. To show firmness at a moment of change. Or at times for mercy's sake. And that is more Christian than the law."

"Special pleading!" The engineer wriggled impatiently and dismissed all this with a wave of his notebook. "That formula would allow any tyrant to break the law at will. And speaking of tyrants—who anoints *them*? The devil?"

Like a fire, running from his hands, along his arms, past his elbows . . . Is she the one?

She is! She is! Of course she is!

Not the slightest hesitation in her voice, in her argument: "What makes man a tyrant is that he flouts the law for his own purposes, not with the authority bestowed on him from above. A tyrant feels no responsibility to heaven, and that is what distinguishes him from a monarch."

When heaven was mentioned seriously as an operative historical force, was any further discussion possible?

"The tyrant is a special case, and we aren't discussing him. A republic too can be destabilized and lapse into lawlessness—and civil war."

The telephone rang at last, and put an end to it.

Ladies looked in from the next room: "Is that Andrei Ivanovich?"

"Dmitriev for me, I expect," Obodovsky said, closing his notebook.

Evfrosinya Maksimovna's voice came from the corridor: "Pyotr Akimovich, it's for you."

Vera flushed bright red. (Andozerskaya saw it without looking at her.) Obodovsky darted to the telephone. Nobody was much interested, until they heard the excitement in his voice.

"Yes, but, I'm sorry, it's a bit late now, there's no point in . . . So let's say tomorrow . . . What? . . . What?! . . . Wha-a-at???"

Ladies poked their heads around the door again, and the lecturer loomed in their rear.

"On Bolshoi Sampso . . . ? So where are you now?"

Obodovsky held the receiver away from his ear, and with a puzzled frown, called down the corridor, sounding bewildered? dismayed? overjoyed? "D'you know, ladies and gentlemen, I almost think . . . it's begun!"

Begun? What had begun? It could have been anything. The casting of a gun barrel? A surgical operation, a difficult childbirth, the flooding of the Neva, war with Sweden . . . ? But no! All present instantly, unerringly, unanimously heard in that colorless word the boom of a great bass bell: IT'S BEGUN!

What else could possibly have begun?

And who could leave now? How could they break up and go home without hearing all about it?

"Is he far away?"

"Just over the Grenadiers' Bridge."

"So tell him to come here."

Nobody would be leaving.

IT HAD BEGUN!

[26]

They were all in the dining room now, the whole group—or a number of little groups—like people waiting for a train.

The same train? Or different ones with different destinations?

And just as when you are waiting for a train your thoughts stray, you can't concentrate on a conversation, because you have to make sure, in case the train pulls in suddenly, that you have everything with you—so the eight guests in Shingarev's dining room lost interest in each other, neglected the conventional flash of the teeth and rattle of the tongue when chance brought them face to face.

They withdrew into waiting. Or looked around for kindred souls.

Not too far away. Will soon be here. At the door now . . .

To the Grenadiers' Bridge, over the bridge, past the Grenadiers' barracks, along Monetnaya—ten blocks, was it?

Just like those last few minutes at the station. Some passengers are relaxed and placid, some are busy with newspapers. Some sit around in the restaurant or the post office. Others, uncomfortable on the benches provided, move their suitcases close to the exit and sit on them, and yet others are in no condition to sit at all once the train is announced, but pace the hall so restlessly that their fellow passengers begin to see double.

Just so, the younger of the two lady militants, the one in the dark green blouse with the brown splashes, found a path around the table, tortuous but just wide enough, and paced restlessly, unceasingly, swerving at exactly the same place, and reversing her course at exactly the same place, on exactly the same parquet block, every time.

Head down, with eyes for no one, sunk in silence, she seemed to be repeating rhythmical phrases in her mind, or in a whisper, as she paced:

To the Russian people! I am the sad Avenging Angel!
I sow the seeds! The centuries of suffering are over!

The older lady did not walk about, did not budge, but sat still with a look of satisfaction, almost of happiness, on her face: the train would be on time, her ticket was in her pocket, she had booked a good seat. Or perhaps she was taking spiteful pleasure in the plight of those who had distrusted the timetable, expected the train to be held up at signals and switches, and now would never get their luggage together in time.

The lecturer, solid character that he was in spite of his youth, sat motionless, his hands lying on the dining-room table before him like separate tools, gigantic pliers or wrenches. The eyes behind the dark-rimmed spectacles were narrowed in thought, as he went over in his mind the next stages of the journey as far as he knew them: were the bridges safe, were the inclines too steep, what was the radius of the curves, was the outer rail high enough? The look on his scholarly young face was tense but optimistic.

The younger lady paced nervously, to a rhythm not her own, to the rhythm of . . . That, That Which Was to Come. She had long been mesmerized by this rhythm, had heard before anyone the clatter of wheels over the switches, the grinding of brake shoes, the steady hum of the rails. These sounds transformed themselves into familiar lines, echoing in her mind, or perhaps no more than a whisper.

Like a blue flame I will race through the soul of the people,
Like a red flame I will race through the streets of the cities.
Through the mouths of each and of all I shall cry, "Freedom!"
And for each, and for all, give "Freedom" a different meaning.

Obodovsky couldn't sit still either. He kept going to the window and raising a corner of the blind—perhaps expecting to see from five stories up whether "She" was already sweeping along Bolshaya Monetnaya.

Nusya let her husband worry for two—her role was to be strong enough for two. She sat stiller than any of them, without a wrinkle on her brow, with no trace of anxiety on her smooth and, yes, still youthful face. Whatever the troubles to come she had seen them before, we weathered the last one, we'll weather this!

Little Vera, whose life was spent quietly between bookcases, had twice in one evening been caught in a whirlwind. First in the street, now here. Her slim form moved restlessly from room to corridor, from corridor to room . . .

The younger lady's hands were clenched, rigid at her side, she could not unclench them, and didn't know where to put them. At last the mysterious brown splashes on her dress seemed to make sense: they were the fires whose light struggled to break through the dark green fog of everyday life.

And I shall write: "My behest is justice."
My enemy shall read: "No mercy will be shown."

As for the colonel and the lady professor, newly met on this station, and still more or less strangers, they looked at each other with something more than goodwill, wondering: Are we traveling to the same destination? Will we find ourselves in the same carriage?

Throughout the evening only one of those present, little Vera, had watched that friendship ripening, although she was not near them much of the time and only half heard what they were saying. She could see farther ahead than her brother, but did not know how to tell him.

The telephone call had left her trembling. It had to happen—this sudden descent of an unexpected visitor on Shingarev's apartment. Mikhail Dmitrievich. It seemed somehow right that he and the great news should arrive at the same time.

She shivered, and asked Evfrosinya Maksimovna to lend her a wrap.

Fronya had children, Fronya had a home to look after, Fronya had guests who had outstayed their welcome, but Fronya was her husband's wife, and knew as well as he did that *It*, alas, was unavoidable, that *It* would come whatever happened, that *It* was imminent, and no one could think of anything else. Fronya too had been a student in her day, and remembered that far-off time when they were waiting for the Other One.

Dusk-to-dawn student sessions, prophesying the bright future. "The student disturbances alone will be enough to shake all of Russian society! The undying student movement will compel the Russian government to yield to historical necessity!" It became the fashionable thing for high school pupils to help those in prison. Even drapers' assistants drafted proclamations in their basements while their masters enjoyed a lengthy postprandial snooze. Even market traders crowded into one of the stalls to read illicit literature: they didn't understand that word "socialism" but whatever was against the government gave them a bit of a thrill. The local constable stood guard outside while they read, so that they wouldn't be caught by the police inspector or informers from among themselves. Wealthy exiles crossed the Volga in motorboats to picnic and sing revolutionary songs—with policemen waiting on them. No action at all was taken against those who sent money to political émigrés or received letters and messages from them. By then, no governor hostile to liberal ideas need expect promotion. It was only when men in butchers' aprons took to the streets and threw stones at windows that some people began wondering where they could get an icon to put on the windowsill for safety. It was a long time since they'd had one of their own. Must borrow the cook's from the kitchen. The universities became autonomous, and on those islets of freedom, where no policeman was allowed to set foot, joint meetings with workers were held and funds for the Armed Uprising were collected! All educated society agreed that the cowardly attempt of the University Council to safeguard its laboratories and museums, rather than convert the university into the headquarters of armed struggle, was disgraceful. Boycott the reactionary professors! Let students, not professors, govern the universities! University buildings offered a warm shelter for all passersby. Sinister characters in fur caps hung around there smoking.

Shivering, Vera drew the Orenburg shawl more tightly around her slender shoulders, looked expectantly, apprehensively at the outer door, and returned to the dining room.

The words promised by the younger lady's expression, and unspoken in all their arguments—were they now radiant in her prophetic face, murmured like the warning of a coming storm?

> To each I say, "Yours are the keys of hope.
> Alone you see the light. For all but you the light is spent."

Only this half-whisper was heard. If they had all begun reminiscing and arguing—the full-blooded lady with the energetic elbows, the lecturer with the quiet bass cough, inexhaustible in argument, yet as wary as Milyukov himself, the anarchic engineer, who looked around from behind the curtains, eyelids twitching painfully, whenever he disagreed with what was said, the lady professor, content to conceal her anxiety with the firmness of her tone and the quietness of her speech, the pseudo-liberal colonel, docile for the moment, but liable to turn and savage you, the young lady librarian, blushing and trying in vain to master her shyness—if they all rushed into speech at once with their memories and thoughts it would be morning before they knew it and they would have missed the messenger and his message.

. . . Talking about revolutions is easy in countries which have never had one. But we lived through one, we saw what it was like.

And what, I ask you, was bad about it?

Subscription banquets, a tidal wave of banquets! A feast of freedom! How copiously the speeches flowed! Never, in all its centuries, had so much been uttered in Russia! All those toasts and speeches, it seemed, were setting the wheels of history turning! Just a shout or two more and the walls would come tumbling down! And no one was guillotined or shot or imprisoned for banqueting.

Not true. In Siberia, for instance, even a banquet could land two hundred at a time in the lockup. (All right, it was only for an hour and a half.)

No, what troubled us was the thought that we were fighting for an illusion. Would revolution ever, at any time, be possible in this hopelessly inert country?

Meanwhile, the immoderately liberal zemstvo men ungrudgingly spent the pennies collected from peasants on revolutionary propaganda.

Every important assassination was greeted with pious approval, gloating smiles, and gleeful whispers.

Don't call it murder! Where there's a party, an ideological basis, terror is not murder, it is the supreme expression of revolutionary energy. Not an act of revenge, but a summons to action, an affirmation of life! Terrorists are people of the highest moral sensitivity.

Educated society moved leftward, both out of conviction and with an anxious ear for shouts from farther to the left. Paralyzed by the clamor to their left, people refused to take a stand: let whoever wants try to stop it, I won't. They would sign any sort of protest, whether or not they agreed with it.

The chief executive of the Nikolai Railway hired the "Vienna" Theater for his striking workers, at his own expense. One factory manager apologized to his workers: "I'm an anarchist at heart myself, but I have no choice . . ."

Ah, but the fait accompli! What an inspiration! The Publishers' Union's proclamation: "I am now in being! And I forbid you to submit so much as a page to the Censorship Committee!" And at once everybody, even the rightists, happily complied! In a flash—censorship was no more! With nary a drop of blood shed.

But then the compositors established their own, revolutionary censorship: what they didn't like they wouldn't set into type.

The green-ribboned transport workers wrecked locomotives—their way of wresting a constitution from the Tsar. Only revolutionaries had the use of the telegraph—and they transmitted what they saw fit.

Why didn't we accept the Manifesto, why didn't we take advantage of it? Wasn't it enough? No, it only exacerbated us. We don't want your Manifesto, we want to crush the serpent underfoot! We don't want Duma elections—but to crush the serpent once and for all!

Come to think of it—this is the eleventh anniversary of the Manifesto.

On the 30th the Manifesto, on the 31st a call from the Soviet of Workers' Deputies: give weapons to the proletariat and the students!

"Down with the whole bunch of them—and it's all ours!" "There will be worldwide rebellion! They'll kill all the cabbies!"

General strike in Moscow. No electricity. Dark nights. Students fell trees, light bonfires, sing revolutionary songs in the university courtyard. Socialist Revolutionaries argue with Social Democrats. One woman student, a colonel's daughter, calls out to her comrades, "Come on, let's go and get food and revolvers!" They steal through the gates onto Nikitskaya Street. "Alms for the students, food and revolvers!" French rolls and hunks of sausage rain into their baskets, there's a rustle of banknotes, here a revolver, there a knife is slipped into a pocket!

Next—pogrom time! Demonstrations with portraits of the Tsar! Any passing student who fails to doff his cap is beaten up!

But in the hospital left-wing doctors treat only revolutionaries and soldiers. Any simple soul who makes the sign of the cross is refused admission.

The Soviet of Workers' Deputies puts out a "financial manifesto": Overthrow the government! Let's take away its gold, and it will fall! Don't pay what you owe to the state, accept payment from the state only in gold! The country lies in ruins! (Though it was pretty well intact.) Trade is at a standstill. (Though it showed no sign of stopping.) We want a Con-stit-u-ent Ass-emb-ly!

Kronstadt sailors agitated for a Constituent Assembly, wrecked a hundred and forty stores and shops, and then calmed down.

The legal "humorous" journals openly threatened the Tsar with assassination. Freedom of speech! Yes—but only for orators of whom the majority approved. Those who were out of tune with the crowd were howled down, pummeled, bundled off the platform.

In Baku one gendarme engaged in revolutionary propaganda, and a secret police agent set up a printshop to turn out proclamations.

The provocateurs in power were driving the people to revolt!

In the autumn of 1905 many people took fright, left the country, and transferred their money abroad.

Two bombs were planted in the café of the Bristol and anarchist proclamations said it was "so that we can see the vile bourgeois writhing in their death throes."

A governor marched in a street demonstration with students, and they flaunted the red skirts of his coat as banners.

All Moscow bristled with barricades, mostly a display of hooligan high spirits—overturned police boxes and tramcars. A lady in a fur cloak rides in a hansom cab with bombs under her seat, and the patrol does not, of course, dare to search her. Nobody stood guard on the barricades, no shots were fired from them. There were only a couple of hundred volunteer militia on the Presnya, and they dispersed without trouble, mingling with the general public.

Intellectuals bought themselves revolvers, although they didn't know how to use them. Later the problem was getting rid of them. Incapable even of burying the things, they abandoned them in lavatories. Or handed them to the servants. "Here, get rid of this."

It hurt to remember: they had held the revolution in their hands and had let it slip away.

In reality there had been no revolution! It was all window dressing. Talking big.

What had happened was something more significant than revolution! Russia was in ferment, caused by an excess of accumulated energy, an excess of wealth. There would have been no revolution if the government had been farsighted and bold enough to trust society and open a channel for those forces. Revolution is always the sign of fundamental error on the part of the government.

What sort of revolution was it anyway? It was all improvisation. Nothing was planned in advance. Two general strikes, sporadic minor mutinies, one urban uprising. All that really mattered had gone before, or began afterward: Terror! Terror! And more terror!

> *The sword of justice I yield to the crowd.*
> *The blind man shall wield it.*
> *With it son shall pierce mother.*
> *And daughter slay father . . .*

In Siberia, though, it had been a bit more serious. Krasnoyarsk was in the hands of revolutionaries for a whole month, administered by the Union of Unions. The troops had to take it in pitched battle. And Chita held out for two months, though it then surrendered to Rennenkampf without a fight. In Vladivostok officers opened fire on a public meeting, and were massacred by sailors. In Elan, and right along the Trans-Siberian, General Meller-Zakomelsky had railwaymen and telegraphers either hanged or stripped naked and beaten with rubber truncheons out in the freezing cold.

A thousand amnestied criminals were moved from Sakhalin to Irkutsk and dumped there. They joined the revolutionaries and formed gangs of armed robbers. These desperadoes even attacked groups of men in broad daylight, on the main street.

A soldier in a punitive company was paid thirty kopecks a day. (Thirty is always the figure, for some reason!) And each company jealously insisted on taking its turn to "suppress."

While certain Academicians demanded the removal from their staircase of soldiers trying to keep warm there.

Back in 1895 a skilled workman of peasant origin, who had educated himself by reading, had argued against strikes at his place of work. This was recalled in 1905, and he was shot in the back.

That year was a testing time for many Russian minds. A year in which it was possible to stop believing that Russia had any future.

Or was it rather a celebration of what life lived boldly could be, a proud hymn to freedom and the open spaces? Was there any hope that it would return?

The revolution ran its course, and bread was still a kopeck and a half a pound, meat was still twenty kopecks.

At the elections to the First Duma, with the police standing by, there were still calls for an armed uprising. And nothing happened.

Later came the "robberies movement": savings banks, post offices, state liquor shops were plundered wholesale. There were daring raids every day.

The Moscow Merchants' Bank was robbed of 800,000 rubles.

Instructions to terrorists recommended that bombs should be made of cast iron, so that there would be more splinters, and packed with nails.

A Rostov "laboratory" even issued an illustrated catalogue with testimonials from purchasers of bombs.

And the field courts-martial? Punitive actions like those against the enemy in a conquered country!

It was bloody work! Done in a hurry, to quench the bonfires of revolution with blood!

The field courts-martial were not an initiative, they were a response. They were used in flagrant cases of murder, robbery, bombing, violent crime generally, when there was no need for investigation and when delay in punishment would contribute to the collapse of society. If someone throws a bomb today, hang him tomorrow, and the next bomb thrower may think twice. They're so brave only if they think they can escape before they're executed, or benefit from an amnesty.

In their haste they executed innocent people! Or people who were guilty but did not deserve the death penalty!

Did that make revolutionary terrorism any more just than field courts-martial? Those clandestine revolutionary tribunals, where sentence of death was passed in the obscurity of the underground, obeyed no code of law but only the dictates of their hatred. Who could see, who could check on those anonymous judges who decided whether a man should live or die?

> *He who has drained the heady draft of wrath*
> *Must either executioner be, or else the hangman's victim.*

The revolutionary deliberately puts himself in mortal danger, sacrifices himself for his cherished ideals.

But then his judge may be killed tomorrow for passing sentence.

It isn't a trial, it's rough justice, dealt out by people beside themselves with anger. A bloody revenge, exacted by the government.

If the revolutionaries kill people, that's Liberation with a capital "L." If the government kills someone, that's hangman's justice. Night arrests and house searches are a loathsome abuse, whereas an underground bomb factory is a house of prayer for the people's happiness?

If you want the bloodshed to stop, if you do not want young men to take up Brownings, don't encourage them with your approval. Why won't educated public opinion condemn robbery and murder? If the

State Duma had just once condemned terrorism, the need for field courts-martial would never have arisen.

Gentlemen, the subject of Robespierre's first speech was: the abolition of capital punishment.

But what sort of Christian regime is it, you ask, that answers terror with terror?

Well, the whole civilized world is Christian, yet capital punishment is retained. There are forces so evil that there is no other defense against them. Abolish the field courts-martial—and you'll get lynch law. After the San Francisco earthquake a man was shot for washing his hands in drinking water.

Overworked executioners could not hang them all, and long trains crawled across Siberia to the penal colonies.

Just look at the figures, gentlemen! During the first year of Russian "freedom," counting from the day of the Manifesto, 7,000 people were killed and 10,000 wounded. Of these, official punitive action accounts for fewer than one-tenth. Twice as many government officials were killed. Who was being terrorized by whom? The rest were ordinary citizens unlucky enough to be killed or wounded by expropriators, revolutionaries, plain hooligans, bandits—or punitive squads.

For example: A priest in church was reading from the Epistle about reconciliation. A student took a shot at him and ran out of the church.

Another example: An artisan entered an apartment where he was known. A five-year-old boy approached him trustingly. He cut the boy's throat and stole . . . some linen.

Another incident: Two old people murdered, for what turned out to be forty-four kopecks.

The record also includes a guest who murdered his hosts because they failed to offer him beer.

Random shots were fired at train windows.

Trains were wrecked for no particular reason.

One terrorist shot and killed a cabby's horse.

In Petersburg a twelve-year-old boy killed his mother because she wouldn't let him go out to play. And a girl of thirteen killed her brother with an ax.

> *I will stir the thrill of killing in the girlish heart.*
> *Awaken bloodstained dreams in children's minds.*

You only have to make a start, start killing, in the name of the rights of man and the citizen, say, and the epidemic of killings soon gets out of control. We, the Russian intelligentsia, had nourished our enlightened intellects on this for some twenty-five years. Remember the letter written by a member of the People's Will Party to his friends, on the eve of his execution: "The pity is that we are perishing to bring shame on a dying monarchy, and for little else. *We wish you a more productive death than ours. God grant you, dear brothers, every success in your terrorist activity!"*

"Tell me, though, tell me, do you or don't you believe in the people?"

"The people by itself is not enough."

"What is more important than the people? What else is there?"

"There's the *roof* under which the people live. A common home for the people, otherwise known as the Russian state. As long as the roof exists, we do not value it. No need, we say, to treasure and preserve anything in Russia—pilfer and burn, as though it all belonged to somebody else."

"But we can't avoid following the universal path of progress either!"

"In the West progress has a powerful mainspring of its own, which governs the whole of Western life. Here it's obviously rather different. Anyway, is progress what we want for ourselves? We say 'progress,' but the word pounding in our hearts is 'revolution.' What makes Europe so interesting to us, so seductive? The fact that revolution emanates from there. Anyway, what is progress? Nobody has yet explained why millions of people crowded together in one place are supposed to be cleverer than people settled at comfortable intervals over a great expanse. Why should the experience of the first group be preferred to that of the second? Besides, whoever takes the lead and moves quickly ahead risks missing the fork in the road and marching on to nowhere. Western Europe has made some very dubious choices since the Middle Ages and yet we are unwilling to try anything of our own, we just follow them, treading where they have trodden."

To keep her post the professor would obviously have to conceal her true views from her students, dealing only with the dim and distant Middle Ages—and in Western Europe at that. If she had taught Russian history she would have been driven out of the Bestuzhev Institute long ago.

Past the Grenadiers' barracks. Then down Monetnaya. Three tram stops—only there was no such route.

But why was Dmitriev so long? Was he unhurt? Was he still alive? Vera shivered.

Beyond the windows—a normal quiet evening. No shots, no fires. Was it all a mistake? Maybe they'd got it wrong?

How could you have a revolution when there were no longer any revolutionaries?

In any assembly, any gathering of educated people, Andozerskaya felt out of things and quickly tired. Making friends was difficult for her. Perhaps she ought not to go out at all?

A marvelous flow of argument. A clever woman! But Vorotyntsev was too tired to go on debating.

There's just one thing I want to tell you . . . But I can't find the right moment . . . But you know what I mean, don't you?

No, no . . . I thought we just had the same way of looking at things . . .

Why don't you ask me, your sister? Why won't you look at me? This isn't a joke. You're putting a rope around your neck!

The younger lady wouldn't sit down for a moment, she was like a new bride sleeplessly awaiting her bridegroom. One moment muttering some outrageous lines by Voloshin, the next shuddering at scenes which only she could see. And suddenly she stopped, there was no one behind her—embraced them all with her eyes, their yearning, the expectation that transcended all differences, the uniqueness of that evening!—shuddered at the beauty of it all, eager to share with them the beauty of this, their own moment, before the knock at the door, before the spell of expectation was broken by crude reality!

She felt with all her fingers for the wall behind her and, propped against it, spoke as if she was delivering a monologue to a piano accompaniment.

"Friends! How beautiful and how terrible is this feeling! Whither are we bound? What is about to happen? Something grandiose and terrifying is imminent. We are rushing toward the abyss—of that there is no doubt! Rushing ahead in a train with an idiot driver! Faster and faster! Faster, ever faster! A steep incline! Derailment is inevitable, the carriages rock wildly, the crash will come any moment, nothing can save us! But ah, the terrible beauty of it! You must admire it! And how thrilled those who survive will be to *know*! Our destruction is inevitable, but what form it will take we cannot even imagine, and in that there is a certain fascination."

Her words found some response. Some of the others were affected.

The atmosphere was oppressive. A brooding calm. If only the storm would break!

It is "fatally inevitable." *Something* is about to happen!

The sooner it breaks, the less dreadful, the less dangerous it will be!

Without the revolutionary will, without the revolutionary deed, there is no hope for Russia!

No one, though, doubts that revolution will come!

Only it is frightening to think of the centuries-wide gulf that divides us from the people.

A country of great and frightening absurdities.

As Petrunkevich once said, wild and unbridled forces are coming into play, but that is a cause for rejoicing. It means that we do not live in a graveyard!

Yes, we are waiting for, hoping for this catastrophe! Thinking Russia is quite ready for revolution.

In any case, the war will not end well for Russia. The country will collapse.

And after the war, we can no longer expect . . . *It* . . . to happen.

In Russia it's always either "too late" or "too soon." Revolution? It's always somehow too soon. Reform? Always somehow too late.

If only those soldiers would plot a little coup. Instead of just talking!

My wish, my ardent desire is that it should be an honorable revolution and carry the war on to the end! That fervent hope makes us choose revolution!

What came next was anyone's guess. They were hushed in delicious anticipation.

The sagacious lecturer—gigantic pincers lying on the table—spoke up, weighing his words. "It's not too late to save the situation even now. By ceding power to a responsible administration."

Enchantment is as fragile as crystal. The younger lady suddenly looked as if she had breathed out the frenzied inspiration which had driven her in circles around the room for the last half hour. Weak at the knees, she sank into a chair.

The older lady was less ready to relax her militancy. "How long must we tolerate their cynical defiance of public opinion? People have been cabinet-making for a year or more. All a waste of time, the Tsar will never fall for it. The parliamentarians have only themselves to blame— they won't do anything decisive!"

Obodovsky, quitting his isolated observation post with an impatient wave of the hand—for it or for the lecturer—said, "A responsible government wouldn't know what to do first either."

"What to do first?" The older lady was amazed. "Save the people, of course."

She would undoubtedly have gone on to explain, but just then there was a ring at the door. And the older lady rushed to meet the messenger.

She clutched at chairs, but her width prevented her from getting any nearer to the corridor. While the younger lady, as if wafted on the breeze—whence this resurgent vigor?—fluttered past and was there first.

No, not quite first. Vera was there already. It was she who opened the door.

The eagerly awaited harbinger of the Unusual, in a cap dog-eared by the wind, and a leather jacket, was surprised himself.

"You here?"

No flush, no strain, no torment in his longish, unremarkable features hinted at the news he was bringing. They expressed nothing but surprise at seeing Vera: "You here?"

He removed his cap from his smooth, dark, neatly parted hair, raised the slender white hand held out to him . . .

And kissed it.

Then he was engulfed in a crowd of women.

"What's happening? Where is it?"

"On the Vyborg side? Have they gone into the city?"

"Occupied the Nevsky?"

"Tell us everything!"

"Take your coat off, and begin at the beginning!"

There was a certain awkwardness or angularity in his movements, perhaps because they were so deliberate. He took off his coat more slowly than the occasion demanded, as though his arms were of different lengths. He wore an engineer's jacket with what looked like crossed hammers in the lapels.

He didn't even know whose apartment he was in, and, after reading the brass plate, was not sure whether he was in the right place. Vera quickly whispered something in his ear. He looked around for his host, but was addressed by the one other person there he knew (and knew very well).

"Come in, Misha, come in." A shake of the hand and a lowered voice for some reason, perhaps because so many loud voices were speaking at once: "Is it serious?"

Dmitriev, wide-eyed and somber, said still more quietly, "Very."

Very! Very serious! Though it was barely a whisper, the ladies had heard, and pushed past the others to surround him.

Obodovsky drew him into the dining room.

"Ladies and gentlemen! Engineer Dmitriev!"

Seeing how impatient they all were, he spared them the handshakes. Some sat, some stood, some propped themselves against the table.

"Come on then! Let's hear it!"

"We're waiting, we're all ears!"

"But begin at the beginning!"

Dmitriev didn't sit either. He stayed by the wall, near the door to the corridor, which seemed to be the most convenient place for addressing nine people. Even there, he stood lopsidedly, with all his weight on one foot and one shoulder higher than the other. And his head bowed.

Begin from the beginning? He seemed to have difficulty finding it.

"Hmm, well . . . There weren't any strikes in the factories all summer, nor in September, nor in October . . . But just lately strange rumors have been going around among the workers. Such persistent rumors, somebody must be spreading them deliberately. First a building is supposed to have collapsed at some factory—where exactly they don't say—and crushed hundreds of workers. Then at some other factory there's supposed to have been an explosion and that's killed hundreds as well. Which factory? you ask. I go around from one to another, on the Neva side, the Narva side, the Vyborg side, and I've found nothing of the kind. But they won't believe me. Then the stories get taller: there's a general uprising in Moscow, the police have refused to suppress it, and so have the troops. A man I know arrives from a

Moscow factory and says there it's the other way around: the rising was supposed to be in Petrograd, the Gostiny Dvor had been wrecked and looted, and the police wouldn't intervene. There are even leaflets going around saying the same kind of thing. This last week there's been such tension that if a piece of sheet metal falls with a crash—nothing unusual about that—they leave their benches and crowd around the exits, they think the whole place is coming down around their ears. Then there are rumors that another call-up is on the way, men previously registered will be taken, and all exemption certificates will be checked."

Yes, yes, but what was happening on the Vyborg side?

"On the Vyborg side they've got the highest wage rates and the biggest range of skills. So they can be sure they won't be fired or drafted. That makes them the cockiest of them all. Think they can get away with anything. And nobody has it in for the police like they do. If an iron plate flies out of the window at Ericsson's it won't land just anywhere but on some policeman's head. The soldiers catch it from the workers. There are workers from the area in reserve units there, and soldiers go out with women workers, so they're all connected one way or another. Say an NCO is marching soldiers to the bathhouse and they see a policeman on duty, they won't go past him quietly, they yell at him from the ranks: 'filthy copper,' 'pigface,' everybody laughs, and the policeman has to grin and bear it, what else can he do? Since last Thursday they've been holding snap meetings at Ericsson's and at Lessner's—the old factory and the new one—the usual sort of thing, when they come off the shift they block the way and start yelling. Last Friday instead of going home after the meeting the men at the Old Lessner factory walked out singing the 'Marseillaise' and got as far as the Finland station before they were dispersed. At the munitions plant they were shouting, 'Smash the merchants, they're hiding their goods.' That's the easiest way to heat things up nowadays: if shopkeepers are rogues and thieves, wrecking shops is legitimate. This morning the day shift at the munitions plant, three thousand workers, came out singing the 'Marseillaise,' and sat down on the railroad track."

Three thousand? Singing the "Marseillaise"? So there is something in it! We did well to wait for him!

To start things rolling, to set the whole mass in motion, just one such episode was needed. Like the beginning of a landslide. From the Vyborg side to Old Petersburg, from Petersburg to the whole of Russia!

Dmitriev was as excited as the rest of them. No one had noticed it till now, though he had been far from calm when he arrived. There are people like that. No sign of agitation shows on those thick lips, that tough, dull skin.

"What demands are they making?" the older lady asked.

"That's just it—they aren't making any," Dmitriev said darkly.

Not making any! That struck a chill. If they refused even to talk, things were as serious as they could be.

"Then this afternoon about a thousand people put down their tools at Renault, and marched up Great Sampsonyevsky. Some of them dashed into the New Lessner works to try to bring them out. They were arrested, but the strike was on just the same, and the Lessner workers joined the march along the Prospect. It was peaceful at first . . ."

You wouldn't have thought so looking at Dmitriev.

"They're right next door, Russian Renault and the New Lessner. And right opposite Renault are the barracks of the 181st Infantry Reserve Regiment. It was about four o'clock when the New Lessner workers set off along Great Sampsonyevsky Prospect, right past the barracks, and . . .

S C R E E N

Factory buildings, dark red brick, seen over high brick walls. The kind of uncomfortable buildings in which cultured people like us never find ourselves, having no business there.

But there they are. Towering. Stretching into the distance. An indeterminate noise.

Down below.

= Workers pouring, streaming out of the gate. Walking down the street, the boring, bricked-in, edge-of-town street, in no sort of order, not walking like an organized demonstration, apparently still unsure themselves where they are going, or why, but carried helplessly along.

Confused voices.

Caps, more caps, caps with peaks, caps without peaks . . . Just occasionally, a hat.

Leather jackets with fleecy collars, autumn coats, tunics, raincoats . . . A mass of black and gray . . .

Faces shaven, clean-shaven, young and old, very few beards, a few mustaches (foppish ones). Differences of age and character evened out by this almost unrelieved clean-shavenness and uniformity of dress.

They are borne along by their shared anxiety. Borne along easily, but with never a cheerful face among them.

= A little farther along the street, a police patrol: perhaps a dozen constables on foot.

Seen closer.
> They have black fur hats, black astrakhan collars, tightly
> belted greatcoats, swords, revolvers, they are more than
> adequately equipped, well-turned-out, strapping fellows.
> Now the local police inspector, wearing a gray officer's over-
> coat with a narrow belt.

Still closer.
> They all wear something orange-colored, the braid on the
> shoulders of the policemen, the tabs on their lapels, the
> piping of the officer's epaulets.
> What, though, is different about the faces of the police? Be-
> cause they *are* quite different. More mustaches? More
> ugly mugs—where did they find them all? No—mainly,
> there's no trace of feeling. Stony-faced discipline.
> The inspector, silver-braided, gives a wave of the hand . . .

We see them in a long shot.
> =   gives the order
We do not hear it.
> A whole bunch of them! Marching now, in formation, march,
> march, marching, in our direction.
> They can! The law! That's what they are! Defy them, and see
> what happens.
Nearby: voices, workers calling to each other, urging each other to line
up, not to lose heart, to remember whatever it was they had promised
each other.
> A squad advancing on us in formation! Only ten men, but
> they mean business!
Timid voices: if you can't walk over it, you have to turn around.
> =   Front of the crowd. Jam-packed. Mostly youngsters. But no
> movement forward. The crowd begins to give ground.
> But then from someone invisible, a single audacious voice
> sings out:
> > *"Like ravening dogs the rich and greedy*
> > *Rend and devour the fruit of your toil."*
> Nobody joins in but it has its effect: resentment is fiercer,
> faces grimmer. But the mouths on the screen remain
> closed.
Two or three voices, whose we cannot see, do join in:
> > *"The sweat of your brow fattens gluttons.*
> > *They snatch the last crust from your mouth."*
> Well, not the last crust—no one quite so emaciated meets
> our eyes. Some of those present have the dignified bear-
> ing of men whose skills are valued. When they unbutton,
> some are wearing suit jackets, or even white shirts. But
> the words of the song are true! That's how we feel! They

steal our last crust, and only in our songs can we make ourselves heard. Sing out, brothers, sing out!

= The police squad draws nearer. They march as if crushing us underfoot.

The inspector, quick to notice, spots something in our midst and yells: "Soldiers! Get out of the crowd! Stand aside!" A few soldiers, convalescents, have, it seems, got wedged into the crowd. Got the bit between their teeth!

One, with one ear bandaged and one arm in a sling, wears a George medal.

Just doing your duty? Tell us about it! Who's shed their blood?

The inspector's voice. Close up. Harsh.

"Soldiers! I'm warning you for the last time!"

The one with the bandages over his ear, an undisciplined lad, answers with his whole mouth, and his whole face.

We can't hear,

but he must have given a robust answer—there's laughter in the ranks! They're laughing! They've found their courage! Now we can see the song leader. Lanky, skinny, no cap (dropped it?), hair ruffled. His face is distorted by the strain of singing for all of them, his mouth wrenched into a strange shape, his Adam's apple jumps.

"*Starve, while they feed their fat faces,*
Starve, while they gamble on 'Change . . ."

His efforts are not in vain! It begins to catch on! A song sets hearts aflame as no amount of exhortation can! Now a dozen throats chorus in support, bawling out words that express their deepest feelings.

"*Starve, while they stuff their fat bellies*
And put up their honor for sale . . ."

= Now the police! We see their swords! Unsheathed!

They advance!

With drawn swords? Perhaps they'll use only the flat of the blade, to turn the crowd and disperse it. Ah, but the policemen's faces tell us that if they have to draw blood they will not turn a hair.

The inspector calls out, as if on the battlefield:

"Soldiers! Mutineers will be put under arrest!"

= The crowd falters, begins to give way. They are frightened. They press closer together, rub shoulders, embolden each other with their numbers, and with their voices, humming the "Marseillaise," they don't know the words, only the song leader does, belting it out fit to burst—in desperation—why are you retreating, boys? remember what you promised . . .

"The Tsar is a vampire, the Tsar's a tormentor.
A vampire drinking the people's blood."
The soldier with the George medal looks black, his wounded
  arm has been crushed, but he won't move! They've
  picked on the wrong man!
= But the swords! Raised swords advancing on them! Fright-
  ening!
= The crowd falls back, the game is lost.
They retreat obliquely, press against a low board fence, about
  three feet high.
With all his remaining strength, as though it was the last song of his
life, the song leader sings on:
"He needs banquets, he needs palaces.
He needs you to pay with your blood."
= The police. Eyeball to eyeball now.
Full screen.
  Those in front wonder: Flat of the blade? Or cutting edge?
  With these devils you never know. One step toward us!
  One more step toward us!
  The hostile faces. Laugh at us, would you? Don't think we
  won't let you have it!
Wider screen.
= We're backing off, only fools defy swords. If they use those
  things we'll run.
  A thousand of us from a dozen of them. It's worse for those
  in front, safe enough in the rear.
The voices have all sunk and died.
  One step! Two steps! They are pushing the workers away from
  the fence, clearing a space along the fence. The police
  press forward with raised swords.
One last cry from the desperate song leader.
"Kill them, the dogs, the rich robbers . . .
Kill the vile vampire, the Tsar."
And again, yet again, there is a brief outburst of muffled voices, like
damp wood bursting into flame.
"Kill them, the dogs, the rich robbers!"
And they've stopped moving! We must not run.
  If we run, we can't call ourselves human beings.
  Demands? We have no demands. The day of reckoning has
  come, that's all!
  And we raise our voices merrily in songs of desperation. Hell,
  we've nothing to lose.
"Smite the villains, let hell have them,
That the day of a better life may dawn."
  At the fence, wedged together now in tight confrontation,
  the front rank of the police and the front of the crowd.

Swords raised, is it? Right—fists forward. Eyes popping,
we sing our own savage song.
    "Smite the villains, let hell have them."
=   Where will it get you—defying armed policemen?
=   And where will it get *you*—defying the whole people?
=   The police have no song. The police need no song. What
      they have is the word of command. The head villain, the
      inspector, orders, "Flat of the blade!" And they lay on!
      They—lay—on! You, you, and you—here's one on the
      head! That's strength for you! Let that jug-eared soldier
      have it! That's the way! Tight-packed, wedged together,
      staggering backward, that's as far as we can go. What
      now? The police move along the fence. Means a lot to
      them, that fence. Determined to clear it for some rea-
      son—just the fence.

Widest screen.
=   Camera swings to reveal the whole length of the low fence.
      Beyond it is a drill square. On the square soldiers drilling,
      with sticks, though, not rifles. Some doing foot drill.
      Some small-arms drill. With NCOs, no officers. Shoul-
      der a rifle? They don't even know how to wear a great-
      coat, but they're still soldiers. Drill or no drill, they can't
      help noticing, heads swivel this way and that.
=   They begin leaving the ragged ranks, moving.
      More and more of them come toward us with their sticks.
      Sticks in hand, just as they were! Sticks, yes! But they're
      uniformed soldiers, fit and well fed!
      "Dirty cops!"
      "Rotten bastards!"
      "Workers, don't give in!"
=   The police freeze, swords raised, don't strike. The inspector
      scans the scene unhappily.

General view of the drill square.
      Hordes of them, hundreds and hundreds, behind the low
      fence three feet or so high. Some still exercising, some
      looking our way, some walking over. Their officers have
      vanished without trace. Just soldiers left, with NCOs like
      themselves.
=   But there's still the fence. The fence is a barrier between
      them.
=   The policemen are still standing with raised swords. The in-
      spector is all alone. He looks right and left. He is alone,
      fated to be the Russian state's one and only defender.
      The foremost ranks of the workers have begun to melt,
      to shrink away. A few still stand there, crouched as if

stumbling. One young apprentice bends down, down. And wrenches out a cobblestone. Hurls it over the heads of several of his fellows. At the head of a policeman! It strikes home, rocks him on his heels, his sword falls from his hand, his cap falls off, and there is

Blood!

At once the order is given:

"Cutting edge!"

The blows fall!

More blood!

Pan shot.

They're running! The soldiers! Running toward us! With their sticks!

The whole broad expanse is loud with their whooping.

"Filthy coppers!"

"Get in there, boys! Help your brothers!"

They rush to attack merrily.

The nimblest are over the fence—call that a fence? Jump. Jump. Jump.

Longer shot.

And the other soldiers, up against the fence? They march into it, push against it, all at once.

The fence is down!

We hear it splinter.

The whole fence stretches in length. The army steps merrily over it! Over the flattened fence, carrying those sticks!

Still longer shot.

Back on the square men are still running, more and more of them! You'll never see such an enthusiastic charge at the front: here nobody is shooting at them, and they know their enemy!

The whole regiment, helter-skelter, upright, brandishing their sticks over their heads!

The broken fence crackles its last under their boots.

The look on the soldiers' faces is one of reckless devilry. We're the ones who have power! We don't have to be afraid!

They run with a will.

"You there, hands off our brothers!"

"Beat the bastard coppers!"

"Hurra-a-a-ah!"

= Some little infantry officer intercepts the attackers, holds up his hand, shouts, tries to stop them. Lots of luck! They don't listen, the comrades rush onward!

A shot. Another. And another.

= The police squad are retreating, firing to cover their retreat. No "hurrahs" for them, it's not in their drill book.
= They blaze away regardless, like doomed men: they're done for, everybody hates them. Now—the rebels are too close to be shot at, all is confusion, it's too late to wield a sword!
= They're singled out from the crowd—their greatcoats, tunics, caps make it easy.
  The inspector is floored, hit on the head by a brick, vanishes under all those feet.
= They are singled out, their swords taken from them, caps knocked off, revolvers wrested from their hands—may come in handy!
= One turns on his captors—savaged, but still bold. He is struck on the head from behind by an iron bar! Got him!
= The song leader seems to have grown a head higher, and he was lanky enough to start with—no, nobody is that tall— is he on stilts? Now he sings out, straining his lungs, sings fit to burst, for all of them:
  "Let us fight the last fight—peace is the prize,
  And our children's happiness, bought with our blood."

We rise above the crowd.
= Great Sampsonyevsky Prospect. A confused mob, thousands of people. Soldiers embrace workers. Flourish their sticks.
A sort of triumphal procession with raised fists.
The song leader seems to be almost the only one singing.
  "And in that bloody dawn shall rise
  The sun of justice and of brotherhood."
Seen as through a narrow tunnel:
= Cavalry—in the distance.
Closer now.
A mounted police patrol.
Closer, larger, widening.
Fifty of them, full gallop, plumed caps, cross-belted, swords drawn!
No flat of the blade from them! They mean to draw blood. And the order has been given.
= But the crowd shows no fear. Men share cigarettes, stand with their arms around each other.
= To one side stand some young men, the sort you see on any street.
Holding bricks, stones, iron bars.
= One busy fellow runs like a madman, holding a burning log, swinging it in a circle.

= The cavalry gallops on, swords drawn.
= The boys wait till they're close enough, hurl their missiles—
we're in this too! Shower their missiles! And take to their
heels!
= The officer is knocked off his horse. Two other men are
dazed, trampled.
  The charge is checked.
= The madman whirls his burning log, ready to hurl it. The
crowd swarms forward, pelting the police with every-
thing, even their sticks!
= Disarray among the mounted police. They turn around.
= The burning brand whirls round and round, giving off smoke,
its trail fuses, becomes a fiery circle.
  A red wheel.

And that voice sings out again, harsh, earsplitting, inexhaustible, triumphant:

> *"Let us fight the last fight—peace is the prize*
> *And our children's happiness, bought with our blood."*

*   *   *

*The monarchic order sails aboard the golden ship of the bourgeoisie over
the shoreless ocean of the people's blood and tears. Smash what little
remains of the illusion that the peoples can be freed by the All-Russian
despot's bayonets! To work, comrades! Long live the Great Russian
Revolution, the second and the last!*

—RSDRP

*   *   *

[27]

It was not just the revolutionary character of the incident on the
Vyborg side that startled Vorotyntsev (though he had not expected
such an outburst of anger—yet another reason to hurry up and change
the conduct of the war), it was also the reminder that Russia meant
170 million people. The Russian army on the far-off southwestern
shoulder of the front, that dense mass of divisions, regiments, people,
with happenings and griefs and hopes of their own, was large enough,
but here on the other shoulder two thousand versts away, northeast of
Petrograd, were other teeming thousands, factory workers and reservists, with griefs and hopes of their own, and the two extremes, unlike
in their experience and their feelings, had only one thing in common,
that they both belonged to boundless Russia.

This made it all the more important for Vorotyntsev to compare his experience with that of others. Nobody was so omniscient and so all comprehending that he could take it on himself to act for Russia. The evening had given him a lot to think about. His mind was in a ferment.

But as they made their way back to Karavannaya Street, he and Vera saw no trace of disorder or unrest. Petrograd by itself was a sizable chunk of Russia.

Georgi fell asleep quickly as usual, but, unusually for him, woke up in the night, and from the way he felt, quite soon: our sleeping bodies somehow measure, let us know how long we have been asleep. He awoke with the pleasurable feeling left by a blissful though now forgotten dream: no, it was not a dream, but a pervading sense of good fortune that filled him with joy. It was a long time since he had experienced anything of the kind. The memory of the national calamity had weighed on him in the daytime and in the intervals of sleep. He had slept a troubled sleep at home in Moscow, and again on the train. Why was his whole body now suffused with a sense of purification, so that, rather than sleep, he wanted just to lie there enjoying this happy state?

He turned over other reasons in his mind, trying to delude himself, but no, it was not because he was on leave, not because he was in Petersburg (he didn't like Petersburg anyway), not because he was staying with his sister and with Nanny, much as he loved them, not even because he had had such an interesting evening—no, the thought seeped into his consciousness: it was because he had met Olda Orestovna.

At the soiree, overcome by happiness, disconcerted by it, he had not had time to wonder, to make sense of it, he had simply been intrigued, delighted that such a clever and well-educated woman showed an interest in him and—on some things—thought as he did.

But now the happiness that welled up in him was like a great sea swell pounding on his chest—and, breasting it, rolling with its surge, he had to confess that it was not the professor's education that delighted him, but the professor herself, not her clever arguments—if she had spoken stupidly or said just the opposite, it would have made no difference—but the way she uttered them and the look on her face.

Nothing had happened to relieve the general gloom—indeed, the reservists' mutiny made things look blacker—yet something (what?) had happened at the soiree to ease his mind and cheer him. He had even lost the urge to argue. Lightheartedness had made him a heavy companion: all he could do was gaze—at the neat, dignified turn of a little head, the subtle play of her eyebrows, signaling what she was going to say, the imperious compression of that small mouth. And that endearing gesture—raising cupped hands and stroking one with the other.

Nothing much had happened that evening, they had not even spoken to each other directly, but it was enough to rob him of the wish to sleep. Sleep was impossible with those waves of joy beating on his chest. After such a long time he had almost given up hope of ever feeling happy again, almost forgotten what it was like, but now he was reluctant to go back to sleep and miss those hours of warmth, of light in darkness.

He smoked a cigarette and tried to turn his mind to the things he had heard at the party, but it was hopeless, he kept coming back to her. Meeting such a woman was something he had never expected.

Yet he couldn't have said what was so unusual about her. She was no conventional beauty, not remarkably graceful or shapely. She talked intelligently, but many others were far from stupid. Was it that she and he thought alike? Not invariably. Sometimes they were diametrically opposed. Was it the way she held herself? Her bearing was unusual in a woman—not pliant and yielding, but upright and sturdy, that of someone sure of her place in the world. Or was it the way she kept glancing at him? There was understanding, recognition, and even unconcealed admiration in her looks, and this alone was enough to make Vorotyntsev feel that he himself was somehow unusual. And her looks said something else, as explicitly as if she had put it into words. Or had he just imagined it?

It was as if something had emanated from her and remained in his possession.

Was it all an illusion? How could he know for sure?

He felt restless in bed. Smoked another cigarette. Suddenly—he knew that he needed that woman! To see her again, talk to her? No, it wasn't a consultation he wanted—what could she tell him anyway? He simply needed her. With a burning desire.

Strangely, he had nothing to compare this experience with, no way of knowing whether he had misunderstood. Perhaps she had just sympathized with his political views, and he would be making a fool of himself?

But if what he thought he had seen in her eyes really was there he could not leave it at that, could not ignore something so extraordinary.

What should he do, though?

He felt restless, uncomfortably hot. No hope of sleep!

"She's unmarried, for some reason," Vera had said.

A foolish, joyous, blazing excitement!

Georgi lay there for hours, not even trying to sleep.

Morning came. Before deciding where to go and how to expend his energy—with so little time for reconnaissance in Petrograd—he made a telephone call as soon as he decently could, and not to Guchkov but to her.

Last night there had been no assumption that he would ring her the following morning. She had given him her number, but for use at some unspecified time during his stay in Petrograd. Standing now before the brown box around the wall phone, Georgi was torn between two anxieties: ringing so soon might be embarrassing, but if he didn't hurry she could be off to lecture!

She was in! And not a bit surprised. On the telephone her melodious voice was like a love song (or was it just for him she spoke like that?). The telephone seemed to remove all that was merely conversational from her speech and accentuate the musical.

"I'm making use of your number sooner than I expected."

"I'm very glad."

He felt drawn toward her through the receiver.

"I somehow feel we didn't finish our conversation last night."

"So do I."

"And since I won't be in Petersburg long . . . would you permit me to see you again?"

"Marvelous idea . . . Come this evening. Come and see how I live."

Tremendous! How readily she had invited him.

But what about Guchkov? What if Guchkov asked him for that evening?

He held the phone, dreading to hear Guchkov answer promptly, in person, and say, "Come this evening."

Luckily: "Aleksandr Ivanovich is not yet back in town."

Anyway, it probably made more sense to see Olda Orestovna first. She had such definite views on everything, and it would be interesting to explore them further.

Meanwhile, he could spend the afternoon delivering his messages to the ministry and the General Staff.

So many, so very many colonels and generals ensconced there, confidently pronouncing on all the things they had never seen for themselves. Long ago, in his youth, Vorotyntsev had aspired to be one of them, but now he felt only revulsion: such posts produced people to fit them.

All day long he carried cocooned within him, hidden from everyone but himself, his secret joy. When evening came he would go to her! How, he wondered, could he have come to Petersburg with no presentiment of such a meeting?

He also had to call in at the Society for the Advancement of Military Science. Their magazine was going to publish an article of his. But that could wait till tomorrow.

A cabby with an officer inside, and a senior officer at that, always goes flat out, without asking whether his fare is really in such a hurry. But Vorotyntsev for once enjoyed the headlong rush. It was last night all over again—the long, open Troitsky Bridge, with pairs of triple lamps at intervals—yet not a bit like last night. Riding so fast that the

Rostral Columns spun around the Stock Exchange. There were the towers of the Peter and Paul Fortress, and there was the angel, barely discernible against the dark sky.

Speeding triumphantly along the damp autumn roadways—a hell-for-leather cabby, carrying an apparently self-assured colonel with a neat beard and a tall fur hat at a jaunty angle. Inside, Vorotyntsev felt not at all sure of himself. His confidence had sagged since morning. Perhaps he was in danger of confusing Olda Orestovna's friendliness and his own liking for her with . . . something else.

The Kamennoostrovsky Prospect again, near Shingarev's apartment. All through the day he hadn't once thought about it, but there obviously was no revolution in Petrograd. Nothing revolutionary had happened. This elegant avenue led to the places of entertainment on the islands. There was the traffic circle at the junction with Ruzheinaya—people said it looked quite Scandinavian.

If he made no move at all he would not go wrong. But he was already in a fever of impatience, and the days were slipping through his fingers. How many such meetings could you expect in one lifetime? One? Two? Perhaps none at all.

There was a bizarre black-and-white house, with turrets, on the corner of Arkhiereiskaya Street. Not there in his time as far as he remembered. There was so much modern construction around now, not a bit like classical Petersburg.

In the daytime you saw the queues, noticed the shortages, but by evening everything was made beautiful by electricity—cinemas, cafés, shop windows with fruit and flowers.

It no longer irritated him, as it had the day before.

He hopped out—bought a bunch of mauve asters. Sped on.

The Sports Palace. The residence of the Emir of Bukhara. Silin Bridge.

But was what he was doing permissible? Such a crude frontal approach to a generally respected woman, on the strength of a few intercepted glances and what he imagined he saw in them? No, it was quite impermissible. All the dictates of etiquette and custom barred the way.

Beyond Karpovka stood a detached house built to resemble an Italian villa. The farther they drove, the denser the lining of trees along the avenue. At Lopukhinskaya there were poplars. What a lovely spot she lived in.

The race there, and the thought that they would be meeting any moment now, exhilarated him.

They turned off along the Pesochnaya Embankment. To the right—the dark brown almost black water of the Little Neva, to the left mansions, villas, lights in the depths of orchards. And there it was—a modest gray house with pebble-dash walls (also fashionable) and "1914" over the entrance. So much had been built in the late prewar years! But for the war just think where we could be now!

Outside it was unremarkable enough, but the interior was something out of the ordinary. There was no stairwell, but instead a rotunda, with a staircase spiraling around the wall. The apartments opened onto a circular landing on the second floor.

Such schoolboy fleet-footedness, such lightheartedness! Where was the settled gloom of so many months, the heaviness which he had carried with him to Shingarev's apartment, to unburden himself with such a struggle? Whence this weightlessness, this sense of renewal? It was a miracle.

It was just as Fyodor, his traveling companion, had said: you are surprised and happy and afraid all at once—love for a woman is like feeling the heat of a flame on your face. Georgi had only half believed him (and felt envious, in case it could be like that!), but now he was experiencing it for himself. The heat of the flame caught him full in the face, there was no defense against it, nor did he wish to defend himself.

He quietly touched the unresisting ivory bell button. And almost closed his eyes as the door opened, so as not to be dazzled.

There she was!

Did she seem taller today? No, she was just as touchingly small and slender. His bouquet hid her altogether. Her hand, slightly sunburned, seemed weightless.

When you find yourself at cross-purposes you listen without understanding, you can't harness your mind to your hearing, perhaps you will remember later on, but you're afraid of asking the wrong questions.

They were in a big room now. Her study? The desk was hidden under leaning towers of books. There were papers everywhere. Shelves crammed with books. A big icon of St. Olga, not in a corner near the ceiling, but flat against a wall, with no lamp before it, as if it was not an icon but just an ordinary picture. There were innumerable toys and figurines, painted and unpainted, on the shelves. Ivan-Tsarevich riding the gray wolf, the battle with the Serpent Gorynich, rams with golden horns and lace-trimmed garments . . . more than the eye could take in.

It was still there! Still there from yesterday! Nothing had happened to dispel it! He didn't know how he knew, but it was still there! Amazing! Nothing had been said but he knew.

There were so many different things on shelves and on the walls that it was easier to note what was missing: the usual lavish display of photographs, framed singly or in dozens. An untypical room. Another picture showed an old man with horns, a streaming beard, and powerful bare shoulders, sitting in a moonlit meadow.

The run upstairs had left him incoherent at first, and his next remarks were hit and miss—his thoughts were shaken and shattered, as in some dazed moment under fire, when you can't get anything straight but the words come tumbling out, endlessly. Hostess and guest were still standing, and Vorotyntsev had paused before some provincial landscape, for no particular reason: water meadows and a little town beyond them. Olda Orestovna's explanation was the first thing Vorotyntsev had clearly understood. It was a view of Makaryev on the Unzha, where her father, a Göttingen Ph.D., had been banished, and become district marshal of the gentry, and where she herself had been born and brought up.

But she broke off in the middle of her explanation, turned from the view of Makaryev to face Vorotyntsev (who only half noticed—he was still looking at the landscape and wondering how an exile could become marshal of the gentry), raised her hand, rested it lightly on his shoulder, on the edge of his epaulet, near his neck, and said in a full, firm voice, "God, how lucky we are to have people like you!"

It was said without embarrassment, not blurted out impulsively, not secretly whispered. She had spoken in a firm, clear voice. It was as though she was presenting him with a medal, hanging it around his neck on a ribbon.

Such a gesture would have been out of place if they had walked into the room in a normal, casual manner and sat down sedately at a polite distance from each other. Who, in those circumstances, would have felt able to rise, cross the room, and lay a hand on a shoulder?

This extraordinary gesture was like a shell exploding soundlessly near Vorotyntsev's cheek, and the thoughts he had failed to express at the awkward moment of his entrance were even more dizzily muddled. Shaken, shell-shocked, derailed, Vorotyntsev, ears aflame, could not call to mind or utter the usual polite phrases. Still, he somehow kept his feet, and did not let slip that unique, that last possible chance to square accounts with the self-assured little general who had decorated him in the eyes of all Russia—the moment when Professor Andozerskaya's hand was already slipping from his shoulder, after which it would be a gross and unpardonable impertinence to reply in the same terms . . .

At that very moment, before he could make the only possible reply, though not to reply was impossible, he caught the delicate hand that had decorated him, pressed his lips to it for longer, and more ardently, than ceremony required . . . rose, plunged again . . . and did the same with the hand that had not decorated him. Only then was it borne in on him that he must not remain silent, but should say something befitting the moment. The words seemed to speak themselves.

"The good fortune is ours . . . That *you* exist . . . That there is someone like you . . ."

Had he done the right thing? And why "our" good fortune? Who were "we"? All Russia perhaps? Anyway, they still stood facing each other, and Vorotyntsev, having made his feelings clear, could, it seemed, go on detaining the hands of that living statue, and did so greedily. Her hands, and her whole person, gave off a faint but distinctive perfume.

The award ceremony had gone on more than long enough. Vorotyntsev released her hands, and Olda Orestovna did not blush, did not sway on her feet, she merely smoothed her hair, and turned back with a little secret smile toward the picture, to finish what she had been saying about Makaryev.

Ah, to walk barefoot in that meadow, when the dew lifts and the ground warms up . . . The flowers that grow there . . . The town's cattle plod past you . . . This is where they hold the fair (which reminded him that chests made in Makaryev were sold all over Russia). There's our school . . . My father was a liberal, contributed a lot of money to local improvements. My nanny was a peasant. (They're everywhere! Peasant nannies made us all what we are.) From her girlhood up she had always been full of questions, and grown-ups got used to telling her things.

They finished viewing the picture and sat down. Olda Orestovna spoke as though lecturing, an orderly exposition in a level voice, but Vorotyntsev had still not recovered from all the surprises of those first crowded minutes. So much had passed between them without a word spoken that the floor under their feet had lost its reliable horizontal firmness. Even in his armchair Vorotyntsev did not feel the normal pull of gravity, the armrests gave him no support, they were handles he gripped to prevent himself from rising into the air. From the first few minutes sound and sense had ceased to correspond, thoughts and sentences passed him by disconnectedly, there were things he didn't hear, others that didn't register, but over all, like a splendid white cloud on a sultry day, floated the assurance that he agreed with whatever she said: about the atmosphere of a lively provincial market town, about the earthenware toys from Dymkovo (those golden-horned rams and motley ducks, for instance), or the Bogorodskoye toys (peasant groups carved from lime wood), or the garishly painted toys from Troitse-Sergeevo; about Vrubel, about Scriabin . . . He nodded back at her, listening to her lilting voice, staring at her lips, the upper one curling slightly, the lower one fuller. And a plump cloud of delight floated serenely over it all.

He had to shake himself out of it, so as not to agree in advance with whatever she was about to say.

Last night at Shingarev's he had felt that he had run himself to a standstill, that he could feebly, cozily just sit, and sit, and today it was worse. He had run upstairs like a schoolboy—what had become of all that energy? Why did his legs feel so pleasurably helpless? He had come here (hadn't he?) for one reason only—to explore further important matters touched on in his presence last night. But before he could summon up the strength to speak Olda Orestovna asked him what he thought of Shingarev.

Vorotyntsev answered that the extraordinary sincerity of the man made him irresistible.

"But it's dreadful to see how the party is corrupting him. He's been a Kadet deputy in three Dumas, and that leaves its mark, so much has happened. There have been times when he's spoken on terrorism and had to refrain from condemning it."

"I was struck by what he said last night about Stolypin."

"Stolypin preys on his mind. Stolypin is even more of an enigma to him than he said last night—he's been much more open with me at times. He's tormented by a paradox in his ideas on right and wrong: he always fought Stolypin as his duty to his party demanded, but Stolypin was doing his best for the peasants, just as Shingarev is. The Kadets made war on Stolypin—but it was he who firmly established our national assembly. They accused him of violating the constitution, but they themselves were capable of much graver violations on occasion. Party politics is a horrible business."

What she said was true enough, but Vorotyntsev was delighted too by her manner of speaking—quiet and womanly, but confident and convincing. She thought clearly and spoke well. And she knew it.

"I was amazed by the Kadets," he replied. "They're so belligerent."

"I never believe in their patriotic alarums and excursions—it's all a bit of a game. The shell shortage actually gave them a boost. All the same, Georgi Mikhailovich"—and all at once her look was both stern and mischievous—"you are closer to the Kadets than you think."

"I am?" He felt himself blushing, foolishly, as though he had been caught in some unseemly act. Though he was quite sure that there was nothing in it. "What makes you . . . ? I'm nothing of the sort."

"Oh, yes, you are," she said, shaking her head sadly.

A treacherous flush gave him away. On the face of it, she was wrong, but deep down . . . she had glimpsed something he would have kept from her.

"The Kadet phenomenon," Olda Orestovna said, still shaking her head, "is not just a political party, it's a poison, a corrosive pervading the whole Russian atmosphere, and we all breathe it in, without even noticing. It is very difficult to hold on to your beliefs and keep them quite separate from the Kadet line. Last night, you, for instance, lightheartedly let drop some remark about a republic . . . That idea buzzes away in our own heads, and in the air around us, as though it was something easily imaginable. Tell me, though—when did the republican idea ever exist in Russia? All right, it was beginning to prevail in Novgorod—and Novgorod perished as a result. All through the Time of Troubles it was a Tsar they were looking for, not a republic. The same was true under the Seven Boyars. Whatever we are, we are not a republican people. The idea of anarchy appeals to us—mob violence, looting, mass disobedience—but not a republic, oh no! If you'd lived for a while in Europe, you'd know that Western states run on fast engines, but they don't wear well, they couldn't stand up to the dangers of three centuries."

Under her disquieting gaze Vorotyntsev wouldn't argue. Anyway, he . . . he hadn't really meant . . .

But she persisted. "Republicanism is a rallying cry for the ambitious: power is there to be seized! So seize it! A republic invites everybody to fight for his own interests, but a republican always risks finding himself under the heel of his own most ruthless foe. And when did the masses, without the guidance of one single will, ever understand correctly where their interests lay and what they should be aiming at? Whenever there's a big fire people get trampled on and trample others. You need a clear, commanding voice—a single one. You're in the army, you ought to know that."

"Of course," Vorotyntsev said with a laugh.

It was all true. But why such fervor? Was this her only reason for inviting him, when he'd been imagining . . . ?

She was looking at him questioningly, challengingly, trying to provoke some sign of life, wondering whether he was dead . . .

"If our present political parties should win power, do you think they'll go on looking for some more just form of society? All they want is to make sure of a majority in elections. A democratic republic in an uneducated country is suicide. It's an appeal to the basest passions of the people. Our naïve and trusting folk will vote at once for those who shout loudest and promise most. It will elect all sorts of rogues and loudmouthed lawyers. And decent candidates will be pushed out and trampled in the crush."

Vorotyntsev tried to excuse himself. "I wasn't really serious. I didn't mean that a republic was something to aim at."

But she had guessed correctly. It wasn't something to aim at—but he didn't reject it.

Her greenish eyes were as bright, and her lips as passionately restless, as if she was talking about something sensual.

"And what is it that democratic republics pride themselves on? A general leveling and so-called equality. Give adolescents the vote—so that a whiskerless lad will have the same rights and as much influence as a wise fifty-year-old. The hankering after equality is a primitive form of human self-deception, which republics exploit, demanding equal performance from those who are unequal. The monarchy, the army, or any good school all depend on a hierarchy of worth, a ladder of values. The whole natural world lives like that. And it's only human society we think we can stir up like porridge. If we cut off, if we topple, all the higher levels . . . We should respond positively to people of high merit, and clear their way to influence in the state, not tear them to pieces."

He was not so much listening as watching her lips moving—and wanting to test their firmness.

She went on, not with last night's easy equanimity, but with eager concern.

"No, Georgi Mikhailovich, you evidently haven't escaped infection by the Kadets. Last night I thought I would find in you an ally, which was why I started talking, but you proved to be more like an opponent. Why? I wonder. Surely all regular officers are staunch monarchists? Aren't you?"

Vorotyntsev had to confess. "I'm . . . er . . . I . . . it isn't such a simple case as that. Not escaped infection—what does that mean? Anyone who is conscious of his duty to the people, must . . . whatever you think. I enjoyed your defense of monarchy in general . . . But here we have the exception to the rule . . . It needs qualification."

"Yes, Georgi Mikhailovich! Ours is indeed an exceptional case: if we lose the monarchy, we lose Russia. Exalted as he is, the people feel that the Tsar belongs with them and is much closer than any of the Duma crowd. I've seen all I want to see of them. Their practice has been anything but constructive, all they're good at is letting off steam in opposition. Give them power tomorrow and they won't be able to run the country. They wouldn't last a minute without the Tsar."

He just listened. Or rather didn't listen, just marveled, just admired her and felt confused.

"For us, losing the monarchy would mean changing not just the state structure but the whole moral order of our lives. It is not given to everybody to be a monarchist, just as not everybody is capable of believing in God, and not everybody is capable of love. You'll find that believers are more likely than not to be monarchists, and the irreligious more likely to be republicans. For a republican, of course, devotion to a monarch is deplorable stupidity. And without such devotion monarchy turns into a sham."

"Yes . . . that's just what I mean." Vorotyntsev had difficulty in getting his words out. He couldn't, he hadn't wanted to tell her in so many words that the Russian monarchy *had* become a sham. But that was the fact of the matter.

"To *have* a monarch at all you must love him. Without your love he doesn't exist. Love him, and be ready to serve him to the end!"

Her eyes shone, as though she was an officer herself, and ready to serve to the end.

Ah, if only it were so simple! But those endless, meaningless parades, instead of getting down to business? Idiotic and disastrous senior appointments by the dozen? And what if the Tsar, though hopelessly incompetent, assumes the Supreme Command? Anyone who had experienced the sacrifices exacted by the war had no choice, he must put the fatherland before the monarchy.

But this was not the time to tell her, and his heart would not have been in it.

"Ah, yes," he said with a laugh, "the monarchist's tragedy. All that's required of him is contentment, jubilation, and gratitude. Never a thought, never an action of his own, just loyalty."

"No! It isn't like that!" Andozerskaya insisted, waving one small hand for emphasis. "A monarchist has the right to speak freely! The right to honest disagreement! In fact, it is his sacred obligation, implicit in the oath he takes! But every subject must at every moment project a ray of loyalty and support: it is from the intersection of those rays that the monarch acquires his strength."

There was a certain beauty in it, of course. But an abstract beauty. If you did not know how sordid and banal modern warfare was.

Altogether, he had heard nothing, here or the night before, except self-contradiction. He would have to digest it all sometime.

Not right now, though.

Right now, he was happy to find, they had drifted into the dining room, and tea was served.

Only then did he wake up to the fact that they were both from the Kostroma region. Zastruzhe was not all that far from Makaryev, yet Georgi had never got as far as the Unzha. Kostroma was in some ways a frontier province. It was precisely the point of transition from central to northern Russia, where Russia's fertility, its modest abundance of vegetation, its limited supply of warmth faltered, where widely separated villages, churches, and mills on bare and chilly, though not yet far northern slopes diffused a sort of melancholy, and houses grew as big and strong as those of the north, fortifying themselves as best they could against longer and harsher winter months. Not that the Kostroma Region was everywhere the same: higher up the Unzha there was trackless forest.

Olda Orestovna was telling him now about her teaching. She was not overly provided with opportunities to speak her mind. Two professors at the Bestuzhev Institute, Vvedensky and Sergeevich, had come to grief already because what they said was not what the students wanted to hear. Still, it had taken Klyuchevsky himself ten years to earn his students' forgiveness for his funeral eulogy on Aleksandr III. The women's courses had become rather healthier since 1905–6. There were a lot of serious students, but they had not learned how to raise their voices, how to argue. There were also quite a few "radical thinkers," and even out-and-out Socialist Revolutionaries and Social Democrats. Those who wanted Russia to win the war were called "social traitors," and openly defeatist talk went on in the students' refectory. Students generally had tilted back toward politics during the war. They would start a "study circle"—on Marxism or the French Revolution— but what went on there was plain, straightforward political agitation.

Olda Orestovna was able to teach at all only because her subject was medieval Western Europe. What's more, the professors themselves filled places on the faculty by co-optation and sometimes took on impostors without the minimum academic qualifications, just as long as they pandered to the taste of the times.

Vorotyntsev listened patiently to her lilting voice, scrutinizing her as though the center of the world had been displaced to sit beside him, rejoicing in his luck and dreading to make some mistake that would blow it all away, as though it had never been.

After tea they felt a common urge to go walking. Outside, they stopped to look at the dark waters of the Nevka, the Little Neva—not at all little from bank to bank—and at sparsely lit Kamenny Island. They walked to the left along the embankment toward Krestovsky Island, which was even darker. The sky was covered by dark clouds, but there was no rain. Apparently there had been heavy snowfalls earlier than usual—on 19 and 20 October—and light frosts. The islands still wore a wintry look. But elsewhere it had all turned to mud.

His fur hat was too hot for his feverish head, but once they got out into the open they were buffeted by a blustering wind from the sea, which stiffened as they went on.

Olda Orestovna was shivering.

"Are you cold?" he asked anxiously.

Taking hold of her other hand, he found that her gloved fingers were indeed cold.

"How warm yours are, though!"

"They always are, for some reason."

"That must be a good thing at the front."

"Not only at the front."

They had left the last houses on the embankment behind, and ahead of them there was nothing but dark, open wasteland, teased and buffeted by the cold, damp wind. They could not see the shoreline, where the tip of Aptekarsky Island merged with the water and Krestovsky Island surfaced beyond it.

She was still shivering.

"You're cold!"

"No, I'm enjoying myself . . ."

They were walking now over broken ground. The last streetlamps were behind them, and their light barely reached that far, but Olda Orestovna knew the place so well that she seemed to see in the dark. She pulled her companion by the hand down a little slope and broke into a run.

"There ought to be a swing here somewhere."

Sure enough, they groped their way to a crude plank suspended by wires, and Vorotyntsev was, by now, not greatly surprised when Olda Orestovna decided she wanted a swing. With just a little help she seated herself on the plank and said, "Push!" He began cautiously, but a merry voice called out, "Harder!" She soared higher and higher, with a mischievous side wind nudging her, threatening to send her spinning or dash her against the upright, and Vorotyntsev rushed to steady the swing. "Why aren't you pushing?" she demanded, more gaily than ever.

Instead, he seized her, swing and all, and said, "You, Professor, are just a little girl! Little Olda! If I had the right to use your first name at all, that's what I'd call you—Olzhenka."

"How extraordinary! I've been given all sorts of pet names, but never that one. Did you ever know a girl called that?"

"No. I've just thought of it."

"I really like it."

"So maybe I can call you that?"

"When there's nobody around to hear it."

"Will there be such times?"

"That's up to you."

And all he could do then was kiss her, kiss the lips he had been looking at longingly all that evening, bending her farther and farther backward on the swing, till her hat fell off, rolled away, and was carried off by the wind.

Vorotyntsev chased the hat, stumbling after it clumsily, in a complete daze.

[28]

It had never happened to him before, and he had nothing to compare it with. Jettisoned, all tumbling away downhill—his main concern, other matters of some importance, his agenda, his return ticket to Moscow, his promises to his wife, promises to his sister—all lost and forgotten, and forgetting them was pure joy.

I've lost nothing! And think what I've found! For the very first time.

Next morning he was at the telephone early: it was hours since they had seen each other. Her voice over the phone. Unlike any other. So musical. Not to be compared with the telephone voices of other women. And there was so much meaning in her slow, deliberate speech.

"Come early. It will make the evening longer."

"How did you sleep?"

"I didn't sleep at all. But I don't feel as if I hadn't slept."

Just talking over the phone was such a delight, he couldn't tear himself away from the receiver.

"A bit weak at the knees?"

"Never you mind."

(A secret smile. He could tell from the tone of her voice. He could see the room, see the telephone, see her standing by it.)

"I can't feel my body at all. It doesn't exist. Light as air! And I haven't a wish in the world."

Just to hear that voice he would be stretched into telephone wire himself!

"What about your work?"

"It's fine, everything's splendid. Come soon!"

And Guchkov? He's pretty sure to be home today. And all the rest of Petrograd?

Aleksandr Ivanovich? Yes, he's back. But he's gone out. Be here this evening. Any message?

Any message? . . . Might clash . . . The evening's taken . . . and all day long. It's all right, thank you.

I'll ring again.

Not yet, though.

Talking over the telephone was tantalizing, but it was an outlet for his burning impatience. However, after another three hours it was such a torment he had to be on the move, to make all possible haste to the far end of the Petersburg side.

Gray, rainy days—but springlike sunshine in his breast! He felt as if he had won a tremendous victory, over vast expanses, one no enemy could wrest from him.

Along the same avenues, past the same palaces, great houses, restaurants and cinemas, but less and less resentful of them, oblivious even of the weather, transported as though by magic carpet, hardly aware of the journey.

Her apartment. Together. Alone.

In her study, looking out on the Pesochnaya Embankment, the swollen, gray-brown Little Neva, and Kamenny Island, where you could just make out, or see clearly through opera glasses, a wooden villa with wooden roosters, Russian style, on the roof, a fantastic stone one with black turrets, and the wooden Kamenny Island Theater.

We *must* go for a stroll there sometime.

But there was simply no time left for strolling. Nor for anything else in Petrograd. Only for those two rooms. Books everywhere—but no time, either, to take them down from their shelves and look at titles, no time to read a single page. Or to inspect all the toys—the carved hussars and ladies of fashion, the troikas, Ilya Muromets and Solovey Razboinik, Jonah and the whale, the bears, pigs and hares, the glazed goblets with animal paws. And that bare-shouldered Pan in the half-darkness, with a bronze sliver of the old moon on the horizon. He wasn't so old as all that. The way he squatted, his midnight look, what he had in mind—all so much easier to understand now!

Just a few days ago Georgi would not have understood, would not even have noticed.

Olda might put that violin concerto by some Belgian on the phonograph, and grip his hand tight. Listen! Listen! This passage now!

Or just talk.

"On the twenty-fifth anniversary of Dostoevsky's death, out of the whole Russian reading public, out of all those in our enlightened capital city, from our proud student body—do you know how many people visited his grave? Seven! I was there . . . Seven people! Russia has followed in the train of his devils. Literally: the Tsar Liberator was assassinated just a few days after Dostoevsky's death. Russia had turned to rush in the wake of the devils. True, many more gathered this year, for the thirty-fifth anniversary. But don't imagine he himself was the main attraction. Oh, no. What attracts them—and the West has already caught a whiff of it—is his description of spiritual corruption, of perversion, seen from within. Dostoevsky is all the rage nowadays. Do *you* like him?"

He couldn't pretend, but felt awkward telling her.

"N-no," he said hesitantly. "He's not my sort of writer. He has too many epileptics, it's all out of proportion. All those superfluous confidants burbling away. And then those inordinately long conversations, all that nit-picking . . . As I see it, life is much simpler."

"So whom do you like? Tolstoy?"

No good pretending. Might as well hang for a sheep as a lamb.

"To tell the truth, nobody after Pushkin and Lermontov. Since then our literature has lacked energy and action. Its heroes are all weaklings or cranks. Take Pierre and Bolkonsky—you keep reading and wondering what they stand for. You can't separate them and you can't understand them. Me—I like strong-minded people."

Her smile acknowledged his right to say so.

It was delightful, sitting there talking to this clever woman about anything and everything—but suddenly conversation is swept away, and . . .

And . . . his hands, unbidden, lifted her—light and little as she was—made to be lifted—lighter still, because at exactly the right moment she flies into his arms!

"Oh, how big you are! My arms won't go around you!"

His legs move of their own accord, he threads his way, swings around, carries her into the other room, to the inevitable place.

Always to the same place—but nothing was ever the same twice—and that was pure enchantment. With Olda there was no foreseeing what would happen, and how: every time, from hour to hour, there was something unexpected, to captivate him and yet flatter his strength. In every gesture some novelty, an interrupted sequence of them. Sometimes—she's in no hurry, and you, you clumsy brute, are left to work out with your own fumbling hands which of those delicate coverings comes next. But another time she would do it herself, in a single motion, wildly, unseeingly, like a gambler throwing down his last card—and he was fired by her recklessness. Then—the doubling and trebling and multiplication of these events. The exclamations of surprise—and that cry that raises you to the height of ecstasy. Is it really true? Not just pretense? You—you're no mere mortal, you're an Atlas!

Everything blurs, walls, shelves, pictures, the world of thought and the world of irreconcilables. No more contradictions . . . So that's what you are! that's what you are! that's what you are! and the more shameless, the closer and the more needed.

Eyes half extinguished, narrowed to slits.

A long interval to rest and recover.

Their talk is languid, perfunctory.

"Do you know the difference between 'loved' and 'desired'?"

"No, I've never thought about it. Aren't they synonyms?"

"O-o-h . . . !"

A woman, even a learned woman, always finds time for nonsensical fishing expeditions of this kind.

"That first evening with me—did you think I might give other men the same sort of welcome?"

"For heaven's sake!"

He hadn't thought so then, or since, but now that she'd asked the question he wondered for a moment. Of course she hadn't treated everybody like this, but there could have been others?

"It . . . just came over me. I mean, when I was listening to you, at Shingarev's, I sensed that . . ."

Yes, yes . . . happened spontaneously. Who knows how? At their first meeting.

"And when I put my hand on your shoulder . . . it meant that you are a Russian knight-errant. It was symbolic. It implied no more than that."

"Symbolic—that's how I took it."

"As a rule, it's just the opposite—I keep everyone at a distance. I even try not to let anyone take my arm. Because the slightest contact may make me lose my head."

"Even if someone just takes your arm?"

"Yes . . . My skin reacts to the touch of a hair. Haven't you noticed?"

He didn't doubt it. His own skin, coarse and insensitive for so many years, felt different, rejuvenated. She had renewed him completely. He had never felt so keenly alive.

He lit a cigarette, still lying in bed, and she asked for one.

They smoked, side by side.

She became serious.

"You know, I'm very rarely as outspoken in company as I was in that outburst at Shingarev's. But lately I've had the feeling that things are coming to a head. And I suddenly had the idea that I'd found an ally in you. Especially when you made your splendid remark about meek acceptance being more useful to society than freedom. But then—you seemed somehow to back down."

Georgi didn't quite know how to put it.

"Look—I'm not against monarchy as such. But *this* Tsar . . . I feel insulted by him."

"There you are, you see, you've caught the same disease as all the others! When did it happen?"

"I can tell you exactly: when Stolypin was assassinated."

"But what could the Tsar do about that?"

"Before it happened—a great deal. And at that moment he could have at least gone to see the wounded man and bowed his head over him. He could have visited him in the hospital. When a faithful dog is killed its master shows more respect for it than the Tsar did for Stolypin. If we forgive him for his treatment of Stolypin, and draw no conclusions, there is nothing to be said for us."

"But everybody, monarchs included, may be momentarily confused by mixed feelings and make a mistake. We can't judge a man by a single incident . . ."

"Look wherever you like. Take those grandiose tricentenary celebrations. Is there any real reason for such vainglorious posturings: O glorious dynasty! The glorious dynasty has had its full share of blunders, palace revolutions, royal nonentities, of wills too weak and wills too cruel."

"No, no . . . you're infected, you're infected!" she wailed, almost despairingly.

"Why couldn't he make a heartfelt pronouncement: 'My subjects! This celebration is your own, it is you who bore the brunt of the dreadful Time of Troubles three hundred years ago. It is you who graciously put your faith in our royal line. I want with all the strength I have to justify that solemn trust.' But he has no such urge to speak frankly to the people at large—and that means that he is not one of us. And what about his pathetic and disgraceful trip to the western provinces? A misconceived attempt to skim the cream of public jubilation, immediately before the enemy began driving us out of Peremyshl and Galicia as a whole. This present Emperor of ours is incapable of coping with this country of ours, and has been so for a quarter of a century. It's terrible! He does not care how much Russian blood is spilled, he thinks there's an ocean of it in reserve."

"But the laws of war being what they are, what can he do?"

"There are more ways than one of waging war. If you have to get involved at all. We should have avoided it."

"I hope you don't go along with the Kadets when they accuse the government of deliberately trying to lose the war."

"Looked at from a purely military point of view, no. In fact, we're gradually beginning to win. But it's impossible to see what we can get out of it. And whatever it is, we're paying too dearly. For the sake of Russia's future, the nation's physical and spiritual survival, the best thing we could possibly do is not to go on with the war."

"But how can we simply give it up?" Olda said in astonishment. "A weightless insect can suddenly change course in mid-flight. But a drowning elephant cannot turn himself around. If we're to give up now, what was the point of all our previous sacrifices?"

"More likely than not they were pointless."

She had not expected this from him! Would never have expected it!

"But it would be a crime against all those who have fallen!"

"We should be thinking of those who are still on their feet," Georgi answered coolly. "As things are, Russia is doomed to destruction—and whatever is blocking her escape must be removed. Once rid of it, Russia will begin to recover."

Olda, startled, asked, "What is it you wish to see removed? Touch the Emperor—if that's it—and we may lose the monarchy altogether. May lose absolutely everything! That's all these people have—their religion and the Tsar."

"But I didn't say *he* should be removed." Georgi wasn't sure himself what he thought. Removed—and replaced by whom? One of the Grand Dukes? Was any one of them worth anything at all? If so, which? Wouldn't it be a worse mistake? "Whatever happens, some major change is necessary."

To tease her and see how far he could go, he added, "But what if in the last resort Russia can only be saved by becoming a republic?"

Olda raised herself on her pillow, twisted sideways, and spoke sternly, enunciating every word slowly and precisely, not a bit like a woman talking to her lover.

"It seems natural to us that there is one God and one only up above . . . and it would be a ridiculous muddle if we had two or three hundred celestial rulers, all at odds with each other, engaged in party strife, like the Olympian gods. To the people, and especially to simple people, it seems just as natural to have here on earth only one individual will above them. That's exactly how the peasant thinks of it—either one single will or no master at all. Monarchy is a reproduction in miniature of the universal order: there is someone above all the rest, equally recognized by all, equally stern or equally merciful to you and your enemy alike."

Hmm, being equally merciful might be difficult. But he should certainly be no enemy to any of his subjects.

Anyway, since he was shamefully neglecting Guchkov and all the inquiries he had meant to make in Petersburg, Vorotyntsev listened all the more readily to Olda, perhaps even hoping to be converted.

"Admit it—this is a wretched dynasty for such a flourishing, such a richly endowed, such a great country. The whole royal family has lost its senses."

"I don't agree! The sum of human wisdom, especially in politics, consists of dealing with what exists, not dreaming up something to put in its place."

She tugged at the sheet, seeking warmth. There was something touching about the flimsy straps of her shift across her bare shoulders. But he was only half aware of this.

He could never have foreseen to whom, and where, he would be trying to explain himself.

He was smoking again.

"There's a Russian word, *zatsarilsya*.* Not used of this Tsar specifically. It's an old word. But that it exists means that the people can conceive of such a possibility. It means that the Tsar has got above himself, ceased to remember what a Tsar should be. Ceased to be aware of the limits to his power. The limits of his function. His people's limits. One must always know how far expansion can go. The people also have their limits."

"We must spare our country! Centuries have gone into its creation," Olda darkly admonished him.

"Indeed we must! That's just what I'm saying! Whoever possesses power, and is caught in the storm of war, must know how to exercise that power."

"But he has been placed in that position. He has his duty to do!"

"If only! If only he thought of it that way, as his destiny, as a heavy burden, and turned to others for help! If he wore the crown with suffering, and not with a sort of inappropriate smile."

He remembered that smile, seen from a march-past.

"But he does feel the burden!" Olda said, with as much assurance as if she had been at close quarters with the Emperor only yesterday. "He does feel it! He suffers. And he's besieged on all sides by slander! You need only remember how he was supposed to have given a ball in the Winter Palace immediately after Tsushima. A lying tale—but it stuck, and the damage it did! There hasn't been a single ball there since 1903. The smile is an attempt to hide his suffering." Her voice

*Literally: "over-Tsared himself." [*Trans.*]

sank still lower. "And his helplessness. He is probably in agony. He's the prisoner of his throne, and a martyr to it." She spoke with as much conviction as if she knew him intimately.

"Well, if it's really so hard for him, if his thoughts on his situation are as you describe them, if he feels too weak for the country's needs, ought he not to . . . ? Shouldn't his supreme duty be to his country? Even if it means . . . abdication?"

Olda sounded grief-stricken. "If you can say that, you're not a monarchist at all. A father, even if he realizes that he's a bad one, cannot renounce his family. He is tied by his status, by his authority, by the subordination of others to him. Your advanced military studies must have carried the germ of progressivism. The Russian monarchy counts for more in the world than you imagine. It holds all Europe together, to begin with."

"Europe? I can't see that. What do we matter to Europe? What I can see is that saving the people, not the monarchy, must be our first priority. We're stuck in a self-destructive posture, and we must wrench ourselves out of it. And what is he doing about it? Nothing. I don't blame him alone. The dynasty as a whole obviously bears some sort of cumulative guilt for a sin that goes all the way back to Peter or even Alexis. They broke faith with the Assembly of the Land, which elected them, they ceased to feel responsible to the Land. So now the moment has come to hand back that responsibility. For the salvation of the people."

Knowing that it might come to this would have been more than she could take. Was it true that only the departure of the Tsar from the Supreme Command could clear the way for the sensible and talented elements in the army, so that they could at least change the conduct of the war, or best of all deliver Russia from it? Alas, there was no legal way of removing the monarch from the Supreme Command. Georgi couldn't formulate the practical implications (he didn't know them himself), but he could try out a proposition on her, expressing it more uncompromisingly than he did to himself, and see how she would correct him.

She clenched both hands, as women do, in a single fist.

"That *you* should think that way is the most terrible thing of all. That I should have to argue with *you* about it. Are you planning an attack on the monarchy as such?"

"No, no, of course not."

"Just think: to renounce the monarchy is to renounce a thousand years of our history. If the monarchic tradition had been a failure a great nation could not have grown from it."

"But what if the regime has become impossibly obtuse? Doesn't listen to argument? Is incapable?"

"You've picked all that up from educated society. But they're just hysterical. Last year they were saying the regime couldn't win the war without them; now they say that the regime's objective is to lose the war. Our intelligentsia is stupid; it has a lot of conscience but no brains."

"So what would you advise us to do?"

"Nothing. Grin and bear it. Lay one finger on the throne—and you'll start a landslide. The consequences are incalculable. You mustn't let short-term aims make you forget more distant goals."

She shook her head, and her whole body swayed with it.

Why keep arguing? He would be only too happy if Olda proved right. It might mean that the crime of lying there beside her was no crime, but just what he should be doing.

"The thing is," Georgi mumbled, less assertively, "he lacks ability. That's what the accident of birth means in this case."

"He doesn't have to be a Solomon, he can choose wise counselors."

"Well, he's chosen the wrong ones. Or if he does listen to clever ones, why doesn't it show in his actions?"

Olda laid chilly hands on him to make him see reason.

"But perhaps even chance happenings are providential, perhaps there is some mysterious purpose in them. If he was born weak—let us strengthen him with our loyalty!"

"Put it any way you like—a monarch has no right to be so wishy-washy. You said yourself that if people do not feel a mystical love for their sovereign, he does not exist. Has he really helped us to go on feeling such love for him, to go on regarding the throne as something sacred? Listening to you now, I can see clearly how sick our monarchy is: our unquestioning trust has been lost and the Emperor is in no hurry to restore it. And that is where his guilt lies. He has done a great deal to make the halo fade. You've said so yourself. So let him refurbish it—by strength of will, by vision, and by courage."

Only a grudging gray twilight filtered through the uncurtained window, but he could see how vexed Olda was, see her disheveled hair.

"It's dreadful! An officer with your record! With such a firm hand! With such ardent public spirit! You're probably a good speaker too. And at such a critical time. But you've lost your bearings, lost your will . . ."

"Will? Will for what?"

Olda lifted one of his hands with both of hers, and dandled it as though weighing it. "In our present extremity only manly hands like these can save Russia."

"That's what I want to be doing! That's all I want! But how?" He was eager for an answer—but inwardly he felt some amusement. She didn't know that by going to bed with him she had at least neutralized him. Didn't know that she had as good as won already.

She let his hand fall and held out her own bare, delicate hands, hands without muscle, hardly the hands to lift two pails—but what she was reaching for was the snaffle, the reins, to control the chariot's wild career herself, if there were no men left to do it.

"We must shore up the monarchy!" she cried out as the chariot flew on. "Give it guide rails!"

Fast as she was traveling, Vorotyntsev swiftly interrupted. "Stolypin tried to! Look what thanks he got!"

"I can't believe it!" She shook her bare forearms like a witch flapping her sleeves in a fairy tale. "You show greater enthusiasm for intimacy with a woman than for your obvious duty!"

"Are you complaining?" he half howled, half laughed, and buried his head, face, beard in her bosom.

They were still.

No arguing, no movement.

Georgi, intoxicated with Olda, euphorically grateful to her, held her slender frame between conciliatory paws. He felt his mentor's whole warm, inviting body beside him, pressed against his own, under the same coverlet. Who would not make his peace, on terms he would reject in the sitting room?

Distant aims should not distract you from those nearer to hand. No argument there!

A little doze . . . ?

Except that the slightest contact . . .

The very slightest . . .

The smallest imaginable hand moving over his skin somewhere. Not even touching. It was as if her fingers could breathe and his skin felt their breath.

One step. Two steps. Lightly gliding . . . but the lighter the contact, the more powerful the effect.

Feeling their way around, getting to know him. His shaggy, battle-hardened chest.

And now the tip of a claw.

Recognizing. Pressing harder. Harder.

What a gift you have been given! Already you are a man transformed! Infused with some new feeling by that featherlike touch! Taken by surprise—you were at rest, inert, oblivious, but now you are transformed!

Her fingers play their little tune and he is on fire—just like that first time.

What would follow? What would follow was always unsure. Every time there was some startling novelty.

As a horse in full stride, if his gallop permitted, might twist his head to stare up at his spirited rider, tossed and bounced in the saddle

—but not tossed or bounced, she holds the bit tight, and with soldierly skill and authority guides her disobedient horse's run to the victory she sees ahead

—but no riding habit disfigures her form—untrammeled, wind-caressed, symmetrical—her legs, drawn up for the leap, tensed in the stirrups . . .

The leap, with lips pressed together, eyes tightly closed as though, like that, her course is easier to see, to whip her way over. Her unbound hair streams in the wind as the rider, losing fear and reason, rushes toward her preordained destruction—she is hurt! she cries out!

She droops, eyes closed, hair hanging limply in the still air, curtaining her face—her hands, too slack to pull on the reins, struggle to hold on, to prevent her from crashing to the ground.

Her faithful steed must finish the gallop for her. Will he hold her safe, will he carry her home . . . ?

That is what a horse is for.

[29]

Half the factories in Petrograd had been on strike, or so they were told after it was all over. Flags, it seemed, had been hung on government buildings (on what was in fact the day of the Emperor's accession) and taken down afterward. Newspaper summaries of military operations had mentioned something "south of Kimpolung," but he had not taken it in. Then a new imperial decree was published calling up category 2 militiamen. What in God's name were they trying to do? They'd gotten it the wrong way around. What had been happening in Petrograd in those . . . how many days was it? Six days were missing, and they couldn't all be holidays. But for Georgi and Olda, as they remembered it later, it had been bed, bed, bed, with an occasional walk when the weather cleared up for an hour or two. They thought of taking a trip to Mustamyaki, where Olda had a little dacha, but they never got around to that either. Some other time.

If I'm still among the living . . .

Anyway, could you really speak of "days" in Petersburg at the end of October? There were only nights. It started getting dark before it was really light; you couldn't call them full days. Daylight was just the fading rays of a veiled sun.

Vorotyntsev had lost sight of his reason for coming to this city, and stopped trying to contact Guchkov after his initial failures. He had no time left for it, although he had postponed his departure three times. It was lucky that he had managed to look in, as promised, on certain people in the War Ministry and the General Staff in his first two days, otherwise he would not have gotten around to it. He had not made contact with the Society for the Advancement of Military Science. Even Vera, dear attentive Vera, who always anticipated her brother's thoughts and wishes—he had hardly seen or spoken to her since that first evening at Shingarev's—and he had asked her nothing about herself. Why wasn't she married? At twenty-five! To ask such a question point-blank was something he couldn't do. He and Vera were in any case always tongue-tied on that one subject, they had never succeeded in opening their hearts to each other, and so he told her nothing about Olda now, but she, clever girl, of course knew all about it anyway. He hadn't found time even for his minimal fraternal duties, and had soon stopped going back to spend the night under Nanny's roof. He just sent for Alina's letters and telegrams instead.

The one thing that marred those blissful days was the need to put together some sort of reply to those letters and telegrams, to explain why he was not on his way back when he had said he'd be gone for only four days (four clear days, or four including travel time?). It wasn't difficult thinking up excuses, he could plead official business, but he remembered Alina calling out as she saw him off, "Write every day!" It was agony, though, trying to put sentences together, searching for the right little word to follow the one before, and stringing them together. The form of address and the ending were particularly difficult: every word looked like an impostor, every single one jarred on ear and eye. And this falsity had to be blurred somehow.

It wasn't just writing his own letters—it was hard, hateful, dishonest work reading what came from Alina. The last thing he needed at that particular time. He was amazed to find that Alina had suddenly become a stranger. Previously, he had gone for a whole year without seeing her, but had not felt like this. And had happily written letters. But now, after just a few days . . .

Alina's latest untimely demand was that they should talk over the telephone—a direct connection between Moscow and Petrograd could be arranged. Luckily, the line between the two capitals was out of order for two days, so Georgi was able to avoid this conversation. His voice, live, even muted by the receiver, would have given him away. Talking to her directly would be unbearable.

The days raced by. He had to be in Moscow on 9 November without fail, for Alina's birthday. And now she had sent a telegram to say that she expected him at least one day before. He consulted Olda. Did one day before mean that he must get there on the 7th or on the 8th? How would it be generally understood? It obviously meant "on the eve," Olda thought, nobody would take it to mean anything different.

Although Georgi was being unfaithful to his wife, he did not feel the least bit guilty of deception or of base behavior. This was simply something quite different, nothing to do with Alina. He had never felt like this with Alina or with anyone else, he was reborn, a different man. That first evening with Olda had cleft his life in two, as a heavy wound might—except that this had not laid him low but raised him to the heights, made him lighter than air, able to soar unaided, and to fall without being dashed to pieces. The Vorotyntsev now afloat with Olda was not the man who had been with Alina, and so there was no betrayal.

He had no wish to think of Alina for the present, but Olda herself returned to the subject several times. He found it both unpleasant and pointless. Whatever they were discussing, Olda was likely to ask, "What does Alina think about it?" "What does Alina do on such occasions?" And once she asked him outright, "Do you love her very much?" He said something evasive.

Georgi had forgotten that it was possible to feel such ease, such freedom. His heart overflowed with gratitude to Olda, and there was no room left for doubt or for guilt.

Throughout those fleeting days and nights, being with Olda, being near her was something innocent, legitimate, yes, legitimate, his due after all those frozen months of trench warfare, after all his unappreciated efforts on the staff and in the field. Well, the Supreme Command had shown no appreciation, so this little woman was his living reward, the best that Russia's abundance could offer, better than any number of medals.

Was she then, *the one*—that nameless, unknown she, never seen, never glimpsed in imagination, beyond the limits of clear vision, but so keenly sensed in his dream at Usdau?

It was in fact Olda who said one day, looking meditatively into the distance, fantasizing, pretending to remember, "We know each other of old. Can't you feel it?"

Not exactly. I could never have invented, imagined anyone quite like her.

But listen. There was that one time . . .

"Where were you on 27 August 1914? Who was with you? What were you thinking about?"

He told her his story.

She smiled. Stroked his mustache, his beard.

"You're very passionate."

"I've never noticed it."

She screwed up her eyes, quizzically.

"You still don't know anything about yourself. Even if you are forty. You didn't make the best of your younger days!"

"If I had I wouldn't have gotten anything done, Olda my love!"

"And what have you done that matters so much?"

She was right. What did it amount to? Plans, rash gestures, defeats. And his fall from favor. Colonels on the General Staff usually dodged regimental postings—no career there, and anyway only one officer in four or five was trained for General Staff duties, and it cost too much for them to be used on regimental service. After two years commanding a regiment Vorotyntsev should by rights be a general. But was not.

In his dream he had not been able to see his unknown visitor's features clearly, but Olda's, seen in broad daylight, seemed just right, and just as attractive. He liked all those toys too—toys not for children, but for herself. (And it pleased him that she hardly ever thought fit to mention children, as if they were invisible from the heights on which she dwelled.) She spoke disdainfully of most women. But with almost childish enthusiasm about nestlings, and animals generally. On Kamenny Ostrov she dragged Georgi back a hundred yards to take a second look at a kitten he hadn't seen properly. Even the professor's belief in astrology, fortune-telling, and good and bad luck signs somehow did not seem incongruous. If Olda dropped some precious object she would silently hug it to her breast—for luck—before replacing it. And he loved the way she sat beside him, with her legs tucked underneath her, gently swaying, and reciting, in a low voice, devoid now of passion but promising its renewal, verse after verse of some fashionable poet or other:

> *"From you, world-weary Anatomist,*
> *I have learned how sweet evil can be."*

Or else she would tell him about something called theurgic art. There was a lot of nonsense in what she said, but Georgi was enchanted by it all—by Olda's favorite pose, her musical voice tirelessly holding forth, being able to hug and touch her while he was listening.

Sometimes they got up and dressed to eat, sometimes Olda would hop out, put on a dressing gown, open or close the curtains, and run, run, run to bring a snack back to bed. They were never apart for long. The sweetest, laziest time was watching light change to darkness, or darkness give way to light. Lying happily in bed engulfed in the flow of time. Most of what they later remembered saying had been said lying down.

But once, at the end of the day, the clouds parted, blue sky showed through the gray, and they went for a long walk. They came across a boatman on the embankment and he ferried them across to Kamenny Ostrov.

It was cold, there was frost in the air, but the sun shone occasionally. Westward the sky had cleared and for Georgi it was as if there was an infinity of light within him. How wonderful it was to be with Olda! They took a closer look at those villas—the one ornamented with roosters, the one with the black turrets, the Swiss chalet. Wind and rain had not yet stripped everything bare, some red-leaved trees, and of course the dark brown oaks, always the latest, had held their own. The Krestovka, sluggish in the cold and hidden under a thick coverlet of leaves, looked as though you could walk across it. Villas, villas, and more villas—wooden villas, with mismatched windows, with spires, with carved woodwork, with pediments like peasant bonnets, with little balconies. By the Elagin Bridge stood the Kamenny Ostrov Theater, an ornate wooden building, now deserted and boarded up. The pathways were firm underfoot, but there was mud to either side of them.

"Do you ever come walking here?"

"I've been known to do so."

He felt no inclination to ask when and with whom. He was content with what he saw and could hold.

"We . . . I lived in Petersburg six years," he said regretfully, "and was hardly ever on the islands. Never had time. Anyway, it's a place for strollers . . . and we weren't . . . I wasn't much of a stroller."

He had corrected himself, not wanting to mention Alina. Though it was no secret that she had been with him in Petersburg, this was not the place to speak of it. But Olda seized her opportunity and gently inserted a sharp claw.

"Did you get on well together?"

What possible answer was there?

She spelled it out.

"Were you friends? Did you understand each other?"

He had to say yes. Blushing.

"You're not," Olda decided, "the sort of person who thinks a great deal about his life and tries to understand himself. But understanding yourself is absolutely essential."

Though not particularly eager to talk politics, Georgi needed to change the subject.

"Tell me," he asked, "is Milyukov really a major historian?"

"How could he be?" Olda answered irritably. "He switched from scholarship to opposition politics very early on, and has rolled and rattled down the easy road ever since. He makes a display of learning, but is not genuinely learned. He has no powerful ideas of his own, and no soul, but he has a great deal of tenacity. Poetically speaking, he's the barren fig tree that . . ."

She interrupted herself to throw both arms around him so that he would see the young moon—already into its first quarter—over his right, not his left shoulder.

Georgi saw the brilliant sickle in the west and said, "It doesn't count if you're made to look."

But all these happy days had taken him into a new month. And he had missed Guchkov altogether.

They walked along the northern embankment, on a simple wooden landing stage, where the cold black waters of the Neva came almost up to their feet.

He began questioning her again about the Kadets, and she answered halfheartedly, as though it was all common knowledge.

"None of them feel any responsibility to the deeper realities of Russian history. It never occurs to them that they do not understand this people's faith, nor its peculiar conception of right and wrong, nor where the main dangers to the national character lie. They boldly assert that 'the people wants this' and 'the people demands that.' But nowhere in Western Europe are radicals so contemptuous of their country's history. If the Kadets had any feeling for our history they would see the war through to the end without a 'responsible government.' "

She looked at him meaningfully in the gathering darkness. She was trying to guess what he was thinking—"see the war through" was meant for him.

"The right-wing thinkers are all discredited in advance and the students won't come near them. So there's nowhere for them to discover a different point of view."

They turned back over the Kamenny Ostrov bridge by lamplight and made their way home. Had they really been walking for nearly three hours, with other people around, instead of staying, just the two of them, in Olda's room? Now they wanted warmth and comfort and the phonograph. Under the moon they had agreed that enough was enough. So Georgi sat in an armchair, telling her how he had once behaved rashly at the front and got away with it. Suddenly—a green flash from Olda's eyes, she sat in his lap, snuggling up to him, whispered one short word in his ear—and their vow of abstinence was shattered.

Time sped by, deliriously compressed.

Then flowed smoothly, slowly again.

The wonder of it.

At peace, triumphant.

If there had been no other indications, the way in which Olda at just the right moment tensed her foot against the floor and sprang nimbly into his arms was enough to show that he was not the first to sweep her off her feet. But his awareness that she was experienced and versatile did not upset him in the least, indeed it pleased him: a late guest cannot be upset to find that others have feasted before him, and is flattered when they hasten to serve him as if he were first at the table. He felt no jealous urge to inquire about his predecessor (or predecessors). They meant no more to him than he did to them. He never asked why she was not married, and whether there was anybody now. She did once remark that divorce had become very common in Petersburg and Moscow lately, that in many marriages one of the partners had previously been divorced, and that Anna Karenina would not need to throw herself under a train nowadays but would get a divorce from a consistory court with no fuss, and marry Vronsky. Georgi listened, and was left wondering: was she divorced? He abandoned himself delightedly to her practiced skills, and if someone else had helped her to acquire them—he was grateful. They could not possibly estrange Olda from him now.

She did, more than once, start telling him about her past, and even about a husband of some sort, though not one to whom she was officially married, but Georgi lost interest before he could get to the bottom of it. Just one of those uninteresting, stereotyped "stories of my life" which everybody was always telling everybody else.

He was still less concerned with her private thoughts as she lay there, eyes tightly closed, spent and speechless. Blissful gratitude to this woman drowned all other feelings. His rampant emotions were like a mountain range beyond which he could not see, and had no wish to see, any other world.

Olda, though, was eager to know more about Georgi's previous love affairs. He reluctantly submitted, started telling her, and at once discovered that there was hardly anything to tell: the few stories he could think of passed like pathetic shadows over that bed of fire. Ashamed of himself, he gave up, there were better things for lips to be doing anyway. Those liaisons were sporadic, haphazard, and left no impression on his mind or his feelings.

In reality Alina had been the only one.

"But was it like this with her?"

"No, never."

Olda tried to draw him out. "Go on, tell me about it."

But what was there to tell? He wouldn't know how to put it. That was then—this is now. There were ten thousand little things—how could he talk about it?

"Is she clever?"

She certainly wasn't stupid. But not what you'd call particularly clever.

"Does she love you?"

"Of course, what a question."

Olda lay, head high, her brown hair, out of curl, straying untidily over a plumped-up pillow, staring sternly not at Georgi but at the top of the wall.

"And is she devoted? To your career?"

Georgi would have liked to say yes, but . . . "Well, it isn't really a woman's thing . . . Not her sort of thing . . ."

Olda had spoken emphatically, as if she did not quite trust him to answer truthfully.

How could he make her understand? It wouldn't fit any logical framework. The things that mattered most would be missing: that he was used to Alina and felt close to her, that they had been through so much together and that their relationship was all the stronger for it. At one time he had thought that Alina shared his commitment, the whole tempo of his life, his sense of predestination. Then it turned out that she put up with it all expecting to be rewarded with a more carefree existence. Well—she was what she was. And all the responsibility rested on her husband's shoulders.

(A husband who couldn't even read her letters? . . . Yes, but no real contradiction there.)

"And do you love her?" Olda for some reason didn't believe it. Her eyes were still fixed on the wall.

"Of course!"

Olda obviously couldn't get it into her head that the two situations—herself and himself here, his life with Alina elsewhere—had no relevance to each other. There he lay, on his back like her, smiling a little at his vision of himself lying there, loved by both of them, by each in her own way—and neither relationship could interfere with the other. His happiness was complete, and he felt too indolent to continue the conversation.

"Would you ever think of putting it to the test?" Olda asked half jokingly.

"What for?"

She smiled. "To make sure. General rules are no help at all in personal decisions. Every case is uniquely labyrinthine. There are no problems on earth more difficult than one's own emotional problems."

"Come, now," Vorotyntsev said, good-humoredly deprecating. "And you a historian! What about the problems of a colossus like Russia?"

"Not to be compared!" she said, and her long eyebrows were a stern straight line over her small features. "Those are problems like mountain peaks, visible from afar, and to many people. Hundreds and thousands of us have an equal right to an opinion on them, and some conclusion can be drawn. But in matters of personal feeling advice from outsiders is inevitably superficial, and no two people will take the same view."

Not so. Vorotyntsev firmly believed that people mature enough to manage affairs of state—and, more difficult still, to carry their fellows with them—were few and far between. Whereas almost everybody on earth succeeded in managing his family. Nothing could be simpler, and it was no one else's concern. He firmly believed it—but in his state of contented repletion he was not going to argue. Whatever she said suited him because she was saying it. Let's leave it at that.

But she was not satisfied. She drew up her slender, girlish legs, her favorite pose, dressed or undressed, hoisted herself higher on the pillow, covered her bare shoulders with the counterpane, and said, "What's more, my dear, one must be incomparably firmer and more resolute in matters of the heart than in matters of state."

"Wha-a-at?"

He was speechless.

She looked at him mockingly, but with a hint of compassion.

"Heaven forbid that you should ever discover how difficult it is. You're in such perfect agreement with yourself, there are no moot questions for you."

She sighed.

"Your new feeling still isn't strong enough."

But what was so special and so marvelous about these conversations in bed was that words were not necessarily followed by more words. Her voice sank.

She slid down from the pillow.

It was late, he was sleepy and his ears could not quite catch what she was mumbling under the counterpane.

"What are you saying?"

A voice from below: "You needn't listen, I'm not talking to you."

They should have been asleep long ago. They hadn't had a single good night's sleep, but they persisted in this drowsy, semiconscious, after-midnight byplay until it reawakened the tempest and Olda, heedless of the nighttime silence, cried out in a piercing voice, the voice of an intrepid huntress.

[3 0]

"You're doomed!" Nusya used to say. "You'll drop dead in harness."

Pyotr Akimovich knew it. And was willing.

He had long ago gotten used to the extraordinary rule that in a country with so many people there were never enough for what needed to be done. So that his own life was stretched to the breaking point, to deal with the expected and the unexpected, and he had learned to accept all these assignments gladly.

Russia's mineral wealth was inexhaustible, and there was a shortage of expertise in the mines as in other branches of Russian industry, but the war had diverted Obodovsky from his normal occupation. Knowing that Russia's future economic might depended on them, Obodovsky *saw* those invisible deposits, was aware of them as most people see the gaily shimmering greenery on the earth's surface. But now there was something else to be done before this subterranean wealth could be tapped—the ground above it had to be saved from the enemy. And so the war was gradually converting this mining engineer into an organizer of other engineering enterprises.

In any case, his passion and his talent for organization had perhaps always come first with Obodovsky. He had realized long ago that good management could double the output of a pit and—so it seemed— triple the carrying capacity of a railroad. Which was why he had been asked by the All-Russian Union of Engineers to form a Subcommittee for Military-Technical Aid, attached to Guchkov's Central War Industry Committee, and was inexorably doomed to become its chairman. This meant that he had to immerse himself in the uncongenial study of military technology, and spend his evenings perusing an endless succession of manuals and monographs.

War on a gigantic scale had brought about such a chaotic proliferation of work in the rear that there was no knowing where you might have to exert yourself next. Today, Friday, 3 November, Obodovsky had been sitting since early morning in one of the poky little rooms of the War Industry Committee, in the depths of No. 59 Nevsky Prospect, interviewing artillery engineers, some of whom were also inventors. The number of those eagerly seeking assistance here after unfortunate experiences with the War Ministry was steadily growing. And you couldn't just brush them off. There might be a diamond among them.

There are few categories of people so difficult to judge as inventors—to decide who is the genius, who the lunatic, who the luckless man of talent, who the trickster. You can know all there is to know in a particular field (Obodovsky certainly didn't know all that much about artillery) and still find it hard not to quail, faced, amid the mists of the unknown, with that fanatical determination, those feverish eyes glowing perhaps with triple vision, seeing farther than you ever could, or perhaps just with the light of madness or the lust for money and fame (neither of which, however, comes the way of Russian inventors). What helped was not so much the extent of your knowledge but having the mentality of an engineer. You could distinguish your own kind from the others.

Obodovsky was conducting the interviews, but without an assumed official manner, without self-importance. Only their positions in relation to a desk lamp under an opaque white shade, and an inkstand, made it possible to distinguish interviewer from applicant.

Kisnemsky was agitated, his tie was awry and his shirt collar turned up, but there was no doubt about him, his previous inventions had proved that he was genuine. He had been unsuccessful with a type of "progressive" gunpowder, and had roped in and brought along a quiet and malleable engineer from the Tambov powder factory whom he had already persuaded to continue the tests.

The progressive gunpowder problem was a by-product of the need for long-range shells. Before the war no one had thought of firing farther than six versts: decisive engagements were not fought in greater depth than that, and as yet there were no means of observing explosions at a greater distance. But over the last year trench warfare had made necessary a range of up to fifteen versts (and aerial observation, already carried out by the Germans, made that possible), as urgently necessary as all the other drastic changes which this extraordinary European war called for, so urgently that if there was no time to design new ones the only thing to do was to increase the range of existing guns. But how? By digging a hole under the trail of the gun carriage, so as to widen the angle of elevation? That added thirty percent to the range, but reduced velocity, and lengthened the time needed to prepare the gun for firing. Obviously, the muzzle velocity of the shell itself must be increased. But how? By increasing the explosive charge? The barrel of the gun was not strong enough to withstand the additional pressure, and the gun carriages wouldn't hold up under the recoil. So they started looking for "progressive" varieties of explosive. Ordinary gunpowder burns out instantly, the shell is launched by a single impulse, and the pressure behind it decreases as it moves along the barrel. Progressive gunpowder must be made to burn in such a way that the quantity of gas would increase progressively every thousandth of a second, which would mean that the pressure on the base of the shell would not decrease, and that on the walls of the barrel would not increase. So, by some as yet unobvious method, you had to devise a compromise between the laws of geometry and the laws of combustion which would tell you what the shape of the grains of powder should be.

Kisnemsky had proposed prismatic bars with grooves in quadratic section, stubbornly insisting that the quantity of gas formed at the moment of ejection would be ten times greater. But it didn't work out! Enough experiments had been carried out on the range to show beyond a doubt that this was not the answer. The grains disintegrated too soon and burned out degressively. Kisnemsky, however, would not admit defeat and leave the field to other competitors. He now needed permission from the War Ministry to transfer the experiments interrupted in Petersburg to the Tambov powder factory, and was asking the War Industry Committee to support his application.

What Obodovsky had to do was weigh the chances of success against the risk of misusing the plant. And to decide how best to explain it to the ministry.

The desk lamp was less and less necessary. The late dawn of autumn in Petersburg had by now revealed the cobbled courtyard outside in all its dreariness, and an anemic gray light was seeping into the room.

Kisnemsky was followed by an engineer from the Commission for the Manufacture of Asphyxiating Gases, also seeking support. Eighteen months earlier it would have been impossible to mention such a thing, and still more absurd to imagine oneself having a hand in the production of poison gas for love of one's country. The chemists had been insistent, but the Grand Duke would not give his consent: un-Russian, he said. But after the German gas attacks at Ypres, resistance collapsed: if the enemy is unfastidious in his methods we will have to make the stuff too! So the relevant commission had been in existence for over a year, two hundred factories were working on it, with senior scientists on their staff, while people in offices and laboratories calmly discussed the effectiveness of particular toxic substances. And suddenly Obodovsky was one of them, heedless of the bone-shaking bump in the road along which logic had taken him.

It was getting on for noon, and by now the feeble light of a dim, drizzly day pervaded the room. At twelve Obodovsky was expecting Dmitriev, who had rung him at home the night before asking to see him on an urgent matter. Meanwhile a railway engineer from the Amur had insinuated himself among the artillery experts to discuss the requirements of a newly opened two-verst concrete bridge, the longest in Russia. After him two bothersome inventors, Podolsky and Yampolsky, no longer allowed over the threshold of the Artillery Committee, and turned down by the Chief Artillery Administration, slipped in and occupied the two vacant chairs. Obodovsky would have turned them away, but they said they needed only three minutes, they weren't asking for an interview, they only wanted Pyotr Akimovich to put their request to Aleksandr Ivanovich . . . who would surely not refuse to take an interest in a grandiose project which promised Russia speedy and complete victory.

Well aware that long-range artillery was the current problem, this duo had abandoned their previously rejected projects and were now proposing to propel shells not by explosives but by electromagnetic power: build a gun fifty yards long operating on the magnetomotive principle and a range of three hundred versts was attainable! The Russian army need advance only a short distance and it could bombard Berlin! And think of all the other advantages—no noise, no smoke, no flash! Casting would be no problem—there was no need for a thick tube. And the weapon would be practically immortal, it need never wear out!

Obodovsky was drawn into the discussion in spite of himself. But although his own expertise was in geology he had a clear enough view of what was involved.

"Tell me, gentlemen," he said with an inquisitorial frown, "won't you need a current of a million amperes? What sort of storage battery will you use? What would the capacity of your power station have to be?"

Although it was pretty obviously fanatical or fraudulent poppycock, they stormed the desk from both ends—how could a miner take it upon himself to reject what was possibly the greatest weapon of the twentieth century?

"Well, gentlemen, couldn't you redesign your model for a range of just fifteen versts, with a barrel one-twentieth as long?"

Podolsky and Yampolsky exchanged glances. They could manage that too, but would still like the present project to be passed on to Guchkov.

Dmitriev came in at this point, with spots of rain on his jacket, and stood listening. The discreetly satirical smile under his big nose finally reassured Obodovsky that he would not be suppressing a major invention by withholding his support.

But it took him a long time to shake them off and rescue a chair for Dmitriev.

Also on the day's agenda was a briefing on a project for modifying other field guns to function as howitzers, using the new idea of a universal detonator with alternating deceleration. But Dmitriev had come to discuss the trench mortar. Not the technicalities: experimental models had been made and tested in battle but they would need a lot of support before they could start mass production. They had meant to discuss it the previous Monday at Shingarev's, but had not gotten around to it. It was only the manufacturing process, not the concept itself, that needed discussion, but Dmitriev's large, stolid face looked weary and sad. He lowered himself onto a chair, with both legs to one side of it.

"Akimovich. The men at the Obukhov factory have refused to do overtime. Some of them had promised me they would come in on Sunday, but now they won't."

It didn't take much thinking about. After all the excited and highly technical talk that morning here was something succinct and simple. Plan and draw and fantasize all you like—it's all just stardust until it is materialized in the form of metal by means of the workshop, the workbench, and workers' hands.

The way he was sitting—was Dmitriev just taking a rest? He probably hadn't done much sitting down since late summer when he got back from the trials of his trench mortar on the Northern Front. It certainly wouldn't do him any harm to sit a while.

His gloomy passivity had communicated itself to Obodovsky. His nervous, sinuous lips were set in a doleful grimace under his faint brushstroke of a mustache.

"What's happened?"

"Nothing's *happened*. It's only that the agitators got around to them, and said, 'How is it that half Petrograd was on strike last Tuesday and Wednesday but not the Obukhov factory?' Said, 'How dared you refuse to support them?' "

That unlucky mortar! The need for it had been realized as long ago as the war with Japan. The Putilov model for a rapid-firing assault gun had been put up for approval in 1910. It was considered, it was approved, but it was not put into production. So they'd spent the ten years after the Japanese war thinking about it and gone into this war without trench artillery. Then, when the initial maneuvering abruptly ended and they settled down in the trenches, there was an outcry: we must have it! hurry up with it! and make it lighter! The three-inch mountain gun that took four horses to pull it was no good. Last year a project for a one-and-a-half-inch trench gun had started making its

leisurely way around the departments, but there were so many Petersburg generals and others in high places whose consent had to be obtained—and no shells were dropping on them, no machine guns
harassing them. The whole year was spent on design and experimental
models and now that they were ready to put it into production the
workers . . .

"And without overtime?"

"The machines would be idle all evening and all night, and the
foundry wouldn't be casting. Anyway, worse things are rumored—
they're thinking of a general strike any day now."

Obodovsky's brows, never at rest for long, shot up.

"General strike? What for?"

"No special reason. They're just thinking about it."

"Some anniversary or other?"

The passion of the Social Democrats for anniversaries and red-letter
days was as full-blooded as that of the royal family. There was a revolutionary calendar showing strike days of obligation: 22 January, 17
April (anniversary of the shootings in the Lena goldfields), 1 May,
obviously, but also 17 November, the day on which their group in the
Duma was arrested, also the day in February on which they were tried,
also . . . also . . . also . . . They tore page after page out of the calendar,
heedless of the effect on Russian industry. And each of these dates
emerging so suddenly from nowhere meant an obligation to strike
which only traitors to the working class could evade.

"Or is there smallpox in Turkestan?"

There had been an epidemic in Baku, in which a dozen workers had
died—and for some crazy reason all Petrograd had to strike immediately.

Dmitriev sat in silence and gave no help with this guesswork.

"At the Metal Factory not long ago some pipsqueak of an agitator
was fired and the whole place was on strike for two days. The management reasoned with them, told them they were halting work on
four minelayers in for repairs. That every day on strike meant a fall of
fifteen thousand in the production of shells. That every shell not fired
for that reason might cost the lives of two Russian infantrymen. Thirty
thousand of your brothers on active service! What do you say to that?
We say to hell with it, give us back our agitator."

Obodovsky's nervous fingers drummed on the desk.

"Can you imagine such a strike in England or France right now, in
wartime? It's unthinkable. If any clear-cut demands are put forward
they can be examined, and some sort of agreement reached. Obviously
people only begin to understand the meaning of freedom at a certain
level of political awareness. Below that critical level—there are only
irrational dark forces . . . a bear rolling a log.

"Free England has militarized industry, and nobody is outraged by

it. But here we get 'betrayal of the workers' interests,' 'tyrannical re-
pression of the individual' . . . If we can mobilize an army, why not war
industry? A soldier obeys orders knowing it may cost him his life, and
doesn't shout about abuse of power. Why, then, should a worker in a
factory of military significance have the right to discharge himself, to
absent himself without leave, to strike? How can we fight with one
hand tied behind our backs? If you judged by the Petersburg factories
you'd think we hadn't begun the war yet. And Petersburg factories
produce half of our arms and ammunition."

But you and I don't need to keep telling each other these things.

This is a strange fate for a civilian who's hated army types and army
ways all his life!

The swarms of bureaucrats who get up in the morning to spend the
whole day at their troughs don't let such things worry them. And the
Kadets and Social Democrats demand liberation from feudalism! As
for Guchkov's committees—they're in no big hurry for militarization
either.

The Guchkov committees had emerged as a new and fresh coordi-
nating mechanism, side by side with the slow and rusty bureaucratic
machine, and seemed capable of getting things moving and producing
results where the old system had failed. Obodovsky had immediately
expected to find in the Guchkov committees those altruistic social
forces which would rally round from all sides to close every breach and
save the day. And he had been wrong. Over the past eighteen months
the War Industry Committees had become just another clumsy, self-
sufficient system, burdened with an inflated staff. It wouldn't have
been so bad if they really had been altruistic. But everyone on the staff
of the committees was desperate to increase his salary, every subcon-
tractor wanted a higher commission, every factory wanted a higher
return, so that the help which the Guchkov committees gave to the
country was becoming an expensive luxury: their three-inch cannon
cost 12,000 rubles, that produced by the government 7,000, and for a
Maxim machine gun, for which the government enterprises charged
1,370 rubles, Tereshchenko was asking 2,700, and expecting the government to supply barrels. In fact, everything that the committees
produced was twice or three times as expensive as its equivalent from
a state enterprise, and Guchkov's activists felt not the least bit
ashamed but, on the contrary, considered themselves the benefactors
and saviors of their country because they delivered the goods quickly
(although not all that quickly). Even Rodzyanko, who supplied birch-
wood gunstocks for rifles, was given an extra ruble per rifle by the War
Ministry, "to keep him sweet"—and Rodzyanko accepted it without
demur!

Where Obodovsky had expected a close-knit group of selfless patriots he was distressed to find a nexus of selfish interests and ulterior

motives. So it was not only people of practical ability who were lacking in Russia but disinterested people too? There were none in the state machine, but there were none among the educated public either, so where were they? Was anyone working all out for his native land with no thought for himself? By a bitter irony, that was the lot of this former revolutionary and outcast. And he saw very few others of his kind around him.

More important, the Guchkov committees were preoccupied not with supplying arms but with reinforcing their own position in society and attacking the regime. This ulterior purpose of theirs did not escape Obodovsky—it was visible even in Guchkov himself. From time to time an unnecessary conference or congress of representatives of the War Industry Committees would be held, at which the main subject for discussion was not technical or organizational but political: the regime did not measure up to the tasks before the country, the government was inspired by dark forces and was leading the country to destruction, the cabinet ought to be composed of persons in whom the country had confidence.

Obodovsky did not need persuading that Russia needed more freedom and an injection of new strength from society at large into the administrative system! But it sickened him to see people digging in and engaging in political struggle while the country was at war. It was dishonorable! And dangerous to Russia.

True, the regime had shown itself to be totally unprepared for the tempo and pressure of events in the war. No other European country had been fully prepared either, but their way of life was more dynamic, and their rulers were not in a complacent trance. Russia was too slow turning herself around. So everybody had to show as much speed as he could. And the more self-seeking Russia's ostensible helpers proved to be, the more desperately the real ones must exert themselves.

Dmitriev's powerful chest heaved a sigh, and he turned his big head to look at Obodovsky.

"I've got one senior fitter working on the trench gun, Malozemov, who says on the quiet, 'Do whatever you can to stop the strike, Mikhail Dmitrievich. None of us old-timers, none of us skilled men want it. We'll work till we drop, we'll do anything you like, only save us from the hooligans. We don't dare go against them ourselves.' And that's just it—we've got good-for-nothings and common laborers giving the skilled men their orders."

That was how strikes always came about in Russia, beginning with the first, famous one at the Obukhov factory. The workers are walking along to the factory with nothing unusual on their minds. But toughs with caps pulled down over their eyes are standing there at the crossroads, some of them strays from other factories, and they stop each one: hold on, comrade, there's going to be a strike. And anybody who won't stop is hit over the head with sticks or stones. Those already on the shop floor are ordered out. Anybody who doesn't come out is pelted with nuts and bolts. By now they've taught the men to move without waiting for that—they just block the doors and shout, "Attention, comrades, we are going on strike."

"Remember that skilled worker at Nikolaev last winter—Voronovoy? He said no to the strike so they did him in—with a revolver. No attempt was made to find the murderer: he'd killed a nobody, not a Grand Duke. Whole factories are lost that way. And cities."

He drummed loudly on the desk.

"No, we can't let this go on! We're just getting cowardly. If we're against abuse of power at all times and in every form, if we've never in our lives given in to the autocratic variety, why give in to any other bully? What was the point of it all if we're just going to change one oppressor for another? It's disgraceful to be afraid of the autocratic regime, but is fear of stone-throwing hooligans any less so? The working class? I'll tell them what I tell you."

When Lysva was in an uproar, and the workers had killed the manager, he had calmed them down. Resistance only made Obodovsky more stubborn. It was the story of his life. He wanted to spring from his chair, sling his topcoat over his shoulders and a scarf around his neck, cram his cap on any which way, and rush for the tram, get down to the factory.

He was pulled up by a sudden thought.

"Isn't it just the same in Western Europe? Only they don't throw stones and hide their faces. They set up picket lines instead. Industry is militarized now, of course, but they used to organize strike pickets: we're on strike, so you people next door mustn't breathe without permission. What's that if not abuse of power? Strike if you want to, I say, that's your right as an individual, but I have a right not to strike, so don't touch me. No, I don't call that civilized. Why bring all that to Russia?"

His anxious brows twitched incessantly. Cooling down a little, he said, "Maybe the very concept of freedom is flawed? We somehow haven't thought about it enough."

When did we engineers part company with the workers? In 1905 we supported them with petitions, and resigned to show solidarity. We used to go down the pit in the same cage. Then a rift opened up and the engineers were left standing on the owners' side, not with the workers. Nowadays it's difficult to cross the divide, there's no mutual trust, we're the gentry. And any engineer who tries reasoning with workers like a human being, like an older brother, is attempting that somersault in which so many gentlefolk broke their necks in the last century.

How can we work together in the same factory without mutual trust?

But, then, what answer had the workers ever been given, except by the police and the Cossacks? How often had anyone addressed them as "fellow countrymen"?

Dmitriev too was disconcerted by this damnable trait in the educated Russian character. But it was impossible to wipe the educated look from your face. You had to act. Do something about the trench gun, to start with. If the infantry battalions were to have it for the spring campaign there was not a day to lose. But the job called for willing collaborators, not hired mercenaries.

"Ye-e-es, well . . ." Dmitriev hadn't moved, he was still sitting sideways, one arm crooked over the chair back. "Suppose we told the soldiers in the trenches that the gun exists but they won't get it because men are striking for some reason or other . . . would it make the slightest sense to any man there?"

To the rescue! Into the fray! Action now! Overturn all obstacles! That was what Obodovsky understood best and usually did, and he was ready to drop everything there and then and set off for the factory. But, mellowed by the years, he was more aware of one unfortunate failing in himself—his impetuosity, his reluctance to believe that others could act in time and no less effectively, that Russia did in fact have good people and plenty of them.

From this bare cupboard of a room, without a single machine tool, or so much as a rough file, littered with nothing but blueprints and newspapers, the Obukhov foundry and engineering shop on the Neva side were not a mere eight versts away but over a mountain. So what could they possibly do to speed up the trench gun?

But just seeing each other had given them all the help they needed. Dmitriev's resolve, made before his arrival, showed in his intent look: "Right, I'll go. And speak to them. I'll get the two key shops together and simply tell them what's what. Tell them what the trench mortar means and why we mustn't go slow with it. I've arranged with the management to address a meeting when the shift ends today. There's just one thing, Akimovich, it's got to be done in agreement with the Workers' Group. They have to help. That's why I'm here."

"The Workers' Group?" Obodovsky thought about it. "You're right, of course. But you don't know how contrary they've become. They're nailed down so tightly by all those party slogans that they can't make a move of their own. The Mensheviks reign supreme, and I can't talk to them. I start swearing at them. Still, having workers' representatives at the center was the right idea. Kozma is sure to be there now, let's go and try our luck."

He shot out of his chair.

They had to hurry along Nevsky, cross the road, and go down Liteiny Prospect.

[31]

Since then the first war had ended, the smoke of revolution had cleared, the country had been flattened by Soviet steamrollers (and the Cheka had shot Obodovsky), there had been another war, no happier for us than the first, and the Soviet steamrollers had rolled again, but all those who saw Gvozdev in the Spassk division of Steplag in the third decade of the captivity from which he would never escape say that even at seventy, with four numbers slapped on him, Kozma Antonovich preserved, in his eyes and on his brow, that peculiar childlike radiance, that look of startled vulnerability.

His early life had been simple and untroubled: want had cut short his childhood games, but as a youngster he had a marvelous time laboring for his father, workdays were good and holidays were good, and it left him with a firm back, strong muscles, and sober ways. He was as much at home in the dance as behind the plow, and loved to lead the singing (when he got to Petersburg he never missed Chaliapin at the House of the People). He married at twenty, and took his wife to Rtishchevo, where he was a skillful and diligent mechanic at the railway junction. Being an engine driver's helper was even better. How they flew along! Then—the revolution, and there was no hiding from it. Everybody became a revolutionary. After that they spent three quiet years in Saratov. Nor did Petersburg disturb their peace to begin with: when war broke out Kozma was already one of the senior turners on the third floor at Ericsson's, where all the finest metalworkers in Petersburg were concentrated. His work always went with a swing: lathe, cutting tools, and metal all did what he asked, and because of that other workers began calling him by his name and patronymic—Kozma Antonovich—before his years required them to do so.

This happy state of equilibrium might have lasted in different times, but not in that strange time of political parties, slogans, and war. A year had now passed since all Petersburg factories were called upon to nominate electors, who in turn would choose a Workers' Group to represent the opinion and the will of the Russian working class employed in war industries. The times were such that there was no avoiding involvement. And since Petersburg had grown used to passing itself off as all Russia (and Russia was used to its doing so), and since Ericsson's was one of the newest and liveliest factories in Petersburg, and the liveliest and most active shop in Ericsson's six-story building was that on the third floor, Kozma was suddenly pushed further and further to the fore, out of the crowd, until no other shoulders and elbows touched his own. First on the list of candidates from the factory, from the Vyborg side, from the city, from Russia as a whole, Gvozdev finally stepped to the front of the stage as Russian worker No. 1.

A step far beyond the stride of any ordinary man. Kozma might have got off lightly, might have sat hidden among hundreds of other delegates, might never have been elected top man, might have remained at ease and obscure, if that first meeting of electors in September 1915 had not been twisted out of shape, denatured and wrecked by the Bolsheviks. The distinctive characteristic of the Bolsheviks is well known: the Mensheviks and the Socialist Revolutionaries were all factions and frictions, there were always thirteen different opinions in each party, whereas the Bolsheviks marched in step, and whether they were voting or just yelling it was with a single voice. Uninvited, unelected, with no mandate at all, they gate-crashed the electoral meeting in force—it was simply impossible to hold the doors against them. They burst in yelling that this meeting should not be happening, that nobody should be delegated—down with the war! down with the imperialist bourgeoisie! One of their people, a certain Kudryashov from the Putilov factory, had wormed his way into the Presidium expecting to become chairman if his side prevailed. But he was recognized, and the workers saw through the trick: he was not Kudryashov and he wasn't from the Putilov factory. The Bolsheviks had sidelined Kudryashov, the delegate elected by the Putilov factory, stolen his instructions and altered them to suit themselves. Their howling and shouting disrupted the meeting, so that no elections took place.

Kozma had always attached more importance to fairness than to anything else. From his early years he liked to see things work out justly, fairly. What most vexed him at the meeting was the unfairness of it. Why did it have to be a shouting match? He described what had happened in a newspaper (helped by literate Mensheviks). He refused to back down, and managed to get another meeting called for November in the Engineers' Club. This time the doors were strictly controlled and only delegates were admitted, no one could just walk in. So Kozma willy-nilly became chairman of the Workers' Group. The Workers' Group was to act in association with the War Industry Committee, to assist it while at the same time protecting workers' interests.

At this second meeting speakers said calmly and sensibly what they thought the Workers' Group was and what it should be doing. Emelyanov, from the Tube Factory, said: We oppose this war, of course, but what must we do to get peace? Russia's salvation, of course, lies not in military defense, but in the triumph of democracy. The government's present to the working class has a sting in its tail, and we must unite all the living forces of the country for the struggle for democracy. Marx tells us that the farther east you go, the dirtier the bourgeoisie is, and it's especially dirty in Russia, but we shall be there criticizing it and egging it on against a regime on its last legs. And through the War Industry Committee we shall also be helping to organize workers' democracy.

Breido, from the Lessner factory, also made a literate speech. Guchkov and Konovalov, he said, are our class enemies, but at certain moments in political life we go hand in hand with the bourgeoisie and give it a bit of a push to the left. It's no good just shouting, "We're against everything," when our nation's existence is in the balance. The Progressive Bloc's demands can do us as much good as they can for them: if all Russian citizens are given their freedom it must apply to the workers as much as to anybody. The bourgeoisie is our ally against the government, and together with it we can revolutionize society at large.

Delegates from Westinghouse said that by joining the War Industry Committee they would be able to prevent increases in productivity at the workers' expense.

A speaker from the Putilov factory: We can't take the view that Germany must be smashed. But we can't let Russia be smashed either. Defending ourselves against the Germans doesn't mean that we support the Tsarist government. Russia belongs to Russian working people. By defending Russia the workers are defending their own road to freedom.

A speaker from the aircraft factory: If we stand aside from the war the cry will go up that we have played into the hands of the Germans and of reaction. Of course, we are joining the War Industry Committee not to manufacture shells but to organize the people's forces!

Another speaker from the Tube Factory: We're joining the committees not to increase shell production but to jolt the country out of its sleeping sickness, to make it end its silence.

They all seemed to be in agreement. Nobody contradicted anybody, yet there was a mounting unease: rack their brains as they might, they weren't really sure why they were joining the War Industry Committee. The guard at the door was as strict as ever, and no Bolsheviks got through into the hall except those elected in the factories, a small minority. Yet everyone who spoke seemed to have a wall of enraged Bolsheviks before him, and tried to speak cautiously and unprovocatively, so as not to anger them. What was said seemed clear enough, yet the fog thickened. They spoke in favor of elections, but the loose ends were not tied up. By then it was Kozma's turn and there was no avoiding it. Speaking not at his workbench, but from a platform, he felt somehow shaky, his ears seemed to be stopped up and only half heard what he was saying, the hall swam, and faced with the Bolsheviks yet again, he felt that this second meeting was all his fault. His mind could not grapple with it all. And what came out was not what Kozma really thought: that we must help our brothers at the front. To say that seemed for some reason impermissible. What came out was somehow apologetic: joining the War Industry Committee is the only way out for the workers, our only hope of emerging from the underground into which we have been driven and in which we are being stifled. The central question in life, he said, was the replacement of landowner power by that of the bourgeoisie, which was now the strongest class economically. (The Mensheviks had given him a few words on a scrap of paper, but he had mislaid it. The few sentences he had memorized he reproduced in a form all his own.) So then, a change of the existing political order was dictated by the infallible logic of life itself. But that did not mean that anyone who defended his country was by doing so refusing to participate in the class struggle. True, the Tsarist government had proved incapable of defending the country, but if Russia lost the war, inasmuch as the German proletariat had betrayed its oath of solidarity, the German Junkers would put a halter around our necks and turn back the wheels of industry in our country. The conditions for successful class warfare would no longer exist, and the workers would be the first to feel the effects. So the choice they must make in spite of everything was to put the weight of worker power into the scales, for the time being, on the side of the bourgeoisie. "We can win freedom only by defending the nation."

The Bolsheviks remained an inconsiderable minority, and in defiance of them a Workers' Group made up of Mensheviks, with a sprinkling of Socialist Revolutionaries, was elected, but they all felt so sheepish, they were all so conscious of the wall of angry faces out there on the street, that having chosen by vote those who would go and assist in defending Russia they went on to vote, under no compulsion, in favor of the directive drafted by the Bolsheviks: in joining the War Industry Committee the workers took no responsibility for its work: the war was being waged not by Russia but by the governing class, for the seizure of markets, the government was irresponsible, the Duma cowardly, hence the aim of the Workers' Group must be not to help factories in defense work but to convene an All-Russian Workers' Congress and prepare themselves to take power as a provisional Soviet of Workers' Deputies. War or no war, the eight-hour workday must be introduced—immediately; complete freedom to exercise trade unions' rights previously won, and also the inviolability of the person, must be guaranteed—immediately; all land must be—immediately—transferred to the peasants; and there must be an immediate amnesty for all political enemies of the government, and for all terrorists still in jail or at hard labor in places of exile.

Shackled by these instructions, and mystified by its own existence— had it been created to help industry defend the country or to fight Tsarist autocracy?—the Workers' Group reported to Guchkov's Central War Industry Committee and was given two rooms with a telephone, and a salaried secretary with an assistant and two clerks, also paid by the committee, in its second building, on the Liteiny Prospect, beyond the junction with Zhukovskaya Street. There it operated openly as the only legal workers' organization in Russia. (Trade unions and workers' clubs had been suspended at the beginning of the war, and there were few factories in which shop stewards had survived, even where the Bolsheviks did not prevent their election.) The Workers' Group was given the right to circularize its branches in other towns, to disseminate its proceedings and resolutions—not in the form of grubby little underground leaflets, but exquisitely printed on the best white paper—to make the rounds of towns and factories, to assemble large bodies of workers for consultation without a police presence. It even, without authorization, proclaimed its own political immunity, equating itself with the party groups in the State Duma! (Left to himself, Kozma would never have thought of that, but he was persuaded to do it by the two advisers who had been imposed upon him.) In wartime conditions these were remarkable achievements.

But Kozma went into his new accommodation with the same blockage in his ears and blur before his eyes. It was like standing at your lathe worrying that the cutting tool might dig too deep and the part jump from the bar. It wasn't at all clear which was the main enemy—Germany or the autocracy? The other fifteen members of the group remained at their places of work, and came in for meetings or to sit around for a while, but Kozma became a fixture—no point knocking around among Ericsson's machines. What he really should be doing, what lead he should give, he had no idea, but the Mensheviks gave him two brisk and businesslike advisers to lean on, Gutovsky and Pumpyansky: they occupied the secretarial posts, and relegated actual secretarial work to the clerks.

Gutovsky was known to Social Democrats as "the Gas" because of the speed with which he expanded in all directions. (His nickname was originally "Acetylene"—a play on his patronymic, Anitsetovich.) There was nothing Gutovsky didn't know about the working class and social democracy! He was simply omniscient, and could answer any question before you'd finished asking. He had brought out a newspaper of his own at one time, and composed leaflets by the dozen. Pumpyansky, though no Gas, was also swift to take off and to take over. Paired, they were better still at explaining and expounding—not always in perfect harmony, but discords were soon resolved. Without those two Kozma would have been lost.

So some sort of order and stability was achieved. Guchkov's committee was satisfied with the group (though it was as helpful to the revolutionary cause as to the cause of defense). In the front room they discussed the organization of the workforce for production, while in the back room they also engaged in conspiratorial activity, drafting and disseminating illegal leaflets, and to everybody who traveled around Russia visiting provincial workers' groups they gave overt instructions to assist defense industry and clandestine instructions to sabotage it. Kozma couldn't keep up with everything that was done and written and circulated in the name of the Workers' Group!

He had bitten off more than he could chew, and wondered why on earth his name was Gvozdev (perhaps from *gvozd*, "nail"). If there ever had been any "nails" in his family he didn't think he was one of them. (More likely than not the Gvozdevs were originally just "smiths.")

For all the wise words he heard, he knew in his heart, if he was honest with himself, that Russia must be defended against Germany. It made no sense to be stirring up revolution in time of war. When his head was in too much of a whirl there was one guiding light: those soldiers—aren't they our brothers? Shouldn't we be thinking of them?

So when, shortly after the election of the Workers' Group, some sort of infectious itch went around Petrograd, with some madman trying to talk workers into a strike on 22 January 1916, a general strike, and not just for one day, intended to overthrow the Tsar, Kozma exercised firm leadership. The men must be restrained from striking, the time was not right. And he himself went around the factories telling them so.

He succeeded in restraining them.

The upshot was that when 22 January came a fight flared up at Ericson's. Auxiliary workers from the lower floors and the yard, egged on by agitators, rushed the third floor and assaulted the skilled men, because they, the "Gvozdevites," had demanded that the strike question should be decided not by a shouting match but fairly, by a clear vote. Hammers, wrenches, steel punches, and iron bars were used as weapons, heavy bolts were hurled around, Gvozdev himself was hit with a stool, a lot of the equipment manufactured on the third floor was smashed, and some of Gvozdev's supporters were shoved down the stairs. But although the whole management had taken flight earlier, the Gvozdevites stood their ground, and prevented the strike.

How the Bolsheviks reviled them, unsparingly and without exception, spat on them and flung mud at them in all the unpaved back streets on the Vyborg side, calling them traitors to the working class, lackeys of the imperialist bourgeoisie, a bunch of political rogues and renegades who had traded their proletarian intransigence for the honor of sitting in easy chairs at the same table as Stolypin's comrade-in-arms (meaning Guchkov). Then they fomented a rowdy campaign among Petrograd workers to recall the Workers' Group: the proletariat must not join bourgeois organizations!

Kozma was in it up to his neck! Nobody had ever abused him like that before. But he understood very well that this was no time to accept "recall," that only by sitting where he was could he champion the workers' rights and privileges. To keep his seat he had to make concessions to the Bolsheviks, whatever their game was, and say one thing while thinking another: say that the aim of the Workers' Group was the complete demolition of the regime, or that the government was planning a Jewish pogrom, when there was no hint of anything of the kind. Or demand things from the factory owners that they could not possibly provide. Or howl that the militarization of the factories meant the reintroduction of serfdom, although it was obvious to everybody that this was the least disruptive way of regulating jobs, the food supply for the workers, and exemption from the draft. You had to join without question in barking at and attacking the regime. The large gatherings of workers, ostensibly "commissions" of the Workers' Group, in the Guchkov committee's main assembly hall discussed not the defense of the country, indeed no, but the government of the future, which must be not just "responsible to parliament," as the Duma demanded, but a "Provisional Revolutionary Government," with democratic socialists among its members. (Though Kolya couldn't for the life of him see why the need for such a government had suddenly become so pressing.) Or else they would be declaring that the people must bypass governments and take peace negotiations into their own hands.

Yes! Yes! said the whisperers in Gvozdev's ear. While outside on the street there were cries of "traitor," and men even broke into the offices on Liteiny to shout it! Whereas Plekhanov wrote from Paris to say that revolutionary activity in wartime was treason!

Yes, Kozma was in it up to his neck.

Nor was it just the Bolsheviks. He was harassed by the quick-footed Interdistrict group and the sharp-tongued Internationalist-Initiativists: "We have certainly not authorized the Gvozdevites to speak for the whole Russian proletariat! They are sacrilegiously usurping the name of the working masses!"

Even Chkheidze and Kerensky shamefacedly shrank from the Workers' Group so as not to soil their hands.

And the workers who had elected the group grew restive and had to be pacified somehow.

The whole Samara section even instructed the central body "not to forge cannon and kill German comrades, but to obtain the separation of the church from the state, the confiscation of gentry land, and a democratic republic." Kozma was by then so befogged that he read this three times without seeing how nonsensical it was. Separation of the church? If they say so—must be right. Confiscation? Those are their orders—must be done. Aha! Fatheads! You've pulled a boner there! You don't forge cannon, you cast them! Probably written by some seminarian.

And where did Guchkov come in? All Social Democratic resolutions and leaflets assured Kozma (who had in fact been provided with a Social Democratic Party card himself) that the Russian bourgeoisie, led by the bloodthirsty Guchkov, was using this war not for the defense of Russia but to line their own pockets and take power by easy stages.

Maybe it was true? How could you look into somebody else's heart? And mugs like us draw in our horns and give way to them.

But when he went to the Workers' Group, there was Aleksandr Ivanovich in person, a shortish man with a slight limp, a rather unhealthy look about him, and a ponderous manner, shaking his hand and saying: "My dear Kozma Antonovich! You're a Russian, and I'm a Russian. We speak the same language, one look and we understand each other. The whole future of Russia depends on what is happening now and how this war ends. If we lose we shall be enslaved by Germany, perhaps for many decades. I know that the workers have long been oppressed and denied their rights. There's a big backlog of accounts to be settled, a lot of sores to be healed. But you and your friends do feel for Russia—of course you do. And you have the political sense to know that this is not the time to settle those accounts, not the time to open those sores. It isn't only you—we too, the whole of Russian society, have a grim reckoning to present to the government. But let us wait, let us finish the war first, we must not let Russia's very backbone be broken. The workers will listen to you. You mustn't tire of explaining to them that every day on strike is a stab in the back for our army, that it means death for our fellow Russians. For your, and our, brothers."

Kozma listened to such speeches, looking closely into Guchkov's eyes, which were not diamonds after all, but like everybody else's, eyes full of entreaty and trust and swollen from illness. (In the first few weeks of the Workers' Group's existence Guchkov was in fact supposed to be dying, and bulletins were published which seemed to anticipate his death.) And Kozma melted, felt that they were soul mates, and agreed with every word.

"No, Aleksandr Ivanovich, we won't nurse our grievances. We were oppressed all right. The owners never gave us a hearing. I'm not talking about Ericsson's, but more out-of-the-way places. It would have been better for them if they'd woken up before the war, of course. But if they've begun to realize, it still isn't too late. Don't think we don't know that if the Germans break through into Russia they'll put a yoke on our necks and gobble up all our bread."

Keep it simple, leave political parties out of it, speak your natural language, and what was there, really, to understand?

As they sat there, on two uncompromisingly hard chairs, facing each other across a simple desk, Kozma could not get it into his head that the man before him was the leader of the imperialist bourgeoisie, and the comrade-in-arms of that man of blood—Stolypin.

"I do understand, Aleksan' Ivanych. You'll have our support. That's why we've come here."

But he was hardly ever allowed such tête-à-têtes, not even for a minute at a time, because he was not just Kozma Gvozdev, an individual and a free agent, he was one of a team, tied by party loyalty to the brainiest, busiest, writing-est, talking-est, indefatigably sharp-eyed secretaries, set to watch over him, and if they missed him for a moment they came loudly flapping in pursuit.

"Oh dear, Kozma Antonych, what have you done now? We'll have the Bolsheviks talking about the Gvozdev-Guchkov Bloc! Have you thought about that?"

Kozma was not his own man. Unlike that other Kozma—Minin—he could not go forth and cry, "Rise, people of Russia, save your motherland!" It was ". . . just whom were you trying to save, Kozma Antonych? The Romanov dynasty? Together with the Black Hundreds and the liberals? Then who's to do our job and stir up class contradictions?"

"Why, the Initiativists will disown us!"

"The Internationalists will back away from us!"

"Especially the Siberian Zimmerwaldists!"

So they didn't allow Kozma to do much talking on his own account. It had to be with a secretary on either side, his shoulders, as it were, pinned between them, his head not free, feeling as if he were in harness.

"Defeating Germany, Aleksandr Ivanych, is of no importance at all to the working class. If they don't want strikes let the factory owners tighten their belts a bit. You say the sores can wait, but our patience is exhausted."

And if Guchkov was leaving for the Crimea to continue his treatment, Acetylene would compose a letter for Kozma, allowing him to sign it, but not to alter a single word. "Our opinion, my own and that of all my comrades, is that 'social peace' is a screen for exploitation, and that as long as there is a class of industrialists the working class will never accept social peace, or even an armistice! Victory over Germany is the path to future conquests for the ruling classes."

Not so very long ago Kozma stood at his bench, picked up his wages on Saturday, and went off home with not a care in the world. He turned out metal parts as he knew best how to, and nobody jogged his elbow. Now he was tied hand and foot by this glib pair. Before a thought could take shape in his head and descend to his throat, Gutovsky and Pumpyansky would feed him an answer, or several answers at once, giving him no time to think. That was what particularly baffled him—that they supplied several answers simultaneously. All of them swift, all different, and all correct.

Take the hardest question of all: Since we're all brothers, shouldn't we—really and truly, between ourselves—be strengthening Russia's defenses?

Well, the first thing to remember is that this war hinders the liberation struggle of the working class. On the other hand, all peoples have the right to defend themselves. And self-defense can lead to revolution. So defense of the country is the same thing as relentless struggle with autocracy—something the Bolsheviks refuse to understand.

A bipartite national policy!

So we are what they call defensists?

Tut-tut! Not another word, comrade! "Defensist" is an opprobrious name used to brand accomplices of the reactionary clique. We are revolutionary defensists, and that term embodies a radically different meaning.

Which must mean that . . . We should work? With all our might?

Sh-sh-sh! You must understand the mobilization of industry, Kozma Antonych, not in a narrowly technical sense, but as social and political mobilization; in other words, we can't allow the franchised strata alone to mobilize. However, the militarization of the factories on the pretense of "mobilization" is a very great danger to the interests of the working class, a new form of factory feudalism.

Wire frames rested on Gutovsky's prominent ears, but even through his glasses his eyes were sharp, quick, challenging.

As he wagged his head over his lessons, Kozma's youthful straw mop flopped over his face and he swept it back with his hand. His teachers were both around thirty, five years younger than himself, but they had found time to get all this great wisdom from books, latched on to it, adapted it for use. Lucky they were there to help, or a man could come to grief in that little room.

If that's how it is, how do we defend ourselves against—what d'you call it? Fideolism? Just by striking?

Well, there are times when the worker is left with no means of fighting for his basic needs except by disorganizing production. But on the other hand, the Bolshevik policy of strikes for the sake of striking and their antiquated, pigheaded boycott campaigns are the least promising method of class warfare. The Bolsheviks ruthlessly exploit the political inexperience of the broad popular masses.

They were both so sharp, those secretaries, that any bit of paper you sent out, any instruction you gave by telephone, they were there first, turning it this way and that, sniffing it all over, sizing it up. How would the Western socialists take it? Would the O.K. bunch approve? What would be the reaction of the Reunionists? the Menshevik Internationalists? the Petersburg Initiative group? And of course the Interdistrict group? Toughest of all—like having a saw blade across your throat and a gag in your mouth—you wondered what deadly response the Bolsheviks would come up with. They, the Bolsheviks, had to be watched more closely than the autocracy.

If some newspaper took it into its head to praise the Workers' Group for its contribution to defense, for its loyalty to the motherland, it was in a way flattering, but the secretaries would be in agonies: if you denied it you'd be damaging your own work, if you didn't the Bolsheviks would have their claws in you.

So every sentence, spoken or written, however well-rounded, must have written into it, tagged onto it, such phrases as "fully conscious of our obligations to the international proletariat" . . . "in the words of the Copenhagen Workers' Congress" . . .

If Kozma could not make a move without his secretaries interfering, they too, and even the senior Mensheviks in the O.K., never took a step independently, never made self-confident decisions, but always looked timidly leftward, worrying about the harsh words the Bolsheviks might have for them.

The Bolsheviks loudly threatened to "run Gvozdev and those other bastards out on a wheelbarrow." Meaning to the rubbish heap—workers used to do that with unpopular foremen, and once dumped they could never reassert themselves. What hurt Kozma, though, was not the Bolshevik pack as a whole, but Sashka Shlyapnikov, their head man. They could say what they liked, but Sashka himself had signed the "Gvozdevite Traitors" proclamation on the very day when Kozma was cracked on the head with a stool. He and Sashka had worked in the same shop, side by side, they were almost the same age, competing to see who could shave metal closest and cleanest. And now . . .

The spilt peas had gone fourteen different ways.

There was no end to the secondhand abuse that Sashka heaped on Kozma: Guchkov had him on a leash, he was a middleman dividing up orders between capitalists . . .

Why, oh why, Sashka, do you daub me with pitch just because I've acted as conciliator and prevented a strike? What's bad about that? Surely it's work, not strikes, that keeps factories going? Suppose we go on striking till German helmets enter Petrograd—is that really what you want? Your trouble is when you get one thing fixed in your head you think you know it all. But what do we know, my friend? Right— our grandfathers lived in the woods and knew every little path. But here there are huge chimneys sticking up, giving off smoke so you can't see through it, and broken stones under your feet that nothing leaves a live trail on. We see only what we see: the policeman at the cross- roads, and the Parviainens, the Aivazes, the Nobels, and the Rozen- kranzes, driving up in their carriages and driving off again. They wouldn't even give us a hearing before, now they show respect, say, "We know your needs, but let's finish the war first." True, they might have come to their senses earlier, but people are all the same, they do nothing till lightning strikes . . . Maybe we should believe them, Sasha? Trying to settle old scores with the German armies watching—what does that make us look like? You and I ought to get together and talk it all over: why are we behaving like enemies? A nail's no good without a cap,* nor a cap without a nail. Haven't you ever stopped and asked

---

*"A nail's no good without a cap": a play on the names Gvozdev and Shlyapnikov. Gvozdev is perhaps from *gvozd*, nail; Shlyapnikov suggests *shlyapa*, hat. [*Trans.*]

yourself, Sasha: What if I've been wrong all along? Can I get inside
somebody else's head and think for him? You've said all those hard
things about me. "The foul ulcer of Gvozdevism!" What's the point
of that, boys? It makes my flesh creep. I've got smart alecks sniffing
around me all the time, and you've got some of your own: they're
mighty quick with the pen and with the tongue, they know it all. Do
you trust *your* group? Watch out you don't burn your fingers."

Gvozdev's counselors were never at a loss. However things went,
whatever awkward turn they took, these people could always twist them
around so that what had happened was exactly what the representatives of workers' democracy had foreseen and pointed to long ago!
Kozma could only listen, eyes popping.

They had a pat answer for everything. A rumor went around that
the strikes weren't spontaneous, that strike funds received contributions from unknown sources—could it be German money?

"No!" said Acetylene heatedly. "German subversive activities have
nothing to do with it, only a stupid know-nothing could think it does.
The reason is the domination of the gentry-bureaucratic clique, whose
whole system of government consists of cynical disregard of the people's interests, and continual provocation. These strikes are a warning
that we cannot go on as we are."

That much was true.

And here they were again, sitting in the back room—Kozma at his
desk, wearing a Russian cross-buttoning blouse under his overall jacket,
Gutovsky and Pumpyansky, each at one end of his desk, in identical
black coats and stand-up collars complete with ties, reasoning with
their president, explaining yet again what he ought to think about a
variety of currently important matters.

The latest hot potato was the Guchkov committee's cavalier treatment of its own Workers' Group. As part of the committee, the group
could not print and circulate any document, resolution, or appeal without the agreement of the other members. (People were afraid that the
group might call openly for revolution, in the name of the committee
as a whole.) "In effect," Gutovsky said, seething, "the committee is
making the need for coordination an excuse for censoring our activities!"

"Censoring our opinions and our views!" Pumpyansky added, wig-
gling his fingers to make it clearer. He had no revolutionary Siberian
past, like Gutovsky's, and had to assert his own importance at every
turn.

"But that does violence to the freedom of opinion of the workers'
representatives!"

"And at once isolates the Workers' Group from the working
masses!"

This was how they always explained things, many times over, as if

Kozma might forget the moment he crossed the threshold. They were particularly insistent that every question was complicated, very complicated, very, very complicated. So that Kozma, for his part, began to fear that he might not understand, might forget, might get muddled over quite simple matters . . . except that there didn't seem to be any simple matters left.

"A definite line has to be drawn," Gutovsky said, drawing it, unwaveringly and precisely, with the edge of his hand on the desk. "A line beyond which we cannot go!"

"Otherwise we will have to ask ourselves whether our presence on the committee is not futile!" Pumpyansky said, wagging his finger for emphasis.

"It's particularly dangerous in view of the recall campaign the Bolsheviks are mounting against the Workers' Group!"

"It undermines the significance which the Workers' Group should have as a class weapon!"

Kozma well remembered how lightly he had moved around the factory, how lightly he had run up the stairs, two steps at a time, only last autumn. Now, sitting day in and day out at this desk, he seemed to have grown heavy, to have taken root, so that he and his chair were like one stubbornly rooted stump growing out of the floor. Growing and unable to rise. He wanted to straighten up, but could only brace his shoulders and stretch backward.

He was under a spell. Bewitched.

"Don't be taken in by sweet talk, Antonych. When you're dealing with Guchkov and his bunch don't forget that they are the tried and tested leaders of capitalism's militant organizations."

"They're out to trap us with their talk of 'national unity,' Antonych—and 'national unity' is transformed into the union of large-scale industrial capitalism with the existing regime."

Yes, things were looking bad for the Workers' Group. They did somehow seem to have fallen into a trap again. Yet Aleksandr Ivanovich seemed to be a decent guy.

"We ought to be checking up on them, not they on us!" Anitsetovich said. "We can't even be sure they're trying to solve problems of military technology in the country's best interests!"

"Against its interests, you can be sure!" Moiseevich, not to be outdone, fully concurred.

Dear, oh dear. Kozma *was* in a quandary.

His upper lip was raised like that of a puzzled child; his hair, newly washed and silky, tumbled over his eyes, which were fixed in entreaty on his teachers.

"Do you really think the danger from outside is what matters?" Gutovsky flapped his black elbows as if attempting to take off.

"Is the danger of a military defeat what matters most?" Pumpyansky's finger emerged from a black sleeve to draw menacing lines in the air.

"What of their predatory scheme to annex Galicia?"

"Their oppression of Poland?"

"Their greedy designs on Constantinople?"

"Their anti-Semitic pogroms policy?"

"D'you call that defending the country?"

"And their criminal scheme to use yellow labor?"

Yellow labor! There was this one melting point at which all working-class parties and groups, and the working class as a whole, fused instead of fragmenting. Beginning last year, it had become fashionable to indenture Chinese labor—originally for the Murmansk railroad, but now, it seemed, for Petrograd as well. What next?

"Will unruly workers be sent into the trenches, and the Chinese into the factories?"

"Which would be the end of the revolutionary movement!"

But the crafty bourgeois had Kozma fooled. Why shouldn't the Chinese be allowed to work? Wouldn't that be . . . you know . . . what they call "internationalism"?

"Oh dear, no! Allowing greedy industrialists to exploit the Chinese even more inhumanely?"

"Not to leave the Chinese defenseless is in fact our prime international duty!"

"Indentured yellow labor is blatant slave-trading!"

"Which is why the Petrograd proletariat cannot allow them into the capital!"

At that point the door was flung open and in burst not the blood-stained Konovalov in person, not Ryabushinsky, but Engineer Obodovsky from the subcommittee for Military-Technical Aid.

A worthy accomplice of the capitalists in question.

Or an unworthy underling.

He came in at a run, in his overcoat, but hatless. He was always in a hurry, with an absentminded look about him except for his sharp eyes.

The absentmindedness was for the Menshevik secretaries, the sharp eyes for Kozma.

Behind him—someone else from the technical team, a big dark hulk in a leather jacket.

Obodovsky hastily introduced him—"Engineer Dmitriev!"—as he covered the space between himself and the desk in one stride to shake hands with Kozma.

Kozma was so firmly grafted onto chair and floor that there was no tearing himself away. He shook hands with Obodovsky but couldn't take a step toward Dmitriev, who in turn greeted him from a distance.

While Gutovsky and Pumpyansky, elbows defensively at the ready, refrained from greetings.

Obodovsky was in too much of a hurry to sit down.

"Kozma Antonych!" he burst out, looking very worried. "I must ask you . . ." Then he turned his eyes upon the startled, battle-ready Mensheviks and his tone became more tentative.

"Perhaps you and I should have a talk."

But why all the secrecy?

What was his imperialist ulterior motive?

"By all means."

"By all means!" Their suspicions aroused, the nimble pair pointed to a seat.

While Kozma, clean-shaven upper lip and sparse eyebrows raised, showed in his light brown eyes his willingness to step outside for a talk—if only he were not vegetating. He couldn't just tear up all his roots.

"What can I do for you, Pyotr Akimych?" Then, more cautiously, more austerely. "Has something happened?"

Obodovsky, still standing, was eager to get on with it.

"The Obukhov factory is holding up the trench mortar, and our infantry is shedding blood unnecessarily for want of it, blood it could save. Help us to persuade the shops working on that order to do overtime and go in on Sundays. And to prevent the strike which could happen shortly. Could you possibly get the factory commission together to handle it?"

Factory commissions, formed by the Workers' Group, were legal organizations. Formally intended to help with defense contracts. But . . .

"But the working class cannot ignore its class interests and turn factory commissions into a weapon against itself."

"That would be a move in the wrong direction, Mr. Obodovsky. But by all means let's look at all sides of the question."

They made themselves even more comfortable in their chairs, spread themselves, and prepared for action.

Obodovsky had known the Gas, then a stripling, back in 1905 in Siberia. He had been one of the loudest mouths in the Siberian Social Democratic Union, determined come what may on armed uprising. But once he was running smoothly he had squandered a great deal of paper on behalf of the Mensheviks, advised the Social Democratic group in the Duma, and now . . . here he was again. Obodovsky hadn't wasted time on such troublemakers in Irkutsk in 1905 and he certainly wasn't going to now.

"Gentlemen," he said, flinching as if attacked by gadflies, "I'm no journalist, alas. And you don't know anything about casting tolerances or turning procedures. So what is there for us to talk about?"

He looked fiercely at Gvozdev.

Gvozdev's tawny eyes answered that he would be glad to help, he even squared his shoulders—but no, nothing budged, all was stuck fast.

The Menshevik advisers were quick off the mark.

"Please, Mr. Obodovsky, don't regard us as supporters of conservative strike-ism flying false radical colors."

"In case you are capable of understanding our point of view, here it is: in present-day circumstances strikes do not benefit the working class."

"A spontaneous flare-up can even damage the working class," was Gutovsky's amendment.

"Spontaneous flare-ups," said Pumpyansky, refusing to be bettered, "only damp down and fragment the growing conflict between Russian society as a whole and the regime."

Except for the twitching of his eyebrows Obodovsky was stock-still. Did this mean that, against all expectations, all present were agreed? That help was at hand?

Dmitriev too, looking gloomily pleased, shifted from one foot to the other.

"But," said Gutovsky with a flash of his glasses and a toss of his curls, "but strikes are the only way out for a working class summarily and cynically dispatched to the front as cannon fodder."

"How indeed," said Pumpyansky, with a toss of his smooth head, "how except by striking can the working class liberate itself from the noose of the police state?"

"Defend the country, yes, but not if it means abstinence from strikes!"

"And no amount of overtime will help in a country where the people's resources are so insanely squandered."

"As so often spelled out in warnings from the revolutionary democrats . . ."

"With whom you at one time had a certain connection, Mr. Obodovsky."

It was against such renegades that the Gas's zeal burned most fiercely. It was self-seeking prodigals like Obodovsky who threw the ranks of the democratic movement into disarray.

Obodovsky was no longer looking at them, but—still standing, perplexed and questioning—at Kozma. No serpentine thoughts darted and wriggled over Kozma's broad candid brow, there was no flapping of the arms or fluttering of the fingers. His hands struggled in vain to tug the chair free of the floor, his thickset shoulders strained . . .

On either side of him they nattered on.

"The answer is not to work overtime but to smash the whole political regime from top to bottom and immediately."

"To wrest power from the irresponsible, reactionary, venal Russian government!"

Obodovsky could restrain himself no longer.

"But not to the detriment of the war effort? Not if it means greater losses for our infantry?"

But they soared out of reach, and with amazing mental nimbleness swooped from the left, then changed direction to swoop from the right. There were kaleidoscopic glimpses of the grotesque Duma's indifferentism, of a workers' democracy issuing appeals to the democracies of allied countries . . .

But what of Kozma?

And the trench mortar?

Could he or couldn't he help?

He struggled in vain to tear himself from the fatal spot to which he was grafted. But . . . but . . . The infantry! Russian infantry needlessly shedding their blood! His two paws pressing down on the desktop, his neck and his whole torso bulging with the strain—as if he were free and could rise unaided with a toss of the straw-colored foliage draped over his temples—the man turned by magic into a tree trunk suddenly spoke out boldly, in a human voice, like a tree in a fairy tale.

"All right, there's a member of our group at the Obukhov factory, Grisha Komarov. I'll phone him right away. He'll do what he can to back you up."

Gutovsky and Pumpyansky blinked, taken aback—but it was over in a quarter of a minute—they changed without changing, their features were as mobile as ever, their speech as rapid and articulate as they hurried to catch up.

"To mobilize industry? That is, of course, a possibility."

"What after all is the point of our activities? To give the working class a legal footing."

"But the working class must be extremely cautious in its choice of methods."

"And effective mobilization is impossible without complete freedom of coalition."

"And the immediate full democratization of . . ."

The engineers did not hear how it ended. They had left.

❊   ❊   ❊

. . . The traitorous Gvozdevites, yes-men of the Kadets, vampires sucking the blood of the working class . . . Government stooges . . . certain engineers who pick up a good 4,000 a year . . . It is our duty, comrades, to take up the sacred struggle, and cry out to the vampires, "Take your bloodstained hands off us!" The workers of Petersburg make known their valiant demands to all the world!

—Central Committee of the RSDRP

❊   ❊   ❊

[3 2]

Board one of the Neva steam trams—three short cars with upper decks—and it will go around the Aleksandr Nevsky monastery and the monastery settlement, then cross the Arkhangelogorodsky Bridge and come out on the Schlüsselburg Prospect. (The bridge's name no doubt means that this was the beginning of the ancient sledge route to Archangel.) Verst by verst it passes the Glassmakers' Quarter, the Empire-style granaries on the banks of the Neva, quaysides, timber barges, hay stores. It passes the Semyanin factory (not your destination), the bobbin factory (an exquisite building not a bit like a factory). Crossing the Horn it skirts the villages of Smolenskoye and Michael the Archangel, each with its own church, and the adjacent Alexander engineering plant (also not your present destination). Now, closer to the shoreline, it rolls on along the Neva where even in the war years villages from opposite banks had met at carnival time on the broad frozen expanses for a fistfight or cockfights or pigeon racing, as if these peasants were totally unaware that Peter's world-famed capital was on their doorstep. The little tram rolls on past the porcelain factory, the third oldest in Europe, set up shortly after the secret of manufacturing porcelain was discovered. Past the few remaining riverside villas built for the magnates of Anna's, Elizabeth's, and Catherine's reigns, now more and more frequently displaced by brick factory buildings and tall chimney stacks, from which black clouds crawl and billow to sully the sky and foul the Neva, drifting toward Little Okhta if the wind is in one quarter, absorbing the smoke from Okhta and from the powder factory if it is on the other. Then, passing Kurakin's villa, it finally reaches what was once Princess Vyazemsky's manor house and grounds, of which few traces have survived half a century of the steelworks founded by Engineer Obukhov, after the wretched Crimean campaign, in which much of our artillery proved useless. This works, which makes armor plating and big guns, and has its own workers' settlement of well-equipped modern two-story houses, is your destination, and you alight. (The tram will trundle on past several cemeteries, several German settlements, the Cenobitic Monastery, a few more factories—and finish up at Murzinki.)

And although you live in Petersburg—not, it is true, in one of the more pleasant quarters, but in Stremyannaya or some such place— now that you have trundled so many versts, with constant changes of scene, of people and of ideas, traveling not as an idle sightseer but with carefully planned business to transact, understanding what is done in this place and indeed eager to lend a hand—suddenly, from the far end of the Schlüsselburg Prospect, you see and feel about the famous city quite differently. Hefting this long, long Neva end of the lever, wriggling it in your hand you discover that the fulcrum of the whole system is not there but here: that the center of gravity of this much lauded Palmyra or Venice of the North is not the glittering Nevsky Prospect, nor the splendid stone-built Morskaya, nor the gilded spires, nor Rossi's colonnades, nor Felten's grilles, past which our legendary poets absently strolled, but the wrought-iron railings themselves, the multitude of lions, the chariot of Victory on its great arch, the very bridges with their cast-iron (or are they living?) horses, the Anichkov Bridge, the Nikolai Bridge, the Blue Bridge, the Chain Bridge, all cast and forged here, far beyond the Neva Gate, here at the Alexander engineering plant. From here you know for sure that the real weight of Petersburg does not lie in what the world at large sees as, and means by, Petersburg. No, that huge agglomeration, gaudy by day, ablaze with light by night, that great, greedy huddle of palaces, theaters, restaurants, shops, seen from here is a wanton, reckless, cynical overload at the far end of the lever, dangerous just because it is at the far end of the arm and threatens to tip the balance.

This was where the important, the sensible work was done, producing not only those so entertaining wrought-iron railings and chariots but many sensible, necessary things; the first Russian locomotive, the ships on the Neva, iron and steel castings of all sizes, from the most enormous to the minute, had first acquired their definitive size and shape, first become mobile and usable here.

Dmitriev always entered the Obukhov or any other factory yard conscious that every minute something on the drawing board was taking shape and becoming a reality. He loved all that was eternal and beautiful in the faraway cluttered center of Petersburg, but was never bored or repelled by these unbeautiful surroundings, the dreary blankness of the walls, the bareness, the litter, the scorched earth with never a blade of grass, the soot, the heat, the foul smells and harsh noises, for these were not manifestations of ugliness, but a necessary accompaniment to the birth of things. To the inexperienced, an engineering plant is a rackety accumulation of workbenches, materials, and finished goods, but those working there know that this apparent disorder is in reality the best sort of order, that everything fits in beautifully, and that every man is in his proper place, working to plan, a necessary part of the whole.

You enjoy going into a factory yard because it all means something. To you, an insider, the cutoffs heaped against a wall are not just so much scrap iron—you know just what job a metalworker was doing to produce each bit of waste. You can read the shavings around the turners' shop just as readily. Brass? Copper? Steel? How wide? How thick? The finished pieces at the forge tell you what its last job was or what its next order is. In fact, the noises from the forge, the look of the smoke over the iron or steel smelteries, the fiery reflections in the windows, their color or lack of it, the fresh heap of slag at the door of the cupola furnace, what the wheelbarrow men are carrying from one shop to another, even the sort of boards piled up outside the drying room, tell the experienced eye everything before it leaves the yard. Before you set foot in the first building you are geared into and magnetized by the work in hand, it is decided for you where you're most needed, and your feet automatically turn in that direction.

The day was dying without ever really dawning. An hour earlier there had been snow or rather a fine, frozen drizzle, and where no one had walked, and the heat from the buildings and the underground steam pipe had not melted it, a thin white coating remained to give the evening a wintry look. And it was getting chilly.

Dmitriev was ill at ease. He wasn't used to making speeches. True, they would be men he worked with, men he knew well, but they would have been assembled in this unnatural way, two hundred at a time, specifically to listen to him. Still, there was no other way of getting them to rally round and join in what needed to be done. He had already figured out what he would say, but hoped to pick up hints from their faces and from the way things went and improve on it as he went along.

He also had to look for that man Komarov to find out whether Gvozdev had telephoned him and what the workers' leaders had decided.

Dmitriev was told in the office that they hadn't forgotten, and that half an hour before the siren went off everybody entitled to be called an engineer—molders, smelters, smiths, fitters, turners, and milling-machine operators—would be brought together in the machine shop.

Unluckily, the duty police sergeant was sitting there in the room while they were talking and of course overheard. He must have known about it anyway. Dmitriev frowned at the thought that this fishface would certainly turn up to make his presence felt, exhibiting his fat rosy cheeks like a signboard, to worry the workers with an unspoken question: why aren't these ugly customers in the trenches? Nothing could have been less welcome. If it upset Dmitriev, what effect would it have on the workers? But he couldn't ask the policeman directly not to turn up. That would only put ideas into his head. Invite suspicion. Just have to see how it goes.

Dmitriev changed his best jacket for a greasy overall tunic with elbow patches, matching trousers with knee pieces, and a different cap— the things he wore to poke around in every nook and corner of the workshops, in storerooms and foundry lofts, as and when necessary. He needed this outfit, so much more appropriate, so much more at home in the factory, as never before, to cross more easily the penitential line between workers and gentlemen. Wearing it, he set off with firmer tread in search of Komarov.

He found him sitting in a draft in the unheated anteroom to the materials storeroom, and they got talking. The day was dark, but it was darker still in the anteroom. The lamp had not been lit, and Komarov himself with his black stubble seemed a darker person than he really was.

"We're calling a meeting then, Grigori Kiryanych?"

"Looks like it."

He seemed to agree. But not very enthusiastically.

"Did you sort things out with Kozma Antonych?"

"We spoke."

Could he expect help from him? Or just neutrality? Or would the man get up and say that the working class did not need this war? The way to the worker's heart was narrow, there was just room for Dmitriev alone: but on one side he would have the policeman elbowing him and on the other some party orator. If this man couldn't help he'd do better to keep quiet. But asking him would be awkward.

They strode across the yard. Komarov was wearing a dirty, cloth work jacket, the sleeves of which ended well above his wrists, but he didn't seem to feel the cold, and his big hands carried metal pieces from the storeroom without freezing.

He was a metal planer, a local man, trained at the Obukhov factory, and that was all to the good. He was, though, also a party man, a Socialist Revolutionary elevated to the Workers' Group, the only Obukhov worker on it—for some reason or other. Probably had the gift of gab.

But he was a sturdy, solid-looking old boy, so he probably wouldn't make too much of a nuisance of himself, like those pushy little busybodies who would do anything to attract attention.

But if, while Dmitriev talked about the trench mortar, Komarov came out with proletarian solidarity, and the policeman sat in the corner scowling, the workers' minds would stray in three different directions—and Dmitriev's speech would go down the drain.

"Grigori Kiryanych," Dmitriev asked point-blank, "we call the meeting—then what?"

Komarov tilted his head and shrugged one shoulder. "Whatever is wanted."

They halted. A shunting engine was backing across their path, pulling two flatcars, each bearing a brand-new 48-line Obukhov gun, heavily greased but not yet under wraps, toward the factory gate for dispatch.

Newly designed long-barreled, medium-caliber beauties, not yet seen at the front.

Where the train had passed, the rails had a wet metallic gleam, ahead of it they were coated with white frost.

The dull, heavy, rhythmical pounding of the steam hammer could be heard from the forge. Dmitriev loved that sound. The whole power of the factory seemed to be concentrated in it.

Komarov looked at the flatcars, at the purplish porous slag strewn on the track to dry it—anywhere rather than at Dmitriev.

While they were still held up Dmitriev turned to him, trying in vain to catch his averted eyes. "Grigori Kiryanych, when you're at your bench you don't try to make one side of a part stronger and the other weaker, do you now? But that's what the Workers' Groups do. They say we'll join the committees, not to make shells, but to rouse the people's forces from their lethargy."

The locomotive had come to a dead stop before them, perhaps to switch tracks.

Komarov held the iron pieces on his open hand. But he was no more forthcoming than before.

"Suppose I keep quiet. What will the workers say? They'll say what do you mean, overtime, when two shops out there are on strike already? For time and a half."

The locomotive moved on again, and Komarov's eyes watched the slow-moving flatcars go by.

Nor could Dmitriev tear himself away. His gaze followed those guns (122 millimeters by European reckoning), those magnificent, perfectly shaped, new Obukhov guns, already ballistically tested, guns which at the beginning of the war were not even at the experimental stage. But plant them all along the front line now, equip every infantry division with them, and they'd shove the Germans back where they came from in no time.

"What can they say? Remember when we produced the first of those guns? It was December last year. And how many have we made since? If it's three dozen we can think ourselves lucky. Is that any way to work? We, the working class!!! Democracy—the regime, giving the bourgeoisie a bit of a shock, that's all you worry about. You ought to start by showing that you *can* work. The working class . . ."

"It doesn't just depend on us."

"On you as much as anybody. Time and a half! Of course, if you've got proclamations all over the walls, on workbenches, wheels, tree trunks, if the watchmen sweep them out in heaps and there are fresh ones up the next morning—who cares about work? If the Germans heard that a factory like this turns out two of these guns a month they'd rupture themselves laughing."

"But why should we be the only ones tightening our belts? Why can't other people make do with less? Those who've got money? What do they care about the war? They spend their whole time playing cards."

It was no good trying to answer that. From down below this was what they could most easily see. And in that other world Dmitriev wouldn't get a hearing.

The steam hammer was pounding away.

The guns proceeded. The two men walked on.

"Grigori Kiryanych, I'm grateful to you, and to all the reasonable people here, for making this meeting possible. But don't spoil it. If you speak, don't give them the official line, tell them honestly what you see with your own eyes."

Whether or not he had taken the point he made no reply. He went off into his workshop.

Dmitriev felt himself getting more and more agitated. There were still forty minutes or so to go, but it was getting dark early, and he wouldn't be at ease until he was with his *own people*, the handful of men who had been working with him for months past on an experimental model of a trench mortar. They had carried out tests together, rejected some features and adopted others in their place. Dmitriev had initiated them, taught them what was what, got them to think about it and make suggestions, and some of their advice had been useful.

He went looking. He would spend the remaining half hour putting them in the right frame of mind. And trying to get an inkling of what awaited him at the meeting. He went into the metal workshop looking for Malozemov, dear old Evdokim Ivanych, a careful and conscientious worker, but he was not around. His fellow workers assumed, as Dmitriev had surmised anyway, that he was in the old foundry with his friend Sozont.

He didn't see Sozont in the foundry. Laborers were raking molding clay, enriching it. He ducked into the coremakers' shop, a lean-to built on to the foundry. Yes, there he was! They'd often gathered in this secluded spot to sketch movable parts so that their gun could be dismantled for transportation and reassembled as rapidly as possible. They were all there. Gray-haired Evdokim Ivanych, sitting on a log as usual, which made him look even shorter than he was, puffing at a cigarette clumsily rolled in newspaper. Sozont Bogolepov, a hefty, broad-shouldered, big-headed man, stood propped up against a cupboard full of molds, looking even bigger than he was, with his hands behind his back—he did not need them for smoking. He liked standing that way, swiveling his polished pumpkin of a head to look at whoever was speaking. There were two corers, one busy molding, the other slumped idly in his seat. Then there was a youngster carrying trays loaded with dry cores from the drying room and ranging them on shelves. At one of the benches a weedy carpenter was briskly completing some job, and rattling away just as busily in a light, thin voice. A hollow-chested, consumptive-looking molder sat dejected on a workbench, doing nothing. Another bench was unmanned. There was one unoccupied stool, but Dmitriev chose to sit on the vacant bench to show that he belonged. He was so tall that his dangling feet touched the floor.

The old foundry was not heated from the factory boiler room, but here in the coremakers' shop there was a cast-iron stove, devouring wood chips and shavings and glowing dull red as always. The air was dry, warm, cheering. It was a pleasure to go in there. Dmitriev wasn't chilled to the bone, but he was glad of the warmth.

They were used to him by now, and each of them carried on with what he was doing.

"The thing is, he's sold all our secrets for three million gold rubles. And collected the money from the director of the bank in person," the lively, small-toothed carpenter was saying, working on his mortise. "So now Wilhelm can take a look at all our plants anytime he likes."

The carpenter, with his gauge sticking out of his overall pocket, deftly loosened the vise, turned the piece around, tightened the screw again, and didn't stop talking for a moment.

"Know how it started? The Germans sent the Tsaritsa some medicinal herbs through him—you know, for the Tsarevich. Some that grow in Germany and we don't have in Russia."

"Nonsense!" Sozont said. "There aren't any herbs that don't grow in Russia."

"I'm telling you there are!" The carpenter gripped his plane, which was almost half his own height—from waist to brow—and started planing in a great hurry. "Otherwise why would she be selling us out?"

"I wonder," said the molder with a sigh. "Maybe they've got something for TB growing there!"

"Anyway, they sent these herbs. Through that Rasputnik. And every time he presented them to the Tsaritsa she gave him a little envelope sealed with her own seal. And inside she'd written down everything the Tsar had told her, and shouldn't have, since the last time. *And* she kept asking Wilhelm what ministers to fire. His Imperial Majesty isn't like his father, he's as soft as soft. Another time they arranged it so that whichever front her hospital train was going to would show where we'd be attacking. And Rasputnik had some Jew working for him, Ruvim Shtein or something, and this Jew had a horse that was as good as invisible, could gallop all the way to Wilhelm and back in one shot."

The others looked disbelieving.

"Well, maybe he didn't get as far as Wilhelm. I don't know. But he ended up a millionaire as well. Now they say he's been found out. And put in the clink."

Dmitriev was surprised to find that the Rubinstein story, or a rather odd version of it, had gotten so far. It wasn't the first time he'd heard such talk from workers. It was like the rubbish and brushwood and logs swept along by a swollen, turbid river after a heavy rainstorm. No good trying to stem the flow, you could only wait for it to pass. He didn't even try to intervene. He knew that he couldn't possibly change anybody's mind. But he was horrified by the depth of their ignorance. And their anxiety. How could they possibly know what was going on? It was horrifying, the wall after wall of incomprehension erected across Russia.

"Anyway, the Germans have given our ministers a billion to kill off a million people—a thousand rubles per person, soldiers or otherwise. And Count Frederiks has picked up the money for all the rest, so here in Petersburg they're starving us to death. There's another rumor going around. A wounded officer in the clinic at Tsarskoye Selo is supposed to have taken a shot at the Tsaritsa. Because she sides with the Germans. Only he missed."

Dmitriev would have liked to go and sit by Evdokim Ivanych, but there was no room, nor could he get up and stand by the cupboard with Sozont, and asking them to come outside would be awkward. Anyway, he didn't feel that he could ask a straight question. What he did feel was the inevitable embarrassment, familiar through the ages to those about to address an audience of workingmen; he felt guilty for no good reason, and somehow vulnerable. He belonged there, he was frank and honest with them, he knew his job, wore a worker's tunic, was physically sound and articulate . . . yet he still envied that little ferret of a carpenter who would jump up and harangue a thousand without turning a hair.

"So you see it's all up with us!" the carpenter said, planing for a while, then suddenly loosening the vise again. "His Imperial Majesty's advisers have all been got at. We've been sold out all the way to Petersburg. Orders have come from Wilhelm to take Russia apart." But the thought seemed to inspire in him malicious glee rather than fear.

"What's this baloney you're talking, snaggletooth?" Dmitriev said.

Not that anybody completely believed the carpenter.

But it would be hopeless trying to convince them that there was nothing in it all.

Carefully inspecting his joint with the help of an oak T square, the carpenter said, "Besides, there's another secret order—it's St. Elisei's night for all the officers."

"Whose night?" the molder asked.

"St. Elisei's night."

"That can't be right," the molder said doubtfully. Probably literate. From reading blueprints.

"What kind of a night do you mean?" the corers wondered.

"Well, all those who haven't got a special piece of paper will all be done in at one time, whether they're at the front or in the rear."

"Who's given that order?"

"I'm telling you somebody has," the carpenter said knowingly.

"Hold on." Dmitriev had suddenly realized that this sort of thing must be going on all over the factory, and at all other factories, not just here in the molding shop. "Where on earth did you get all this from?"

"Go anywhere you like, everybody says the same. We've got people going around telling us things. Socials of one sort or another. And Jew boys. Just you wait, they say, it's all going up in flames."

These horror stories had spread like the plague. Nothing to be done. It was the same everywhere. Higher up too, only in different words.

"They muddy the water like in a fishpond in the spring," Malozemov, sitting on his log, barked angrily. You could tell from the way he talked that some of his teeth were missing, but his gray mustache concealed the deficiency.

"The people are defenseless," Sozont pronounced from his cupboard.

Sozont and Evdokim were from the same place. Like many Petersburg workers not registered as "townsfolk" they were described in their residence permits—and loudly proclaimed it at each reregistration, or whenever the police came around—as peasants from the province of Novgorod, one from the Zalutsk, the other from the Gubin rural district. This in spite of the fact that they had worked uninterruptedly at the Obukhov factory for many years (Sozont twenty, Evdokim twenty-five). They socialized with their compatriots in the factory, there were family ties between them, and when they spoke of "our place" they didn't mean the factory but their native place, where there were seven streams all called "the Robya," and to which Evdokim intended to work his way back, in time to be buried there. He was determined not to end up in a Petersburg cemetery.

The conversation droned on, and moved to the other inevitable, eternal, inexhaustible theme—prices. People in Russia had for years been used to stable prices, prices that seemed to be embedded in the goods for sale, an intrinsic part of them, and they were flabbergasted by the unchecked rise in prices in wartime. Like a child just learning to talk, painstakingly trying over and over again to utter some extraordinary, unmanageable word, these simple people uttered the latest prices over and over again, looking hard at each other as if to make sure that it was all true, that it really could be that way. Bread up from four to six kopecks a pound—the great globe itself reeled. Tea! You won't be drinking it like you used to. Herring, once four kopecks a pound, now thirty! Or take shoes and clothes! Galoshes used to be one ruble thirty, now—can you believe it?—they're four rubles fifty. And how are you going to keep warm? That's one thing that won't wait till the war ends. Birch logs were seven and a half a sazhen, now it's twenty or more. For someone watching this unstoppable, this diabolical escalation from day to day, what explanation could there be except that some wicked, greedy hand was raking in the money? What else could account for the fact that things had ceased to cost their proper, immemorial price? Some invisible, wicked plotter was getting rich at the expense of ordinary folk, and those up above were all in on the plot. Why is there nothing to buy? They're hiding it, that's why, making a fortune out of our tears, getting fat in their hideouts. And you can't get your hands on them, you don't know where they are. They ride by in carriages, you can't catch up with them.

If yesterday's prices left you aghast, they were nothing in comparison with the latest sensations. What should have been frightening became almost funny: those crazy prices can't affect sensible people like us, let's watch them skyrocketing and gloat!

In a way they were right. It didn't affect them. It affected their women. *They* didn't have to shell out the extra rubles at the counter— the women did. Theirs was the heartbreak.

"What d'you mean, shell out?" Evdokim retorted from his stool. "That's if they get as far as the counter. We go to work, and we're warm and dry, we eat in the co-op canteen. It's called work, but it's a cinch. But a woman has to wrap herself as warm as she can in her shawl and go and stand out in the freezing cold, two or three hours at a time—and there's still no knowing if she'll get anything. And who's looking after the kids? And the house is going to hell."

Evdokim Ivanych spoke with a depth of feeling for his wife that comes only with age. When you can put yourself in her place. His fine wrinkles were darkened by iron dust, his eyes were dim, he always looked and sounded glum, even when he was half smiling under his mustache.

"Warm, hooray!" one of the apprentices said cheerily, moving over to put more wood in the stove. "There's not much coal at home, you can't get really warm."

He had the stove door open, but the wood was too big and needed breaking up.

"Haven't you got eyes?" Sozont asked sternly. He had taken his time about checking the young man.

Whether or not the kid understood, he obediently dropped the wood, already charred, and threw in some skimpier, rougher cutoffs.

They were in favor of sugar coupons: what's fair is fair. Not so long ago the rich hogged the sugar whatever the price, and the poor got sweet nothing. Now every consumer got the same, and that was the right way to do it.

If everybody was equally hungry, nobody need feel aggrieved. There'd be no cause to moan. The really vexing thing was that people weren't equal, that some did well at the expense of others. They ought to put meat on coupons as well. They had it all fixed once, why did they drop it? Beef, now? Who'd believe it? Makes you giddy to think of it. Forty-five kopecks a pound! Have we gone crazy? Who could keep up with that?

They ought to do the same with milk. Life in Petersburg is all haywire: if no milk's brought in, there's none for the kids, and you can't go out to the stall and milk the cow. There are some skinny cows in the village of Michael the Archangel, but there's never enough hay in this present mess. It takes more than twenty-five years to get used to living like this.

Yet nowhere in Russia could workers' wages compare with those paid in Petersburg. At first they used to add up the figures on the quiet and tell each other, "We'll make a bundle out of the war." Since then wages had more or less doubled. But prices had beaten them to it and raced out of sight.

But whatever position you're in, some are better off, some worse. The soldiers envy you, Dmitriev reminded them. Here you only have to lift a shell off the bench and load it; there they put their heads in the way of it. Want to join them, for half a pound of meat?

True enough. Life in Petersburg was terribly hard, but just about bearable. Try living bent double in the trenches. Here you might have to put in ten or even twelve hours at work, but you went home and slept under your own roof at night.

"Only they'll be packing us off out there soon."

"The more we strike, the sooner we'll be there."

"Oh yes—and who's going to take our place?"

"The Chinese, that's who!"

"Chi-nese?" The agile carpenter left his bench for the first time and opened his arms wide. "What can they do, the Chinese? Which bench can they work at?"

"They can be taught," Malozemov said, from down on his log. He'd seen all sorts of people taught in his time.

"He'd fold up in no time, your Chinaman would, even just on unskilled labor," the carpenter said, shrill with indignation. "D'you think two Chinamen could lift your ladle in the foundry?"

"What about you—are you tougher than a Chinaman?" Sozont asked, from above.

"I don't do any lifting," the carpenter said, seizing the gauge and starting in on some new lengths of wood. He was hard at it, because he was on piecework.

The others were in no great hurry.

They all knew that there was to be a meeting, and who would be there—but they avoided the subject, and the engineer was gleaning less than he had expected from their conversation.

Should he mention it himself? He somehow couldn't get the words out.

Malozemov, from his log, kept glancing at the engineer with his knowing old eyes. He realized that Dimitriev had come looking for support but that the conversation had taken the wrong turn.

The conversation floundered while Dmitriev sat among them for half an hour, getting, if anything, more timid all the time. This was their life. What hope was there that five hundred hands would suddenly take hold of the trench mortar?

Only when they were summoned by a shout, and started moving, did Evdokim Ivanych take the engineer by the elbow, out in the foundry, and speak with feeling as he had a little while back about his wife and the cows in the village of Michael the Archangel.

"The main thing is, Mitrich, talk boldly, like the agitators do. Don't let anybody interrupt. If they shout, you shout back. With us workers, you see, it's this way—all for one and one for all. We're like a single block of stone, we're all either to one side or to the other. To split is something we just can't do. You can win us over—but it has to be one and all. So let's see you do it."

[3 3]

Thus encouraged, Dmitriev went into the big engineering shop, where the crane hook, detached and drawn up into the roof, would still be oscillating for some time. He had to exchange a few words with the chief engineer and return greetings from foremen, but his mind was elsewhere. He was carefully studying the gathering.

Every worker there, left to himself, would probably respond to a simple approach. But when five or six hundred at once poured out into the yard at the end of the shift, black-faced, indistinguishable, mysterious, alien, it was no good trying to remember what you could say to or expect from any single man. Instead, you automatically looked away, lowered your eyes, and helplessly acknowledged the undeniable gap between "you" and "us."

An indelible line had been drawn. Would he ever learn to cross it effortlessly, or at least without letting them see the effort it cost?

It was no different this time as they crossed the floor and found seats, jumping up onto the ledges of their workbenches or other flat surfaces, or placing benches across the trolley track in the central aisle for those coming from other shops. He had no experience with them in such numbers, and in this context, and found them rather intimidating. Massive pieces of iron, cast iron and steel lay around and were moved from place to place, in this shop as everywhere in the Obukhov factory, but there were established formulas, immutably fixed engineering procedures, grips and cranes, to deal with them. Two hundred or two hundred and fifty live, soft-bodied, loosely packed people became a huge, unknown object governed by unknown formulas. This was different from engineering. It was wrong to call politicians empty wafflers. The tension made them talk so much.

And Evdokim Ivanych was right. Workers could only be thought of in the mass, that was what you had to take into account. A single peasant can do two hundred jobs, he and his family together have two hundred skills, and he is most complete when he is alone. A single worker is nothing, even the most skilled of metalworkers, like Evdokim: whatever the job, he has only one operation, or part of an operation, to perform, and for completeness two hundred must gather together.

The policeman was there, of course. With his fat face and the self-importance of one who knows it all better than any of them. Without a word to anyone he sat down on a stool to the side and slightly to the rear of the speaker.

He spoiled the whole scene, spoiled Dmitriev's appearance in the eyes of the workers.

The foremen sat in a little group of their own.

Komarov, dark-skinned and unshaven, sat aloof, leaving it to someone else to open the meeting.

They were all taking their seats now, men in dark blouses, worn outside and unbelted, in tunics, or in old jackets, whatever they wore to work. Except for the caps, which they all wore while working, but had now, even those who were at home here, removed, as custom dictated, without being told or asked to. Someone had started it, the rest had followed suit, and now they were bareheaded to a man. But what did you do with your cap? Hold it on your knees. Or knead it in your hands.

The doffed caps and the silence hardly broken by subdued conversation showed that they realized the exceptional importance of this gathering.

Of the bared heads a few were close-shaven, soldier fashion, some were balding, perhaps the result of soft living, most had the bushy hair of a still inexhaustibly vigorous stock. There were haircuts of all sorts, some done with the kitchen scissors to save money on barbers.

No, they weren't prospering. They looked careworn, anxious, sullen. When prices raced ahead of wages, what good was overtime to them? Just a waste of effort. From their point of view they were right to refuse it.

But only from the point of view of one who could pull his sheepskin tight around his chest, ram his cap down over his eyes, and run against the biting wind from the Neva home to his own apartment.

Dmitriev had been rehearsing his opening words in his mind and so missed the beginning of the proceedings. He stood there, upright and braced, aware only of his eyes fixed on the workers and the hammering in his breast. They were all waiting, looking at him, and he had forgotten to seek advice on the very first step, hadn't even thought about it. This assembly, two hundred strong. What should he call them? Comrades? No, that would be cheap toadying, and anyway with the policeman there it was impossible, he didn't want to strike the revolutionary note. Gentlemen? That would sound ridiculous. The Russian language was immense but there was nothing for it except: "Brothers! Some of us . . . ." He glanced at his *own people* sitting in a bunch. Little Malozemov was invisible, screened by the man in front, but Sozont's austere, hairless pumpkin of a head shone out over the crowd. "Some of us know that the factory has produced a successful prototype of a trench mortar and is about to go on to mass production. The time has come for some machines and some whole shops to be put on this job exclusively. So I have asked the management . . . and the representatives of the Workers' Group . . . to assemble you, who will be taking part in this, in order to . . ." (Was this really necessary? Why all this "in order to"? Why not just say, "Do what you're told"?) "In order to explain to you what sort of gun it is and what it is for."

They pricked up their ears. Men with shaggy heads, heavy jaws, knitted brows, nearly all beardless, here and there a mustache, but mostly barefaced, cheeks sucked in, mouths pursed distrustfully, wondering what there was to explain. What's this pig in a poke they're offering us now? Better watch out.

How could they be any different in stony Petersburg? Neither strength nor refreshment nor sound counsel seeps through its stones to you. And your ears are assailed with tales of . . . "Elisei's night."

But Dmitriev was pleased with the sound of his own voice. It had a clear, firm ring.

"You have to realize that in this war things have often taken a turn that no army ever expected. And that goes for the artillery. Ever since it was first invented it has led a sort of separate existence: it always stood apart from the other arms, it fired from a distance, it didn't get mixed up with the infantry. But in modern warfare the battlefield is so congested, and the situation changes so rapidly, that the artillery cannot stand apart and at a distance from the infantry. Machine-gun posts, for instance, spring up and disappear so quickly, they have to be dealt with in a few short minutes, so that an artillery observer, even if he is in the thick of the infantry, cannot inform a battery well to his rear over lines that keep breaking, find the range and pinpoint the target."

Was he making it too complicated? Apparently not. Some faces showed interest: might as well listen, can't get skinned for that.

"We do have our three-inch field gun, as you know. A splendid gun, very good for grazing fire, does a beautiful job." (He demonstrated with his hand how effective it was.) "So a single battery can wipe out a battalion of infantry in close formation, or a cavalry regiment, in a matter of minutes."

(A beautiful job!)

"But because it's a low firer it has to keep quiet when our infantry closes to within a hundred and fifty sazhens of the enemy, so as not to fire on our own troops. That means you can neither position it close nor fire over the heads of our own infantry. The result is that at the most difficult and dangerous moments, when our infantry is being mowed down by enemy machine guns, it is denied the support of our own artillery."

How was it going? He thought he was getting through to them. They were all looking fixedly, silently, more and more gravely at the engineer. Who wouldn't be affected? It could be the fate of any one of you . . . any one of us, tomorrow. They'd been on war work for over two years, and for over two years the threat of punishment hanging over them had been—the draft, the training depot, relegation to the trenches. Yet what did they know about this war? About the cannon produced in their factory? How they were positioned, how they were shifted from place to place, how they fired?

"Or more difficult and dangerous still: when our infantry, with a great effort and heavy losses, breaches enemy lines and breaks into his trenches, at the very moment when all is muddle and confusion, when nobody is in the right place and not everybody has an officer of his own at hand and there is no hope of communication by telephone— at that very moment the infantry is deprived of artillery support: with no communications link, unable to see from a distance because of the smoke and dust, and amid the general confusion—who would ever dare open fire? The upshot is that as a reward for its victories and all the losses it incurs our infantry lands in a particularly vulnerable situation, and may easily be rolled back with heavy casualties."

Best of all, the glow and the steady beat in his chest told him that he had almost surmounted the barrier of excruciating embarrassment, more or less unthinkingly, self-assuredly even, as he saw first one face, then another, a fifth, a seventh, brighten. He had after all stolen nothing from them, he was guilty of no offense against them, why shouldn't he look them in the eye?

More and more eyes were fixed on him. With interest, and close attention. The kitchen haircuts were endearing. Out there, brothers, you get your head shaven—and maybe lose it altogether.

"So it's been demonstrated, in combat and at the cost of blood, that we need an artillery escort, to accompany its infantry as closely as possible, able to open fire immediately, and with perfect visibility whatever the circumstances. How can we manage that? Our three-inch gun is not adapted to the purpose. Dismantled for transportation it weighs over one hundred and twenty poods. Which means that on a firm, smooth road it takes six horses to pull it. And if the going is just a bit more difficult—where there are ruts or mud or furrows—you need eight or even ten horses, and the gunners still have to give an occasional push. What would you expect the road to be like on a battlefield? As bad as can be. You'll never get all those horses, and if you did they'd all be wounded in no time. In short, if the artillery is to accompany its infantry in battle it can't rely on horses."

They were a very good audience. Those whose view was blocked craned around from behind other men's shoulders. Openmouthed, or frowning, or drawn and tense, they were all receptive, they all understood, and Dmitriev saw no sign of resistance or mockery. He could draw support not only from his own little group but from almost any face in the crowd. How to account for the viciousness, the wild cries, the shaking of fists, in those street clashes, like the one five days earlier on Great Sampsonyevsky Prospect? Their faces were not particularly intelligent, they were rather duller, less varied than peasant faces—but they were faces with Russian features and responsive to Russian speech. What kind of contemptuous or callous treatment had it taken to alienate them so completely?

"So then, our artillery must become still lighter and smaller. Easier to dismantle and reassemble. Our guns must learn not to ride behind, but to march shoulder to shoulder with the infantry and do what is required immediately. Our guns must be such that the men can spring off them like goats and slip into the same trenches as the infantry. In other words, we need a trench gun. Just such a gun as we, our group of skilled workers, have now made."

They smiled. Not his own men—they knew it all of old—but the other two hundred. Because they were given a clear and simple message: see what clever fellows there are in our factory, just look what we can do.

"Our gun is precisely that, easy to dismantle and reassemble. Dismantled for transportation it weighs seven poods. Any three of you could move it, right? In a tight spot maybe two could handle it?"

The engineer seemed to be asking their opinion. There was a subdued buzz of interest and men turned to look at their neighbors: would it take three? or only two?

"The gun carriage weighs another four poods, which two men can manage at a run if necessary. Add a pound and a quarter for the shell—you can practically put that in your pocket! And this gun can fire eight rounds a minute."

"And what's its range?" one of the youngest skilled men asked brightly, unaggressively.

"It can manage as much as three versts!" Dmitriev answered unhesitatingly.

A buzz of astonishment went around the shop.

"But it doesn't need to. More often than not it will be firing at targets visible to the naked eye, up to three hundred sazhens away. And as soon as the Germans spot it our gunners can dismantle and shift it, bent double along the bottom of the trench if necessary."

They showed their approval of the gun. A cheerful murmur spread through the audience and grew louder.

By now Dmitriev had got into his stride and would have gone on to explain how this gun differed from ordinary mortars. And tell them that the Germans and the French already had small-caliber trench artillery and that only the Russians were lagging behind. But he sensed that this was superfluous and might even put them off: knowing that only Russia was without such artillery might arouse either eagerness to compete or—who knows?—the bitter thought that Russia was . . . like that.

He was brought up short by something else he had not thought of before he had tasted success. How were they to make their decision? They could hardly vote on it. Or could they? Such a large body of workers in which even the most skilled man was dependent on all the rest—how did they generally go about it?

Komarov must know the answer. Dmitriev turned to look at him for the first time. Nothing to worry about there. He was listening with every sign of approval, not disguising the satisfaction he felt simply as a man, not a party member. He was another of those who had not really known about the new gun. This was the first he had been told.

Dmitriev also glanced at the policeman. He would have done better not to. His eyes would not have reminded his listeners of the man's existence. The policeman was as placid as ever, neither angered nor moved by Dmitriev's story, but gazing steadily at the assembly as if he expected no good to come of it all.

But now that you and I, brothers, are as one . . .

"This gun, then, is overdue at the front, it should have been there long ago, last spring. Can we manage it by next spring? We need lots of them! Hundreds in fact! And only our Obukhov factory can produce them."

But however good-naturedly you speak or listen, there are limits to what you can say, and to what you can believe. However honest you want to be, you can't blurt out the whole truth. Complete honesty would mean giving reasons for the delay. Why weren't we ready last spring, or last summer? Well, it was because . . . because . . . higher authority took a long time scrutinizing the blueprints. They were dozed and grumbled over by ancient ruins of generals with one foot in retirement but reluctant to part with the office chair. Dozed over by people in no danger of being sent to the trenches themselves and with no feeling for the faceless herd stuck there. They're the ones who've wasted nearly a whole year. But you, brothers . . .

"It's up to us now, brothers, to get these guns out in a hurry. Not a single production line must be idle . . ."

(Though you too, brothers, are all in essential occupations and not many of you are in danger of being sent out there.)

"I got back from the Dvina last August. We'd been trying out the gun. The soldiers were simply overjoyed with it. 'With a gun like that we could get somewhere,' they said. 'Be quick about it! Hurry them up back in Petersburg!' Just think how many lives this gun can save, lives of Russian soldiers, our brothers!"

Then, in a ringing voice, looking from face to face.

"But you . . . just the other day you decided not to work overtime. Just tell the men out there, on the Dvina, that the skilled workers in Petersburg are clock-watching, that they can't stomach staying on after their shift, so there'll be no trench gun . . ."

It was true. He had just returned from the Dvina trenches, where he had told the men about it and shared their shocked resentment.

"Let the rest of the factory do what it likes, but you, brothers . . . I beg you. We beg you. The Workers' Group as well . . . Spare them some of the bloodshed."

He was begging them, but confidently, sure of their support, of their openhearted, generous sympathy.

"The workshops singled out here must start working around the clock, on Sundays as well. Overtime must be shared among shifts."

His impatient mind was already assigning them to work stations, he knew already who would be doing what, saw already how, tomorrow morning . . .

No—no resistance. But—some hesitation. But—the high spirits of a moment ago had sagged. They exchanged sidelong looks. Glanced at Komarov. At the policeman.

Well, of course, not one of them was an independent individual. How could they make a decision? The trench gun was a good thing, to be sure they could see that, and the brothers would gladly . . . if only someone with authority would first put into words what it was they all wanted, they would all agree immediately.

Komarov was in no hurry. He did not feel himself to be the most important man there. He was looking around for someone.

And suddenly someone invisible behind all those backs, and a metal stanchion, cried out, in a voice at once harshly imperious and insolently mocking, like the crowing of a cock: "Let those who started it stem the bloodletting! Riga is nothing to us, let the Germans have it!"

He hadn't expected this! Dmitriev hadn't expected it! This was the cry Evdokim had . . . He must answer it at once! Shout louder! Something apt? What, though? It was so stupid . . . "let the Germans have it." He had tried his hardest to explain. How could he answer this?

Too late. He couldn't pull himself together in time. It had to be done on the instant. And he had lost his head.

The policeman, though, sprang nimbly to his feet, stood on tiptoe, spotted his man, and made a beeline for him.

Only to find himself looking at an unbroken row of hostile backs. Talk about a needle in a haystack!

He'd only made things worse.

The two hundred and fifty sat silent. Heads bowed.

[3 4]

The workers of the night shift were all in the factory by now. For ten short minutes, the day shift, a dark crowd denser than at any demonstration or jollification, flooded the wide roadway of the Schlüsselburg Prospect outside the factory, then trickled away. In such a throng anything might happen. But nothing did. Some walked off toward the two-storied Obukhov housing development, others dispersed along side streets. Those who had no farther to go than the Glassmakers' Quarter walked along the Prospect. Others packed the steam tram, all three coaches, inside and out, and still others were left waiting at the stop. The area in front of the factory, brilliantly lit by many electric lamps, was cleared. Now you could see the tricolor flag flying over the factory gates (for the anniversary of the Tsar's accession). The policeman at the crossroads. A patrol (introduced after the disturbances) passing slowly along the Prospect. A belated carter with an overloaded wagon and a horse that nodded its head at the whip without quickening its pace. There was light in the windows of Zhakhov's "porter shop" (alehouse to us) and the door opened frequently. The butcher and the baker had bolted and barred their shutters and doors. On the other side of the Prospect there was a church porch, and the lights from the narthex showed that vespers was in progress. On this side stood a pharmacy. And a shack housing the mutual aid society, jammed up against the long factory fence.

The evening was still almost wintry, with a fine drizzle, scarcely visible in the lamplight, and a light dusting of snow on untrodden parts of the roadway.

People were going into the mutual aid building, in full view of the sentry and the police patrol, and not only men from the factory, but a young lady in a waisted fur coat, unlike anything worn at the far end of the Neva Quarter. But checking up on all this was not the job of the police. They had no instructions. If someone else saw any need, let him get on with it. Both police and factory management knew that the mutual aid and insurance offices, introduced two years before the war, were a hive of illegal activity, and that people with no business there were forever coming and going, but it was thought politically inadvisable to pick on these particular institutions. And after what had boiled up at the beginning of the week in the Vyborg Quarter the policeman was all for a quiet life, and not poking his nose in: if you're standing sentry, and nobody bothers you, continue standing.

Apart from the vestibule the mutual aid office had only two rooms. In the first abacuses were indeed at work, and sick-pay vouchers and disability pension forms were filled in (though even in these the clerks inserted the latest propaganda leaflet, copied in their own handwriting). But the clerks in the second room were not in the least surprised when Mashistov—an Obukhov man like themselves, an ordinary worker, but not all that ordinary, known for his connections and his activities—turned up and dismissed them with a nod. Which meant that there was to be a conference, a conspiratorial meeting. The two clerks grabbed papers, pens, inkstand and blotter, and moved into the first room. They were replaced immediately by a stern young man in a thick woollen overcoat, sand-colored, and a stout, warm reddish-brown peaked cap, together with the young lady in the expensive winter coat, but with a simple Orenburg scarf on her head.

Mashistov, a forty-year-old with a wooden, rectangular face, greeted the young man as "Comrade Vadim."

The young man took off his damp cap and put it on the sheet of cardboard covering the main desk, shook Mashistov's hand, and introduced him to "Comrade Maria." "She will take my place from time to time. Make a note."

Controls were not all that strict at the Obukhov gates. When necessary Comrade Vadim could get in even there, and as many as twenty men could be squeezed into some cubbyhole, but there was no need for that today, and they had arranged to meet here so as not to invite trouble by flitting in and out. What made the mutual aid office so useful was not so much the miserable handouts tossed to workers— free medicines and doctoring, two-thirds of wages in case of illness or accident—but the legitimate opportunity they gave to assemble under one roof, disseminate propaganda, organize and conspire unhindered. Such opportunities expanded from year to year, with the establishment not only of more mutual aid societies but of workers' cooperatives, factory canteens—an ever-growing number of convenient places for conspiratorial gatherings, assignations, transmission of messages, and simple proselytizing. In spite of the war this kind of work was becoming easier every year, more like what older comrades (not Vadim, he was only twenty-two) remembered from the revolutionary years. They had survived even 1914, that turbid year when everyone was intoxicated with the stinking fumes of chauvinism, when, so it was said, you couldn't breathe a word against the war in the presence of ordinary workers, when nobody would accept a leaflet and those who wrote them gave up in despair, and when a man concealed his party affiliation even from his neighbors at the next bench, for fear of being beaten up. There would never be a worse time than that.

"What about the others?" Comrade Vadim asked. He didn't take off his overcoat, just tugged the scarf from around his neck and placed it on the main desk. He smoothed down his hair, which was ash blond with a sprinkling of ginger, and so wiry that even his cap couldn't flatten it. And sat at the desk. Young as he was, his deportment commanded unquestioning respect.

"They should be here shortly," Mashistov said, stiff-jawed, weighing out his words deliberately, importantly. "Uksila will be a bit late."

Uksila would be a bit late, and Makarov was also missing, but in came Efim Dakhin, a man who moved briskly and seemed to be frowning heavily, but only because his little eyes were so deep-set.

"Hello, Vadim!" he said curtly. He scowled at the girl, but was introduced and shook hands with her as if she was a man.

"Hello, Comrade Maria."

Maria greeted each of them with a respectful handshake, a little bow, and a voice hushed by emotion. She undid the top button of her coat, but did not remove it, and threw back her wet scarf, revealing a black blouse, fastened at the side with shining student's buttons. And although her dark auburn hair was smoothed back close to her head, and although the men behaved as though they had no thought for any such thing, it was impossible not to see that she was—a beauty!

Dakhin had not come alone. He pointed to his companion. "This is the pride of our engineering shop, Akindin Kokushkin!"

The young man standing before them, cap in hand, was obviously no party member, obviously inexperienced, a simpleton. His hair, tossed back from his brow, had been smoothed over neck and ears by a careless hand, his face was thin and beardless, and his mouth half open with joy.

"Come on, Kesha, let's hear how you told the engineer where to get off," Dakhin said, looking at him with grim satisfaction.

"Well, er . . . it's . . . um . . . I . . . er . . . like . . ."

Kesha smiled still more happily, showing his crooked teeth. But telling his story was beyond him, so Dakhin took it on himself.

"It's like this," he said in his hoarse, toneless voice, "the lackey Komarov, the policeman, and the management pulled us in for one of their prayer meetings. In the name of the ace of hearts and the sack of gold. Then this engineer starts plucking our heartstrings—says we've got to work nights and Sundays to make another new gun for them . . ."

Mashistov knew all this, but Vadim listened carefully, and as for Maria—Maria's eyelashes rose higher and higher, her dark hazel eyes opened wider and wider in amazement at the engineer's brazenness and the daring rebuff it had met with.

"They all know my voice, so I told Kesha what to do. 'Stand behind that pillar,' I said. 'Shout what I tell you loud as you can, and I'll cover you.'"

Kesha had no voice at all now, not even that insolent cockcrow. He could only bare his crooked teeth in a smile as he saw how pleased with him all of them, the visiting gentlefolk included, were.

There was a thoroughbred quality about Vadim. Imposing to look at, he was perhaps not much good in a fight. His skin was white and delicate; you wouldn't need a gauntlet to draw blood, the touch of a bare hand could do it. White, but not smooth, it was dotted with little pink spots asking to be picked.

"Good. Very good," he said, smiling at Akindin. "Thank you, Comrade Kokushkin."

He hesitated, then rose and shook Akindin's hand from across the desk.

Whereupon Maria also rose, went over to Kesha, and shook his hand. Tenderly? Tentatively? Whichever it was, Kesha's heart raced and his head was in a whirl. He had never remotely dreamed of meeting such a fine young lady, let alone of touching her.

Maria went back to her seat. Mashistov then lowered himself slowly, deliberately onto a chair. Akindin decided that he too was allowed to sit, and anyway the room was too small for five people to walk around. So he sat by the nearer desk, placing his cap before him. Still smiling.

Only Dakhin was left standing. And frowning.

Vadim looked from the one to the other, noted a certain embarrassment, and judged that all was as it should be.

"Well done, Comrade Kokushkin," he said, measuring out each word clearly and precisely, as if it were a reward. "Always follow your instinct as a worker and it will not let you down."

"He's not a bad metalworker either," Mashistov added.

"No, it won't let you down. If somebody comes collecting for aid to the wounded, or the families of men killed in action, or refugees, what do you say to them?"

Perhaps Akindin knew, perhaps he would have found the right answer to the collector, but—here and now? He couldn't put his finger on it, he was lost for words, with half an eye on the amazing young lady.

"What does your instinct tell you?"

Akindin stared at the pale, solemn little gentleman, lips still apart, teeth bared, spellbound.

But Vadim didn't expect an answer. Listening carefully to his own voice, gazing at Kesha with shining eyes, he patiently explained. "What you have to say is: 'Did the government ask us before it started this war? Is it our fault if there are widows and orphans and cripples and refugees? Let those who started it and made them that way, let them pay for it. Anyway, what can the workers' few pennies do against a sea of national calamities?' But if anybody comes collecting for political martyrs or exiles, for wreaths, or for their families, that's our collection, there's nobody else to do it, only us workers."

Although Vadim was no longer rejoicing or praising him, the half-smile remained fixed on Akindin's face.

Maria sat there with a composure unusual in one so young. Hers was the serene beauty often seen in Russian women's faces. She listened to Vadim without missing a word, glancing at Kesha to make sure that he understood, and turning friendly looks upon the others.

"Patriotism is the hook on which they hope to catch us. Catch those whose hearts are not forged on the anvil."

What a metaphor! Maria could not take her wide, dark eyes off him. How true. How apt. Mashistov sat facing her across the desk. It was not just his face that seemed to have been hammered into shape— with no narrowing at the jaw or widening at the brow, with its hard, unmoving eyes—the palpable hardness of his nature must come from that anvil-forged heart.

Vadim ungrudgingly continued, for the benefit of Kesha alone. To the others these matters were rudimentary. "We have to open our eyes, Comrade Kokushkin, to the fact that our enemy is not in some far-off country, not abroad, but right here, among us. How long will we go on falling for the line that the Russian soldier is our brother and must have his gun in a hurry—what about the German soldier, the German worker, isn't he our brother too? Does it really matter to the proletariat who the exploiter is—a Russian or a German capitalist? Those who too importunately call on you to save the fatherland you must answer with the old Obukhov slogan of 1901—your very own slogan. Do you remember it?"

It wasn't just Kesha, who was only a youngster; the others didn't seem to know it or to have read of it either. Ah, but Vadim, though not an Obukhov worker himself, did know, and spoke for all of them: "Where there is bread—there is our fatherland."

Right, right . . . Akindin, flattered, blinked eager agreement. He had no thought of leaving.

But Dakhin loomed over him, looking angry. He had made a point of not sitting down.

Enough had been said, but, perhaps because the others had not turned up, Comrade Vadim wiped the corners of his mouth with a white handkerchief, and continued, in the same clear, even, unemphatic voice. "We are supposed to die, but for them it's a banquet, they won't mind if the war goes on for ten years. You get paper money, while the bigwigs plunder the people's gold. What, for instance, have you got to eat nowadays? Nothing at all."

"Soup, potatoes," Kesha remembered. "Fish."

"Is there any meat in the soup?"

"Sometimes there is."

"There you are, then. And rye bread, you can't buy wheaten bread. Who has the strength to cast cannon on that sort of food? And what do the factory owners eat? Have you any idea?"

No, on that subject Akindin had no ideas at all. Nor had any of the others. Maybe grouse or something, swimming in sour cream, indescribably delicious, out of this world.

"Or take a shirt," Akindin said, plucking up his courage. "Used to cost three quarters, and never wear out. Now you're lucky if it's less than three rubles." He became still more animated. "I used to pay two rubles for a corner, now the landlady asks eight."

"There you are, then. And on top of that they want to treat you like cattle, take away your rights, forbid you to move from one factory to another. And what's more, send you to training units and to the front."

Lanky, fair-haired, wooden Uksila had come in and was standing behind Akindin.

"Right then, Kesha," the morose Dakhin said impatiently, "you can be off now."

Kesha collected himself, jumped up, seized his cap, bowed and bowed again, beaming, to his fellow workers, to the strangers—nobody shook his hand this time—and left.

And Dakhin finally sat down. Heavily.

Comrade Vadim smiled.

"You mustn't get impatient, Comrade Dakhin. Don't ever begrudge time spent on agitation, it always pays. Anyway, you did the right thing. You didn't prepare Kokushkin in easy stages, did you? Went straight at it, am I right?"

Vadim was referring to the various current methods of recruiting and educating a worker before admitting him to the party circle: observing him at his bench, studying his attitude in apparently casual conversations, giving him minor tasks to begin with, like collecting money, then getting him to carry leaflets from one shop to another.

"Yes, you boldly omitted the preliminaries, broke through the defensist cobwebs, and tried your man out at the same time. Then brought him here, which was also correct."

Dakhin remained just as gloomy, no hope of widening those sunken eyes or relaxing those grimly set lips, but there were some slight signs that he was gratified by this praise.

Maria noticed how everybody hung on Vadim's words. He was so much younger than the others, yet how readily they recognized his superiority in speech, in intelligence, and in experience.

Now that there were no outsiders present, only party members (Maria was obviously one, since Vadim had brought her), they became more businesslike.

"Comrades," Vadim said crisply, no longer in the smooth expository voice he had used on Kesha, "I bring instructions directly from the Pe-Ka."

The Pe-Ka! The Petersburg Committee! That had a thrilling ring!

"The Petersburg Committee has a serious grievance against the

Obukhov workers. How could you fail to support the Vyborg Quarter on the thirtieth and thirty-first? You didn't lift a finger."

They could only sigh. Mashistov more heavily than the others. Mashistov was the factory *organizer*. He had to bear the brunt of the rebuke. The rectangular jaw dropped slightly.

"We do what we can. We refused overtime. Two shops are on strike at present. For time and a half."

"So why not all of them?" Vadim asked sternly. "When the Pe-Ka looks at the Neva Quarter it sees us going over to the liquidators."

"That's too much!" Dakhin burst out angrily. His eyes were needle sharp in their deep sockets.

Vadim spread his big, soft white fingers. (He was not embarrassed that his hands were not those of a workingman—the work they did was more important.)

"Is it, though? What about 22 January? The whole of working-class Petersburg was on strike. Only the Neva Quarter was at work. What was our excuse? That nobody told us to put down our tools, nobody came along to lead us out? That's what makes them say there's no militancy beyond the Neva Gate."

Lanky Uksila, bent double over a desk, grinned as much as to say, "They're right." It was shaming. That they weren't militant had been obvious long ago.

She saw all those hands—honest, strong, sinewy, hardworking hands used to gripping tools—lying on a desk or gripping the back of a chair—and to think that she was admitted to this circle! Veronika (Maria) could hardly believe it, but there she was, sitting for the first time with these men of iron, these true hearts, quite at home with them, except that she was embarrassed by her fur coat (she should have changed it; it was the correct wear for a visit to the Alexandra Theater, but here it might draw attention to what should be a secret meeting) and also by her luxuriant hair, which looked as though it was meant to invite admiration, and her far too delicate hands. She was so proud and so happy to be accepted as an equal by these people, and to be of use to them, that she had sworn to renounce, was there and then renouncing, her previous frivolous life of idle chitchat.

Busy renouncing, she paid less attention to what was being said.

"It's the influence of the Alexander plant," Mashistov said thoughtfully. Thoughtfulness shone out from his staring, almost immobile eyes. "They've become petty bourgeois, they've built themselves little houses, they keep cows—and our men would like to keep up with them."

"Right now they're getting ready for the holidays," Dakhin snapped. "They'll be off to church in droves!"

"What holidays are those?" Vadim asked in surprise.

"Our Lady of Kazan. Then Our Lady Comforter of All the Afflicted," Dakhin snapped. "She's their patron saint."

"The things these priests think of!" Vadim said, surprised and amused. "All the Afflicted! Crafty, eh? They've hit the nail on the head there! Only what we have to do is get all the afflicted to revolt, instead of bowing down to their silly old God."

"Our men have become very passive," Uksila said with a strong Finnish accent. "They're afraid of the training company. They put their hopes on the co-ops."

Uksila himself, being a Finn, didn't have to worry about the draft whatever happened. The Finns were exempt.

"Co-ops!" Vadim's big, soft pink lips parted in a grin. "You'll soon see how they'll feed you . . . Gvozdev's Canteen Center . . . You at least must understand that all this hullabaloo about co-ops and canteens is just a way of stepping up exploitation, to squeeze more out of you."

Yes, they could see it now. The workers' leaders looked sheepish. So it was just another swindle.

"You plod along behind the Duma Mensheviks, behind Chkheidze, that Marxoid lackey of Guchkov and Puryshkevich, and even he is more revolutionary than you."

They were silent. We don't know any better.

"Anyway, comrades, the Petersburg Committee has met and given me instructions to pass on to the Obukhov factory. The main thrust of our propaganda now must be inequalities of consumption, the high cost of living, food shortages. We must persistently exploit the dissatisfaction and indignation of the masses along these lines. You, however, have missed out on the whole cost-of-living campaign."

They were lost for an answer.

"But it is not too late, even now."

He took a sheaf of papers, folded into four, from his inside pocket, and opened them out.

"First you must arrange a short meeting and adopt a resolution along these lines. What I have here is a specimen resolution drafted by the Pe-Ka for workers' meetings on the food crisis: 'We, the workers of such and such a plant . . . fill it in . . . having discussed the food crisis . . . ' " He read briskly, without pauses, but the words did not fuse or collide. " 'First, that it is the inevitable result of the interminable imperialist bloodbath . . . second, that in Russia it is complicated by the supremacy of the Tsarist monarchy, which has put the country's economy at the mercy of capitalist predators . . . third, that the prolongation of the war will bring hunger, poverty, and the physical degeneration of the masses . . . fourth, that cooperatives and specifically workers' dining rooms, wage increases, and similar half measures only segregate the workers in separate supply systems, turn the rest of the population against the working class, and split the forces of revolution . . . and fifth, that the only recourse against hunger is all-out struggle against the war itself. Therefore the whole working class and all democrats must rise up in revolutionary struggle and civil war under the slogan 'Down with the war!' "

And all this—his ability to read and understand written matter quickly, and to make it comprehensible to others—was only a small part of his talents. Veronika had already learned that her director in this new life could write just as rapidly! Comrade Vadim—Matvei Ryss—was a member of the Petersburg Committee's literary board. He specialized in leaflets. He could sit down and produce in little more than an hour the final draft of a fervent and cogent appeal to the masses, urging them either to "take to the streets" ("Abandon the stifling dungeons of labor!") or, conversely, to stay off them ("Do not let them spill your precious workers' blood on the paving stones of Petersburg before the time is ripe!"), directing their wrath by turns against the "Romanov gang of hereditary bloodsuckers," the "sharks of our national industry," or the "hopeless petty bourgeois obtuseness of the socialist-liquidators." Admittedly these stock expressions were not in the best literary taste, but their impact was breathtaking. Of course, Matvei hadn't invented these expressions himself, they existed already, to suit a particular audience and a particular objective. Matvei's cleverness consisted in memorizing hundreds of them, letting them circulate freely in his mind, surfacing and submerging, so that the exact words he needed attached themselves spontaneously to the nib of his pen—"chariots of militarism," "traveling salesmen of chauvinism," "crowned murderers," "brothers worn out by their hard fate"—words to frame and reinforce the latest demands and exhortations of the Pe-Ka.

And not just the Pe-Ka!

"I also have instructions from the Be-Tse-Ka!" Vadim announced, looking sterner and more important than ever.

The Be-Tse-Ka? They all turned to look at him, and Mashistov spoke, more sharply than usual. "The Bureau of the Central Committee? It doesn't exist."

"It was reestablished just the other day," Vadim said mysteriously. And added more mysteriously still, "Comrade Belenin returned from abroad the other day."

Those words "returned from abroad" baffled the imagination. The battle zones were pitted with craters and crisscrossed with barbed wire, the frontiers were sealed—how could a member of a clandestine organization, a wanted man without a passport, transport himself? On the breeze, perhaps? Yesterday Switzerland, today Petersburg—what sort of supermen were these?

"Belenin? Who's he?" the impetuous Dakhin couldn't help asking.

Don't know who Belenin is? Lanky Uksila grinned sardonically,

Mashistov looked more wooden than ever, Vadim licked his lips pity-ingly, and even Veronika, who didn't herself know the answer, was embarrassed by the impropriety of the question.

Dakhin drew his eyes still deeper into their dark sockets.

"Well then," Vadim calmly continued, "these are the Be-Tse-Ka's instructions. To fight the Gvozdevites with all our strength. To sabotage all war industry consistently and on a broad front. Understood?"

Perfectly. Anyway, we're doing a bit of that already.

"But be warned. Remember that our strongest weapon is the strike. There's a shortage of fully qualified workers, so you won't be sent to the front, and you can make big demands. You can strike, organize meetings, adopt strongly worded resolutions, but under no circumstances must you let yourselves be provoked into premature bloody clashes. If you have to take to the street you must avoid any sort of collision. The time has not come. The final attack will take place when we establish a firm alliance with the army. Also understood?"

Veronika remembered that distant time—how far away it now seemed!—at the beginning of August 1914, when students had sung patriotic songs on the Nevsky, and knelt before the Winter Palace, and she and her friends in the Bestuzhev Institute had rejoiced in the war as a refreshing storm! When even people sitting in tramcars took off their hats if they heard demonstrators in the street singing "God Save the Tsar." Things had changed so drastically since then—when exactly?—that people couldn't be driven out into the street even to celebrate the taking of Erzerum or the Brusilov offensive. And here they now were, talking seriously about the final assault, as though it was imminent. And saying quite openly: we want nothing to do with your cannons, we declare war on your war!

It was this feeling of certain strength, steadily growing and sure of itself, that had won her over, brought her to this place, flooded her with the happiness of belonging. She marveled at her old self, blindly unable for so long to find the true path.

"And one final thing. By order of the Be-Tse-Ka, we must call a general strike for 8 November, when the trial of the revolutionary sailors begins. A strike in protest against the trial."

"What sailors are those?" Dakhin asked, undeterred. He had burned his fingers once, but still meant to know everything.

"You've been told—revolutionary sailors," Uksila snapped.

Mashistov had never heard of them either, but the look of dogged devotion on his face seemed to say that he had spent his life grieving for these sailors and could bear their suffering no longer.

Vadim nonetheless explained. "I'll tell you what sort of sailors they are. Last autumn they spread propaganda among ships' companies. About . . . about the food, about officers with German names . . . never mind what. Anyway, they caused unrest on the *Gangut* and the *Rurik*, and we regard them as revolutionaries. They were kept in various jails for some time. Now they're about to get rough justice. You'll be given some leaflets tomorrow. Comrade Maria here will deliver them, that's why I brought her along."

Maria (Veronika) blushed, with everyone looking at her.

"If you want to know what it says in the leaflet . . ." Vadim promptly unfolded one and read excerpts. He read as a hare or a kangaroo hops, barely touching the ground, carrying off crumbs of soil on its paws. "Because in their stifling barracks they have preserved their revolutionary consciousness undimmed . . . refused to be an unprotesting instrument in the hands of . . . The government is powerless to put the cadres of the working class, millions strong, in the dock, but its despicable courts are always at the service of . . . To mark the alliance of the revolutionary people with the revolutionary army we are bringing our factories to a standstill! Let the hangman's hand falter at the people's protest! Down with the death penalty!"

Down with the death penalty! Tolstoy's dream! The dream of all the noblest hearts! To think that she had wasted so many years, as a Bestuzhev student, astray in the "world of the arts," before catching up with these people, whose breadth of vision left her gasping!

Matvei's fair skin had turned pink. But he wasn't going to read it all the way through. He folded the papers and looked hard at each of his comrades.

"But this will simultaneously be a strike in protest against the arrest of soldiers of the 181st Regiment. And against the high cost of living. By taking part in this strike you will wash away the disgrace of your previous inaction. Prepare yourselves. Are you up to it?"

They had to be up to it. Uksila rose to his full height. Mashistov also stood up, raising his boxlike head.

They settled the details and put on their street clothes.

Matvei wound a dark red scarf around his throat, and finally put on his cap. While Veronika pulled up her Orenburg head scarf, hiding her neatly dressed hair, and becoming slightly less pretty. Handshakes all around—and the three workers all shook hers. She touched those honest, toilworn hands with respect and reverence, and they pressed hers in an iron grip, painfully—but pleasurably.

They were showing their trust in her. Initiating her.

How desperately she wanted to do well by these people, to be useful if only in a small way to them and to their noble cause: the movement to end the war! To end all wars on this earth, once and for all! And all forms of capital punishment! No one must be oppressed! All must be freed from servitude!

They left the mutual aid society's shack in full view of the sentry, and with a patrol somewhere around, so Matvei took the young woman's arm, to make it all look innocent, and they set off like that slowly along the Schlüsselburg Prospect.

And although Veronika knew that Matvei had taken her arm only for the sake of appearances, and that he was not particularly concerned for her, she walked along as if he really meant it.

"I'm so grateful to you for taking me with you. And entrusting me with this task. You'll see that I'm just the right person for it."

Matvei's thoughts were elsewhere and he said nothing.

It was a pleasant, not too wintry evening. A fine moisture, not quite snowflakes and not quite raindrops, settled on the forehead and the cheeks. An endless vista of streetlamps drew them along the Prospect, that long carriageway without sidewalks. Scraps of newspaper littered the road. It looked neglected. It couldn't always have been like that. There weren't many people around. The shops were all shut, the side streets dark. They moved aside for a newish American truck heading for the city. Veronika retreated instinctively to save her fur coat from splashes, but Matvei also gave way.

Twenty long blocks ahead of them lay the city that was dark for half the year, built all of stone, but so well adapted to illumination at night, to entertainments of all kinds, balls, theaters, horse racing, trips to the islands, a city equipped to ensure the felicity of the few, and at this evening hour just beginning to live its real life, youthful guardsmen erect in swift cabs to show off their manly forms, slapping the cabby's shoulder with their gloves to speed him up, rushing toward their appointed pleasures, with not the slightest desire to know anything whatsoever about the workers' world on their periphery or the strikes which had already hit the city and were to hit it again.

Veronika had to take the steam tram, then an electric tram, and travel right across the frivolous, elegant part of the city, across its bridges to the outer edge of Vasilevsky Island, where the Nikolai Embankment ended at the 21st Line.

But she was in no hurry to get away. Matvei lived with his lawyer father on Staro-Nevsky, but also rented a room locally—sharp left at the Bekhter Clinic, not far from his own Psychoneurological Institute. The institute was presently in danger of losing its autonomy and was seething with indignation. Matvei had to be on the spot.

When they were safe from police surveillance he took his arm away and stopped steering her. She looked sideways at his bold, self-assured, energetic face, and timidly tucked her neatly gloved hand under his elbow. Afraid of seeming like a mushy schoolgirl, she said quickly, "Tell me, Matvei. . . ." What she most wanted to ask was who Belenin was (a nom de guerre, obviously).

But it would be wrong to press him too hard. Idle curiosity and superfluous actions had no place in conspiratorial work. And this rule of strict confidentiality within the party, and Matvei's own uncompromising rigidity, had fused in Veronika's mind into the single virtue of manly steadfastness. His party did not go in for jokes, for loose talk, for pointless blather, and was very different in this from the decadent and ineffectual milieu in which Veronika had languished till now.

"Tell me . . . I still don't really understand . . ."

"What?" he asked absently, looking straight ahead.

Veronika very much wanted to believe with all her heart, like the rest of them, and as quickly as possible, but doubts would nonetheless arise and multiply, so she asked, and indeed Matvei encouraged her to ask.

"That slogan—'Convert the present war into civil war.'" She was speaking of awesome historical phenomena, but her voice was soft and casual. "Might not that have the opposite effect, and prolong the food crisis? I mean, if the war in its third year threatens the people with physical degeneration, what will happen if it goes on much longer, even as a civil war?"

Matvei listened attentively, then burst out laughing. "As soon as we knock this thieving government and all those scoundrelly Guchkovs and Ryabushinskys off their perches, as soon as the democratic republic is established, there will be no more of these queues, these price increases, every consumer item will appear immediately."

"But where from?"

"There's plenty of everything. In Petersburg, right now, there's plenty. The merchants and industrialists simply keep things hidden till they can rip off their super-profits. This long fence we're just passing—you couldn't jump over it. But what's on the other side? Pretty certainly some sort of warehouse, and that warehouse is most probably full of foodstuffs and other goods, but you can't get at them. No-o-o," he said, laughing at her incredulity, "the whole food crisis is caused by the interplay of supply and demand, by speculation. Establish tomorrow a socialist system of distribution, and right away there'll be enough and to spare for everyone. Hunger will cease the day after the revolution. Everything will appear, sugar, meat, white bread, milk. The people will take everything into their own hands—the existing stocks and the management of the economy—they will organize things according to plan, and an age of abundance, even, will set in. People will start producing all that is needed with such enthusiasm! I'll go farther; the solution of the food crisis is impossible without socialism, because only then will social production begin to serve not the enrichment of individuals but the interests of all mankind!"

Veronika was not looking where she was going. By now her other hand was holding Matvei's elbow while she gazed at his rapt expression. She loved hearing about his dreams of the future—though "dreams" was the wrong word. She trembled at the vivid picture of the dream already made flesh. At the sheer power of this man. She must introduce him to her brother—if Sasha was ever transferred to Petersburg. They were sure to take to each other from the start. She could see them together: they were just like each other. Not so much in appearance, in something else, more important.

"And anyway, when we say 'civil war' it's just a manner of speaking.

War with whom? How long can a handful of exploiters stand up to the whole united working class? A month or two, perhaps? And then if the proletariat immediately seizes power all over Europe and holds out a hand to us? Just think what power the German proletariat represents!"

"And the war with Germany will end?"

"Certainly it will! Certainly! Once a socialist order is created all wars will cease at once. Surely two socialist countries would never make war on each other? Can you imagine it?"

It was obviously absurd.

"No one can ever force a socialist state to make war! Wars are started by the rulers, not by their people. When the capitalist order ends, human suffering will end with it."

Heavens, how good it sounded! And what a good thing she had not been too bashful to question him, and could now see for herself how neatly it all fitted in.

Meanwhile: "Here's your stop, off you go. You'll come around for the leaflets tomorrow, right? What time?"

He only had to turn left, along Fourth Circle.

"I'll walk you home," she said, bending forward.

They walked down the dark, potholed street, toward the park at the other end.

They were silent for a while. Suddenly Matvei stopped. He put one arm around her, and though no look, no movement of his had prepared her for it, began kissing her, greedily, again and again, crushing her lips with his own, forcing her head backward.

Her head scarf slipped back, but she didn't feel the cold. Nor the bend in her back, nor the prickling.

She just felt happy.

*   *   *

Let us destroy the decrepit despotism of Nicholas II, let us sweep the filthy scum of landowners and priests from the land of Russia, and oppression will be no more, wars will cease forever. The forward contingents of the International have already entered the blood-drenched arena. Comrades—do not delay! Beware of arriving too late! Long live the Federal Republic of Europe!

—RSDRP

*   *   *

[3 5]

The nickname your village inflicts on you is rarely so inoffensive that you would not wish to change it. It is meant to rankle. Those who invent it have suffered in their time and want to see you squirm. From your infancy. Whether you are a boy or a girl, the street watches you closely, peers through its windows, hoping to see you miss your footing or drop what you are carrying, hears you, from over its fences, whimper or invoke high heaven. Whether you are out in the field working or on the road with your cart, it will not lose track of you. If your axle is ungreased, or your horse is unfed, you're Layabout Lyova or Sasha Slugabed. As for the women, they keep a ten times sharper eye on each other. Leave the kneading trough uncovered, or the oven cloth lying around, sit awkwardly at your spinning wheel, and in no time you're Slovenly Slava or Mucky Masha, a lazy lump or a fumbling fusspot, you're not sure which is worse. Someone catches you in the act and flings a name at you, and either it falls away like a lump of dry mud or, carried by the street wind, it hits you right on the cheek and sticks and stings forever. In the cradle, in nursery school, everyone has a nickname but it rarely follows them as they grow up. But if a name is stuck on a grown girl she will wear it when she rocks her grandchildren, if a name is stuck on a grown boy he will carry it as a grandfather. It may even be handed down to your posterity. Blub's descendants may be Blubbiches, Stodger's may be Stodgerkins, never mind their real surname. Your surname is for the rural council, the clerk, the draft officer, the zemstvo paramedic. The surname passed on like a worn coin from your great-grandfathers and great-great-grandfathers indicates your lineage, no more. A nickname alone reveals your true lineaments to your fellow villagers. A single clumsy moment, a single careless mishap—and you are branded for the rest of your days.

It's true what they say: one thoughtless hour and you're a fool for life.

It's the same with the gentry. Take Tsirmant. They started calling him Squire Patches—and however spacious your marble halls later on, however many troikas you own, however much silver you stash away— once you're Patches you're Patches forever. No good trying to hobnob with the Princes Volkonsky. There is always something in these thumbnail sketches. Nicknames are never given at random. If a sharp eye has spotted it—it's a part of you. It's a lucky villager who is given a not too offensive sobriquet, such as Marrow Bone, meaning he makes a fat living (snarling and snatching, like a dog at a bone), or the Block, meaning he's strong (but wooden-headed and cross-grained).

Kamenka had chosen to call Elisei Blagodarev Stalky. There was not the slightest hint of an insult in it.

He was already a man of thirty when he first appeared in Kamenka, before the war with Turkey, married Domasha Opolovnikova, and was taken into his father-in-law's house. His native place was beyond Baikal, although his forebears had not always lived there. He had been given a nickname there too, but had not brought it with him to Kamenka, and had disclosed it to no one. Nor, for that matter, did he ever say anything about his previous life, except perhaps to Domasha occasionally. His sons were told nothing about it by their father. He must have been doing something, lived or wandered around somewhere before he was thirty. Perhaps he had had some setbacks, but he arrived on the river Savala undamaged, and Kamenka had quickly adopted the homeless loner under the name of Stalky.

Here too things had not been easy for Elisei Blagodarev, in a family without men. The years went by, and he and his first son were not given an allotment. He had to begin by buying land with borrowed money, repaying it in installments, then leasing a little more. Only later was he given an allotment for two, then a little more for his second son, Arseni, but by then there were five children, as well as two orphans left by Domasha's sister, who herself had lived with them until she was married. Elisei had now lived in Kamenka for more than thirty years. He didn't drink or smoke or covet other people's property or brawl. He simply pulled his load. But his wagon was so overloaded, and its wheels so clogged, that, straining for dear life, he could not straighten out and pick up speed. Like many others, Elisei was harnessed to a load beyond his strength, and the most vexatious thing of all was that the road was potholed. In spite of it all, he had managed to set up his older son, Adrian, on a farm of his own, at Blue Bushes. And he had preserved his upright figure, the alert poise of his head, and sharp, bright eyes which gazed steadily into the distance and which he screwed up to look at anything nearer, as though it caused him pain. He saw as far and clearly at sixty-six as if he was still a young man and felt that his prime still lay before him.

Arseni Blagodarev's street name was Moaner. He grew up to be as big and strong as his father, but neither he nor his brother Adrian had their father's slender grace. Their hair and complexion were somewhat darker, their noses a little broader, their cheekbones rather more prominent, Tambov cheekbones, their lips fuller, and their heads not so neatly poised on their necks. Elisei grumbled sometimes: "You've spoiled my bloodline, Domasha."

Whereas the youngest son had been the image of his father, just as bright and slender (stemlike). He would have been eighteen now, but had drowned in his early teens, watering horses in the pond, and clinging to their tails when his feet couldn't touch bottom. Both daughters had married away from home, one at Korovainovo, on the Mokraya Panda, the other even farther away, at Inokovka, a stone's throw from

Kirsanov. And so only Arseni was left behind with his parents, and they had been about to give him a holding of his own when along came the war.

Nothing had prepared his father for Arseni's arrival that day. But from the open cart shed he heard the latch of the farmyard gate click and his heart skipped a beat. Nothing had prepared him until Quacker yapped (the whole village kept its dogs chained until the sheep were brought in for the winter), gave another half-yap, this time of welcome, and was silent, probably frisking around someone. Elisei went into the yard just as he was, saddle in hand (he had been about to hitch up), and realized in a flash.

"Senka! You here?!"

Was he even taller than before? Must be his soldierly bearing. As soon as he lowered his knapsack from his left shoulder to the ground, his father seized him, and pressed his face against his son's cheek, above the yellow-edged shoulder board with the grenadiers' insignia— crossed cannons and a fiery shell burst—on it.

His father's sheepskin hat pushed Arseni's service cap askew, and the forgotten saddle bumped against him. Mustache and beard prickled Arseni's face before he could draw back. The fresh smell of wind and hay and leather told him that he was at home, where he belonged.

Neither of them had to stoop. They were almost the same height.

"Papa! You're straight-backed as ever!"

"Me?" Flinging his arms wide, admiring his son. "I can thresh a sheaf without a flail. Five swings and you've got fine flour."

You could believe him. More like a poplar than an old man. Firm hands gripping Senka's shoulders. Firm voice. Eyes clear.

"As soon as I get a forkful it's a sheaf, and while the others are bringing the second, mine's on the rick. I can't see any end for me, Senka. I could go and fight right now, if you like, just as well as you can."

He had not been called up for the war with Japan because of his age. But in the war with Turkey he had won a George Cross. Now Senka had two stripes, and two medals on his chest (were they giving them away more freely?), one a George Cross of his own, all shiny and new, with a clean ribbon—it was a pity to wear it except on special occasions. His father couldn't resist running his hand over the medals.

"So, so. You're a pretty good soldier? So why can't you finish it off without us?"

They embraced again.

That was when Senka's mother caught sight of them. She hadn't noticed Senka through the window, and the cottage had a blank wall on the yard side. She must have heard them from the entrance hall, and now she came around the corner of the cottage like a shot. She was much shorter than her husband and her son, but as strong as she had always been. She pushed her husband aside and hugged her son, surrounding him with the smell of stove smoke and the baking oven, and said, or rather breathed voicelessly, "Senka, my love! My little son!"

Better cover him with kisses quickly. He'll be too shy to bend down again. Kiss him again and again, this gift of God, preserved and restored to you by Our Lady of Kazan for her very own feast day.

His mother's face was very smooth, with few wrinkles. She was quite unlike his father in build and looks, but her dark eyes were just as clear as his.

All women shed tears on such occasions, but Senka's mother refrained. She took his cheeks in her hands, looked at him admiringly, without so much as a whimper.

She looked hard, inspecting him closely.

"So you haven't been wounded, not one single time? Haven't kept it quiet?"

"No, Mama, I'm in one piece, you can see for yourself."

"And you aren't thin in the face either."

"All the grub we get, Mama, you'll never see anything like it in the village. And we don't have all the worries you have, the officers do our thinking for us. You couldn't ask for anything more."

His mother laughed with him.

"You've come just at the right time, for the festival. Why didn't you write? Never mind, I've got till this evening and all Friday. I'll get some baking and brewing done, you'll see."

Arseni clapped his mama on her plump shoulders. "You're such workers, both of you, so young!"

His mother gave his father a stern look. "Thank God, we can't say we haven't got a man in the house. Some people kill themselves working, or ask for prisoners of war, but we're all right!"

His father laughed under his fair mustache. "Ask them for an Austrian if you like, and I'll go off to the war. Look at this milksop with his two Georges, and I've only got one."

He was still holding the saddle. But he wasn't going to saddle up now.

Arseni's father was fourteen years older than his mother, but even so, he said he'd married too young, a man should hold out till thirty-six. He had scolded Senka, tried to prevent him from marrying at twenty-four. There had been rows. Adrian too had set up on his own, left home too early.

But where was Katya, his own little Katya? His mother hadn't said, and it wasn't for Senka to ask.

They went to the rear porch, his father still carrying the saddle, as well as Senka's knapsack and Senka's cap, which had landed on the floor.

Through the wide-open door from the hallway onto the porch, no longer on all fours, but upright, though he still had to steady himself with a hand on the lintel, out he toddled, wearing nothing but a little shirt, barefoot, bareheaded, flaxen-haired—

"Se-va-styan!"

He looked goggle-eyed at this stranger. And puffed out his lower lip, just like his daddy.

Come here, let me get hold of you—and up you go!

No, he wasn't happy about it, he didn't know this new uncle, he wanted Grandma. "Look how he's shaking me, look how he's tossing me around!"

Senka fussed the little boy and set him down.

"Off you go, small fry, you're a good walker. We'll get acquainted later, plenty of time for that."

"He's run outside! He'll catch cold! Fenya!"

Out rushed young Fenya, Senka's orphan cousin. She stood trans-fixed. Sharp-featured and quick-moving, she had to stand almost on tiptoe to kiss her cousin.

"Hey, you're quite a young lady!" Arseni declared, and kissed her head, where her hair was parted.

"How you've grown in a year! You'll soon be as big as Katya!"

Where is my Katya? Why hasn't she come running? Why hasn't anybody said a word about her?

But it wasn't for him to ask. He would feel embarrassed.

His mother saved him the trouble. "Fenya! Run and fetch Katya!"

Fenya hadn't waited to be asked; head scarf on, shawl on, felt boots on, and off she dashed to the threshing floor.

"They've been braking the flax. Fenya came home for a bite to eat. We finished chopping the cabbage and put it up for pickling yesterday. Today it's the flax."

They trooped back into the cottage, little Sevastyan leading the way. His grandma opened the door for him. He rested a hand on the high step, swung one leg over, then the other, straightened up, burst out laughing, and ran off. Arseni remembered from his own childhood how warm the unpainted, broom-scratched yellow boards were to bare feet.

A startling realization: this is me, the spitting image of me, from his little forehead down to his little toenail. Not just my son, a son of mine might look different from me. There aren't any words to say just what it is, but it's a shock to see just how like me he is, it's me all over again! A second me!

Through a gap in the partition he could see a cradle, still gently swinging.

Asleep.

The little daughter I've never seen, look how tiny she is! No size to her at all yet, her eyes closed, no bigger than little fingernails, her nose just two turned-up nostrils, no telling whether she's like me or Katya, only women are good at that. But still my heart beats faster. This is my flesh and blood.

My daughter. I have a little daughter too.

He ran his finger over her cheek, so gently she didn't feel it.

He didn't know which one of them to look at. He'd tried to hold his darling son, but the child wouldn't have it, there he was now hiding behind Grandma, peeping out from behind her skirts.

Elisei stood silently, shifting from one foot to the other, staring at his bombardier, just as the bombardier was staring at his own precious son. Maybe wishing he could hoist Senka in his arms just once more.

That's how it goes: you don't make much fuss over the old folks, and when he's grown up your son won't make much fuss over you.

The soldier took off his greatcoat, and his mother perched on a bench to light the lamp before the icon. Joy had come among them one day early and caught them with the house still unprepared for the feast of Our Lady.

Senka's mother got down from the bench, looked around at her family, and a movement of her hand told them to kneel.

Senka's father sank to his knees behind her. His head was an elongated oval, egg-shaped. But not bald, he had quite a lot of hair, flattened now by his cap, grayish but with a sprinkling of yellow.

Senka too knelt.

Domasha began reciting a prayer. She didn't drone, didn't stumble over words like someone struggling through bushes at night. She made the few prayers she knew meaningful, not so much praying to the Virgin as conversing with her, heart to heart.

Little Sevastyan too—would you believe it?—without being made to, knelt next to his grandma, waved his little hands in the air when the others crossed themselves, and stared unblinkingly at the icons. How had he learned all that? He was barely two years old.

They rose from their prayers, and it was one mad whirl. Where did you start? With the presents perhaps? But what presents could you buy on a soldier's pittance? A kerchief for one, a ribbon for another, lump sugar saved from his rations for someone else. What mattered was the thought, the ceremony, not the present itself.

But his mother was ahead of him.

"No, you'll eat now, Senka, my dear. Sit down and eat first. I've got onion pie. And baked bream. And there's beetroot wine already brewed, only it really needs to stand a bit longer."

Yes, he'd seen it, Senka had, coming through the hallway, pitchers stopped with twists of straw, and the fermenting froth oozing through.

Ah, here she was at last! She flew into the cottage like a bomb into a dugout, just one flash of a black-and-yellow skirt, her feet hardly seeming to touch the floor, then she was butting Senya, in his ribs,

here, there, everywhere, fit to break his bones. He still hadn't got a
look at her face, she was pressing it against his ribs, and he couldn't
tell whether she was crying or just out of breath, but he could see the
white nape of her neck, see that her sleeves were gathered at the shoulders, see the black squares and yellow stripes of her skirt, see the homespun girdle high on her back, with tassels on either side.

Like a little bird, all that there was of her no higher than his elbow,
Katya, my little Katya! I would like to pick you up and toss you in the
air like little Sevastyan, but not with my parents looking. When I got
off the train at Rzhaksa, when I walked down the highroad and saw
Kamenka looking down on me, when I lifted the latch on the gate—
all that was in a dream. I didn't feel that I was at home. Now I know
I'm home—with Katya under my arm.

He breathed hard.

Tipped her head back. She blushed, said nothing.

Soldier's wife—neither widow nor wedded woman, that was the saying.

They kissed.

Nothing for it—had to let her go.

All together now, under one roof, and Senka could have held them
all in one embrace, except that his mother was too wide. Back in the
battery Senka had felt at home—but no, this was the only place for
him.

"Have you had a look at Proska?"

"Yes."

"Well, take another look."

They went to the cradle behind the screen. The little girl was asleep,
her cheeks bright red, she meant to go on sleeping. Nine months—
how far back did that make it?

"She can crawl already," Katya boasted, uncovering the child's head,
so that he could see her better.

Senka was looking at Katya, though, the gathered sleeves, the tas-
seled girdle.

"Why are you all dressed up today?"

She raised her head and looked into his eyes. "I just felt like it."
Then quietly: "I dreamt about you."

Just that—and his heart was on fire.

But little Sevastyan had toddled over to his mama and was clutching
her leg.

And Domanya was ordering them to the table. Why hadn't he written? Why hadn't he sent a telegram? Your father would have been at
the station with the buggy, I would have baked sponge cake and pies
. . . Never mind, it'll all be there tomorrow, I've got the dough made.

"See, Mama, it all happened in a rush, in a single day. They'd turned
me down already, and I'd written to tell you. Then that same evening

the lieutenant sent for me and said hold the letter, maybe they will let you go, then the next day he calls me in and says it's been granted, go and get some paper from the letter writer."

The months and years had washed over Senka, none of them empty, you might think, it was all service orders, the Germans, never a minute's rest, forever on the go, but he'd never felt pushed so hard, so ready to burst as now, at home! Two eyes, two ears, two hands, one mouth not enough to eat your mother's food, answer your father's questions, reach out to caress the children, all at the same time. Katya had fed Proska, and was holding her out to him. He took his daughter in his arms for the first time, and she wet him. All this was so new, and he had to take care not to upset anybody. Katya didn't seem altogether at ease either, she kept eyeing him as if he was almost a stranger, watching to see how he looked at his daughter, and how often he would hold out his hand to little Sevastyan, wondering whether he really loved them or was just pretending.

No good, though, these women would keep you talking forever if you let them. What Senka wanted to know was: How are you managing by yourself, Dad? What jobs are marking time, what hasn't gotten done? I'm here now, and I'll get cracking with you! Double harness, you know what a team we make! That's what I came on leave for— not to fool around.

They went out of the cottage.

His father had been thinking along the same lines. I can still pull my weight, and my back isn't too stiff. Your Katya's a big help—even with the pitchfork—or carting.

Need help? I certainly do! But the time for work will be after the holidays. We can look around now, though, while the women are busy in the cottage.

They went out into the yard. Quacker jumped up to lick Senka's hands.

His father's woodpile had not dwindled during the year: he had replaced all that he had used. Anyway, they used mainly dung bricks for fuel—the black earth of Tambov needed no manure. Where forests are thin you burn dung.

His father explained things. Look, you have to understand our situation here, before you can get to work. For a start, there may be nobody to take a job on, it's mostly women now, or say the plows aren't right, we've got nothing to mend them with, and the ground doesn't get sown. For another thing, why do we need to grow so much grain, why should we sow if we're worse off for it?

What could be more galling: to plow and sow, knowing before you started that you would only be worse off by doing it? Arseni felt hot under the collar. But his father went on.

"We can get by, for a year, or maybe two, on our own grain, without sowing. We're not in such a hurry to sell grain as we used to be. The whole village has cut down on autumn plowing. We've got money nowadays. We got paid for the horses taken over by the army and for the stock. We pay taxes with the same money, and money has gotten cheaper, so our taxes are a lot lower than they were. The same goes for the Peasants' Bank. Lord above, all this crazy money will destroy the people."

The words reached Senka's ears, but it was all strange to him. The village had never before had to ask itself why it should grow so much grain. He couldn't make head or tail of it. He couldn't remember ever hearing anything like it.

His father hadn't finished yet. The state vodka shops were no longer there either—another reason for people not to break their necks for money. Then again, soldiers' wives got their allowances. Some women had gotten out of hand as a result, and didn't give their fathers-in-law anything toward expenses, but blew the whole bundle on fancy clothes and dainties. To hell with the holding, it won't run away. If our husbands come back from the war in one piece we'll start earning again. If their husbands do come back they're not going to like it.

"What about Katya?" Senka asked anxiously.

"Katya? No, never. She hands over her money, every last kopeck. I give her her share afterward. Besides, she has to help her mother out. Not just with money but with her hands."

Their yard, strewn with gravel from the river, was not muddy, although out in the street you had to walk on duckboards in some places and the whole road from Rzhaksa was a black morass after the recent rains. Hens wandered about the yard, and a bay foal came over to butt his master and nuzzle his hand. Arseni tickled him behind his ears.

"So how many have you got left altogether?"

"Well, there's Strigan here—he's one of Kupavka's—Kupavka herself, and a gelding. And Kudesy."

Two workhorses and a trotter, then.

"You handed the other two over?"

"Yes."

"Hmm, we'll have to stock up again after the war."

"We'll have to make a fresh start with a lot of things after the war, Senka, but where do you begin? I handed one cow over as well, and a bullock, they made me."

"So how many are left?"

"Two cows. An eighteen-month bull. And a yearling calf."

"We've come down in the world, Dad."

"Suppose we save that money—what's the good of it? It's rubbish. Easy money, money for nothing, but you can't buy a thing with it. Money's got so light you can change it into coppers and empty a mountain of them onto the scales, it won't weigh as much as a piece of calico, let alone a pair of boots."

Their cowsheds, pigsties, and henhouse covered an area of twelve by twenty arshins* under a single roof, while the horses occupied the space between the mangers and the water trough. There were horses at the front, with the battery, and Arseni knew and loved every one of them, but there were none so dear as his own here at home. His heart thumped at the sight of them.

The gelding stood still and didn't look around. Kudesy started, pricked up his ears, and a shiver ran down his spine. But Kupavka knew him! She recognized the young master, snorted, smiled. Arseni felt a warm glow as the horse greeted him, embraced her head, caressed her.

He fed the horses some hay from the open shed.

"Remember, we used to get seven poods of nails for a pood of grain. Now you get one pood. Shoeing nails were always ten kopecks—and suddenly it's two rubles. So we didn't market much of the summer crop even, and surely we won't take much of this crop in. It's over there in the bin, and the other's in ricks by the drying barn. We'll thresh some more for seed before snow comes."

"Has it all been brought in?"

"Yes."

"So now the mice will be nibbling it!"

"They will. But that's the problem—where can we store it? Why should we keep more than we need for food and seed? We've never kept more than eighty poods over the winter. We aren't equipped to keep it. Some people have started leaving it in the field, in stooks, instead of threshing it."

"What do they do that for?"

"Well, some people say you can have your grain taken from you by force at train stations or river ports, or if it's going from one province to another."

"But you get paid for it, don't you?"

"If you call it paid—at fixed prices. It's less than nothing. We've got these government agents dropping in on us all the time, prowling and prying, say they've got to write down all we've got in stock. So they write what's in my granary—and likely as not come and take it from me tomorrow."

The light was poor outside, it was dimmer still in the barn, and Elisei's face was shaded by his well-worn, shaggy cap, but his eyes were bright and keen. From the beginning of time being a peasant had meant having a hundred things to do, wondering at every turn: Rain or drought? Windy or calm? Dew or ground frost? Sand or soil? The birds, the worms, the state of the roads and the barn, the market. And when you've taken all this into consideration and invested your labor it's a toss-up whether you have a profit or a loss. And the way things

*Arshin: A unit of length equal to twenty-eight inches. [*Trans.*]

were now, rack your brain as you might, there'd never been anything like it, and Senka didn't know what to advise.

After the cowshed they looked into the pigsty, the empty sheep pen—the sheep were out on the common field—and the hen run. The geese walked around freely, fending for themselves.

Some people make it a rule never to bring the crop to market right away. Better careful than quick, they figure. Maybe the fixed prices will go up? And what if we get a famine on top of everything else? The grain will come in handy then, for us and our cattle. How long will this war go on? Should we really be in a hurry to move the crop? And what's it going to be like after the war? We've lost so many cattle already, and a lot more will be slaughtered.

They went outside. Early that morning the sky had been clear, and it looked as if they were in for a fine day. But now it was overcast, darker. Was that rain? Not yet, just a few drops.

There had been two spells of morning frost, before and after the feast of the Intercession of the Virgin. But the weather had become milder again.

"So what are we going to do, Dad?"

"On your way here, was the road in bad shape?"

"For the first five versts after the Likhovat gully the horses nearly left their shoes in the mud."

"No good trying to get anywhere. Now, at hay making we had lovely summer weather, got a bumper crop in. How long are you going to be here?"

"I'll be staying till after Michael's day. But not till the Presentation. About a month."

"Aha," his father said happily, "so we'll have you till the first sledging, and you and I can go down to the meadows and get the hay in. We'll get thirty sledge loads or maybe more."

The hay barn beyond the fence stood empty, waiting. There was only a scattering of hay on the loft floor, where somebody had been sleeping.

"And then we can stook the hemp and bring it in. We'll caulk the barn, there'll be time before the big frosts."

What about the roof? Senka took a quick look at the cottage from this side—he'd already seen it from the street, no sign anywhere of damage to the thatch—neatly trimmed bundles of straw "under clay."

"You're keeping on top of things, Dad, no doubt about it!"

All the letters written to Arseni consisted of greetings and best wishes. There was never anything specific about how they were making out, never any details. But now, walking around and casting an eye, you saw that things were going well! They were managing!

His father was flattered to hear it from his son, as from an equal.

Not as well as that, though. The fairs weren't as lively, not so many people showed up at those two dozen yearly fairs.

From Tugolukovo to Sampur, from Tokarevka to Rzhaksa—horse fairs, wood fairs, potters' fairs, honey fairs . . . In Kamenka too the fair had come and gone quietly that year. You didn't get carters teaming up for long-distance jobs, they were just roped in for compulsory local transport duty. Life was turning in on itself, retreating into its own backyard, its own four walls.

"Another thing—we'll do some drying and threshing, there's a lot waiting to be threshed after the wet summer. And maybe we can dig a trench for the pig food while you're here. We've got to stock up for the bad weather."

"Of course, Dad. We'll get it dug. In no time."

All that strength—alive, your own son's, ready to work for you. But it all depended on whether one little jagged piece of shrapnel flew past. An inch nearer—and your son's no more. You're left to howl alone. And that one inch, that one metal splinter, won't make Tsar or zemstvo spare a thought for you. It's all in God's hands, and for now— your son's alive.

"You're a bit low on manure. Remember how we used to have piles of it?"

"They've taken so many cattle, dung's worth its weight in gold."

"Yes, a lot of cattle have been slaughtered with this war. We eat meat in the army like we never did in all our born days. Fresh-killed meat every day, Dad."

His father was surprised. "They never fed us like that when I was a soldier."

"They say the army's changed for the better in a lot of ways these last few years. Anyway, what are we going to do for the holiday?"

"I killed a wether yesterday. I can kill another if you like."

They stood for a while at his father's bench, looked at his work, and were on their way to the orchard when a sudden thought struck Arseni. "What about the bees, though? Are they settled?"

"They're settled!" Question and answer made father and son happy. Not just a matter of husbandry. Beekeeping stirred deeper feelings. "Yes, they're in the winter hive now."

Katya dashed toward them, her black-and-yellow skirt fluttering. The cape she had hastily thrown over her shoulders did not meet in front, and was rucked up at the back.

"Senya, Mama wants to know what you want done about the bath."

Ordinarily the family would be heating a bath the next day, in time for the holiday, but for Senya it had to be done now. His mother said well, yes, only she had more than enough to do, with just the one pair of hands. Katya spoke up quickly. "It's got to be today, Mama, of course it must! After all that traveling! And when do they ever get a real wash back there? I can make the fire while I'm doing other things, it won't hold me up."

And off she dashed to the bathhouse.

Senka was eager to help.

"Should I fetch the wood, or water?" His father, of course, had the wood all ready, and the water came from the well right by the bath-house, but it would give him five minutes for a chat with his wife somewhere along the way.

Fenka, coming home from the threshing floor, was also eager to help, but Katya shooed her away: "Mama's told you what to do! Any-way, it's time to steam the mash for the horses.

Fenka had learned to do a lot of jobs, she could milk a cow properly, she was at the age when a girl must pick up these skills. But she hovered around, clung to them, wouldn't let them out of her sight, because she was growing up fast, and she was curious: how would husband and wife behave on his first day home? She wanted to see for herself, to take note for the future.

It was no use! The gate banged once, twice, three times—neighbors dropping in to take a look at the soldier and touch his medals. Nobody had been invited, nobody had been told, but one neighbor had spotted him from a window, another over his fence, a little bird had told an-other . . . you can't keep anything secret in a village. First came Yakim Rozhok, a man bent double at the waist, the one who always had to be the first to know. No neighbor, he had toddled over from the far end of the village, the part called Past-the-Church. Then came Agapei Derba, a dark, lanky man, walking as stiffly as if he had poles for legs. He was the only one Quacker barked at, but he didn't turn his sullen head. He listened to everybody, staring morosely at the ground. You'd wait a long time for a word from him. Next was old Ilyakha Bayunya, wearing striped shalwar with a gaudy tobacco pouch tucked under his belt, leaning heavily on his walking stick nowadays. And Nisifor Stre-moukh—hey, not called up yet, and his brother already back home on crutches?

"Come on, soldier! Let's have a look at you!"

"What's it like being in the army?"

Fatheads! Only one way to find out. Go and try it yourselves.

"What's it like? Nothing to it. You lay your head on your fist and your ribs on whatever. Wondering what the quartermaster will dish out tomorrow—a pinch of tea or a lick of sugar. You're short of every-thing, we're short of nothing."

"They say it's a good life, being a soldier, but nobody much wants to join."

"Look at him, the guy's getting ahead fast—more stripes than last year. So what are you now?"

"Bombardier."

"Come on, show us your medals."

The medals were on his greatcoat, and the greatcoat was in the cottage. You couldn't sit around outside. Anyway, it was too cold. But it was a bad time to ask them in—there was nowhere to sit them, the cottage hadn't been tidied up, the women were busy cooking, bustling about like mad things. But the men were already rolling cigarettes, flint grated on steel, and the sparks were caught on tinder—matches were saved for the stove these days, and the menfolk didn't get any. Only old Ilyakha had crossed himself before the icons as they entered. Now they had started raising a cloud of smoke in the cottage. The Blagodarevs never smoked, not one of them.

So many men still at home in Kamenka. Not only old men either.

"Dammit! Why are you all hanging on at home here? It's your fault we just can't get on top of Fritzy."

"It's coming along, though, isn't it?"

"Who's winning?"

"A lot of *his* have been knocked off," Arseni answered easily. Then more heavily: "Quite a few of ours as well . . . The number of little birches we've chopped down for crosses, the number of holes we've dug. And we're not one little bit further on."

Now something was bothering little Proska. She suddenly let out a wail, and Arseni, unused to it, was worried—that's my daughter, not somebody else's, crying. But Katya was there like a flash, plucking the child out of her cradle, changing her diaper, washing her, rocking her a bit, making her a pacifier by chewing some rusks and wrapping them in gauze, popping her back into the cradle again. While the men of the village laid siege to Arseni, hoping to hear that there was some promise of peace. Had he heard tell of it?

"No, never a whisper, not a whiff on the breeze. Poison gas is all you can smell."

"Gas? How d'you mean? What gas?"

"I can tell you, boys, I wouldn't even wish it on the enemy. If you get hit by a piece of shrapnel—well, you expect that in a fight, you don't really mind all that much. But swallow enough of that other stuff and it'll tie your innards in knots."

They wouldn't let go, they wanted to know this, they wanted to know that . . . What did you get your second George for? Tell us everything that's happened to you.

Arseni started telling them about his battery, about the Dryagovets forest, about the communication trenches, how you couldn't stand up straight in them, and hardly dared hope you'd reach the dugout. He began lightheartedly, occasionally catching Sevastyan and hugging him to his knees—the little rogue was wandering about among all those legs, staring wide-eyed and prattling to himself. Began lightheartedly, but couldn't keep it up. There wasn't much to laugh about. Back there in the battery, among themselves, there was never a whimper, except perhaps when they thought of home. They took things as they came, without thinking about it too much, but here, in his native village, talking to his neighbors, he could not help seeing that other life in all its sadness. Back there they were used to the idea that a soldier's tears are cheap, but here, in his own home, with little Sevastyan by him, stealing glances at the cradle and at Katya, looking at his mother and father, the sadness of it all could not have weighed more heavily upon him. His brother Adrian, twice wounded, was back at the front line. Nisifor's brother was on crutches. Old Ilyakha had been robbed of his two sons. War was only bearable so long as you knew you had a home to return to, wooden walls of your own to rub your back against, a wife to take hold of at night. But back there at Dryagovets, where the sergeant major gave out the sugar, to lie down while the priest swung his censer, to go to sleep forever under a cross made of sticks—that was a thought to wipe the grin off anybody's face.

Yakim Rozhok, squatting against the wall, chimed in from down below: "Still, Adrian's been wounded twice and you never have, thank God, have you?"

"Well, a bullet doesn't always hit bone, it may hit a bush."

Talk like that grated on Arseni's father. He rose and left the room.

The visitors started in on another subject. There's a rumor going around that we're exporting sugar, grain, and leather to the Germans, through Finland or somewhere. Is it true?

That was not one of the things Arseni knew about. His battery got no more news than Kamenka did.

"I only know," he said with a sigh, "that the Germans can't keep it up forever."

Domasha herself confronted the guests. She was always firm and outspoken, famous throughout the village for it, and the menfolk respected her.

"Now then, neighbors, I need more elbowroom! Let me have my son for the first day at any rate! There'll be plenty of time for chatting when you come to church for the festival."

No harm done, the men weren't offended, they collected themselves and went out, taking some of their smoke with them: first Rozhok, bent double, craning his neck to look up and back, then Stremoukh, old Bayunya, tap-tapping with his stick, and Agapei Derba, looking gloomier and more morose than when he had come, still hiding both hands in his cap, eyes fixed on the floor, high-stepping over the threshold and catching his foot in his shalwar.

Arseni's mother held the door open behind them for a while, to let the smoke out. Then she set about preparing for the holiday, first scraping the table white so that she could knead dough on it.

Arseni saw the visitors off and made for the orchard. His path crossed Katya's as she hurried back from the bathhouse in her cape.

"How's it going? Want any help?"

"No, Senya love, it'll be hot soon."

She was like quicksilver, but he kept hold of her. So she started talking about little Sevastyan: what d'you think of him, do you love him?

She knew the answer was yes or she wouldn't have opened her mouth.

"He's very much like me, I can see it now. He even sticks his lip out like this."

"You haven't seen anything yet. He's as simplehearted as you are. And he's going to be big and strong. Look at the size of his little paws already, just like yours, finger for finger, and what a grip he's got! He always wants to try out your father's pitchfork! He's got a back just like yours as well."

His back? Arseni didn't know his own back all that well, and would never have thought of studying Sevastyan's. How could you tell whether his back was like his father's, at two years old?

Takes a woman to remember her husband's back!

Katya wriggled and shook off his hold without another word.

He caught up with her for a moment as she reached the yard.

"Katya! Remember how we felt that time we didn't sleep separate for Lent?"

She blushed and looked down.

Nobody had any thought of war as yet, and the rule was that even newlyweds had to take a break after Shrovetide. But Katya wasn't pregnant yet, and they were both hungry for it. So they told each other in whispers, "If we are committing a sin, maybe God will forgive us." And they kept it up till Palm Sunday. But God must have forgiven them, because look what a fine son she'd borne! If they'd bowed to the law Katya might still have been childless when the war came.

Father Mikhail had frowned over his calendar and threatened Katya. Quick-witted as ever, she said, "It's the honest truth, Father, I've been carrying him past my time! Just didn't seem to want to drop out somehow!"

"During the Great Fast! And that's how he's turned out! A great big boy!" Arseni wouldn't let her run away. "Anyway, all my leave is before Lent now. So we're all right for a long way ahead."

And nights were longer in autumn.

"Senya love, don't be in such a hurry, let me go, Mama's waiting, Fenya's waiting!" Then, looking back at him: "We won't be in the house. And the storeroom's full up. If I make our bed in the hayloft, will it be too cold?"

"Cold? Never!" She had vanished before the words were out of his mouth.

He went walking again with his father. To the winter hives. Around the orchard. Discussing which trees and bushes to transplant. His father had a lot to tell him, and no other listener could have given him such pleasure. The day before yesterday I was fishing in the fen at the Savala—bream longer than your forearm, you were eating one of them, you know. And this week the red sandpipers will be on the wing. What about it?

Elisei was one of the best hunters in the village. And he had fired Senka with his own enthusiasm.

You don't get much of a day at the end of October. It wasn't so far into the afternoon, but the light was already draining away. Senka and his father stayed out a bit longer, sizing up the digging to be done, but smoke was rising from the bathhouse, and Katya was calling, "Senka! Come on!"

The floor just inside the bathhouse was strewn with clean straw, and Katya had laid out clean linen for her husband on a bench under the little window. Arseni stripped off his army shirt, his boots, and his foot rags—and dived into the steam room. She hadn't overheated. Senka didn't like it too hot.

Back in the battery they'd built a bathhouse in a dugout, a roomier one—but no, it wasn't like your own at home. Here, your foot knew every floorboard, every plank of the sweating shelf, that tub, those buckets, those dippers—one of them no good, but it didn't get thrown away.

She showed him where everything was, and turned on her heel.

"All right, Senya, I'm off."

In a twinkling she could have slipped through the door, but no, another twirl, another quick glance.

"What d'you mean, you're off?" Arseni said, slowly reaching out to take her by the shoulder.

Katya looked sideways and downward. "We will have all night."

"Na-a-a," Senka heard himself say, "I'm not waiting till night!"

Katya looked up at him demurely. "Fenya's all worked up, can't take her eyes away. She'll be on tenterhooks, counting the minutes till I get back."

But Senka wouldn't take his hand away.

Katya pleaded with him: "She'll be asking questions. I'll be ashamed."

This girlish, womanish "shame," supposing it really still lingered and wasn't just invented, Arseni had never been able to understand.

"So what!" he roared, wide-mouthed, as if yawning. "Just tell her. Who else can the poor girl find out from?"

Head lowered again, very quietly, in a whisper: "And the bench is too narrow, Senka love."

"Who needs a bench?" Senka retorted cheerfully. He grabbed her with both paws and pulled her close.

Katya raised her head slowly, slowly looked her husband straight in the eye, and (she sounded frightened. Why? He had done nothing to frighten her: some woman's game perhaps) said, "Aren't you going to thrash me with the birch twigs?"

"No, I'm not," Senka said.

"Maybe you will, though?"

What had gotten into her? One minute she was afraid of being thrashed, the next she seemed afraid of having to go without it. Senka laughed even more heartily.

"All right, I'll thrash you! Right now if you like."

Katya, just as she was, still fully dressed, reached for the birch twigs. And holding them in front of her, raising them carefully above her head, but not as high as Senka's, held them out to him!

She looked up from under the twigs, waiting to see what he would do. Silently pleading—thrash me then, thrash me, lord and master.

Senka was dumbfounded. He felt frightened himself.

"Whatever for? You mean you've . . . ? You haven't . . . have you?"

The hell you have!

[3 6]

Arseni was not a cruel man, he was never hard on anybody, and with Katya he was as gentle as could be. So that their relationship was loving and serene, pure joy, with never a thing to complain about.

The days of Arseni's courtship, and those first few months before the war, when she was carrying Sevastyan, had been warm and sunny— never a harsh word, not a single blow from his great paw. Not that she had ever done anything to anger him; she always knew his wishes before he did and was quick to carry them out.

Then the war had gnawed holes in everyone's life and left it in tatters. His first leave had been a fleeting dream, this was his second, and in between she had been husbandless: carrying a child, giving birth, feeding her baby, and all the time, wondering what her husband would be like when he returned and how they would get along. Wondering above all whether he *would* return. And pining, pining, pining for the man of her choice, whether she was getting the stove ready, milking, feeding chickens, harvesting, raking hay, retting flax, combing wool, spinning, weaving—whatever she was doing she would picture his return, now one way, now another. What time of year would it be? At what hour of the day? What would he find her doing? Would his first kiss be on the threshold, in the hallway . . . ?

But deeper down and more insistently another feeling smoldered, one she wondered at herself. One she couldn't put a name to.

Something ungraspable, something you couldn't ask even a true friend to help you understand. Something so elusive you had to fathom it for yourself or give up and resign yourself to not knowing. She couldn't put her complaint into words. Their life together could not have been sweeter. Too short, that was all. And their time apart so terribly long. But during that second separation, after his first leave, Katya got it into her head that she would like her husband to come back from the war . . . not quite as he had been. She wanted him to be just as serenely good-natured, just as kind and loving . . . But . . . there must be something more. He would sweep her off her feet like a child (she was no heavier to him than little Sevastyan). But then— that something more.

Pluzhnikov's wife, Agasha, was two years older than Katya, but they had gone to the same dances as girls. Agasha had always been such a dolled-up show-off, and she was just the same after her marriage—the same, yet, with a husband at her side, completely different. It was a mystery—she was the same, and she was completely different.

One day Katya couldn't help saying something about it.

Agasha showed her big pearly teeth and said, "Well, you've got a husband yourself, haven't you? Only you've hardly lived together yet. Just wait a bit till he starts feeling his oats and comes down a bit heavy on you—and you'll change like I did."

Comes down heavy? What does that mean? Comes down heavy!

But those words lodged in Katya's head. A mystery—but there, somewhere, was the answer.

She had been worried about it ever since, sure that there was something worth knowing.

What if Senka came back not just the dear man he had always been but somehow . . . frightening? No, not frightening. More masterful, say. . .

Before the war it sometimes happened that a gang of boys would go girl hunting, and when they caught one they would lift her skirt and rope it around her arms and above her head. Sometimes it was just horseplay—making a girl run around blindfolded and half naked, just for fun. But sometimes it was to punish a girl who, as they saw it, had misbehaved. In such cases they would also whip their victim with their belts. When word of it reached the other girls, they would cluck like frightened hens. There would be such oohing and aahing. Could any punishment be more dreadful and more shaming? They asked God to spare them such rough handling, and cursed and vilified those young men. Whoever they might be: their captive would not have recognized them in the dark. Katya joined in the chorus, throwing up her hands, clutching her head, screwing up her eyes in horror, but behind her closed eyelids, in a secret place that nobody else could see, she wondered: What if *he* were the one? What if she knew him by his voice or his hand, or because her heart told her? Told her he was doing it not to shame her in the eyes of the village, but to make her know her future master? Her arms would be pinned, her eyes would see nothing, all she could do would be to run—but what if her legs wouldn't work, what if her will failed her, and she just crashed to the ground?

Delicious terror.

We see how furiously the cock treads a hen, anyone would think he'd claw her to death . . . but she picks herself up, shakes herself as if after a bath, and effortlessly lays an egg.

Arseni, big and strong as he was, far from using his strength on Katya, was afraid of crushing her in his great paws, and anyway he used to say, thinking of others as well as her, "Women, even while they're girls, have to be treated gently." Katya sometimes said, "Senya, you're too easy on me! If you overdo the kindness, I may turn bad," but he would only laugh: "Turn bad? Never, not you."

It was true, of course—all the tricks she got up to, all her anxious efforts, had one purpose only—to win his approval.

But in the second year of the war Katya had got that funny idea into her head. Would she ever dare mention it when her husband came home? Mention what? She couldn't have said herself.

When he did come, it was out of the blue. No letter. All of a sudden—there he was, on the doorstep. Too big to fit in any doorway, head higher than any lintel—her lord and master! Katya was in a spin, she rushed around three times faster than usual, finished her chores, got the bathhouse ready, and all the time she was tripping and skipping her heart was pounding. What now? What should she expect?

She didn't think for a moment that he would thrash her. It was to have been a joke: "You aren't going to thrash me, are you?" But what came out was: "Aren't you going to thrash me?" She lifted the twigs slowly, suddenly numb with horror, she didn't really mean it, her hands were shaking, but they raised the twigs of their own accord.

"You mean you've . . ." Senka yelled.

As if she would! How could he think it of her! It was a game she was playing.

"No, don't!" Katya screamed, shaking her head violently, hair flying.

But he was already taking the birch from her. Now he was holding it.

"No, no!" Katya screamed again and again, but she had closed her eyes tight. Closed her eyes. Why? If she had looked him in the eye he would have believed her! As it was . . .

He did not believe her!

The voice she heard was a new and frightening one, not Senka's voice at all.

"All right, pull your dress up!"

She only had to open her eyes and speak up, say no, I never did . . . But her voice had gone. Her head went down, lower, lower, without her willing it. Her hands too—down, down, gripping her skirt.

Then Senka was saying still more harshly, "Higher! Higher! And get down on the floor!"

A voice so ferocious there would be no pity.

At the last moment, her head still uncovered, she looked into his eyes . . . eyes dilated with rage!

"No, Senya love, no! There never was anybody else!"

She didn't know whether it was a shout or a whisper.

"Get down, I said," he thundered, brandishing the birch twigs.

He didn't push her, though. Didn't press her down onto the floor. If he had she would have sprung up. But he didn't.

Submissively, covering—and uncovering—herself, she sank to her knees, then lower until she was prone, her unseeing head and her elbows on the bathhouse floor.

Then—a searing sensation, this way, that way, a scorching pain, not like the glow you get from the twigs on the bathhouse shelf. She hadn't expected it to be so painful, to burn like that! Again and again and again! And she couldn't defend herself with her hands, her hands had gone into hiding! She resented being beaten, and for nothing, but she did not cry out again.

He went on whipping her, without a word.

She was sorry for herself, her defenseless self, and she shed silent tears. But she did not cry out. She wept into her hands, and into her skirt, just wriggling slightly at each broad, stinging stroke of the forty-twig broom, but not trying to dodge it.

From hamstring to midriff she felt a burning, tearing pain—for offenses never committed, for others yet to come—or rather so that they wouldn't. For no fault at all. Humbling herself to her master.

She wept and waited for him to stop, for his anger to pass.

For mercy to prevail.

He paused. Said, still furiously, "Why don't you tell me? Who was it?"

She wept. She sobbed.

He waited.

Brought down the birch twice, more gently. Straight along the spine, more like a bathhouse caress.

"Who've you been with? Why don't you tell me?"

She went on sobbing. Couldn't get a word out in answer.

He bent down low, close to her, and said, no longer angry, but frightened, "Katya, little one?!"

He it was who drew back her skirt from her head. He turned her face toward his—and she said, "There wasn't anybody, Senya love! I shut myself up all the time you were away."

Senya was stupefied.

"So why didn't you say so?"

"I did, I shouted to you!"

"Well, you didn't shout loud enough!"

Katya turned to lie on her skirt with her cheek against the floor.

"So why didn't you jump up? Why didn't you get out of the way?"

Katya went on crying.

Then he bent right down to the floor, his face close to hers, and said in a low voice, "Why did you lie there so quiet?"

"Quiet? You ought to try it!"

"So why was I beating you?" he asked, frowning.

She smiled through her last tears.

"It's all right. You're my master. I know now I have to obey you."

She brought her lips close to him and began kissing him. Over and over again.

As for Senya . . .

He picked her up and carried her like a child.

Nursed her.

Kissed better the place where the birch had hurt her. Her dress had clung to her back and softened the blows.

. . . They forgot that Fenya might be waiting for Katya, and that her mother-in-law might want her help at the stove, but they no longer cared what the others might think, or whether neighbors had gathered . . . they just stayed on and on in the bathhouse.

It had never been like that before. That fierce glow from head to foot.

Days are short after the Feast of the Protection, dusk comes early. By now there was little light through the small bathhouse window. They could have lit the wicks standing in saucers of mutton fat on the window ledge, but the reflected light from outside was enough for eyes accustomed to it, and more than they needed.

It was dark when they left the bathhouse and went over to the hayloft. No one had looked for them, and no one noticed. There was no light in the cottage now, nor in neighbors' houses. Almost the whole village was in darkness.

The children were left in the cottage for Domanya to look after. In the hayloft Katya made up a bed on a feather mattress she herself had stuffed, and laid a sheepskin coat on top.

The sheepskin alone was enough to make them feel unbearably hot, and they uncovered themselves again.

There were no gaps in the roof overhead and it was darker up there than outside. But the light slanting through cracks lower down showed that there was a moon behind the clouds.

They felt no desire to sleep. They talked far into the night. It was a rambling conversation. Katya kept interrupting Arseni to tell him about the children's little ways and how clever they were and how much Sevastyan, young as he was, was like his father in character. Or else to ask him something about army life.

But what they talked about most, and agreed on most readily, was their future. The war was bound to end someday, and Senka, God willing, would come home unhurt. What sort of life would they make for themselves then? Senka had brought with him a rumor that George medalists would be given allotments after the war, seven desyatins a man. Life would really be worth living! Yes, but, Senya, people around here are saying every peasant will be given a bigger allotment after the war. But where will they get all the extra land from? From the land-owners, of course, and the Crown Lands Office, and all those different banks. They'll find it all right. Who says Russia's short of land? It's just that those who've got it don't want to let go of it. But even if they cheat us again we won't sit back with our arms folded. We'll move onto a spread of our own, maybe buy a bit more land, it'll be paid for sooner or later, and the two of us together, loving each other, and with the children God's sent us . . . it'll be pure happiness, working to pay the debt off first, then to make ourselves comfortable. All good things have to be worked for. And what you work hard for isn't a rolling stone—it's brick laid on brick. Katya was saving up her family allow-ance already, she didn't spend what her father-in-law handed back on gewgaws, it would all be kept and would come in handy. Only—money was worth less all the time. They had to have a separate holding—nothing else would do, had to have their land around them, within a single boundary, not in different strips moving around every few years. They were young and healthy, and they had every chance if, God will-ing, Senya came through unhurt. Maybe his father would like to join in and make it a bigger holding? Well, there was time to think about that. He'd most likely want to stay put, but he'd help just the same. That would be safest. Starting a separate holding would take a lot of money.

Was there anything Katya didn't know about farm work? She could do it all. But what she liked best was geese. They would build their home close to a stream, or at any rate a pond, or in a pinch they'd dig themselves a pond. And raise lots of geese.

Katya could go on about geese till you told her to stop. What clever birds they were! If, say, a goose was sitting on eggs and the stove hadn't been lit for two days, she wouldn't drink! She had the sense to know that if she had to go out into the yard the eggs would get cold. Geese never made water indoors. Katya knew the right time for everything. At first snow, you fed male goslings grain for twelve days, then killed them right away. Let it go a single day longer and feathers started forming, then you'd have to wait another twelve days, twice as long. Once a goose started laying, you had to feed her chaff, no hard grain at all. The proper way for geese to live was three females to a male. Four, and the gander would wear himself out. For five geese you needed two ganders. Where the real skill came in, though, was in choosing your ganders, judging their points as males. If a gander's got nineteen feathers in his tail, he's fine; if he's got eighteen, don't keep him. Open his wing feathers out: little black spots at their base mean he's strong, white patches mean he's a weakling. The layers of feathers under the wing—it could be two or three or four—showed you how many geese he can tread.

"Listen—what made you remember my back?"

"I remember every bit of you."

"If I get killed, will you still remember?"

She snuggled up close, as close as she could.

It was late, and they were at peace, and should have been going off to sleep. But no. The itch was there again.

"Only, Senya dear, my back hurts terribly," Katya said.

"I'm not surprised!"

"Only, Senya dear, what if . . . what if there's another one?"

"He's just what we need," Senya said lightheartedly.

"What if it's a girl again?"

"Let them all come!"

"And another one after that?"

"Why not!"

Life could be beautiful!

*   *   *

IF HEART AND HEAD ARE STRONG,
YOU WON'T WANT FOR LONG.

*   *   *

[3 7]

Their meetings in the Stüssihof restaurant were known as the Skittle Club, although there was no skittle alley.

". . . The Swiss government is the executive committee of the bourgeoisie . . ."

"Skittle Club" was somebody's idea of a joke: their politics made no sense, but plenty of noise.

". . . The Swiss government is a pawn in the hands of the military clique . . ."

But they had cheerfully adopted the name. We'll knock the capitalists down like ninepins!

(He had educated them. He had cured them of religion. He had implanted in them an appreciation of the historical role of violence.)

". . . The Swiss government is shamelessly selling out the masses to the financial magnates."

It was some years now since Nobs had started the discussion table in the restaurant on Stüssihof Square. He had brought together the younger people, the activists. Then Lenin had gradually started coming.

(How many humiliations he had had to endure in this conceited country! The Social Democrats in Bern had always looked down on him. When he had moved to Zurich last spring he had tried to get a few Russian émigrés together for lectures—but the few who came at all had soon drifted away. Then he had transferred his attentions to the young Swiss. Some men of forty-seven might think it beneath their dignity—fishing for baby-faced supporters and working them over one by one—but if you could wrest a single one of them from the opportunist Grimm it was time well spent.)

"... The Swiss government is toadying to European reaction and encroaching on the democratic rights of the people."

Across the table sits simpleminded, broad-faced Platten, the fitter (since he had broken his arm he had been a draftsman, but fitter sounded more proletarian). His big face is busy absorbing what is said—it is all so difficult. His brow is knotted and his soft ripe lips pursed with effort, helping his eyes and ears not to miss a word.

"... Swiss Social Democrats must show complete lack of confidence in their government ..."

The table has been made longer for a jolly Swiss gathering. No cloth covers, its planed surface pitted with knotholes, polished by a century of elbows and plates. All nine of them have arranged themselves on two benches, giving themselves plenty of room, and one place is blocked by a pillar. Some have ordered snacks, some beer, just to keep up appearances, and because the Swiss always do. (Everyone pays for himself.) A lantern hangs from the pillar.

That elongated, triangular face under the unruly lick of hair, the keenest face there, belongs to Willi Münzenberg, the German from Erfurt. He is very quick on the uptake, and in fact it's all much too slow for him. His long restless hands reach out for more. These are the clichés he rings out himself at public meetings.

(He'd had luck with the younger people in Zurich. There were half a dozen of them here—all youth leaders. Not like in 1914, when he had sent Inessa to see the Swiss leftists—Naine was fishing, Graber helping his wife to hang the washing out—and nobody wanted to know.)

"... We must learn not to trust our governments ..."

Lenin is at the corner of the table by the pillar, which conceals him from one side. Nobs is at the far end, diagonally opposite, as far out of range as possible, watchful, ingratiating, catlike. He started it all—does he now regret it? In years he is one of them—they are all around thirty—but in party status, in self-importance, and even in girth he has ceased or is ceasing to belong.

Over every table hangs a lamp of a different color. The one over the

Skittle Club is red. A reddish light plays on every face—Platten's broad open features, the black forelock and starched collar of the self-assured and foppish Mimiola, Radek's unkempt and tousled curls, his irremovable pipe, his permanently parted wet lips.

". . . In every country stir up hatred of your own government! This is the only work worthy of a socialist . . ."

(Work with the young was the only thing worth doing. There was nothing humiliating about it. It was simply taking the long view. Grimm wasn't so very old—he was eleven years Lenin's junior—but he already had a handhold on power. He wasn't stupid, but theory was over his head. He didn't want an armed rising, yet he had leftish hankerings. When Lenin had entered Switzerland in 1914, mentioning Greulich's name, and established himself there with Grimm as his sponsor, they had met and talked far into the night. Grimm had asked, "What do you think the Swiss Social Democrats should do in the present situation?" To see what he was made of, Lenin had answered in a flash, "I would immediately declare civil war!" For a moment Grimm was scared. But then he had decided that it was just a joke.)

". . . The neutrality of Switzerland is a bourgeois fraud and means submission to the imperialist war . . ."

Platten's brow is convulsed, his eyes strained and bewildered. How difficult, how terribly difficult it is to master the lofty science of socialism! These grandiose formulas somehow refuse to fit in with your own poor limited experience. War is a fraud and neutrality is a fraud—so neutrality is just as bad as war? . . . But a sideways glance at your comrades shows you that they understand it all, and you are ashamed to admit that you don't, so you pretend.

(It was not just facile phrasemongering. He had brought forth these ideas in a fit of inspiration on his journey across Austria, written a definitive summary of them when he reached Bern, introduced them in a Central Committee manifesto, then defended them in his tussle with Plekhanov at Lausanne. You could know your Marxism inside out and still not find the answer when a real crisis burst upon you: the man who finds it makes an original discovery. In the autumn of 1914, when four-fifths of Europe's Socialists had taken a stand in defense of the fatherland, while one-fifth timidly bleated "for peace," Lenin alone in the ranks of world socialism had pointed the way for the others: *for war!*—but a *different* war!—and immediately!!)

Lenin too has a mug of beer in front of him. The Swiss politician at the tavern table is a species he can't endure, but this is the ritual. Bronski looks sleepy and imperturbable as always. But Radek, with the black whiskers that run from ear to ear under his chin, with his horn-rimmed glasses, his quick glance, and his buckteeth, restlessly switching his eternally smoking black pipe from corner to corner of his mouth—Radek has heard it all before, and now finds it too elementary, too tame, and too slow.

". . . The petty ambition of petty states to stand aloof from the great battles of world history . . ."

Platten is quietly floundering, trying not to give himself away. The idea of world revolution is easy to understand but it is so difficult to apply to his Switzerland. His mind consents. Since they have avoided the universal bloodbath, they mustn't sit calmly by but summon the people to class battles. But his heart is unreasonable: it is good that in those houses clinging to the mountain ledges peasants can live in peace, that the men are all at home, that grass is mown in the meadows four times in a summer, however steep the slopes may be, that the tall barns will be filled to the roof with the store of hay, that the tinkling of hundreds of little bells, sheep bells and cow bells, sounds from spur to spur, as though the mountains themselves were ringing.

". . . The narrow-minded egoism of privileged small nations . . ."

The plodding walk of herdsmen. Now and then, the deafening crack of a bullwhip on the stony road, echoing through the folds in the hills. Water troughs at mountain springs, long enough for twenty cows to drink. Shifting winds over swaying grass, shifting mists steaming over wooded gorges, and when sunlight breaks through the rain, there may be no room for the rainbow's arc, and it will stand upright like a pillar on the mountain. The quiet inscription on a hostel in the wilderness: "The motherland shelters her children with her forest cloak."

". . . Industry bound up with tourism . . . Your bourgeoisie trades in the beauties of the Alps, and your opportunists help them at it . . ."

Platten gives up his attempt at concealment, and innocently, trustingly, his face reflects his doubts.

Lenin has noticed! From where he sits at the corner of the table—the only older man among all those youngsters, looking well over fifty—he strikes home with a swift, shrewd, sideways thrust.

". . . A republic of lackeys! That's what Switzerland is!"

The keynote of his harangue.

Radek guffaws happily, deftly switches his pipe—the fingering is different every time—and sucks in imposing quantities of damp smoke. Willi mischievously tries to catch Teacher's eye, his long hands writhing impatiently: encore! encore!

Platten isn't arguing. Platten is merely puzzled. Perhaps his country is like an ornate hotel, but lackeys are obsequious, fussing and fawning, while the Swiss are staid and dignified. Even ministers' wives don't keep lackeys, but beat their own carpets.

(But it had never been known for a letter to go astray in Switzerland, and the libraries were magnificently run: books were sent without charge and immediately to remote pensions in the mountains.)

". . . Sops for docile workers in the form of social reforms—to persuade them not to overthrow the bourgeoisie . . ."

It has taken three weeks of effort to arrange this meeting and they have finally got them all together on the evening of Friday, the third—

the eve of the Party Congress. Radek has been a great help, made himself very useful.

(When Radek was nice, he was really nice, a super pal. At present there was no living without him. And how well he spoke and wrote German! He took the sharpest bends in the road with ease—there was no need to waste time explaining. A scoundrel, but a brilliant one—such people were invaluable. But at times he was loathsome. In Bern they had avoided meeting, communicated through the mail, and in February broken off relations forever. At the Kienthal Conference he had spoken like an out-and-out provocateur.)

". . . The Swiss people are more cruelly hungry every day, and risk being drawn into the war and killed in the interests of capitalism . . ."

Nobs's skeptical amber cigarette holder balances unaided on his nether lip.

(What a business it had been, starting, without a single supporter in Europe, the struggle for the renewal of the International, or rather its demolition and the construction of a new, Third International. At one minute scraping together any of the Bolshevik émigrés who would agree to come; the next, rallying with Grimm's help three dozen women—the International Conference of Socialist Women—and, since he could hardly attend in person to give them the guidance they needed, sitting for three days in the café of the Volkshaus while Inessa, Nadya, and Zinka Lilina ran to report and ask for instructions.)

". . . Will you go to the slaughter for interests which are foreign to your own? Or will you instead make great sacrifices for socialism, for the interests of nine-tenths of mankind?"

(Then there was the International Socialist Youth Conference. They had mustered fewer than a score, mostly people who had evaded the call-up and were sure to be against the war, and again he had sat in the same café for three days, while Inessa and Safarov trotted to him for instructions. This was when Willi had appeared on the scene.)

If you're twenty-seven, with ten turbulent years of the youth movement behind you—meetings, organizations, conferences, demonstrations . . . And if, among your peers, you discover that you have a voice, courage, luck—people listen to you, you rise step by step as though to a platform where you can be seen better, and suddenly find yourself in demand as a public speaker, delegate, secretary . . . And the party leaders immediately try to draw you into their orbit, and urge you not to listen to that Asiatic with his wild ideas, yet it is from him and from the incendiary Trotsky that you always learn what is right and what matters!

". . . 'Defense of the fatherland' is a fraud on the people, and can never be 'war for democracy.' And Switzerland is no different . . ."

Twenty-seven! The things he'd been through! His mother's early death, beatings from his stepmother, beatings from his father, serving in his father's tavern, playing cards and talking politics with the customers, at the washtub under his stepmother's eye, always suffering because his clothes were ragged and his boots the wrong size, drawn into propaganda work while he was apprenticed to a shoemaker, emigration to Zurich when he was only twenty to work as a pharmacist's dispenser and join in all the class battles . . .

In the reddish light from the lamp Münzenberg's devoted and determined face is trustful and expectant. The tempered strength of his will shows in the sharp jut of his narrow chin. His brows are knit in an eager frown of welcome for revolutionary ideas. He has already often done as Lenin said and the results have been good. He rallied more than two thousand people for a Youth Day on the Zürichberg and led them through the city singing the "Internationale," waving red flags and shouting, "Down with the war!" He had earned an invitation to Kienthal and joined Lenin in signing the resolution of the left.

". . . In Switzerland too, 'defense of the fatherland' is a humbugging phrase. It paves the way for the massacre of workers and small peasants . . ."

Schmidt from Winterthur, an ungainly figure at the far end of the bench, is puzzled and peers past his neighbors to say, "The war can't affect our country, we're neutral . . ."

"Ah, but Switzerland may enter the war at any moment!"

Nobs chews his amber holder under his fluffy blond mustache. He smiles like an amiable cat, but his eyes are mistrustful and a tuft of hair stands up like a question mark.

"Of course, refusal to defend the fatherland makes exceptionally high demands on revolutionary consciousness!"

(All his life he had been the leader of a minority, pitting himself with a handful of followers against all the rest, and aggressive tactics had been essential. His tactics were to whittle down the majority resolution as far as he could—and then still not accept it! Either you record our opinion in the minutes or we leave! . . . But you're in the minority, why are you dictating to us? . . . All right—we're leaving! A breakdown! A public brawl! A disgrace! . . . That was how it had been at all those conferences, and there had never been a majority that hadn't weakened. *The wind always blows from the far left!* No Socialist in the world could afford to ignore that fact. That was why Grimm was so unsure of himself, and why he had hurriedly called the Zimmerwald Conference.)

". . . Not a single penny for a regular army, not even in Switzerland! . . ."

"Not even in peacetime?"

"Even in peacetime Socialists must vote against military credits for the bourgeois state!"

(Lenin had had to wait a long time for his invitation to Zimmerwald, and had been very depressed. Grimm might not summon him, and it would be quite unseemly to force himself on them. What sort of conference would it be anyway? A bunch of silly shits would get together and declare themselves "for peace and against annexations." *For peace*—he couldn't bear to hear those words! . . . Meanwhile, he had discreetly used his influence to insinuate as many of his supporters as he could into the list of delegates. Those who were against their own governments—they would be the nucleus of a left International! . . . But they could muster only eight: himself, Grishka, and Radek, that was three, Platten, one Latvian, and three Scandinavians. Still, the *whole* of the "old" International, fifty years after its foundation, had barely filled the four wagons that carried the participants into the mountains so as not to attract the attention of the authorities, who in fact noticed neither the arrival of the delegates in Switzerland nor their dispersal. They had learned of it only from the foreign press.)

"But the special character of Switzerland . . ."

"Special character nothing! Switzerland is just another imperialist country!"

Platten recoils. His brow is an open book. He struggles to bring the creases of astonishment under control. His unregenerate heart rebels: our Switzerland may be a tiny country, but surely it is a very special one. Since the three cantons were first united, have we ever annexed anybody? With intense mental effort he strives to accept these advanced ideas. His big, strong, helpless hands lie palm upward on the table.

(Platten was good material to work on. Through Platten alone he could bring the whole Zurich organization into line. If only he would work harder at educating himself.)

"And so we, the Zimmerwald left, are now completely unanimous: we *reject* defense of the fatherland!"

Some of the awkward squad didn't understand.

"But if we reject defense of the fatherland, are we to leave the country defenseless?"

"A radically incorrect formulation! The right way to put it is this: either we let ourselves be killed in the interests of the world imperialist bourgeoisie or, at the cost of fewer casualties, we carry out a socialist revolution in Switzerland—the only way to deliver the Swiss masses from rising prices and hunger!"

(In Zimmerwald he had hardly spoken at all, but had directed his left-wing supporters from the shadows. That was the most effective way to deploy his forces. The speechmaking could be safely left to Radek—he'd be witty, resourceful, relaxed, self-confident. His own duty as leader was to weld his small group more firmly together. An ordinary enemy is only half an enemy. But the man who used to be with us and suddenly wobbles off the line is doubly our enemy! We must hit him first and hardest! But it is better to anticipate trouble and prime your followers in caucus between sessions.)

". . . The disgusting thing about pacifists is that they dream of peace without a socialist revolution."

Radek is always ready for marching orders. His pockets bulge with newspapers, books, all he needs for a day: if he has to hurry off to a revolution he can go as he is. How interesting he finds it all!!!

(But the rogue needed watching. He might change sides, might betray, at any minute. And he sometimes got things wrong—trying to reconcile Grimm and Platten, for instance, when it was important to keep them quarreling.)

". . . Revolution is absolutely essential for the elimination of war . . ."

Just look at Bronski, dozing again. He might as well not be here at all. He is only needed so that we have enough people. When his vote is wanted, it will be there. And when required he will say what is required. (Yes, he is stupid. But there are so few of us that every one counts.)

". . . Only a socialist system can deliver mankind from war . . ."

Difficult to say whether Nobs really approves. His eyes and lips sympathize, but his ears are still and his brow is unruffled. Yet he is editor in chief of the main left-wing paper and is effortlessly advancing to the commanding heights of the Party. They all have great need of him.

He needs them too, though. Nobs knows perfectly well that the wind always blows from the left. Small as their group is, it may change the course of the whole Swiss Party. Only he doesn't want them to be a millstone around his neck.

". . . It is illogical for anyone who aims at ending the war to reject socialist revolution . . ."

(When Liebknecht's letter was read to the Zimmerwald Conference, Lenin had sprung to his feet shouting: "CIVIL WAR IS A SPLENDID THING!" Caution is all very well nine times out of ten, but the tenth time you must overstep the mark. Take the proletarian slogan—"fraternization"—to the trenches! Preach class struggle to the troops. Tell them to turn their bayonets against their fellow countrymen! THE AGE OF THE BAYONET IS AT HAND! It was risky, of course, for an émigré in a neutral country to carry on like this, but he had always gotten away with it. At Zimmerwald, though, that foul German crook Ledebour had said, "You can put your name to it here, because you're safe. Why don't you go to Russia and *send* your signature?" That was the level of debate with such people!)

". . . The Swiss Party is stubbornly stuck in the rut of strict legality and is making no preparations for revolutionary mass struggle . . ."

From the counter with its two potbellied old barrels and its dozens of colorful bottles a waiter with blunt Swiss features is slowly carrying golden tankards and dark red glasses and tumblers to the table. From the serving hatch another waiter brings yellow trays with thin brown slices of smoked sausage and plates of roast meat or fish. Swiss bellies are unhurriedly packing away inordinately lavish Swiss helpings, each enough for four. And at every glutton's elbow a second helping is keeping warm over a little flame.

". . . The socialist reorganization of Switzerland is perfectly feasible and urgently necessary. Capitalism is completely ripe for transformation into socialism—here and now . . ."

(At the last session of the Zimmerwald Conference, from midday on all through the night, the left had raised a storm over each amendment, demanded at every turn that its dissenting opinion be recorded, and by these means shifted the revolution considerably to the left. They hadn't, of course, succeeded in putting through either the "Civil War" or "A New International" resolution. Still, the Zimmerwald left had emerged as a new wing of the international movement, and Lenin was no longer a mere Russian sectarian, but its chief. The official leadership, however, had remained with the centrists and the hero of the conference in newspapers throughout the world was Grimm. Though not much more than thirty, he was already on the Executive Committee of the International, because he was hand in glove with the opportunists. Lenin had been visiting or living in Switzerland for twenty years on and off, long before Grimm was ever heard of.)

Willi's thin, eager face. He agrees, agrees completely; but it is essential for him to understand exactly what must be done, and where to start.

"In Switzerland it will be necessary to expropriate . . . a maximum of . . . thirty thousand bourgeois at the very most. And of course to seize all the banks right away. And Switzerland will then be a proletarian country."

From his place by the pillar, Lenin observes them obliquely, his domed brow inclined, bringing the full pressure of his mind and his hard gaze to bear on them, skillfully checking how much each of them has taken in. His thinner hair is a richer red in the light from the lantern.

"Strike at the roots of the present social order *by concrete action.* And *now!*"

That is the step which Socialists everywhere find so difficult. Nobs screws up his eyes as though in pain. Even the proletarian from Winterthur looks a bit down in the mouth. And Mimiola's high starched collar is choking him.

A fine fellow, our Ulyanov, but much too extreme. Nowhere on earth, let alone in Switzerland or Italy, would you find anyone so extreme.

It is hard, so hard on them.

Lenin's gaze slides rapidly, restlessly over all those heads, so different, yet all so nearly his for the taking.

They all dread his lethal sarcasm.

(When you can't force something through a narrow opening it often helps to pile on extra weight.)

He addresses the table at large, simultaneously pursuing each of the six Swiss in his thoughts. His voice is tense, but lacking in resonance—it seems always to get lost in his chest, his larynx, or his mouth, and it slurs the *r*'s.

"The only way to do it is to *split the Party*! It's a bourgeois affectation to pretend that 'civil peace' can reign in Swiss social democracy!"

They shudder. They freeze.

But he goes on: "The bourgeoisie has reared the social chauvinists to serve it as watchdogs! How can you speak of *unity* with them?"

(Keep hitting the same spot, over and over again, varying the words just slightly—that's the first rule of propagandists and preachers.)

"It's a disease that affects Social Democrats not only in Switzerland, not only in Russia, but all over the world—this maudlin hankering after 'reconciliation'! They're all ready to renounce their principles for the sake of a bogus 'unity'! Yet short of a complete organizational break with the social patriots, it's impossible to advance a single step toward socialism!!"

However unresponsive they are, whatever they may be thinking, he has the assurance of a teacher confronting his class: the whole class may disagree, but Teacher is right just the same. His voice becomes still more guttural, more impatient, more excited.

"The question of a split is of fundamental importance! Any concession here is a *crime*! All those who vacillate on this are *enemies of the proletariat*! True revolutionaries are never afraid of a split!"

(Split, split, and split again! Split at all stages of the movement! Go on splitting until you find yourself a tiny clique—but nonetheless the Central Committee! Those left in it may be the most mediocre, the most insignificant people, but if they are united in a single obedience you can achieve anything!!!)

"It is high time for a split at the international level! We have excellent reports on the split in the German Socialist Party. The time has come to break with the Kautskyites in your own and all other countries! *Break* with the Second International—and start building a Third!"

(A method tried and proven at the very dawn of the century. He had pierced and slain the Economists with the death ray of *What Is to Be Done?*, his scheme for a band of professional conspirators. He had shaken off the clammy clinging incubus of Menshevism with his *One Step Forward, Two Steps Back*. He did not want power for its own sake, but how could he help taking the helm when all the rest steered so incompetently? He could not let his incomparable qualities of leadership atrophy and go to waste.)

Yet the idea might have been born there and then, at the table, might have been an instantaneous and irresistible revelation: *split* your party—and thereby ensure the victory of the revolution!

Nobs, stiff with delicious fear, doesn't even murmur. If you refuse, who knows, you may be the loser. Perhaps the best place to be is right here, at this table?

Platten's paw has frozen on the handle of his tankard.

Mimiola has triumphed over his constricting collar, risen clear of it. But he looks gloomy.

Willi wears a little smile of startled enlightenment. He is ready. And he will carry the young with him. He will repeat every word of it from the platform.

The heavy brow batters away at the breached wall.

"My book on imperialism proves conclusively that revolution is imminent and inevitable in all the industrialized countries of Europe."

There are still a couple of them who want to believe, but can't quite see it.

There you are, living in a room you've grown used to, and one morning you go out into the street, with familiar buildings all around you, and you start a revolution. But how? . . . Who is going to show you how? There has never been anything quite like it.

"Yes, but this is Switzerland . . ."

"What of it? That was a glorious strike in Zurich in 1912! And what about this summer? Willi's marvelous demonstration on the Bahnhofstrasse! A baptism of blood!"

Yes, this was Willi's proudest boast.

"All those casualties!"

Even the first of August hadn't been as good as the third, in honor of the fallen.

They hem and haw . . . In Switzerland? . . .

How can they disbelieve him? He treats every youngster as his equal with perfect seriousness. Not like those leaders who snub their juniors once they get one foot on the ladder. He never begrudges the effort spent on conversation with the young, wearing them down with questions, questions, questions, until he can slip a noose on them.

"Yes, but in Switzerland . . ."

While they are clearing up this little matter, Radek has found time to read two of the newspapers from his bulging pockets and leaf through a book. And still they don't understand!

Radek pokes the stem of his pipe at them. "Your own Party Congress last year . . . adopted a resolution on revolutionary action by the masses! What about that?"

Well, what about it? . . . All sorts of resolutions are passed. Passing resolutions is easy enough.

"Then there's Kienthal!"

Five of those present had been at Kienthal, including Nobs and Münzenberg. Among the forty-five delegates they had been part of the minority of twelve. They had threatened once again to wreck the meeting by walking out, had in fact left the hall and returned. So the majority had given way to the minority, and they had pushed the resolution further and further to the left: "*Only the acquisition of political power by the proletariat can ensure peace!*"

True enough, but you can say anything in resolutions . . .

"No, but here in Switzerland . . ."

The most patient of men couldn't listen to these numskulls without exploding! Then—he amazes himself with a fresh revelation, which comes out in a hoarse cracked whisper.

"Don't you realize that Switzerland is the most revolutionary country in the world??!"

They are all rocked back in their seats, clutching tankards, plates, forks . . . The lantern on the pillar sways in the wind of his voice. Nobs grabs at his cigarette holder as it falls from his mouth.

???????????????? . . .

(He saw it all! Saw the barricades that would soon rise in Zurich, not, perhaps, on the Bahnhofstrasse, where all the banks were, but over toward the working-class district by the Volkshaus on the Helvetiaplatz!)

And with a caustic flash of the Mongol eyes, in a voice without depth or resonance, but with the cutting edge of a Kalmyk saber, catching only on the *r*'s: "Because Switzerland is the only country in the world where soldiers are given weapons and ammunition to take home!"

So . . . ?

"*Do you know what revolution means?* It means seizing the banks! The railway station! The post office and telegraph! The big enterprises! And that's all! Once you've done that the revolution is victorious! And what do you need to do it? *Only weapons!* And the weapons are there!"

The things Fritz Platten hears from this man, who is his fate and his doom! Sometimes his blood freezes . . .

Lenin has abandoned persuasion and is rapping out orders to these recalcitrants, these incompetent muddlers.

"So what are you waiting for? What more do you need? Universal military training? Well then, the time has come to demand it!"

He is improvising, thinking between sentences, picking his way among his thoughts, but his voice never falters.

"Officers must be elected by the people. Any group of . . . a hundred can demand military training! With instructors paid from the public purse. It is *precisely* the civic freedom of Switzerland, its effective democracy, that makes revolution immensely easier!"

Bracing himself against the table, he looks as though he were about to spread his wings, fly up from the dining room of the Stüssihof restaurant, and soar above the five-cornered, enclosed medieval square, itself no bigger than a good-sized public hall, glide over the comic warrior with a flag on the fountain, spiral past the jutting balconies, past the fresco of the two cobblers hammering away on their stools three floors up, past the coats of arms on the pediments five floors up, and over the tiled roofs of old Zurich, over the mountain pensions and the overdecorated chalets of the lackeys' republic.

"Begin propaganda in the army *immediately!* Make the troops and young men of call-up age see that it is right and inevitable for them to use their arms to liberate themselves from hireling slavery! . . . Put out leaflets calling for an *immediate* socialist revolution in Switzerland!"

(Rather rash words for a foreigner without a passport, but this was the one time in ten that made the difference between victory and defeat.)

"Take executive control of all working-class associations immediately! Insist that the Party's parliamentary representatives publicly preach socialist revolution! The compulsory takeover of factories, mills, and agricultural holdings!"

What? Go and take people's property away from them, just like that? Without passing a law? The Swiss blockheads couldn't blink fast enough.

"To reinforce the revolutionary elements in the country, all foreigners should be naturalized without charge. If the government makes the slightest move toward war, create underground workers' organizations! And in the event of war . . ."

Greatly daring, Münzenberg and Mimiola, leaders of youth, finished it for him: ". . . refuse to perform military service!"

(Luckily Münzenberg and Radek, deserters from the German and Austro-Hungarian armies, respectively, cannot be deported under Swiss law.)

Not one little thing have they understood! A mocking smile but not an unfriendly one, passes over Lenin's face. He has no other choice— down, down he comes, past the cobblers hammering away at their work with slavish diligence, over the blue column of the fountain, to alight with a rush in his old place in the restaurant.

"Under no circumstances must they refuse; what can you be thinking of? In Switzerland especially! When they give you arms, take them! Demand demobilization—yes, but without giving up your arms! Keep your arms and get out into the streets! Not a single hour of civil peace! Strikes! Demonstrations! Form squads of armed workers!!! And then *an armed uprising!!!*"

Broad-browed Platten is bowled over as though by a blow on the head: "But with all Europe at war . . . will the neighboring powers . . . tolerate a revolution in Switzerland? They'll intervene . . ."

This is the nub of Lenin's scheme—the utter, unreproducible uniqueness of Switzerland.

"That's what is so splendid! While all Europe is at war—barricades in Switzerland! A revolution in Switzerland! Switzerland speaks three major European languages. And through those three languages the revolution will overflow in three directions and flood all Europe! The alliance of revolutionary elements will expand to include the proletariat of all Europe! A sense of class solidarity will be aroused in the three neighboring countries! If there is any intervention, revolution will flare up through Europe!! That is why SWITZERLAND IS THE CENTER OF WORLD REVOLUTION TODAY!!!"

Singed by the red light, the members of the Skittle Club sit fixed as the words chance to find them. The narrow triangle of Münzenberg's intrepid face is thrust forward into the glow. Nobs's fluffy mustache is also touched with the flame. Mimiola looks as if he was about to pull his tie off and lead his hot-blooded Italians over the ruins of Europe. Bronski in his sad, sly way is trying to look eager for battle. Radek wriggles, licks his lips, and excitement flashes behind his glasses: if that's how it's going to be, what fun he will have!

(The Skittle Club is the Third International in embryo!)

"You are the best part of the Swiss proletariat!"

Radek has a resolution ready and waiting for tomorrow's Congress of the Swiss Party. If only Nobs will print it . . .

Hmmmmm . . .

But who will put it to the Congress?

Hmmmmm . . .

Since the restaurant would soon be closing, the party broke up.

There were three streetlamps on Stüssihof Square, and lights shone from the windows of houses all around. You could easily read the plaque telling how in 1443 Burgomaster Stüssi had fallen in battle not far from here. His family home had stood for sixty years before that. That must be Stüssi too, the comic Swiss warrior in armor and blue hose standing in the middle of the fountain. You could hear the thin jets of water splashing into the bluish basin. The air was dry and cold for this part of the world.

They were still talking as they took leave of each other and walked away over the smooth cobbles. The square seemed completely shut in, and unless you knew where to look for the crevices which were streets, you might wonder whether you would ever get out. Some of the company went off down a bumpy cobbled slope, and took the side street which led to the embankment. Others turned off at the tavern called the Franciscan. Willi, however, accompanied his teacher along the same street in the opposite direction, past the Voltaire cabaret on the next corner, where the arty set raved the night away, and on the narrow pavements they encountered prostitutes who were still waiting for customers. Past the Voltaire they turned steeply uphill, under an antiquated lamp on an iron post, along a street like a stairway, so narrow that with arms outstretched you could almost touch both walls at once, and there was hardly room to walk two abreast; up and up they went.

The heels of Lenin's stout mountain boots clattered on the cobbles.

Willi wanted his teacher to reassure him over and over again. He had not forgotten the fight on the Bahnhofstrasse that summer, but every trace had been hosed and swept away, the shopwindows were as dazzling as ever, the bourgeoisie strolled around as comfortably as before, and the workers placidly obeyed their accommodating leaders.

"Yes, but the people aren't ready for it . . ."

At a sharp turning in the alley, in the dim light of someone's sleepless upper windows, the voice from under the dark cap was quiet but as sharp-edged as ever.

"Of course the people aren't ready. But that doesn't give us the right to postpone the *beginning*."

In spite of the platform victories behind him, the yells of assembled youth in his ears, Willi persisted.

"But we are such a small minority!"

Lenin stopped, and out of the darkness came something not revealed even to the select gathering at the Skittle Club.

"The majority is always stupid, and we cannot wait for it. A resolute minority must act—and then it becomes the majority."

The Congress opened the following morning, across the river in the Merchants' Hall. Lenin, as leader of a foreign party, was invited to deliver greetings. Radek was also there, ostensibly representing the Polish Party. Two from "our" side, speaking in succession.

On the first morning not all the delegates had arrived, and the audience was no larger than at a good lecture. (Lenin, in fact, was not used to large audiences; he had never known what it was like to address a thousand people at a time—except just once, at a mass meeting in Petersburg when he had lost his tongue.)

As soon as he looked out over the hall caution overcame him. Just as at Zimmerwald, just as at Kienthal, he had no overpowering urge to speak his mind fully—no, the full fervor of his conviction was naturally reserved for a closed meeting of his supporters. Here, of course, he did not call for action either against the government or against the banks. Standing before this nominally Social Democratic but in reality bourgeois mass of self-satisfied, fat-faced Swiss, lounging at their little tables, Lenin sensed immediately that they did not and would not understand him, and that he had practically nothing to say to them. He somehow couldn't even bring himself to remind them of the highly revolutionary resolution which they themselves had adopted last year—and anyway it might spoil everything.

So his salutations would have been quite short, if he had not gotten painfully entangled with the Adler affair. (Two weeks earlier, Fritz Adler, Secretary of the Austrian Social Democratic Party, had shot and killed the Prime Minister of Austria-Hungary—killed the head of the imperial government in time of war!) This assassination had captured everyone's imagination, there was a lot of talk about it, and before making up his own mind Lenin had inquired carefully into the circumstances. Who had influenced Adler? (His Russian Socialist Revolutionary wife, perhaps?) Because he was secretly preoccupied with this problem, a perpetual source of disagreement with the Russian SRs here at the Congress, he had devoted half of his speech to an irrelevant discussion of terrorism . . . He had said that the greetings sent to the terrorist by the Central Committee of the Italian Party *deserved full sympathy*, if the assassination were understood as a signal to the Social Democrats to abandon opportunist tactics. And he had defended at length the Russian Bolsheviks' opposition to individual terror: it was *only* because terror ought to be a *mass* activity.

Meanwhile the Swiss munched and swigged and mooed and tippled—there was no way to understand them.

Still, the Saturday session had gone well and raised his hopes. Platten was applauded by the majority, and Papa Greulich, a seventy-five-year-old with a luxuriant gray mop of hair, started joking about the Party's "adoption of new pets." (Nothing to the round Schweizerdeutsch rudenesses we'll heap on you when the time comes! When we come to power, we'll hang you!) It had worked, it had gone off beautifully! Lenin had cheered up and felt like an old warhorse in the swirl of battle. Moreover, the circumspect Nobs had not refused to put forward the Skittle Club's (i.e., Radek's) resolution: that the Congress should adhere to the Kienthal decisions. (The stupid Swiss might vote for it just to be in fashion, without really knowing what the Kienthal decisions were—and then they'd be caught! After that, you could bait your hook with their own resolution and catch the whole bunch of them! Grimm as well!)

Trivialities? No! That is how history is made—from one hard-won resolution to the next, through the pressure of the minority, you push and push every resolution—leftward, ever leftward!

Then the next step. That Saturday evening, on the Skittle Club's initiative, by individual invitation, a separate, secret, private meeting of all young delegates was held away from the Congress building; they gambled on the normal sympathy of the young for the left. The plan was simple: to work out with their help a resolution (or rather submit a ready-made one brought along by Radek) for them to put forward and force through the Congress on the following day, Sunday.

At this private conference of young delegates, Willi, of course, was in the chair—making lavish use of his commanding gestures, his bold, cheerful voice, and his tumbling hair—and Radek was at his side, smothered in curls, wearing his merrily militant spectacles, reading his resolution, explaining it, answering questions. (He was a good speaker too—but his pen was beyond price.) Lenin, as he always preferred to, had sat inconspicuously among the rest, and contented himself with listening attentively.

All might have gone well. The young delegates listened closely to their Russo-Polish comrade and seemed in agreement.

All might have gone well if something extremely unpleasant hadn't happened. They had not had the sense to lock the door. And through the unlocked door, unnoticed at first, came two malicious tale-bearers, two horrid old bags: Madame Blok, who was Grimm's friend no less, and Martov's lady friend, Dimka Smidovich. Once these wretched females were in, there was no getting them out: they'd scream and make a scene! And the whole meeting could hardly move elsewhere! Anyway, they'd already seen and heard Radek speaking, and realized, of course, that a resolution for the Swiss Congress was being drafted by Russians.

What an infernal nuisance! What a colossal fiasco! Loathsome creatures with their filthy little intrigues! Of course, they'd rushed off to Grimm and whispered in his ear. And he, the brute, the blackguard, the utter swine, had believed the silly bitches. He'd tried to start a vulgar brawl by printing vile innuendos in his *Berner Tagwacht*, which were absolutely incomprehensible to ninety-nine percent of its readers: "A *certain small group of foreigners*, who look at our workers' movement through spectacles of their own, and are utterly indifferent to Swiss affairs, are trying in a fit of impatience to provoke an artificial revolution in our country! . . ."

Poppycock! Unmitigated hogwash! And that is what they call a working-class leader?

Then at the Congress they'd laughed down Nobs's resolution. When he proposed making it a rule for the future that only those opposed to national self-defense should be nominated for parliament, Greulich had been greatly amused. If we elect such deputies, he said, their hotheadedness may land them in the *skittle alley*.

The Congress roared with laughter.

Moreover, consideration of the Kienthal resolution had been postponed—until February 1917.

What a tragedy it all was! So much effort, so many evenings, so much conviction, lucid thought, and revolutionary dynamite had gone into it! And the result was—a heap of vulgar, stupid opportunist debris, like dingy cotton wool, like the dust of junk rooms.

In musty Switzerland the bacillus of petty bourgeois cretinism reigned triumphant.

And the bourgeois world still stood, unexploded.

*   *   *

FOR FOLK LIKE YOU WITH NIMBLE TONGUE
             THE ROAD AHEAD IS NEVER LONG.
FOR FOLK LIKE ME WITH NO BOOK LEARNING
     IT'S THE LONG, LONG LANE THAT HAS NO TURNING.

*   *   *

[3 8]

On the afternoon of 7 November, Vorotyntsev looked in at General Staff HQ once more to deal with unfinished business, and emerged onto the Nevsky. He had a ticket for the late train in his pocket, and had said goodbye to Olda that morning, so that at last he would be able to spend an evening with Nanny and Vera. All he had to do was walk along the Nevsky one last time, as far as Karavannaya Street. He felt full to the brim with some luminous, ringing substance, triumphant yet at ease, as if his body was supported not by his skeleton but by the pressure of that substance from within. He seemed not to have lost anything in those last few days, not to be in any way depleted, but rather to have taken in more and more of that triumphant substance, so that now he was filled with a tingling vibrancy the like of which he had never experienced, and would have thought impossible a week ago.

One of the objects on Olda's walls was a dark metal gong. One stroke with a horsehair-headed stick and its deep booming note went on and on, a lingering, muffled joyous resonance. Georgi felt now that he was vibrating like that gong. He had thought of himself as having mass, as a thing of burnished metal, but had not known till now that such sounds could be drawn from him. But there it was—that steady, booming sound in his breast. The world seemed new—especially the women in it.

He had spent eight days in Petrograd, it would soon be nine, and he had not achieved the sole object of his journey, had not arranged a single serious interview. He could not remember neglecting his duty in this way at any time in his life.

His mind reproached him, but his body felt only gratitude. Time was running out, in a few months, a few weeks, it might be too late to save the situation. But he too had only one life, and was living, perhaps, the last month of it—how could he decline the gift that fate had put in his way? Without it he would be a pauper, without those eight days he would never have known what life could be.

He reproached himself, but there were excuses. For a start, he had tried several times to telephone Guchkov and had left messages. He had picked up the receiver that very afternoon and missed him yet again: yes, he is in town, and will probably be back this evening. They were evidently fated not to meet. Then again, while distracting him from his duty Olda had left a little cloud of doubt in his mind. It was all a lot more complicated than he had thought in his impetuosity, it needed careful consideration. Somehow, his eagerness to look people up and clarify matters had cooled in those eight days.

He had taken off from Romania like a shell from a gun, but had gradually lost his destructive velocity in flight.

Walking along the Prospect, Vorotyntsev, as soldiers do, kept half an eye open for other soldiers, to be sure of returning their salute. On this occasion, crossing the Politseisky Bridge, he saw from the corner of his eye a powerfully built officer with a tall fur hat and major general's epaulets. His hand shot up, to salute smartly, before he looked the general in the face and recognized—Svechin.

Svechin replied with the same mechanical gesture before looking Vorotyntsev over and recognizing him.

Although he had read in *Russky Invalid* that Svechin was now a major general, he had only vaguely remembered it, and failed to substitute the new for the old Svechin in his mind's eye. He stood, now, blinking in surprise.

They turned, walked toward each other, and their hands met.

"Ye-gori?"

"Your Excellency!"

"That's enough of that!"

Svechin gave him a little hug. "You could have been the same, only you chose not to. Remember the old definition: What's a general? A colonel who's become stupid enough."

"Glad you remember. But you still haven't said no?"

Svechin's heavy lips parted in a smile.

"Doesn't apply to me, as far as I can see. Besides, refusing would look ungracious. Anyway"—touching the gold hilt of Vorotyntsev's sword—"isn't that just as good?"

Was he merely being polite or did he mean it?

Vorotyntsev had, in fact, felt no envy when he first read of Svechin's promotion, and felt none now that he saw him. Envy and resentment were two feelings he had never known, perhaps because of his supreme self-confidence. Never once in the past two years had he regretted relieving his feelings in the presence of the generals at GHQ and ramming the truth down their throats.

Still—there had been a little pang when he read the *Invalid* and another one now.

"Maybe this isn't you, though? Can there be two of you? You're at GHQ, I've got your letter in my pocket, inviting me there."

"Maybe there are two of you as well? I wrote thinking you were with your regiment and here you are in Petersburg."

A lucky meeting! Vorotyntsev hadn't known how seriously to take Svechin's letter, received just as he was setting out. Should he or shouldn't he look in at GHQ on his return journey?

"I'm leaving tonight."

"And I'm off in three hours' time. Pity we can't travel together."

Svechin's left hand held a little crocodile-skin case, too small to be called luggage or a burden, so that even a general could carry it without a breach of regulations.

"But when did you get here? I wish we could have gotten together!" Vorotyntsev blurted out. He couldn't really regret it: how could they have met, with Olda around?

There was a cold glint in Svechin's black eyes. "This morning."

Vorotyntsev was puzzled. "You got here today, and you're leaving today?"

"I . . . er . . ." Svechin's big lips set in a grim line. "I only came to break it off with my wife."

Vorotyntsev couldn't take it in. "Between getting here this morning and leaving tonight?"

"One day's more than enough," Svechin said curtly, looking past Vorotyntsev.

In the meantime, they had unthinkingly turned around and Vorotyntsev was walking in Svechin's direction. They crossed the Moika, stood for a while, crossed the Nevsky to the Businessmen's Club, and stood there a bit. Then, letting their feet decide for them, they went off along the Moika toward Gorokhovaya Street.

The sky had been overcast all day, and the heavy clouds were darker still as the early northern dusk approached. Rain was setting in, and the spots crinkled the gray surface of the Moika.

"It's like this," Svechin explained gloomily. "A few months ago I discovered that my wife was hanging around with the Rasputin clique. I warned her. But I'm not like the Evangelist—I don't give seven and seventy warnings, just one. Especially when it's a woman."

Vorotyntsev was mildly deprecating. "Why be so much harder on women?"

"I'll tell you why," Svechin said heavily. "Any other way you're done for. You can forgive your orderly ten times, you can forgive a volunteer for running from the battlefield, there's some chance he may improve. But if a woman doesn't take your first warning to heart there's no hope for her."

A strange, a merciless judgment. It was good, though, to meet an old friend unexpectedly and find that you were as much at ease with each other as ever. But could anything have failed to please him, now that there was Olda? Everything was splendid, everything was just right, even the rain.

"What exactly happened?"

"Nothing much. The Holy Man came to tea a time or two, that's all. He was in my apartment—drinking tea!" Svechin's long lips writhed. It was a sign that he was enraged. That habit and the brilliant blackness of his eyes had earned him his nickname—"the Mad Mullah." His rages, however, never affected the way in which he discharged his duties.

"So he came to tea! I ask you! Just ordinary hospitality!" Vorotyntsev retorted, still more cheerfully, almost teasingly. "Probably there were other guests as well, all talking about spiritual matters."

Svechin refused to see the funny side. "If they want to pray, that's what a church is for," he answered sternly. "And if you can't do without holy men, take a trip to the Optina monastery. You get a different sort of holy man there anyway . . . But when half a dozen silly women dress up in see-through frocks to rub themselves against a hulking great country bumpkin . . ."

"Come on, not half a dozen at a time!"

"If not a dozen! People say they go to the bathhouse with him—countesses, princesses, every one of them somebody's wife, like mine—and take turns sponging him down."

"Come on, not all of them. Not every time," Vorotyntsev said dubiously.

Still . . . here we are sedately strolling along the embankment but—one false step and . . . splash!

"I'm not condemning those countesses wholesale. My one reservation is that it's no place for *my* wife. She ought to consider her husband. Even if all they do is collect black rusks to wrap in their scented hankies, and beg Grishka to give them his dirty underclothes to wear. They took tea at my table, after she'd been warned—that's quite enough."

"What does she say about it?"

"I don't know. And it makes no difference." He pursed his lips as if to whistle. "I didn't find her at home, you see. And I wasn't going to wait, because I have to be at GHQ tomorrow. I wrote her a note, packed this case—and the rest is up to her."

Vorotyntsev was taken aback. Just like that? Ending a marriage as if you were rushing into a cavalry charge!

"My sons are both cadets. They'll go on to officer training school."

The rain was heavier now, and the big spots were wetting their fur hats and greatcoats. They walked on along the Moika and turned into Kirpichny Lane. It was getting dark, and the air was raw. Lamps would soon be lit.

"Where are you going now?"

"Nowhere much. To have dinner."

"Let's dine together, then. We can go to my sister's if you like."

"No, let's go to a restaurant. Cubat's is quite near here."

They walked along Kirpichny Lane. Past the triple-arched plate-glass window of the restaurant, already curtained and cozily lit from within. They turned onto Bolshaya Morskaya Street and walked toward the stuccoed building's marble portico. As they turned the corner, a hansom cab with pneumatic tires stole past them and pulled up at Cubat's. A young man got out and handed down his lady. A slender girl in a reddish-brown coat and a black hat which did not quite cover her hair, she jumped lightly down, lost her footing, and was steadied by her companion in what looked like an embrace. They went in before the two officers, and a whiff of perfume followed the girl into the vestibule.

The friends took off their greatcoats under the pink-shaded lamps, enjoying the warmth, and unbuckled their swords. The other two were dealt with by the next cloakroom attendant. The girl's coat had concealed an exquisitely molded form clad in a golden ankle-length dress, with long luxuriant hair falling in two cascades down her back. Her companion called her Likonya.

Georgi, sated, you might suppose, with feminine charms, nonetheless looked at her attentively. Even her he would not have noticed earlier. But now, when their eyes met, he did not find it improper to let his gaze linger just a little longer, as if trying not just to show admiration but to give her some special message.

"Did young ladies like that come here in the old days? Wasn't Cubat's a place for talking business?"

"When we get back a lot of things will be unrecognizable," Svechin replied darkly.

The first thing that was unrecognizable and unpleasant was her companion, with his neat tiers of gray ringlets, a hint—could it be?—of lipstick, and his indolent, self-assured manner. He glanced at them haughtily, showing no more interest in two senior officers wearing the aiguillettes and silver badges of Staff Academy graduates than in the cloakroom attendant.

"Imagine it—a milksop like that—when we're at war. I'd like to double him through the communication trenches with his head between his knees."

"Yes," Svechin muttered. "They read their somnambulist poetry, they listen to those hysterics Severyanin and Vertinsky. We have no idea what's growing here while we're away."

The ground floor of the restaurant was a long carpeted room with warm-colored silk curtains at the big, triple-arched windows, dim overhead lighting, and shaded table lamps. But Cubat's had certainly changed its character: glitteringly ornamented ladies sat smoking cigarettes with long mouthpieces. And in the far corner, at several tables placed together and laden with dishes, a large party was celebrating some great civilian triumph. The excessively loud voices of the well wined and dined could be heard across the restaurant, and on a platform behind a curtain some sort of spectacle was being contrived for them.

Vorotyntsev had never been a lover of restaurants—partly because money had been tight for so many years, but also on principle: restaurants slow down the work in hand and increase the share of pleasure in life disproportionately—something which Vorotyntsev had never permitted himself and had long ceased to want.

But it was pleasant for once to sink into a comfortable chair, facing Svechin, sit lapped in a subtle combination of appetizing smells, and while you waited for the menu—what? Smoke, of course.

A lucky chance all right! An excellent opportunity to talk to a friend about anything and everything without constraint. Although all Vorotyntsev's conversations in Petrograd so far had not helped him to order his thoughts, but left him more confused.

Svechin too had settled himself comfortably, to make the most of the time until his train left, and was contentedly lighting his pipe. No one could have guessed that this was more or less the moment when his wife would enter their apartment to be guillotined by the note from a husband whom she had supposed to be seven hundred versts away.

Astounding that he could be so peremptory. And control his feelings so effortlessly.

They were so much at ease with each other because there was no need for them to go into details: although they had not met for two years, and hardly ever written to each other, one word was enough as a rule for each to understand at once, and as a rule completely.

If the word was "Champagne"—it meant not the homeland of the wine, but the sector in which the Allies had promised all summer to launch an offensive and relieve us, but instead of doing so they had left us to perish for lack of shells in last year's disastrous retreat. They had sent us no shells either, but once we were done for, had fired off three million of their own—in Champagne, where else?—all to no purpose.

What, come to that, had the Allies achieved in the whole of 1915? How much fighting had the British infantry done? Since the beginning of the war it had advanced a few hundred yards. They knew how to look after themselves.

Then again—why did we fling the Caucasian Army into an unnecessary and hopeless offensive over the Turkish mountains? Could anything be more senseless than our assault on Turkey? Mountains, snow, heroes, and miracles like those of Suvorov's campaigns—and

Erzerum is taken! But they could make no use of it, it was all for nothing.

Ah, but it rescued the Allies at Salonika. It made things easier for England in Mesopotamia.

No need for lengthy expositions. A name was enough. The pulverizing of the Guards in September at Svinyukhi-Korytnitsa ("Pigs' Trough"—the name of the place told you just what the operation was worth). Or the absurd March offensive near Lakes Naroch and Drisvyaty, which never had the slightest chance of success. In their hurry to get it over with before the thaw they advanced heedless of casualties, roads became impassable, there was water knee high in the trenches, the artillery and supply trains were immobilized.

And all that just to save the Allies at Verdun. And even the battle at Verdun was started by the Germans, the Allies would never have brought themselves to do it. Vorotyntsev saw everything in the same color, that of despair.

But Svechin, looking at it all from GHQ, could afford to be fairer.

"Verdun was a massacre. The French also lost a hundred thousand men there."

Vorotyntsev wasn't so easily won over.

"Well, their fame will resound throughout the world, they'll go down in history. But how many men did Evert lose? Must have been . . ."

"Seventy thousand."

"You see! And never a peep. That's how we die."

Svechin knows a lot. It'll take time to drag it all out of him.

And the arms they send us! All their rejects. They don't refuse our crackly new leather harness or our hardwood caissons. But we need three hundred locomotives—and they won't provide them. Their standard excuse is: "The needs of the Western Front are enormous, and we cannot deprive it of anything."

But that's nothing! Think of the men! . . . Shortly after Samsonov's disaster the Allies had the barefaced cheek to ask us to send four army corps to France via Archangel. Then their crack Senegalese troops had heavy losses and from March this year onward they have been shamelessly demanding four hundred thousand of our soldiers, at the rate of forty thousand a month, to fight on their front.

Vorotyntsev did not exactly hiss his next words, but spoke like a locomotive letting off steam. "Tha-a-at's why they came here, Viviani and Thomas, why their handsome mugs were in all the picture papers. And they did get their Russian Expeditionary Corps! Anything crazier it was impossible to imagine: Russian peasants stuck in somebody else's trenches, at the back of beyond, as if they were colonial troops from Senegal.

"I would never, never have given them that corps!" Vorotyntsev said, seething. "No, they'll fight to the last drop of blood, as long as it's

Russian blood. No, the Emperor is incapable of firmness, quite incapable."

His eyes searched Svechin's face, for *his* opinion of the Emperor. He ought not to have changed.

"What could we do?" Svechin countered, with his usual calm pessimism. His head was shaven bare, his face clean-shaven except for the small, close-clipped black mustache under his big nose. "Alekseev haggled with the Emperor and with the French, but in the end we had to let them have six brigades, each ten thousand strong. The Allies argue with iron logic that as long as a shortage of arms prevents the Russians from using all their forces, it's not for them to let us have additional arms, but for us to assign our surplus personnel to their front." He gave a short laugh. "As a fashionable poet puts in his public readings: 'With Russian dead the foe must pave the way, or ne'er set foot in Paris.'"

Looking past Svechin's shoulder, Vorotyntsev's eyes fell upon the couple sitting three tables away. And for some reason the "fashionable poet" merged with the ringleted decadent sitting with his back to the officers. Likonya was sitting half turned toward him and could be conveniently studied.

Vorotyntsev had long ago dismissed them from his thoughts—his conversation with Svechin was vitally important, he wanted only to plunge more and more deeply into it—and yet some residual awareness of them lingered in his eye and in his mind. What could they be talking about? What kind of lives did they lead? And why should he concern himself with this girl, whom he would never see again? Some piquant essence emanated from her, it was impossible not to feel her presence. Women, it appeared, were not all feminine in the same way. This girl seemed to Vorotyntsev like a concentrate of all that he had drunk in such deep drafts those last few days. But from the way in which she had jumped from the cab into the young man's arms, her display of affectionate abandon at the cloakroom counter, the most disinterested observer could only regretfully conclude that this Likonya, with the slow, watchful eyes and the double cascade of hair . . .

"They're quite frank about it: give us your soldiers and then we'll give you arms. They are mildly excited by our feats but they demand payment like usurers: for all the arms we order we pay on the dot, we deposit gold in a London bank, we get nothing on credit. And now that our hard cash has run out we can't order arms, we're having to cut down."

Svechin wrinkled his big rugged nose as if at a bad smell.

Not even on credit? Well, there'd been enough warning signs, you'd learned to expect the worst—yet there were still things you would never anticipate. They demand forty thousand Russian bodies a month, and still want payment on the nail, and in gold, for every scrap of iron. No, Western business methods are something we will never understand! How long will we let ourselves be fleeced?

"Damned hucksters! They don't see us as comrades in misfortune, but as a handy cudgel. France has simply bought us. How could we, rich as we are, fall for it? How can we make war on such unequal terms?"

And all the time he was asking these questions he saw in his mind's eye the same imperial face—looking at once embarrassed and apathetic. *He*, of course, knew all this. Why, then, did He give way so easily? Why had He put his head in this noose? Why did He not tell His allies straight . . . either you . . . or else we'll get out of the war?

"We're all alone, really," Vorotyntsev said, pouring out the bitterness that had fermented in him for so long. "What good have the English or French ever done us? Why, when you think of it, are they our allies? How lightly we forgave them for the Crimean war! And what about the war with Japan?"

England had, after all, been Japan's ally, had made that country a gift of two battleships with British crews, sold her thirty or so auxiliary craft, supplied the Japanese fleet with coal—Togo fought all his battles on their coal. And France had an *entente cordiale* with Japan, while, needless to say, keeping up her alliance with us against Germany. What were we to make of that? What were we thinking of? Even now the Allies are at it all the time, seeing who can bellyache the loudest about "us democrats having to put up with foul reactionary Russia as an ally." Last year Lloyd George publicly gloated over our retreats and losses.

"And this is the second war in which their friends the Americans have been undisguisedly hostile to us. Why, and to what purpose, are we their allies?"

They had resumed what used to be their customary roles: Vorotyntsev hotly denouncing, Svechin sometimes reminding him with grim sarcasm of the hopeless facts, but as a rule saying nothing and smoothly pursuing his career.

Vorotyntsev hadn't finished yet.

"And what about the Balkans? Was it worth our taking Plevna or freezing on Mount Shipka for the Bulgarians? The whole idea of making ourselves the leaders of Slavdom is a false one—Constantinople or no Constantinople! It was for the sake of Slavdom that we clashed with the Germans. They were moving into the Balkans, and looking toward Mesopotamia—but why should we care? Let England worry. And all we've done for the Serbs—where has that got us? We've been fighting over two years for Serbia and Montenegro—and what's the result? They're wiped off the face of the earth. And we ourselves are getting shaky. Millions under the ground, two million POWs, if not more, fortresses destroyed, whole provinces surrendered—all for our allies! How is it that England could take a whole year transferring troops to the Continent—and we're supposed to get ours into position in a couple of weeks? After Samsonov, couldn't we have stopped pressing on Germany—contrary to our own military doctrine—and putting our standing army through the meat grinder? And it's the French who saddled us with the Romanians as allies!"

Svechin neither agreed nor disagreed but laughed cynically between two puffs of smoke. "Yes, and we get blamed because our armies aren't making a big enough effort in Romania. And our setbacks in that country are put down to Russian treachery."

"Is that what they say? Well, there you are! And all because of the Constantinople mirage!" Vorotyntsev snapped. "As if our dear allies would ever cede the Straits to us poor fools! What are we using for brains? Such stupid greed! Almost everybody is infatuated with Constantinople—damn the place, I say! Even Dostoevsky had his eye on it. All the way from the extreme right to the Kadets, Shingarev included—without Constantinople they don't think life is worth living."

"Well, what about our Golovin?" Svechin said with a laugh. "Remember? 'Russia's like a house boarded up so that there's no way in except through the chimney.'"

"They've forgotten where the doors and windows are! Our own windows are blocked by heaps of junk! I've spent a little time in Kadet circles while I've been here. You can't let out a peep against England, they're up in arms immediately. When we were with Golovin eight years back we kept saying expand the defense industry so that we won't be dependent on anybody. But the mothballed elders and the Duma alike begrudged the gold. The same gold they've now shipped abroad—all of it."

The prices on the menu were incredibly high. But there was a wide choice. Vorotyntsev couldn't very well afford it . . . Still, what were they going to drink? A general's stars had to be christened, surely? They must be able to rustle up some vodka here—on the q.t. no doubt.

Just as religious discipline is always rigorously enforced on the common people, whereas polite society is permitted certain indulgences, so here there were bound to be exceptions.

Svechin, much as he might agree, merely gave his little laugh. Svechin knew where to draw the line. He was a critic of a special sort, you had to get used to him. He could have told Vorotyntsev even more distressing things about the Allies, but he was not one for jumping stone walls. Grumble all you like, but do your job in your own little patch.

"Did you know, by the way, that Alekseev recommended making peace with Turkey and doing away with that front altogether?"

"You amaze me! You mean even he's clever enough for that? So what came of it?"

"Nothing at all. What would you expect of us? . . . But is it your idea that we should have allied ourselves with the Germans?"

"One retired corps commander said the moment war was declared, 'That's it, then, two empires are doomed, the Russian and the German.' I didn't attach enough importance to it at the time. I'm not saying we should have allied ourselves with them, but we could have confined ourselves to friendly neutrality. They suggested it more than once, in 1907 for instance."

"But we had to break loose from Germany's stranglehold."

"We could have done that without necessarily going to war. Rapprochement with the Central Powers was something you dared not even mention out loud! The Kadets made it difficult for us to arm ourselves, but at the same time didn't want reconciliation with Germany! Of course, once we had a treaty with France we had to come to her rescue. But we should have realized earlier that we didn't need that treaty *or* that alliance *or* any additional territory. What we needed was simply to get on with developing our country. Stolypin understood that, and was doing it."

A great hulk like Svechin was not so easily shifted.

"Yes, but Germany also intrigued against us during the Japanese war. The purpose of their alliance with us was to strangle us with a trade agreement, so that they could get our grain for nothing. And while we're remembering the past, who was it who denied us the Straits at the Congress of Berlin? Why did Skobelev say that the road to Constantinople runs through Berlin? The Germans have always looked on Russia as manure for their own crops."

True enough. Whenever you looked back you saw nothing but humiliation. So much for Russian policy.

"In any case, there were ways of dodging this war. And we should have done so."

"No. Once Germany had made up her mind to go to war with us we couldn't have dodged it without humiliation. They'd have forced us into it, and it would have been one disgrace after another. If we were to remain on an equal footing with Germany, an alliance with France was essential. Which is why Aleksandr III accepted it. If he hadn't we would have been facing the enemy alone."

"And what of it? Is Russia's back weaker than Germany's? No, it is not! Yet another Fatherland War? Our people would have stood together, united, to the last man, not like now. Put yourself in Germany's place—isn't she alone? What allies has she really got? None. But they're standing up to the whole world. If they can stand alone couldn't a gigantic country like ours have held out? Why should we care about what is really a commercial conflict between England and Germany?

It's no concern of ours. Why are we bogged down in it? If Russia gets involved abroad, it's only because she doesn't know where her strength lies. If we knew what was good for us we'd never go barging in on their childish games. Why do we feel bound to get into every dustup? Our policies are thought up by idiots. Or rather not thought about at all. The firmer our footing within our own boundaries, the stronger we are. Yes, you're right, the Turkish war was meant as a lesson to us: we fought and died while others remained neutral, never lifted a finger, and managed things to suit themselves. Yet all we had to do was not to get mixed up in that war, say, 'Keep on fighting, it's got nothing to do with us,' stand by peacefully for a couple of years—and there would have been no power to compare with ours."

"Come on, Yegori, what can't be cured must be endured. Right or wrong, you can't remake history. Why get so hot under the collar?"

"Because we can deduce from all that what we should be doing next," Vorotyntsev said stubbornly.

"And that is?" asked Svechin, preparing to laugh.

"We-ell . . . we must change our views on the conduct of this war. Stop banging our heads against a wall regardless of lives lost."

"Too bad they didn't appoint you instead of Alekseev! But how would you go about it?"

"Me?" His answer was ready, there was no hesitation. "At the very least I would have slept through 1916 and not stuck my neck out at all."

At that moment the noise from the banqueters grew louder. An announcement was made, and all of them—racketeers still at large, pharmacists who had gotten rich selling opium and cocaine—clapped their beautifully manicured hands. Someone bowed. (What was it all about? A wedding? No. An anniversary, then? A profitable deal?) The curtain was twitched aside, and behind it . . .

Behind it hung a wheel. Two staff members quickly lit the wheel at various points and hastily jumped out of the way.

The wheel started revolving, self-propelled, spraying a shower of sparks while the flame spread to envelope the whole disk. There were three colors—silver at the center, blue over most of the circle, red around the rim. Like the national flag, but revolving. A revolving, a spinning flag.

Oh, what fun! What a marvelous idea! The racketeers laughed, cheered, applauded. But there was something the pyrotechnicians had not allowed for. The silver color faded, the blue faded, both were exhausted, and still the surrounding red was not the least bit dimmer. The blazing rim went on spinning by itself.

Red.

Crimson.

Blood red.

Fiery.
Spinning and spinning, scattering sparks.
It reminded him of something not quite the same, but . . .
Of course! The burning mill at Usdau!

[3 9]

Their vodka was served in a mineral water bottle. The devil is ingenious. How was it done? Obviously Cubat's had bribed the police to turn a blind eye.

If these uniformed guests ordered salty snacks with their mineral water it was obviously an eccentric whim of theirs.

At one table "white tea" was served in an obese teapot. Yes, they were managing all right.

All right, shall we start?

A shot at a time. They were out of practice, and the drink warmed and cheered them immediately.

In that hour with Svechin, Vorotyntsev's complacent triumphalism had deserted him. The reverberations of the gong had died away. His body had reverted to its normal state and his dreamy mind was clearing.

The war had to be fought differently. Instead of hoping that it would be over by next summer—change its whole character.

Svechin agreed. Yes, we must change our methods of making war. Bogged down in the trenches the way we were, it wasn't easy to break out, we could be stuck there for ten years. There was, however, one idea which nobody at GHQ would listen to: instead of trying to push forward all along each front, deploy well-trained and superbly equipped shock troops, all on horseback or on wheels. Open up a breach, however narrow, in the front, if only for a few hours, and throw in one of these groups in a raid deep behind the lines. Jerry wouldn't stand up to this sort of warfare, it would be better than the partisan warfare in the Fatherland War. And he couldn't use the same tactics in reply, because our raids into territory inhabited by our own people would find support, whereas he wouldn't.

No. They had gone over the ground where there was no disagreement, but now their views diverged sharply because their experience in the past two years had been so different.

"It's not a question of method, Andreich. Certainly not of tactical method. I'm trying to tell you that we must change the whole character of the war."

The view from GHQ was not the same as that from a regimental dugout. Those who held staff jobs too long ceased to feel for those who died in battle. They could tally up all those zeros at the end of the number. But . . .

"Think back and try to realize how many of our people we have slaughtered already. Among the officers, all the best, and all the middling good ones, have been killed already, don't forget. How many regiments are there like the 1st Siberian, with not a single officer left? Instead of regular officers you've got ensigns "with ideas." We destroyed the majority of our NCOs in 1914. More Russians have been killed than at any other time in our history, in all the wars you care to mention. And it is precisely and almost exclusively Russian blood. We don't draft the Caucasians—fair enough. The Central Asians were unwilling to serve even behind the lines, and we accepted that—fair enough."

"You wouldn't find the non-Russians much help in this war. They won't join infantry regiments if they can help it, they're cavalrymen, and in a war like this one you need to cut down on the cavalry, as you well know. Besides, nobody is as staunch in battle as Russians are."

"So it's flog the willing horse, eh? Just think what we're doing! Sending militia into the thick of it, defenseless old graybeards. Driving Russia to her death with our own hands. If we spare other people, why can't we spare our own? We're losing more than the war—we're losing the Russian people! It sounds unbelievable, but we've drained the country of how many millions? Thirteen? And we go on pumping. It's boys of nineteen now. Yet there aren't even three million in the trenches—where are all the rest? And we round up the horses, we ruin the civilian population. Why? The Germans had an interval of forty-three years between wars, we had a mere nine. But which side is fighting more skillfully?"

"For all their skill they're now feeding their horses on ersatz fodder, a mixture of straw and sawdust. They're well organized, of course, but they're suffocating for lack of men, provisions, and munitions, whereas in their eyes our army in the field is a most formidable force."

"Really? But what about the home front? We in the front line still don't have a very clear view."

He said "we" out of politeness, knowing full well that Svechin at GHQ had too exalted and detached a viewpoint.

"We in the field can only look straight ahead, at the enemy. And if you travel around all you hear is 'We need to beat the German within first,' and 'If you don't know how to fight, give it up!' Workers are already rebelling and drawing in reserve troops."

"Come on now! Those are just scare stories."

"It's true, I tell you! Just the other day in Petrograd, there were very serious disturbances on the Vyborg side. The police were there . . . And the 181st Reserve Regiment was involved . . . If fighting had crossed the bridges there'd have been trouble all over Petrograd . . ."

"Oh, come on!"

It was always "Oh, come on" when something had not quite happened. And when it did happen it would be "What else would you expect?"

The highway robbers at the other end of the hall were noisily enjoying themselves, laughing explosively. And they were all, of course, legally entitled to squander money and live it up in Cubat's even on ordinary weekdays.

Svechin was disinclined to believe him, but Vorotyntsev had felt the same himself ten days ago. How could anyone coming straight from the army in the field believe such things?

"Even flour is getting short in some places. This is perhaps a more dangerous time than the summer of 1915. Last year, however far we retreated, the home front was always well fed and steady."

"What do you mean, however far we retreated?" Svechin said angrily. "It wasn't beyond Moscow, like in the Fatherland War, was it? Or all the way to Poltava, like Peter? It wasn't even to the Dnieper—we retreated that far from the Poles on more than one occasion. No, we are just stationary on the edge of Poland. All right, we've lost Poland, Galicia, part of the Baltic provinces . . ." (Poland, Galicia, the Baltic provinces . . . but Olda was still there. With Olda you didn't feel that you were in such a soundly defeated army.)

"I would have liked to see you retreating backward up the Carpathians to escape from the Hungarian plain."

"In 1915 the situation looked frightening because we had no shells. So we drew back five hundred versts, but we didn't let them surround a single Army Group or corps. Now we have all the shells we need, and then some, and it gets better every month. The army is steady and strong and doing its duty—I know of no cases of insubordination. Without realizing it you're letting your impressions of Romania get you down. Besides, Germany and Austria are no longer capable of a major offensive at any point, they're going over to the defensive. And they're doomed to exhaustion, because they have no reinforcements coming from anywhere. The morale of Germans taken prisoner lately is low."

Svechin's too large head, always close-cropped because his hair was so sparse, was not a rounded oval like other people's but had prominent, asymmetrical bumps, which you could think of as marks of stubbornness. His hair was scanty, but his head was rock hard.

"We, on the contrary, have already won the war." He rammed it home with his bumpy head. "It doesn't matter whether those valiant little allies of ours—damn them—win the odd battle or not, the war is ours in any case. Don't forget, the Central Powers produce six hundred thousand shells a day, the Entente eight hundred thousand, that's bound to tip the scale sooner or later."

But it only takes one such shell—right in the middle of one of our trenches . . .

Vorotyntsev crouched over the table, eyeball to eyeball with Svechin. As soldiers crouch poised to attack.

"Our *root* is destroyed, Andreich!" he said, his voice muted but firm. "In these twenty-seven months our root has been destroyed. Don't bother counting the Allies' shells. Go and look at our regiments. They're not the regiments they were when they marched through Prussia in Samsonov's day. We're left with a substitute army, Andreich! No victory will compensate for the Russia killed in battle! And now we're beating the last spark of life out of the people's body. Don't bother counting the Allies' shells, or our own. The people were promised a three-month war, the people are at the end of their tether, all the people want is an armistice! The soldiers' attitude is: the gentlefolk started this war, but it's peasants they're killing! If Russia is utterly changed and we're left with a substitute—what good is victory?"

It had some slight effect on Svechin.

But he was not persuaded. Startled rather.

"You mean you no longer even want victory?"

"I simply see things as they are," Vorotyntsev said, recovering his breath after his tirade. "We both remember that splendid bit of logic: 'He who endures to the end shall be saved'—don't we? If we're not annihilated that will obviously be victory, after all our stupidities. Victory in Europe does nothing for us. Well, what does it do for us? Allow us to seize more land? Or are we talking about Constantinople again?"

By now Svechin was looking at him in amazement. No, he couldn't accept this.

"So what do you propose? To hoof it out of the war right now, or what? A separate peace? But if Russia parts company with the Allies now she'll end up among the defeated. A premature peace would bring Russia to disaster. To revolution even."

"Quite the contrary!" Vorotyntsev calmly asserted.

But a separate peace—just like that—was not what he wanted, or at least he was not yet ready to say so.

"Listen," Svechin said, "I can agree with you that it might have been cleverer not to get involved in this war. But once in we have to finish it, not keep changing direction. An aborted war, a war brought to an untimely end, threatens us with worse consequences than the present tension. How, I ask you, could we possibly withdraw from the war without damage to Russia?"

"But don't you see that continuing it, dragging it out, will do even more damage? We can discuss the practicalities. One possibility, as I see it, is to shut our eyes and take it easy."

"And what will the Allies say to that?"

"It isn't the Allies we should be thinking about, but the salvation of our own people. That's the sort of talk we hear from Kadet intellectuals—that Russia will bear an indelible mark of shame if she wrecks her union with the Allies. But the Allies have ridden on our backs too long, we've had enough of it. All their wars have been waged solely for their own advantage, and only we are such blockheads as to stick our necks out for no good reason. I sometimes think, to tell you the truth, that when we got involved in this war we fell into a cunning trap of theirs: the Allies needed to put Germany in her place, and thought it would be a good idea to do it with Russian hands, because—remembering her inability to hold out against Japan—Russia would crack up internally at the same time. So they would be the winners, they would usurp the victory—with Russia as their cat's-paw. So let them have their victory—all we need is to escape destruction, to stop losing people. There is, after all, a stage of sickness, or of tiredness, at which you cannot go a single step farther."

From similar facts they had drawn different conclusions. Such passionate disagreements between people so much alike may be vexatious at first, but are always fruitful in the end.

"No, you're wrong, it's quite the other way around," Svechin insisted, "1917 will in fact be the most important year of the war, and it's precisely because of all our sacrifices that we cannot relax our efforts now. In fact, we must enlarge the army now that the front extends to the Black Sea. People previously exempt are being brought before the draft boards again. We expect an extra six hundred thousand from that. Add another hundred and fifty thousand category 2 militia. And add to that the normal annual intake. With these resources . . ."

Resources! God help us!

"We just can't tax the people's patience any further, I'm telling you!"

"You've started talking like a Narodnik, instead of an officer on the General Staff!" Svechin said, with a smile in his lustrous black eyes.

"No, like a doctor. Like a doctor who puts his ear to someone's chest and hears the creaking of mortality. Believe me! I'm not speaking idly. I know."

Till that minute Vorotyntsev had been saying all that he meant to say, without toning it down, and however much Svechin disagreed, there it was, for both of them to contemplate, out in the open. But to go on from there, to suggest solutions, ways out, was beyond him. He knew, he felt, only that action was necessary. And meeting somebody like Svechin—what could be more natural? He was clever, strong, quick, completely trustworthy, and now a prominent figure, a general at the heart of GHQ. Not much less grand than Guchkov. He had met, and would meet, no one of equal importance on his present travels.

But Svechin was all soldier. However understanding he was, he would not cooperate.

"Here in Petersburg everybody has this crazy idea that we're losing.

Where do they get it from? And they all get each other worked up. Guchkov, of course, is at it too, right out in front. That shitty letter he wrote to Alekseev, have you read it? He latched on to things of no real substance, for the sake of abusing the government and creating as much of an uproar as he could. Exaggerating, distorting, spreading his fictions far and wide—a womanish trick, the sort of hysterical behavior you can expect from everybody here. And what does the letter prove? Nothing. Just another literary exercise in the Petersburg manner."

The conversation had taken a strange turn: Svechin himself had homed in on the central figure, and Vorotyntsev was at a loss how to defend him. Back there in Romania that letter had been the drop that filled his cup, the spark that fired his impatience. Perhaps, he thought, we sometimes make up our minds too hastily. Now it did seem a peculiar way of doing things.

Svechin was continuing with his demolition. "Guchkov, of all people, ought to be ashamed to miss the point as he has. He thinks of himself as a military man, he's made flying visits to the front, he supposedly knows the supply situation, and indeed is personally concerned with it. Although it's difficult to know whether those War Industry Committees do more to help or to hinder supplies—it's no good having so many masters, all of them dashing off to the front so that they can give the generals pep talks and distribute cyclostyled speeches to the officers."

At this point the fish soup was served, momentarily distracting them and calming them down. Their vodka was running out. They attacked the soup without waiting for it to cool.

Somewhat fortified, the beardless, black-browed bashi-bazouk could smile again.

"I wish you could see the effect it's had on Alekseev. He's been ill ever since, he can't get over it. He's a true Russian if ever there was one. What he fears more than anything in the world is his superiors. What if the Emperor started thinking that Alekseev really is corresponding with Guchkov!"

Vorotyntsev immediately asked himself whether Svechin too was not afraid of his superiors, and if you got right down to it, how did he now feel about the Emperor? That was the key to everything.

"Anyway, if you worked like he does you too would fall sick. That one head has to hold everything that affects the civilian population, as well as all army business: stockpiling foodstuffs and fodder, the metal shortage, fuel, even the militarization of factories. He carries on just as before: doesn't look for assistants and will never find himself a good staff. Half of those at GHQ are little better than drones. His one and only adviser was Borisov, an unkempt, unwashed éminence grise, who was just as idle as the rest. Alekseev wants only robots like that fool Pustovoitenko, people who keep the papers in good order and don't interfere. The old boy doesn't even want to look at the operational plans of our department: his view is that if decisions have to be taken by one man, that man ought also to draw up the plans by himself. Unaided! If you suggest something to him—raids, say—he just waves you away, says spare me these newfangled notions!"

"Well, even if he does make his decisions all by himself, from what I've seen of them they're not too bad. If, as you say, he's in favor of peace with Turkey. And if what I've heard is correct, he didn't want to get tied up with Romania, but to give priority to the northern sector of the front. And then, I suppose, the Emperor is still putting spokes in his wheel?"

Svechin, hovering over his soup, answered calmly. "What about the Allied diplomats? And the Empress? Even that swine Rasputin advises Alekseev through intermediaries."

Although his eyes added nothing to what he had said, he had taken the point, of course. But he brought the conversation back to his old theme.

"You can't channel all the concerns of the army and the country as a whole through a single head. To try to do so is the distinctive characteristic of a man of meager talent. With us it's the accepted thing to grumble at the Tsar, and abuse the government unsparingly, but not to say a word against our old man, who has become one of Russia's recognized assets. Just between ourselves, though, is he really fit to be the commander in chief of a great army?"

That's just it: he isn't commander in chief. The Supreme Commander is right beside him—sleeping, strolling, dining with the generals and the diplomats, listening to hunting stories, going to the cinema.

"Of course, it's easy to idolize Alekseev, after Yanushkevich and Danilov. But he is the proverbial shovel set up instead of an icon."

Vorotyntsev felt bound to acquiesce here: "That, Andreich, is the depressing result of decades of ineptitude. Even when they genuinely want to appoint a man of talent they are no longer able to find one. So they appoint people on the hereditary principle, people bearing the same stamp of mediocrity as themselves. If we wanted to stick our noses into this war we needed to be a strong power, otherwise it would have been better to keep out. The home front too would have stood up to four times as much, just as it does in Germany, if it was under a strong hand."

Svechin might not have been listening. "I don't really want to speak ill of him. He isn't greedy, isn't ambitious, he has a sensible view of things, he won't reject the correct solution, if it's on the plane he's accustomed to, and within the bounds of moderation, and he won't go to bed at night until he's given all the instructions he has in mind. Only he's begun to loom over Russia like a monument of priceless experience. Anyway, what I've been meaning to say is that the old man is now seriously ill. It's obviously going to be a lengthy business and he'll obviously have to take sick leave."

"I had no idea! What's wrong with him?"

"Something with his kidneys. And he has a high temperature all the time. When we're feeling spiteful we say it's caused by the fright Guchkov's letter gave him. Anyway, the old man has gone into a steep decline. But what I'm getting at is this: previously you couldn't so much as hint that so-and-so knew his business and ought to be taken on by GHQ. The old man would say, 'If we spent less time sleeping we could manage ourselves.' But now, if he's absent for a long time, they're bound to take on new people at GHQ. Are you on leave at present? Or are you here on business?"

Vorotyntsev's heart beat faster. "I plan to be back with my regiment in five days' time."

"And you'll rot there for a bowl of Romanian gruel." Svechin laid a fine hand on Vorotyntsev's and spoke in a matter-of-fact way, as though anxious to forestall his friend's gratitude.

"Don't think I've been forgetting you these past two years. It's just that circumstances were unfavorable. You couldn't possibly return to the Grand Duke's staff, you know that yourself."

It would be marvelous! If he wanted to have a hand in crucial changes at the center, GHQ was the best place to be.

"Two new armies are presently being deployed to your left, all the way to the Danube estuary."

"When did this happen? I saw nothing."

"Starting on 30 October. And you'll be pulled out of the 9th Army and stationed down there, where you'll be further off the map than ever, and so deep in the mud you won't be able to lift your feet. They've started the redeployment already. How long do you intend to hang around on the frozen fringe?"

That was indeed one of Vorotyntsev's grievances: being a regimental commander was fine, but why in such a godforsaken place? Toward the Danube? That must mean against Bulgaria? And that meant chasing the old Byzantine dream again. He would resent dying for Constantinople when the main battle line was drawn along the Dvina.

"I want to try to get you into GHQ quickly while the old man's away." And as if he thought persuasion was necessary: "We can always find more regimental commanders. But you're a strategist—where ought you to be?"

As if he needed persuading that he was a strategist! That had been his nickname at the beginning of his career as a young officer. Only a few officers from his Military Academy days really knew Vorotyntsev's capabilities. He would never drop the slightest hint of it, but he would not have considered even the post of army commander beyond his deserts. GHQ? Yes, he had need of GHQ, and GHQ needed him.

But . . . "Isn't there an order that only officers in category 3, the semi-disabled, are to be given staff jobs?"

As the commander of a regiment in the field, Vorotyntsev thoroughly hated the grossly inflated staffs usual in the Russian Army. He would have been perfectly satisfied with a transfer to a regimental command on the Northern Front.

"HQ staffs are one thing, GHQ another," Svechin retorted, with friendly abruptness. "Anyway, there are perfectly fit officers on HQ staffs, you can't throw them out. Don't be so awkward, Yegor, don't fight it. Just tell me where to send the orders and I'll get them off in two or three days. Or maybe you can call in at GHQ now, on your way back."

"Good enough, Andreich," Vorotyntsev said, thinking it over, "that's just fine."

But if it had come to this, did he have the right, would it not be ignoble, to conceal from Svechin his present way of thinking, and those vague schemes which as yet could hardly be called a plan of action, but all the same . . . ? Svechin ought to be aware of whom he was recommending. Putting it all into words was, however, very difficult, it still needed consideration. Yet those mutinous thoughts of his were a refusal to accept the state of mesmerized paralysis in which the Emperor conducted, or rather let himself be carried along by, the war. Mutinous thoughts, which some might think could help to save Russia—yet with a slight shift of accent they could perhaps be called treasonable.

Vorotyntsev was, in any case, not the only one who thought that way. It was in the air, and others of course thought the same.

But did Svechin?

"It's all very well, Andreich. But let me tell you that the condition of the state as a whole is ruinous. Which means that something more is required of us than service at GHQ."

He looked hard at the bashi-bazouk.

Who went on eating his fish, watching out for the bones.

Vorotyntsev bent forward, elbows on the table, concentrating on his big-eyed, big-eared obstinate friend all the pent-up mental energy which had catapulted him out of Romania. Just one or two sentences, correctly or incorrectly worded . . .

But from somewhere over their heads . . .

"Ah-hah! So this is where the Young Turks are meeting today!"

They looked up with a start: Aleksandr Ivanovich Guchkov was standing by their table!!

Dark gray frock coat, stiff stand-up collar, black tie. He was smiling, and there was even an endearing shyness in his smile. He blinked at them through his pince-nez with obvious pleasure.

Vorotyntsev jumped up, overjoyed. "Aleksandr Ivanych! What a miracle!"

Svechin rose less demonstratively.

Guchkov's handshake was rather limp. And in general he looked rather lifeless, though he tried to make up for it by holding his head high.

"What is a miracle?"

"That we've met you here!"

"I come to Cubat's quite often. It's more of a miracle that you are here. And both together."

"I rang several times. I wanted to see you!"

"So I was told."

The expression in his prominent eyes was grave and sad. There were bags under his eyes, his cheeks sagged, and there was a great tiredness in his puffy face.

No need to ask, really, but . . . "How are you feeling now?"

His shoulders were hunched. The lines of his body were slack and weary. There were gray hairs in his close-cropped tonsure, the hair combed back at his temples, his small, rounded beard, and his side whiskers.

"How d'you expect me to feel? Illness doesn't improve anybody."

Civilian dress. Sedate and handsome, unhurried, cautious even, in his movements. An average educated member of the merchant class, the sort who might spend his surplus money on building an art collection, or supporting a boarding school for gifted children. Physically somewhat underendowed, a bit pudgy, a sedentary type.

But wasn't he one of Russia's greatest daredevils and most reckless duelists? The inspiration of the Young Turks? The organizer of a unique circle of Duma deputies and young army officers in the Third Duma?

So much like the average educated businessman frequenting Cubat's restaurant. Yet at the same time the soul of Moscow. A man feared by the Tsar! The object of the Tsaritsa's unquenchable hatred! But himself crowned with glory, and so immune from punishment.

"Gentlemen," he said with a laugh, "from the way you're talking anybody can see from the far end of the room that you're hatching a plot. And what sort of supper are you getting here? If you've got time to spare I've ordered a private room. Shall we go upstairs? I am expecting guests, but I still have time to telephone and make it for later."

Svechin and Vorotyntsev exchanged a glance. Nothing could have suited them better. One of them had left at home a final note breaking off his marriage, and was only waiting until it was time for his train to leave, and the other had come to Petersburg to see this very man.

Guchkov beckoned them toward the staircase to the second floor.

He wasn't exactly limping, but the foot wounded in the Boer War, and now concealed in a high shoe with a built-up heel, seemed heavier than the other.

[4 0]

In the private room it was just like home, there was the same free-dom and ease, but you were also free from women, and could have a serious man-to-man conversation safe from unwanted eyes or ears. More surprising still, compared with the monotonous fare in the trenches, or that in the officers' mess at GHQ, was the food on offer here. As they entered, they found a table laid for six, and on it smoked sturgeon, poached sturgeon, pink salmon in gleaming aspic, and Shu-stov's rowanberry vodka—so it hadn't yet vanished from the face of the earth. Nor was that all: on the stool in the corner stood a promising ice bucket with a napkin. The whole scene was simply unreal.

While Guchkov went to the telephone Svechin gave his verdict: "I'll say one thing—he's no hypocrite. With his money and his business connections, why should he pretend?"

They'd finished their fish soup downstairs, but now the true soldier's appetite—it can wolf down three dinners—showed its teeth.

Guchkov, returning, saw from their faces that the two friends had cheered up. He laughed.

"You see, gentlemen, Russia isn't down and out yet. Russia has everything, only not in the right places. The government can't keep the goods moving but *we* are coping so far. What can I have the pleasure of offering you? No, never mind that, I'm an invalid and a slow mover, so let's be informal, just help yourselves! Viktor Andreich! Georgi Mikhalich!"

He hadn't forgotten, though it was so long since they'd met.

Svechin did not wait to be asked twice, but went over to the bucket, plucked a bottle of vodka from the ice, and grabbed a jar of caviar at the same time.

"What's all that about an explosion on the *Maria?*" Guchkov sud-denly asked Svechin.

Svechin raised his eyebrows. "Why, was there something about it in the papers?"

"Yes, in today's."

The friends hadn't seen it.

"It happened a while ago, on 20 October," Vorotyntsev volunteered. "I heard about it on the way here."

"There you are, you see, and we ordinary citizens only get to know these things from the newspapers," Guchkov said with a disgruntled look, which was the perfect complement to his present appearance.

Svechin's look was truculent. "No explanation has been found. No one knows what caused it. We've lost a battleship. And five hundred sailors."

"It's strange, though, that it coincided exactly with the German offensive against Constantsa," Vorotyntsev pointed out.

"There's a sequel," Svechin said darkly. "There's just been a big explosion on a ship in Archangel harbor. Have the papers mentioned that yet? There's an explosives warehouse there—it could have blown up the whole port."

"Whew!"

"What is going on? Is it all the work of one gang? Are we really so helpless?" Vorotyntsev was horrified. He suddenly saw another wall confronting him, a wall of hidden dangers from secret enemies. Something you never think about at the front. How do you fight such people?

Guchkov snorted. "With this government? Is there anything at all it can do?"

He's right, Vorotyntsev thought. Even if it were not so battered and bruised, a government like ours couldn't deal with this.

They were using only half of the table, Guchkov at the head, the two friends on either side of him, leaving three places for the guests due later.

Svechin poured for Vorotyntsev and himself, and asked if their host would have some.

"Just enough to wet my lips," Guchkov answered sadly.

"We've been following the doctor's reports," Vorotyntsev said sympathetically. "All Russia has, Aleksandr Ivanych. At New Year we were afraid for you. And you only fifty-four! But God was merciful."

Thanks to those bulletins on what looked like a fatal illness Guchkov had enjoyed an unusual display of affection. He had heard for once the voice of Russia, not that of the parties, and had received an avalanche of unexpected letters from every corner of the country, from people unknown to him, all saying, "Live, Guchkov! We need you!" (There was even a rumor that he had been poisoned by the Rasputin gang.) At the nadir of powerlessness he felt more powerful than ever before. In a country of meekly submissive subjects, without official status or authority or soldiers of his own, bombarded with anonymous hate letters from left and right ("Hang yourself, before we polish you off"), under police surveillance though chronically ill, he was the only person in all Russia who could strike fear into the royal couple and their rotating ministers.

The instant flood of sympathy from all educated Russia may well have been what revived him on his deathbed. But when everybody you meet looks at you with pitying eyes and asks about your illness... sympathy from people in robust health, for whom illness is something outside their experience, and difficult to imagine, can become tiresome. And what if fate has mockingly burdened your indefatigable body not with one illness but with several, to be borne like penitential chains beneath your European dress, and while you smile sadly in reply to words of sympathy, they weigh more heavily, gall you more cruelly than the royal family's hatred or your quarrels with the Kadets?

"I spent last spring convalescing in the Crimea," he said. "I wouldn't want to give Alix the pleasure . . ."

He obviously felt that he had played a dirty trick on the Empress, and was proud of it.

In Vorotyntsev's eyes Guchkov's was a character of a kind seldom met in Russia. He combined two types of courage which are hardly ever found together in Russians: that martial courage which is natural to them and that civic courage which is so unusual. (Vorotyntsev, however, knew that he too possessed both.) Only this combination could shift Russia's inert bulk. Moreover, Guchkov's will was unshakable. His views were a little fuzzier: for all his clashes with the Kadets he had a tendency to merge with them. Still, it was a long time since Vorotyntsev had last seen him, and he could have changed greatly in those years.

He studied Vorotyntsev closely through his pince-nez, and said calmly, casually, "Regimental commander, are you? Stationed where at present?"

"In the worst place you can think of. On the extreme left of the 9th Army," Vorotyntsev said gloomily. "I've got out of the habit of thinking of it while I've been moving around. It seems like the back of beyond now, nothing to do with anybody here."

Guchkov demurred, with a few cautious shakes of the head. "You shouldn't say that. There are worse places."

"Where?"

"The Caucasian Front. I'm on my way there. People write to me privately that typhus is rife. Medical services are inadequate. The food and fodder situation is bad. And the reason for all this?" he asked with heavy emphasis. "Why are they in particular experiencing these problems?"

Only then did Vorotyntsev dimly understand what he was driving at. Somebody's revenge on Nikolai Nikolaevich?! The Tsaritsa's? Could it really depend so directly on her? Could you really imagine her or anyone else wreaking vengeance on the whole Caucasian Front because of a single Grand Duke? On every soldier there? No, it was a calumny, a gross exaggeration. In his hatred of the Empress, Guchkov too was losing all sense of proportion.

It left a bad taste.

But Guchkov persisted, with no trace of doubt in his expression. "I'll be there shortly, and I'll see for myself. I hope to God that people have exaggerated."

He took a pickled mushroom and nibbled it tentatively.

Was he perhaps putting on weight? No, he was just rather puffy.

Still unwell. His illness had sapped his strength. That he was still so far from being fit troubled Vorotyntsev. Perhaps the man no longer had the strength for anything?

But his position was still unique. He was at the center of public life, and on easy terms with the commanders of Army Groups, as also with the Supreme Commander's Chief of Staff. If anything was to be done, he, and no one else, was the one to do it! But if he was too ill? . . .

"Ah, yes!" Vorotyntsev suddenly remembered, "as I came through Moscow there was a persistent rumor that you were under arrest."

Guchkov smiled, looking complacent.

"For my letter to Alekseev? Have you read it?"

Vorotyntsev said yes, without enthusiasm. Svechin simply nodded his hairless block of a head. He was busy serving himself, rising from time to time to visit the ice bucket, drinking rowanberry vodka, eating copiously, chomping vigorously.

Vorotyntsev joined in. He felt his trench-cramped frame relaxing. The slowly melting saltiness of the salmon. How good it was.

Another five days and he would be sloshing around in the trenches again, sending men into hopeless battle. Did Guchkov, or didn't he, have something in mind?

Guchkov interlaced his fingers on the slope of his prominent belly and resumed his grumbling.

"That's how things are nowadays. You draft a letter to an official personage, you show it to one or two people you know, ask them if you have the right to send it. . . . Rodzyanko, for instance—who could be more loyal to the throne? He's so loyal he'd burn down Tsarskoye Selo if that was what it took to protect the Tsar's honor. But then the secret got out, it took wing, first it went around the Duma, then all over Russia, people are reading it as far away as Samara and Nizhny. As for Moscow and Petersburg—it might as well be pasted up on the walls." A faint, mischievous smile did nothing to modify the misery written all over his face, or to gladden his listeners.

"That tirade of yours at GHQ—you should have written it down at the time and showed it to a few friends," Guchkov said.

Guchkov's gratification that his outburst had become common knowledge jarred on Vorotyntsev. It still gave him a certain pleasure to hear his own exploit recalled, but he would never have dreamt of behaving as Guchkov suggested. He would leave that sort of thing to the sensational press.

"What right would I have had to do that? It was a military secret."

"That secrecy of theirs is what's stifling us." Guchkov sighed, a shadow of what may have been physical pain passing over his face. "State secrets. At that time it was not yet too late to save the situation. People still believed implicitly, and Russia was ready to take the whole burden on one shoulder."

So was it now too late? . . . Whoever was crowned with the people's trust should know the right time for action, know when the time had come to speak for all Russia to hear.

"It was great the way you pitched into them. You spoke for all of us. You don't regret it, do you?"

"Not in the least. Never," Vorotyntsev said, darting a glance at him.

It was true. He had never regretted it.

Svechin's lips were set in a wry line.

The maître d'hôtel came in to make sure that he had understood Guchkov's instructions about wine: should he serve the Château Lafite with the foie gras and the Pichon-Longueville with the *mouton nivernaise*? These questions obviously related to the second dinner, not to theirs: such fare would be too recherché for a front-line soldier's palate. Theirs would be a different class of dinner.

The thrust of Guchkov's utterances was vigorous, his tone weary. "It's secrecy that's landed us in this situation—left us without shells. I warned the Duma about it in '14, but they wouldn't believe me. So Russia is right to want openness at last."

"If there isn't enough openness for you in Russia," Svechin retorted, "I don't know what you mean by the word."

Guchkov was amazed. "You mean you think there is enough?"

"You mean you think there isn't?" Svechin rolled those enormous eyes, which would never need spectacles and would look ludicrous behind pince-nez. "The newspapers here are far more undisciplined than they could ever be in France or England in wartime. Completely irresponsible. Print grossly exaggerated news items, nobody ever checks, and they're always subversive. According to their lying tales, we're hopelessly behind, hopelessly short of arms. They ignore our industrial miracle completely. For the government they have only unrelieved abuse. On any subject, things couldn't be worse anywhere than in our country, nobody could be more stupid than our ministers. All is lost, according to them, and the only hope of salvation is to transfer power to the Kadets and Zemgor. That isn't freedom of speech—it's verbal diarrhea. They get all Russia in an uproar, the army included. And all the papers are left-wing."

Every blow was well judged, but why was he so exasperated with Aleksandr Ivanych? Something had been riling Svechin ever since Guchkov's arrival. His jest downstairs, about "hatching a plot," perhaps? Or his mention of the Young Turks? Svechin did not like to be reminded of them. He lashed out again, unsparingly.

"You and your little brothers, the Kadets, are so proud of the way you're rocking Russia and throwing her off balance. Watch out it doesn't all come crashing down on your heads."

Guchkov didn't take offense but spread his fingers, silently appealing to Vorotyntsev for justice. How could anyone call the Kadets his brothers, when he had been fighting them for eleven years without a break? He knew too much about the subject, and it was far too complicated to be discussed one-dimensionally. His status didn't permit him to make excuses for himself to these officers, and it would look like malicious gossip if he said that Milyukov lacked the courage of his convictions, was not straightforward in his actions, and would ruin anything he put his hand to. And if he said that the Fourth Duma was capable neither of cooperating with the government, as the Third Duma had, nor of quarreling with it effectively, it would look as if he felt aggrieved that he had not been elected himself. (You can't always keep up with your own motivation: perhaps what had prompted his rebellious moves, and made a conspirator of him last autumn, was precisely that—the failure of the Moscow public to elect him even as a member of the proposed deputation to the Tsar. A year ago almost to the day, 7 November, Guchkov had proposed that he and those "little brothers" should unite to provoke the final breach with the regime. But to no avail. The Kadets' desire to form a government themselves always prevailed over their readiness to take risks. It had taken a whole year of whispering in private apartments just to save the Progressive Bloc.)

Guchkov had a characteristic pose: he held his hand, palm downward, like the peak of a cap, over his eyes, as though shading them from the excessively strong overhead light, or to aid concentration, rested his elbow on the table, and sat looking at the officers.

In this posture the energetic Guchkov looked even more ineffectual than the Kadets. Perhaps in a career of uncompromising awkwardness he had bumped his head against too many walls?

Svechin, red in the face as only a stout fellow who has drunk a little too much can be, showed no mercy.

"They and you alike are destabilizing Russia. I don't know which of you is worse. You're all patriots, you all want victory, and want it without risk to yourselves. Those letters of yours bode no good, anything but."

Vorotyntsev's heart-to-heart with Svechin had just been getting underway when Guchkov had interrupted. And now that the three of them could be having the most interesting of discussions Svechin had gone berserk. Still, his harsh words had helped Vorotyntsev to see *the* letter in a different light—to see its affinity with the Kadet newspapers. You could say that the Kadets and Guchkov were trying to outshout each other.

Confused and uncertain, he did nothing to restrain Svechin. The two officers had been drinking and Guchkov had not—and so there was a difference in temperature and in loudness.

Svechin went on, louder than necessary: "It's the same with Sukhomlinov. He's an idiot, of course, and a fly-by-night, and he was out of his depth at the War Ministry, but you stopped at nothing to bring him down, in a fight you use fair means or foul, hit wherever it hurts most."

"It can be like that," Guchkov said with a faint smile.

"You don't stop to think about Russia herself! And then what was all that Myasoedov business, the spy who wasn't a spy? In the middle of a war you played spy games around the War Ministry—just to topple the minister. How could you bring yourself to do it?"

"The man's been proved to be a spy," Guchkov said, looking colder, sterner.

Vorotyntsev could see that Svechin was about to launch into a heated argument. He himself knew nothing much about the Myasoedov affair, what he had read in the papers was pretty vague, and he would have been interested to hear more about it, but he did not want the whole conversation to break down at that point.

"The important thing," he said, cutting Svechin short, "is not who is denounced by Guchkov, but what Guchkov has done in real terms for the army."

Svechin was, as a rule, a self-controlled skeptic, but once roused there was no holding him.

"Another thing, Aleksandr Ivanovich, you'd do better not to pamper the War Industry Committees the way you do. You're always cooking up some congress or other."

Guchkov, looking hurt, lowered his shading hand.

"And who do you think is performing your industrial miracle if not the War Industry Committees? I'm proud of my participation in them."

"But why do you rip us off? Why do you charge us double? Why does a gun from a state factory cost seven thousand and one of yours twelve? All you civic-minded people are busy forcing up prices, via the ministry. You build factories where they aren't needed, so as to ruin state enterprises. And what concern of yours are the railway plans for 1922? Why have you got Social Democrats on your committees? Don't tell us they're rooting for victory! Maybe they're nosing out the best way to blow everything up?"

"You mean the Workers' Group? The whole idea is that it's better to let them sit in with me as assistants and consultants than to have them tramping the streets with red flags. What are we supposed to do if the regime . . . I know this regime of ours: the government is incapable of doing anything itself, yet doesn't want help when it's offered. With a regime like this, victory will be impossible if we don't intervene."

What did he mean by "intervene"? Was he thinking only of the War Industry Committees? Vorotyntsev was all eyes, trying to see beneath the surface, to miss nothing. But there it was again! How it grated! "Everything for victory!" But "for victory" did not necessarily mean "for Russia." (And if the war effort is as badly organized as Guchkov's letter says, *dare* we continue?)

"Put yourself in the government's place and you'll really have something to howl about!" Even the chair was too stationary for Svechin and he started rocking it onto its back legs. "The government wouldn't be worth a damn if it gave way to you all along the line. And that still goes whether the ministers of the day are out-and-out reactionaries or ultraliberals. They're the ministers—they have to govern, not the parliamentary speechmakers or the War Industry Committees. As things are, every congress you arbitrarily convene meets only to put pressure on the government and demand the universal franchise. When you people talk about fulfilling your civic duty to your motherland you mean working to overthrow the regime."

Like a great round boulder rolling downhill and coming to rest right under your feet, blocking your way, Svechin had cut across and ruined the meeting with Guchkov to which Vorotyntsev had so eagerly looked forward. Hopeless to try to check him now that the drink was going to his head. And—damn it—much of what he said was right. The government really was incompetent, and that was what was so horrible.

Guchkov answered calmly, apparently oblivious of Svechin's brusqueness.

"However, if organized society is engaged in serving the motherland, it naturally demands political rights for itself at the same time."

Svechin, in a dark fury, rocked back on his chair and said, "They have simply sensed that the regime lacks support and started scrambling for power. If the regime shows weakness—seize it by the throat! Change the state structure to suit them, right in the middle of a war; that's what they're asking! They must be out of their minds!"

Svechin's answer was for Guchkov—but perhaps it was meant for Vorotyntsev too? Perhaps Svechin was answering in advance the thoughts he was not ready to voice?

Well, if it isn't the system that needs changing, what is it? Suppose that, without a change of monarch, we have a new government—should it be composed of Kadets? Not worth exerting yourself for them. These were the important things they should be discussing, but the conversation had gone off the rails. Now that a lucky change of circumstances had brought them together he must not part from Guchkov with nothing resolved. But, given Guchkov's unique situation, only he himself could broach *the* subject.

Guchkov adjusted his pince-nez before his prominent eyes and said, "Well, winning the war with such an incompetent government is indeed impossible!"

Of course he was *thinking of something*! A plan for some sort of coup must surely be ripening in such a mind!

"What must we do to win, then?" The legs of Svechin's chair struck the floor with a sound like the gnashing of teeth. "Set thatches on fire?"

This was where the bouillon was brought in, with a dish of hot pies. Those smells! Vorotyntsev and Svechin had each downed a bowl of fish soup earlier, but they happily ladled out the bouillon. And took a swig of that long-forgotten ice-cold vodka to help it down. Gr-r-r-r-reat!

All this had a soothing effect on Svechin. He stopped rocking.

Guchkov also sipped a little hot bouillon, with an invalid's enjoyment.

"Of course not," he said when the waiter had left. "I'm completely against arson and that sort of thing. That is just what the Kadets won't understand—that you must not sow thoughts of revolution among the masses."

Vorotyntsev could not have been more pleased: Guchkov was not passively waiting for upheavals, as the Kadets were, he wanted action to prevent them. Just what Vorotyntsev had hoped to hear.

Svechin spoke in a more conciliatory tone. "They don't understand some things, Aleksandr Ivanych, but others they understand better than you. I can tell you from personal experience that we sometimes act on other people's ideas without realizing it. We don't notice that we are under their influence. You, now, imagine that you are carrying through a bold, independent program, whereas in reality you are unthinkingly acting in accordance with some Masonic scheme. Honestly and truly now—although I don't suppose you'll tell me—are you a Mason yourself?"

He was joking, of course. Or was he? He stared hard at Guchkov.

Guchkov's face was guileless, his brow untroubled, and he laughed in turn.

"Honestly and truly, I personally was never invited to join or if I ever was it wasn't meant seriously. I sense that some people are joining something or other for some reason. But I would never join myself. I am a monarchist, and that in itself is reason enough for not being a Mason. Freemasonry is moral corruption: you look people in the eyes and lie to them. An unmanly game. Whatever it is you want to do you should act openly, straightforwardly—why all this hole-and-corner stuff, why the masks? As I see it, you can make history and you can explain history without Masonic secrets. You can strive to bring about great historical changes by straightforward, clearly visible actions."

Well said, indeed! And if Guchkov had really not been invited to join those only dimly visible and vaguely frightening Masons, they dwindled into something cowering in a corner.

It was always the same with Svechin. After a drink or two with friends he became more contrary than ever, and used rougher language than he would have permitted himself on duty.

"Still, you mustn't be so pleased with yourself, Aleksandr Ivanych.

Without ever joining them, you can, involuntarily and unconsciously, support a line which, Masonic or not, is certainly Jewish. You think you're independent, but . . ."

"M-e-e-e?"

"You-ou-ou! It's a knack the Jews have. Every crucial situation, every important person—they'll be there manipulating. That nobody Rasputin—once he became influential, there they were, all over him. As for you . . . Think about it. Is your attitude toward the government any different from theirs? And they don't give a damn what becomes of Russia."

Guchkov planted his elbows firmly on the table.

"That, in fact, is one of the things which divide us from the Kadets."

"How, exactly?" Svechin asked challengingly.

"I'll tell you. To hear the Kadets talk, the Jewish question is just about the most important political question of all. It stands at the head of their political program. According to the Kadets, the main aim of the war is equality of rights for the Jews, not the continued existence of Russia, her very survival. On that point all Kadets are as one man. In the first three Dumas they blocked legislation on equal rights for the peasants—demanding a simultaneous grant of equal rights to the Jews—and ended by scrapping the whole thing. The Kadets can't get it into their heads that these two reforms are not equally urgent for Russia. Nor equally overdue. Whereas we . . ."

Svechin dismissed all this with a wave of his big hand. "You're no less obsessed with them. All the lawyers are Jews. All those in the press gallery of the Duma are Jews. If they are so downtrodden, how is it that the task of expressing and influencing public opinion is entrusted to them? A few puny right-wing papers are financed by dubious money, but does the whole liberal press rely on clean money? Where does the money come from? It's Jewish money, of course. Which means that they control the papers. Just look at the names of the publishers. It's not quite two years since the Pale of Settlement ceased to exist and the two capitals and all the other towns are teeming with them. As of this year sixty or even eighty percent of the students in some universities will be Jewish. Commerce has thrown its doors wide open to them, and all trade passes through their hands. Take the Putyatin works—rotten shrapnel, by the way, it's produced by Rabinovich, who's paid Putyatin for the use of his name. How many factories like that does your War Industry Committees have? And Jewish sugar merchants are shipping Russian sugar to Germany on the sly! Oppressed? The hell they are! They're like a compressed spring. It will snap back one of these days—and the impact will be terrible!"

Guchkov raised a restraining finger. "A spring snaps back," he said, still carefully excluding all trace of excitement from his voice, "when it is compressed too far. Just don't press too hard."

"There you are, you see." Stubborn, mocking, impossible Svechin was rocking on his chair, and on his hobbyhorse again. "You pander to them. You join them in lambasting the government and the Sovereign. Would you ever have the nerve to say one-eighth as much against *them*? No, never! And why? *That's* what should be called 'Judophobia'! Downtrodden, are they?! They'll show us who's boss one of these days! Whoever lets the chosen people on board soon finds himself shipping water. Russia will be another of their victims."

"No, no, no!" Vorotyntsev felt it was time to butt in. "No, no. Don't try to twist the facts. If we're losing our way and heading downhill fast, we have ourselves to blame." He was vexed that this rare occasion was again taking such a futile turn and looked like ending nowhere. "I've observed for many years past that the Jewish question is such a thorny one, with so many ramifications, that whatever the subject there's no avoiding it. There's no solution either, yet nobody is indifferent to it. At the same time . . ."

Guchkov took off his pince-nez to wipe them. Painstaking inspection of them seemed to absorb his attention completely. Without pince-nez he looked sicker and sadder, but also more profoundly thoughtful.

"It is," he said, "a subtle peculiarity of the Jewish question that you are drawn into it willy-nilly, and find yourself helplessly admitting that it is the greatest, the most acute, most urgent, and most characteristic of all our problems. No other subject so conclusively determines our judgment of a person, of his political and even his moral profile. We find ourselves thinking that when, and only when, the Jewish problem is solved the state's other problems will all be easy to resolve." Guchkov smiled. "The Kadets, now, have let themselves be taken in, and swallowed all that. But you too, Viktor Andreich, have fallen victim—to the opposite way of looking at it."

The simplest way of distracting them from this argument was to hurry them along to a simple solution. Vorotyntsev took up where Guchkov had left off, speaking quickly.

"Everybody is in such a hurry to occupy one of two extreme positions on the Jewish question, ignoring all others. For some people the Jews are an undifferentiated mass of noble sufferers, who must be loved without exception. Not even individual Jews may be censured, since any reproach will reflect on them all. For others, all Jews are sinister and malicious conspirators, you must hate them in the mass and may not like even individuals without arousing suspicion. Any attempt to qualify these judgments, any reluctance either to detest heartily or to love dearly every single one of them, is indignantly repulsed by both sides. But there are thousands of questions on which only the middle view is fruitful. Surely, gentlemen, this is a question on which we should take a middle position. I for one claim to stand firmly in the middle. I will most decidedly never consent to hand

Russia over to the condescending leadership of the Jews—even if it is only intellectual leadership. But I have no ill will toward them, and no desire to oppress them."

"In other words, you'd give them their head?" Svechin thundered, with undiminished asperity. "They'll soon show you who's boss! That's the secret, don't you see? They cannot and never will accept equality. Give them an inch and they'll be on top of you in no time!"

"I think, perhaps," Guchkov said, concentrating on the problem, contemplating his pince-nez as though they were the greatest of riddles, "that I too occupy the middle ground. What I and . . . certain like-minded people think is this. The Jews have been sent to us for a purpose. Not every country has six million of them, but we have. The destinies of the Russian and the Jew were meant, for whatever reason, to intertwine. Whether they will ever be disentwined I do not know. The spiteful glee of a Herzenstein, who called the burning of manor houses 'rural illuminations,' makes him of course an alien soul. What made that so painful for us was that those Russian peasants didn't realize what they were doing, didn't realize that Russia was burning and wrecking herself, while a member of the Russian parliament . . . well, he's dead now . . . Then again, I shall not claim that the Jews in general love us. And for my part I confess that I have no great love for them. Still, they have been sent to us. And since the state is ours we have to make this entwinement generally acceptable. But in Europe, you say . . . Europe has treated them more harshly than we have. The Pale of Settlement? When it existed it did nothing at all to hinder the rapid growth of Jewish trade, industry, and banking. Our country is dependent in time of war on international Jewish money. And, oh yes, they are all-powerful in the periodical press. Art criticism and theater criticism are both in their hands. They must not be admitted to officer rank—that would endanger the national spirit. Not that this is one of their ambitions. Nor must they be allowed to own great landed estates. But none of this means that we should oppress them."

Black eyes blazed to either side of Svechin's nose. "You refuse to realize," he said, "that you are giving away all along the line. The War Industry Committees, for instance, have let themselves be diverted from helping the army in the field to sapping the regime. In your own way you too, Aleksandr Ivanych, are trying to set thatches on fire."

Guchkov did not close his mind to inquiry into his mistakes and no heated retort followed. Still holding the eloquent bridge of his unfathomable pince-nez in one hand, and shading his brow with the other, perhaps against his noisy interlocutor rather than the light, he spoke as though he was trying out the thought on himself.

"But we cannot renounce the Liberation movement just because the Jews like it and have joined it . . ."

And Vorotyntsev told Svechin, "You're like the Kadets yourself, only the other way around. You're stuck in an extreme position—it's always the Jews, you have no eyes for anything else. If I'd wanted to talk about that I needn't have left Bukovina. But I can mention a number of problems more important than that of the Jews. I've come two thousand versts and met the two of you so unexpectedly, and I want to . . ."

Want to what?

Guchkov withdrew his shading hand and looked up at Vorotyntsev. His hazel eyes were not those of an eager young man, and their prominence was perhaps a symptom of his illness, but his expression was still that of a fighter.

Why this sudden alertness? It must mean something.

. . . Want to . . . what?

Surely he must need people like Vorotyntsev.

But a little doubt crept in, did they both have the same thing in mind?

. . . Want to . . . ?

Well, gentlemen, here we are. Don't tell me that determined, intelligent, and energetic people like us can't think up some way of saving the situation?

A large joint of roast beef, surrounded by greens, had been brought in.

Guchkov didn't want any, but the waiter carved for the friends, and they got busy.

They were silent while the waiter was in the room, but even when he left, the conversation was not resumed. Svechin's silence was as decisive and uncompromising as his words had been before. He ate with enjoyment. Guchkov was obviously saving his appetite for the dinner to come—or perhaps he never ate much. He moistened his lips with red wine from time to time. And also remained silent. Vorotyntsev could not speak out directly, but he had to keep the conversation on course.

"I've been wondering, Aleksandr Ivanych—did Alekseev reply to your letter?"

Guchkov thoughtfully tapped his pince-nez against a finger.

"No. But Stürmer answered for him."

"What did he say?"

"He forbade me, in the Emperor's name, access to the army in the field. Or even to hospital trains. And above all, of course, to GHQ. Or to Army Group HQs. It was a cleverly calculated blow." He frowned. "Without the army—what am I?"

This was too much for Svechin, and he was ready with his objections again.

"So what would you do in their place? If you were the head of state, and some public figure with no official post wrote to the Chief of Staff of your armed forces, telling him that your wretched, rotten, slimy

regime was decaying at the roots—would you let him go around de-
moralizing the army still further? Anyway, they aren't stopping you
from visiting the Caucasian Front."

Again Guchkov was in no hurry to reply. Without his pince-nez his
face was defenseless. His expression was half rueful, half ironic.

"Stürmer also warned me that I might be banished from the capital.
And the Police Department is keeping me under observation . . . I
doubt whether any of the bombers were ever so closely watched . . . I
take care not to mention names on the telephone or in letters. When
I am talking to friends or to my brothers we use code names for some
people. I shouldn't be surprised if you too are under observation,
Georgi Mikhalich, since you've telephoned me several times. A record
is kept of all visitors to my house. Right now, I don't doubt that plainclothesmen have followed my Packard here in a hansom cab and are
keeping watch at the entrance."

"Well, Alekseev was in trouble too, don't think he wasn't," Svechin
said obstinately. "He had to do some explaining to the Emperor of
course."

"Explain how he could exchange letters with a swine and treacherous spider like me?" Guchkov said sadly, trying hard to smile.

"Probably. Something like that. And Alekseev presumably disavowed
you."

Guchkov raised his eyebrows. Lowered them. Accepted it. What
could you say? Politics was like that.

"And that's one of the main reasons for his illness."

"Come on, you said that wasn't altogether true!"

"I have heard that he is ill," Guchkov said with a nod.

"So now he'll probably take a lengthy leave, to recover."

"Leave?" Guchkov was all ears, and immediately wanted to know
who would take Alekseev's place. He obviously had some special reason
for asking.

Who indeed? Nothing could be more important.

Svechin obliged. "I don't mind revealing what I've heard. In confidence, of course. They could, obviously, appoint any blockhead they
like, but the rumor is that two candidates are under consideration—
Golovin and Ruzsky."

Golovin? Surely they won't promote him? Our very own Golovin!

Guchkov put his pince-nez back on. They seemed to have acquired
a more cheerful gleam.

"Golovin—that would be marvelous."

For Vorotyntsev every word Guchkov spoke had to be scrutinized
twice. Marvelous? For what purpose? In what sense?

"He'll move the army around boldly," Vorotyntsev prophesied, "but
he himself will move very cautiously. He's changed a great deal, gentlemen. He's with us now, QMG of the 9th. He acts only with the

permission of his superiors. Without it his abilities seem to be paralyzed."

"Would it be for long?" Guchkov asked, keenly interested. "And
what would you do in that case, Georgi Mikhalich? Go back to GHQ?"

He had guessed . . . Vorotyntsev rubbed his beard vigorously. His
eyes said more than his words.

"In the first place, will Golovin want that? And will it be Golovin
anyway? Second, Alekseev would be very unhappy about it. And in the
third place—am I needed there, Aleksandr Ivanych? Is that where I'm
needed? How can I decide?"

He looked at Guchkov expectantly, hopefully.

"Ruzsky?" Guchkov said as though running over a list of his own
subordinates. "He's a bit sluggish. And too full of himself. Who else
could there be?"

Guchkov no longer wore that look of "civilian sitting sadly at home
with nothing to do." He had pulled himself together, come to life
again. He was thinking hard.

"Why don't you smoke, gentlemen? You'd no doubt like to."

Their fingers had in fact been itching for some time, but they had
spared Guchkov. Now Svechin reached out and opened the ventilation
pane. They started smoking—Svechin his pipe—lolling comfortably.
Guchkov carefully ran a stiffly starched napkin over his lips, around
his lips, under his mustache, and over the top of his beard. He laid
the napkin down.

Rose. And with one hand under his coattails, limping slightly, almost
imperceptibly, started pacing the confined space of the private room.
Just a few steps, this way and that. He seemed to gain strength, and
even to look younger, before their very eyes.

He sat down again and locked his hands before him.

"Gentlemen. I hope I can rely on your silence in all circumstances?
Have I your word of honor?"

Of course, it went without saying.

And suddenly, with his head tilted challengingly, they had before
them the famous duelist. There was a sprinkling of gray, no more,
at the front of his close-cropped hair and around the edges of his
beard.

"Gentlemen, I see nothing to prevent me from sharing with you
some ideas which it is still not too late to . . . carry out."

At last! The moment Vorotyntsev had been waiting for! He was not
too late. He was *there*.

Guchkov was looking mostly at him.

Conscious of his fame and of his authority in their country.

And fired by that daring, that eternal need to take risks, which had
driven him all his life.

"What I would like your views on is this: What ought patriots to do when, in their country's time of distress, they see it ruled by court favorites and buffoons? What must courageous people with position, influence, and weapons do? People to whom everything has been given, but from whom history will demand a strict accounting?"

[41]

(ALEKSANDR GUCHKOV)

Fyodor Guchkov, Aleksandr's grandfather, was a house serf whose mistress owned land in the Maloyaroslavl district. At the end of the eighteenth century, aged thirteen, he found himself in Moscow, apprenticed to a cloth merchant for twenty kopecks a month (ten for his owner, ten for himself). He married a serf, redeemed himself and his family, and set up a mill with English looms at Preobrazhenskoye. According to family tradition, it was his idea to set fire to Moscow when Napoleon was advancing into the city. All that he had was destroyed in the fire, but he replaced and expanded it. He nonetheless handed over his factory and his business to his sons while he still had years to live, and was later banished to Petrozavodsk for contumacious adherence to the Old Belief. His son Ivan fell in love with a married French woman, stole into her apartment through the kitchen disguised as a coachman, took her away from her husband, and married her, thereby breaking with the Old Belief. There were four sons of that marriage, one of whom was Aleksandr. He was in some ways an embodiment of the Moscow merchant type, and was on the boards of various banks and joint-stock companies, but was not rich: he made over his inheritance to his brother Fyodor and was not in his father's view much of a businessman. The pattern of Aleksandr's life was, indeed, unusual for one of his origins and milieu, proving yet again that character is fate.

He began to take a passionate interest in social matters while still a schoolboy. His family, descended from serfs, revered Aleksandr II, and when Zasulich shot Trepov, Sasha Guchkov took the side of the government at school: the would-be assassin had raised her hand against a trusted servant of the Emperor! His schoolmates beat him for it. But shortly afterward he felt the irresistible attraction of terrorism himself. After the humiliation of the Berlin Congress, and the appearance of a British fleet in the Bosphorus, Sasha decided to kill Disraeli with his own hand, punishing him for his anti-Russian policy, and so vindicating Russia's honor. He bought a revolver, learned to shoot, saved money to run away to England, and was enraptured by the thought of dying for Russia on the scaffold. But he confided in his brother, his brother betrayed him to their father—and the whole plan was in ruins. (Thirty years later, as the head of a Duma delegation in London, he stood before Lord Beaconsfield's monument: "And to think you might have died at my hands!")

He left the Moscow high school with a gold medal, and Moscow University with a "candidate's" degree (also a mark of distinction), and went to Germany for five years to finish his education, attending courses in philosophy and economics, after which he wrote a number of works on social landownership, on insurance, on the economy of ancient Novgorod, and carried out research (how we unconsciously anticipate our future selves!) on the possible involvement of Catherine II in the Mirovich plot.

At twenty-three Guchkov passed the examination for enrollment as an ensign in a grenadier regiment, and this was not just a matter of performing his military service in the manner expected of a university graduate, no more of a formality than his election at twenty-six as an honorary justice of the peace in Moscow, and at thirty-one as a member of the Moscow Municipal Board. Active participation in civil and military affairs always intersected and interacted in Guchkov's life—he was at once a parliamentary orator, a statesman, the defender of the army, and a crack shot.

We can be sure that early in life he was painfully conscious of a tendency widespread among the Russian intelligentsia not to be unduly fond of action, to prefer talk and argument, and, if something was undertaken, not to carry it through to the end, but to excuse yourself and others from the conclusive stages. Perhaps because he came from sturdy peasant and merchant stock Aleksandr Guchkov felt within himself the will and ability to act and to carry his actions through to completion. So while his former fellow student Pavel Milyukov was finding lectures and debates more and more enjoyable, Guchkov's impatience tore him from libraries and lecture rooms, and drove him to fight student duels in Germany, to the battlefield, to the life of action. He was never a spectator but always a participant, and sometimes a reckless one.

When he heard about the famine in Russia he abruptly left Berlin University and plunged into the wilds of Nizhny Novgorod province, to work as a rural district clerk and help feed the countryside. When the Turks were massacring Armenians, Guchkov rushed to the scene. Guarding the Manchurian Railway while it was under construction was a dangerous business, but Guchkov gave up his municipal activities in Moscow to serve as an officer out there, always eager for a fight. From there it was not far to Tibet, and he journeyed to that country's holy places. He was tormented by a yearning for heroic action. The Boer War—remote and romantic—broke out, some people got excited over newspaper reports, some sang "The Transvaal Is in Flames," but Aleksandr Guchkov and his brother Fyodor served as volunteers with the Boers, and even the brave Boers marveled at his coolness in battle: he stopped, under case-shot fire, to disentangle the traces of mules pulling an ammunition cart, saving them from certain death. In those years he wrote more than one farewell letter to his parents, in case death proved unavoidable. He almost lost a leg in the Boer War, and was lame for the rest of his life. He was also troubled by angina from the age of twenty-six. But when the rising of the Macedonian Chetniks against the Turks flared up, Guchkov was on his way to volunteer immediately. Too restless to marry until he was forty-one, he was away again at forty-two for the war with Japan—though this time not with rifle in hand, but as a representative of the Red Cross and the Moscow Municipal Board (which did not save him from a short spell as a prisoner of the Japanese).

That would probably not have been the end of his instant responses to distant world events, had not the most important events of all (though no one as yet foresaw how profoundly they would affect the world at large) boiled up in the very heart of Russia.

Everything that Guchkov had done so far, all his eagerness to rush to the rescue, now looked like nothing more than youthful excitability, the preparation of a man who could measure up to great events in the state. The time had come to try him out, to see what feats he could perform for Russia.

His name was already quite well known, and he was a person of note in Moscow. On his return from Manchuria in the spring of 1905 he learned that he had been chosen by the Moscow City Duma as a delegate to the Conference of Zemstvos in May. More and more of those achieving prominence in that context were not real zemstvo men at all but people like Petrunkevich, Milyukov, Rodichev, the Dolgorukov brothers. The red-hot revolutionary mood of the conference astonished the newly arrived Guchkov. A deputation was elected to advise the Tsar to introduce a constitution, and many delegates fervently hoped that it would be refused an audience, so that they could foment revolution without qualms. The group of moderates around Shipov, Guchkov among them, found themselves a vilified minority. But Guchkov, who was not elected to the deputation, received a personal invitation, while the conference was in progress, to Peterhof to see the Tsar (who had been told of his work for the Red Cross and of his disputes with Milyukov). He was received, conversed with the Tsar for a whole hour, and the meeting took place in the gracious presence of the Empress (who could not possibly foresee that this lowly tradesperson would someday be her fiercest foe). This was immediately after Tsushima, and before the zemstvo deputation was granted an audience. Guchkov spoke as he thought he was entitled to: he was the man of courage offering advice to a timid stay-at-home monarch, shut off from real life; advice not to let internal weaknesses get the better of Russia, and in no event to make peace with Japan, which would mean that the machinations of outside powers would decide Russia's fate, but, having committed himself to the war, to hold out against Japan, and at home to convene quickly, and without complicated elections, an Assembly of the Land, from the gentry, the peasants, and the townsfolk, to appear before it in person, and address it boldly, saying that many mistakes had been made in the past, that they would not be repeated, but that this was not the time for reform, what was needed was to finish the war, and if the country was united Russia could not lose to Japan, and would not lose! The strength that was missing at present would be drawn from the Assembly, and this would be felt by the army, whose spirits would soar, and also in Japan, which based all its expectations on social collapse in Russia. "Yes, you're right, the Emperor said thoughtfully, and over and over again: "You're absolutely right." (While to another person more or less simultaneously advising him to the contrary—that an Assembly of the Land would strengthen the revolutionary movement, that continuation of the war threatened Russia with destruction, that peace must be concluded immediately, and at any price— the Emperor also repeatedly nodded agreement: "You are quite right. That is exactly how we must proceed.")

Basking in the Emperor's favor, Guchkov was also called that summer to the Peterhof Conference, to help draft proposals for the Duma. All present proposed a complex system of election by classes, to ensure their own leadership, except Shipov and Guchkov, who wanted nationwide elections, but in stages, not direct, which would ensure that at each level candidates were sufficiently well known to the electorate.

Surely the holders of supreme power, shown a rational road forward, would take it. No—they had blundered into this war and bungled it, and were now in a stupid and costly hurry to extricate their feet from the accursed Asian morass. At home, in Russia, instead of taking bold steps they made do all summer with small, cowardly, belated ones, and when they realized that the water was up to their necks rushed out the muddled 30 October Manifesto. The Manifesto was wrested from the regime not because it lacked physical force (the force was there, and was exhibited two months later in the suppression of an armed uprising in Moscow), but because the Tsar's seldom used willpower gave way at times to fits of uncertainty, and at such times people could take from him whatever they pleased.

The Manifesto was condemned by right and left alike. The attitude of the educated public was: he's taken fright, the Tsar's backing down, let's extort more from him, what we've got so far is nothing! (When, in November, Guchkov proposed that the Zemstvo Congress condemn violence and assassination as means of political struggle the "constitutional" majority rejected his wording!) The Kadets refused to join Witte's cabinet, half of which he suggested should be drawn from the "public."

Others who were invited and refused were Shipov, Guchkov, Stakhovich, president of the Orel zemstvo, and Prince Evgeni Trubetskoy, believing that they were invited only for the sake of appearances, that they would be mixed in with the old administrators, and that there would be no real reform of policy. Shipov, indeed, insisted that they were a minority, and that the leftists, who were in the majority, were the ones to be invited if the public was to support the government. However, in the course of long conversations as they traveled together from Moscow to Petersburg and back, to advise on the establishment of a legislative Duma or discuss their entry into the cabinet, Shipov, Guchkov, and Stakhovich identified and confirmed the basis for a new party.

New parties proliferated after the Manifesto. More and more of them, smaller and smaller. This problem of party alignment caught Shipov's group at a disadvantage. They were, of course, against all forms of adversarial politics. But now they had to accept constitutional government and political parties as necessary evils, given that they had already been introduced by the will of the monarch. There was no other choice: they had to bear their share of the burden under the new system. Then again, now that a constitution and the rule of law had been adopted—and these were for practical purposes the only matters on which Shipov was at odds with the zemstvo majority—there was no practical reason why he should not join the Kadet Party. What kept them apart was, in his words, the remoteness of the Kadets from "the fundamental characteristics of the Russian national spirit."

Guchkov, however, was in favor of a constitutional monarchy of the very sort promised by the Manifesto, with a government responsible to the monarch, not to the political parties. He did not approve of the aggressive attitude of the left zemstvo men, of the Kadets' overinsistence on parliamentarianism for its own sake. As far as he was concerned, the Manifesto was good enough as it was, and his worry was that the regime might stealthily retract it bit by bit.

Shipov and Guchkov agreed that the time had come to unite politically all those who wanted to put the Manifesto into practice, and to establish a new system of government while preserving the authority of the monarch—in other words, all who rejected both immobility and revolutionary upheavals, who had some feeling for historical roots, for what had endured the test of the ages and must be preserved in this new phase of development. This required the creation, not of a party, but of an alliance of parties, so that electors would not form excessively small groups, aggravating party divisions with their disagreements on particular questions, though they were at one on the main issue. The first such alliance would not oppose the government, but support it.

Early in November 1905 its sixteen founding members announced the formation of the Union of 30 October, which invited small parties to join it without abandoning their programs. Entry was denied only to supporters of republican democracy. The main planks in the new Union's program included: all the usual civil rights and immunities; equalization of the rights of the peasantry with those of other classes; state and crown lands to be declared a fund for the relief of land hunger; confiscation of private land to be permitted, but only in exceptional circumstances and with fair compensation; insurance for workers, limitation of the workday to eight hours, and even the right to strike, on condition that it did not harm the rest of the population or the interests of the state; direct progressive taxation (the richer you are, the more you pay), and the reduction of indirect taxes.

The organizers of the Union of 30 October wanted the Duma to be convened as soon as possible—imagining that this would be the beginning of a close union between monarch and people. But the weeks went by quickly, bringing with them new shocks and new ordeals for Russia: the drunken mutiny at Kronstadt, the naval mutiny at Sevastopol, disturbances in the provinces, assassinations, other terrorist acts, all Siberia paralyzed, the armed uprising in Moscow, and in reply a "state of emergency" instead of "the unshakable foundations of the civic freedoms" promised by the Manifesto. The left and the government seemed to be trying to anticipate and outdo each other— in toppling the ill-starred Manifesto and trampling it underfoot. And the Union of 30 October, which had hoped to base all its activity on the Manifesto, had to contend for its most cherished principles before it was fully established itself.

The organizers explained their complicated, pacific middle-of-the-road line as follows:

> **Shipov:** Anyone who holds dear the peaceful transformation of the state order must acknowledge that the Manifesto marks the end of the revolutionary movement in our country, and show his goodwill by contributing to the implementation of the new principles. We distance ourselves both from the left-wing and from the right-wing parties. From the right because they strive to preserve the old system of ministerial command, which brought us to Tsushima. From the left because the whole Russian people is devoted to the idea of monarchy, and not to the despotism of an oligarchy or of the masses. The monarch is above all political parties and the freedom and rights of every citizen are best assured under constitutional monarchy. Unlike the parties of the left, we believe that man must be not only free but imbued with a moral ideal.

Here the chairman of its Central Committee was greatly exaggerating, attributing his own lofty program to the motley alliance which constituted the Union. For Shipov, the objectives of the Union coincided with his own old dream of eliminating bad temper, prejudiced suspicion, and mutual distrust from political struggle and reducing the political struggle as far as possible to amicable elucidation of debatable questions in order to reach agreements acceptable to the opposing sides.

Guchkov: We cannot take a negative attitude toward what was created by old Russia. The monarchical principle also must be carried over in revised form into the new Russia.

In the Huntsman's Club on Vozdvizhenskaya Street, with three hundred beautifully dressed people listening to the self-assured orators, the "Octobrist" Congress might look like a triumph: the complicated middle road of social development was clearly expressed in the speeches and unquestioningly accepted by the audience. But when the Duma elections began soon after, the minor parties and their candidates quickly split off from the Union of 30 October and joined whichever opportunist bloc might get them elected. So that the Union, apparently so strong and solid, proved to be jerry-built. While educated society, more and more exasperated, more and more convinced that no agreement with "that regime" was possible, did not vote for the eccentric preachers of the middle line—whatever that meant—and of compromise. At the Duma elections early in 1906 the Octobrists were crushingly defeated, even Shipov and Guchkov failing to win seats. It looked as though their efforts during the preceding months to implant their high principles in a receptive political body had been in vain.

It was a critical moment for both of them, but although the difference in age between them was only eleven years, for Shipov it marked the beginning of a sharp political decline, whereas Guchkov rose swiftly to higher things. It was not so much because of their defeat as for a number of other contributory reasons that they parted company, and indeed were estranged, at this point. Shortly after their failure in the elections, Shipov ceded the presidency of the Union of 30 October to Guchkov. Their parting can be seen as the passing of an age and the beginning of a new one, but in any case it is one of life's rules that no one should linger on the stage once he has played his part to the full. For Shipov that time came when he was fifty-five. The lucky ones are those whom it overtakes at seventy. Some are squeezed out at thirty.

Our reason for devoting so much attention to Dmitri Shipov in our survey of events is not that he influenced the course of Russian history, but rather that once the cruelest years, the years of great convulsions, set in he lost all influence. Once the social upheaval began, the beneficent, moderating activities of earlier, quieter years, which had brought some success for his patient, deep-laid plans, and given him influence throughout Russia, were succeeded by a series of defeats, honorable retractions, and complete withdrawal into inaction, a recoil into helplessness. Our reason for looking so attentively at the lessons Shipov teaches us is in fact that in a quarter of a century in public life he seems not to have diverged by a single degree from a moral concept determined by his religious beliefs, seems never at any stage to have become embittered, to have lost control of himself in the heat of the battle, to have sought revenge on rivals, to have been underhanded, or self-seeking, or greedy for fame— never! Instead, his calm, meticulous mind applied that moral concept to Russian history, not somewhere behind the scenes but at the center of events, and in what were Russia's most dangerous and fateful months he was called in to advise the Emperor and offered a post in the government (in July 1906 that of Prime Minister). But the advice he gave was never taken. And he refused all governmental posts, after weighing the balance of forces and of feelings. This was the curious fate of so many Russian men of action: for a variety of reasons they nearly always refused to act.

The case of Shipov raises an awkward question: Does history admit of consistently moral activity? Or at what level of moral maturity in a given society does such activity become possible? Even seventy years later, in the most open of countries, with centuries of political maturity and flexibility behind them, how often does agreement and compromise result from a higher understanding, a friendly willingness to give way and oblige another, rather than from an equilibrium of selfish interests and forces? Hardly ever.

On an imperceptibly bending path our eyes assure us that the way lies straight ahead, and we belatedly realize that we have described a circle. So it was in Shipov's political life: in this last, too stormy year he had rounded a bend without noticing it. Only a year earlier he had thought that the constitutional path would be a disastrous one for Russia. Then, in obedience to the monarch's will, he had become one of the proponents of the Manifesto of 30 October, a stauncher one than the Emperor himself. Now that victory—just about, still precarious—was with the regime, Shipov, without realizing it, began siding more and more frequently with the Kadets: "The regime must give up its struggle against society."

In those very months hundreds of officials were killed or received death threats. (A meeting of Moscow tramway workers "officially" voted to kill Guchkov's brother Nikolai, mayor of Moscow, for his actions against strikers.) Yet Shipov did not go on to say, "And society must give up its struggle against the regime." He recoiled from Stolypin's vigorous measures, claiming that he "does not acknowledge the moral principle in the state order and state life," and was inclined to put the latter at the mercy of the Kadets, the very ones for whom morality would always dissolve in expediency.

When Shipov and Stolypin met to discuss the possibility of forming a joint government, circumstances were conspiring in their favor. There was, however, never a glimmer of agreement between them, but instantaneous antipathy, which provoked Shipov, usually so mild and peaceable, into making an incoherent, offensive statement, later spelled out in more logical form. Stolypin (he said) was not sincerely committed to the Manifesto, but in fact opposed to it; he wanted to run the country in the tradition of the old absolutism; he was contemptuous of representative institutions, and bore the main responsibility for the dissolution of the First Duma; he had a limited political horizon; and in general a superficial worldview; he did not aim at the general good and the higher truth; he was, moreover, conceited and domineering, and he had succeeded in subjugating the Emperor to his pernicious but potent influence.

For his part, Stolypin probably thought that Shipov, loftily surveying the scene with saintly eyes, lacked a practical grasp of things, tactical resourcefulness, speed, and energy, that he was a marvelous talker, but incapable of any action whatsoever at moments of crisis—and so was not up to the task of saving Russia.

What makes Shipov's case all the sadder is that in his last years, when he was no longer elected to the Duma but more and more unceremoniously sidelined, excluded even from minor posts, even from the district zemstvo and the Moscow City Duma, and while he dawdled over his memoirs, his vision became not keener but weaker, as a half-tearful film of loving kindness and inflexible faith clouded his view. Finishing off his reminiscences in the autumn of 1918, he informs us that the last great war in history is over, that no such bloody catastrophe will ever happen again, that the ideas of militarism and imperialism have been discredited forever, that religious consciousness has triumphed, especially in the United States, that the God-bearing and God-seeking Russian people will in the near future rise again from its knees, and that the intelligentsia will bring its views into line with the people's ideals—witness the conversion of the terrorist-socialist Savinkov to Christianity.

That Shipov ended in this way makes us wonder how quick and accurate his assessment of events and his decisions would have been if he had agreed to head the Russian government in June 1906. (This is not a purely imaginary exercise. Prince G. E. Lvov, a close political associate of Shipov, took part with him in the same discussions. Lvov showed in 1917 just what their whole policy was worth.) If you regard the people as a stalwart God-bearer—why indeed not entrust them to the caprices of a Kadet Duma? Nothing can harm a God-bearer, he will rise to his feet whatever happens. From our distance it is easier to judge which of them, Shipov or Stolypin, was more right or more wrong. They themselves, in those hot weeks, could only rely on intuition.

For Guchkov too, after he parted company with Shipov, Stolypin was a fateful figure. One who sundered the recent allies as though with a saber stroke. At their first meeting, thanks to that intuition which is so often our salvation, Guchkov took an instant and unqualified liking to his strong, confident, brave contemporary. We often fail to realize how much our likes and dislikes are determined not by beliefs but by temperament. Guchkov recognized in Stolypin a man of action, strong-willed and clear-minded, with a definite view on every question, straightforward in all his pronouncements—and one in whom "things Russian are at the center of everything."

Guchkov himself had returned from his travels and his wars at forty-five, still to all appearances a young man. His one aim, his one eager ambition, was to set public life on a new course. He took the helm of the Union of 30 October from Shipov when it was on the rocks, and sought to carry forward the plan which they had launched together: that of amicable collaboration between the regime and society. Guchkov found it strange to hear from Shipov that, though politically active, he condemned political strife.

> For me, on the contrary, it is always very satisfying to give my opponent a good drubbing!

The fight itself, the cut and thrust, the excitement of combat, were Guchkov's passion. Even in the most turbulent months, when Russia was threatened with collapse and disintegration, he rejected as absurd Shipov's advice to cede Russia to a Kadet Duma and let both of them realize their mistake later. Guchkov could not stand the Kadets, and missed no opportunity to hit out at them: even at a provincial zemstvo board meeting, discussing a turn of phrase in some minor local matter, the Kadets must be made to choke on it.

But in spite of this attitude, and for all his sympathy with Stolypin, Guchkov could not bring himself to join his first cabinet: that would have meant crossing the gulf between government and society. On Aptekarsky Island, a few months before the explosion, Stolypin offered him the post of Minister of Trade and Industry, and Guchkov showed his approval of the government's policy, but doggedly made his acceptance conditional on invitations to various other representatives of society to join the government. No agreement was reached, but Guchkov promised support for Stolypin from "society's" side.

At about the same time the Emperor also felt a need to talk to Guchkov again and received him at Peterhof. This was during the Sveaborg mutiny, but what struck Guchkov was Peterhof's dreamy tranquillity. The Emperor was in a good humor, affable and charming, as so often, irresistibly charming. He also invited Guchkov to join the government. But it was obvious that he did not realize the seriousness of the situation. He might have been the monarch of some other country. On some other planet. In his view any updating of domestic policy was superfluous and he was unwilling to tie his hands with any definite program.

> I cannot tell you how dismayed I felt. The impressions left by Peterhof were nearly the end of me. I see no hope in the near future. We are in for still ruder shocks. But at the same time, there is a consolatory feeling that no one is innocent, that all the victims of the impending catastrophe have only themselves to blame, that a great act of historical justice is being accomplished. I feel painfully sorry for some individuals, but not for those same people in the mass, for whole classes, for the whole system.

Guchkov said this in a letter to his wife, when the impressions left by his audience at Peterhof were still fresh. Russia's baffling plight, Russia's helplessness, were encapsulated in this strange, courteous Tsar, who could think of nothing to ask a soldier except where he had previously served, and after hearing a famous pianist play asked only whether he was the older or younger brother of a sailor with the same name.

Guchkov, though dismayed, did not weaken, but waded against the current on his strong warrior legs. In August 1906 the introduction of field courts-martial was explained in a government communiqué as follows:

> The revolution aims not at reform (to which the government also considers itself committed) but at the destruction of statehood and the monarchy.

Society at large was, of course, indignant about the courts, but Guchkov was not afraid to be the lone voice of approval in the press:

> A strong government, which has to protect a newborn political freedom, must resort to rapid and severe repressions. In certain localities in our country internecine war is in progress, and the laws of war are always cruel. Robbery has become more and more frequent, and has reached the stage where it has lost its revolutionary character and become mere brigandage. The introduction of field courts-martial is a cruel necessity. Repressions are compatible with a liberal policy: only the suppression of terror can create normal conditions. The government must respond to revolutionary violence by energetic measures to suppress it. I believe implicitly in Pyotr Arkadievich Stolypin. Persons as able and talented as he is have never before held power in our country.

Then a year later:

> If we are witnessing the last throes of revolution, we owe it solely to Stolypin.

Guchkov's supporters fell away, and the left reviled him. But with this declaration he had set foot firmly on the path he would follow for the six years which were the height of his career—those crucial years in everyone's life for which all the rest is just a backdrop.

The way ahead was not easy to begin with. Society thirsted for leftism and revolution, and the Octobrists had no more luck in the second Duma election than in the first. But in the spring of 1907 Guchkov resigned his safe but too peaceful seat in the State Council to fight for the Duma and rally the Octobrists, assailed by curses and threats from the left.

Were the conditions in which the Union of 30 October could function a thing of the past, as Shipov believed, or were they only now beginning to emerge, as Guchkov confidently maintained? Was this the time for

> the reconciliation of the Russian state and Russian society, those age-old enemies, friendly cooperation with the regime, and a painless transition from the condemned system of government to the new one?

Russia could cope with its new tasks at home and in the world at large

> only under the leadership of a strong monarchy. The Constitution [of 1906] makes the governmental power transparent to society and so liberates it from dark and irresponsible forces

but not in order to put it

> at the disposal of political parties and their central committees! We are opposed to those revolutionary elements who thought they could exploit the difficult situation in which the government found itself in order to seize power by means of a coup. In the struggle with sedition, at the moment of deadly danger, we unhesitatingly took the side of the government

while retaining the freedom both to condemn the government's mistakes and to defend its sound actions.

Perhaps the Manifesto itself—issued by a Tsar at first too unyielding, then excessively frightened—was a leap beyond the power of a country completely unprepared for parliamentary life? Perhaps the law of 16 June 1907 promised a smoother evolution toward a parliamentary system?

> The coup d'état carried out by our monarch meant in fact the establishment of a constitutional order. I am sure that calm and loyal work on the part of the Third Duma will reconcile even our opponents, that in a year or two the venomous sting which has for so long poisoned the body of the nation will have been drawn, and that the surplus energy of the revolution will be transferred to constructive work.

And that was what happened. The year 1907 was when incontestable signs of recovery were first seen in Russia. People who, in earlier years, were scurrying from one emergency meeting to another were now working on economic programs, and the engineer became a more and more considerable figure in public life.

In the autumn of 1907 the Octobrists were elected to the Third Duma as a firmly united group, and their leader, Guchkov, now had to show in practice whether or not it was possible to follow the middle line of balanced reconstruction in Russia. The first two Dumas had only one aim—to harass the government and inflame the public. Would the Third succeed in shaping the country's future political course?

The first fresh impulse we feel here is the relationship between the leader of the Duma majority, Guchkov, and Prime Minister Stolypin. Their collaboration was based not on collusion, on a common scheme, but on service to a common idea, on a contest to decide which understood it best. Unity of purpose went with debate and competition. One of Guchkov's first parliamentary interventions (in May 1908) was his attempt to block the naval credits: to reinforce Russia by denying her battleships! Otherwise

> how can we get away from the specters of the past? The government must come clean and name for all to hear those who are to blame for the catastrophe.

This speech greatly annoyed Nikolai II, who dearly loved the navy, and he began to see Guchkov, whom he had greatly liked until then, in a much poorer light.

From the platform of the Duma, Guchkov was free to tell the whole unhappy story of the war with Japan.

> The main blame for our failures does not lie with the army—the culprits are our central government and our educated public. The government thoughtlessly contributed to the outbreak of this war, did not take the trouble to put our defenses on a proper footing during the long years of peace, and when the danger arose did not realize the seriousness of the situation. The assumption was that this was a distant colonial war, which we could conduct without exerting our strength to the full. Only much later was it realized that what was at stake was not just southern Manchuria but the very existence of Russia. And when we did become strong in the Far East, and the army was still in good spirits, the government lost faith in itself and in its people, and concluded that peace which for a long time to come reduced our standing in the world to zero.
>
> But while the government came to realize its mistakes—if only at the end of that unhappy war—our educated public remained blinkered to the end. It proved to be not the least bit more farsighted than the government—each was as bad as the other. The unpopularity of the excuse for the war made the public close its eyes to the vital interests at stake in that distant place. And there was a constant flow from here to the army—in the press, in letters from family and friends, in what visitors told them—of words which tended to sap its morale, to deprive it of what was left of its belief in itself and in victory. Throughout the war our public had a demoralizing effect on our army. ("True!" from the right.) And at the end of the war it compounded its error.

In the army too, however,

> bureaucracy was all-pervading, it subordinated the fighting men, deadened their energies, damaged their morale. The High Command could not have been feebler. As in the Crimean and the Turkish wars, most of our generals were not equipped to deploy the whole range of weaponry. Throughout our

country the unnatural system of selection which allows the weak and worth-less to float to the top, and rejects the bold and talented, is still in force to this day.

When Guchkov spoke it was never to show off on the Duma platform, but, with every speech he made, to bring about some improvement in his country, and more particularly in the army, to which he had devoted his political career. At one time he spoke up for funds to improve the conditions of the soldiers in the ranks, who were living on short rations, at another for increased allowances for officers, a caste despised by "society," overlooked by the treasury, yet obliged at critical moments in the country's life to show the highest martial valor on behalf of all the rest.

The shortage of officers in the army is assuming menacing proportions. There are units in which it reaches fifty percent. Even in the past officers' pay reduced them to poverty. But in recent years while many social groups and classes, in the hurly-burly of the so-called Liberation movement, have more or less assured their material well-being, poverty does not just stand on the officer's threshold but has entered his dwelling, officers' wives do the meanest of jobs, officers' families have to eat from the company cooking pot, and in the far-off borderlands the life they lead is one not fit for any human being. The future holds no promise for any army officer . . . Impossible to provide for your family even at the end of your days.

The only claim to privilege in the army should belong to education, military expertise, and talent. (Applause, but not from the right.)

Whereas, in fact, the Guards, those with the right pedigree, sufficient means, or con-nections in the capital, enjoyed unearned and unjustifiable privileges.

The millstone of garrison service grinds chivalrous sentiments and noble characters to dust. A sense of honor, and self-respect, are not cherished: instead the honorable ambition which is one of the main stimuli to heroism in a military man is destroyed by bullying, by ill treatment and humiliation of subordinates. Officers leave the army and become land surveyors, bailiffs, bookkeepers—anything to get out of it. Only the few genuine enthusiasts for the soldier's trade, and men unfit for any other employment, remain in the army.

And still the inroads of reform upon the War Ministry were too timid.

And when you recall how other peoples have behaved after heavy defeats, sorrow and envy steal into your heart. Do you remember how France was reborn after 1871, and what sacrifices she endured, up to the moment when the breeze of socialist doctrine stiffened and completed the work of destruc-tion of which the Germans had proved incapable?

As long ago as 1908 Guchkov had realized and said quite publicly that

our arsenal of cartridges and shells is quite inadequate to the changed con-ditions of warfare. In the event of a major war our factories are not equipped to cover the expenditure of ammunition, and there are some weapon systems which our industry does not manufacture at all.

He also spoke of the need to transfer factories, while there was time, from what might become Russia's Western Front. (In the event, nothing was shifted before the retreat of 1915.) And of the weakness and dilapidation of our fortresses. (Which were left just as they were.)

There was an occasional gleam of humor in Guchkov's bitter speeches.

> In my view no minister should be more concerned for the freedom of the press than the Minister of War. In his place I would be badgering the Minister of the Interior every day of the week to put forward legislation to broaden the freedom of the press.

The point being that we would never be able to improve the War Ministry, and in particular its legendary Supply Departments, until the army's voice made itself heard and public opinion could exercise some control. On one occasion the Minister of War (Rediger) undertook an unprecedented inspection of the Supply Departments.

> Confronted with the materials produced by this inspection, I find myself helpless, for whenever I ask whether this or that abuse is known to the War Ministry I can be sure that the department's answer will be "I know of much greater abuses." (Laughter in the center and on the left.) And if the department says that it lacks adequate punitive powers, I feel sure that the Duma will set no limits to those powers: where thieving supply officers are concerned we are ready to go even as far as field courts-martial. (Applause in the center and on the left.) I feel sure that on this question even the gentlemen on the left abstain only because they are too shy to vote. (Noise on the left.) And then—all those stories about cardboard soles for the heroes of Shipka, about frostbitten feet and a barefoot army, will recede into the realm of legend. (Tumultuous applause. Puryshkevich: "Good for you, Guchkov!")

Guchkov went into matters concerning the War Ministry with particular thoroughness. He himself headed the Duma Defense Commission (excluding socialists and Kadets alike), to which Rediger, the minister, readily disclosed all the defects of the system. They tried to examine conscientiously the state of Russia's armed forces. Guchkov formed ties with General Vasili Gurko and with naval circles. The Commission made no attempt to reduce military credits but now always increased them, and succeeded in raising officers' pay. "Up above" it was a cause for dissatisfaction that the Duma was trying to make itself popular with the army by increasing war credits and meddling in what was none of its business. But, viewed from the Duma, the top people themselves might give cause for dissatisfaction, and Guchkov resolved to detonate this explosive theme in a sensational speech. To forestall possible obstruction he concealed his intention from everybody, including the president of the Duma. He began by expressing himself in favor of the budget estimates. Then, speaking as quickly as he could to avoid interruption, he attacked the Grand Dukes.

> The State Defense Council, presided over by Grand Duke Nikolai Nikolaevich, has usurped the power and responsibility of the Ministry of War and is holding up all improvements in military matters. (Cries of "Bravo!" Applause.) To give you the complete picture of the disorganization bordering on anarchy (cries of "Bravo!" and "He's right!") which now prevails in the War Ministry, I must add this: the post of Inspector General of Artillery is held by Grand Duke Sergei Mikhailovich, that of Inspector General of Engineers by Grand Duke Pyotr Nikolaevich, that of Supreme Head of Military

Schools by Grand Duke Konstantin Konstantinovich. Which means that responsible branches of the armed services are headed by persons who by virtue of their position are in practice responsible to no one. ("Bravo! Bravo!") It is our duty to call these things by their proper name, but at the same time we have to acknowledge that we are powerless. ("True! True!") Deputy Puryshkevich was right; we cannot afford any more defeats! Another defeat for Russia would mean not only ceding territory, not only paying reparations, it would be the poisonous sting that would bring our motherland to the grave. (Applause, cries of "True!") And if we ask the country to make heavy sacrifices in the cause of defense, we also have the right to address just one request to that handful of irresponsible persons: that they renounce some of their earthly blessings and some of the pleasures of vanity! (Prolonged, stormy applause on the left, in the center, and here and there on the right.) We have the right to expect this sacrifice of them.

The flustered president closed the session. The Duma was shaken. Milyukov approached him in the lobby.

"Aleksandr Ivanych! What *have* you done? After that the Duma will be dissolved."

"No, the army and the people are on our side—they won't dare!"

Nikolai II's remark to Stolypin was: "It would have been all right for him to say it in a private conversation, but not from a public platform." But in a private conversation the answer would have been: "Yes, you're quite right," with a smile, and everything would have remained just as before. Guchkov was sure that only thoughts expressed in public would have any effect. No one refuted what he had said, and the prestige of the Grand Dukes was undermined. In spite of which they remained in similar positions until 1917. The Defense Council, however, was disbanded, to everyone's relief.

Guchkov was losing the Tsar's former goodwill. And that was not at all what he wanted. Early in 1909 he forced Rediger to admit, in reply to a question in the Duma about the efficiency of the High Command, that

> in selecting candidates for the highest posts we have to take the existing structure into consideration

and for that answer the Emperor dismissed the Minister of War and appointed a new one who was to be there for many long years—Sukhomlinov. This man was already an enemy of the Duma Military Commission, and only his deputy, Polivanov, supplied Guchkov with the secret information he needed. Sukhomlinov himself would often be the subject of embarrassing disclosures by Guchkov.

Shingarev says in his memoirs:

> Guchkov's speeches could not possibly have been made by anyone else among us. Uproar, and suspension for fifteen sessions, would have resulted. But he was listened to.

The right, however, listened uneasily. They saw in Guchkov's invariable sympathy with the army a desire to draw it away from the imperial regime and toward the Duma. In right-wing newspapers, and from the Duma platform, Guchkov was accused of "Young Turkism," of "opening wounds" in our defense system, undermining confidence, washing the dirty clothes in public. This was his answer:

> When we saw incompetent commanders we said, "These are incompetent

commanders." It is not we who call them by their proper names, who should be blamed but those who keep such commanders on. Ritual incense burning and cover-up tactics have done us so much harm that we have to make use of the Duma to speak the truth. Deputy Puryshkevich has rebuked me. "We need trust," he says, "and you sow distrust." But there is something worse than distrust, and that is misplaced trust. And we mean to destroy that wherever we find it.

Puryshkevich spoke of my "cotton-wear patriotism," repeating a shopworn witticism. Those gentlemen cannot forgive me for my mercantile origins. To give them material for further witticisms, let me add that I am not only the son of a merchant but the grandson of a peasant, a serf who won his freedom and rose in the world by dint of hard work and determination. (Applause.) And in my "cotton-wear patriotism" you may, perhaps, find an echo of another sort of patriotism—the black-earth, muzhik variety, which knows exactly what little gentlemen like you are worth.

Can it really be said that Guchkov did not remain true to the original program of the Union of 30 October? The lifetime of the Third Duma presented, as he saw it,

a picture of Russian life as it has not been since the 1860s: the regime and society, which had always been irreconcilable enemies, now drew closer. The main role in this act of reconciliation was played by Stolypin, with his quite exceptional combination of qualities. It was only thanks to his fascinating personality, and to the noble qualities of his intellect and character, that an atmosphere of goodwill and trust on the part of society gradually formed around the regime, in place of the hatred and suspicion that had been there before. The Third Duma's levelheadedness and moderation had a profound educational effect on Russian society. An unprecedentedly favorable situation was created, holding the promise of renewal in all areas of our life.

Ah, but the old stick-in-the-muds who had grown moldy in office were not going to crawl out of the nation's way so quickly. By the spring of 1909, as soon as the rumblings of revolution had died down, these phantoms, these monsters, rallied round the throne—to help get rid of Stolypin. Plans for his retirement were in hand when Guchkov said, in a press interview, that

the constitution is under threat from rightist groups, emeritus bureaucrats out of office under the new system, the right wing of the State Council. While Stolypin was waging war on revolution, the right could live in peace. But once the age of reform set in, the rightists realized that their triumphs were nearing an end. As the revolution subsided, forgetful people who had hypocritically tolerated the Manifesto as a thoughtless concession now raised their heads. Those who had brought Russia to unprecedented humiliation, and who somehow vanished when the deadly debt was to be paid—these people are now creeping out of their old manure piles and taking over important positions.

Furthermore:

Stolypin forgives no one for theft, bribe taking, or greed. In such cases he is merciless. When the menacing round of senatorial inspections began, the dark kingdom of bribe takers and peculators was in turmoil. Ripples of fear for their existence disturbed those marsh dwellers.

(Stolypin nonetheless outlasted that spring. The Emperor was not yet too sick of him, and apparently did not yet feel dangerously overshadowed.)

The special feature of the center was that Guchkov could just as forcefully impugn the left.

> If in the past there could be any illusion about the moral significance and political effectiveness of terrorism, if in the past in certain social circles terrorism was surrounded with an atmosphere of sympathy, and even empathy, the puddles of blood and mud have by now deprived terrorism of that aureole. And our state and social system has proved stout enough to withstand the mindless onslaught of mindless people. Who can deny that terrorism has degenerated into savage, mindless malice? The last few years, marked by the activity of the Liberation movement, have made their modest contribution to the growth of hooliganism. Just remember how the revolutionary movement began in Russia. With the Decembrists. And where it ended. (Cries from the left: "It hasn't ended yet!") Terrorism pitilessly destroys not only those who are its real and dangerous foes, it kills blindly, randomly, anybody and everybody. Earlier it may have been possible to suppose that a modicum of self-sacrifice and heroism was to be found in the ranks of revolution, but heroism has long ago migrated to the opposite camp. We have to acknowledge that the policemen, the soldiers, the generals, governors, and ministers who have bravely remained at their posts year after year after year, exposing themselves and their families to danger from one minute to the next—they are the true heroes! (Applause in the center and on the right.)

Guchkov urged the whole Duma to support the bill on aid to families whose breadwinners had been killed by revolutionaries, which would help to cure the moral malaise in the country and would

> put an end to, or reduce, the bloodshed which is the misfortune and the shame of our motherland.

His urging, needless to say, was in vain. The Constitutional Democrats, as well as the socialists, would have been untrue to themselves if they had ventured to condemn revolutionary terror out loud. Heads incorrigibly slewed leftward could not return to a midway position.

> From the extreme left groups we hear nothing but speeches full of suspicion, full of poison, full of hatred. This shows just how sincere is their participation in the onerous work we are carrying out.

There were other opportunities to confront the left later on. Terrorism was always the issue. Later in 1909, Karpov, chief of the Okhrana in Petersburg, was blown up in an apartment rented by the police themselves on Astrakhanskaya Street. There were noisy questions in the Duma, in which both the left and the Kadets insinuated that this was a put-up job, alleging that the apartment was a police bomb-making factory. Why, the center retorted, would the police need a bomb factory, and a secret one at that? To cause explosions? No, the left ingeniously replied, they needed bombs to plant when they made a search.

Such was the ardor on both sides of the Duma, each of them ever eager to prove that it was in the right and "the others" eternally at fault, that speakers ignored the factual details as well as their opponents' arguments. The inexhaustibly flowery Rodichev, whose tongue had brought him fame, and very nearly condemned him to death, now recited from the Duma platform an article in a French newspaper by the émigré Burtsev (such things were possible in this "conservative" Duma),

> whom the Kadet faction trusts more than it does the chairman of the Council of Ministers.

But he had omitted—unintentionally, no doubt, Guchkov said sarcastically—the passage in Burtsev's article confirming that the man who carried out the explosion (Petrov-Voskresensky) was

> an agent of the revolution, an executioner acting for the revolutionary tribunal and assigned to the Okhrana camp as a double agent.

This prompted Guchkov to assert:

> Representatives of revolutionary parties often present themselves to the police, offering their services for money. Moral decay has gone a long way in the revolutionary camp. So far that they have moved on from the old slogan "All is permissible in political struggle" to a new one—"All is permitted in all areas of life." The idealistic and heroic period of the revolution, known to us all by hearsay, has long ago receded, and the brigand period has now set in. Deputy Chkheidze over there will probably not contradict me. In the days of the Liberation movement I got letters from the Caucasus telling me that every so-called political expropriation was simply robbery with violence, to raise funds for the revolution, and always accompanied by lavish binges in the best restaurants in Tiflis. Whenever one of these binges took place people knew that there had been a political expropriation.

Then, turning to the left:

> If you expose police procedures which really are meant as provocation you will always find allies in us. But if what you want is to disarm the state and the government in the struggle with revolution—it's no, thank you.

In this way he stood up firmly against loud and furious onslaughts from the left, from the right, and at times from the left and right simultaneously, sometimes winning support, sometimes roundly abused, but always in the belief that he was steadily steering a middle course, trying to keep the peace between Russia's rulers and Russian society, so that they could work creatively, and always in the hope that both the rulers and society would someday limit themselves and renounce their inordinate demands.

This was the special characteristic of the parliamentary center:

> There are groups in the Duma who are not at all concerned to make our legislative labors bear fruit. Our "comrades" on the left constantly insist, and hope, that nothing will come of the Duma, and that what we need is a great catastrophe,

while the rightists raised the threat that the Duma itself would cause the catastrophe, and the regime looked on the Duma with contempt and saw no need to reckon with it. But both sides will be disappointed. The Duma will succeed in reestablishing truth and justice in our country.

Sound legislation was more important to the center than to anyone else. Its special characteristic was its need to cover its flanks, sometimes with the right wing, sometimes with the left, joining now with the right to outvote the left, now with the left to outvote the right, so as to make some progress and defend the country's interests.

In alliance with the left, Guchkov

—(in 1908) supported the protest against the unprecedentedly high-handed behavior of the Governor-General of Moscow, who had the effrontery to demand that books banned by the censors should be confiscated, and indeed handed in to the authorities;

—(in 1909) supported the right of the Old Believers to preach their faith openly (the socialists, of course, were all in favor, but the Orthodox Church tried to deny them this freedom);

—condemned the harassment of attorneys (when the Ministry of Justice—just imagine!—attempted to withhold permission to visit prisons from lawyers who passed forbidden items to prisoners);

—(in 1910) asserted that "the need for a system of pacification has passed. We no longer see any obstacles which could excuse delay in granting civic freedoms. We are waiting!";

—(in 1912) was for investigation of the shooting of strikers in the Lena goldfields, where "conditions of slave labor prevail which happily belong to the vanished past as far as the greater part of Russian industry is concerned," and where the authorities had "panicked and lost their heads because they feared for their lives";

—stirred by a telegram from Korolenko, interceded for and saved a man condemned to death for a political crime.

But it was also characteristic of the center that none of this won it any political allies.

At times Guchkov sounds a little weary:

We feel rather isolated, both in the country and in the Duma.

It would have been better not to have to depend on anybody, not to join any kind of bloc: the fruitful parliaments are those with an independent center, the weak ones those with an unstable center. There, one of the unexpected things that can happen is a union of right and left against the center. And it did happen—in surprising circumstances. The Octobrist group proposed that the 1912 session of the Duma should deal first with two questions of the greatest importance to peasant Russia: order on the land and order in the courts—the regulation of land use and the reestablishment of elected local courts independent of the administration. The right wing of the Duma was, of course, against this. But would the left be for it? Not at all. The Social Democrats opposed it, because it "wouldn't help" (wouldn't help them). But what of the Kadets? The flower of the Russian intelligentsia? The Kadets were also against: inviolability of the person was a much more urgent and important matter.

So the Octobrist center was short of votes.

Gentlemen, we are confronted with a red-black bloc and that is the curse that bedevils Russian life. (Laughter on the right and the left, applause in the center.) Never before has this bloc behaved so cynically. We all, of course, need to score off our opponents, but the living body of the people should not be our battleground. We shall wreck the bill and leave the population without effective courts for long years to come.

And what of it? Let them do without.

Back in March 1910, Guchkov had preferred to be elected president of the Duma—so that, in accordance with the custom, he would have regular audiences with the Emperor. He had high hopes of directly influencing the Emperor and indeed of changing the course of Russia's history.

> You will forgive me, Your Majesty, but I have made it my specialty to tell you only worrisome things. I know that you are surrounded by people who communicate only what it is pleasant to hear.

He interested the Emperor, fascinated him even. His aim was to break the ice between Duma and Emperor. The Emperor listened attentively (in passive mode he always carried conviction) but also often spoke his mind animatedly. Guchkov suspected at times that other wills voiced through the Emperor—from behind inner doors, or in his oppressed mind—the likes and dislikes, the caprices and the intrigues of elusive shadows, lurking, whispering. Then again, there was a difference of six years in age—and from his higher rung Guchkov could look down with compassion on this amiable semblance of a Tsar devoid, alas, of any positive ambition.

Guchkov shared with Stolypin the tragic role of defending the monarchy against the monarch, the authority of the sovereign power against the holders of power.

> My life belongs to the Emperor, but my conscience does not belong to him, and I shall fight on.

Sukhomlinov kept the Emperor entertained by inventing new military uniforms (the Emperor took a childish delight in them, he would have become a prey to melancholy if the whole army had been dressed alike), was careful not to weary him with boring reports, and concealed shortcomings. Above all he hindered the replacement of the existing High Command with generals capable of waging war. In his audiences with the Tsar, Guchkov complained that all measures to reform the army had been slowed down, that the arms industry was not expanding, and that technical improvements depended entirely on imports from abroad. But what he read in the Emperor's eyes was: "Trying to get even with the minister?"

Guchkov was irrepressible, forever issuing challenges—even in his year as president of the Duma he could not restrain himself, but fought and survived one of his many duels, this one with a fellow Octobrist, Count Uvarov, and left the Duma to serve a four-month sentence in the fortress, but was pardoned by the Emperor after serving less than a month. (Guchkov's duels should have included one with Milyukov, for insulting him in the Duma.)

But then Guchkov slipped up. After a very warm reception by the Emperor he shared his triumph and his hopes with too wide a circle of Duma colleagues, and this got into the newspapers. The next time, the Emperor received Guchkov coldly, did not even sit down, and did not even say goodbye to him. And that was that.

Rash impulses and erratic behavior of this kind also troubled the course of cooperation between Guchkov and Stolypin. And when in March 1911 Stolypin put through the Western Zemstvo bill by suspending the Duma and the State Council for three days, Guchkov found it necessary to dissociate himself vehemently and show the whole world that he was not a party to it. He gave up the presidency of the Duma, which had become a tedious chore since his breach with the Tsar, and went on a fact-finding mission for the Red Cross to plague-stricken Manchuria (where he was too far away to be in danger of recall). Steeling himself, he thought up an explanation of his drastic overreaction for the benefit of the astonished Stolypin:

> You know how much your victory always meant to me and how I loathed your enemies. But the step you are taking is a fatal one, not just for you personally (I know that you are indifferent to that) but to the renewed Russia which is so dear to you and which, thanks to your own efforts, has begun to emerge from chaos.

Guchkov returned from Manchuria in August, a few days before Stolypin's assassination. He was met by a rumor that the Finnish nationalists were planning an attempt on Stolypin (which may have been true) and managed to warn Kurlov in Kiev (but not Pyotr Arkadievich himself, not wanting to worry him).

In September, with fifty or so other Octobrists, he went by special train to Kiev for the funeral.

Whether or not he regretted not supporting Stolypin at the last stage of his career, he now made the murdered man's cause his own. The Octobrist Central Committee accused the Kadets of deliberately playing on the feelings of the public in a way that made the assassination easier. On the fortieth day after Stolypin's death the Octobrists stated, in a Duma interpellation:

> The revolutionary parties and Russia's enemies have combined to carry out their long-standing threat to revenge themselves on the man who once crushed revolution.

Guchkov, supporting the interpellation, said:

> This was a life for the Tsar and for the motherland . . . The generation to which I belong was born with Karakozov's shot ringing in their ears. The bloody and dirty tide of terrorism washed over our fatherland, and carried away the Tsar Liberator. Terror impeded and still impedes the steady march of reform; terror put weapons into the hands of reaction; terror obscured the dawn of Russian freedom in a bloody mist. All this is fresh in everyone's memory. (Cries of "Bravo!" from the right and the center, and of "Fairy tales!" from the left.) Now terror has removed even the man who did more than anyone to put representative government on a firm footing in our country.
>
> Worms pullulated around the open sore that was eating into the living organism of the Russian people. They made our sickness the source of their health. (Shouts on the left: "The Okhrana!") For this gang nothing existed except career considerations and calculations of personal gain. ("Bravo!" from the right and center.) These were the big bandits, "greedily thronging," but with a supporting cast of petty crooks. When they found their tail being trodden on, their claws clipped, their restaurant bills queried, they facilitated by direct action and willful negligence the murder of the chairman of the Council of Ministers.

The interpellation named Kurlov, Spiridovich, Verigin, and Kulyabko—all four of them—and Guchkov in his Duma speech gave further details: they had taken bribes and purloined letters of credit. He spoke of

> the vicious circle in which the government flounders helplessly. The regime is the prisoner of its own servants. If you tread on the head of the snake (Puryshkevich: "Don't expect support from us!") it will sting whoever dares to, and for some it may be a fatal, farewell sting. If you pension off the guilty, and otherwise everything stays as it was, you are doomed. There is another way—the complete reorganization of our political police. Have you the strength of will for that?

Needless to say, they had not. Doomed, they left things as they were.

When he spoke of the "serpent" Guchkov had in mind Rasputin, among others. Another of the heavy burdens he had inherited. But this was a situation as complex as it was dangerous. How could Guchkov, unpardonable as he believed his own treatment and that of the slighted Stolypin to be, reveal to the Russian people at large that the autocratic ruler of Russia himself was involved? He looked to the ministers for help. And found none. Then, in January 1912, an article exposing Rasputin as a member of the Khlyst sect appeared in Guchkov's newspaper, *Moscow Voice*. The issue was, of course, confiscated, and the editor prosecuted. This gave the Octobrists the right to raise the matter in parliament. The question read:

> How long will the Most Holy Synod remain a silent and inactive observer while the scoundrel Khlyst, sex maniac, and charlatan Grigori Rasputin enacts his tragicomedy? Why are the bishops and archpriests silent? Why are all the newspapers in Petersburg and Moscow instructed to print nothing about Rasputin?

Guchkov, speaking in support of the vengeful interpellation, said:

> Things are not well with our state. All that our people holds sacred is under threat. The prelates say nothing, the state does nothing. In such circumstances it is the patriotic duty of the press and of the people's representatives to express society's indignation.

Subsequently, in the debate on the budget estimate for the Holy Synod, he said:

> Never have I risen to speak from this platform with such a heavy heart. It takes a temperament different from mine, and a spiritual makeup foreign to me, to concentrate on the insurance of church property, the equalization of episcopal stipends, or even the preparatory steps toward the convocation of a provincial church council, when all these things are fading into insignificance and I feel like shouting aloud that the church is in danger and the same danger threatens the state. This fanatical sectarian, or rogue and vagabond, whichever he is, this figure so bizarre in the bright light of the twentieth century (voice from the left: "Electricity and steam!"), by what means has this man usurped such influence that the highest authorities of state and church bow down before him? (From the left: "You may kiss my hand!") Just think who is master up above there, who turns the handle that brings about changes of policy and of personnel, the fall of some and the elevation of others. (Markov II: "Old wives' tales!") Behind Grigori Rasputin stands a gang, a whole motley crew, with some surprising members, who have pur-

chased an interest in his personality and his magical tricks, marketing the holy man! They are his prompters, they tell him what whispers to pass on. It is a whole commercial enterprise, and it plays its game skillfully and subtly. Years of revolutionary and antiecclesiastical propaganda could not have done what Rasputin can achieve in a few days. The Social Democrat Gegechkori is right from his own point of view when he says that "Rasputin has his uses." Indeed, for Gegechkori's friends, the more of a "Rasputin," the more debauched he is, the better. At this dreadful moment, with despair and dismay on one side and malicious glee on the other, where do we look for authority? In church or in state? And where were you, the Procurator of the Holy Synod, to be found? When we were discussing legislation to guarantee freedom of worship, the right to convert from one denomination to another, and on Old Believer communities, all this to correct an ancient wrong, we saw you among our opponents. But the ulcer gnawing at the core of the nation's soul you have ignored completely!

I have often noticed that those who have obtained a large share of life's blessings are least inclined to part with them. I know that we cannot always demand heroism. But there is an ethical minimum, obligatory for all who are invested with power. There are occasions when serving and timeserving are two different things. When civic heroism becomes an obligation. Under the years 1911–12 some future Russian chronicler will record that "while Vladimir Karlovich Sabler was High Procurator of the Holy Synod the Orthodox Church sank lower than ever before!"

It was after this speech that the Empress pronounced hanging too good for Guchkov. He was by now not just a political but a personal enemy of the imperial couple. And that was just how he saw it himself.

The more outspoken he became, the harsher he was and the less fastidious in his methods. Early in 1912 he disseminated hectographed copies of letters written by the Empress and the Grand Dukes to Rasputin and supplied by the monk Iliodor (some of them turned out to be forgeries). At about the same time Guchkov's secret informant Polivanov, after reading some official letter to Sukhomlinov, reported to Guchkov his conclusion that there was a German spy in the ministry and close to the minister—one Myasoedov, to cap it all a former officer of gendarmes whose current assignment was to look out for political disaffection in the army. (There had been no such invigilation for quite some time, informants had been called off, and this was a recent and private venture on the part of the minister.) No more tempting combination of circumstances, no better target, could have been contrived. If the attack succeeded, the War Minister (whose post Guchkov most wanted to control) would be toppled, and his own man, Polivanov, appointed. He was not slow to strike, with sensational articles, in Suvorin's two newspapers and in his own: "Espionage and Detection," "Who is in charge of counterespionage in Russia?" and a reproduction of his own statement in the State Defense Council. There was no precedent in Russian history for such an accusation against the War Ministry! It was all the more effective because it invoked the antipathies of the public: a gendarme officer! political surveillance! espionage! See what they're like! The public was duly perturbed and demanded that the War Ministry reveal its secrets. By now the rumor that Polivanov would replace Sukhomlinov was making the rounds. But Guchkov himself, under interrogation by the investigating magistrate, had nothing more substantial than rumor to offer, and Polivanov's information proved valueless. (Guchkov refused to accept this to the end of his days.) Sukhomlinov himself, however, like the coward he was, was slow in countering the allegations. Then Lieutenant Colonel Myasoedov struck the newspaper proprietor Boris Suvorin in the face with a riding crop, in the stands at the racecourse, and challenged Guchkov to a duel. For that Guchkov was of course ever ready! They met with pistols on Krestovsky Island, and Guchkov appeared in the Duma later with a bandaged hand, to thunderous applause. (He had not fired at his opponent, but Myasoedov was forced to resign for disgraceful behavior.)

These speeches resounded throughout the country, and it sometimes looked as though the whole state was changing because of them.

In reality there was no change at all. The Supreme Power was still the same towering, insensate wall, and people despaired of finding any force to breach it and let it in light and fresh air. Had the Manifesto ever existed? Had it been left as a memorial to the Tsar's panicky impulsiveness? Had the Octobrist Party itself ever existed? (Shcheglovitov, leader of the right, would shortly call it "the party of the lost charter.") Presumably it had, since it constituted the stable center of the Third Duma. But in the elections to the Fourth Duma, in the autumn of 1912, the party suffered defeat, characteristically under attack from left and right. The left saw it as the party of landowners and the big bourgeoisie, the right as the party of "October Christ-sellers." After the party's defeat a great exertion of the imagination and the voice was required to maintain that it still existed. Once again, it fell to Guchkov to make most of the effort. He had suffered torment on the hustings: soliciting votes from the electorate was always humiliating, not at all like speaking in the Duma, where his position was secure. And after that he was rejected—a nationwide sensation!—by his very own Moscow, its favorite son, its idol no longer. The fickle public looked around for other candidates.

Neither right nor left could forgive him for his speeches and his middle-of-the-road policy. The most difficult line of all to follow in a developing political system.

Only yesterday you thought that your party, and you yourself, *were* Russia. And suddenly you find that you most certainly are not. You are cruelly wounded, but realization of what has happened is slow in coming. No man instantly understands the meaning of what has befallen him. But when change means success, means victory, we are quicker to appreciate it. It is more difficult to discern that life has taken a sharp turn downward from a high plateau, that there is nothing to be done, that if it drags on for another thirty years it will be downhill all the way.

Guchkov was only fifty when this defeat overtook him. Though disheartened, he neither understood nor accepted the verdict. He still believed in his powers—believed that he could, by himself, reverse his own fortunes and those of his party. He resorted to his well-tried method: went off to the war in the Balkans and remained there for a year. He spent the year thinking over what had happened, and in the end took it as a sign that he must change his strategy.

At the unveiling of the Stolypin memorial in Kiev in September 1913, Guchkov laid a wreath and silently bowed down to the ground. It would have been yet another surprise to the dead man to know how Guchkov interpreted loyalty to his murdered contemporary, fellow spirit, and rival. In November, unbroken and intransigent, Guchkov rounded up his disintegrating party and presented its conference, and the country, with a complete volte-face.

> Our program, condemned by some in 1905 as too moderate and backward-looking, was a natural expression of the optimism of the age, a challenging call for reconciliation. It was a solemn pact between the historic regime and Russian society, a pledge of mutual loyalty. And Russian society would have had no excuse if at a moment of dreadful danger to the state it had refused to support the regime.
>
> But the struggle in which a giant like Stolypin wore himself out proved far too much for his successors. For them the price of remaining in power is self-effacement. The Manifesto of 30 October has not been formally rescinded, but the regime's creativity has dried up, there is no broad plan, no common will, there is complete paralysis. The goodwill of society toward the regime, the trust so carefully built up in Stolypin's time, collapsed in a flash. The regime is incapable even of inspiring fear. Even the harm it does is often unreasoning, a reflex reaction. The government's policy is leading us to inevitable dire catastrophe. But those who look forward to the enthronement of order on the ruins of the vanquished system will find themselves mistaken. I see no elements of stability in those destructive forces. Are we not in danger of lapsing into a period of prolonged anarchy, with the collapse of statehood? Are we not living through another Time of Troubles, but this time in a more dangerous international situation?
>
> The attempt to reconcile state and society has not succeeded. It would now be an inexcusable mistake to prolong a pact which the regime itself has torn up.

Does history change direction while we stand still? Or is it really we ourselves who unconsciously make these abrupt turns, in desperation because we—of all people—are rejected? When some coherent form of words is found for it, it all looks logical enough. That for which Guchkov had condemned and detested the Kadets no more than six years earlier was, it seemed, now the right course for the Octobrists, though the system of government had not changed. The Octobrists were now bringing up the rear of the Kadets. The disoriented Guchkov was turning 180 degrees, and making a very good attempt to prove that not he but the circular walls of the carousel had turned.

> At one time, in the days of national insanity, we Octobrists raised our voice against the excesses of radicalism. Now, in the days of governmental insanity, it is our duty to warn the regime. Faced with catastrophe, we must make one last attempt to bring the regime to its senses. Will our warning cry reach the heights on which the fate of Russia is decided? Can we infect the regime with our own excruciating anxiety? Can we rescue it from its somnambulistic state? They must not let themselves be lulled by superficial signs of calm. Never before were the revolutionary organizations so shattered and so en-

feebled, yet never before was Russian society so profoundly revolutionized—
by the actions of the regime itself.

That was the new twist Guchkov gave to the argument, but no one was there to
be turned around except the Octobrists in the Duma, of which he himself was no
longer a member. The right wing and the center of the old Octobrist Party had broken
ranks. Only a score of left-wing Octobrists supported Guchkov, calling themselves
"progressists."

No one was asking to be converted. Russia was not for turning. And Guchkov himself spent most of his time in the Commission for the Reorganization of the Petersburg
Water Supply.

Had he perhaps become overexcited and made such a silly fuss just because he
himself had been thrown out?

Still at the height of his powers, he was denied any chance of using them; renowned throughout Russia, he was suddenly of no use to anyone. Observing the pusillanimity of Russian policy, abroad as well as at home, Guchkov despaired. "They"
had failed to remain on friendly terms with Germany, which was what both countries
needed, but failed also to confront that country effectively. There was one, and only
one, possible argument in favor of the coming war—a breakthrough to Constantinople—but the Balkan countries, and especially Bulgaria, were precisely the ones that
Russia had alienated and lost in those last prewar years. Guchkov arranged a meeting
between a Bulgarian general and the Serbian minister in his Petersburg apartment, in
an attempt to reconcile the two Balkan countries. For almost a hundred years Pan-
Slavic policies had been a dead weight on Russian minds, even that of the otherworldly Dostoevsky. Who could expect Guchkov to free himself from it and realize
that Russia's welfare depended only on her internal and not her external development? Every age has its ceiling of comprehension, and Guchkov was no more capable
than Milyukov, or than the whole Progressive Bloc, of renouncing the dream of Constantinople. As soon as the fatal shot was fired in Sarajevo, Guchkov, in a state of
high excitement, and anxiety that Russia would not go to war, wrote to the Foreign
Minister, Sazonov:

> This, then, is the latest—but is it the last?—stage of humiliation to which
> we have inevitably descended thanks to the faintheartedness of the Emperor.
> I believed in you once, hoping to find at least some reflected glimmer of
> Stolypin's great Russian soul. Now my hope is that the cup of the Russian
> people's patience will run over, and they will shrug you off, each and every
> one of you.

(Ah yes, his wish would be realized! More fully than he could ever have expected!)

Guchkov's reaction to the first day of the war was: "Now we're for it! The bills are
coming in!"

He was taking a cure at Essentuki when war broke out. He rushed off by the first
army train. Heading for the front! But the only place open to him was in the Red
Cross, of which he had remained a very helpful member all those years. He got as far
as Soldau, where the clouds of disaster were gathering over the 2nd Army. He was
with the 2nd Army (doomed by its number? doomed by the ill luck of those still
serving in it? doomed more probably by the hopeless incompetence of General Yuri

Danilov—"Black Danilov") when he and it were once again almost completely surrounded near Lodz in November 1914. A narrow corridor had been kept open, and its fate was in the balance. But the route for evacuation of the wounded had been cut off earlier, and Guchkov decided to stay with them, to stand up for them when they fell into German hands and share their fate. When the corridor was nearly closed he sent Prince Volkonsky with a written request for aid:

> The number of wounded has mounted to 12,000 and we have only the most meager resources to help them. We are extremely short of everything—personnel, dressings, fuel, bread. I am pretty tough, but even so this is hard to take. Today, 22 November, appears to be the critical day, and only a miracle can save our army. But the fate of the campaign, indeed the fate of Russia itself, is bound up with that of the army. And all this is the fault of the gang of scoundrels who have installed themselves up above.

The pincers, however, were prized open, and on this occasion the 2nd Army was saved. Guchkov wrote both to the government and to the Duma while he was still at the front, and arrived in Petrograd in person shortly afterward. He told his story to each influential minister in turn. And came up against a brick wall. He succeeded in getting an interview with Voeykov, the Palace Commandant, urging him to "open the Emperor's eyes" and tell him to dismiss Sukhomlinov at once—otherwise supplies to the army would cease altogether. (Whether he did, or, as seems more likely, did not, realize that disruption of supplies to the army was the common experience of all the warring countries, it was a good stick with which to beat Sukhomlinov.) But to no effect. Addressing a group of Duma deputies—Kadets, centrists, *and* right-wingers—he represented the situation as already hopeless. They all refused to believe him: Guchkov was playing the fool again, courting notoriety as always. They were, all of them, still under the spell of the national unification in August, which was supposed to mean that Russia's victory was assured.

Not until early 1915 did it dawn on Petrograd that things were going badly at the front. Then fate handsomely compensated Guchkov: others, not he himself, now accused Myasoedov of espionage, and he was promptly executed. Guchkov's earlier efforts had not been in vain. His prestige was reinforced, and Sukhomlinov's was terminally low. Galicia and Poland had to be surrendered for the government to become scared enough, for society to be sufficiently worked up, and for Sukhomlinov to be replaced at last by Polivanov.

Throughout the war Guchkov felt himself to be the man Russia most needed, preferably as Minister of War, but he remained an ineffectual busybody, an outsider, with no official standing—a Russian destiny! Becoming more and more convinced that the government would not budge, would not change its ways for the better, from the summer of 1915 on Guchkov successfully presided over the War Industry Committees, set up to supply the army with arms and munitions (correctly, it seems, assuming that it could outperform the government in this area). Polivanov, who enjoyed his confidence, was now War Minister, so that Guchkov could be sure of learning all the details firsthand, and exercising his influence from within the government. But now that he had the bit between his teeth, he was not going to trail behind the Kadets. On the contrary, he would outdo them in aggressiveness. And so, at conferences held in Sep-

tember 1915, after the dissolution of the Duma, he proposed that the dismissed deputies continue the fight by extraparliamentary methods! Once again, he was cruelly
rebuffed and not even included in the deputation elected by those conferences. The
Progressive Bloc, discreetly intent on self-preservation, settled down to await the next
convocation of the Duma.

The restless Guchkov had always been ahead of the Kadets in his development (one
horse ahead on the carousel?) and in more of a hurry than they were to break with
the accursed defeatist regime. But in 1916 he was quicker than the Kadets to take
fright at what he had previously urged.

> Our methods of struggle are double-edged, and given the high feeling of the
> people at large and especially the workers, they could be the spark to start
> a conflagration the dimensions of which no one can foresee or localize.

When the regime is utterly impervious to persuasion, and society's conflict with it
threatens to ignite and blow up Russia as a whole—what then? What else is there left
except a conspiracy, well hidden and confined to a small group, actively working for
a palace revolution?

By the autumn of 1916 Guchkov's plans and aspirations were more and more sharply
focused on one thing only—a palace revolution.

[4 2]

Neglect an opportunity like today's and your conspiracy would never
take shape. But it was no good just talking in hints. Svechin's irasci-
bility was, to be sure, a reason for caution. But he was too decent a
man to blab—no doubt about that. And Vorotyntsev's ready responsiveness made up for Svechin's recalcitrance. Vorotyntsev was one of
those gratifying listeners who draw you out, make talking enjoyable as
you gaze into their eyes.

"A month ago a sort of unofficial conference of various . . . thinkers
. . . took place here. Kadets, most of them. In a private apartment,
which is where public life in general is carried on nowadays. I was
one of those present. Just listening, most of the time. I sampled all
imaginable points of view. Let's sample what they say again, you
and me.

"They're all agreed that the regime rests on nothing. It would need
one push. And that events are moving inexorably in the direction of a
great popular upsurge—in other words, a revolution. But nobody
makes the slightest move to prevent it, to reach out and stop this
upsurge. All they can think about is what will happen when the blow
falls. Can the government, contemptible, will-less, and unsure of itself
as it is, successfully resist? No. They are all agreed about that. So then
they consider two alternatives. The first is that the helpless government, when it really starts drowning, will cry out to the educated pub-

lic, to the legislative institutions, for help . . . Meaning, of course, to Milyukov and the Progressive Bloc. And that's all they're waiting for! Educated society, needless to say, will agree to help the dying government, will, needless to say, not shrink from responsibility, but will take over the reins, while preserving the monarchy—they have sense enough for that. Perhaps with a change of Emperor—they'll have to see when the time comes. The second alternative is that the regime holds out stubbornly to the last, fails to see reason even at the moment of destruction, which incidentally is more its style."

Vorotyntsev's eager face clouded over.

Guchkov allowed himself to digress. "It's human nature. It's the cause of all the cataclysms in history. You'd think it would be enough to say come to your senses, get out before you're thrown out, how many hints do you need, how often have you been shown the door! But no! Can you see them yielding because common sense demands it, and not because they're coerced into it? Not for anything in the world!"

He thought a moment and qualified this.

"It's different in Europe. Here nothing will make them step down until an almighty fist crashes down on their damn silly noggins. They gave way just once, with the Manifesto, and they were hopping mad, and started snatching it back like the dirty thieves they are."

Svechin quietly smoked on. He seemed less inclined to argue, but also less attentive.

"So, in the second version, the regime collapses ingloriously without summoning the franchised classes to its aid. For a while the elemental forces prevail. What do the franchised classes do? They refuse to side with the mob, and calmly await their moment. After the joys of anarchy and the street celebrations a moment will inevitably arrive when a new form of government must be organized, and then they say it will be their turn—the turn of people with experience in state matters, who will inevitably be invited to govern the country—because who except themselves is capable of doing so? In both versions, then, all "we" have to do is sit quietly and await the call—right?" Guchkov laughed, inviting their reaction.

Vorotyntsev also laughed. Svechin showed no interest.

"Milyukov is sure that he's drawn the winning number—whether the regime gives way voluntarily or is knocked off its perch by revolution—the ministers, the anarchists, the Allies, or whoever will inevitably come and pay homage to the Kadets."

Vorotyntsev's eager upturned face twisted in a grimace.

"What's wrong?" Guchkov asked.

"Why are you so sure, Aleksandr Ivanych, that there will be a revolution? Where do you see it coming from? I see no sign of it anywhere."

"Oh dear, how mistaken you are. I decided that revolution was inevitable back in the spring of 1914. The war prevented it."

"I don't think that's true. There's no such thought in the heads of our soldiers."

(There was, though, that business the other day on the Vyborg side . . .)

Svechin was expressionless. There was no trace of feeling in that rugged, big-nosed face.

Guchkov explained further. "They dream of something like what happened in respectable France in 1848. But even in France one revolution was never like another. The only way in which they are alike is that it would have been better if none of them had happened."

He twisted his triangularly folded napkin.

"I told them straight: Gentlemen, whoever starts the revolution will take command of it and assume power. You are profoundly mistaken if you think that one force will do all the hard work of revolution, then summon another to govern Russia. If we allow our monarch to be overthrown by re-vo-lu-tion-aries, it's all up with us! Get your necks ready for the guillotine! It's no good sitting around waiting like drooling idiots for a dainty little revolution. We must use our minds and our will to stop revolution! Or get around it." He extended his short hand obliquely, gripping the napkin as though it was the rein of an invisible horse. A stubby hand, but skilled in handling firearms. And with no little experience of shooting.

Vorotyntsev's quick eyes absorbed the scene, but he did not interrupt. Svechin enveloped himself in smoke, so that he looked like a balding, dark-haired idol in a cloud of incense.

This time Guchkov pressed the napkin to his breast, acknowledging with feeling: "If we have let Russia get into this hopeless state it is for us, the upper classes and educated society, to find a way out that will not shake her to her depths. If the masses start moving the state will come tumbling down and all Russia with it. Revolution would mean the collapse of the front. We must make sure at all costs that nothing sets the great boulder in motion."

Surely that much was beyond doubt. Not among the Kadets perhaps. But what objection could anyone else find to it?

Hold back the boulder? Vorotyntsev was ready to put his shoulder to it. It would take not one but twenty like him of course. Why not try?

"All that would be needed is to address that thought—of a possible upheaval, an overthrow, to the crowd and afterward . . ."

He glanced at Svechin. Sparks on the thatch? Sorry, sorry. I used to get carried away at times with Kadets. Sometimes in the heat of the moment, I brought things to the surface I didn't really want to see there. Only a year ago I was trying to get them to come out and fight openly.

His heart was like that . . . sometimes beating fit to burst his rib cage. But now he understood things better . . .

"Once the mob is allowed to rise . . . (they'll force their way in here, into our private room at Cubat's, into our comfortable and orderly way of life) . . . you'll never drive them back where they belong. The mob must have no part in politics, it must be fed only what others have prepared. That is the rational lesson of all history."

Was he expecting objections? There were none.

"But whose task is it to prevent the conflagration from engulfing Russia? Who has to be on the alert, to forestall the elemental forces, who if not ourselves, the leaders of Russian society, the strong and active? It is our duty. And it is also in our interest politically."

Up to this point it was just one of those conversations you might hear anywhere and everywhere in Russia—between friends or chance acquaintances, in drawing rooms, even those of Grand Dukes, among Guards officers, or Duma deputies, zemstvo councillors, first-class passengers, patients taking the waters at Kislovodsk. But a barely perceptible rephrasing, a few elusive words, a tone of voice that could not be recorded, and instead of the stiff collar of your shirt or tunic you would begin to feel around your neck the tickling of a well-soaped noose. The walls of your cozy study would dissolve into those of a casemate in the Peter and Paul Fortress.

The words they were using seemed just the same, except for a few trifling variations.

"And when nobody's words of warning have any effect on the highest level . . . And if the personal characteristics . . . of those people who . . . on whom the burden of guilt for Russia's misfortunes rests most heavily . . . er . . . leave no hope of including them in any salutary political arrangement . . . ?" He glanced again at Svechin. There was a sort of enigmatic hostility about the man. Yet how useful he would be, there at GHQ! Why keep up this game of nods and winks? Out loud, irrevocably:

"The Emperor, who cannot be parted from his witch of a wife, must be made to give up the throne. A palace revolution is Russia's only salvation."

The words had been spoken. And there was no hint of fear in the hazel eyes.

He looked at Svechin.

Vorotyntsev leaned forward expectantly. His gaze followed Guchkov's, questioning Svechin.

The hush of one of those tremendous moments when the pistons of history start silently moving but have not yet set the main shaft in motion.

Thick-skinned Svechin, though, seemed insensitive to the solemnity and the significance of those moments. His large mouth was twisted in a half smile that was not a smile. He looked like a Ukrainian, standing by his cart in the market and being offered a ridiculous price for one of his pots. "Hicks from the sticks, gentlemen! A coup d'état in wartime? It'll cause a landslide, total collapse."

Vorotyntsev wasn't with him. "All you know," he said thoughtfully, "is duty—duty today and duty tomorrow. Just doing your duty will land you in a hopeless situation one of these days. Right now . . ."

No, Svechin couldn't see why they were treating him as an idiot, pretending his goods were worth nothing. He turned on Vorotyntsev, lowering his head like a bull about to charge, meaty lips turned outward: "Aleksandr Ivanych wants to save us from revolution, but he's calling for it louder than anybody. If our system of government is rotten, as Aleksandr Ivanych and his friends have been chanting for the past ten years . . ."

"Five," was Guchkov's curt correction.

". . . we couldn't have gone on fighting a war like this for three years. We would have caved in by now."

Five years! Guchkov had deliberately drawn the line there? Meaning "from Stolypin's murder"? Yes, ever since that day it had been clear that the monarch was incorrigible and that any attempt to help him was wasted effort. And now that the villain Kurlov was the clandestine Minister of the Interior, hiding behind Protopopov, while the slimy Spiridovich and all the others involved in the cover-up infested the higher levels of government . . . Everything had changed.

It was a vibrant moment. Everything was in the balance. Who knew which side the scale would come down on? A gentle change of regime to save Russia from an upheaval—but what if another upheaval followed? Could you save Russia simply by overthrowing the Tsar? Just like that?

Vorotyntsev felt the ground move under his feet.

One thing he was certain about: "You're at GHQ tallying figures," he told Svechin. "You don't see the men doomed to die, you don't feel it."

"How does that come into it?" Svechin asked, through clenched teeth.

"I'll tell you how!" A tremor passed over him as the pent-up and suppressed tension of the twenty-six months sought release.

"A government that can send its subjects to destruction for no good cause, smashing whole divisions to smithereens, like someone sweeping crockery from a table with a careless sleeve . . . That government's subjects are in fact released from their obligations."

But he was cooling down as he spoke. The unfortunate thing about speaking without thinking is that you always speak crudely and imprecisely.

The Mad Mullah trembled violently, struggling to contain himself.

His big lips writhed. "So you . . . so how can you call yourself a monarchist?"

Vorotyntsev mopped his tense brow.

Guchkov rushed to his aid. "Don't confuse monarchism and legitimism. No sensible person objects to monarchy."

(Though for all anybody knew Guchkov himself might be a republican.)

"Your starting point must be Russia's situation, not the abstract principle of monarchy. If the monarchy can only be saved by removing the monarch, I show that I'm a monarchist by doing so. There's no better way of proving yourself a loyal monarchist than by taking part in such a coup. The monarchic system will not only survive, it will be reinforced. It will be precisely that—a monarchist coup."

Svechin made no further response. His gaze was fixed steadily, grimly, on a point somewhere between the two of them.

"And another thing," Guchkov reminded him. "This should fit in with your convictions, if you're consistent. There's another reason for hurrying up with a palace coup to forestall revolution: so that it is carried out by Russian hands alone. Do it without the plebs, yes, but also without the Jews. So that the country will develop along Russian lines."

A weighty argument?

Svechin remained expressionless. Just sat there, shrouding himself in smoke again. He needed, after all, to relax—after the meal, after all that drink—before his journey.

Perhaps they shouldn't have begun this conversation in his presence? They had let themselves be tempted by the fact that he was at GHQ.

Vorotyntsev did not disguise his eagerness to hear what would come next.

Neither his eye nor his memory had let Guchkov down: this officer was just as he remembered him, his loyalties were not those of a mediocre garrison captain. Five colonels and fifteen captains like him was all you would need.

Various plans had already been discussed. Except for his occasional descents on the front—and it was difficult to foresee and exploit these trips—the Tsar was always at either Tsarskoye Selo or GHQ. At Tsarskoye there would be serious resistance and therefore bloodshed. At GHQ it would be impossible without the participation or at least the acquiescence of the High Command.

But perhaps this was not the time to stir up these depths?

Although . . . Svechin, fed and resting, looked more and more peaceable. He was drinking Narzan. The stolid *khokhol* was homeward bound from market with all his pots.

For Vorotyntsev's sake Guchkov had to go on talking. "So, then, there is no need to involve a large number of soldiers. The fewer, the better. It should be on a smaller scale than the Decembrist affair."

If Guchkov thought of himself as following in the Decembrists' footsteps, surely he must feel the rope lightly tickling his neck. The neck which the Empress had already measured and lovingly marked for her own.

In conspirator's language: a gentle palace revolution. In the language of authority: a grave treasonable act.

Noticing, or anticipating, some reaction of this sort in his companions, Guchkov smiled understandingly. "There is some risk in every fight. But people usually exaggerate it."

Where there was no risk at all he himself felt limp and weak.

"An open appeal to the soldiers, explaining our objectives fully, might result in mass revolution. We need just a few of them—say, one or two units—behind us at the last moment, to march them out in a public demonstration perhaps. That's what we need to be sure of."

And this was just what Guchkov found most attractive in officers of the Vorotyntsev type: they could, at the crucial moment, quickly and forcefully carry the soldiers with them, perhaps explaining, but if necessary without a single word.

Vorotyntsev was someone to whom Guchkov felt he should disclose almost every detail of his scheme there and then: precisely which unit he would be commanding and where he should immediately get himself transferred for that purpose. This was to provide for a third possibility—that the coup would take place not at GHQ or at Tsarskoye Selo, but somewhere between them. The Emperor, who found the boredom of GHQ oppressive, and hankered after the peace and quiet of home, was forever darting back and forth between GHQ and Tsarskoye, always by the same route, and always ordering the train to slow down at night so that the clatter would not disturb his sleep. That would be the best solution: to seize the Emperor en route, at night, when he was almost defenseless, using a small force of railroad troops or auxiliary units stationed along the line. Guchkov was already studying these units and trying to select reliable officers (though so far without much success).

But, in Svechin's presence, how could he possibly . . . ?

The way he was sitting, Svechin might as well have been absent. He was sufficiently absent for it to be impossible to read him. And sufficiently present to be in the way.

So Guchkov could only speak more generally.

"One thing we rule out completely is the 23 March variant." And, seeing raised eyebrows: "You know, when Paul I was strangled. The murder of the monarch is not to be contemplated whatever happens. The new regime must not be based on blood."

No, indeed! Vorotyntsev had not yet weighed the implications fully.

A coup? That still needed thinking about. Assassination? That was not even to be thought of.

"Besides, if his son or his brother is to succeed him, neither would wade through his blood. So what we must achieve—suddenly, quickly, with a small group—is simply abdication. In favor of his brother or his son. A manifesto is to be prepared in advance; all he has to do is sign it. The King of England will gladly give his cousin hospitality, to help ensure future victories . . ."

He had put his foot in it. Vorotyntsev turned cold: "To ensure future victories?" To go on laying down peasants' lives? Was that what he called a "purely Russian coup"? Would it not after all be an Anglo-French coup?

Vorotyntsev had of course always known that Guchkov was all for the war, but look how devoted he was to Russia! Surely, to save her, he would come to think differently?

To come right out with it, speak of an armistice, of withdrawing from the war, was absolutely impossible. His uniform forbade it.

Guchkov's brown eyes flashed behind his pince-nez. He was too excited to notice.

"As few casualties as possible among the bodyguard in the exchange of fire. If a coup of that sort took place tomorrow, all Russia would greet it with exultation. The whole army! The whole officer corps!"

He looked at Svechin reproachfully: come tomorrow you'll be rejoicing too, you bashi-bazouk you! But join in? Not likely.

"Don't overdo the rejoicing too soon," Svechin said darkly. "What if he won't abdicate?"

"I can't imagine that. His character being what it is, he'll go quietly. He'll give in right away."

"But what if, after all, he refuses to give way?"

Guchkov sighed. He swung his pince-nez on their ribbon. Yes, there was that one weak spot, others had pointed it out to him.

"No. No blood will be shed whatever happens."

Svechin raised his great eyebrows. "So there'll be nothing for it but to hang yourself."

"He'll give in immediately!" Guchkov pronounced firmly, looking through his pince-nez. "Really, gentlemen! You must try to understand his psychology. He dismisses a minister and is afraid to tell him to his face, he thanks him, makes a fuss over him, says see you tomorrow—and then comes a little note: 'I am relieving you of your post.' Look at his behavior throughout his reign! . . . And how afraid he is of that woman! Away from her he'll sign whatever is put before him."

He looked to Vorotyntsev for approval. What he liked about the colonel was his obvious lack of commitment to this particular occupant of the throne. No trace of awe. He could just see this colonel moving quickly along the train to post his men between carriages.

But Vorotyntsev's eyes were for some reason evasive.

It would be good if Svechin had the tact to leave. But he stayed put. Smoking and sipping. (Liqueurs had been brought with the coffee.)

There was not much else that Guchkov could say explicitly. Just that the heir to the throne would not be despised by the public, as the present ruler was. Who would be regent? Mikhail? Or would there be a regency council? Guchkov delicately hinted that he did not seek power for himself.

"I fear that there is no unique, providential individual of the sort we need in Russia at present. We will need a regency council, a collective. We must bring back the good ministers—Krivoshein, Samarin, Shcherbatov . . ."

But why calculate a hundred moves ahead? First—the deed itself.

Action! That was always the factor that divided those close to Guchkov from the others, the windbags. But the deed itself was still vague even in his mind. He had traveled to the Caucasian Front recently, partly with the idea of talking to Nikolai Nikolaevich, sounding him out, finding out what he would do if . . . Earlier, Guchkov had made use of his work with the Red Cross to make contact with the military. Now that he was denied access to the main fronts he could catch officers only when they were on leave or on some mission behind the lines. He had talked as he had today in company on various occasions, and they all seemed more or less sympathetic, but when it came to joining in, the younger officers were still with him, but their seniors declined. Out of loyalty? Or fear? So far he had recruited no one above the rank of captain. The two men most firmly committed to the conspiracy, so it seemed, were one political intriguer, the Kadet Nekrasov, and one pampered millionaire, Tereshchenko, neither of them capable of any military action themselves. Was Russia really so short of people?

But perhaps he had not been wasting his time today. Perhaps he had found his man.

Meanwhile, he had to think of something to say. Ah, yes . . .

"I regret very much that when General Krymov visited Petersburg last winter it was at the height of my illness. He saw other people here, but not me. While he was fighting on the Northern Front, I was taking the waters down south. When I got back north he had been assigned to the south. Did you meet him there, Georgi Mikhalich?"

"I saw him. Only briefly, to tell the truth."

"Is he near you down there?"

"Don't you know what's happened to him?"

Guchkov didn't know. So Vorotyntsev started telling him, feeling relieved.

"Krymov was Chief of Staff of the 3rd Cavalry Corps, and its creator. Then he took command of the Ussuri Cavalry Division, in the same corps. The corps commander was wounded, and Röhrberg was put in his place. Röhrberg and Krymov got on badly from the start—not many people find Krymov easy . . . Krymov is no respecter of rank, he's capable of telling an army commander to go to blazes. In July, Röhrberg packed off his Ussuri Division into the Carpathians, it was raining heavily, there were no roads, supply wagons could not get through, they weren't part of any operation but could not get permission to withdraw. So Krymov pulled his division back twenty-five versts on his own authority and sent a dispatch asking 'in view of my inability to carry out instructions, to be relieved of my divisional command.' Then the fat was in the fire! But he still wasn't sacked."

Guchkov was delighted. "Tough nut!" he said with a chuckle.

Krymov? As he sat there cheerfully and sympathetically telling that stony-faced, awkward customer's story, he remembered that day and night at Usdau . . . Krymov? A man full of surprises. Maybe . . . Who could tell? Perhaps we don't always recognize our own kind.

But that last time in autumn Krymov had not looked to Vorotyntsev like the audacious hero of the Carpathian incident, the man who had served with Artamonov back there, the man whose will and intelligence had enabled the 4th Siberian Corps to hold out at Liaoyang when the others were collapsing. His impression had been that Krymov, though not finished, had worn badly. He had been a rock, but now the virtue had gone out of him. All living things have their breaking point. Failures mount up, until you can no longer heave your legs over the barriers. That autumn Vorotyntsev himself had almost reached the limit. Only his present journey had brought a postponement and a remedy.

Vorotyntsev's busy hand had come to rest on the tablecloth, and Guchkov sympathetically laid his own soft palm on its weather-beaten roughness.

"Look, Georgi Mikhalich, you really must think about getting a transfer. To somewhere nearer. Up here . . . We need to talk."

Svechin still refused to understand. And to go away. Very well, then . . .

"I live on Furstadt Street, corner of Voskresensky Prospect. Could you possibly come and see me? You'll find . . . a few others there . . . The day after tomorrow. I would like you to meet them."

Wasn't that just what he had wanted from Guchkov? Wasn't that what he'd come for?

But Vorotyntsev's bright, expectant gaze seemed suddenly to switch off, to become different. His stubborn determination had flagged. It was as though he had just woken up, or been given a surprise.

"Sorry, Aleksandr Ivanych, I just can't. I've overstayed already."

His hand was still under Guchkov's

"Come on, that doesn't matter." Guchkov thought about it. "We'll wangle you an extension. Who's your corps commander? It's only for two days—and then you're on your way. We can't let you disappear into the distance quite so quickly."

The Vorotyntsev whom Guchkov had imagined lifting himself lightly onto the step outside the Tsar's carriage was suddenly no longer there. His frostbitten and weather-beaten face, his clean-shaven cheeks, his bare temples, and his brow, were invaded by a flush so deep that it almost matched the russet brown of his tunic.

He clumsily withdrew his hand from under Guchkov's, searching for words as though he was about to tell a lie, or trying not to.

"I have to leave for Moscow this evening, without fail . . . And spend tomorrow and the next day there . . . I've got my ticket."

He blurted it out haltingly, shamefacedly blushing deeply.

"Ticket, ticket—what does that matter? You can exchange it. Send a telegram, say you'll be two days late." Guchkov good-humoredly refused to understand the seriousness of the situation.

But serious it was.

"What if I come back in, say, four days' time?" Vorotyntsev asked, miserably, hopefully.

"In three or four days' time the people I was talking about won't be here. And I will have left."

His retreat was cut off. He couldn't think of any more excuses. Would that the earth would open up and swallow him! "The truth is, it's my wife's birthday, and she's angry with me already." An impasse. Barrier breast high. Rope under chin.

No, he couldn't lie his way out of it.

"You see, it's . . ."

He would have been less ashamed parading naked in front of them. His lips parted in a grimace, he lowered his eyes, shrank.

". . . my wife's birthday. And she and I . . ."

She and I? Was he going to describe the whole ritual? The Chinese bell? All her grievances? It would all have been possible if he had been writing long, affectionate letters throughout that week, but as it was . . . he would have to say he had been ill.

"I promised faithfully . . . and now I'm in a desperate hurry."

When there was only one woman, she was no hindrance, he could always get by. But now there were two, and it was a deadlock, there was no room to move.

He had not realized till this minute that he was tied hand and foot.

What a disgrace! One he could never get over, unlike anything he'd ever known. If only he could get the blush off his cheek, but it wouldn't go away, and it betrayed him.

He looked up.

Svechin was grinning, but it was a cheerful and evidently friendly grin.

"Hey!" he cried, pulling out his watch. "I'm going to miss my train. Gentlemen, goodbye. Aleksandr Ivanych, I am most humbly grateful!" He stuffed his pipe into his pocket. Sword? In the cloakroom. He looked as happy getting ready as if he had been waiting for this all along. Why hadn't he looked at his watch earlier? "Yegor? Isn't it time you went?" A hug and a kiss for Vorotyntsev. A vigorous handshake for Guchkov.

Vorotyntsev felt less ashamed, but more unhappy, now that he was alone at last with Guchkov. He had looked forward so much to meeting him, had tried so hard to track him down, had finally found him and was now letting him escape. It was something he hadn't felt in forty years: getting ready to jump, and then not jumping; walking up to the mark, and turning away.

It was so big a turn he had no name for it. He had not yet had time to understand it.

But how could the next two wretched days affect such a great design so seriously?

The clear-eyed colonel looked hard at the sick leader's mournful features.

"Aleksandr Ivanych! It doesn't matter. I can be wherever you like in as short a time as you please!"

Abandoning his place in the ranks of Russia's defenders? All that mattered now was to be home by tomorrow for his wife's birthday . . .

Guchkov took off his pince-nez, and examined them at a distance, then between the fingers of both hands . . .

He had found his man. They had been talking for two hours. A fighting colonel, full of energy, one who *understood*, no Blimp, some-one eager to tackle Russia's problems, to all appearances a fellow spirit, with his hand already on the hilt of his sword, ready to leap into action . . .

And then . . . his wife's birthday?

In all those months while Guchkov was talking conspiracy, more clearly with some people, more vaguely with others (he himself still had only a vague picture of it, and was still not absolutely sure that he was fully committed, that he was beginning something he meant to carry through), this was one of the first officers in whom he had found a resolve set harder perhaps than his own. He had felt for almost the first time that here was someone in whom the idea had firmly taken root. And then, because of some woman's whim . . .

Why, oh why, was Russia so short of serious people?

"Aleksandr Ivanych! I'm on the Southwestern Front. Do you want me to look up Krymov?"

Well, why not? This was a mission he wouldn't entrust to anyone else.

"How much should I tell him? Where and how can the two of you meet?"

With Svechin gone they could speak openly. Fill in gaps, call things by their names. But something had snapped in Guchkov too. It wasn't just that he was tired, and that it was almost time for his postponed guests and for another serious conversation. No—when you're getting on for sixty you don't get worked up, or calm down, quite so quickly.

Nonetheless, they went on talking for a while. Was it in principle feasible? Where should they look for recruits? They settled one or two things. Where to send letters, and how to word them. They parted feeling that they had not altogether wasted their time.

Guchkov's other meetings had been no different.

When Vorotyntsev had left, he still had some time before his guests arrived. He took off his dinner jacket and lay on the sofa. Covering his face.

He had stumbled again—and his short-lived spurt of energy had drained away. It seemed so simple to intercept the imperial train at some small station, lay before the weak wearer of the crown a previously drafted manifesto—and the fate of Russia, the fate of the whole world, would follow a different course . . . But where did you find the five colonels capable of detaching themselves from all that was warm and live?

It was not—as the colonel had gone away thinking—contempt that Guchkov felt for Vorotyntsev. We are quick to despise others when we are young and have everything still to learn. But as our experience of life grows we realize that contempt is not something a wise person feels. For a long time Guchkov had gone forward surefootedly, chosen freely, been invulnerable and inflexible, and a succession of transient women had nourished his martial ardor without enfeebling or poisoning him.

But then he had tripped up. Clearheaded though he was, he had married badly, acting on someone else's prompting. He had eyes, he had experience, he understood women—and yet he had married impulsively, foolishly. Now he knew, no one knew better, how a woman can drain and unnerve and suffocate the strongest of men. Guchkov had lived, not during his apprenticeship but in the years of his military maturity, with a woman spiritually alien to him, incapable of appreciating his activities or assisting him in them, so that over and over again he had wasted on her precious reserves of strength. Because his family life was ruined beyond repair Guchkov had flung himself all the more desperately into the political struggle, behaving indeed at times with excessive ferocity, simply to break loose.

It is a fact often hidden from history, and viewed with skepticism by historians, that great political decisions sometimes depend on trivial personal circumstances: had he not broken yet again with Masha (it was always—and never—for the last time) Guchkov's grievance against the Tsar might not by itself have so inflamed him that he slammed the doors on the Duma and dashed off to Manchuria, to help with another country's epidemic. Which had meant that he was not close enough to Stolypin in his last harried months, had not been there to hold out a hand when, God knows, it might have helped. But his existence was so galling, so burdensome, so suffocating, that he had to pull up stakes in a hurry and get as far away as he could.

At other times his ill-starred marriage had so shackled him that he lacked the strength to move at all. But the most terrifying time was when he had been on his deathbed in January: his wife had sent all the nurses packing, asserted her incontestable rights for all Russian society to see, and taken possession of the dying man in an enjoyable frenzy of hysterical fussing.

So Guchkov did not judge Vorotyntsev too severely. Before you can disdain what may look like petty family problems you need to know the depth of the pit and how difficult it can sometimes be to climb its slippery sides.

Death had indeed struck a month back—not father or mother, but their oldest son, Lyova, lowering its black lid on their years of crippling tension. (If he had known that it was to be that one of his three children, how carefully he would have guarded him, how tenderly he would have cherished him, while there was still time!)

The death of a son is death for the father—but a living death. A son's death is a hand placed on your shoulder from *out there*, to remind you!

He felt as though he was losing his balance: previously he had leaned too far forward, and begun to sway, now he was rocking backward.

This instability was dangerous. It had shown itself in Stolypin in the last year before his death.

What had hurt him most in Svechin's reproaches that evening was the idea that he, Guchkov, himself was shaking the whole structure, threatening to burn it down. How could you strike a balance? If you courted publicity, the whole edifice was rocked. If you chose silence, the result was stagnation.

He was beginning to feel that his zenith was behind him. That his epoch was ending and another beginning. As when he himself had superseded Shipov. Russia's perspective was long, that of any individual life short. You served your turn—and made yourself scarce. Shipov had been fifty-five. Guchkov was now fifty-five.

Here he was, chief conspirator, and he couldn't wait three or four days for Vorotyntsev. Why? Because before going to the Caucasian Front he had to take the cure at Kislovodsk. Mounting this conspiracy had been an uphill struggle against illness and enfeeblement.

For four years now he had battled on, and he no longer had the strength for it. He had never recovered from that breach in 1912, from the ingratitude of the public, the way in which it turned its ugly mug away, all the betrayals . . .

How many attempts like today's had he still to make, every one of them mortally tiring? How could he manage, with only a few months in hand? He was not, after all, even at the preparation stage. Only discussing underlying principles.

There had been a whole year of talk about conspiracy, but there was no conspiracy.

*   *   *

MAY THE DEVIL FLY AWAY WITH YOU— THESE WHEELS AREN'T GREASED!

*   *   *

[43]

The Ulyanovs lived exactly halfway between the Cantonal Library and the City Library, and it was only slightly farther to the Center for Socialist Literature: all were between five and seven minutes away at average walking speed. They all opened at nine, but today he was driven out of the house forty minutes earlier: stupidly, humiliatingly fleeing from that shock-headed ragamuffin, Zemlyachka's nephew, so as to spare himself, to avoid impertinent chatter which might enrage him and ruin his whole day.

Objectively speaking, there was no avoiding such figures in émigré revolutionary circles—slovenly, vacant-looking young men with unformed minds but ever ready to pronounce on any subject, just to show that they had opinions. They were everlastingly hungry and penniless. You might think that they would try to earn a bit by copying—there was a total lack of copyists in Zurich; think of all the trouble he'd had getting his lost *Imperialism* copied. But no, they could neither spell nor write legibly—and anyway they all wanted nothing less than an editorship, and immediately! Their constant preoccupation was where to find a free meal. On the Ulyanovs' budget this was an intolerable imposition: Zemlyachka's nephew was capable of wolfing down two eggs, and four sandwiches for good measure. They had firmly banned him from the dinner table, so he started appearing early in the morning, always with some flimsy excuse—returning or borrowing a book or a newspaper, but really with an eye to breakfast. ("Whatever you do, don't feed him," he had told Nadya as he left the house just now. "He'll soon stop coming.") It wouldn't be so bad if he meekly ate and then went away, but no, he thought it necessary to show his gratitude in a gush of pseudo-intellectual drivel, to elucidate fundamental questions and always in the same aggressive, know-it-all fashion.

These visits, that knowing, superior smile on the face of a milksop, made Vladimir Ilyich ill for the day. In general, any unexpected upset to his daily routine, especially an uninvited and untimely guest, any pointless waste of time, so exasperated and unsettled him that he was incapable of work. Nothing was more vexatious than expending your nervous energy and your cogency in argument, not at a conference, in a pamphlet, in debate with an important party opponent, but, for no good reason, on a lout who didn't even mean what he was saying. Most émigrés had to count their pennies, but a whole day frittered away was no loss to them. A single wasted hour made Lenin feel ill! Even if in retrospect some unforeseen meeting, conversation, or piece of business proved important and necessary, the unexpected always irritated him at the time.

But the émigré world has its own code of behavior and you are defenseless against such visitors, you cannot simply show them the door or refuse to let them in: it would set malicious tongues wagging and seriously damage your reputation. You would instantly be accused of arrogance, lordliness, overweening conceit, "leaderism," dictatorial pretensions . . . the émigré world was a nest of vicious snakes, forever writhing and hissing. So that whenever one of these impudent rogues saw fit to leave Russia—and even escaping from Siberia was the easiest thing in the world, so that everybody fled abroad, expecting to be kept at the Party's expense—you must not only welcome him but invent something for him to do. And within a year you might find the swine actually working on some journal, though probably only one number would ever appear.

Take that born troublemaker Evgenia Bosch. Why didn't she go to Russia, as she was supposed to? There was absolutely nothing for her to do *here*, but she would try to invent something, and expected others to think up work for her. One of the plagues of émigré life was having to devise occupations for émigrés.

Of course, once the revolution began, its ramifications would provide work for every one of these little boys and girls, indeed each of them would be indispensable, there would be only too few of them. But while there was no revolution, cramped and pinched as everyone was, these brats were unbearable.

It was an exhausting state of affairs. How long had it been going on? Was it nine years since they had fled from Russia, fled from defeat? Sixteen since that first unhappy meeting and clash with Plekhanov? Twenty-one since that stupid bungle in Petersburg? That tormenting state of mind when every sinew craves action, when you feel that you could move mountains or continents with the energy pent up and tense inside you, but there is nothing to exert your powers upon, no fingertip contact with people, when parties, crowds, and continents will not bow to your will but chaotically, senselessly whirl and collide, not knowing where they are bound—you alone know that!—while all your energy, all your plans go for nothing, and you burn yourself out converting half a dozen Swiss youngsters in the Skittle Club. Still, even they were something. Earlier, when no one came to meetings except two Swiss, two Germans, one Pole, one Jew, and one Russian, who sat telling each other jokes, things were really bad, it was pathetic, he was ready to call it a day!

Now that he had reached the Limmat Embankment without meeting Zemlyachka's nephew he could assume that he was safe. His self-defensive irritation gradually subsided.

Ragged gray clouds with whitish edges gave the day a cold, severe light.

Big plate-glass windows encroached upon the lakefront, blatantly displaying on a background of silk and velvet all the ingenious handiwork of idleness—jewelry, perfumes, haberdashery, linen. The lackeys' republic was flaunting its luxury, untouched by the war, as provocatively as it knew how.

Moving away in disgust from these perverse fantasies in gold, satin, and lace (he hated the things themselves, and still more the people who loved them) Lenin waited for a tram to pass (a dog ran right in front of it but reached the other side unhurt), then crossed the road and set out along the riverbank.

By the Münster Bridge he let a car, a hansom, and a cyclist with a long basket on his back go by. The City Library was right in front of him, and he would have liked to go in at once, but it was still closed.

If he went on, he would have to make a detour: there was no way between the library and the water. The library building was the former Wasser-Kirche, so called because it jutted out into the water. Four hundred years ago, the resolute Zwingli had taken it away from the priests and handed it over for civic use.

There he stood in person, before the requisitioned church, on a black marble pedestal several steps high, with his snub nose, his book, and the point of his sword resting in the space between his feet. Lenin always spared him an approving glance. True, his book was the Bible, but, all the same, for the sixteenth century he had shown splendid resolution, today's Socialists could take a lesson from him. An excellent combination, the book and the sword. The book, with the sword as its extension.

Clausewitz: war is politics, with the pen finally exchanged for the sword. All politics lead to war, and that is their only value.

The river added dampness to the cold of the morning air. They said that it never froze. Somehow he always associated Russia with winter, and emigration with perpetual winterlessness. He leaned over the railings. Here, where the river mouth widened, there was an array of boats several rows deep along both banks—boats masted and unmasted, boats with cabins and boats with tarpaulin covers. The masts were swaying.

Kesküla was complaining that someone close to the Central Committee had stolen the money intended to pay for the publication of a pamphlet. It would have to be paid again. Outrageous!

The water was dark, but quite clear. Gray stones could be seen on the bottom.

The three aspects of war according to Clausewitz: the operations of reason fall to the government, free spiritual activity to the commanders, and hatred to the people.

The neat square stones of the embankment pavement were thickly strewn with maple leaves (it was the custom not to sweep them up). That tree there—what was it?—had not yet lost its spiky cones.

Everything was getting wildly expensive. They would soon have nothing to live on. The price of paper was rising faster than anything! Shlyapnikov was no good at all at extracting money from Gorky and from Bonch. He should wrench it out of them with pliers! Let them pay up and pay handsomely.

All his life his mother had helped him out from family funds. On his foreign travels or in Petersburg, however much he overspent, he had never had to think of earning money. He had been able to afford a balanced diet in jail, to shorten his journey to Siberia, to avoid transit prisons. In emigration he could ask for money at any time, and by some miracle she had always managed to send it. But since the summer he had had no mother, and he would never be able to ask again.

A flock of black ducks with white heads bobbed on the lake, suddenly took off, scuffing the water, flew low over the surface, and settled. Then they flocked together again and swam sedately back to their old place.

But although Clausewitz seemed to have explained the basic laws of war in general, it was impossible to understand the law of the war now in progress. Or that of the war which must be started.

Surely the Swedes at least could make him a loan! Shlyapnikov must drop a hint to Branting: it would come more naturally from him, as Russia's representative.

A professional revolutionary ought to be relieved of the need to worry about his livelihood. Party funds should guarantee the leading members of the Central Committee a maintenance allowance for some time to come.

The wives of solid Swiss citizens were crumbling bread and dropping it from the big bridge.

The ducks quickly gathered, and others—with green heads and yellow beaks—joined them. And yet others, with blue-gray plumage.

If we are to publish in *Letopis*, the alliance between the Machists and the Menshevik Organizing Committee must be split. People around Gorky are intriguing against us.

Two or three ducks skimmed the lake, chasing each other and churning the water with wings and feet.

To think that he must look to Gorky for money and, what was more, humble himself before that incredibly spineless shilly-shallier, beg his forgiveness for assailing Kautsky, discard the most telling and enjoyable knocks in the whole book just to please him.

What would be nice now would be to go for a brisk row. They'd often talked about it, but never gotten around to it. Now it would have to wait till spring. Walking and scrambling about in the mountains or tramping the streets of Zurich were the only ways Lenin had of dissipating and soothing the ache of unused muscles. But he still felt it in his shoulders and the best thing for that was rowing.

Another great worry was the loss of his *Imperialism*, sent off in manuscript last summer. The most mysterious thing about it was that a responsible post office could find no clue as to how it had vanished. The British censorship had become ridiculous, and the French had lost all shame, so that it was not surprising if *Imperialism* had attracted attention—its author was no longer an ordinary émigré, one of the thousands here in Switzerland whom the police ignored. Perhaps he was already under surveillance? Perhaps he was being watched at this very moment, here on the embankment? His position was precarious. At the first—or anyway the second—hint from the Russian or the French ambassador he might be hauled before a military court or deported from Switzerland for infringing its neutrality. They would only have to listen in from a neighboring table to one speech at the Skittle Club.

He stretched himself and trudged on downstream along the railings, near the water's edge, looking like the neediest of Zurich's inhabitants with his shabby bowler hat, his threadbare coat, and his waterproof shopping bag (his, though, held notebooks, abstracts, clippings). Reaching the big bridge, he patiently let pass someone's opulent phaeton, a slow four-horse dray, and a one-horse tram with three big plate-glass windows and a uniformed driver up in front.

He would, therefore, have to burn dangerous drafts, give all important documents to respectable Swiss citizens for safekeeping, start signing himself "Frei" again, or something like that, and on occasion use invisible ink, even for letters between Zurich, Bern, and Geneva. All this in a neutral country! Just like at home, under the noses of the police . . . And *Imperialism*, written out all over again, must be done up in the covers of a book so that it would get through.

He crossed the big bridge and came out on the broad paved path along the lake, which was also unswept and carpeted with brown maple leaves.

The air from this wider water was stronger, fresher, colder.

Swans, white and gray, were floating there. Or rather, not floating but sitting statuesquely on the water. In the shallows, now one, now another of them dipped its head to peck at something in the depths, its white behind sticking up, its feet treading the air. Then it lengthily shook the water from its snaky neck.

Behind, to the left, a pale sun was peeping from beyond the Opera House. But it was a cold sun, its light held no warmth.

It was soothing, all this water. All this space. The pressure in his chest eased. It was only when it released him that he realized how hard pressed and harassed he normally was.

The broad expanse of the lake. Scattered about it, fishermen rode at anchor. On the other side, and to the left, the elongated, gently sloping wooded bulk of the Uetliberg stretched to the far end of the lake. There were white spots on it in places: a light snow had fallen on the high ground and had not melted.

A spacious lake, reminding him of Geneva.

The fresh, lapping waves of Lake Geneva would stay in his memory as long as he lived. That was where he had suffered the greatest disaster in his life: the shattering of his idol.

How young he had been, how full of youthful rapture, how infatuated when he had come to Switzerland for that first meeting with Plekhanov, to seek his recognition. It was then, sending "Volgin" (Plekhanov) his declaration of friendship before leaving Munich, that he had first thought of signing himself "Lenin." All that was needed was that the old man should control his vanity, that one great river should acknowledge the other, so that together they could encompass all Russia.

Young men full of vigor, who had served their time in Siberia, escaped great dangers, and broken out of Russia, were bringing these elderly, distinguished revolutionaries their plans for *Iskra*, for a journal, for working side by side together to fan the flames of revolution! It was incredible in retrospect, but he had still believed in a general reunification, including the Economists, had even defended Kautsky against Plekhanov. It sounded like a bad joke! They had naïvely supposed that all Marxists stood for the same things and could work in harmony. They had seen themselves as bearers of glad tidings: we, the young, are continuing what you began.

They had run up against something different: a calculating concern with retaining power, remaining in command. The *Iskra* plan and the fanning of flames in Russia were matters of complete indifference to Plekhanov: all he wanted was to be sole leader. So he had cunningly represented Lenin as a comic conciliator, an opportunist, and himself as a rock-hard revolutionary. And he had taught Lenin where the advantage lay in a schism: the one who calls for a split is always on firmer ground.

How could he ever forget that night in the village of Vésenaz, when he and Potresov had disembarked from the Geneva steamer like whipped schoolboys, smarting and humiliated, when they had paced the village from end to end in the darkness, shouting their resentment, seething, ashamed of themselves—and all around them over the mountains and the lake an electric storm had walked the night sky, without breaking out in rain. They were so outraged that at moments they almost burst into tears. And an infernal chill had descended on his heart.

On that bitter night Vladimir Ulyanov was born again. Only since that night had he become what he was, become his true self.

This harsh lesson Lenin took to heart, never to forget it. He would never believe anyone again, never let sentiment tinge his dealings with others.

Somebody nearby started feeding the gulls, and they shot up from the water, greedily, impatiently swooping and wheeling, catching the bread in midair, screaming, fighting, even venturing onto the parapet, flying almost into the faces of Lenin and his neighbors. He waved one of them away and walked on.

How memory catches at chance coincidences, sentimental associations. Lake Geneva again, nothing more, had been between them before they had known each other, when he was beginning to come into his own, receiving the delegates to the Second Congress, carefully studying each one, testing him out, making a bid for his support, and she was bearing her fifth child, to a husband younger than herself, and also reading for the first time *The Development of Capitalism* by somebody named Ilin, with no idea of what lay ahead.

Five years went by, and they still did not know each other, although she had been in Geneva several times. It was in Geneva too, at an unforgettable performance of *La Dame aux Camélias*, that he had been pierced with anguish, had first doubted the meaning of his life. At that very time her husband lay dying in Davos. Then, only a few months later, in Paris, she had come to him.

The wind, noticeably chillier here, crinkled the waters in a frown. He put his bag down by the embankment railings, raised his collar, and stood there peering down at the lake. It was already quite cold. Even according to the stupid Russian calendar it was 25 October, which meant 7 November European style. And Inessa was still freezing at her Sörenberg villa, doing her best to catch a chill. Or to make him angry.

Or to punish him.

She made him wait for her letters. She was denying him news of herself. Either she didn't answer at all or else she wrote late. So that you had to choose your words carefully: of course, if you don't feel like answering . . . or if you feel like not answering . . . I won't pester you with questions . . .

In all his personal relationships Lenin was careful to assert his superiority, was always on his dignity. But here it was impossible: he
could find no vantage point. He could only hide his embarrassment in
jokes. Only beg.

He must learn to meet silence with silence. To wait for her answer.
But nothing could be more difficult: it was when you didn't see each
other that you needed most of all to write, to share your thoughts!
And anyway, there was business which could not wait.

It would be quite simple, here and now, without waiting for her
answer, to write a few affectionate and unresentful lines. (No, they
mustn't be affectionate, there must not be the slightest breath of affection; all letters in wartime were subject to censorship, and you had
to write as though you were making a statement in a police station.
Mustn't give them a weapon against yourself.)

Yes, he was at her mercy if she chose to punish him. He acknowledged dependence on no one in the world except Inessa. He felt it
least when he was smarting from one of their fights. Most of all when
they were together.

No, when they were not . . .

Everything he had ever had in life—food, drink, clothes, house and
home—had been not *for him*, indeed he had wanted nothing of all
this except as a means of keeping himself going for the sake of the
Cause. His month off in summer, his mountain walks in the Carpathians, or from Sörenberg up the Rothorn, the Alpine view before his
eyes, the slab of chocolate eaten while stretched out on the slopes of
the Zürichberg, the smoked Volga sturgeon sent by his mother—none
of this was self-indulgence, mere gratification of the flesh, it was a way
of making himself mentally fit for his work. Good health was a revolutionary's main asset.

Only his meetings with Inessa, even their business meetings, were
just for himself, for the sake of the foolishly happy, free and easy,
lighthearted state of animal contentment in which they left him, although they could be a time-wasting and debilitating distraction.

All the men and women Lenin had ever met in his life he had valued
only if, and as long as, they were useful to the Cause. Only Inessa,
although she had entered his life through the Cause—and there was
no other way, no outsider could have gotten near him—existed as if
for him alone, complementing his existence with her own.

Inessa revealed to him things he would never have thought of, never
imagined, and might have lived his life without discovering. In their
arguments about free love he had an unbreakable net of logic for her
vague ideas. Slip through it if you can! But it was hopeless. The dark
water from the depths of the lake runs unhindered through the fisherman's net, and Inessa with her concept of free love was not to be
caught in the net of class analysis. Slowed down for a moment, she

slipped easily through the mesh. Her arguments were defeated but she was invincible.

Long ago, when the whole world was carefully measured, appraised, and regulated, she had shaken his certainties, bidding him to break bounds and follow her through a world which was the same yet unlike anything he had imagined, and he had gone with her, like a timid but delighted schoolboy, anxiously clinging to her guiding hand, full of childlike, doglike gratitude toward her, worshipping her right down to the blue veins of her slender foot for all that she had revealed to him, and made to last as long as her love for him.

From where she was, from Sörenberg in the southwest, over the frowning autumn waters, even in the whistling November wind, he felt her love calling to him. He remembered the flutter of eyelids over half-closed eyes, the quick gleam of her white teeth.

Why was she punishing him? Why hadn't she come down to Clarens, where it was warmer? Last year the first snow had fallen on Sörenberg at the beginning of October. It had been very cold.

Over the roof of the theater, which was dotted with mythological winged trumpeters, the sun suddenly shone out full strength. The sunlight was cold here, and orange-colored where it had encroached on the heights of the Uetliberg, but the lower slopes, where buildings towered around a gray-green dome with a belfry, were still in gloom.

Those were happy days—in Longjumeau, Brussels, Copenhagen, Cracow. In Bern too. Happy years. Seven of them.

He, who was incapable of wasting five minutes without finding idleness an exasperating burden, had spent hours on end with Inessa. He had not despised himself for it, not been in any hurry to pull himself together, but had abandoned himself completely to his weakness. It had reached the point where he had confided everything to her, wanted to tell her everything—much more than he would tell any man. How quick and fresh was her response and her advice! And how he had missed them in the last six months! Since April. Since Kienthal.

Had something snapped at Kienthal? He hadn't felt it at the time.

He had been forced to leave Bern: Grimm was the dominant influence there and he would never have been able to get together a circle of sympathizers. He had been right to go away. But how could he have imagined when he left that they would never meet again?

In Kienthal he had noticed nothing. In the thick of that wonderful six-day battle.

The one person whose feelings he could not afford to hurt: he might lose her forever. This fear of upsetting a delicate equilibrium which he had experienced with no one else sometimes put him in a comic position. He had to humor her unfortunate passion for writing theoretical articles. Frank criticism was impossible, and he had to choose his words carefully or sometimes simply lie. "What could I possibly have against publishing your article? Of course I'm for it." Then, afterward, he would pretend that unforeseen circumstances prevented it. Rebukes, and even political correction, had to be softened until they almost became praise. He had to endure her arbitrariness as a translator: at times, instead of translating his text, she would amend the sense, or even censor it, rejecting ideas which were not to her liking. No one could be allowed to do that! But to Inessa his reproaches were mild and courteous. His courtesy was a way of ingratiating himself. If he wrote a longer letter than usual, he would immediately apologize: "I shouldn't be rambling on like this."

But even his eagerness to please did not make him feel small. With Inessa, nothing was humiliating.

This was her way of punishing him, not writing. Not answering his letters.

Once she dug her heels in there was no persuading her. A white steamer moved away from the landing stage, sending waves toward him. Two white swans, immune to the cold, their necks gracefully arched, apparently set in their pose forever, were rocked by the waves.

He felt cold. He took his bag and walked on along the railings.

With Inessa beside him he had painfully bent his will to hers, but now that she was far away he could attain almost complete freedom from her.

Here in the severe light of an autumn morning, with sunshine chasing shadow over the cold lake.

For as long as he could remember he had been aware of a safety device in himself. Any setback, any waste of time, any display of weakness depressed the catch further and further until suddenly it sprang back, flinging him into action with a force which nothing could withstand.

You must economize on idle sentiment or your work will stagnate.

With Inessa far away his natural caution was coming back to him. Caution forbade any additional stress in his life. A permanent union with Inessa? Life would be chaotic. She was too mercurial, too much a person in her own right, too distracting. Then there were her children—and a way of life quite strange to him. He could not, he had no right to let himself be slowed down and taken out of his way by those children.

The best solution was to live with Nadya, and he had been right to adopt it all those years ago. Yakubova had been more vivacious, and nicer-looking, but could never have helped him as Nadya had. Nadya was much more than a fellow spirit: on the most trivial of subjects her thoughts and feelings never differed from his own. She knew how the whole world frayed and fretted and irritated him, and she herself not only did not irritate but soothed and protected him, took all his worries upon herself. However sharp his revulsions of feeling, however sudden his outbursts, she was there to share and soften them. And how quick she was to take her cue! When Radek was behaving like a swine, she was curt and hard with him, and if he made some excuse to call, she stopped him at the door. But when Radek became a model comrade, a congenial adviser, how warmly she welcomed him. If she had needed to rehearse, to make an effort, she might sometimes have gone wrong, but she merely felt for Ilyich with unwavering loyalty. Living with her made no excessive demands on his nerves.

Then again—and this was not to be ignored—Inessa was not economical, not capable of living sensibly and modestly. She often behaved erratically. She would suddenly, for instance, take it into her head to dress in the latest fashion. Whereas Nadya had no equal for orderliness and economy. She understood instinctively that every extra franc in hand meant extra time for thinking and working. What was more, she never let her tongue run away with her—a rare thing in a woman—never boasted, never said a word to outsiders when she had been warned not to. For that matter, she knew when to keep quiet without being told.

In view of all this, it would ill become a revolutionary to be uncomfortably conscious in company that his wife was far from beautiful, not outstandingly intelligent, and a year older than himself. To succeed in the world he must be as free as possible from inner doubts and outside distractions, must narrowly concentrate all his efforts on his goal. For Lenin the politician his union with Nadya was all that reason could require.

True, there had always been the three of them. Leaving their homes in adjoining streets to meet in the forest around Bern; going for mountain rambles on Sörenberg to pick Alpine roses or mushrooms (although sometimes he and Inessa had gone off by themselves to remote mountain refuges); at some pension, where he and Nadya had sat reading in the shade, while Inessa spent hours at the piano; sitting on tree stumps on the warm slopes, he and Nadya at their books as always, and Inessa gracefully sunning herself like a little girl out with her elders; best of all, those long hours when he had talked to both of them about his ideas, his plans, his future articles. How often he had taken in at a glance, and marveled at, his incomparable, incredible, impossible good luck, wished that it would last for years. And it had lasted! If Nadya ever wrote a long, detailed friendly letter, it was to Inessa. If there was one person whom she tirelessly praised to all their comrades, it was Inessa. Only in letters to Volodya's mother—her own mother saw how things were—in letters from daughter-in-law to mother-in-law, describing their life together and their walks, did she write as though there were just the two of them. Very tactfully.

Now their mothers had both died within a short time: hers after an attack of influenza last spring, his that summer in Petersburg. The mail reached their mountain pension at Flums by mule, so that the telegram announcing his mother's death had arrived late, on the second anniversary of the outbreak of war, which was also Swiss Union Day, one of those innumerable, chaotic Swiss festivals when beacons were lit, fireworks shot off, and guns fired on every mountaintop. They had sat together that evening looking at the beacons, and paid their last respects to his mother to the sound of those salvos. It was probably easier like that, at a distance.

If you are both getting on for fifty, and your mothers, yours and hers, both die, it makes you still older. And brings you closer. Besides, you are both revolutionaries. So that perhaps . . .

A motorboat was traveling diagonally across the lake, from that very direction, from Sörenberg, tossing its prow as it swiftly plowed the water, leaving behind a triangular patch of foam and shattering the silence with its metallic coughing.

There was something about it, as it sped on, cutting a swift furrow through the water, pointing its pitiless beak, harshly chattering, which broke his train of thought, jolted his mind—and forgetting social analysis, forgetting logical argument, he suddenly saw very, very simply what he had never seen before.

If she stood for free love in theory, and could not be dissuaded, what reason was there to think that she did not practice it? . . .

He had mentally reviewed, anticipated, and enumerated for her benefit every point that could be made about relations between bourgeois and proletarians, but he had overlooked just one little thing: if they had not seen each other since Kienthal—and they were so near—if for half a year she had neither come nor summoned him, and had now almost stopped writing . . .

Perhaps this summer she had been with someone else?

Why had he invariably pictured her alone, and never imagined that it could be otherwise?

On this side of the lake there was still wan sunlight, but on the other side thick gray clouds were streaming over the Uetliberg, packing the valley with mist. The mountain, the lower slopes, the bell tower were quickly swathed, and the mist crept on toward the Zurich shore.

What could be simpler? And how was it that he had examined the question from every angle—except this one?

No, it was impossible! His comrade and friend! After their glorious fight against the centrists at Kienthal!

He gripped the cold railings, and felt like howling—through the railings, across the lake, over the Uetliberg, over all the mountains between them. Inessa! Don't leave me! Inessa! . . .

He must write, immediately, swallowing his pride, write anything so long as it would bring an answer. Of course, the post office opened earlier than the library; why hadn't he thought of it before? It opened at eight: he should have gone there and written a letter. Now it was too late.

Yes, it was too late now. They were banging and clanging their bells like madmen, like idiots! As though every bit of old iron in the city was under repair. The bells of the Frau-Münster clanged out over the post office, the double-belfried Gross-Münster crashed out the hour up above the shop signs on every floor of Bellevue . . . How many more churches were there in Zurich?

The mist and cloud had rolled over to his side of the lake and it was suddenly gray and cheerless.

He drew his watch from his vest pocket with numb fingers. If they were banging on their buckets it must be nine o'clock. He hadn't been to the post office, he'd lost track of time, he'd come too far—however briskly he walked now, he would reach the Cantonal Library well after opening time. A bad start. And he had set out with such good intentions.

Very well. The letter must wait. He must work now.

He bowled along, a short, stocky figure, scarcely troubling to avoid those in his path. There, nearby, was the City Library. He could go there, but he had the journals and books for today's work on call at the other one. He hurried as fast as he could along the loathsome bourgeois embankment, where the smells of delicatessen and confectionery wafted from doorways to tickle jaded appetites, where the shopkeepers had performed miracles of ingenuity to offer their customers a twenty-first version of sausage and a hundred-and-first variety of patisserie. Windows full of chocolates, smokers' supplies, dinner services, clocks, antiques flashed by . . . It was so difficult on this smart embankment to imagine a mob with axes and firebrands someday smashing all that plate glass to smithereens.

But it must be done!

Everything here looked too solid and permanent—the houses, doors, doorbells, bolts.

Yes, it must be done!

From every corner of the city came the clanging of bells, frenzied and hollow.

[4 4]

Here, too, Zwingli had laid about him with almost proletarian resolution, setting a good example by bisecting the Predigerkirche midway between its spires. Half of it had been occupied for centuries past by a library. It was a source of particular satisfaction that both the main libraries of Zurich had triumphed over religion.

He went into the hushed room. Nine windows with pointed arches rose to a height of five or six stories. At a still dizzier height, the ribs of the vaulted roof met in bosses.

All this soaring space was entirely wasted, except for a two-storied wooden gallery attached to the walls. On the walls, between bookcases, hung many somber portraits—haughty municipal councillors and burgomasters in doublets and frilled shirts. He had never had time to look at them carefully or read the inscriptions.

As he passed through the heavy doors Lenin saw that his favorite place in the gallery by the central window, and another which he found convenient, were both occupied. He was late. The day had begun awkwardly.

He signed the register, but the librarian with the glasses and the ex officio smile could not make out what had become of one of his three piles of books on reserve.

These petty vexations, one on top of another, could rob him of hours of working time.

The success or failure of a working day may depend on trivial events at its outset. Now he had started late. There was less than half a day, only three hours in fact, between opening time and the lunch break, and part of that was already wasted.

Imperialism had been fully drafted in twenty exercise books, written up, lost, and rewritten—but Lenin had taken out yet another heap of material on the same subject. He felt that something more was needed. Yet it was difficult to see what. He had had all his findings clearly in mind long before he reached his twentieth copybook. His prevision had become so acute of late that he knew remarkably early, before he sat down to write, what his conclusions would be.

Now it looked as though he must take out the sweetest knocks in the whole book. Stinking, slimy, sanctimonious old creature! Nowhere, in the whole history of social democracy, had there ever been a more loathsome and despicable humbug. The missing pile was on Persia. He had already begun making extracts. Nobody had thought about socialism's Eastern Front properly, and it needed study.

Never mind, his swipes at Kautsky would not go to waste—he would put them in somewhere else.

He was also drafting an important and detailed summary of policy for the Swiss leftists, so that they could systematically correct their failures at the Congress. But this could be more conveniently done in the Center for Socialist Literature than here.

No, she had always helped, always translated for him. Any day now she would leave the mountains for Clarens, and might come to him. Why imagine the worst? He had not been thinking straight.

He had arrived feeling that he had also left something undone, overlooked something in his article against disarmament. He had finished it once (it was there in his bag), but doubt still nagged at the back of his mind. The main ideas were all there: disarmament is a counsel of despair; disarmament means renouncing any idea of revolution; those who look for socialism without revolution and dictatorship are no Socialists; we will have women and children of thirteen and upward fighting in Russia in the coming civil war. All true enough, but he was still left with a feeling that some statements were inadequately qualified. You must be super-cautious, never give your enemies a thing to quote against you. You must equip all dangerous sentences with protective subsidiary clauses, make sure that every sentence is defended at all points, hedged with qualifications, carefully balanced, so that no one can find a vulnerable spot. The article, then, could do with some re-examination—and in fact he had already started. Here, for example, was something written in the heat of the moment: "We support the use of violence by the masses." They'd pounce on that! Tack a bit on ". . . against their oppressors."

But this was something he could do elsewhere, and time was going by.

He started looking over the theses for the Swiss leftists. Still a lot of work there. Everything had to be chewed up very small for them. House-to-house distribution of leaflets—to whom? To the poorest peasants and farm laborers. Which agricultural holdings should be subject to forcible expropriation? Let's say those over fifteen hectares. After what period of residence should foreigners qualify for Swiss citizenship? Let's say three months—and gratis, that's important. What is meant by "revolutionary rates of taxation"? Too general. Must compile a table showing concretely what percentage is to be paid on property over 20,000 francs, 50,000 francs, and so on. How should people in guesthouses be assessed? Draw up a precise scale for them too—nobody ever seems to get down to practical details. A guest paying five francs a day is one of us—one percent is enough—but anyone paying ten francs should be charged twenty percent immediately.

His gorge rose as he thought of Grimm's and Greulich's latest dirty trick. Filthy opportunists, sneaking scoundrels—just you wait, we'll have you in the pillory!

He seemed unable to escape these vexations and distractions. It's always the same: let them get out of hand and it's impossible to concentrate, to work methodically, or even to sit still.

Then there was that frantic and still unsettled argument with the "Japanese," which had wasted so much of his energy and was still interfering with his work. He had thought that after several articles and a couple of dozen letters the conflict was resolved, but it was still not quite dead!

He could never manage to concentrate all his efforts on a single major objective. He was forever discovering enemies in secondary sectors which might at present look quite unimportant; but no front was ever unimportant—at some future moment these secondary fronts might be decisive. So that you must furiously round on those snapping at your flanks and show them your teeth. It wasn't just the "Japanese" (Pyatakov and that Bosch woman of his, who had escaped from Siberia via Japan). Bukharin was siding with them too. They, who hadn't an ounce of brains between them, had reduced themselves with Radek's assistance to a state of collective stupefaction, to the ultimate in cretinism—if it wasn't "Imperialist economism" it was the self-determination of nations, or "democracy." These little rosy piglets, this younger generation of Party members, were so self-satisfied, so very sure of themselves, so ready to take over the leadership at any moment, and yet they were thrown by every sharp turn, not one of them had the trained skill and flexibility to swerve instantly to left or right, anticipating every fall with which the tortuous road of revolution threatened them.

Take democracy. Bukharin undervalued it in a primitive, adolescent fashion. He wrote openly that "we will have to dispense with democracy in the period of the seizure of power." Not at all! *In a general way* socialist revolution was impossible without a struggle for democracy, and the piglets should have their little pink snouts rubbed in this truth. But, of course, it must always be remembered that this was true only in a particular situation, in a certain sense, for a certain period. A different time would come when democratic aims *of any kind* would only be a *hindrance* to socialist revolution. (Double underlining here!) Suppose, for instance, when the battle is already raging, when the revolution is underway, we need to seize the banks—and they call on us to wait, to put the republic on a legal basis first?

Lenin had explained it over and over again, in letters many pages long, but they had turned up their noses. He had bothered so much with these troublemakers and intriguers only because the "Japanese" had money for a journal. *Kommunist* could not have been started without their help. All the same, the alliance made sense only as long as Lenin had a majority on the editorial board. (Equality with such fools was unthinkable. To hell with them! It would be idiocy, it would ruin everything!) It was better to drag the fatheads through the mud. You wouldn't accept a peaceful solution, so we'll bash your ugly mugs in!

He had confined his argument with Bukharin to letters, and not let it come into the open. But he had been too furious to answer the letter Bukharin had written before his departure. Now he had gone off to America—probably he had taken offense.

To himself Lenin acknowledged that Bukharin was very clever. But his constant resistance was exasperating.

All opposition exasperated him—especially on theoretical questions, where it implied a claim to leadership.

Radek was another matter, and it would be well worthwhile thrashing the little shit as a lesson to the rest. Radek's lowest trick yet was surreptitiously egging on the piglets while hiding behind the Zimmerwald left. (At Kienthal he had tried to make Lenin quarrel with all the leftists, and had caused him to fall out with Rosa.) Radek's political behavior was that of a barefaced, impudent Tyszko-type huckster—the only politics such snotty-nosed guttersnipes had ever known. After the way he had slung Lenin and Zinoviev off the board of *Vorbote* the only thing to do was to punch him on the snout or turn your back on him. If you forgive this sort of thing in politics, people regard you as a fool or a knave.

In the present case the right thing was to snub him. Especially as there was no disagreement on general matters, but only on Russo-Polish problems. Where Switzerland was concerned, Radek had no choice. Since he opposed Grimm, he was forced into alliance with Lenin—and what an ally he was!

Zinoviev, too, had acted like a scoundrel in this business of the "Japanese," and urged him to give in. They were all unstable. You couldn't rely on the closest of them.

To put a stop to Bukharin's capers it was necessary to carry the argument to Russia too, and finish off the "Japanese" on Russian soil. Shlyapnikov had been ordered to do so. But Shlyapnikov was another muddlehead, and his girlfriend Kollontai was worse. (Incidentally, he mustn't forget that it would be a good idea to sneak her into the Scandinavian Conference of Neutrals, perhaps as interpreter to one of the delegates, and sniff out their plans!)

There were so many of them, these pseudo-Socialist muddlers, everywhere, in the warring countries, among the neutrals, in Russia. Was Trotsky any better, though, with his pious fatuities—"neither victors nor vanquished"? What rubbish. No, of course he was seeking cheap popularity, but let's see to it that Tsarism is nevertheless vanquished, don't let it wriggle out of the present free-for-all! You can't be "against all wars" and remain a Socialist.

Where Shlyapnikov was at present he didn't know. Still in Stockholm? Or had he already gone to Russia? Letters reached Sweden through Kesküla and his people as occasion offered, but did they get any further? There was nobody with any sense there, no system. There was no end to Shlyapnikov's delays; he went to Russia only rarely, and once there always stayed too long, the sluggard. If you said anything to him he took offense. And if he didn't go, there was nobody else. So to make him look important they had had to co-opt him to the Central Committee.

At this point the librarian came up to Lenin's desk and with a whispered apology and an apologetic bow laid the pile of material on Persia before him.

Many thanks! Half an hour or so to the lunch break, and along comes Persia! Should he make a start, or not?

Of course, Shlyapnikov was not yet ripe for membership on the Central Committee, he lacked Malinovsky's maturity. But he had taken Malinovsky's place, and the titles "member of the CC" and "chairman of the Russia Bureau" had turned his head, given him a taste for power. First he was shouldering Litvinov aside to get in on talks with foreign Socialists, then he was giving idiotic advice in practically every letter he wrote: "Why don't you move to Sweden?" He was sickeningly sure of himself, but he couldn't be cut adrift, he was doing a serious job, and he had to be answered, formally at least, with respect.

Somehow he couldn't settle down to his work. His brain was in too much of a whirl. He couldn't concentrate, couldn't adjust to the leisurely movement of Persia's feudal economy.

Malinovsky, Malinovsky! The Russian Bebel manqué. How he could work! How well he had handled the masses! What a remarkable type, what a personality! A natural leader of workingmen, a collective symbol of the Russian proletariat. Lenin had long felt the lack of such a working-class leader in the Party at his right hand, to complement him, to convert his ideas into mass action. What Lenin had particularly liked in him was that he molded himself to his allotted place, carried out orders with alacrity and without demur—but brilliantly and effectively. He had what is called in bourgeois terms a criminal record—a few thefts—but this only threw into relief his proletarian intolerance of private property and the colorfulness of his character. So that, when excessively suspicious comrades began casting aspersions, Lenin's confidence in him grew stronger all the time. Imagine him as a provocateur? Impossible! (And it was still impossible.) After his incendiary speeches in the Duma, and his skillful management of the split between Bolsheviks and Mensheviks in the Duma group, Lenin not only had been glad to introduce Malinovsky himself to the Central Committee but had brought in others solely on the strength of Malinovsky's recommendation—Stalin, for instance. When they were living in Poronin, no guest from Russia was more welcome than Malinovsky. Except for that last, dreadful night in May, when he had appeared unexpectedly after his sudden and unauthorized withdrawal from the Duma. But still, he had put in an appearance and not run away. Would he have dared to do so if his hands were not clean? . . . Their discussion had gone on all night. It was in any case impossible to *prove* anything against Malinovsky. (And what good could it do?) Who could believe the stupid tale that the secret police themselves had found it "embarrassing" that one of their informers was among the best orators in the Duma and had ordered him to withdraw? What rot! Were the secret police stupid enough to work against themselves? He, Kuba, and

Grishka had constituted themselves a sort of party tribunal, found Roman Malinovsky not guilty, and vouched for his innocence before the International Socialist Bureau.

Nonetheless, they had quietly parted company for the time being. For personal reasons.

Lenin would never have another such helper! . . . Shlyapnikov? No, no.

Now the lunch break was upon him. How on earth did these Swiss manage to work up an appetite for lunch by twelve o'clock?

However, Lenin had noticed that the librarian on duty today did not always go to lunch. He went over and inquired. No, he wasn't going. Was it at all possible to stay through the lunch break? It was.

Here was a bit of luck. Lunch wasn't worth the disturbance it would involve. It was easier to work on an empty stomach. And he would gain time.

He needn't hurry now. The best thing in fact, though, would be to stock up with newspapers right away. To save money, Lenin never bought them, never took out subscriptions, though he needed to read thirty or forty of them—all the various *Arbeiters* and *Stimmes*.

He collected all there were and carried them over to his desk.

Reading the papers was one of his most important daily tasks, his entrée to the world outside. Reading the papers heightened his sense of responsibility, his firmness of purpose, his militancy, helped him to feel that his enemies were alive and real. Socialists, social patriots, and centrists from every spot on the face of the earth, not to mention all the bourgeois donkeys, seemed to crowd around you in the reading room, gesturing, babbling, all speaking loudly at once, and you seized your opportunity to strike back, to note their weak points and hit out at them. Reading the papers meant making abstracts at the same time. By analogy, by association, by contradiction, sparks of thought were continually struck off, flying at a tangent to left or right, onto loose scraps of paper, onto the lined pages of exercise books, into blank margins, and every thought must be stitched to paper with a fiery thread before it could fade, to smolder there until it was wanted, in a draft summary or else in a letter begun there and then so that he could forge his sentences red-hot. Some of these thoughts were intended to clear his own mind, others for use in argument, to sting or to stun, others as a more effective rehash of things which the stupid found difficult, others again to keep distant comrades, perhaps as far away as Russia, theoretically attuned to him.

Vandervelde and Branting, Huysmans and Jouhaux, Plekhanov and Potresov, Ledebour and Haase, Bauer and Bernstein, the two Adlers, even Pannekoek and Roland Holst—Lenin felt as though all these exasperating opponents were close enough to touch. No matter where their nests were, in Holland, England, France, Scandinavia, Austria, or

Petersburg, he felt them to be within sight, within hearing, he was connected with all of them in a single complex of throbbing nerves—asleep or awake, at his books, at table, or out walking.

There were no readers left. Evidently the lunch break had begun. The librarian went through a glass door into the depths of the book stacks. All the desk lamps were extinguished and the reading room was lost in the soaring dimness, the tomblike silence of the church it once was. Taking advantage of this rare opportunity to discharge his excess nervous tension, Lenin began briskly pacing the longest straight walk in the building, the central aisle from the entrance under the wooden gallery to the two long transverse steps before what had been the altar. A distance of fifty paces unobstructed by bookshelves or desks.

He was used to walking in city streets or in the mountains, and he had always lived in poky little places with no room to move around. Now, pacing faster and faster with his hunter's stride, brushing aside the Hilferdings, Martovs, Greulichs, Longuets, Pressmanns, and Chkheidzes, abruptly choking them off in mid-sentence, pulling them up short, routing them—in this frenzied, pendulumlike oscillation he beat off wave after wave of enemies.

He was liberating himself from his enemies.

And he felt more and more ready for methodical work.

At a certain moment, halfway along the aisle, he suddenly felt that it was enough.

And sat down to work.

He had been wrong to think like that about Inessa. He had nothing at all to go on.

No! He had been sitting at the wrong desk. Now he would have to move it all—books, newspapers, notebooks—into the gallery, to his usual desk. He had to make two trips.

The steps creaked slightly in the gray Gothic hush.

And suddenly he felt very weary. He almost collapsed into his chair. His head was . . .

Although he had missed lunch he did not feel at all hungry. He could make do with very little food: he generated energy almost without eating.

Right by the window, without lamplight for the time being. But it was a gloomy day.

He started reading the newspapers. He read about the general military situation. There was nothing there to cheer him.

Not so bad, of course, as in August, at that terrible moment when a still fresh Romania had suddenly joined in, enormously reinforcing her allies, and it had seemed that Russia would extricate herself after all. But Germany had proved strong enough to smash Romania almost effortlessly. It was astonishing—no one could have prophesied it two months earlier. Nevertheless, and also contrary to all predictions, Germany was not winning the war in Europe as a whole. On the Western Front there was an unbreakable and hopeless impasse. On the Eastern Front too—and this was the greatest shock—1916 had brought no victory. A year ago Tsarism had already been close to collapse, was *already* shaken to its foundations, yet now it was on its feet again and holding its own. The greatest hope, the greatest victory, had ebbed, seeped away, vanished.

In one corner of his head, just in that one little spot, near his left temple, it was as though a vacuum had formed. That was bad. He had let himself get too excited.

In no country did it appear that even the third year of this bloody war had awakened the people to reality. The Russians, as always, were the most hopeless of all. It was they who were suffering the most extravagant losses, they whose stacked bodies barred the way to German efficiency and German technology. Reporting on the Eastern Front was generally vague and inaccurate, there were no war correspondents there, people knew and cared little about it, and of course the press in the Entente countries tried not to say much about an ally of which it was ashamed. But it often gave figures of Russian casualties. Lenin always looked for these figures and made a mark by them—with surprise and satisfaction. The bigger the figures, the happier they made him: all those soldiers killed, wounded, or taken prisoner were stakes falling out of absolutism's fence and leaving the monarchy weaker. But at the same time the figures drove him to despair: no people on earth were so long-suffering and so devoid of sense as the Russians. Their patience knew no bounds. Any abomination, any filth dished out to them they would lap up with nothing but reverent gratitude for their beloved benefactor.

Should he put the lights on after all? The words seemed to swim before his eyes.

This damp Russian firewood refused to catch fire! The best blazes were all ancient history—the salt riots, the cholera riots, the copper coin riots, the Razin rebellion, the Pugachev rebellion. Except perhaps to seize the estate of a neighboring landowner, which was there before their eyes, neither proletariat nor professional revolutionaries would ever set the dark peasant mass in motion. Corrupted and emasculated by Orthodoxy, the peasants seemed to have lost their passion for the ax and the torch. If a people could endure such a war without rebelling, what could be done with it?

The game was lost. There would be no revolution in Russia.

He covered his eyes with his hands and sat still.

Whether from tiredness or from depression something seemed to have sagged inside him.

The readers were reassembling. Chairs were moved. A book fell. Lamps were turned on.

There might be worse to come. Was Tsarism already wriggling out of the trap? By making a *separate peace??* (Treble underlining.) And what else could Germany do, if she couldn't win a war on two fronts?

That was really frightening. The worst thing possible. All would be lost. The world revolution. Revolution in Russia. Lenin's whole life, two decades of ceaseless effort.

A report that a separate peace was in the making, that secret negotiations between Germany and Russia had already *officially* begun, and that the two powers were already agreed on the main points, had recently been published by Grimm in the *Berner Tagwacht*. It was signed K. R. Without asking the rascally Radek you could safely guess that it was he. (But how had he managed to persuade Grimm?!) And if you knew his gift for sparkling improvisation you could safely assume that he had not eavesdropped on diplomats, sneaked a look at secret documents, or even picked up a stray rumor, but that as he idled the morning away in bed, with newspapers on top of and under the blankets and books on the floor, he occasionally composed such items "from our own correspondent" in Norway or Argentina.

What mattered was not where this particular report had originated. Nor that the Russian ambassador in Bern had denied it—what else could he do? What did matter was that it had the piercing ring of truth: for the Tsar this really was *the right way out!* Just what he ought to do! Just what Lenin would do in his place!

So they must strike and strike again at this weak point! Raise the alarm! Put a stop to it! Forestall him! Not let him pull his feet out of the trap unharmed!

Of course, you could expect only utter stupidity from Nikolai II and his government. You wouldn't have expected them to start this war if they had had any sense at all. But they did start it—and what a wonderful present they've given us!

So perhaps it was still possible to frighten them with publicity and avert the danger?

A separate peace! It would of course be a remarkably neat way out. But still, they weren't clever enough for it.

In any case, there was nothing to be done in Russia for the time being. Nobody there read *Social Democrat*. All eyes were on the Milyukovs and Shingarevs. All anyone ever talked of was the Kadets. And just look how their delegation had been received in the West. The Tsar might take it into his head to move over a little, let Guchkov and the Kadets have ministries—and then you'd never get them, never break through.

How could you knead sad Russian dough into any sort of shape! Why was he born in that uncouth country? Just because a quarter of his blood was Russian, fate had hitched him to the ramshackle Russian rattletrap. A quarter of his blood, but nothing in his character, his will, his inclinations made him kin to that slovenly, slapdash, eternally drunken country. Lenin knew of nothing more revolting than back-slapping Russian hearties, tearful tavern penitents, self-styled geniuses bewailing their ruined lives. Lenin was a bowstring, or an arrow from the bow. Lenin could size up a situation, and the best or only means to an end, at half a glance. What then tied him to that country? With a little more work he could have mastered three European languages, as he had mastered that semi-Tartar tongue. He was tied, you say, to Russia by twenty years as a practicing revolutionary? Yes, but by nothing else. Now, after the creation of the Zimmerwald left, he was sufficiently well known in international socialist circles to step over. Socialism made no distinctions of nationality. Trotsky, for instance, had left for America. He had made the right choice. Bukharin was on his way there. Perhaps that was the place to go.

No, there was something wrong with him today. The day had started wrong, and had never got going properly. It was as though the working of his mind was too fast for his body, his physical frame, his breast. And there was that little pocket of emptiness near his left temple. He felt hollow with fatigue, and the tissues of his body seemed to sag around the cavity within him.

Too much had happened at once, and he suddenly felt that he would not get through a good day's work, but would roll on downhill, enervated, ineffectual, dejected.

A true politician is not at the mercy of his years, his feelings, circumstances, but brings at all seasons and times of day an unvarying mechanical efficiency to bear in his actions, his speeches, his battles. Lenin, too, was a remarkably smooth-functioning machine, with inexhaustible drive, but even he experienced one or two days in a year when his drive slackened, leaving him despondent, exhausted, prostrate. On such a day there was no choice but to go to bed early and sleep soundly.

Lenin might seem completely in control of his mind and his will, but even he was helpless against these attacks of despair. His certainties, his firm perspective, his proven tactics would suddenly become blurred, indistinct, elusive. The world would turn its stupid gray backside on him.

And the disease which sat inside him, ever watchful, would suddenly make its sharp corners felt, like a stone in a sack.

He felt it in his temple.

Yes, he had always followed the path of refusal to compromise, to smooth over differences, and by doing so had created a conquering force. He had a prophetic certainty that it would conquer. That it was important to preserve a strictly centralized group, no matter how small, no matter who its members were. The conciliation and unification movements had long ago shown that they spelled ruin for a workers' party. Reconciliation with disarmers? Reconciliation with the *Nashe Slovo* gang? Reconciliation with the Russian Kautskyites? With the swine on the Menshevik Organizing Committee? Become a flunkey to social chauvinists? Embrace the village idiots of socialism? No, to hell with that! Give him a tiny minority which was firm, sure, his own!

However, he had gradually found himself almost isolated—betrayed and deserted, while all manner of unifiers and disarmers, liquidators and defensists, chauvinists and antistatists, trashy scribblers and mangy timeserving petty bourgeois riffraff had gathered elsewhere in a tight bunch. Sometimes he was reduced to such a small minority that nobody at all remained at his side, as in 1908, the year of loneliness and misery after all his defeats, the most dreadful, the hardest year of his life—also spent in Switzerland. The intellectuals had abandoned the Bolshevik ranks in a panic: so much the better, at least the Party was rid of that petty bourgeois filth. Among those foul caricature intellectuals Lenin had felt particularly humiliated, insignificant, lost. It filled him with despair to feel himself sinking into their mire. It would have been idiotic to become like them. In every gesture, every word, every oath even, he was determined not to resemble them! . . . But it looked as though soon there would be no one at all left. It reached the point where he was desperately clinging to his last ten or fifteen supporters! And simply in order to capture fifteen Bolsheviks, and to deny them to the Machists, he had dashed off to London for material and written a philosophical work three hundred pages long, which no one had ever read; but he had discredited Bogdanov and dislodged him from the leadership! Then throughout the damp autumn those endless chilly walks by Lake Geneva, endlessly assuring themselves that they were not downhearted, and were on the road to victory.

Even with the cleverest of them, like Trotsky or Bukharin, he could find no common language. Of the few who stayed near he could never be sure for more than a month ahead—Zinoviev, for instance, with his weak nerves and his precarious beliefs. (Grishka really had no beliefs at all.)

So that, after all, no "conquering force" had been created. His whole career, twenty-three years of uninterrupted militant campaigning against political stupidity, vulgarity, opportunism, his whole grim life under a constant hail of hatred, had brought him—what? Only isolation. The force of inertia carried him on along the same line—splitting with one, branding another, dissociating himself from a third—but he wearily realized that he was in a rut, that he could no longer look forward to real success.

The loneliness.

If only there was someone to tell, someone to share it with, so that he would hear his own voice.

What a day . . . Everything had fallen apart in his hands. He had sat away the hours to no purpose.

Piles of books. Piles of newspapers . . . In his years as an émigré he must have read, scanned, written, stacks, reams, pillars of paper.

When he was young, the scent of imminent revolution was fresh in the air. The path toward it seemed simple and short. He told everyone, again and again, that "the universal belief in revolution is in itself the beginning of revolution!" A time of happy expectancy.

But these last ten years, since his second emigration, had been filled, stuffed, packed tight with—what? Nothing but paper—envelopes, packets, newspaper wrappers, routine letters, express letters—so much time was spent on correspondence alone (not to mention the cost of postage, but that came from Party funds). Almost his whole life, half of every day, went into those endless letters. Nobody lived near him, his sympathizers were scattered to the four corners of the earth, and from a distance he had to keep their loyalty, rally, direct, advise, interrogate, beg, and thank them, coordinate resolutions (all this with his friends, at the same time never interrupting for a moment the fierce struggle with his enemies), and nothing was ever more urgent and important than the letter of the moment (though tomorrow it might seem trivial and too late, and anyway wrong). You exchanged articles in outline, proofs, criticisms, corrections, reviews, summaries, points for discussion, excerpts from the press, newspapers by the cart-load, sometimes issues of your own journals, which never got beyond the first few numbers—and all the time you felt that none of it was serious, you couldn't believe, couldn't imagine, that a social movement could force its way up through the heaps of paper and newspaper wrappings littering the earth to the cherished goal of state power—where you would need qualities quite different from those required during your dozen years in reading rooms.

He was nearing the end of his forty-seventh year, in an anxious, monotonous life of nothing but ink on paper, enmities and alliances, quarrels and agreements that sprang up and faded in a day or a week, all terribly important, all requiring enormous tact and skill, and always with politicians so much inferior to himself, all of it water into a bottomless bucket, instantly lost and forgotten, labor in vain. In a life of constant agitation, twisting and turning, his whole achievement was to fight his way into an impassable rubbish heap.

His arms dangled limply, his back would not straighten, he looked utterly played out.

Meanwhile his disease grew heavier, fitfully stirring and nagging inside him. It made not a sound, entered into no disputes, but no opponent was more powerful.

An evil which now would never leave him.

His vocation—he knew no other—was to change the course of history, and fulfillment had been denied him.

All his incomparable abilities—appreciated now by everyone in the Party, but he set a truer and still higher value on them—all his quick-wittedness, his penetration, his grasp, his uselessly clear understanding of world events, had failed to bring him not only political victory but even the position of a Member of Parliament in Toyland, like Grimm. Or that of a successful lawyer (though he would hate to be a lawyer—he had lost every case in Samara). Or even that of a journalist.

Just because he had been born in accursed Russia.

It was his habit to carry out even the most laborious and thankless tasks conscientiously, and he was still trying to draft his detailed theses for the education of the Swiss left Zimmerwaldists on the cost of living, on the intolerable economic position of the masses. What should be the maximum salary for office workers and bureaucrats? What to watch for in the Party press? How to rid the Party of Grütlian reformists . . .

It was no good. His work would not take shape. The heart had gone out of his routine and left a hole. His head was beginning to ache. Breathing was difficult. The very sight of his papers sickened him. By tomorrow the attack should be over, but at present he felt such a loathing for everything that he could have lain down and died.

Guiltily deciding not to sit through the working day (not that there was much of it left), he stuffed the notebooks and manuscripts into his shopping bag as best he could, slammed the books shut and stacked them, made a neat bundle of the newspapers, put some things on their shelves, and took the rest back to the librarian, treading carefully on the steps so as not to come crashing down with that great pile.

At the door he pulled on his heavy overcoat, carelessly crammed on his bowler hat, and shuffled off.

Walking the same way, day in and day out, gave neither legs nor eyes enough to do: it had become automatic.

It was beginning to get dark, and there was some mist too. Electric lights were already lit in the windows of shops and restaurants.

A huge barrel was being rolled along the narrow side street, and behind it came a wheelbarrow. There was no way around them.

He might easily, very easily, never escape from this cramped, apathetic, petty bourgeois Switzerland, and end his days here with the Skittle Club.

Through the window of a food shop he could see a nickel-plated machine rhythmically cutting an appetizing ham into even slices. The grocer, looking as smug as all Swiss, came out onto the threshold of his establishment, and—whether he knew them or not—presented a grötzi free of charge to one passerby after another. In the third year of war the shops still importunately flaunted their plenty, though prices had risen by leaps and bounds because of the submarines. The bourgeoisie could still pick and choose.

Luckily it was too cold to put café tables out on the pavement, or they would be sitting, lounging, sprawling there, goggling at the passersby, making you step around them with a curse. Through all his years as an émigré Lenin had hated cafés, those smoke-filled dens of logorrhea, where nine-tenths of the compulsive revolutionary windbags were in permanent session. During the war Zurich had drawn in another dubious crowd from the belligerent neighbors. It was because of them that rents had gone up—this mob of adventurers, shady businessmen, profiteers, draft-dodging students and blathering intellectuals, with their philosophical manifestos and artistic demonstrations, in revolt against they knew not what. And they were all there—in the cafés.

America was no doubt just as well off. The upper stratum of the working class everywhere would sooner get rich than make a revolution. No one, either here or there, needed his dynamite, the sweep of his ax.

He, who was capable of taking the world apart, or blowing it up and then rebuilding it, he had been born too soon, born merely to be a torment to himself.

At its midpoint the Spiegelgasse rose in a hump, riding over a little hill of its own. Leaving home, wherever bound, he half ran downward. Coming back, wherever he had been, he faced a steep hill. If he had gotten into his stride, or was in a good humor, he thought nothing of it. But now he could scarcely drag himself along. He seemed not to be walking but scraping the ground with his feet.

The steep, narrow staircase of the old house held the smells of many years. It was dark now, but the lamps had not been lit, and he had to tread cautiously.

Third floor. A polyglot babble. The oppressive smells of the apartment.

His room was like a prison cell for two. Two beds, a table, chairs. An iron stove, with its pipe running through the wall, no fire in it (although it was getting cold enough). An upturned crate that had once held books served as a dresser. (Because they were forever on the move they bought no furniture.)

In the last rays of daylight Nadya was still writing at the table. She looked around. She was surprised.

But her eyes were used to the poor light, and when she saw him looking sixty, saw his yellow-gray face, his fixed dead gaze, she did not ask why he was so early.

She had some experience with these attacks, which could prostrate him for days at a time or sometimes for several weeks, when he was burnt out with excitement, or the strain of battle was too much even for his iron body. He had suffered nervous attacks of this sort after 1903, again after *One Step Forward, Two Steps Back*, and more than once after the Fifth Congress.

The bowler hat weighed heavily on his head, the overcoat on his shoulders. It was a struggle to rid himself of them . . . Nadya helped him . . . He dragged his feet and the shopping bag with books across the room.

He found strength to look at what Nadya had been writing and raised it to his eyes. Their accounts.

A depressingly long column of figures.

Though 1908 had been gloomy and lonely, they had been rolling in money after the Tiflis expropriation. They had an account with the Crédit Lyonnais. To escape from their misery they went to concerts in the evenings, had a holiday in Nice, traveled, lived in hotels, took cabs, rented a Paris apartment for a thousand francs, with a mirror over the fireplace.

He sat down on the bed.

Sat, slumped, shrank. His body sank into the mattress, his head sank onto his shoulders, his neck disappeared: his chin rested on his chest, the back of his head on his spine.

With one hand he held on to the edge of the table in front of him.

One eye was half closed. His mouth was half open. A tough, untidy stubble bristled on his upper lip. His flat-tipped nose was pushed outward.

He sat like that for one minute, two, three.

"Do you want to lie down? Get undressed?" Nadya asked in her soft, toneless voice.

He was silent.

"Why didn't you come back for lunch? Were you working too hard?"

He nodded with an effort.

"Will you eat now?" But her voice held no promise of carnivorous delights. She just couldn't learn to cook.

How different from Shushenskoye! Then there was always a fire in the stove, pots on it, a roast in the oven (a whole sheep was meat for a week), tubs of pickles, snipe, grouse, you could bathe in milk if you felt like it. And everything was washed sparkling clean by a little servant girl.

His dome was completely bald now. He had kept only his back hair, and that was thinning. (They themselves had made things worse in 1902: they had begrudged the money for a good doctor, and a half-trained Russian medical student prescribed iodine for a rash on his head, which caused his hair to fall out.)

Nadya came closer, gently, timidly stroked his head.

Several long, deep lines furrowed his brow from temple to temple. He sighed loudly, jerkily—more like a man pulling a heavy load than a deskbound intellectual. Without raising his submerged head, looking not at his wife but straight ahead, over the table, he said wearily, oh so wearily, "When the war ends we'll go to America."

She couldn't believe her ears.

"But what about the Zimmerwald left? The new International?" She stood there, forlorn and frumpish.

Her husband sighed, and answered in a hoarse, flat, weak voice. "It's obvious which way things are going in Russia. The Tsar will make a deal with the Kadets, and they will form a government. Then we'll have twenty or thirty years of boring, vulgar, bourgeois evolution. With no hope at all for revolutionaries. We won't live to see the day."

Very well, then. They would go. She stroked the thin hair on the back of his head.

Suddenly the landlady knocked at the door. Someone had come to see them.

This was all they needed. Whoever it was had chosen a fine time! Without even asking, Nadya went to send the visitor away.

She came back looking bewildered. "Volodya! It's Sklarz! From Berlin . . ."

*   *   *

IT CAN GO ON FOUR LEGS—
AS LONG AS IT LAYS EGGS.

*   *   *

[4 5]

On the eve of the feast of our Lady of Kazan, a Friday, the women were hard at it boiling and baking, their cheeks flushed all day from the heat of the stove. And from all the neighboring villages—Izobilnaya, Torchki, Bredikhin, and even Zhuravlino-Vershinskoye—guests dressed in their best and drawn by high-steppers assembled for their kinsfolk's high holiday. After more than two years of culling it was astonishing how populous their volost was. Men in early middle age were still all at home, and the region's famous horses were as handsome and spirited as ever, with their burnished holiday harness sparkling and jingling. The men wore two-piece or three-piece suits, delivered from the depths of clothes chests, and creaky new boots, no one was ill shod. While the women went to church in frills and flounces all colors of the rainbow, if not in beaver capes, Mother wearing a Turkish shawl, Katya in Romanian lace-up bootees.

Among those who arrived was Adrian's wife, Anfisa, bringing her three little ones from the farm at Blue Bushes to visit the Blagodarevs. Though a guest herself she helped with the cooking and serving, as other guests poured in to view the soldier. Anfisa was a good sort, and one of the family, more or less—but she couldn't hide her envy, and who wouldn't feel sore? Adrian had been wounded twice, but didn't have a medal, Senka not even once, and he had two.

Well, it had just happened that way, and what could Senka do about it? He felt embarrassed himself. Ever since his homecoming his hands had been aching for work, to make up for lost time. Never mind all those years he had spent manhandling gun carriages, ramming shells into the breech, digging holes in the ground—none of that work counted, it was as though he had never done it, he was eager to put his back into it as never before, but this was not the time, he had arrived on the eve of a holiday, three days on end of feasting and friendly faces, going from table to table, showing himself.

The festivals dovetailed one into the other. On Saturday it was Our Lady of Kazan, their patron saint's day. The local authorities never failed to raise the flag on the eve of the feast, which was also the anniversary of the Emperor's accession. This year, St. Dmitri's Saturday, the day of remembrance of dead relatives, fell on the same day as the parish feast. On Sunday, the second day of the parish feast, there were prayers from house to house, the reveling knew no bounds, night was falling when guests went their ways. Monday was the feast of Our Lady Comforter of All the Afflicted, with yet another service in the church, yet another whole day of holiday, this time among your own folk, the villagers of Kamenka.

So every morning the Blagodarevs doused their heads with ice-cold water to clear them after yesterday's jollification, and went off to morning prayers and mass, leaving Mother or Katya or Fenya at home with the little ones.

Summoned by the bells, the villagers walked down from their homes on all the hills of Kamenka, and uphill again to the church, all in their best clothes, the women wearing bright red or dark blue head scarves and shawls, jackets, or even pelisses, which they could always hang up in the narthex should they feel too warm. The men too wore bright clothes. The old women were in their Sunday black. Even the boys had their boots on, picking the drier places to strut around and show off. Why dress up otherwise?

Arseni was eternally indebted to Father Mikhail. His father would not have let him, any more than Adrian and their sisters, go to school, he couldn't afford it, and anyway going to school wasn't the rule at the time. Senka's father wanted him to go and work for the village herdsman, but when Father Mikhail got wind of it he talked to Elisei and gave him ten poods of rye to let his son attend the church school. (There was as yet no zemstvo school in Kamenka.) That was the old Father Mikhail, the present one's father, who used to call grown-up parishioners his "little ones," he was dead now, and his son had taken his place. Also called Father Mikhail Molchanov, he performed the rites just as punctiliously—mass could take more than two hours on

Sunday—officiated at services by request just as zealously, was just as meek, and people consulted him on matters of conscience just as willingly. The only difference was that he didn't call grown-ups his "little ones." He was always in the garden with spade and shears, following his father in this respect too, and had let the lilacs around his little house grow even more profusely.

In the past Arseni had said the responses for him, and sung in the choir. So Father Mikhail sent word that he should walk straight up and take his place in the choir for the holidays, and receive communion on Our Lady of Kazan's day. It was as though the last two years and a bit had never been, as if Arseni had never been wrenched from his village, snatched away as though in the jaws of a wolf, to drag himself along with fires and explosions all around him, hide from cross fire in trenches and shell holes, and return the German bounty in kind. There it was, the church of his childhood, his very own church, unchanged, the icons and candelabra still in their old places, the same chancel rail, and Father Mikhail standing in the same chasuble before the same wrought-iron sanctuary gates. Arseni had attended services and requiems at the front, standing before a collapsible field altar, and the liturgy had been sung to the same chant, but there, as with everything else in a soldier's life, it somehow wasn't the real thing. You got used to it, and stopped noticing, it was only when you went home to your village that you felt the difference. Now Arseni could sing out again, heartily, without constraint. And listen with the people of his own village to the festival hymn: "Mother of God, unworthy as we are we will never cease to proclaim Thy power: for if Thou didst not intercede and pray for us who would deliver us from such great troubles? Who would have kept us free unto this time?"

Whether it was sung or chanted, whether it could be understood at once or its meaning was dark, whether you followed every word or started thinking your own thoughts about what it would be like after the war, say, and what a fine life you and Katya would have together, the words of the prayer still lifted you above life's rough-and-tumble, as did the church itself. Humbly adorned as it was, the best of the cottages could not compare with it. It was open to everyone, and treated all alike. As they stood through the service of their patron saint, they were conscious all the time of what would very shortly follow, the general merrymaking, the heavy drinking, the horse racing, the horse trading, the brawling, with young men confronting each other in pitched battles, and even grown men in a fighting frenzy, but here in church you were reminded that all this was froth and scum, that we, all of us together, are the *mir*, children of the same God, and that it is not meet we should bear malice one toward another. All stand quietly, all bend their heads when they should, even the proud and quarrelsome, and when it is time to kneel, all kneel, and if a man's mind has room only for his everyday concerns, if all he asks from God is to give his children or his cattle good health, or to help him in his plans for his holding, that too is as it should be, there is no harm in it. But hope you choke! Bust a gut! Die, why don't you! Nobody here will pray for anything like that. "We have no other help, save only for Thee, Queen of Heaven. Be Thou our help: Thou art our hope and our glory. For we are Thy servants, and we shall not be shamed."

If he turned his head slightly Arseni could see Katya out of the corner of his eye, standing on the left, the women's side of the church, in the throng of holiday worshippers, and praying. So meek and mild, so neat, so quick in her movements, gazing so devoutly at the Mother of God, bowing from the waist so eagerly and easily, with a little flutter of her head scarf. And to see her cheerful devoutness, her eager obeisances, nobody would have said, nobody could imagine, that she had ever had sinful thoughts, in the bathhouse just now, or before, or that she harbored any for the future. Arseni dutifully sang along with the choir, but in his heart there was a song of praise: I thank Thee, Lord, for sending me such a wife, good to look at, good worker, good-tempered. Little wife of mine, none could be better!

Afterward people poured out of the church, scattering downhill, to their festivities. Previously no one in Kamenka had taken strong drink except at holiday times—anyone who did was not a man, no head of household, and when the war came distilling under license had been suspended anyway. But they were not left without strong drink. They had always brewed braga and beer, but now they learned how to distill, from grain, a liquor stronger than vodka. It lifted you out of this world, left you ever so merry. By now there were maybe seven phonographs in Kamenka and the fashion was to stand them on benches outside the gates, or at a window, to entertain the world at large, and keep the accordionists quiet for a bit. The young people would dance in front of the fire station where the ground had been trampled down. They sang songs at the tops of their voices, sang fit to burst, hill answering hill.

After the jollifications of the patron saint's day the young men always fought, village against village, and even grown men were drawn into the fray. Nowadays there was noticeably less jollity than usual and fighting went on with or without the parish feast. This year there was a fight almost to the death between drunken conscripts—Kamenka versus Volkhonskoye. They couldn't save it for the Germans. The two constables from the big town and the village had a hard time breaking it up and had to turn the fire hose on them. And the mischief the village boys got up to beat anything ever heard of. Eighteen-year-old Mishka, son of a respected father, got together a band of youths and the village had never experienced anything like the malicious damage they did. They stole poultry, blocked chimneys, broke branches in orchards belonging to other peasants. That was definitely out of order—the rule had always been that you could steal the squire's apples but nobody else's. Not one of them was caught red-handed, and Mishka Rul's father could do nothing with him, he was due to go into the army anyway.

The three days merged into one, you went from cottage to cottage, from feast to feast, until you couldn't say whom you'd seen, where, or what you'd scoffed down—meat or fish, pies or galantines. Arseni made the rounds, jingling his two medals, removing them from his greatcoat to pin them on his tunic, gladly telling his listeners for the umpteenth time how he had won them, how things were generally at the front, what the Germans were like, yelling across the table, above the roar of voices, and the strains of the accordion. "What every soldier should know: spit on your rifle, but don't wet the barrel!!" "A soldier doesn't need a fur coat, marching will keep him warm." There was another saying, that "a soldier on leave means shirt outside breeches," but he himself was always tightly belted, if only because he would have been ashamed to let his belly sag and hunch his shoulders with such a fine figure of a father beside him. Whatever anybody asked Senka, yelling above the hubbub, plucking at his tunic, planting a hand on his shoulder, he answered confidently, whether he knew or not. Was it true that the Germans weren't just throwing bombs anymore but belching fire? And was it true that the Frenchies had black devils fighting for them, in the flesh, not hiding themselves? And why were we fighting the Germans, a Christian people like ourselves, so fiercely? With the Turks or the Japanese it was different . . .

Then, of course, they sang, at the tops of their voices.

For three whole days they were living on top of one another, indoors the whole time, and it was only as he walked from cottage to cottage, or went outside to cool his head in the damp, chill air that Arseni saw the sky, through clouds sometimes stretched to the thinness of fine linen, with the sun shining through, and saw his village spread out before him from the hill on which Davydov the landowner's house stood, and from which the main street ran down to the bridge over the stream, then on beyond the bridge and past Pluzhnikov's brick house, to another hill, beyond the crest of which the road ran down again all the way to the river Savala and to another hill over against the Prince's Forest, or else you could turn aside toward the hill on which the church and the priest's garden stood, together with the cemetery, the parish school which Arseni had attended, the zemstvo school, the hospital, the horse clinic, and the copse. There was also a broad view of the rolling water meadows along the Savala, and in the distance the bend where it rounded the village, retreating here and there to touch outlying farms, then, farther up, the highroad, where it turned around on itself and vanished in the direction of the station at Rzhaksa. After surveying all this, and picturing his own future farm growing up there somewhere over the Savala, it was back to the table, where dishes not yet sampled had appeared, and you were invited to dunk limp wheaten pancakes in cream or wash down buckwheat cakes with tea.

After which the festive meal was crowned with golden slumbers.

During the holidays he also found time to overcome Sevastyan's shyness: he never passed the child without patting or stroking him. But the little boy still wouldn't come to his father's arms—he hid behind his mother or his grandmother. He could say "grand-da" and liked pulling the old man's mustache, but didn't know the word "daddy" yet. Never mind—three weeks would make all the difference. It was amazing how acutely aware Arseni was of the blood tie with Sevastyan. He didn't just know that this was his child, the child his wife had borne him. If the child had been hidden from him, if they'd told him that it was someone else's child, he would still have sought him out, blood would have called to blood. The little boy himself seemed to sense it—staring wide-eyed at his father, and once, just once, quietly snuggling up to him.

It wasn't just Sevastyan, though. Proska too, when she caught sight of her father from her cradle, dropped her pacifier and followed him with her eyes as far as she could.

Proska's eyes were like the sky on a spring day.

Today was the feast of Our Lady Comforter of All the Afflicted, and they went to mass again, but the service was shorter. In his sermon, as befitted the day, the priest told them that we all have sorrows, no one escapes sorrow, and things still worse, but that sorrows should unite us before God, not divide us, unite us more surely than our successes, our joys, and our festivals.

The congregation dispersed, and as they left Elisei and Arseni were approached by Pluzhnikov himself, a fine figure of a man with a pitch-black cowlick, an expensive dark blue serge coat, nipped in at the waist, and patent-leather boots with stiff, non-crease tops. He invited father and son to dinner in two hours' time.

Honoring the George medalist! And his father no less. Pluzhnikov was perhaps the most important man in the *mir*, not in terms of wealth or years, but in the estimation of the community. He had reached that position in the few years after the troubles. At one time no one could have foreseen that he would rise in the world: he had been a bit of a troublemaker, one of a handful of peasants whom the landowner Vasil' Vasilich, and Alyoshka Khersonsky, the deacon's son, surreptitiously incited against the Tsar. Vasil' Vasilich himself had gone off to France, but seven peasants from that district and two neighboring ones, Pluzhnikov among them, were rounded up and banished to Olonets province. In addition to this they had some sort of link with Socialist Revolutionaries in Tambov. Moreover, Pluzhnikov was at the time the elected head of a mutual aid society which collected money to buy land—money for which the SRs were supposed to have exchanged counterfeit notes on the very steps of the bank. Nobody really knew the ins and outs of the affair, but Pluzhnikov had spent two years in exile. When he returned he was unrecognizable: still a leader of men but a sensible one. He built himself a brick house, made his own farm profitable, with two hundred hives, bought extra land, and also started a credit cooperative, which gave peasants a chance to make good and greater freedom of action: instead of the bother of seeking out purchasers, and making long journeys themselves, they could dispatch produce through the cooperative, which would also make loans. Good? They had never known anything like it. In the few years before the war Pluzhnikov's efforts, his good judgment, and the advice he gave the commune had earned him, scarcely forty, the title of "bat'ka," but it hadn't stuck, it never became a street name, and people went on respectfully calling him Grigori Naumovich. He was recognized as a leader far beyond his own district.

Although Pluzhnikov had always shown his esteem for the older Blagodarev with a word of greeting, a bow, or by consulting him on some matter concerning the credit association, they had never eaten at each other's tables, and Elisei Nikiforovich understood that Pluzhnikov was inviting him mainly because of his son. This was still an honor, not an affront, for it was truly said, "Don't pride yourself on your father, pride yourself on a fine son": you don't choose your father and don't rear him, but your son is your own stock through and through, the fruit of your loins, for him you will be blamed and for him you will be praised.

With a dignified inclination of his head Elisei accepted the invitation for himself and his son.

A fine head, the old man had, and he carried it like a youngster. His gaze had become placid over the years, but was still so piercing that even Pluzhnikov abandoned that air of conscious superiority which he usually wore with peasants. Yes. Pluzhnikov had invited him because of his son, his son was becoming an important figure in the village, with his two George medals, he was literate, a high flyer. Pluzhnikov was looking forward to the rural reconstruction so close at hand, he already had a multitude of innovations and improvements in mind, and men like Arseni would be beyond price. But the father too was splendid. The Russian village was still as strong as ever, two years of war had not undermined it. Pluzhnikov had made it his duty to consolidate that strength.

Another man stood nearby, waiting for Pluzhnikov, dressed in a three-piece worsted suit with a silver watch chain showing over one pocket. This was their fellow villager, the greatly respected merchant Evpati Bruyakin, nothing much to look at, but worth thousands. The time had come for them to resume an important, not to say earth-shaking, discussion begun some time ago. Bruyakin had disclosed to Pluzhnikov his decision, not yet made public, to wind down his business and eventually stop buying and selling altogether. Pluzhnikov opposed the idea outright. He couldn't see the sense of it—the village's very own merchant ceasing to do business, for no reason at all, when things were going smoothly? Pluzhnikov had to go home, where a visitor from town was waiting, so he and Bruyakin walked off with all eyes upon them, to continue their discussion as they made their leisurely way down the dry slope and turned to pass the zemstvo hospital.

Evpati's father, Gavrila, had started the business, but Evpati had made his first excursion as a buyer, under his father's supervision, at the age of eight. At thirteen he already had a granary license—in his father's name to begin with, in his own from the age of sixteen—and had later obtained a license to deal in groceries and haberdashery. For thirty years now the whole district had known that Satya (his street name) "had everything." His shop was on the main street of Kamenka and the approach to it was strewn with shingle from the river. To one side of the building there were stacks of beams, panels, posts, laths, and planks, and hired hands sawed off lengths as required. Before the entrance stood a scale that could take up to forty poods, and a kerosene tank with a pump. The stout outer door and the shutters were secured by iron hasps and ring bolts. When only the glass doors were closed callers tugged at the bell rope and one of the family would come down from the second floor of the half-timber, half-brick house to serve them. The air in the roomy shop was heavy with smells to tickle a peasant's nose, and you didn't know where to look first. There were barrels of tar and linseed oil, crates containing axle grease, chalk, and lime, if you weren't careful you'd trip over boxes full of horseshoes and nails of all sizes, and sheets of glass stood in boxes against the walls. There were steelyards, with sets of weights of one pound and upward. There were felloes and yokes. Painted wooden tableware. Pottery—earthenware or china, dyed and glazed or unglazed—was ranged on shelves. Ovenware, jugs, pots, teacups, bread dishes. Farther along there were enameled saucepans, teapots, and mugs, cast-iron cooking pots, frying pans, and braziers. The other side of the shop was the place for barrels of herring and boxes of dried and smoked roach. On a landing up three steps, where they could more easily be lowered onto the scales on their way to a cart, were bast sacks containing salt, and bags of flour, granulated sugar, conical sugar loaves wrapped in blue paper and tied with string, packets in all sizes from the whole sugar loaf to an eighth of a pound. There was also small lump sugar in little boxes but there was no call for that, it melted too easily. In drawers that tilted outward there were slabs of gingerbread, gingerbread rings, bonbons, lozenges, toffee, chocolate coins, half ruble and ruble size, wrapped in golden paper, raisins, dates, figs, and prunes. (In summer there were also watermelons, muskmelons, and grapes.) As well as other provisions. There were cigarettes too—Shurymury, Uncle Kostya, and Koz'ma Kryuchkov, machines for rolling your own leaf tobacco, coarse-cut *makhorka*, cigarette paper, writing paper, exercise books, indelible pencils, colored pencils, writing slates.

But what Satya liked best was the drapery side—selling calico, satin, and even fine linen and silk. These goods brought him into contact with women, of whom he was terribly fond, and all the more so because he was no oil painting himself. He would load two carts with fabric and ride out to all the fairs in the neighborhood. These goods occupied the most eye-catching shelves in his shop. Shelves crammed with broadcloth, plush, and twill. Cloth for trousers, jackets, and suits. Woolen shawls and angora shawls, Orenburg and Penza shawls. Head scarves, and ribbons of all colors. You got goods down from the upper shelves with the aid of a ladder, or you might only need a pole with a fork on the end. On the counter lay rolls of oilcloth, each with one edge turned out to show the pattern. Under the glass lids were buttons of a hundred colors and sizes, pieces of lace, pins, hairpins, knitting needles, fine combs, large-toothed combs. Lined up on a stand, there were felt boots—ordinary ones, soft ones, hairy ones, black, gray, or white, and even some embroidered with red and green thread. There too were shiny rubber galoshes, men's and women's, shoe high or boot high. The one thing Bruyakin didn't sell was leather footwear. But he stocked dressed leather pieces. And this smoothly running machine, thirty years in the building, this source of wealth for himself and of comfort for the whole village he now proposed to run down, to shut off, to destroy. All at once to abandon his own way of life and deprive the village of its character. But why? What would become of all these good things?

Pluzhnikov was up in arms. But sure that he could talk Evpati out of it, nip his plan in the bud.

Evpati Bruyakin's expression was mild, almost obsequious, with never a stubborn line in it—no foothold there for contrariness. The merest wisp of beard, the merest wisp of mustache. He always looked the same—willing to listen, ready to learn, eager to oblige. Ah, but those eyes were shrewd, crafty, quick to see the main chance.

"Oh dear, Grigori Naumovich," he said with a sigh that summed up many nights of thought. "Ask a bird how it knows bad weather is on the way. Why it hides beforehand. When if it didn't it would be done for. Well, that's how I am. I have this feeling."

"Where do you get it from? Why haven't I got it? What signs are there?" Pluzhnikov, as was his habit, spoke with the voice of authority. "Business isn't falling off, is it?"

"No," Evpati agreed. "Not yet, not so you'd notice." But his eyes were prickly, resentful. "I can feel it, though. Like when they looted Anokhin's place in '05. And the Solovovs'. We're headed down that same road again."

"That's not the way things are going at all!" Pluzhnikov said. Stubborn as a mule! "Bigger and better opportunities for the peasants, that's what's just around the corner. We'll really get started after the war, just you wait and see!"

"Oh dear, no. Dear me, no, Grigori Naumych. Don't fool yourself. Business likes freedom. And there won't be any."

"Won't be any freedom?? Where d'you get that idea from? Won't be any? That's exactly what's on the way—freedom for the likes of us!" Black-haired Pluzhnikov's eyes flashed.

"Oh dear, oh dear, don't fool yourself, Grigori Naumych. Bad times are upon us."

"All the more reason to serve the *mir*! Having a merchant of our own makes the people stronger."

"Business and friendship are strangers." Evpati spread his hands, nimble, prehensile hands with strong fingers. "Best to shut the gate while the street's empty."

Pluzhnikov pierced him with a look. But there was puzzlement in it too. One of them was barking up the wrong tree. And Pluzhnikov wasn't used to being wrong.

He turned his mind to practicalities. "So then, who's going to take over? The cooperative?"

Bruyakin smiled briefly under his soft fair mustache. "Goods without a master are orphans."

"What about you—what are you going to do?"

"I might just buy an extra piece of land and expand my farm." As it was, he had never given up farming.

"Well, just wait a bit, don't make your mind up yet, let's think about it! What will you do with your stock? And all the rest? How will Kamenka manage? No, I just don't believe it!"

They stopped talking as they neared Pluzhnikov's house—a brick-built "five-waller" with a tin roof and brick lintels. It stood by the river, fronting the street, close to the bridge.

Bruyakin wanted to go home, but Pluzhnikov asked him in for a chat with a visitor from town. This was Zyablitsky, who had once worked for the zemstvo, but had since spent some years with a cooperative association and was one of its accredited buyers. He had set out for Kamenka on business early Monday morning with nothing further from his mind than Our Lady Comforter of All the Afflicted, unaware that the parish holiday had not yet ended—and so the only business he found himself doing was with beer and sterlet.

Pluzhnikov's wife, Agasha, and his mother-in-law were busy about the house, and the children were at home, so the men walked through to the best room. The man from town sat looking glum for a while, but suddenly cheered up. He was wearing town clothes—a suit and the whitest of white collars. Small spectacles framed his bright gaze. A puny fellow with a thin neck. He introduced himself. "Anatol Sergeich . . ."

Bruyakin could put on airs too. "Evpati Gavrilych."

Pluzhnikov laughed. "Go on, talk to him a bit, he'll entice you into the co-op as well."

The best room was seven arshins by seven, with three windows looking out on the street and three onto the stream, and even on a dark day, and through the flowers on the windowsills, and the lace curtains, there was light enough. The eighteen-inch floorboards were smoothly painted, with not a bump or a crack, and the walls were plastered and whitewashed like those of a town house. The room was furnished in town fashion too—not a single bench, but an oak wardrobe, a cupboard for the best crockery, a tall mirror with a carved frame—you could see yourself full-length in it—and a bedstead with hollow, nickel-plated posts (but, in country fashion, the coverlet had a flounce of homemade lace, there were two counterpanes, one showing from under the other, two pillows at the head of the bed and two at the foot). The table was not in the icon corner (indeed, there was no icon corner) but moved out into the middle of the room, covered with a deep red embroidered cloth and surrounded by bentwood chairs. There was also a hard sofa with a felted back, and a phonograph aiming its horn at the room from one corner, with an armchair beside it.

Pluzhnikov's motto was "Old is best—best got rid of."

In Zyablitsky's view it was Pluzhnikov and his like who gave the intelligentsia, and enlightened ideas, their entrée to the village. He himself had worked for over ten years first as a zemstvo statistician and economist and then in the cooperative movement, a representative of the "third element" so detested by the government for its "revolutionism," and no less despised by committed revolutionaries for choosing the anthill of "little deeds," worrying about grants and arrears, about goods bought or sold without excessive profit, but too soon consumed or worn out. Who could think of that as a worthwhile alternative to the enormous upheavals which would bring about the rebirth of mankind, brushed instantaneously by the fiery wing of salvation? Many leaders of public opinion and many progressive writers ridiculed those stuck in the dim bog of "little deeds" with no wider horizon beyond it. True, there were revolutionaries of the older school like Chaikovsky, who remained true to the doctrine that the one reliable means of access to the village for an intellectual was via peasant cooperatives. And the zemstvo intelligentsia, caught between the harassment of officialdom and the scorn of progressive youth, bravely and stubbornly stood their ground, labored patiently on, and lived to celebrate, with becoming modesty in the years immediately before the war, the steady expansion, indeed the full flowering of their patient activity, to succeed at last in capturing the villagers' imagination. For Zyablitsky the great reward had always been a chance to expound his cherished beliefs to enlightened villagers like those now before him. Pluzhnikov had not stopped at establishing a credit association, but had invited agronomists to lecture the villagers in the winter, and was now trying to organize an office for the leasing of agricultural machinery and a permanent agricultural advisory service. With allies like these, Zyablitsky believed, the village, and hence Russia as a whole, could be transformed.

"But one thing I must say to you, Grigori Naumovich, and to both of you gentlemen, is that practical people like you do not fully appreciate the significance of cooperation. It is not just a commercial mechanism, not just a means of maximizing profits by achieving economies. Cooperation is a broad movement, whose limits are the ideals of humanity. An elected cooperator is, in a manner of speaking, the people's first minister. The people instruct him, and the people call him to account. Cooperation teaches the masses to stand up for their legitimate interests in a state where the rule of law does not obtain. It is the spontaneous path to freedom."

He turned his smoothly brushed head to look at Pluzhnikov's big-boned face in its frame of black beard.

"I've always been for cooperation," Pluzhnikov said. "If anybody is, I am. But you can't pull all peasant Russia out of the mud with just cooperation, it'll take a stronger horse than that."

Zyablitsky was upset to meet with a rebuff even from this quarter. "Cooperation," he said more insistently, "must produce its own peasant intelligentsia. It must refashion customs and characters, continue the efforts of the populist school. That was the idea of our founder, Robert Owen. Any social order can choose as its base and its support either the best people or the rabble. And cooperation is there to help it choose the first."

That was a strange look on Bruyakin's face. Not cantankerous exactly. Withdrawn, unseeing. Zyablitsky had seen that look on peasant faces so often, and despaired. You could never read them, never get through to them.

"That's all very well," Pluzhnikov said, scowling, "but all we want co-ops for is to protect us from the towns. And people from the towns use them to get at us, and educate us. We don't need them. We can teach ourselves all we need to know."

"Of course you can," Zyablitsky said eagerly, lacing his fingers. "That's just what I'm telling you. But for the time being, how can you refuse help from the towns?"

"Help?" Pluzhnikov, wolfish, said. He appealed to Bruyakin. "When did we ever see any help from the town? Or anything except beggar-my-neighbor? The town's no friend to us. The town is the enemy!"

Bruyakin, with his "I'm not arguing but I'm not looking either" gaze, again silently assented.

Zyablitsky, alarmed, rocked back in his chair and threw up his hands. "Grigori Naumovich, I implore you! How can you set the two against each other in that way? Just read the newspapers, look at the debates in the Duma, see what they say at Zemgor congresses."

Pluzhnikov might look stolid but he could fly off the handle. He pushed his chair back from under himself, using his feet, not his hands, and rose.

"Martyn coveted nobody's riches, but kept his cash in his own britches. It's time the peasant spoke up for himself. I've read your Duma debates! All those arguments about how ministers should be appointed, that's all over our heads. The most literate of us can hardly make out what your Duma's saying, and it just irritates us. Now if we had a rural district zemstvo, that would be something. Those newspapers of yours, what Zemgor says—I read it all! And what do they write? That the village must be curbed, that the village is getting too rich, that's what those sons of bitches write! Hit the villages with lower prices!"

Prominent brown eyes ablaze under his forelock, shoulders squared, fist like a hammer.

He started pacing the roomy parlor in his creaky patent-leather boots, wide breeches, and embroidered silk shirt, held tight by a plaited cord, about-facing with military precision. He spoke from near the window.

"Rich, you say? Oh yes, everybody's got paper money, and they all deposit it with the association, but when it's been lying there a while what will you be able to do with it? Rich? With rye at a ruble and a half? Wheat at two-thirty? When boots"—he slapped his boot top—"cost seven rubles before the war, and now they're twenty-five? Meaning seventeen poods of rye."

The impassive Bruyakin sat motionless, hands together on his knees.

Pluzhnikov, now by the smooth-tiled stove, spoke from his full height. "Because the town has lost its conscience! If it ever had one. Who started it? The town! Who wouldn't let us have sugar? The town. So we started holding on to our eggs. Grain is cheaper now in Russia, not ten times dearer, like everything we get from the towns. They skin us alive, and then they gnash their teeth at us."

Zyablitsky, following Pluzhnikov's movements, fidgeted as if there was a hedgehog on his chair.

"Come, come, Grigori Naumych!" he implored. "You go too far, you mustn't draw such extreme conclusions! It simply isn't right to say that the town is the village's enemy!"

Pluzhnikov went back to the table and tapped it gently with his fist. "That's just what it is, though—the enemy!" The vase tinkled assent. "Take yourself—you're a good friend, a nice fellow, but you're only here for our grain, aren't you? To 'take inventory of our stocks.' For the zemstvo, of course, between friends, not to confiscate any of it. But then the governor will issue a decree saying confiscate it all, and you'll roll up to do the job."

"Come, come, Grigori Naumych," Zyablitsky implored, "how can you! You're much too harsh! Who would ever dare forcibly remove grain from your barns?"

True, it almost defied belief: to take by force what it had cost blood to grow? And anyway, would the peasants let them do it?

What—that flimsy, dainty little man with the rooster's neck—take grain from the village? Laughable!

Pluzhnikov, still on the march, by the door now: "I'll tell you this much, the army we don't mind feeding, of course. But the towns? The profiteers, the banks? No, we do mind! The crowd that's gathered in Russia's towns now, all sorts and conditions of people, the whole of the western provinces, all stepping on each other's toes, none of them are doing any work—and the Tambov peasant is supposed to feed them all? Think again! When you get back, you can tell them that we won't give up our grain as easily as that! Get it into your head: the peasant's like a bear spear—once dug in there he stays. We'll give grain for the army, of course, but for Petersburg—no, we won't!"

That was when Agasha came in, still in her holiday best, just as she had been in church, except that she had tied an apron over it, as fresh and brightly colored as the rest—and still wearing brand-new seamless galoshes over her indoor shoes. She had brought a linen cloth, to lay the table, and also a message: "Evpati Gavrilych, your son's come for you, he says come home, you've got guests."

Time for Evpati to go, then. And he still hadn't said a thing. Might as well not have been there. Ah, but he'd listened carefully, heard every word.

The woman had something else on her mind. She called to the boy in the hall: "Kolya, come on in here."

Fourteen-year-old Kolya came in, looking sheepish. His auburn hair stood in curly tufts. He was big for his age.

"Some ladies' man you are, can't even comb your hair," Agasha declared. "Evpati Gavrilych, did you know this boy of yours had started going with grown women?"

Kolya gave himself away by blushing furiously.

"Still," Agasha said approvingly, "you can see he has some shame left."

Evpati shot a shrewd glance at Kolya, then at Agasha, and said simply, "Oh?"

Dubiously. But not looking for an argument.

Kolya's cheeks were on fire. He couldn't help it.

"You didn't know, then?" Agasha seemed happy about it. There's no game women enjoy more. "Make him tell you himself. People have seen him going there."

"Well, that's soon fixed," Bruyakin said, laughing. "Lie down on the bench, get your backside smacked, and marry the wench."

They took their leave.

Women are nasty creatures! Kolya was frightened and angry. Always spying and prying and their tongues are sharp as razors. We've been careful—how did it get out? He was cold with fear, expecting his father to pitch into him at any moment, and still not sure whether to own up or lie his way out of it. Just as long as the old man didn't tell his mother. She wasn't his real mother, but better than a real mother to him. He would be ashamed if she knew.

They were outside now and his father still hadn't said a word. Kolya was very surprised. They walked on side by side, in step—still not a word. Would the storm break at home? Did he mean it, the big stick? That would be worse still. After Marusya, whose husband was away in the army, Kolya Satych felt more or less grown up. But against his father and the big stick he was still powerless.

His father remained silent. Miraculously. Nothing could be surer to rile him than Agasha's revelation. But he was bottling up his anger.

In fact, Kolya's father had other things on his mind. He was going over again his decision to go out of business. It would be a breakneck swerve, a sort of betrayal of his own father and of himself, putting an end to something handed down from generation to generation. And nothing told him clearly that he ought to stop. This or that was in short supply, but it would sort itself out once the war ended. Still, a kind of tightness in his chest warned Bruyakin of troubles as yet unknown, and he was half afraid that he might not be in time to wind up his affairs. That would take a year, if not two. Some of his best goods, those that weren't perishable, he could keep back, to make a killing when better times came. Have to find a good hiding place. Talking to Pluzhnikov, and even listening to that outsider, had only helped to convince him in some obscure way that life was about to change completely, and that freedom to do business was a thing of the past.

As for the boy, yes, it was news to him, he hadn't known. At fourteen? A bit early. Still, he recognized his own flesh and blood in his younger son. The older one wasn't like that, but his own father, Gavrila, had had the same weakness, and used to mend looms and distaffs and sharpen spindles for village women, more often for love than for money. Evpati's own first name, in fact, meant "sentimental." He had been about Kolya's age when he started sniffing around women. And from that day to this he hadn't lost his liking for them—not with his first wife, nor with his second—he liked making presents of fine cloth on the sly, and had his own reasons for liking weddings, and dances at the fair, where you could slip the women a few drinks (he never touched spirits himself) and have fun with them when they got tipsy. But Kolya? At fourteen? Oh well, good for him. Let him get on with it, the sooner he grew up, the sooner he'd be able to help out, though he'd been able to harrow and reap and mow since he was ten.

Kolya still couldn't feel the ground under his feet, but began to take heart: his father was saying nothing!

Swarthy Marusya was twenty-two, and came from near the Tambov powder mill, but had married into Kamenka. She had heard from her husband during his first year in the army, but not after that. She must have gotten bored and restless as soldiers' wives do. She had taken notice of the boy first, and she had sent him messages, through a woman friend and the friend's young man. She could have chosen an older boy, of course, but he was the one she took a fancy to. Which was when Kolya Satych first realized that there was something special about him. He knew what it was all about, he'd known since he was seven, playing weddings with little girls, but before Marusya he hadn't tried it for himself. Her cottage was on the edge of the village, over toward the Savala. He made his way there furtively, his heart beating wildly, and abandoned himself to her tyrannical passion. She wouldn't even let him undress himself, she took off all his clothes, kissing him here, there, and everywhere, petting and teasing him, taking her pleasure in every way she could think of. Her eyes were like glowing coals, her lips brick red, and there was a deep flush on her cheeks. She licked the boy into shape and taught him all sorts of diabolical tricks.

Kolya Satych began to feel grown up. And although nobody in the village knew—Agasha was the first to let the cat out of the bag—he noticed that girls seemed to sense something in him and he could now see right through them and treated them differently, affectionately. His head was in a whirl, he craved excitement, and forbidden pleasures. As Marusya once told him, with her rippling laugh: "That's when we're happiest, my little Kolya, when our eyes show no shame. Now you're like that too." It annoyed him a lot that his father still made him go to the zemstvo school even though he was older than his classmates. And he was never going to cope with all he was supposed to learn.

What he most wanted right now was to latch on to a gang of young toughs, all of them at least two, some of them four years older than himself. The leader of this gang was Mishka Rul, the champion prankster, brawler, and daredevil. Rul's father still sometimes tried to beat him, but Mishka fought him off: "Lay a hand on me one more time and I'll stick a knife in you." To gain entrance to this gang Kolya had already started stealing from his father's shop—cigarettes for the boys and goods he could exchange for moonshine liquor, to treat them to a bottle. He listened enviously, slavishly, to stories of the wild tricks they had already played or were planning. Rul made fun of all who objected to his behavior or threatened to cut him down to size. Now they were trying to think of tricks they could play to exasperate the priest. The boys listened openmouthed to Rul's tales of his exploits.

"Remember when Mokei Likhvantsev's Thoroughbred stallion got loose? Nobody knows it, but that was me. Know why? He was too eager to establish order in the village, so I decided to get my own back on him with his lovely Lipa, and enjoy myself with lovely Lipa while I was at it."

The boys could only gasp at his daring. But how had he managed it?

"I was on the lookout for when he and Lipa went to the bathhouse. It was nearly dark, and I sneaked into his yard and let the stallion out. Then I knocked at his niece Lushka's house, two doors away, and said run to the bathhouse and tell your uncle the stallion's gotten loose and run off to the meadows! Then I watched from behind the bushes while Mokei got dressed and rushed off to look for the stallion. I knew he'd be at it a good two hours. So I walked into the anteroom of the bathhouse slow-like and got undressed. Lipushka was splashing about on the other side of the door. She thought her husband had come back. I went in and said, 'It's only me, Rul, don't be afraid.' There was a dip burning, she saw me, cried out, and scrambled onto the sweating shelf to get away from me, 'Get out of here,' she says, 'or I'll scald you.'

" 'Splash me just once,' I said, 'and I'll stick your head in the boiler, and that's where you'll stay.' 'Get out! I'll tell Mokei!' 'When I go you can tell him,' I say, 'but while we're waiting—come down from there, Lipushka, onto the floor.' 'I'll scratch you to pieces!' 'And I'll rip you to bits!' Then I pulled her down from the shelf, and she's really soft. Women can be like that—really soft. She tries to struggle. 'Look,' I say, 'if you thrash about like this I'll tell Mokei myself, and say it was you who put me up to letting the stallion out!' 'I'm done for,' she moans, 'it's curtains for me. What have you done to me, you villain? Well, the sin will be yours.' 'All mine,' I said, 'all mine.' So then she relaxed and gave in to me."

The boys howled with glee. What a hero! If only we could do the same!

Kolya felt faint with envy, with a jealous yearning to do desperate deeds of his own.

Rul pointed up the moral. "So remember, boys, when you get married don't trust your wives. There's always some bachelor hanging around to take advantage. You can never be sure of them. And she didn't tell Mokei, of course not."

[46]

Pluzhnikov, wearing an embroidered shirt and baggy breeches like those of an officer, was waiting for the Blagodarevs on his front porch. He shook hands, yet again, first the father's, then the son's, and led them into the long entrance hall. While they were taking off their hats and coats outside the parlor door Agafya emerged from the back room to pay her respects. Agafya Anastasyevna to some, plain Agasha to others, was not much older than Katya, and they had gone to the same girlish get-togethers. Small children peeped out from behind her. But the master of the house invited his guests into the parlor.

There they were introduced to a guest from town, who tentatively offered a soft hand. "Anatol Sergeich."

The Blagodarevs settled for the sofa, Pluzhnikov pulled up an arm-chair and sat cross-legged, and the man from town found himself a seat. Agasha came through the other door, from the living room, to set the table: there was a clatter of gleaming spoons, she deftly distributed forks with black-and-white bone handles and shiny town-bought knives, placed heavy glazed tankards, tumblers, and wineglasses on the table, and came back with jugs, decanters, a fat Caspian herring on an oval platter, looking for all the world like a sterlet in aspic, and other cold dishes, together with a tomato salad, mushrooms of all descriptions, and homemade cheese—enough to feed a dozen. After all they'd eaten those last few days you wouldn't think there was room for another morsel, but their eyes took note of it all as they talked. It eased conversation and favorably disposed them toward their host.

Agasha was wearing her Sunday best—a light blue cloth sarafan, with the puffed-out white linen sleeves of her petticoat showing from underneath it. She was sturdy, robust, and not too thin in the arm. Her back was unbent, and her head, with its thick straw-colored plaits gathered at the temples, was held high as she carried in the heavy trays. She walked quickly, but not with mincing steps, quickly but noiselessly in her galoshes.

Pluzhnikov took the lead, warmly declaring that what Kamenka needed was more fine young men like Arseni. The war, he said, will not go on forever, and when it ends all those heads and hands, with all they've picked up in far-off countries, will come in handy here at home, life won't be the same after the war, it won't go on in the old way, we'll be like somebody who recovers from a mortal illness and is a completely new man afterward, seeing and doing many things as he never did before.

The elder Blagodarev eyed him closely. That keen gaze from under the corn-colored eyebrows had always been able to sight a distant sail on Lake Baikal, or a mouse a hundred sazhens away in a field. In that room his vision was so much better than it need be that he squinted to avoid seeing too much. Or perhaps he was trying to look through the man and decide whether he meant what he said.

He did. Pluzhnikov thought about life in the round, not just what to do next as he rose each morning. He did the thinking for the whole community.

He had a lot of questions for Arseni about the war. Did they have enough arms? Enough shells? Was it true that they now had plenty of everything? Men as well? Companies and batteries at full strength?

Maybe a bit too full, Arseni said. It's terrible in the trenches, men falling over each other's feet, a single mortar shell can finish off five at a time. Truth is, so many of us Russians have been knocked out they're filling the gap with non-Russians and non-Christians.

What do the soldiers think about it all? What do they talk about among themselves?

What do they talk about? What we talk about isn't worth knowing: it's who's been under bombardment or in a gas attack or caught some shrapnel lately. Or else they talk about the old woman, wonder whether she's playing around back home, or else about the farm, and how they're getting along back there without enough working hands, or about how the Germans shoe their horses differently from us, or about how the Belorussians . . .

All right, but what do they say about the war in general? When do they think peace will come? Have we got the strength to fight on to the end?

The thing is, the Germans on the staff will be too much for us. If there weren't any traitors . . .

Are there any?

Actually, maybe there aren't. It would be mighty hard to take if there really are. Then there's a lot of mud slung at Rasputin.

Both Blagodarevs were angry with Rasputin. After all, he started out as a peasant himself, and look at him now, shows how much we can rely on our own kind. Once a peasant rises in the world he gets too big for his boots, forgets his own people, he's worse than any gentleman. Just think, somebody who's climbed so high he may have humped the Tsaritsa herself still won't stand up for the peasant. Here you're hit with fixed prices, you can't get a nail or a scythe—and back there he's gorging and swilling?

Pluzhnikov dismissed it. "That's all silly gossip." He wanted to get at the root of things. Rasputin or no Rasputin, Grigori Naumovich refused to believe that it was no good putting your hopes on the peasant. The peasant was the only hope! He, and no one else. Peasants could only be saved by peasants, by themselves! And it was time they woke up to the fact.

Next month, November, there was to be—just imagine—what they called a congress of small landowners in Petersburg. Maybe something sensible would come of it.

Was Grigori Naumovich invited?

"I don't know, I'm waiting to hear. They promised to send me a ticket from Tambov, but I don't know if they will."

And so—to the table. Each had a side to himself, Arseni facing Pluzhnikov, his father facing the guest. Town fashion: a large plate and a small one before each of them, spoons stuck in the food on the serving dishes, but watch your manners, no helping yourself from the dish straight into your mouth, load the food onto your plate first (funny idea all the same—dirties the plate and lets the food get cold). Eat what you've put on your plate, and don't take more until you're asked: "Please, help yourself, it's not there just to look at!" Arseni had seen these town ways among the officers, and only hoped his father wouldn't let himself down. No, it was all right, the old man was treading cautiously, taking no risks, looking neither to right nor to left. But the worry of it all tied his tongue and his thoughts as with ropes.

The host took hold of a big jug of home brew and filled and refilled tankards with thick, brown, oily-looking braga, and the braga was all froth the moment you took a pull at it.

"All right, first toast to the one who counts most! Agasha, come on in! To our George medalist! May he get through the war with glory and come back whole to his children, his wife, his parents, and all of us. Many are no longer with us—and we need heroes!"

There was a hollow clatter of earthenware as tankard met tankard. The braga was made from honey, not grain. Brewing it had kept Agasha busy for several days. You could drink yourself silly on it. It was strong all right!

Agasha didn't sit down. She drained her tankard standing up while the men remained seated, and bowed to Arseni. As to an elder. Although they had joined in the same fun and games at one time. That was how much the war had changed things.

Oh, how it warmed the blood, that braga! Bursting with his own strength, replete with the honor shown him, Arseni didn't know what to do with all those hands, all those heads . . . Ah, well, might find a use for them sometime.

The guest from town, who had sat down at the table without crossing himself, now turned gleaming spectacles on the Blagodarevs and paused between mouthfuls to ask, "How do you, gentlemen, feel about cooperation?"

Arseni kept silent. His young memory was so cluttered with -ations and -utions and -itions—cooperation, mobilization, revolutions, requisitions—it was like trying to force your way through a plantation of young fir trees.

His father, though, was an old hand. He rose to the challenge immediately.

"How d'you think we feel? When nails were two rubles a pood before the war, and now they're forty? We can't mend a plow or a harrow, we haven't even got the wherewithal to shoe a horse. Or grease an axle. And you can't get a harvester or a winnowing machine at any price."

The visitor looked like a child never yet beaten or pulled by the ears and expecting nothing but kindness from life.

Agasha had been bustling around quietly, visiting the stove in the kitchen, revisiting the table, encouraging them to eat up as she came and went, but taking care not to interrupt this men's talk. But when she heard the bit about prices she flew off the handle, and attacked the townsman as if it was all his fault.

"And what about sugar? A ruble and a half a pound—who ever heard of that before? An arshin of calico used to cost twelve kopecks, now it's ninety! What gets us down is that townsfolk jack up prices whenever they feel like it, and hide the goods somewhere." Agasha flared up quickly. One minute she was watching every twitch of her husband's eyebrow, the next she was up in arms. Once she got started she'd tell a few home truths.

Pluzhnikov chuckled, and seemed to be enjoying it. He rested his black beard on the strong arch of his folded hands, and explained to Arseni in his booming voice: "Cooperation means an association. It can be a credit association, like ours. Or a savings and loan association."

"A-a-ah . . . It's like an artel, you mean?" Arseni still wasn't sure. It was a lot to take in all at once. Never a good idea to hurry things.

The man from town showed his white teeth and spoke in still more honeyed and complacent tones, trying to soften the older Blagodarev's stern gaze, but not forgetting the son.

"An artel, yes, but one embracing the whole district, the whole province, all Russia in fact."

Grigori Naumovich put it more simply: "If we had right now one strong, unified cooperative system we would know where to buy cheaply, whether it was in Nizhny or in Moscow. And the profiteers would be out of business. And artels would exchange goods directly— ours, Ponzari, Panovy Kusty. An artel could make its deliveries to the War Ministry directly—and the requisitioning officer would also be out of a job. What's more, an artel could register reserves in its own locality, which is something the plenipotentiaries will never manage."

Elisei Nikiforovich reacted to the word "plenipotentiaries" with something like a groan. "This winter they took our cattle off us just at calving time. Cows were calving out on the roads. They were slaughtered. But there wasn't enough salt, and the carcasses rotted when the thaw came."

Who needed to be told all this? Who was he arguing with? He and

Pluzhnikov weren't differing about anything, and this empty-headed little pouter pigeon cutting his food into smaller and smaller pieces, eating, stowing it away—we aren't having such a high old time of it in the towns, says he. Strip him of his glasses and his starched shirt, give him a haircut like ours, country style, and he still wouldn't look like a peasant, just a weedy slip of a boy. Anyway, he's not a town merchant, he doesn't make things of his own in a factory, all he's brought with him is his soft talk. So maybe he's here to spy on what grain we've got?

There was nobody to argue with, but Elisei Nikiforovich, once launched, poured his heart out, eyeing the townie with a piercing, angry look that would have reached far beyond the walls of the parlor, challenging him to understand.

"Why do we have to give up our grain for nothing? Those jabberers in town are out of their minds. There's a fixed price for everything the village lets the town have—why no fixed prices the other way? There's a war on, you say, so let's all behave like brothers. That's all right. We muzhiks have got nothing against being brothers: take our grain, all of it if you like, without money, only give us your goods without money as well! Like we used to before—a pood of iron for two poods of grain, a scythe for a pood of grain—that'll suit us fine! Prices can be firm or otherwise just as long as we don't have to break our backs for nothing. The peasant will slog away as long as he can put one foot in front of the other. But this way he's going to bust a gut for nothing!"

Arseni was no longer familiar with all these different prices, he had no idea what cost what, all that had slipped his memory: you paid for nothing in the army, and you paid for nothing on leave. He felt remote from all that the three of them, his father included, were saying. His body, and not just his head, was still back there in the trenches. They had still not come home. He was a guest blown in by the wind. He sat quietly, filled up his plate, and went on eating with never a word. The other men, though, were becoming heated.

Agasha came and went quietly over the smooth, snugly fitted board floor, never a heavy step, never a shuffle, brought in an egg-and-cabbage tart, hot from the oven, gave each of them a portion, carried out the empty plates, and hardly another word was heard from her.

Pluzhnikov meanwhile poured drinks—a quick glance, a quick tilt of the bottle—braga, cordials, liqueurs were all on hand. Elisei had the bit between his teeth now, expanding his chest, like a trotter rushing uphill.

"Handfuls of paper—what kind of money d'you call that? That's not being rich! We're rich when we've got grain in the barn, cattle in the stall, and our fields seeded. When spring comes around, will we have enough seed to sow with? And if—God forbid—they start calling up more men before spring, who'll be doing the work?"

The townie was so hot under the collar that he stopped eating and drinking and sat twisting his fork like a bradawl in a piece of pie crust, eager to answer back.

Agasha, just as quietly as she had moved about the room, now placed a chair at the townie's side of the table—he didn't take up much room—next to her husband, on his right. And sat down demurely. She took little sips from a tumbler, and listened.

Pluzhnikov had not frowned at any of her comings and goings, or checked her with a gesture, and he showed no surprise when she sat by him: clever woman that she was, she had not fallen down on her job, so let her sit in on our men's talk. A man's wife is his crowning glory.

Arseni looked and learned.

Pluzhnikov, just back from Olonets province, and widowed earlier, had singled out Agasha when she was no more than eighteen, but already a handsome and competent woman. So that although he had married only a little earlier than Arseni, he was more than twenty years older than Agasha, and his older daughter by his first wife had married before her. But as husband and wife sat side by side, more or less the same height, you could see from their whole demeanor, from the way they held themselves, that she was not a daughter to him, but all that a wife should be, his prop and, if need be, his replacement. Pluzhnikov was tough and a go-getter. Why shouldn't he have a young wife? Take more than that to frighten him.

The townie, who perhaps wasn't to blame for any of it, had by now twisted his bit of pie crust into a shapeless mess. He put down his fork.

"Tell me, though, Grigori Naumych, what you mean by saying you won't give grain to Petersburg. And why Petersburg in particular?"

Agasha pushed the suckling pig and the horseradish closer to him.

Pluzhnikov poured him some liquor. And helped him out.

"That's only a manner of speaking, of course—saying we won't give grain. Right now the peasant is giving everything for the war, you know that yourself, Anatol Sergeich. Tambov province always used to market fifteen poods per desyatin, now it's twenty-five, and the co-ops have helped quite a bit there. The cattle—they've taken thirty thousand head from our district. They took a pair out of every four, without stopping to think whether they were pedigree or dairy cattle. *Our* cattle, I'm talking about—they don't touch the gentry's pedigree herds at all."

The townie wasn't looking quite so aggrieved. "But that's as it should be: they're the best of their kind, the best breeds . . ."

"As it should be—maybe. But it says in the paper that in our district Count Orlov-Davydov—a member of your State Duma, remember . . ."

"Ours, Grigori Naumych," the guest implored, "yours and mine equally . . ."

". . . concealed two hundred and forty head of cattle. Now it's come
to light, and they've put the estate manager on trial. The count's supposed not to have known. No, if it's everything for the war, let it be
from everybody. Why does it always have to be just from the peasant?
They've gotten used to our patience."

The town! Pluzhnikov went there often enough, he wasn't long back
from a trip—and there were still so many young men there, crowds of
idlers! Hordes of directors of this and plenipotentiaries extraordinary
for that, every one of them exempt from military service. Did they
think the peasants were blind, couldn't see what was going on? Gentry
landowners had extra help sent to them, but when did we ever get
any? Except maybe a few women on their own, with five children. And
there was one fellow always in the tavern. And they've started paying
crazy wages in the towns—a laborer pulls down five rubles a day, so
our girls have started running off to the towns . . . Everybody wants it
easier.

Elisei chimed in again. "Cattle, horses, harness, carts—we hand all
of it over, and for less than it's worth. And they make us supply transport free, just like the old days. No, they don't spread it around fairly.
They strip the village naked and haul everything to the towns."

Pluzhnikov's turn again. "That Duma of yours shouldn't have split
into left and right, they shouldn't spend all their time picking on one
another and voting each other down. Every deputy ought to be his
own man from his own place, and whatever his own place tells him,
whatever he can see with his own eyes needs to be done, that's what
he should say. If you divide up into parties and keep rooting for your
own party all the time—that can only divide Russia and bamboozle
people."

Well, well! Wasn't he an SR himself at one time? Seems you can't
go through life without shedding a few feathers.

Elisei had listened dutifully, but had something to add. "The Duma
ought to be helping the Tsar. The Tsar's there to put our lives in
order."

Pluzhnikov hadn't finished. "We peasants will never get justice from
a Duma like that. In fact, we'll never get justice from the town at all."

Zyablitsky was more and more dismayed. He looked utterly despondent. He couldn't have been more dismayed if his wife had run away
from him. He hung his head, propped it up with his hand so that his
glasses would not fall off. Or perhaps he was a bit tipsy: our braga's
strong, and you never get a snootful in town nowadays!

"But what do you mean by justice?" he asked in a thin voice.

Pluzhnikov, big-boned, and not short of flesh either, went on drinking as though he hadn't taken a single swig. His gaze was sober and
steady. With his lustrous eyes and his pitch-black beard he could have
been a Gypsy—many Tambov people have such looks.

"That's just it: where does the peasant look for justice? I've thought

about it a lot. Is the canton ours? No, it isn't ours. The canton headman isn't *our* chief, all he knows how to do is carry out orders from
the constable, the inspector, and the superintendent. He and the canton administration are there to meet the endless demands from higher
up. That's what keeps all those clerks busy scribbling. For starvation
wages, by the way. What drain do our canton and zemstvo dues go
down? And when they rope us in for village meetings it isn't for something vitally important to us, it's for some business of their own, which
we don't always understand. We aren't allowed to decide anything.
We just stand there trying to keep our feet from going to sleep. Am
I right, Elisei Nikiforych?"

The elder Blagodarev confirmed it, looking fierce.

Pluzhnikov could have been freshening his thoughts for the forthcoming congress of small landowners. "The zemstvo? How can it be
our zemstvo when we only elect candidates, and the land captain graciously makes his own selection from them? Anyway, since the war
started the zemstvos have had the same itch to give orders. What do
they send us from the district zemstvo? Nothing but orders to deliver
so many cattle, so many horses, so many carts. And now here you are,
Anatol Sergeich—I'm not criticizing, you're a good man and you sympathize with us, I know, but you've never in your life had anything to
do with grain, and now they've sent you all looking for grain, counting
up what stocks we've got, am I right?"

The townie couldn't look him in the face. His glasses were about to
slip off.

"A canton zemstvo, where we, not the gentry, get together and decide things for ourselves, like in credit associations, they won't allow.
Or if they do, they'll twist it into something like the canton board,
and we'll be no freer."

Elisei waved the word away. "Free? All our lives—no freedom."

That little word "all" came like a heavy groan from deep inside him.

Pluzhnikov looked around the table expectantly. Agasha started—
had she forgotten something?

No, his hand rested briefly, tenderly on hers.

Agasha blushed furiously, flattered by her husband's open show of
affection. But raised herself by a head, pretending that nothing happened.

"The commune?" Pluzhnikov shook his bull-like head. "They've
been trying to make it work for fifty-odd years now, twisting it into all
sorts of shapes, this way and that. But no. That's not the cart that can
get us a thousand versts from here. Thanks be, Stolypin released us.
So—they murdered him straightaway. Who? What for? Take your
pick. There was a whole bunch of them, all in it together. He improved
our lives, and took the landlords' cheap labor from them, so they killed
him. Who d'you think killed the Tsar Liberator? The peasants could

never have done it. But the landlords—there again, he'd taken their unpaid labor away, and they couldn't swap serfs for hounds anymore. That's the way it is—the town's our enemy, and the landlord's our enemy."

"They wreck all the Tsar's good wishes," Elisei said sternly, weightily. "They don't carry out orders."

Pluzhnikov, relaxing, propped up his heavy head with both hands. "The village is losing heart. Our peasants are being killed in their thousands at the front. All these call-ups, requisitions, and fixed prices will be the death of us. The town organizes its congresses, conferences, committees, political parties—but there's nothing like that in the village. Who's ever going to do anything for us? Anatol Sergeich here and his friends? Don't take it amiss, Anatol Sergeich, but you aren't strong enough by a long shot to carry us with you."

"So there we are, Grigori Naumovich, there we are, gentlemen." Zyablitsky was coming back to life. He had mended his smile. He looked around at each of them in turn, including Arseni, and even Agasha, as though asking them to be his guests. "So you and I have agreed that cooperation can be a great help in our lives."

Pluzhnikov demurred. "That's not the point. We don't say no to cooperation, why should we? In fact, after the war we will band together to buy expensive machines, we can't avoid it, nobody can get by with a sickle and a flail anymore. After the war working hands will never be as free again as they were."

But that was just what Elisei Blagodarev couldn't get into his head. Why should everything change so completely after the war? We remember other wars—nothing changed then!

"Nothing changed after the Turkish war, of course. But after the Japanese—didn't it just . . . in ten years the village was unrecognizable. Think how much extra land we bought, how much building we did. Remember how we used to dress."

True enough.

"After this war there'll be even bigger changes. Russia's never fought a war like this in all its existence. I'm telling you the country will be as different as if it was getting over a deadly illness. We have to use our heads, and get ready for it."

He looked hard at Arseni.

And this time Arseni didn't feel superfluous. The drink had made his feet hot and his legs weak, but his hands felt as strong as ever. This is where I may prove useful, he thought. Must learn to listen and understand.

Pluzhnikov sat up straight on his chair and tugged at his shirt, pulling it close to his back under the braided belt. He was halfway between the two Blagodarevs in years, in his prime, as they say: he had lived long enough to acquire wisdom, but was not yet losing his strength.

"What does our class amount to—the peasants? How are we treated? The moment anybody rises in the world through education or as a reward for service he's promoted to 'personal honorary citizenship' and no longer counts as a peasant. Anybody who gets on in life is lost to us. But anybody who's deprived of his rights, any ex-convict, is lumped in with us. To turn us into a herd of cattle. And we're subject to separate authorities. Subject to the landlords again, through the land captains." Hands on hips, solid, a fighter, and intelligent. "That freedom you talk about—they're supposed to have given it to us fifty years ago—so why don't we just take it?"

Elisei suddenly cleared his throat and spoke in a deep bass voice that his son had never heard before. "I tried to. It wasn't to be had."

When was that, Dad? I never knew.

Pluzhnikov snapped back at him. "You have to take it. Nobody will force money on you—and it's the same with freedom. If you're offered the chance. No help is forthcoming. Neither from Petersburg nor from Moscow. Neither from the town nor from the landlord. Nor from the SRs. Because the SRs, however much they try to ingratiate themselves with the peasants, don't think like peasants, they just sing along. And what do we do? We keep on dreaming, we wait for the powers that be to tell us what to do. And what *they* do is send us papers and papers and papers. And there's nobody to shout"—Pluzhnikov raised his voice till the parlor was too small for it, the walls couldn't hold it, it could be heard in the Prince's Forest—"nobody to shout, 'Hey, Russia, take hold of it yourself!' "

Agasha's lips parted, showing her pearly teeth, as she gazed, fascinated, at her husband.

Zyablitsky recoiled, alarmed by this roaring. But Pluzhnikov had nothing more to say. And Zyablitsky plucked up his courage to argue.

"You have distressed me greatly today, Grigori Naumovich. You don't like the Duma. You don't like Zemgor. Or the parties. And you say cooperation is weak. Criticism is always easy. But what positive proposals have you got?"

No more theatrical voices from Pluzhnikov. With his hands at his sides, his fingers in his belt, he said, "One thing's clear: the townsfolk—all those officials and bigwigs—let them look after themselves as best they can. We aren't asking for equal rights with them, so why don't they just leave us alone . . ."

Who'd be a woman! She didn't want to miss anything, but everything had been eaten and drunk and it was time to clear the table for tea. She rose, saw at a glance what to pick up, and carried it away.

". . . and those of us who live around here can take matters into their own hands! And look after ourselves. The canton? It can cope. The rural district? It can manage without the *uyezd* center! And even the provinces—why not peasant government, without the towns? We can live our own lives, and the town can do what it likes, we aren't hindering it. Why do we have to let somebody else govern us, instead of doing it ourselves? Who gets the power, who has the last word? Anybody rather than the peasant. They must think we're a lot of utter blockheads. Mushrooms grow in the country—but the town knows about them too!"

His lustrous eyes flashed.

Devil take it—he's got it all worked out! A village boy like the rest of us!

Elisei Nikiforovich stared straight ahead, stern and unsmiling. He sat squarely on his chair, without a word.

Zyablitsky, however, cheered up a little, waved his small hand, and complacently laid out his wares. "That's your typical peasant utopia! It's five hundred years old, and nowhere, neither in Europe nor in Asia, has it ever been realized. Just think, Grigori Naumovich, how would it work organizationally? Given the unity of the state's functions, how can you possibly have peasant autonomy without the framework of a modern state? In a war with external enemies, for instance? And when you need a single economy and a single administrative and transportion system? Can't you see it's utopian?"

"What it would be like we don't yet know," Pluzhnikov said, rejecting Zyablitsky's sympathy with a shake of his head. "It needs thinking about. Such a big country needs a lot of different governing bodies. And somewhere among them there would be room for peasant self-government."

That was his sticking point. And he was right. What d'you think we are, blockheads? Arseni felt the rightness of it keenly. Something would come of it, there must be a breakthrough someday.

His father, however, wasn't at all pleased. He gave their host a rather dark look. But there was more to come.

"We aren't short of people even now, we're still strong enough, even with this war on, think of all the men with good heads and strong arms we could get together to discuss things and give advice! Paramon Kryzhnikov, Aksyon Frolagin, Kuzma Opolovnikov, Mokei Likhvantsev. Am I right, Elisei Nikiforovich?"

Arseni had noticed already that his father was worried, uneasy. But he had never been one to react hastily. When he spoke it was in measured tones, and without a nod of the head.

"There's no shortage of fools among our folk as well. All right, the gentry have their fair share, but who says we don't? When the gentry's estates were plundered in '05 some people who only had twenty desyatins more than the communal allotment were plundered just the same. And all those who aren't ashamed to do it still help themselves to Davydov's wood and hay. We graze our cattle on his meadows. He doesn't fence himself in, so we trample all over him. If you give people like us a free run—you'd better look out!"

He thought for a minute, and summed up in ringing tones before Pluzhnikov could reply. "People's faith has been shaken, that's what. And letting them govern won't help matters."

The little guest from town was determined to make his own point. "Very well, then, let's suppose that the right forms of government can be found. By what route do you propose to get there?"

"By what route?" Pluzhnikov answered, arms still akimbo. "We're not going to put bombs under provincial governors, that's for sure. But you'd have to be more than human to know in advance. Just wait a bit, and things will start going that way without our help. When they do we mustn't miss the crucial moment."

Agasha, meanwhile, had brought in the samovar, with some rich buns and pastries. She filled glasses with strong dark tea.

Zyablitsky's spirits were rising all the time.

"You can't base realistic calculations on such hopes. You have no realistic means to suggest, Grigori Naumych. And I'm glad it isn't bombs. You should return to the original way—lively cooperative activity, in the broadest possible sense!"

The tea had come at the right time to wash down the fish and the cold meats, and there was white lump sugar on the table, with cakes of all sorts. But there was a knock at the veranda door.

Agasha went down to see who it was, came back and said in a low voice, "It's Panyushkin, the clerk. Wants you."

Pluzhnikov hesitated. Should he go outside?

"Oh, all right, ask him in."

Semyon Panyushkin came in, wearing a short velveteen jacket, without overcoat, clean and tidy as always. His own unaided efforts over a number of years had raised him to the position of canton clerk. He had grazed cattle in summer and studied in winter, and had been promoted because of his good sense.

In stature and bulk he was much like Zyablitsky. His hair was greased and smoothed down. His manner was modest, with no trace of self-importance. He bowed, wished them a happy holiday, and was invited to the table, but hesitated, obviously wanting to speak to Grigori Naumovich in private.

"Is it a secret?" Pluzhnikov made as if to move into the other room.

The clerk, first repository and custodian of secrets, sighed. "No, certainly not. It has to be announced anyway. I just wanted to let you know first."

Pluzhnikov had no official position of any kind. But he was "the old one," so the clerk had come to tell him first. Out of respect. They sat him down, gave him tea, sugar to go with it, and a layered bun.

He wasted no time in telling them, taking a piece of paper out of an inside pocket. It had just been delivered.

A decree dated 5 November announced the call-up of category 2 militia, men aged thirty-seven to forty, together with all those omitted in the previous drafts. Enrollment would begin on 7 November (tomorrow).

A bolt from the blue!

The day was nearly over, the revels were ending. Another hour or two and inviolable darkness would descend upon the village. There would be loud voices in cottages, and people would be late putting out their oil lamps and dips and wax tapers, but nobody would be touched till morning, no need till morning to shoulder those white bags with provisions, harness the cart, and set out, with the womenfolk seeing you off, for Sampur to report to the recruiting officer. The night is ours. One last, sad night, sleeping beside the wife of your bosom. Only she mustn't sleep, she has to stitch your food bag together. The night is ours, but maybe get the stove going again? No, everybody's got enough baked already.

That's war for you, that's how it makes its entrance, like an iron wedge straight into your chest. In its third year now, it had become a fixed and familiar feature of their lives. Those who had been killed were already dead and buried. The living had, as best they could, been holidaying, storytelling, playing accordions, then suddenly a piece of paper from a canton clerk's pocket is unfolded—and the whole street is stricken! Its future had begun unfolding right there, on Pluzhnikov's table.

Who would be taken?

They were picking off men up to forty, the very prime of life for a peasant. Nobody forty-one or over would be touched just yet.

Pluzhnikov began reading out names. Some quickly, some more thoughtfully. He had only Christian names, patronymic, surnames, and dates of birth before him, but saw each name ringed with questions: how many would be left in this family, how many children in that, how would they manage the farm?

The recruiting officer was giving them a close shave. He was taking the miller! The miller, would you believe it! Who would replace him? Would the mill stop grinding? It was a trade that had to be learned, after all.

They were taking boss-eyed Afonka. Not such a great loss to Kamenka but still . . . You gave him your hemp straw and didn't have to bother with it, he'd twist your ropes for you and you settled up later. Would everybody have to do it himself now? You'd never get around to it.

Nikifor Big-ears was hitting the road too! Held on as long as he could . . .

What about the Snooper? Wasn't he about the same age? Yes, they were taking the Snooper.

What about Long-fallow, then? No, he was just above the cutoff.

Look at this, though! They're taking the blacksmith! Kuzma Opo-lovnikov!

"What!" Like a burst of flame from Elisei. "Are they out of their minds?"

"He's the right age."

"Only you can't measure everybody up just by age, who's going to mend our plows? Or shoe our horses? What are we going to do, the whole village? Do they ever stop to think?"

The stupidity of it riled Elisei so much that he rose. And paced the room. What were they going to do? Letting Kuzma Opolovnikov go was like losing your own son. (They were in fact related. He was Do-masha's second cousin.)

"Senka!" he said loudly, as if Senka was to blame. "I thought you said you had plenty of men."

"They're sitting shoulder to shoulder in the trenches."

"What about blacksmiths?"

"The brigade's got enough blacksmiths. We could spare you one."

He and Katya had an elaborately patterned wrought-iron bedstead made by the same Kuzma—not a store-bought bed, like the Pluzh-nikovs'—one that would sleep six, or you could dance a bear on it. This Kuzma, nicknamed Pile-driver, a bit of a cutup but a good worker, was always whiskery, but when Senka had sat next to him at table yesterday he had been, for once, clean-shaven. Senka had teased him, telling him he ought to be in the army, but not really meaning it, not envying him.

Senka never envied those who had avoided the war. You couldn't change things anyhow. If everybody went, things would still be no easier. It was the luck of the draw.

The blacksmith, though—you couldn't help being sorry. He was a first-class blacksmith, not everybody had one like him.

"Aren't they taking Wet-leg?"

No, they weren't.

Wet-leg, Vasya Tarakin, was younger than Arseni. He had been sub-ject to regular military service in 1914, and when war broke out was called up with the first draft. Off he went, with the rest of them, but he was home again in less than a month. How come? Got a full set of arms and legs, haven't you? Caught some complaint, perhaps? No, nothing like that. I told them I wasn't going to kill people.

How d'you like that! If he'd been called up in peacetime and re-fused, it might have made sense. But before the war he hadn't said a word, hadn't let on, then when everybody had to go and fight, he backs out. Kamenka didn't like that. It wasn't what the *mir* expected: if the others were all going, you should go—what makes you so special? Till then nobody had noticed anything bad in Vaska Tarakin. He was the oldest of six children, his father had died when he was fourteen, and he had started farming and tailoring like his father before him. Then his sister had grown up and brought a husband home. Vaska, no longer the sole breadwinner, was called up. Of course, you could feel for him, with all those mouths to feed. Still, others had enough of their own, nobody was particularly enthusiastic about the war, but if everybody had to go—then let it be everybody, if it's good enough for them it's good enough for you. Ah, but with the tailoring he'd gotten into the habit of reading—those little books that cost two or three kopecks apiece. Count Tolstoy, says he, has opened his eyes to the idea of Jesus Christ. We all live because the Father of our life wills it, and no one except the Father may take life.

So that was how Wet-leg had managed not to go to war. He was called up on two other occasions—and was very soon back home again. So anybody could act the holy fool and sit pretty till the war was over. "What about pigs, then?" Grandpa Bayunya had asked him. "Or sheep? They're living creatures as well, given to us by the Father of our lives." Vaska acknowledged it, and stopped slaughtering and eating animals. His brother-in-law carried on slaughtering, though, so the family didn't want for meat.

The situation now was that they had given up trying to draft Wet-leg. They had decided to leave him in peace.

Pluzhnikov gloomily pored over the list. He could not take his eyes off it. They were draining the village of its strength—those he had mentioned a while ago, Paramon Kryzhnikov, Kuzma Opolovnikov, Mokei Likhvantsev, and all the others. Making a clean sweep. He himself was close enough to the broom. Just another year or two. One more draft like this . . . Who, then, would there be to win *freedom* for the peasant? Whose efforts would help the village to stand on its own feet? They were like wolves, carrying off lambs between their teeth, and whenever they came again, in six months or one month, whoever they singled out, Kamenka would have to surrender him.

There was no one to cry out to, no one to tell that it was not sensible to drain the village to such an extent. Should they summon a village assembly? Send delegates to the police superintendent? What resistance could the village offer? Where could it make itself felt?

Elisei and his son, meanwhile, were trying to work out which of Domasha's distant cousins, or relatives in neighboring villages, would be roped in. They shouldn't sit there drinking tea, it was time to go home, the holiday had abruptly ended.

Semyon, the clerk, told them something else. A clerk is more than the papers he receives, he can see what is coming. In a few days' time, he said, there would be a decree calling up the 1898 class. They would not be taken till next spring, but the order would be promulgated now.

You mean they won't even leave the boys at home till they're nineteen? They'll be drafted before that?

So that means Zinovi Skuropas?
And Lyoksa Tevondin?
Both good boys!
Mishka Rul, though, let him go and fight!
Time to leave.
"Elisei Nikiforych!" Agasha said. "Senya! Your tea!"
"Thank you, from both of us, Agasha, you've made us very welcome," Senya's father said. "But you know what they say—guests and the harvest should be brought home in time."
The holiday was at an end.
While they had been sitting with Pluzhnikov it had gotten chillier and darker and the wind had grown stronger. The mud churned up in the middle of the street had hardened and frosted over and the beaten tracks in front of houses had frozen hard. The wind was picking up dust and gravel, carrying them, whirling them, sweeping them from one end of the village to the other.
Elisei had this to say about their host: "He's a useful man. But mark my words, Senka: if a crock's once had tar in it there's no burning it out."
The wind rose, slamming garden gates and doors more and more loudly. Or perhaps they were banged by people running from house to house with the news.
Bad news does not rest, does not leak out gradually, it rushes through the village, as if borne by this wind. Semyon would have needed only to whisper it to one or two before going to Pluzhnikov, and every cottage would know it by now. In some there was already the sound of women wailing. In others they were still wondering—is ours among them?
Next morning would come the upheaval—everyone on the move, a long line of men straggling along the Sampur road, with women wailing. And those interminable songs. The creaking of wheels.
You couldn't get on with your life. They wouldn't let you settle down to anything.
The way the weather was—cloudy, frosty, a ground wind—there would be snow before long.
"If the snow sticks on frozen ground we'll get down to the meadows, Senka."

*   *   *

Fall in round the flag, brave boys,
All who're fit to tote a gun.
Let 'em have it hot and strong, boys.
Get old Jerry on the run.

Stock Exchange News

[4 7]

To establish regular secret contact with anyone you please, without ever meeting face to face, you need only set up a chain of intermediaries—at least two, but preferably three. Your immediate contact habitually meets twenty people besides yourself, only one of whom is the next link in the chain, and each of these meets twenty others. This gives four hundred possible combinations, and no secret police, no Burtsev, can ever investigate all of them.

The ultra-cautious Lenin had several such lines of communication.

Last summer, after meeting Parvus in Bern, Lenin had released Hanecki to join him in Scandinavia, as director of his agency for trade and revolution. However, the line between Copenhagen and Zurich was down, so they had chosen a new intermediary—Sklarz, a Berlin businessman, who also had shares in Parvus's agency and could travel freely both to Denmark and to Switzerland. They had, however, agreed that when he came to Zurich he should follow the rules about intermediate links and not meet Lenin personally, but use Bronski's lady friend, Dora Dolina, as his go-between. The fact that he had come to Lenin's lodgings in person meant either a breach of conspiratorial discipline or that something extraordinarily important had happened.

How untimely it was, though! Lenin was exhausted, he could not think clearly, his heartbeat was irregular. But since Sklarz had come, since he had been seen on the street, on the stairs, at the door, it was too late to turn him away.

To greet Sklarz he had not merely to rise from the bed but, with his enfeebled legs, to project his hollow body upward from the bottom of a well. And only then, with his head thrust forward, could he see the energetic little Galician Jew.

Very conscious of his own importance he was, too, more expensively dressed than ever—that overcoat, that hat (he had placed it on the one and only desk-cum-dining table, but still, there was nowhere else), and he was holding a light traveling salesman's case made of crocodile skin or maybe hippopotamus hide.

At least he refrained from the ritual German *"Wie geht's?"* and the forced how-nice-to-see-you smile. He gave a businesslike bow and extended his little hand with dignity. He looked around to see that it was safe, that there were no witnesses. Nadya had left the room, and they were alone.

Why, though, had he come straight there and in person?

Here it came. From a deep inner pocket he produced an envelope.

Expensive pale green paper, with an embossed crest. A fat envelope, a positively obese one.

How shamelessly Parvus displayed his wealth even in little things! This envelope, for instance. And on his visits to Zurich he stayed in the most expensive hotel, Baur au Lac. In Bern he had ambled about a cheap student canteen (dinner sixty-five rappen) in search of Lenin, puffing the most expensive of cigars.

To think that this was the man with whom in Munich long ago he had started *Iskra*.

All right, he had a letter. But why couldn't he have sent Dora with it? These lightning visits had to be explained to *comrades*.

Sklarz was surprised to find Herr Ulyanov so ill educated. That was no way to do *business*. He had been told to destroy the letter before leaving.

His finger went through the motions of striking a match and holding it to the envelope.

Tell me something I don't know. What d'you *think* we do? The letters we've burned in our time! . . .

All right, let's read it. A familiar situation for anyone in the underground. Lenin too would have to ensure that his reply, once read, was not preserved. One such scrap of paper could destroy a whole political career.

Neither knife nor scissors was handy. The table was bare. And Nadya was in the kitchen. Tearing off one corner, Lenin inserted his thick index finger and used it as a paper knife. It left jagged edges like dog's teeth on both sides of the tear. So much for you and your blasted money! How much pleasanter to handle the cheapest of envelopes, to write on the cheapest paper.

He took out the letter. That's why it was so fat, because the paper was even thicker and more opulent than the envelope. And the letter was written in bold capitals, with wide spaces between the lines, and on one side only. Now here was the way not to do *business*. Parvus had forgotten how they used to send *Iskra* into Russia on super-thin paper.

Careful. He must pull himself together, clear his mind. (He had eaten nothing since breakfast time.) Must examine it thoroughly.

Sklarz made himself unobtrusive. He was not troublesomely familiar. Without superfluous talk, without even removing his coat, he went over to the other chair, by the window, leaving, however, his soft gray hat with its elegantly dented crown on the table.

He did not carry his case over to the window either but put it down on the floor in the middle of the room.

Polite of him, of course, but on a dull day the best place for reading was over by the window. Sklarz, however, had already occupied the other chair, taken a crumpled illustrated magazine out of his pocket, and solemnly unfolded it.

Should he light the lamp? No matches in sight. And Nadya was in the kitchen.

But the lamp was already lit! It was half hidden by the hat, and its wick was turned all the way down. Had Nadya lit it? He didn't remember her doing so. Perhaps Sklarz really had struck a match? Could he have . . . ? Strange.

Thick vellum, crested. Three pages of writing altogether. And a fourth, empty except for one line.

There was nothing special about Parvus's handwriting—it was not noticeably hostile, or imperious, or impertinent, and his signature, "Dr. Helphand," was unrevealing.

But Parvus's hippopotamus blood spurted from the letter into Lenin's feverish hands, poured into his veins, swirled threateningly in his bloodstream. To prevent it from rising above his elbows Lenin dropped the letter on the table as though it were heavy. And flopped down helplessly on his chair.

In twenty years of life and struggle Lenin had experienced every kind of opponent—the haughtily ironical, the sarcastic, the sly, the base, the obstinate, the persistent, not to mention the spluttering-rhetorical, the quixotic, the effete, the slow-witted, the lachrymose, and other miscellaneous shits. With some of them he had been engaged for many years on end, and not all of them had he sent flying, laid out with a blow, but he had always been aware of the immeasurable superiority given to him by his clear view of the situation, his firm grip, his ability to floor any of them sooner or later.

With this man alone he felt unsure of himself. He did not know whether he could stand up to Parvus as an enemy.

But there had hardly been a day of enmity between them. He was Lenin's natural ally, had offered an alliance many times in his life, insistently, importunately, last year in particular, and now of course was doing it again.

But alliance with Parvus was something which Lenin had hardly ever been able to accept.

He read. His eyes moved along the lines, but somehow his head would not take in the meaning. He was too unwell.

Lenin knew the key to open every Social Democrat in the world, knew the shelf to put him on. But Parvus would not open, would not be put anywhere, and he stood across Lenin's path. Parvus did not fit into any classification. He had never joined either Bolsheviks or Mensheviks (and had even naïvely attempted to reconcile them). He was a Russian revolutionary, but at nineteen he had come here to Switzerland from Odessa, and immediately chosen the Western path, decided to become a purely Western Socialist and never return to Russia. He had said jokingly, "I'm looking for a homeland which doesn't cost too much." All the same, he hadn't found himself a cheap one, but had knocked about Europe for twenty-five years like the Wandering

Jew, never acquiring citizenship. It was only this year that he had finally become a German subject—but at too high a price.

His eyes happened to fall on Sklarz's case. It was so heavy, so tightly
packed. How did he lug it about? He was so small himself. Why did
he need it?

Ah, that was why he didn't seem to be able to read—there wasn't
enough light.

Two points at the end were clear enough. Both complaints. One
against Bukharin and Pyatakov for their overzealous investigation of
the German network in Sweden: these silly little boys must not be
allowed to get out of hand. The other against Shlyapnikov: he is very
self-willed, refuses to collaborate, goes his own way, although unity is
essential to our forces in Petersburg. Write and tell him not to rebuff
our representatives.

He called himself Parvus—"little"—but was indisputably big. He
had become one of the outstanding publicists in the German Social
Democratic Party. His capacity for work was no less than that of Lenin.
He had written brilliant Marxist articles, which had delighted Bebel,
Kautsky, Liebknecht, Rosa, and Lenin himself (how he had lambasted
Bernstein!), and had brought the young Trotsky under his sway. Then
he had suddenly abandoned his newspapers and the position he had
won for himself in the journalistic world, and fled, first to peddle
Gorky's plays (and of course rob him), then to sink out of sight altogether. His vision was keen and far-reaching. He had been the first,
back in the nineteenth century, to start the fight for the eight-hour
day, the first to hail the general strike as the main method of struggle
for the proletariat. But it could hardly be said that any proposal of his
had started a movement, won him followers: instead of organizing
them he would detach himself and drop out after a while. He had to
be first, and alone, on the road he followed.

Lenin had now read the letter all the way through, without even
noticing whether it was written in Russian or in German. It alternated
between the two from sentence to sentence. There were spelling mistakes in the Russian.

Parvus was full of contradictions. A desperate revolutionary, whose
hand would not tremble while overthrowing an empire; and a passionate trader, whose hand trembled as it counted out money. At one time
he went around in broken shoes and shiny trousers, but back in Munich in 1901 he was forever dinning into Lenin the need to get rich,
the immense power of money. Earlier still, back in Odessa, while Aleksandr III was still on the throne, he had come to the conclusion that
the liberation of the Jews in Russia was impossible until Tsardom was
overthrown—and immediately lost all interest in Russian affairs, left
for the West, returning clandestinely only once, as the companion of
a doctor specializing in the study of famine, after which he had pub-

lished *Starving Russia: A Traveler's Impressions*. Then he seemed to have immersed himself completely in German Social Democracy. But at the very beginning of the Japanese war, which was almost ignored in Geneva émigré circles, Parvus had been the first to declare it "the bloody dawn of great events."

There was not enough light. He kept screwing up the wick, but it only smoldered and smoked. Of course, it was empty, she'd forgotten to put kerosene in it.

There and then, in 1904, Parvus had prophesied that the industrial states would end up waging a world war. Parvus invariably leapt or, rather, with his unwieldy bulk, stepped forward to prophesy earlier, and farther into the future, than anyone else. Sometimes his predictions were very accurate, as, for instance, that industry would destroy national boundaries, or that in the future revolution would be the inseparable companion of war, and world revolution of world war. He had, in essence, said before Lenin all that there was to be said about imperialism. Sometimes, though, he talked the wildest nonsense: about Europe as a whole declining and being caught in a vise between America and Russia; about Russia needing only schools and freedom to become a second America. Another time, showing scant respect for the central tenets of Marxism, he had suggested that private industry should not be nationalized, because it might prove unprofitable. Then there was his grotesque fantasy about the possibility of a socialist party winning power and turning it against the majority of the people, suppressing the trade unions. But, right or wrong, his massive, elephantine figure always moved to a position so distinctive that he half blocked the Social Democratic horizon: though he had never wholly blocked the true path, he had always been so much in Lenin's way that there was no passing him without collision. Never an opponent, always an ally, but one who, if you were not careful, might crush your ribs. He was, uniquely, incomparably, Lenin's rival—and more often than not successful, always ahead. Yet in no way his enemy, always extending the hand of an ally—but it was quite impossible to take it.

What did Sklarz want with that case? It looked as big as a pig.

Things might have gone very differently between them, but for 1905. Lenin had taken no part at all in the 1905 revolution, done absolutely nothing—entirely because of Parvus: Parvus with his heavy and unerring tread, never straying for a moment, had filled the road ahead, and robbed Lenin of the will to go forward, of all initiative. At the first thunderclap of Bloody Sunday, Parvus had made his proclamation: *Set up a workers' government!* His quick-sightedness, his impetuosity had taken even Lenin's breath away: surely decisions could not be taken so swiftly and simply! And he had retorted in *Vperyod* that Parvus's slogan was premature and dangerous, that they must act in alliance with the petty bourgeoisie, with the revolutionary democrats, because the proletariat was too weak! But Parvus and Trotsky had scrawled a hasty pamphlet and flung it at the Geneva émigrés, Bolsheviks and Mensheviks alike, as a challenge: Russia had no experience with parliaments, the bourgeoisie was feeble, the bureaucratic hierarchy was insignificant, the peasantry was ignorant and unorganized, so that the proletariat had no alternative but to take command of the revolution. Those Social Democrats who recoiled from the initiative of the proletariat would become an insignificant sect.

The whole Geneva émigré community, however, had stayed lethargically where it was, as though to make this prophecy come true—all except Trotsky, who rushed to Kiev, then to Finland, drawing closer to make his jump, and Parvus, who charged in at the first signal of the October general strike, which, once again, he had been prophesying back in the last century. Neither Bolsheviks nor Mensheviks, these two were free from all discipline, and fellows in audacity.

Yes, it was the size of a large pig. Its swelling bulk blocked the whole room. While Sklarz, by the window, seemed surely to have grown smaller?

It's not something I could put on paper, or say at the most restricted conference—but yes, I did make a mistake. Belief in yourself, political maturity, skill in assessing situations, all come to you gradually, with age and experience. (Though Parvus was only three years older.) Yes, I made a mistake, I was shortsighted, and I wasn't bold enough. (But you must not talk like that even to your closest supporter, or you may rob him of his faith in his leader.) Yet how could he have avoided making this mistake? The months had dragged by in that year of turmoil and confusion, everything was in ferment, there was thunder in the air, but it never looked like real revolution was going to break out. There in Geneva, still unable to travel, he was filled with indignation: couldn't those dolts back home get a move on, couldn't they start a proper revolution? He wrote letter after letter to Russia: energy is what is needed, frantic energy! You've been babbling about bombs for half a year now and haven't made a single one! Let everyone arm himself at once as best he can—with a revolver, a knife, a gasoline-soaked rag for starting fires, anything! The combat groups should not hesitate, there would be no special military training. Let each group begin training itself—if only by beating up policemen! Or by killing a plainclothesman! Or blowing up a police station! Or attacking a bank! These attacks, of course, might degenerate into reckless extremism, but never mind! A few dozen casualties would be handsomely repaid if the Party gained hundreds of experienced fighters!

No, his tired mind would not take in this untimely letter. He read on, understanding nothing.

. . . It had all seemed so obvious. Knuckle-dusters! Clubs! Gasoline-soaked rags! Spades! Guncotton! Barbed wire! Nails (for use against mounted police)! These were all weapons, and good ones! If one Cossack is accidentally cut off from the rest, attack and take his sword from him! Climb to the upper stories of buildings and rain stones down on the troops! Pour boiling water on them! Keep acid up there to pour on the police!

Parvus and Trotsky had done none of these things, but merely arrived in Petersburg, issued a proclamation, and convened a new organ of government: the Soviet of Workers' Deputies. They asked no one's permission, and nobody hindered them. A pure workers' government! Already in session! Although they had arrived a mere two weeks before the others, they had taken control of everything. The chairman of the Soviet was their man of straw, Nosar; its outstanding orator and general favorite, Trotsky; while its inventor, Parvus, directed it from behind the scenes. They had taken over the struggling *Russian Gazette*, which sold for one kopeck and was popular in style and tone, and suddenly its sales rose to half a million and the ideas of the two friends flowed out to the masses.

Over by the window, Sklarz had slid lower in his chair, shrunk till he looked like a little bird with its beak buried in a picture paper.

During those last days in Geneva, Lenin's pen had raced to spell out the whole theory and practice of revolution, as he had learned it in libraries from the best French authorities. He had kept up a rapid fire of letters to Russia. They needed to know how large a combat group should be (from three to thirty people), how to maintain communication with Party military committees, how to choose the best places for street fighting, where to store bombs and stones. They must find out where the arsenals were, and the working routine in government offices and banks, get to know people who could help them to infiltrate and take over . . . To begin an attack under favorable conditions was not just the right but the direct duty of any revolutionary. Fighting the Black Hundreds would be a splendid baptism of fire: beat them up, kill them, blow up their headquarters!

He had gone to Russia on the heels of his last letter, and found things there very different. No combat groups were being formed, no one was laying in acid, bombs, or stones. He found instead that even the bourgeois came to listen to the Soviet, with Trotsky on the platform spinning and whirling and coruscating like a Catherine wheel. He and Parvus, as though born for a life in the public eye, dazzled all Petersburg—the editorial offices, the political salons—they were invited everywhere and received with applause. There was even a group of people calling themselves "Parvusites." Instead of sneaking around corners with gasoline-soaked rags, Parvus was preparing a collected edition of his works, Parvus was buying up tickets for satirical shows and distributing them to friends. A fine revolution, if in the evening there was no measured tread of patrols on deserted pavements and theater doors were open wide . . .

He couldn't run over to the window—the swollen black case stood big as a trunk in the way. And there was no strength in his legs.

In that revolution Lenin had been bruised by Parvus, as though he had stood too near an elephant. He had sat at meetings of the Soviet, listening to the heroes of the day with his head in his hands. Parvus's slogans, repeated and read out over and over again, were perfectly correct: after the victory of the revolution the proletariat *must not let go of its weapons, but prepare for civil war! It must regard its liberal allies as enemies!* Excellent slogans, and he himself was left with nothing to say from the platform of the Soviet. Everything was going almost as it should, indeed so well that there was no room for the Bolshevik leader. His whole life had been adjusted to the demands of the underground, and his legs would not carry him up into the broad daylight. Lenin had not gone to Moscow when the rising began there, no longer caring whether the insurgents were following his own, earlier instructions from Geneva or someone else's. His self-confidence had failed him, and he had skulked through the revolution in a daze, sitting it out in Kuokkala, forty miles from Petersburg and over the Finnish border, where he was safe from arrest, while Krupskaya traveled to the capital every day to gather news. He couldn't understand it himself: all his life he had done nothing but prepare for revolution, and when it came his strength had ebbed and deserted him.

Next, from the shadows—he always tried to operate behind the scenes, not to get in front of cameras, not to provide material for biographers—Parvus had fathered an anonymous resolution on the Soviet, its Financial Manifesto. What looked like a set of uncouth and primitive demands from the illiterate masses was really the program of a clever and experienced financier striking at the foundations of the hated Russian state, to bring it down in ruins at a single blow. Give Parvus his due—it was a superb, a most instructive revolutionary document. (But the government too had seen its significance and arrested the whole Petersburg Soviet on the following day. As it happened, Parvus was not present, and had survived to set up a second Soviet at once, with a different membership. They came to arrest this new body, and again Parvus escaped.)

There was no kerosene in the lamp, yet it had been burning for an hour, giving no less light than before.

It took years for the ribs dented by Parvus to straighten out again, for Lenin to regain his assurance that he too was of some use in the world. What had helped most was seeing Parvus's mistakes and his failures, seeing this hippopotamus, this elephant, crashing blindly through the thickets, his hide punctured by broken branches, seeing him stumble into holes in his headlong charge. He had been expelled

from the Party for misappropriation of funds, become a ruthless profiteer, boozed with his bosomy blondes in public—and ended by openly
supporting German imperialism: he had expressed his views frankly in
print and in speeches, and defiantly left for Berlin.

The hat behind the lamp shifted and revealed its satin lining.

No, it was lying quietly, just as Sklarz had left it.

Rumors had already reached Lenin, through Christo Rakovsky in
Romania and David Ryazanov in Vienna, that Parvus was coming to
him with *interesting proposals*—so careless was he about covering his
tracks. But Parvus's reputation as an undisguised ally of the Kaiser had
preceded him, while he was boozing in Zurich on the way. They were
all used to poverty, year in and year out, and suddenly their former
comrade turned up in the role of an Oriental pasha, something of a
shock to the émigré mind, but also a source of largesse. When he had
found Lenin in the canteen at Bern, wedged his enormous belly behind
the table, and loudly declared in the presence of a dozen comrades
that they must have a talk, Lenin, without hesitation, without even
thinking about it, had replied with a curt rebuff. He had come from
warring Germany to chat like a peacetime tourist, had he? (Lenin was
no less eager for a talk!) Well, then, Lenin must request him to *take
himself away again!* (It was the only possible thing to do!)

The handle of the big case flopped to one side.

But they had to see each other, of course! They couldn't keep putting things on paper, in case one of their letters fell into the hands of
enemies. So Lenin whispered to Siefeldt, who ran after the fat man
and gave him the address. (Lenin told Siefeldt afterward that he had
sent the shark away unfed.) And in the Ulyanovs' spartan room the
broad-beamed Parvus, with diamond studs in his dazzlingly displayed
cuffs, had with some difficulty seated himself on the bed next to
Lenin, lolling against him and pushing him toward the pillow and the
iron bedstead.

Snap! The suitcase had finally burst open . . . and, freeing his elbows,
straightening his back, he unfolded, rose to his full height and girth,
in his dark blue three-piece suit, with his diamond cuff links, and,
stretching his cramped legs, he came one step, two steps closer.

There he stood, life-sized, in the flesh, with his ungovernable belly,
the elongated dome of his head, the fleshy bulldog features, the little
imperial, looking at Lenin with pale watchful eyes. Amicably, as ever.

True, true—they should have had a talk long ago. They had always
talked in hasty snatches, been out of touch or at loggerheads, and it
was so difficult for them to meet: with enemies, and friends too, on
the lookout. The utmost secrecy was necessary! But now that he had
found his way here, this was better than writing letters. The critical
moment for an eye-to-eye talk had arrived.

Izrail Lazarevich! You surprise me! Whatever has become of your remarkable intelligence? Why are you so indiscreet? Why have you put yourself in such a vulnerable position? You yourself are making it quite impossible for us to collaborate.

No hello, no proffered hand (and it was just as well, because Lenin lacked the strength to rise and greet him, his hand seemed paralyzed, and a hello would have stuck in his throat), Parvus simply slumped, not of course on the chair, but on the bed again, his unwieldy bulk sprawling against Lenin and squeezing him into the corner.

Training his protuberant, colorless eyes directly on his companion's face, he spoke with casual irony, teasing a friend, not addressing an audience.

"I'm surprised too, Vladimir Ilyich. Have you still nothing to occupy you but agitation and protests? What's the use of all this childish noisemaking? All these so-called conferences—thirty silly women in the Volkshaus one day, a dozen deserters the next?"

He unceremoniously pushed Lenin farther along the bed, and his unhealthily enlarged head loomed close.

"Since when have you sided with those who want to change the world with a broad-nibbed pen? What children all these Socialists are, with their eternal indignation! But you mustn't be like them! If you want serious *action*, should you really be hiding in holes and corners, not letting it be seen where your sympathies lie in this war?"

Although speech was still difficult his head was clearer, as though he had drunk strong tea. Even without words they understood each other perfectly.

Well, of course, this was no pathetic Kautsky, demonstrating "for peace" and refusing to meddle with the war.

"Neither of us looks at war like a sister of mercy. Casualties, bloodshed, suffering are inevitable. What matters is the outcome."

Well, of course, Parvus was utterly right. If Russia was to be shattered, Germany must be victorious, and they must seek German support. So far, so good. But Parvus had overstepped the mark. Not for the first time.

"Izrail Lazarevich, if a Socialist has one real asset, it is his honor. If we lose our honor, we lose everything. Between ourselves, the closeness of our positions naturally makes us allies. And of course we will need each other and help each other very much. But nowadays you are politically in such bad odor . . . It would take just one Burtsev to ruin everything. So we will have to make a show of disagreement, attack each other in the press. Not a full-time controversy, of course . . . just occasionally . . . so if I should call you . . ." (even face to face Lenin never moderated his language: the more harshly you speak, the better you understand each other) ". . . if I should call you, for instance . . . Hindenburg's morally degenerate toady . . . that renegade, that filthy lackey . . . you can see for yourself that you leave me no alternative . . ."

"By all means, it doesn't matter a bit." A bitter smile creased Parvus's puffy face. "In Berlin last spring I was given a million marks, some of which I sent at once to Rakovsky, to Trotsky and Martov, and to you here in Switzerland—did you get it? . . . What? You weren't aware of it? Do please check with your treasurer, maybe he's pocketed it . . . Trotsky took the money . . . although he'd already publicly disowned me. 'Falstaff in politics' he called me . . . He's written my obituary before I'm dead. I say nothing. It's all right, of course, I understand."

A fixed, glassy stare from under the faint raised brows. Parvus and Trotsky had parted company earlier over the theory of permanent revolution. He had loved Trotsky like a younger brother.

But now he had high hopes for Lenin, and leaned on him with all his pudgy immensity, forcing him farther and farther along the bed, until he was sitting on the pillow and could feel the headboard against his elbow.

"Aren't you afraid that mere slogans will be a dead letter without money? With money in your hands, power will be yours! How else will you seize power? That's the unpleasant question. And if you don't mind my saying so, I seem to remember you in 1904 taking what looked very much like Japanese money for the Third Congress and for *Vperyod*. That was all right, wasn't it? And now I'm Hindenburg's lackey, am I?" He did his best to laugh.

It was just like the last time. Perhaps it *was* the last time? . . . In Bern, in the room he had rented from a housewife? Or was he in his room in the Zurich cobbler's house? Or not in a room at all? He seemed to be hearing it all for the second time. No table, no Sklarz. Just a massive Swiss iron bed, with the two of them upon it, great men both, floating above a world pregnant with revolution, a world which looked up to them expectantly, as they sat with their legs dangling, and the bed sped again around its dark orbit. There was just enough light from some invisible source for him to see his companion, just enough sound for him to hear.

"Never mind . . . It's all right . . . I understand."

Parvus despised the world. That world, far below, under the bed.

"As I see it, if you want to *convert the war into a civil war*, one ally is as good as another. At present you have—*how much?*" He was being funny. "I won't ask you, it isn't done. But I have—not for myself, but for the *Cause*—well, I got a million last spring, and I'll get another five million this summer. And there's plenty more to come. What do you say to that?"

He and Parvus alike had always despised the émigré community for its unreality, its ineffectualness, its driveling intellectualism—it was all talk, nothing but talk. But money was something more serious. Oh, yes.

Lenin was sickened by his self-assurance, but fascinated by the reality of his power.

Parvus opened his pale eyes wide and smacked his lips under the straggly mustache.

"The Plan! I've produced a master plan. I've submitted it to the German government. And, let me tell you, I can get as much as twenty million to carry it out. Only I have reserved the most important place in my plan for *you*. What are you . . ."

A gust of marsh breath, right in his face.

". . . going to do? . . . Go on waiting? . . . Well, I . . ."

His dome was no smaller than Lenin's, half his face was bare brow, half his head a thinly covered backward slope. Ruthless, inhuman intelligence in his eyes, as he spoke.

"I AM SETTING THE DATE OF THE RUSSIAN REVOLUTION FOR 22 JANUARY NEXT YEAR!"

[4 8]

How are great yet simple plans born? Ideas are conceived and grow in the subconscious before you have any definite purpose for them. Then, suddenly, elements long familiar perhaps to others as well as yourself spontaneously converge, and it is in your head that they fuse to form a single plan, a plan so clear and simple that you wonder why no one had arrived at it before.

Why had it not taken shape earlier in the minds of the German General Staff, who should have been the first to think of it? True, they did not understand Russia very well. Since the autumn of 1914 and the battle on the Marne, they had realized that their plans for a quick victory had failed, but until the autumn of 1915 they had gone on hoping for a separate peace with Russia, busily putting out feelers, never imagining that the Romanovs would rebuff them. This was what had distracted them.

Parvus, insulated from the main events, stranded in bronze-and-blue Constantinople, in possession of the riches he had so desired, and with them every imaginable carnal delight—the East knows how to sate the male soul and slake male desire—remote from the great battle ("in the reserve socialist army," as Trotsky had put it), and in no danger of experiencing its consequences, had never, even at his most jaded and dissipated, abandoned the quest which had begun in his distant youth on the diagonally opposite shore of the Black Sea.

He had not abandoned it when, earlier, he went to the Balkans, where he was more widely read than Marx and Engels. He had not forgotten it when he was earning his bread in the low dives of Constantinople and rallying dockside beggars for a May Day demonstration. He had been still more mindful of it when he rose in the world under the Young Turks and converted his financial genius from an ax hacking at the Russian trunk to a gardener's spade mulching the Turkish sapling. The millions which so mysteriously flooded in on him and carried him along on their tide had not dazed him or made him forgetful. He did not forget while he was founding banks and trading with mother Odessa or stepmother Germany. The shot at Sarajevo had stung him like the lash of a whip. Parvus had a seismographic sense of movement in the depths, he knew at once that the landslide was coming! That the stupid old bear would be trapped! At last it had come, the Great War, the World War! He had long foretold it, described it, evoked it—the most powerful locomotive of history! The first chariot of socialism! While socialist parties all over Europe were in an uproar over war credits, Parvus made not a single speech, published not a single line. He wasted no time, there was not a minute to lose, but scurried about his secret passages, trying to persuade Turkey's rulers that only by siding with Germany could their country break loose from the endless chain of "capitulations." He hurried up the delivery of equipment and spare parts for Turkish railways and flour mills, to supply the towns with grain and put Turkey in a position not only to declare war in the autumn but to begin serious military operations in the Caucasus as soon as possible. (He was working just as busily on Bulgaria, which he also succeeded in preparing for war.) Only after these essential feats could Parvus allow himself to settle back comfortably into his favorite and long-neglected occupation—propaganda: this time in the Balkan press, with the slogan FOR DEMOCRACY! AGAINST TSARISM!

This needed explanation, careful argument, to convince as many as possible—and the sparks rained merrily from his unblunted pen. Why ask who bears the "war guilt," "who attacked first," when world imperialism has been preparing for this fight for decades? Somebody had to attack first, and it might have been anyone. Don't look for meaningless "causes" but think like Socialists: how are we, the world proletariat, to make use of the war, or in other words, on which side should we fight? Germany has the most powerful Social Democratic party in the world, Germany is the stronghold of socialism, and so for Germany this is a war of self-defense. If socialism is smashed in Germany it will be defeated everywhere. The road to the victory of world socialism lies through the reinforcement of German military power, while the fact that Tsarism is on the same side as the Entente reveals even more clearly where the true enemies of socialism are: thus, the victory of the Entente would bring a new age of oppression to the whole world. So workers' parties throughout the world must fight *against Russian Tsarism*. Advising the proletariat to adopt neutrality (as Trotsky does) means opting out from history, it is revolutionary cretinism. So the object of world socialism is the crushing defeat of Russia and a revolution in that country! Unless Russia is decentralized and democratized the whole world is in danger. And since Germany bears the main burden of the struggle against Muscovite imperialism, the revolutionary movement there must be suspended for the time being. At a later stage victory in war will bring class victories for the proletariat. THE VICTORY OF GERMANY IS THE VICTORY OF SOCIALISM!

The first to come and consult Parvus in response to this publication were members of the League for the Liberation of the Ukraine, based in Vienna (there were old acquaintances from *Iskra* days among them), then the Armenian and Georgian nationalists. His door in Constantinople was open to all engaged in fighting Russia.

Thus Parvus's dynamism magnetically attracted people of different experience, and from this explosive combination of socialist and nationalist interests the Plan was born. Until then socialist programs had always babbled about autonomy. But no! Only the disruption and dismemberment of Russia could bring down absolutism, and give the nations freedom and socialism simultaneously.

While the first Ukrainian and Caucasian expeditionary groups were collapsing (in their haste they had recruited all sorts of braggarts and adventurers, the conspiratorial scheme was suddenly made public in the émigré press, and Enver Pasha stopped the expeditions), the magnetic combination of iron components into a single plan was gradually perfected in Parvus's grotesquely capacious head. Just as engineers like triangular supports because of their resistance to deformation, so Parvus found that the nationalist and socialist components lacked a third partner—the German government. The aims of all three very closely coincided!

Parvus's past life might have been deliberately designed for the faultless creation of the Plan. It now only remained for him—happy amalgam of theorist, operator, and politician that he was—to formulate the Plan point by point in December 1914, give the German ambassador an inkling of it in January, receive a hospitable summons to Berlin, and stagger the higher-ups at a personal interview in the ministry. In nineteen years that country had not even tossed him a set of naturalization papers, it had closed down all his journals, hounded him from city to city, contemplated handing him over to the Russian secret police, and now the highest in the government gazed deferentially into his prophetic eyes. In March 1915, on presentation of a definitive and detailed memorandum, he received his first advance of a million marks.

The Plan was to concentrate all their potential, all their forces, all their resources under a single command, to control from a single headquarters the activities of the Central Powers, the Russian revolutionaries, and the border peoples. (He knew the strength of this ox, and he had chosen his ax to match it.)

No uncoordinated, private improvisations. The Plan was insistent that German victory could never be final without a revolution in Russia: until it was carved up, Russia would remain an unabated menace. The Russian fortress, however, could not be destroyed by any one of these forces in isolation, but only by a single-minded alliance of all three. There must be a simultaneous explosion of social revolution and national revolution, with German financial and material support. His experience with the 1905 revolution—as its author he should know, and what induced the imperial government to take their adviser seriously was that he was no mere footloose businessman but the father of the first revolution—made it clear that all the symptoms were recurring, that all the conditions for revolution were still in being, and that it would indeed proceed more quickly in conditions of world war, but only if it were given a skillful push, only if the catastrophe were speeded up by action from outside. The Putilov, Obukhov, and Baltic plants in Petersburg and the shipyards at Nikolaev would be made ready to serve as centers of *social* revolution (the author had particularly strong links with southern Russia). The date was set—one which already had a painful significance in Russia, the anniversary of Bloody Sunday—in the first place for a one-day strike in memory of the victims, and a single street demonstration in support of the eight-hour day and a democratic republic. But when the police began to disperse the demonstrators they would resist, and if there was the slightest bloodshed, the flame would race along all the fuses! The one-day strikes would merge into a general strike "for freedom and peace." Leaflets would be distributed in the biggest factories, and weapons would be ready for use in Petersburg and Moscow. Within twenty-four hours a hundred thousand men would be set in motion. The railwaymen (also primed in advance) would join them, and all traffic would be halted on the Petersburg–Moscow, Petersburg–Warsaw, Moscow–Warsaw, and Southwestern lines. To ensure a total and simultaneous stoppage, bridges should also be blown up at several points along the Trans-Siberian trunk line, and a team of skilled operatives should be dispatched for this purpose. Siberia was dealt with in a separate section of the Plan. The forces stationed there were extremely weak, and the towns, under the influence of political exiles, were in a revolutionary mood. This made it easier to organize sabotage, and once the disorders began the exiles should be transferred en masse to Petersburg, so as to inject into the capital thousands of practiced agitators, and bring millions of conscripts within range of propaganda. Propaganda would be carried out by the whole Russian left-wing press, and reinforced by a flood of defeatist émigré leaflets. (It would be easy enough to get them printed in bulk in Switzerland, for instance.) Any publication which sapped the Russian will to resist and pointed to social revolution as the way out of the war would be useful. The main target for propaganda would be the army in the field. (Parvus also envisaged a mutiny in the Black Sea Fleet. He had established links with the Odessa sailors on his way through Bulgaria long ago. He had always strongly suspected that the Japanese were responsible for the *Potemkin* mutiny. It would certainly be possible to blow up one or two battleships.) Experienced agents would also be sent to set fire to the Baku oil wells, which presented no difficulty since they were so inadequately guarded. The pace of social revolution must be further accelerated by financial means: counterfeit rubles would be showered on the Russian population from German planes, while banknotes with identical serial numbers would be put into simultaneous circulation abroad, in Petersburg and in Moscow, to undermine the exchange rate of the ruble and create panic in the capitals.

For all their Clausewitzes, Elder Moltkes, and Younger Moltkes, for all their self-confident strategy, for all the haughty precision of their staff work, limited Prussian brains had never risen to a concept of such grandeur!

Germany had never had such an adviser on Russia and its weaknesses. (So much so that even now she did not fully appreciate him.)

And that is by no means all! The *national* revolutions will begin simultaneously. Our most important lever is the Ukrainian movement. Without the Ukraine to buttress it the Russian edifice will soon topple over. The Ukrainian movement will spread to the Kuban Cossacks, and the Don Cossacks too may prove shaky. There will naturally be collaboration with the Finns, who are the most mature of the empire's peoples and almost free already. It will be easy to send weapons to them, and through them to Russia. Poland is always just five minutes away from rebellion against Russia and only awaits the signal. With Poland and Finland in revolt the Baltic lands in between them will be stirred to action. (In another version of the Plan, Parvus provided for the voluntary union of the Baltic provinces with Germany.) The Georgian and Armenian nationalists are already actively collaborating with the governments of the Central Powers and in their pay. The Caucasus is fragmented and will be more difficult to rouse, but with Turkey's help, by means of Muslim agitation, we'll stir them up to a *gazawat*, a holy war. And with that all around them the Terek Cossacks will scarcely want to lay down their lives for the Tsar rather than break away themselves.

So the highly centralized Russian empire will collapse, never to rise again! Internal struggles will shake Russia to its foundations! Peasants will start taking the land from its owners. Soldiers will desert the trenches in droves to make sure of their share when the land is divided up. (They would mutiny against their officers, shoot all the generals!

But this part of the prospect must be tactfully concealed—it might stir unpleasant forebodings in Prussian breasts.)

Wait a bit, though (catching his breath), that's not all! That's not the end of it! Shaken by destructive propaganda within, Russia must simultaneously be besieged by a hostile world press. An anti-Tsarist campaign will be mounted by socialist newspapers in various countries, and the excitement of Tsar-baiting will spread to their neighbors on the right, the liberals—that is to say, to the dominant section of the press throughout the world. A newspaper crusade against the Tsar! In this connection it is particularly important to capture public opinion in the United States. And by exposing Tsarism we will simultaneously unmask and undermine the whole Entente!

This, then, was Parvus's proposal to Germany: instead of the desperate butchery of infantry and artillery warfare—a single injection of German money, and, with no German losses, the most populous member of the Entente would be torn away in the space of a few months! Not surprisingly, the German government jumped at the program!

Parvus, indeed, had never doubted that they would. He was, however, anxious about the reaction of others in Berlin: the Socialists. How would his project be received by his stepmother party? His ideas had always been too deep for use in their mass agitation, and too far in advance of his time to seem practical even to the leaders of the party in which he had been knocking his head against the wall and wasting his ideas for nineteen years now, without ever holding office or voting rights at a single congress. He had, for a short time, been one of its heroes—when he had just returned from Siberia and everyone was devouring his memoirs, *In the Russian Bastille*. Then he had dirtied his hands in the unfortunate Gorky affair, a secret party commission had condemned him to expulsion, and five years of excommunication had still not wiped out the stain. Worst of all, though, was his legendary and inexplicable rise to riches in a single year—something people in general, and democratic Socialists in particular, are too narrow-minded to forgive. (It was a psychological puzzle: had his wealth been inherited no one would ever have reproached him with it.) His wealth alone was bound to make them hate and reject him, but they had also found nobler grounds for indignation: he had become a henchman of imperialism! Klara and Liebknecht he could understand, but Rosa! Rosa, with whom he had once been on intimate terms (though even then she had been ashamed of him—because of his appearance perhaps—and always concealed their relationship), Rosa too had shown him the door. In the meantime, Bebel had died, Kautsky and Bernstein had split up and impaired their authority, and a complacent new leadership was looking for weaknesses in the position of this Socialist drifter. How, they asked, would the Prussian government behave after victory? Why should revolution in Russia make Prussia look more tolerantly and kindly on socialism? Would it not see its chance to put the lid on English and French democracy?

Of course, there was some truth in their objections, there were grounds for doubt—but there was nothing here of that bold and perfect vision that can shake and remake a world! No one, or hardly anyone, in Europe could lift himself far enough out of his rut to see that *the destruction of Russia now held the key to the future history of the world!* All else was secondary.

Meanwhile the Socialists of the Entente were mounting a campaign to expose Parvus.

The bitterness of their reproaches poisoned the pleasure that his success should have given him, although the majority of European Socialists were neither well versed in theory nor effective in practice. They could not rise to a general view of the terrain, they lacked the skill to match each turn of events with a tactical twist. They were merely bureaucrats of socialism, stuck fast, coffined in the corridors of dogma: they no longer moved, no longer crawled along these corridors, but lay down in them, not even daring to imagine a turning ahead. When Parvus first openly called on them to help Germany he had filled them with maidenly horror. How nice it would be for them to sit the war out as innocent neutrals, salving their consciences with moral indignation, both against war and against those who dared to interfere with it.

But the decisive role belonged to the Russian Socialists, and they were the subject of careful analysis in the Plan as submitted to the German government. They were broken up into scattered groups, and thus impotent—but not one of these groups must be neglected, each must be turned to use. It was therefore necessary to lead them along the road to unity—arrange a unification congress, for which Geneva would be a suitable venue. Some groups, such as the Bund, the Spilka, the Poles, the Finns, would certainly support the Plan. But unity could not be achieved without reconciling Bolsheviks and Mensheviks. And that would depend entirely on the Bolshevik leader, who was at present in Switzerland.

Various difficulties might arise, and it might even turn out that some Russian Socialists were patriots and did not want to see the Russian empire dismembered. But there were grounds for confidence: these beggarly émigrés had been short of money for decades, both for everyday needs—they had never known where their next meal was coming from, and they were quite incapable of earning a living—and for their incessant journeys and congresses, and their endless scribbling of pamphlets and articles. They would not be able to resist if a fat purse were held out to them. Why, even the strong, legal Western parties and trade unions rose readily to offers of financial help, for their workers, of course, but still—who in this world does not want to eat well, be better dressed, live in a warmer and more spacious house? (Discreet help for leaders who live modestly also greatly reinforces our friendship with them.) How, then, can the émigrés refuse?

On his way to Switzerland, Parvus had anticipated with particular relish a successful meeting with Lenin. Their collaboration in Munich was a thing of the past, they had not seen each other in years, but Parvus's keen eye had never lost sight of this unique Socialist, who had no equal in all Europe: uninhibited, free from prejudice and squeamishness, ready in any new situation to adopt whatever methods promised success. The only hard-nosed realist, never carried away by illusions, the greatest realist in the socialist movement except for Parvus himself. All that Lenin lacked was breadth. The savage, intolerant narrowness of the born schismatic harnessed his tremendous energy to futilities—fragmenting this group, dissociating himself from that, yapping at intruders, petty bickering, dogfights, needling newspaper articles—wasted his strength in meaningless struggles, with nothing to show except mounds of scribbled paper. This schismatic narrowness doomed him to sterility in Europe, left him no future except in Russia—but also made him indispensable for any activity there. Indispensable now!

Now that Parvus's younger comrade-in-arms, Trotsky, whom he had so dearly loved, had abdicated once and for all, now that Trotsky's vitality and clarity of vision had deserted him—the cold gleam of Lenin's star summoned him irresistibly to Switzerland. Quite spontaneously, Lenin had been saying the same things; that it did not matter who was the aggressor, that Tsarism was the stronghold of reaction and must be shattered first, that . . . Nuances in parenthetic remarks, buried in subsidiary clauses and noticed by hardly anyone else, told Parvus that Lenin had not changed, that he was still as demanding in some matters and as undemanding in others as he had always been, that he would not balk at an alliance with the Kaiser or the devil himself if it helped to crush the Tsar. Parvus had therefore warned him in advance to expect interesting proposals: there was no reason to doubt that an alliance would be concluded. The only trouble was those miserable artificial disagreements with the Mensheviks, about which Lenin was particularly stupid and stubborn. Still, a million marks in subsidies should carry some weight. In his memorandum to the German government Parvus had specifically mentioned Lenin, with his underground organization throughout Russia, as his main support. With Lenin at his right hand, as Trotsky had been in the other revolution, success was assured.

Sure of success, Parvus had traveled to Bern, paced the student canteen, cigar in mouth, and been surprised at first by Lenin's resounding refusal, but quickly appreciated the other's prudence and tact. Sitting on the cramped bed, he had used his bulk to squeeze the lightweight Lenin into a corner.

"But you must have capital! What will you use to seize power? That's the unpleasant question."

Tha-a-a-at was something Lenin understood very well! That bare ideas will get you no further forward, that you cannot make a revolution without power, that in our time the primary source of power is money, and that all other forms of power—organization, weapons, people capable of using those weapons to kill—are begotten of money. All very true, nobody would deny it!

With his incomparable mental agility which made reflection unnecessary, his expression changing from one moment to the next—Parvus even glimpsed a smiling hint of complicity—Lenin coolly shifted his ground and answered in his burring voice.

"Why unpleasant? When people take the right Party attitude toward money the Party is pleased. It is displeased when money is turned into a weapon *against* the Party."

"That's all very well, but you can't help giving yourself away." Parvus spoke with friendly irony. "*Social Democrat* costs something to publish. Or maybe"—his Falstaffian belly shook with laughter—"maybe you tell the Swiss tax inspectors that on the contrary you live on your fees from *Social Democrat?*"

Lenin often wore a mocking look, but very rarely smiled: instead he screwed up his naturally deep-set eyes, hiding them completely. He chose his words carefully. "Philanthropic donations keep coming from somewhere. It is perfectly correct from the Party's point of view to accept charity—why shouldn't it be?"

(Money, in fact, was not so short as all that, they could all have lived more easily if they were as shameless as some of those through whose hands it flowed. Bagotsky threw money about in a scandalous fashion, and nobody would think of checking the Austrian money held by Weiss. It was no use putting pressure on them, that might spoil everything. But it ran through their hands like water.)

Parvus's eye found no comfort anywhere—not in Lenin's frayed jacket, nor in his patched collar, nor in the worn-out tablecloth, nor in the bare room, where two boxes, one on top of the other, served as a bookcase. But Parvus felt not in the least apologetic about his diamonds, his cheviot coat, his English shoes: this parade of poverty on Lenin's part was all a game, the Party line, intended to set the tone and serve as an example of a "leader beyond reproach." In this adopted role, faithfully performed for years on end, could be seen the narrowness and drabness of his mind. But this could be corrected, and even Lenin could be taught to cut a figure.

(But no! No! A deep antipathy, an instinctive protest made Lenin *spontaneously* always shut himself off from any luxury, however easily

available. To have sufficient was a different matter, that was reasonable. But luxury was the beginning of degeneracy, and Parvus had been
caught that way. Let the money pour in by the million, but for the
revolution, while he himself kept within the limits of the necessary,
counting every rappen and proud of it. It was not at all a pose, and
only partly by way of example to those whom he could not coerce.)

Glancing swiftly sideways and upward, Lenin spoke without hostility
or resentment. "Izrail Lazarevich! Your undying faith in the omnipo-
tence of money is what has let you down. You know what I mean."

(If your expenses are small it is like being in a locked room, your
secrets are safe: nothing leaks, you feel secure, you will never recklessly
let yourself go, all is firm and fast. But riches are like uncontrolled
chatter. No! There must be discipline in this as in everything. Only
self-limitation makes it possible to build up a powerful drive. Thus,
although he could afford to put down the 1,200-franc security for permission to reside in Switzerland—which was essential to his safety and
his work—he just wouldn't pay, but chose instead to make a fuss, write
letters, declare himself destitute, beg for a discretionary reduction to
one-tenth, waste precious time calling on the chief of police, sometimes accompanied by Karl Moor, who had a well-stuffed wallet in his
pocket, so that he need only hold his hand out and extract a banknote
from him. When he was finally granted a reduction to three hundred,
he still paid only a hundred, and went on haggling. Then when he
moved to Zurich he wouldn't pay at all, but wrote begging to be excused, and corresponded with Bern, requesting the transfer of his hundred francs to his present canton. Lenin was good at this: good at
lacing himself tight: only tight-laced did he breathe freely.)

The purpose of any conversation is to understand your partner fully
without unnecessarily exposing yourself.

With a sharp, probing look and a skeptical grin, he asked, "Why do
you need wealth of your own? Come on, tell me! Explain yourself."

A child's question. One of those "whys" it is ridiculous to answer.
So that every wish can become reality, of course. The feeling it gives
you is probably like that which a physical giant gets from the play of
his muscles. Affirmation of his rights on earth. The meaning of life.

Parvus sighed. "It's only human to like being rich. Surely you understand, Vladimir Ilyich?"

But looking at that bald brow, at the aging skin of his temples, at
the too sharp, too tense vee of his eyebrows, Parvus suddenly suspected
that Lenin really didn't understand, that he wasn't pretending. His all-
penetrating gaze saw only what was in front of him.

Parvus spoke again, more gently. "How shall I put it? . . . It's pleasant
to have perfect sight or perfect hearing, and it's just the same with
wealth . . ."

But was his decision to get rich really the result of conscious thought, of a theoretical belief? No, it was an innate necessity, and his commercial impulses, his flair for *Geschäft*, his reluctance to let slip any profit which loomed in his field of vision, were not a matter of plans and programs, but almost a biological function which proceeded almost unconsciously yet unerringly. It was a matter of instinct with him always to feel the movement of economic life around him, the emergence of disproportions, imbalances, gaps which begged him, cried out to him to insert his hand and extract a profit. This was so much a part of his innermost nature that he conducted his multifarious business transactions, which by now were scattered over ten European countries, without a single ledger, keeping all the figures in his head.

(Lenin, of course, accepted that in the final analysis personal wealth was a *Privatsache*, a private matter. But his eyes bored into Parvus, probing for an answer: was he or was he not a Socialist? That was the problem. Twenty-five years of socialist journalism—but was he a Socialist? . . .)

Parvus hurriedly returned to the point. "Let me tell you—wealth means power. Power is what the proletariat aspires to, isn't it? I was a big name for twenty-five years, better known than you, and it did nothing for me. But all roads are open to the wealthy. Take these negotiations, for instance. What government would believe a beggar and give him millions for a project? Whereas a rich man obviously won't take it for himself, he has his own millions."

The inordinately large, asymmetrical head tilted trustfully, and the colorless, philosophical eyes gazed amicably and peaceably at Lenin.

"Don't miss your chance, Vladimir Ilyich. Life offers you opportunities like this only once."

Yes, this he understood. At the beginning of the war he had enjoyed an unaccustomed luxury; a friendly eagle (Austrian in this case) had taken him on its wing and carried him in a twinkling where it was bidden. (There was no passenger transport to Switzerland, and the Ulyanovs had traveled on a troop train.) Lenin had discovered with a thrill that it might be better not to hover helplessly, to drift on a sea of words and ideas, but to abandon once and for all his helpless and uneasy émigré existence, and cling instead to real material forces, move in unison with them. As always, and in everything, Parvus had been ahead of him.

"To make a revolution takes a lot of money," Parvus insisted, his friendly shoulder pressing against Lenin. "But to hold on to power when you get there will take even more."

An odd way of putting it, but strikingly true.

The innermost nucleus of Parvus's thought was undoubtedly correct.

But the innermost nucleus of Lenin's thought was also undoubtedly correct.

"Just think, if only we combined your capacities with mine. And with such powerful support! With your incomparable talent for revolution! How much longer do you want to go on kicking your heels in these émigré holes? How much longer can you go on waiting for a revolution somewhere ahead—and refusing to recognize it when it arrives and grabs you by the shoulder? . . ."

Oh dear, no! Nothing, neither shared joy, nor fervent hope, and still less flattery, could dim Lenin's vigilant gaze. He had a quicker and keener eye for the narrowest chink of disagreement than for the broad expanse of converging platforms. He might be an outcast and a failure, but he had invariably known that Parvus in all his successes, all his prophecies, was wrong, or at least not altogether right! Although he himself had achieved nothing—right was on his side!

Now Parvus was amused. Laughter was shaking that unwieldy body which so loved its bottle of champagne before breakfast, its leisurely bath, its little suppers with the ladies, when it was not chained to its couch by rheumatism.

"Do you intend to go on in the same way, raising money through bank raids? What are you going to do next—rob the Crédit Lyonnais? You'll be deported to New Caledonia, comrades! To the galleys!"

He was overcome with laughter.

Lenin's brows twitched slightly in disagreement. But his searching gaze considered the problem dispassionately.

There was no theoretical objection to raiding a bank before general expropriation was legalized—it was, so to speak, borrowing against your future. But in practice it might or might not be worthwhile. If there was one thing the Bolsheviks had undoubtedly been good at in the revolutionary years it was the "exes." They had begun with raids on ticket offices and trains. The first 200,000 from Georgia had simply transformed the life of the Party. And if only they had succeeded in taking that fifteen million from Mendelssohn's Bank in Berlin in 1907 . . . ! (Kamo was arrested en route, and it fell through.) It was a risky method, but very effective, and in any case it dirtied the Party's hands less than dealings with the general staffs of foreign countries.

"Don't like dirtying your hands? Afraid of getting found out?" Parvus too narrowed his eyes to slits, deliberately, contemptuously, shaming and reproving him. "You can rely on my experience: in *big* enterprises you'll never be found out. It's those who balk at little ones who get caught."

What a pachyderm! He didn't give a damn what people said, just clumped about the world on his great flat feet, crushing everything in his path.

Lenin's right eye darted an angry glance at him.

Parvus became sympathetic. He took both of Lenin's hands in his own jellylike paws (an unpleasant habit of his) and spoke like the closest of friends. (At one time they had almost been on first-name terms.)

"Vladimir Ilyich, you must not neglect to analyze the reasons for your failure in one revolution already. Perhaps the fault lies in you? It is important to recognize that for the future. Be careful you don't lose next time."

Where did he get his brazen self-assurance? Where the hell does he get off setting himself up as a teacher? Was this another attempt to impose his leadership? Self-infatuation must have blinded him.

Lenin wrenched his hands free and spoke with a savage grin, one of those grins of spontaneous mockery that forced up his eyebrows and brought a flush of joy to his face as he savored his triumphant retort.

"Izrail Lazarevich! It's you who should rather be analyzing your *own failings!* I didn't lose last time, because I wasn't running the revolution! You were the one who lost! How did you come to grief?"

So far he had said nothing irreparable. Just a businesslike argument. He could still stop in time. But all those years of gasping for breath with that great hulk crushing his ribs, and the spontaneous urge to tease, made him go further than he had to. (And was there anything to the man except ambition? Except the thirst for power? Except wealth?)

"Why did you lose heart so quickly in the Peter–Paul Fortress—was it the solitary confinement, the dampness? Why such tender concern for your miserable carcass? How do you explain that diary full of cheap pathos for German philistines? All those delusions about amnesties? How you came as near as all hell to petitioning the Tsar? Is that the behavior of a revolutionary leader?"

And he himself? A baldheaded, spiky-browed, flinty-eyed little man with fussy, fidgety movements?

Yet, except for the two of them, there was no one left to do the job.

Parvus never blushed, as though the fluid coursing in his veins was not the usual red, but watery green, like the color of his skin. There was no reason at all for him to lose his temper, but when Lenin thrust that sarcastic grin in his face, and shook with mocking laughter, and went on shaking, Parvus suddenly forgot his great qualities and foolishly retorted, "Anybody would think you had fought on the barricades! Or that you had marched just once in a street demonstration with Cossack whips waiting for you! At least I escaped from a transit prison on the way to Siberia! But why should you run for it, when you had a false medical certificate and got yourself sent to the Siberian Riviera instead of the north?"

(There were plenty of other things on the tip of his tongue. All very well for you, he thought, to give the call to arms from neutral Switzerland, especially when you've never been called up in your life!)

If anyone insulted you like that in public you would have to commit political murder, fatally blacken his reputation, but when it happens in private you have a choice. You can even suppose that this criticism is not wholly unsympathetic. Or admit that you have been unnecessarily rough yourself, as you often are in discussion.

No, thought Parvus, it was stupid of me to speak like that! I didn't come to Switzerland just to quarrel.

Parvus, thought Lenin, may be very useful. He is in a unique position. Why quarrel with him?

Lenin is the pillar on which the whole Plan rests. If he deserts me, who will make the revolution?

Another smile from Lenin, but a different one, not at all caustic, but infinitely knowing, a smile to be shared between the cleverest people in the world. His hand fell on Parvus's shoulder, and he spoke in a half whisper. "I tell you what. Do you know what your main mistake was in 1905? Why the revolution was a failure?"

Parvus responded with selfless objectivity, like a scientist ready to admit error however painful it might be. "The Financial Manifesto? Was I in too much of a hurry?"

Lenin wagged his finger in the little space left between their heads, and smiled like a Kalmyk extolling a melon in an Astrakhan bazaar. "No, no, no. The Financial Manifesto was a stroke of genius. But those Soviets of yours . . ."

"My Soviets united the whole working class instead of splitting it up like the Social Democrats do. My Soviets were gradually becoming the center of power. If only we'd succeeded in getting the eight-hour day—that and nothing else—there would have been risings in imitation of us throughout Europe, and there you would have had your *permanent revolution!*"

Slyly, slit-eyed, Lenin watched Parvus erecting defenses for his vanity, and was in no hurry to interrupt. This damned muddle over permanent revolution was another reason why he, Parvus, and Trotsky had quarreled. As though they were riding behind each other on a merry-go-round, they had all at different times moved to this position, and as each of them emerged from its shadow he had insisted that the other two were wrong. The other two were always somewhere ahead or still far behind.

Lenin parried in a confidential whisper, with the same slyly good-natured Asiatic smile. "Not at all. As you yourself so rightly said at the time, there must be uninterrupted civil war! The proletariat must not lay down its weapons! Where *were* your weapons, though?"

Parvus frowned. Nobody likes remembering his blunders.

Lenin had thought so much about it, never thought so much about anything, and now, still gripping his companion by the shoulder, bending toward him, narrowing his eyes to a piercing squint, he was in the mood to share his thoughts.

"You shouldn't have waited for a National Assembly in addition to the Soviets. Once you'd convened the Petersburg Soviet you had your proletarian National Assembly. What you should have done . . ."

He leaned forward as though sharpening the focus of his gaze, his mind, his words, and spoke still more confidentially. "What you should have done was to set up the very next day an armed punitive organization under the Soviet. That would have been your *weapon!*"

Then he sat silent, with Parvus fixed in his searchlight beam. Nothing seemed so important to him.

A typical armchair philosopher, a dreamer. After years of thought he had made his discovery, and although it was a decade late he thought it incomparably important. The crippling frustrations of émigré existence, remote from the scene of action, from the real forces— what a miserable fate! All his energy for years and years had gone into quarrels and wrangles, and schisms and squabbles, and now Parvus had flung wide the gates into the world arena! But all he did was sit curled up on his bed like a gopher and grin.

The second most powerful mind in European socialism was going to waste in an émigré hideout. He must be saved—for his own sake.

But also for the Cause.

For the Plan.

"Well, then, do you understand my Plan? Do you accept it?"

How to break through that frozen fixity? Had he dozed off? Was he in a trance? He wasn't taking anything in.

Parvus moved still nearer, and spoke right into his ear, so that he could not help hearing. "Vladimir Ilyich! Will you join our alliance?"

Like a man deaf and dumb. His eyes were unreadable. His tongue did not answer.

Holding on to his shoulder, Parvus tried again.

"Vladimir Ilyich! Your hour has struck! The time has come for your underground to work and conquer! In the past you had no strength, I mean no money, but now I'll pump in as much as you like. Just open the pipes for it to flow in. Tell us which towns we should give money, and to whom. Give us names. Who is to receive leaflets and literature? Transporting weapons is more difficult, but we'll take weapons in too. And how are we going to coordinate our actions? I can't imagine how you manage from here, from Switzerland. Should I arrange a move to Stockholm? It's very simple . . ."

On and on. Pushing. Pumping in his hippopotamus blood!

Lenin wriggled his shoulders and shook off Parvus's hand.

[4 9]

He had heard and understood it all perfectly. But a candid answer would not have passed the barrier of distrust and distaste in his breast.

His frankness about 1905 was quite enough to be going on with.

Of course he saw the merits of Parvus's Plan. If he couldn't, who could? A splendid program—a *sound* program! The offensive tactics were practicable, the means chosen reliable, the forces enlisted adequate.

Now he could admit it: there was no third thinker of such power, such penetrating vision in the International. Just the two of them.

And that was why he must be immensely circumspect. In political negotiations, always suspect a trap where the ground looks smoothest.

Had Parvus, then, stolen a march once again? No. Theoretically, and in a general way, Lenin had formulated the same ideas when war first broke out. But what was impressive in Parvus was his businesslike attention to concrete detail. Parvus the financier.

Faced with this grandiose program Lenin could question neither its soundness nor its desirability.

It was all well thought out. On the simple calculation that my worst enemy's worst enemy is my friend, the Kaiser's government was the best ally in the world. That such an alliance was permissible he agreed without a moment's hesitation: only an utter fool disdains serious assistance in a serious struggle.

An alliance—yes. But the dictates of caution must come before the alliance. Caution not as a merely negative measure, but as the condition of any effective action. Without super-super-caution, to hell with your alliance and to hell with your Plan! We don't want the chorus of Social Democratic grannies all over Europe tutting and spluttering! Lenin too admitted to himself—cautiously—that he had no qualms about France, the *rentiers'* republic. But he always knew where to stop, what to leave unsaid, where to keep an emergency exit open. Whereas Parvus had paraded his wild views, and irredeemably compromised his political reputation.

This was when Lenin had realized the other man's weakness and his own superiority. Parvus had always been first to discover new ground, and tramped on ahead, blocking the way. But he lacked the stamina for a long race. He hadn't been able to lead the Soviets more than two months. Twenty years and more of trying to reeducate the German Socialists was too much for him—he had come unstuck, fallen by the wayside. Whereas Lenin felt that he had the stamina to run forever, without ever losing his breath, to run as long as he was conscious—if need be, he would collapse into the grave with his race unfinished. But he would never drop out.

An alliance—certainly, with pleasure. But in this alliance he would be the coy bride, not the eager bridegroom. Let them run after *you*. Behave in such a way that even when you are weak you keep the upper hand and your independence. In fact, Lenin had already done something of the sort in Bern. He had, of course, not gone knocking on the door of the German ambassador, Romberg, the way Parvus did in Constantinople. But when he had made his theses public he knew very well whose ears they would please—and the theses had reached the right ears. Romberg himself had sent the Estonian revolutionary Keskula to discuss things with him and discover his intentions. And, of course, while remaining within the limits of his actual program—the overthrow of Tsarism, a separate peace with Germany, secession of the non-Russian peoples, renunciation of the Turkish straits—he felt entitled to offer a slightly juicier bribe: without being untrue to himself, or distorting the line, he could and did promise Romberg the invasion of India by a Russian revolutionary army. In this there was no betrayal of principles: an assault on British imperialism was necessary, and who if not Russia could mount it? One of these days we will invade. Of course, it was a concession, a sop, a swerve, a skid, but there was no danger in it. True, Keskula had a wolfish look and wolfish ways, and he was stronger-minded and more effective than any wishy-washy Russian Social Democrat, but here too Lenin sensed no danger. Since Estonia must in any case be released, like all the subject peoples, from the Russian prison, there was no distortion of the line: each of them used the other without fear of stumbling. They introduced Artur Siefeldt and Moisei Kharitonov into the chain, and Keskula went off to Scandinavia, where he was most helpful, especially with publications. He found money for pamphlets and helped organize contacts with Shlyapnikov, and so with Russia.

All this lacked the grandeur of Parvus's Plan, but in its quiet little way it was politically sound. And Lenin had kept his nose clean.

Parvus had now begun to show impatience. (Another of his faults.) Seeing that the conversation was not going as he wished, that he was not making a sale, he said bitterly and contemptuously (which could do no good at all), "So you are like all the rest? Afraid of getting a smudge on your nose? Waiting for something?"

He had placed such hopes on Lenin! He at least, he had thought, is with me! If I can't get together with him, who else is there?

In some agitation, losing his millionaire's complacency altogether, he haltingly produced his last arguments. "Vladimir Ilyich, you must not fall behind the times. With other people it doesn't matter, but in you it would be unforgivable. Surely you must see that the age of revolutionaries with parcels of illegal literature and homemade bombs has gone, never to return. The new type of revolutionary is a giant, like you and me. He counts everything in millions—people and money alike—and he must be able to get his hands on the levers by which states are overthrown or established. Getting at those levers is not easy, and at times it is even necessary to join the chauvinists."

Also true. True enough. But . . .

(Should he ask what price the Russian revolution would pay for German help? He refrained from doing so, but kept the question in mind for the future. It would be naïve to expect such help for nothing.)

When you enter into an alliance the first rule is not to trust your ally. On the treacherous ground of diplomacy always regard every ally as, above all, a potential cheat.

Lenin had not been dozing at all. He had been weighing things in his mind. If anyone had been dozing, it was probably Parvus in his Berlin negotiations. Lenin finally opened his eyes and radiated anxious inquiry, rattling off his questions like a drumroll.

"Will Wilhelm's government really want to overthrow the Russian monarchy? Why should they? All they need is peace with Russia. They would happily go on living in friendship with the Russian monarchy. They only need our strikes to scare the Tsar and force him to make peace, that's all."

As though Parvus needed to be told! No one should be deceived by the way he looked—rich, well fed, with a carefully groomed imperial on his pendulous double chin. To speak frankly (and sometimes, with some people, he would go so far), the shadow of separate peace had troubled all his negotiations with the German government. Peace between Russia and Germany would be the graveyard of the Great Idea. All the while there was a suspicion that, although the Germans were giving money for revolution, in their hearts they thought only of separate peace with the Tsar, and were surreptitiously sending people to make contact.

These muffled secret tunnelings must be detected, and frustrated by timely ridicule. The Tsar is *no longer* in a position to make peace! If he suddenly decides to make peace with you, power in Russia may pass to a strong right-wing nationalist government, which will not respect the Tsar's undertakings—and you will only have reinforced their position! . . . It must be drilled into Prussian skulls that only a government having the people's confidence could sign a *real peace* with Germany. Let "Peace" be the revolution's first slogan, the first concern of the new government! That government would find it easier to make concessions because it would bear no guilt for the war. From such a government Germany could expect *much more* . . .

He could already see the treaty, and was ready to sign it himself in advance.

And he caught a gleam in Lenin's eyes which meant that he could see it too.

You couldn't go into every detail (nor should you). There were various schools of thought among the Germans. The majority were inclined to view England as the main enemy, and were prepared to make peace with Russia. And unfortunately Secretary of State von Jagow, the most Prussian of Prussians, although he considered the onslaught of Slavdom a greater danger than England, did not, you know, much like the plan to break up Russia by revolution. (It was impossible to understand him fully: with his aristocratic mannerisms and his effete skepticism, he did not conceal his distaste for the diplomacy of secret agents, *hommes de confiance*, dubious middlemen. It was, of course, a great hindrance that such a man should be the head of the German Foreign Office.)

Parvus, however, in spite of his exquisite ugliness, could be captivating. The German ambassador in Copenhagen, Count von Brockdorff-Rantzau, enchanted by Parvus's incomparable intelligence, was his already.

All arguments must be used to prevent the catastrophe of a separate peace with the Tsar. They must strenuously try to convince the Germans that revolution in Russia was inevitable, that the whole country, and the army with it, was in ferment, that educated society was seething with discontent, not to mention the workers, including those in arms production—a single match would be enough to blow everything up! Why, it was even possible to set an exact date—and keep to it!

But the sharp little man with the big head, the bald brow, and the grin which hardly ever left his lips seemed even less convinced than von Jagow, and showed no mercy. "So you have in fact no agreement with them? Just the semblance of one? Still just talking?"

The eternal privilege of those who never act themselves: to interrogate, be dissatisfied, find fault.

Paddling with both hands to prevent his body from collapsing backward like an overstuffed sack, Parvus straightened up. "Not on crested paper, of course! It's all very fluid. And you have to keep its contours in view at every moment and determine its direction."

Try even to determine the direction of strategic offensives. Explaining, urging, insistently advising that whatever happens they should not advance on Petersburg! That would cause an upsurge of patriotism, Russia would unite, and the revolution would lose steam. At the same time, the Tsar must be denied any success in the field, and in particular must not be allowed to reach the Dardanelles, which would irreversibly reinforce his prestige. The best place to strike was on the southern flank: make the Ukraine your ally, detach the Donets coalfields, and Russia is finished.

Then again, they were afraid that the earthquake might set up tremors in Berlin. So that he also had to persuade them that revolution in Russia would not spread to Germany.

The little man jumped. "What's that? What did you say?" Steadily pushing his obese companion away, and winning more room for himself on the bed. "What do you mean? Have you reconciled yourself to the idea that the revolution will not go beyond Russia? Do you really think that?" His eyes were hard and inquisitorial. Suddenly—he would never mince his words when a principle was threatened—he burst out indignantly: "Why, that's treason!"

(No, Parvus was simply not a Socialist. He was something quite different.)

He, who never ventured outside Switzerland, never set his hand to anything *practical*, had been proved right again, must attack, must denounce.

"How shortsighted! What poverty of vision! How could the revolution survive in a single country?"

It was the same old *permanent revolution* all over again, the enchanted carousel on which they were doomed to circle forever, eternally following and fleeing, hurling yesterday's or tomorrow's reproaches at each other, neither of them ever in the right.

Did Parvus not want revolution in Germany? Was it really not his aim? Was it true what they wrote about him, that he had become a German patriot?

Parvus, though, was no longer a child, to go on riding that carousel. A revolutionary of the new type, a millionaire revolutionary, a financier and industrialist, can afford to express himself more frankly.

"World revolution is not at present feasible, but a socialist revolution in Russia is. Tsarism is the enemy against which *all* workers' parties everywhere must unite!"

More frankly does not mean frankly. It was a ticklish problem, one which you could not put into so many words in public discussions among Socialists. Even tête-à-tête you wouldn't mention it to every fellow Socialist.

You never knew where you had him—this mercurial creature with the bullet head and the sharp tongue. You could hardly ever tell what his next slogan would be—he always surprised everybody. You could never discover at all what he was thinking. Did he not understand that Russian socialism had special tasks to perform? Did he not accept them?

It was easier to discuss this problem with Brockdorff, even. (Indeed Parvus had noticed that you could discuss anything more straightforwardly and simply with diplomats than with Socialists.)

All he could do now was emphasize the elementary.

"It is Tsarism which must be destroyed here and now, by any means possible, and that's all we must think of!"

And so to the main question—how do you destroy it? The whole point of his visit and of this conversation was to find out what underground organizations in the capitals and in the provinces Lenin was willing to assign immediately to the preparation of a rising. Who and where were these people, with their iron unity and their invincible battle-readiness? Parvus knew what he was doing when he recommended this man to the German government as the most fanatical of Russian revolutionaries! He knew why he had come now to enlist him as an ally! For decades Lenin had seemed merely a mad sectarian. He had cast off all allies, fragmented all his forces, refused to hear of a "party of professors," would have nothing to do with "smooth economic development," cared for nothing but the underground, always the underground, and his party of professional revolutionaries! In peacetime Parvus and everyone else had thought this absurd, but now that there was a war on they began at last to see clearly how provident, how farsighted, and how clever he was! The time had finally come to use his powerful, well-trained secret army! Now at last it would prove its worth. Parvus was counting on this army in his negotiations in Berlin, he was counting on it when he had drawn up his Plan.

But Lenin was not to be diverted, not to be thrown off his stride like that. He had his own end in view and stubbornly pursued it.

"And how can you equate the revolutionary situation of 1905 with the present situation in such a primitive fashion?"

Well, obviously this war was more destructive and more protracted, the masses incomparably more exhausted and embittered, the revolutionary organization stronger, the liberals also stronger, while Tsarism had utterly failed to reinforce itself.

Lenin, however, persisted. His eyes seemed never to look directly at the other man, but to zigzag around him.

"Very well. But how can you so confidently set a starting date from outside?"

"Well, Vladimir Ilyich, we must have some date to aim at, if we are to concert our actions. Suggest a different one, if you like. But 22 January is best, because it is symbolic, everybody remembers it, and many will begin without any signal from us. It will be easier to bring them out into the streets. And once the first few are out there'll be no stopping it!"

Lenin was being very difficult. Understandable, though: to uncover his beloved underground would be like handing it over to someone else. Of course he didn't like the idea.

If Parvus was so ardently persistent, it meant that he was trying to take advantage of you.

"So what do you say, Vladimir Ilyich? The time has come to act!"

(Oh yes, I understand your Plan! You will emerge as the unifier of all the Party groups. Add to that your financial power and your theoretical talent, and there you are—leader of a united party and of the Second Revolution? Not again?!)

From the inscrutable eyes, from the set lips, through the impenetrable bald dome, Parvus, himself extraordinarily percipient, seized Lenin's thoughts, opened them out, read them, and answered at a tangent.

"My reason for suggesting that you go to Stockholm is so that you can be in charge from beginning to end. You need give me no names, tell me no secrets—just take the money, the leaflets, the weapons, and send them on! I'm not, you know"—Parvus sighed weakly; so exhausting, these political discussions—"I'm not the man I was ten years ago. I won't be going to Russia. I consider myself German these days."

(All the more suspicious. Why in that case did he think of nothing but Russia?)

"I only want to see the Plan carried out."

. . . But perhaps we see the Plan too in different ways?

He was quicksilver: no argument could hold him. "You mean that I too should be seen dirtying my hands, like you, on the German General Staff? A revolutionary internationalist can't afford that."

Two more pulls at his invisible oars brought Parvus alongside his armor-plated companion.

"You needn't get dirty! Why should you? I'll take all the dirty work on myself—I already have. The millions I give you will be clean. Just show me how to pipe them in. Once we've tied in your subterranean, submarine, secret connections with mine we'll touch off the Second Russian Revolution! Well??"

The eyes, which at the expense of color in the iris, lashes, and brows were pellucid concentrations of pure intelligence, tried to understand. Why this refusal?

But Lenin's eyes themselves were piercing gimlets. There was no way into them.

With his gimlet eyes and his crooked little grin—suspicious, shrewd, derisory—Lenin resisted these enticements.

"And for this purpose, you say, we need a conciliation conference in Geneva?" His voice was silky and venomous. "We must make peace? With the Mensheviks?" And he recoiled, as though from a shock, as far as the bedstead would permit. "What are you thinking of? What does making peace mean? *Giving in to the Mensheviks???*" He tossed his head violently, as though he was butting someone. "Never! Not for the world! Peace with the Mensheviks? I would sooner see Tsarism survive another thousand years than give a millimeter to the Mensheviks!"

And anyway—was he or wasn't he a Socialist?!

Lenin went on butting the air after he had stopped speaking, as though he was finishing someone off. As though he was finishing what he had to say soundlessly, with frenzied pantomime.

Parvus didn't understand a thing. This, after all, was not what he had come for. The greatest, most indefatigable, and most extreme of revolutionaries—in the most favorable of situations, with assistance lavished upon him—would not make a revolution?

Parvus, losing hope by now, asked point-blank, "So why have you spent thirty years on theoretical battles and border disputes? Where is your logic? You built up an underground, didn't you? Here is the best possible occasion for using it, there'll never be another like it as long as you live! Surely you weren't just playing a part?"

Lenin was never stuck for an answer.

"If we're going to accuse each other of inconsistency . . . You used to say that a handful of people cannot revolutionize the masses. Do you still say so?"

Parvus's chin was suddenly too heavy for his head, his head for his neck, and his neck for his body, his hands drooped between his knees. "We-e-ell . . ."

With Lenin's refusal the Great Plan was almost in ruins.

"All right then . . . Good . . . Or not so good . . . There's so little time . . . I'll have to create my own organization."

Lenin has miscalculated! He'll be sorry someday.

"You might at least let me have one of your men, our mutual friend perhaps?"

(No good burning bridges, no good quarreling, Parvus might turn out to be very useful.)

"Whom do you mean?"

"Hanecki."

"He's yours."

"I've already got Chudnovsky and Uritsky. What about Bukharin?"

"No, that's not for him."

"All right. But you yourself, will you go to Scandinavia? I can get you there quickly."

Lenin's eyes were gimlets. "No, no, no!"

Parvus was helpless under the burden of his own weight. He heaved a deep sigh. "Ah, well . . . There's one other thing I've dreamt of all my life and can now afford: to bring out a socialist journal of my own." He tried to throw back his swollen head proudly, in imitation of the bold and ardent spirit who had first thought of it. *"The Bell* I'll call it."

Four feet felt a jarring bump as the bed landed on the shoemaker's floor.

[5 0]

The revolutionary who succeeds underground is not the one who hides like a mouse under the floorboards, shunning the light of day and social involvement. The successful and resourceful underground worker takes an active part in the everyday life of those around him, he shares their weaknesses and passions, he is in the public eye, in the hurly-burly, with an occupation which everyone understands, and he may spend much of his time and strength on his daily routine—but his main, his secret activity goes on side by side with his out-in-the-open daily round, and all the more successfully if they are organically connected. The wisest way is also the simplest: to combine your secret and your out-in-the-open activity easily and naturally.

This was how Parvus saw it. (His experience with underground work was short—the few months in 1905, between the suppression of the Soviet and his arrest, then between his return from banishment and his departure abroad.) He understood still better that a man's natural occupation is one for which he has a vocation and talent. So, in May 1915, as he prepared to carry on alone after Lenin's disastrous refusal to join him in making a revolution, he had decided, with as little conscious thought as he gave to breathing, that he and his collaborators would make commerce their first and chief occupation, and that revolution would run in tandem with business.

That same summer he set up in neutral Denmark—which retained the main prerogative of all free Western countries, to trade without impediment—an import-export agency, which in present circumstances would naturally be prepared to deal with firms in any country at all—Germany, Russia, England, Sweden, the Netherlands—buying and selling where prices were most favorable. With Lenin's agreement, Hanecki at once became business manager of Parvus's new concern. The combination of two such ardent commercial spirits does not merely double their power, but increases it many times over. Then they were joined by a third, who was very nearly their equal—Georg Sklarz. (Not, it must be said, blown along by a whim of fate, but obligingly sent to cooperate with them by the intelligence branch of the German General Staff.) This Sklarz (who achieved notoriety in postwar Germany, among other things in a succession of court cases in which he showed himself to be a remarkable actor) proved to be an indispensable member of the trio—a business genius like his partners, resourceful, quick-thinking, reacting silently and swiftly to any assignment or any twist of events, and always emerging successful. (He had brought with him two other Sklarz brothers: Waldemar, who went to work in the trade-and-revolution agency itself, and Henryk, who, under the pseudonym of Pundik, and in partnership with Romanovich and Dolgopolsky, already ran a secret office in Copenhagen, investigating illicit exports from Germany on behalf of the German General Staff.) The idea of combining business with political activity soon proved its value: *Geschäft* served politics, and politics smoothed the path of *Geschäft*. Support from the General Staff made the agency's transactions easier and its profits greater.

Within a few months of its foundation the import-export agency was a flourishing business, buying, selling, and shipping, with no thought of narrow specialization, copper, chrome, nickel, and rubber, transferring from Russia to Germany mainly grain and foodstuffs, from Germany to Russia mainly technical equipment, chemicals, medicines, but the range of goods exchanged included also stockings, contraceptives, salvarsan, caviar, cognac, and used motor vehicles (in Russia, they were able to stipulate that these should not be commandeered for military purposes). In trade with Western countries this was one of many such agencies uncomfortably jostling each other, but in trade with Russia, which for him mattered most, Parvus's agency had a monopoly. Some goods were shipped openly, with legal export licenses, others were shipped under false bills of lading, or even smuggled. This required ingenuity in packing and loading, and there had to be someone to take responsibility if caught, but it was Hanecki and Sklarz who involved themselves in all this, letting Parvus remain quietly in the shade, his favorite place, to deal with matters of high policy.

What made the combination of commercial and revolutionary activity an idea of genius was that revolutionary agents posing as business representatives, with the Petersburg lawyer Kozlovsky playing the main part, could travel quite legally to Russia, inside Russia, and back again to Parvus. But Parvus's brilliance was seen still more clearly in his arrangements for sending money. To pass money from the German government quickly and without hindrance into the hands of Russian revolutionaries might seem an impossible task, but the import-export agency performed it with ease. It sent to Russia goods and nothing but goods, and always in excess of what it bought there. The earnings of collaborating firms, such as Fabian Klingsland, were banked in the normal way (in the Petersburg branch of the Bank of Siberia), and it was then entirely a matter for the agency to decide whether or not to withdraw the money from Russia—in fact it was to Russia's advantage that it stay there. In Petersburg, the Bolshevik lawyer Kozlovsky ("the Sword") and Hanecki's people could withdraw any sum at any time and hand it over to the revolutionaries.

This was where Parvus showed his genius: the import of goods which Russia badly needed to wage war provided funds for knocking Russia out of the war.

Parvus's method of selecting the agency's revolutionary staff showed the same insistence on combining the overt and the covert. He set up for this purpose yet another subsidiary organization in Copenhagen— the Institute for Research into the Consequences of War. To recruit its personnel he frequently and openly sought the acquaintance of Socialists and met them for discussions. Whenever a candidate was eager, and qualified, to plunge into the depths, he did so and became a secret agent. Those who proved unsuitable or intractable were kept in the dark—the conversation followed its natural course, and they might be kept on as overt members of the legal institute. The institute itself was not fictitious, but gratified Parvus's besetting passion for economic research, just as the heavily subsidized *Bell*, published in Germany, gratified his passion for socialism. (One who longed to join the institute was Bukharin—and there could have been no better place for him, nor could the institute have found a more useful member— but the fastidious and puritanical Lenin forbade his young comrade to associate with the shady Parvus, just as he forbade Shlyapnikov to go near the dubious Hanecki.)

All this Parvus managed brilliantly, because here he was in his ele- ment. But what came next was more difficult. To whom should this money be given in Russia? And how could you bring about a revolution in that huge country with a dozen business representatives and a few Western Socialists like Kruze? It was easiest in Petersburg, where he had many contacts, where the lawyer Kozlovsky could receive clients without arousing suspicion and recruit the necessary people in the factories, and where the fanatical Interdistrict group was active—fol- lowing what had always been Parvus's own line—recognizing neither Bolsheviks nor Mensheviks, and readily accessible to him through one of their members, Uritsky. Although the socialist forces in Petersburg were split, Parvus had put together a strong group of activists, espe- cially in the Putilov plant. But although it has been truly said that revolution in any state succeeds or fails in the capital, there was no assurance that the initial shock would be effective in such a large coun- try without disturbances in the provinces. Parvus, however, had live connections of his own only in Odessa, and through Odessa with Ni- kolaev. There was no one to stir up this inert, mute country as a whole. A few agents, however freely they spent, could not create a network in the few remaining months. Whereas Lenin had a ready-made net- work—and had treacherously concealed it.

But Parvus, from his memories of 1905, understood very well how disturbances begin. To start a strike, or a riot, to bring the people out on the streets, you do not need the unanimous consent of the majority, or even one in four; indeed, it is wasted effort to try to prepare even a tenth of them for action. A single shrill cry from the thick of the crowd, a single orator at the factory gates, two or three toughs bran- dishing fists or sticks are often enough to keep a whole shift from their workbenches or bring them into the streets. Then there are neighborly conversations condemning the government, the transmission of alarming rumors (which with no further effort can be left to strike at a distance like a charge of electricity), the scattering of leaflets in factory rest rooms and smoking rooms, under workbenches—for each and any of these preliminary blows you need no more than five men to a factory, and if you cannot find five who will do it out of conviction, you can buy help in the nearest tavern—what tavern scrounger refuses money?

In any other circumstances sporadic troublemaking in factories would not have been enough, but now, in the second year of a war which had already devoured so many, with hunger suddenly threatening, with the army losing battle after battle, with the whole country in ferment, with revolution still fresh in the minds of the present generation, a few such jolts—Parvus was convinced of it—could set off a landslide. That was his strategy—to start an avalanche with a few light snowfalls. Without Lenin's help in the remaining months he could do no more. But the date itself was fraught with menace for Tsarism: even if there were no agents at work, if not a single ruble was spent, 22 January could still not pass quietly. All the same, it would be as well to give a helping hand. So Parvus, who had Count von Brockdorff-Rantzau completely under his spell, and practically dictated his dispatches from Copenhagen to the German Foreign Ministry, confidently promised revolution in Russia on 22 January 1916.

He hoped, at least, that it would be so. Lavishly endowed with the gift of far-reaching and penetrating prophecy, he was nonetheless a creature of earth, and could not always distinguish a flash of prophetic insight from the uprush of desire. He longed so violently for a devastating revolution in Russia that he could be forgiven for misinterpreting his emotion.

This was not, however, something which the German government, and especially Secretary of State Gottlieb von Jagow, would readily forgive. Always the ironist, always contemptuous of this grubby Socialist millionaire, von Jagow now concluded that Parvus had been deceiving the German Reich all along, that he had never seriously tried to bring about a revolution, that he had most probably simply pocketed the millions given to him. Intelligence services have a rule that such expenditure is not subject to audit. But for the rest of 1916 the Ministry of Foreign Affairs paid Parvus not a pfennig more.

This didn't mean total defeat, and outwardly it was not a defeat at all. The wheels of the import-export agency went on turning and making money. The General Staff compassionately filled the gap left by the Foreign Ministry. The research institute continued collecting information and studying it. Parvus took an active hand in supplying Denmark with cheap coal, won over the Danish trade unions, was treated as their friend and equal by the Danish and later by the German Socialist leaders. He finally obtained German citizenship, which he had been begging for since 1891, and there seemed to be no doubt that at the first postwar elections he would take his place among the leaders of the Socialist group in the Reichstag. His *Bell* continued to appear, exhorting Germany to patriotic socialism. His exorbitant personal wealth grew and grew, and he had holdings in almost all neutral countries, as well as, of course, in Turkey and Bulgaria, where he had founded his fortunes. His house in the aristocratic quarter of Copenhagen was furnished with the flamboyance of the nouveau riche, guarded by savage dogs, and an elegant Adler carried him from his door. He even managed to preserve intact his influence on Count von Brockdorff-Rantzau, and to impress on this constant partner-in-conversation the full complexity of the revolutionary's task, the intricate mechanics of his difficulties. Through Brockdorff, too, as far as tact allowed, he tried to obstruct the renewed German quest for a separate peace with Russia.

You might suppose that the long procession of successes which came to meet him would have more than satisfied him. Not so! His uneasy consciousness of a mission unfulfilled—although he no longer had any intention of returning to *that* country—secretly teased and tormented him. In his leisurely suppers with the Prussian aristocrat he expounded a variant, adapted to the German outlook, of what was now not so much a program as his political testament, a hazy outline of the future. How the revolution, once begun, must quickly broaden its scope, like the Great French Revolution, by trying and executing the Tsar: only such an inaugural sacrifice could show the revolution that it need recognize no boundaries for itself. How the peasants must feel free to take the redistribution of land into their own hands—which alone would open the floodgates of anarchy. And when anarchy was at its height, in full flood, that was the very moment when Germany, by military intervention, with minimal losses and enormous advantages, could rid itself forever of the threat from the East: sink Russia's fleet, take away her arms, raze her fortifications, forbid her ever again to form an army or establish war industries, or, better still, any industry at all, cripple her by amputating all that could be amputated—leave her, in short, a *tabula rasa*, so that she could forget her ten centuries of nastiness and begin her history all over again.

Parvus never forgot an injury.

But he could not see at present what more he could do.

Meanwhile the government of the German empire was disgracing itself by seeking a separate peace with this still undestroyed power.

But Secretary of State von Jagow's health was steadily declining, and in the late autumn of 1916 he was happy to retire, giving up his post to the more active Zimmermann, who did not take over with it his predecessor's Old World distaste for secret agents and political hucksters. New plans of action soared into view! And Parvus's old grudge against Lenin raised its head. *Why* had he done it? What did he mean by it?

The bed hit the shoemaker's floor with all four feet, and Parvus was catapulted upright on his fat columnar legs. Painfully stretching, he shuffled across the room, carrying his pampered body like a heavy sack. He went around the table and sat on the other side, taking no care not to soil his snow-white cuffs on the Ulyanovs' dirty oilcloth.

His smile now was not for a man of power and an equal, but for a pathetic little animal in a hole.

"That's it, then, is it? Zimmerwald? . . . Kienthal? . . . Getting the leftists to vote correctly? . . . And what has the great Party done at home in Russia these past two years? . . . Why isn't there a single bubble to be seen on the surface?"

Lenin just sat there, sinking into the bed, and bent his heavy head without answering.

"Didn't you say you had no need of money?"

Lenin was embarrassed and almost inaudible. "We never said that, Izrail Lazarevich. We need money very, very badly. Desperately."

"But I offered you money! And you refused!"

Lenin's voice was parched and strained. "What do you mean, refused? A sensible offer of help, without strings, we never refuse. We're only too glad . . ."

"You're just playing children's games here in Switzerland." The fat hulk would have liked to gloat, but there was nothing to gloat over. Russia was not losing the war, Germany was not winning it, Germany's main ally, and his own, was giving up the fight.

Lenin's words seemed to stick in his throat.

"For serious games you have to pay a serious price."

He looked sick. His eyes, less secretive than usual, were full of pain, and his next words were spoken without vehemence, with no other motive, it seemed, than to distract himself from his pain.

"After all, Izrail Lazarevich, your revolution too was a will-o'-the-wisp, a soap bubble. It was naïve to expect anything else."

Parvus heaved indignantly, and the lamp flame flickered, leapt, and smoked as his breath played on it.

"We had forty-five thousand on strike in Petersburg! Do you think you, sitting here, could bring forty-five thousand out?"

He forestalled Lenin's retort that the forty-five thousand included some of *his* people.

". . . The Putilov workers got the date wrong—but they were marvelous! What a rumpus they kicked up! But the Nevskaya Zastava let me down—why didn't you bring them out? I staged a splendid strike in Nikolaev—ten thousand came out! With impossible demands, so that a rising was certain! But they too were four days late. It's not so easy from this distance to tie them all to the same day. But how is it that Moscow never stirred? What was your Moscow committee doing?"

(Lenin only wished that he knew!)

Parvus warmed to his theme, crooking a finger for each of his successes, as though he was boasting about his wealth.

"I brought out the Ekaterinoslav ironworks! And the Tula copper plant! And the Tula cartridge factory! . . ."

All these strikes had indeed broken out in January, though not on the 22nd—but who had started them, who had led them there on the spot? It was not clear at this distance, and everybody claimed credit, including the Mensheviks.

"We came very close—but where were your people? The Interdistrict group gave me wholehearted support, they've got fire in their bellies, but they're a mere handful. While you and the Mensheviks are still tossing balls to each other! Russia is flooded with leaflets—are you going to tell me they're yours, not mine? It was I who blew up the *Empress Maria*—or didn't you notice it?" Parvus thundered on, his eyes staring wildly. "The Black Sea battleship—didn't you notice it???!"

He threw up his manicured white hands—look at the hands that blew up a battleship!

"Why wouldn't you join us, Vladimir Ilyich? Where are *your* strikes? Where are your riots? Which factories can you bring to a standstill at a predetermined date? Which of the nationalist organizations are you working with?"

Does he really not understand? . . . For all his cleverness? My façade is a success, then! I must keep it up!

Why hadn't he joined in! . . . Of course, he could have gotten around the Mensheviks somehow. Made some arrangement to share the leadership (although this, yes, this, was the most painful and difficult thing of all). Only . . .

Only—everyone's abilities are limited. Lenin was—a writer of articles. And pamphlets. He gave lectures. He made speeches. He carried on agitation among young leftists. He trounced opportunists everywhere in Europe. He believed that he had acquired a thorough knowledge of problems connected with industry, agriculture, the strike movement, trade unions. And now, after reading Clausewitz, of military matters too. He understood now what war was, and how an armed uprising should be carried out. And he could explain it all, with tireless clarity, to any audience.

There was only one thing of which he was incapable—action. The one thing he could not do was—blow up a battleship.

"But all is not yet lost, Vladimir Ilyich," said Parvus, consoling, encouraging, from across the table. He took his gold watch from his vest pocket and nodded at it approvingly. "We'll postpone the revolution until 22 January 1917! But let's do it together! Shall we be together this time?"

Why on earth shouldn't they? The perspicacious Parvus simply couldn't see it.

Lenin could not keep his end up in this conversation. He was lost for an answer. How could he talk about entering or not entering into an alliance, when his position was so ridiculously weak? Dignified concealment of his impotence was what he must aim at: hiding the fact that he had no functioning organization, no underground in Russia. If it existed at all it was a law unto itself, and he had no control over its actions or their timing. He simply did not know what *was* there—he was not in uninterrupted communication with Russia, had no means of sending instructions or receiving a reply. He was only too glad if Shlyapnikov, who was all by himself, managed to pitch a bundle of *Social Democrats* over the frontier. His sister Anya was in Petersburg, doing whatever she could, and they had corresponded in invisible ink, but even this link had snapped. How could he stir up rebellion among the national minorities? It would be something if he could preserve a fragment of his own party . . .

Parvus, flabbily draped over his creaking chair, had not exhausted his generosity.

"How do your collaborators cross the Russian frontier? Surely not on their own feet, or in rowboats? That's all out-of-date, nineteenth-century stuff. It's time you forgot all that! If you like, we'll provide them with splendid documents and they can travel first-class, like my people . . ."

Parvus, no doubt, was ugly—as seen by women, or a public meeting. But his colorless, watery eyes were irresistibly clever—and cleverness was something Lenin appreciated.

If only he could get away from them. Parvus must not guess the truth.

Must not guess that *action* was just what Lenin could not manage. All the rest he knew how to do. But one thing he could not do: bring the great moment nearer, make it happen.

Parvus, with his millions, with his weapons probably already in the ports, with his conspiratorial skill, with various factories already securely in his grip—Parvus clapped his hands, the hands of a man of action, white and pudgy though they were, and continued his interrogation.

"What *are* you waiting for, Vladimir Ilyich? Why don't you give the signal? How long do you intend to wait?"

Lenin was waiting for—for *something* to happen. For some favorable tide of affairs to carry his little boat home—to a fait accompli.

Ludicrously, all the ideas on which Lenin had based his life could neither change the course of the war, nor transform it into a civil war, nor force Russia to lose.

The little boat lay like a toy on the sand, and there was no tide to float it . . .

All this time the letter on expensive greenish paper lay there asking him: What do you say, then, Vladimir Ilyich? Will *your* people cooperate or won't they? Where are your meeting points? Who takes delivery of weapons? Tell me what you have there of any real use.

Precisely the question Lenin could not answer, since he had nothing. Switzerland was on one planet, Russia on another. What he had was . . . a tiny group, calling itself a party, and he could not account for all its members—some might have split off. What he had was . . . *What Is to Be Done?*, *Two Tactics, Empiriocriticism, Imperialism*. What he had was . . . a head, capable at any moment of providing a centralized organization with decisions, each individual revolutionary with detailed instructions, and the masses with thrilling slogans. And nothing more, no more today than he had had eighteen months ago. So that tactical caution and simple pride alike forbade him to reveal his weak spot to Parvus, any more than he had eighteen months ago.

But Parvus hung over the table, his fishy eyes full of mockery, his brow no less steeply terraced than Lenin's, and awaited, demanded an answer.

He had very cleverly seized the initiative, asking question after question so that he need do no explaining himself. But he must have his own reasons for this approach at this particular time, after eighteen months of silence.

Avoiding the puzzled hovering gaze from under Parvus's upturned hairless eyebrows, rolling his head as he perused the letter, Lenin tried to think how he could refuse help without giving offense, without losing an ally, how to conceal his own secret while divining that of his companion. Skipping what was in the letter and looking for what was not there.

Lenin was always eager above all to seize on weaknesses which offset his own. If there was no chink in Parvus's armor, why was he making this second approach, and so insistently? Had his strength failed him? Or his funds perhaps? Had his network broken down? Or perhaps the German government was no longer paying so well? They made you work for your money, once they had you hooked.

How good it was to be independent! Oh no, we're not so weak as you think! Not nearly as weak as some!

His right hand as usual made pencil marks in preparation for his reply—straight lines, wavy lines, squiggles, question marks, exclamation marks . . . While his left hand restlessly rubbed his forehead, and his forehead gathered in the points he would make.

Trotsky's complaints against his former mentor—that he was frivolous, lacked stamina, and abandoned his friends in time of trouble—were so much sentimental rubbish. These were all pardonable faults, and need not stand in the way of an alliance. If only Parvus had not committed gross political errors. He should not have exposed himself publicly by rushing at a mirage of revolution. He should not have made *The Bell* a cesspool of German chauvinism. The hippo had wallowed in the mire with Hindenburg—and destroyed his reputation. Destroyed himself as a Socialist once and for all.

It was sad. There were not many Socialists like him!

(But although he had destroyed himself, there was no sense in quarreling. Parvus might still be enormously helpful.)

Regaining his confidence, Lenin raised his eyes from the letter, from the edge of the table, and looked at his indefatigable rival. The contours of his head, shapeless enough at the best of times, and of his pudgy shoulders blurred and trembled.

Trembled as though they were shaking with grief. Grief that even with Lenin he could not make himself fully understood.

His features faded, till he was no more than a lengthening streak of bluish mist. He bowed, drifted across the room, and seeped through the window.

But while there was still barely time Lenin shouted after him, not crowing over him, but just so that the truth should not go untold: "Let myself be tied to someone else's policy? Not for anything in the world! That's where you made your mistake, Izrail Lazarevich! I'll take what I need from others—of course! But tie my *own* hands? No!!! It would be absurd to speak of an alliance which meant tying my own hands!"

The whole scene vanished like smoke, leaving no trace of Sklarz or of his case. His hat, too, belatedly whisked itself off the table and flung itself after them.

Lenin had proved to be the more farsighted of the two! Though he had made no revolution, though he was helpless and ineffectual, he knew that he was right, he had not let himself be misled: ideas are more durable than all your millions, I can soldier on without them. Never fear, even the conferences for women and deserters will prove to have been worthwhile. Under the crimson flag of the International I can wait another thirty years if need be.

He had preserved his greatest treasure—his honor as a Socialist.

No, it's too soon to think of surrender! Too soon to leave Switzerland. A few more months of purposeful work, and the Swiss Party will be split.

Soon after that—we will start the revolution here!

And from Switzerland the flame of revolution will be kindled throughout Europe!

Document No. 2

7 November

Tsarskoye Selo

To His Majesty.

My own angel, once again we are parting! . . . Seeing you in our home environment after a six-month absence—thank you for this quiet joy!

I hate letting you go there to all those torments, and anxieties and worries. And now there's this business with Poland. But God does all for the best, and so I *want* to believe that this too will be for the best. Their troops won't want to fight against us, mutinies will break out, a revolution, who knows what—that is my opinion. I shall ask our Friend what he thinks.

I don't like Nikolasha coming to GHQ. I only hope he won't cause trouble, with his adherents! Don't let him go calling anywhere, let him return to the Caucasus, otherwise the revolutionary party will be cheering for him again. They have gradually begun to forget him.

I am very heavy at heart. But in my soul I am constantly with you and I love you dearly.

Forever, my dear, my darling, your old

Wifey

8 November

Mogilev

To Her Majesty.

My priceless, beloved darling! With all my loving old heart I thank you for your dear letter. We both felt so sad when the train moved out. I prayed with Baby and played dominoes for a bit. We went to bed early. . . .

Aleksei's cat ran away and hid under a big pile of planks. We put our overcoats on and went looking for her. The sailor found her immediately with the help of an electric torch, but it took us a long time to make the wretched creature come out, she wouldn't obey Baby.

Oh, my treasure, my love! How I miss you. It was such genuine happiness—those six days at home!

God keep you and the girls.

For ever and ever, My Sunny, all yours, your old

Nicky

[5 1]

On the train back to Moscow the wonderful lightheartedness which had kept Vorotyntsev afloat through those nine days in Petersburg gradually left him. His triumphant mood had evaporated before he reached Moscow and he was having to drug himself more and more heavily with tobacco smoke.

He stepped out onto the platform with feet that seemed numb. He felt dejected, anxious, full of confused forebodings.

Why this heaviness? He had nothing at all to fear. His unease could not be a presentiment of disaster. He wasn't even late for Alina's birthday: he'd arrived as expected, on the eve. Late in the day, to be sure.

He was, though, beginning to realize that he would soon have to shoulder a crushing burden: the need to dissemble. His smile, his eyes, his words must proclaim that nothing out of the ordinary had happened in Petersburg, that this was just one of those holdups you come to expect.

They were economizing on street lighting in Moscow and the city was quite dark in places. But trams trundled by like glittering chariots, and some shopwindows were radiant.

He sensed a certain unease abroad in the streets. The cabby went fast. They always did when the fare was an officer. Hopeless trying to slow him down.

She could not possibly *know*. So I'm late. That's the army for you.

He could explain, defuse the situation. And, after all, he *was* back in time for her birthday.

His feet, so light on the Pesochnaya Embankment and on Aptekarsky Island, dragged like iron weights as he climbed the stairs to his third-floor home.

Alina came out to meet him in the hall, looking as if she had been lying down with a bad headache. Perhaps she really was ill.

With one foot over the threshold, still in his overcoat, he took her by her fragile elbows instead of embracing her, and asked in alarm what was wrong. He had always felt her aches and indispositions as if they were his own.

Pale-faced, eyebrows raised, she said, "I would think you know better than I do." And looked at him searchingly. There was a deathly finality in her manner, an air about her of having gone beyond all possible limits.

He quickly bent down to kiss her. His lips found first her forehead, then an ear.

She could not possibly have heard, and there was nothing to give him away, but for one moment he was assailed by a feeling that she did know, and that he might as well not try to hide it. He must not give in to that feeling, must not let it show in his words or his looks.

"Are you ill?" he asked anxiously. He had never felt so awkward with her, so guilty, and so sorry for her all at once.

She threw back her head and stared at him silently, from half-closed eyes, as though he was lost to her.

"Yes," she said. "Because of you." And walked away without waiting for him to take off his sword and greatcoat.

"But I'm here now, I'm home in time!" Georgi called after her.

His protestation went unanswered.

He took off his sword and coat quickly, hung his coat any which way on a hook, and quickly followed her.

Alina was standing at the dressing table, with her back half turned to him, rummaging in one of those big chocolate boxes she liked to collect and find a use for later, looking for some small object. With her back to him, and her head bent so that her neck looked pathetically vulnerable below those newly curled ringlets. Even her shoulder expressed her hurt.

Georgi had been so intoxicated with happiness those last few days— why had it never occurred to him that she was having such a hard time? And why, oh why, couldn't he have managed to write her just one decent letter? When she had begged him to write every day, and always looked forward so much to hearing from him.

He had never once taken pity on her. On that defenseless neck.

But, still supposing that it was no worse than that, he took her by the shoulders, gently, so that she would not twist out of his grasp, and repeated from behind her, "Alina, my dear, don't be angry. Don't upset yourself. Please forgive me."

She half turned, looked at him sorrowfully, and answered, emphasizing every syllable, "You have disgraced me!"

Georgi was shaken. This couldn't be a coincidence. She knew!

She slowly turned her head away. And stood with the back of her neck to him again.

She knew! How, though?

Still she didn't try to free her shoulders.

Which must mean that she didn't know after all!

Whatever else was wrong could not be as terrible as that.

He stood looking at her neck, at her delicately sculpted ear. She had beautiful ears.

It had sometimes happened that he had carelessly or clumsily or impatiently done something to hurt her, put himself in the wrong without being aware of it. And the best way to get out of these upsets and back into smoother waters was simply to beg forgiveness. Saying sorry was a ritual that had always worked for them. But this time his guilt was too great for that. It would be better to distract her with some powerful excuse. Alina always listened readily to powerful excuses.

First, though, he needed to know exactly what the situation was.

"Look, Alina, my love," he murmured, "I did get back on time."

She flared up, flung down the chocolate box, and turned on him. "On time? You call this on time? After three telegrams! And four letters! I expect you'll say they didn't reach you!"

Alina's eyes blazed, and her face was suddenly younger, and no longer looked languid and unwell. Her face always changed with remarkable rapidity! At least she wasn't ill! So he was late—was that all there was to it?

He held her by her shoulders, facing him, feeling more sure of himself.

It had been ten days instead of four, yes. But those dunderheads on the General Staff had lost touch with the army in the field, and didn't seem to want to know about it. (Not enough to account for a whole week.) At the ministry too, they kept promising to see me, and putting it off. (Still not enough.) Then Svechin kept me waiting, telegraphed saying he was on his way to Petrograd, and it would be worth my while to wait. To discuss a possible assignment to GHQ. (Would this mention of GHQ cheer her up? Not one little bit. And she still had to be told that because of GHQ he would be leaving earlier.)

Georgi spoke fervently, gazing innocently into her eyes, trying hard not to look shifty. It was the first time that anything like this had happened to him, and it was unbearable. He felt himself blushing, blushing so that she could not fail to notice.

It's all over, then! She's guessed . . .

The corners of her eyes narrowed. Ironically? Suspiciously?

"I telegraphed telling you to come—when?"

"At least one day early."

"And what did you do?"

"Came one day early."

"You call this one day early? This is the night before, not the day before."

She was wounded, she was suffering acutely, poor girl, but—oh!— Georgi was relieved of his first, stupefying impression that she knew everything.

If all I've done to upset her is arriving late on the eve of her birthday—that's easily fixed.

"I thought when you said the day before you meant not on the day itself . . . Forgive me!" He raised her delicate, weightless hands, and put his lips to each in turn.

Yes, her birthday was a great, joyous day (her name day meant less to her, she did not like her saint) but there were another half dozen great and joyous and truly sacred days in their calendar, a whole string of them. And he had never missed one!

She smiled wryly.

"So here you are! Thank you! Now that I've canceled the guests."

Nothing terrible had happened after all.

"Well, it still isn't too late—why not invite them again first thing tomorrow?"

The hurt helplessness in her bright eyes gave way to a look that pierced him to the depths of his soul.

"Not too late? You *really* think so?

"Couldn't you have written just once to encourage your 'little pearl'? Why were your letters so short and offhand?"

Well, yes. Common prudence should have told him that writing would have made things easier. He was certainly at fault there. Which made it all the more easy for him to ask forgiveness now.

He asked, but without using his hands too much, without drawing her close and kissing her. Now that he knew she did not know he was sickened by a sudden thought: I'm beginning to feel sleepy, and we should be going to bed soon. The very idea was bizarre, revolting, unnatural.

But it was late, he was so very tired . . . and doing his best to look more tired than he was.

He needn't have bothered. Alina proudly raised her head. There was no sign of illness or exhaustion as she looked into his eyes and said slowly and clearly, "It's my birthday. You've ruined it for me. And it was to have been such an important one."

She turned away, slipping out of his slack hold, walked, heels clicking, over the parquet floor, and disappeared into the bedroom, noisily turning the key left there in readiness.

What a relief! How good to sleep alone, at ease, unconstrained, with no need at all to pretend! He could have his sleep at last.

He would have liked a bite of supper. Should he raid the sideboard? Look in the kitchen? No, it would be safer to put the light out quickly, and not risk a replay of their conversation.

One last cigarette—in the dark. In one sense this birthday had come around just in time. He had disgraced himself with his response to Guchkov. But Guchkov might have been even more upset to be told that the Russian soldier was the least of his concerns. How could you expect him to think of anything except a brilliant victory? Besides, there was no knowing what Guchkov might have involved him in. Was that really the path he wanted to follow? Surely not.

It was very easy to be mistaken about those you thought were on your side.

He felt just as much at odds with Shingarev.

It was only on the train on the way home, not last night at Cubat's, that Vorotyntsev had seen the trap he was falling into. The Emperor was boundlessly devoted to the Allies, whatever the cost in Russian blood, but so were the Kadet opposition, and so were the conspirators—just as devoted to the same Allies, and at the same price.

He had imagined himself at one with them—but had quickly reached the parting of the ways. He had found no cause worthy of his efforts. And now there was this other problem: what did the future hold for Alina and himself?

It was sickening to have to lie—lie with his looks, even with his hands. And it was a dirty trick to play on her.

He wouldn't be able to stand it for long. He would have to slip away and get to GHQ.

All that she had suffered that week could not be so easily forgiven. It wasn't just a red-letter day, an annual celebration, it symbolized their togetherness.

After that evening at Muma's, when Georgi, without doing or saying anything very much, had unexpectedly made such a favorable impression on everybody, Susanna and others had insisted on seeing him again when he returned, and this had given Alina the idea of inviting lots of guests on her birthday to hear all that he could tell them. They had all been given advanced notice.

It would not have been like her to spend that week passively waiting after he had fallen silent, broken contact, trampled everything underfoot. She was temperamentally more inclined to rush in impetuously and demand an explanation. He was still less than two days late when she bought a ticket for Petrograd, and imagined herself confronting him there—how abjectly apologetic he would be! But suddenly she felt unwell . . . a chill, a heavy cold, a headache . . . she lost her appetite . . . took to her bed . . . and the days in which she might have reassured herself ran out. Her pride left her with only one course of action—to put off her guests, pretending that she and her husband had decided to celebrate by themselves, away from Moscow. It was not too late, perhaps, but she could not possibly renew the invitations now.

Georgi had become infinitely rougher and more bearish as the war went on. She had realized it last year, when she visited him in Bukovina. It had been her birthday then too—an important one, her thirtieth—the end of a decade—and that too had been a dismal event. Her husband had forgotten how they used to cherish and revel in all their family anniversaries: the day on which he had proposed, the day of their first kiss, the day of their betrothal, their wedding day. He had become insensitive, and it was her womanly duty, no matter how long it took, to soften him and humanize him again.

She had heard a musicologist say, in an interesting lecture, that Pushkin had shown his psychological insight in crediting Herman with no emotions except those of the compulsive gambler: Lisa, to him, was no more than a front-door key. It was the Chaikovsky brothers who had, implausibly, introduced Herman's love for Lisa, and ruined what had been a straightforward story line.

Maybe Georgi was like Pushkin's hero, except that his passion was not cards but—but what? Maps, perhaps.

She could, of course, leave it at that—act as though nothing had happened. His delay was unpardonable, but still, he had returned, and it was still the day before her birthday.

Alina was certainly not one to look for quarrels and lengthy arguments. She liked domestic harmony, with nothing to disturb the orderly and comfortable routine which she had created. But with this went a need to feel, to be constantly aware, that she was appreciated.

[5 2]

The light of the morning sun rising over the Moscow River found its way through two of their windows. The last two days had been cold and dull—indeed the weather had been foul throughout the autumn months. But suddenly, on Alina's birthday the sun had peeped out. A good omen! A symbol! Time to shed the cares that weighed so heavily. To behave as if last night had seen the end of all that was bad, and only good things could happen today. Alina had no wish to nurse a grudge.

She emerged from the bedroom fully dressed, wearing a dress with a high collar.

Georgi had already shaved and put on his uniform, complete with sword belt. He sat waiting for her in the living room. When he was anxious to please he could be very sweet, and even found it in himself to be gallant. He rose to meet her with a friendly smile. And carrying a present.

He embraced her tenderly, and kissed her.

The present was nothing very much, not something planned long in advance, just a little thing picked up the other day in Petersburg—an expandable bracelet in finely wrought gold. In a pretty little case.

He put it around her arm himself.

No good comes of prolonging quarrels. Alina did not want to dwell on her grievances. She was determined to be happy. Georgi couldn't help the way he was—why be annoyed with him.

Shortly afterward the little Chinese bell summoned him to breakfast.

A quiet, cozy breakfast. With the sun shining. Alina was as cheerful as a little bird. Her very own, special day. Today she had to be merry, had to be happy.

"But you see, Georgi, I told everybody that you and I would be away today. We simply can't stay here now, we'll have to go somewhere."

He frowned slightly. He didn't much like the idea. A cloud passed over his brow.

"We can invite people some other day."

"Grumpy! You just want to sit at your desk the whole time. It's your own fault you were late. And just look at the weather! Let's go out of town!"

"Where, though?"

They exchanged suggestions. Alina wanted somewhere with a hotel or guesthouse, so that they could stay overnight if they felt like it.

"Maybe S . . . ? There's an idea! The lake, at S . . . !"

"Lake, you call it? More like a pond!"

"Well, you used to call it a lake!"

They agreed on that.

But although they wasted no time getting ready the sun was shining less brightly when they left the house, and the sky was grayer all the time.

In spite of the weather, the canceled party, and the guests forgone, Alina had resolved not to sulk or show resentment, but to act as though it was all for the best. He must, sometime or other, be made to feel what it meant to have a wife. Back with the army he would soon get hard and cross again.

But as they traveled in the suburban train a keen wind sprang up, chasing dark gray rain clouds until they covered the sky.

Alina thought of a game to while the time away: they would both try to recall all their birthdays, wedding anniversaries, Christmases, and New Years—where they were, in what circumstances, and with whom they had celebrated.

Alina did most of the remembering. Georgi seemed rather half-hearted about it. She noticed again, as she had earlier that morning, that from time to time he sighed heavily.

"Why are you sighing like that?"

He was surprised. "Was I? I wasn't aware of it."

"Very deep sighs. You were the same after East Prussia. You kept sighing just like that all the time you were in Moscow."

He shook his head in surprise.

She took pity on him, and laid her hand on his to soothe him.

"Have you got a lot of worries? Was your trip a disappointment?"

He frowned.

"Y-yes, I suppose so . . . yes . . . it was disappointing."

Alina had looked forward to boating on the lake. Not a chance! The rowboats were all beached and upside down, there were no oars, and the sky was now so dark that no one would wish to go out on the water.

But she so much wanted to do something out of the ordinary!

Their one stroke of luck was with the guesthouse: it was open, there were vacancies, and meals were served. There were several rooms to choose from, and they took a pleasant corner room on the second floor, with one window looking out on a forest, and a view of the lake from the other. It was warm in the room too. And the chambermaid had stoked up the Dutch stove from the corridor side—wood was plentiful there, not like in town. Hurrah, let's stay the night! It will be so cozy!

Once settled in, once thoroughly warmed—what next? A walk?

They went for a walk.

Alina took it into her head to gather a bouquet of autumn leaves, a medley of beautiful autumn colors. But there were no red leaves to be found anywhere. And hardly any pure yellow ones. Nothing but withered brown things, and twigs with cones.

What was to have been a thing of beauty never took shape.

Anyway, it's no fun unless both of you have your hearts in it. If you are like a frolicsome child, and your companion like a severe and humorless nursemaid who doesn't want to hop and skip and climb trees, and won't let you do any of those things . . . She had forgiven him, but he wasn't grateful, there was no break in the clouds. Something was weighing on his mind.

More sighs. Why had he gotten into that habit again? Just for today he might try to restrain himself.

The weather was steadily worsening, the wind was freshening, driving the clouds into a compact gray mass. Chilled to the bone even with her fur collar up, Alina started shivering. Her husband did then put one arm around her. And they went back to the guesthouse.

I know—maybe there's a piano here? I could play for you, I would love to play for you!

Yes, there was an upright piano. But it was badly out of tune, it jarred on the ear. Alina was so annoyed that she flared up and scolded the landlady.

"How can you keep an instrument in this condition? Why have it at all if this is the best you can do? Some guesthouse this is!"

She was as distressed by the plight of the out-of-tune piano as if it were a neglected living creature. Which was what she was beginning to feel like herself . . .

On her special day. She had meant to enjoy it at all costs, and now it was almost in ruins.

How could she make it enjoyable all by herself? It took two. But Georgi was gloomy, as gloomy as could be. He had spoiled everything, upset everything. He'd been forgiven—and now look at him.

Swirling showers, not very heavy, and soon over, swept the guesthouse, coming from different directions, as they could tell from a multitude of rapid, oblique drops on the windowpanes, more and more conspicuous as they began to turn into sleet or snow. Whenever such a flurry of rain and snow, whipped up by a gusty wind, lashed and bespattered the guesthouse, it seemed that foul weather had set in for a week.

Left with nothing else to do, they went downstairs to dine. There wasn't much choice, but the food they had ordered an hour earlier was ready for them. Port wine was served.

Georgi started proposing a toast, to her. All that was lacking was a sparkling table, and a dozen guests, like those she had previously invited. But even with just the two of them, and even in that half-dark dining room, he could have said something more eloquent and more heartfelt. Why, when there was no one else to hear, when he was almost whispering in her ear, why was it costing him such an effort, why was he speaking so clumsily, so unlike him—words tumbling over each other, sentences unraveling, as if he'd completely forgotten how to do it? He rambled, said nothing explicit about their love for one another, or their future, or, really, about his wishes for her on her birthday . . .

Instead of being happy she felt sick at heart.

Then the dinner turned out to be an unsavory mess, not a bit birthday-like. The rice that came with it was sticky, soaked in something brown, and, even so, quite dry.

"Do you remember," Alina asked, "we read somewhere that in China a man suspected of a crime is made to eat dry rice, and if he's too agitated to salivate, and can't swallow, that's taken as proof of his guilt?"

The untouched heap of brown rice on her plate suddenly seemed to swell as she looked at it—like a symbol of her ruined and ravaged birthday. And perhaps of something more. From now on, whenever she found herself remembering birthdays, those dark flurries outside and that brown rice would surface.

Alina's eyes filled with tears. But she held herself in check.

Her husband seemed not even to notice. He was smoking. The blustering wind hurled spinning snowflakes in waves against the windows. By now it was so dark inside that lamps were brought in with the dessert.

When they went up to their room the lamp had been lit there. But it was not yet night: there was still a long, long evening ahead of them.

A small square room: two beds, two bedside tables, a chest of drawers, and a dressing table. The dreariness of it. If only they were in town! Should they go back? . . . In that storm and in the dark?

If only there had been a piano! I'd have played and played for you, all evening.

Yes, oh yes! He wished it as fervently as she did, he always liked that. Liked to soften his harsh nature with music.

What, though, what could they do to pass the time? If they hadn't been in too much of a hurry to think of it they could have brought some roast nuts. She would lie down, and he would sit by the bed and crack them: one for you, one for me, bad ones don't count.

At home they could think of lots of things, and they both had things of their own to do, but here, alone together and with nothing on hand, what could they think up?

Georgi found a nail and hung his sword on the bare wall, not in the closet. He wandered around like a lost soul, pausing now and then to press his forehead against the windowpane.

Alina sat before the mirror. For a birthday girl she looked pretty miserable.

"Well—this is some birthday we're having, thanks to you. Worse than a bad joke."

He just stood there, pressing his forehead against the dark windowpane.

She felt like crying. It cost her a great effort not to burst into tears.

Georgi came over and sat on the bed, arms folded. Saying nothing. Sighing again.

"Look at you!" Alina burst out. "Why are you so gloomy? Why do you keep sighing all the time, as if you'd just come from a funeral?"

She could see the tragic look in his eyes reflected in the mirror—and suddenly, without knowing why, she was afraid, she recoiled from the mirror, and screamed, beside herself: "Wha-a-a-at is it? What's wrong?"

He was not surprised by her scream—and that frightened her all the more. He averted his eyes, rested one hand on the bedstead, and sat there hanging his head.

His sword hung like a threat on the naked wall behind them.

Alina faltered. Perhaps she ought not to ask, perhaps it was better not to look for an explanation.

But how could she hold out till morning, cooped up in that poky little room with those funereal sighs?

"Georgi! What *has* happened?" Alina asked, fearfully, urgently. "Why aren't you looking at me? Look at me!"

He looked. As though every bit of him ached, as though his lips could not form words. His voice was muffled, hollow, broken.

"I . . . I . . . don't know how to tell you . . ."

If Georgi had ever lived through such a luckless day it was so long ago that he had forgotten. Every movement, every word cost him an effort. How he longed to be out of it, the very next day, to take the train and be off to Mogilev. But no, he had to do something to make amends for his lateness and for the wrecked birthday. Had to stay on in Moscow for a while. He dared not say a word about GHQ just yet.

For the first time in his life he had to pretend to his wife, show emotions which he did not feel, celebrate, when he felt numb all over, let his tongue utter words which came neither from his heart nor from his head.

For one day it might be possible—but must it now be forever?

A ball and chain too heavy to drag.

But he was conscience-stricken, and sorry for Alina. He had sincerely wanted to be kind and attentive today. But he felt completely lifeless.

He was sorry for her, and his pity was especially acute when she had almost burst into tears over the brown rice that was impossible to swallow. Surely she deserved a better birthday than this?

He could see everything falling apart, everything going to rack and ruin, and there was nothing he could do to put it right. He could not alter his looks, his tone of voice. (Lifeless he felt, yet deep, deep down in his breast, though no longer full of her, he clung to Olda, cherished her, felt her stirring within him.)

If only we could get out of here and back to Moscow, this very evening! But no, we have to wait for good weather.

Shut up in a little square room, condemned to togetherness, tête-à-tête.

So lifeless that pretending was the hardest thing of all. And anyway, how could he go on hiding all his life? He would not give up Olda for anything in the world, so was this how it would be for the rest of his life?

No, he must brace himself! How much more noble it would be to tell her himself, straight out, and be rid of secrecy once and for all!

He remembered fleetingly the story he had heard on the train—how Zinaida, from Tambov, had made her engineer tell his wife everything at the very beginning. And how, there on the train, when it had no relevance at all to him, he had thought her behavior only right.

Right, yes. But was it the conventional thing? The conventional thing in such situations had always been to lie. But why? How much easier your conscience would be if you told the truth and stood up straight again. Surely one human being was capable of telling another the truth?

His feelings had brought him to the brink of confession, but he might not have gotten around to it. If they had left for the city perhaps nothing would have happened. But as it was, locked in by bad weather even more securely than yesterday, with Alina relentlessly questioning him, and realizing that any moment now they would be going to bed together . . .

His tongue could not utter it, he could not find words, and there was another stumbling block. What had she done to deserve all this? She was less to blame than anyone—yet she must bear the brunt.

But he had to tell her.

There was no change of expression in Alina's eyes—neither "Go on, go on!" nor "Stop, I don't want to know!" They only opened wider, and took it all in. Her quick, clever gray eyes, always so understanding.

He in turn directed his full gaze on his wife (he could still see his sword on the wall out of the corner of his eye).

She did not cry out. No emotion contorted her features. There was no puckering of the brow even.

She was smiling! Her lips were parted in a smile of incomprehension. You mean you . . . ? You mean she . . . ?

That Alina did not jump up, did not cry out, did not rage at him, pierced Georgi to the quick. Suddenly she was so dear to him that the estrangement of the last twenty-four hours was forgotten. He moved to sit beside her, on her bed, and smoothed the ends of her hair on her temple.

"But it doesn't mean that I have stopped loving you. It doesn't mean that at all."

Good God, could it really be over with so little fuss? Could sensible women really be made to understand things as simply as this?

Alina bent away from him, slowly, gently, until her head was resting on the pillow.

His hand could still reach her. He stroked her shoulder. Her hair was freshly curled. A new, quite new tenderness toward his wife flooded his being. And gratitude that she could understand. What a woman! What lofty feelings they could share!

A tender reconciliation seemed to steal over them, like a protective shadow.

She wept. But quietly, unprotestingly. No sobs, no reproaches.

"But did it have to be Petersburg?" Alina suddenly complained, in a thin, almost childlike voice. "The city where you and I were so happy together? Which has so many memories for us?"

In the soothing silence he felt all at once such relief, such relief, such an easing of body and soul—as if the woman lying beside him was one he had fought ten years to win, and now at last . . . How dearly he loved her again! The deadness he had felt last night, and today, might never have been.

"Was it . . . very nice for you being with her?" Alina asked, not even in a whisper, in a mere breath.

"Yes, very," Georgi answered honestly, simply.

"Just—that way, or generally?"

"Well, yes, generally. She's so lively."

Alina lay there without speaking, eyes closed, for a long time. He moved even closer to her, tenderly stroked her temple, touched her delicately shaped ear, the youthfully smooth skin of her cheek.

She was exquisite.

It was so quiet in their room that they could hear every breath of wind outside, and the sloppy fumbling of the sleet at the windows.

"What do you mean by generally?" Alina whispered, without opening her eyes. "Does she play the piano?"

"No," Georgi answered calmly, quietly. "But she talks very interestingly about music, she has a discerning taste. She's generally clever, with a broad education." He should not have gone on talking about Olda, but he was carried away. "She's complicated. Highly charged. Doesn't give way too easily to prevailing opinion. She has such deep-rooted, independent ideas about history, about society . . ."

He was praising her so freely to defend and justify himself. Alina liked clever people, and Olda was so brilliant! Even another woman could not help being enchanted by her. How easy, how loving life on earth would be if only people were a little more understanding, a little more tolerant, a little readier to make allowances for one another.

"Who is she?" Alina asked, in the same quiet, caressing voice, opening her eyes, but not seeing his.

That was something Georgi hadn't thought of. He hadn't expected to be asked straight out, and so soon, who she was. But then he hadn't expected Alina to take it so meekly, to show such an honest desire to understand. Now that he'd started he would have to name her sooner or later. So why not now? When to speak her name aloud would be music to his ears.

But for some reason it stuck in his throat. Something prevented him from saying it.

From her pillow, Alina, now dry-eyed, turned a calm, deep, searching look on him.

He lowered his eyes.

She must have looked away. She lay there without a sound, her cheek against the pillow.

And, following his own train of thought, he said out loud, "Alochka! I've never for a moment thought of leaving you . . . I don't . . . But I . . . I can't really . . ."

He absentmindedly stroked the roll of hair at the back of her head.

She raised her head again. No trace of tears! Nothing could make her cry today! Her proud face was burning. Her half-closed eyes were tense.

"Tell me," she said, "does Vera know?"

He suppressed a shudder. A completely unexpected question. Vera did know, of course, and understood, although it had never been mentioned directly. She knew! But—it cut him to the quick—this was something he could not tell Alina! Just when he had begun to revel in his truthfulness he suddenly had to renounce it, to start lying, start quickly, and make it sound convincing with that interrogating gaze upon him.

"No," he said, boldly, firmly, "how could you think so? Of course she doesn't!"

Well, if it had never been directly mentioned, she didn't know, and he was right. He had told her a bigger truth—surely she could believe his half-truth?

Did she?

He broke into a sweat. He was trapped. This was where telling the truth got you.

She sat up slowly, and said austerely, "Well . . . it's better that way. It's better than the unfeelingness I thought I saw in you lately."

Then, deliberately: "I'm glad for you."

There was silence throughout the guesthouse. Profound silence. The fires had been banked, the pokers had rattled their last, the stove door had been slammed with one final cast-iron clang. There was no more shuffling in the corridor.

The steady stream of water drumming on the tin window ledge outside could be heard all the more clearly. The snow must be thawing as it fell.

In the same toneless voice she said, "Go outside while I get ready for bed."

He showed his surprise.

With the look of a woman much older and wiser than he was, she explained, without anger, sounding almost friendly: "With you there I used to behave as if I was by myself. But it won't be like that anymore."

[5 3]

She felt like a small child. The disaster that had crashed down upon her was so huge, so merciless that her childish hands lacked strength to lift it off her or to claw out from under it: she had so longed for things to go well, for a nice smooth, comfortable sunlit life, and suddenly disaster had come crashing down on her and crushed everything.

Worst of all, this was the side of things which she never wanted even to talk about, it would be shaming, demeaning, improper, and now it had so ruthlessly forced itself upon her. Making it impossible to exist only for the higher things in life.

Tears flowed gently, copiously.

What was she to do? How was she to behave? There is never anyone to ask: you cannot bring yourself to admit ignorance.

She had been deposed from her pedestal. She was no longer the Incomparable! No longer his One and Only!

Her tears were shed for the sweet life that was over, that could never be restored to its former self. Even the morsel of happiness left to her that morning, modest and subdued as it was, had gone, never to return.

The day had begun so well—and look how it had ended! The wreckage had been there to see yesterday but Alina had not realized it. Since morning she had tried so hard to be cheerful, to forgive him, to mend the broken cup with tiny patches, so that she could drink her birthday happiness from it. She had taken such pains all her life to create conditions for love, and it had been the same today. How eagerly she had hurried to the lake, into the woods, like a winged creature!

Who would have thought he had it in him? His feelings were so atrophied—was he actually capable of a Great Love?

The tears poured down—and outside the heavens too were weeping. Weeping inconsolably, lashing the windows with their tears.

She had ceased to be his Pearl, his Meadow Dewdrop!

Others would inevitably notice and understand—how could it possibly be concealed? His unfaithfulness would make it plain to all that she was no longer "the best of best wives."

He did not even realize what it was that he had destroyed! How he would yet regret it! And that he would never find a replacement for what had been!

Vera did know, of course—Georgi had lied. Vera must have seen something, or made a very good guess—it was something she couldn't help noticing.

It would creep all around Petersburg, find its way to Moscow, reach her own mother and the people at Borisoglebsk—that was a thought she couldn't bear! To be seen as a deserted wife? How could she possibly survive such a humiliation?

And . . . on the other side . . . what did it amount to? A flare-up? A conflagration? There was nothing she could do against that. She would not have the strength to fight it.

All that was left to her was to withdraw.

Withdraw from . . . life?

Oh, how unbearably, how excruciatingly he would suffer! She could imagine exactly how he would feel! How remorseful he would be, how he would regret it!

He had not known how to value what he possessed.

Why had he told her? If it was just an unimportant, casual affair, why had he said anything? "Pious lies"—wasn't that what they were called? He should have kept quiet, suffered in silence.

No, it was good that he had spoken. It meant that this was the first time. Other husbands deceived their wives lightheartedly, as a matter of course, but he never had, not once, in all those years.

After all, his Little Pearl was not just any woman!

But what if nothing could be saved from the wreck? What if he was lost to her forever?

He lay there on his bed, across the room, motionless, never once heaving one of those deep sighs she had heard so often in the last twenty-four hours. (Had he been sighing for that woman? Or at the thought of the explaining he had to do?) Surely he couldn't be sleeping! How could he possibly sleep after all that!

He had become such a stranger—and all at once closer than he had ever been. She couldn't live through the next hour, through this night, without him, she would die!

He was lying so near, showing not the slightest inclination to come and lie beside her, to stroke her forehead, ask what he could do to help her.

He had wounded her mortally and would not come to her aid.

He was lying so near—but was no longer hers. Close beside her, but she could not call him to her.

She was trembling violently.

She had never known any torment like this. This mixture of intimacy and inaccessibility, of repulsion and attraction, of hopeless loss and hope that all might yet be regained—this confused sensation seemed to become a crimson glow in the darkness, its incandescent rays filling the room, scorching her breast, drawing from her . . . one long wail!

Yes, he had done well to make a clean breast of it: he had earned the right to be open from then on. The numbness he had felt on the journey back to Moscow had vanished without a trace. His mind was perfectly at ease, indeed he was happy, as he stretched out in his bed and went to sleep.

It took him some time to wake up. He had heard it in his sleep, that loud, long-drawn-out moan that filled the whole room, and had known that it was Olda crying out—the ecstatic cry that filled his breast with such pride. What awakened him was a heartrending moan that must surely be heard out in the corridor. Though he could still see nothing in the gray half-light, he knew that this was Alina wailing, an agonized wail he had never heard before! Not a cry that prolonged the joy of realization.

He called out to her, but she went on moaning, just as loudly, not responding. He half rose in bed, called out to her again, more alarmed this time. Alina just went on moaning more and more pitifully.

Georgi swung his feet onto the floor. Went over to her bed. Bent over her. Asked what was wrong. The light from the window was faint, but the rain had died down, and there was a hint of moonlight from behind the clouds. He could see that Alina was lying on her back and trembling from head to foot.

Did she need medicine? Something to drink? Fear and pity clutched at his heart. Poor little girl! What have I done to you?!

Bending low, he asked her again and again, and through her despairing moans, her excruciating sobs, at last made out her whispered reply: "Come to me! Come!"

At first he could not believe that he had heard correctly. Was he not defiled?

But that was what she was asking, painfully pleading for.

He lay down beside her. Her face was very wet, and her whole body was like that of one snatched from a fire. He did not remember her ever being like this, in all their years together.

In a little while she was silent.

And, with his arms gently around her, she fell asleep.

[5 4]

And that was how they began the following day, treating each other with tender solicitude. As though what had happened between them yesterday was something very good, which had left them lovingly at one. They had always been at ease with one another, but on this dreamy, dawdling day they crossed over into a new stage of intimacy, of unconstraint such as they had never experienced before.

Somehow they knew at once that they would stay on, not go back to Moscow that day. Alina's movements were so carefully controlled, her looks so faraway, it seemed that traveling by train, or horse-drawn carriage, might shatter her.

The rain had stopped, and at first there were even occasional glimpses of blue sky. Then it clouded over. Then there was a little sun again.

They wandered around for hours, slowly, cautiously, as if afraid that Alina might trip on a root. Wandered through the late autumn forest. The oaks were still shedding their last discolored leaves but underfoot was a dark brown, russet, and yellow carpet.

The expression on any woman's face changes quickly, and Alina was no exception, but Georgi had never seen such a complete transformation, and could not believe his eyes. Alina had become younger, prettier, softer, and something more sublime than sadness shone in her gray eyes—a tender melancholy. She had become simply irresistible.

He told her so.

Enchanted by this sudden radiance, Georgi fussed over Alina, guiding her with tender care, wrapping her up carefully to shield her from the wind. There was no explosion, no quarrel, no reproach even in her looks! What a woman! How strong her love for him must be, and how little he had prized it! For this unexpected, otherworldly Alina he felt not just compassion, but gratitude, as if he was falling in love with her all over again, felt a tenderness which had ebbed long ago but now flooded his being once more. It seemed natural now to find all the time for her he had never found before, to lead her with slow steps, walk with her, keep her warm.

Since she was capable of such suffering for his sake.

The whole world was hushed and still. Nothing was happening anywhere in the world, nothing could call Colonel Vorotyntsev away, nowhere under the sun was there room for anything but his wish that all this would end well. With no thought at all of giving up Olda, he must now do all he could to support Alina.

A smile so subtle that no earthly creature would have been thought capable of it. Eyes filled with tender renunciation, in a face suddenly thinner, suddenly younger, freed from the power of vain cares.

Georgi simply could not believe what he saw. Resignation? Was it possible? Georgi, surely, had always treated Alina with loving care, but never so much as today! She had lost none of her beauty over the years, but never had it been such a spiritual beauty.

"You are irresistible!" he repeated.

He spoke now and then, and she barely answered. She just shone with that strange light, and smiled dreamily. All day long she neither started nor kept up a conversation. He would begin and give up after a while.

They walked and walked. Lingered over dinner. And the day, a short one, was ending.

Would he please read aloud to her in the evening? From one of her favorite books. He borrowed *Jane Eyre* from the landlady. Alina was happy.

She lay still for three hours while he sat beside her on the bed and read to her.

It was a story about the loftiest of sentiments, written by a woman of noble sentiments, for other women of noble sentiments about yet another such woman, eager to do justice to the lofty sentiments of others and exhibit her own noble nature—and although Georgi found it pretty strange to be sitting there reading a sentimental story aloud, he felt that for all the dissimilarity of plot it was all relevant, that it was right for him to be reading it, and to affirm these noble and sacrificial sentiments.

But he suspected once or twice and finally saw for sure that Alina herself wasn't hearing any of it.

It was happiness enough for her to have him sitting there, reading to her.

Later, lying in the dark beside him, she was a long time going to sleep. Suddenly she spoke. Her longest speech all day.

"You know what? . . . The very young ought to be taught not writing or arithmetic or needlework or scripture . . . But how to love."

"How can you teach them that?"

"There has to be a way. It isn't something we're born with, so it has to be taught."

He thought she'd fallen asleep. But no. She put her arm around his neck.

"If you'd been different on my first night I would have felt different too. Ever afterward."

Georgi, already half asleep, was mystified. What did their first night have to do with anything? That was ten years ago.

"I didn't realize it myself till today."

It cost him a great effort to remember that first night.

But it was as if this new friendship between them had given Alina a certain detachment and she reminded him how it had all been—that room in the dusk, the last light fading, Georgi leaving the room, herself undressing while he was away, lying there feeling frightened, and then he . . .

Hmm . . . maybe it had been like that . . . Maybe . . . She hadn't convinced him, but he was moved by the live pain of her recollection, her effort to exchange confidences with him. Strange as it would once have been to speak of these things, never before mentioned between them, it now seemed simple. This extreme candor filled them with an extraordinary warmth: it was as if their whole life together had been make-believe, and suddenly, for the first time, it was all real, all as it should have been from the first moment.

But they would have to leave tomorrow, without fail, they had stayed too long already! This was Vorotyntsev's seventeenth day away from his regiment! Throughout his service career he had felt like a cat on hot bricks if he was a single day overdue. And he still had to look in at GHQ! How much longer was that going to take? Could he really find time?

Alina, however, had no thought of leaving. She didn't even realize what the situation was. She wore still that rapt expression of blissful renunciation, looking so fragile that it was impossible to hurry her; try shaking her out of it and you might break her.

A dilemma. He didn't want to put off his departure but he had to spare his wife's feelings.

The news had not been easy for her to take. And it was of course true that he had started letting slip by, throwing away, wasting one day after another in Petersburg. The crucial days he had squandered with Olda. Once you had set foot on the slippery slope . . . Now it was time to show Alina some consideration.

As before, they took their time over breakfast. Then went out for another deliberately unhurried stroll. A hard frost overnight had left a fringe of ice around the pool. The weather remained cold and windy, but the sun was shining. It brought a smile from Alina. Her smile was at once compassionate and mechanical. A smile that seemed to have been borrowed from somebody else.

From time to time she touched him gently and pointed to something—a leaf trapped in the ice, a belated bird.

Georgi felt a pang: all this was his fault.

He had meant to insist on leaving before dinner, but his strength had failed him. She wanted to stay on—and of course it was for her to say.

Some sort of healing process was going on in her mind.

It got warmer in the afternoon. A lovely autumn day. They walked and walked—most of the time without speaking, as before. He made an occasional remark, but more often than not she did not reply. She screwed up her eyes in the bright sunshine, but uncomplainingly. Letting herself be led, hand under his arm, without argument, wherever he chose, back to the guesthouse if he wished, drifting with the current.

The silence they shared, and her meek submissiveness, made Georgi more and more sure that he would never leave her.

He knew it was imperative for him to move, to act decisively—but he was duty-bound to hang on in this ridiculous guesthouse doing nothing.

Instead of staying in Petersburg for another meeting with Guchkov he had shamefacedly hurried home for a family celebration—to find himself a prisoner in this place!

But it wasn't Alina who had started it. He had. And he had to take responsibility.

More procrastination, another delayed departure—it was just as it was with Olda in Petersburg, but his feelings were very different.

Another whole day of this strange, upside-down second honeymoon of theirs went by.

Toward evening it was no longer freezing and the sky was clouded over again.

Neither of them wanted to talk, and there was nothing to stop him from thinking. Yet he could not make room even for thoughts about Olda, though deep within him the memory of her was a song of gratitude and happiness. He could not think freely.

What did the future hold for him and Olda?

At dinner Alina wore an absent smile. But something was different—this was not the sublime resignation he had seemed to see the night before. The corners of her mouth looked very tight.

That evening she insisted on hearing her schoolgirl favorite, *Jane*

Eyre, all over again. And although Georgi knew that yet again she would not be listening, he could not get out of reading to her.

He read without himself understanding a single word of what he was reading. He was racked with worry about the time he was wasting. And worry for Alina. He stole anxious and fearful looks from time to time at her strange, mindlessly blissful smile.

And felt that he was shackled to this woman.

What terrible thing had he done?

*   *   *

HE MAY HAVE SET OUT FOR LADOGA,
BUT HE LANDED IN TIKHVIN.

*   *   *

[5 5]

One thing's for sure, no matter how many marvelous people you meet later on, there's no one like the friend of your youth. No one else will ever be so close. If only because there's no one else with whom you can relive your past in such detail. Your friend knows all about it, has shared it, and when memory is suddenly jogged two pairs of eyebrows twitch at once, and you are both roaring with laughter, convulsed. "Those were the days!" Or: "Remember what we had to put up with in Cadet School? 'Heads up! Straighten that leg! This isn't the u-ni-ni-versity!' "

In fact Cadet School had left them less to remember than anything else. Their time had been wasted so idiotically! Those uncouth senior cadets! Practicing saluting when they would have been better occupied with their training manuals. Folding their clothes at bedtime—no more than five inches high or eight in width, or you'd be woken up in the night to fold them again. Cramming regulations irrelevant in battle. (While no one taught them the essentials. Indeed, the teachers themselves still had it all to learn.)

I've just thought of something! Remember when we were sitting in the big room at the Rumyantsev Academy, up in the corner by the bookcase with the encyclopedias, looking at Vladimir Soloviev's thoughts on the theocratic state being the realization of the Kingdom of Heaven? Which got us absolutely nowhere. Surely the Kingdom of Heaven is not merely an earthly institutional ideal, achievable by practical social measures? Surely it presupposes a world transformed, in which the flesh and the disembodied spirit are governed by other laws, and surely it has no relevance to human historical reality? Would you believe it—our brigade chaplain has just given me an article by Evgeni

Trubetskoy to read, one we missed. (None of this had yet been said, but it would be, without fail, when next they met.)

And all that they had seen of the war, all that they had gone through separately in the last eighteen months—who could be told about it, and expected to understand, if not the friend of your youth? They had experienced it separately, but their thoughts about it would be identical. So many different roads traveled, different binoculars looked through, but their angle of vision was the same. If we get through the war alive we two will be doing something or other together, that goes without saying. As things are, we can find ways of meeting without waiting for the war to end: across a table planted in the ground under a pine tree, or lying on the pine needles, prone on a cape with room for two, looking into each other's eyes—could any two people in the world understand each other better! To talk and talk for hours on end! Cleansing your soul! Time more precious than that you might spend with your beloved. (Might—because *you* have no such person, and neither do I.)

Back in Artillery School, sitting beside each other in topography lessons, learning to draw maps with universal coordinates, they had thought up a marvelous scheme: you could indicate every square verst on the continent with a single Roman letter followed by six figures. Add a seventh figure and you were down to one ninth of a square verst—one hundred and seventy by one hundred and seventy sazhens. With such precision they would never have any difficulty in locating each other. Simply insert those figures at intervals among the words of a letter, and the army censors will never guess that I have told you in code on which square my battery is located. The names of units can be mentioned openly, they are common knowledge. (For that matter, you could identify the square openly, and they still wouldn't notice. The camouflage was just a precaution.) Of course, if one of them was somewhere near Vilna, and the other in the Carpathians, this wily scheme wouldn't help. But if they were near enough, say twenty or thirty versts apart, and told each other, one of them could surely manage a visit sooner or later.

Although they had both graduated from the Heavy Artillery Department there were no suitable vacancies (there was hardly any heavy artillery) and they were assigned to different divisions. At first they were too far apart, but then Kotya was moved closer, and that May, after a light shower of warm spring rain, which the earth returned in perfumed vapors, in a Belorussian village overburdened with the horde of soldiers billeted on it, Sanya had asked one officer, then another, if he knew where Second Lieutenant Gulai was, Kotya had heard about it, charged down the street, caught sight of his friend—and the two second lieutenants ran into each other's arms, laughing aloud to think how cunning they had been, how cleverly they had contrived it!

In August, Kotya had found his way to Sanya here in Dryagovets. So today he had no need at all to consult the map. He even knew exactly which dugout to head for. Reining in his horse by a pine tree, he dismounted and gave the reins to his orderly. As he set off on foot, Sanya appeared from an unexpected direction. So here we are! An unlooked-for holiday for some hours!

They embraced. Gripped each other hard. Kotya had grown stronger. He clasped Sanya around the ribs till it hurt. (Sanya might have done the same—you don't realize you're doing it yourself.) His lips seemed to be all muscle. His small clipped mustache pricklier.

They embraced—but with no trace of their old eager, laughing ardor. Let's see now—how else have you changed? Cheeks hollower? Look a bit sterner? Even the dome of your head and the shape of your temples seem different. What has happened to you? All this in the space of a few months?

No, my friend—in just a couple of days.

His head seemed longer, less rounded. His eyelids rose and half closed again, tremulously, as though he was taking aim.

"So how are things with you?"

"I'll tell you shortly."

Sanya, holding him by the shoulders: "You'll stay the night, won't you?"

"That's what I came for."

"Good!"

"Can you do something about the horses, and put the orderly up?"

"Yes, of course. Tsyzh! Let's have some fried potatoes! And some of the emergency ration, all right?"

Sanya was falling over himself to make his guest at home. But while he was bustling in and out making arrangements something impelled him to change his tunic, complete with George medal, for another, unadorned one. Kotya was brave and more of a soldier than Sanya, but the chance to win a medal had not yet come his way. They both knew that it was not a matter of derring-do, but of luck—whether the commendation was effectively worded, whether it landed on the right desk and at the right moment—and that someone who had never caught a whiff of battle might receive a decoration "with swords," but Sanya was nevertheless determined that no awkward shadow would come between them. Sanya was as proud of his new medal as a little boy, but when he stopped to think, it seemed absurd and unfair that his friend had only the red sword knot of St. Anna and the Order of St. Stanislav.

Evening was drawing near, and Sanya suggested a walk before supper. There was something they hadn't gotten around to on Kotya's last visit, and had agreed to do this time—take a look at the way in which the grenadiers had positioned their antiaircraft guns: their own carpenters had fashioned swiveling bases, tilted each gun carriage, and dug a circular trench under its trail. Strangely, all this now intrigued them as much as sweet philosophy once had. All these binoculars and compasses had become part of their lives and conversation.

Kotya went along without demur. But to all appearances mechanically. They buttoned themselves up against the wind. There were still ragged clouds overhead, their western edges fringed with red and violet—the sky was clearing, and it would be getting colder. The ground was freezing already, hardening into irregular ridges.

Last time Kotya himself had said that if you have to make war do it properly, learn all you can. He had talked about 35th Corps's Gvozdev platforms (made of railroad ties) which one man could maneuver unaided: they scared off enemy planes, though there were no direct hits. Now Sanya said, as if apologizing on behalf of the grenadiers, "Some batteries, of course, now have antiaircraft guns mounted on armored cars, or so we're told. That's the kind of thing we need. At present it's all rather primitive."

Kotya said nothing.

Sanya went on to complain that the Germans coordinated aerial and artillery strikes, that they had spotters to correct the line of fire, captive balloons and aerial photography, while Russian planes broke down, no balloons were issued, and communications were inadequate. And insofar as reconnaissance was carried out at all the results were not passed on promptly.

They were walking on the edge of the forest, stumbling over frozen hummocks. Kotya suddenly woke up, and stopped.

"Why are we behaving like children? Or idiots? It'll soon be winter. What kind of soldier goes charging around in the cold when he could be sitting in the warmth?"

They went back. Somewhere soldiers lined up for their supper were singing the last words of the evening hymn.

They had not reached their destination, but they were already tired, and conversation flagged. Kotya was not his old self, best hurry back into the warmth.

Coats off. Chernega won't be here today, there's a spare bunk. When Ustimovich turns up he won't be in our way.

Now's the time to say all the things you can't put in letters. Things for which a whole night's talk would be too little.

But now that he had looked more closely Sanya hardly recognized Kotya. It wasn't just absentmindedness or automatism, it was as though nothing he saw meant anything to him. He seemed to be completely at a loss—he never had been in the past. And although there was nothing gladdening about any of this, Sanya somehow felt that his friend was closer than ever in this new, melancholy frame of mind.

Kotya's hair was close-cropped—not for him a stylish haircut—and that made him look almost like a common soldier, rough and ready, prepared for anything.

He stared at Sanya, eyebrows raised.

"Why are we standing?"

They sat down.

"How much have you people here heard about our battle at Skrobotovo?"

"Ah, so that's where all the racket was? At Skrobotovo again, like in the summer? We don't really know much about it . . ."

"No, of course not." Kotya's stiff half-shaven lip twisted in a wry grin. "If a battle goes badly the rule with us is to hush it up, conceal it from those up above and from the neighbors. But you did hear the guns?"

"Yes, there were a lot of big bangs to our right. Let's see, when was it, the day before yesterday?"

"And the day before that. I barely came through alive, brother, I can tell you. I don't know how I survived."

Sanya saw it all now: Konstantin had come back "from the other side." And had begun to feel so much at home there that returning gave him no joy. His heart was a cinder. He sat with one leg over the other, clasping his upper knee with interlaced fingers, and looking despondently, fixedly past his friend, past the table, down at the floor.

Kotya had told his friend last time that the Russian command had decided to launch in that sector what was to be an offensive all along the Western Front, throwing in three army corps. They tried to breach the German positions at the village of Skrobotovo. And what do you think? No sooner had they taken two lines of German trenches than an inexplicable order was given to withdraw. Then when the Germans were back and well dug in, our troops were sent to retake the trenches, but were made to look silly. To their right the 46th Division, instead of just making a demonstration, advanced deep into enemy territory and entrenched itself, but there was no backup and it had to withdraw. In short, there was no breakthrough at Skrobotovo, no objective was taken, but they did occupy a depression, advance along it right up to enemy lines, and go to ground there. They were as close as they possibly could be, as close as you are always ordered to get but never do. So the top brass thought it would be a pity to abandon such a position and ordered them not to go home to their own cozy trenches but to dig in, thirty paces from the enemy. The ground was too soggy for deep digging, so under cover of darkness they hauled in bodies to make a parapet—there were more than enough of them—covered it with earth, and there you were, a strongpoint. They stayed there in that stench, and a cloud of blowflies, for a month, got used to the smell, made themselves dugouts—shallow holes in the ground, half walled around with sacks filled with earth. It was a deadly place. The 81st Division dragged out a dozen or two dead men every night. But the deadliest spot of all was the right-hand trench, where Lieutenant Colonel Kupryukhin's battalion was stationed. The trench was right at the foot of a slope occupied by the Germans, no more than a few dozen paces away, there was no cover at all, the Germans could even empty their slops on them. The regimental commander asked permission to evacuate that trench, because the Germans could simply jump on them from above, but General Parchevsky, the corps commander, replied, "The rule for Russians is: not one step backward!" Kupryukhin was a little man, bald-headed, nothing much to look at, but he knew his business. He had to stay where he was, but did his best to fortify the position. From the artillery observation post on Lapin Hill you could see infantry with no hope of survival in the trench digging themselves foxholes in the sloping sides of the depression, ramming themselves in up to the waist or beyond, and leaving their legs to be riddled by enemy bullets. The dead remained there in those ready-made coffins until they were pulled out by their legs. Or in some cases were not.

All this "closing in" was incredibly stupid. If you don't intend to attack there's no point in drawing nearer. That only makes the counterattack easier, which is what happened. At such close quarters German losses were also high, though they don't pack as many men into a trench as we do, and with them every man counts for more. They suffered losses, and lost patience. So they decided to dislodge us and win themselves a quieter line.

The most humiliating and horrible thing about this battle was that we were forewarned! A German soldier came over to our side in the night—interestingly enough, not a Pole, nor an Alsatian, but a pure German. Cowardice? Battle fatigue? Anyway, he warned us that there would be an attack the next morning. It didn't, in fact, begin till midday, but this still didn't help us. We had from midnight till noon the next day to reorganize and get ready, but couldn't manage it. We lost as many men and retreated as far as if we had not received advance warning.

Anyway, there's no use trying to put things right if your faults are the air you breathe, if your faults are *you*. Germans rely on heavy artillery, Russians on God. When we draw the boundary lines between divisions strictly with reference to natural landmarks, just to make writing orders easier, and have no reserves ready to reinforce the junctions, what is to stop a whole battalion from strolling through a gap to take us from the rear? What if our sappers establish strongpoints not in concealed places but on hilltops, where they are more easily defended but can be safely bypassed on the lower slopes—and that's the end of them? The war's in its third year and we still can't put steel helmets on our soldiers' heads—think how many unnecessary casualties that has cost us. They send us the bare minimum of Zelinsky gas masks, strictly according to our nominal strength, so that if a man loses one, or is transferred or left for dead, there's no mask for his replacement. We pack soldiers into our trenches two rifles to a sazhen, so close that firing is awkward. You'd think they were tightly packed on purpose, so that German shells won't land in vain. But perhaps analysis of the battle of Skrobotovo isn't worthwhile outside the 35th Corps. In any case, it is not an event of any significance for the Western Front, still less for the war in Europe as a whole. But for anyone who crawled through blood and over dead flesh there, and had no hope of crawling to safety, that battle divides his life in two: there's before Skrobotovo and there's after Skrobotovo.

The Germans brought up, or realigned, guns from several other sectors, and were apparently planning a gas attack on our flank, from Lake Koldyczew. But they had to call it off because the wind obstinately favored the Russians.

It had all made painful listening for Sanya, rocked him on his heels. But when he heard about the gas he clutched his head in both hands. Say what you like, there is something demoniac, diabolical about asphyxiating gases. Earth is no place for this form of warfare. Those who kill with poison gas are no longer human. They don't even look human, especially at night, lit by shell bursts—those white rubber skulls, with square goggles and green proboscises.

Yes, but did Germans carrying flame throwers look human: one man in front with a fire-spraying tube, one behind bent double under the gasoline tank?

As it turned out, the Germans had made allowances for an unfavorable wind. They began their attack in an unorthodox way, bombarding our rear with gas shells, where we least expected them, so that the horses in particular suffered heavy casualties. (It was lucky that Chernega was not in the dugout!) And the wind had then carried the gas toward our positions. Our battery was one of those bombarded with chemical shells for two hours on end, the gas hung in the air, we were all suffocating in our gas masks. Nobody could hear the words of command, so Staff Captain Klementyev tore off his mask, barked out an order, and was gassed. Then they started peppering our forward positions with shrapnel, fragmentation bombs, fougasses. They raked Kupryukhin's battalion with fire from above, then jumped down into their trench. They attacked seven times in a matter of hours, with intervals for bombardment. Two battalions had flame throwers. They took the whole of Lapin Hill, the "copse with the handle," and the "Austro-Hungarian trench," as we called them. The Soligalich Regiment was on the receiving end of all this. Then the Oka Regiment was sent in to counterattack.

Our artillery brigade hadn't done its sums correctly. They blazed away heavily at first, then suddenly realized that there weren't enough shells, so many horses had been gassed that deliveries had fallen off. The need to economize left the Oka Regiment without adequate artillery support. As a result, although individual companies had advanced in bounds, by the end of the day the regiment as a whole had achieved nothing. Anyway, it was not in our power to lead an assault. Everything depends on whether the men will follow or not. You never know until the last moment. They'll charge as one man when it's a sure thing. But another time a company commander may have no more than a dozen soldiers behind him. And what kind of attack can you expect from a unit exhausted by confinement to the trenches and defeat? So that's how the day went.

In the night, our neighbors, the 55th Division, took the manor house at Skrobotovo. Next morning, Colonel Rusakovsky led the Oka Regiment into battle himself, got a bullet in the belly and was mortally wounded—but they retook the Austro-Hungarian trench.

Retook it and packed it full of men. And there they—we!—were pounded all day long with shellfire. And we had nowhere to set up an observation post except right there, in the Austro-Hungarian trench. Lieutenant Gulai was sent to take a look. There really was nowhere else to put it, but with a temporary cable, broken every hour, and broken again before they finished mending it—there was no permanent, buried cable—the observer was of no earthly use. Communication was by exchange of notes, with a runner struggling to reach the battery via a communication trench which was caving in and filling up. That's how our gunners had to operate while the men stuck in the trench were being pulverized. And then the Germans charged.

One corner of Kotya's pursed lips twisted in a grimace. He had managed to grab a dead man's rifle. A hefty German had jumped down beside him. Kotya's bayonet got there first. What's it like, bayoneting somebody? Not at all difficult. Like sticking a knife into butter. But pulling it out, that's something! Thought I'd never manage it. The hilt of the bayonet won't let it come out—you see, in your ignorance you've driven it in too deep—and there you are with the man you've stabbed to death, he hasn't closed his eyes yet, and you're inseparable, you can't get away from him. And there's no room to turn around in the trench. But you must get your bayonet back quickly, before another of them lands on top of you.

The savage look on his friend's face frightened Sanya. (I could never kill anyone like that!) They were used to bloodshed by now, but this . . . Had you ever . . . was it the first time? (And there I was trying to distract him with trivialities!)

"Yes, my friend." Kotya slowly nodded his newly close-cropped dome. "Anybody who comes out alive from a hand-to-hand battle . . ."

They had crawled out of the trench on all fours, over the wounded and the dead. It was this last picture that loomed large in Kotya's memory: crawling along the trench over corpses and wounded men. Some of them, it seemed, were not wounded, but just lying down: let them all come, just as long as we don't have to mount another attack. Then the machine gun wouldn't go around a bend, because the bottom of the trench was too narrow, and they had to dismantle it while those crawling behind waited. Then men came crawling from both ends into the same communication trench and tried to shove each other out of the way. Those who stayed behind in the trench alive were no better off: they were sprayed by flame throwers and burned to death in black smoke, while suffocating fumes drifted over the whole area.

"It must have been terrifying!"

"D'you know, you get so desperate you don't care whether they kill you or not. As if you've accepted death already and there's nothing more to be afraid of. And nothing more you want."

That was the end of the battle. Toward evening they abandoned the Austro-Hungarian trench and were fortifying a new line—from the "left gas trench" up to the manor house. The battle may have had some other significance for observers on the sidelines, but to Lieutenant Gulai it meant no more than this: that they had sat there half a day, helpless victims, without doing anything, and that only a handful of them had miraculously survived. Their losses over two days amounted to 1,253 men. That was just for the 81st Division. General Parchevsky should have been set down there himself, together with those who had contrived that battle at Skrobotovo.

So that (for them) the European "World War" was divided into two parts: before Skrobotovo and after Skrobotovo. "After" was only just beginning. Kotya had come to see Sanya before he had quite recovered.

The first consolation for those at war, though only for officers, was obtainable from the shop at the Brigade Club, or supplied in a medicine bottle by the doctor. (Common soldiers never got a sip from one end of the war to the other.) Feel like a drink? Come on, then, while it lasts. The potatoes have stopped sizzling, they're getting cold. Half a tumbler full of the liquid that looks so much like water simplifies the world's problems. And consoles you.

Sanya had a story of his own to tell. Things have been happening here too. On 31 October the Moscow Grenadiers had carried out a reconnaissance raid. The reason for the raid was that a whole German regiment had withdrawn to Romania, and our feelings were hurt: weren't they taking us seriously? So we shelled their wire barricades by daylight, breached them in a few places, and, still by daylight, went in to the attack. Another fiasco. To begin with, they hadn't cleared the passages completely, and the infantry had to finish cutting the wire. Second, the German machine gunners were never silent. They were obviously sitting comfortably in blockhouses. We broke through to the German trenches in a few places, but some companies of the Moscow Regiment lay flat on their faces in the mud, right by the wire barricades. They were ordered to retreat singly, but couldn't get to their feet, because the firing was fiercer than ever. This went on till it was dark. So much for the raid: they took one wounded German, and one machine gun. Of the grenadiers 18 were killed, 203 wounded, and 147 left lying there for another twenty-four hours, till it grew dark and they were helped back.

Of those two engagements it was impossible to say which was the more absurd. But the friends were not in competition with their stories, because Sanya had not been in the Moscow Regiment's sector and had not lain in the mud all day, whereas Kotya had returned from the other world, and they might easily have never seen each other again. And anyway, Sanya wasn't bursting to pass on news about the grenadiers. He had hoped that Kotya would take his mind off all that.

Kotya had much more to tell him. After his spell in the Austro-Hungarian trench he had somehow become acutely aware of things near and not so near, of the war, of the whole world, in a way quite new to him. Before, it had been just the opposite. He hadn't liked talking about the way things were going generally, what he called "politics," he would talk only about his regiment, his brigade, about what was nearest to him. His new, keen insight made him no happier, it made him miserable, but at least he felt that now he *knew*.

Knew that the generals and GHQ did not share our griefs, didn't really care what happens. Some of them must have heads on their shoulders—what were they thinking of, why couldn't they see what was going on? Nowadays too many officers had an eye to the main chance, and heroism had come to mean wangling a George medal without undue risk. (A good thing I changed my tunic, Sanya thought.) As for the six-week ensigns, they weren't officers at all. And the whole army wasn't what it was when we first knew it last year.

He had acquired a peculiar new gesture: an oblique chopping motion, always with the right hand, as though he was slashing at something with his sword. Cutting away deadwood.

For all Kotya's hacking Sanya was not so easily convinced. Tentatively, not wanting to cross him, to offend him, but astounded to find that Kotya seemed not to feel the most hurtful thing of all: "My dear Kotya . . . How can I put it? In a sense defeat is easier to bear than victory . . . I mean, it's terrible to die, in the meat grinder, a helpless victim . . . when you want to live! Especially if like us you haven't yet lived at all! But to be all in one piece yourself and kill others—surely that's more terrible still. You wouldn't want to go on living after that anyway . . . Would you?"

Sanya looked hopefully at his friend. His thinking was painful and confused, no one in the army understood it, but surely the friend who had shared his youthful sessions in the library must understand.

But Kotya's expression hardened into a savage glare, he stared at Sanya like a madman, as if he was forcing his way with difficulty through—what? The shell-shocked daze in which the battle at Skrobotovo had left him? The blatant stupidity of what Sanya was saying? He dismissed it angrily, with an oblique sweep of his hand.

"Spare me Dostoevsky!"

He struck the same pose again—one leg over the other, laced fingers clasping one knee, staring past Sanya, past the table, at something on the floor, and said with a look of black despair, "We're a pair of fools, you and I. What the devil impelled us to volunteer at the very beginning of the war? We could very well have waited till we graduated from Moscow University and gone on to officers' school afterward. That's what bothers me the most—that we put our own heads in the noose. We'd have been wrong to shirk it? Wrong to wait a while? That's all nonsense. It was our own crazy idea."

He seemed to be recalling Sanya's arguments at the time, remembering that it was mostly Sanya who had dragged the two of them into it.

Well, perhaps it was true, perhaps it had been that way. Kotya hadn't the heart to reproach his friend directly. But the effect was the same. And Sanya felt called on to find new arguments, a new justification.

Only his head was buzzing after the drink—he wasn't used to it—and he wasn't sure whether it eased his misery or aggravated it. Every word that passed between them that day chipped away at, eroded their friendship, more and more irreparably dividing their foolish student past from the hopeless future.

Sanya had not expected this. Indeed, he had never been conscious of such a divide. Quite the contrary. On long, sleepless nights he visualized his life as a single luminous path extending into the future.

But he had no ready answer. In the ever-flowing stream of humanity some people, for whatever reason, were destined to achieve great things, in long and eventful lives. And others to die young, without making any contribution of their own, their good intentions and ambitions unrealized.

"There's nothing we can do about it, Kotya. We can't regard our own lives as more important than the general scheme of things. I suppose that even the soul of one who has departed life early with nothing achieved is no less precious in the eyes of God, and that its place is not lost."

Kotya looked at him uncomprehendingly, as if he was a half-wit.

"Oh, well . . . God, now . . . that's something I can't talk about seriously."

He closed his eyes tight, opened them again and burst out: "Where is it, then, this place for the departed soul when the bullet has finished off the body? Am I supposed to believe in those fairy stories about the Second Coming, believe in the resurrection of the body, with Scipio Africanus, Louis XVI, and I myself, Konstantin Gulai, one of these days individually resurrected? Nonsense."

They were scraping up the last of the potatoes, cold by now, with their forks.

"We mustn't oversimplify . . . But the soul cannot, of course, be killed by a bullet . . . It will return in one way or another to the region of . . . to the bosom of the World Spirit."

Konstantin snorted and made no attempt to answer.

At that point Ustimovich came in, lowering his head under the narrow beams that held up the ceiling. An absurd, clumsy figure, looking older than he was, with a big nose and big ears, harassed beyond endurance, not so much by the war itself as by military discipline and separation from his family, Ensign Ustimovich spent every waking moment of his life in the army more dead than alive. He was introduced to Kotya and sat down to help finish the potatoes and swig what was left of the vodka.

Sanya had meant all along to warn Kotya—but hadn't gotten around to it—to make allowances for the "gas commandant," not to laugh at him, or show the contempt which talented young people often feel for misfits and failures: the man had been torn from his family and his teaching job, he hadn't been trained as an artillery officer, he couldn't shoot, he knew nothing about field guns, and he had seen only a few months of active service.

But it all went smoothly. Ustimovich began questioning Kotya in his unassuming, pleasantly hoarse voice, and Kotya, still reliving the grimness of what he had been through, told the whole story to Ustimovich, as he would tell it over and over again. He needed to do this, to unburden himself, to rid himself of it, and Ustimovich made a good listener, gasping and groaning in the right places, sympathizing—it was terrible to imagine *his* large defenseless body in that shallow, corpse-carpeted trench. They leaned toward each other at the corner of the table, and Sanya suddenly realized that they were somehow alike, although Ustimovich was getting on for fifty, and Kotya half his age, and although Ustimovich had a narrow head and luxuriant black hair, while Kotya's head widened at the temples and cheekbones, and his hair was reddish. But there was the same harsh shadow of despair on their faces. Ustimovich had looked like that since his first day there.

Neither of them had learned to enjoy his war, as Chernega did.

Kotya insisted, and he was right, that no one need resent dying in a worthwhile action, one that influences the course of events, but that it was an affront to have to die in a shambles for no reason worth mentioning, the helpless victim of sheer muddle. You were in the grip of despair—it wasn't cowardice—at the futility of it all, stuck there like helpless sheep.

It was, however, Konstantin's firm conviction, never before expressed so clearly, that a man dies the death decreed for him, and that there is no escaping your fate.

"Staff Captain Sazontsev served in the same battalion from the beginning of the war, in the front line throughout, and never got a scratch. An excellent soldier. Then the division commander took pity on him and transferred him to division HQ. On his very first evening there a shell exploded nearby, Sazontsev opened the door of his dugout to see where the explosion was, and was killed instantly by shrapnel from a second shell."

Ustimovich nodded. He wasn't a bit surprised.

"Then again, there was a volunteer named Tilicheev in our battery, who had a very serious heart condition and wasn't expected to live. He had bent our commander's ear back in 1914, and been taken on contrary to regulations. And what a soldier he was! He seemed to court death: 'Better me than you—I'm dying anyway.' And he came out in one piece every time. Then, not so long ago, he was lying on the grass and a lieutenant from another unit came along and asked him the way to the battalion commander's dugout. 'It's difficult to explain,' Tilicheev says. 'I'll take you there.' He jumped to his feet awkwardly, took two steps, and fell down dead."

Of course, just as Ustimovich had expected.

"Or take Bombardier Denisov. He was fearless, stood his ground with shrapnel falling around him, didn't even keep his head down. Then one day he suddenly went crazy and dashed for cover in a munitions trench. He had to run quite a way. He lay down flat—and a shell landed right behind him. It should have killed all of us. But it didn't go off. Denisov, though, was fatally concussed. Oh no, you can't escape your fate!"

Ustimovich nodded repeatedly.

Sanya felt bound to contradict: "Just think what you're saying! It can't be like that! If it were, what would become of our freedom of will? There would be nothing left of humanity."

But the two of them were so involved by now that Sanya was more or less excluded from their conversation. Ustimovich described the grenadiers' reconnaissance raid, and Kotya listened patiently. Then it was time for tea. They had some biscuits in their ration tins. The tea warmed and enlivened them. The main subject of conversation now was the State Duma: for all its fine talk it gave no help—real, substantial help, that is, not trains fitted out as bathhouses. Kotya began chopping the air again.

"I would plant all those Milyukovs, Maklakovs, Puryshkeviches, and Markovs in our Austro-Hungarian trench for half a day, give them a taste of what 'fighting on to a victorious conclusion' means. If they still feel like ranting in the Duma after that—let them!"

Ustimovich agreed completely. It was impossible to imagine anything more alien to him than this war. As far as he was concerned, the war could end in complete defeat tomorrow—just as long as he was discharged and sent home.

While he was having tea Ustimovich cleared his throat repeatedly, and his voice became warmer. He made some incoherent remarks about teaching school, how difficult it was to explain things to dunces, then switched to the common soldier, how he munched away at his rusks on the march, sitting down, lying down, until he fell asleep, and was incapable of saving anything for later.

Sanya started feeling melancholy. The conversation had developed as if Kotya had come to see Ustimovich, not himself. They would have only a few hours together, and there was so much he wanted to share, but as things were, they probably wouldn't notice if he went away.

Sure enough, when they'd finished tea Ustimovich suggested a game of sixty-six or chemin de fer to the man he'd never seen before. (Chernega played for laughs, but Sanya couldn't stand the sight of playing cards.) Kotya had begun to seem so much like Ustimovich that it was easy to imagine him agreeing. But not at all. He suddenly seemed to come to his senses, drew out his pocket watch, and looked at Sanya. And it was as though the veneer of harshness which had covered his face all evening had peeled away. The eyes that looked at Sanya now were as friendly as they always used to be—not just ordinary brown eyes flecked with yellow, eyes like no one else's, if you covered the rest of his face you would know him, they were unique. Meditative eyes.

You couldn't imagine him playing cards. That was a variant of drunkenness.

Sanya took him for a walk before they turned in.

Now that Kotya had unburdened himself—twice, holding nothing back, and that was a good thing—he said no more, just strode along in silence. Yawning from time to time. As you do when you gradually calm down after an outburst.

It was a dark, but starry night. The sky had cleared. Beyond Golubovshchina there was a reddish glow where the moon was rising. Every day it rose one hour later, and farther to the left. When you live in the same place for a long time and your eyes are used to it, you know where, over which trees, the moon—full, almost full, waning—will rise. On quiet evenings, if the weather was fine, Sanya liked to leave the dugout for a stroll, near the battery or over toward Golubovshchina. These solitary walks by moonlight made him feel younger, cleared his thoughts, raised them to higher things.

This too was a night flooded with moonlight, and they could have strolled over the hardening ground till midnight if they had wished, but Kotya was too dazed, too tired, he could not stop yawning.

He was in a pitiable state.

Sanya did return to the fact that they had burdened their consciousness by volunteering. "You're right, Kotya, it weighs on my conscience the whole time. But our brigade chaplain has a very convincing way of putting it. He says that logically the opposite of war is not peace but absence of war. The opposite of peace is the world's bad conscience."

He paused between phrases, giving Kotya time to join in with a word of protest or assent. But Kotya said nothing. He scraped the ground with his boots at every step. Something else in common with Ustimovich. Something he never used to do. He said nothing.

"So that war is not the worst form of violence. So you and I have not committed such a very grave sin in going to war . . . It was not such a great mistake as all that."

No, Kotya would not be tempted to join in assembling and testing this ladder of arguments. His response, in fact, was one of irritation.

"Who's talking about sin—it's our lives we're going to throw away here! We've made a present of them—to whom? For what stinking reason? You and I have read and reread everything the world's philosophers have written—and I ask you, where does it get you? It's all rubbish, waste of time. Words lead nowhere, do no good. Only action counts. The word is completely bankrupt, all over the world. And all those humanitarians, your Tolstoy included, and all those Dostoevskys, are just so many gasbags."

The words came out in short, sharp bursts.

There was nothing more to be said.

The moon had risen over Golubovshchina, shedding its eternally mysterious, eternally enthralling light. Sanya could have talked the whole night through. But it wasn't working out that way. They strolled around for a while in silence and went home to bed.

Ustimovich had already stretched his ungainly frame full length on the solid bank of earth that served him as a bed—on his back, of course, to help him snore. The only free time Ustimovich had in the army was in bed.

Sanya put Kotya to bed down below. He himself would be climbing up onto Chernega's bunk.

While Sanya, stripped down to his underpants, was on his way to blow out the lamp, Kotya, perhaps seeing that he was upset, relented and said, with his old, good-natured laugh, "Listen—d'you remember going to a tavern with that old eccentric, the Stargazer? Well there's a pretty good library left behind in the manor house, the owner was obviously a reader. And would you believe it, there's a little book by our Stargazer . . . Miscellaneous articles on the Ideal Society, how to inculcate virtue. I leafed through them all—bah, these people who've never been shot at . . ."

Kotya was lying flat on his back, with his head on two pillows. "Why," he asked, "should you have to inculcate virtue? That's nonsense. If goodness is part of human nature it will show itself without anyone inculcating it. And if it is not part of humanity's makeup there's no point in pretending it is."

That was Sanya's last sight of him as he blew out the lamp and climbed aloft.

Anyway, Kotya had changed his tune.

Sanya could hear in the darkness that Kotya was not asleep. He thought regretfully that he had expressed himself badly, and wanted even now to strike up a worthwhile conversation. Hanging over the edge of the top bunk in the darkness he said, "You can't settle it with a stroke of the ax and say either goodness exists or it doesn't. It does—and it doesn't. It is there in our nature—and it isn't. It is what we have to evolve toward. Otherwise what is the sense of our earthly existence?"

Kotya did not reply. But he was not asleep.

"I started telling you about Trubetskoy's article on the dispute between Tolstoy and Vladimir Soloviev on the meaning of the Kingdom of Heaven. It is very instructive. Some of the finer points of Christianity are not highlighted in the Gospels, but only hinted at, and they get lost sight of completely in everyday life. For instance: 'Render unto Caesar the things that are Caesar's.' Are we to take this to mean that Christ is expressing approval of the Roman Empire, and of the state in general? Of course not! But he knows that people will not be able to live without the state for a very long time to come. That the state, with all its deficiencies, its law courts, its wars, and its policemen, is still a lesser evil than chaos. But a time will come when every state will have to depart this earth and give way to a higher order—the Kingdom of Heaven. Only here Trubetskoy himself loses sight of the problem. Because if we place our hopes on the transformation of the world by the Second Coming, it does not matter whether or not we gradually evolve toward it: the transition cannot be effected gradually."

Kotya had had enough. "Stop talking crazy, Sanya old friend. What's this Kingdom of Heaven you keep on about? We could burble about it in our student days, when we were young pups who hadn't seen war. But now that all the nations of Europe have been making mincemeat of each other, gassing each other, spewing fire at each other for nearly three years, does this look as if the Kingdom of Heaven is at hand? You and I will be polished off well before that, never fear!"

*　　*　　*

Dear (Frau, Fräulein)
The office of the Commandant at Altdamm POW Camp regrets having to inform you that your (husband, father, son,

*brother, fiancé), prisoner of war . . . born . . . 18 . . . died on
. . . 1916 in the local military hospital at . . . and was buried
with full Christian rites in the local cemetery.*
Lieutenant Colonel . . .

Commandant Altdamm, . . . ember 1916

[5 6]

Sanya and Kotya went to sleep still at cross-purposes. But when they
woke up a new day was beginning, they were full of life, there were
the usual horsey noises. They bounded out of the dugout stripped to
the waist, outside there was a light frost, the sun was rising, they
poured water from mugs down each other's backs. No more perplexi-
ties. No time for them, duty called. And anyway, if your head's only
too likely to be blown off why overtax it? It'll all come right in the end
if we get out of this alive.

Tsyzh brought them buckwheat, braised just enough, every grain
separate, smelling of lard. They scraped the dish clean with their
wooden spoons.

Then the battery commander's telephone operator came running to
warn the gentlemen officers that Brigade HQ had rung—some kind of
inspection team was on the way, better get ready for it. Get ready—
how? I don't know. Who gave you your orders? The senior telephone
operator. They all laughed.

Kotya told the story—acting all the parts—of the captain from the
General Staff who had grilled an elderly colonel in the presence of his
juniors: How would he deal with a gas attack? But what if this, and
what if that? Radiating modesty throughout, the honest old colonel
was sweating blood: he always knew what to do in a combat situation,
but confronted with this popinjay in shiny harness . . . Joking aside, if
there was one set of people Kotya disliked it was General Staff officers:
those gods of war imagined heaven knows what, as if it was possible
to theorize about this hopeless muddle, understand it and control it.
Who could make any sort of prediction when the behavior of a whole
company might be affected by one soldier tripping up?

But they weren't allowed to drink their tea in peace. Captain Sokhatsky wanted to see his gentlemen officers! Don't leave yet, Kotya,
we won't be long! . . . No, friends, they mean to keep you hopping.
The best of luck to you! Where's my orderly, where are the horses?

So they didn't even say goodbye properly, Sanya couldn't see Kotya
off, they embraced hurriedly, left yesterday's discussion in the air. But
what did it matter? They had gone through so much together.

Captain Sokhatsky, the oldest officer in the battery, an even taller man than the battery commander, as long in the leg as an artillery range finder—no infantry trench was deep enough for him—and as bright as a new pin, from his boots to his cockade, was waiting with one foot on a tree stump too high for other feet, nervously plucking at his sword knot and anxiously surveying the battery positions as if expecting an attack. All right. He had sent for them because of the upcoming inspection, Lieutenant Colonel Boyer being away on a mission, it was always the same at critical moments.

"All we know is that there's one general and one colonel, that they are theorists, but theorists of what we haven't been told. Why in God's name did they have to start with No. 3 Battery!"

In the pale early light of a low, almost wintry sun, Sokhatsky's eyes wandered anxiously over the battery's untidy comings and goings. They had only very recently changed into winter uniform, there were still adjustments to be made, and Sokhatsky was wondering what faults could be detected and corrected in half an hour. His troubled gaze passed over their heads, and he did not at first notice that only two, not three platoon commanders stood before him.

"Where's Chernega?" (Damn his eyes!) "Why is he absent from roll call? If he thinks this is a tea party he's in for a rude awakening!"

They were getting into bad habits, sitting around, lying around, discipline gets sloppy. It didn't matter when all was quiet, but in an emergency . . .

Ustimovich, his bushy black eyebrows in a frown of concentration, did his best not to stoop in the captain's presence. That was all he could do to help.

The gunners, in army issue, fur caps with flaps, jerkins and padded trousers, went to and fro on their normal business, but their sharp eyes had spotted the commotion among the officers, and they knew that the other ranks would shortly feel the effect of it.

"Zakovorodny!" The captain's long arm swung the battery sergeant major around as he was tiptoeing by. This bustling, round-shouldered Ukrainian rarely strayed from the gun carriages and the baggage train, where he was as busy as he would be at home on the farm. He had turned up by chance, but joined in the officers' discussion.

There had been inspections before—of the commissariat, of medical services—the object of each inspection team being to spend just enough time "under fire" to collect medals—but the thought of this "theoretical general," whatever that might mean, gave them gooseflesh. The supply side, which was the captain's main concern, presumably didn't come into it; although that too had its theoretical aspect. In any event, the general appearance of the battery, its manpower, the smartness of its turnout, the state of its weapons and of the dugouts, would not be irrelevant, whatever the commission's concern.

Things which seemed quite normal when you took your daily stroll past gun emplacements and dugouts were suddenly flagrant examples of slovenliness, of neglect, of incorrect placing, of general disorder—and most glaringly unsatisfactory of all was the appearance of the soldiers. It was not humanly possible for Sanya to pull up Khomuyovnikov, say, day in and day out, to nag him because his collar was always unbuttoned and awry, his belt was not straight but fastened slantwise, his cap did not sit squarely and firmly on his head but perched precariously to one side, ready to fall off any minute. Or there was Sarafanov, who kept his belt slack, like a pregnant woman, afraid to wear anything tight around her belly. While Ulezko and Gormotun didn't feel themselves to be soldiers at all: they were "locals" taken from nearby villages, bypassing the recruiting officer, and behaved as though they were not performing military service themselves but waiting on temporary guests. They liked retailing local lore, they knew the history of every apple tree. ("Why plant that tree when you've got no children?" "There were people before us, weren't there? And there'll be people after us.") After a year in the army they still weren't used to the fact that it was always on the move, eastward or westward, and that they too had to tear themselves away from their brick cottages and storks' nests. Anyway, Sanya himself heartily disliked military punctilio: why bother if belts were slack or awry, why not let the men enjoy a bit more freedom while they can? Then there were the touchy ones like Pecherzewski, and the educated ones like Barou: Sanya would have been too embarrassed to rebuke these people. Barou wore a university badge on his greatcoat—his whole uniform was merely a dismal temporary backdrop for it. You couldn't even ask him, politely, to keep his thumbs along his trouser seams—his eyes frankly reminded the second lieutenant that he, Barou, was not just his equal, but his superior.

"Well, we've still got twenty minutes. Dis-miss!"

The captain kept Lazhenitsyn back.

"The most likely thing is firing procedures. If so, you're the only one. If I get a chance I'll point to you, bring you forward, and if I don't—take the initiative and step forward anyway."

But maybe they would focus on their equipment? The gun emplacements? Shelters for the gun crews? Camouflage? Storage trenches for shells? Or perhaps defenses against gas? Ensign Ustimovich—get over here!

Never mind, here he comes, fresh from his Gustava, the rascal Chernega, looking guilty and sly, still in a daze, but replete and pleased with himself, bowling along like a loose cannonball.

He raised his hand to salute with feigned contrition.

But this was the one man to get everybody ready! He was an officer now, but was as close to the men as if he had never ceased to be an NCO.

They had to step lively now, as if for battle. Sanya rushed back to his platoon. All at once he was seeing things with different eyes, less indulgently. Only a quarter of an hour to go and how far from perfect his battery was! Still time to sew a button on that slovenly Zhgar's shoulder strap, remove the mess gear left outside the dugouts to dry in the sun, and all the tin cans saved for future use, take down the footcloths washed and hung out on branches to dry, but no time to strew fresh sand on the footpaths (which no one used anyway)—and there was no knowing what might be hanging up or lying around in the dugouts themselves. Or whether the mattresses were dry or damp. And what if the inspection team made them turn their undershirts inside out and found you know what in someone's underarm seam? What a disgrace that would be for No. 3 Platoon!

But before the second lieutenant had finished explaining to the bombardiers what must be checked and put right (while his own anxious thoughts raced past them: What was being done about the gun carriages? Were the horses well groomed—on a dry day when there shouldn't be a spot of mud on them?), the captain's orderly was after him: officers to report to their senior officer on the double!

Lazhenitsyn set off at a trot, one hand steadying the map case at his side, to join Captain Sokhatsky. Chernega was rolling and Ustimovich wearily loping in the same direction.

Once again, long-legged Sokhatsky was standing with one foot resting on the tree stump, and one hand on his elevated knee, fingering his sword knot even more nervously than before. He gave them further information. Another telegraphic message had arrived from headquarters; they had not managed to find out why the inspection team was coming, but were able to supply the names of its members: a Petersburg general from GAU, a staff colonel from AAICF Upart, and for good measure one of their own generals, the Corps Artillery Inspector.

In the cryptic slang of Russian staff officers who had given up after three weary years of grinding out long, tongue-twisting appellations, this meant Lieutenant General Zabludsky, from the chief Artillery Administration, a colonel from the Artillery Administration of the Inspector General in the Field, and one of their own generals, the Corps Inspector of Artillery (bringing with him an artillery specialist attached to the brigade).

This made things a little clearer. It meant that superficial appearances—objects untidily scattered around, damp mattresses, the state of the cookhouse and the bathhouse—would be ignored. The inspection would definitely not be of the "lice we slay, to God we pray" variety. And it would most probably have nothing to do with tactics, since the Corps Inspector of Artillery, like the Chief Artillery Administration, was responsible only for artillery technology, not tactics. So among things that did not arise and need not be worried about were horses, liaison with the infantry, communications, camouflage, outer trenches, precautions against gas . . . the condition of their guns? Expenditure of shells? Storage of ammunition? And . . . ?

"Fuses? Detonators? Effectiveness of fire?" Lazhenitsyn wondered helpfully.

Impossible to foresee, too late to put things right. The object of this inspection remained a mystery, a menacing mystery; since it had been kept secret even from Brigade HQ, where the team had spent the night.

Broadly speaking, the object of the inspection was nevertheless perfectly clear: to find irregularities and to nag, so that the counterobjective of No. 3 Battery's officers was also perfectly clear: to conceal all conceivable irregularities by all possible means, and to encourage the inspection team to depart and leave them in peace. Captain Sokhatsky had no need to brief the platoon commanders on this—they understood very well. The difficulty lay elsewhere: the really crafty inspection teams made a point of bypassing senior and even junior officers and unearthed faults by interrogating NCOs and common soldiers.

"Put the brighter ones up front! Once you see what they're getting at, put the best people in their way. It's very easy to get mixed up and play your trumps badly. Hey! Why aren't you wearing your swords, gentlemen?"

But at that very minute a telephone operator came running to say that they should parade without personal weapons (and Captain Sokhatsky quickly unbuckled his own sword). In fact, they were not to parade at all, because the battery was not supposed to know about the inspection.

So everybody was to go about his normal business, to do whatever he would be doing before the routine exercises. The platoon dispersed looking exaggeratedly casual.

But no more than two minutes later Sokhatsky, strolling casually along, suddenly, much to his surprise, saw the inspection team approaching: they could not all get into one car, and the Corps Inspector of Artillery and the brigade adjutant were trotting on horseback. (From the farm at Uzmoshye to the battery was less than three versts, a nice little outing on foot or by droshky. Motor transport had been provided to enhance their importance.)

Captain Sokhatsky, as delighted as he was surprised, ran at the double to receive the visitors, but even before he had raised his right hand to salute he had flapped his left at the sergeant major, who did not fail to notice it, the bugler sounded the call to fall in, and the whole battery, though taken entirely unawares, lined up by platoons with extraordinary rapidity, and looking more or less presentable, in two rows behind their guns, which were camouflaged with fresh pine branches.

The Corps Inspector of Artillery and the brigade adjutant swung nimbly from their saddles (men had run forward to hold their bridles) and the inspection team began awkwardly extracting their legs from the car.

The Petersburg general was a disappointment. Instead of standing at attention he hovered awkwardly while the captain made his report, and suddenly took off his cap to mop his brow and his crown (revealing a narrow head with a wrinkled brow and hair receding from the temples). He lacked not only the dignity of a general but the solidity you expect in any officer: his greatcoat did not hug his figure but hung loosely, and his mustache was so inconspicuous that his face looked bare.

The colonel from the Artillery Administration, however, was very tall and very handsome, with two carefully cultivated beards, mirror images of each other, each at an angle of forty-five degrees from the vertical and ninety degrees from the other. From his great height he turned on everyone a piercing and annihilating look, as much as to say, "You're all scoundrels, out to trick me, but I'll soon show you up for what you are."

Then there was the staff captain, young, lively, incapable of standing still, always eager to be on the move.

And, finally, a rather subdued lieutenant. He immediately took out a big notebook and prepared to make notes.

At the sight of that notebook their hearts sank into their boots.

The general ambled, the colonel strode, and the staff captain bobbed along behind in the direction of the battery, with all the others following. Captain Sokhatsky ventured, as though duty-bound, to catch up with them, run on ahead, and give his orders in a high thin voice: "Battery—atten-shun! Dress by the . . . ! Officers . . . !" After which, rigidly at attention, he reported yet again to the Petersburg general.

The general waved him away, embarrassed by these unnecessary formalities. He took his pince-nez from his pocket, put them on, cast a casual glance at the ranks, and a less casual one at No. 1 Platoon's (Chernega's) No. 1 gun, and turned to his retinue. "Er . . . let's see . . . how long have they been continuously in action?"

The Corps Inspector of Artillery leaned toward him and whispered something in his ear.

"Of course, of course, stand at ease," the general said, smiling past the battery commander, addressing the soldiers directly. "Stand at ease, friends."

Captain Sokhatsky relayed the order and, still standing at attention, listened in to what was being said in the general's party.

While the rest of them were standing there, the lively staff captain bounded over to No. 1 gun, hopped onto its bipod, removed its cover, opened the breech, and looked along the barrel.

Whatever the general's party were discussing it was obvious by now that guns were what interested them. (Had the barrels been cleaned properly the last time?)

The inspection team went into a huddle at this first stop, near No. 1 gun, and Captain Sokhatsky, looking rather guilty, answered their questions (every word was promptly recorded in the big notebook), but the junior officers were not called in. Chernega, who was nearest, could no doubt hear everything, but Lazhenitsyn, over by No. 3 gun, heard nothing.

Meanwhile the staff captain had transferred himself from No. 1 gun to No. 2 and was peering into it.

The men could see that their officers were worried, and many of them felt uneasy (nobody expects anything good from an inspection). Zhgar, a candidate for martyrdom, stood in the front rank with his eyes popping out, but stock-still. Unfortunately Sarafanov had also strayed into the front rank, with his belt, as always, slack. Behind him, lazily ironic Barou stood with his weight on one foot, while from the rear rank Beinarovich's brilliant black eyes shone with pleasure to see the officers in difficulties.

Suddenly, the towering, double-bearded fine figure of a colonel broke away from the team and strode over to the left flank so rapidly that Lazhenitsyn in his confusion was of two minds as to whether to call his men to attention again, but remembered in time that with the whole battery on parade and senior officers present it would be wrong. The colonel did not even notice whether there was an officer with the platoon or not. Walking more slowly, he scrutinized the soldiers' faces closely, repeatedly, with his clever and very sharp eyes and came to a halt in front of Zhgar—who else? The colonel, towering over the hangdog soldier lowly in stature, rank, and function, gently interrogated him. "Tell me, my friend, when a cannon is fired, is the barrel sometimes so hot you can't touch it?"

Never in Zhgar's life had a colonel—and such a gentleman at that—entered into conversation with him, man to man! Zhgar stood at attention, eyes bulging, threw back his head, and made a supreme effort. "Yes, sir!!"

"But how hot exactly?" the insidious colonel asked, more gently and disarmingly than ever. "If you put your cap on the barrel, will it start smoking?"

Zhgar had spoken indistinctly all his life, even when he was at ease, and you had to be used to him to understand him. He blurted out an answer. The colonel did not understand it, but he patiently renewed his question. This time he did understand.

"No, sir. Putting a cap on a gun is not allowed."

"But supposing you did?" the colonel asked with a smile.

"No, never, it's strictly against orders." Zhgar had dug in his heels now. It was as if the battery had regularly received orders on the subject.

Lazhenitsyn's mind was racing as he tried to see some sense in all this.

Beinarovich, at ease in the rear rank, took advantage of the general relaxation to steal a malicious glance at his second lieutenant and speak out without being asked. "It would catch fire!"

The colonel looked around and located this supporting voice. "You mean if a lot of shells were fired in quick succession?"

"That's right!"

"So how much time is there between one shot and the next?"

Beinarovich looked lost. He hadn't been ready for that one.

The colonel's eyes moved on, to . . . where next? Barou. And once he saw the university student's badge on his greatcoat, it was Barou he addressed. "How many shots a minute is rapid fire?"

He knew that the question was meant for him, but since he was not addressed by name, he ignored it, stood there unconcerned, with his weight on one foot and his eyes turned away.

As bad luck would have it, Sarafanov, standing in front and a little to one side of Barou, thought that the colonel was questioning him. He jumped, threw back his head as if shot, and stammered pitifully, "No, Your Honor, we don't know the minute!"

"Don't know the minute?" The colonel was surprised.

Undaunted by the fine gentleman's persistence, Sarafanov repeated, "No, sir, we just can't tell what's a minute, Your Honor."

Come to think of it, how could they? When they'd never in their lives worn a watch, how could they know what gentlefolk meant by a minute? And how valuable it could be.

The colonel's piercing gaze swept the ranks again and came to rest on Mottele Katz, a little, round, dark man with eagerness to oblige in his eyes. "You tell me, bombardier."

Katz, flattered by his attention, and anxious not to disappoint, made himself as tall as he could and said, "Three or four shots, Your Honor."

"No more than that?" The colonel, looking surprised, seemed anxious for him to do better.

Meanwhile the diligent staff captain was clambering around behind the backs of No. 3 Platoon.

Katz, one of nature's diplomats, tried hard to think of an answer that would make everyone happy—himself, this colonel, his own officer, and the whole battery. He glanced quickly at the second lieutenant, but was given no hint.

"Well . . . er . . . maybe . . . er . . . maybe sometimes five."

"Only five?" The colonel was not at all happy.

"What about when the order 'drumfire' is given?"

"Well . . . er—mm—of course . . . it's . . . er . . . more in that case," Katz said, retreating step by step.

"But is such an order—'drumfire' or 'uninterrupted fire'—ever given?"

The colonel's question was now directed to the whole formation, not just Katz alone. He hung over them, obviously willing them to answer yes.

"Ten rounds a minute—is it ever that many?"

"Yes, it is." Beinarovich shouted triumphantly.

Whether the muttering in the ranks amounted to an answer it was hard to say. Certainly no one else gave clear confirmation.

They couldn't see that it was any disgrace if the battery fired a lot of rounds, but it was better not to answer, just in case: whatever you said or didn't say, nothing good could be expected from the brass.

The second lieutenant was at long last beginning to suspect what kind of trap was being set, and wanted to intervene, but feared that interrupting the colonel might be a breach of discipline.

At that moment a loud voice could be heard from No. 1 Platoon— not a soldierly bark, but a naturally, comically loud voice, that of Chernega. Sanya did not catch what he said, but it was greeted with a burst of laughter from the main group, and the Petersburg general called out to the officers what sounded more like an invitation than a command: "Over here, gentlemen, please."

The probing colonel was put out. He wanted to stay and ask a few more questions. But he had to go.

The nimble captain jumped down from his sixth cannon to join them.

"No," said the Corps Inspector of Artillery, still chuckling at Chernega's sally. "No such order has ever been given in our corps—neither 'uninterrupted fire' nor 'drumfire.' "

His chuckle told the officers where they stood. Drumfire, once the artilleryman's pride and joy, was that no longer, but for some reason a bad thing.

When the platoon commanders reached the improbable general— a lopsided figure with pince-nez—the gaze he turned on them was anything but stern.

"Tell me, gentlemen," he asked with a confidential air. "You regularly observe where and how your shells explode, don't you?" His eyes came to rest on Lazhenitsyn.

"Tell me, Lieutenant, do you ever notice that at a given elevation the distance a shell carries slowly but surely decreases? And that you have to raise your sights above what your initial calculations prescribed?"

This clever question, so subtly worded, those narrowed eyes scrutinizing him—it was like facing an oral examiner—warmed Sanya's heart. It was as though this war, these guns (although they were the subject of the discussion), the uniforms the general and he were wearing, ceased to exist, and this was an experienced professor testing a student's powers of observation, and a student eager to help establish the truth to the best of his ability.

"Yes, I have!" Sanya was surprised, surprised at himself—he had never drawn any general conclusion from all those particular instances, never talked even to the battery commander about it. "Yes, I have noticed that happening."

The double-bearded colonel gave a loud cough of approval from somewhere behind Sanya's head.

And down it went in the notebook.

The Corps Inspector of Artillery, though, raised his eyebrows, greatly surprised.

But before he could speak Chernega's voice boomed out from beside Sanya. "Permission to speak, Your Excellency? I've never observed anything of the sort. It's just normal dispersion. Sometimes past the target, sometimes short of it. Due to the wind and various other things."

He spoke so forcefully that his voice alone was enough to dispel Sanya's hazy notions. He would naturally be believed: he was probably the one who never left the observation post, and the lieutenant the one who was seldom there.

No one contradicted or showed surprise, so this too was recorded.

Ustimovich did not even try to look as if he ever visited an observation post. He stood as if standing in silent submission to his fate was hard labor in itself.

The professorial general squinted at gangling, doomed Ustimovich, at Chernega's smooth round face with its crafty white mustache, and again at bashful Sanya, then gave his questioning another twist. "Now, Lieutenant, how would you estimate this systematic shortfall as a percentage of the total distance? What, very roughly, would it amount to?"

Sanya could not have been more eager to answer. He found it very interesting himself. But it required thought. He needed to picture to himself certain memorable occasions, remember where he had aimed and where the explosion had actually occurred. Then get out his maps and measure distances. That way he could calculate the percentage.

But his pause for thought made it look as though he was unable to answer, and the Corps Inspector of Artillery condescendingly made excuses for him to the Petersburg general.

"Unfortunately, Your Excellency, none of the junior officers you see here are regulars, nor is the battery commander, and it requires great skill to draw conclusions from such observations. And you must be used to observing every explosion very carefully."

He pursed his lips regretfully.

The two-bearded one acquiesced. "So let's go where we can find some regulars!"

The professorial general would still have liked to ask more questions, but the others were poised to leave. They turned on their heels. The notebook was closed.

Sanya could not see Chernega behind him. He saw one thing only:

that the nice, tired professor gave the flunked student the faintest of smiles, but could do nothing to improve his marks—he was forced to leave with the others. As they walked away, the restive staff captain was urgently trying to prove some point to the double-bearded colonel, with the brigade's technical officer raising objections. For three minutes a whiff of the lecture room hung over the scarred and cannon-studded scorched earth of Dryagovets—a forgotten aroma, so unlike that of warfare, quickly dispersed in the cold autumn air.

But this incursion, this inquisition must have some object, there must be some idea behind it! No. 3 Battery of the Grenadier Brigade had been innocently fighting, never imagining that their activities had some arcane significance that people racked their brains over at GHQ and in Petersburg.

Sanya found himself trying to catch up with the professorial general before he left. Chernega—probably—gripped him by the elbow to stop him, but Sanya broke loose without looking around and reached his objective.

"Your Excellency, please excuse me! But couldn't I be of some use? I could carry out observations . . . If you would kindly tell me what you're looking for."

The professor did not mind being detained, and the two of them walked side by side, letting the quicker ones go on ahead. The professor, shoulders hunched, explained: "It's like this. Excessive use of rapid fire wears out the barrel and makes the gun unusable before its time. In theory the permissible firing rate of our guns is, as you know, up to ten rounds per minute. This, however, is as a last resort in an emergency. If you want a gun to last, the optimum firing rate is one or two a minute—that way the gun will bear up under as many as ten thousand rounds. But some senior commanders who don't know much about artillery make unreasonable demands—continuous intensive fire for hours on end, just for the sound effects, the roar of cannons is meant to put heart into the advancing infantry, and they don't care if the guns get red-hot and wear out twice as quickly. What's more, the qualifications of officer personnel have gone down a lot since the war began"—the professor gently touched this particular second lieutenant's arm to show that he was not included—"and they don't notice the loss of distance and accuracy. So not only are shells foolishly wasted but the guns themselves have to be taken out for reboring after four thousand rounds. And the fact is, we don't have any reserve supply of guns."

Sanya saw it all now! Evidently staff officers up at the top didn't waste all their time on bureaucratic nonsense.

The Corps Inspector of Artillery and the brigade adjutant were already in their saddles, the others had taken their seats in the car, its door was open, with Captain Sokhatsky beside it, and they were only

waiting for the general—but he paused to speak to the second lieutenant.

"So does all that mean that even if you have a lot of shells you
should use them sparingly?" Sanya asked.

"You should never economize if using them saves lives. But you
should never fire just to deafen somebody. 'Drumfire' means loss of
self-control, excessive anxiety among the artillery officers."

With this the general held out his soft, strengthless hand for the
second lieutenant to shake.

Sanya walked back deep in thought and did not notice that Chernega had taken it upon himself to dismiss the whole battery, and was
stumping over the hard frosty ground toward him. They drew level.

"Eh, Sanya, you silly son of a gun," Chernega said, digging him in
the ribs. "Why do you talk such nonsense? If you'd looked around at
me you'd have known what to say."

"What d'you mean?" Sanya said, surprised. "It really is like that,
the range does decrease."

"What do I mean?" Chernega said, pushing his barrel of a chest at
Sanya. "I mean they'll take our guns away from us, give us rifles instead
and put us in the infantry, while they're fixing them. Where would we
be going without our guns? Have you thought of that?"

Amazing. Chernega hadn't heard what the professor had said, hadn't
heard him saying that there were no replacements for the guns—but
he knew without being told.

"How did you guess?"

Chernega smiled from under his pudgy cheeks—the smile of a man
bursting with health, strength, know-how, and regret that these were
not granted to everyone.

"With top brass around, it's better to watch out, keep to your side
of the line—then everything's fine."

Document No. 3

Leaflet in Moscow University

November 1916

Comrade Students!

Faith in truth and reason is perishing. Hopes of a splendid free life are perishing.
And oh, horror! In this triumphal celebration of death the intelligentsia occupy the
place of honor, like the betrothed at a banquet.

How Russia's reactionaries rejoiced when clever heads laid all their sins at Germany's door. They have converted the war "for the welfare of the people" to an
unprecedented drive to dupe the people and strip them bare. Comrade students!
Why are you silent? You have deluded yourselves too long with the thought that you
are the people's brightest hope. At this fateful moment it is shameful for you, the

leaders and teachers of the people, to cherish the comfortable delusion that you are performing a great service to the people. The people has been waiting for centuries for those who will set it free from its heavy shackles, help it to straighten its numbed limbs, and point the way to a bright and joyful life. And behold, the liberators have arrived at a tragic moment, have bent their backs to carry firewood, and by doing so condemned the slaves of a thousand years to be butchered. They have arrived—and enthusiastically adopted the slogan "Everything for Victory!" And nothing for freedom.

But the people does not need a victory that turns the people's teachers into beasts of burden. Comrade students! You have studied so that you can teach the people. Show it the path of salvation: peace and the convocation of a Constituent Assembly. Organize the people, lead it from the darkness of the grave into the sunshine!

[5 7]

The next morning the atmosphere in the two-windowed corner room was oppressive. The air itself seemed heavier. Through one window they could see the dense, dark spruce forest struggling with the wind, through the other a gloomy autumn scene, bare branches swaying, and the pool swollen by the heavy rainfall overnight.

Alina's eyes had changed completely. It was difficult to face their hard brilliance. She rose looking not fragile and defeated, but proudly self-sufficient, asking nothing from him. Austere and remote, she sat silently before the mirror, interminably brushing her hair.

Georgi was now completely out of his depth. How ought he to behave, to look, to address her? For two days they had been under a spell. Now it was broken, and what came next was uncertain. The simplest plan would be to leave for Moscow as quickly as possible—and then on to Mogilev. And gradually . . . it would take time, of course . . . everything would turn out all right. That still left some hours to get through before the train was due.

But Alina announced from before the mirror that they would stay on for one more day.

Didn't just suggest it. Announced it.

Weird! There was nothing at all to stay on for, absolutely nothing to do, they couldn't even go for a walk in such weather. Talk? They had said, over and over, all that there was to say. With relations between them as they were, Georgi would have found further delay intolerable even in Moscow. So much time had elapsed already—this was his eighteenth day of absence from his regiment, and now . . .

He must, somehow, steel himself to tell her about Mogilev.

But Alina had made her declaration with such calm assurance, such a bright, austere look that Georgi, guilty as he was, criminal that he was, the Georgi who had not stopped to count the days squandered with Olda, had to give way. The woman sitting before him was suffering incarnate, and it was because of him, because she loved him. How could he feebly hint that "duty calls"?

He had no choice, then. Another long, empty, pointless day to be faced.

He lit a cigarette, and they went down to breakfast.

Vorotyntsev never drank wine at breakfast time, but now he did. Alina never took wine at all, but this was where she started. The day before the day before yesterday—was it?—she had gulped down her birthday drink with a grimace, but now she tossed her wine back with an unpleasant gleam in her eyes.

"If we must die, let's die to music."

His eyebrows shot up. It was only a vulgar catchphrase, of course. She couldn't mean it literally. Could she? No, she just wanted to hear how it sounded. But she went on.

"The thought of death no longer disturbs me. You said something like that in one of your letters from the front."

Oh, no! A chill ran down Georgi's spine.

She poured herself a second glass from the decanter and drank it down.

Then, like a wasp homing in to sting—but lightly, teasingly—she said, "Maybe I should commit suicide. What do you think? You wouldn't mind, would you? You'd be all right."

This was brazen provocation, of course. But Georgi, sighing heavily, said, "Alina, don't . . ."

Yes, their misunderstanding had swollen overnight like the waters of that pool, and threatened to submerge them. He had thought it was all over but things were not to be so simple.

She reached for the decanter again. He covered her glass with his hand. She took another, empty one, and filled it, splashing wine onto the floor.

"Right now—I have to!" she said with a stubborn gleam in her eyes. "And I'm going to!"

The omelette she left untouched.

"Lively—was that the word you used?"

He did not understand at first.

She squinted at him. "Come on, tell me, explain to me. *How* exactly did she cast such a spell over you that in just a few days you were head over heels? What made her so irresistible?"

He looked into the alarming brilliance of her gaze and lowered his eyes.

"Complicated. Highly charged," Alina repeated thoughtfully, word-perfect. "Doesn't give way too easily to prevailing opinion. Well, that's easy to see. What else, though? Tell me more."

There was so much more he could have told her. But he was silent, head bowed.

"She's a prodigy, that's what! But *who* is she?"

He was painstakingly gleaning the last elusive specks of his omelette.

"Tut-tut, why are you so afraid to mention her name? Why are you such a coward? Is she the same?"

The wine was taking effect quickly. Alina was gradually losing her self-control, speaking louder than necessary, so that almost the whole dining room could hear her.

Georgi gently urged her to come back upstairs.

"No!" she rapped out, louder still. "This is too much! You enjoy singing her praises! You go into raptures over her! I want to see her, I want to know her, so that I can share your enjoyment!"

He gripped her elbow firmly and with some difficulty steered her out of the dining room.

"So I'm no longer wanted?" she said loudly on the stairs. "Henceforward surplus goods? Couldn't wait to get rid of the poor silly creature?"

Then, in the upstairs corridor: "Is this what I get for all my sacrifices? For my loyalty? Just like that?"

He guided her into the room, released her arm, and sat down. She flung herself backward, planted her back against the door and looked down on him, beautiful in her wrath.

"What have you ever given me? In all your life? *What*, I ask you? When I could have"—she waved a supple pianist's hand—"could have become . . ." She let her hand fall in a gesture of regret for what might have been.

Whatever she said now, however loudly she shouted, he had started it all. Served him right. She was the one who was hurt.

She had calmed down a little. Suddenly seemed quite sober. Her eyes pierced, her words probed him.

"Tell me what you intend to do. Look at me, please. What did you mean by praising her like that? Did you mean you won't give her up? Is that it? Do you want a ménage à trois? Or what?"

He was lost for an answer. He had meant no more than he had said. He was quite unprepared for this. He had praised Olda because . . . Because he was hoping that . . .

"How can I put it? The two of you belong to different spheres of life . . . they don't overlap."

She finished the sentence for him. "So they can be combined?"

No, of course not, what he meant was . . . But why should he be expected to have his explanation down pat?

He felt sick at heart, and no longer understood what was happening to him. Yesterday and the day before things had looked so much brighter—now suddenly everything was hopeless.

And then . . . he still had the war to get through . . . and there was no knowing whether he would come out of it alive.

But Alina's outburst had exhausted itself. She had barely strength enough to reach a chair and sink into it, sideways, with one arm dangling loosely over its back, and her head sunk onto the other shoulder.

In the look she turned on him, there was more sorrow than anger.

A long, long look.

Then she said, in a quiet, clear, placatory voice, "Yes, that's it. It has to be taught. Instead of mathematics if necessary." And sadly, tenderly: "You needed teaching more than anybody."

Was she giving the story a new twist? Making it look as if the wrong he had done her dated not from his recent trip, but from long, long ago? He found this hard to understand and felt indignant.

"What makes you say so? You've had some good years since then."

"You mean you have!"

Her reasoning was becoming too subtle for the ordinary male mind. But at least the storm was over. Who could say who was to blame and who wasn't . . . ? He sighed.

"Love is something for women to think about." He lit a cigarette and inhaled. "You have more insight into these things, you can make sense of them. We're here to fight and to work, it's you who must analyze."

A wryly superior smile expressed her pity for him, for herself, for the world at large.

And all the time he felt sorry for her, so very sorry!

But also tense, breathless. His world had become narrower, shallower. He could not go on sitting there, pointlessly bickering, quibbling.

One thing was clear: they would not be traveling today either.

"Look, I think I'll go out for half an hour, take a walk. By myself, don't you come, there's a sharp wind, you'll catch cold. I just want to blow the cobwebs away."

She made no objection. So without the usual ritual (a peck on the cheek or forehead, even if he was only going to be away for an hour or so) he left.

Buffeted by the wind's fitful fury, muffled up in his trusty overcoat, steadying his trusty sword with one hand, Vorotyntsev at once felt easier. Buffeting him, hugging him, the wind blew away all the sticky nonsense for which he himself was responsible. Vorotyntsev walked in the piercing cold as though doomed to do it by orders from above and felt no chill. He marched with a light step along the little path around the pool and uphill into the spruce forest. Though things had gone so miserably awry in Romania lately, he would much rather have been back there, in that muddy, flea-ridden hole at Kimpolung, stepping out like this, under orders to choose a line to defend and work out a battle plan.

If Georgi could have foreseen that confessing to Alina would cause such an upset and that he would be so hopelessly, helplessly bogged down in this place, nothing in the world would have induced him to speak.

He was not used to solving problems of this sort, or to self-examination. His life and his activities until then had never given rise to self-doubt or inner conflict: all the conflict, all the uncertainties, had always been with or about the world outside, and he could bring his big guns to bear on them.

That Zinaida—what was she thinking of when she made her engineer confess? Would that come as less of a shock to the engineer's wife? Perhaps Zinaida was just cutting off his retreat, to keep him for herself?

Women! When they start bothering your head with their trifling problems it's time to pull stakes, move out! Stepping briskly, left, right, left, right in the cold, against the wind, you feel stronger, start thinking straight again, begin to make sense.

He had come out for half an hour, and it was already time to return. Or had he said an hour? Time to go back, anyway. But he walked on.

The road curved around the spruce forest and came out at the station. A pleasant surprise! He had imagined himself bottled up in the guesthouse, completely immobilized—and now . . .

He seized a telegram form, quickly wrote in the address—General Svechin, GHQ, Mogilev—and felt himself a soldier again.

The message read: "telegraph Moscow address officially summoning urgently Yegor."

Otherwise it seemed likely that there would be no getting away from Moscow either.

An abrupt about-face and back to the guesthouse. Too late, he thought, "What about Olda? Why didn't I telegraph her?" He still wasn't used to the idea that every telegraph office, every post office linked him with Olda, Olda was there for him! (He had, however, found time on his last evening in Petrograd to ring her and tell her that he was going via Mogilev and she could write to him there.)

Yes, Olda was there but her image seemed to have dimmed in those last four days, to have receded into the far distance. He no longer felt that hot current in the middle of his breast, that wave emanating from her. It cost him an effort to remember her vividly. With her he was an entirely new man. But others insisted that he should be as before.

The wind had blown away the stale feeling stagnating in him, and Georgi returned patiently, in a mood to talk to Alina as gently and lovingly as he possibly could.

But the landlady, whom Alina had rudely rebuked for her out-of-tune piano, intercepted him on the ground floor and said, "Your wife is very poorly!"

He had forgotten the threat she had made that morning, but now it came back to him like a blow on the head.

He took the stairs two at a time, rushed along the corridor like a whirlwind, found the door open, and a maidservant by Alina's bed, who said, "She's a little better now."

Alina was lying on her back, pale, fully dressed, but with her collar undone. She had a hot-water bottle under each hand, and another at her feet.

It was a heart attack. The guest in the next room but one was a doctor, and he had examined her. She was well enough now for him to leave.

The maidservant also left the room.

Georgi dropped his fur hat on the floor and knelt at his wife's bedside.

"Alina, darling! What is it? What happened?"

He caressed her hand, her shoulder, her forehead.

She looked pale, bloodless. And she still had difficulty in speaking.

"Don't think that I wanted to . . . It just came over me . . . like ants running over my shoulders, my arms, and my hands started getting numb. I tried to write you a note. But I couldn't finish it, I collapsed . . ."

It was there on the table, a note on a scrap of hotel paper, written with a blunt pencil that doubled every stroke. Every letter was deformed, as though writhing in pain, her numb fingers had struggled to produce the least little mark, nothing could have been less like Alina's proud, bold hand.

"Georgi, dear," he read, "I feel very poorly. You mustn't think that I wanted . . ."

She had thought that she was dying. And had been in a hurry to write, telling him not to think that she . . .

My precious one! My touching little wife!

He quickly slipped off his greatcoat and went back to sit on the edge of her bed.

"Have they given you any medicine?" (She nodded, with a look of childlike contentment.) "Are you feeling better now?" (Another nod. Glad that someone was taking notice of her, looking after her.)

"My poor girl!"

He stroked her hair back from her forehead.

"I'll never leave you, don't even think it! I never had any intention of leaving you."

His heart was wrung. He had never felt such pity. And such warm affection. My poor darling, I was almost the death of you!

Alina lay there with a soft light in her eyes, looking almost happy.

[5 8]

Later she was her bright self again. She readily agreed to return to the city. On the way back she was subdued and absentminded.

But as they drew into the station she suddenly clouded over. "I don't want to go home!" she said. "I can't go home."

She began shuddering violently. Tremors of anxiety ran obliquely across her cheeks and her brow.

Was she afraid that crossing the threshold of that familiar apartment would be too much of a shock? She could not carry her present hard-won equilibrium safely across the threshold of her everyday existence: something would collapse in ruins. The contrast between her old surroundings and her new circumstances would be too great. That was understandable. But what was to be done? Georgi could not get stuck there forever for the sake of marital harmony.

He himself did not find crossing the threshold of his home at all difficult. On the contrary, he was eager to get there—just for once in the course of this pointless excursion to do what he liked best, sit at home, rummage in the desk drawers he was so fond of, find little things he had just thought of. It was evidently not to be. He was denied his own home, his treasure, as if a spell had been cast over it.

Perhaps he should set out for Mogilev that evening? No, it was obviously unthinkable to leave Alina alone. He wondered whether she would let him go the next day. His only hope was that telegram from Svechin.

A fine mess he had landed himself in, and he saw no way of extricating himself.

But the tremors running over his wife's face told him that they could not possibly spend the evening at home without some sort of explosion. With Alina in her present state it would be like carrying a grenade at your side with the pin removed. Better, even, to kill time in the Daisy patisserie, two steps from home.

Suddenly an idea. Passing through Moscow two weeks earlier, he had run into Lieutenant Colonel Smyslovsky on Ostozhenka Street. Smyslovsky, himself an artillery officer, had been at Usdau with Vorotyntsev, had been wounded, and was now living in Moscow. He had invited Vorotyntsev to visit him. He lived, with a whole nest of Smyslovskys, not far away, on Bolshoi Afanasiev Street. What might otherwise be a sticky evening could be spent there. They could drop in at home briefly, to change.

Alina brightened up again, grateful to her husband for this respite. She was once again the docile, painfully thin little girl she had become in these last few enchanted days.

Vsevolod Smyslovsky's answer when Vorotyntsev rang him was affirmative: he was at home, he would be glad to see them, one of his brothers, Aleksei, who had just arrived from the front, would also be there, and Sunday was a particularly convenient day.

Yes, of course, it was Sunday! In the vacuum of the guesthouse the Vorotyntsevs had lost track of the days.

Alina put on her best shoes, silk over fine leather, a red-and-white frock, and a brooch suitable for the company: a small enameled copy of an officer's epaulet.

The Smyslovskys lived near Sivtsev Vrazhek, directly opposite the little church of St. Athanasius and St. Cyril, with its un-Russian portico and columns, all on a small scale. Its apse backed onto Filippovsky Lane. They occupied a spacious eight-room apartment on the raised ground floor of an old building, with windows looking out on one side on quiet Bolshoi Afanasiev Street and on the other facing the courtyard. In this apartment, a long time ago now, their father had died, their mother had passed away quietly in her sleep, and all seven children had grown up. The four who were unmarried lived there still and the others came visiting, bringing their grandchildren. There were distinct strata of furniture deposited by several generations, all of it respected not for unity of style, as in the house of latter-day lawyers and other nouveaux riches, nor because of its usefulness to the present occupants, but simply for old times' sake—it had always stood exactly where it stood now.

There were many such apartments on Moscow side streets. The one surprise was the composition of the household. Not one married couple, not a single child, just a spinster sister and three bachelor brothers younger than herself, but not at all young. Since their father, the headmaster of an academy for young gentlemen, had been a mathematician, all five sons had chosen to study his subject, but, after leaving the 1st Cadet Corps in Moscow, had, like Vorotyntsev, made amends for their father's departure from the family's military tradition and entered the Mikhail Artillery School in Petersburg. Only Pavel had then chosen not to serve as an artillery officer but to teach mathematics in the Aleksandr Institute, which meant so much to Vorotyntsev. The other four were all well known in the army. Evgeni, in fact, was a lieutenant general, and the inventor of a new type of field gun.

The Vorotyntsevs were received by the youngest, Vsevolod, limping from his wound (the wound itself had not been very serious, but it had reopened twice and refused to heal), and by Elizaveta, who was over fifty and the oldest of the family. She already had a visitor, a university student, a young lady who, however, treated the elderly teacher very much as an equal, and turned out to be not a former pupil of hers but a fellow teacher in a free school for workers. Elizaveta Konstantinovna had spent her whole life teaching, anybody, anywhere—the children of the poor, neighbors' children, nephews, grand-children, draymen, and most recently factory workers. This was perhaps not the most interesting company for Alina just now, but as long as there were several new faces and the evening passed without incident . . .

As the Vorotyntsevs arrived, the student was heatedly describing the campaign against Professor Modestov, Deputy Rector, and, in his person, the police regime which was gradually being established at the university. A week earlier a student named Manotskov had been expelled. His call-up papers were not in order, and they had made this an excuse to harass him. But after his expulsion he often slipped into the university to attend student meetings. When Blagov, the porter at the Chemical Institute, a bullying sergeant-major type, high-handedly took their entrance permits away from three of those who were scheduled to speak, Manotskov charged at him heroically, seized him by his shirtfront, shook him, and took the permits from him! Since then Manotskov had been a hunted man. Every possible excuse was used to trap him. And Deputy Rector Modestov, flouting the constitution, academic freedom, and the universal canons of morality, had seen fit, with his own hand, to remove Manotskov's overcoat from its peg in order to search the pockets and determine who owned it!

Elizaveta Konstantinovna shook her head and closed her eyes in horror, reluctant to believe that *a person could take another person's coat from its peg.* Look what an autocratic system without checks and balances can lead to!

As when he was listening to Engineer Dmitriev's account of the riot on the Vyborg side, what struck Vorotyntsev was not so much the event itself as the vastness, the inexhaustibility of Russia: wherever you went, however many thousands of versts you covered, every place had its own particular crowds, its own unique worries, its own reasons for rebellion.

They sat at the oak dining table and a bowl of apples was produced. Vorotyntsev was happy to see Alina take an apple, peel it with her knife, and cut little pieces from it. Thank God, she had eaten nothing since morning, she'd been living on air. Things would somehow gradually settle down, fade into the background.

The students had been so furious with Modestov after this that they vowed to get him dismissed. The next time he broke the rules—by entering the lecture room during the break wearing an overcoat and galoshes—the whole student body rose in spontaneous protest. Medical students in the senior classes voted for a general strike—until Modestov was removed! They raced around lecture rooms to bring other students out. They were generally successful; most students showed political awareness and solidarity. They were, however, unable to break through into the Law Faculty building: the porters had locked all the doors. But the most outrageous event occurred in the History Faculty: Professor Speransky refused to interrupt his lecture and simply expelled the invading students from the room. More scandalous still, Professor Chelpanov's students themselves drove the agitators out, shouting such things as "We don't want to grow up to be idiots!" And this in the History Faculty, where you'd think social problems would be of more immediate concern than anywhere else! The spineless mass had succumbed to the influence of the students from the aristocracy.

Vorotyntsev burst out laughing, but glanced at Alina and restrained himself, so as not to hurt her feelings. He visualized the irate professor stepping to the edge of his platform and raising his little finger, at which the rebels, daunted by his courage, retreated, backed out of the room, stepping on each other's toes, and closed the door behind them. A truly martial moment! All that stuff about the power of the crowd was a fairy tale: the crowd is always weak because there is no unity of hearts and minds, no one wants to be the first to sacrifice himself. Nothing in the world is stronger than the spirit of a single human being: if it resolves to sacrifice itself it can stand firm without fear of cracking. This was not a story about bravery in battle, but as a rule educated people were more cowardly when confronted by left-wing loudmouths than in face of machine guns.

There was worse to come. Students who had reached the age of twenty-one were to be drafted into the army by lot. And just recently an unauthorized student meeting had been raided and hectographed copies of speeches by Kerensky and Chkheidze, pictures of Zhelyabov and Gertsenshtein, and pamphlets on "War and the Tasks of Social Democracy" had been confiscated. The two students most deeply implicated had been banished!

"To Siberia?" cried Elizaveta Konstantinovna.

"From the Moscow province! They have been cut off from their alma mater!"

Vorotyntsev was curious. "Forgive me," he said, "but what are the tasks of Social Democracy with regard to the war?" He truly did not know.

The student looked at him scornfully. "Everybody knows that," she said. "If you still don't . . ."

This gate-crashing colonel had ruined the atmosphere.

She went on to describe how there had recently been a tremendous scuffle in the Assembly Hall, and several students with monarchist sympathies had been beaten up.

After which she took her leave.

Every minute that passed eased the stifling pressure that had built up around the guesthouse and the pool, when there were just the two of them and the whole world was compressed into that little space. Sitting there among the others, Alina was her old self, without that eerie look of renunciation on her face. She asked, with normal feminine curiosity, how such an unusual household was managed.

(That's it, Alina dear, hang in there!)

The answer was a surprise. Although they had a cook and a maid, and the Smyslovsky brothers' orderlies gave a hand, the family was unusual in that boys and girls alike had been able to cook from an early age, and the brothers in fact were more expert than their sister. If they ate in some restaurant and liked a specialty of the house, instead of following the usual practice and buying the chef's secret, they analyzed the dish with their eyes and their palates, and when they got home one of the brothers would have worked out how to prepare the dish just as well.

The guests smiled.

"That's not all. Aleksei is a baker too."

The colonel? Was it possible?

Well, he had had one of Filippov's bakers assigned to his brigade, to teach his men to bake black bread, and had taken the opportunity to learn himself. Aleksei was extraordinarily talented, he could pick up any craft.

Vsevolod limped in with a decanter and canapés. From the first words he and Vorotyntsev had exchanged each of them had recognized that the other was genuine and that, belonging as they both did to such a different world, neither of them was really at ease sitting around in a Moscow apartment. Such men had no need to beat about the bush. It was easy for them to talk about what was uppermost in their memories. They could leave sentences unfinished: Yes, I know just what you mean—here's to you.

But Georgi was still concerned for Alina. He kept half an eye on her as she left the room with their hostess and shortly returned. The situation was precarious. Nothing really interested her.

Pavel came out into the dining room. His health was poor (chest trouble).

"Social problems" crept into the conversation again over tea, but Vorotyntsev had had more than enough of that in Petrograd. At least the talking there was done by those who had to deal with things, whereas here it was endless expressions of sympathy for all that was progressive and endless condemnation of the government.

An old gentry family. All the men were officers. And yet . . .

Vorotyntsev did not know Aleksei Smyslovsky, but had seen his wife, the beautiful Elena Nikolaevna, daughter of General Malakhov, commander of the Moscow Military District, on several occasions. She looked Japanese, and liked to emphasize the resemblance—in the pattern embroidered on her dress and by wearing kimono sleeves, or at fancy-dress balls appearing in full Japanese costume. He had been looking forward to seeing her again.

But Aleksei arrived, or rather burst in, without his wife. Charged in like a schoolboy home for the holidays, rather than a balding, fiftyish colonel, hurriedly embraced them all in turn, including Vorotyntsev when they were introduced ("Heard a lot about you"), and prevented himself only just in time from embracing Alina. He was below average height, had a long, wispy gray beard like a fairy-tale wizard, and joyously shining eyes. He inspected them all eagerly, then the room, to see if all the objects were where they should be, asked his sister whether this, that, or the other was still around . . .

"Even the rats' trapezes are still there in the pantry," his sister said. She couldn't suppress a smile, which greatly softened her stern features.

Aleksei, it seemed, was seized by fits of enthusiasm like summer squalls, violent while they lasted, but short-lived. He had once had a passion for white rats, and had set up cages for them in his room, with runs, and trapezes for them to swing on. The passion evaporated, he forgot the rats, and one by one they died. But this was only one of his crazes. He had taken up bookbinding and photography. Even petit point—and he was not in the least embarrassed when people laughed. "It's not one of the heavier trades. And suppose I land in jail one of these days?"

"What a crazy notion. Why should you land in jail?"

He had a full set of carpenter's tools, and against and on the wall there were plant stands, shelves, and little cupboards of his making. When he married he had left everything at Bolshoi Afanasiev Street, as if acknowledging that this was the home he would never really leave. By now he had five children, and the family had moved from one apartment to another, from town to town. But this was still the nest in which he was most at home.

What with his display of explosive high spirits, the warmth of his welcome, and the stories of his lively versatility, Alina herself cheered up. (What a good idea it had been to bring her here! This was how it should be. Life goes on, and we mustn't let ourselves stagnate.)

They reminisced briefly about Usdau and Rothfliess—events which now seemed almost as remote as the war with Japan. They remembered Aleksei Konstantinovich holding out there, at the station in Rothfliess with Nechvolodov. "A remarkable soldier," Aleksei said of him, "but a monarchi-i-ist! A national-i-i-ist!"

It turned out, however, that Aleksei's older son, Boris, who was now an officer and had been at the front for a year, was also a monarchist and a nationalist, and displeased with his father.

Well, well.

Aleksei's father-in-law, Infantry General Malakhov, was a courageous man. In 1905 it was he who, as commander of the Moscow Military District, had restored life to normal in the shattered city, and he had twice been a target for terrorists. Had none of this rubbed off on his son-in-law? Those disparaging remarks about Nechvolodov . . . !

But there is a time for everything, entertainment included, and Aleksei did not intend to go on talking about the army in the field.

"What about a little music?" he said.

Was he a musician as well as everything else? Yes, he even composed, and wrote the lyrics for love songs.

Alina was all smiles, eager to hear him. She was almost herself again—unconstrained and poised, and she even had color in her cheeks.

"No, not that, Tchaikovsky would be better, what a pity Mikhail isn't here."

He said it as though Mikhail was not away commanding a grenadier artillery brigade in the middle of the Great War, but had simply slipped out for an hour. As though the primary and permanent thing in the world was their family, and all else was incidental. What Aleksei meant was that Mikhail's absence disrupted their trio: he played the cello. Vsevolod came limping in with his violin, and Aleksei skipped over to the piano and raised the lid.

Tchaikovsky? He had written all sorts of romances. Heaven forbid that Aleksei should play one of the tragic ones, "Alone once more . . ." Alina was quite capable of bursting into tears before the whole company (and who could blame her? "After all that's happened? I couldn't help it!"). But whether it was just his cheerful nature, or because he was so glad to be back, or because he sensed that the lady visitor needed it, Aleksei struck up a cheerful, rollicking tune and sang in a rich baritone, emphasizing the humor with his intonations.

Alina was laughing helplessly. And Vorotyntsev blessed his luck—she had no competition, since the "Japanese" lady had not arrived, and there were no happy couples for her to envy. This household of detached persons was ideal. Alina was enjoying herself, and had moved to sit at the piano with Aleksei Konstantinovich and turn his pages.

The second love song was also a playful one, and Aleksei contrived to play and to sing while pretending to address his declaration to Alina, with the aid of the expressive bushy brows under his mirror-smooth scalp.

"I shall say not a word, trouble you no more . . ."

A splendid family, no doubt about it, and so versatile, with all their scientific, artistic, and practical skills. Why, then, as soon as the conversation turned to politics, did they echo so unoriginally the Kadets and the zemstvo hussars?

The five brothers—one a general, the others colonels or lieutenant colonels—were all exceptional people, all experts. Five brothers! And just the kind of people who should be taking the initiative! Yet—could any one of them be relied on?

"The night flowers sleep the long day through.
But when the sun sinks behind the copse . . ."

But perhaps this was how it should be? They were all ready to sacrifice their lives. What more could you ask?

Next there was a duet, violin and piano. (An "ensemble," Georgi remembered. Just what was needed.)

They asked Alina to play. She sat at the piano, erect and solemn, and played three virtuoso pieces in succession, with backward jerks of the head.

They congratulated her loudly. Aleksei clapped, and Alina looked like the happiest person on earth.

Yes, it would all work out. This lively, comical character with the beard and the bald head had jolted Vorotyntsev too out of his anxiety. During those days at the guesthouse the world had not shrunk, not contracted, and one must not allow oneself to be constricted either. The tribulations which an hour ago had seemed intractable now proved to be in part imaginary. What, in reality, had happened? No one had died, no one was sick, no one had lost a limb or an eye—things that happened every minute in the front line. He hadn't even suffered a flesh wound in the leg.

He looked on as Aleksei, at the piano, recited one of his own poems. Alina listened with exaggerated attention, head bowed over the music rest. Vorotyntsev accepted another cup of tea from their hostess. He even felt drawn to the taciturn Pavel (who had uttered not a word—but had written a manual with Przewalsky).

If only he could slip away without further explanation, without further delay, avoid a row—and leave for GHQ tomorrow.

He had completed his tour of the two capitals. And found . . . Found whom? Found what?

[5 9]

From the Smyslovskys' they hadn't far to go: along Tsaritsyn Street to Prechistenka, then by Vsevolozhsky Street, past the headquarters of the Moscow Military District (Vorotyntsev's own) to Ostozhenka Street, and they were home. By himself Georgi would have walked faster and been there in five minutes. But with the present awkwardness between them, and Alina deliberately dawdling, and Georgi adjusting his pace to hers, as she always wanted him to, progress was neither quick nor comfortable. Silence would have been oppressive, so he had to say something. But what could he possibly talk about?

Well, their evening with the Smyslovskys, obviously. Who had done and said what. One sentence at a time. With pauses. Remarkable family. How versatile Aleksei Smyslovsky is.

Alina listened. Said nothing, walked on.

As they entered Tsaritsyn Street, Vorotyntsev suddenly saw a brilliant light directly ahead of him. He looked up. Dark cloud covered the sky, but you only knew that because it was pierced by a deep hole with pitch-black edges and a luminous interior. Through this rift you could see not the moon itself but a subdued light like that from a mysterious lantern, or an opaque window in the wall of a dark castle.

He halted, and held Alina back.

"Just look at that!"

Ordinarily she would have been thrilled, deeply moved even, and would have stood admiring the sight. But now she gave it one indifferent stare, said nothing, and stirred impatiently.

They walked on. Things looked bad.

Good, here was Prechistenka. Cabbies were converging on an all-night tearoom, leaving their vehicles lined up along Ostozhenka Street. They gave their horses oats in nose bags, and, whip handle lodged in boot, went to warm themselves with a glass of tea and exchange a few words.

The Sunday evening quiet was broken by a rumbling, distant at first, then gradually, alarmingly louder. It was an army truck, empty of course, except for two soldiers in the back. It emerged from the square, rounded the corner with squealing tires, honked earsplittingly at a cab and a bunch of slow-moving pedestrians outside Military District HQ, and drove on just as noisily toward the Supply Depot.

Vorotyntsev had noticed more than once, in Moscow and in Petersburg, this new habit of driving empty trucks at high speed (loaded they were slower), as though the outcome of the war hung on their pointless careering. Soldiers not sent to the front charged around out of sheer joie de vivre: Look at us go! Look what a punch we pack! Out of our way! Their officers for some reason did not try to restrain them. Civilians were exasperated and alarmed by their behavior. It made them feel that something dreadful was about to happen.

Alina did not turn her head, did not notice the truck. But her neck was unbent and her head held high.

They entered Vsevolozhsky Street, and it was impossible not to see that the way ahead was brightly lit: the castle in the sky had been blown away, nothing was left of it, and the moon, already beginning to wane, and chipped on its right side, floated freely among the bright little clouds.

It was the same moon that Olda had pointed out to him when it was new.

"Do look!" He could not help himself, though it might seem like an attempt to distract her with a weather report.

She gave it the briefest of glances, and this time did not even pause.

As they reached the end of Vsevolozhsky Street a black paw stole across the sky and clutched the moon in its claws.

"That duet of theirs was really nice. And to think they can even manage a trio."

"So how did I play today?"

Hmm, yes, missed a trick there. Should have started with that. Georgi was out of practice, and had forgotten that he was expected always to take note of what she played, and how. Not that he ever failed to enjoy her playing. He had loved her for that first of all, from the moment they met. He had always enjoyed it without reservation. But today there had been a nagging doubt. He could, of course, say "marvelous," "better than ever," but petty deception weighed upon him. More honest, surely, to speak his mind? Keep up the candor, the complete honesty, which had so unexpectedly begun to color their relationship at the deserted guesthouse? It was like shedding a burden and finding that you could straighten your back again.

Something bothered me a little, my dear girl. Let me tell you about it in the friendliest possible way, it will make things easier for both of us.

"Do you know what I particularly like about the way the brothers play? It's their demeanor. They're quite good players, of course, but they know very well that they aren't geniuses. So they behave in that half-humorous, unbuttoned way. As if they were making fun of themselves and apologizing for their inadequacy."

They were passing under a streetlamp at that moment and he could see that Alina was frowning.

Should he go on? Now that he had started . . . But try to let her down lightly.

"Whereas you . . . there's none of that jokiness in you. You sit there looking every inch the virtuoso, completely absorbed in your playing, assuming that everybody is listening with rapt attention."

"Yes," Alina said, with a toss of her head, "because I take music very seriously. Because it's *my life*."

They were too far from the streetlamp now for him to see her clearly, but her speech was clipped and toneless.

More gently still: "That's true, Alina dear. But good taste demands that even at serious moments we mustn't look pretentious."

Alina, upset, missed her step.

"This is something new! Are you saying that I have poor taste? Till now our tastes seemed to coincide completely, which was why we got along so well." Alina's voice hardened. "And now you've realized that I don't have good taste! It's since Petersburg, is it?"

"Petersburg has nothing to do with it. It's not something new. You don't always realize, Alina dear, how . . . positive . . . you are in your opinions . . . in company you're sometimes just a little . . . uncompromising . . ."

Now you've put your foot in it! Talk yourself out of this! . . . What possessed you to start bringing up such trifles? When all he need do was to hold out for a few hours until Svechin's telegram came.

"No, it's since Petersburg!" Alina insisted, almost affectionately, placing her hand on the lapel of his greatcoat. "Admit it, you can see now what you couldn't see before."

They were now completely out of step. He gripped her arm and hurried her along.

"Petersburg doesn't come into it . . . All right, it's since Petersburg, but it's really since . . ."

Alina had started walking briskly, there was no need to draw her along. She started speaking in short bursts, as if she was slashing him with a whip.

"Tell me. Is she really such a remarkable woman, such a prodigy of a woman, that she could completely change your whole outlook in a few days? Transform your tastes?"

Georgi was careful not to sound irritated himself. But he could not leave such a blunt question unanswered.

"Well, you know . . . we learn something from everybody we meet in this life . . . it isn't just her . . . but in a way it's partly her . . ." (A thrill ran through him at the memory of Olda, even when her name was not mentioned.)

"She has nothing but good qualities? Broadly educated, a genius? Effortless expertise in absolutely everything, not just history? Only she can't play the piano!"

They were now crossing Ostozhenka Street, and nearly home. The sky was dark. The little church half hidden among the houses was in darkness. But a gas lamp projected just enough light to the middle of the street for him to see that Alina's face, from chin to temple, was contorted by suffering. Oh, God—what had he done now, idiot, clumsy oaf that he was!

Their path was briefly barred by a horse pulling, with head held high, bell jingling, a cab on pneumatic tires, and seated in it a dignified lady wearing an enormous hat.

"And I'm a nonentity, is that it?" Alina asked, standing in the middle of the street, her voice rising to a shriek, as if she hoped for, demanded confirmation.

He drew her away, led her to the sidewalk, but made up his mind to say no more. This only made matters worse, but he couldn't truckle to her, couldn't say, "You're brilliantly talented."

They had reached the front door of their building. They went upstairs. Silently. Entered the home they shared—strangers to each other. Second floor. Still without a word. Third floor. What a stupid conversation.

"Please forgive me, Alina dear. I didn't mean it. Of course I don't think anything of the sort. You know that I just . . . Oh—a telegram . . . For me. From GHQ. Urgent recall. Report without delay . . . That's it, then. I'll have to go. Wasn't expecting this. Please forgive me, Alina, love . . ."

She seemed not to have understood or even seen the telegram.

He helped her off with her coat. She wrenched herself out of it as if it were on fire.

She rushed across their little dining room into her own room. But she returned immediately, lit the big lamp in the dining room, went up to her husband, who had barely had time to unbuckle his sword and was still holding it in his hand, and said in a strained voice, "Let me look at you! Let me look at you!"

Pent-up anger flared in her eyes. Where now was that spellbound docility, that trancelike indifference? That emanation of a spiritual radiance acquired by bitter suffering?

What did it mean, this "let me look at you"? He simply could not understand. She had something extraordinary in mind, but what? She stared at him, he stared back. As well as her blazing anger and the harshness of her expression he could see the bitterness welling up in her defenseless slender neck. She was utterly unlike herself—the self that he knew. Looking at that painfully swollen throat, he felt a sharp pang of pity for her helplessness. And although he had already begged her to forgive him—why, oh, why had he hurt her so unnecessarily. He held out his hands again, and took her elbows, to say it all again, more fully, more eloquently.

"Compare us all you like! If she really is such a superior person she won't want to share her life with a mediocrity, a failed army officer!"

She freed her elbows, turned on her heel, and went back to her room. He heard her lock the door.

He stood there, lost in thought, still wearing his greatcoat. Yes, what she had said was probably true.

He took off his coat and hung it up. Share his life? But when, if ever, had Alina ever shared his way of looking at things?

What should he do? Knock on her door, crawl to her? He had begged her forgiveness, that was enough.

He put out the light in the dining room. All the lights.

All right, then, get some sleep on this last night, instead of listening to her sobbing and whispering, and trying to soothe her.

He stretched out on the sofa in his study and lit a cigarette.

Things would look better in the morning.

He slept a deep, dreamless sleep, without once awakening, even when he turned over.

He woke up later than usual. Instead of jumping out of bed at once he lay there in the unbroken silence.

Whatever happened he would not stay there another day. No matter what new twist she thought up. Not even if she clung to him in the doorway and screamed. Perhaps he could slip out quietly, without breakfast, while she was still asleep, and catch the first train?

He rose, walked on tiptoe, and put on his slippers—boots might creak.

But the door from the dining room to Alina's room was open. In the dining room everything was as it had been the night before. No preparations for breakfast had been made.

In the middle of the table stood a photograph of Alina wearing a broad-brimmed hat, and there was a sheet of white paper propped up against its inclined frame.

A note written in her mannered hand, with curlicues like the tails of comets. But with a new savagery about it.

"I despise myself for humiliating myself, for tolerating, for wanting a show of affection from you in that wretched guesthouse! It was like committing incest!" The upstrokes and downstrokes were like so many sturdy stems onto which the letters were grafted. But Georgi knew that their sturdiness was only apparent and that they would scarcely support those word clusters for another five minutes.

"When I was leaving our little home for the lake four days ago I imagined that I was the only one, and incomparable. Now here I am, home again, second best. How dare you compare us? And will you go on comparing us at every turn?"

She must have gone out very quietly. She'd been too clever for him, leaving first.

It had come to that: each of them trying to trick the other.

Perhaps in fact she had left last night, as soon as he had fallen asleep.

There was more: "I am going to Petersburg to take a look at your fair siren, and decide whether it is worth my while committing suicide on her account. Don't try to follow me, and don't wait at home for me—I don't want to see you when I get back!"

Aha! But how would she know where to look? Although, although . . . He began striding anxiously about the room, flexing all the muscles of his back as he rounded the table . . . although, yes . . . "highly educated"—"something to do with history" . . . he had given away far too much . . . Maybe she would find her?

Should he send a telegram to Olda to warn her?

Warn her? Tell her that he had given away their secret, mentioned her name? That he had given her name away on the very first day? That the world would shortly collapse about her ears?

A telegram to Vera? Telling her to intercept his crazy wife if she could?

No, she would not go anywhere near Vera. And anyway, what could Vera do with her in her present state?

He paced the apartment more and more rapidly. He felt as if he was on fire.

In her bedroom drawers had been pulled out and emptied. Two frocks lay in a heap on the unmade bed.

A crumpled sheet of paper lay on the floor.

It was in the same handwriting, the size of the letters growing with her fury.

O-o-oh, when he was walking Alina around the pool, tucking the scarf around her neck to protect her from the wind, he had decided too soon that it would all work out.

Ought he to rush off to Petersburg again himself? What about GHQ? And his regiment? He was impossibly late already! He had made a big enough fool of himself as it was.

"You thought you had found a meek little idiot, did you? But I have a way out! Just wait, you'll see how brill . . ."

She had crossed it all out and thrown it away.

Here was another sheet crumpled and tossed toward the window.

"For whose sake was it that I sacrificed my musical career . . ."

It dawned on him that she could hardly have left for Petersburg last night—she would have been too late for the last train. And it was still too early for the first.

An idea! Susanna Iosifovna had for some reason given him her telephone number, without being asked.

He put his greatcoat on over his shirt and went out of the apartment—in such a hurry that he almost forgot the key and slammed the door behind him—and rushed down to the telephone on the lower landing.

She answered. How much softer women's voices sounded over the telephone.

"Susanna Iosifovna! Please don't be surprised, and please forgive my intrusion. Alina Vladimirovna may possibly turn up at your apartment shortly. Or"—a sudden thought—"or maybe she's with you already?"

There was some hesitation at the other end.

Evidently she was there.

"If so, I beg you, even though I have no right to . . . you have a good influence on her. If she is thinking of going to Petersburg, please try to dissuade her . . . It can only cause trouble . . . For her too . . ."

A pause at the other end. Then, cautiously but amicably: "Very well, Georgi Mikhailovich, I'll try."

An intelligent woman! A delightful woman! He was glad that she was at Alina's side. Couldn't have wished for anything better.

That's it, then! Enough women for now!

To the front!

*　*　*

SOME TRUTHS ARE BEST KEPT
FROM WIVES.

*　*　*

Document No. 4

PRINCE G. E. LVOV TO M. V. RODZYANKO

11 November 1916

The chairmen of provincial zemstvo boards, meeting in Moscow on 7 November to discuss the state of the food supply . . . Government policy has borne fatal fruit . . . All the measures adopted by the central authorities seem to be designed to complicate even further the dire situation in which the country finds itself . . . It is high time to realize that the government now in power is incapable of bringing the war to an end while safeguarding the true interests of Russia. Agonizing and terrible suspicions of treachery and treasonable acts have now given way to a clear realization that the hand of the enemy secretly influences the course of government policy. Indignantly rejecting all thought of an ignominious peace . . . the chairmen of provincial zemstvo boards have unanimously concluded that the government at present in power, openly suspected as it is of subservience to sinister influences inimical to Russia, cannot govern the country and is leading it along the road to ruin and ignominy . . .

[6 0]

When the decree calling category 2 militia to the colors as of 7 November appeared in the press, Roman Tomchak, lounging in his rocking chair, felt as if his legs had been cut from under him. He could neither go on rocking nor rise to his feet. This time he would inevitably be among the first called.

The news extinguished all will to resist. Hunched, head bowed, he cowered in his last refuge, his rocking chair.

That was how Irina found him, a small, swarthy, crumpled figure, with his bald patch to the fore and a newspaper on his knees. One look, not at him, but at the newspaper, told her everything.

Throughout the war years Irina had felt deeply ashamed that her husband was not in the army. True, there were other steppe farmers of his age, in their thirties—the younger Mordorenko, Nikanor, or the youngest of that family of Molokans—but they were running large estates themselves (and the Molokan sect were in any case exempt as conscientious objectors). Whereas Roman, at thirty-eight, had not been allowed by his difficult and indefatigable father to take part in the business. He had in fact shown little inclination to do so, but was content to sit out the war down on the farm, with occasional trips to the big cities.

But last summer, in the darkest days of the Russian retreat, when Irina was dismayed by her country's losses and fearful for its future, she had come across newspaper reports of the nurse Rimma Ivanova's heroic death. What particularly affected her was that Rimma too was from Stavropol, and had attended the Olgin School, next door to Irina's boarding school. She was a few years younger than Irina, but . . . When all the officers in her company, the 10th, had been killed, Rimma herself led the soldiers in a counterattack, took an enemy trench, was killed, and was posthumously awarded a George medal, fourth class.

Even before this Irina had liked handling her Winchester, trying out her (unfailing) marksmanship, and imagining how fearless she would be in battle. But now she was ten times as eager: she had always admired the way Russia had fought in the First Fatherland War. She had a detailed knowledge of it from pictures, but had never expected to land in a time just as heroic. But when the menacing storm clouds of the Second Fatherland War had filled the sky, there was no place for Irina around army campfires, nor with the partisans, nor at the side of Vasilissa, the headman's wife. She would gladly have given up tending her cinerarias, cyclamens, and Japanese chrysanthemums, and arranging and rearranging the seven dozen changes of dress hanging uselessly in her closet, to experience for the first time the exhilaration and heroism of army life. "Romasha!" she would say. "Let's join up!" "Why, do you want to get me killed?" "Let me go by myself, then." "To do what?"

Irina could see it clearly. She would be using her rifle. She had a vivid and unembarrassed vision of herself in simple, soldierly dress, perhaps even wearing breeches, lying on the ground, or up a tree, like her beloved Natty Bumppo. Even if Russia were not in such danger she would not have been sorry to escape from the inactivity which had become so wearisome. (Though if Russia had not been in danger there would have been no means of escape.) But she had not dared to horrify her husband with the role she saw for herself. "I'll go as a nurse," she said. "So that you can cheat on me with the officers?"

He didn't mean it, of course. He knew how strictly she had been brought up, that she had passed directly from her father's to her husband's governance, and had enjoyed so little independence that she had never even bought a railroad ticket, and wouldn't know where and how. She never left home for town unless accompanied by one of the Cossacks or a maidservant, she would not wear a sleeveless dress, and would leave the table immediately if her husband thought one of the male guests was paying her too much attention. She regarded Anna Karenina as the vilest of women. He would certainly not suspect her, but could not face the double disgrace of letting his wife go while he stayed at home himself.

She had thought of joining the 1914 Society: the very name of it was a trumpet call, it made her think of 1812. They sent her tickets and pamphlets, and invited her to meetings at Ekaterinoslav, but Roman would never let her go. Then it transpired that the Society intended to combat German encroachment in Russia. A good cause! Irina had long been distressed by German inroads. Even before the war she had impatiently wondered how long Germans would be allowed to rule Russia. But now, for all the Society's efforts, if you looked at the pictures in the press every fifth general, officer, senator, or member of the State Council had a German name, and since spring a man named Stürmer, undisguised, had taken control of Russia. What a humiliation! Wilhelm, with the Tsaritsa's help, had conquered after all!

Then the Society had turned against German landowners. But, needless to say, nobody had dared to let out a peep against their mighty neighbor, the richest rancher in the whole North Caucasus, Baron von Shtengel. Instead they set about harassing, trying to ruin and drive out other neighbors of theirs, ordinary German settlers, decent people and clever farmers, from whom the Tomchaks had borrowed ideas, among many others about the construction of their cattle barn and their laundry—iron-hooped tubs on casters moved directly under the taps, and wringers were fixed to the rims of the tubs, so that linen never dried outside, but in a cross-draft under cover.

Irina sided with the settlers and was expelled from the Society. Roman laughed. He himself never played such childish games. The Unions of Zemstvos and Towns were hard at work all over Russia (there were, however, no zemstvos in the Caucasus), but Roman, sitting in his rocking chair with the newspaper, found their activities just as comical. Any activity more serious than these pathetic yappings would, he assumed, be possible only after the war.

But now, dismayed by the latest mobilization decree, he realized that he had miscalculated: he would not be able to sit out this endless war at home, he would have to seek refuge in the Union. After twenty-seven months the war was as bloodthirsty as ever. Out there you could meet your end in less than a month.

Irina kissed her husband's bald patch and tried to reassure him. They might not take him. And if they meant to it would not be just yet, there would be time to think of some way out. The simplest and most obvious thing, of course, would be for him to take a full part in managing the estate. That would suffice. Irina would beg and beseech his father . . . but . . . even to save his son's life the old man would never agree. It was so unfair, because Roman had great managerial talents— if only he was allowed to develop them. Look how shrewd he had been, on various occasions, in predicting what would attract the most buyers that year, what they should sow, and it had happened just as he had said. There was that season—when was it?—when he had rented five thousand desyatins, at Gulkevichi, from Fedos Mordorenko and sown flax, which was hardly ever seen in those parts, and it was just as he had foreseen—a big harvest and a big demand in autumn. Other steppe farmers drove in to see and to marvel. He had repeated this one more year, again successfully, then given up in time, and his imitators couldn't get a good price. He could do anything if he turned his hand to it!

This reminder of his coup with the flax gave Roman new strength. He was, after all, a man of parts—why lose heart? (It had always been like that with him: any setback was followed by a spell of black depression.) If circumstances threatened to overwhelm him, he must devise some plan of action.

It was Irina who had given him the idea: why not make a speech at the meeting? An unprecedented meeting of all the neighboring farmers was to be held, at their house, on Sunday, 12 November. Previously they had gotten together only for name-day celebrations, or card parties, but now they had taken it into their heads to do what the rest of Russia was doing, and hold a meeting. Roman had ridiculed this enterprise, and said that he wouldn't even go downstairs to say hello. But now he saw his mistake. The more deeply steppe farmers sank into the wartime morass, the more problems there were. He had not wanted to involve himself, his own money was in the bank, but now, with his abilities, his education, and his eloquence, and also his invariable sobriety among those debauched pigs, he had every chance of assuming a leading role. Once he was authorized by the conference to negotiate on its behalf with other such groups of steppe farmers, with Ekaterinodar, Rostov, and so on, it would be the beginning of a period of furious activity, with excursions here, there, and everywhere, he would be in general demand, and he could forget about the draft. You're right, Irina my love, you're absolutely right, my precious, let me give you a big kiss . . .

From that moment on Roman was a new man. He shaved immediately, cheered up, changed his dressing gown for a frock coat, hurried down to the countinghouse, where he had not been seen for a long time, asked to be shown the books, questioned the steward and the clerk. This was on Saturday, but he did not stick his nose outside the countinghouse on Sunday either, and on Monday he toured the fields with the shaggy-headed bailiff, as far as the boundary with Tretyak's spread. Tuesday he spent at home, on the upstairs veranda, calculating and writing.

Such unusual activity could not escape the older Tomchak's notice. He didn't make any difficulties, gave not a single bark, didn't try to stop his son from copying figures from the ledgers, didn't even ask what it was all for. Roman himself explained that he was not trying to interfere in the business, just writing an address.

Never, but never, had Zakhar Fyodorovich's tongue trotted out that word in that sense. Ad-dress? Sounds like the piece you'd give to the tailor to sew on. But he had read in the newspapers that ministers addressed reports to the Tsar. And that learned gentlemen addressed learned gatherings. So, contrary to custom, he refrained from interfering or giving instructions, and sat quietly at an empty desk, leaning on his cane, and quietly observed his son's work on the address and his interrogation of the staff. But he did not ask what line the address would be taking.

Roman was quite happy. His father's presence did not disturb him. Let him see that anything could be entrusted to such a son, that his was a safe pair of hands.

Right then, when Roman had become so brisk and efficient, and the whole household and the whole yard were busily preparing for the grand reception, old Tomchak, who had always been so loud and boisterous, suddenly became very quiet. He stopped shushing and shouting at people, gave his orders quietly and laconically, drove nowhere, but just walked about slowly with his favorite gnarled stick. His old woman was worried—maybe he was ill? The staff spoke in hushed voices, dreading some novel display of anger. But the old man was simply lost in thought. And he told no one what it was he was thinking about.

So there he sat, in the office, stealing glances from under his bushy brows at this surprising sight—his son working. If only he had had such a son, able to work like that, ten years ago, and if only that son had gone on working for those ten years, he could have handed it all over to him without anxiety. But it couldn't be done all at once, not just like that. Irina was sweet-talking him, and Tomchak realized why, he knew about the call-up. But the business, built up from nothing, back there on the Kuma to begin with, then at Maslov Kut, and for the past twenty years in the Kuban, with two thousand desyatins, and sales as far away as Kharkov, and even to the French—a business like that was very much bigger than Tomchak himself, and could not be spread out like a bed of straw so that his son would not hurt himself falling. The business had a life of its own, it was no longer merely a family concern, it involved many other people, and produced vast quantities of goods for Russia. It was in effect no longer Tomchak's personal property, and he was simply not at liberty to place it in unreliable hands—he would as soon hang himself. If he had had a sensible son what was there to stop Zakhar Fyodorovich at the age of fifty-eight from taking it easier, allowing himself a little leisure? He could still have kept half an eye on things, but spent time mostly reading the Lives of the Saints, and maybe he could have gone to the Monastery of the Caves in Kiev to say a few prayers, or even to Palestine. But with this son Tomchak was determined to carry on and not to relax his hold for another twenty years if necessary. He'd given in to his daughter-in-law over Ksenia, but Ksenia would be finishing school that year, and they would get her fixed up with a husband. And before the twenty years was up he would rear himself the sort of grandson he needed. Then he could finally get around to the Lives of the Saints. But this son of his—he might as well go and fight the Germans. It had all been handed to him on a platter, and he'd turned up his pig's nose at it. (But in his heart of hearts he still hoped that with God's grace this son of his would mend his ways.)

Roman worked away feverishly at his address. On the eve of the gathering, when he had all his figures ready, and the whole household was caught up in a frenzy of cleaning and cooking, he did not stir from his aerie, but ordered the old manservant, Ilya, to bring his evening meal up to the veranda—which was what he had always enjoyed most. He cleared the card table of papers for the time being, and the servant ceremoniously flapped a stiffly starched tablecloth over it, and carried in glassware and silverware. Nowhere else, and with no other company, was it so enjoyable to dine as at home and by yourself. With no one to hurry you, no conversation to distract you, you could concentrate on enjoying the food, you had time and occasion to recall similar combinations of flavors, in the restaurant of the Europa Hotel, at Baden-Baden . . . By yourself you could drink a tot or two, you could even carry your glass into the bedroom, stand before the mirror, and . . . "Your health, Mr. Deputy!" Russians destroy themselves by drinking when they're miserable. The time to drink is when you're happy, and then only a little at a time.

You could take a stroll around the bedroom, with an agreeable buzzing in your head. The room was big enough to serve as Roman's study in winter and to house their library. Half of the books were Irina's, half of them Roman's. Irina's were a miscellany, in their original bindings. Roman had his rebound in uniform black covers, so that Pushkin and Gogol and all the others looked like volumes in one enormous "collected works." The spine of each volume bore in gilt lettering the initials R. T., and on the front cover his full surname, R. Tomchak. Some six hundred identical volumes made a most impressive sight.

Yes, in the Fifth State Duma his radical program would astound them all. The autocracy must be whittled down—until it was little more than a plaything. Second, the philosophical work of the giant Tolstoy must be completed by administrative measures: the Church must be demolished! It must be stripped of its capital and its lands—property which lay idle and only hindered progress. The Church must become a mere appendage, to provide christening and burial services for those who wanted them, nothing more. Third . . . but you couldn't of course turn everything upside down single-handed, you would have to create a party of capable people unlike any that Russia now possessed. In comatose, undifferentiated Asiatic Russia, while the so-called Kadets exchanged blows with their near neighbors to the left, the Social Democrats, there was no major party capable of action.

In came Irina, in a pinafore, flushed and happy.

"Well, how are things? Do you need anything?"

"Everything's fine! D'you know, I might even say I'm glad the storm has broken, it's woken me up! I'm even thinking of making this conference the beginning of a sort of movement, purely commercial to begin with, and only here in the Kuban at first, but later . . . It would confront the authorities with tough conditions. We're the ones who feed them, so they would have to accept. Have you had lunch, by the way?"

"Have I! When you're standing in the kitchen in that heat, tasting everything . . . Do you realize that, not counting snacks, but desserts included, we will have ten dishes tomorrow!"

"Whew!"

"Well, we can't let ourselves down. Not on an occasion like this! And on your debut."

"Another thing—I've been thinking about the car."

She knew how it rankled. Last year when automobiles were requisitioned they had without so much as a by-your-leave taken the Rolls-Royce. It had cost him 180,000 rubles, and now it had ended up with Grand Duke Nikolai Nikolaevich, after his transfer to the Caucasus, or perhaps with some mere general, who could tell. For years Irina had pleaded with Roman not to provoke people by keeping a car.

"I'm thinking now that if this business gets off the ground perhaps I should put myself in the hands of Borée and Co. They sell only British cars, apparently with guarantees of exemption from requisitioning."

"Just as you like," Irina said, all smiles because he was so active and so nice to her. "I'll always prefer trotting horses, you know that. But if things go as you expect you'll shortly need a car, of course."

"You are a darling." He kissed her hot, pink cheek.

"I'll come back and consult you on what I ought to wear tomorrow."

"Do, please do."

She was clever, Irina. And devoted. Young. And beautiful. For public appearances, for show, for his travels, he could not imagine a better wife. Everybody admired her, everybody envied him. But a glamorous exterior could be very deceptive: deep down there was something missing, that vital disturbing something that you might find in a homely girl in a bedraggled skirt. If only you had that little something, my darling, you wouldn't need your weird and wonderful ideas, or your Winchester, or the 1914 Society.

Never mind, his political activity would necessitate frequent trips without his wife.

Irina meanwhile, happier still after her tête-à-tête with her affectionate husband, hurried away to the cold larder to see that the cakes had been put away carefully, then to the cellar to check the salted dishes, then back to the kitchen. It was a long time since she had been so preoccupied with tasks that were not of her own invention but obligatory. They had all been taught to cook at boarding school. You'd never make a good wife if you couldn't. But in the Tomchak domain, to take a hand in the kitchen would have demeaned Irina herself and offended her mother-in-law. It would also have shown distrust of the servants: a regular visitor to the kitchen could not help noticing—as Irina had—how they put things aside for themselves and their families. So wealth had deprived her of the simple enjoyment which a woman can find in her kitchen.

These last few days had been different. She was planning the whole affair: the decoration of the dining room, the arrangement of dishes, and the order in which they were to be served. She had chosen and sampled everything on the menu, sauces and garnishes included. As the war went on, the possibilities had become more limited. Their stocks of certain items, now unobtainable elsewhere, were exhausted. (But there was still abundance and superabundance!) There was also a shortage of female help—some of the women servants had replaced full-time workers who had been called up, and there was only one housekeeper to look after the house and the yard, with no pantry maid to help her. So that today everyone was fully stretched, and Irina felt all the more needed—especially to help stuff the birds.

Tomorrow's conference of steppe farmers differed from their usual gatherings in that only the farmers themselves were invited, no wives or daughters. Irina and her mother-in-law would be the only women at table. But it suddenly occurred to them that old Darya might take it into her head to appear. That would make a number of changes necessary, beginning with the placement.

Although old Darya, Foma Mordorenko's widow, had divided her whole estate between her three sons, who themselves now had grown-up children, her power was still so great that her sons considered themselves accountable to her. She might very well want to come and listen, and even make herself heard. She kept an even tighter rein on the servants: none of them had rooms of their own, they slept higgledy-piggledy in the marble vestibule, and personal attendants on the floor outside the master's or mistress's door. Old Darya was indomitable, and even the authorities at Armavir danced attendance on her. On one occasion 500 rubles were missed in her office. A police inspector, two policemen, and a tracker dog were summoned from Armavir. The servants were made to stand in a ring, the dog was brought out of the office, and they all shook in their shoes. The dog sniffed around for a while, went up to Avraam, the clerk, and placed its paws on his shoulders. (His was of course the only scent it would have picked up in the office.) The clerk, a gangling, sickly fellow, turned pale. The inspector struck him repeatedly. They strapped a sack of bricks on his back and sent him off to Armavir, eighteen versts away. There he was beaten and grilled, while the inspector sat enjoying the old lady's hospitality, inquiring from time to time by telephone how the interrogation was going. The clerk confessed, saying first that he had hidden the money in a barn, then that it was near the latrine, and Darya had all the servants digging. Meanwhile the clerk died from the beatings he had received. (Some years later one of Darya's daughters-in-law, dying young of tuberculosis, confessed to the crime: "I'm being punished for Avraam: I was the one who stole it.")

But Darya's power was fraying at the edges. Her widowed son had imported a replacement for his wife—a cabaret singer. The family ceased visiting him, and the chanteuse received other guests in lacy negligee, with nothing but a knitted bodice underneath.

Whether she had really been a chanteuse, whether she had ever sung little ditties somewhere, Irina did not really know, but she used the odious word "chanteuse" to describe, collectively, the whole category of women of ill repute who sapped the foundations of family life. She stigmatized them, willed them out of existence, would not hear them mentioned, tried not even to think of them, but that scene which someone had once described to her—the chanteuse receiving her guests—had etched itself on her memory and continually returned to trouble her. Nothing but an undergarment and a lacy negligee! She shuddered.

She still had to decide what to wear tomorrow. There would be no other women present, so she must dress austerely. A waist-length jacket with astrakhan trimming.

She still had to visit the laundry, where the head laundress was ironing, on a special table made for Irina's voluminous duvet covers, the tulle curtains for the main reception room.

The sun had almost set when Irina, tired out, left the house for her usual evening walk across the park.

The weather, in early November, was still warm and mild, and, as usual in the southern autumn, windless. But for the fallen leaves and the early sunset, it was more like summer, and Irina felt too warm in her woolen blouse. Nor was there any dew.

The first, crooked avenue was strewn with big, violet pods. A twig fell into the oval ornamental pond, and expanding circles wrinkled its surface, then, rebuffed by the concrete rim, splashed backward, forming strange patterns in which reflected treetops danced, the unshed leaves of plane trees, inordinately large, and other leaves, green and yellow, elongated and drooping like the ears of some strange creature.

As soon as dusk fell the silvery Himalayan firs quickly changed color. They became dark. And a large bird of some sort could be seen darting about in them.

Looking back through the firs toward the house, she could see that, upstairs and downstairs, lights were going on, variously colored by lampshades and curtains. Out there walking it was easy to imagine that this was not her house, the uncommonly comfortable house which had nonetheless palled on her, in which she knew where every object stood or lay or hung, and just what every person was doing or was about to say—no, this was the fascinating abode of chivalrous and high-souled strangers, and the life lived there was noble, radiant, dignified, such a life as you would rarely meet even in books.

There was more light in the outermost avenue, lined with chestnut trees. Big chestnuts in spiky shells lay uncollected underfoot.

The chestnut avenue led into a pleached corridor of Chinese acacias, with little chains of poisonous-looking fruits. There too it was dark again.

This, on the westernmost edge of the park, was where Irina always walked in the evening, passing from light to twilight, and back again from twilight into the light. There she indulged her fantasies about yogis, theosophists, and the transmigration of the soul. She was very ready to believe in the transmigration of the soul, and found that some Oriental ideas fitted in beautifully with Christian truths, and saw it all as so many hypostases of beauty. Irina liked imagining who she had been *before*, and who she was going to be *afterward*, and wondering whether she would reach the stars before she was reincarnated. She liked thinking about a tremulous, unrealizable beauty meant not for us but for liberated souls.

A pure sky, without a single pink cloud, was making way for a still night, waiting for the stars and the Milky Way to show through, and the moon, past its full and veering leftward each day, to rise. As the light waned, bonfires stood out clearly here and there. They were burning the haulm of sunflowers out on the steppe, making potash. There was a labor shortage, and tasks unfinished were left for autumn nights. All through the endless war, which could not be seen or heard from here, the steppe, God's bountiful tablecloth, continued to yield its gifts to mankind as generously as ever, asking only that their hands should not forget it.

Anyone looking out from the second-story balcony would see the steppe lit by these sporadic fires. Suddenly—a vision: out there, countless nomads advancing on Russia like a plague of locusts had halted for the night, and these were their campfires.

[6 1]

Zakhar Tomchak had spent his early days in beggarly adobe huts, with roofs so low that he had to bend double in the doorway, and even inside could not quite straighten his burly frame, which was why he had taken such a liking to high ceilings. He might never have imagined what it was like to have such a thing if he had not visited some of Rostov's more notable buildings, the Bank and the Exchange in particular, just when he was about to build himself a new house. He had decreed then that both floors of the house on his new estate should be seven arshins (nearly fifteen feet) high—unheard of in these parts— and the main reception room on the first floor eight arshins, which meant raising the floor of the upstairs family living room, to which all the old furniture was relegated.

The main reception room was decorated with pink and gold paint, made to look like wallpaper. The ceiling was not the same color all over: plump white clouds floated there, with little cherubs winging their way between them—mischievous little things, not the kind you see in church—and peeping down at the guests. A chandelier with twenty electric bulbs hung from the ceiling, and there was a curved bracket with three lamps on the wall between each pair of windows. In one corner of the room—as a concession to Tomchak's daughter and daughter-in-law: all respectable people had one—stood a grand piano with a mahogany frame, flanked by two palms. Another corner, by contrast, was decked with icons; this was, after all, a Christian household. In a third corner stood a palm tree so large that it took the combined exertions of all four Cossacks to move it. One wall was adorned with a huge mirror, three times the length of a man's outspread arms, with a carved and gilded frame—the gilt, though, was dull, not shiny (another sign of good taste)—and the mirror itself had been made at His Imperial Majesty's own glass, porcelain, and crystal works. Against the other long wall, between the wide double door of the entrance and the dining-room door, loomed a huge pink-tiled stove. One of the shorter walls was glassed, to give a view of the winter garden with its exotic hothouse flowers, while the other short wall had been removed, leaving only an archway through which guests could pass four abreast if they so pleased, into the drawing room. The drawing room was painted blue, and whether you chose an upright chair, an armchair, or a sofa they were all of highly polished rosewood. The floor of the drawing room was permanently covered with a French carpet. When autumn came around they laid a Turkmen carpet in the main reception room, as they had now for the meeting.

That room was so vast and so beautiful that they couldn't think what to use it for. Dine in it? They dined elsewhere. A ball? The steppe farmers weren't much for dancing. They might want to play cards, but it was too cavernous, and the family living room was the place for that. In the six years of the estate's existence there had probably never been a better opportunity, never been any occasion to assemble all the neighboring steppe farmers, whether friends or outsiders with whom they had never drained a glass at the same table, and to talk business. That spacious hall was the reason why they had agreed to assemble at Tomchak's.

On yet another fine day of sunshine and cobwebs, toward noon, describing an arc on the front courtyard and another on the ramp up to the front porch, the steppe farmers began arriving in a steady stream, in cars, phaetons, traps, and four-wheelers. The Stundist came in a two-wheeled charabanc, without a coachman—a wonder it wasn't an oxcart, funny folks those nonconformists!

Zakhar Fyodorovich, wearing a lilac-colored cheviot suit and a tie (damned piece of string around your neck, enough to choke you!), stood on the porch and was kept busy shaking hands, descending to greet some guests in their carriages, and retreating up the steps to await others. Three Mordorenko cubs, all hefty fellows with topknots, two sons of Foma and one of Akim, arrived separately. Darya, to everyone's relief, did not appear. Little Tretyak lowered his rotund person from a high seat, as cautiously as a spider moving about its web, looking around as if he expected to be stung. As always, even in summer, he was wearing his old black overcoat, unbuttoned, with its skirts sweeping the ground. Chepurnykh drove in behind his mettlesome troika. His head was shaven so close that it shone like a mirror (he used to wear a Cossack pigtail but people had made fun of it in Rostov, so he had recently shaved it off), but his mustaches stuck out sideways like Cossack lances. After him came the Myasnyankins, uncle and nephew, as thick as thieves, both purple in the face—they must have been knocking it back since morning. There were also two Molokans from distant homesteads. And of course the Stundist.

As for Vladimir Rudolfovich von Shtengel, not only did he not deign to appear himself, he didn't even send his bailiff. He wanted nothing to do with peasants.

They trooped into the vestibule, where Ilya, the footman, wearing gray side whiskers, by order from above, and full-dress livery, stood waiting. He accepted hats, coats, and canes and, with a low bow, showed each guest the way to the main reception room.

Where, though, should Roman position himself? Pride had prevented him from telling his father anything about the substance of his speech, and pride had prevented his father from asking. But they had also omitted to discuss how they would receive their guests. Ought Roman to station himself beside his father on the porch? If he did he might cease to look important in his own right. In the vestibule, then? Impossible, with the footman there. So Roman received the guests in the main reception room itself, looking austere and businesslike, with no trace of a smile (he knew, from the mirror and from Irina, that smiling did not suit him—it made him look somehow menacing). He greeted them, showed them to seats there or in the drawing room, and made a few quick businesslike remarks intended to put the steppe farmers in a mood for strenuous intellectual effort rather than the usual gabbling and gobbling.

But what most surprised hosts and guests alike was the correspondent! Yes, a real live reporter from the Ekaterinodar newspaper! Nobody had expected him, nobody had thought of inviting him, he just happened to be in Armavir and had got wind of the conference (or rather scented a feed on the scale usual among steppe farmers) and had come down by train, walking from the station. He had a white face (perhaps the only one in the Kuban) and was so thin you'd think he had worms.

Roman saw at once how useful he could be. Just what he needed—why hadn't he thought of it himself? He was very polite and attentive to the man, and assigned him a place next to his own at the great table, which was covered with a blue cloth for the conference.

The other steppe farmers were ill at ease with him. How did you behave with someone like that watching? He'd write it all down! Best not to open your mouth at all.

They went on talking at a safe distance, but fell silent the moment he approached. The subject of conversation was Rostov's mills, which had always processed Kuban grain, but now the steppe farmers had been ordered not to take it there, so some mills were idle and others had started hulling coarse grains. While in the Kuban grain was spoiling. "Yes," somebody said, "and a man came down from Petersburg and reckoned there's nothing at all to eat there." "But if we could get the grain to Rostov, would they give us a decent price? Might as well feed it to the cattle for free, make more of a profit that way." "Binder twine always used to be four and a half rubles a pood, now it's fifteen." "Never mind twine, what about shoe leather?" "What about the cost of labor, then? One time you could hire a good all-around worker for the whole summer for fifty rubles, now he wants two hundred!" "That's nothing, come harvest time a woman would work from sunup to sundown for seventy kopecks and think herself lucky. Now *you're* lucky if it isn't three rubles." "Wouldn't be so bad if anybody did an honest day's work, but they're just after the money, they aren't there to work. Say you pay what they ask, all the good workers have been mopped up, there's only cripples left, all those fit to serve have been taken. Yet down in Rostov every little farting engine has a draftee working it. They might at least give us enough prisoners, but they even begrudge us prisoners. And those they do send are barbers or book-keepers, because prisoners've got their own specialties, see. And it wouldn't be so bad if we could keep the ones they did send, but when the harvest is at its busiest they pull them in and whisk them off the Lord knows where."

There was some truth in their complaints, but they were leading nowhere, they were a distraction from Roman's report, and they could spoil everything. Dark and dapper, he moved swiftly about the hall, urging his father and the other older men to get the proceedings started.

But how? How did you go about "holding a conference"? They went to the big table with the blue cloth, and even the Mordorenko brothers, even Yakov, with the platinum teeth, were reluctant to occupy the best places. They hung back, showing unprecedented deference, not fighting as they usually did over who should occupy the limelight, but contesting who should hide behind the others.

And all the time keeping a wary eye on the correspondent.

Roman's father, as host, made an introductory speech of sorts: here we all are, then, so let's talk things over, let's hear what everybody thinks about it all . . . But he did not propose electing a chairman. Roman was waiting for him to say, "My son here has a report for you!" But he didn't.

Oh well, he'd have to do it himself. The two dozen uncouth, fat-faced, red- or copper-complexioned clodhoppers sitting around the spacious table, on chairs you could lose yourself in, with no glasses or playing cards to hold, didn't know what to do with their hands, but were careful not to paw the blue cloth. They looked merely vacant, but they felt embarrassed. There was not a single scrap of paper on the spacious blue oval. Nothing at all except a large ledger in front of Roman, and a notepad in front of the correspondent. But these were enough to put them on their guard, and they stole apprehensive glances at Roman. He rose without further ado, surveyed the assembly and said, "Gentlemen, to make our conference a fruitful one, would you perhaps find it convenient if I present a report analyzing the main problems confronting us, and suggesting practical steps to be taken, after which you might like to express your own views?"

They were all flabbergasted: they had no idea that such a fine talker had been raised in their midst! The words he used! The Stundist with the little black beard, sitting in the far corner there, might know them, but nobody else did.

There was no need for a chairman after all. A confused murmur of assent, followed by silence, left the way clear for Roman's address. He opened his ledger, and occasionally, but not too frequently, glancing at it, he spoke firmly and fluently, looking to his right and to his left in turn.

"First group of problems—prices for our produce, and above all, of course, for grain."

Rustling the pages of his book now and then, underlining or circling something there in pencil, he spoke to the steppe farmers about cereals and maize and wool—telling them what they knew already, but could not have put together so quickly and neatly to save their lives. (And who would have the patience to write it all down!) Roman spoke indignantly of low fixed prices but reminded them that prices for requisitioned cattle had been fixed too low to begin with, then raised at the farmers' insistence, so that the state began paying four or five hundred rubles for a yoke of oxen.

The reporter began taking notes.

Irina contented herself with occasional peeks through the half-closed door of the dining room.

"Second group of problems—the prices of manufactured goods."

He read out the current prices for plows, threshing machines, shovels . . . They were so incensed by these prices that Chepurnykh burst out in his thundering bass: "And the towns want everything for free! They ought to try working like we have to!"

Others chipped in: "If the factories didn't keep striking, prices would be all right."

Most of them just listened. Some of the listeners turned up their noses, but were disarmed by the sight of those not quite birds, not quite humans flying over them. Roman himself was amazed by their attentiveness and the success of his first venture into public life. He became more fluent and self-consciously superior.

"Third group of problems—laborers. As you know, the situation was catastrophic before, but now they're calling up category 2 militiamen under forty. In a couple of months production on our farms will come to a standstill."

The Molokans with the prominent cheekbones batted their eyelids: he was right!

Fedos Mordorenko called out, "They'll ruin us farmers completely!"

"And let's not forget how it corrupts the workforce. The workers know they're in demand, so they don't work as hard as they did before the war. They know they can always quit and find themselves a higher wage."

The correspondent was getting it all down. (And whenever the door to the dining room opened slightly he tried to hear what was happening in there. He really was remarkably thin, in contrast to the steppe farmers present.)

They listened without the usual babel of contradictions. Roman had always been conscious of his superiority to the locals, but was surprised to find how effective his speech was proving. Taking care not to let their attention wander, he cited instances and figures, but not too many, then passed on to further problems: the government's failure to give agricultural producers credit, so that they either had to stop producing or accept whatever prices the market offered, even if it ruined them completely, because they could not afford to wait for better ones.

Here there were many shouts of approval, and Roman, more and more confident that he was now their acknowledged advocate, concluded as follows: "Only medium and large-scale agriculture is advantageous to the state: there is a larger return on capital, and labor input is more effective. The peasants lack the means to improve their farming methods. Nor are gentry estates run as well as they might be: the landowning gentry themselves are work-shy, they are poor businessmen, and their bailiffs rob them right and left and have no proprietorial interest in the estates. Only the big commercial farms like ours represent the highest type of modern agricultural enterprise. The state ought to realize that—and we mustn't forget it ourselves. The time, therefore, has come for us to adopt a different tone with the powers that be. Instead of waiting for blessings to descend upon us, instead of begging, we must start demanding. Remind them what we mean to the state, how much we produce—and *demand*."

Yes, yes, the meeting was won over, he could feel it, by his proud self-confidence and his unspoken offer to do the demanding for them. They held their heads higher (some curled their lips haughtily) when they were told for the first time in their lives that they could . . . make demands on the authorities?! Treat them like we treat our clerks?!

Roman then spelled out a number of proposals. They should adopt a resolution, elect a representative with full powers to connect with other groups of farmers, and then enter into negotiations with the authorities and offer terms on behalf of all of them. If there were not enough prisoners of war to go around, workers should be brought in from the east or the north, the government should be able to do that, but if not, let it think of something else. Let the government make credits available to the steppe farmers, at less than the eight percent charged by the robbers at the Volga-Kama Bank. If the official prices for cereals were unfavorable, the steppe farmers had the option not to sow grain crops at all, or to reduce the sown area, at once, that autumn, and switch their capital and labor to something more profitable. It went without saying that they should have nothing to do with *belo-turka* and *girka*, cereal crops for which the government did not offer a worthwhile price.

It had been an undoubted success. When they elected a "plenipotentiary," as he had suggested, he was sure to be their man. And it would be reported in the newspaper. Modestly, he resumed his seat. Took a cigarette from the golden case, Irina's gift, and lit it. Glanced at a few faces.

They had been so absorbed in Roman's trenchant speech that when he concluded, closed his heavy ledger, and sat down they seemed to be waiting for him to say something more, to make it easier for others.

For one thing, the chairs were too comfortable, they swallowed five- or six-pood bodies, sucked them into the depths, so that with the tabletop almost touching his chin a man couldn't say much even if he wanted to. And getting to his feet would be even more difficult.

Gloomy little Tretyak placed his palms on the table and pushed, straightening his elbows, preparing to prop himself up while he spoke—but the effort was too much for him and he remained seated.

Yakov Mordorenko clicked his platinum teeth.

Someone sighed. Someone else cleared his throat.

The Myasnyankins knit their brows importantly and exchanged glances, but said nothing.

Surely someone else ought to say something? What did people do at these meetings? Nobody seemed to be coming forward.

Roman was so pleased with himself that the one person he had lost sight of was his father. And anyway, the old man was sitting on the same side of the table, two places away, and Roman would have found it awkward to screw his head around in that direction.

Nor was anyone expecting the senior Tomchak to speak. They assumed that he and his son had concerted their ideas in advance.

Zakhar Fyodorovich had sat through Roman's speech in silence. And when, supporting himself on both armrests, he now rose, they still supposed that he meant only to attend to some domestic matter, perhaps check preparations for dinner. But no. He remained standing, a sturdy figure, unbowed by age, but pressing his knuckles against the solid oak beneath the blue cloth to steady himself.

And if it resembled a conference at all it was only because Zakhar Fyodorovich had taken it into his head to stand while the others, though no grander than himself, remained seated. He began in a subdued, unemphatic voice, more quietly indeed than he usually spoke. It was quite unlike Roman's address.

"So there it is, masters . . . We can switch to wool and cattle and clover and sunflowers, and get by that way for a couple of years. We'd make a profit all right. And by then, maybe, this pesky war will be over, it can't go on till the Second Coming. But can anybody tell me here and now *how* the war will end? Maybe the Germans will get to Armavir? Supposing we all agree now not to sow wheat—what is our army going to stuff in its mouth this coming year?"

He wasn't just quiet, pensive was the only word for it, as he had been for some days past. Could this be the Zakhar Fyodorovich who was so good at barking and flourishing his cane? Could this man ever have hurtled over the steppe, whipping his horses to a gallop? He was silent for some time, as if he had said all that he meant to say. But he remained on his feet, and they all waited. Then he began again, still speaking quietly, in tones that sounded almost affectionate and were seldom heard in the family circle.

"Yes, things are going badly. This last year has been ruinous. And the one that's coming will be just the same. But whoever we send to talk to the government and whatever they manage to think up there— maybe they're all fools anyway—we've got to do some thinking for ourselves, that's why we're all here."

He paused as he reached the most difficult part, in no hurry to stick his neck out.

"Maybe just for a year or two we ought to forget that damned word 'profit.' Pretend we haven't known all our lives what it means. Never mind if more flows out than in next year, just as long as the work gets done, men! Just as long as the wheat gets grown and people get to eat it. No credit bank is going to give us money for that. And we're not going to ask them! Just as long as I've got a scrap of fatback and a whole loaf a day to eat . . . I can go all through Lent eating nothing, you might say. My belly might cave in a bit, but I'll live, and from Easter to Trinity I can grow it again, and a bit extra. Same for all of us—a couple of years' work and we'll all be back where we were. The land's saved us before and it will again. Don't forget—money didn't make us, we made money! If we let a bit slip through our fingers now we'll get it all back again after the war."

Roman was horrified. What nonsense was his father talking? What kind of mischief was this? Should have spoken to him beforehand—if only I'd known. But who'd have expected anything like this from the old man!

What a pity Darya wasn't there! She'd have answered Zakhar with her walking stick. Then all those Mordorenkos—instead of getting flour for their laborers from their own mill, with its forty-two pairs of grindstones, they'd set up a little steam engine on the farm to grind middlings—surely they wouldn't stand for Zakhar's "no profit" talk? Or Tretyak—true, he didn't begrudge his workers a lamb or two, but if there were a few sardines left in a can when guests left he'd have it put away for next time. What would he make of this "never mind if more flows out than in"?

Still, no one interrupted the madman, and he had something to add: "Nobody's going to bring us workers. We have to find them ourselves. And that means we have to pay. If it costs two hundred for the season, that's it—two hundred. On top of selling our grain at a loss we've got to pay laborers more, and bear the loss. Because they've got to live through this war as well, it's no easier for them than for you or me. Or for my seventy-two draft oxen, if there's nobody to look after them."

He spoke with affection. For his oxen.

By now Roman could see that a storm was about to break. Across the table they were baring their teeth, every one of them except the Stundist, who was too timid to get involved. Evstignei Mordorenko, the horsey one, looked as if he'd dislocated his jaw. All Yakov's platinum was displayed in a savage grin. The Myasnyankins had turned purple. Tretyak again placed his puny little hands on the table as if he meant to draw his legs up after them and scramble across it on all fours.

[6 2]

(THE PROGRESSIVE BLOC)

Of all the warring countries Russia alone refrained from thinking about the food supply beforehand, or even when the war began. Russia's average annual grain harvest was 4 billion poods. It reached 5 billion in 1913, was 200 million poods above the average in 1914 itself, was normal in 1915, and even in 1916 was only 200 million poods lower. Russia exported 600 to 700 million poods of grain annually—more than any other country in the world. Export of grain was suspended when war broke out, and with a cumulative surplus of half a billion poods a year in prospect there was less reason than ever to fear a shortage. In 1914 orders from the War Office amounted to less than half of the surplus. The country's cup was running over. Demand for many other products—sugar, for instance—also fell far short of increasing output. As late as 1916 the number of cattle, sheep, and pigs had not decreased, and the War Office's horse census showed that there were 87 percent more foals than in 1912, before mobilization began. The area of arable land, including that not presently cultivated, exceeded the country's requirements by half as much again.

Germany made coarse grinding, and the addition of potato meal to flour, compulsory from October 1914, and introduced rationing—225 grams of flour per person—in February 1915. In the summer of 1915 the whole crop, once it was harvested, was requisitioned by the state. In every European country bread was baked with additives. The Western Allies were supplied with grain by America. Only Russia did not feel the pinch and no one there—neither her benighted rulers nor the enlightened Duma economists—supposed that she ever would. They could not even be bothered to take stock of the country's reserves.

The first surprise came early in 1915, when suddenly there were no oats. There were hundreds of cavalry regiments galloping away or champing at the bit, the whole artillery was lugged around by horses, all our supply wagons and transports were horse-drawn—and suddenly, for reasons unknown, there were no oats. There was fodder enough for the army that year, but Petrograd and Moscow couldn't get it at any price.

Everybody had lightheartedly ignored the problem, but now everybody woke up to it, some because they were officially concerned, others looking for profit, and yet others out of a sense of civic duty. Not a single item of foodstuff escaped public scrutiny, and the government was swift to intervene: this was the year in which the Russian army found itself without shells and the public began to wonder whether "that government" would also reduce it to hunger. It was indeed strange that, although exports were suspended and production had increased, prices for some reason had begun to rise.

A new term now appeared for the first time in Russia—"food procurement." The problem arose so suddenly and so alarmingly that there was no time to consider whether to let it work itself out or to draw up a general plan—and if so, who were the best people to do that? Those who had been buying foodstuffs for decades—brokers, wholesalers, merchants, the zemstvos, cooperatives—were now ousted by the "plenipotentiaries" who descended on the countryside like a plague of locusts. The Ministry of Agriculture, which previously had always occupied itself only with land use and amelioration, was now required, without extra staff or funds, to procure foodstuffs. It hurriedly dispatched unqualified people to buy up farm produce, while the army authorities, and even individual units, also lost no time in sending out procurement agents and commission agents of their own. With government agencies and public organizations zealously competing, many ad hoc committees, loosely supervised by "special plenipotentiaries," were soon operating.

The situation became so alarming that as early as 2 March 1915 a law was enacted authorizing local officials to prohibit exports from or even requisitioning within their districts. Governors invested with full powers were not slow to take advantage of this authorization. They girded their provinces with checkpoints and prohibitions, and stemmed the flow of grain and foodstuffs generally to other areas. So that if, say, the cooperatives of Shuya had previously been quick enough off the mark to buy grain and send it to Kineshma to be ground, nothing could now be brought out of Kineshma and Shuya could not get its own grain back. In a matter of months the restrictive laws destroyed the natural connections between producers and consumers which had existed for many years, and the work of a hundred-thousand-strong network of grain merchants, large and small, with a lifetime of experience, some of them carrying on an inherited business. The plenipotentiaries were given the right to spy on the grain dealers' movements, threaten them with requisitioning, reduce their prices, or simply close down their business. Honest trade was crippled and disappeared from the market, ousted by speculators prepared to flout restrictions and carry goods through roadblocks, resorting if necessary to bribery.

As a result, food prices rose rapidly. By the beginning of 1916 they had doubled all over the country. The public convened conferences to discuss the fight against price inflation, while the government set up committees to combat it. Every provincial and every town governor fought against it to the best of his ability within the limits of his jurisdiction. The hyperactive Minister of the Interior, Khvostov (the nephew), devised a measure that would become only too popular in the years ahead—"relieving congested railway junctions" by rounding up black marketeers.

The problem confronting Russia loomed so large that the regime balked at it and, instead of bypassing the distrustful public, in the summer of 1915 invited its most farseeing and best-educated representatives to take part in a Special Conference on Food Supplies, presided over by the Minister of Agriculture. This new body naturally reinforced itself with its own Price Inflation Commission, its own provincial and district committees, and its own plenipotentiaries (by now plenipotentiaries in chief) for particular products—sugar, butter, leather . . . Thus, in all the big cities—Kiev, Kharkov, Samara, Saratov, Nizhny—the food supply passed into the hands of Progressists.

The Special Conference could and should have looked into other possibilities. They might have noted that in some provinces—Saratov and Voronezh, for instance—much land belonging to the Peasant Land Bank was lying idle, and turned it over to homeless and jobless refugees as temporary settlers. They could have directed their efforts to Volynia, by then recovered from the enemy but still not rehabilitated after the ravages of war, because the Ministry of Agriculture refused to provide funds, or to the lands previously owned by Germans resident in Russia, which had ceased to be productive as soon as they were confiscated—these too could have been handed over to the Peasant Land Bank, or to the zemstvos, or to the war-wounded, and put to work again.

But no, working along these lines was too slow to appeal to the Special Conference, in which not a single ministerial decision was taken without approval of the lay members. These representatives of the liberty-loving Russian public, brought up to think mainly in terms of class and economic warfare, had been given an inspiring opportunity to defend the interests of the patriotic urban population against the greed of the benighted "agrarians"—a term which had come from the West, but was readily adopted by the Russian intelligentsia: agrarians were those in possession of the land, meaning in the first place the gentry landowners, but for want of anywhere else to put them, the peasants, with four-fifths of the land under cultivation, had to be included in this category. The agrarians could be curbed, and Russia saved, only by *fixed prices*. The landowners must not profit from rising grain prices, even it this meant stifling the peasants.

Who first suggested price fixing? The government and the politically conscious public were rival claimants to the honor, but whoever it was could point to the example of Germany, which had begun to fix prices a year earlier. It might be thought that there was no need for fixed prices in a country like Russia, where food was abundant and the producers would themselves bring prices down to undercut each other. But the Special Conference, the political activists among the public, and the lazy government plenipotentiaries began loudly demanding fixed prices, and in 1915 Krivoshein, then Minister of Agriculture, was reluctantly compelled to introduce them—for oats to begin with, then for other cereals. Prices, however, were fixed only for government transactions—the purchase of supplies for the army—somewhat above current market prices, and at just the right time, toward the end of the harvest, when the crop was, in accordance with age-old custom, already on its way to market. Private traders could maintain cereals at less than the fixed prices, and the plenipotentiaries did not try to put a stop to it, enjoying as they did lower prices themselves. The army was adequately supplied, and the free market was able to obtain all the grain it needed, transport it to its own mills, grind it, and satisfy the whole of northern and central Russia. The country got through the winter of 1915–16 without a food shortage.

Throughout 1916, however, prices rose steadily and the purchasing power of the ruble was halved between January and August. The "public" bestirred itself, and resolved that grain prices must remain fixed whatever happened; the enrichment of the agrarians and the impoverishment of the towns must be blocked.

So as early as the spring of 1916 heated and confused arguments broke out in the

Duma, in the press, and everywhere else, about the level at which grain prices should be fixed for the coming year, and how to prevent them from rising. Answering these questions required the widest possible consultation. Zemstvo statisticians interrogated producers and analyzed production costs, while gatherings of landowners and cultivators at the district and provincial level produced their own estimates. Conferences of urban activists—officials and ordinary citizens—arrived at figures much lower than those produced in rural areas. The independent (liberal and financial) press publicized this disparity, inveighing against the prodigious appetites of the agrarians. Agrarians were simply greedy! Landowners were self-centered! These were the charges leveled against them by left-wing (in other words by all) urban activists. They were out to grab all they could, to batten on the people's sufferings. They were incapable of subordinating proprietorial interests to those of the state.

The Progressive Bloc's main thinkers and orators in the Special Conference on Food Supplies were Voronkov and Groman. Voronkov, adhering to his class principles, opined that the peasants would gain by selling more cheaply and that only the landlords wanted higher prices. If fixed prices were raised, how would the peasants in non-grain-growing areas, who had to buy from elsewhere, manage? Only concern for the peasants dictated his demand for the lowest grain prices—at the level set in Poltava province—throughout Russia. The like-minded Groman, a liberal academic economist who had nonetheless done a great deal of damage when working for the Penza provincial zemstvo, found different theoretical arguments to support the same conclusion. Since the purchasing power of money had declined, the peasant would not be seduced by high prices. He would be able to satisfy all his needs by selling two or three poods. (There were no taverns now, so he wouldn't sell grain to buy vodka.) He would not need to take grain to market, and might well stop sowing. Whereas low fixed prices would create want in the countryside, and the towns would get enough bread as a result. (A great future lay ahead of Groman. He was to be Zinoviev's "supply dictator" and would concoct the First Five-Year Plan for the Bolsheviks. That, however, was not a great personal success for him—it landed him in jail.)

The Voronkov-Groman line was supported by representatives of commerce and industry (themselves bread eaters and nongrowers) and by the urban middle class choir in unison.

The chorus muffled and drowned out the voices—so few and far between in the Duma and so hateful to the public ear—of landowners and peasants protesting that fixed prices were a means of forcibly confiscating grain, that once you set foot on that path you would never leave it. They pointed out that while the ruble had fallen to half its previous value the price of grain had risen only by a quarter or a third: in real terms grain had become cheaper, not dearer. (Ah, but we townsfolk still have to dig deeper into our pockets!) Low fixed prices would affect the peasants just as much as the landowners, and were equally unfair to both groups. If an oak provides acorns you shouldn't ask for its roots as well! The pursuit of cheapness by fixing prices at the Poltava level for Russia as a whole would lead to the ruin of agriculture, or to the disappearance of grain from the market. (Is that a threat? Do you mean that it will disappear? Or that you won't surrender it? If that's it, say so! Anyway, the peasants will readily surrender theirs—the market will be flooded with it!)

Prices must be fixed at a level such that they will readily market their grain, since to devise artificial, let alone forcible measures for extracting grain from the 18 million holdings in which it is located is too difficult a task and perhaps beyond our capabilities.

Landowners sought to disguise their "greed" with all sorts of petty special pleas that prices should take into account the rising cost of transport, that it was absurd for unknowledgeable townsmen to slap unreasonable prices on seed grain, for instance, of which you got half a pood to the pood; that a local crop failure, as in Kursk province, automatically doubled production costs—and how could fixed prices compensate for this? Not just prohibitions but measures to strengthen the rural producers were needed to stabilize production, bearing in mind that 11 million workers had been taken from rural Russia into the army, and that it had been given only 600,000 prisoners of war in return, yet was required to produce the same harvest as before and at unchanged prices.

The rural population's defenders (meaning the right) said:

> Russia is made strong not by a poverty-stricken but by a rich and efficient peasantry. How they dread overpaying the peasant! How they dread pouring into the reservoir which they are forever draining!

In educated Russia it had, of course, been the case for half a century past that defense of the rural economy meant exclusively defense of the peasantry. And that was now the tenor of speeches made in the Duma and the Special Conference by landowner deputies. Apart from public statements there was, of course, clandestine resistance. The whole of 1916 was abuzz with discussion of fixed grain prices (but prices refused to settle down). Naumov, the Minister of Agriculture, who favored them, was supported by the Bloc, but was dismissed in June, and Count Bobrinsky, who succeeded him after an interval, was against them, and in no hurry to act.

The argument was not just about the principle, and the level, of fixed prices but also about how widely they should be applied. They had originated in 1915 only for army procurements. For some time afterward other transactions were unaffected and the old disincentive system remained in being. Anyone who could conceal his grain from the plenipotentiaries, from requisition orders, and from provincial boundary patrols, and so avoid selling at fixed prices, could bide his time and sell his grain quite legally at higher free-market prices.

The insufferable agrarians took the argument still further. Why was only grain under discussion? Why should prices be fixed only on grain? In Germany, fixed grain prices were low, but then so were the fixed prices for all manufactured goods. The village could buy as cheaply as it sold. In America grain was even dearer than it was in Russia, but manufactured goods, on the contrary, were cheaper. Whereas in Russia kerosene, iron, and agricultural implements now cost ten to fifteen times their prewar prices. That was why the Russian village felt as if the town was snatching the food out of its mouth. The agrarians had the nerve to point out that their entrepreneurial profit never exceeded 3 percent. While the incomes of industrialists (for instance, that of Konovalov, one of the most prominent members of the Progressive Bloc) had soared out of control during the war, reaching a 200–300 percent return on basic capital, or in some cases 500 or even 1,000 percent. Where, one might ask, could such profits have come from, when the cost of raw materials and labor had risen? Only from robbing the consumer. There was no other conceivable source. Oil companies, if they wished, could hold up production in anticipation of a rise in oil prices, undeterred by the fact that mills were brought to a standstill. While Russian banks, pawnshops, and joint-stock companies, unlike their German counterparts, could keep goods of any sort whatsoever hidden in their repositories until a rise in prices made it profitable to sell. In short, price control should apply to industrial goods as well as to agricultural produce. If profits were to be limited, why should banks be an exception?

The main orators of the Progressive Bloc turned a blind eye to the doings of industrialists, bankers, joint-stock companies. The industrialists were lashed by the Social Democrats and upbraided by the rightists, but never by the liberal center and its leading economists.

So the problem grew and grew, until it affected every aspect of life on the home front. To Russian minds it was difficult, and frightening, to imagine their country tied hand and foot like Germany, but now that the country seemed to be suffering from excessively lax rather than too tight controls, it found itself pushed by events in this direction. A concept previously strange to Russia began to creep in—that of dictatorship. The parliamentary democracies of England and France were ahead of us and already introducing it, but here even our rightists objected that "attempts to regiment a country like Russia are futile," while the Progressive Bloc stood out against extralegal coercion of a free society. In July 1916 the Chief of the General Staff, General Alekseev, presented the Emperor with a plan to establish a "civil dictatorship," to which the ministries and the military alike would be subordinate. The defense industries would be militarized, and so free from strikes, while workers' families would be guaranteed soldiers' rations at low prices, and so released from the daily struggle to obtain food. The freedom-loving Russian factory owners, supported by the Kadet and socialist elements of the public, indignantly repudiated the intrusion of military high-handedness into industrial matters. The Emperor was in any case incapable of taking any firm and wholehearted decision. He wavered a while and then set up a few ineffective interdepartmental committees.

While all these arguments were going on, as month followed month in 1916, fixed prices for cereals and only for cereals struck deep roots in Russian life on the home front. The military, the civil authorities, and the urban public all agreed that they were essential. Their scope widened from month to month: purchases at fixed prices could be made by the plenipotentiaries of arms factories, those of the two capitals and other major cities, and suddenly the dual price systems became intolerable. Congresses of plenipotentiaries, Duma deputies, people active in local and municipal government demanded that the absurdity of free trade should be banned completely, and even the rightists saw no other solution, now that free trade had in any case been fatally disrupted.

The introduction of fixed prices in 1916 went like this. All Russia—literate or illiterate—knew that prices were to be fixed, but their level was a matter of dispute. It should have been announced early in the summer, as grain procurement begins in the south at the end of June and gradually moves northward. But the whole summer was spent in argument. The prices were finally announced in September (at the insistence of the consumer members of the Special Conference they were quite moderate), but right from the start no one had any faith in them. Battle was joined: the town side claimed that a ruble and a half for a pood of rye was inordinately high, the landowners insisted that it was unfairly low. Since the newspapers hinted that three ministers thought the prices too low, rural Russia was not at all sure that the argument was over and that it could not expect higher prices. The landowners' grain was coming in because they had no way of interrupting the traffic, but supplies from the peasants were suddenly at a standstill. Before prices were fixed millers could replenish their stocks at local markets and feed the population. But as soon as the prices were announced the peasants cursed and turned their carts homeward.

The psychological moment, at which for many years past grain had been taken to market, had been missed. And once it had been missed, there was nothing to be done. Even a price increase would not conjure up grain again. The producers were not so much in need of paper money that they could not wait for a further increase.

The army's plenipotentiaries requisitioned the grain they needed, but the wholesale purchasers did not succeed in moving grain by river in summer or in autumn. In 1916 they let the whole navigation season slip by, though rivers were the arteries of the Russian grain trade. The Nizhny Novgorod barge train, which traditionally collected 10 million poods of the new crop from the lower Volga, returned to its winter moorings empty. In the autumn of 1916 the first-class mills of the middle and lower Volga, which used to mill a hundred thousand poods a day for the whole north, came to a standstill and dismissed their workers. At railroad stations too many freight cars stood empty waiting for grain that never came. For the Novgorod, Pskov, and Archangel provinces buying grain became more and more of an impossibility. In autumn, as always, Russia's dirt roads were washed out, and although there was still a month of navigation left, it was impossible, with the best will in the world, to transport grain to the docks or to a railroad.

A full crop was harvested by soldiers' wives, old people, and adolescents in 1916. But it was not where it was needed: in the depths of rural Russia it languished in barns and ricks out of reach of mills, bakers, and bread shops. There was bread in Russia—but there might as well not have been. There was no need for famine in Russia—but by the spring of 1917 the threat of famine might become reality. Before autumn was out even provinces as far south as Kharkov and Rostov-on-Don had begun to experience interruptions in grain supplies, while Moscow and Petrograd had laid in no stocks at all, and were living on deliveries organized from day to day by the government.

The progressive public should have been triumphant: it had obtained low fixed prices and so succeeded in damaging the hated landowners. But, contrary to the predictions of Kadet economists, and to Groman's amazement, it was not the village that found itself in dire difficulties—forcing it to market its grain speedily—but the towns, further burdened as they were with refugees from the western provinces. They had denied the agrarians the chance to get rich quickly. But they had handed it to the urban profiteers instead.

Only an unusually firm government would have dared to think and decide for itself, ignoring the loud self-confident voice of educated society. The Russian government's response to the reproaches and importunities of the public was to give way, to vacillate, and sometimes to retract the concessions it had made. Its will was eroded, churned into a fluid mess like the Russian dirt road in autumn. The opposite ends of an invisible rope were in the hands of the educated public and of the government, and each side tugged away, sometimes gaining, sometimes giving ground, never noticing that the rope had formed itself into a noose, and that the noose was not just anywhere, but around the gullet of their country.

After the dismissal of the Duma in September 1915 the Kadet leaders were deeply disillusioned. The word was, of course, that now events would bypass the monarch, that he had put himself in the position of having to make amends, but payment had to be postponed until Germany was defeated. Even the restrained Maklakov made these transparent remarks in *Russkie Vedomosti*:

> If you and your mother are being driven along a narrow mountain road by a chauffeur who doesn't know what he is doing, but, having taken the wheel, refuses to surrender it, would you, I ask you, try to wrest it from his hands? No! Indeed, you would give the driver helpful advice and put off the reckoning with him until that longed-for time when you were back on level ground . . .

The right wing of the Bloc did not see what had happened as a disaster.

> We regarded the replacement of the Supreme Commander as a tragedy, but the Emperor was more farsighted and the change proved to be for the best. We insisted on the replacement of ministers, yet the most undesirable of them, Goremykin, remained—and the war went better. The flow of refugees was stemmed, Moscow will not be taken—and that is infinitely more important than who is going to be a minister, or when they convoke the Duma. So if we shake our fists at the government we will only weaken our own authority.

The Kadets felt even worse. Maybe they should not have joined the Bloc at all? A long line of left-wing parties was forever tugging the left-leaning Kadets in their direction. The more to the left a party was, the more the intelligentsia respected it, and in that noble array the Kadets were a mob of opportunist office hunters. The Kadet Party itself had its own left wing, led by Nekrasov, Margulis, and Mandelstam, who accused Milyukov of leading the party into a bog, demanded that it get into line with the left, adopt illegal tactics, unite with the socialists, and, of course, leave the Bloc.

The center of the Bloc also acknowledged the collapse of its hopes.

> Efremov: Society is dismayed by the Bloc's failure to assert itself. The Duma session was ended—the Bloc was silent.

> Prince G. **Lvov:** The Bloc wanted to make a sacrifice, share the responsibility, but obtuse people explained this as an aspiration to carry out some sort of coup. The Bloc has made no mistakes. But Russia is left in the air.

In 1915–16 Milyukov needed great resourcefulness in argument, and great sureness of foot, as the Bloc teetered on the brink of the abyss. No ordinary eyes would discern it, but their outstanding leader discerned, and revealed to his intimates, that the Bloc's time was at hand. Once the war ended, France and England would not give a single kopeck to any government which was not answerable to the Duma. The nearer victory came, the more anxious our stupid government would be to compromise. It could not appear at a peace congress with its daggers drawn against the Duma. It had wedged itself into a dead end more constricted than itself by going to war with Germany. But it must not be allowed to make peace with Wilhelm, it must be forced to carry the war to a victorious conclusion! And victory would deliver the Russian government into the hands of the liberals. Hence, their strategy must be to wait, and be patient.

On the other hand, of course, the threat of revolution was growing, and here the Kadets must deploy all their skill: they must restrain their just indignation and remember that accounts with the government could be settled only after the war. They must endure the humiliations, the harassment, the contempt they could expect from the government, but make sure that no social explosion took place before the war ended. Otherwise Wilhelm would emerge victorious and deliver us into the hands of an all-powerful Nicholas. If a social explosion was in fact inevitable, it would come on the day *after the war*, and the cowardly government would capitulate instantly, enabling the country's educated and liberal circles to seize power without bloodshed, especially as they would have the support of England and France.

In either case, they argued, we will soon be in power.

Throughout those months they met frequently in private apartments, and Milyukov, methodical as ever, diligently recorded those wearisome ding-dong debates for the benefit of history. (He subsequently abandoned his notes in Russia, instead of taking them with him into emigration, where he would probably have destroyed them. These notes look fresher to a modern reader than his cunningly crafted, polished memoirs or his published speeches.)

> **Astrov:** The social strata below look on us with hatred and exasperation. The people's anger is vented not on the government but on the social organizations.

> **Maklakov:** The leftists are mounting a disgusting attack on the franchised classes. I'm afraid we are in for a radical disagreement with the left.

> **Milyukov:** We must prepare our defense against accusations from the left.

> **Maklakov:** But from the moment when we enter into conflict with the crown I have no fear of the left. How can we arouse the public? Should we devise a compelling slogan and call for strikes? We are afraid to go down that road. I put my hopes on 23 March (date of the Emperor Paul's assassination).

> Prince G. **Lvov:** If we put too much emphasis on conflict with the crown the result may be complete failure. We unite people by an appeal to greed.

> **Chelnokov:** I'm afraid the so-called upsurge will be a weak and ineffective one. How many times do we have to adopt the same resolutions?

Guchkov somehow or other got into the act:

> I would be prepared to await the end of the war, if we could be sure that it would end favorably. But we are being led to total defeat and collapse. Your silence, and ours, will be interpreted as acquiescence with the regime. We must break off peaceful relations with it.

> **Meller:** We are a threat now because we are silent. Our position is very strong.

VI. **Gurko:** If we remain silent Grishka (Rasputin) himself will become Prime Minister. Only fear has any effect. We must frighten the wits out of them. Should we appeal to the streets? Perhaps as a last resort we should.

Stempkovsky: Supplies to the army are now running smoothly. So price inflation and the chaos on the railways are the sticks we must use to beat the government.

Efremov: We must set the press on them.

Shidlovsky: And include in a future Duma resolution patriotic phrases and ideas to indemnify ourselves. To preserve the Bloc we have to avoid raising thorny questions.

Milyukov put forward a draft resolution for adoption by a Duma which had yet to be convened. It contained all the demands without which victory over Germany was—supposedly—impossible: first and foremost, an amnesty for the revolutionaries, then equal rights for the Jews and conciliation of the non-Russian peoples, and finally "a government made up of people strengthened by the confidence of the country at large." Once again they were brought up short by the intractable problem of identifying such people for the benefit of the Emperor. How could they be sure that a particular person really did enjoy the country's confidence? What if the Emperor agreed tomorrow—and asked, "Where are they?" Would it not be tactless to mention names at this point?

Dmitryukov: Public confidence is a concept not mentioned in constitutional law.

(So perhaps it should be?)

Efremov: It is dangerous to attach too much importance to a change of faces. What is needed is a change of system. The formula "an administration enjoying confidence" is a mistake, the administration must be *responsible*. Ministers should not be driven out from above but should depart when they are denied the confidence of the Duma.

Milyukov: That means changing the whole state structure. No one does that in wartime. You don't change horses in midstream.

But they all agreed that the Bloc had one main, indisputable, immediate task:

—To make a scapegoat of Goremykin, blame him for everything.

—But we said that the Duma could not be convened with Goremykin still there—and now we're agreeing to it?

—Serious conversations with Goremykin must wait till after the war. We must arm ourselves with patience.

—No, we can't let Goremykin sign the peace treaty.

—If it comes to complete victory over Germany we won't be able to rekindle hostility toward Goremykin.

—We must sound the alarm: the Council of Ministers is the only unpatriotic group in the country!

Shulgin: We must run the whole show so we can say as much as possible before we're sent packing!

But the government, feeble and sluggish as it was, outmaneuvered the Bloc yet again. In mid-January the superannuated Goremykin was dismissed. This was three weeks before the Duma was due to assemble: their sacrificial victim had been spared. Only to be replaced by . . . By whom? Was Nicholas II deliberately devising a farce? With the World War at its most intense, and Russian society seething, whom did he single out from among his gifted subjects, from among Russia's 170 million people, to serve as Prime Minister, and by what ludicrous criterion? A dutiful hack from the General Affairs Department, born to supervise the ceremonial side of government, with a German name to boot—Stürmer, the High Chamberlain of the Imperial Court. (He was perfectly honest and reasonably active, but a mediocrity. But the worst of it was that the Emperor had no ear for the insulting ring of the name.) Goremykin's two widely separated prongs of beard were replaced by a single long, limp mop which looked as if it was glued on like Santa Claus's whiskers. And whereas the odious Goremykin in his time had wanted to govern alone, without the Duma, the new All-Russian Master of Ceremonies not only did not object to its protracted sittings but did his best to get along with the Progressive Bloc, and even invited the deputies to a social gathering!

The flabbergasted deputies conferred in secret.

Shidlovsky: Why shouldn't we go to his party?

Milyukov: Never, come what may—we would be letting ourselves down.

Efremov: We must not play a waiting game: that will make the government feel more sure of itself. We must say right away we have no faith in the government!

Maklakov: How can we—on its very first day—say that we have no faith in the government? That just looks like blind prejudice.

At this point, however, the Zemgor militants arrived in Petrograd and presented their note to the Duma. They asserted not only that victory was impossible under the present government but that the country should not go on fighting one day longer while it was in power.

N. Kishkin: Transport, the food supply, refugees must all be taken away from the government and handed over to the social organizations. Otherwise we must break with it completely!

N. Shchepkin: Should we preserve this semblance of a Duma simply for the sake of a free platform? Or in its present inglorious existence has it already lost all significance and would final dissolution of the Duma serve the country better?

Astrov: We sought to set out our impressions in the memorandum. No amendments are necessary. An objective formulation is not what concerns us. What we want from the Bloc is an assured and stern tone. The inner core of the social organizations is getting tired of waiting.

The Duma met on 22 February 1916. They wanted originally to put it off for another two weeks and meet on Forgiveness Day—the last day of Shrovetide, which is dear to every Russian, the day when Orthodox Christians bow low to each other and beg forgiveness. The Kadets were so remote from Orthodoxy that Forgiveness Day was most unlikely to mollify them. The throne, however, was conscious of some mistake or tactlessness on its part, and Russia's most imposing fatty, Rodzyanko, scored a success: he talked the Emperor into taking an unusual step—attending the opening of the Duma and in fact visiting it for the first time in his life. The turbulent deputies assembled in the Catherine Hall greeted the Emperor with prolonged "hurrahs." A solemn service was held, and the members of the Duma, the far left excluded, sang "Save, O Lord, Thy people." The Emperor looked very pale as he first set foot in that tigers' cage, but gradually recovered his composure.

But for the stiffness to which his lack of self-assurance condemned him, that man might even then have changed the history of Russia: a frank gaze, a big smile, a man-to-man handshake with the deputies, then perhaps he could have mounted the rostrum, stood under that frigid portrait of himself, and opened his heart to his Russian subjects, tell them of his own anxiety, his sadness, but say at the same time that together with the people's representatives (never mind for the moment whether they really were that) he hoped to get the better of Wilhelm, that there would never be a separate peace, that in truth he had never entertained such a thought, had never made a move in that direction, because to do so you would have to be a traitor to Russia, and he, her Tsar, who owed her most, strove to serve her to the best of his abilities. All this, not just in words but in a voice that was loud and steady. He should have gone on to replace the Master of Ceremonies with some competent person as Prime Minister—almost any change would have been for the better.

But the energy of the dynasty, and its ability to speak out boldly and frankly, had died with Aleksandr III.

On that day, as always, the looks, words, gestures, and actions of the monarch were as constrained and as evasive as could be. He said a few vague words to the circle of deputies immediately around him, peeked for the first time in the ten years of the Duma's existence into the chamber, asked which party sat on which benches, signed the distinguished visitors' book, chatted amicably with the Duma clerks, with whom he felt more at ease, and took his leave. (His brother Mikhail at least stayed on through the boredom of the Duma session.)

Then the limp old Master of Ceremonies with his long brush of a beard mounted the rostrum holding an exercise book, to read out in his feeble voice a government statement.

He was answered by **Milyukov:**

> At some point lack of expertise seems to have become a qualification for appointment to a ministry. This is a government with no confidence in the Russian people. I leave the rostrum without an answer, and with no hope of receiving one from the present government.

He had mastered as well as anybody the tactic of pretending to break relations and not going through with it. His cautious hoof could always feel the brink of the abyss before him.

Restraining himself and others was the main effort Milyukov had to make throughout 1916: restraining the Progressive Bloc, restraining the rabid Zemgor Alliance, and above all restraining the left in his own party. At the Kadet congress late in February the leftists savaged and sought to annihilate Milyukov. His harshest critics were the Kadets from Kiev and Odessa and the Moscow attorney Mandelstam.

> **Mandelstam:** Milyukov is sure that he is saving the party from disaster, but he is in fact destroying it. We must, before it is too late, cross over to the

other side of the abyss, and form a bloc with those to our left, not with those to the right. Our political calculations must start from the fact that there will be a reckoning, a stern judgment by the people, after the war. Let us be frank: there are many in our midst who see revolution as another Pugachev rising and nothing more. But if we do not want a senseless rebellion we must endeavor to play the leading role in the popular movement.

Shingarev was inclined to agree with him in part:

Our whole object must be to prevent an explosion of popular despair from thwarting victory over Germany. But we must also insure ourselves against the possibility that after the war, when this criminal government stands before a stern tribunal . . .

The government was already in the dock, that was settled in advance . . .

. . . we cannot be reproached with having given it our support. We must once and for all establish the fact that Stürmer is in our eyes a hundred times worse than Goremykin.

(So there! Not so long ago it was impossible to imagine anyone worse than Goremykin. They thought they had to pin the blame for everything on him and knock him off his perch—now there was someone a hundred times worse!)

In Goremykin we at least had someone straightforward and honest in power. (Not what they used to say about him.)

That was just an insane wager on the part of reaction—it would conquer or perish. Whereas Stürmer is provocation incarnate, the fox in place of the wolf. His function is to delude us and to win time. But we will not help Stürmer to correct the regime's terrible mistakes: let it perish! We cannot throw so much as a rope's end to a regime like this! There must be no negotiations with them!

Milyukov, however, his self-assurance unshaken, persisted:

The mere existence of the Bloc has pinned the regime in a corner. By extensive publicity in the press and vigorous criticism in the Duma we will compel this regime to submit to supervision by the social organizations!

And, of course, the tactical calculation of the Kadets had to be kept in mind: the nearer they got to the peace congress, the more certain it was that the Tsar's government would be delivered into their hands . . . The Bloc's hour would come.

He held his own, and obtained a majority for a considerable time afterward, almost the whole of 1916. The Bloc, so to speak, lay low in the trenches, waiting for the terrible conflict to come, and occupying itself in the meantime with routine Duma business. Nor did Stürmer—provocation incarnate—move to dismiss them, so that the Duma worked peacefully on for the two months before Easter, and for one month in the summer. Indeed, its sessions had a sleepy air about them. There was no major retreat at the front that summer, and there were some successes against Turkey. Things began to look much better, and the government, instead of falling, seemed rather to be strengthening its position.

But the subdued Progressive Bloc was more and more frequently outshouted by the rabid Unions. Guchkov's War Industry Committees had scarcely ended their congress—denouncing "the present criminal regime which is working to bring about the complete defeat of our country" and urging "the State Duma to commit itself resolutely to the struggle for power"—when the delegates of the Unions of Zemstvos and Towns assembled in Moscow. These congresses were held on the clamorous insistence of the provinces, especially Kiev, Odessa, and the Caucasus. The circumspect Chelnokov did his best to put off the congress of the Union of Towns but in the end had to declare it open:

> Having made no preparations for war, the government reveals at every step how damaging its role is. When we saw that the government was leading the country to destruction, and condemning the army to a shattering defeat, we were compelled to take matters into our own hands. We had no wish to dabble in politics, but we were forced to. As we did in September, we again demand: A pardon for political offenders! Equal rights for all nationalities! A responsible government!

Here the irrepressible Astrov broke in:

> The government is in the hands of clowns, crooks, and traitors! Come to your senses! Get out now! We will shortly smash your ally Germany!

Milyukov rushed in to reason with them:

> The resolution of this congress could be the spark that causes a conflagration. We must not risk breaking with the government completely.

The star most rapidly rising was that of Prince Georgi Evgenievich Lvov. He had been elected to the first two Dumas on the Kadet ticket, and indeed had made the trip to Vyborg, but had slunk off without signing the appeal. ("We felt that he was not really one of us," said Milyukov.) By 1915–16, however, every educated Russian not directly involved in government saw clearly just how Russia could and must be saved. Prince Lvov, president of the Union of Zemstvos, was infected, carried away, exalted. He presided over a lavish joint banquet at the Praga restaurant, where the most important participants came together after their congresses.

Over the dazzling tablecloths, glassware, and silver the finest traditions of 1904 resurfaced. The representatives of Poland, Finland, and especially those of the Caucasus were demonstratively, tumultuously feted—most especially the mayor of Tiflis, Khatisov, who repeated over and over again, at the congress, at the banquet, and in the lobbies:

> Let me tell you that in the Caucasus there are no rightists! In the Caucasus there are only moderate leftists and extreme leftists! And the whole Caucasus does not request—it demands!

Never mind the resolutions, never mind the declarations, in all these hobnobbings a grandiose new plan evolved: it was time to start ignoring the government completely, time for the organized public to take all Russia's affairs, all Russia into its own hands. We are at present few in number, of course, but we are the nuclei around which the whole of Russian society can be united!

Burly Konovalov, a factory owner with a European polish, a great liberal, and an amateur pianist, but not one to waste words, said:

> The rebirth of the workers' organizations is taking place under the flag of the War Industry Committees. The forthcoming workers' congress will see the birth of an All-Russian Union of Workers. This compact organization will be crowned, as it were, with a Soviet of Workers' Deputies.

Oh, how he longed for that Soviet of Workers' Deputies! But, together with Guchkov and Ryabushinsky, he was in more of a hurry to set up something else, the Central Committee for Food Supplies, to take the procurement and distribution of foodstuffs out of the government's hands.

The creation of an All-Russian Peasant Union was rather more complicated, but they laid the foundations for it in the shape of the All-Russian Cooperative Union.

Yet again they were beset by the sacred shades of that first, decisive Union which had given birth to all the others and fused them in one awesome Union of Unions!

> Nekrasov: And when these Unions are all in being they will generate a supreme body to act as the general staff of Russia's social forces.

All the national organizations would rally round it. And, with the support of the mobilized people and the mobilized army (there was now no difference between the barracks and the street—a propitious circumstance), "all Russia is in our hands."

It sounded so wonderful at banquets, and it was all going so smoothly and so quickly—they need only sit back and await results without letting on to the press. They began quietly working on the composition of a "cabinet of confidence." The Prime Minister designate was no longer Rodzyanko, who had too seldom pitted his bovine bulk against the crown. Indeed he was suspected of despicable conservatism, and had even accepted a decoration from the Emperor in December 1915. He was supplanted by that spiritual giant, Prince Georgi Lvov, whom all the evidence showed to be a great man born to be the leader of a free Russia. Foreign Affairs must unquestionably go to the outstanding expert, Milyukov. Trade and Industry, of course, to the hardworking Konovalov. Defense probably to Guchkov . . .

Alas, the spring and summer of 1916 proved inauspicious for the Russian Liberation movement. The "government of confidence" was approved but not called upon to govern. The Unions were conjured up—but somehow refused to materialize. Greedy traders did not want the movement and prices of goods to be determined by the Kadets, with shop assistants leaving their counters to make speeches. Ignorant peasants did not rush to join the Cooperative Union. No one took orders from the Food Supplies Committee. Meanwhile the "criminal regime of rogues and traitors" had launched an offensive (Brusilov's), against its "ally" Germany, the army let itself be carried away and attacked successfully, and it even began to look as though Russia would not necessarily lose the war, that the devil would play one of his pranks and let her win! In March it had seemed that the situation was strained to the breaking point, but Stürmer, who was a hundred times worse than Goremykin, was still inexplicably in place. Most alarmingly, the public's hostility toward the government seemed to be weakening, and there were signs of a willingness to cooperate with it.

What is more, the government decided to apply ruthless pressure. In April an unprecedented ministerial instruction prohibited unauthorized congresses. As if Zemgor could help the army by day-to-day work alone! It had to have frequent provincial and all-Russian congresses! Then the authorities decided to send a vice-governor to every congress, with the power to terminate any meeting that went beyond the bounds of a strictly businesslike program. In other words, the educated public was deprived of its one remaining right: to assemble at the state's expense and browbeat and blackguard the government to its heart's content! An outrageous example of state terrorism!

The Police Department next deliberately leaked its survey of nongovernmental organizations. It made a brief appearance in the press, was passed around, and many public figures were not at all pleased to learn that their plans and their utterances at supposedly secret meetings were very well known to the Police Department. Since the speeches they made as good, freedom-loving citizens did, according to Adzhemov,

> fulfill all the judicial requirements for proceedings under the statute on at-
> tempts to overthrow the established order . . .

and since only the incomprehensible naïveté of the government had so far prevented it from invoking this statute, many public figures began behaving more cautiously.

The mood among the most progressive elements in society was one of profound disenchantment.

The State Duma made not the slightest bid for power at its tedious June session, and deputies often failed to turn up. The Progressive Bloc simply took a nap while it "awaited its hour," and its most effective leaders were absent throughout: they had gone off to Europe for some months as members of a parliamentary delegation.

This outing was, to be sure, a convenient way of doing the only thing left to the Russian middle class: to complain to the Allies about the imperial government, exhibit themselves to parliamentarians in democratic countries, seek their aid, and try to dissuade them from calling in their loans to Russia after the war. (Konovalov, inde-fatigable as a factory owner should be, begrudging neither time nor money for political ends, suggested to the progressive elements in Russian society that they should publish a special magazine in English and French, in which the Western public would be enlightened as to the nature and the course of Russian liberalism's struggle against its reactionary government, and profiles would be provided both of useless ministers and of the major figures in the left camp waiting to take over. Such a publication, pub-lished in the West and distributed gratis, would help greatly to capture the hearts of the European and American public.)

Milyukov was not just happy about his European trip, he was in raptures. After all that futile wrangling between parties in Russia anyone would blossom anew in Euro-pean air! He went home in time to address the Duma before it dispersed. Then—now that he had acquired a taste for it—he hurried back to Europe for the summer, to lecture in Christiania and Oxford and to take a rest from the horrors of war on the shores of Lake Geneva. It was September when he arrived back in Russia—to be greeted by a number of political shocks.

The year had run on without conflict, and the Bloc seemed to have been sitting still since the dramatic days of its creation. The feeling abroad in Russia's September air was that the Bloc had missed its chance, that while it sat and waited others were pushing into its place. The unthinkable thought was noised around—that the Duma was a bourgeois mob of Stürmer stooges!

Milyukov had to reestablish his reputation in democratic circles, and quickly! Willy-nilly, he had to launch some sort of offensive. Otherwise even Pavel Nikolaevich Mil-yukov could lose his position as leader.

What particularly galled him personally was that when Sazonov—who might almost have been a member of the Bloc—was dismissed, the precious Ministry of Foreign Affairs had been entrusted to . . . yes, the old floor mop Stürmer.

And then there was Protopopov, causing confusion and doing the Bloc a great deal of harm. The marshal of the Simbirsk nobility, who also owned a textile mill, Proto-popov had followed fashion and become a member of a War Industry Committee. More important, he was an old, prominent, politically respectable member of the State Duma. In the Third Duma he had questioned the government about the illegal activities of the Union of the Russian People. In 1914 he had been elected to a vice presidency of the Duma by an overwhelming majority—and no one had ever found any serious fault in him. Because of his seniority he had headed the Duma's delegation abroad, so that he was formally Milyukov's superior, and on his return was received by the Emperor. That meeting had a consequence which left Milyukov thunderstruck: in September a member of the Progressive Bloc, and one of the Duma's leaders, was appointed Minister of the Interior!

What had happened? The Bloc had scored a victory in an unexpected direction and at an unexpected moment. A colossal victory for society, a capitulation on the part of the regime, such as no one would have dreamt of. This was it, the first step toward the creation of a government of confidence. A man assured of the Duma's confidence, and hence that of the whole people, had become a minister! Further invitations could now be expected. Once you had an Octobrist minister, a Kadet minister was perfectly possible. The whole press welcomed Protopopov's appointment, and the Stock Exchange responded with a rise in share values.

Alas, the regime and Protopopov himself promptly shattered the public's hopes. Protopopov started saying that he was enchanted by the Emperor, ready to exert himself to strengthen the autocracy, and in one interview he went so far as to admit that his program was based on struggle with the social organizations. In short, his appointment proved to be not the beginning of a new era, but a reward for a contemptible turncoat. The Duma deputies had evidently not scrutinized carefully enough those colleagues whom they had chosen to speak for them. Now that they saw him for what he was, they were surprised: he had no education, no special knowledge, no affinity with any stratum of society, he was just a decayed landowner and an impecunious manufacturer, with no serious influence in the Duma, who had made his way under the fashionable flag of left-wing Octobrism. In himself he was an excessively nervous, mercurial, hysterical person, far too impressionable, and mentally so unstable that he had once abandoned his family for treatment by a Tibetan medicine man and even taken to coming downstairs backward. He had no talents whatsoever, was unused to systematic work, had no definite views on matters political, no sense of direction in his activities, "no Tsar in the head," as the saying went. People began to remember that he had been friends with Sukhomlinov and realized that he must have found favor with Rasputin. So the appointment of this unbalanced person and low traitor was not the welcome inspiration of a certain person whom discretion forbade them to mention but a cunning maneuver intended to split the Bloc.

For about a month the contempt and loathing of educated Russia was concentrated on Protopopov, until he could stand it no longer and began behaving ridiculously. When the Duma refused to hear his answers to its accusations he changed his ministerial seat for that of a deputy, and sought a hearing from there. A few days later he went to meet the Duma leaders wearing gendarme uniform, fatally damaging himself in their eyes. Though he had been twice chosen, by the Duma and by the throne, his actions and his plans alike were impetuous and misconceived. At one moment he was reinforcing the run-down provincial police force, demanding reports by telegraph on political speeches at zemstvo meetings, drafting a plan for preliminary censorship (which Russia had managed to do without all through the war), secretly monitoring the dealings of the Bloc's leaders with Buchanan, the British ambassador. At the next he was preparing to complete the abolition of Jewish disabilities, or else contemplating a law on the expropriation of gentry lands (which greatly alarmed the Duma because it was in danger of losing a revolutionary weapon). He created chaos in his ministry by neglecting to read papers. He called in the old police dog Kurlov to assist him, but for fear of the Duma's reaction hesitated to make his appointment public, and this caused yet another scandal. At the end of October 1916 he was half inclined to cancel the forthcoming session of the Duma.

Nor did the grain problem escape Protopopov's attention. He associated himself with (and so helped to discredit) those who favored free trade and the abolition of fixed prices. A Ministry of Agriculture circular came out against the general system of procurement and distribution of grain, involving local committees and cooperatives (suspecting with much justice that the committees would direct their efforts to stirring up the population, as the congresses on price inflation had done), and banned committees at the rural district level. There were hints in the press, which he denied, that he aimed at transferring the management of all food supplies to his own Ministry of the Interior. The grain problem, however, was left up in the air, suspended between two ministries (of the Interior and of Agriculture) and further from resolution than ever.

The Kadets were less troubled by the grain problem than by the disgrace of their previous association with Protopopov, which had tarnished the Progressive Bloc at a time when even the left of the Kadet Central Committee had begun to deride it.

Konovalov, feeling the support of an indignant public behind him, and bold as always in his methods, introduced a novel form of consultation.

The "Konovalov Conferences," held at his Moscow home, were intended to "quicken the pulse of Moscow life" and start building a bridge between the Kadets and the Social Democrats. This is the sort of thing said there:

> The day after peace comes, a bloody civil war will break out in our country. Even now Russia has no government whatsoever . . .

True enough, the intimidated government was less and less able to make its existence felt.

> The next session of the State Duma must put decisive pressure on the regime. There is unlikely to be a more favorable moment for taking power by storm.

This was something the Kadets had realized already.

> We have arrived at a moment when patience is finally exhausted and trust used up completely.

The patient liberal public had been offering for more than a year to take over the government and save the country—but there was no persuading the blind self-serving maniacs whose hands convulsively gripped the rudder! Should the liberals put off their action yet again? And risk seeing the Duma itself dubbed a Black Hundreds organization? However reluctantly, however much it went against the grain, they had to act.

On 5 November an all-Russian conference of the Kadet Party gathered, without inviting the press. Yet again the intransigent provincials visited their leftist indignation on the metropolitan compromisers. Milyukov's caution is destroying the party in the eyes of a public moving steadily leftward! Traveling so much abroad, he no longer knows the mood at home! Remember that the Fifth Duma is due to be elected in 1917! If we do not emerge from the final session of the Fourth Duma with greater authority, if we do not show the people that we are no less determined than the left . . . As it was, they had missed an opportunity when they failed to obtain autonomy for Poland—and now Wilhelm had declared Poland independent! Should the Kadets really be uniting with the moderates? No, with the Unions of Zemstvos and Towns! With the cooperatives! With the workers! With the trade unions! The fight should be carried on outside the Duma! And their best platform was . . . the food supply problem!

They were right in thinking that the supply problem was a very effective way of stirring up the public and hammering the government, but the trouble was that the Kadets themselves did not know how to solve it. In the supply problem and price inflation lurked a menacing conundrum. The unenlightened man in the street was more preoccupied with them than with the war itself, with victory and the Turkish straits, but the Kadets, a party of intellectuals, could not sink so low: all problems must be viewed from the perspective of Russia's future greatness.

Milyukov was becoming more of a stick-in-the-mud, more stubborn and more circumspect all the time, and he resisted the trend yet again: they should confine themselves to struggle through the Duma—no illegality, no underground activity!

> In the last resort the terrified government will try to cling to us, and our task then will be not to complete its destruction but to establish a constitutional order. That is why we must preserve our sense of proportion in the struggle with the government. As it is, the mind of the people has a dangerous inclination toward anarchy, and in the darkest recesses the idea of the state is totally discredited.

He stood firm and collected the support he needed, but in the Duma itself he could not avoid going over to the attack.

He was on the horns of a dilemma: either they will win the war without us (if we are too restrained) or revolution will trump us (if we are too rebellious). Could the government be overthrown without a mass movement? But what if the mass movement escalated into a revolution? It was easy enough for the provincials to assemble, clamor a while, and disperse. But things were different for the parliamentarians, who had no power, whichever way they voted. Perhaps one thing and one thing only gave the Duma any power at all: that it could not be summarily dissolved. If that happened, there would be such a hullabaloo! Long-suffering Russia would rise to a man!

But what if it did not?

There was only one thing to do: Stürmer must be brought down at all costs. The prolongation of the war for a third year was not dangerous, and the Progressive Bloc used all its eloquence to push the Russian state farther and deeper into it. Nor were the shortages, the high price of grain, and the possibility of famine so very dangerous. The main danger was Stürmer. If Stürmer was dismissed and replaced by someone from the Progressive Bloc, the path to salvation would open up for Russia.

In early November there was less and less daylight in Petrograd. Whether the Bureau of the Progressive Bloc met in private apartments during the long evenings, or in Room 11 of the Tauride Palace on mornings when dawn never came, their tangled and troubled discussions were held under electric light. White papers lay on green plush cloths in the pools of light from desk lamps. Milyukov, busy now bending, now defending his difficult line, still found time to record these discussions for us.

Milyukov: We must concentrate our attack on Stürmer.

Shulgin: The most effective way to get at Stürmer is the struggle against German domination. I'm in favor of breaking the government's neck, but we must have some measures of an organic character in place at the same time.

Kapnist: I agree. To reassure the country we must break the government's neck! Let's not start discussing "German domination"—by doing so we put a weapon in the hands of the rightists.

Shingarev: On that matter we need to find formulations aimed against the rightists. We must show that we can work as well as talk. Raise important questions, like that of the rural district zemstvo.

Efremov: Yes, we must break the government's neck! In the first week there must be no peaceful work at all, we must concentrate on trying to bring down the cabinet! Trying to formulate advice for this regime is a waste of time, they are incapable of doing anything. In any case, it is not for the legislature to propose concrete plans and introduce projects of its own. That would be a risky business, it would mean accepting too much responsibility. The critic's role is more profitable.

Shulgin: What if they say, "All right, you take over"? You wouldn't be ready, wouldn't know what to do instead.

Maklakov: You claim to believe in responsible government, yet you're unwilling to offer advice to the executive. I'm afraid we may discredit the parliamentary principle.

Rostovtsev: The country won't understand it. It'll say, "They're good at abuse, but they've got no advice to offer."

Rodzyanko (he had not felt free to join the Bloc formally, but sometimes attended its meetings secretly): The government is utterly useless. That must be the starting point for the Bloc's representatives. There are, of course, various things that can't be said: about the conduct of the war, about our diplomatic failures. We must not revolutionize the country. But to keep quiet altogether is equally impossible.

A pretty puzzle for Milyukov. There was nothing you could talk about, but silence was impossible. You couldn't offer advice, but not offering advice was impossible.

Shidlovsky: We won't tell them what we want, or else they'll accept our amendments and write them into their draft bills.

As had already happened with fixed prices. The Bloc, blessed with an abundance of ideas, had thrown out this one, and the government had snapped it up and emerged so much the stronger. Now the traitor Protopopov would snap up their thoughts on the supply problem—inspection raids, roadblocks, obligatory deliveries—and once again the results would be something of an improvement. That was the tragedy of it all.

    Stempkovsky: Fixed prices alone are not enough. We must go on to requisitioning with fixed quotas.

    V. Lvov: We have already set out along the road to state socialism. What we need is a dictatorship over the food supply exercised by the social organizations.

    Shingarev: We must decide whether we want to support state socialism or say no to it. We may find ourselves falling out over this.

    Stempkovsky: If we suddenly switch to practical efforts to improve the food supply, the army will not understand.

But what was this talk of practical steps? The thing to do was to draft a shattering Declaration.

    Milyukov: The main theme must be our patriotism: *they* cannot bring the war to a victorious conclusion.

Another difficulty was that the threat of military catastrophe had receded: it no longer loomed as large as it had the year before. In fact, Russia was now stronger than when the war began. But this must not be said, this was not the note to be sounded in Duma speeches—or else the whole policy of the Bloc would be in ruins.

    Efremov: The situation is most alarming. Society's energy is visibly declining. Our situation is tragic, because it is our duty to carry out a coup to make sure of winning the war. But a coup in wartime is an act of treason and, if we love our country, impossible. I won't say, "Brothers, overthrow the government!" Let us phrase our speeches so that no call for revolution is implicit in them. Let us draw the boundary lines beyond which we must not go.

    Stempkovsky: Without a sharp change of direction we will have lost anyway. If we are less aggressive, too peaceable, the country will leave us behind. Away from the capitals people are talking of treason, saying that the Empress is more or less Wilhelm's friend. If we don't make a decisive move, if we allow the Duma to be dissolved, we will only have ourselves to blame. In my mind there is no doubt at all: another few months of this regime and Russia will perish.

    Kapnist: Should the Duma be dismissed, a tidal wave will overwhelm us. We must follow Pavel Nikolaevich's lead and content ourselves with pinpricks. Only if a separate peace is signed can we take the revolutionary road.

    Shingarev: I don't believe that a separate peace would cause a revolution. All those tired people would simply say, "Let's have a good sleep, a good wash, and something to eat." Of course, the blow to our national pride would have serious consequences. But if ill-wishers are working for a separate peace, they are what we must attack. We must declare such activities treasonable— and the State Duma will put itself in an unassailable position! This will give satisfaction to the army, which talks about nothing else. We will hit the regime where it hurts most.

    V. Lvov: There is no more patriotic slogan than this: save the country from the government!

Yes, they would put themselves in a very strong position if they declared that they were the patriots, and the government defeatists and traitors. The main danger was Stürmer's government! Milyukov spent day after day drafting and redrafting declarations to be made by the Bloc. Some of them, when he listened too much to his colleagues, were very strongly worded. Then he would have second thoughts, or let himself be dissuaded, and tone his draft down. With every revision some caustic and toxic expressions were grudgingly dropped and replaced by others.

> The treasonable behavior of the regime . . . The steep moral decline in government circles . . . Privileged predators . . . A regime hated and despised by all . . . None of this is a secret to our enemies . . . The State Duma disowns responsibility for the wanton shedding of the nation's blood and for the army's sufferings, and points the finger at the real culprits . . .

Day after day was spent discussing drafts. (Shulgin also submitted one.)

> **Krupensky:** We must not use those terms "treason," "betrayal." The throne is surrounded by a gang of criminals, yes, but we must not say so out loud. Excessively severe criticism will demoralize the country. We must not flaunt the truth, or we might check the upsurge. It is not a question of evil intent but of total incompetence. The main thing is to destroy Stürmer. Accusations of treason and incompetence must be directed against *him* personally. And we shouldn't exaggerate England's merits as Milyukov does.

> **Shulgin:** Blaming everything on particular ministers and depicting them as criminals is just trifling with the problem. I recognize that it is politically necessary for us to say only damning things. But we can't have it both ways: if the system is to blame, what's the point of talking about criminals? We ought to be telling the truth about the Supreme Power itself, but we can't.

> **Kapnist:** The burden of our declaration must be that Russia is great and rich in resources. The rest must be an onslaught on disorders.

> **Rodzyanko:** Softly, softly, or they may dissolve the Duma.

> **Efremov:** But there are profiteers and money grabbers among the general public too. If we reprove them, we'll weaken our attacks on the government, which is also out of the question.

> **Shingarev:** The government knows exactly how things stand. They don't give a damn for Russia, just as long as they can hang on. Judged by results, the government's performance is tantamount to a crime. If the Duma does not take a strong line the country will say, "There goes our last hope." We can't paint things blacker than they are in reality. Any minute now there will be no bread in the shops and the workers will take to the streets in a rush. The country is already itching to take justice into its own hands. Are we to wait for the street to find its voice? Or openly cry, "Treason!"

They managed somehow to agree on a text. Six copies were typed and distributed, one to each parliamentary group, for approval. And suddenly—betrayal! a leak! The venerable Krupensky took fright and showed it to Protopopov, who showed it to Stürmer and word came from the government that the Duma would be dissolved! The only possible answer to their Declaration was immediate dissolution!

What a debacle! Three days before the next session opened! When it was already too late to change the thing! And just think of the danger they were in!

On 12 November, although it was Sunday, an emergency meeting was called—all members of the Duma Bureau (except the traitor, of course) and senior members of the State Council.

> **Shidlovsky:** The word "treason" will make the greatest possible impression. If it is uttered from the rostrum of the Duma the people will take that as a guarantee of its truth. The result will be rejoicing in Germany. We must not give way to threats, but "treason" must take a back seat. People down below demand that we "cry out" but sometimes silence is required. After all, we are not trying to start a revolution but to prevent it.

> **M. Stakhovich:** It will damage the government, of course, but it will help the country. We shouldn't come right out with accusations of treason, but should say that "such a system of government leads to rumors of treason." If we let the possible danger deter us from mentioning treason at all, members of the Duma will kick themselves when they realize that they have waited too long to speak. We shouldn't try to get by with a compromise. And they won't dissolve the Duma anyway.

> **Milyukov:** Dissolution is not at all impossible.

Yes, they had got themselves in a tangle with that word "treason"—they could neither leave it in nor take it out. It would have been more sensible to drop it, but the public was incensed and would say that the Duma had taken fright and connived at treason.

> **B. Golitsyn:** If there is a dissolution we must try to ignore it! We mustn't all take off for home! Otherwise there will be repressions and the country will be plunged into darkness. But it's better not to provoke dissolution. To word it more cautiously: *either* they're idiots or they're traitors, make your choice.

This idea rather appealed to Milyukov.

> **Shingarev:** News of the government's threat will get around, and if the Declaration is not read out people will say, "The Duma lost its courage." Even at the price of dissolution we must preserve the moral standing of the people's representative body!

> **Stempkovsky** (on second thought): Of course, the threat ought not to influence us. The Duma must be above reproach. But it's equally evident that we are in too much of a hurry. What if our action is followed not by any sort of storm, but just normal Petrograd weather?

(Meaning gray black clouds and dirty drizzle?)

> Suppose the public puts up with all the government's affronts and the war ends in Russia's favor? Suppose they say, "There you are—we won even without the Duma"? Shouldn't we postpone out-and-out condemnation until it's clear that all is lost?

> **Shulgin** (also backing down): A Duma that can be influenced by threats is one we don't need anyway! But if we can possibly get an adjournment instead of dissolution, that would be great!

(Many members of the Duma would appreciate the difference: adjournment meant that deputies' stipends would still be paid, and they would not be called up into the army, dissolution would mean that some of them would have to become soldiers.)

If the passage about treason is unnecessarily dangerous we can withdraw it. (They had no idea that the crown would be even more alarmed than they were.)

VI. **Gurko:** Spreading the notion of treason simply aggravates unrest in the country. The masses pick up the general drift and get the impression that there are traitors at the top in Russia, so let's drive them out. But the government is not guilty of treason in the strict sense—that is a false suggestion. We can, however, emphasize even more strongly that the government's stupidity is such that it gives rise to false rumors of treason.

(True—Milyukov accepts the point.)

They dispersed to consult with their various parliamentary groups. They met again on 13 November, the day before the opening of the Duma. Anxious moments! It was now or never!

Shulgin: We have to fight—this government is rubbish. But since we have no intention of going to the barricades ourselves we mustn't incite others. The original program of the Bloc, on which we all agreed, was to support the regime, not to overthrow it. The Duma was to be a safety valve, letting off steam, not building it up. The paragraph about treason should therefore be removed.

Stempkovsky: We don't want to summon anyone to the barricades, and we won't be there ourselves. We must not talk in such a way as to stir up the crowd even more. We must draw a line between the government and the Supreme Power—and not accuse the latter.

Kapnist: But surely we don't want to break up the Duma majority. Not to make a Declaration shows signs of disintegration.

But it was too late to do it all again.

Shidlovsky: Without the Bloc what is left? Underground activity? No use at all. And anyway there are no fundamental differences between us. It's just that we aren't used to working as a coalition.

Milyukov: The Bloc was in danger of splitting right from the beginning, but it's less serious now than it was.

Efremov: The fissure is a fundamental one. The Declaration is too weak and mild. Treason, if proven, is a capital crime. We must insist on the establishment of a commission of inquiry. Only a trial, and retribution, can pacify the people's conscience and prevent the people from exacting vengeance! (After an interruption:) The Progressist group is leaving the Bloc.

Thus, the Progressive Bloc had failed to take a single positive step since its creation, and at its first attempt to do so fell apart at the seams.

*   *   *

Instead of the Stürmers—the Milyukovs? Replace one set of murderers with another? Down with the black-and-yellow flag of the Progressive

*Bloc! Down with the stinking monstrosity of a misbegotten constitution!
Let us forge a genuine hammer of revolution!*

—RSDRP

*   *   *

[6 3]

You have to be born with eyes in the back of your head. And ears
on your cap. You don't have to smell him, or see his shadow, you just
know without knowing how. Your back feels his presence. You're being
shadowed! You walk along, apparently without looking back, but you
always know, you are always quite sure whether you're being followed
or not. That shabby bundle of rags on the bridge yonder, idly spitting
into the water or eyeing the passersby . . . At the tram stop you know
who is simply waiting for a tram and who has been standing there too
long.

And, of course, you need good legs. If your legs are weak it's no life
for you, you'll fold up in no time at all. Don't go in for work underground if your legs are weak—especially in a city like Petersburg. Like
my old mother, Khionia Nikolaevna, says: "It's his legs that feed the
wolf." Same with the underground worker: it's his legs he relies on.

Then things work out as awkwardly as they can, just to spite you,
to wear you to a frazzle. You arrange meeting places well in advance,
but choose a place to sleep at the last minute, according to circumstances, according to whether you're being watched or not. You knew
last night, of course, that you would be meeting Lutovinov this morning, that there was a place nearby where you could spend the night in
an emergency, and headquarters in the Pavlovs' house on Serdobolskaya Street was not far away—but not only must you not give away
the hiding place by showing up there, you must take care not to compromise a single individual by letting your guard down. So last night,
with two of them on his heels, and unable to shake them off, he had
to zigzag all over the city, and rather than spend the night out in
gardens (as he had last winter at temperatures below zero, wandering
around and freezing till daybreak) he had to make a beeline for the
Grazhdanka, through a dense copse where the sleuths would give up
for fear of a knife in the ribs, or else make for the Galley Port.

It was there, in the Galley Port, that he shook them off, on a dark
patch of wasteland.

But today he had had to drag himself right across Vasilevsky Island,
right across the Petersburg side, across Aptekarsky and Kamenny islands and the suburbs of Novaya Derevnya and Lanskaya. Gorky's
apartment was more or less on his way, but he could not be visited
until the day after tomorrow, and Serdobolskaya Street was close by,

but that must wait till the evening, and in the meantime he must not even squint in that direction. All this for his morning meetings and then he would have to go from Serdobolskaya, where he was already expected, traverse the whole city again, past the Nevsky Gate, to the Glassmakers' Quarter. And only then, if he was still in the clear, would he come back here to Serdobolskaya. And all this would have been a piece of cake, but for the lockout, blast it.

The lockout was something he hadn't expected.

He hadn't expected those people to make such a bold move. You got used to them shilly-shallying and then giving way.

Could he possibly have made a mistake?

It preyed on his mind—the thought that he had blundered. Overstepped the mark.

Lenin had been so insistent. Mass action must be avoided! Concentration on small underground conspiratorial cells!

He had slept badly. His head was heavy. Muzzy. And he had a long, hard day before him.

Some people like Petersburg, some don't. It's a matter of taste, but when you're plodding along like this, with stone to the left of you, stone to the right of you, stone underfoot, sometimes the pavement comes up to hit you and you feel like howling: Mama, why did I ever leave green Murom, why did I ever set out to see the wide world?

Just a joke, of course.

It was a lot quicker by tram, but trams day after day would rattle the soul out of you, shake your head to bits. Anyway, you didn't always have the five- and ten-kopeck pieces for your fare. And just imagine if one of the sleuths hopped on, you'd have to get off right away and your money would be down the drain. On foot you had more of a chance, you could maneuver.

The old laws of conspiracy no longer held. Many had ceased to observe strict rules: they did not take precautions with hideouts or even with underground printing presses. They said you only get caught because of "inside information" anyway, not because you've been shadowed, it's always because of traitors, and you never knew who they were. The police won't pick you up on the street very often, and if they do they'll only send you out of town for a while. You'll just wear yourself out with this conspiratorial nonsense.

No, as a rule they won't pick you up on the street. But you carry a Finnish passport just in case (to show you're exempt from military service). Your Russian passport is kept in reserve. You'd need one if you applied for a residence permit. So you don't. No such person. No fixed abode. Free as a bird.

Many of them did in fact get away with it. And of course we don't want idiots like you to get hit—if you do we'll be stuck there with you. But we would still like to see hopeless idiots like you taught a lesson. Say you're expelled for a short time. It doesn't seem long to you, but afterward the whole setup needs rebuilding.

It may not seem long to you, but to me any interruption is too long. I won't sacrifice a single day of freedom without good reason. I'm ready to die. I'm ready to go to Siberia, but only if I know there's no other way. But to go into the Kresty if only for a month—for no good reason? Find yourself another fathead, I'm not your man. Never skimp on conspiratorial precautions. Overdoing the precautions always pays off.

Self-discipline means freedom, freedom means you can carry on working for the Party.

You'd know if you'd run around as much as I have. I stuck it out in Petersburg all last winter, with never a scratch. Traveled all around the provinces unscathed myself, and never got anybody else caught. Left for Scandinavia—got there safe and sound. Smuggled "literature," bales of it, sometimes around the North Cape even, and it got through. And back I came—safe and sound. And here I am walking the streets of Petersburg again. What d'you think of that? No doubt there's still the odd speck of dust from the sidewalks of New York and Copenhagen on the soles of my shoes. Maybe a granite chip or two from the Finnish north. And if I get through safely until February I'll be back there.

But this time around, who wouldn't have been found out? The way I arrived! Storm clouds over the Vyborg district, everybody expecting a blinding flash of lightning. On the trams, in the street, in the shops, at every turn people openly vilify the powers that be, with Little Mother Empress and Rasputin getting their share. And the police spies didn't turn a hair. They'd heard it all so often. The uniformed police were laughed at and abused to their faces. Then a reserve regiment mutinied. When the army gets restless it means the end isn't far off. After the sickening inactivity, the frivolity and pettiness, the contemptible squabbling of émigré life, and after a week in Arctic darkness, deafened by the roar of a waterfall, you're suddenly faced with all this and have to make your mind up. All by yourself.

You could easily get it wrong.

Maybe you already have.

Have you? Haven't you? It's as if somebody had your soul on a lathe, planing it down.

The rules you made for yourself are clear and immutable. You have to know all the working-class districts down to the last cul-de-sac. Have to know every little path through the backyards of the Vyborg, Neva, and Narva districts. And, of course, all the yards with two entrances. You must never follow the same route more than once. Never sleep in the same apartment two nights running. Nor, if the sleuths are closing in, must you hole up in the same apartment for two or three days on end. When the hunt thins out you must leave very early in the morning, while it's still dark. Or another thing you can do is go into one place late in the afternoon as if you mean to stay the night, then move to a different apartment late in the evening. (The Glass-workers' Quarter, where two sisters live next door to each other, is a good place for that.) And you must never tell even your most reliable comrades where you may be spending the night. The less they know, the better.

Another good dodge is to keep changing your hat and overcoat. You can always shake the sleuths off that way. Remember last winter, when they were right on your heels, in broad daylight? Where to hide? The baths, of course! Took a private cubicle. Sent for a messenger: listen, go to such an address, there's a girl there, Tonya, she's called, tell her on the quiet, not while her mother's listening, "Uncle Sasha's taken a room, he wants you to go to him." She came. "Uncle Sasha, you've disgraced me, people will say a man sent for me from the bathhouse. Suppose the street finds out—who will marry me after that?" "Never mind, Tonya dear, never mind, it's for the Revolution. I'll find you a suitor like you never saw! . . . Here, take my hat and coat, wrap them in the sheet. And bring me your daddy's, we'll swap them back in a day or two . . ." And I got clean away.

Your Petersburg worker will always get you out of a hole.

These same nieces, and young girls in general, are good at counter-surveillance, you can send them out into the open to keep an eye on the sleuths.

Now, if you stayed with your sister two days in a row that would be a real rest. You could catch up on your sleep. And on your food. The most aggravating thing about these conspiratorial hideouts is always having to make fresh arrangements for one night at a time—and having to put up with the politeness of your hosts. They're never expecting you till the last minute, they're put out by your arrival, but don't like to show it. There may be three small rooms for six people, and not enough beds—thank you, I'm grateful to you for whatever it is, give me any old thing to lie on, I can go under the table there, I'll soon drop off, you just carry on as usual! But no, they give up their best bed, they feel obliged to entertain you, the man of the house insists on showing how educated he is politically and keeps you up half the night discussing Party programs. By then you're incapable of taking any more hospitality, or conversation, or even talk about Party programs, you just want them to take pity on you and leave you in peace, your head is buzzing, you'd give anything just for a spell of silence . . . Just to be silent, stretch out without sheets, without even undressing, over there by the slop pail, anywhere, as long as your head gets a rest and your tongue can stop working.

Besides, an underground revolutionary's head is cluttered with three times as many worries as any ordinary person's. Apart from the usual, everyday concerns—moving around, jobs to be done, what to say to people—other cares weigh heavily on his brain: the safest way to dress, what to carry and what not to carry in his pockets, in what order to visit particular houses and meet particular people, so as not to lay a trail from one to another, what to leave where, who can be asked to hide something for him, pass something on, keep a secret.

Then, when your head is in this state, and after a poor night's rest, you find that nuisance of a lawyer, Sokolov, pops up: the sailor revolutionaries are facing trial, they're threatened with execution! It was all happening at once! The ferment, the smell of powder in the air, a regiment mutinies, soldiers fraternize with workers! A number of soldiers have been arrested and are awaiting trial—and suddenly these sailors are threatened with the death sentence! What should the party of the proletariat do? Why, hit back fast with a general strike! The decision was made in three minutes, without hesitation. When is the trial? On 8 November. So on 8 November—it's everyone out!

A big thank-you to the workers and their families. The more poverty-stricken and joyless their lives, the more ready they are to share their shelter, to move over and make room, as long as you're not fussy. During the war apartments belonging to the gentry and the intelligentsia ceased to be available for conspiratorial purposes. The change had set in before the war, in fact as soon as the tide of revolution turned.

These people liked calling themselves Bolsheviks, of course, Mitya Pavlov had visited one of them quite recently. On general Party matters they had the friendliest of conversations, but as soon as Pavlov got to the point—"A representative of the Central Committee has arrived from abroad, he needs somewhere to stay the night"—the other man beat a hasty retreat: "Simply impossible, I'm being watched!" Pretending that he was concerned for the CC's representative, not for himself. As if anybody would think it worthwhile watching a worm like him. Luckily, Pavlov was up to the occasion. "You're all good at talking. But we can't get our literature released." "What? You mean, you've got no money either?" He was amazed! He would never have imagined it! "How much do you need, then?" Pavlov: "A lot." (He should have said "three hundred.") The other thought quickly and paid his ransom. "I can manage a hundred."

All in all, it's been a useful lesson. They started bolting as early as 1908, all those bigmouths. Soon showed what sort of revolutionaries they were. Even before the war the only professional revolutionaries left were workers. There were barely enough intellectuals to form a Bolshevik group in the Duma and run the newspaper. Now even they have disappeared. As things are now, the Petersburg committee has not a single journalist left, and there's no one to write leaflets. Militant students, novices, have come along to help out.

Never mind the liquidators, nobody expects anything from them.

But where are the former *Pravda* group? They used to be so much more reliable—but they've swerved from the *Pravda* line. They've "had their eyes opened to their fatherland." They've lapsed into patriotism or rather—to avoid that odious word—they've squeezed into any old bolt-hole, just to escape the call-up, to avoid being sent to the front. They've flocked into statistical departments, the Unions of Zemstvos and Towns, the War Industry Committees, serving side by side with the Guchkovites and the Gvozdevites, showing the underground opposition away with both hands, giving any sort of underground activity a wide berth. Krasikov? Shary? What sort of Bolsheviks are they now? True, Podvoisky still keeps in touch, cautiously. They're all in "important positions." We and they are no longer marching in step. Crafty Bonch has kept his ugly head down: "I'm just a student of religious sects, an ethnographer." Steklov-Nakhamkes is a secretary in the Union of Towns. Kozlovsky has his own law office on Sergiev Street and is making his pile.

Most annoying of all is Krasin. He used to be the very soul of the *Pravda* group, now he's taken off, vanished into the blue! Become a businessman, a chief executive more or less, earning a hundred thousand rubles, rolling in it, and not a single kopeck for his old comrades. Well, to be frank, it's no use expecting him to. Gorky is right: those people would sooner give you money to get tanked up at Cubat's than for underground work.

They've thought up a group label for themselves—"unattached" Social Democrats. So that they need not accept conspiratorial Party discipline or account for their behavior. Their attitude is: "We know what we're doing, no need for you to stick your nose in."

There was some thought of sending old *Pravda* supporters an ultimatum: come over to us immediately or we'll never accept you later.

Which meant that Sokolov, the little lawyer, isn't one of the worst. He's obliging. He even helps with money now and then. He passes on all the information he picks up in journalistic and legal circles. And on occasion he has made his apartment available for meetings with those jittery parliamentarians—the Chkheidzes and Kerenskys—you needed a place in which you could put the screws to them as Lenin demanded: the Russian Kautskyites must be brought to account by the workers' underground! And sure enough they tied themselves in knots trying to excuse themselves.

The workers' underground. But is there such a thing? The trouble is that the reflux has gone much deeper. That sort of life, with spells of imprisonment and banishment on top of it, wears people out. Last year when you went around to the old places, you saw more than enough. There was a smell of wormwood in the fields. Don't look, Sanya! Take Ryabinin, the geologist, a native of Murom, like yourself. One of your own, of course, he smiles and smiles, but it's no use trying to recruit him for the Revolution anymore, he's a dropout. Or Gromov, from Sormovo. A Social Democrat since 1900. Jailed and banished over and over again, till finally he got tired of it. He'd aged and gone gray, and withdrawn into his own little house, into his family circle . . . At best, a mere sympathizer. Or Grishka from Novgorod. We were fellow prisoners in 1904, and again in Vladimir Central in 1905. Poverty, unemployment, family cares had crushed him. What a propagandist, what an organizer he used to be! Now all that is lost. He agonizes over it, it gives him no peace—but he still says leave me out of it, boys, find somebody younger.

But what if the men all give up, one after another? Who's going to train the new recruits? Who will bond them with the Party?

You can forgive the workers. But not the intellectuals.

But at bottom that's how it's bound to be. Where can you find a genuine proletarian politician—not proletarians in name only—and can such a person exist? The main problem for him is how to become a politician without ceasing to be a worker. Otherwise, how can you call yourself "proletarian"? You'll just be an intellectual, a semi-bourgeois. That's why this new species of "educated proletarian" has recently appeared on the scene—our best hope for the future. There are very few of them, very few of us, but only our kind can carry on the workers' cause. We must inevitably take responsibility for every form of revolutionary activity—journalism, writing and distribution of leaflets, clandestine correspondence, that in particular we must not entrust to other hands.

It's difficult of course. Standing at a factory bench for ten years, occasionally thumbing through a pamphlet or two. Or if you live your life on the run, in hiding, forever coming and going, when do you have time to read? When do you have time to think? The smarty-pants émigrés can afford that luxury, they needn't fear a knock on the door. Yet they've been studying the "theory" of the workers' movement in their discussion groups for twenty-odd years, quarreling and splitting all the time, never able to agree on anything. Then we came along and showed them right off how to put it into practice.

Because you can't put it to the test just in your head, you have to find out whether it gives your hands work to do, or is it just something that slips off one tongue to be taken up by another? Those bigheads, however hard they struggled to wedge themselves into the workers' movement, you would never in your heart be at one with them. You would always be strangers.

Only . . . don't forget Sashenka Kollontai. She it was who had educated Sanka Shlyapnikov when he was an uncouth youngster unused to wearing a shirt, let alone debating, helped him with his French, which he had just started learning in a self-education group. Sashenka—a member of the upper class, an intellectual, dazzlingly beautiful! Such clothes, such hairdos! Yet so sound, and so bold, so trenchant! At Larvik, lying beside her on warm stones at the water's edge, lying there for hours on end, listening and listening, storing up every word . . .

And what about Lenin?

No-o, until you had absorbed what they had to offer, you would never be really clever.

But now you can steer a straight course without help from anyone. Shlyapnikov—what they call a "Central Party official," isn't he? He is. And among the few so called he occupies a special position. Lenin writes to him with what looks almost like respect: "You are in charge of the situation. I will not interfere, let the proper authority decide." And how have you risen so high? By using your hands and your feet, that's how, but also by missing no opportunity to work with your head, to read, to write, to educate yourself. So all these things can be managed at once? Evidently they can. And the title "Central" hasn't dimmed your wits or puffed you up. Above all, you aren't out of practice, you still love more than anything using your own hands, machining weighty, distinctively shaped, precisely measured, darkly gleaming metal parts. And, what's more, getting money for it, and using it to buy a little extra food for all those émigré sages, as if they were your little brothers, all those other Central Party workers on their uppers without a kopeck to their name, struggling to make enough for four dinners, wondering which article to translate for which distant editor, transferring lines from one bit of white paper to another just as indecipherable.

And—if he admitted what his memory knew to be true—when he was overtaken, with no one else beside him, by the events of July 1914 in Petersburg, wasn't it Shlyapnikov who sized up the situation accurately and unaided? Had he not instinctively understood—at once and unambiguously—that working-class solidarity would never give way to patriotic hooliganism, that we would never basely and slavishly bow down to it as the intellectuals did? Where was the logic of it? Why, after showing your contempt for the Japanese war, support war against Germany? Is it the Dardanelles you want? And when the Mensheviks invited him to a late-night banquet at Palkin's restaurant, in honor of the visiting Belgian socialist Vandervelde, undaunted by the fact that he was in a hopeless minority, in fact all alone, he had lambasted—in excellent French—those always in the majority at such banquets and always stubbornly determined not to submit to the true majority in the factories. "Who started it?" they asked. What a bogus argument! As if it mattered who had attacked first. The blame for the war rested on the world bourgeoisie, and on the Belgian just as much as the German bourgeoisie. Instead of talking about "poor little Belgium" or "poor little Serbia" they should be saying "Down with the war!" "Long live the Revolution!" "Amnesty for political prisoners, martyrs for freedom!" (He had written the leaflet himself.)

A World War was, of course, a hard nut to crack. Neither humanity at large nor the working class had been prepared for anything of the kind. No wonder they were at a loss! Those whirlwind months confused minds, threw them off balance, robbed some people of their wits altogether. It wasn't only the worldwide Workers' International that split, the closest of friendships collapsed in the general madness. When they managed to get to Sweden in October, how happy he and Sashenka had been to find themselves at one in their loyalty to the cause! The war had caught them far apart but their thoughts about it all were identical! How eagerly he had listened, how readily he had understood her account of the first days of the war in Berlin. The German socialists had voted for war credits!! After a lifetime of ramming their exemplary social democracy down our throats, they had stupidly blundered into a blind alley! The German women workers, tried and tested activists, were a dead loss too: with their bourgeois "help for the wounded," their concern for orphans, they didn't understand that it was nobler, braver, and indeed cheaper—to revolt! To lose thousands on the streets, rather than millions at the front! But then there were outbreaks of chauvinism among Russian socialists caught by the war in Germany and interned: a malicious glee at the thought that "our side" would break through from East Prussia to Berlin. Our side? Meaning the Russian generals? The Cossacks? What is Russia anyway? Russia thought of as somehow "our own"? What does it mean, "the defense of our unfortunate fatherland"? "If there's one thing that doesn't move me at all it's the fate of Russia. The fate of the Revolution is my burning passion!" Sashenska said fervently, "If there's one thing I don't want it's victory for Russia! Who's going to get killed on the other side? Aren't they proletarians, just the same as ours? Certainly not the spoiled sons of the bourgeoisie. No, no, there are no Russias for us, no Germanys. We want nothing to do with your defeats or with your victories, it's all the same to us. What the proletariat needs is peace!!"

They had been so pleased with themselves, yet the two of them together had not gone far enough. It was, as always, Lenin, with his trenchant mind, who had surprised them, convinced them, dazzled them with the last and most important word. What do you mean, it's all the same? There's no comparison. Tsarism is a hundred times worse than Kaiserism!! We are not just indifferent to patriotism—we are anti-patriots! The "peace" slogan? Incorrect! That's for the hoi polloi. For the priests. What the proletariat needs is *civil war*!!!

Sanka was, secretly, taken aback. Why civil war? Why yet worse devastation? But Sashenka, eyes shining, grasped it at once. Of course, of course! Civil war! she cried, and covered him with kisses.

Yes, but what about now? What would Lenin have done? In Petersburg, on 8 November?

I somehow think, no, I feel sure that Lenin would say just the same: hit them with a general strike! And don't take three minutes over it—make it fifteen seconds! Lenin has that incredible characteristic—his ability to see everything at a glance, in a flash of lightning. And not to vacillate at the critical moment, nor feel regret later.

Yes, but how would he respond to a lockout?

Lucky you've got a good head on your shoulders, because it all depends on you—the fate of all those workers, 120,000 of them. You've never in your life had to make such a far-reaching decision. You've got maybe five seconds to think about it. If you wait for the next issue of the Party newspaper, with its comments on today's events, to reach Petersburg—assuming it comes out at all, and the editorial board hasn't finally been wrecked by its petty squabbles—and instruct you how you should have proceeded, four months will have gone by. Anyway, the bale containing that issue of the paper won't sneak through unaided, you'll have to make the effort to get there and give it a helping hand.

But why talk about 8 November when it's already 13 November? Whether you should have or not you've already placed the plank over the stream and stepped onto it, it's already threatening to break under your weight . . . and the decision you have to make now is a different one. Which way to jump? Back where you came from—or do you go forward? That's all you have to decide. Which way to jump (with responsibility for 120,000 workers on your shoulders).

There's no one you can turn to for advice. Neither at the "Center," in Switzerland. Nor here in Petersburg. It all depends on you. On one single person.

And you have only till the end of the day. You haven't slept, you haven't eaten, you haven't sat down for a minute, but you have to make up your mind which way to jump. Forward? Or back again?

In the meantime, an outlay of ten kopecks and his trusty legs had taken Shlyapnikov as far as Lanskaya Street, to a region of cart tracks and vegetable gardens, ten minutes late. His boots strode through sticky mud and hopped over ditches to where on this damp, misty day, before the first frost came, workmen who owned plots occasionally made their way by narrow paths skirting boundary stones or stands of young trees, to dig up what remained of their crop. No one was shadowing Shlyapnikov now. He was "clean" when he reached the plank shed which was his rendezvous. Inside the shed two firm hands, his and Lutovinov's, met with a loud smack.

"I'm clean. What about you? Haven't come straight from Shurkanov have you?"

"No."

"Thanks."

If you're underground it's no good being the only one of many to follow the rules strictly. He'd taken all these precautions, but if Lutovinov had come straight from Shurkanov's he might easily have brought a tail. Shurkanov's apartment was "a lantern for the Okhrana," a fine young fellow from the Aivaz factory had told Shlyapnikov the last time, but other people had shown up before he could explain, and he had been arrested shortly afterward. So Shurkanov had remained an enigma. True, Shlyapnikov himself did not suspect the man, and that was what mattered: you can always smell treachery, in fact that's the only way you ever find out who the traitors are. Shurkanov had even been a member of the Third Duma, though he was nobody much, just an average metalworker. His place had been searched more than once, he was under open surveillance on the streets, but nobody had been trapped as a result. He was fond of drink, liked to get the "old hands" together and reminisce about the revolutionary days, and one of the old hands, also a former Duma deputy, had whispered in Shlyapnikov's ear that "he lives beyond his means, there's something funny about it." (Suspicion creeps like a serpent from one worker's heart to another—that's what they've brought us to!) Shurkanov's house was conveniently situated, many people used it as a contact point, and Lutovinov actually lived there. Shlyapnikov had been offered a room too, but said no, thank you, I can manage. Shurkanov had also procured a Russian passport for Shlyapnikov, a "safe one." Fine, let it wait a while.

Your discipline means your freedom, and freedom means you can work. If you've taken on the leadership of the Party's All-Russian Center you mustn't get caught. When you're the one and only plenipotentiary of the Central Committee at large in Russia you have to be a bit careful how you tramp around Petersburg.

The upturned peak of Lutovinov's cap shaded a yellow forelock, a sloping brow, and a rugged, naïvely honest face framed by big ears. His jaw was one you wouldn't dislocate with a single punch but his huge brow made it look small. His size was impressive—but he had used up all his strength growing, you couldn't see him as a blacksmith's striker.

He says they've managed to get an old copying machine written off at the factory, then stolen it and dispatched it to Yuzovka.

"Good work! And what are they printing there?"

"What's her name . . . Kollontai, *Who Needs the War*."

"Good!"

"And old revolutionary songs."

"That's a bit of a luxury."

"Well, people don't know them, Gavrilovich. Revolutionary songs aren't very well known these days. They turn out for a demonstration, and don't know what to sing."

"Maybe you're right . . . But be sure to send them the leaflets. Current tasks, what needs doing today . . ."

Lutovinov himself was from Lugansk, and was responsible for liaison with the provinces. When Shlyapnikov was going abroad in February he had left them his connections with the whole provincial network—with Nizhny, Nikolaev, Saratov, and Rostov. When he got back things had changed beyond recognition, all the contacts had been lost, and the provinces were crying out for literature, for information, nobody was explaining to them what was happening and what they should do about it. Moscow—Moscow of all places!—had no oblast committee of its own, they were either afraid to establish one or didn't know how. Smidovich, Skvortsov, Nogin, and Olminsky were all sitting in their own small corners, working at something or other—so they said. But how on earth could you expect to see any work done at the national level when they couldn't manage to set something up in Moscow? So much of the network was in ruins, so many contacts had been lost—he might as well not have worked all last winter to build it up for them, and now he had to begin all over again. What a helpless group they were! The only contacts were those Lutovinov had with the Donbass. The Petersburgers were no better. If a batch of literature got stuck on the Swedish border, or somewhere nearer in Finland, instead of going to rescue it they'd wait for it to crawl home itself, or for Belenin (Shlyapnikov) to make the trip and chase it down. (You'd die laughing! Last year in the far north of Norway he'd found bales of literature dumped there in 1906 and never sent on, just forgotten. Who would want to read it now? It was so out of date it would addle your brains just trying to understand who was against whom and where everybody stood.) The Petersburgers hadn't even managed to preserve their printing press at Novaya Derevnya. But when it came to bellyaching about the Central Organ, and how late it was in sending instructions, they all joined in the chorus.

That's how it was; "there" was one thing, "here" another. In the two and a half years of the war, life here had diverged so far from life out there, the two sides had drifted so far apart that it was impossible to imagine from *there* what things were like *here* . . . Out there people were surprised and angry. What, they asked, are they all doing in Russia? Are they still alive or aren't they? Why have they clammed up? Why no reports from them? What work are they doing, if any? They aren't sending any money either, how are we supposed to carry on our work abroad, where can we get money from if not from Russia? "You are to go there, Comrade Belenin, but all you're to do is establish connections, get some money out of them, and then come back as quickly as you can, you can't stay there long without coming to grief yourself and damaging the cause." So—you get here, and what do you see? You see that workers are striking after all, that they're gradually wising up, that there's no trace of the crazy patriotism we saw in 1914, but: "We're short of literature! Why aren't they sending up-to-date articles, their latest thoughts? Why are they so closemouthed? Why do they sit there doing nothing, with no surveillance, no emergencies to worry about? You mean to say they can't rustle up some money in wealthy Europe, and we've got to pitch in our hard-earned coppers?"

It was almost impossible for the two sides to understand each other. Shlyapnikov alone divided his time between both places, carrying the vital concerns of each as if in two heavy wicker baskets from Murom, suspended from a yoke on his shoulders, careful never to take his mind off either (neglect either for a moment and the whole contraption would topple over), plodding steadily on, whatever the ground underfoot was like.

Lutovinov was goggling at him like a bumpkin who comes to town and sees an automobile for the first time, wondering if this can be the same Belenin who was here before, gave his instructions, and vanished. The same Belenin back again? From over the sea, with such a war on—and with not a scratch on him? How is it possible? They all looked at him in amazement, not just Lutovinov. It was hard to believe that the man sitting here with you in a garden shed had been in Christiania two weeks back, and in September returning from America on an ocean liner (second class, not third), admiring the ocean waves to the cheerful strains of a brass band.

You couldn't tell the whole story in detail, no one must know more than was necessary. Some things you could tell them, but once you got started . . .

Crossing the river Torne at Haparanda, walking under the bridge to avoid the police watch, with your feet sinking through the ice . . . Then, with Finnish guides and disguised as a Finn yourself, taking roundabout ways through the forest to bypass the gendarmes' checkpoints.

Or jolting over snowdrifts on a Finnish peasant sledge for eight nights on end, resting up in woodcutters' huts by day. The virgin snow. The silence. The aurora borealis. Forest paths with overarching trees. The trees dwindle to dwarf size and you are crossing a mossy bog on skis, though you have never learned to use them. Long detours to bypass the checkpoints . . .

It helps, of course, that the whole Finnish population is hostile to the Russian authorities, ever ready to transport our literature, provide guides for our revolutionaries, spy on the Russian army, and help German POWs return to their homeland . . . while the Finns themselves volunteer for the German army by the thousand.

Lutovinov pulled out of his pocket a crust of rye bread and half a dozen tomatoes. The bread had rested in his pocket unwrapped and the tomatoes were unripe and a muddy green in color, but very welcome, since Shlyapnikov had spent a hungry night, not wanting to eat his hosts out of house and home.

"This is great! Any salt?"

There was salt too. They both had knives. There was no paper to serve as a tablecloth, but the bench was clean anyway. They moved to opposite ends of it, and arranged the food in the middle.

"Better take a peek, Yura, see whether anything's happening out there."

Yura looked out. The mist was thinning, and you could see farther. All was well. Even if it hadn't been, you could give the police spies a taste of your fists in a place like this.

Not much of a meal, those tomatoes. Not enough to line the bottom of a hungry belly. But sliced up and salted, a piece for you and a piece for me, you've got something that draws you closer together than the cause itself.

That last crossing, his third, was the hardest of all. A test not so much of patience this time as of how much your feet and your heart could stand. Not everybody could have managed it, and that was a fact. Yet again, he finds himself far to the north of anywhere. A sledge and a driver, but it isn't free this time: one mark per kilometer. The polar night. But you can see a long way—maybe there's a moon behind the clouds? Along a river valley tumbling into ditches. Then over the river on foot, you and your guides clinging to opposite ends of a long rope. The frontier guards who pass that way several times a day have worn a track through the snow along the riverbank. Another sledge. You sleep a while. Change sledges at farmhouses. All around—the wilderness. Not a single stranger passing on foot, not a single cart. At Rovaniemi—another river, this time a dark, noisy, ice-free river. Loud voices calling for a boat.

(You tell your story, but all the time your heart is not in it. You should be thinking of other things. What's going to happen? What should you do about it? Though your mind is almost made up. Jump! And—then what?)

Among the Finns you're like a dumb man: don't know a single word of Finnish. They take you where you want to go, and that's good enough. They won't betray you. In fact, you're glad you don't have to converse when you stop for the night. It's good to be able to rest and plan ahead. Suddenly—you're stopped. Searched. The Finns gabble away in their own language, their Russian is very poor. It turns out that your captors are a sort of army unit in the heart of the forest, consisting of old soldiers and raw young men. These are the so-called activists—Finns who have taken up arms against Russia. (In effect, they're fighting for Germany, but that needn't worry you right now.) They aren't too fond of their own Social Democrats—regard them as aliens. But when they're told that you're a revolutionary they let you pass. After which it's southward again. There's less and less snow. A thaw has set in. Time to take extra care. Must be on your guard now.

But the bolder and more casual you are, the less you are suspected. Sometimes it's a matter of seconds—you dodge a patrol by nipping up a fire escape onto the station roof. Another time a gendarme manages to grab you and asks to see your passport. You search your pockets with alacrity and suddenly realize: "I haven't got it! Anyway, I live locally and we don't bother with them." (Though everything you're wearing is of foreign manufacture. But then the Finns dress better than we do.) The gendarme arrests you anyway. Takes you into the station waiting room, turns around to look for backup—and in one second, no, half a second you're gone with the wind! Through the door! Bowling someone over and away into the forest! Keep to the forest. You've gotten away with it. But don't go in circles. Where's the railroad track? And how can you decide whether a train is going your way or in the opposite direction? The sky is overcast. You guess correctly. Then it's on foot again. It's dark. Warm. Hurry it up! You must put maybe forty versts behind you by morning. Thirsty? There's snow. Hungry? Do without. You search the trackmen's sheds, but find nothing. Suddenly—look out! A railway bridge! There'll be sentries, obviously. Must go the long way around. Make a detour—an extra ten versts. Next—talk a boatman into ferrying you across. By morning you're asleep in a barn, in straw, with mice squeaking in your ear. Next night—all the way to Uleaborg by forest road. But avoiding passersby. You've covered seventy versts in two nights! When you arrive at the editorial office of the Social Democratic newspaper and sit down, you can't get up again. Your legs are like lead, your toes are galled and bleeding. Later, the comrades will concoct a false document and a photograph and take you through to Helsingfors, but right now it's doubtful whether you can even stand up and go to the farm to rest. (The blisters still haven't healed, and they make walking difficult.)

"Yes, they're good tomatoes, these."

All this explained why the members of the Central Committee abroad, Vladimir Ilyich and Zinoviev, were, putting it bluntly, not keen on such excursions. Shlyapnikov, though, had never been a stay-at-home anyway. Besides, here in Russia he knew a lot of workers personally, which was a big help with communications. So off he went on his rounds, with his yoke over his shoulders, sympathizing with the émigrés when he was abroad, and with the natives when he was in Russia.

Comrade Belenin, dear friend, tell them in Piter we must have money, they'll have to get up a collection! Get it from *Letopis*, from Gorky, from Bonch, from *Volna* if need be—from anywhere as long as it's money! Then when I get here I find *Volna* is quite the wrong sort of publication—they're against us and I won't get a kopeck out of them. And Bonch begrudges every ruble, as do all the once-upon-a-time Social Democrats. True, Gorky always gives—we'd starve without him. As for those coppers from members in the Petersburg factories, it pains me to take them. Then there's the extra 10 percent we take from local organizations for the All-Russian Bureau of the Central Committee. But send that money abroad with my own hands? Oh no.

Money, money, that's always where you have to start. He produced a wad and counted out fifteen red notes into Lutovinov's clumsy paw.

"Here you are, Yura. That's all for the time being. You'll have to manage somehow."

The hundred and fifty looked even less in Lutovinov's fist.

"It isn't much, Gavrilovich. What can I do with this?"

What could he do with it? Was that all he needed to move around, to organize things, to buy "material"? Plus something to live on?

He sighed, thought a bit. Should I make it another twenty? But what about Nizhny? What about Ivanovo–Voznesensk? And Tula? And what if somebody had to go to the Urals?

Can't be done.

The previous year his budget had been bigger. He and his photographer brother-in-law had the idea of printing postcards with pictures of the imprisoned Duma deputies in convicts' smocks. They had done a brisk trade in the factories. In addition to which Shlyapnikov had brought in several numbers of *Sotsial-Demokrat* and two of *Kommunist*, which were loaned to readers for a fee. Whereas now . . .

(Now . . . his heart sank: he had to decide.)

"You may not believe it, Yura, I went off to America to try to earn some money and I could hardly pay for my passage."

Lutovinov stared wide-eyed. "What, you? You really went to work for money?"

It's no great secret, I can tell him about it.

"When I was leaving, a certain person here . . ."

(Gorky. But no need to tell him that . . .)

". . . gave me some documentation on the persecution of the Jews. What's been happening since the war broke out. I was supposed to get the stuff published in the West. Not to give it away, though, to sell it. The Jews were supposed to pay good prices for it! Nothing's done except for hard cash in the West. In Copenhagen, for instance, half the town are black marketeers and profiteers nowadays. And the Social Democrats are as bad as the rest."

"What, *our* comrades?"

"Everybody gets corrupted there. There's a black market in canned food meant for the army, in German pencils, in medicines . . . If they get expelled from Denmark they set up in business in their next place. There's somebody called Parvus—he's amassed several million already. And now he's a benefactor, the scoundrel."

At the very mention of that ambiguous figure, Parvus, the Social Democratic moneybags, a dark cloud descended on his heart. He put the man out of his mind. Not his business. Lenin would see to him—with his iron nit comb.

"Or take America nowadays. I needed a passport for the voyage back. They're issued by the Russian Consulate. But I couldn't let them know who I was. I had to pretend I lived in America. They advised me to get confirmation from my parish that I belonged there. I went to see the priest, and for two dollars he gave me a certificate. That's how it is with them."

(With my people, the Old Believers, you'd never, never get that.)

"That's America for you. Everybody's on the make. If they aren't making it today they're dreaming about it tomorrow. But living is cheap there, and easy. Our comrades there tried hard to persuade me to stay, said it's the same working class here, you know, you can be just as much a help to the International here as there. But I wasn't having any of it. So all right, they've got two Russian newspapers. And a few in Yiddish. There's one called *New World*, with a Menshevik running it. I submitted a report on the situation in Russia, thought I could topple that Menshevik, wanted to put a Bolshevik in his place, but there was nobody suitable, not a single one, can you believe it?"

He laughed.

"So what papers did you use to get in there?"

Good thinking, Yurka. He had a good conspiratorial head on his shoulders.

"Getting in was still more difficult. They've got immigration control in New York Harbor. They don't let sick people in—don't need them. They check your money, your income, your prospects, whether you've at least got well-off acquaintances. Paupers are turned back."

"So what could you show them?" Lutovinov's blue eyes were popping, but he was enjoying Shlyapnikov's success in advance.

"What I showed them was"—with a catch in his voice, he always spoke of it with pride—"was my turner's papers. Turner, first class, in English. I qualified in England."

He put an arm around Lutovinov, a shabby figure in his skimpy gray-brown-ginger overcoat (it had lost its original single color) with frayed buttonholes which would soon look like—just holes. Shlyapnikov had exchanged his own European coat in Piter for one so threadbare that it was almost white. He had kept only his good boots.

"Last summer I asked the Central Committee for permission to leave Norway and go to England. They wouldn't let me at first. But once I was standing behind a machine I was earning money for the Party as well as for myself, and sent some to them in Switzerland. The working class is what everything else is based on, brother. A workingman will survive anywhere. And let me tell you something—you shouldn't let Party business take you away from your machine too much, mustn't get out of practice. You're a real craftsman. You must try to become an educated proletarian. Without such people we will never build the Party. Or else it won't be the right sort of party."

Yurka, with Shlyapnikov's arm around him, listened trustfully. Like a younger brother, though so much bigger. There were only three years between them, but Yurka had seen so much less of the world.

"Or what can easily happen to people is they get too big for their boots and turn into God knows what—useless windbags. Now take Gvozdev—we're fighting him, but I'm fond of him just the same. Standing at the next bench to his is a real treat! A good pair of hands— no two ways about it!"

The shed door was wide open, so they could see anyone coming. It was a gray day. The air was hazy, and there were patches of fog close to the ground. Potatoes had been lifted and lay along the furrows. The red-brownish haulm was drenched.

Somewhere over there all those foreign countries . . .

"So did they?"

"Did they what?"

"Let you into America?"

"Oh yes! A turner, remember! Not a squeak out of them."

"But when they were interrogating you and all that, where was the Jewish printed matter?" Lutovinov's mind was still on track.

"In the engine room, with a comrade," Shlyapnikov said reassuringly.

"So did you sell it?"

"At a ridiculous price. I really disgraced myself. The Jews back in Stockholm were eager to buy and offered a good price. But I was afraid it would all go straight to the German General Staff and be used by them . . . There are German spies at every turn, you know, in Sweden and Denmark. A revolutionary activist risks dirtying himself on the German intelligence service from time to time. Things don't look very strict in Europe, but you have to be on your guard. If they manage to plant money on you, you'll never shake them off. So what I suggested to the Swedish Jews was give us the money for a press and we'll publish your stuff first, then our own. But no, they wanted to be sole proprietors of the material. I got suspicious, that's why I lit out for America. The Jews there won't begrudge the money, I thought, they're all millionaires. What to use for travel money, though? I had to use Party money for the voyage, traveling in the cheapest class. And what was the result? I arrived in July, the worst time possible: all the rich Jews had left town for the summer, and the others haggled. So I sold the stuff for five hundred dollars, I'm ashamed to say. And two hundred and fifty went on the return fare and living expenses. You see what happens when a workingman goes into business."

At moments like that a juicy swear word often helps. But Shlyapnikov was not in the habit. Never had been, on account of his religion.

"New York is just stone, iron, and smoke, I don't know how people live there. In Piter at least we've got copses and vegetable gardens, but there's nowhere you can just sit like this in New York."

Mustn't sit here for long either. This drizzly day was deceptively quiet. Right behind their backs along the Sampsonyevsky Prospect, along the Vyborg and Pollyustrovskaya embankments, the factories had been silent for three, four, or five days now. The strike had closed some, the retaliatory lockout had slammed the gates of others. Ericsson's, the Old and the New Lessner works, the Old and New Parviainen works, Aivaz, Renault, Phoenix, Nobel, Ekwall, Prometheus, Baranovsky's, and yet others all over Petersburg, 120,000 workers, maybe a few less . . . and who would be deciding their fate? He would, Shlyapnikov would. It should really be the Bureau of the Central Committee and the Petersburg Committee, but it was impossible to get them all together, and he wasn't going to consult that pain in the neck Molotov, somebody from the Petersburg Committee would come along to Pavlov's apartment that evening and the two of them would decide. (We'll decide—but the leaflets have most likely been printed already. We'll decide—but it's already decided.)

"Listen, Yura"—Shlyapnikov's arm was resting still more heavily on his shoulder—"you know what we want to do, don't you? To disrupt the lockout we want to call a total general strike, starting tomorrow, all over Petersburg, right down to the last small workshop, the very last worker—everybody!"

His arm pressed harder still. A somber face, dark as if blackened by smoke, with sick eyes and drooping mustache, looked out from under the workman's cap.

"What do you think? Will the proletariat support us? Will it catch on?"

Lutovinov was silent.

"Or won't it?"

Yura thought it over.

"What can I say, Gavrilovich? In the little places, those where there's no firm hand to organize things, it's always anybody's guess. It may catch on, and it may not . . . People are chickening out."

Shlyapnikov shrank into himself, looking darker and sicker than ever. He knew all that. That was where he had begun: as a fitter's mate with other young workers, in the Obukhov strike in 1901, stuffing their pockets with nuts and bolts, metal cutoffs, stones, rushing from the Semyannikov to the Obukhov plant, to drive the know-nothings who didn't want to strike away from their machines.

"Yes, but it isn't all rabbit punches, there's got to be solidarity. If one group are in a fix the others must help them out. If there's no solidarity, what kind of proletariat are we? We'll never, never . . ."

"They're chickening out," Lutovinov said. "They need pepping up.

It all depends . . . I don't really know . . . Now if somebody could slip the strikers a bit of money . . ."

"All right, then. It'll be decided this evening, we'll send a runner sometime in the night . . ."

A sensible fellow, Lutovinov. And one of us.

"Listen, maybe you ought to take the whole south over, what do you say? Add Voronezh, Kharkov, and the North Caucasus to what you've got now? Let's think about it—how many are on our side in those towns, what connections we have, how many people do we need? What d'you say, shall we meet in a week's time and discuss it? D'you want to bring somebody else with you?"

They agreed on the details: where, when to meet, how they would recognize each other, how they would get through the door, the password.

All right. Time to leave. Separately.

Palm smacked palm. Shlyapnikov strode away between the rows of potatoes, muddying his boots.

The mist had settled, and the air was damper than in the morning.

If he could have communicated with the CC by telegraph, he could have tapped out his message, they would have answered, they could have discussed the situation. But they weren't in communication even by letter—you could do what you liked, use invisible ink, write code, conceal the message in the covers of a book, there was no one to take a message of any sort. At one time all clandestine correspondence had been carried on via the Duma group, but that arrangement had collapsed when they were arrested. A certain amount had trickled through via Lenin's sister, but she had been detained for three months. Now, if she wasn't banished to Astrakhan (her husband was pulling strings to keep her at home on health grounds and he was a company director, so she would be allowed to stay) she would still be under surveillance and a spent force.

No contact at all! Until you go yourself. Right, you can feel the yoke on your shoulders. Show that you're up to it!

If only the Central Committee Bureau really meant something. As things are, what does it amount to? Three of us strolling down the Lesnoy Boulevard when it gets dark, and making our decisions as we go. It's called the BCC, but liaison with abroad and with the provinces and all the real work fall on me, on Shlyapnikov. Zalutsky is supposed to be our link with the Petersburg Committee. To all intents and purposes he *is* the PC. That drip Molotov is responsible for literature. Nominally. Try reading one of his leaflets, you'll doze off before you're halfway through. He might as well be writing for sheep or cows. If you want something with fire in it you commission the youngsters, the students, to write it. Molotov was only taken on because there was nobody else. And because he fitted Lenin's specifications: the leadership must consist solely of people who understand that our prime tactical objective is to distance ourselves from Chkheidze. In no circumstances must we join forces with Chkheidze. If we did cooperate with Mensheviks we would find ourselves chained to them, helpless lackeys. Molotov had taken the point.

The ears in the back of his head told him that he was clean. No reason why anybody should be following him anyway. He'd only just arrived, they hadn't been expecting him, and were not yet used to seeing him around. Yesterday, they'd been trailing the man he was to meet, not Shlyapnikov himself.

At least relations with the Petersburg Committee were now more or less friendly. All last winter the Petersburgers had been at daggers drawn with the CC. When Shlyapnikov, newly co-opted onto the CC, had turned up they had been reluctant even to recognize him. From their own point of view they were right. But the immediate result was the sort of squabble you always got with intellectuals. Who should be put on the Bureau of the Central Committee? The Petersburgers wanted to pack it with members of their own committee. Shlyapnikov had other ideas. There was more to Russia than just Petersburg. He didn't just put forward names he'd thought up himself, he had brought a ready-made list of candidates from abroad, but he found on arrival that either they were not in Petersburg at all or else they were lying low somewhere on the outskirts, like Steklov at Mustamyaki, and wouldn't be drawn in. Or else their line was "different from ours." The Petersburgers made even bigger demands: wanted him to reveal his means of communication with the Party abroad and with the provinces in case he, Shlyapnikov, got caught. That's asking a lot! We'll get caught one of these days, but you'll come to grief before we do. Then the Petersburgers started throwing insults around: Shlyapnikov's playing the dictator! Shlyapnikov wants to be in sole command! No, I don't want to, but I'm compelled to. That's how these squabbles always started. Shlyapnikov had seen it happen to others, but hadn't managed to avoid it himself, it began with personalities and developed into a *theoretical* argument. The dispute devolved on *Problems of Insurance*, as if the whole future of the Russian Revolution depended on that moribund journal. The Petersburg Committee passed a resolution condemning the journal's editors. The *Insurance* men barked back like mad dogs. The Petersburg Committee passed another resolution, this time against Shlyapnikov. The Bureau of the Central Committee spoke out against the Petersburg Committee. The Petersburgers chose new editors for the journal, and accused Shlyapnikov of bypassing the PC in his dealings with members of the organization (so what am I supposed to do, sit around twiddling my thumbs?), of taking no steps to convene an all-Russian Party conference (and a fat lot you've done about it!), of distributing consignments of literature from abroad without reference to the Petersburg Committee (and who lugged the bales around on his own back that time in Norway?). There was no end to their nonsense. The whole of last winter had passed them by while they were wrangling. There were only a couple of dozen activists, all of them workingmen, yet they were incapable of making peace with each other.

That was one of the reasons for his sudden flight abroad in February. That, and the fact that the sleuths were hard on his heels, so that he could go out only at dusk and meet people only by night. Besides, he had itchy feet—he had this constant urge to be where he might be needed more.

When you walk and keep walking your worries weigh less heavily, you walk off all the things that were troubling you, and relax.

Shlyapnikov had time to spare before his next meeting, so he trudged steadily up Great Sampsonyevsky Prospect, which runs in a straight line for many versts.

The ears in the back of his head still told him that no one was following.

There were more people than usual on Great Sampsonyevsky Prospect. The workers were not at work. Some of them were loafing around in the street, others were standing in line for their womenfolk at butcher shops and dairies.

He covered the ground steadily and was soon approaching the hallowed places where he had worked for so long. In 1914, for instance, when he was the "Frenchman."

Such an amusing idea! A French turner with a French passport showing up in Petersburg to earn the big money. If they docked five kopecks an hour from his pay he threatened to walk out: we've got laws in the West, let me tell you! He concealed his identity from most of his fellow workers, but at Lessner's and Ericsson's they crowded around to listen when—suppressing his broad northern Russian accent, and amazing them with his rapid progress in Russian—he talked about Lenin or Martov, almost legendary figures to them. It was easy for him, taking advantage of his position as a "foreigner" to pass through the cordons of policemen, who saluted as they offered their solicitous warnings, and plunge into the outer darkness of the Vyborg side, into a raging storm of revolutionary songs accompanied by accordions, where the police themselves feared to tread. What a 14th of July that was! How high were their hopes! And a few days later, still the same "Frenchman" with the dyed mustache and the bowler hat, he had clenched his fists until his nails dug into his palms as he watched, with mingled pride and pain, workers reporting to recruiting offices, carrying red banners, and also, alas, imperial flags, the banners of the proletariat capitulating to international chauvinism. The only retort the "Frenchman" could make was to keep his hat on when "God Save the Tsar" arose from under the banners.

Yet again his feet measured the Petersburg pavements. This time nobody was looking for him, comparing him with photographs, he was clean. Anyway, his mustache was different and he was dressed differently. Even if he bumped into somebody who knew him well he would not be recognized.

There's the "Russian Renault," over to the left. To the right there, beyond Flyugov Lane, is the low fence damaged the other day by the mutinous 181st Regiment. The fence has been mended and reinforced with new posts.

Reservists drilling on the parade ground again, as if nothing had happened.

It was a very close thing. Almost looked like the beginning . . . But wasn't. As you say, Yurka, it's always a gamble . . .

As it turned out, there was never any intention of court-martialing those soldiers. Nor were the sailors ever in danger of capital punishment under Article 102. Sixteen of the twenty had been acquitted outright. As Shlyapnikov had since been told, it was just that Sokolov, their defense counsel, needed a helping hand to wangle an acquittal. So he had . . .

While you . . .

Ah, Sanyok, Sanyok, Sasha would say, with a reproving tap on the cheek, your naïveté will be the death of you, you'll come a cropper one of these days, with that simplemindedness of yours. A revolutionary can't afford to be so simpleminded.

(Lenin had said the same: "Aleksandr, you're too trusting, too much of an optimist.")

You and Sokolov met quite by chance. And Sokolov must have made it all up as he went along. And it took you three minutes to fall for it. Hook, line, and sinker.

Got overexcited, didn't you!

The Petersburg proletariat had responded to the Party with a strike at all the main enterprises. The Party had decided—so the proletariat struck! Just how it should be! Just what was needed! The proletariat rose up as soon as the first leaflet reached them. We're a power in the land!

Now sixteen of the twenty sailors were at liberty. But the factories were closed down. Closed down by you, the representative of the Central Committee. Better not admit your mistake out loud; there would be a great howl of triumph from the Gvozdevites, now rabid defenders of the fatherland. They'd have a field day.

The idea had been to give the military court a bit of a fright: stay out a day or two, then go back.

But then came the lockout. There was nowhere to go back to. If workers did show up at their factories the police drove them away.

That was not the worst of it. Sheets of yellowish paper, the wretched stuff you got in the third year of the war, were pasted up on the locked gates of the Renault and New Lessner factories and all the others. People walked up to the gates and stood just long enough to read the message. You could join them without attracting attention ... but you already knew it by heart.

CHIEF OF STAFF OF THE PETROGRAD MILITARY DISTRICT

10 November 1916

TO THE DIRECTOR OF THE ... FACTORY

By order of the Commander of the Military District workers in your factory born in 1896 and 1897 and eligible for military service are hereby deprived of deferment and are to report immediately for active service in the armed forces. You are to forward lists of the workers concerned to the military commandant and to the local police station, and give severance pay to those liable for call-up immediately.

That was three days ago, but there were no festive send-offs, no white bundles, no wailing women to be seen, and it was very doubtful whether men really were being paid off: what kind of idiot would go along to a closed factory to collect severance pay? And even if the list had been sent to the area commandant, that was not the end of it, since area commandants had their own job to do, and could grant draftees deferments to go and work in another factory. (This was where Gvozdev's group could be useful for once.) Even when conscripts were in their army greatcoats employers might have second thoughts and send them back to their benches.

True, only the two youngest age groups, who hadn't really had time to become workers anyway, were being called up. But if you did nothing about it, if you gave in to the military jackboot, the workers' movement in Russia was done for.

So we didn't give in—and the result is all these gloomy men wandering up and down the Great Sampsonyevsky Prospect at loose ends.

It's a lockout! Get out, all of you!

The decrepit regime has dug in its heels. Has dared to act for once.

That was the real surprise: that they had screwed up their courage. It was so long since they'd shown any.

He had miscalculated there.

He trudged along, on legs as heavy as they had been when he reached Uleaborg.

He was proud all the same. What strength they had! You couldn't count exactly, it changed every day. There were factories, and strikes, and nothing was known of them two hundred yards away except by the factory inspectors. So what if it was only 60,000, not 120,000—

that was still a hell of a lot! Could those pencil peddlers in Copenhagen possibly imagine anything on this scale in Russia?

The sensible thing for the victorious proletariat to do now was to
retreat in good order. But no, they were paralyzed by the lockout and
the call-up.

It was terrifying. He had never faced an ordeal like this. One move
could wreck everything. He had tried to tell them that it was too soon
to fight, that they weren't ready. And then rushed into battle himself.

Threading a screw was slow and painstaking work. Gauging the diameter. Gauging the speed. A few turns in reverse to clear away the
swarf. Then greasing it.

A fool could easily make a mess of it. Just one twist too many.

So what was the solution? Beg for mercy? From the factory owners?
From the authorities? Sacrifice the conscripts? And those who had
been fired?

That was no solution. Right or wrong, there was only one way to go
now, straight ahead.

Once battle is joined, the only way out is straight ahead!

But the worm gnawed at his guilty breast, though he alone knew his
guilt. Sanka, Sanka, you should have kept your cool!

His feet felt heavier all the time. And they were wet through.

And he was short of sleep. *And* his belly was empty. It was about
time he ate something.

Litovskaya Street, Helsingfors Lane, the Moscow Regiment's Barracks. Walk a little faster past Ericsson's—somebody might recognize
you . . . The same notice was there, outside Ericsson's . . . He knew
every alleyway in that area without looking at names. And every courtyard without looking through the entrance.

Yes, and that was why he felt so miserable. Not because he, the
chairman of the All-Russian Bureau of the Central Committee, had—
probably—made a mistake, not because of the consequences this
might have for the Party, and indeed for Russia as a whole—no, simply
because those factory gates were closed. Closed against the workers.
Closed by you, Sasha. Closed to the workers by you.

Before he had known a single socialist, before he had read a single
brochure, he already had one dream: someday, God willing, I'll be a
fully trained craftsman. Just let me master the use of the lathe, and
I'll get by anywhere! This hope had taken him to Vacha, to Sormovo,
to the naval dockyards on the Neva (adding a year to his age on his
passport), and to the Semyannikov factory. But he had been driven off
course—sent to inculcate political awareness in older workers by
bouncing bolts off their heads. He was fired and blacklisted. After that
it was downhill all the way—into the revolutionary movement, into
one jail and another. Downhill the going was somehow easier, but his
dream still urged him upward. To become a metalworker, first class!
To work with his hands till the day he died!

And here you are with eyes always watchful, ears on the alert, a good pair of legs, a head on your shoulders. *And a good pair of hands*— that's the main thing. Your happiest days are still those spent not on committees, at strike meetings, in demonstrations, or with émigré politicians, no, it's when you walk into some place that's all cheerful noise and cogs and pinions and crankshafts and helical gears, and you know every move you need to make, and do it your own way, and hear simple words of praise from the old hands, then from the foreman—that's where you really feel at home! And every Saturday you slide into your pocket coins as heavy as only those earned by honest labor ever are.

Later, you worked with German, French, and English turners. A different International from the one that attends congresses in dickey shirts, this was the grass-roots, the original International, in smocks and work jackets and gaiters, covered with grease spots, shuffling through metal shavings along workshop aisles, and what your ear didn't catch your eyes would make up for, and you walked proudly about the Wembley factory—"first turner," qualified mechanic—a fine craftsman with the whole world as your fatherland.

And now you've closed the gates to others.

How? Why?

Ah, at last. Baburin Street. So where's that café? Hunger gnaws at your belly like a wolf!

The café is full of warm smells—cabbage, meat, fried onions, bread fresh from the oven—lovely! Nobody takes his overcoat off in this place. You sit with your cap on your knees. Is he here yet? Ah, there he is, against that partition. Fellow with restless eyes, rather a stupid face, Kayurov is his name. Eyes wander to the trays on the tables. What do they eat here? Croquettes and potatoes. Macaroni with meatballs. Thick soup. Goulash. Eat all you can. Don't begrudge yourself. If you get hungry on a day like this you could foul everything up.

"Hello there."

"Hello."

Ordinary type, this Kayurov, narrow-shouldered, middle-sized, just a pattern maker, not a real craftsman. But grab you by the throat as soon as look at you. And he can yell as loud as the next man.

Doesn't matter what we say, or how loud. At the other tables they're all busy with their own conversations, eating, adding up the bill. Not listening to us, we're just two friends, no different from the rest.

"You clean?"

"Yes."

"Sure?"

"What d'you take me for?"

Kayurov was as offhand about that as about everything else. So cocksure he might not have noticed. And a bit too excitable. You'd never think he's eight years older than me. Close-shaven. Or maybe he can't grow a beard.

Huddled over their plates, Kayurov already eating, Shlyapnikov waiting, they get down to business, keeping their voices low.

"There's no other choice. We call a general strike as of tomorrow.
All over Petersburg. Our demands are: end the lockout and cancel the
call-up."

"The men know already. Word's gotten around."

"So will they go for it? Can we pull it off?"

"Ericsson's is all right, of course. And both Lessners."

Goes without saying. They're locked out anyway. Can't do anything
else.

"I mean those who're still at work. The factories around them.
Which do you know about?"

"Gerhard's. Morgan's. Rosenkranz."

"Small fry!"

"Maybe, but it all adds up! Then there's Lütsch and Tschescher,
electrical appliances. Kmyadt's, dyes. Grigoriev's, cooked meats."

"But will everybody join in?"

"You bet they will."

If anybody else had said it Shlyapnikov would have believed him.
But this one was too fond of big talk.

"What about the Arsenal?"

Kayurov wouldn't risk a guess.

"I don't know."

"And the textile mills? Sampsonyevskaya, Nevskaya?"

"We're waiting to hear."

Waiting, that way it can all run into the ground. And you will be
held responsible. You personally. And you have half a day left to make
up your mind. You always think an appeal to the political awareness
of the workers will suffice. But the stakes are high, you'll be saying
"just one last time" yet again.

Then, firmly, in his voice of command. "We must pull it off at all
costs. If they won't walk out you'll have to drive them out—with nuts
and bolts if necessary. The leaflets will be ready this evening, send
somebody around to the Pavlovs' after eight. Distribute them overnight. The morning shift must be held up everywhere. In the street,
at the factory gates, on the steps—anywhere, just as long as you stop
them. If you don't we'll lose everything."

"It's as good as done!"

Kayurov sounded confident. This was right up his alley. When
strong-arm stuff was needed he was first off the mark. Some things he
might make a hash of, but not this . . . !

"I've heard they're giving strikers a handout in some places."

"Oh? Who is? Where do the funds come from?"

"Lord knows. The Interdistrict group maybe, or the Initiative
group."

Internationalists? Socialists outside the rival parties? Well, well! A mystery. Still, it's all grist for our mill.

Vaska Kayurov likes a chat. But there are things you can't tell him . . . That your heart is heavy, that you wonder whether we've made a mistake. Just tell him what you've decided. That's enough for him.

It's a general rule anyway. Everything you say is meant for one particular listener. Five minutes later you may be talking to someone else. The words will be different, and so in some respect will you.

Kayurov's a good man to talk to if you want to relieve your feelings by abusing someone. Everything about Kayurov is sharp. From his restless, piercing eyes to the biting language he uses. He lashes out at Chkheidze again: he's a liar when he says he sympathizes with the Zimmerwald declaration, he just wants to hitch us to a bourgeois government. Suppose Milyukov does replace Stürmer—where does that get us? He had harsher words still for Gvozdev; know him myself, from Ericsson's, I'd like to get my teeth in his throat! Strikebreakers! Want to force arbitration hearings on us, Gvozdev's boys do! They've decided saving the country means saving the monarchy. A harmless little mistake! Our Minins and Pozharskys nowadays don't lay their purses on the altar, nowadays they're out to pinch what's there already.

If we want to go on talking without attracting attention we ought to drag the meal out. But the spoon's in such a hurry to empty the plate. Braised meat, cabbage, potatoes . . . Food problem's bound to come up with those people staring you in the face. Doesn't take much to· set Kayurov off anyway. Action's what he's good at, but he likes airing his views. Which are sometimes quite sensible.

"There ought to be fixed prices for all food, of course. But the government mustn't be given a monopoly on the grain trade! That can't be allowed! The government must not control the grain supply, or they'll have us at their mercy. We aren't making enough of the food problem in our agitation. We must stir up housewives to wreck the shops. If the women take to the streets they won't let the Cossacks loose on them!"

Kayurov has a separate group of his own, men originally from Sormovo, among whom he passes for a wise head. They wanted to do it all themselves—make the plans *and* carry them out, maybe launch the whole second Russian Revolution. They refused even to recognize the Petersburg Committee for quite some time: you do your thing, they said, and we'll do ours. Partly because they're distrustful: the committee might include informers who could land them all in jail. But you have to draw the line somewhere: the secret police, bless them, also try to infect us with suspicion so as to disunite us. When Chernomaz, of the Petersburg Committee, smeared the "expats," said they're just sitting it out comfortably, all they do is send orders, and expect us to treat them like holy writ—Kayurov's group lent a ready ear. And when

Shlyapnikov had arrived in person last autumn—here you are, a real live member of the Central Committee, right here, not "sitting it out"!—there had been an outcry from Kayurov's group: That's impossible! We never elected him! He's a provocateur!

Impossible! Nobody else can manage it, so you can't have managed it either. Obviously, the Okhrana must have escorted you over the frontier. True, you didn't elect me. Present circumstances being so difficult. But which of you could be named in my place?

They talked it over and sorted it all out, with Gorky as intermediary: he was from their part of the world, from Nizhny Novgorod, and so the only one whom the Sormovo group looked up to and trusted. His apartment was the one place where they all met—to wag their tongues and sob on his breast, remembering the collapse of the first revolution, the glorious "red years" up to 1907, and the subsequent decline of the working class. (Gorky liked shedding a tear or two himself.)

Now that my feet are warmer they feel wetter than ever. I can feel the water gathering inside my boots. How nice it would be to take them off and dry out! A homeless man can never find a place to do it.

Gorky keeps open house in his apartment on the Kronverksky Prospect, and all sorts of people flock there—ordinary workers, Social Democrats, revolutionary democrats in general, and he's always hospitable, you always get something to eat there, and the atmosphere could not be more cheerful if beyond those walls Tsarism had ceased to exist, or was already on its way out. The apartment is kept under observation, there are often plainclothesmen on duty outside, but since its occupant is not engaged in clandestine or illegal activities, and since people flock there in such numbers—as many as forty at a time—visiting Gorky need not breach the rules of underground activity, and Shlyapnikov permits himself to go there.

"When will you be at Aleksei Maksimych's? Tell him I'll stop by the day after tomorrow."

To pick up the news from the Duma. The Duma opens tomorrow and the next day Gorky will have all the news from the lobbies. And where else would you get all the news from bourgeois circles, and even from the ruling clique, and all the printed matter that was making the rounds? That secret meeting of factory owners with the city governor? Here's the typed report. Protopopov's secret meeting with the Duma deputies? Here's the record, send it abroad if you feel like it.

"Aleksei Maksimych has gone off to Moscow."

"Oh? When?"

All those messages Lenin gave me for Gorky. Getting him to cough up money—I can handle that all right. But some of the other jobs are a bit trickier. Like cutting out the "Okists" by joining up with the "Makhists." Can't make any sense of that at all. Sweep them all out with the same broom—that would be easier to understand and to do. Lenin's always trying to play one group against the another. But Gorky's best of friends with both groups. And with all the others. Though at bottom his position is the same as ours.

Kayurov echoed his thoughts. "Aleksei Maksimych and I had an argument about what line we should take if things started happening quickly. The Revolution will begin at the front, that's obvious. But that means that the front will be weakened immediately and Russia will lose this blasted 'second fatherland war.' Which is a good thing. Lenin writes that the defeat of their own country is to the advantage of the proletariat. So one or the other of the two imperialist groups will win a temporary hegemony over Russia. Well, then—which of the two is preferable? Aleksei Maksimych always claims that the Franco-British combination is better. And I tell him that capitalists of all nations have factories in Piter, even the Swedes, even the Finns, and they rule us. So we have plenty of chances to compare. Your Englishman is always the most savage and most spiteful of the lot. At the Nevsky cotton mill they let in a yardful of women looking for work, and he comes out on the porch with a pipe between his teeth and stares at them contemptuously as if they were cattle. The Germans aren't so barefaced. A bit more human, you might say, more like our own. All those German foremen we've got in the factories—you can have words with them and make it up afterward. What do you think?"

What Shlyapnikov thought was that this kind of talk made him sick. He'd had his fill of it *there*, he hadn't expected to have to listen to it *here*. But should he answer back, should he try to explain? Start an argument here and now? He had filled his belly, and a sluggish warmth was spreading over his whole body. He would have liked to go on sitting there languidly and could easily have gone to sleep in his chair. But an underground agent cannot permit himself to lie down or even sit still for long, except at times of extreme danger. His tea drunk, he was pressed for time. It's his legs that feed the wolf.

"Besides," Kayurov said, warming to his theme, "they're neighbors. How can you jump over them?"

"Know what, Vaska?" Shlyapnikov beckoned to the waiter for his bill. "Don't go spreading that stupid talk around, even at Gorky's. Our line is to slip by under the Germans' jaws without them vomiting all over us."

Shared words, separate bills. If you work for your kopecks you count them carefully. Each of them paid his own tab.

Shlyapnikov left feeling worried.

But he had his wits about him. He walked down the lane in the other direction toward Mezhevaya Street. With nobody in tow, apparently.

Once there he jumped onto a moving tram, which quickly picked up speed. Now he was sure that he was clean. Couldn't afford to make mistakes today.

He thought it best to take a connecting ticket. Didn't want to walk for a single block along the Nevsky, where he was likely to be noticed. Besides, it would save him five kopecks.

If the Petersburg militants all think like Kayurov, how can we avoid getting our hands dirty? From day one of the war the German General Staff has seen the Russian socialist-internationalists as more or less its allies. More or less is right! And pigs may (more or less) fly!

But Lenin keeps his weather eye open! He won't let it go too far!

Sashenka—smart girl—had smelled a rat when some socialists interned in Berlin in 1914 were offered the chance to return to Russia. Who was rolling out the red carpet, and why, and where the money was coming from no one knew. All those Chkhenkelis and Nakhamkeses and Luries and Gordons jumped at the chance, and authorized her to speak for them—so off she went and refused on behalf of herself and all the others! How they'd scolded her!

Then that snake Kesküla turned up, the self-styled Estonian revolutionary. He arrived in Scandinavia from Switzerland with loads of money to dish out. What about you—need some money? To publish your brochures? To transport your literature? For Party purposes generally? "Pliss, ve ken alvays find some!" Printing presses? Weapons? We can get you anything provided you're fighting against Tsarism. He was warmly recommended by Lenin—they know me, I see so-and-so and such-and-such regularly. Kollontai was almost taken in, but this time Shlyapnikov was more suspicious and saw right through him. Of course, they'd cooperated with the scoundrel to some extent, because of his credentials, and Shlyapnikov had told him more than he should—but then a sobering thought had occurred to him. Homeless émigrés do not have checkbooks or friends in Russian banks. On your way, brother! While the going's good!

He'd told Lenin all about Kesküla, in a letter, told him not to trust the man. Brainy people, with their heads buried in books and newspapers, don't notice such trickery. You have to look where you're putting your feet, or you'll step in something . . .

At the end of Nizhegorodskaya Street he got off and waited for the city-circle tram, the No. 6, with the green and blue markings. He was standing a step or two away from a policeman, but in a close-packed, faceless crowd. They were at the bottleneck on the Vyborg side, where the road suddenly rears up to cross the Liteiny Bridge. Massed workers had so often stormed that bridge to irrupt into the city—only to be brought up short by policemen of one kind or another.

And would of course storm it again?

Must storm it again.

Strolling around Stockholm is one thing. This is something different. Our own Petersburg paving stones under our feet, our own Liteiny Bridge, fated one of these days to open up to our marching columns.

Never mind the policeman standing there.

Europe has split apart at the scarlet seams that were its frontiers! And such very clever people are so mixed up about it! Perfectly decent German socialists are puzzled by ours. Look—you're against Tsarism! And there's no more dreadful danger in Europe than Tsarism! So why don't you want help from Germany? Do you really want to see Tsarism defeated or not?

Well, we don't want help from you via Wilhelm, and that's all there is to it. Don't *help* us by shelling our brothers with six-inchers! We can do without that sort of proletarian solidarity!

That should be clear enough. But it still wasn't. Not to anybody. Take the Finnish "activists" getting arms from Germany. Why had they let Shlyapnikov pass instead of killing him back there in the polar darkness? Why, because he was an ally of sorts. And Shlyapnikov wasn't going to argue, wasn't going to say in sign language, "Go ahead, shoot me, I don't want your help."

Incidentally, running guns to the Finns was one of Keskula's games.

The tram shuddered and rattled its way over the Liteiny Bridge, over the cold, dark gray Neva. Now it was stopping outside the District Court. How those inside would love to lay hands on whoever was stirring up all the strikes.

Now that his belly was full he found himself nodding off to make up for all those sleepless nights. There was a confused buzz in his head. He could have dozed a while in spite of the jolting tram.

Chased away from one door, Keskula had tried another. Shlyapnikov wouldn't take his money, but Bogrovsky, secretary of the RSDRP group in Stockholm, did. Signing blank receipts sent by Lenin, and putting Shlyapnikov's seal on them! Neat, eh?

Then Bukharin and Pyatakov had charged in to investigate.

Keskula had been repulsed abroad, but—not to worry—Russia was within his reach. When Shlyapnikov arrived in Petersburg a dubious Dane of some sort named Kruze, a Social Democrat needless to say, but representing a commercial firm, had approached him, saying that what puzzled him most was why the Russian Social Democrats were not preparing for armed insurrection. Did they want arms sent in from abroad? There was no difficulty about that. Or type fonts for their printshop, in whatever quantity.

Well, it was tempting. And difficult to know what to make of it. (They might have taken the bait, but Kruze was in a hurry and dashed off to see Bukharin's wife in Moscow. What—no one preparing for insurrection in Moscow either? He also wanted to know whether they could locate various Estonians for him—he had a note for them from their comrade Keskula.)

Meanwhile, Bukharin and Pyatakov were hot on Keskküla's trail. They succeeded in unraveling the whole story. Keskküla was an agent of the German General Staff, and a whole web of intrigue had already been woven around the Russian revolutionaries in Switzerland.

You might have expected neutral Sweden to ignore the émigrés' tidying-up efforts. But no. They had been patient in the past, but now they arrested the self-appointed sleuths and deported them. And the Bosch female with them. *And* Aleksandra Kollontai. So much for Swedish neutrality! Don't dare touch German spies! (Shlyapnikov had rescued them all when he returned from Petersburg: in the West he was regarded as the only real representative of Russian Social Democracy, and Branting had helped him.)

The tram clanked on along Kirochnaya Street and onto Znamenskaya, not very far from the Tauride Palace, where tomorrow the Duma windbags would be holding their festive and fatuous gathering. Some of them taking the workers' name in vain, since they were really and truly afraid of the workers' movement.

Afraid of this latest escalation from strike to lockout to counterstrike—with who knew what consequences? Would Petersburg hold out? While they were deliberating, cooped up in the Tauride Palace, would Petersburg still stand firm?

The plank had broken as he made his leap forward! (He couldn't have said at what particular moment, but jump he did.) Would he land on his feet on the other bank? Or headfirst in the stream? The next twelve hours would decide, and he must collect his wits, make certain adjustments . . . But his head was buzzing and incapable of thinking straight.

He couldn't think straight, but all sorts of nonsensical thoughts crowded into his mind . . . The "Japanese," so-called (Pyatakov with his Bosch woman, and Bukharin) . . . their investigation of the German agents was their one and only success. Otherwise, they had always been tadpoles—ludicrous creatures with big heads, incapable of achieving anything. Amidst his books and his papers, in debate, Bukharin had a voice of thunder, his eyes blazed, he never conceded a single point. But in any real-life situation, and especially when traveling—at the station in London, or on the quayside in Denmark, with a forged passport in the name of Moishe Dolgolevsky, though he looked as Russian as could be, unable to speak a single foreign language, incapable of answering officials boldly and confidently—Bukharin was laughably helpless, he became a shapeless item of baggage, and as such Shlyapnikov had toted him around, onto ships from England to Norway, or from Denmark to Norway, had sprung him from a Swedish jail, and, taking pity on his discomfiture, sent him on tour around America "on Party business." Any attempt to retool the "Japanese" resident in Sweden, on Russia's borders, for the really important tasks of transmitting literature and maintaining communications, had proved quite hopeless, they were so awkward, and everybody, they themselves included, recognized it. They had in fact set off in the direction of "Russia," but by what route? They had been on the road for nearly two years— via Switzerland, France, England, Norway, and Sweden—until in the end their strength had failed them. Any farther and they would have been hoofing it over the ice. Their expertise was in rushing out articles: Here, print this! Send that off! They were just as skillful at whipping up disagreements on theory.

He got off the tram. His route ran along Rozhdestvenskaya and Khersonskaya streets, but he kept to the backyards, making for the Arkhangelogorodsky Bridge.

Life in emigration was such that a single match could set off an explosion. Disagreement on theory instantly became personal enmity. The "Japanese" had disagreed with Lenin as to whether self-determination should or should not be promised to all nations unconditionally. (Lenin used to say it should be promised to nobody! Now he said, "Promise away!" While the "Japanese" went on saying "no" as before.) Between them they had wrecked the editorial board of *Kommunist*. If they quarreled on one little point everything could go to the devil, workers' cause included!

Shlyapnikov could neither understand nor accept that a difference of opinion must inevitably make people enemies. Well, that's our intelligentsia for you. There's no mistaking them. They'd sooner see the whole movement collapse than give way on a matter of principle. But why should the workers' cause suffer? If it was to get anywhere in Russia, surely they ought to make peace?

As though he hadn't enough to do, on his last visit to Russia he had to set about making peace between the "Japanese" and the "Swiss." He had wasted two months acting as a buffer between them. He had tried to explain to both sides what *Kommunist* meant to the Russian worker. They stood in line for it! Snapped it up! Waste of breath. Bukharin left for America unreconciled.

Ah, the Schlüsselburg Prospect. Workingmen like me walking around here. I won't stand out. Needn't take the steam tram. It isn't far, and I've got time.

But Shlyapnikov's role as peacemaker had not ended there. As he set off back to a Petersburg seething with industrial unrest in that third autumn of the war, Lenin had ordered him, as his first priority, to convene the Bureau of the Central Committee to discuss disagreements among the editors of *Kommunist* (Comrade Belenin's report), express their solidarity with the basic (i.e., Leninist) line of the Central Committee, and send their resolution in writing to Switzerland immediately.

Lenin didn't say with whom. Petersburg would look after that. It had nothing else on its mind.

All the same, Shlyapnikov tried to strike a balance. Differences of opinion on particular questions among members of the Central Organ should not be used to prevent them from contributing to the Central Committee's publications. Their cooperation on uncontentious matters should be welcomed. (They would jump at the chance.)

So he carried out his mission and got the "Japanese" condemned, but, in his heart of hearts, when he turned his gaze from Petersburg to the world out there, to all those Russian Social Democratic colonies teeming with theoretical and literary talents, the Americans, the English (in England alone Litvinov, Chicherin, Peters, Kerzhentsev, and heaven knows how many others were taking their ease), the French, the Swiss, the Swedish, the Danish, all those Chudnovskys, Uritskys, Trotskys, Volodarskys, Suritsys, Zurabovs, Luries (or "Larins"), Levins (or "Dalins"), Gordons, Dermans, all of them waiting there for the end of the war or for world revolution—and you're the one "co-opted" to rush back and forth and shoulder the yoke. Carry this in and bring that out, to shake Tsarism to its foundations. Carry this in, bring that out, and deliver your report for us to discuss.

On arrival abroad you have to ask Lenin which country you can live in. Can I go and work as a turner in England? Am I allowed to meet Branting, or would that be treading on Litvinov's toes?

You arrive abroad and all the dithering soon gets you down. What you really want to do is bask on that pebbly beach, or plunge headfirst into the water. What difference would it make?

Shlyapnikov didn't resent the yoke: his broad shoulders, his indomitable spirit, his tireless legs were made for it. He did not mind the whole burden being placed on him alone. It rather amused him. But on a worrisome day like this he really ought to be able to consult other Central Committee members: there were decisions to be made, action to be taken. And sure enough there was no one on the spot.

By now he was making his way through the Glassmakers' Quarter. He crossed Porcelain Street, and found himself on the little square in front of the Church of All the Afflicted. There were crowds around the church and the shops as always, and it was easy to keep out of sight. He would not arouse suspicion entering Kovalenko's studio, which was open to all.

Kovalenko, Manya Shlyapnikova's husband, was not a court photographer or a famous one. He had won no medals at exhibitions to emboss on his business cards, but he was just the photographer the workers' cause needed to help fill the Party's coffers (though spicier cards—"Rasputin and the Tsaritsa," "Rasputin and Vyrubova," also sold well in Petersburg).

If you needed to enlist others for clandestine activity, who better than close relatives? There were no more willing helpers. And you never felt safer than when you were resting in the dark, windowless back room of a relative's house, lying low like a hunted beast in its lair.

Iosif Ivanych was photographing a client under the studio lamps. A lower-middle-class woman with two children, and two young ladies, sat in the waiting room. Stepping quietly, Shlyapnikov slipped discreetly behind the curtain. His sister Manya was in the inner room.

"Want something to eat?"

"Not just now."

"Will you be staying the night?"

"No, no. I'll just sit around until it gets dark. What time is it now? I'm not late, then. A student should be coming here shortly. Fellow with big features and sticking-out ears, won't be wearing a uniform. Ask him what kind of photograph he wants. He'll say, 'I would like one in Caucasian dress.' Then bring him in here."

He took his overcoat off, and passed behind a chintz curtain with lilac-flower pattern into a back room. It had no light of its own, and that which reached it from the dining room was stolen from the Petersburg grayness outside. He sat down on the bed. His head slumped heavily into his hands.

What he would really like to do was lie down and stay put till morning. For some reason he often found himself short of sleep when the day ahead was particularly difficult.

The bed sagged under him, his knees rose and his head sank toward them . . . Had he been asleep? Manya touched his shoulder.

"He's come."

He rubbed and rubbed his unshaven face with dry hands. It seemed to refresh him. He left the room.

Matvei Ryss was sitting at the dining table. He had placed his student cap on the bright blue embroidered tablecloth, but was still wearing a stylish overcoat and a reddish-brown scarf. He had a luxuriant thatch of ash-blond hair, and everything about him—ears, cheeks, and lips—was fresh, pink, and bright.

Youth to the rescue. This student group—Anya Kogan, Zhenya Gut, Roshal—this new intake of young people marked a break with the old intelligentsia. These were the cadre of the future. We can manage better without their sleepy elders.

"Well? How are things?" he asked, doing his best to sound brisk and cheerful as he shook hands with the student.

"Fine, Comrade Belenin!"

"Fine, you say? So why didn't the Obukhov factory support the strike?"

"They've adopted our resolution on the food shortage. And I can guarantee their support for a general strike against the lockouts."

"You sure?"

"We'll see to it."

"It's very important, young man. The Obukhov factory carries a lot of weight."

"They can't get out of it. Can't go against workers' solidarity."

"Fine, you make me happy. Anything else?"

"There's unrest in the university."

"You don't say! That's marvelous!"

It was catching on! It *was* happening after all!

"They all got together on the main staircase the day before yesterday to discuss food prices and the troops refusing to fire on workers at the pipe factory. Did that really happen?"

"No, it didn't."

"Well, at the meeting they said it did. Then they sang revolutionary songs in the corridors and stormed the lecture rooms."

"Great! Good for them!"

"The university, the Bestuzhev Institute, and our place, the Psychoneurological Institute, are ready to strike. If there's a general strike we'll support it."

Shlyapnikov, facing him across the small dining table, showed his pleasure. "Good work, boys, well done!"

Support comes from where you least expect it. While the workers were following those "defensists" like a flock of sheep.

He gazed at Ryss approvingly. "Right now the main battle is the strike against the lockout."

"I realize that."

"And we're getting your leaflet ready. Not like in the old days underground, when it would be handwritten, or rolled off on a duplicating machine, but in a proper printshop."

Ryss shook his head incredulously.

"You'll see! I'm not going to mention names but a handpicked bunch of trustworthy men get together on the night shift and instead of their newspaper they print our leaflet. All we have to do is carry the bundles out."

"It's simpler still for the Interdistrict group."

"How's that?" Shlyapnikov asked jealously. This was a group, somewhere between the Bolsheviks and Mensheviks, which thought that it alone could . . .

"They just pay to get their printing done in a legal printshop. The owner takes fifty rubles for a thousand copies, paper supplied."

"Well, well . . ." Shlyapnikov sounded a little put out.

"And where d'you think the printshop is? On Gorokhovaya, right next to the city governor's offices."

"That's pretty good." Shlyapnikov looked glum. "I've noticed that their paper and typeface are good. Anyway . . . We'll distribute the leaflets this evening. I'll try to send some here by night for the Nevsky district. Pick them up as early as you can in the morning and distribute them. This is a battle we must win. We've never fought one like it before."

"Understood," said Ryss with a twitch of his ginger eyebrows. "We'll put our backs into it."

Stout fellow. Without his sort you wouldn't know where to turn next. If you had to do all the writing and everything else yourself *and . . .*

"So what about the other one?"

"That's ready as well," Ryss said, shaking his head without further disturbing his hair, tousled as it was. He took a piece of paper with a new text from his pocket, unfolded it, and laid it on the table.

New jobs to be done and old anniversaries trod on each other's heels, gave him no peace. Before they knew about the lockout this leaflet had been ordered for 17 November, the second anniversary of the arrest of the Bolshevik Duma deputies. Although they hadn't behaved as they should in court—Kamenev particularly—this anniversary had become a recognized occasion for fomenting working-class resentment.

Matvei's writing was bold and irregular, with long tails to the letters. Legible enough. But Shlyapnikov wanted to hear how it sounded.

"Don't say it too loud, though, or they'll hear it in the studio."

Ryss began reading happily, keeping his voice down, but with as much feeling as he could muster.

". . . in the persons of those five deputies the whole Russian proletariat was on trial . . . At that time the war was only just beginning to sink its talons into the bodies of the peoples of Europe. Many listened with their eyes shut to the deafening drumrolls of the servile bourgeois press . . ."

A ringing voice, demanding to be heard from political platforms. He would make a fine orator. The man who writes his own speeches knows where to put the emphases.

"Marvelous style you've got!"

Lenin was correct when he wrote that the leaflet was the most important and the most difficult form of political literature. Not many of the émigrés had such a good style. Bukharin was drier. And Shlyapnikov himself, for all Kollontai's coaching, was not up to much, his writing lacked punch.

". . . Let us mark the day on which we were robbed of our workers' representatives by intensifying agitation for our demands . . . With the hiss of the conveyor belts in our ears we reach out our muscular hands to you! In serried ranks reborn in the Third International, we will step up the struggle to end the war by means of civil war . . ."

"Great stuff. Great. There's just one thing, don't go writing for the Interdistrict crowd."

"I've never written anything for them!" Ryss protested.

"You can't fool me! I recognize your style!"

"That's not me, Comrade Belenin. They're all handy with the pen."

"Let's leave it at that. But if you did it wouldn't be honest."

He picked up the paper. There were damp finger marks where Matvei had held it.

"Tell me, was Solomon Ryss, the Maximalist, your brother?"

"Cousin."

"Quite a family. Fighters all."

When Shlyapnikov had said goodbye to the student, his brother-in-law came in. He had finished work but was still wearing his smock. He looked at Shlyapnikov with a peculiar smile on his face.

"Aleksei Gavrilovich, in all the times you've been here you've never let me take your photograph. Neither this autumn nor last. One of these days you'll wonder where the years have gone to. Let's do it now. I've got some room left on a plate."

Shlyapnikov stared, momentarily at a loss. He was used to the crowd outside, which meant that anyone could enter the studio without arousing suspicion, and whenever he arrived someone was having his photograph taken, yet it had never occurred to him that he could do the same. Indeed, that he needed a photograph of himself.

Or that maybe Sashenka would want one.

A slight shrug. Lips pursed. His hand rose to rub his cheeks in a masculine gesture of apology.

"But I haven't had a shave, Iosif Ivanych."

"So shave now. Manya will get you some hot water in a jiffy."

But being unshaven was just an excuse. He wasn't in the mood. He felt depressed and anxious to be elsewhere, not wasting time sitting for a photograph.

All the same he went over to the mirror suspended at an angle over the table between the windows. It was in an awkward place, and you had to bend double to see yourself in it. Besides, it was tarnished, chipped and flaking around the edges.

He looked every day of his thirty-two years, and could have been taken for forty. His face was Russian, but not strikingly Russian: looking at the group photograph taken in a French factory, when he had trimmed his mustache differently and parted his hair, you would have been hard put to single out the one Russian from his French fellow workers. In a decent suit he could pass, say, for a French traveling salesman.

He himself would have liked to look a bit more heroic, to have more of the revolutionary about him. But maybe he was better without it—that way the police would be quicker to pounce on him. As it was, he looked like your average factory hand—one whose mind was on payday, and if he drank at all, knew his limit. Modest mustache, modestly close-cropped hair. But what made the man in the mirror a stranger, a mystery to himself, was something different: he looked like someone who *knew*, rather than someone who did things. (Whereas he had always honestly put into practice all that he knew.) The eyes were wrong, not those of a fighter, and so was the smile—a sad one. Why, whatever pose he struck for the photographer, did he always end up looking so strange? Not a bit like a real revolutionary. Even that mere boy Ryss looked much more like the real thing.

It was worse today. His eyes showed that he was short of sleep, unrested, his mustache drooped, and he looked so downcast—not a bit like the "lover boy" whom Sasha was always so eager to go walking with along the slopes at Holmenkollen, where they could watch the trains go by from the edge of the cliff. What had become of his youth, his strength, his nimble legs? Was all that really less than two years ago?

"No, thank you, Iosif Ivanych. Some other time. I don't feel like it."

"Just as you please. Let's eat, then."

Kovalenko went off to wash his hands.

How different the young Aleksandr had looked at seventeen, before his first spell in solitary, before he had come under surveillance, before he had done time in Vladimir Central. In fact, before he was a revolutionary at all, in one of those cheap Russian shirts worn in the provinces, with arms restlessly eager to work, however tightly he folded them on his chest they were like living things struggling to escape. And eyes full of the will to believe and to do great deeds.

His faith had been that of the Orthodox Old Believers. They were still persecuted in those days, but these genuine Orthodox Christians staunchly defended their beliefs, and Aleksandr, like all the others, was ready to die for them. But persecution was abandoned, it was no longer possible to suffer for the faith, the more adaptable members began truckling to authority and the energies of the young flowed into other channels. Aleksandr was converted to Social Democracy. A completely different cause, on the face of it, but the enemy, the persecutors, were the same as before—except that they were now on the other flank.

He was still not much older, although he had been arrested several times, still the same awkward provincial, still uncertain what to do with his hands or with the rest of himself, the same sober, shy, taciturn youngster when he went abroad for the first time and something wonderful, something he could never have dreamt of happened: a woman, a lady, as he would have called her a little while ago at home in Russia, a beauty (although she was rather short and twelve years his senior), experienced and seductive, had taken him under her iridescent wing— and sometimes he felt as if his legs had lost all feeling and he was no longer standing on firm ground, his emotions were in turmoil with the strangeness of it all. As the saying goes: a fine lady's favors are like honey on the knife.

Honey, yes. On a knife. But gradually things took a different turn. Gradually he drew himself up to her level. So that, in spite of her advantage in age, her German, French, and English, her exquisite manners, her facility with the pen, when she had shaped him in her own mold, transformed him, she finally admitted that in comparison with him she was "a Finnish bumpkin." "Your bumpkin, my darling dear! Hurry back to me!"

Lenin too was always hurrying him up—hurry home, hurry back to report. If he hurried back now he would find himself snowbound yet again in a lonely guesthouse, with northern pines standing like tall, pointed candles in the drifts. But Scandinavia was just a fiction, "a mirage." Reality was this dying Petersburg day, the loud ticking of the wall clock and the clatter of spoons scooping up the last drop of soup.

He had forgotten that he had sat down to eat with them.

His sister and brother-in-law had a question for him, but he hadn't been following their discussion and was lost for an answer.

"No second course for me, Masha. I think I'll have a bit of a nap now."

His poor head tried to work out how long he could afford to sleep. Two hours, say. Maybe two and a half. They won't be ready any earlier. I'll go as soon as you wake me up. Later on in the evening I'll send the leaflets for your district, and you can hand them out as people come for them. That young man who was here . . . you can give him . . . let's see . . . yes, a quarter of what I send."

He left his hosts to finish their meal and drink their tea—economizing on sugar for them—stepped back through the flowery curtain, and collapsed on the bed.

You've gone around all day with a head as heavy as lead, with one thought relentlessly nagging: Am I doing the right thing? Am I doing the wrong thing? What will come of it? So belly-flop onto the bed, bury all your troubles in the pillow, lie there for a couple of hours like a log . . . What luxury!

But all at once he was wide awake again! Damn! They were still at the table, he could hear the teacups rattling. The turmoil inside him had called him back from the brink, wouldn't let him sleep. Hey, look alive! Get on with it! There's a lockout, remember! You started this— now finish it! Mama, mama.

Mother of mine, Khionia Nikolaevna, let your little boy sleep, let him stay in bed a while, he's so warm and cozy! Don't get me up yet, it's too early to go to the factory. Too early to go to work, I'm too little, the four of us are only little, we'll get our fair share of work when the time comes, bending our backs from dawn to dusk for a few kopecks. Daddy got drowned, with only me there to see, the others don't remember, but anyway it's too soon for us to be going to work, the woods and the pond are the places for us. We're lining up beside you, crossing ourselves with two fingers in front of the true old-style icons, chanting "The prophets had prophesied for a thousand years" and other psalms we knew by heart in our quavering voices.

At school the scripture teacher punishes me for the true faith, every church holiday he makes me kneel for two hours and go hungry till the evening, all because I don't go to their unclean church. But God's truth is ours alone, there is no other truth in this world. So many martyrs remembered in the Lives of Saints were gladly martyred for it, so many were burned to death, like your Belenin forebears, or frozen to death in icy water, or thrown into dungeons, so many had their ribs broken with tongs, and we, your little children, will as we grow up endure all kinds of torments for our faith and proclaim it even on the pyre, even on the cross, if that is God's will. But now I'm so warm and cozy, Mama dear, let me linger a while, let me sleep a little longer.

No. I can't sleep and leave something started by me unfinished.

No, Comrade Belenin, you mustn't sleep, this is no time for it. The proletariat has no right to give in to sleep, that would be too incautious and indeed criminal.

Of course, of course. To ruin things would be a crime . . . But where has this devil's advocate come from, to attack me on the very first day?

You, Comrade Belenin, failed on your first visit to establish the firm links we need. And that is how we will measure the success of your second journey—by the number of connections established. Furthermore, Comrade Belenin, you have failed to arrange a reliable means of exchanging conspiratorial letters, and that is a great nuisance to us. Nor have you collected in Petersburg the money the CC needs.

"With the hiss of the conveyor belts in our ears we reach out our muscular hands to you."

Another thing—you mustn't keep absenting yourself so often, traveling to Denmark, Norway, England, America . . . Stockholm is where you are most needed. Until you organize transport and communications with Russia . . . security . . . meeting places . . . Comrade Kollontai can easily join you in a village near Stockholm.

Whatever you do, Yurka, don't ever quit your workbench for Party business. Or else our Party will just be . . .

Make a round trip to two or three Party Centers, establish links, return to Sweden immediately, and pass on all your contacts to us so that we can discuss further developments with you . . . Make the trip a quick one, and bring us all the contacts—that's your objective! After that you can go back to Russia again.

And there you were, tongue-tied, with your head like a lump of lead, paralyzed, incapable of explaining that it wasn't quite so simple, that you have to walk until there are bleeding blisters on your feet, that on the frontier the ice is likely to . . .

Yes, you need reliable documents to show at the frontier. Do you have any? You must obtain them. I have no doubt that there is still a reliable stratum of workers who follow the *Pravda* line in Russia, there's the Central Committee Bureau, you could even reestablish the Central

Committee itself. And even bring one or two influential comrades back with you to Sweden, to establish firmer ties with us. To make sure we are singing the same tunes.

Yes, but, Comrade Lenin, when you're crossing the frontier the ice is always likely to give way . . . and even if you're holding on to a rope . . . and if the ice is melting you're in this dugout canoe and it's . . .

Don't exaggerate the difficulties, Comrade Belenin. And don't underrate the importance of ideological uniformity . . . that is a tendency of yours, you mustn't mind my mentioning it, but you always do underestimate it! Believe me, it really is absolutely essential to our work at such a difficult time.

Yes, but . . . you hear the ice cracking, you grab the piers of the bridge with both hands. (Lucky you have the use of your hands at least . . . your head is a dead weight, paralyzed, but your hands are free.) Your feet slip and slide farther and farther apart as the crack in the ice widens . . .

Yes, of course, you must take care of yourself. You are in great danger in Russia, and you can best further the cause by making a quick round of a few Russian centers and returning to Sweden to consolidate contacts with us. And then we can exchange letters. In general I would be interested to learn what questions are uppermost in Russia now. Who is asking them? At what level?

"Comrade Lenin, I've had this idea for quite a while. I wrote to you about it. Why don't you and Grigori move to Sweden? You'd be so much nearer to Russia, and it would speed everything up . . . I can arrange everything for you at this end through Branting . . ."

Branting? But he's a social patriot. Don't do any deals with him. You can make use of him, though, as an official person with an address of his own . . . and to protect our interest . . . and to raise loans . . .

"What I mean is . . ." (My tongue won't obey me and my head's a dead weight.) "What I mean is, you've been so far away these last two years, why couldn't you yourself move a bit nearer here? I'll arrange absolutely everything here . . . and right off you'll have all the contacts."

No, no, Comrade Belenin! That would be very imprudent. Getting there would cost too much, and the cost of living there is too high . . . and mainly, you can't be sure about the police, they can be troublesome in Sweden. And what if the Swedes suddenly decided to join in the war? No, such a change of place would be premature.

"But, Comrade Lenin . . ."

"No, Comrade Belenin!!"

But all the same . . . What if the sledge driver lets me down? What if I wake up tomorrow and find the horse gone . . . snow, forest, northern lights . . . stare at the lights till your eyes pop out . . . Wait—maybe they've killed me? . . . They must have, cracked me over the head with an ax . . . or why can't I raise my head?

You, Aleksandr, must avoid groundless optimism! Above all, beware of the intrigues of liquidators! Beware of social chauvinists! Don't trust revolutionary chauvinists like Kerensky either, our paths are not the same! You are too trusting.

Yes, Vladimir Ilyich, but he had such an honest face. I never thought for a moment . . . The Finns too are all against Tsarism, how could I suspect that . . . They must simply have hacked me to death in my bed . . . in my sleep . . .

Your nerves seem to be getting the better of you. I sent you the Kienthal materials quite a while ago. I've written to you three times and got no answer. You are very stingy with your letters. Aleksandra Mikhailovna—please tell Aleksandr that he's very stingy with his letters, and it just isn't good enough! We can't keep in step if we go on like that!

What am I to do now? What's going to happen with the lockout? What a fiasco—if they'd killed me just a little bit later. We could have won this strike . . . Instead of cutting me off halfway . . .

What's wrong, Aleksandr? Have I offended you? You have my warmest best wishes! I wrote you a big, fat letter! And got no reply. Please let me have your criticisms of my draft manifesto.

Vladimir Ilyich! Inasmuch as I have been murdered . . . I beg to report that . . . This business of the lockout . . . I don't know whether I have acted correctly or not, there was nobody I could consult . . . And nothing of the sort has ever happened before . . . But abandoning those revolutionary sailors, when they risked being sentenced to death, or so I was told . . . But on the other hand we must not squander the forces of the proletariat prematurely . . . I can see now, all right, that I did make a mistake . . .

Aleksandr, if you have taken offense I am ready to make any apology you like. My dear friend! My dear friend! My dear friend! You aren't angry with me anymore, are you? I'm very grateful to you! A thousand best wishes!

Yes, I've made a mistake . . . That was my weakness when I was alive, being too ready to believe in success. Taking risks I couldn't afford . . . But now I can't put it right . . . it was so unexpected, you see . . . it was obviously the blunt end of an ax. Or maybe they used a pistol . . . a bullet in the back of my head . . .

With your permission I am sending you my theses, and I await your reaction with interest. On the question of self-determination—which Radek and Pyatakov have made such a wretched, stupid, filthy, driveling mess of—I hope you're on my side. It is very important to me to know whether Belenin and I differ on this subject and if so how. And how we can eliminate this difference before the lovers of faction— those foul Kautskyites, and all the opportunist scum—get hold of it. I hope that you will be as tactful as possible when you frame your questions to Bukharin.

So you'd better send somebody else urgently, Vladimir Ilyich . . . Because there's nobody here worth mentioning. Molotov simply isn't . . . well, you know what he's like . . . And the rest just squat in their holes. Who can you send, though? There's nobody there either . . . Here, you have to be able to fight off the sleuths and keep running around the gardens all night if necessary, at temperatures below zero.

I really am very anxious to know what questions are coming up in Russia. Who is raising them? And in what precise conditions? In what circumstances?

Should I perhaps try to lift my head? If I don't no one will do it for me. All right . . . here goes.

The "Japanese" have overdone it, you know, with this investigation of Keskula, they've only succeeded in scaring left socialist circles. They shouldn't have been so tactless!

It's not a head, it's a Finnish boulder. I'm too weak for anything. My body wriggles like a lizard on a rock . . . on those warm rocks at Larvik . . . Sashenka . . . Sashenka . . . A bumpkin you called yourself? I never saw a more beautiful woman than you! I'm the bumpkin . . . I'm the one who's made a mess of things . . . Sashenka, I'm coming back to you! I'm coming, give me your hand. Come on now! Pull!

Oo-oo-oo-oof!

Still alive?

The blood had gone to my head. My head had slipped off the bed and the blood rushed to it . . .

On the other side of the curtain the lamp had been extinguished in the dining room, but there was a faint light from the third room. From time to time he heard a pleasant humming and rustling.

Manya using her sewing machine and straightening the material.

That was the only sound.

She wasn't ready to awaken him. It was still too early.

He had saved his head from bursting, but his body felt bruised and battered. And his head was no fresher, in fact it felt heavier. Sleep was all he wanted now—twenty hours of it.

But no one will lift that boulder for you.

You must go and raise it.

Raise all Petersburg.

Only first you must get out of bed somehow or other. And don't sink back onto it, get over to the washbasin. Washing in cold water always makes you feel better. Then . . . Go part of the way by steam tram. Then two ordinary trams. Then a long haul on foot. The sleuths haven't spotted you yet. But all these detours are essential, just make sure, when your goal is the headquarters of the Bureau of the Central Committee, where Maria Grigorievna keeps the official seal and certain papers. So you'll have to hang around for another half hour on the Vyborg side.

I'm shattered, though. Can't get my watch out of my pocket to look at the time.

She still hasn't called me, though. So I can lie here a little longer.

I've simply got to hold out! If I die now or end up behind bars the whole thing will collapse, and that's a fact. The yoke would snap, one basket would fall on this side, one on the other side, there would be no communication, no clandestine mail, the Central Committee abroad would be on its own, at loggerheads with the International, and Russia, or rather every single city in Russia, would be isolated. And all the stuff we write in our leaflets, all the threats we make, would be just empty boasting, with nothing behind it.

Must make the effort to rise . . . But will the whole city rise? Will half a million workers follow the lead of half a hundred Bolsheviks at odds with each other?

If this doesn't come off, it's all over, for a long time to come.

Suddenly, though no one had knocked on the outside door, he heard steps in the anteroom to the studio—rapid, firm, masculine steps! Not the master of the house, he felt sure! It could be one of *them*!

Quick! On your feet. Boots? No time. A weapon? Grab the pressing iron! If he's alone—hit him. If there are three of them—jump out the window! Whatever happens, don't give yourself up. Not at a moment like this!

"Where is he, Manya?"

A voice he knew. Whose? His head wasn't working. Would you believe it—Mitka Pavlov! In person? Had it misfired? Were the others under arrest?

He pulled the curtain aside—and there he was—cold, dusted with snow, but cheerful.

"Gavrilovich! We've won!"

Then he was embracing Shlyapnikov, kissing him, though the bundles under his arm got in their way.

As did the pressing iron. Shlyapnikov put it down on a stool.

"What? Won? How?" Unshod, in his socks (the European socks he wore instead of foot rags).

"The owners have given in! And the government!" Mitya roared in a voice too loud for the room. "The lockout is off! The call-up is off!"

"What are you telling me?" So weak he staggered back against the lintel, and got tangled in the curtain. "When did you hear, and how?"

Pavlov wouldn't be diverted. "So I decided not to distribute the leaflets just yet. Was that right? I sent the men away till morning: told them we'd most likely be calling the general strike off. Is that right?"

Mitya Pavlov was one of those who didn't like striking: he was much too fond of his pattern maker's job at the Russo-Baltic factory. And of his engineer boss, Sikorski—they were building Ilya-Muromets tanks.

He was thrusting his bundle into Shlyapnikov's hands as he spoke.

"Yes, of course . . . Only why did you . . ." Shlyapnikov gave a weak laugh. "You could have made the decision yourself. Why make the men turn out twice?"

Mitya was insistent. He had to take the parcel.

"What's in it?"

"Pies."

Sure enough. He could smell them now.

"Why?"

"Still warm. Masha's sent them for you."

"Why ever . . . ?"

"She just did . . ."

"What's in them?"

"Take a bite and you'll see."

"Oh, but there are two bundles here. What's in the other one?"

"The leaflets, of course! I've brought a batch of leaflets to show you. We printed them at the *Evening Times*. A beautiful job! It's a terrible pity to waste work like that!"

"Manya, call Iosif! These pies are still warm! What's in them, onion? How did you get them here?"

They relit the lamp. He ate standing in his stocking feet on the strip of coarse matting. One of the leaflets lay on the table. Coarse, yellow wartime paper, but the printing was superb, clear-cut, with no smudges, no irregularities. He gazed at it admiringly, and even ran the back of his hand over it (his fingers were greasy by now). He read out a few passages.

" 'The way in which your strike has spread . . . to draw in about 120,000 workers . . . has shown all those who are waiting hopefully for a salutary upheaval how closely linked are the revolutionary army and the revolutionary people. Is this why we are turned out of our factories? The government has treacherously signed . . . To send the young and turbulent to the front? Turn the factory into a barracks? Are we meekly to give our lives under this iron heel so that a handful of parasites may prosper?' "

"A great job of writing, Gavrilovich. Whose is it?"

"I've got a young man worth his weight in gold. Nice pies, how did you manage to carry them? . . . So then, the ruling classes are making the job of overthrowing them so much the easier! 'In reply to the closing of the factories we call upon . . . while all those who have been thrown into the street . . . will . . . to the last man . . . ' "

A pity, yes, it was a good leaflet. But we'll be writing and printing plenty of others.

"Oh, yes. They're shitting themselves! Shit-scared, the whole crooked gang of them! Let's be honest about it, boys, we're putting the pressure on—but the whole caboodle is collapsing anyway!"

You see two men at a beer stall on the street corner, they plant their elbows on the counter, grip each other's hands, and each tries to bend the other's wrist, to see which hand will touch the counter first—and suddenly there's no contest: one of the hands has gone down without a struggle: Too weak? Owner too drunk? Wrist broken? . . .

He was giving way before the might of the working class—that midget of a Tsar named Nikolai II!!!

[6 4]

That Thursday would be his oldest daughter Olga's twenty-first birthday. Had she not been a Tsar's daughter she would probably have been married by now. But, imprisoned as she was by palace protocol and dynastic convention, she could form only imaginary attachments, which she concealed even from her mother. This was all the more necessary because she resented admonitions, sulked if she was chided, was the most obstinate of all four daughters, and at the same time volatile and unpredictable. What she found particularly tiresome was to be told how young ladies were taught to behave in times gone by: she was apt to flare up and answer back with a defiant stare. But her presence was striking: tall, with golden curls and blue eyes, she had been colonel in chief of one of the hussar regiments from the age of sixteen, and very proud of it, especially when she could ride out in hussar uniform. She was a quick learner, for that very reason indolent, and so not particularly well educated.

The Empress had long refused to recognize that her daughters were grown up, but even she could no longer deny that the two older ones were adults.

In whatever free time was left from her agonizing preoccupation with affairs of state and the ever-pressing need to write, communicate, receive visitors, give instructions, she thought hard and fearfully about her daughters' future. What fate awaited them? Whom were they destined to marry? To what foreign lands would they depart, never to return? Life was an enigma and the future was hidden behind a veil. Above all, would it be their good fortune to find the unquestioning and uninterrupted love which Aleksandra herself had now enjoyed with her angel Nicky for twenty-two years? Alas, such a love was becoming more and more of a rarity.

Then again—what sort of world would they be living in? Once the present war was over, would ideals exist, or would people remain the desiccated egoists they now were? What an age to live in! People's mental landscape changed continually. Machines and money were destroying art. There were no great writers, musicians, artists left in any country in the world, and those who were considered gifted showed symptoms of depravity.

There was another Olga in their inner family circle—the Emperor's sister. After years of entreaty she had finally been allowed to divorce the Duke of Oldenburg and was to marry his adjutant, a captain in the cuirassier regiment. They were to be married quietly that Friday, in a little church at Kiev, overlooking the Dnieper just where the image of the pagan god Perun had once stood. The Empress had serious misgivings about this marriage. There were already three ugly morganatic blots on the dynasty, and this was one more. But who did not long for private happiness? Who could have the heart to deny it to them?

The girls had been brought up by Aleksandra Fyodorovna herself—which was why for many years she had so little time to help the Emperor with his duties. In the small and modest court of Hesse she had been brought up to know the value of money, to be thrifty, and to make herself useful. She followed the same course with her daughters: garments and footwear were passed down from older to younger sister, and there was a limit to the number of toys allowed. This system was essential to the mental equilibrium of the Empress. (She herself was no slave to luxury. She could wear the same dresses for years on end and had to be reminded that she needed new ones.) Aleksandra Fyodorovna shielded her girls from friendship with the flighty daughters of the aristocracy, or with the other Grand Duchesses, their cousins and second cousins, whose upbringing seemed to her deplorable. (This created fresh fault lines of resentment within the dynasty.) She herself was skilled in various forms of needlework, had mastered the use of a sewing machine, and could embroider. She tried to pass on these skills to her daughters, and would not allow them to sit around doing nothing. Truth to tell, only Tatyana took it all in and was clever enough with her hands to become a good needlewoman. She made blouses for herself and her sisters, embroidered and knitted. She also often dressed her mother's hair, which was no easy task. She was always busy with something. In many ways she was like her mother: she was hardly ever naughty, she was reserved, proud, secretive, but she also knew better than the others how to make her authority felt and earned her nickname of "the little governess" by continually reminding her sisters of their mother's wishes. This patient, affectionate girl was born to be the consolation of her parents in old age.

The Empress had been surprised to find that in Russia upper-class young ladies were interested only in officers. She had tried setting up sewing circles in which matrons and young ladies would make things for the poor, but they had quickly lost interest and the circles had collapsed. The Empress's more successful initiatives included a school for children's nannies at Tsarskoye Selo, a home for veterans of the Japanese war in the palace park, where they were taught a trade, and a school of folk art in Petersburg, where girls from all over Russia were taught handicrafts. (She was guided partly by her belief that the strength of the throne was in the common people and that encouraging folk art would help her to know the country, the people, and the provinces more intimately, and to form a real union with them.) She built sanatoria for tuberculosis patients in the Crimea at her own expense, and organized bazaars for their benefit: she had stood for hours on her weak, swollen legs selling articles which she and her daughters had embroidered themselves.

As soon as this horrible war erupted the Empress busily set about organizing a network of medical facilities—field clinics, hospitals, and hospital trains—funding many of them herself, including the nearest, that inside the Great Palace at Tsarskoye Selo, known as "Her Majesty's Own Clinic." Olga presided over the Committee for Aid to Soldiers' Families, Tatyana over the Refugees' Committee. The Empress, her two older daughters, and Anya Vyrubova all attended special wartime courses for nurses, took lessons from a surgeon, and did their practical work as ordinary nurses in their own clinic, removing bloody bandages from the wounded, washing them, helping with dressings, assisting at operations: Aleksandra Fyodorovna even handed the surgeon his instruments, she was not afraid of blood, pus, or vomit, and was untroubled by the thought of losing for the moment her royal aureole. She learned to change bedding quickly, without disturbing patients, to prepare complicated dressings (and to put them on herself), and she was immensely proud when she earned her nurse's certificate and her Red Cross chevron.

Of the four of them, the haughty and capricious Anya got tired of hospital work first, and began begging off, but some six months later she was involved in an accident and landed in the hospital herself. The two girls had been working there regularly and seriously for over two years. Tanya had made particularly good progress—she was shortly due to administer chloroform herself for the first time. Aleksandra Fyodorovna genuinely liked helping the surgeons and dressing wounds, and was happy when she could do this work. It helped to settle her nerves. But she had been able to work to her own satisfaction only in the first year of the war, 1914, and for part of this summer. The limiting factor was her health. Long operations were sometimes too much for her legs. Sometimes she was bedridden—for four months on end last winter. She had been unable to visit the military hospital in the Great Palace even once. And, of course, she had several others to inspect—emergency hospitals set up in the most surprising places—banks, the auditoriums of theaters . . . Some of them were in other towns, and there were also hospital trains . . .

Above all, there was her son. Her only son's chronic illness. Aleksei's cruel disability had shown itself in his infancy. The joy which the birth of an heir had brought was shadowed almost at once by continual anxiety. Not only was the slightest cut dangerous to him, he only had to bump a hand or a foot against a piece of furniture and an enormous, livid swelling would show that he was bleeding internally. The little boy would have to spend several days lying down. His mother bathed him herself, never left the nursery, forgetting at times that she was still also the Tsaritsa. All children's games and high-spirited romps were forbidden him from the start: he could not ride a bicycle, or play tennis, or even run about. Every mother feels her child's pain as her own, every knock, every misstep he took hurt Aleksandra. Most agonizing of all was her unremitting awareness that she was to blame: without willing it, she had brought all these sufferings on him! She had known about this defect in her family: relatives of hers, her uncle, Queen Victoria's son, and her younger brother, had died of the disease. Several of her nephews also suffered from it. She had known, but to hope is human, and Aleksandra had hoped that it would miss her son. She had been punished for it—or, rather, her boy had been punished.

He had terrible experiences, and the most terrifying thing about them was that the best and most experienced doctors were sometimes at a loss and admitted their helplessness. But then the Holy Man had appeared. One touch, or at times a single look, a single word, from him sufficed and the boy would begin to get well again. His mother knew by now for sure that he only had to visit her son and her son would recover. Four years ago Aleksei had lost his footing jumping into a boat at Skierniewice, and had hovered between life and death for three weeks, lying with one leg raised up, unable to straighten it, crying out in pain. His face was shrunken, waxen, his little nose sharp, and the doctors, Fyodorov and Derevenko, were inclined to think that his condition was hopeless. The boy, although he was only eight years old, realized it himself and asked his mother to "put up a memorial to me in the park at Tsarskoye Selo when I die." All this was in Poland, and their Friend was in Siberia at the time They sent him a telegram, a last despairing cry for help, and he replied by telegram: "The illness is not as dangerous as it seems, do not let the doctors torment him." That was all! And as soon as the telegram arrived the Heir to the Throne began to recover! Surely it was a miracle?

Then, last autumn, Aleksei had gone with his father to GHQ (letting him go had filled her with dread, but she could not condemn the Emperor to the horrors of loneliness at GHQ), and while he was there his nose had started bleeding so persistently that the doctors could not stop it. The Emperor had to leave GHQ immediately and hurry back on the royal train. The little boy was brought home, his mother knelt at his bedside . . . but the hemorrhage continued, and could not be stanched, and it seemed certain that he would bleed to death! Then they sent for Grigori Efimovich. He entered the room, made a sweeping sign of the cross over the Heir, and said, "Don't be anxious— nothing more is needed!" and left. With that the bleeding stopped. (And there had been no major hemorrhage since.)

They knew now that what their Friend had told them was true: "If I am not near you the Heir will not live."

If this had all happened in Europe they would have been looking for doctors and super-doctors. (Aleksandra herself did not like the famous ones, and preferred the humble Evgeni Botkin to his eminent brother Sergei.) Everywhere on earth people are treated with whatever local remedy is available—polar lichens, wild herbs, waterweeds. In Russia there have always been itinerant holy men, "God's people." Peculiarly Russian, they are not necessarily priests but are nonetheless styled "elders" (like venerable monks). They are endowed with God's grace and the Lord pays special heed to their prayers. It was a holy man of this sort, an "elder," whom Orthodox Russia, the simple Russian people, had sent to save their son, and so perhaps the throne itself. What was the point of being an Orthodox Tsar if you did not commune with and heed such men from the depths of the people? The royal couple had found him immediately after their first Friend, Monsieur Philippe. The Montenegrin sisters, Grand Duchesses both, had invited the Empress to their home to meet the man of God. She had taken one look and believed in him at once. There was nothing in his appearance, nothing at all, that could possibly be thought contrived or bogus. He was tall, very tall, with a slight stoop. He wore a Russian blouse, and high Russian boots. His pale face was gaunt, emaciated even, his blue-gray eyes piercing, searching, compelling, his eyebrows shaggy tufts, his hair untidily plastered down. There was about him an iconlike austerity and an assured strength. It was his self-assurance that particularly impressed her. His utterances were those of one with authority. It was as if a figure in a village painter's picture had come to life: a picture of a holy man, a man of the people, not a symbolic figure, not a generalized abstraction, but a living human being. You could reach out and touch him, you could listen to him, and when he spoke the fact that he was semi-literate only made his speech the more vivid, made what he said more extraordinary than anything the Empress had ever heard, so interesting were his stories, so spiritually profound his thoughts. He knew a great deal of scripture, had walked all over Russia on his own two feet, had visited many monasteries, great and small. He had educated himself by prayer and fasting—meat and dairy products he no longer ate at all.

Frequent meetings over the years had made the Empress more and more certain that he was indeed chosen by God to save their threatened dynasty. The power of his prayer was vast, and effective not only in restoring the Heir to health. It had saved the lives of many soldiers at the front, the lives of all those he had prayed for. His prayers protected the Emperor himself on all his travels. During the war, the Empress had kept their Friend informed in advance of the Emperor's movements, the secret routes he would be following, so that his blessing would be accurately oriented and reach its goal more surely. She sought his blessing on every journey the Emperor undertook. When the royal couple visited hostile Odessa their Friend had prayed so hard that he scarcely had time for sleep. But it went much further than that. His voice was tirelessly raised in prayer and benediction, by night and by day, blessing all Orthodox warriors, calling on the heavenly host to be with them, summoning angels to fight in the ranks of Russia's soldiers. When the situation at the front was particularly serious, or a great offensive was planned, as now, on the Southwestern front, the Empress would reveal to him the General Staff's latest orders, so that he could reflect on them and pray. Last winter he had been very annoyed when they launched an attack without consulting him. He would have advised delay, telling them that he was continually praying and trying to decide when the right moment would come, to avoid squandering lives to no purpose as Brusilov had done. He always advised them not to be forever on the offensive: if they were more patient less blood would be spilled. When our forces were held up by persistent mists Anya sent a telegram to their Friend asking for sunny weather (and he promised it in his answering telegram from Siberia). He gave presents of religious pictures and icons to the Emperor himself and every member of his family, and that summer, when the Empress visited GHQ, he had sent an icon to General Alekseev. (Provided that Alekseev had accepted it sincerely, in the appropriate frame of mind, God would undoubtedly bless his military labors.) And even when they were considering whether or not to grant Olga, the Tsar's sister, permission to divorce, it was to their Friend that the Empress first turned for advice.

She always felt more troubled when he left for Siberia, more at ease when he was in Petrograd and she could send messages through Anya and ask his advice. Whenever something was done against his wishes Aleksandra's heart bled. She felt frustrated—and afraid.

Such a gift of words he had! What lovely telegrams he sent! What courage, what wisdom they imparted!

"No matter what is used to cut down the impious tree, it falls just the same. St. Nicholas is with you and his miraculous manifestation always works miracles."

"The well is deep and their ropes are too short."

"In tribulation joy is more radiant. The Church is invincible."

"An evil tongue is worthless, praise is of little worth, there is joy beside the throne."

"God's light is over you, let us not fear the insignificant."

"You must never be too worried. God will help you anyway."

"Be holy, as I am holy."

It was difficult to reproduce the things he said, words were powerless, you had to respond to the spiritual fervor that went with them, the fervor that suffused his reminiscences of Palestine. And how generously he gave to the poor! Every kopeck he received went to them. He was as greathearted, as kind to all men as was Christ himself. Many bishops, even, looked up to him. (The Empress was dreadfully displeased when some people called him simply "Rasputin." She was trying to break her intimates of the habit.)

What happiness it was when they could also make use of the advice and wide experience of the man sent by God in the business of government, receive with gratitude the fruits of his spiritual vision, and invoke his blessing at every step they took. Aleksandra had read in a certain French book that "the state cannot perish if its ruler is guided by a man of God."

Their Friend spent his nights not in sleep but in getting ready to advise the Emperor. He could peer into the distant future, and his judgment could therefore be relied on. He told them that they must always do as he said, for such was the wish of the Lord God. How many sober and sound counsels he had given over the years! He had urged them not to intervene in the Bosnian conflict: things had to be put in order at home. He had gone down on his knees to the Emperor to restrain him from entering the Balkan war: their enemies were only too eager for Russia to get bogged down there. He had also tried to hold them back from this present dreadful conflict: the Balkans were not worth a World War, and Serbia would prove ungrateful. He might have prevailed if he had not been lying wounded in Siberia. (Even so, he had sent telegrams urging restraint, but the Emperor had angrily rejected them.) He had advised against marching to Serbia through Romania, against calling up category 2 reservists, or men over forty, but had recommended drafting Tartars as well as Russians, after carefully explaining the situation to them. The Emperor should not visit Lvov and Peremyshl—it was too early: and as it turned out, shortly after his visit he was humiliated by having to surrender them. So many things would have gone better in this war if they had always listened to their Friend's advice! He it was who had suggested organizing a day of prayer and religious processions throughout the land—and soon afterward the recoil of the Russian armies had been halted. He again, having no faith in Nikolasha, bade the Emperor assume Supreme Command himself, and never surrender it to others who knew less than he did. On a number of occasions he had opposed the convocation of the Duma—and that body had never done any good. When it was convened in February 1915 he had advised the Emperor to put in an unexpected appearance and so disarm the deputies. He constantly warned them that a government answerable to the Duma would spell ruin. Again, it had been his idea to publish information on the waste of government funds by Zemgor (the Empress's heart ached when she thought how much more good the state itself could have done with a quarter of that sum). God had inspired all these salutary ideas of his. Again, because he remained close to the common people Grigori saw many things with their eyes, and gave valuable advice accordingly—as, for instance, not to raise streetcar fares from five to ten kopecks; not to prevent wounded soldiers from using streetcars; to order bakers' shops to weigh bread in advance, so that people need not stand in line; to bring firewood into the city by water before the first frosts set in.

Their Friend confidently predicted that the glorious days of the reign were at hand. Happier times were coming, and the war would soon take a turn for the better. He joyfully persuaded the Empress that her appearance, and that of the Heir at the front, brought good fortune to the troops, and accordingly bade her visit GHQ to review the troops, and also provincial towns and hospitals, more frequently. The Empress felt ashamed that she was unable, in return for their Friend's blessing and for the light and joy he brought into their lives, to grant his own small request: not to take his son, a category 2 reservist, into the army, or, if there was no avoiding it, to enlist him in the Combined Guards Regiment formed to protect the Tsarskoye Selo palace.

But to take full advantage of their Friend's wisdom regular communication with him was necessary—by letter, by telegram (or by the newest medium, the telephone). He also had to be seen frequently. This, however, was not at all simple for the royal couple. To associate with him too openly would invite the ridicule and malice of high society, and of educated people generally. Shunning publicity, they had to meet their Friend discreetly, and as far as possible in secret, to prevent all those tongues from wagging. A Tsar does not live the life of a free man. He is much more restricted than his subjects. He has no right to intimate relationships. Every request for an audience goes through a chain of courtiers who will probably let the whole world know about it. So when, several times a year, the royal couple received Grigori Efimovich at home in the palace, he was ushered not into the big official reception room, but by a side entrance into the Empress's study. (The servants knew, of course, and there might have been less gossip if she had received him in the grandest of the staterooms.) They would kiss three times, in the Russian fashion, and sit down to talk. It was always in the evening, and Aleksei would come along in his little blue dressing gown to keep them company until his bedtime. They talked a great deal about his health, and about the royal couple's other worries. They also discussed the Divine, and their Friend filled them with hope, and entertained them with stories about Siberia. (In fact, he felt offended: he longed to be received openly. It gratified his pride when the royal couple had the courage to send telegrams directly, and not through Anya.)

The Empress did not invite their Friend to the palace in the Emperor's absence. People were such unbelievably vicious gossips. (They had, for instance, concocted a slanderous tale about Grigori Efimovich which no one in his right mind could possibly believe: he was supposed to have been appointed by the Cathedral Church of St. Theodore to light the icon lamps—in every room of the palace.)

She needed to see him and to question him frequently—in the terrible last year it had been almost every other day, and there was no other choice but to meet in Anya's "little house," a separate establishment, but still in Tsarskoye Selo. Sometimes it was at her request, sometimes he summoned her. She would try to get there unnoticed, and he might be accompanied by his wife, or his daughters, when they came from Siberia to visit him. The Emperor himself had been known to go there, when their Friend urgently needed to see him, and the Empress occasionally visited him in Anya's absence. They also invited potential ministers along for him to get to know them better, or their Friend might bring some bishop or other with him. The conversation would always be both edifying and soothing. Sometimes their Friend would come to see the Empress at the hospital. Such were the subterfuges forced on royalty by spiteful and suspicious eyes. He might inform the press that he was leaving for Siberia—and then stay put. Whenever she visited GHQ the Empress had to receive their Friend's blessing first. She would have refused to leave without it. In Lent this year their Friend had taken communion in the same church and at the same time as the whole royal family.

But calumny was the life breath of the world in which she lived. Listen to the slander and lies they spread about that Holy Man, and he was the greatest of evildoers. Even the Empress's sister believed these slanders—and they had parted forever as a result: our Friend's enemies are our own enemies. (The Empress had even banished the Tsar's onetime confessor, Bishop Teofan, for the same offense.) He had inevitably become the victim of envy on the part of those who had hoped and failed to draw near to the throne. Like every saint, he had to suffer for righteousness' sake—suffer above all from calumny. People came to hate him, and bespattered him with lies. One slanderous tale was that he was a drunkard—he who would not even drink milk! The Holy Elder was called a debauchee and a lecher, the royal family themselves were supposedly involved in his debauches, and these filthy slanderers went so far as to say that he had the entrée to the bedrooms of the young Grand Duchesses! They had fabricated a police report on an alleged brawl in a restaurant, which had supposedly led to the dismissal of the head of the Corps of Gendarmes. If anything of the sort had happened, why hadn't the police been called immediately, to catch him red-handed? True, our Friend kisses everyone, men and women alike, as people did in olden days. Read the apostles—their usual greeting was a kiss. (The Empress's faith had been shaken, briefly, only once, when she read the letters written by the embittered

Iliodor after his dismissal: annoyed with herself, she had quickly rejected stories which at first sight had looked plausible.) To cap it all they had accused the Man of God of links with the Germans! There was no limit to their malice and stupidity, though they were a great help to the revolutionaries.

The Empress had nevertheless sent Anya to Grigori's native village, Pokrovskoye, beyond Tyumen, to check up on him. She was able to confirm their best assumptions: the village fished with nets like the apostles, chanting psalms and prayers the while. Huge icons hung around the walls of the two-story cottage. True, the local priest disliked Grigori—that was to be expected—and his fellow villagers did not think that he was in any way out of the ordinary.

The Empress had given a great deal of thought to their Friend. A prophet is, of course, always without honor in his own country. Wherever there is a servant of the Lord the Evil One lurks to instill his venom. Our Friend lives for his sovereign, and for Russia, and endures all slanders for our sake. So many of his prayers have already been answered! Russia will be deprived of God's blessing if we allow the man whom God has sent to aid us, the man who prays for us unceasingly, to become the victim of persecution in our country. God would not forgive us for our weakness. Whenever they step up their attack on him the state's fortunes take a turn for the worse! Let them all rise up against you, I shall never abandon you!

During the past year, since the Emperor had been spending more time at GHQ, and she had to manage in Petersburg alone, their Friend had actively helped her to choose ministers and to give them guidance. To assess a man's worth immediately is the thorniest of problems, the heaviest of burdens, and sometimes the curse of those in the royal trade. But their Friend possessed this skill in full measure. He had long, pleasant, and fruitful talks with Stürmer (and ordered him to report to the Empress weekly), he had dined with the Finance Minister, and with the Minister of Trade and Industry. (They were getting more used to the idea that Grigori had to be consulted on important matters.) On one occasion, to decide whether Khvostov (the uncle) was a suitable replacement for Goremykin (how could they find out? How could they get a close look at him?) it was their Friend's idea to approach him in the guise of an ordinary petitioner and size him up in that way. He did so, and found the man unsuitable.

She was so accustomed to consulting their Friend on the choice of ministers that she sometimes sought his advice on the appointment of a city governor. He had approved of the Moscow governor. But with Obolensky's appointment as governor of Petrograd there was a hitch. The incident demonstrated Grigori Efimovich's goodness of heart and his spiritual responsiveness. He had been the first to urge dismissal of this particular governor, on the grounds that he was causing great hardship to the population, was completely mishandling the provisioning of the city, and was responsible for the bread queues. True, Obolensky had never shown hostility toward Grigori, which made it painful to call for his resignation, but the well-being of Petrograd demanded it. Perhaps he could be transferred to a provincial governorship somewhere? But then Obolensky invited Grigori to dinner, showed his guest, list in hand, that he always carried out his requests, wept copiously—and Grigori Efimovich departed deeply moved. In a spiritual sense it meant a great deal that a man with such a soul had come over to him without reserve. That man must not be demoted, but appointed governor-general of Finland, which was his dearest wish, or else Vice-Minister of the Interior.

The defense of their Friend, which she saw as her highest duty, was sometimes uppermost in the Empress's thoughts about the Duma—if they were left sitting there too long with nothing to do they would start talking about him, or about Archbishop Varnava of Tobolsk, who had been appointed at his request. And she always considered his interests in her choice of ministers. (Last year's contingent, forced on them by Nikolasha, were a bunch of contemptible cowards, and all of them hostile.) The Empress's ambition was to produce a unified cabinet in which the ministers to a man would support their Friend and heed his advice. The need to protect their Friend from persecution, attacks, and unpleasantness influenced the choice of the Procurator-General of the Holy Synod in particular: persecution of their Friend and those bishops who supported him by other churchmen was only to be expected (and particularly dangerous). The quest for suitable candidates made the Empress's head ache. Samarin was insufferable, but it took them a long time to find someone to replace him. There was no one! Their first choice was Volzhin (and their Friend approved him), but no sooner was he appointed than he showed himself to be a coward in his dealings with the Duma, and in awe of public opinion. He had not dared to help Metropolitan Pitirim, or even to rusticate that swine Archbishop Nikon of Vologda. As long as Volzhin was there, church business would never go smoothly—he had proved completely incapable of understanding it. Pitirim had written to the Empress to tell her what should be done, and she had informed the Emperor, so that he could give Volzhin his orders. Then they were lucky enough to find Rayev, a splendid person and one familiar with matters ecclesiastical from his childhood. Stürmer praised him highly, and when the Empress received him he made an excellent impression. He was given Zhevakov as his assistant, and together they would be a real boon to the Church. There was no longer any resistance to the things the Church needed to do. Above all, the metropolitans must be "our" people: Pitirim was transferred from Georgia to Petrograd, Makari from Tomsk to Moscow, and Vladimir, who had done his best to harm all "our" people, was transferred to Kiev, the best place for him. All just as their Friend had wished. To reinforce Pitirim's position, the Empress arranged a special trip for him to GHQ to see the Emperor. The priest Melchisedek was elevated to a bishopric, and their Friend destined him for a metropolitan archbishopric some time in the future. Varnava, of course, still had opponents in the Synod—animals, there was no other word for them. The Synod was still unruly and likely at any moment to produce some bombshell, like its decision to establish seven archbishoprics in Russia instead of the existing three. The Synod got as far as publishing this, but then their Friend objected: how can we agree to seven of them, when even now we can scarcely muster three decent metropolitans? The Empress succeeded in quashing the decision.

And then the agonizing search to find Russia a worthy Prime Minister! There was no such person. The Empress often exclaimed, "Lord God, where in Russia can we find the people we need?" She could never understand why, in such a great country, you could not find suitable candidates for every post. You could sometimes feel bitterly disappointed in the Russian people. Now that the Emperor had left for GHQ, and was fully occupied with military matters, it had become more and more obvious that Goremykin was getting weaker, and that the job would prove too much for him. The Duma detested him, and there was reason to fear that it would hiss him off the stage. The Empress spent her sleepless nights agonizing over every possible candidate for the post, then discussed them with their Friend. In the end they had hit upon Stürmer. He was loyal (loyal also to their Friend!) and his head was still uncluttered. Could they risk appointing someone with a German name? He had a high opinion of Grigori, which was very important. At any rate, he would do for the present, and if the Emperor decided someone younger was needed he could be replaced. The Emperor agreed, but then Stürmer himself took fright, and asked permission to change his name to "Panin," his mother's name. Both their Friend and the Empress vigorously opposed it. If people objected to his name—let them! There would be objections whoever was appointed. Dozens, no, hundreds of loyal servants of the crown had already been dismissed in the ludicrous campaign against German surnames—and where were suitable replacements to be found? Stürmer's first action as Prime Minister was to declare that Russia would not lay down her arms until she and her allies together had emerged victorious. And for all the raving of the liberal and revolutionary riffraff, he had now presided over the cabinet satisfactorily for nine months.

Choosing a Minister of the Interior had been a more tragic experience. One candidate, Makarov, had previously served in the post after Stolypin, and had valuable experience, but was completely disqualified by his behavior in the Iliodor scandal. What is more, he had not only failed to stand up for the Empress, but had dishonestly shown her letter to outsiders and was in fact hostile to her. (Unfortunately, he had nonetheless been appointed that summer to the Ministry of Justice—no good could come of that.) The Emperor had to explain to the new Minister of Justice as soon as he was appointed that if he persecuted their Friend himself, or even allowed people to write or say disgusting things about him, it would be as if he were acting directly against the royal couple.

Khvostov (the nephew) had enchanted them to begin with, and they had appointed him to Internal Affairs, but what a grievous error it was, alas how easy it was to be mistaken in people! What was wanted was a man of resolute character, someone who was utterly unafraid of leftists. Their Friend, and Anya, had interviewed him first, and praised him highly. He had then successfully sought an audience with the Empress. She had looked forward eagerly to seeing him, and when she saw and heard him she was greatly impressed! This was a man, not an old woman, one who would not allow anything to hurt them. For the Emperor he was ready to be cut into little pieces. He believed in the Empress's wisdom. He would stand up for their Friend and allow no gratuitous reference to him. He had a Russian name, he was a member of the Duma and so knew them all, how to talk to them, and how to defend the government. He was confident that he had the skill and good sense to put things right. He would prevent the publication of misleading articles. Working with him would be sheer delight! He was remarkably clever. A good speaker. The Empress urged her husband not to hesitate to make this young man a minister. The Emperor, as it turned out, was against him, but took him nonetheless on her insistence. Only later, much later, did the Empress, desperately disillusioned, recall that she had felt certain misgivings, wondered whether the candidate was perhaps too sure of himself, and whether in some contexts he might not be less than loyal. Meanwhile, something dreadful had happened: the devil had entered into Khvostov, and he had abruptly changed, he had not only turned against their Friend but had accused his circle of espionage, and asked the Emperor's permission to exile him to Siberia. For five terrible months, while Khvostov was still in power, with the police and money at his disposal, the Empress had seriously feared for the lives of their Friend and Anya. When Khvostov was dismissed, the Empress and their Friend had felt that this was too lenient, that he should have been stripped of his embroidered uniform and put on trial. (Grigori's wrath was fearful to behold—she had never seen him like that before!)

After this sad setback the Empress had become apathetic, and in the early months of 1916 intervened very little in state affairs. Her confidence in her own judgment was shaken. But after a while she returned to the fray. How could she refrain from intervening? You would have to be mindless, soulless, heartless, not to grieve over what was happening in Russia. Events did not stand still, but demanded action—and whether she liked it or not the responsibility fell on her while the Emperor was at GHQ. Many ministers, the best of them, sought audience with her, while the poorer ones had to be eased out. How would she ever find for every office people who would carry out her instructions? The search for a Minister of War had given them a great deal of trouble. The sarcastic Polivanov, a friend of Guchkov and a traitor, and also the choice of the old General Staff, could not remain in office! (Now *there* was your traitor—not Sukhomlinov!) Replacing Polivanov would clip the revolutionary party's wings at once! It must be done quickly—for the sake of the throne, for their son's sake, for Russia's sake! But month after month went by and they could not find a successor. Shuvaev, the replacement dreamt up by GHQ with the Emperor present, was someone of whom the Empress could not possibly approve: she doubted whether he could cope with the duties of the office—making a statement in the Duma, for instance. Their Friend, and the Empress herself, pressed the claims of the highly respected elderly General Ivanov—now there was a man with both experience and authority, the Duma's hearts would undoubtedly go out to "Granddad" Ivanov. But the Emperor kept Ivanov on at GHQ, with nothing at all to do, and refused to make him minister. The Empress then began insisting with renewed fervor on the candidate she had most favored in Polivanov's time, the meticulously efficient Belyaev. (She knew him from one of her Committees of Trustees, on which he had never created difficulties.) That would have been a sensible choice. Transferred from staff work and given ministerial independence he would be very good. He was so hardworking, and such an absolute gentleman, he had answered the English King and Lord Kitchener so cleverly, as a member of the Russian delegation. Besides, she knew his old mother. He would never think of attacking their Friend. But alas, instead of promoting him the Emperor had for some reason relieved him of his post as Chief of the General Staff and had now sent him off to Romania somewhere. But the Empress went on hoping that she would finally prevail, and that this noble general would become Russia's War Minister in a very short time.

Amazingly, even with their Friend's advice, the selection of ministers was very far from satisfactory. It was such a difficult task! (Because ministers, of course, had to be not just ministers but friends!) She had first asked the Tsar to appoint Naumov Minister of Agriculture, and then herself requested his dismissal when he did not live up to expectations. She had doubted whether Bark was a good Minister of Finance (many sensible people were against him) and suggested Count Tatishchev as a replacement, but had then backed down, perhaps rightly.

She had insisted on dismissing Rukhlov from Communications, because of his age, but again with unfortunate consequences: Aleksandr Trepov was appointed without their Friend's opinion being sought, and turned out to be his enemy. (She remembered now that she herself had found him rather off-putting!) Then Count Ignatiev, at Education, had seemed at first a decent sort, but was too much a popularity seeker, with his liberal speeches in the Duma. All in all, he too was unsuitable, and must be removed. But their longest campaign had been to make Sazonov's position at the Ministry of Foreign Affairs untenable. Ever since the ministerial revolt last year they had detested that long-nosed nuisance, that uncongenial mischief maker, but could find no diplomat with a wide enough knowledge of foreign countries to replace him. Finally, their patience had snapped, and in July during one of the Empress's visits to GHQ, they had dismissed Sazonov and simply passed his portfolio to Stürmer: there was no question of visiting other countries during the war anyway. But it was because of this that they had let Makarov into the cabinet, as Minister of Justice, and transferred Internal Affairs from Stürmer to Khvostov (the uncle). He hated both Stürmer and their Friend, but there had been no real opportunity to dismiss him. He had finally left of his own accord, when the Police Department was removed from his control.

Their Ministers of the Interior were, it seemed, a punishment inflicted by fate. She would have been finally reduced to despair, but for Grigori's bright idea: he had recommended, in September, the gifted Protopopov, whom he had known for years, and spoken so warmly of him that the Empress was persuaded before she had even seen the man. Here was someone who would paralyze and silence the Duma! Truly, in his person God had sent them a real man!

Protopopov seemed to complete a well-balanced and harmonious cabinet (with only Belyaev missing, and a few minor adjustments to be made). From early autumn onward everything appeared to be going well, and no crisis was expected. All year round Stürmer had regularly visited the Empress to report, requesting audience through Anya, and he was only too glad when she traveled to GHQ in his place. His confidence in her was simply touching. The Empress was gradually training the other ministers too—the older Khvostov, Count Bobrinsky, Prince Shakhovskoy, Bark, even Grigorovich, the Navy man, to come and report to her. Some of them even addressed their requests for audience with the Emperor to her. The Empress set herself the task of making them work as a team, she even pressed Shakhovskoy and Bobrinsky to cooperate with Protopopov. And she was stubborn enough to get her way.

The food shortage made this particularly important. Cunning Krivoshein had created confusion by annexing responsibility for the food supply to what was then his own Ministry of Agriculture, where there was no specialist staff (only a lot of supporters of left-wing parties), whereas the Ministry of the Interior had staff in every province, and their Friend had long ago insisted on making these people responsible for grain collection. He had long been worried that a shortage of food-stuffs in Petrograd would lead to disturbances and other unpleasant-ness. And anyway, it was shameful to make the poor people suffer! It humiliated Russia in the eyes of the Allies! We have plenty of every-thing—it's just that they won't bring it to market, they've let prices rise out of reach, they've made a complete muddle, above all by pro-hibiting export and import of grain between provinces, and by forcing the peasants to surrender their grain. A month ago, prompted by the Empress, Protopopov and Bobrinsky (Agriculture) had sent a joint cir-cular to all governors, urging them to observe extreme caution in using measures of coercion. Protopopov had said, with fervent conviction, that "when evil people want to ensure success they always appeal to the people, and the people listens to them. We must do the same: send around people to explain to the peasants why they should not hold back their grain. And the peasants will obey them!" Protopopov had seemed quite prepared for his ministry to take full responsibility for the matter—but for some reason, had started dragging his feet in the last few days.

His meeting with leading members of the Duma in a private apart-ment ten days earlier had given him a terrible shock. Those scoundrels not only had no further wish to cooperate with their former colleague now that he was a servant of the throne, they even had the imperti-nence to demand his resignation. After the meeting he had rushed to see their Friend in a state of extreme agitation. As it happened, the Emperor was at home in Tsarskoye Selo for the first time in five months, and Grigori, no less agitated himself, telegraphed directly, not through Anya, which would have taken longer.

> Heart-to-heart talk with Kalinin they order him resign he be-side himself firmness God's pedestal Grigori Novy.

(All correspondence passed through other hands. The imperial couple had no privacy. They were so tightly hemmed in by watchful eyes that they were obliged, like underground revolutionaries, to use safe pseu-donyms. Thus their Friend called Protopopov "Kalinin" in letters and telegrams. Grigori himself had, with permission from on high, long ago exchanged his hateful surname Rasputin for "Novy.")

Needless to say, Protopopov would not be surrendered to them—but what villains they were! Members of the gang reared their heads in many different places, but especially in the Unions of Zemstvos and Towns—shameless wretches, living at the state's expense, but acting solely against the government! Though hers was no longer a young head Aleksandra sometimes had ideas in the course of her agonizing sleepless nights. Organize propaganda against Zemgor at the front!

Organize surveillance of its agents, and send packing all those—doctors, paramedics, and nurses especially—who filled the soldiers' ears with all sorts of pernicious nonsense! Protopopov must find good, honest people to keep watch.

Mischief no less serious was brewing in Guchkov's War Industry Committees, politically no less dangerous than Zemgor. They were supposedly concerned only with supplies, but the agenda at their meetings often amounted to a direct attack on the dynasty. It was the same with the so-called Committees on Price Inflation, which served only to inflame antigovernment feeling. Guchkov, Rodzyanko, and the rest of the scoundrelly Duma deputies were intriguing to wrest as many matters as possible out of ministerial hands, and to make it look as if only they themselves were capable of working effectively. Guchkov had been seriously ill last winter. Because her concern was for the throne and the good of all Russia there was nothing at all sinful in the Empress's wish to see him depart for the next world. Alas, he had recovered. And now he was trying to stir the passions of the Supreme Commander's Chief of Staff, filling him with all sorts of vile allegations, trying to win him over—and Alekseev, always too trusting, might end up in the net of that clever scoundrel.

Now they had all attacked at once! Look what they had thought up for the opening of the Duma: that abominable declaration, not unexpected, thanks to Krupensky: he had attended their meeting, then brought that obscene piece of paper to Protopopov. The Empress also had received him to express her gratitude. The odious piece of paper proved to be undisguisedly revolutionary in character, replete with grotesque and shameless declarations: for instance, that they could not work with the ministers (whether the ministers could work with them was what they ought to worry about). Stürmer was most alarmed, afraid of what might happen at the forthcoming Duma sittings. The Empress, on the contrary, was always able to triumph over her ailments in such circumstances and to steel herself: we are at war with the Duma and we must be firm. How can we respond? After careful consideration it was decided not to suspend the Duma if it misbehaved too seriously, but to dissolve it outright pending the next elections in 1917. That would give them something to think about.

Only five days had passed since the Emperor's departure from Tsarskoye Selo, but so much had happened and there was so much to be done!

When she had seen Protopopov just three days ago he had nothing new to say. But yesterday he had urgently requested a meeting and had arrived looking extremely agitated. He was as svelte and light and ethereal as ever, and his quick eyes and mobile features even more eloquent. This time they expressed penitence and despair: he had just seen their Friend and their Friend had explained to him why his reluctance to take over responsibility for the food supply was completely mistaken. Now he was convinced and ready to take it over. But with only two days to go before the opening of the Duma, it ought to be announced in advance—could they hope to obtain the Emperor's signature from Mogilev in good time?

His agitation affected the Empress. She had long been thinking along the same lines and had been surprised by Protopopov's temporizing. Now that their Friend had spoken so firmly, what further doubt could there be? She acted with lightning speed. The day was half over, but in what was left of 12 November, Stürmer would have time to draft a decree transferring full responsibility for the food supply to the Minister of the Interior, effective immediately. The Empress herself rushed a letter to her husband explaining matters. If they sent it by courier that evening it would be in Mogilev on the morning of the 13th. And if she asked the Emperor to sign without delay and return the decree by the four-thirty train from Mogilev it would be back in Petrograd on the morning of the 14th, two or three hours before the Duma met! She had plenty of time! Provided only that the Tsar got back to Mogilev from his visit to Kiev by the evening of the 12th, according to plan. With God's help it will be so, and we will be in time!

The Empress herself was greatly stimulated by this operation: she liked resolute action. The weather was dull and depressing, with a sprinkling of rain in the air, but she had overcome her depression by acting effectively. One should always act energetically and speedily, and head off the enemy! She looked sympathetically at Protopopov as his too expressive features gradually relaxed. (She thought he looked honest, upright, pure.) He was a newcomer to the Council of Ministers, and needed strong support when the Duma baited him. The Empress had already asked the Emperor not to receive other ministers at Mogilev, but to communicate with them through Protopopov. This would greatly improve his standing and strengthen his position, while he would be able to share his plans with the Emperor and seek advice.

"Oh, yes," she said, remembering, "they tell me there have been disturbances of some sort at factories in the city."

"Nothing special, Your Majesty." Protopopov smiled enchantingly, as usual, while meaning to look adamant. "We have firm hands, we will keep them in order."

Good enough, but Stürmer's suggestion shortly after he took office back in March had been sound: it would be sensible to militarize the munitions factories and treat the workers as if they were army conscripts—then there would be no more strikes. (But the industrialists and the Kadets had stood in the way, said it would be trampling freedom underfoot.)

Protopopov departed, but action had left the Tsaritsa pleasantly excited, and the feeling remained with her until late in the evening. God willing, everything would be in one pair of firm hands and Protopopov would put an end to the Unions of Zemstvos and Towns. Their Friend would help him, and point the way. The Duma, of course, would be furious: it would want to split management of the food supply among a dozen pairs of hands and create confusion.

Then the Minister of Industry, Prince Shakhovskoy, took the wind out of her sails. She received him thinking she could rely on his loyalty, but he displayed his disrespect for Stürmer and his disapproval of Protopopov, and prophesied that they would have to go. To think that there was such disharmony inside the cabinet itself! The Empress listened unsympathetically and dismissed him ungraciously.

She attended a concert in her hospital, and knew when she returned that she was as usual condemned to a sleepless night. Five hours of unbroken sleep amounted to a holiday for her. It was always better with Nicky. It was during his absences that insomnia tormented her most. There were many nights when she lost consciousness for a mere two hours just before dawn. Some nights—there had been one such three days ago—she slept for a mere half hour. These sleepless nights meant that Aleksandra Fyodorovna's permanent exhaustion and listlessness aggravated her numerous ailments—the list would run into dozens: every known variety of migraine, neuralgia, cardiac disorder, lumbago, from time to time hellish headaches, dizziness, dyspnea, palpitations, enlargement of the heart, cyanosis of the hands, kidney stones, swelling of the face when the weather changed, inflammation of the trigeminal nerve, failing vision (the result, she said, wryly, of unshed tears), a pain in her eye as though she had stuck a pencil in it, pains in her jaw, inflammation of the periosteum, numbness all over her body, back pains, colds, coughs, bruises from falling down. Last year, 1915, she had begun with three months in bed. This year she had never been free from illness, and at any given moment had four or five ailments. Regularly, three or four times a year, she suffered total collapse. After a sleepless night, exhausted and racked with pain, she was unable to rise before midday. She would lie in bed with closed eyes for a time, then continue her repose on the sofa. She would lie on her side, put on her spectacles, and write with one of her fountain pens her interminable daily letter to the Emperor, trying to make up for the lack of contact while they were so far apart. She could never say anything in a few words, she always needed a ream of paper. After lunch in bed around midday she would rise, because audiences had been arranged, or she had to visit a hospital, her own or some other (where she would be carried upstairs in an armchair because her own legs could not manage steps), the rapid motion in a carriage would give her palpitations, and she would always have to dose herself with drops for her heart and with many other medicines, undergo massages and rubs, electrotherapy of the facial nerves, and, when she was alone, swathe her head in a thick shawl and avoid direct sunlight, much as she loved it.

Yesterday, again, she had spent lying down, exhausted, her nerves in shreds—and that night she had slept hardly at all. All these sleepless nights were filled with winged thoughts, they raced past, dragging her sick body after them, aged beyond its forty-five years, thoughts sometimes proudly soaring, sometimes mercilessly clawing her breast. During those sleepless nights she had many ideas about affairs of state. But by morning her head would be wearier than ever and, with no relief from sleeplessness to be had, the whole world looked black and hopeless.

But she must never give in! Must she believe that evil people would seize control of the earth? Why, when bad people actively fight for their cause, should good people merely complain, sit with arms folded and await events? No! Although the Empress was permanently and seriously ill, although her heart functioned badly, she could not sit still and watch what was happening, she could always summon up more energy than the whole clique of them together!

The summer of 1915 was the most terrible time of all. The struggle in progress was in reality a struggle for the throne itself. Their Friend had revealed this to them, but it had cost a great deal of effort to make the Emperor accept it. In the Duma wagers had been made that the Emperor would be prevented from assuming Supreme Command, and then that he would not be allowed to dissolve the Duma. That summer the Empress had intervened more insistently than ever, until her strength failed her and she was so weary at heart that she just wanted to sleep and forget the daily nightmare. But this was also when her interventions were most successful. Everybody was against it, droning voices all around warned that if the Emperor took over GHQ there would be a revolution. Only their Friend and the Empress insisted that he must take over. And they were proved right. But the direct result of their victory was that once the Tsar had left for GHQ they could no longer be constantly at his side, helping him to stand fast. Alone at GHQ he was always likely to relax his hold: he was surrounded by outsiders and he gave in to them. Ought he perhaps to come home more often? The military situation did not permit it. Perhaps the Empress should go there more frequently? (She would gladly have moved to GHQ altogether.) Again, the situation did not permit it. Besides, it was only too annoyingly obvious to the public that the Emperor's most important decisions, on appointments and dismissals among other things, were taken when his wife was visiting. She could only do her best to carry conviction in the long letters she wrote daily, repeating the same thoughts, differently worded, over and over again. Sometimes her advice prevailed, sometimes it was too late, sometimes it had no effect: mild, gentle, affectionate Nicky could be stubborn. But Nicky had faith in her, and entrusted many important discussions, and the task of receiving ministers, to her.

She relayed their Friend's advice to the Emperor without demur, and understood much of it herself. But as she looked more deeply into things, her mind expanded—she had spontaneous ideas of her own, and slipped them into her letters. She was, for instance, very worried about separate Latvian regiments—this was a force which could be difficult to control, and she thought it would be safer to disband them and disperse the men among other regiments. She saw the need for a special militia, to be kept in reserve for use if there were disorders in Petrograd: the police were not trained to deal with such things, and were not even armed. She suggested sending members of the Emperor's personal staff to factories to watch developments and to make people feel that the Tsar, and not just Guchkov's bullyboys, had eyes everywhere. But the Tsar's suite had grown fat and lazy, and not one of them traveled anywhere. She realized that they had handled the State Council badly. They had appointed to it the very people they wanted to be rid of: the throne was helping to undermine itself. (The President of the Council must be replaced.) They could further reinforce their support by raising the salaries of poorly paid officials all over the country. She asked the Emperor to see to it that all the alleged incidents during the evacuation of the Jews were cleared up without unnecessary scandal. One should always distinguish between good and bad Jews, and not treat them all with the same severity. The Tsar might have been inclined to make hasty concessions to Poland when that country was surrendered to Germany had she not stayed his hand; he must not make promises and gifts which would cause difficulties for Baby later on. Whenever the question of German prisoners of war in Russia arose, the Empress was embarrassed and hurt by the widespread suspicion that she sympathized with the enemy, when all she wanted was that they should be kept in humane conditions so that Russia could be seen to be superior to Germany in this respect, and after the war people would speak approvingly of her treatment of prisoners. She asked the Emperor—shyly, almost whispering in his ear— to send a commission of inquiry to POW camps for Germans in Siberia, and to allow the prisoners to celebrate Wilhelm's birthday. In Russia some people called her "the German woman," but she was now hated in Germany too. Everyone, of course, has affectionate ties with his or her birthplace and blood relatives, and every scrap of news from Germany, whether through her Swedish or English relatives, or in an unexpected letter from Darmstadt passed on by German nurses, disturbed her, flooded her being with poetic memories of her youth. When she heard that the Germans had suffered heavy losses, she, of course, thought of her brother and his troops and her heart sank. But her blood boiled when people in Germany gloated over Russian losses. Her grief over this bloody war knew no bounds. How Christ must suffer, to see all this bloodshed! The world was growing more and more depraved. Humanity had perished, replaced by Sodom and Gomorrah. This war was the beginning of a universal, an enormous, an immeasurable catastrophe, heartbreaking for her too. No, it was not out of sympathy for Germany that the Empress pleaded with the Emperor to rein in *Novoye Vremya* (which did all it could to inflame hatred of the enemy) or to forbid ruthless persecution of the Baltic barons—it was because such absurdities harmed Russia itself, weakened the throne and the army. "We" brought the German "takeover" on ourselves: it's because of our indolent Slav nature that we failed to keep the banks in our own hands—nobody noticed in time. Our people are talented, gifted—but lazy and incapable of showing initiative. Aleksandra sincerely loved this country which had become her own, and it grieved her to see huge Russia dependent on others, while its disorganization gladdened German hearts. In Russia people rarely carried out their duties properly unless they were watched. Order was lacking in our poor country, because it was alien to the Slav character.

Aleksandra could never do things by halves. She took everything too much to heart. God had given her such a big heart that it consumed her whole being. As things now were, she could no longer ignore even purely military problems, could not help sharing her husband's fortunes in the field. It had begun with her anxiety about Alekseev and whether or not he would suit the Emperor: he seemed to have little energy, he was jittery, he lacked soul and sensitivity, he was a thing of paper. Add to that his secret ties with Guchkov . . . if he was also inclined to oppose their Friend he certainly would not do his job well. Alekseev openly disregarded Stürmer and made sure that other ministers realized it. That was a grotesque state of affairs. The Empress was well aware that Alekseev disliked her personally. She had also started inquiring into the performance of the navy, and Grigorovich, the Navy Minister, sent her operational reports, which she read avidly and then returned under seal. But once she began paying close attention to military matters, her heart could not accept the futile bloodletting which was the only name for Russia's many unsuccessful offensives, and she implored the Emperor to halt them. Why go on knocking your head against a wall, why sacrifice men like flies? This is a second Verdun! Our generals are sacrificing lives without counting, out of sheer obstinacy, with no faith in victory, they have grown callous because they are so accustomed to losses. Spare our fighting men, stop it now! We must await a more favorable moment, not press on blindly, everybody feels that, but no one can bring himself to tell you. I should be wearing the trousers at GHQ too, instead of those idiots!

She had started looking closely at the generals. Devil take them!

Why are they so feeble and useless? Be strict with them! Look—in wartime you have to select generals for their competence, not by age and seniority! Kaledin, for instance—can he really be the right man in the right place, when things are so difficult? She racked her brains: how could Nicky learn the whole truth about his armed forces? And she had an idea: let him summon regimental commanders to GHQ for a two-week spell of duty! They would be able to tell the Emperor many truths unknown even to the generals, the Emperor would have a live connection with the army, and the generals would be afraid of what the regimental commanders might say about them. But for some reason nothing was done about it.

The Empress saw many soldiers in hospitals, and those from regiments of which she was colonel in chief were always presented to her after their recovery. As a result, she had been able to put forward many regimental commanders for promotion herself. She had once even recommended a naval captain of her acquaintance for the post of Chief of Staff of the Black Sea Fleet. When the General Staff Academy wanted to take over the building which housed a certain hospital, she had asked the Emperor if the request could be denied: were Academy-trained officers really so much needed in time of war?

Four days ago she had received at his own request General Bonch-Bruyevich, former Chief of Staff of the Northern Army Group, who had been removed, through no fault of his own, in favor of "Black" Danilov, an unscrupulous person, a desk soldier and undoubtedly an enemy. The Empress was glad to receive the courteous Bonch-Bruyevich and listened to him carefully. Afterward, she described the profound and pleasant impression he had made on her for the benefit of the Tsar, and told him what needed to be put right on the Northern Front, without letting Alekseev know where this information had come from. Old Ruzsky was unwell, a cocaine addict, and reluctant to act, but he could stay where he was, provided he had an energetic chief of staff. At present, however, good people were being removed. As a result, on the Northern Front there wasn't even any reconnaissance in depth of enemy positions. Better still, the Emperor ought to see Bonch-Bruyevich himself: he was very clever, he was honest, and he had a lot of information to give. He wanted nothing for himself, he was acting only for the common good.

Against the background of all these failed generals the Empress saw more and more vividly as time went on the cruel injustice which she and the Emperor had allowed to befall the unfortunate Sukhomlinov. She had so thoughtlessly permitted them to dismiss him and to strip him of his aiguillettes last year, and now she regretted it. Especially when she remembered who had demanded it. Her enemies! And how they had exulted afterward! It was his young wife—a vulgar creature, divorcée, adventuress, and bribe taker—who had spoiled everything for

Sukhomlinov, it was she who had wrecked his reputation. But since then there had been a yearlong investigation—and no real crime had been discovered, no one had proved anything, he was not only not a spy but had never harbored any criminal intent. He spent too little on the army? That was because Kokovtsov had not provided the money. And we've had the unhappy Sukhomlinov locked up for six months now—he's old, he's a broken man, those months of imprisonment are punishment enough. True, the Emperor had let him go with a heavy heart, and written him a kindly letter of dismissal, and Sukhomlinov had dishonorably shown it around, and even allowed copies to be made, to make his fall less painful, not stopping to think how the Emperor's enemies might exploit this. But the Empress had forgiven him this weakness, she had intervened on his behalf as soon as the investigation began, asking for the replacement of a senator who was prejudiced against him (he had been punished by Sukhomlinov for surrendering Peremyshl), and she had seen to it that the Emperor himself was the first to read Sukhomlinov's diary and his letters to his wife, before the investigation, so that he could decide for himself whether the general was guilty or not. The senator, bent on revenge, had consigned Sukhomlinov to the Peter–Paul Fortress, although the investigation did not require that. Now she felt more and more sorry for him: he'll die in a dungeon, he'll lose his mind, and we will never forgive ourselves. And he was in jail partly to cover up the bribes taken by Ksheshinskaya and her lover, Grand Duke Sergei Mikhailovich (Inspector General of Artillery)—which was the reason why an open trial was too risky. But one should never be afraid to release a prisoner, to help the sinner to be born again and to lead thereafter an upright life: as their Friend said, prisoners, because of their suffering, stand higher than we do in the eyes of God. Their Friend was very eager to see Sukhomlinov released on bail. It could be done without a lot of publicity, almost secretly.

The night dragged on, interminably, excruciatingly. Two o'clock, three, four, and still the Empress could not sleep. Thoughts, anxieties, passed through her mind in an endlessly tedious procession. It was suddenly obvious to her that they could not delay with Sukhomlinov any longer. The Emperor had either said nothing all this time or delayed answering petitions for his release. Difficulty in making up his mind was part of Nicky's character. But their Friend was insistent, and the Empress resolved to write to her husband the next day demanding that he telegraph Stürmer immediately to say that, having acquainted himself with the materials of the investigation, the Emperor saw no grounds for the charges against him, and his instructions were to terminate the proceedings. This would forestall the obscene statements which could be expected from Guchkov and the Duma crowd. Once convinced that he was not guilty, it was unthinkable to keep a man in jail just because you were faintheartedly afraid of the outcry your enemies might make.

There was one other prisoner whose cause their Friend insistently pleaded. This was Rubinstein, a rich businessman. He had contributed to charities and had been raised to the rank of State Counselor. He had some shady financial deals to his name, but after all he wasn't the only one. He had been arrested by General Batyushin's counterespionage commission, which was directly subordinate to Alekseev, and it was impossible not to suspect that Guchkov had put the military up to it in the hope of finding evidence against their Friend (since he and Rubinstein were so close). Batyushin's commission had previously come under Bonch-Bruyevich, and in those days had been a good thing, but since it had been transferred to Alekseev's jurisdiction it had escaped sensible control, had operated clumsily and unfairly, and had interfered in matters which were not its concern. It was time to put a stop to all that. She felt sorry for Rubinstein. His health was poor, and he might not be able to stand imprisonment. Their Friend and Anya were both pleading for clemency. The important thing was to transfer him at once from the front-line prison at Pskov to Petrograd, to the jurisdiction of the Ministry of the Interior—the Emperor must telegraph the order himself, or through Alekseev, without delay, and once he was in Petrograd, Protopopov could release him immediately, or if doing it so openly could cause embarrassment, send him, say, to Siberia and discreetly release him there.

Both things must be done immediately. Their Friend's instructions could not be flouted. The Man of God would guide the Emperor's bark safely between the reefs—and old "Sunny," staunch and unwavering, was ever ready to fight loyally and doughtily for her loved ones and for their, and her, country.

It was only when she had made up her mind to perform these two acts of clemency as a matter of urgency that the Empress gradually grew calmer and, toward morning, finally fell asleep.

Had she managed two hours' sleep this time? She woke exhausted and, as usual, her gradual return to life took several hours. In the meantime, she lay on her side hastily writing to the Emperor, telling him all that her sleepless night had yielded. Her eyes sometimes failed her in that position, and she could not always see clearly what she was writing.

But she could not stay in bed too long: as on every previous day, appointments had been made for her—to make arrangements for the wounded, to discuss supply trains, a number of ladies had to be received, and a minister—and suddenly she was told that Protopopov had telephoned urgently begging for audience to discuss a very important matter.

Oh God! They had reached complete agreement only yesterday—

what could have happened since? She would have to receive Protopopov before doing anything else, but even before that she would have to go for a drive in a car, just for half an hour or so, to clear her head.

The weather was quite as dismal, as depressing, as unrelievedly gloomy as yesterday. And there were occasional bursts of rain.

The first frost had come early that year, on 2 October, and there was even snow. The leaves were falling, and the Empress could now see the church of the Great Palace from her windows.

She went for her drive, but her head was just as heavy when she returned.

Protopopov came in looking dreadful. His eyes were unsteady, wild even, his mustache quivered—it was strange to see such a bewildered expression on a face always so self-assured and triumphant.

What did it mean? What could possibly have happened?

His beautiful voice trembled with emotion, his words as always poured out in a swift stream. It seemed that the banks were reluctant, that there was no support anywhere, that all the ministers were perturbed when they heard that Protopopov was assuming responsibility for the food supply. This was a very sensitive subject for the Duma, and if Protopopov's appointment were made public tomorrow it would cause a storm in the Duma of unforeseeable magnitude.

The Empress heard him out quite coolly. Her manner seemed to say, "Very well, then, we are prepared for a fight, however savage, in fact that's the way we want it!"

"No, no," Protopopov protested, squirming in agony, he wasn't the least bit afraid, only the outcry might take on such proportions that Stürmer would have to dissolve the Duma immediately, on the very first day in fact, and that would be most awkward.

What, then, should they do?

Delay. Delay announcing his new responsibility just for a little while. Two weeks, say. Give the Duma a chance to calm down. It could be more conveniently dissolved later on. Protopopov was making this request not just on his own behalf, he was ready to fight on to victory (although he knew very well how destructive raging storms in the Duma could be), the request came from a majority of the ministers, it was in the interests of the cabinet as a whole!

If the Empress's state of mind had been painful before, her perplexity now made it doubly so. She could see no sense in going back on a decision taken so enthusiastically only yesterday. Why be frightened of uproar in the Duma? That would happen anyway, on one excuse or another.

But the light of absolute certainty shone in Protopopov's soulful face, a face for the brush of an artist, so strikingly expressive with those bushy brows, those shining eyes, those thick lips under that heavy dark mustache—every feature expressed a conviction still more profound than that of yesterday.

Perhaps she had not understood him properly.

But to begin with, it was their Friend's desire that Protopopov should take sole responsibility for the food supply. And second, even if they changed their minds yet again, the Emperor would just have received yesterday's letter and would be signing the order, which would arrive by tomorrow morning. (Though in such an emergency—and the tension this month was as great as it had been last summer—the Empress could of course take it on herself to countermand the order. Her endlessly indulgent spouse would forgive her.)

"Telegraph the Emperor!" Protopopov's entreaty came from the depths of his being.

But how could she possibly entrust such a delicate matter to a telegram? Dozens of people would read it, and these tergiversations would become common property immediately.

"Send it in code!" Protopopov croaked.

But even messages in official cipher passed through several pairs of strange hands. Oh dear, oh dear! The Empress had completely forgotten until now that she and her husband had agonized over the need to have some means of discreetly communicating important news to each other, and done nothing about it for far too long, but had finally ordered a cipher to be designed for their use. And still had never once used it.

"I'll encode it myself!" Protopopov exclaimed.

He was taking it so much to heart that it was practically impossible to refuse him: how could he possibly carry out their former decision against his will?

And after all, they weren't canceling the appointment, were they? Just postponing it for two weeks.

But then again—she couldn't possibly go against their Friend's instructions.

She had made up her mind. "I tell you what, Aleksandr Dmitrich," she said. "Go as quickly as you can to Petrograd to Gorokhovaya Street, to see Grigori. If he says no, then we leave things as they were yesterday. If he permits us to change it, come back quickly, we will still be in time to send a coded telegram, and the Emperor will be in time to cancel the order by tomorrow morning, two hours before the Duma meets."

Protopopov started from his chair and sped on his way.

Such a dear man, such a nice man, she was sorry for him, she wanted to relieve him of his too, too unbearable anxiety.

That was how she was, in love and in all her attachments: once she had made up her mind about someone it was forever. This was the man to whom she had entrusted the protection of the throne. Friends must always come to the rescue of friends.

[6 5]

(THE STATE DUMA, 14 NOVEMBER)

In the White Hall of the Tauride Palace, the floor of which was occupied by leather armchairs, each with its desk, arranged in terraced semicircles, some 450 deputies had assembled under the glass roof for the opening session of the State Duma. At the far end of the hall diplomats of allied countries were ceremonially ensconced on little balconies between Corinthian pillars. The galleries to left and right were packed with supporters of this or that party. At each corner, in the foreground, were low-ceilinged press boxes, uncomfortably full. In the ministerial box to the right of the rostrum Stürmer himself, with a beard so long that it looked false, sat with some of his colleagues. Everyone knew that he would leave for the State Council immediately after the opening ceremony, on the pretext that he was attending a church service.

The president, flanked by his two deputies, mounted a central dais as high again as the platform beneath it. The president was a burly, robust fellow, bursting with a rustic vigor which he had, however, not acquired by tilling the earth, twisting oxen along a furrow. Instead, after his schooling in the Corps of Pages, he had served as a Horse Guards officer, then as a chamberlain, he had held all sorts of presidencies, marshalships, trusteeships, and, lo and behold, he was now at the head of the nation's elected representatives. He mounted the most honorific platform in Russia, elevating it yet further with his own height, conscious of the impression his every movement must make on those present and of its importance to his fatherland. He gripped a hefty bell with his hefty paw.

The Duma fell silent before him—each "fraction" seated in its own segment of the hall: the far left, the numerous Kadet group, the Progressists, the thinning ranks of the Octobrists (the upper rows in their section were sparsely occupied), the Russian nationalists, nationalists from the non-Russian areas, rightists.

Rodzyanko knew that his unusually resonant voice could easily fill that hall, or one four times as large. But the historic significance of the occasion must ring out today—not just his voice—and that too he would have no difficulty in expressing.

This was not just the opening day of a normal annual session. Down there at the president's feet the Progressive Bloc were tensed like tigers. Sometime in the next hour or two they would pounce. That they were about to spring was an open secret, known to the journalists waiting no less tensely, to the spectators, and to the gaggle of apprehensive ministers, bent on slipping away at the appropriate moment through a door left half open for them. (There was also a concealed alarm bell in their box with which they could summon the guard.) Even the Empress had heard about it, out at Tsarskoye Selo. The Unions of Zemstvos and Towns had already proclaimed that the hour of decision had arrived. The president himself, who was more or less privy to the Bloc's plans, knew the secret as well as anybody. He stood there now on his eminence like a monument, looked down on only by the portrait of the Emperor behind him (twice Rodzyanko's height, standing stiff and straight, cap in hand), but one wrong word and the president might fall under the claws of the predators. One very wrong word and they would be upon him there where he stood, to drag him down and rend him.

Rodzyanko had recently warned the leaders of the Bloc repeatedly:

> The Duma, in the person of its President, is the victim of a whispering campaign. The object is to demoralize us all. I may be brutally interrupted during the speech I am due to make at the opening session. But I do not intend to mince my words. I may be brutally interrupted because of the influence of certain persons, and my further *tenure* will become impossible. In that case I will appeal to the Duma.

They promised to support him. However, the Bloc's support was not everything. The position of president of the State Duma had no parallel. He was unique, as the chairman of the Council of Ministers was not, since *he* was frequently replaced. In the last analysis, the president of the State Duma was the second personage in Russia, after the Emperor. He was the intermediary between the Tsar and the people's representatives, holding the balance even between the monarch and the Duma. To retain this eminence he had to take care to preserve both the majesty of the monarchy and the passion of the Duma. He had himself to utter words of warning to the Emperor. In his frequent reports to the Emperor he showed remarkable boldness and greatly influenced him, but always in such a way that his own great mission would not be hindered. (Just the other day, however, the Emperor had been so tactless as to deny the president an audience.) However angry the Emperor sometimes made him, he exercised restraint for both their sakes. Yet, if a miracle happened tomorrow and a "ministry of confidence" was created . . . in the Bloc's present plans Rodzyanko would not even be a member of that cabinet! Milyukov had made a point of telling him so. Rodzyanko, however, did not intend to take this lying down, feeling as he did that he was obviously a more important figure than Milyukov. He was the representative in chief of all the people's representatives, Russia personified as it were, and no other public figure was so well suited to the premiership. Current rumors mentioned him in this connection. (Some said he had been in line for the post in 1915.) Grand Dukes were among those who spoke of it . . . And this was another reason why he needed to emphasize his independence of the Bloc, and reinforce his special position between the Bloc and the throne.

> **Rodzyanko:** Gentlemen, members of the State Duma! We are about to resume our activities after a long, indeed an excessively prolonged interval. (A dig at the government. Applause. Cries of "Bravo!" "True, true!") The prime duty of the State Duma is the immediate removal of that which . . . (voice from the left: "Not that which, those who!") prevents our country from achieving the sole aim which it has set itself.

He had leaned to one side sufficiently, now he must tip the balance, say something firm to prevent the Duma from going to pieces and losing its grip on power. He went on in a ringing bass that defied contradiction.

> This nightmare of a war bears down on our motherland with crushing weight. It has to be won, whatever the cost to the country. (Prolonged, tumultuous applause except from the extreme left.) Our national honor, our national

conscience demand it, the well-being of future generations imperatively demands it. (Stormy applause. Cries of "True!" "Bravo!") We have surprised
the world with our unanimity and the strength of our resistance. What, then,
are the paths to our goals? Calm inside the country, stoutheartedness in our
trials, and *insistence on speaking the truth here*, within these walls. (Stormy
applause.) The government must learn from you what the country needs. (A
voice from the left: "Their resignation!")

Stepping firmly, balancing cautiously:

> In time of struggle, when the people's forces are fully stretched, no one
> should stifle the people's spirit with unnecessary restrictions. (Applause in
> the center and on the left.) The government cannot follow a path separate
> from that of the people, but, strong in the *confidence of the country* . . .

A very subtle passage this. Rodzyanko did not say that the present government was
following a path separate from that of the people, nor that it did not have the confidence of the Duma, but he was at one with the Duma in his longing for a government
which would

> . . . take over the lead of society's own forces, go forward in agreement with
> the people's aspirations on the path to victory over the enemy. (A voice from
> the left: "Down with them! Tell the government to get out!")

Careful! Time to bend the other way!

> The country will never aid the enemy by internal strife.

A glorious sentence—it called for a follow-up in verse.

> *Russia, Holy Russia! None shall overcome thee!*
> *Thy awesome cliff defies the battering storm!*

His deep bass might have been ordering a regiment into the attack.

All chasms safely skirted—time now to cross the firm bridge of ritual. Rodzyanko
looks upward, out across the hall, toward the diplomats, hailing

> the family of nations fighting side by side with us, in the name of lofty
> principles . . . And the ally who has newly rallied to us, the valorous Roma-
> nian people!

The whole Duma is already on its feet, turning to look at the diplomats, and the
Kadets shout: "Long live England! Hurrah!"

The Kadets take particular pleasure in honoring England, and applauding her ambassador, Sir George Buchanan, to spite the German Stürmer, who in their view shows
insufficient respect and gratitude to that country. Rodzyanko obligingly alludes to
this:

> There are no cunning ploys which the enemy will overlook in his insidious
> efforts to loosen and overturn our alliance. But the enemy's machinations
> are futile. Russia will not betray her friends (general applause) and will reject
> with scorn any idea of a separate peace!

This passage was a sure winner: it showed his loyalty to the throne and at the same
time was to the taste of the Duma since it seemed to be aimed at Stürmer.

We recognize you, our brave Russian gray-clad fighting man, you who in the

> simplicity of your soul look for neither profit nor reward . . . Intrepid warriors, our prayers are with you!

It had gone well. The inaugural address was over. One further gesture was necessary: to send greetings to the Emperor, assuring him that the Duma . . . And to prevent an outburst of protests—we don't want to talk to the Tsar!—he gave it this twist.

> . . . send greetings to our valiant army and navy in the person of their Supreme Leader, the Emperor!

Nobody would argue with that. Agreed unanimously. (But through shouts from the left of "Stürmer out! His presence here is a disgrace!")

The Prime Minister could hardly go on sitting there with people shouting insults at him. He was in fact ready to leave, but these hostile voices made it difficult for the government to exit from the hall in a dignified manner.

Before all other business the tactful thing now would be to call on a Polish deputy to speak, out of turn. As long ago as summer 1914, the then Supreme Commander had promised the Poles, in imprecise terms, the realization of their fathers' and grandfathers' dearest ambition, the resurrection and reunification of the Polish nation (though under the scepter of the Russian Tsar). On second thought, Russia had seen no need to hurry. Then, a year ago, Poland had been surrendered to Wilhelm, and Russia had missed her chance to make an official declaration. The Germans had waited a year, and then proclaimed Poland independent—most probably so that they could draft Poles into their army. So now a deputy from a Polish constituency declared:

> The Polish people will not accept this German solution, which runs counter to its aspirations.

Meaning that Poland did not desire independence as a gift from Germany, without a Polish seaboard, and without Galicia.

Next, it seemed natural to allow the Progressive Bloc onto the rostrum to make a declaration. (Markov II: "The Progressive Bloc minus Progressists." Laughter.) Yes, the committed Progressists had split away, alas. And the declaration itself, after endless compromises—how limp and colorless it was! What had become of Milyukov's original militant draft? The declaration was read out in a flat monotone by Shidlovsky.

> Just one year ago . . . the impotence of a government which did not rest on . . . the unanimous wish of the whole Duma that Sukhomlinov should be brought to trial has not been carried out. (Stormy applause, except from the extreme right. Shouts of "Traitors shield traitors!" "Rasputin won't allow it!")
>
> Distrust of the regime has given way to a feeling close to indignation. The populace is ready to believe the most grotesque rumors. The government has used every possible excuse to deny the public any say in things . . . A completely undeserved insult . . . The censorship's activities are meant to protect the nonexistent prestige of the regime . . . The precious trust of the Allies is being squandered . . . Warm sympathy for the great English people. (Applause.) The government as at present constituted cannot cope with the danger. Persons whose continued presence at the head . . . make way for people who . . . Rely on the support of the majority in the State Duma and carry out its program.

The declaration was read out in temperate tones and the walls of the Tauride Palace did not quake. But who was to follow the declaration, to outbid it and trump it? Which deputy's seat always felt like a pincushion under him? Who regarded speechifying from the rostrum as the whole point and purpose of his activity? Who jumps the queue, gets his note in quickly, is called first, and is already scurrying past the stenographers, an untidy figure, no longer young, but oh so very agile? He reaches the heights.

> Chkheidze (Social Democrat): I shall, of course, be repeating myself, but, gentlemen, who can avoid repeating himself when his subject is the war? I too shall reproduce certain thoughts which we have expressed earlier. The World War was caused by materialistic rivalry between great powers. Objective interests . . . Contradictions of the capitalist system . . .

For Chkheidze, Russia had never really existed. Chkheidze had the butterfly lightness of a tiny group which had no influence on events, no responsibility for anything at all, but did have its legitimate allotment of parliamentary time. And what else was the Duma for? Precisely for that, to compel people to listen to you for an hour, and then another hour. No need to sit in working parties, no need to sit studying Duma papers, but when it comes to speaking—by all means, as long as I don't have to stick to the point or help the meeting get anywhere.

> Not the solution of old nationality problems, but their aggravation, not the abandonment of militarist oppression and dictatorship on the part of the reactionary classes, but their reinforcement . . . Subjection to a capitalist oligarchy . . . Deputy Milyukov says that the whole thing rests on Germany's conscience, but there is no escaping facts. What sort of liberation did you bring to Galicia, gentlemen, when you were the victors there? Gentlemen, hand on heart—what entitles me to reassure Georgians with talk of the blessings which their nation can expect from the war? And what, gentlemen, am I to say on the Ukrainian question? The treatment of the Uniate metropolitan? What about Finland? . . . And Poland?

Chkheidze's enunciation was unclear—a guttural clucking—but this did not trouble him, did not curb his flights of oratory. For the hour allotted to him he was the first and most powerful man in the Duma, fearlessly pulverizing all those landowners, capitalists, and financiers, from the monarchists to the Progressists, and not omitting to bare his teeth at the Kadets. The assembly wasted an hour of mental freshness listening to this sort of stuff:

> You keep repeating that the war is creating conditions for consolidation, for unification—but what does this unity amount to? And how is unity faring in your Bloc? (Milyukov: "Stürmer will thank you for that.") Unity between landowners and peasants? Unity between labor and capital? With an eye to the militarization of labor? And what about the slogan "universal disarmament"? (Laughter.) We demand, gentlemen, the liquidation of this horrible war, we demand peace! But not a peace concluded by irresponsible diplomats! Never! In the name of Russian Social Democracy, in the name of the proletariat throughout the Russian lands, we demand a peace which . . . by coordinating the forces of European democracy . . . without forcible annexations!

(Labor in vain! Lenin will call him a chauvinist revolutionary: "If he wants revolution it is not to bring about the collapse of Russia." In Shlyapnikov's words: "The struggling proletarians of Russia found in Chkheidze's speech nothing to guide them, none of the revolutionary tension which animated the working class.")

The Duma's procedural rules supported Chkheidze as air supports a bird. The whole Duma, having been denied a Social Democratic education, was now forced to give ear to the sermonizing of this far-out orator. There was nothing to hinder his soaring flight. But tactics forced Chkheidze to come down to earth and suddenly close ranks with the Bloc.

> Such a struggle of course requires great circumspection and foresight. (From the right: "And better brains!") But there is one obstacle which we must remove immediately—and that, gentlemen, is the government which holds the fate of our country in its hands.

But then, after siding with the Duma majority, the fiery publicist (failed pupil of the Kutaisi high school and the Kharkov Veterinary School, occasional student of Odessa University) goes on immediately to express his pity and contempt for these class-conscious cowards and reprimands them like backward pupils.

> In this respect you, gentlemen, have long deluded yourselves, or else have deliberately pretended not to understand. Can you say that this thought has ripened in your heads? It seems to be the case that you share this thought, but are you capable, gentlemen, of taking any decisive step, of joining us in carrying out this first of many tasks? . . . We know your temperament and your tempo, and we call for no more than legal means of struggle. But you were not courageous enough, that is your normal characteristic: you're always about to set the world on fire—and the results are always pathetic.

If a speaker was of medium height, his head would be just slightly higher than the president's dais. As for Chkheidze, he was lost to sight somewhere below there. He made a lot of noise but his was not the speech which made the majestic president nervous. Who paid any attention to Chkheidze? Nor, when Kerensky jumped up to put on the show expected of him, would that be the most embarrassing scene. No, looking down the list of speakers, Rodzyanko saw Milyukov's name inexorably drawing nearer. The contents of his speech were already known to a narrow circle of deputies, and the president himself had spent part of yesterday urging Milyukov to omit passages which concerned august personages. To no avail. But merely to preside while such a speech was delivered was doubly dangerous: to interrupt or object meant damning yourself in the eyes of the whole of the Duma, and so to suffer inevitable defeat at the presidential elections in two days' time. But to remain neutral would mean finally damning yourself in the eyes of the imperial family.

How could a man surrender an office which had become so much part of himself that no one could even imagine them apart? With someone other than Rodzyanko as president the Duma would, in effect, cease to be the Duma. Russia would be a different Russia. And what would he himself be if he was not reelected? Separated from Russia, no longer a pillar of his country but a stepson. Besides . . .

> This office is a sacred cult, an honor attainable by only a few happy mortals in this earthly life of ours.

He had thought of a simple ruse. He whispered to his deputy Varun-Sekret, installed him in the place of honor, and stepping noiselessly, for all his bulk, his whole demeanor showing that this was not for long, but alas he simply had to, and on such a solemn day . . . he left the hall.

> (On the eve of the session. I caught a chill. I was feeling poorly, I had difficulty in finishing my speech, and I handed over to my deputy immediately afterward.)

But—surprise, surprise!

This unimportant fact proved to be fraught with serious consequences!

Next Professor Levashov made a statement on behalf of the right, boringly written and uninspiringly read. His audience neither applauded nor booed him.

> Our fatherland is being flooded with persons of German origin, who have taken possession of our best land, all our commerce and industry . . . They have every opportunity to provide our ferocious enemies with information on . . . To damage bridges, blow up storage depots, artificially provoke popular disturbances. The majority in the State Duma systematically avoids discussing the struggle against the German takeover.
>
> The rapacity of the black marketeers who have appeared everywhere on the home front, the banks and joint-stock companies . . . We on the right, more than a year ago . . . The State Duma has confined itself to . . . Nor has the government shown . . .

Only toward the end did he touch a live nerve.

> We condemn those who endeavor to exploit the government's blunders to seize power for themselves, mouthing loud phrases about serving their motherland. We reject the charge against the government of repressing so-called public opinion. The government's mistakes are in a very different area: in the absence of firm authority, in its fear of stern measures. The government is guilty, rather, of a desire to please everybody at once.

(In 1916 this was by no means obvious. You would need to live a lot longer to make comparisons.)

> When hundreds of millions of government money have been allocated to the Unions of Zemstvos and Towns, when tens of thousands of people have been excused from military service to carry out their work—can it be said that the government is obstructing the activities of these organizations?

(Nobody knew exactly how much had been allocated—it was 550 million rubles of government money, as against 10 million in private donations—because the whole of the widely read free liberal press unanimously refused to publish this inconvenient information.)

> We call on you to put an end to the struggle for power or at least to postpone it until the end of the war.

That was not the sort of thing the Duma wanted to hear—and it didn't listen.

Kerensky had awaited his turn in an agony of impatience, but it had come at last. The proceedings thus far had been sheer boredom, but now things would begin to happen. Hag-ridden by ideological frenzy, by the sweet torment of his personal responsibility to Russian society and to the Duma—the state's fourth, his own first— confident in his combination of extreme political boldness with superb oratorical skill, Kerensky let slip no opportunity to speak—in debate, in questions to ministers, in explanation of his vote, to explain his conduct on expulsion from the chamber. It seemed that he had no sooner left the rostrum than he was putting his name down to speak again, and as soon as his turn came up he skipped, up he zoomed again, light on his feet, neatly nipped in at the waist, dressed up to the nines. (Shouts from the right: "Best man at a wedding!" "Ask him whose best man he was!") But what did all that matter, with turns of phrase one more beautiful than the other, impatient to trip smoothly off his tongue three times faster than any other orator in the hall could speak.

> **Kerensky:** The bloody vortex into which European democracy has been drawn on the initiative of the dominant classes must be brought to an end! But, gentlemen, how can we leave the preparation of the peace for which democracy longs to those people who are systematically destroying the organism of the state? Did last year's terrible thunderclap on the San and outside Warsaw . . .

(here a slight twist of his tightly buttoned torso, one elegant hand swinging to the rear and to the right, pointing at the box which the ministers have already vacated)

> bring them to their senses and compel them to leave those places? They were soon themselves again, and for a whole long year inflicted new indignities on the Russian people. Everything possible was done to crush its enthusiasm and its spirit.

He dwells on that word—enthusiasm! enthu-zi-azm!—with special force even when the rhetorical torrent is in full spate. The stenographic record will read most impressively in a few days' time. Kerensky's group, like that of Chkheidze, is small in number, and has no influence on Duma voting, but between them they fill almost a quarter of the Duma's time with their speeches.

> Gentlemen! The government ridicules the demand for an amnesty, which has swept the whole country! A regime of what can only be called White terror has been created over the past year! All the prisons are filled with representatives of the toiling masses!

(Even according to Chkheidze there were only 7,000 political prisoners, and most of those were in places of banishment from which only the lazy, and those who didn't want to end up in the army, did not escape.)

> And is it not sym-bol-ic that our comrades, members of the State Duma, Social Democrats, remain in places of banishment in the Turukhansk territory while Sukhomlinov strolls around Petrograd? (Voices from the left: "Shame!")
>
> Who has damaged and disorganized Russia to such an extent that the urban masses are forced to demonstrate in protest, and their call for bread is answered with leaden bullets?

(No one could recollect any such incident. But from the Duma platform anything would serve.)

> Who, gentlemen, is to blame for the fact that throughout the country despondency and dread are gaining ground from day to day? The government's actions are controlled by hints, instructions from unaccountable persons controlled by the con-temp-tible Grishka Rasputin!

Any mention of that name was forbidden—but Kerensky was not easily restrained. It was an e-mo-tion-al shock to the nerves of his audience. The elegant, beautifully turned-out best man flourished his fists—his little white fists—at the ignorant, snuffling bearded peasant!

> Surely, gentlemen, all that we are experiencing must make us unanimously proclaim that the main, the greatest enemy of our country is not at the front! He is here among us! And there is no salvation for our country until we compel those who are destroying, who despise and make a mockery of our country to depart!

But just suppose that one of these days Aleksandr Kerensky himself . . . oh, how different it would all be! Apple blossom would fill the dizzy air! How very different things would immediately become!

> Tell me, gentlemen! If Russia was at the present time ruled by . . .

(This was not his own idea, rather one of Guchkov's, and it had been around for quite some time, but why not repeat it if it slipped so easily off the tongue?)

> . . . agents of enemy powers—could they possibly present their servants with any other program for creating anarchy in Russia?

> Ministers are reluctant to come here and discuss the situation with us face to face, because they know very well what they are doing! They know what a storm of indignation awaits them! (Applause from the left.) Having tied this great people hand and foot, and blindfolded it, they have cast it under the feet of a powerful enemy, while they themselves, protected by the machinery of censorship and banishment, prefer, like hired assassins, to strike the fatal blow surreptitiously! (Stormy applause from the left.)

Varun-Sekret, a native of the steppes around Kherson, was also a staunch liberal, but . . .

> Duma member Kerensky, I call on you to . . .

> **Kerensky:** Where are they, where are those people . . .

he cried more shrilly than ever, pointing at the empty government seats. He knew that Milyukov was getting ready to make a powerful attack, and he had to strike first and more effectively.

> . . . *these people suspected of treason, these fratricides, these cowards?* (Stormy applause from the left. The center is silent. Cries from the right of "What's he talking about?" "This can't possibly be allowed!" "Shame!")

> **Varun:** Member of the Duma Kerensky, I must warn you that any repetition . . .

But Kerensky didn't need to repeat himself. He had fired off his main salvo, and smoky flame still hung in the air.

> I cannot refrain from saying here that all attempts to save the country will be fruitless as long as power is in the hands . . . I maintain that at the present moment we have no greater enemy than those who, at the summit of power, are leading the country to disaster! I maintain that this above all is what must be told to those who pay tribute in blood and imprisonment . . . and who are not allowed to know the truth! We must tell the masses this: before you can conclude a peace worthy of international democracy you must destroy those who are oblivious of their duty! They . . .

(for the third time he repeats his dramatic gesture, swiveling to transfix the ministerial box with his forensic hand)

      . . . must go! They betray the interests of . . .

Alas and alack! Rodzyanko is still missing—and he only went for a minute! And Kerensky still had a long way to go to the end of his allotted hour—time enough to vilify and demolish the earthly Tsar and the Tsar of heaven. The inexperienced Varun-Sekret takes fright and rings his bell over the orator's serpentine head.

> Member of the State Duma Kerensky, I withdraw your right to address the assembly. Please leave the rostrum.

Suddenly—the fight goes out of him and he meekly submits. His punitive eloquence evaporates, he sags like a pricked soap bubble. A moment ago there was no restraining his wrath. Now, suddenly, with an elegant wriggle, shoulders slightly bowed, display handkerchief showing in his breast pocket, he descends, or rather saunters down the steps to admiring murmurs from the ladies in the gallery, applause from the left and howls of fury from the right.

He had stolen a march on Milyukov and that was all he wanted to do. He had exhausted his stock of gestures and accusations, and he had no practical suggestions to make. He had in fact counted on being cut short, the sooner the better.

Who, though, would speak for the other side? Where, on the right, is his equal, ready to rush into the fray? Alas! there is no one. Another flat, dreary, boring voice, that of a retired Hussar Guards officer, now a lean and hungry chamberlain, reading a prepared statement on behalf of the Russian nationalists.

> **Balashov:** Conscious of their responsibility to Russia and the throne . . . enthusiastically salute the mighty and valiant . . . Regretfully, the government has no plan of action . . . constant replacement of personnel, promulgation of insufficiently thought-out and incoherent measures . . . A favorable situation for looting . . . But the legislative institutions, which have assumed responsibility for military supplies and provisions, are also . . . Creation of a greater Romania, friendly to Slavdom . . . How naïve and shortsighted are those who think that the end of the World War is near. Until the unification of all the ancient Russian lands and possession of the Black Sea entrances are achieved . . .
>
> We call upon all classes to show patience and self-denial in the struggle against luxury. We believe that as a result of the world conflict . . . moral rebirth of the people . . . triumph of Russian culture . . .

Boring, boring. But there had to be a breathing space before the explosion. It was annoying that the smart-aleck Kerensky had filched and flaunted the most resounding themes. But that was the custom and the privilege of the left. Besides, what was said was less important than by whom. Even if the leader of the parliamentary majority spoke more moderately, the effect would be multiplied by the size of his majority, of the whole Progressive Bloc.

The leader of the parliamentary majority (by Western norms certain to become head of government) was entered in the list of speakers not just anywhere, but so that he could bring the Duma's day to a climax. He inspects the stenographers with a semicircular stare, something no averagely well-known deputy would do. He knows before he looks around at the hall that there are no eyes absently gazing elsewhere, that they are all fixed expectantly on his imposing nape, his broad neck, his solid back, knowing that he has not come empty-handed, that his very ascent to the rostrum marks an epoch in the work of the Duma, a stride forward in Russian history. (The French press describes him as "the great leader who in the very near future will play an outstanding role in his fatherland.") When he turns to his audience his graying forelock, his plain, forbidding spectacles, the long untrimmed mustache which holds no promise of conciliatory words, when, between tirades read from the text before him, he treats the hall to a glimpse of the excellent manners which make it possible for him to perform in European circles without demeaning himself, he sees that the Duma majority is gripped and unanimously behind him, while the reactionary right is convulsed with fury.

It is always the same. But today the leader of the People's Freedom Party, also leader of the Progressive Bloc, mounts the rostrum with a task of more than usual importance. He had made no real speech there since March. He had missed a whole Duma session traveling in Europe. Now two sessions on end had passed too peacefully, out of tune with the boldness of the congresses of the Unions of Zemstvos and Towns. People were getting the impression that the Duma was forfeiting its authority, that its conflict with government was at a standstill. Pavel Nikolaevich himself had prudently slowed down the activities of the Bloc as far as possible, but he was guiltily aware of his growing indebtedness to the left, and could no longer afford to fall behind revolutionary public opinion. The time had come to blow up the position which they could not take by siege. Without an honorable alliance with the left, without support from the left, the Liberals would cease to exist. The more offensively the left tried to provoke a split, to deprive the Kadets of a life-giving union with the people, the more sensational his speech must be, to wring cries of approval from the left benches too, and to put the schismatic Progressists to shame.

> (The Duma was lagging behind. Public pressure was increasing. People awaited a new word with growing impatience. It had to be spoken on 14 November. It was clear that hitting out at Stürmer was insufficient, one had to aim higher, and not spare the source to which all rumors ascended. I realized the risk I was running but felt that I had to disregard it.)

So as he mounted the rostrum he carried with him an invisible forty-pound bomb, which he placed for the moment at his feet.

Milyukov: It is with a heavy heart that I mount this rostrum today.

On the contrary—with a very light heart. In two Dumas he had read out some fifty speeches, each an hour long, and with great enjoyment. How much more prestigious was the Duma rostrum than the professorial chair which he had been denied in his younger days. Students might, or might not, take notes when you lectured, but the deputies would eagerly snatch them from the stenographers and in a day or two dozens of trains would carry thousands of copies all over Russia. In his mind's eye he could already see tomorrow's newspapers: "Milyukov's brilliant speech produced a tremendous impression—one of his best parliamentary speeches. He bombarded his audience with searching questions. We were left with the feeling that we were living through one of those moments when word becomes deed." This speech would shake even those who never read speeches. And, someday, excerpts from it would be included in textbooks of Russian history. This for instance:

> You remember the circumstances in which more than a year ago ... The country was calling for a government of persons with the confidence of the ... Influenced by our setbacks in the field, the government made certain concessions. Ministers detested by the public were dismissed, and legal proceedings against the Minister of War were initiated. How different things are now, gentlemen, in the twenty-seventh month of the war! I will say openly that we have lost all faith that this regime can lead us to victory. All the Allied states have brought the best people of all parties into government.

(We have people just as good!)

> But our rulers have sunk even below the level at which they were at more normal times in the life of Russia. We used to appeal not to the intelligence and knowledge of the regime, but to its patriotism and its conscience ...

(Nothing of the sort had happened. It was just a manner of speaking.)

> But can we do that now? Gentlemen, if the Germans had decided to use the opportunities they have to influence and suborn ... in order to disorganize our country ...

(That thought again—originally Guchkov's, already appropriated by Kerensky—but why should Milyukov not restate it, more vividly, of course?)

> ... they could not have done a better job than the Russian government has. On 26 June ...

(It was actually a week later, but the professor of history, no mathematician, always got dates—damn them!—mixed up.)

> from this rostrum I uttered a warning that from one end of the Russian lands to the other sinister rumors of treason and betrayal are rife. Then three days ago the chairmen of provincial zemstvo boards also declared that "the nagging suspicion has become a clear realization that an enemy hand is secretly influencing the course of state business."

Quoting each other was, of course, not conclusive proof, but it froze the blood: enemy hand secretly influencing ...! People would not be saying that if there was nothing to it. Dark forces—fearsome, many-faced, hydra-headed, insidious—menace Russia and we have foolishly succumbed to them!

> Gentlemen, I have no wish to encourage morbid suspicion, but how can anyone refute these suspicions when a handful of dubious persons manage the most important state business in their own base interests?

Now the chairmen of the provincial zemstvo boards could boldly quote Milyukov.

In drafting this speech he had sought to use experience acquired abroad in recent months and to disguise the gap in his experience of his own country during that period. His tactic—convenient, highly effective, and tactical—was to quote from the foreign newspapers which he had read assiduously on his travels and to relay the rumors they contained.

> I have here a copy of the *Berliner Tageblatt*. The information contained in this article is partly outdated and partly incorrect ... You may well ask who

Manasevich-Manuilov is. Well, until recently he was Stürmer's private secretary at the Ministry of Foreign Affairs.

Fascinating stuff! Shortage of bread in Russia, you say? The leader of the Bloc is about to lay bare for us the deepest root of Russia's suffering.

> I will not be telling you anything new, I will be repeating what you already know. That he was arrested for taking a bribe. Why, then, was he let off? That too is no secret: he informed the investigators that he had shared a bribe with the chairman of the Council of Ministers, Stürmer! And was promptly released! (Applause. Uproar.)

Others had answered an affront in the Duma by challenging the offender to a duel—but not Stürmer: Milyukov had nothing to fear there.

Chkheidze and Kerensky, who did not read the foreign press, were completely eclipsed! . . . True, it subsequently emerged that the "bribe" was a put-up job. Who had given how much and for what Pavel Nikolaevich would never discover, and Manasevich had shared it with no one, certainly not with Stürmer, because he had been arrested on the spot. (But never mind that, the story was

> not something learned directly, but conjecture: isolated, often minute details had to be pieced together, like a mosaic. It would be difficult to frame an accusation for a court of law, but for ordinary purposes it looks highly probable.)

And anyway, this was not a university lecture room, where historical events must be described exactly as they happened. Here, you were no longer describing but making history, and you had to shout louder than mere facts allowed, so as to make things plain to the public and frightening to the enemy with your noise. Stürmer had to be removed, everybody loathed him, and Milyukov especially, because he had tactlessly and ineffectually usurped the post of Minister of Foreign Affairs, to which he was so ill suited.

So how was Russia to be saved?

> Permit me, then, to dwell on Stürmer's appointment as Minister of Foreign Affairs. In my mind this is bound up with impressions gathered during my trip abroad. I shall simply recount the things I learned on my journey there and back.

This made it easier for him, doing it stage by stage, having a route to follow. It would also be statesmanlike. And, of course, the deputies would find it interesting: they did not travel abroad, did not have confidential conversations in the private offices of our ambassadors in Paris and London.

> The *Berliner Tageblatt*: "Stürmer belongs to circles which view the war without special enthusiasm." *Kölnische Zeitung*: "Stürmer will do nothing to resist the desire for peace emerging in Russia." *Neue Freie Presse*: "However Russified the elderly Stürmer now is, it is still rather strange that a German will be in charge of a foreign policy which originated in Pan-Slav ideas. He has made no promise (take note, gentlemen!) that he will never conclude peace without Constantinople and the Straits."

> What makes German newspapers so sure that Stürmer, carrying out the wishes of the right, will act in opposition to England? Reports in the Russian

press. At about the same time, the Moscow newspapers published a note from the extreme right . . .

The speaker's voice hardened. The extreme right! Those same dark forces which stood in the way of freedom, victory, and England.

> Yet again, gentlemen, a note from the extreme right (Zamyslovsky: "And it always turns out to be a lie!"), delivered to GHQ in July. This note declares that although we must fight on to final victory we should bring the war to a timely end, otherwise the fruits of victory will be lost as a result of revolution. (Zamyslovsky: "Signatories! Signatories!")

Milyukov knew nothing about signatories, he had seen no such newspaper. He would have to borrow a plausible piece from the mosaic:

> This is an old theme with our Germanophiles. (Zamyslovsky: "Signatories! Let him tell us who signed it!")

The unhappy Varun, unsure from which side the threat was coming, tinkled to himself:

> Member of the Duma Zamyslovsky, please do not speak from the floor.
>
> **Milyukov:** I am quoting from the Moscow newspapers.

Which newspapers? For what date? Why won't he say? There are many newspapers, and still more dates in the calendar, you can't look through all of them. Anyway, Pavel Nikolaevich had been abroad, and was short of time on his return. So please make do with the *Neue Freie Presse* for 25 July.

> **Zamyslovsky:** Slanderer, name the signatories, don't slander people.
>
> **Varun:** Member of the Duma Zamyslovsky, I most humbly beg you . . .
>
> **Zamyslovsky:** Name the signatories. Slanderer!
>
> **Varun:** Member of the Duma . . . I call on you to . . .
>
> **Vishnevsky I:** We demand to be told who signed it. Tell him to stop slandering . . .
>
> **Varun:** Member of the Duma Vishnevsky . . .

They meant to go on badgering him about those signatures. The Progressive Bloc were sitting quietly, the left were sitting quietly, they weren't calling for signatures, they were being objective about it all. The majority in the chamber were against the "dark forces," and anyway there was no turning back, he had to show how sure of his facts he was by the firmness of his voice. Milyukov puffed out his bristly mustache and said:

> I've told you what my source is. It is the Moscow press, excerpts from which are reproduced in foreign newspapers.

He would not say in so many words "in the newspapers of the other side in this war." That would be embarrassing, but the Germans were meticulous people, surely they would not be misquoting? Something must have filtered through to them. Not, perhaps, precisely in that form . . . But let's take a leaf from the archaeologists' book. Don't show your ignorance! They start with a few nondescript shards, fit them together and reconstitute . . .

> I am relaying the impressions I formed while abroad . . . I tell you that the consensus there is that a note from the extreme right was delivered to GHQ . . .

(And, like all documents at GHQ, promptly published in the Moscow papers?)

> . . . to the effect that we must put a speedy end to the war, otherwise there will be a revolution . . .

> **Zamyslovsky:** You're a slanderer, that's what you are!

> **Markov** II: He's simply repeating something he knows to be false.

> Voice from the left: Is such an expression from the floor permissible, Mr. Chairman?

> **Varun:** I repeat, Member of the State Duma Zamys . . .

> **Milyukov:** I am unmoved by Mr. Zamyslovsky's language. (Voice from the left: "Bravo!") Who, we may ask, is supposed to be carrying out this revolution? The Unions of Towns and Zemtsvos perhaps? The War Industry Committees? The Congress of Liberal . . .

What a ridiculous charge! The things they thought of! But best move on quickly from the rightists' note:

> Gentlemen, you know that besides the note I have quoted there exist a number of others. Their idée fixe is the imminence of revolution, from the left!

Well, really—what an absurd notion! Revolution—set off by the left! Who ever heard of such a thing?

> An idée fixe, which every member of the cabinet is required to be obsessed with. An idée fixe to which the upsurge of national spirit and the beginning of Russian freedom are sacrificed! . . . Continuing my journey . . . I reached London and Paris . . . Firmness of trust which unites us with our allies . . . Agreement on Constantinople and the Straits . . . When Sazonov was in charge of the ministry . . .

—and under Milyukov's influence . . . Till suddenly the post was occupied by . . . by whom? Not by Milyukov, but by Stürmer.

> What confidence can Russia's envoys feel when behind them stands— Stürmer? The delicate business of diplomacy calls for fine needlework. But sometimes things are dealt with ham-handedly. I, gentlemen, have seen the damage done to the most delicate fibers . . . That is what Mr. Stürmer has done—and it is perhaps no oversight on his part that he has not promised us Constantinople and the Straits!

In this context it was to be hoped that they would not remind him how he had toured the country preaching pacifism before the war. Youthful follies couldn't be held against him.

> Then I went on to Switzerland, for a rest, not to engage in politics.

On reading the Duma reports, how pleased the Russian soldier in the trenches would be to find that the leader of the People's Freedom Party had not had to go without a summer holiday, and had even enjoyed a quick look at some of Switzerland's spas. (For the Christmas holiday he would be going to his nice little dacha in the Crimea!) Incidentally, Switzerland is full of émigré Russian revolutionaries! . . . I met one or two of them.

> But even there the same dark shadows dogged me. On the shores of Lake Geneva I could not get away from the Russian Police Department. You

know—those "special assignments" which call for special attention on our part.

So undercover sleuths were treading on Milyukov's heels? No, they were there to enjoy themselves.

> It appears that officials of the department frequent the salons of Russian ladies well known for their Germanophilia.

With Milyukov treading on *their* heels, sacrificing his holiday.

> Gentlemen, I shall not tell you the *name* of the lady . . .

It sounded intriguing, and much more ominous than if he *had* mentioned the name. At the same time a delicate hint that he was received by great ladies himself . . . However, to make it more concrete:

> . . . the lady who progressed from a tenderness for an Austrian prince to a tenderness for a German baron.

These personal details were unavoidable, women always brought them into politics . . . The speaker would shortly be surrounded in the corridors by a congratulatory crowd eager to shake his hand, to thank him effusively—and, of course, to interrogate him . . .

> Her salon on the Via Curva, and later at Montreux, was well known for the pro-German sentiments of the hostess. This lady has now moved to Petrograd. Her name appears in the newspapers. Passing through Paris, I found . . . Parisians were scandalized, and I must add with deep regret that this was the very same lady who launched Mr. Stürmer on his career . . .

The "great ladies" theme was handled with such delicacy that even the extreme right refrained from bellowing in protest. Yet this was just where Milyukov was guilty of a few (venial) errors. (In the summer of 1917 he would—honestly and magnanimously—admit that

> it subsequently became clear to me that the lady in question, E. K. Naryshkina, was innocent.

Not least because *that* Naryshkina, Lily, had never returned to Petrograd, and the Petrograd Naryshkina mentioned by newspapers was another person altogether—Zizi, an aged lady-in-waiting, left almost heartbroken by Milyukov's speech. Pavel Nikolaevich would arrive at the truth in the end. But *at the time*, speaking from the rostrum of the Duma, only a disrupting suspicion, only a red-hot rumor could give History a push—and what political benefit would conscientious doubt have brought? The masses, all Russia, the whole world was looking to the Duma for something or other that would . . .)

> What is my object in pointing to these matters? I do not, gentlemen, assert that I have incontestably chanced on one of the channels of communication. But this is one link in the chain . . . To lay bare the routes and methods . . . judicial inquiry is needed . . .

It might have been treated as a joke—but his audience listened with bated breath. No detective drama could have gripped and excited them like this. It seemed that at any moment now a corner of the curtain would be raised and dreadful secrets disclosed! How penetrating this Milyukov was! He obviously knew much more than he was saying! Now he *was* mentioning a name—an ill-omened name, and not that of a lady.

When we accused Sukhomlinov, we also, of course, lacked proof. We had then what we have now—the instinctive *voice of the whole country and its subjective certainty!* (Applause.)

Oh God! We sit here or rot in the trenches—and we are betrayed! Russia is betrayed! Where are they leading us?

(The truth about Sukhomlinov would shortly become clear, and Pavel Nikolaevich would say, in a confidential context, when his words would no longer have any political effect, that Sukhomlinov had

> not acted in accordance with the seriousness of the moment. It was not so much treachery as complete imbecility, inability to rise to the situation. I personally was far from supposing that there was more to it than simple stupidity: treachery, and treason, never entered my head ...)

> ... Gentlemen, I would probably not have decided to speak about each particular impression I formed if, taken together, they did not constitute ... After leaving Paris for London ... That for some time past our enemies have gotten to know our most precious secrets, and that this never happened in Sazonov's time. (Exclamations of "Aha!" from the left.) In communicating this important fact I apologize for my inability to name my source.

(A certain Allied diplomat had been afraid to show a certain Russian envoy a certain scrap of paper.)

But the fact that the name was withheld made it all the more frightening: our innermost secrets had been betrayed to Wilhelm!

The word "treason" had been struck from the Bloc's declaration, but Milyukov had, oh so cleverly, pinned the label on the government, which had fled from the chamber. Now came the most explosive passage in his speech. But—just in case—he had to cover himself.

> Gentlemen, without harboring any personal suspicion I cannot say exactly what role this affair played *in a certain antechamber already well known to us*, through which Protopopov also advanced to a ministerial chair. (Hubbub on the left: "Splendid! He means Rasputin!")

He had phrased it subtly and elegantly. But, friends, there's a whiff of something stronger than Rasputin here—the shouters still had no idea of the full force of Milyukov's explosion. The clever trick he'd thought of was to read from the German press—in German, rapidly, easily, just to get it across, never mind if they didn't understand, as long as they didn't interrupt.

> This is the very same court party which appointed Stürmer. As the *Neue Freie Presse* puts it: *"Das ist der Sieg der Hofpartei, die sich um die junge Zarin gruppiert."*

He had gotten away with it! Varun was transfixed, too shocked to blink. Anyway, not many of those in the chamber understood—but that didn't matter, it had been said and would be translated in the Duma record. They would spread the word in spluttering Russian: court party grouped around the young Tsaritsa!

He had gotten away with that—so he could strike again! Nonchalantly, he reverted to Russian.

> In any case, I have some grounds for thinking that the proposals made by

the German counselor to Protopopov in Stockholm were repeated through a more direct channel and from a higher source.

The deputies rubbed their brows, they still had not understood. This was where the professor had the advantage of the semi-literate Chkheidze and the platitudinous Kerensky. His language was so smooth, no loose ends to pick at, yet everything necessary was said! "From a higher source" obviously meant "from somewhere no lower than the German Ministry of Foreign Affairs," and "through a more direct channel" meant to the Russian government, or even the Tsar, directly.

> And when we hear from the British ambassador a grave accusation against the same circle . . . (Translate for yourselves "court party grouped around the young Tsaritsa") . . . paving the way toward a separate peace . . .

Behold, the power of parliamentary oratory! However gratuitous, however disingenuous it is, once pronounced it hardens into granite: the Tsaritsa was working for a separate peace!

Nobody is given time to think about it, to cry out, to let out so much as a squeak: but what actually were Milyukov's "some grounds for thinking"? . . . What led you, Pavel Nikolaevich, and you, Sir George Buchanan, to the conclusion that . . . ?

(At a later date, a much later date, Pavel Nikolaevich would kindly explain:

> There is one puzzling circumstance which I have not succeeded in clarifying. Someone once sent me an American magazine with an article entitled "Russia's Peace Proposals." There was a picture of Jagow, a picture of Stürmer, and the text summarized an article in the Swiss newspaper *Berner Tagwacht*. The agenda for peace talks allegedly proposed by Russia seemed plausible enough. How they found their way into the *Berner Tagwacht*, what source of information the newspaper has, I have not been able to discover. There were no official traces in the Russian Ministry of Foreign Affairs. There were, however, frequent allusions, *so that there may have been something to the story.*

Yes, of course there was: the *Berner Tagwacht* article was signed K. R. Karl Radek could not pay his coal bill at the time, and anyway it was such fun!)

Obviously, once hints were dropped, the leader of the Duma opposition had the right to accuse the Russian government of treason!

Now for the bomb in readiness at his feet! Raise it, very gradually, from the ground.

> Yes, gentlemen, our legislative problems are now a matter of secondary importance. With the present government we cannot lead Russia to victory! (Cries of "True" from the left.) In the past we have agreed that you should not wage war inside the country while you are fighting at the front. Everyone, I think, is now convinced that it is useless trying to argue with them: fear of the people seals their eyes so that their main aim is to end the war as quickly as possible, even if the result is a draw. Just so long as they are relieved of the need to seek popular support.

But at whom should the bomb be aimed? The government had taken flight. Rodzyanko had fled. The Tsar was out of reach, and would not come along to defend himself. But hear me, all Russia!

> We say to this government, "We shall fight you . . .

(A little caution, however, does no harm.)

    . . . by all legal means, until you go away!" (Shouts of approval from the left.)

The Bloc had not authorized him to speak directly of *treason*, but in preliminary meetings Milyukov had seized on the formula: "Either complete idiots or traitors, take your pick." Now, in full spate, he flung out the words:

    And for practical purposes, does it really make any difference?

The bomb was thrown! It was in the air!

    Are we dealing with stupidity or with treason? When *the regime consciously prefers chaos and disorganization* . . .

The bombshell had exploded!

    . . . what is that? STUPIDITY or TREASON? (Angry noises, indignant cries on the right. They pound their desks. Jubilation in the center and on the left.)

The bombshell had been thrown not by an irresponsible socialist but by the leader of educated and responsible people, people with the vote! He would not say such things without good reason!

    When in conditions of general disquiet the authorities deliberately provoke popular unrest—the involvement of the Police Department in disturbances at factories is well attested . . .

(Make up your own minds just how well attested—as with all that has gone before: with the Germans outside Riga the Petrograd police are distributing leaflets in munitions factories calling for rebellion simply in order to bring about "peace by provocation"?

    . . . which is it? Stupidity or treason? (Shouts of triumph and of anger.)

(And if in forty years' time archival records are used to establish what is even now obvious to any simpleton, that it is the Germans above all who need these strikes, that they have the money, they have the agents, they have taken the appropriate steps—that, and not now, will be the time to demote the professor.)

    You ask why we have begun the fight in time of war? The answer, gentlemen, is that only in wartime are *they* dangerous. That is why we are fighting them now, while the war is on, and for the sake of the war. (Cries of "Bravo!" Applause.) *Victory over a perfidious government is tantamount to winning the whole campaign!!* (Prolonged, stormy applause except from the extreme right.)

Go ahead, then, applaud, while I quietly leave the rostrum and resume my seat. Applaud—but you yourselves do not yet realize the full significance of the speech you have heard today. It will come to be regarded as

    the storm signal for revolution!

The newspapers will be forbidden to print it in full, but the country will instinctively fill in the blank spaces. The country will be galvanized by

    the electric spark running through it from your speeches in this white chamber. Hitherto Russia has been blindly astray, feeling its way in the darkness. It was losing sight of the objective. It was beginning to tire. The country was beset by phantoms. But now the State Duma has shown the country a ray of light! And already there is a glimmer of hope! The country's sense of purpose is reborn!

Modesty dictated the words "from your speeches." Not, however, from the speeches of the rightists. Nor from the prancings of Chkheidze and Kerensky. A process of elimination left one speech only.

> Truly, gentlemen, occasions like 14 November do not repeat themselves.
> Make a note of the date: 14 November marks the beginning of an era!

And when I say

> the country is ready to acknowledge you as its leaders

after the necessary process of elimination you must understand this to mean

> acknowledge me as its leader.

As for the government, after its *treason* we have nothing more to say to it.

So, then, it had been openly proclaimed from the Duma platform that the country's monarch was a traitor, involved in a conspiracy with its enemy. Whose punitive hand would fall upon the traducer's head tomorrow?

No one's.

What storm would break over him?

No storm. They had long ago grown used to public dissatisfaction and the public's urge to attack, and would consider it bad form to lower themselves by answering.

But if the ground on which the throne rested had been churned to "treacherous" mud, though lightning had not struck, the throne was already tottering.

[6 6]

Mogilev was like an enormous hotel for officers, with guests continually arriving and departing. Colonels and generals fresh from the front could count on an invitation to lunch or dinner with the Emperor, but had to apply and wait their turn. Vorotyntsev had no intention of doing so. He had seen the Emperor from a distance, outside his residence, inspecting a squadron of Terek Cossacks newly returned from the front, and would content himself with this glimpse.

In the mess at GHQ officers rarely had time to get to know each other. They would arrive for a brief stay, and leave as soon as their business was done. The company changed from breakfast to lunchtime, and from lunch to dinner. From one meal to the next you found new neighbors at your small table. Yet an observer unfamiliar with the ethos of these people would never have guessed that they were not all close acquaintances, comrades of old. Three years of war had intensified the regular officers' esprit de corps (ensigns were never seen in the place), which showed itself unmistakably in similarity of uniform, of behavior, and even in the way they saluted. The trivial differences which had once existed between the Guards and the army at large, between various arms of the service, between training establishments, and between regiments were now much less marked. Any two officers who had seen front-line service and now found themselves sitting side by side were at once bound together in friendship, fellow feeling, even solicitude, as though they were old regimental comrades—that special kind of friendship which flourishes in the absence of any official relationship. They shared the same bitter experience, and the same expectation: "colonel today, corpse tomorrow." Whenever there was a chance to advise, explain, help, make life a little easier—every man there would hasten to do so, out of a more than fraternal feeling. Their ranks had been thinned by two-thirds or three-quarters since the war began, and the duties and tasks of those who had gone rested now on the shoulders, on the rectangular epaulets, of those left behind.

Thus, the captain, the lieutenant colonel, and the heavy-headed colonel of engineers who sat down to lunch at Vorotyntsev's table had never met before, but they knew each other well. They had not yet exchanged names, or mentioned units, but from the moment they sat down they behaved like old acquaintances and good friends.

Vorotyntsev happily adopted this tone, which after his brief excursion full of strange encounters made him feel that he was home again, back with the army, his regiment, and the familiar routine of the front. He promptly joined in the desultory conversation. The lieutenant colonel and the captain were grumbling about the mess, the setup at GHQ, its location, the accommodation for officers—but all this was just in fun, extolling by contrast the superior attractions of life in the trenches. It sounded particularly amusing and lighthearted from the lieutenant colonel with one gold tooth showing between his sardonic lips. He insisted that if he survived he would find it impossible to live in a town and would make himself a bunker somewhere on the outskirts, with a good field of view, and would sometimes climb a tree to reconnoiter further.

How strange it was, Vorotyntsev reflected, that on his travels around the two capitals he had never once been able to relax and laugh. What a salutary human trait it was that the worse things became, the readier people were to laugh. It was no laughing matter—but you couldn't help it.

The conversation turned to the Mogilev ladies, locals and refugees, and the lieutenant colonel with the gold tooth and the yellowish-white mustache said jestingly, "I was in the hussars as a young man, but I was never as successful as these *zemstvo hussars* are now. The ladies are more calculating than they used to be. These fellows won't get killed, they have big salaries, and their khaki uniform looks almost military—they wear broader shoulder straps and sword belts than we do. The moment Milyukov is made Minister of War we'll all be cashiered and replaced by an army of Whigs."

The engineer refused to fall in with the facetious tone of the younger men and shook his head gloomily. "It's an orgy for scroungers at the state's expense. They arrive here with warrants by the thousand, worm their way into the confidence of front-line commands, and go around telling everybody that the government is utterly useless. And this in time of war! Leftists almost to a man, and Jews, many of them. And the way they throw their weight around in rural areas and in district capitals! Putting the local authorities out of business!"

"Just draft dodgers," the captain opined. "Strutting around, fit as a fiddle—if they love Russia and victory so much, why don't they pay the *blood tax*?"

"Yes, and then there's the Red Cross! A neutral power! All those private hospitals they've set up everywhere, just to demoralize the army. They mollycoddle the men, dress them up in good linen, feed them delicacies, fine ladies fuss over them and sometimes plant political pamphlets on them. And after all that it's: What, me go back and fight? No, thanks!"

"There's a Red Cross flag on practically every fourth house in Moscow," Vorotyntsev recalled, "thousands of little private hospitals, civilian doctors, no army supervision at all."

Whatever subject you touched on, so many problems had accumulated in three years of war that it was difficult to see any way out. Great skill would be called for.

"And what about these refugee committees all over Russia? Also staffed with people of call-up age. Now there's a good place to make a start with equal rights for women!"

"There you are again," said Gold Tooth. "Suppose the government had taken charge of refugees, and suppose one little girl had died, the whole press would be screaming its head off, all the papers would be full of half-page or full-page pictures of the girl on her deathbed, and earlier with her mama and her brothers. As it is, the refugees are the responsibility of unofficial committees, and if two thousand die the papers and the public will say, 'That's not many! Considering there are three million refugees!'"

The conversation became more general. Loud voices were heard from the next table but one, and they all turned around to look. The officers concerned obviously did not mind attracting attention. A lieutenant colonel in the supply service, with pince-nez and a rather nasal voice, was retailing with relish his telephone conversation with Petrograd an hour earlier. The newspapers, it seemed, had appeared with blank spaces, and you could only guess at what had been omitted from reports of Duma proceedings by trying to supply missing links in the argument. But everyone present in the Duma gallery yesterday had been shaken by the speeches, especially that of Milyukov.

"Not one of the four Dumas to date has ever heard a speech of such historical importance! What he said was quite unprecedented! He tore off all the veils!"

Veils? What veils? Vorotyntsev could not imagine. But it left him deeply uneasy. "Tore off all the veils!"

God help us! Here we all are, doing heaven knows what, while back there things are happening fast!

"Don't worry, Zemgor will exert itself, all those typewriters and duplicators will get to work, and we'll have all the forbidden speeches here in the army, probably in the form of lithographed leaflets."

Those sitting farther off asked each other what it was all about, and the news sped from table to table. Someone called out loudly, determined to be heard above the hubbub, "It's comforting to know that there is in Russia a forum in which someone can speak for you!"

Uncertainty about what Milyukov had actually said encouraged the most varied conjectures.

"Did Shingarev speak, do you know?" Vorotyntsev impulsively asked the unprepossessing supply officer. He had begun to regard Shingarev as an ally.

"What's going to happen now?" people asked. "Will they dissolve the Duma?"

"Nobody will do any dissolving. The government will shrug it off and stay just where it is."

The engineer colonel had paid little attention to this commotion. Hunched over the table, he muttered almost to himself, "I don't know, gentlemen, why you think it matters who lets out a fart in the Duma, whether it's Milyukov or Rodichev. Just ask yourself: Is there one single thing they really know about? I'm not talking about the engineer branch, say, or the artillery, but more generally—industry, say? Or the mines? Or agriculture? So what business have they got trying to foist themselves on us as a 'responsible government'?"

Those at the next table overheard him and were indignant.

"They aren't foisting themselves on anybody! They're expressing the free opinion of Russia!"

Others joined in, all speaking at once. But supporters of the Duma seemed to be louder and more numerous. The engineer made a despairing gesture.

"The ministers we have now are a lot of turds, but they can do their job, they'd trained to it. Those characters in the Duma are good at jabbering and that's all. Put them in charge of Russia tomorrow and it will never get out of the shit."

Lunch over, they went their different ways. The dining room rang with the jingle of spurs.

Outside, the day was dull, but warm.

On the roof of the Quartermaster General's Department there was a machine gun under wraps, for use against enemy aircraft. A sentry stood by it.

Vorotyntsev went over to the Operations Section, up to the second floor, to visit Svechin. Since arriving he had seen him only in passing.

Svechin had an office to himself with maps on the walls, stacks of files everywhere, and three telephones on his desk.

"Hm-m-m," said Vorotyntsev, looking around, "not like our office at Baranowicze: three desks in one room of a hovel, and one field telephone for us all."

"We're growing, getting more important," Svechin said, lolling back in his semicircular padded desk chair. Here in his own office he was no longer the devil-may-care swashbuckler he had been for a few hours in a Petrograd restaurant. "Anyway, that fooling around in peasant huts and railroad trucks at Baranowicze was all Danilov's idea. We might just as well have lived quietly in tents."

There was another comfortable chair for a visitor, and Vorotyntsev seated himself.

"And who's going to be in charge of all this? How's Golovin getting on?"

"He's finished, our Golovin. His stock's worthless."

"Ruzsky, then?"

"Ever hopeful. But it won't happen."

"So who?"

Svechin bared strong, very large teeth in one of his rare smiles.

"Well, to tell the truth, His Majesty would like to make do with Pustovoitenko. Who could ask for more in a general? Polite, efficient, never contradicts, won't get any big ideas. What about operational orders? I hear you asking. Before he leaves, Alekseev will write out enough to last him three months. Ah, but His Majesty often has to go to Tsarskoye Selo—does that mean Pustovoitenko will deputize as Supreme Commander? Doesn't seem quite right, somehow."

The dim light from outside was augmented by a desk lamp under a green glass shade. Svechin, relaxing, filled a pipe and offered Vorotyntsev another.

"Fill up, it's good stuff."

"So who's it going to be?" Vorotyntsev asked, taking the pipe.

"You'll never guess," said the idol, with a flash of his black eyes. "I'll give you three guesses. Try one of those nobody would even think of."

"You!" Vorotyntsev blurted out.

"Or you!" Svechin retorted. "The Emperor did say, 'Once I had a colonel named Vorotyntsev, he almost won Samsonov's battle for him, perhaps I ought to appoint him!' 'Well, Your Majesty, he's still alive,' I said. 'Really? Where?' 'Near Moscow somewhere, the postmark is illegible.' Well, I couldn't very easily send for you, could I?"

The last time they had met, a spark of something like anger had leapt between them. Now things were as they always used to be.

"Just as long as it isn't Nikolai Nikolaevich. He's on his way, you know."

"On his way *here*? Is this the first time since he was dismissed?"

"Uh-huh. A historic moment. He wanted to be here for the 6th—his birthday, and the anniversary of the Tsarskoye Selo Hussars. Uncle once commanded that regiment, Nephew also served in it, and they both love fancy uniforms. What Uncle really wanted was to make his peace, or talk to the Tsar face to face, without Alix around. But he was refused permission. His orders are to come the day after the anniversary."

"Anyway," Vorotyntsev said, shaking his head, "what does Uncle amount to? He's just an old windbag, Uncle is. All spit and polish."

Svechin had said as much before him. He repeated his earlier demand. "No, come on, think of something impossible! Something stupid if you like—but just make a guess!"

He gave Vorotyntsev a meaningful look.

Vorotyntsev in a flash of inspiration blurted out, "Krymov?!"

Svechin bared his big teeth and wagged one large finger meaningfully. "Still haven't forgotten, still haven't put it behind you? I'd begun thinking you'd finally come to your senses and wouldn't put your foot in it again."

Even now Vorotyntsev couldn't help blushing, remembering how ashamed he had been.

"Yes, well, I was a little upset . . . but there were other considerations too, don't imagine that . . . Anyway, I haven't entirely given up the idea . . ."

Svechin's thick lower lip curled. "In that case you're an idiot. And there I was, glad that you'd found a good excuse."

"Good excuse? It was a disgrace. But then again . . ."

Svechin leaned forward across the desk. "But what's good about this coup they're planning, Yegor? It'll all come to nothing . . . The Guchkov crowd and that so-called Yellow Bloc imagine that the most difficult problem at present is how to topple . . . them . . . But you just show me whom and what you'll put in their place. If it's something worse, or you just don't know, it may be better not to do it . . . let things take their course. Of the house of Romanov—whom would you substitute? The little boy? He would be a plaything in the hands of the regency council. Besides, he's not strong, and he's backward—what sort of behavior is that for a twelve-year-old, drenching generals with water? They're all doing their best to spoil him. Mikhail Aleksandrych? A less than average colonel, very much inferior to you and me. Nikolai Nikolaich? We've dealt with him already. One of the Vladimiroviches? One's a coxcomb, the other's a drunk. The Konstantinoviches? They'd best stick to poetry. So we're left with a republic? A Kadet government? You'd have to lose all self-respect to take orders from them. To hand over Russia to their control."

It was all true. But it wasn't for Vorotyntsev to solve all these problems in advance.

"And would you want Guchkov as regent?" Svechin asked, black eyes ablaze. "Or Prime Minister?"

"He doesn't aspire to it. Remember what he said about a Man of Providence . . ."

"Said, yes. But how sincere was he? I can't believe that he's altogether . . . Would anybody start a stunt like that if he wasn't looking for a share of the power? The man who gets mixed up in this sort of thing obviously must 'aspire' . . . Wouldn't you? Can you see yourself standing aside immediately afterward?"

Vorotyntsev smiled briefly. He had absolutely no aspirations of his own. Word of honor! He wanted only to act for the salvation of Russia. But when it came to the point you'd have to start reorganizing. That much was true.

Svechin caught him smiling. "Aha!"

"No, I . . ."

"Tell me—they all accuse the government in chorus of not respecting the rule of law, of trampling on their rights, yet they themselves are plotting a coup d'état . . . Where does that leave rule of law, eh?"

Vorotyntsev thought a moment, puffing hard—he was not used to smoking a pipe.

"Then again, Guchkov has Myasoedov's death on his conscience. What a nasty business that was. A lot of wild nonsense to blacken the whole imperial government."

"Yes," said Vorotyntsev. "But what exactly was at the bottom of the Myasoedov affair, do you know?"

"I know exactly. The Warsaw city commandant told me, he was there when the trial took place. Guchkov set out to expose Myasoedov in 1912, but got nowhere. He proved nothing, and there was nothing to prove, it was just demagoguery. But there was a lot of hoo-ha in the papers, and the mud stuck—Myasoedov was a spy. Then in December 1914 a son of a bitch named Kolpakovsky came along to the General Staff—he was a second lieutenant in the 23rd Regiment, taken prisoner in your Samsonov campaign, but got out of it by posing as a Ukrainian separatist, and the Germans hired him to spy for them, or so they thought, but when they slipped him back over the Russian frontier he unmasked himself. He thought he'd make his story more plausible by claiming that the Germans had told him, told the new boy, how highly they thought of their spy Myasoedov, only they didn't know either his address, which was in the Petersburg directory, or where he now was. This Kolpakovsky had simply remembered what he'd read in the papers. Guchkov's old lie had worked. Well, a report on Myasoedov was duly sent to the Northwestern Army Group, where he was serving as an interpreter in the 10th Army. Even so, nothing would have come of it, nobody would have treated it seriously, if the 10th Army hadn't lost a corps in East Prussia just one month later.

This sent a shock wave right across Russia. Then there's that other bastard, Bonch-Bruyevich, you know who I mean."

"I should say so!"

That asshole! He'd submitted a dissertation to the Academy three times over, failed every time, and been given a job in administration.

"Well then, it was his idea, he put Ruzsky up to that third thrust into East Prussia. Now Bonch had to find a culprit, so he grabbed this spy and traitor with both hands. They arrested him and court-martialed him in a hurry in the Warsaw Fortress. The main informer, Kolpakovsky, wasn't even present in court! Nor was there any defense counsel. There was no proof of guilt whatsoever, although a secretary-observer had been attached to Myasoedov for two months previously. Just to make sure, they imposed a second death penalty—for looting: he was supposed to have walked off with some statuettes from a German house. The trial began in the morning, sentence was passed in the evening, they wouldn't let him send a telegram to the Emperor, wouldn't let him say goodbye to his mother—she was in Warsaw— they hanged him the same night, five hours later. Covering their tracks?"

Vorotyntsev could only gasp. In cases like this you couldn't help imagining yourself wrongly condemned. He remembered Vereshcohagin's son. "Didn't anybody try to stop them?"

"Nikolai Nikolaich confirmed the sentence by telegram. And Bonch afterward became chief of staff of an army, then of a whole Army Group. And Guchkov not only did not back down, he's been trying lately to revive the whole business—to topple Sukhomlinov."

If a close associate of the War Minister was a spy, maybe the minister himself is a spy? Where would that leave the Tsar?

Well, that was Guchkov. That was how politicians behaved.

"What are they like, the people around Guchkov nowadays?" Svechin was anxious to know. "A lot worse than he is, I would imagine?"

"Yes, the Kadets have thrown him off course. Guchkov today isn't the Guchkov of old."

"What about the conspiracy?" Svechin swathed himself in smoke from his big pipe. A shifting bluish haze. "The conspiracy is just a big joke! Anybody he runs into in a restaurant he tells all about it."

"Come on—he knew he could depend on us."

"But how many times must it have happened before? D'you think nobody knows about this plot of theirs? All Petersburg is talking about the plot Guchkov is hatching. The Police Department must have received a hundred denunciations. What sort of conspirator is he? He's capable of botching anything. It's just that our government is too timid, never knows whether to go left or right around a post."

"So when it comes to action Guchkov is obviously neither here nor

there. It's just talk. But there may be complications . . . oh, yes!" Vorotyntsev's pipe was out, and he put it down. "Anyway, his program
seems a bit peculiar. All in all, Russia might be even worse led than
she is now . . ."

"And where did they get the idea there might be a revolution? I
can't see where it sprang from. These politicians have done so much
hollering they've ended by scaring themselves. If you listen to them,
Russia's always doomed, in fact it met its doom long ago, its fate was
sealed from Rurik on. Of course, His Most August Majesty is more to
blame than anyone—he's the one who gave them their head. He keeps
changing his mind, never settles on anything, and he's never had the
courage to curb them. God forbid he should ever directly command
so much as a single division. He'd dash around all over the place, and
end by leading them into machine-gun fire, just like his great favorites
always do. Well, that's not what he's there for. He's been on the throne
a long time, and that's a good thing in itself. Thank God for it."

"It isn't just one division! He's led the whole army into a trap!"
Vorotyntsev said weightily.

"This is what Romania's done to you—you're hallucinating. You've
spent too long on the front line, that's all."

"Why don't you go and do a bit of fighting?"

"Why should I? Why don't you come here instead? It's ridiculous!
Those swine are undermining military discipline in time of war and
pretending it's to ensure victory!"

Vorotyntsev leaned closer to him across the table. "It isn't a question
of victory, Andreich! Maybe the politicians are trying to scare people,
blindly. But those who really know see good reason to be scared. You
should go and take a look. You can't see a thing from this office."

Svechin, determined to go nowhere, wedged himself more firmly
into his chair. "You've got rebellion in your blood. You're a born rebel.
Come on, tell me, what's your program? Sleep through it all? Is that
realistic when the front lines are so close together?"

Well, no, if you were honest about it you couldn't just escape into
dreamland. He hadn't been able to come right out with it at Cubat's
. . . but here . . . after all that had been said . . . Very quietly . . .

"The thing is . . . to get out of this war altogether. We got stuck
with it for no good reason."

All the time he had been traveling this thought had been on the tip
of his tongue, but he had never succeeded in expressing it. It was not
at all easy for an officer to say such a thing. And now that he had—
it was probably too late and in the wrong place.

Svechin goggled, looked as if he was about to yell. Instead, he said
quietly, with his head close to his companion's, "You mean . . . in spite
of everything . . . a separate peace?"

"What else is there? If you're ruptured right across your belly, can you go on pulling? I'm telling you—they've knocked the stuffing out of us. We missed our chance to opt for neutrality in 1914—let's do it now."

"And let them chop off a chunk of our territory?"

"Not one little bit. The Germans will be only too glad of a respite. What little of our land they have, they'll evacuate. Including Poland, you ask? We have to liberate Poland anyway—let the Germans sort it out. As for the polenta eaters, we'll be glad to get away from them."

Instead of bellowing about oath breaking and treason, Svechin said, "Look, you're a soldier. Just think! Sit in my chair a bit and you'll see things more clearly. Except for that Romanian shithouse of yours we haven't retreated anywhere for nearly two years now. What's wrong with you? Aren't you aware of it? That's Zemgor's line, making out that the war is lost. It shouldn't be yours . . ."

"Not the war! I've been trying to tell you that we've lost our people!"

"We're holding on to Riga, we've got bridgeheads beyond the Dvina! Dvinsk, Minsk, and that whole area as far as Pinsk is in our hands! Arms and equipment? We're better off than in any month since 1914. This is for your ears only: right now we have as many three-inch shells in stock as we have expended all through the war! Machine guns? The Tula plant used to produce seven hundred a year, now it's a thousand a month! Artillery fuses—it used to be fifty thousand a month, now it's seventy thousand a day! Have you heard of SPHA?"

"No, but the number of units produced still doesn't prove . . ."

"Special-Purpose Heavy Artillery. We're bursting at the seams with it. And it already has its reserve supply of ammunition. The Artillery Directorate is getting it ready for a breakthrough next spring. We've never been able to put on such a show of strength before. The Germans will be flabbergasted. This is all secret! The spring offensive will be a tremendous affair! With the Baltic Fleet—we've got Nepenin, he's a fighter. No other country in Europe has young admirals like him and Kolchak. Kolchak wants to make a landing in the Turkish straits in the spring of 1917." His hand skimmed lightly over the rough wall map beside him, as far as the Black Sea. The wrong bait for Vorotyntsev: those mad enough to want the Bosphorus could have it!

"And even if we had nothing, even if we really did fold our paws and doze off, we would still win the war. The Americans have an election this month. Then the president will have a free hand and before you know it he'll be joining in the war, and it won't be on Germany's side. What sort of idiot would go for a separate peace when Germany's already caught a cold?"

Vorotyntsev dismissed all this with a wave or two of his hand. "An American victory is not a victory for us. They never gave us any money to carry on the war. What sort of victory are we looking for? We don't need any more land. We do need to save our people."

Well, of course, the view from the Supreme Commander's HQ was more cheering, indeed entirely positive. Anyone sitting there might succumb to such arguments. But once back in your trench you'll find the load heavier than ever.

All the talk Vorotyntsev had heard in those three weeks, and all the talking he had done himself, had made things no clearer. We make our own idiosyncratic patterns of today's events, our own predictions for tomorrow, but there is only one sure way for things to go and none of us can see it clearly.

"Yegor, Yegor! How many times have I told you—if you want to make history you mustn't kick out wildly, you mustn't try to struggle out of harness. You're too restive for your own good. Pull the load you're harnessed to! Let history take its course."

Vorotyntsev studied his rock-solid friend. The shiny metal of the telephone receiver. The dead ash in his half-smoked pipe. He drummed on the arm of his chair.

Sighed.

It had ripened in him in the trenches. Out walking. Out riding.

And had never ceased to nag at him in these last three weeks.

But his question had still not been answered.

"Who *will* be appointed then?"

"Give up, do you?" Svechin said with a smirk. "Can't guess?" He rubbed his big hands together, enjoying every moment. "No one would ever guess. It's one more thing that goes to show we can't possibly lose the war." Then, almost shouting: "It's Gurku!"

At first Vorotyntsev did not recognize the name, long forgotten in this facetiously modified form. He stared at his friend, stupefied. Then he asked, "You mean Gurko? Vasili Osipich? Gurochka? It can't be true!" It lifted him from his chair and he rushed around the office, striking his chest with one hand, then the other. "How on earth did that come about? How, how . . . ?"

"I'll tell you," Svechin said, beaming. "Mikhail Vasilich insisted. Just imagine that! I take back half of what I've ever said against the old man. The Emperor, of course, wasn't at all eager to take such a boor, such a barbarian—not one of us, quite wrong. He'll be telling us home truths. But the old man was in bed with a hundred-degree temperature, and the Emperor gave in to him. The order isn't signed yet, but everything points that way."

This was indeed a departure from the Emperor's usual anemic style of leadership. He was not appointing some blockhead of a guardsman, or some grand duke, he had bypassed all the sycophants and self-seekers, all the doggie dancing masters, tellers of funny stories and court favorites, all the puffed-up adjutant generals, and arrogant hoary ancients, passed over all the Army Group commanders, disregarded all claims to seniority, and given control of the Russian army to a desperado, a genuine fighting soldier, a clever, indefatigable, uncompromising general at the peak of his powers. And—what was more—in days long gone the leader of the Young Turks!

Svechin read his thoughts and pulled him up sharply. "Don't get too excited! You're back on your hobbyhorse, aren't you? If it's that infantile Young Turk game, say goodbye to it, forget it, drop it. But you haven't heard yet what a brave show he put up at Vladimir Volynsk. He's in excellent form. With a general like him we can . . . ! And you will be back here again!"

A Chief of Staff like Gurko, with a Supreme Commander like the present one—yes, please! They would add up to one authoritative Supreme Commander! Such a meteoric rise could not fail to make any true officer's heart beat faster! This had always been how truly great war leaders rose to the top! Only thus could he emerge—the new Suvorov for whom Russia had longed ever since the war began. If he had been slower about it he would have been no Suvorov!

Could it change the whole course of the war?

Had the change already begun?

It meant . . . Once Gurko was in place it meant that to all intents and purposes the coup had already been carried out. No better choice could be made. Whatever happened.

Power, then, is almost in *our* hands?

*　　*　　*

I HAD FARTHER TO GO
BUT THE HORSES WERE SLOW.

*　　*　　*

[6 7]

In the meantime he had to pay for this summons to GHQ by putting in a few hours' work in the Intelligence Department, supplementing their information.

He got busy but was so thrilled with the news that his mind kept returning to Gurko. Could they really appoint him? Over the heads of so many others? If only they would! It would change everything, put right so much that was wrong!

At first he had been taken aback by the unexpectedness of it. Yet, when you thought about it, was Gurko's appointment really so unforeseeable? Once upon a time, in Stolypin's best years, Vasili Gurko had supplied Guchkov and his Military Commission of the Duma with military consultants, and it was in Gurko's apartment that they had met the politicians to help coordinate their views on legislative proposals. Alekseev himself had been one of the earliest of these advisers. Always circumspect, he had later distanced himself and avoided the disparaging label "Young Turk." But now (perhaps Svechin and I should not have spoken ill of him?), mindful of the past and free from envy—had he listened to his conscience and refused to overlook merit and talent? Gurko had been promoted to corps commander after his swoop on Allenstein and successful withdrawal with a single cavalry division: it had come too late for Samsonov (and had shown Rennen-kampf up: he and the rest of them should have acted quickly), but in itself it was a daring and faultlessly executed raid. Since then he had marked time until last year Alekseev had promoted him, a mere lieutenant general, to command an army, with full generals under him, and given him, temporarily, the Northern Army Group, then the Guards Army. Now Alekseev apparently saw Gurko as the only possible successor to himself, and had summoned him for that reason. Noble Alekseev!

So thrilled was Vorotyntsev by the news that everything now seemed to depend on Gurko: his own immediate prospects, where he would be tomorrow, the future of his secret plan, which had become so blurred during his travels that he now hardly understood it himself. His belief in it had been badly shaken by Svechin, and in some respects by Olda, but he was still seeking the formulation which had so far eluded him.

He badly needed a letter from Olda. How he missed her! It was so long since he had seen her. Did she really exist? He hardly knew: that weekend with Alina at the guesthouse was like a wall between them. His heart, his body were aware of Olda every minute of the day, but his mind sometimes forgot her altogether.

In the past few hours the warmish, dull day had darkened. A storm was brewing. A brisk wind had sprung up and was chasing black clouds across the sky, though as yet no rain was falling. Sudden powerful gusts whipped off hats, billowed garments, tousled the manes and tails of horses, and even held back pedestrians breasting it on Governor's Square. Unusually for that time of year, and with a sky so dark, the wind had brought excessive, almost summery warmth. It could not last long, but in the dying hours of the day it troubled breathing and feelings. Work over, and on his way to the post office, Vorotyntsev, feeling hot and overburdened in his greatcoat and his tall fur hat, regretted not bringing raincoat and forage cap.

To his right the wind was whistling loudly around a white fire tower with a gilded top like a fireman's helmet. He enjoyed bracing himself and battling against the wind as he crossed the close-fitted cobble-stones of Governor's Square, making for the old Town Hall, a five-story building topped by a bell tower, more or less Polish in inspiration. He came out on Bolshaya Sadovaya Street, behind the Town Hall, where Jewish traders were still selling petit fours, "radish fritters," and other confections to children, from stalls set against the stone wall of the monastery.

Mogilev's best pharmacies, photographic studios, and shops were all there on this long street stretching beyond the monastery and its blue belfry. Shop signs showed red gloves, golden boots, festoons of Ukrainian sausages. Dusk was falling and the after-school promenade was beginning. Girls in twos and fours wearing porkpie hats with a ribbon fluttering over one ear: brown ribbon with golden rosette, blue with silver, pink with gold. Some of the girls were very pretty, and almost adult. The boys, also in small groups, sauntered behind them: high school pupils wearing dark blue caps with white piping, stylishly crumpled like those of cavalry officers, modern school pupils in green caps with yellow piping. Mogilev too was now a capital city of sorts, with a bustling life of its own, and people were stimulated, not deterred, by the boisterous warm wind.

Vorotyntsev was on his way to the post office in the hope of finding a general delivery letter from Olda. The nearer he got, the tighter his chest became, the more insistently his heart hammered her name. He had lived through so many pointless days, useless explanations, futile crises since he had last seen her. He had put her in an intolerable position, and had put his little sister Vera in a stupid one if Alina descended on her looking for explanations. Why had he been in such a hurry? How could he have behaved so idiotically? He had almost been simpleton enough to let Alina worm Olda's name out of him. Even without it, she had punished him for his candor.

It was three days since he had heard anything of Alina, but that was something of a relief: the less you saw and heard, the less you ached. Just as long as she had not gone off to Petrograd for a showdown with Olda. Perhaps dear Susanna had made herself useful and held Alina back?

Alina was suffering, of course (by now probably less than at first). He would still have to meet her, spend time with her, but just now it cost him a mental effort to remember that. Just now what he wanted was not to think about her at all.

He went first to the telegram window. It was in his hand as soon as he asked—a telegram from Petrograd. He almost tore it in his haste to open it. From Vera. All was well, Alina was not with her. She had been sensible enough to stay away, thank God. But what sort of ordeal had it been for dear Vera? What was she thinking now? It was all horribly unpleasant.

Lighter at heart, Vorotyntsev went to ask for his letters with pleasurable anticipation. The clerk behind the highly polished oak barrier began sorting through the "V" pile with careful fingers, in no hurry at all to find what he was looking for, but determined not to miss it.

Vorotyntsev's eyes tried to wrest the expected envelope from the clerk's fingers, though he had no idea as yet what it would look like, since he had never received a letter from Olda and did not yet know her handwriting well enough to recognize it at a distance and upside down, but longing for, loving in advance her envelope, her handwriting and what she had written—whatever it was it would send the hot blood coursing through his veins, he could feel it already!

The clerk, good man, had found it! A smallish envelope, but not at all ladylike, slightly elongated, of stout corrugated paper, white but with a grayish tinge. Its delicate silky lining rustled as it changed hands. The handwriting was upright, the letters as small and compact as Olda herself when she sat with her arms tightly folded and her legs tucked up under her on the sofa.

He was in a feverish hurry, but afraid that he might carelessly tear the precious envelope. The clerk, excellent fellow, observed the colonel's predicament and offered him a pair of scissors. All this with no trace of a smile. Before slitting the envelope Vorotyntsev looked hard at the stamps. They belonged to the "Help Our Fighting Men and Their Families" series. He was familiar with them, had often seen them, but this particular combination heightened his excitement. Was it coincidence? One showed St. George, Bringer of Victory, mounted, lance leveled, the other a woman wearing the headdress of a boyar's wife, and embracing infant orphans. This great lady, pictured from behind, was tall and quite unlike Olda in appearance, but her queenly persona, at once majestic and kindly, was of course that of Olda!

Vorotyntsev slit the envelope, taking care not to cut off the least little strip, and carried the letter over to an oak reading desk quartered by diagonal partitions, which made it impossible for anyone standing beside him to look over as he read. How he had longed to take Olda's tiny hands in his own! To hear her low, lilting voice! Now it was as though all this was happening at once. This was not a letter he was holding, but her hands. He was not reading the words, he was hearing Olda's voice. He read random snatches, making no sense of them, happily skipping sentences and looking back at them, reading the same passage three times in succession and still not taking it in. Shielded by the partitions and the slant of the desk from the eyes of his neighbors he was completely absorbed in Olda, plunging his face into her, chattering with her, and the tone of their happy chatter was more important than the half-understood and quickly forgotten sentences. There would be time for them later.

Little by little he began to realize that she had written the letter as confusedly as he was reading it. She had paced and paced, as full of him as if he had not left her the night before, but was still beside her, and she was walking and conversing with him. Then, tired out, she had sat down five minutes before midnight to write what little re-

mained in her mind—just those few sentences—of all that she had
said to him. Sat down? Or was she walking, as if she had never seen
it before, around the room she had paced so often, with open arms,
as if to say, "Are you here? Where are you? Sweep me off my feet!
Lift me in your arms!"

Vorotyntsev half closed his eyes, the better to see her walking toward
him with open arms, as if she was playing blind man's buff! Lift me
in your arms! Yes, my darling! Light as a feather!

Walking? Letter? Talking? Kissing? It was all mixed up in his head.
Where was it all happening? Who was talking to whom? He stood
leaning on the desk, reading it over and over again, feeling faint . . .
What was all this? . . . When the war's over . . . we'll go somewhere . . .
walk barefoot through the meadows . . . he could see her little bare feet
clearly. He kissed them, kissed the soles, kissed every tiny toe in turn.

Vorotyntsev put the precious letter away and walked off, his feet like
those of a drunken man, cautiously aware of the smooth, flagged floor.
He had reached the door before it occurred to him that there might
also have been some serious message in the letter. He had read it, but
nothing had registered. Read it carefully later on? No, right now.

Back he went. As far as the lamp on the wall there.

No, better go all the way back to my cozy little section of the reading
desk.

As he drew the letter from the envelope again, another scrap of
paper, with a postscript, fell out. How had he failed to notice it before?
It might have gotten lost!

"Written this morning. For no particular reason. Just reluctant to
part with it! I shall be lonely! Listen to the wind! That will be me!
Listen to the rustling of the boughs! That will be me!"

A scrap of paper, two lines. But again his heart leapt, filled with
youthful eagerness, yearned toward her. Olda! My gift from heaven!
My recompense!

Yes, but *was* there any serious message in the letter? Ah—there it
was:

"Now that you are there—I beg you to look around you, look carefully, talk to people, find out with whom you can do the things I so
wanted to inspire you to do. Seek out men who are loyal and true!
Our life together, the life of all of us, depends on it, we must not let
anything cut it short!"

Still scarcely feeling the floor under his feet, he walked to the broad
heavy door, which closed itself behind him.

As he stepped out, the crazy wind buffeted him in the chest—a
strong wind, but its unusual warmth made it seem merely playful.

Listen to it! That will be me!

While Vorotyntsev had been in the post office evening had set in.
It was still early, but dark. The lamps at short intervals along Bolshaya

Sadovaya Street had been lit. It must have been raining a little, there were fresh puddles, and the roadway and the sidewalk gleamed near the streetlamps, brightening the Mogilev evening. The light shower had made the embrace of the gusting wind all the warmer. What weather! Spring in November!

Vorotyntsev wanted to walk and keep walking, and this wind was a joy. His greatcoat and his tall fur hat were no longer a burden. He felt weightless. It cost him no effort to return the salutes of passing soldiers. The evening promenade was in full swing. Besides the high school pupils there were now couples on the street, with here and there a soldier and his girl, some of them withdrawing from the brightly lit street into darker corners. Vorotyntsev, feeling as young as any of these young lovers, strode on at a brisk, businesslike pace, footsteps loud on the flagstones, spurs jingling, borne along and buoyed up by his happiness.

Just now, in the post office, it was his Olda he held by her hands, and now he was carrying her, little thing, in his bosom.

How easy it all was: all yours, held tight against your breast, all there, carried with you!

And you yourself borne along like a hot-air balloon!

Riders, army automobiles, supply wagons went by, a detachment of soldiers marched past—yet somehow these things were not reminders of war. This town, burdened as it was with all the soldiers billeted there, and the worries they brought with them, seemed, perhaps because it was new to him, perhaps because of the blustering of that crazy warm wind, or the lamplight reflected in the puddles, a place of beauty and carefree youthful happiness. No more than that.

He wanted to stay with those young people, not to return to his dreary hotel. He had reached Governor's Square and, enjoying his struggle with the wind, straddling its gusts, he began crossing the square again, not toward the Quartermaster's side, but bearing right toward the little square with the sundial, beyond which lay the path to a little public park, known as the Rampart, because it loomed steeply over the Dnieper, and might once have been a man-made embankment. He walked on, greedily inhaling that hot, moist, joyous air!

A second life. It might soon begin. Olda was like a new galaxy, with an infinite number of unexplored worlds still awaiting discovery.

He strode across the Rampart without slackening his pace, forgetting how short the path was and that it would end abruptly against a wooden fence above the embankment. There were few lampposts here, and no places of entertainment—the open-air stage to one side was dark, it was out of season. On the fringes of the park the courting couples, freer from constraint, kissed without concealment, swelling Vorontyntsev's joy.

Listen to the branches rustling—that will be me!

He ranged the Rampart, taking first one path, then another.

In the light from the streetlamp he saw the tall figure of a general advancing toward him. The general was entering the pool of light, walking slowly, hands behind his back, head bowed, as if unhappy. Vorotyntsev was some distance away, but was borne briskly along so that they met directly under the lamp.

Even at a distance he had thought that there was something rather familiar about that lean figure. As he approached, he effortlessly exchanged his loping stride for a more soldierly step, raised himself to his full height, and turned slightly toward the general, who also drew one hand from behind his back and turned toward the colonel. And then, directly under the lamp, Vorotyntsev could not fail to recognize him.

"Good evening, Your Excellency!"

He stood and waited. There was nothing else to do.

The general had also stopped, though he had not yet recognized his companion.

"Good evening, Colonel . . . Oh, oh, it's Vorotyntsev, isn't it?"

He held out his hand. He looked and sounded old, but his grip was firm and tenacious.

"Don't tell me you're back at GHQ again?"

"What, me-e? Certainly not, Aleksandr Dmitrich," Vorotyntsev said cheerfully. "Just here for two days, more or less by accident. And you?"

"Me-e?" Nechvolodov's "me-e" was as long-drawn-out as Vorotyntsev's, but not at all cheerful. He seemed to be choosing his words carefully.

"I've been staying here in reserve. For over a month now. They can't find me a job."

Vorotyntsev was so elated, and this unhappy note was so much out of tune with his own feelings that he felt like leaving it there and hurrying on, although this one-man race of his had no real objective.

Nechvolodov saw him wavering.

"You're in a hurry?"

"Er . . . no. I'm in no hurry. Just taking a walk."

"Well then, would you mind if we walk together?"

"Of course not . . . Let's do that."

He turned around, lost his momentum, and fell in with Nechvolodov's funereal step.

There, on the gravel of the Rampart, his boots, his greatcoat turned for him, but the hot-air balloon that was his breast sailed on, riding the playful wind, through the darkness, to no matter where.

[6 8]

He had turned around and almost come to a halt, but, after his happiness striding headlong into the darkness with Olda in his arms, falling in with the general at his pace and finding him apparently deeply depressed left him at a loss for a moment. He answered his companion's questions, and even asked some of his own, but at first without making much sense.

(Sweep me off my feet! Lift me up!)

Nechvolodov's story, however, claimed his attention. He had been relieved of his command by Brusilov a month earlier, because of serious misunderstandings with the Unions of Zemstvos and Towns, with which Brusilov had no wish to quarrel. As a major general he was automatically put in reserve, and summoned to GHQ to await a new assignment. But there was a surplus of errant generals relegated to GHQ, to await pardon and a new senior command. More than a month later, Nechvolodov had not been offered a division, brigades were being abolished, and it was beneath his dignity to accept a regiment. His case had apparently gone astray in the GHQ underbrush. Nobody, it seemed, had any use for him. At the height of a great war he was apparently superfluous to the Russian army.

Vorotyntsev himself could not endure that sly fox Brusilov, and personal feelings apart, he knew that the man's reputation was inflated, that he was hopeless as a commander in the field.

As for Nechvolodov, Vorotyntsev thought not for the first time that in their young days he and the general had been much alike: the same uprush of talent, the same exaggerated sense of their own strength, the same impatience to reform the Russian army from top to bottom, almost single-handed. But Nechvolodov had happened upon a less favorable time, and really had found himself quite alone. There were only twelve years between them. An age difference of less than a generation. But of a whole reign. Then again, Nechvolodov had risen more rapidly and spectacularly, had become an officer at an earlier age, and entered the Academy a good twenty years before Vorotyntsev. So that where their friends, their memories, their service records were concerned they were in effect a whole generation apart.

(When the war's over . . . we'll walk barefoot through the meadows . . .)

Though not much over fifty, in the lamplight Nechvolodov looked . . . not exactly old, but very weary. Unlike most officers, he was clean-shaven, so that his sunken cheeks were difficult to ignore. This was only too obviously a man who had never succeeded in anything. Vorotyntsev found the comparison with himself chilling. In the summer of

1914 he himself had still been proudly confident that he would acquit himself brilliantly. Two years of war had dimmed and dismissed his hopes. Yet in occasional brighter moments he began believing again that he was destined to do great things: he had not been wounded, he was not enfeebled, he had not aged, his talents had not lost their fine edge. But his morale was sometimes low. (Perhaps that was why he was so eager to find an occupation with more scope than that of an officer in the line.)

No, even now Vorotyntsev refused to believe that he too, as he grew older, would find himself unwanted and unused, and would fade away ingloriously like Nechvolodov.

They walked on at a funereal pace, with the general complaining bitterly.

"The left, though, can get away with anything. As soon as they kick up a fuss everybody gives in to them. It's plain sailing for anybody who's out to damage the regime. When Hannibal was threatening Rome the mighty senate itself took the field against the plebeian Varro, who was already responsible for disgrace and disaster—merely in order to reinforce the authority of the military. While our State Duma, in time of war, openly incites the people to disobey ministers, and the army in the field reads insulting reports in the newspapers."

Walking slowly between lampposts, they entered what seemed to be a long tunnel under the trees and were suddenly invisible to each other. The sides of the tunnel swayed overhead, the trees sighed, struggled in the wind, lashed themselves and shed their last leaves. (Listen to the rustling of the boughs! That will be me!)

"Actually, all they care about is the triumph of their own party. What all those Kadets fear is not that the government will lose the war but, on the contrary, that it will win, and without their aid. That's why they are so eager to form a Kadet government right away. They have always assumed that the war cannot be won without them. But we now have shells, the front is firm, we can get on very well without them—and they're back where they started. What will they use for a springboard after the war?"

Vorotyntsev had seen something of the Kadets, and his impressions had been different. It obviously wasn't true of Shingarev. But Mili Izmailovich? It might be. And Pavel Nikolaevich?

Other muddles incensed the general more than his stagnant career.

" 'Reactionary internal policy'! I ask you! Who's talking about policy at present? Win—that's the only policy for us. It's reached the point where local governmental bodies in the towns are in opposition to higher authority. Who ever heard of such a thing? And the press? It's all leftist. All destructive. Vilifies the Church, vilifies patriots—they narrowly avoid mentioning the throne directly, they've learned to yap about what they call the regime. Every fly-by-night journalist speaks in the name of Russia. They shower us with sewage, but never print our denials, that's their idea of freedom. And any newspaper that stands up for the government is called reptilian or said to be on the government payroll. Nobody has yet managed to create a great Russian national newspaper. Nor even an official government newspaper, for that matter. Russia must surely be the only country which hasn't gotten around to it. Why do we have to listen year in and year out to nothing but abuse of the government?"

"Yes, but look . . ." Vorotyntsev, feeling the superiority of the happy man over the unhappy one, mildly demurred. "There has to be freedom of speech. Things have to be called by their own names, abuses must become public knowledge, so that rogues will tremble in their hiding places."

"Yes, of course! But do you really think they'll publicize the misdeeds of their own Zemgor people? Or the industrialists? Or the black marketeers who corner the food supplies? Those people they cover up for, the biggest rogues of all have nothing to fear from them. Their abuse is reserved for the government."

True enough.

"And the people learn what is going on in the country only as malicious detractors portray it. The majority of our people, thank God, are untouched by this plague. But only because they do not read the newspapers."

"If it was only the majority of our people, Aleksandr Dmitrich . . . But the fact is that the majority of officers too have no real understanding of what's going on. All we think of is rank, promotion, medals, sword knots, traditions of the unit, traditions of the training school, how the last parade went off—but as far as social problems are concerned we're nothing but lamebrained ignoramuses. We think things will look after themselves and can carry on very well without us."

"Yes! Yes!" said the general in a brisker voice.

"Anyway," said Vorotyntsev, not quite sure where his thoughts would lead him, "the majority never decide anything. It's always a minority. Those who *act*."

"Or those who shout loudest."

"All the same, Aleksandr Dmitrich," Vorotyntsev went on in the same calm tone of voice, "people must be free to express their opinions. And there must be some outlet for it. The Duma, the newspapers . . ."

"Yes, but whose freedom are we talking about?" To judge from his voice in the darkness Nechvolodov had halted, horrified. Vorotyntsev also came to a standstill.

"There is in Russia some sort of 'education league,' teeming with hundreds and thousands of teachers. But what does 'education' mean to them? To them there is nothing sacred in Russia, it has no historic rights, no national foundations. They hate everything Russian, everything Orthodox, everything that goes back into the depths of time. Education, to them, means revolution. They call it 'freedom' to make it less alarming. But what sort of freedom do they have in mind? Eight out of ten of our fellow countrymen are peasants, and one in every ten belongs to the urban lower middle class. These 'parties' never speak for them. Nor for the clergy. At best they represent some section of the gentry. But they really speak only for themselves. It's all one gang. When they talk about 'the people's rights' they mean power for themselves. You can open as many parliaments as you like—those sitting there will be lawyers. Start all the newspapers you please—you'll have nothing but journalists. Each and every one of them yapping at Russia. While Russia is voiceless. The country consists of peasants, but its Duma is packed with lawyers from the two capitals."

"If that's so, our electoral law is useless. Let's change it."

"That won't help, the lawyers and journalists will worm their way in just the same. Parliament is an institution specially made for them. And if they ever get their 'responsible government' they'll go completely berserk. We simply must not let Russia fall into the hands of such madmen! Surely you don't expect anything good from our Duma? What is it they're asking for? Ministers accountable only to them. In other words, they want to undermine the fundamental laws of the state. Also an amnesty for terrorists and revolutionaries. In other words, they want to free the enemies of the state, so that they can start all over again. One more thing—they don't want the least little law to be enacted without the Duma's consent. And they can, of course, sink any law in a morass of verbiage."

"So where does that leave us? What's your solution?"

"Dismiss them immediately!" It sounded like an order.

So there! Vorotyntsev began to feel uncomfortable.

Nechvolodov's voice took on a solemn tone.

"Dissolve the Duma! The Tsar has only to lift his hand and say, 'Hear me, my country! We are restoring Russia to herself!' "

Such grandiloquent extremism, which caused the listener to smile or to doubt, had always embarrassed Vorotyntsev. Such pontifications floated somewhere above the humdrum concerns of today's society and could never capture its imagination.

Because of the wind his words were louder than their meaning required.

"Wouldn't dismissing the Duma mean more and worse disorders?"

Out of the darkness Nechvolodov's hand descended unerringly on Vorotyntsev's shoulder.

"A cowardly argument. Quite the opposite. It's the first sure step away from revolution. How feebleminded can you be—trying to combat revolution with concessions? The state only weakens itself by giving way to windbag civilians. The revolution is already upon us. Can't you see that? It took over I don't know how many years ago. It's bouncing and knocking us around as we speak. It has almost triumphed! Yet here we are, so afraid of stirring it up, of provoking it, that we do nothing about it!"

So! Revolution was no longer *imminent*—it had arrived already! Vorotyntsev himself had seen no sign of it. He had argued with Guchkov about it. Then, earlier in the day, Svechin, wreathed in fragrant pipe smoke in his comfortable office, had laughed off talk of revolution as mere fantasy. But now, in the wind-torn darkness with the general's firm hand resting on his shoulder, he was struck by the coincidence: Guchkov and Nechvolodov had arrived at the same conclusion from opposite poles. All the pessimistic things he had heard on this trip crowded into his mind again, and he asked himself—could it be true? Was revolution already at the door?

They had stood long enough. Nechvolodov took Vorotyntsev by the elbow—a downward movement, given the difference in height between them—and steered him farther across the Rampart. The hot, crazy wind gamboled among the trees, hugged them, buffeted them, wrestled with them, sent fallen leaves scampering noisily along the ground. The walkers occasionally stepped on something hard, a pebble or a chestnut, and crushed it underfoot.

We have traveled by different routes, Vorotyntsev thought, but are not Nechvolodov's anxieties for Russia and my own identical?

"Surely, Colonel, you can see what Russia has been reduced to? The war is not to blame for the catastrophe which has befallen us! The reason isn't our casualties, and it isn't the breakdown of the supply system. It is the fact that we were defeated in advance by the leftist spirit! Long before the war the country was badly shaken by wild talk as well as by bombs. For a long time now it has been dangerous to stand in the way of revolution, and risk-free to assist it. Those who have renounced all traditional Russian values, the revolutionary horde, the locusts from the abyss, vilify and blaspheme and no one dares challenge them. A left-wing newspaper can print the most subversive of articles, a left-wing speaker can deliver the most incendiary of speeches—but just try pointing out the dangers of such utterances and the whole leftist camp will raise a howl of denunciation. All honest people have a panicky fear of this word, so they pass by in silence any incitement to unrest. Certificates of honesty have to be obtained from the left. The whole press, the whole academic establishment, the whole intelligentsia all mock the regime. The gentry follow suit. And we too are dumbstruck in the face of the leftist Russophobe clichés which everyone finds so natural and so modern. Utter just one word in defense of Orthodox Christianity and they will howl you down, cry shame. The Pirogov Society holds its congress, and you expect these doctors to behave like doctors—but what do they talk about? In wartime, remember. The wounded and how to treat them? Oh no. It's the same old subject—how to change our governmental system!"

The voice that brooked no contradiction reached Vorotyntsev from some invisible location in the darkness.

"The whole life of Russia is caught in a spiritual trap. Three stigmata, three infectious fears have reduced us all to impotence: if you argue with the left you are a "Black Hundreder," if you argue with the young you are a die-hard conservative, if you argue with the Jews you are an anti-Semite. By these means they are forcing us to surrender Russia not only without a struggle but without argument, without demur. And what follows will be the triumph of *progress*! On the face of it Russia is still ruled by the Emperor. In reality it has long been ruled by a swarm of leftist locusts."

Now he was going too far! It was not yet true that the left ruled Russia. But, of course, the Tsar ought not to be a nonentity. You had to know how to rule.

(He kept this to himself, however. Open disrespect for the monarch would be embarrassing.)

Nechvolodov gripped his elbow more firmly and strode on with a firmer step across the Rampart into the chaotic darkness, into the unseemly vortex of the wind.

"It's a sickness—this muddying of the nation's spirit. Think how thrilled the educated class was with the bomb throwers, and how it exulted in our defeats in the Far East. We were no longer ourselves, usurpers had supplanted us, some sort of airborne pestilence had come upon us. It was as if some creature of the depths had uncoiled itself when we liberated the serfs, and writhed upward, eager to wrestle Russia into the abyss. A handful of prancing horned devils appeared and all Russia was in turmoil. There is some kind of universal process at work here. It isn't just a political trend, it is a cosmic turbulence. Perhaps these unclean spirits, though they have appeared first in Russia, are meant to sweep across the entire world. It fell to Dostoevsky to observe the earliest years of this visitation and he understood it at once and warned us. But we ignored him. Now the ground is being snatched from under our feet. The doughtiest defenders are losing heart and giving up."

The walk, begun out of pure sympathy, had already jolted Vorotyntsev out of his amorous mood, and was beginning to disorient him still further. A malaise borne by an ill wind? Was he catching the general's sickness? A new way of looking at Russia—ugly and extreme—such as Vorotyntsev had never encountered before. But it too was concerned with the country's roots—and he had heard them snapping while he was at the front. Three weeks ago he had been traveling to the main centers of Russian life, his ideas, or so it seemed to him, all of a piece, unfragmented. But at each encounter he had changed, begun to doubt, swerved, stumbled. All that he had learned for sure was that things were much more complicated than he had thought.

He was stumbling again. But he tried to argue.

"Still, we had centuries in which to prevent it. To ensure that no backwoods village would be short of pickled cabbage for the winter. Where were our eyes? Where were our hearts? And what of the august fingers that wrote 'reject' on every bold proposal? Why didn't we liberate the peasants a hundred years before the visitation? And when we did get around to it, why couldn't we have been more generous, why did we leave them short of land? What sort of despicable greed on the part of landowners prevented peasants for decades from resettling in Siberia, and forcibly brought them back if they did, just to push up the price of land rented from the gentry? What sort of sense did it make, not allowing resettlement in Siberia, which was all ours, and empty?"

Start brooding about the past and the image of the thwarted and murdered Stolypin loomed at every turn.

"There was a man capable of dragging Russia out of the slough by sheer force. And who started hounding him first? Wasn't it the right? Wasn't it they who murdered him? He knew how to get things moving—so they tied his hands."

No rightist, however far to the right his views, had the understanding of the peasant mind which Vorotyntsev had been lucky enough to absorb in Zastruzhe. The rightists skimmed the surface, but were ignorant of the depths.

"All those leftist academics, of course, have no real sympathy with the peasants. But what a splendid boost their flights of rhetoric were given!"

They moved so slowly into the lamplight, and out of it again, that Vorotyntsev had time to imprint his companion's image on his mind and afterward connect it with the voice in the darkness: the greatcoat with no claim to elegance buttoned tightly around the tall, sturdy frame, the bearing—that of a man despondent but unbowed, the face gaunt, yet every feature infused with energy. From the grip on his elbow, and the occasional pressure on his ribs, Vorotyntsev could tell that his companion's body was still muscular and supple. There was nothing except his bitter words to show how much he had aged.

"Yes. True. The professors don't feel for Russia, the revolutionaries still less. But what of us? Where do we stand? Why are we paralyzed in the face of the plague of locusts? Why are we overcome by lethargy? Why are our forces so scattered? Why are we, each and every one of us, so isolated?"

His "we" confidently bracketed Vorotyntsev with himself. But what made him so certain? Perhaps this whole conversation was meant to establish a basis for joint action?

"We can't even find a pen to defend us, let alone a sword. We have nobody who can write. We're all inarticulate."

Why, indeed, had they no writers? Why were the right-wing newspapers so feeble, and always sniping at each other? Why could none of them take a broader view?

People speak of "the right." But do we really have a "right"? There's no such party, no stable structure. No orators. No leaders. No funds. That is the reality of the mysterious visitation: those who should resist it are impotent. (Or cretinous? Why are they all so clumsy, so hamfisted, so crude, so impatient, why are they doomed always to fail?) They lack the perspicacity to realize that the struggle is inevitable, and that it can be won only by spiritual strength and purity. (Ah, but where is that "high personage" of yours? And why have you allowed the very word "rightist" to be made into an insult?)

"Let us behave in such a way that we have no cause for shame. I myself am not in the least ashamed. I will openly admit, anywhere you like, that I am proud to be credited with membership in the Black Hundred. The term, by the way, originates with the 'black hundred' monks who successfully defended the Monastery of the Trinity and St. Sergius against the Poles, and so saved a Russia in turmoil. Then, in 1905, the name Black Hundred was bestowed on the bewildered 'dark' (uneducated) millions who rallied to the defense of the regime when it proved incapable of defending itself. But today—today, find me a hundred if you can! Just one hundred, ready to act—where are they?"

They had now reached the point on the outermost path at which the Rampart was interrupted by a steep footpath down to the embankment below. Facing them across the gorge, the governor's gardens occupied a slope just as steep. There was no lamp near them here, but from beyond the fence around the governor's gardens electric lights blinked through the second-story windows of the Tsar's residence, as though swayed by the rough wind blowing through the bare trees.

In the Tsar's residence the evening was probably taking its usual carefree course, untroubled by problems of state. Were they enjoying a leisurely dinner, or sitting over a late cup of tea, or playing cards, or exchanging stories of army life?

While here, a hundred sazhens away, unsummoned, unwanted, forgotten, a servant of the throne stood and waited. In the weak light from afar his face was not clearly visible, but if you strained your eyes you could see his tall, upright figure, and the hand resting on what might be either a tree stump or a post.

It looked as though Nechvolodov was resting on his sword.

His idle sword. Unwanted in battle. Driven into the ground.

The revolution is here already? All around us! One knight stood out against it, ready to do battle. But he was never called upon to help. Now his sword had sunk so far into the ground that no hand will ever draw it.

And if it were drawn its point would have rusted away.

Over there, behind the closed doors of the brightly lit house, from which any decision taken would be relayed within a quarter of an hour by ticker tape, were they also painfully preoccupied with state problems?

As were the two men standing there on the Rampart, jostled by the warm wind. But no one looked to them for decisions or asked for their help. The slighted general had found his place on the wrong side of the Tsar's garden fence. (Had he perhaps been coming to stand here every evening for a month? He had certainly known today just where he was leading Vorotyntsev.)

"We must unite! We must act!" Nechvolodov rapped out, apparently not doubting for a moment that he was speaking to a kindred spirit, or perhaps simply unable to keep his thoughts to himself any longer. "We must restore the people's pride in its nationhood! That is more vital and more urgent than attacking the enemy without."

This last idea coincided precisely with Vorotyntsev's own. It fitted in exactly with the message he had carried around for the past few weeks, without being able to convince anyone.

Olda had written, "Seek out men who are loyal and true!" She was right. That was what he had to do.

As Nechvolodov saw it, we began the war supposedly in defense of Serbia. But that soon faded, and we found ourselves fighting against powers with the same kind of government as ourselves, in alliance with powers whose form of government is just the opposite.

Well, Vorotyntsev was not the one to stand up for the Allies.

Confronted with a way of thinking like his own, he nonetheless saw one possible objection: the Central Powers are afraid that we may unite the Slavs, and so they feel compelled to fight against us. Why have we ranted so recklessly about the Slavs, generation after generation? Why do we go on carrying this burden when we lack the strength for it?

Nechvolodov was equally uninterested in the Slavs. His thoughts too were for Russia alone, and how she was to be dragged out of the mire.

"We need to create a new and reinvigorated right-wing force. Drawn from the sources of our national history. And offer ourselves as a prop to the enfeebled regime. The days of decision have arrived! United under a strong hand we can by our fortitude save Russia at the last moment. We must step forward and say courageously—and saying it is even more difficult than stepping forward—that Russia cannot exist without monarchy, such is her nature."

And nothing more is needed? Vorotyntsev had been led along that path before. The same old rhetoric, the same helpless floundering. Whenever he heard these monarchist extravaganzas Vorotyntsev was astonished to see how independent-minded, levelheaded, educated people could acquiesce so blindly in all the actions of their infallible Tsar. The strength of their sentiment might excite admiration—but where was their plan of action?

Vorotyntsev did not spare his companion. "Under whose firm hand?" he asked. "If the sovereign himself is incredibly weak, whose hand is it to be? If the nation's spirit is troubled, doesn't the trouble start at the very top? And if the monarch consorts with Rasputin, isn't that trouble enough? Should the Emperor be free to order his private life just as he pleases? What then becomes of the mystique of monarchy?"

"What does Rasputin matter?" Nechvolodov said indignantly. "The whole Rasputin legend has been blown up out of all proportion by the enemies of monarchy. How can they best undermine the throne? All their talk of 'the curse of autocracy' doesn't get much of a response. But if the Empress is the mistress of a debauched peasant and a German spy into the bargain—that's all they need. Rasputin fits in beautifully. They can fight against the throne and pretend they're fighting for Russia."

"But what if there is really no firm hand up above? What if the Emperor is steering things the wrong way or just letting it all fall apart?"

As far as he could judge through the gusts of wind Nechvolodov's voice faltered for the first time. Not because he was wavering in his loyalty, but because he was taken aback: here was a high-ranking officer with a record of bravery, surely incapable of being anything but a loyal servant of the throne . . . and yet . . . nonetheless . . .

"Yes, our Emperor is too softhearted at times. But a monarchist must not regard himself as a blind executant of the monarch's will. If he did, all the mistakes and failures of the regime would be . . . whose responsibility? The monarchist must say, 'The Tsar is always right, but I am responsible for all I do, and if anyone is to blame, it is I.' The Emperor needs loyal people, not slaves. The monarchic power is greater than the monarch! To doubt a monarch is to doubt not just one individual but monarchy as such. The Tsar is the embodiment of the people's hopes."

"Not this one!" Vorotyntsev retorted harshly.

"Yes—whoever occupies that position," Nechvolodov said, horrified. "The Tsar and Russia are inseparable concepts."

"No! Only a Tsar worthy of his country. You can reinforce the state if you have someone of character at the center. But you can't reinforce it around a vacuum, which is itself ashamed of its excessively loyal supporters. We take for granted the bizarre fact that in our country people loyal to the throne not only have to put up with ridicule from the public but are despised by the regime itself. It behaves as if it had no need for them. Or perhaps it is ashamed of them."

"That's something only God can judge. It is not for mere men to do so," Nechvolodov said in a deep voice.

"I don't agree. It's a practical problem. I would go so far as to say that the regime itself has become so disloyal that to serve it too honestly is now dangerous. Instead of protecting you in return, it may betray you. That is probably why many people serve it only at half strength. Just go through the motions. And so the throne is surrounded, hemmed in by a rabble of 'excellencies' without conscience, without sense, with none but selfish interests, and all of them there by courtesy of the Tsar, who else? Crooked money-grubbers, not monarchists."

For the first time Nechvolodov was lost for a reply. He stood there upright, facing the Tsar's residence, gripping the rusted sword lodged in the ground. So that's the situation. Guchkov wants to do one thing to avoid revolution. Nechvolodov wants to do the opposite—also to avoid revolution.

They're all at cross-purposes. All pulling different ways. And meanwhile Russia is slithering down the slope.

"Say what you like, Aleksandr Dmitrich, I can't rally round a mere symbol. There has to be a head worthy of the name. With no atmosphere of corruption around it."

Nechvolodov sighed heavily. "One of these days, one of these days, we will realize how very worthy he is! The purity of his heart. His love for all that is sacred in Russia. His angelic simplicity."

Yes, his angelic simplicity was indeed moving. Had he not sent—in return for guns or for gold or simply to vindicate his imperial honor—sixty thousand Russian souls to the French front?

No, Vorotyntsev was not prepared to accept what he was offered. But still, this "comradely bravery controlled by a firm hand," was there anything to it?

They walked back along the avenue. And Nechvolodov, head lowered, ceased pontificating and disclosed conspiratorially (secretly plotting to save the existing regime!) a plan already in existence. Not his own, but that devised by a monarchist group in the capital led by Rimsky-Korsakov.

They envisaged only the simplest, self-evident, and logically necessary actions. They would scrutinize afresh all ministers, commanders of military districts, and governor-generals, and would leave in place no one judged unqualified or slack or spineless, but only bold and decisive people devoted to the throne. Each of them would be required to take an oath affirming his readiness to die in the impending struggle. And each one would name a worthy successor, someone like himself, to replace him in the event of his death.

Vorotyntsev expressed his doubts. It would be extremely difficult to find so many people of that caliber in the upper levels of the establishment. The very stratum in which selfless, self-sacrificing, fiercely loyal monarchists were in short supply.

"If you mean there aren't three hundred loyal and staunch people left in the upper class, the throne is indeed beyond salvation," the general gloomily agreed.

Here, though, was one of the three hundred—a future governor, commander of a military district, distinguished soldier—pacing the Rampart each evening, watching over the Tsar's residence like a supernumerary sentry.

Perhaps he thinks he's found another?

The Duma, as previously stated, would be dismissed by royal proclamation, with no date set for recall. A state of siege would be proclaimed in major towns. Part of the Guards Corps would be brought back to Petersburg, and cavalry units would be stationed in Moscow.

"Aleksandr Dmitrich, you must know very well that the Guards have been put through the meat grinder. Not by the Masons, but by Brusilov, Raukh, and the Emperor's old and best friend, Bezobrazov."

Munitions factories must be put on a war footing so as to eliminate strikes. Government commissars should be appointed to all Zemgor and Guchkov committees, so that their activities could be brought under government supervision, and a stop put to revolutionary propaganda.

This didn't seem too much to ask. It was all perfectly sensible.

Beyond that, we must be ready to fight, and to give our lives, instead of putting our trust in God's mercy alone and waiting for the state to collapse. The main thing was not to give ground. Not to waver. Half measures only exacerbate the other side's virulence. We mustn't let ourselves be frightened into concessions. We must act circumspectly, but decisively, as if at the bedside of a mortally sick patient. And then there would be no revolution.

"I thought you said it had arrived already?"

"It will retreat. What has arrived is a crisis, but it can be resolved to our advantage. As long as we don't shut our eyes on the brink of catastrophe!"

The tormented wind had still not blown itself out. It rushed at them furiously, sometimes from above, sometimes from under their feet, sometimes buffeting them in the chest and pulling them up short, then just as suddenly subsiding.

Trying to persuade me? Trying to dissuade me?

There was no denying that the general's plan was both bold and simple—perhaps too simple. Simpler and clearer than Guchkov's. And all its demands were natural. (It did nothing, however, to deliver the people from the war or from the Allies.) But there was one gaping hole, which seemed to vitiate the whole concept.

"Who, though, is going to try out and appoint and move around these governors? Who administers the oath? Surely *he* can't do it?"

Nechvolodov was silent.

"He is incapable of such decisive action, as you very well know. Just think what strength of character, what resolve, it would take to prepare his immediate circle to die for the cause!"

Nechvolodov remained silent.

But Vorotyntsev persisted.

"What has the Emperor said about this project?"

They walked on.

"The project has been passed to Stürmer. So far he has been afraid to put it into the hands of the monarch."

"Afraid, eh? There you are, then!" Vorotyntsev said briskly, almost as if he was glad to hear it: good or ill he had his result. "There we are, then! What does he have to be afraid of? Tell me. Afraid he himself might have to swear he would lay down his life. So there we are! The throne is encrusted with layer upon layer of nonentities! How are you ever going to clean it? And where are your three hundred loyal servants?"

Even Guchkov had been more realistic.

"So why doesn't one of *you* submit the plan?"

The general, up aloft, nodded at the house.

"How, though? The Emperor's eyes are dimmed. And all means of access to him are closed."

So there it was. The Tsar's residence stood there before them. What was he doing, the inscrutable monarch, somewhere beyond those brilliantly lit windows so near at hand? Listening yet again to boring hussars' stories? Playing solitaire?

Whatever it was, he had no time to read a plan devised by his monarchist supporters.

He could not even find places and jobs for his most loyal and intrepid generals.

The lonely colonel had saddened and disheartened the lonely general. But he too—just as a little while ago he had made an about-face and his rapid flight had become a funeral march—he too had lost, had gone on losing from week to week, something of the velocity which had catapulted him from Kimpolung to Petersburg. In the course of his discussions Vorotyntsev seemed to have come full circle. He was back almost where he had started. Looking, perhaps, in the opposite direction.

Is it thinkable—rocking the boat?

Well, Gurko will soon be here. Then we will see.

[6 9]

That year the Emperor had been detained at GHQ by military operations for five months. He finally found time for a quick visit to Tsarskoye Selo around 2 November, the anniversary of his father's death, then, after attending the annual memorial service in the Cathedral of St. Peter and St. Paul, felt impelled to go and see his mother at Kiev. So, on his return from Tsarskoye Selo to Mogilev, instead of settling into the governor's residence again he rejoined the train for a leisurely journey southward.

Kiev, Kiev! It held unforgettable memories, sacred memories for him. Whenever he entered the city a lofty, austere, ancient feeling filled his heart. Before all else he felt the need to go and worship in the Cathedral of St. Sophia. This time he took Aleksei with him, as soon as they left the station, and before going on to the palace to see Mama.

At this time of year you could usually expect cloudless, golden autumn weather in Kiev. But no, there was mist—a warm mist—in the air. In the brooding, opaque hush the ranks of soldiers and cadets lining the streets looked particularly imposing. That same day he had to attend a graduation parade of officer cadets in the palace yard, and the next day visit four training establishments and show himself to the public by driving through several streets with Mama and the Heir. But nothing made a stronger impression than those soldiers lining the streets of Kiev under the brooding mist.

At first the Emperor did not realize why they were there. Even as he drove past the theater he did not at first remember: the times, the people, and much else had changed so. It came back to him only as he entered the well-remembered rooms of the palace, where they had spent several happy days in September 1911. He had a sudden vivid recollection of those Kiev celebrations, the general rejoicing, flags and garlands and the imperial monogram everywhere, bands playing, the streets, then as now, lined with rank upon rank of soldiers, the same loud cries of "Hurrah!"—but it was in these very rooms that he had come home to Alix that evening and told her that the unhappy Stolypin had been wounded in the theater. Here too they had been told of Stolypin's death on their return from Chernigov.

Suddenly, five autumns later, Stolypin's image loomed larger and clearer in the Tsar's mind than at any time since his death. After five barren years seeking, and firing, ministers he suddenly realized with a shock that there had been no one since to compare with Stolypin. In the present war, in the present dearth of leaders, what a decisive force Stolypin might have been!

Why had the Emperor been so dissatisfied with him? Why had he intended to dismiss him? For reasons so trivial that he could no longer remember them. The war years were a mountain barrier hiding them from him.

So those two days spent in Kiev, those two cozy evenings when the three of them sat together and he and Mama helped Baby with his jigsaw puzzles, and decided to let his sister Olga marry her cuirassier, were nonetheless tinged with sadness.

The return journey gave him further food for thought. They passed four troop trains en route from Riga to the south, carrying reinforcements for the Romanians. What joy it was to see all those cheerful young faces at the window, to hear their singing! Russia was not running short of fighting men!

They arrived back at GHQ in a dreadful downpour—but that was supposed to be a good omen.

Then, two days ago, he had received a message from Alix that Protopopov had now been given full responsibility for the food supply. (There had indeed been a telegram while he was at Kiev, from Grigori, but as always it was so awkwardly worded that the Emperor did not understand it.) He had no hesitation in signing. He had wanted to do this for some time, and would have done it before leaving Tsarskoye if Protopopov had not demurred. All we need now is God's aid! A couple of difficult months and everything will sort itself out! We must just be firm!

No sooner had he dispatched the courier with his reply than a telegram arrived from Alix—in code, which they very rarely used. She asked his permission not to announce Protopopov's appointment for the present.

This telegram came as a shock. She was simply putting things back where they had been the day before, without suggesting any alternative, and the Emperor, in Mogilev, could not be expected to know what snags had been encountered in Petrograd. The reversal did seem much too abrupt. A little more thought before the original decision might have helped.

The incident inspired some doubts—not his first—about Protopopov. Was he in fact a well-balanced person or was there some truth in the Duma's malicious gossip? But it was Rodzyanko who had first recommended Protopopov for the post of Minister of Trade and Industry. It pleased the Emperor to remember that he himself had singled out Protopopov, without any preconceived ideas. At their first meeting Protopopov had pleased him, as a former officer in the Horse Guards. No, no one had foisted Protopopov on him. Alix's advice (and Grigori's) had fallen on receptive ground: Nikolai himself had always dreamt of a Minister of the Interior who would work in harmony with the Duma. This had been his hope with Khvostov (the nephew), but it had been tragically disappointed. Protopopov, however, had once been the Duma's prime favorite, and as the head of its parliamentary delegation he had been praised and recommended by the Allies' press without exception. Which meant that the Duma, in its present vicious attacks on Protopopov, was only showing its own true colors.

And yet . . . And yet deep down the Emperor was resentfully aware that it was not he who had decided on Protopopov. As in the unfortunate case of Khvostov (the nephew), whom he had opposed to begin with, but in the end unsuccessfully. It had been the same with Shuvaev, Volzhin, and many others, who, once chosen, had been removed with some difficulty. How many times had Nikolai told Alix, "I can't change my mind every two months, that's simply intolerable!"

Looked at another way, whoever had the task of choosing would not be infallible. Those accursed shortages—fuel, ore, food—were a perpetual source of worry. There came a time when you no longer knew what to believe, and the stuff you heard from this or that minister made your head spin. It wasn't easy if you had never been in business yourself: prices kept rising, and the country had to be supplied somehow.

His anxieties had been aggravated in Kiev by Mama. She had told him sternly that he should not listen to his wife so much. The public at large was dangerously incensed. Why must he always defy public opinion, why exacerbate the conflict?

That he was always ready to heed his wife's advice was true enough. But her advice was more often than not remarkably sound. She was nearly always right!

He loved her for it. But at times he found it irksome that she, and not he, was always right, and that she made up her mind more quickly and more positively than he did.

But for all her assurance she too could not be infallible. The two feelings lived side by side in his breast, feeding on each other. When he left Tsarskoye for GHQ, or saw her off from GHQ on her way home, he suffered the torment of parting, and simultaneously the relief of a soldier returning to his free and easy masculine world. After which he would immediately begin inviting her back and hurrying her up, and as the day of her arrival drew nearer, so his impatience for her dear presence, her approval, her sweet caresses grew. With her arrival, his agitation gave way to a profound calm, and he was ready to dismiss all cares and vexations from his mind. But she herself was the first to remind him of them—and decisions were more easily taken when they were together. Afterward, though, it made Nikolai uncomfortable to think that major decisions were always taken in that way, and he would feel tempted again to assert his soldierly and masculine independence, and to make further decisions unaided. (That was how he had come to appoint Samarin last year—after which he had stayed on at GHQ for an extra two weeks, waiting for his wife's anger to cool.) New informants, new ministerial reports helped him to see things from a new angle, often differently from Alix. But sometimes the Emperor made his own decision and it turned out to be the wrong one, his courage failed him, and he could not wait to see her again.

Alix's advice often bore the distinctive stamp of Grigori's approval, and might indeed have originated with him. To Nikolai it seemed only right—this desire to listen to the sober voice of the people, to a man of the people. And it was an endearing trait, Alix's eagerness, which he understood and treasured, to get below the specious surface of things, to peer into their occult significance and explore the workings of hidden forces. This was, perhaps, the right way for human beings to achieve understanding. But Alix's longing for esoteric knowledge had become so passionate that Nikolai had begun to feel uncomfortable and uneasy about it. Grigori would send the Emperor a bouquet with fervent greetings, or perhaps a single flower, or wine from his own birthday party, to be taken as medicine, and Alix always asked the Emperor to thank him. (And to telegraph Easter greetings to him at Pokrovskoye.) Grigori had begun by presenting him with an icon of St. Nikolai, then given him other icons and images (to be held in his hands at crucial moments), and even an icon for Alekseev (presenting it to him for no particular reason was horribly embarrassing, but Alix had insisted), and to cap it all, a comb, with which he was to comb his hair before every difficult conversation and decision. Perhaps such a comb really did have some mysterious power. (At least it was more credible than the claim made for an icon presented by M. Philippe: a little bell attached to it was supposed to ring whenever a nasty visitor arrived.) Alix had gone further, and insisted that before every journey he made, and before leaving for GHQ, Nikolai should be blessed by Grigori himself, in his capacity as a sacred personage, and that after a long absence he should make a special visit to Tsarskoye for the renewal of the blessing: contact with Grigori's breast would lighten his woes and instill in him wisdom from on high. Nikolai experienced nothing of the sort, and was unable to believe in it. "You are, after all, just a man!" Alix reminded him. She insisted that when he referred to Grigori in correspondence he must begin the words "he" and "Friend" with capital letters. She exhorted him to "think about Grigori more often," and at all difficult moments to beg him to intercede with God. We must, she said, heed his advice, it is never given without deep thought, God reveals all to him, God had some good reason for sending him to us. His prayers are needed by Baby and by us, for the sake of our reign and for Russia. Alix often reproached Nikolai with inattention to his words and reluctance to follow his advice. She prayed that the Emperor would come to feel more deeply: but for Grigori, anything might happen. She was very insistent that the Emperor should invite Grigori to GHQ—which would bring immediate and decisive success to Russia's armies. Again, Nikolai did not believe that his presence would have this effect, and was too nervous about what people would think, and about his generals and officers, ever to invite Grigori, but could not forbid him to send telegrams direct to GHQ, sometimes addressed to the Empress during her visits, sometimes to Vyrubova or Voeykov, sometimes to "GHQ: Deliver to Chief."

These original telegrams contained a mixture of popular speech in all its crudity and enigmatic pieties. The meaning of the whole was sometimes unfathomable. These sentences sometimes had a pungent, folksy flavor like that of rye bread or fermenting apples. There was always something in them, but it wasn't always easy to understand: "Your victory and your ship." "All fears nothing time of firmness will of man must be stone." (This for the edification of the Tsar in particular.) "You said no one shall offend my people but why all this." "I love you retain mine even on Gorokhovaya Street." "What is for your profit give like wolves sheep oh, no need the fortress is God." "Write to them all that they should speak more often give power to one alone so that he can work with reason." (This last referred to the ministers, and was well said.)

Embarrassment was a state of mind to which Nikolai had become more and more accustomed: he felt acutely every awkward situation that arose. But he was always so paralyzed by his embarrassment that he could not break out of it. He could see that his relationship with Rasputin was becoming too close for comfort, and that it did not always look good (though it was at times very good), but by now it was impossible to withdraw. Natural tact, and concern for his wife's feelings, prevented him from speaking to her frankly. What troubled him was not that his spouse saw Grigori as the supreme authority, herself second to him, and the Emperor only in third place. No, what perturbed him was that Grigori's authority continually manifested itself in behests which quite often went beyond the limit of the permissible. His prayers, visions, intuitions, even sometimes his dreams, might suddenly indicate that an offensive must be launched in the vicinity of Riga without delay, or that they should not climb the Carpathians, or alternatively that they should climb them before winter came, and all were prophetic revelations because, as Alix wrote, "God has given him more insight and more sense than all the military put together." Grigori always knew better than anyone the point at which an attack should be made (he had scolded them for beginning the big winter offensive without seeking his consent) and who should be appointed to which office. He might draft and forward to the Emperor a paper "on five urgently important questions of policy" or submit a telegram drafted in his own idiom, to be sent to the King of Serbia. At one moment he would be asking the Emperor to be firmer with ministers. At the next, opposing the Emperor's departure for GHQ, or reproaching him with his long absence from Tsarskoye Selo, and saying that he must return if only for two days for a consultation. Overseeing his every move with affectionate concern, Grigori had complained that when the Tsar was last at Tsarskoye he had found so little time to talk, and had not disclosed what changes he would be making and what subjects he meant to raise with ministers. On one occasion (while Stolypin was still alive) he had insisted that the Tsar must receive him openly, so as to quash all the malicious gossip about him. (The Emperor had, however, never granted him an audience in this way.) Alix continually urged him to make it a rule that whoever was against their Friend was against the Tsar. She demanded that the Emperor should not just serve and love him privately, but should show ministers and others of importance in the state that he did not look down on Grigori so that they too would listen to him. Whenever Grigori's predictions remained unfulfilled (when, for instance, the war did not end as and when he had prophesied) Alix promptly forgot them, and to spare her acute distress the Emperor refrained from reminding her. Grigori's less fortunate testimonials she could always explain away: Khvostov (the nephew), for instance, had, she said, been a good choice, but had subsequently changed, and their Friend could not be held responsible for that.

Grigori also sent on, or put in the Tsar's hands when they met, a great number of petitions—people asking favors or appealing against punishment, more often than not expecting the Tsar to circumvent the law, which he could not do. Even more irksome than these petitions were Grigori's requests, passed on by the Empress, to be allowed to send a new icon to reach him on the day when an offensive was to be launched, or to say a particularly fervent prayer on the day itself— which meant that he needed to know the date in advance. The Emperor, a soldier first and foremost, knew that he could not possibly disclose his strategic intentions, with dates and locations. But he was afraid that his skepticism might upset his wife's psychological equilibrium, and anyway it was sheer fantasy to suppose that a semi-literate Siberian peasant, who genuinely wished the royal couple well, might misuse this information for the benefit of the enemy. He undoubtedly did wish to pray—and prayer might help! And Nikolai, grudgingly, against his own better judgment, sometimes gave Alix such information in his letters: the date when a lull in the fighting would end, when a diversion would be carried out around Pinsk, when the Guards would be thrown in. Or revealed the decision to cancel completely a planned northern offensive in order to conserve their forces. But as a rule he implored Alix to keep such things to herself, not to let another soul, not even their Friend, know about them. Even so, the thought that he had let a secret leak out left him irritable and uneasy.

This perpetual self-doubt—this uncertainty that relations were what they should be, and his feeling that there was nothing to be done about it—was what had perturbed Mama so often in the past, and again when they last spoke.

No sooner had the Emperor returned to GHQ, and endured the exasperating confusion over Protopopov's appointment, than his uncle Grand Duke Nikolai Mikhailovich, who had been seeking an invitation for some time, suddenly appeared. The Emperor received him on Tuesday evening.

The imperial family had grown inordinately. Besides various uncles still in the land of the living, the Emperor had numerous first and second cousins, and although he was younger than many of them, because of his position, and the failings of many grand dukes, he had long considered himself burdened with responsibility for the dynasty as a whole.

As for Nikolai Mikhailovich, the Emperor was unable to think highly of him. His salient features were an almost feminine inclination to fuss and an irascible vanity. He had set out more than once on the path of state service, but always unsuccessfully. For the past year he had been dinning into the Emperor the need for a commission to work out the peace terms which Russia would dictate to Germany (should Germany be partitioned, or only Austria?) with himself presiding over it. Finding no outlet for his talents in the service of the state, Uncle Nikolai had confidently declared himself to be an outstanding historian. The Emperor, however, could not see it. He had a great love of Russia's history himself, and indeed there was nothing he so enjoyed reading and thinking about, but he could not find in it so much to fuss about and to criticize as Uncle Nikolai did. Add to this that Nikolai Mikhailovich was jealous of his cousin Nikolai Nikolaevich's martial fame, and always spoke ill of him to the Emperor. All in all, the Emperor was inclined to treat Nikolai Mikhailovich as something of a joke.

There he was wrong. The visit on 14 November proved to be a bitter pill. Nikolai Mikhailovich, completely bald, short-necked, head squashed on shoulders, mustache and beard sculpted with extraordinary precision, had turned up at dinner looking grim and self-important, and afterward, when they were alone, his trembling hands had shown that he was under a strain. Before the relaxed atmosphere that was usual between relatives could be established he launched into a lofty harangue.

Was his nephew confident that he could discharge his historic task and bring the war to a victorious conclusion? Was he aware of the real situation in the empire? Did people give him truthful reports? And did he know where the root of the trouble was? No, everybody was deceiving him.

His manner and his tone signified that he, Nikolai Mikhailovich, did know the real situation in the empire, did know the whole truth, did know the root of all the trouble.

They both lit up to steady their nerves. Nikolai Mikhailovich smoked a Russian cigarette, while the Emperor used his pipe-shaped meerschaum holder.

The Emperor's heart sank in anticipation of another blow from Nikolai Mikhailovich on the spot still sore from Mama's pressure. Just as he had expected. His uncle even mentioned that he was speaking at the instigation and with the support of Mama and of the Emperor's two sisters. (His sisters too? What business of theirs?) He had the temerity to speak directly of the Empress and of Rasputin. They, as he saw it, were the root of the trouble. In fact, the root of the trouble was that the public had gotten to know the procedure, previously hidden from them, for appointing ministers—namely, that it was done through Rasputin. To become a minister in Russia you had to find favor with the peasant Rasputin.

Nikolai Mikhailovich was so ill at ease that his cigarette kept going out. He had mislaid his matches and while he fumbled the Emperor moved closer to oblige with his cigarette lighter. Outwardly the Emperor betrayed no feelings. But feeling there was—the intense hurt caused by pressure on a sore spot. Putting aside all the exaggerations which Nikolai Mikhailovich heaped up so unsparingly, there was no getting away from the embarrassing and humiliating fact that there was much truth in what he said.

The Emperor's impeccable upbringing had, however, taught him not to show his feelings (one of the rules of the royal trade) and he remained disarmingly courteous.

While Nikolai Mikhailovich used such expressions as "the systematic insinuations of your dear spouse" and "what comes from her mouth is the result of skillful juggling of the facts." But what good would it do if the Emperor protested? Given his uncle's prejudices and his insensitivity in his dealings with others, it would be pointless. Order him to be silent? Hardly the way to win an argument with an older relative. And, anyway, he would feel awkward trying to assert his authority.

So the Emperor listened to it all without protest, tendering the cigarette lighter when necessary.

"You always used to say that all those around you deceive you. What makes you think that you are not deceived by your wife, who is deceived in turn by her entourage? The immediate decisions you make independently and on impulse are always remarkably sound" (this was diplomatic flattery, not what the Grand Duke really thought), "but as soon as other influences make themselves felt you begin to vacillate, and your decisions are not so good. If you could only put an end to the intrusion of these dark forces, Russia's renaissance would begin at once."

That was something which the Emperor took leave to doubt. When it came to dark, anti-Russian forces he saw more of them on the side of the Duma and the Unions.

But he voiced no objection. He had in fact no skill in argument. He was effective in discussion only with those whose views he shared. With others he was dumb.

By "Russia's renaissance" Nikolai Mikhailovich, it seemed, meant no more than making ministers responsible to the Duma.

Meeting no opposition, he pressed harder and in strange language.

"Hear this! You are on the eve of an era of new disturbances! I will go further: on the eve of a new era of assassination attempts!"

Where had he picked this up? From whom had he heard it? How did he know?

Uncle went on with rising excitement: "You have your Cossacks here, and plenty of room in the garden. You can order them to kill me and bury my body. No one would ever know. But it was my duty to tell you all this."

He had evidently rehearsed his harangue in advance. But he suddenly realized that these solemn tones were out of place in polite conversation. He took another pull at his cigarette, sighed, and still hearing no protest from the Emperor, reproached him for his silence.

"You are a great charmer, you know. You remind me of Aleksandr I." He found a great deal more to say in the same reproachful vein, and still meeting with only the vaguest response. Nikolai Mikhailovich left behind a letter written in advance. It contained all that he had just said, but he had wanted to deliver it in person.

It was not until he said goodbye and was seeing Uncle to the door that the Emperor began to feel sick at heart.

The very idea of opening and reading the letter repelled him.

He would have to tell Alix about this visit in his daily letter, but hated the thought and wished he could avoid it.

Bedtime came—but sleep did not. He had always slept soundly, but it looked like this was going to be a wakeful night: he was too worked up, too agitated to sleep.

He knew that Mama agreed with Nikolai Mikhailovich—indeed that she had authorized him to speak as he had. His sister Olga too (although she had said nothing when she asked his consent to her divorce and remarriage). As well as his sister Ksenia and her husband, Sergo, once such a close friend. He could think of other members of the royal family who would join this hostile semicircle.

"An era of assassination attempts!" This from the lips of a Grand Duke!

Many letters denouncing Rasputin reached GHQ, but all of them anonymous, which did not enhance the credibility of their authors. The imperial family itself was not spared in the insinuations, but no noble person could believe such slanders, which must rebound on those who spread them. True, Dzhunkovsky had once reported that Rasputin had been seen drinking heavily in a restaurant, but if that was made a reason for punishment, how many members of the upper class would remain unscathed?

Rasputin, of course, might have his faults, like any other human being. But he laid claim to no official post, nor to a stipend (such as the Grand Dukes all received). It was a private matter for the imperial couple. She had a right to her private attachments, even if they were weaknesses, and who was any the worse for them? Why did everyone attach so much importance to them? It was as if a volcanic eruption of hatred for Grigori had set high society and the educated public ablaze. Their own furious malice was the only possible explanation. Such violent hatred could have no other. The Emperor could not in reply lower himself by making excuses, could not tell anyone how important this man was to the Empress's morale. Nikolai himself was not sure whether Grigori was responsible for healing the Heir's sickness on various occasions, but Alix believed in him passionately, and her belief sustained her. In any case, the Heir's sickness was never named. Its nature was a jealously guarded secret. So that this could not be advanced as a reason for Rasputin's position.

In fact, after his conversation with Grigori the Emperor was firmly of the opinion that this peasant had a sounder view of things than very many public servants, courtiers—or Grand Dukes. He was a guileless and upright representative of the real people and one who knew what the people needed. Listening to him was very instructive and refreshing. How often he had urged the Emperor to beware of futile losses, not to beat his head against a wall, something which many bemedaled generals failed to understand. Grigori had, for instance, recommended halting the Brusilov offensive just at the right time—after which there had been heavy losses at Kovel and no further advance. (Russia's generals were sometimes so thoughtless, irrational, idiotic even, ignorant of the rudiments of military science, that the Emperor was almost reduced to utter despair. But what could he do with them? They were all that he had.)

Then again—Grigori spoke so eloquently, so beautifully even, about religious matters.

But very shortly the Emperor would not be able to avoid another interview with a Grand Duke, this time with Nikolasha (Nikolai Nikolaevich). He was determined to visit GHQ—and the commander in chief of the Caucasian Army Group could hardly be forbidden to do so after a fifteen-month absence. (Alix was very much against his visit, told her husband to receive him coldly, to be firm with him, and not to be trapped into making promises.) It had in fact been longer than fifteen months since they had met. When the Emperor took over from Nikolasha at GHQ, instead of meeting him he had written a letter to say that he forgave the Grand Duke for all his mistakes, for all the losses, the setbacks and disasters at the front, and that the Emperor's love and trust remained unchanged. In reality, as they crossed the barrier of flame which was the summer of 1915, the feelings of both men were exposed to great strain and great heat. The scars which both bore were still clearly visible.

Although the Emperor's decision to take command of the army was his own, the realization of an ambition long secretly cherished, his will might have failed him in the uncertainties of that August and faced with universal opposition. Even now it was embarrassing to remember the disproportionate part Grigori had played in supporting him. (Alix was forever reminding him that it was Grigori who had then saved Russia.) Nikolasha also remembered all this only too well, and as one of those who hated Grigori most violently, was very likely to hark back to it when they met.

The Emperor's heart ached. The next grand-ducal visit promised another unpleasant conversation, in which he would be unable either to reply or to express his own feelings.

Such conversations, interviews, audiences were the main content of the monarch's hemmed-in and hard-pressed existence. Supposedly all-powerful, he could not choose to whom or about what he would talk.

He had been left very little room for maneuver. Among other things he could not remove useless generals: there were no replacements, and he must not create chaos. Nor could he flout the opinion of Alekseev and the Army Group commanders in directing military operations. Nor was he free to leave Mogilev when he pleased, particularly when there were setbacks, as at present in Romania. How pleasant it is not to feel tied to one spot! But such freedom was not for the Emperor. In Mogilev itself his routine was fenced in by lunches, dinners, tea parties with his staff and with representatives of the Allies, by audiences with a steady succession of visitors, and by the cramped garden in which he had too little room to exercise his strong, young, and splendidly healthy body. (Dr. Botkin had recently pronounced him even fitter than he had been two years ago.) Compelled to live in the stone cage of Mogilev, the Emperor found real relief and enjoyment only in his daily outings: in three seasons of the year driving out of town to walk to his heart's content out in open country, and when the Dnieper was in flood indulging in his favorite sport—rowing. Although he was nearly fifty years old, it was not until last spring in Mogilev that Nikolai had witnessed that awesome spectacle—after three days of fog over the floodlands the thawing ice sailing majestically down the Dnieper. A sight to be remembered as long as you lived. And who then could deny himself the pleasure of rowing against the swift current? A thrilling challenge! Nikolai was a first-class oarsman. Two pairs were formed—the others were sailors—and they raced each other throughout the spring months. How supple his limbs felt after rowing! Then for a spin on a fast motorboat. He spent as much time as he could outdoors, to get a tan and not look like those pale-faced staff officers.

This was an unusually warm day, not a bit like November, windless but also sunless, in fact dark under a leaden sky, but without so much as a sprinkle of rain. Such weather is depressingly gloomy when you are indoors and in town, but out in the country it is soothingly poetic: almost all the leaves had fallen, and faded from yellow to leaden gray, but here and there a few clung to the last invisible threads, awaiting the first assault of wind. Under that sky, under those clouds, the expanse of fields, scarcely visible at a distance, looked like God's dwelling place, spacious and welcoming. It was silent, deserted. The peasant's work was all done. The summer birds too had flown away. The soil had been loosened for winter—the ground was warm and soft to the touch. If you came upon a potato left unpicked you could dig it up without a spade, light a fire of dry stalks, and bake it. The fire would be not too big, not too bright, a quiet part of that quiet day. Good to sit around in silence.

At such moments Nikolai forgot accursed politics altogether. Not the war—he was keenly aware of it, and of those faraway trenches in ground just like this, and of the exploding shells inaudible from where he was. But, oh God, how readily he would have surrendered his throne—if there was anyone to take his place—returned the Supreme Command to Nikolasha, and become an ordinary soldier in one of his glorious regiments, just for the right to sit like this by a campfire, burning his fingers on a charred potato, free from mental and emotional torment, engaged in ordinary human conversation, while he waited for orders telling him exactly what to do.

Nikolai not only got no enjoyment from power and pomp—the more simply life was organized, the more he liked it.

A light breeze sprang up, fanning the hot embers. They finished the potatoes, strewed earth over the ashes, dusted off their hands, and made for the town.

As they drove there, the wind freshened. The weather was changing. That brooding calm could not be expected to last.

His son had not accompanied him out of town. His leg was painful. But today he had his own way of amusing himself: a direct line to Tsarskoye Selo had been experimentally installed and he was trying to talk to his mother. His efforts were not very successful. The Emperor himself hated telephones and never used them if he could help it.

Aleksei's leg was no better. He had pulled a tendon, and the slightest injury always resulted in a disturbance of the circulation and an internal swelling. The doctor's orders were that he should lie down. (Five days earlier he had suffered a dangerous nosebleed but fortunately they had managed to cauterize it.)

The moment he arrived the Emperor learned that Alekseev was far from well and went to see him. Alekseev had been warned of his visit and had managed to rise. The Emperor chided him, and ordered him back to bed at once. The old man was reluctant to obey while the Emperor was in the room. He was suffering the lingering effects of an old kidney infection, combined with a high fever, and it was now obvious that he could not carry on working but would have to go away for treatment. The question of his replacement had been under discussion for some days—and he now unexpectedly suggested the commander of the Guards' Army, General Gurko. There could obviously be no question of taking one of the Army Group commanders from his present post.

But the Tsar regretted having to part with Alekseev. He had grown used to the general in the last fifteen months. Their daily conferences and the whole business of the Supreme Command had passed without disagreements. The Tsar, too, had grown used to Alekseev's unmartial appearance—he looked like a lean and hungry high school teacher, Chekhov's Belikov perhaps—to the cap with its peak jammed down over his spectacles, to his inelegant, untrimmed mustache and his querulous voice. There had never been a flare-up of anger between them, or an acute disagreement. Alekseev always gave convincing reasons for his actions, and he could not be expected to feel affection for the ministers appointed in rapid succession by the Emperor. True, Alekseev had to concern himself continually with the food supply, with transport, with metal production, so that last summer he had lost patience and recommended that the Tsar create the post of Supreme Minister for State Defense. He would be in charge on the home front, as GHQ was in the field, so that GHQ would have only one minister to deal with. This plan made good sense—but if it were adopted what would become of the Council of Ministers? And the four special consultative committees involving members of the public? There was the danger of fresh quarrels with the Duma and what was the point of irritating them unnecessarily? The Emperor vacillated for some time, but in the end shelved it. This had, however, not damaged relations with Alekseev.

"Come on now, Mikhail Vasilievich, lie down, just as you are, with your boots on, or I won't stay and talk to you."

"I'll stay sitting down, Your Majesty, it would be harder for me to get up."

Alekseev's armchair was a rather crude, well-worn, uncomfortable piece of furniture, but there was always a knitted cushion on the seat.

Relations between them might have been damaged in the last few months by Guchkov's letters to Alekseev. Though reluctant to believe that Alekseev had ever answered them (but perhaps?) the Emperor was hurt by his concealment of these disgusting mendacious letters: instead of showing them he had hidden them in a drawer and protested that they had not reached him. Meanwhile one of Guchkov's letters was circulating so widely in both capitals that Alix was finally able to get hold of it and send it to her husband. And that was the first he had known about it.

They had both felt aggrieved, but this had not spoiled their relationship. The Emperor loved this old general. (Not so very old at that—there were only eleven years between them. Yesterday was, as it happened, Alekseev's birthday. The Emperor had remembered it and had a present ready.)

The Emperor was vexed to think that Alekseev's illness and departure would mean that he himself could not possibly go away. So Alix would have to come to him next week.

They talked a little longer, and Alekseev, who had been reading the day's newspapers, said that the Duma had behaved badly at its opening session yesterday.

He mentioned no details, and the Emperor would have hated to ask—as much as he would have hated crossing the room to take those loathsome newspapers in his hands and scan their columns for signs of the Duma's favor or disfavor. But he was distracted, put out, and had lost the thread of their conversation.

He left.

What was that wretched Rodzyanko (a court chamberlain, recipient of many decorations and honors) thinking of? Why couldn't he keep them in hand?

Stürmer had indeed urged him not to convene the Duma at all that autumn, to prolong the recess for another year, or to dissolve it and call fresh elections for next autumn.

But the Emperor had considered any such measure improper and demeaning. He had nonetheless hoped that the deputies would be patriotic enough not to aggravate dissensions and difficulties at the present juncture, but to hold their peace until the war was over.

He was upset. And worried. He could easily imagine the speeches made there, without having read them. He anxiously wondered how he was to hold out against them. What was he to do with the government? Would he be able to hold out with his present ministers? Or would he have to sacrifice someone to appease the Duma?

There was a lack of fellow feeling and mutual trust within the government itself. His ministers, selected singly at different times and by different methods, did not all approve of each other. Perhaps old Trepov (Aleksandr), to whom the Emperor had talked on the train journey back from Tsarskoye the other day, could take over as Prime Minister. He was ready to replace Stürmer—but only on condition that Protopopov was also dismissed. And, no doubt, Bobrinsky. (Nikolai had not seen Alix since this conversation, and had not yet ventured to write to her about it. He wanted to think it over by himself first.)

He had once placed such hopes on Stürmer! He had hoped that his appointment would be like a thunderclap. He had sternly tried to show all the ministers that Stürmer must be respected! The old man had done his best. He was honest and good and not at all stupid. But was there anybody who could please the Duma gang? Anyone who could stand up to them?

Trepov, perhaps. He was tough enough.

But he dreaded to think how angrily Alix would protest. She would not sacrifice Protopopov for anything in the world. (And as for Grigori . . .)

He would be sorry to let Protopopov go himself, he was remarkably easy to talk to and to work with, he was never brutally importunate in word or deed (as Stolypin had been: every conversation with him had been an excruciating strain). Protopopov knew how to leave room for conjecture, for contingencies, for uncertainty, for the unspoken. An admirably smooth fellow.

In any case, would such concessions really strengthen the government and the throne? Would they not be another admission of weakness?

He sadly reviewed in memory the long succession of ministers whom he had sacrificed in his efforts to satisfy the insatiable Duma: dear Nikolai Maklakov, clever Shcheglovitov, honest Rukhlov, cheerful Sukhomlinov. He had even gone so far as to put his War Minister on trial in wartime! Which was as bad as indicting himself! (And had delayed Sukhomlinov's release on bail until the very last moment.)

And still he had not done enough to please them. Instead their importunities had become fiercer and more frenzied than before. So why had he made any concessions at all?

The situation had begun to seem to him as hopelessly fraught with problems as it had been in the summer of 1915.

Absorbed in these gloomy thoughts, and with no one at all at HQ to confide in, the Emperor still got through his daily routine and received people without betraying his feelings. These formal audiences, however, occupied his time and his attention completely, and left him exhausted.

Meanwhile, the swelling in Baby's leg was worse, he had difficulty in turning over, and he looked at everyone with those big eyes (his father's eyes) accustomed to grief. He had grown used to his sad fate too early in life.

When it was time for Aleksei to go to sleep, Nikolai stood by his bed and said a prayer, which the little boy repeated lying down.

They slept on adjacent beds in the same little room, with religious pictures and crucifixes on the walls, and all night long the father could hear the little boy's groans, mingling with the howling of the wind outside.

Those groans made the father want to sob out loud or to take flight.

The buffeting wind gave way to a steady downpour, in which there seemed to be snowflakes mingled with the rain.

[7 0]

It was unbelievable how everything had changed overnight. Yesterday's crazy wind had cooled down, released a downpour, then blanketed Mogilev with snow, then subsided toward morning with the temperature below freezing. The snowfall had been so heavy that pedestrians had left diagonal tracks across Governor's Square, but the yardmen were still behind with their task. The first swift sledges could be glimpsed here and there, but wheeled carts were still making ruts in the snow, and motorcars hooted impatiently, throwing up a fine spray of snow and skidding on their back wheels.

The unexpectedness of winter's incursion heightened its psychological effect. In this whiter, purer, sterner world Vorotyntsev could not remain troubled, perplexed, and happy all at once, as he had been only yesterday. It was in any case time for him to come to his senses after his fecklessness during his journey. He had resolved nothing, achieved nothing. Once back with his regiment he would be himself again—but not before.

He awoke feeling strong and energetic, and, full as he was of Olda, his first thought was of Gurko. He must, somehow, see the general and talk to him, but could not afford to wait much longer.

Had he not been so eager he might not have recognized immediately the stocky figure crossing the courtyard to the officers' mess: the once familiar back, the firm, purposeful step, the somewhat exaggerated swing of the arms. Yes, it was Gurko! Busy as ever, preoccupied with serious matters, incapable of weakening, or wasting time.

Having failed to catch his eye, Vorotyntsev went on into the mess hall.

It seemed to be just as Svechin had said. But could it be . . . ?

The officers' mess was abuzz with a fresh item of sensational news, received this time not by telephone but from someone just back from Petrograd: the day before yesterday, in the Duma, Milyukov *had proved with the documents in his hand that the Empress was a traitress!* And Milyukov was obviously the last man to say such a thing without proof. As a scholar, a historian, he knew the importance of evidence as well as anybody!

Newspapers were passed around. There was nothing in them, of course, but the gaps in the printed columns, at once sinister and un-availing, were like so many gunshot wounds in the sides of the regime.

The mess buzzed. The loyal and the uncommitted alike were shaken: if the Empress makes a habit of passing on the Supreme Command's secrets to the Germans, how can we be expected to fight on?

Some maliciously gloated. The Empress was unloved.

Some remembered Nikolai Nikolaevich saying long ago, "Put her in a nunnery!"

Vorotyntsev remembered the somber talk among ordinary soldiers, based on insidious rumors and distorted by unschooled imaginations. What sort of commotion could be expected now, when it reached the soldiers' ears that the Empress had been called a traitress in the Duma, and their officers had to admit that it was so? Officers could assemble at headquarters, discuss what to do next, reach for their swords, but an ordinary soldier could not put his head out over the parapet of his trench, he had nowhere to go. How would he take it? He would surely throw down his rifle. Why should he go walking into machine-gun fire now?

People were talking freely, mutinously even. Did the Emperor know? they asked. What would he do now? There must obviously be a change of government. Milyukov must be very sure of his position to have spoken so bluntly. The palace would have to back down! Then there would be changes!

But what could they themselves do about it? Nobody knew which way to turn, nobody had any practical proposal, it was just talk, talk, talk . . .

Vorotyntsev raised his voice so that he could be heard at several neighboring tables.

"But where is this treason? What does it amount to? Has anyone of us, gentlemen, witnessed any actual instance of treason? If so, when?"

No one chose to answer. They had heard what he had to say—and the hum of conversation resumed, every man talking to himself.

If the idea of a coup had never previously occurred to Vorotyntsev he might have been more worked up than any of them. But he had been thinking it over for some weeks now, had pondered the arguments for and against and was still undecided, indeed was perhaps much further from a decision than when he had left Romania.

The intractable engineer colonel had heard all he needed. "Milyukov should be indicted for making a speech like that, the scoundrel! People can get away with anything in this country. They're a lot of scandal-mongering old women, not representative of the nation."

A lieutenant colonel said, with the air of one in the know, that the Duma was in fact to be dissolved in a few days' time. Stürmer, he said, was already on his way to GHQ to get the Emperor's signature.

Again, no one inquired how he knew. Things were like that now.

Everyone had heard something. And most of them repeated accurately what they had heard.

Vorotyntsev had a secret source of his own. Immediately after lunch he went to see Svechin.

"So good old Gurko's arrived! I've seen him myself!"

"Yes, late last night. He sat up with the old man." Svechin shook his bumpy boulder of a head. "The old man's in a bad way. He has a high temperature. But there's even worse news. The Living Corpse has also arrived. Yesterday."

Vorotyntsev felt sick. It was as if he had swallowed something slimy.

"Where's he sprung from? He's supposed to be in France!"

"Must have been in Petrograd. With some cock-and-bull report. About how he'd pinned medals on the mademoiselles."

"After Alekseev's job? Thinks there's a vacancy?" Vorotyntsev roared.

"Indubitably. These carrion crows can smell things a long way off."

"The insolence of the man! The shamelessness of it!" He strode around the little office. "Zhilinsky! At a time like this! In command of the whole army! That really would be the end! Life wouldn't be worth living! We couldn't put up with that a single minute! And you sit there talking! We've got to do something about it ourselves! If we don't he's sure to be appointed!"

All his hopes were dashed. Knocked on the head.

"Don't get too excited. Zhilinsky's reputation is pretty shaky anyway. With Stürmer and Rasputin up there already they won't want him as well. We're getting more of a nose for reputations. Anyway, I don't think Mikhail Vasilich will permit it at any price, he'll outmaneuver them. He'd sooner forgo his sick leave and stay here and die at his desk."

They went into another building, to the orderly room, looking for Gurko.

They found him in one of the less important offices. Just as they remembered him: the spiky mustache, the sharp eyes, the quick movements of that restless head.

He was sitting at what could hardly be called a desk, and was certainly not his, blocking the aisle, looking like someone who had dropped in for a chat. He was wearing two George Crosses, one on his chest, one on his collar, and no other marks of distinction, such as Academy aiguillettes—superfluous clutter, in his view, although he had been on the General Staff for a quarter of a century. A few other senior officers, unconnected with that room, had gathered, out of friendship, not on business. There were no files, no stapled orders, no maps even, none of the usual paraphernalia of staff work—just a casual heap of clean sheets of paper, for anyone who felt like it to write, do calculations, or make drawings. Gurko—with the first sprinkling of silver in his mane of stiff, dark hair—looked around, half rose from his chair, greeted Svechin and Vorotyntsev with a quick handshake, showing no surprise, asking no questions, and in a clear but subdued voice—hardly the voice you would expect from someone with the general's build, or in that room: elsewhere it could blare like Joshua's trumpet before Jericho—continued his animated discussion with the officers, the tone of which the newcomers quickly grasped and adopted. Careful not to inquire why these matters were being discussed there, on that day, and with General Gurko, they were examining, with figures, the general's idea, accepted in principle before Svechin and Vorotyntsev arrived, that it would be possible during the few short months of the winter lull to reorganize the Russian army. How should they proceed, and what reserves would they call on to convert the whole army, from the Baltic to the Black Sea, into three-battalion instead of four-battalion regiments, without letting the enemy feel any relaxation of Russian pressure? The advantages of the concept were obvious. The Germans had fielded three-battalion regiments from the start, thus avoiding overcrowding of the trenches with inactive manpower vulnerable to enemy fire. In this way the Russian army could gain forty-eight extra divisions, or release from the front line alone more than a million men.

Vorotyntsev's own favorite notion! To reduce the size of the army! He's caught on! Put his mind to it!

The advantages were obvious. But only a daredevil general, one not anxious for a quiet life, unconcerned with promotion, not susceptible to wilting under the burden of office, and so able to demand a free hand, to assert his independence of the Emperor, and of all those swarming like importunate midges around him—only such a man could act like this in the third winter of a war between huge and unwieldy forces.

The fifty-two-year-old younger son of the famous Iosif Gurko, field marshal in the last Russo-Turkish war, who had taken mountains by storm, was just such a one. What marked Vasili Gurko out as a genuine commander was the fact that he never limited himself to carrying out orders, never confined himself within the bounds of his responsibilities, and never failed to draw general conclusions from every engagement, from the experience of his unit, and to pass them on to everyone else. Thus, his training manual based on the waging of position warfare on the Russian front was already in its seventh edition, and was eagerly snapped up. And now, though he was not yet the Supreme Commander's Chief of Staff and might not be for some weeks yet, he saw no point in his rapid elevation unless he could proceed full speed to reorganize the army from top to bottom! At once, without delay, to reduce losses today, win the war tomorrow, without waiting for civil servants and committees for postwar this and postwar that to shake off their blissful lethargy.

Such a scheme was sure to captivate! Svechin had to leave after a while, but it had taken Vorotyntsev only five minutes to find himself a stool, move it up to the table, and sit with the others, writing, calculating, drawing diagrams on the same sheets of paper, arguing with them as if he had been invited expressly for that purpose. They smoked, talked, reasoned with each other, without regard to rank, as if all the others were the equals of the full general and his aide-de-camp. Gurko's earnest gaze quickly weighed up possibilities, his clear, clipped voice summed up the alternatives and expressed his preferences in measured tones. Vorotyntsev felt hot—he was glowing with happiness. It was so long since he had taken a hand in staff work worthy of the name!

What a joy it was to work with a man of talent!

Gurko was remarkable for his grasp of essentials, his readiness to be persuaded instead of obstinately clinging to his own ideas, and his refusal to interfere in details once he had accepted a clear and definite decision in principle.

The problem expanded rapidly, there was no easy way of limiting it. Having reorganized regiments, should a division be left with four regiments? Or should every formation comprise three units? Should infantry brigades be abolished as superfluous? What about the artillery? The number of pieces to a battery should long ago have been reduced from six to four: as it was, cannon were underused and shells wasted. But could the reorganization of both services be managed simultaneously? You couldn't leave an infantry division with an artillery brigade reduced to twenty-four guns. Double the number of brigades perhaps? They would have to ask the Allies for more guns—and wouldn't get them. What about field glasses, stereotelescopes, compasses, telephones? . . .

All his life Vorotyntsev had been drawn to decisive people and repelled by ditherers. Anyone more decisive than Gurko it was impossible to imagine. The concentration in his lean, expressive face, and his laconic judgments, told you all you needed to know. He was not taken aback, not awed, not flustered by the abrupt enlargement of his responsibilities—far from it. He was growing quite naturally into his new post, even before he was appointed, as a plant grows simply and silently, because it cannot help growing. Just as long as Zhilinsky's intrigues did not succeed, just as long as the disloyal and easily swayed Emperor did not change his mind! Here at last was a man of the twentieth century, assuming the position he was born to fill! If he could only go on acting as speedily and boldly for one year! The possibilities open to a commander were much reduced, but the country's need of him was not. If this general lasted a year at GHQ the Russian army would bring the World War to a victorious conclusion. It was beginning to look as if Svechin was right! We have lost nothing yet!

Why, after all, had he been so ready to give up? Vorotyntsev asked himself. He was made of the same stuff as Gurko, but looking at him across the cracked varnish of what had once been the table—not meant to serve as a desk—of the District Court, he could size the general up with no feeling of rivalry, merely with the desire to attach himself to the powerful tail of this comet.

On his way here Vorotyntsev had clung to his secret scheme, and had even devised his opening move. He would say that he had met Guchkov in Petrograd, they had reviewed all the obvious names, and Guchkov had questioned him about Gurko with particular interest and enthusiasm. (It would be no lie, but a justifiable inference, that they had been talking about candidates for Alekseev's post, and if Svechin had felt able to mention Gurko on that occasion, would Guchkov have been any less excited? Would he have paced his office any less excitedly? Would he not have thought of Gurko in that same context? Have wanted to meet him, with the same thoughts in mind? This supposition was something he owed to Guchkov, an undischarged obligation.) Ought he, perhaps, to tell Gurko about it, with due emphasis, and look for signs of a similar inclination on his part?

And, immediately, he asked himself whether there was any point to it. He was so gripped by the technical problems of reorganizing the divisions that Guchkovian memories, which had been fading gradually since Petrograd, now finally flickered out. The real work to be done lay before him on the table. It restored him instantly to his normal alertness and readiness for action. Gurko, of course, must feel the same—ten times over. Even to hint at the other matter would be embarrassing, shameful, impossible. Do your duty, bear the burden, and don't get underfoot!

The determined set of the general's mouth, his natural austerity, sternly forbade any hint that an oath once given could be broken.

Svechin's departure was followed by that of a second officer and a third, then another officer came into the room. Vorotyntsev stayed on. He was free all day and could have wished for no better way of spending it.

By now they had thought through all the details of the reorganization. Several sheets of paper were covered with particulars of the tasks to be carried out, the names of those responsible for each of them, the numbers of personnel affected, and the composition of each unit. They could have gone on in greater detail, but they were already beginning to count in millions—and who said that Russia's manpower was inexhaustible? What had become of her millions? The Quartermaster General was feeding six million at the front—yet there were only two million fighting men in all. In other words, four million were noncombatants, supply troops? How could they be siphoned off? Or look at it this way: The home front believed that it had given the forces fourteen million men. Losses in all categories amounted to six million. There should then be eight million left. There were in fact six million. Where were the missing two million? Then—with a cavalry general presiding!—they discussed the future of the cavalry. It was less and less needed in warfare, it gobbled up grain when there was a shortage, and there were millions of horses which would be more useful on the home front. They also discussed the provisioning of the army—there were still enough groats, sugar, and meat, but the supply of flour was inadequate.

Finally, they turned to Romania. Gurko, it turned out, was anything but indifferent to events there, in fact they weighed on his mind. His own Army Group (known as the Guards Army—otherwise it would have been the 13th!) was after all stationed on the Southwestern Front. He understood the Romanian problem only too well. How could the front be held by Russian units interspersed with unreliable Romanian units? How much longer could they hold out? Gurko was acutely conscious that Russia's alliance with "gallant Romania" was a disaster and a curse.

The Tsar's lunchtime was drawing near. Gurko, for some reason, had not been invited. Vorotyntsev was alarmed. Was this the result of Zhilinsky's intrigues? Could he have squeezed Gurko out already?

Vorotyntsev refused to believe it. It surely meant only that someone had not been told, and had not made the arrangements.

But think of the trouble the Emperor would be having with him! He could not be swayed, could not be bent, could not be sweetened by an invitation to the table of the Highest, and the Emperor would always hear the unvarnished truth. Every day of his temporary tenure this refractory character would behave as if he had been appointed for life. The Emperor would be deafened by the sound of his voice. Please, please, appoint him, and appoint him quickly!

Meanwhile, the cavalry officer aide-de-camp had obtained two plates of something dry and the four of them chewed away as they worked. This was when Gurko first mentioned directly the appointment they had been taking for granted. He deplored the fact that he was always having to work with new people. That year he had been forcibly dragged from one command to another—from his corps to the 5th Army, to the Northern Front, to the Guards Army, and everywhere he had found and attracted invaluable officers, many of whom had asked to be taken with him each time he was transferred, and there were many he would have gladly brought to GHQ, such as General Miller from the 5th Army, whom he had mentioned before, but it couldn't be done, it would be improper, it was too much trouble.

Vorotyntsev realized at once that he would not be summoned to GHQ, that this one happy day of total absorption was all he could expect.

Looked at another way, this was only reasonable, and indeed necessary: now that he knew the rationale and procedure of the reorganization Vorotyntsev was indeed best back where he came from, on the periphery, to work on this program—but at the headquarters of the 9th Army, which would shortly be reinforced by several corps, because the Romanians were so ineffectual. Gurko would give the order as soon as he took over.

If he ever did.

Anyway, as part of the general reorganization the spotlight would fall on the distant Romanian corner too.

This was a man who would not squander Russian blood.

Vorotyntsev had, in any case, not really been looking for a post at GHQ—Svechin had thrown him off course by trying to talk him into it.

Not so long ago he had supposed that he would never leave the front line until the war ended, nor indeed would he wish to. But this trip had weakened his resolve, and he had rejoiced in the new opportunity which seemed to be opening up. He had, truth to tell, been heartily sick of his regiment.

When they were about to leave together, and Gurko was donning his greatcoat (with an ordinary officer's gray lining, not a general's, in red), Vorotyntsev, moved by a feeling that he was both neglecting his duty and letting Gurko down, found himself blurting out a version of their encounter in Petersburg, and passing on Guchkov's greetings, almost involuntarily—but looking hard at the stern general as he did so, wondering whether he would react . . . accordingly.

In fact, Gurko showed little emotion, indeed hardly any. He pursed his lips under his mustache.

"Aleksandr Ivanych . . . Aleksandr Ivanych is . . . very bold . . . very persistent. Whatever his beliefs"—he made a wobbly movement with his hand—"at the time . . . But . . . because he has traveled a great deal as a volunteer, and on private visits to various fronts, he greatly overestimates his understanding of warfare and of military problems. He has a great many acquaintances in the army—not always the best of the people, that journalist Novitsky, for instance. They all have stories to tell him, he gets to hear about everything . . . And then he . . ."

Vorotyntsev found himself thinking that Guchkov might very well be an embarrassment to Gurko in his new post. A man might attach no importance to his position, might show disrespect for the Tsar—but only in the line of duty, only for the good of the cause. And if Guchkov had cast a shadow over Alekseev—how much worse was Gurko's case, given their close ties in the past. If Guchkov turned up at GHQ now—what would people make of this appointment, this substitution arranged by Alekseev?

Vorotyntsev blushed—not externally, but in his mind. It was too stupid! How long would he carry around with him this outdated Young Turkism?

But Guchkov had nonetheless left a little dent on the surface of his conscience.

Krymov. Should I go and see him? Or shouldn't I?

[71]

(THE STATE DUMA, 16–17 NOVEMBER)

The proceedings of the Duma on 14 November appeared in the newspapers with blank spaces. Passages were omitted even from the speeches of Levashov and Balashov. Apocryphal, and contradictory, versions were passed from hand to hand—tricksters were selling them for a few rubles apiece. Even the government could not obtain the authentic text of Milyukov's speech from the Duma, though this was the one disseminated all over the country (sometimes with additions). "Society" said with one voice that the Duma must be protected. (Burtsev, the great unearther and savorer of secrets, later asked Milyukov where he had found his facts, which looked more like fibs. Milyukov replied that he had taken them from the *Neue Freie Presse*, that perhaps they needed checking but he was in a hurry to use them before the socialists did.)

In absenting himself from the chair Rodzyanko had shown foresight. On the evening of 15 November he received a note from Stürmer, who was waiting to hear what the president of the Duma meant to do about the insults to the imperial family at yesterday's sitting, and, simultaneously, a letter from the Minister of the Court reminding him that he, Rodzyanko, was a court chamberlain, and also asking to be informed what steps . . .

What steps indeed . . . Well, he could have that passage excised from the stenographic record. And sacrifice Varun-Sekret, though that would be a pity. At the same time, he could vindicate himself in the eyes of the public with a statement to the newspapers that he was not responsible for the omissions from speeches, which he always passed to the Press Bureau in full. Rodzyanko was no intriguer, indeed he much preferred to be as frank as possible. But, regarding himself as the Duma incarnate, the Duma on two legs, he was compelled to hedge his bets for Russia's sake. In the Third Duma, when Guchkov was preparing to question the government about Rasputin, Rodzyanko, already president, had secretly warned the Tsar. On this last occasion, he had not done so, but he had now to cover himself.

And so "the greatest—and fattest—man in Russia" (as the Emperor called him), alias "the Samovar" or "the Big Drum" (the Duma's nicknames for him), again ascended the presidential tower, as self-assured as ever. The assembly came to order. The government, true to form, had absented itself, to avoid a clash—times had changed since Stolypin. The ministers' box was occupied only by their deputies. The public gallery was even more crowded than it had been the day before yesterday.

Chaliapin himself was said to be present. Another fracas was expected, and the press gallery was packed.

In spite of everything, it would fall to the previous offender, blundering Varun, to open the session. Various boring announcements were made about legislative proposals received, and the names of negligent deputies who had missed sessions were read out, after which there was no way of avoiding it or putting it off.

> **Varun-Sekret:** Gentlemen, members of the State Duma! On 14 November, Deputy Milyukov saw fit to quote from German newspapers allegations concerning persons who are customarily not mentioned here, and discussion of whom is inadmissible. Not knowing German, I did not exercise the president's right of censorship, provided for in standing orders. This passage has now been deleted from the stenographic report. Nonetheless, I must acknowledge that I was in error, and I tender my apologies to the Duma. I consider it my duty to resign from my office as vice president.

> **Kerensky** (from the body of the hall): Going to Canossa is degrading.

(Such taste—such an apt analogy!) Corpulent Rodzyanko, unscathed and basking in the universal love and joy of the Duma, replaced his deputy in the chair, muting his bell-like bass.

What were they to debate? Whether the government should resign? Whether it was any good? No such question could appear on the agenda. They were to debate a submission from the Budget Commission.

The next speaker was slim and sharp-featured, with spiky mustaches, something of a dandy, but not offensively so. Well mannered and circumspect, the subject of a doggerel couplet by the Duma poetaster, Puryshkevich:

> *Thy voice is soft, thy manner mild.*
> *But, Shulgin, thou'rt the devil's child.*

He had once been on the far right, but was now a "progressive nationalist."

He came forward, looking excited, knowing that this was an important occasion, and conscious of the rapt, theatrical attention of an audience expecting fresh explosions.

> **Shulgin:** It is with no light heart that I begin our discussion today. I do not belong to the ranks of those for whom strife with the powers that be is a time-honored custom. On the contrary, in our philosophy even a bad government is better than no government. We must be particularly cautious in our behavior toward the government in time of war. We would wish, therefore, to exercise the utmost restraint.

Speakers, however, spur each other on, the flame of competition is fanned, and it is almost impossible for a man with a romantic cast of mind to curb his tongue.

> And if we now raise the banner of struggle against this regime it is because we have indeed reached the limit of our endurance. (Cries of "Bravo!" from the left.) Should people who have looked Hindenburg in the eye without trembling tremble before Stürmer? (Laughter and applause, except from the extreme right.) To remain silent in such conditions would be the most dan-

gerous thing of all. Oh, if only this regime were working toward the same end as ourselves, even Russian fashion, which is to say confusedly, we would try to assure the population that it will stagger on to the desired destination. As it is, we have only one recourse: to fight against this regime until it makes itself disappear. ("Bravo!" from the left. Except for the extreme right, the whole assembly applauds.)

This was even stronger and more threatening than Milyukov's statement, since the speaker was a well-known monarchist. Such a shift of opinion meant that patience was exhausted, and that something was about to happen—if not there and then in the chamber, then somewhere else. The atmosphere was electric. ("A brilliant light that acts upon the nerves . . . ah, those speeches . . . to speak is terrifying . . . all Russia is listening . . .")

Such a struggle is the only way to prevent that which we must fear most—anarchy and the collapse of all authority. Such a struggle will mean that officers at the front will lead their companies into the attack more confidently, because they will know that the State Duma is fighting against the sinister shadow. The plenipotentiaries and zemstvos will purchase and ship grain more confidently, in the knowledge that it will not trickle away through the gap between the Ministry of Agriculture and the Ministry of the Interior. The workers too, with Russia's fate partly in their hands, will work at their benches with greater zeal. And even when armed bands burst into their workshops crying, "Strike now and join the struggle against the government," the workers will answer, "Be off with you, provocateurs! The State Duma is fighting for Russia side by side with the government, and if we use the strike weapon we will be fighting for Germany." (Applause.) So then, gentlemen, how are *we* to carry on the struggle? For the present there is only one way: to tell the truth as it really is!

Grave accusations have been made here. But the horrifying thing is not that they were made, but the way in which they were received. The horrifying thing is that the chairman of the Council of Ministers will not come here to make a statement and refute the accusations.

In other words, the government lacked the strength even to defend itself, could not even bring itself to enter the chamber when it was accused of treason.

(We are bound to ask ourselves why. Why *didn't* Stürmer come forward to vindicate himself? Such a gulf had opened up that ministers saw no point in addressing deputies face to face—and speeches in the Duma were all the more violent as a result. Stürmer wrote later:

If I had been there I would have said that I had taken no bribes and shared none. Unfortunately I could not do this. The animosity was so powerful that I could not think of mounting the rostrum and subjecting myself to unacceptable attacks.

The hostility was such that the "oppressor" was even more terrified than the oppressed, and the power holders cowered in the background. Stürmer was guilty neither of treason nor of bribe taking, he had accepted nothing from Manasevich, yet an attempt to sue Milyukov was as far as he dared go.)

Instead of this, he brings vexatious lawsuits against Deputy Milyukov. Gentlemen, Stürmer stands for the total disorganization of the food supply. Stürmer stands for Sukhomlinov getting off scot-free, and we fear that this is only the beginning—only the first line of that diabolical charter in which the program for the disgrace and destruction of Russia will be set out! (Prolonged, stormy applause from the whole chamber except the extreme right. Cries of "Bravo!")

In emigration in 1924 Shulgin recalled:

We showed too much talent in our oratorical exercises. People were only too ready to believe us when we said that the government was useless.

There were 440 deputies in the Duma, but some of them were silent for the whole four years of its existence. Peasants, archpriests, zemstvo doctors, Cossacks, professors, and marshals of the nobility sat stroking mustaches and beards and just listening. While, in accordance with a ceremonial understood by all, leaders of parties and of splinter groups paraded across the tribunal in a circular procession.

Here comes that tempestuous dissident from the Bloc, leader of the Progressists, honorary justice of the peace and superintendent of high schools, the shock-headed deputy from the Don.

Efremov: The pernicious character of the existing political system, the incompetence and impotence of the power holders . . . A government which the country does not believe . . . It may well be that over the whole period of its historical existence the government of Russia has never presented such a picture of horrifying disarray, such unrelieved mediocrity, such total incomprehension of the nation's needs.

(He spoke honestly, assuredly, as he saw the situation. But anyone inquiring into these matters half a century later would just as surely fail to see either the horrifying disarray or the total incomprehension. Contemporary observers were the victims of self-hypnosis.)

At such a critical time to know, yet to be silent and inactive, ignoring what is going on, and still to remain in power is criminal neglect of one's duty to one's country, *bordering on treason*. Rumors about a possible separate peace threaten to leave Russia isolated in the family of civilized peoples. Even to think of a separate peace is in itself a betrayal of Russia. Anyone brazen enough to aim at such a peace will incur the people's vengeance as a traitor to the fatherland!

(Time would tell!)

The people must give careful thought to it all. Intrigues behind the scenes, the surreptitious influence of adventurers, holy men, shady operators, and open or secret friends of Germany . . . (Applause in the center and on the left.) We cannot limit ourselves to a change of personnel . . .

(That was where they parted company with the Bloc.)

. . . what is needed is a radical transformation of *the whole political system*. A government responsible to the Duma! We must unshackle the Russian people! (Applause.)

It got worse as it went on. The speakers were like children taking turns pushing each other on a swing. And they began to swing higher than the leader of the majority could have wished, let alone the monumental president, who was yet again in a state of high anxiety. Onto the tribune bounced a figure in a Circassian coat with cartridge belts and the epaulets of a Cossack captain (alas, the topknot he had worn in the first days of the war had disappeared into a mop of hair), fresh from the front (and eager to show it), a dashing Cossack left-winger from Terek . . . a buffoon, yet by no means unpopular with the Duma, namely, Mikhail Karaulov.

> The crucial fact about our last session was overwhelmed and lost in the turbulent seas of passionate rhetoric: that fact was the nonappearance of ministers at a session of the Budget Commission. The commission came to the conclusion that the total disorganization of the food supply threatens to render futile all the bloodshed at the front. Stürmer, however, replied that he found it impossible to appear before the Budget Commission. We must, as a matter of urgency establish the principle that ministers are responsible to the Duma. The present government, in the absence of such responsibility, will not only never create a great Russia but will ruin the Russia of the present. But I had never supposed that the threat of disaster was so close. We must intervene and break the fatal chain of events!

It was like a gallop on horseback, followed by a cleaving stroke of the saber: it takes your breath away, you no longer feel the ground beneath you—you charge full tilt and your arm swings unbidden . . .

> On Tuesday a terrible accusation was hurled at the government from the tribunal—but what did you then do on Wednesday? You went on discussing with representatives of that same government, in the same Special Conferences, the same questions as before Tuesday. Let me turn your indignant gaze in a direction which may come as a surprise. If Wilhelm has allies within our government, the government too has its allies within us: they are our inaction, our weakness of will, our indecisiveness. The government is strong solely because of our weakness! Was it not from our ranks that the cry went up a year ago: "Don't change horses in midstream"?

The bold warrior from Terek was ready to change them even in the middle of a mountain torrent.

> Was it not from among us that the specious but false argument emerged about the criminal driver steering the car in which our motherland is seated into the abyss?

Maklakov, top of the class, permits himself the faintest of smiles, showing indulgence toward the impetuous Cossack.

> Was it not we who passed the ludicrous Lenten law, while questions concerning political and civic freedom were consigned to oblivion? Gentlemen, can't you see that the present government is a phantom, a flitting shadow, that the source of its courage is our timidity, and that the more time we lose, the stronger it is? The government is fully confident that you will not go beyond harsh words and in practice will deny it nothing. Your indignation is nothing but hysterical screaming. You have surrendered the reins of the state chariot, you have climbed from the driving seat to the body of the

vehicle and are now awakened only by jolts over the potholes. Meanwhile, the country expects you to act, act, and act again. What are we to do? you ask. (Voice from the left: "You tell us!" Laughter on the right.) I'm about to tell you. I have always maintained that, looked at calmly and rationally, there are no hopeless situations. I have always maintained that there are at least three ways out of any situation. (Laughter.) From the present situation I can in fact see four! ("Oho!" Laughter.) I won't speak of a fifth and sixth, which are self-evident—our dissolution or Stürmer's dismissal. The first solution is this: since it has become clear to us that the government is leading the state to disgrace and disaster, we should ask our president to request an audience with the Emperor and submit for his gracious consideration . . . I will be told that this is unconstitutional . . . Have it your own way, gentlemen! The second way out is perfectly constitutional: it is to break off relations with the government completely! To boycott ministers and stop inviting them to the Duma.

Rodzyanko: Member of the State Duma Karaulov, we cannot refuse to invite ministers, that is their right.

Karaulov: It is their right to appear, but we are not obliged to invite them.

Rodzyanko: Please do not argue with observations from the chair.

Karaulov: Very well, sir. So, gentlemen, let's leave the ministers in peace for the time being. (Laughter.) What is in our power is to reject completely the budget for 1917. And all the draft bills presented by commissions! (Zamyslovsky: "And go home.") *You* may go home, I will be going to the front, I will be of more use there than wasting words here.

Rodzyanko: I will be compelled to deprive you of the right to speak.

Karaulov (hurrying to make his main point): The third way out . . . I'm afraid that this third way is the one you will take. Fearing that the Duma may be dissolved, you hand over the boyar Milyukov, bound hand and foot, to the boyar Stürmer, stalk the lobbies for rumors, count kopecks in the Budget Commission, and heave deep sighs because tens of billions are slipping past you unchecked.

The fourth way, gentlemen deputies . . . No, the fourth way is not for you and not to be spoken of here. It is the way which the country itself will take when it finally loses its last hope—its hope in you! (Applause from the left.)

This portentous promise made it obvious that Karaulov had connections, that he *knew* something, and his hearers wondered what strings he held in his hands.

Part of the Duma ritual was to give speakers from the non-Russian nationalities a turn on the tribune. Partly to cool the Duma down a little, Rodzyanko now called, one after the other, a Muslim deputy, a deputy from Kurland, and one from the Jewish community in Kovno. (Not that discussion of the Jewish question was likely to cool the Duma down. Rather the opposite.) But the great disadvantage of an evenhanded alternation of speakers was that there were also rightists in the chamber and the Duma would have to listen to their obscurantist ravings for the time prescribed by standing procedure. What, though, did the rightists now amount to? Their number was steadily falling, their ranks were thinning, fragmenting, coming apart at the seams, they seemed to be degenerating, to be afraid of their own existence and to lack the courage to defend it. Where have we seen before the deputy now mounting the tribune steps? A tall, heavily built, big-headed fellow, wearing a starched collar big enough for a horse, with waxed mustaches and a mop of black curls. Whose silhouette does he remind us of? Of course, of course—in fact that's his nickname in the Duma—"the Bronze Horseman." Nor is the resemblance fortuitous: Markov belongs to the Naryshkin clan (as did Peter the Great's mother), and the family likeness has surfaced after seven if not ten generations! Only his walk is not that of the Emperor, he bobs along as if unsure of his footing.

The universally hated president of the Union of the Russian People affects a defiant hauteur, or infuriated hardness, his face is rigidly set, because he is used to swimming forever against the current, and finding himself among enemies in any gathering of educated Russian people. This manner reinforces their eagerness to oppose him. He exercises a kind of negative appeal: if Shingarev charms even his opponents, Markov repels even those who share his views. His crude bullying can repel even when what he is saying is correct. If the Duma decided to exclude one single member and took a vote on it, Markov would be expelled with no objections from anyone.

    Markov II: Mr. Shulgin has only one recourse left to him: to fight against the government of Russia until it topples into the abyss. We in the Duma will attack the hated government with words—and that will be called patriotism. But when the factory workers strike because they believe what you say, that will be treason. *They* are not mere windbags, and if you say let us fight against the state power in the middle of a terrible war, you must realize that your words will lead to unrest, to a popular revolt, at the very moment when the state is trembling under the blows of its enemy. The ministers you hate will not be put to flight just by your words—that can be brought about only by the *fourth way* which Deputy Karaulov did not dare mention here. The fourth way, which that gentleman with a medal from the Tsar on his chest suggested to you, is indeed capable of routing the government, but it is also capable of destroying Russia. (Noise and laughter on the left. "It's not funny! Russia is weeping!" from the right.) You Shulgins are defeatists, because you have caused the people and the army to lose faith. If they cease to believe that they have behind them a regime governing with the best intentions no one will want to fight.

    Shingarev: They're fighting for Russia, not for the government!

    Markov: We on the right are in a difficult position. (Laughter on the left, cries of "True!")

It was indeed true. He was pretty sure that his cause was lost, both in this assembly and in Russia at large.

    A grave charge has been leveled at the chairman of the Council of Ministers from the rostrum. We remain silent—and Mr. Shulgin is able to pretend that we agree with him. But the reason for our silence was that cries of indignation are not the right argument against such direct accusations. I have heard that this affair will be the subject of legal proceedings: it will be de-

cided in court whether the chairman of the Council of Ministers is guilty or
the deputy who accused him is a slanderer. Mr. Shulgin is not happy about
this: you're trying to wriggle out of it with forensic chicanery, he says. You
would have the chairman of the Council of Ministers mount this rostrum
and say, "It isn't true that I've taken bribes, it isn't true that I'm a traitor."
And if he did you'd be yelling, "Down with him! Off with you!" (From the
left: "True!") You hoped that the whole issue would be blurred by the dissolution of the Duma. So that you could appeal to the people, and to those
in the trenches who are giving their lives for you, and tell them, "We accused
him of bribe taking, so they dismissed us." That didn't happen, you're threatened with a lawsuit, so now you're prevaricating and complaining about legal
chicanery.

(The First Department of the Senate requested Milyukov to explain the grounds
for his accusations, but, having none, he answered evasively, saying that he would
present "all the evidence" when a commission of inquiry into the actions of the minister was set up. *Russkie Vedomosti* approved of this answer, arguing that if Milyukov
consented to explain himself it would create a precedent which would limit freedom
of speech in the Duma. Deputies, of course, must be completely free to slander.)

You have heard the heroic words of the Cossack deputy Karaulov. He has
promised to overthrow all that we now have by a "fourth means," of which
he will speak in some other place. But there are only technical differences
between his speech and those of Milyukov, Kerensky, and Chkheidze, or the
amiable utterance of Mr. Shulgin: they all point in the same direction—to
revolution! (Karaulov: "It's the government that's pointing us toward it!")
You do not realize what it is that you want to do: you want to destroy all
that constitutes the Russian state, the good together with the bad!

To the annoyance of the majority, Markov was not really much inferior to the orators
of the Bloc in clarity and coherence. He had received an education of sorts, at the
Institute of Civil Engineers. Although the hostile bulk of Rodzyanko hovered suspiciously over his head, Markov knew that, regardless of the president, he had a right
to the time allotted by standing procedure. In full command of the situation, he stood
firm on the rostrum, reinforced by his many years of acting in a hostile milieu.

We on the right will do all we can to frustrate you in this. We are not
courtiers in white breeches and ostrich plumes. But we are subjects loyal to
our oath.

Milyukov's speech, as usual with that deputy, was carefully planned in
advance: he read almost the whole of it. It was not like Kerensky's frenzied
speech—forty-four words a second. Milyukov spoke most seductively, and
his less educated listeners would not have been able to appreciate fully an
exposition so brilliant in form and so bad in content. Its whole structure was
based on excerpts from foreign newspapers. One Moscow newspaper—title
unknown—printed a report that a note had been sent to GHQ by extreme
rightists—names not given—stressing the need for a separate peace, this was
reprinted in Europe, and this *proves* that the extreme right are traitors to
their fatherland. From primitive mentalities this procedure is excusable—

but from a professor, a historian, a politician? And afterward, when the question is asked, "Is this stupidity or treason?" the chorus from *Aida* answers, "Treason!" (Laughter.) This is very picturesque, it would be extremely effective in the theater, but imagine it the other way around. A member of parliament in England reads out a clipping from *Russkoye Znamya* about Deputy Milyukov and asks the British parliament, "Is this stupidity or treason?" Only pure stupidity could consider this proof. (Applause from the right. Laughter and cries of "Bravo!") If he had any proof, which I very much doubt, he should have tabled a parliamentary question, complete with documents and statements from witnesses. (Noises on the left.)

The same is true of what he says about ministers. Absolutely nothing is proven, no one is shown to be guilty. What has brought you to such a pitch of indignation with the government? Its incompetent organization of the food supply. As far as that goes, we agree with you completely. But it is you who have contrived to bring about this absurd situation, and you should have the courage to admit it, and not to shunt the blame onto the government. The government is now almost excluded from the management of the food supply, you have planted your own progressively minded activists everywhere as plenipotentiaries. If it's truth you're after, confess that instead of helping the government you have aggravated the muddle which the government was making before. And then join us in thinking how to get out of this impasse, instead of fostering rebellion in the country.

The vice-governor of Kharkov, Koshura-Masalsky, received a message of gratitude from the workers: he had combated rising prices, but not by means which you would find altogether acceptable. The poorer inhabitants of Kharkov all saw him as their champion, fighting the moneybags, the black marketeers and profiteers. And what did you do? You promptly hounded him out of office. So that now all other governors will be wary of the progressive State Duma. You, gentlemen, do not really want to combat high prices—if you do you should renounce profiteering yourselves! There are too many black marketeers and profiteers in progressive circles—that's the whole trouble. You lack the courage to target your own shady dealers.

We on the right can see only one way out: an economic dictatorship exercised by the government.

(Which sounded to the progressive Duma like something conjured up from hell.)

Without it we will have people standing in line, and we will have the speculators and racketeers who elected many of you.

Gentlemen, I have enjoyed reading the so-called progressive, leftist—meaning Jewish—newspapers. I was simply delighted to see how people land themselves in complete contradiction of their fundamental beliefs. The further to the left the papers were, the more insistently they demanded that the peasants should be brought under control and forced to sell their grain. I disagree with that profoundly, but I am delighted to see these newspapers and these parties revealing their true nature, showing what their love of the people really amounts to. They pitch into the poorer peasant—that ruthless profiteer! He doesn't want fixed prices—he wants higher prices! This is typical: as soon as the town, which has always lived at the expense of the village, has always eaten at the village's expense, always shortchanged the village— as soon as things became the least little bit difficult for the town the urban bellyachers immediately obtained the support of the whole progressive camp, and the progressive camp had no hesitation in attacking the everlastingly wronged peasant in the village.

When people speak of the lofty patriotism of those in public life, I beg you to consider a little more carefully and coolly. The Chief Artillery Administration has just made public the comparative costs of unpatriotic government shells and patriotic private shells: a 107-millimeter shell from a state factory costs fifteen rubles, from a private factory thirty-five; six-inch mortar bombs cost forty-eight rubles from state factories, seventy-five from private factories. The author of the memorandum concludes that if there had been less patriotic public spirit in Russia, and a few more state factories, the country would already have saved more than a billion rubles. Of course, if we had had no private factories we would not have been able to produce all the shells we need. Nonetheless, the public figures concerned are now busy robbing the people of a second billion, they do not work free of charge, they are in a great hurry to get exceedingly rich. But when the government, after allotting five hundred million rubles of the state's (the people's) money to the public organizations, says please, gentlemen, permit us to introduce one modest government auditor into each of your committees—what sort of outcry do we hear from the progressive activists? "This is police supervision, you insult us!" How can auditing by the state be described as "refusal to trust" them when five hundred million rubles of state funds are involved? (Hubbub on the left. Cries of "Police rule!") Last year, when the budget estimate for the Most Holy Synod was under consideration, and you learned that five kopecks was collected from worshippers bringing their own little yellow candles to church, you called for state financial supervision of bishops of the Orthodox Church, in case they inadvertently expended the money of the faithful in some way uncongenial to such zealots for the Orthodox faith as yourselves. Yet the billions of state funds flowing through your nongovernmental bodies must not be subject to audit?

He goes on to speak of industrialists who resell army permits for the use of freight cars. The time allotted to speakers is generous, but Markov's has run out. He asks for more.

>**Rodzyanko:** I cannot put this request to the vote. (Shouts from the right: "It's been done more than once before!" and "It's been allowed often enough!")

Markov's speech could damage Rodzyanko's relations not with the Emperor, like those of Milyukov, but with the Duma, which that very evening would be deciding whether to reelect him for the following year. However, everybody was listening attentively to this calm speech, which had robbed the attack on the government of much of its impetus (voices from the left as well as from the right called, "Let's hear him!") and Rodzyanko took the plunge:

Is the Duma minded to grant an extension? I put it to the vote.

Markov then spoke of the abuses of nongovernmental organizations, and particularly of the way in which the Unions of Zemstvos and Towns shielded deserters.

> Remember the well-known trial of Paramonov at Rostov, remember that ultraprogressive public figure's profiteering and extortion, and how the local administration assisted him. Remember the arrest of the Kiev sugar kings, who operated under cover of the flag of public service for the salvation of the fatherland. When you denounce the government, do not forget all these people. Many dirty deeds and many obscenities are committed under the flag of public service.
>
> If we really see ministers betraying the Russian state, we will deal with them more ruthlessly than you would! But we will not put our faith in unsupported allegations, in mere excerpts from foreign newspapers. There are strikes in the factories, and you accuse the police. But why the police, when there are members of the Duma who send people in for this purpose, and say that striking is the way to obtain peace? Campaigning for peace when the Germans have a stranglehold on Russia—now that *is* treason. Those members of the Duma are traitors, and you do nothing to eliminate them from your midst. So, then, let us indeed fight against treason, we are with you there, but first make the effort to expel the real traitors from your midst, because until you do you have no moral right to accuse others. (Applause from the right.)

Shortly afterward, the Duma's silver-tongued orator, a barrister more famous for his eloquence and insufficiently respected for the profundity and precision of his thought (the Faculty of Mathematics had left its mark on him) mounted the rostrum, looking gently reproachful, with his gaze turned, it might seem, inward rather than on the chamber.

V. **Maklakov**: Gentlemen, I do not intend to denounce anyone.

(This was a dig at Milyukov, as usual.)

> Although things are going well at the front just now, and Germany's war-weariness is becoming obvious to all,

As was the weariness of the speaker himself, so offhand and cheerless was his demeanor, so low his voice, though clear enough. No showy "Roman" rhetoric here, he spoke in casual conversational fashion—you would never guess that his speech had been carefully rehearsed.

> we are confronted with a new and terrible danger, and it has nothing to do with the food crisis, but with the fact that something has happened to Russia, that her spirit has somehow changed. Some people already make so bold as to talk of peace, others—with the enemy looking on—to say, "The worse the better, let the catastrophe happen, it will get us somewhere or other." While others lock up their barns . . .

(So he too had in mind hoarders other than the industrialists and the banks.)

> . . . get rich, speculate, and make merry. While the fainthearted and those of little faith lose all hope and say, "Russia will not hold out for long." And this hopelessness is transmitted to the soldiers at the front. That is where the danger lies.

And this is the same Russia that two years ago belied the hopes that Germany placed on our internal dissensions; the Russia that last year, at the moment of sudden disaster, had the courage not to lose her head; the Russia that instead of indulging in contemptible rhetoric set her shoulder to the wheel! What has happened to that endlessly patient, long-suffering Russia of ours?

Maklakov, incidentally, was one of the few who before war broke out, as early as the spring of 1914, had prophesied Russia's defeat. He had prophesied it, but had not opposed the war, in fact he had wanted it.

Over the length and breadth of Russia people ask despairingly, "Where is our government? Who is governing Russia? Where are they leading us?" And it is not we who ask these questions, not the State Duma, nor yet the revolution, for which we are allegedly calling—that revolution is at a standstill. No—the regime itself, before our very eyes, and the eyes of all Europe, persists in destroying whatever confidence we might have in it with kaleidoscopic changes of personnel which give us no time even to discern the faces of ministers as they fall. Incomprehensible promotions, incomprehensible falls from grace—a political conundrum. And the end result is what? Stürmer's government! They are used to telling lies around the throne, they can deceive their Emperor, but they will not deceive Russia! ("Bravo!" Applause from the whole chamber, except the extreme right.)

We are advised to avoid damaging the prestige of the regime—then everything will be all right. Remember the Kovno fortress. Desperate cries for help reached us from the officers at Kovno: Grigoriev, the commandant, they said, would not defend the fortress. We too cried out—but in muted voices; on this tribune we were silent, not wanting to damage morale in the army, and fearing that anything we said might reach the ears of the Germans. Russia paid for our silence with the fall of a first-class fortress. Grigoriev is a symbol: a single commandant paralyzed a whole army. In the same way our government paralyzes all Russia.

Russia asks in alarm why she has had imposed on her a government which will destroy her. It is not much to ask for—that the country should be able to have faith in those who presume to lead it.

No, it is no accident, it is the regime—this accursed, senile, decrepit regime, which has outlived its time but still lives on. Let every minister choose now whether to serve Russia or the regime, since to serve both is as impossible as serving both God and Mammon! (Prolonged applause. Cries of "Bravo!") Should we be surprised that a spirit of rebellion has swept the country, which all Markov's eloquence, all Stürmer's repressive measures, and all the new lies, the fresh mud which will be slung at the majority in the State Duma, are alike powerless to dispel? No gentlemen, Russia's patience is as great as Russia herself is great, but this war has shown that it too has a limit. Our obedience also has its limit!

This was his second (minor) climax—after which he relapsed into doleful recital of the sad facts which Russia had charged her orator to reveal.

Let Markov II not think that we are calling for revolution. The imminent danger is quite different: no one can compel Russia to fight against her will. She will not want to make sacrifices for the greater glory of those people, for the privilege and satisfaction of having them at the head of the state. (Prolonged applause, except from the extreme right.) Russia's answer to you will be not revolution, but dismay, despondency,

(conveyed by his tone of voice)

and indifference. And if this happens, and we are led to peace by way not of victory but of a draw . . .

What had become of the meekness and niceness of a moment ago? Now his anger flared, his voice soared to indignant clangor.

Oh, then, I say unhesitatingly—beware! For Russia will forgive no one for a drawn war and a shameful peace. (Prolonged applause. "Bravo!")

(Like all the leaders of the Kadet Party, Maklakov knew for sure just what the country was thinking. But a draw would not have been so bad, Vasili Alekseevich. What if it comes to total surrender at Brest-Litovsk? What emotional reserves have you left yourself?)

Russia at present is like an army unit about to panic: the guns go on firing, initially the soldiers still obey orders out of habit, but once the cry of "every man for himself" goes up they will all take to their heels. There is, however, still time. If a government is appointed consisting not just of servants of the present regime but servants of Russia.

In other words, Pavel Nikolaevich, Vasili Alekseevich, Fyodor Izmailovich, Nikolai Vissarionovich, Moisei Sergeevich.

Russia will eagerly accept such a government. She will rouse herself, and when she does, woe to Germany!

The moment of choice has arrived: it is either us or the government, we cannot go on living side by side! (Prolonged, stormy applause.) And if the Duma is dismissed—as if it were possible to dismiss the whole country!—if the pyre is lit on which they would consign to the flames the future of our motherland as a nation, then, gentlemen . . .

Here, but for his habitual coolness, Maklakov would have lost control of his emotions.

. . . the Duma may become the only bulwark of order!

The session should have ended on that powerful prophetic note, but questions to ministers had been drawn up, signed, and tabled, so now they were read out.

Question from thirty-three members: Russia has awaited the truthful and free words of its representatives with tense anxiety. However, on 15 November the speeches delivered here were not fully reflected in the newspapers. The declaration of the Progressive Bloc was in large part suppressed. Not a single periodical publication printed the speeches of Kerensky, Chkheidze, and Milyukov. There were blank spaces in the speeches of members of the State Council.

This occurred even though "public speeches delivered in the performance of official duties are not subject to the operations of wartime censorship." What measures have been adopted to ensure observation of the above-mentioned . . .

Question from thirty-one members. The commander of the Moscow Military District has issued an order introducing prior censorship of "materials which might harm military interests." Have steps been taken to cancel this illegal . . . ?

(There was no prior censorship elsewhere in Russia, so why should there be in Moscow?)

They went off to dine and returned that evening to elect the next president of the Duma.

President: To explain his vote—Chkheidze.

He leapt to his feet! He had a tiny opening! Only five minutes but in five minutes what couldn't you . . . !

Chkheidze: After the Act of 16 June we were always certain that the majority in this Duma would do the bidding of the government. It was a barrier beyond which the people could not pass to continue *the work of 1905*. In the last two Dumas the walls of this white chamber have of course heard no speeches of this kind, and we may welcome this. But I beg you, gentlemen, not to delude yourselves, do not think that you have said anything new. What you have said is a repetition of much that has been said before, and more inspiring and substantial speeches were heard from this tribune in the First and Second Dumas.

But, gentlemen, in spite of all your fervent speeches, I still ask myself how long can things go on like this? . . . I am not, gentlemen—God forbid!—summoning you to revolution, there has never been any question of that. But one thing, gentlemen, I will say: revolution has never destroyed a single people or a single state. It did not destroy England, whose praises you now sing. It did not destroy France—remember the Commune of 1871. And Germany's might dates precisely from 1848. Nor has it destroyed China.

So what I have to say to you is this: the squabble between you and the government interests me greatly. How long can that squabble continue?

President: Member of the Duma Chkheidze, your time is up.

He had in any case explained exhaustively the reasons for his vote. If he could just slip in another couple of phrases!

Chkheidze: . . . this very day . . . apologized on bended knee . . . on this very spot . . . and proposed that . . . (Applause from the left.)

Chkheidze, relieved, made his escape.

The votes were cast and counted. Rodzyanko, to his great delight, was elected—though only by half of the Duma.

He opened the next session at midday on 17 November. But if it was not a challenge, what else could explain such odd behavior—this time the government box was not vacant. Two ministers sat there, both in uniform: Grigorovich, the Navy Minister (and the only one for whom the public had any liking), and the War Minister, Shuvaev (a quartermaster who got nobody's back up). These ministers were inoffensive in themselves—let's not hiss them for the moment, but what are we to make of their appearance here after yesterday's thunderbolt, the charge of treason against the government? Let's wait and see.

The previous agenda was now abandoned, in favor of questions to ministers. But whatever name was given to the proceedings they always came to the same thing.

    Adzhemov (Kadet): Put yourselves for a moment in the position of an ordinary Russian citizen, who turns eagerly to the morning papers to see what his elected representatives have said on his behalf. Right-wing deputy Levashov said . . . a long row of dots. Markov II speaks . . . and even him we see only in miniature. You, gentlemen, shut up in this chamber, in this ancient Potemkin palace, may shout and wax as indignant as you like, Russia will never hear a single word of it anyway! The government has never before sunk to such a level of stupidity as it has now: to show for all Russia to see that there is not a single political current able to support this pathetic, worthless government. But Moscow is outside the theater of war, and, as the law stands, should not be subject to military censorship.

    Instead of words there are blank spaces. That's where the revolution is, and those are the people making revolution!

    Skobelev (Social Democrat): Our tormented and humiliated land was waiting for the Duma to sit, so that it could hear the truth. But no sooner did the first words of truth ring out than this white chamber was overlaid with the white paper you see here. Gentlemen, you must tear this scrap of paper—document No. 16672—from your heads, otherwise your presence here will have no purpose.

    You have been told here that there are several ways out of any situation. But you are taking the line of least resistance—heaping all your indignation on Stürmer, although he merely reflects the nature of our state system. Gentlemen, what can the citizen read into blank spaces headed with the names of Count Kapnist or Shulgin? He may think that they were calling for the overthrow of the autocracy and the establishment of a democratic republic when all they were talking about was the overthrow of Stürmer.

    Gentlemen, provocation is a factor inseparable from the greatness of our state system and its continued well-being.

But oh how nimble he is, taking over the rostrum yet again, in one single bound. Who? Who but . . .

    Kerensky: Are we not in fact living in an occupied country, like Belgium or Serbia? In which the state has been seized by a hostile power, and every possibility of national political activity suppressed? . . . Gentlemen, does not the never-ending replacement of particular ministers on these benches raise in your minds the question: who is putting on this puppet show, who controls the entrances and exits of these scoundrels, sometimes . . . ?

    Rodzyanko: Member of the State Duma Kerensky, I humbly beg you to choose your words carefully.

A bit late to be choosy! He'd already said it.

    Kerensky: Gentlemen, when the benighted masses, ignorant of the truth, sometimes lose control of themselves and stampede in the wrong direction, you are apt to say, "There's no patriotism in this country." But there are people for whom the country has been not a mother but a source of profit, people who have lived for centuries on the blood and sweat of those same masses, and when they betray the interests of the state to protect their personal position . . .

    Rodzyanko: Member of the State Duma Kerensky, please return to the question.

    Kerensky: What I am saying is relevant to the question. I intend to show that the rulers of Russia never could and never wanted to conceal its military secrets from hostile powers.

    Rodzyanko: I humbly beg you to return to the question. If you do not comply . . .

It is his duty to interrupt, but he does so halfheartedly, because the Duma is drifting, reeling leftward at his feet. The press holds its breath, the public gallery holds its breath, thrilled by this burst of machine-gun fire from its favorite orator.

    Kerensky: Yesterday, one of those whose names I do not mention, but who tirelessly defends those who . . . informed me from this rostrum that I am a traitor to the state. (Markov: "And I repeat it.") But do you not remember, gentlemen, that on 10 March 1915, when the Duma majority was still full of the spirit of "unity with the regime," I sent the president a letter . . .

(which was already making the rounds in the capitals and in the provinces)

    . . . in which I said that "treason had built its nest at the summit of the Russian government," and that the Myasoedov affair was only a symptom? And was it not I who then asked . . . ?

    Rodzyanko: Member of the Duma Kerensky, please restrain yourself . . .

    Kerensky: I would be happy if the problem posed by the present position of the state could be reduced to one of treason on the part of individuals, if we could find evidence against individual ministers,

(which in fact they could not)

    but if we remove them by the thousand, the old regime has through the centuries nurtured thousands of lackeys to serve it . . .

At this Rodzyanko finally decided to silence him.

Other speeches are made, boring documents are read out, and for half a minute the dashing Karaulov bounds back onto the rostrum.

    Karaulov: I rise, gentlemen, to say just a very few words.

> *Where strong deeds are what is needed*
> *Waste no time on idle speeches.*

But I must supplement this by voicing my extreme indignation. Is it really to be tolerated that statements by deputies, which are not relayed to the country at large, should be heard by members of the public who pack the galleries to overflowing, but not listened to by deputies themselves?

They had left the chamber for the buffet. (Laughter, noise.) Then, yet again:

    Markov II: Yes, Aleksandr Fyodorovich Kerensky, I do regard you as a traitor to the state on the strength of your pronouncements from this rostrum. Anyone who in the present situation has the temerity to *campaign for peace*, and, what is more, by violent means, is a state criminal and a traitor.

If ministers are committing such terrible crimes, why do you legislators not address questions to them in the chamber? Why, because questions to ministers must have some basis in fact, quotations from the German press are not enough, you have to produce evidence, so you are afraid to ask questions, and you should be ashamed of yourselves! History will decide who was right, and you will not be able to falsify it. When you hurl such accusations at people you should treat the matter seriously. If you can offer proof we will not be against you, we will be ahead of you. But prove your statements first.

Yes, gentlemen, the blank spaces in the papers are disturbing and annoying, that much is true. But if they were occupied by the speeches you made on 14 November and today, in the middle of such a war, they would have much more dangerous consequences, they would rob our defenders of belief in the need for self-sacrifice. You will deprive the Russian soldier of all desire to resist the enemy. Why should they, if all that you have said from this rostrum is true? You are Germany's prime accomplices. However vexatious it may be to see these derisive blank spaces in the newspapers, which reduce our speeches to absurdity, they are better than that systematic campaign by which you seek to turn all Russia upside down, and to bring about war between nations inside Russia itself, here and now. (Gasps of indignation on the left.) Yes, gentlemen, there should be no blank spaces! Fill them with advertisements, but let's have no blank spaces! I will go further: if our newspapers continue to upset the people and perturb the army—shut them down, each and every one! (Laughter on the left.) In time of war, one wise nation, the Roman republic, used to jettison the usual freedoms, and choose a dictator. When the whole male population is going into the trenches, when all the freedoms are impaired by the very nature of military operations, don't talk to us about freedom of speech and freedom of the press, tell us how to defeat the Germans. You are still reluctant to understand how great are the dangers threatening Russia. If you succeed in implanting the conviction that there is treason in the rear and treason on high—that day will see the destruction of the Russian army and the Russian people, which will be torn to little pieces, and *the first to perish will be you, the little people!* (Applause from the right.)

Markov had prepared the ground for a counterattack by the government, and the War Minister now mounted the rostrum. The Progressive Bloc braced itself and closed ranks: No surrender! No concessions! We won't even listen to your pathetic arguments! The government has betrayed the country, the throne has betrayed the country, that has been loudly proclaimed and we will allow no one to refute it.

    Shuvaev: . . . to share a few thoughts on the times we are living through. When we would have prevented the universal conflagration we met with no response from the enemy camp . . .

So far, so good. There were shouts of "True!" Next, the minister talked for a time about traditional German inhumanity and that was also found acceptable. (More cries of "True!") Then:

Every day we draw closer to victory! (Prolonged applause from the whole chamber, cries of "Bravo!")

And that is because the war is being fought not by the army alone but by the whole state! All who can have joined in supplying the army.

(Meaning that "society" had. Fine!)

Here are some figures. In the past eighteen months the number of three-inch cannon has increased eight times ("Bravo!"), howitzers four times, heavy shells seven to nine times, three-inch shells nineteen times, fuses nineteen times, land mines nineteen times, some explosives as much as forty times ("Bravo!"), and poison gases seventy times ("Bravo!").

Such is the result of working together in harmony. Permit me to hope and to request that you will continue helping to equip our valiant army. ("Bravo!" from all parts of the chamber.) The enemy is fatally weakened—he will not be equal to the situation. Every day brings us closer to victory. Victory at any cost—such is the imperious behest of our Sovereign Supreme Commander. The well-being of our motherland, which must take precedence over all else, demands it. (Stormy, prolonged applause from the whole chamber.)

Nothing wrong with that! In fact, apart from the intrusive obligatory "Sovereign" it was not just not bad—it was simply splendid. True, it made no allowance for a military defeat, but it did acknowledge that responsibility for supplying the army was borne entirely by the nongovernmental organizations! Nor was there any hint of solidarity with Stürmer, Protopopov, and that whole nest of traitors and supporters of a separate peace!

Grigorovich: I consider it my sacred duty also to speak and to state openly that your continuous support over many years in defense of the state . . . (Stormy, prolonged applause from the whole chamber, and shouts of "Bravo!")

What did it all mean? Why, that the army and navy had dissociated themselves from the loathsome, rotten, traitorous government and were uniting with the Duma opposition!

(The two ministers had in fact been sent by the craven government to play on the patriotic feelings of the Duma and so bring about a reconciliation. But when they took the stage with nine hundred unblinking eyes fixed on them they could not summon up the courage to mention the accursed government, or resist the temptation to solicit applause for themselves.)

Nonetheless, this at once necessitated a whispered consultation around Milyukov. Twenty-minute recess! (During the interval Shuvaev thanked Milyukov for his earlier patriotic speech.)

Rodichev: It rarely happens that what needs to be said is said so powerfully. To fight on to the end is of course the one thing we want, that after all is the only reason we are sitting here. (Applause on the left and in the center.) We have behind us the universal enthusiasm of the whole country, and more than two hundred years of heroic sacrifices, which Russia has not begrudged. But if we are not to begrudge such sacrifices, we must have faith in our leaders. Russia needs to have faith in her rulers. This has been her need of old—honest and conscientious rule. And when noxious air pours through every crack we say clean up the atmosphere!

Deputy Markov spoke one great truth: when he asked how your speeches could be allowed to circulate throughout Russia without refutation. That is the unfortunate thing about our speeches—that they have indeed gone without refutation. In this we see the tragedy of the impossible task which *they* have set themselves: defeating the enemy while despising their fatherland.

One belief in Russia remains unshakable—that is belief in the State Duma. ("Bravo!" from the left.) It is the only place in Russia where free speech—the power of which knows no bounds—is heard. (Applause from the left and in the center. "Bravo!")

We will hear more from this Duma later.

Document No. 5

Petrograd, 16 November

CIRCULAR TELEGRAM TO RUSSIAN AMBASSADORS
From Minister of Foreign Affairs Stürmer

Rumors recently spread by the press of certain countries concerning separate negotiations allegedly conducted between Russia and Germany with a view to the conclusion of a separate peace . . . only play into the hands of hostile states . . . Russia will fight hand in hand with her valiant allies against the common foe without the slightest wavering to the hour of final victory.

[7 2]

The Empress was attached to her private hospital not merely by the fact that she worked in it but by far deeper feelings: she went there to sit at the bedsides of patients, sometimes silently holding the hand of a grievously sick man, or laying her own hand on his head, and speaking words of comfort, taking the place of his absent loved ones. She had her favorites among the wounded, would sit beside them day after day, until they recovered or died, and would subsequently remember the dead as if they had been members of her own family. At the bedsides of the less seriously ill she would do embroidery while they told her their stories. She would take them flowers. One wounded young man had said, "I'm so happy now—I don't want anything more." Sometimes she came across officers who had seen her ten or fifteen years ago at a distance, reviewing troops, while newer acquaintances became friends never to be forgotten. The gratitude of the wounded restored and sustained the Empress herself. She was drawn to the hospital when she most missed her husband and her son. Once there she forgot her loneliness. She was drawn to the place whenever she felt particularly depressed and unhappy. When she was unable to sit in a chair she would still go to the hospital and lie on a sofa, and even so would enjoy the comfort and tranquillity which those surroundings instilled in her.

She felt closer than ever to the wounded when she prayed with them. This she saw as one of her womanly duties—to try to bring people whenever possible closer to God. And the souls of common soldiers (though not the souls of officers) are childlike. The Empress attended church services with convalescents. She prayed with the dying. Prayer always helps a departing soul. Behold—yet another brave soul is abandoning this world to become one with the shining stars! And every dying man helped her to understand more clearly the awesome significance of what was happening.

Faith was an even greater help than work. The Church is an incomparable help for those who are sad at heart. Tears shed there bring relief. In earlier days, when she was more mobile, the Empress liked to ride with Anya, incognito, in a one-horse sled, to some obscure, sparsely attended church, and to kneel in prayer on the stone floor. For so many years now she had petitioned God for her son's health. Once she had set a candle in the Church of the Sign and prayed for the Emperor, the throne, and the Heir as she did every day, Aleksandra felt calm. She took communion several times a year, and this was more than anything else a source of spiritual strength. M. Philippe—all those years ago—had persuaded her that she enjoyed the protection of the Mother of God and had special ties with her. She had faith particularly in the Feast of the Protection, as a day which should confer special favor. It made a great impression on her when their Friend also said that the day of the Nativity of the Virgin was her special day. Not all conversations with their Friend were alike, but when a truly *magical* conversation arose, about miracles and the inexplicable, the Empress's soul thrilled: such conversations helped her to rise above earthly cares, to look down on them from on high. She also read books about the religions of India and of Persia.

It was easy to see that all the present turmoil on earth—this monstrous European war, all that was happening in Russia, the struggle of the Russian throne against its sworn enemies—had a much profounder significance than was immediately obvious. "We who have learned to look at things from another side too can see the true nature and meaning of the struggle."

And perhaps expect it to end horribly.

Last summer, in the most grueling days of the Russian retreat, Varnava had suddenly telegraphed from Tobolsk to say that people had seen a cross in the sky in broad daylight.

Now, overnight from Thursday to Friday, the Empress had had a strange dream in which she seemed to be undergoing an operation.

She was lying on the operating table, fully conscious. Her right arm was being amputated, but she felt no pain, only acute regret: how can you fight the good fight without your right arm? And how would she now cross herself? And write to Nicky?

She awoke with a violent start.

She fought against the fear that oppressed her. Unfortunately she remembered feeling like that for the first time when she was a young bride-to-be. She had arrived in Petersburg, to become Empress of Russia, accompanying the coffin of the late Tsar from the Crimea. The funeral was followed by several memorial services, and, except that the bride was allowed to wear white, the wedding was like a continuation of the burial service.

And now—with all her ailments and anxieties—she felt so old and so downhearted! Since this unhappy war had begun her heart had never been free from anxiety for a single day.

The war had started in the suite of rooms adjoining her own, but the Emperor had told her nothing that day, had not once sought her advice, so that she knew nothing about the general mobilization—and had wept bitterly when she learned of it. She had felt that something irreparable had happened in the world.

Once the war began, what was the right thing for the Emperor to do? They had decided that his place was with the troops, and that he ought to visit fighting units as often as possible—something he liked doing anyway. If it was such a comfort to him to see these great bodies of devoted and happy subjects, what must it mean to them? A priceless recompense! Imagine their feelings when they saw the Emperor so near, so much one of themselves, and, what is more, accompanied by Baby! What valor this precious manifestation would inspire in them, what sunny memories would remain with them all for the rest of their lives! They would see for whom they were fighting and dying, that it was not just for GHQ, not for Nikolasha (who, incidentally, had let himself down badly by never visiting the troops in the field). The Emperor must inspect as many units as possible, and the papers must report these occasions. The Empress thought of herself as a soldier's daughter and a soldier's wife, and would have liked to go with her husband, nearer to the front line, to give the soldiers new heart. She would have liked to see the faces of those brave men when they saw for whom they were going into battle.

Cruel separation was the price which husband and wife now had to pay for Nicky's decision to assume the post of Supreme Commander. In the preceding twenty-one years their loving hearts had never been separated. Now a single week apart seemed an eternity—and at times they were separated for several weeks.

How desperately unhappy it makes me not to be with you! How dearly I wish that I need never be separated from you, that I could share everything, see everything with you! I have cried my eyes out! But this wife of yours is always with you, and within you! I cannot endure the knowledge that you are continually overburdened with anxieties, and so far away from me. I hate letting you go where all those torments and troubles await you. It is a dreadful thing to spend month after month after month at GHQ, never leaving the town. You spend all your time reading dispatches, my poor boy. And what a trial those ministers are, whom you have to receive even when it is terribly hot. How hard you have to work, what an awful life you lead.

These continual separations wear out the heart. I will never get used to the moment of parting. I see your big, sad eyes, full of love, before me, afterward they haunt me. And the horrid consciousness of your absence never lets up. You and I are, and always will be, a single whole. It is amazing, the love my old heart is still capable of! I love you more and more with every day that passes! I love you as few have ever been loved. Even beyond the grave I shall still be your wife and your friend. My poor, big Lambkin! My brave little boy! Dear little boy with the big heart! My sweet! My sunlight! Sunshine of my sick soul! I am enclosing some little rose petals—yes, I have kissed them! I envy them because they will wing their way to you. You must kiss them too. The place circled in my letter is where I have left a big kiss. I have perfumed this letter, to take away the nasty smell of ink. And I am sending you the flowers that were in our room, your old Sunny had breathed in their fragrance. How I love to get flowers from you! They are a pledge of tender love. I shut myself up alone to delight in your dear letter. I read it over and over, crazy old woman that I am, and kiss your dear handwriting. In my imagination I lay my head on your shoulder, and lie quietly on your breast. When I go to bed I always bless and kiss your pillow. I go over and over your words in the darkness, they fill me with quiet happiness and I feel younger. I want you to dream about your little wife. Feel my arms entwining you—always together, forever inseparable. These separations only cause the fire to burn more fiercely. Telegrams cannot be hot—they pass through so many hands. Feel me beside you, I am warming and caressing you. I long to feel that you are my very own, I kiss you all over—I alone have a perfect right to do that, haven't I?

I don't want to boast, but no one loves you like your old Sunny. *She** has the audacity to call you her own, *she* complains that she gets too little affection, *she* thinks that she alone misses you. *She* is completely shattered, she who has never in her life been put to the test. You are her life, for her everything is concentrated in her own person and in you, but you are mine not hers, as she dares to call you. You burn her letters, don't you, so that they will not fall into anyone else's

*Referring to Anna (Anya) Vyrubova (nee Taneyeva). [*Trans.*]

hands? I will gladly pass them on myself, although Anya does not understand how little interest her letters hold for you. But it will be better if she writes through me, rather than through her servants. See—she kisses your hand. Here is another loving kiss from her. Here is her voluminous love letter to you. She sends you lots of loving kisses. She is out of her mind with joy that you are returning to Tsarskoye. Send her your greetings, she grieves if there is nothing for her. Send her a kiss, that will make her happy. (I can't bear begging for kisses, like Anya.) But don't allow the lady of your heart to write too often. You must train her to be moderate, because the more one has, the more one wants. You must always pour cold water on her. Of course, if you need these exchanges with her, that's another matter. But unless we are firm now we will have trouble and lover's tantrums, like in the Crimea.

Anya Taneyeva had become a lady-in-waiting, and been given permission to wear the Empress's monogram picked out in diamonds, back in 1903, when she was a girl of nineteen. But she had quickly risen above her nominal station, and within two years the whole court was so jealous of her relationship with Her Majesty that, to avoid arousing the envy of other ladies-in-waiting, she was sometimes taken to the Empress's study by way of a service room (which, however, gave rise to other misinterpretations). Their friendship was reinforced by music, they played pieces for four hands, took singing lessons from a professor at the Conservatoire, sang duets (Anya had a high soprano, the Empress a fine contralto), but this had come to an end because the Emperor did not like his wife to sing. Moreover, Anya shared the Empress's religious sentiments, her general perception of reality, and her feeling that the world is full of mystic auguries and awful warnings.

The Empress's need for an understanding womanly soul close to her was all the greater because from the moment she set foot in Russia she had been at odds with the notables of St. Petersburg, and the breach had since become unbridgeable. From her very first days in Russia she had felt that she was for some reason not liked there and never would be. If she had acted quickly she might have put things right, but for Aleksandra this would have been excruciatingly difficult. She was, at the best of times, reserved and painfully shy, and, feeling that the public was prejudiced against her, she withdrew still further into herself. It was her misfortune always to look constrained in company, and this made her unprepossessing. She was incapable of pretense, of those insincere little smiles that beguile the crowd. She had no winning wiles. Nothing was more painful to her than hobnobbing with people whom she had no wish to know, and in public she seemed cold, stiff, bored—and was indeed bored—all this, moreover, in contrast to the smiling, gracious dowager Empress, with whom she was unable to compete. (*She* loved receptions, and always took precedence, arm in arm with the Emperor.) Then, soon afterward, came children, and illnesses, one after another, and she had to spend a lot of time lying down—she could not even stand comfortably, so that balls and receptions, even private ones, were out of the question, and such events were canceled. Many people were eager to be received privately, and those who were granted this favor were at once enrolled in the ranks of her friends. People would forgive her everything in return for such an interview, but even this became too much for her, and she refused one request after another. She could not plead serious illness as an excuse because this too had to be concealed, and so the explanation found for the Empress's behavior was her pride, her coldness, her unsociability. When the house of Romanov had celebrated its tricentenary the pomp of the occasion had been matched only by the coldness and hostility of the glittering ranks of socialites toward the imperial couple!

Anya Taneyeva, then, had become no mere courtier but the closest of friends. She was twelve years the Empress's junior, twelve years her daughter Olga's senior, and so like a younger sister or an older daughter. Anya shared the imperial family's favorite private outings, yachting among the Finnish skerries, where they could wander the island paths without fear of terrorists, mushrooming and blackberrying like ordinary people. It was there that the Empress had once embraced her and said, "God has sent you to me, and I will never be alone again." In 1907 Anya had married Vyrubov, a naval officer who had escaped with his life when the *Petropavlovsk* was blown up. Their Majesties had blessed the couple with an icon in the palace church, but they had soon parted and divorced. Anya's experience of married life was simply her husband's ungovernable rages, and she had run away from him, retaining for the rest of her days only his surname. At court she did not resume her position as lady-in-waiting, but was simply the Empress's one and only intimate friend.

Gradually, however, she had become more than that—a third party permanently attached to the imperial couple, so that they were never allowed to be quite alone or to belong only to each other. Are we ever safe from human ingratitude? They had given her their hearts, a home, a share in their private life, how could they not feel aggrieved when she had behaved in a manner so unworthy of herself in the autumn of 1913 in the Crimea, and again in the winter and spring of 1914? There had been warning signs as she had gravitated toward the Emperor, and distanced herself from the Empress, treating her indeed with inexplicable rudeness, hauteur, coldness, and withdrawing completely from their previous intimacy. The Empress had sent her packing from the Crimea.

Separation had not lasted long. The Empress had forgiven Anya and recalled her. But something had gone forever. Their relationship was strained, they could not feel as close and as easy with one another as before. Anya's caprices ruined quiet evenings, and it became obvious how spoiled and badly brought up she was. Anya thought only of herself, and was constantly in need of novelty, so that the Empress lived in fear of her sudden changes of mood.

Then, in January last year, Anya had suffered a terrible blow. She had been involved in a train crash, broken both legs, suffered injuries to her head and her back, vomited blood. She had spent six months lying on her back and undergone several operations. Now she was a cripple, and always had to use a crutch. This might have led to a complete renewal of their former friendship: the Empress had sat at her bedside for hours on end, but, heavens, how far Anya now was from her! Illness had not improved her, she was more capricious, more demanding, than ever, she showed her spite in cryptic but wounding remarks, she hoped that her disability would earn her more attention, more visits, more affection from the Emperor, hoped to recover her old position. She refused to recognize that the Empress had too many other obligations, was jealous of the attention she paid to the wounded, wrote five notes a day requiring her presence, considered two visits a day insufficient, although there was nothing to talk about. In the hope that a result of the accident would be peace, and to take Anya's mind off herself, the Empress read the Lives of the Saints to her, but those hard eyes were a long time softening, and she still wanted the Emperor to visit her frequently. "You have your children, I have only him!" She took to visiting in a wheelchair, and wanted to live in the palace so that she could meet him in the garden without the Empress present. Only by consistent firmness and cautious handling did they finally cure her.

But as month followed month of dreadful war, and enemies multiplied on all sides, Anya remained in spite of everything a loyal and trusted soul, unreservedly devoted as no one else was. She shared the imperial couple's veneration of their Friend and was a party to all their dealings with him, which were concealed from the rest of the world. It was only in Anya's little house that they could meet their Friend unobserved, only through her could they remain in communication with him. As soon as she could get around on crutches she started going to see him in his third-story apartment on Gorokhovaya Street. She shared his tribulations, and received anonymous threatening letters, telling her which dates she should fear. Even her medical attendant received threats that he would die a violent death, and for a time she was protected by the palace guard. Their Friend invariably praised her, calling her the "heavenly adolescent," would have no other intermediary, and bade the Empress take her along on her visits to GHQ. Moreover, her aggressiveness diminished, and she was once again a nice girl, a good-natured and loyal helper.

We are so few. Together we shall have more peace, more strength.

So few of us and so far apart. My poor, suffering darling, my sunny, big-eyed dear! You are doing a great and wise thing, but when will you be freed from alarums and excursions, when will they honestly carry out your orders, serving you for your own sake? How I wish I could help you. How I wish I could help you to carry your cumbersome, clumsy cross! It is terrible, having to let you do all the heavy work alone! How can I soothe your weary head? A woman can sometimes help, if men will only listen to her. You are always so busy you may forget that I am your notebook. I am sending this scrap of paper to remind you—keep it before you when you receive a minister, why, oh, why are we not together to discuss it all! My pen flies over the paper like a mad thing, unable to keep up with my thoughts, but I cannot write about all the things I would like to write about. It would be good to install a direct line—so long as it was not tapped.

With her sense of duty, her love, her compassion for her harassed husband, the Empress had found in herself a manly strength of will and manly understanding—much needed in the last few years when it seemed that the men had all started wearing skirts. Once she no longer had small children on her hands, she formed definite opinions on matters of policy, and her opinions were invariably correct. And of course she was so close to the center of power that she could not permit herself not to intervene! At first, she had come to the aid of her imperial spouse hesitantly, her advice had been tentative, apologetic—she hoped he would not mind her offering some ideas of her own. She prayed to God daily that she might be a true helpmeet and a sound adviser.

I feel that I am being cruel, tormenting you like this, my gentle, patient angel. My letters must often irritate you. But if I have ever given you pain it was not deliberately. You know that never in our lives has there been any friction between us, or so much as an angry word. But I have always been your alarm bell, and warned you against bad people. I know that I may cause you pain and grief, but you, Baby, and Russia are too dear to me. If only because of your love for me and for Baby, do not let what anyone says or writes to you discourage you. It makes me furious sometimes to know that people deceive you and recommend the worst possible things. Do not take any big step without warning me and discussing the whole thing calmly. I would obviously not write like this if I did not know how likely you are to waver and to change your mind—and what it costs to make you cling to your own opinion. I am so afraid for your kind and gentle nature, always so ready to give in to others. I feel that it is cruel of me to be writing this, but I suffer for you as if you were a gentle, softhearted child who listens to evil counselors and needs guidance. To be apart at a time like this is unbearable, and enough to drive anyone mad. How much easier it would be if we could share everything! (Would you like me to come for one day to give you courage and firmness?) It is our duty to pass on to Baby a strong state, and for his sake we dare not be weak, otherwise his reign will be still more difficult, since he will have to correct our mistakes and pull hard on the reins which you have held so loosely. We have been raised to the throne by God, and must safeguard it with a firm hand and pass it on inviolate to our son. It is my duty, as the mother of Russia, to say this to you.

At first the Empress had felt that the ministers disliked her (as did the whole of Petersburg high society and the Tsar's relatives), but as time went on she grew more and more confident in her efforts to be of help. The time came when Nicky was grateful that she had found something worthwhile to do—to discuss things with the ministers and try to preserve harmony among them. No longer ill at ease, she conversed with them in torrential Russian and they were too polite to laugh at her mistakes. The ministers could see that the Empress was energetic, and that she passed on to the Emperor all that she saw or heard, everything that was happening—that she was the Emperor's eyes and ears and a stout wall behind him. Bobrinsky told her that "the leftist clique hates you, Your Majesty, because it feels that you stand up for Russia and for the throne!"

Yes! And she was more Russian than some others in that country, and would never be indifferent to the dirty tricks of the left!

It is more difficult for me to make you show firmness than to endure the hatred of others, which leaves me cold. Oh, how I wish that I could infuse my willpower into your veins! Do not listen to people who are not from God, but are cowards. You have spoiled them with your kindness and your readiness to forgive everything, they do not know the meaning of the word obedience. Do not bow to them! Let them feel the power of your hand and your spirit! If they know that you can always be forced to make concessions we will never have any peace.

The lord and master himself always wore a shy smile. But Aleksandra understood the immense significance of the present reign and all the dangers that beset it. Nicky lacked the ability to size up people quickly, but Aleksandra found that she possessed this skill. He suffered many difficult moments, not knowing who was speaking the truth and who had an ax to grind. The Emperor's weakness was that if anyone put excessive pressure on him he always gave way in the end, and supposed that it would be for the best. But that was just what he should not do: every concession inevitably led to further demands. If ministers were changed to suit every whim of the Duma, the Duma would start imagining that it was dismissing them itself. His advisers and his entourage misled him, and sometimes forced him to behave unfairly. He was always slow to make up his mind, and had to be spurred on by his little wife. Oh, those vacillations of his! That inexhaustible gentleness! Such gentleness, such meekness was sublime—but its place was in heaven, not on this earth! Such gentleness was, of course, a Christian ideal, but out of place on the throne! On the throne, a tight rein was needed, and an iron will.

What torment she had endured because of his unpardonable mildness! To instill in him courage, resolve, and energy was his wife's main aim. How I wish that I could make you believe in yourself! There are no words for your patience and your forgiveness. Speak to me freely, weep if you wish—you will feel physical relief. Perhaps I am not clever enough, but I have strong feelings, I listen to my soul, and I only wish that you could listen too, my little bird. My spirit is bold, and I am ready for anything that you may need. I have energy enough, even when I feel ill. I want to look into everything, so that I can wake people up, impose order, and unite all forces. Let all work shoulder to shoulder for the one great cause, and not for personal advantage. Trivial people often spoil a great cause. Such people find me troublesome. Am I wearying you by talking like this? I hate being a pest. How I long for a time when I can write you nothing but sweet, funny little letters about our love, our affection for each other, our caresses. If only we could go to the south for a few days! But business won't go away, it is a strict taskmaster and you must be strict too! Let them feel your might! Silence those who contradict you—you are their sovereign! Whoever makes mistakes—punish him. And when you punish do not immediately forgive, as you are inclined to, do not immediately give good new posts to those you have just dismissed. You are not sufficiently feared. Be firm and inspire fear, you are a man! Be like iron. Let them feel your will and your resolve! Bang the table! Be master! The Tsar rules, not the Duma! Be Peter the Great, Ivan the Terrible, Emperor Paul, and crush them under your weight! Be a lion against that small bunch of rascally republicans! We are at war, and at such a time internal strife is treason. Why can't you see it that way? (When the war ends, our enemies must be called to account. Why should those who planned to dethrone their Emperor remain at liberty? Or Samarin, who has given us so much trouble?)

Why do they hate me so? Because I am your rock and your support, and this is something they cannot endure. The unrighteous and the evil hate our Friend's, and my, influence on you—but that alone is beneficial. I rely completely on our Friend. Thanks to His guidance we shall weather these difficult times. Our Friend's prayers give you the strength of which you're so much in need. If we did not have him all would have been over long ago.

The atmosphere at home was wholesome, and there Nicky saw things as they were. But when he was at GHQ the Empress lived in fear of sinister machinations. She had visited GHQ several times in recent months, taking all her daughters with her on her private train and proceeding from the station to the governor's residence by car. After lunch, they changed their clothes and went out for a walk, after which they changed again for tea, then returned to their train. The Emperor and the Heir would come to dine with them. Wonderful, unforgettable visits, and a real meeting of minds, though it was not quite the same as at home. For some days past the Empress had been living for her next visit to GHQ, already arranged and due shortly.

But even the few days remaining were hard to bear: there was danger in the air, more menacing from day to day, just as in the summer of 1915. If they were not careful they might find themselves sliding into revolution. What a life Aleksandra now led! She hardly slept, just two hours or so night after night, her soul was on fire, her head was weary, she felt exhausted from early morning on—only her courage never flagged, her will to fight for the Emperor's throne and for Baby. And then there were two weeks of heavy, damp days under an impenetrable canopy of cloud, with never a ray of sunshine. It was in such weather that the malevolent Duma had opened.

But next day, Wednesday—oh joy! Bright, unbelievably bright sunshine! Such delight, such a hopeful omen: God will help us out of even this situation! Perhaps this change of weather is a sign that everything will change for the better? And there was another reason for rejoicing, another omen: they had finally installed a direct line to GHQ, and Baby had come to the phone at the other end, only the connection was so poor and his voice seemed so far away and so faint that it was impossible to make anything out.

The whole world was sunlit, and the bad news from the Duma on Tuesday—some sort of vile speech from Milyukov—somehow melted away and looked quite unimportant.

Stürmer, however, was greatly disturbed by that sitting. The Duma simply wouldn't hear of legislative activity, and was intent only on its struggle with the government. It wouldn't even point out what it thought was wrong. It was simply "us or them," bring down the government and replace it with people of our own! In the middle of a war like this! Madmen! If they're allowed to appoint and remove ministers it will destroy Russia. They're all obsessed with it, but we mustn't let it happen!

Stürmer was also depressed because he himself had gotten it in the neck, poor fellow: Milyukov had called him a bribe taker and a traitor, citing Buchanan as his authority, and Buchanan had remained silent! What a shabby way for the ambassador of an Allied country to behave. He was not such a blabbermouth, nor such an idiot as the French ambassador, but he wasn't very clever either, and worst of all he was arrogant: he had started speaking insolently to the Emperor and trying to dictate to him.

So then, because they could not get at the throne they had attacked a defenseless old man—and it was agony to Stürmer to think that he had brought all these troubles upon the Emperor. He had hoped for a collective protest from the government, but the ministers had declined—let the old man disentangle himself as best he can. Stürmer thought that Rodzyanko should be deprived of his status as a court chamberlain, for not stopping speakers when they began making insinuations. He had instructed Frederiks, as Minister of the Court, to reprimand Rodzyanko, but Frederiks was so very old that he understood nothing and had written something useless. An impossible situation had, then, arisen: the Prime Minister was left defenseless against a slanderer. He could only sue the offender, like any private citizen.

True, Shuvaev and Grigorovich had spoken on behalf of the government, but they had blurred the issue, sounded the wrong note: it was as if they were distancing themselves from the rest of the government and ingratiating themselves with the Duma. Shuvaev had, in fact, behaved much worse: he had shaken Milyukov's hand in the lobby, shortly after his attack on us.

No, Shuvaev is spineless, of no use at all. We desperately need a new Minister of War—that real gentleman Belyaev!

So there we are! The left are furious because everything is slipping away from them: they see that a firm government is being formed at last, and that when it is they will get nowhere. They can shout as much as they like, we will show them that we are not afraid, that we are firm. The Duma crowd are revolting, with their attitude toward Russia: they do her so much harm, they couldn't care less about her.

It is sad to have to realize that the ill-intentioned are often braver and quicker off the mark, and so more successful, than we are.

But we must look ahead, not just sleep, as people usually do in Russia. In reality, things generally are getting better. Slowly, yes, but surely, things are improving.

An unfortunate situation had also been created by Protopopov's change of mind over the food supply problem. Stürmer's belief that Protopopov was too inclined to fuss had been reinforced by this recent abrupt reversal. But it was not Protopopov who fussed too much, it was Stürmer who dillydallied. He was too slow in answering his enemies, and could not keep a firm hand on his ministers. No, Protopopov was cool and collected, and above all devoted, he was honorable in his support of *us* and he reveres our Friend.

But this rapid and muddled change in the management of food supplies did, of course, greatly trouble the Empress too. The Emperor himself was dismayed by it, and far from home as he was, alone and vulnerable, he ought not to have to endure such wavering. But don't upset yourself—she had written at once—the first decision was the correct one, and it will shortly be implemented.

In this tense situation the Empress found her meetings with their

Friend—often two in one week—particularly uplifting. That Wednesday evening their Friend arrived at Anya's little house with a bishop. His manner was most dignified, majestic, and he had spoken serenely. He was, though, distressed by the news that Nikolasha was to visit GHQ—for the first time since his replacement. Nikolasha was an evil spirit. Their Friend was also annoyed with Protopopov, and said flatly that he had backed down out of cowardice, delaying the decision on the food supply for two weeks was sheer stupidity, there was no sense in it at all. As far as the Duma was concerned, their Friend was not excessively perturbed: it always made a noise, whatever happened and whatever you did. We're releasing Sukhomlinov—and that's good. But what about Rubinstein? The Emperor still hasn't sent a telegram ordering his release. Has he fallen prey to doubt again? Has he been told some other story at GHQ? Why is he being so slow? (Appeals on behalf of Rubinstein had reached the Empress from many quarters.)

Stürmer himself was partly to blame for all that had happened: he had taken fright, gone a whole month without seeing their Friend, and so lost his balance. Their Friend had been right when he said that the premiership was enough for Stürmer, and that he should not take over the Ministry of Foreign Affairs as well—that was when the worst of the sniping at the government had begun. Their Friend's view now was that Stürmer should give up Foreign Affairs. He should plead sickness for a couple of weeks until the Duma yelled itself hoarse, take a brief leave of absence, but certainly not think of retiring—he was a devoted, honorable, loyal man, and could resume quietly as soon as the Duma went into recess. In the meantime, the senior minister, Trepov, would deputize for him, as the law prescribed. (And Stürmer would instruct him to take good care of their Friend.)

If the Empress had not been protected by their Friend's wisdom anything might have happened, he was a rock of faith and of succor.

She could not, of course, feel toward Trepov as she did toward Goremykin or Stürmer. They were people of the older, better sort, they loved the Empress, and came to her with every worrying problem. Whereas Trepov was a hard man, did not love her, and did not believe in their Friend. Working with him would be difficult.

But it was only for a little while! Both Stürmer and Protopopov would, of course, remain in their posts. There were so few honest people that if you did find someone who was devoted to you, you had to cling to him with all your might. They're trying to take the devoted and conscientious people away from us, and to replace them with dubious characters from the Duma who are no good for anything. It's not a matter of individual dismissals and appointments—what's in question is the prestige of the monarchy. *They* would not stop at one individual—they'd force them all out one by one, followed by the imperial couple themselves!

Only a few days remained before the Empress's next visit to GHQ, but they were turbulent days, and—such was the pressure from the Duma—the Empress was very much afraid that in those few days the Emperor might be led astray and induced to yield. Every day she wrote letters several pages long, each more ingenious and more forceful than the last, helping her spouse to steel himself and shielding him from fresh dangers.

She had dispatched her strongest argument, and felt that what might prove a fateful week was nearing its end, but instead, she had received, that Friday, a letter with an enclosure: Grand Duke Nikolai Mikhailovich, who for some reason (why? her heart sank, fearing some new mischief) had arrived at GHQ on Tuesday, and not only taken it upon himself to lecture the Emperor but had left with him a disgusting letter, and Nicky, who had suspiciously failed to mention the occasion at all on Wednesday, on Thursday enclosed the letter so that the Empress could read it for herself—and now it was burning her fingers.

Miserable old blabbermouth! Filthy, loathsome person! This stuff he was peddling—against his Emperor's wife and in time of war—was obscene filth, treason! For the whole twenty years he had hated the Empress, spoken ill of her in his club, so that even complete outsiders were shocked by the things he said. He was the incarnation of all that was vile, he could not bear the fact that people were beginning to take notice of the Empress's opinion. How easy it is to give advice when you are uninvolved and unburdened with responsibility!

She lit a cigarette, although smoking dilated her heart.

Was this what her dream about the severed arm had portended?

On Friday, after two fine days, the weather became gloomy and terribly oppressive.

What hurt her most was that Nikolai Mikhailovich undoubtedly had the backing of the Emperor's mama and his sisters—they had given a ready ear to malicious gossip and no doubt approved of his action! It hurt her that in the course of their conversation Nicky had not once pulled the insulting old windbag up short (and maybe was even swayed by him to some extent?).

Why did you not tell him that if he said another word against me you would send him to Siberia, since what he is doing borders on treason? You are too kindhearted, my dear one. I am your wife, and they cannot be allowed to do it. How dare he try to turn you against your Sunny? Even a private individual would not tolerate for a single hour such attacks on his wife! It makes not a scrap of difference to me, such worldly things, such dirty little tricks have no effect on me, but my dear litle husband should have stood up for me. Many people may think that you don't care.

Nasty people everywhere were bandying the name of the Empress about. She was receiving the most scurrilous anonymous letters. A poisoned fog of rumor rose from Petrograd and Moscow. By no means all the details of this vicious tittle-tattle reached the ears of the imperial couple, but what they did hear was inflammatory enough. The Empress was English by upbringing, but there were asses who called her "the German woman" (just as the unfortunate Marie Antoinette had been "the Austrian woman"). (As if a single Tsaritsa in the past two centuries had been Russian!) Now, at the height of the war, foreignness was more or less equated with treason! The man of God had come to symbolize all that was hated by Russian educated society, which itself did not understand a quarter of what it read. In the two corrupt capitals reckless talk about the imperial couple was rife. To begin with, they merely laughed at all this gossip. Who are these critics of ours? A handful of Petrograd aristocrats who spend their time playing bridge and don't know the first thing about Russia. And anyway, in the middle of the greatest of wars, should we really be paying attention to contemptible scandalmongering (which was now spreading like wildfire even in the diplomatic corps!)? It only encouraged them to shut themselves up more closely in their immediate family circle and not to see or listen to anyone else.

But their privacy was breached by direct approaches from insolent persons, some of them wearing court uniform, who wrote ten-page memoranda brazenly telling the monarch what he must do. (This Frederiks of ours is a dotty old ditherer, long past his prime as Minister of the Court, incapable of punishing the Master of the Royal Hunt for slander, but Nicky keeps the old man because dismissal would upset him. Never mind, they'll be made to pay for it when peace comes, and many of them will be struck off the register of courtiers.) Even the archpriest at GHQ had offered unsought advice.

The noxious mists of slander steamed around them. Everyone was free to lie, to indulge in innuendo, to sling mud, and nowhere in Russia did anyone rise up to defend the Empress.

She wore the Russian crown and whole regiments bore her name— but had she any means at all of defending herself against these slanders? The awesome power and the wrath of her imperial husband were her only protection.

But he had not come to her defense even when, at the former GHQ, Nikolasha had discussed with the Emperor's officers, and with some of the Grand Dukes, the possibility of locking up the living and reigning and still not dethroned Empress as if she were an inanimate object or wild beast.

[7 3]

Pavel Ivanovich had a dream. He was lying with Lyoka on a wide bed, not to make love, but engaged in one of those exhausting conversations of which there had been so many in their last few years together. Then she started soliciting his caresses and although he sensed even in his sleep that it was unnatural and forbidden they began kissing each other's cheeks. Suddenly he felt that his cheeks were very wet. What could the reason be? It was then that he suddenly saw Lyoka's face clearly (until then he had not seen it at all). There were bloody marks in two or three places on her cheeks, not subcutaneous bruises but wet patches as though from deep cuts, and in the shape of two rows of teeth. Then he realized that the wetness on his own face was also where he had been bleeding freely. They had not been kissing but biting each other, unintentionally, and at first unaware of it. He got up and went to wash himself. When he got back he saw in the light from some invisible and inexplicable source that Lyoka was lying just where she had been, fully dressed. Her face was washed clean and showed no trace of those cuts but was contorted into the grimace of pain and self-pity which he had often seen before they parted. Some invisible mischief-maker had given her a piece of paper and something to rest it on, and Lyoka was reluctantly signing it with the same miserable expression, full of pity not for him but for herself. He knew that she was doing something shameful, that she would be horrified when she realized it. "Why are you doing this?" he asked. "People will find out!" She laughed bitterly. "Ah, what does it matter?"

He awoke, sick at heart, as always after a vivid dream of her. There had been no pleasant ones for a long time now.

Pavel Ivanovich dreamt of no one else so frequently. It was extraordinary. So many years since they had lived together, or even seen each other, yet Leokadia intruded on his dreams as importunately, as vengefully as ever. It had not been like that when they were falling in love, nor when they were husband and wife. These relentless dreams must be of her doing. She must be able, when she was experiencing strong emotions, to project them. And Pavel Ivanovich was receptive and a frequent dreamer. So that although he had not seen Lyoka in years, and no longer exchanged letters with her, he sometimes knew almost exactly what she was feeling or doing. He had only to extract the underlying meaning of the dream, and by now he was used to that. Once she appeared to him in what had been an evening gown, now completely threadbare, bedraggled, and in holes. On another occasion he saw her with a twisted spine, and bent at the waist as though doubled up by illness or a stab wound. Another time they were riding in a hired phaeton, but facing backward, so that they could not see whether there was a coachman or a horse, and the phaeton was rolling backward. He had said, apparently sincerely, "I was hoping to see you at home," meaning here, at Maly Vlasievsky. And she had replied quite mournfully, looking younger in her sadness, "Have we really still got a home?"

Today, as always after such dreams, he awoke with an aching heart. An ache that never went away.

He turned the dream over in his mind, and could not get to sleep again. It was already light. Perhaps he had slept long enough.

As he got older, Pavel Ivanovich had started piling the pillows high. If he didn't, the blood went to his head during the night, and it ached the whole day afterward. He had long ceased to jump out of bed, eager for action, as soon as he woke up. Nowadays he shifted slowly, very slowly, into his daytime mode, gradually pushing himself higher until he was half sitting.

And all the time he could see—ever since the bed had been moved to its present position, nine years ago now—the same familiar scene, the view he saw first every morning: of a small window in an old wooden house (single frame in summer, double frames, with cotton wool and tumblers filled with salt on the ledge between them, in winter). In the bottom right corner of the picture was the ornamental carving above the gable of an outbuilding, part of a roof, and most of a brick chimney (with smoke, sometimes transparent, sometimes dense, streaming from it, sometimes vertically, sometimes in ragged wisps chased sideways by the wind). Higher and to the left he could see a stout elm branch—in leaf, or bare, or snow-covered, still, or swaying gently with its twigs shining independently, under overcast skies or in slanting sunlight. Beyond it and from behind the neighboring building he saw the little church of St. Vlasi, the upper ridge of its brickwork, but not its dome. Beyond this there was a wooden wall and part of another roof.

This view had faced the bed for nine years, and had indeed not changed for as long as Varsonofiev could remember—and he had been born in this house, sixty-one years ago. Previously he had been vaguely aware of its existence, but now that it took him so long to get out of bed, the view, colored by his mood and by the weather, prepared him for the sometimes cruel day ahead.

Over the years rising had become a problem. This time it was still very early, and the gray November morning was just breaking through wet bare branches and over a wet sheet-iron roof. What he would have liked to do was to sleep a little more, his body felt so feeble and so listless. Ever since his former mother-in-law, Lyoka's mother, had died, she too had sometimes appeared in Pavel Ivanovich's dreams, just as vividly as Lyoka, and with all the energy she had displayed in her lifetime. Shortly after her death he had dreamt of her walking quickly along the Arbat, with her gray hair loose and untidy. Pavel Ivanovich could hardly keep up with her, passersby might just as well not have been there, they were like disembodied spirits, and there was no risk of bumping into them. His mother-in-law gesticulated as she walked along, urgently pointing to something, and muttering inarticulately about things in shopwindows, or even the cinema signs. Suddenly, the Arbat vanished, there was no more traffic, and she was sitting like a matryoshka doll, wearing a peasant head scarf and very red in the face, saying plaintively, "Pashenka! I have something to ask you—please take me in!" But even in his sleep Varsonofiev realized that she was not asking to be allowed into his house, because she was dead, and it was good that she was not inviting him to join her. He demurred. "How can I, Maria Nikolaevna, it's impossible." She looked downcast and said, "I get visitors here, you know"—meaning visitors from earth. Even in his sleep he felt puzzled. "What is that supposed to mean?" he asked. She answered coldly, "Make what you like of it."

Varsonofiev was used to treating such dreams not as kaleidoscopic jumbles of incoherent fancies but as genuine spiritual encounters with the living or the dead, but always in code: we sometimes find it difficult to decipher, sometimes we refused to waste time trying. No one from the other life can express his thoughts satisfactorily to the living, and our occasional communications with the dead are inevitably imprecise, a matter of guesswork and tentative interpretation. But character and mood are always expressed in dreams almost without concealment. Tearfulness and grief were evidently dominant in Maria Nikolaevna's state beyond the grave, as they had been toward the end on earth, during her long illness. He had twice dreamt of her weeping with bitter resentment, and both times (on different nights) it had something to do with a fish—indeed, she was slumped across the table with her chest touching the plate of fried fish she was eating. She was obviously weeping not so much for herself as for Lyoka. On another occasion, Pavel Ivanovich seemed to see himself lying in bed, with Maria Nikolaevna, in a hospital smock, standing at his feet and twisting his toes painfully. As if revenging herself on him.

The wrong you have done to someone constantly changes its character as long as that person lives. Not just your actions, but fleeting thoughts of the past day, or something you have just learned, can change the complexion of your offense and your relationship with the injured person. But once that person is dead your offense is fixed forever. Sometimes it is black, and burns cruelly. Sometimes it is a gentle glow, a persistent signal, a greeting from one world to another.

Pavel Ivanovich's life with Lyoka remained in suspense somewhere, now neither his nor hers, where beginnings and ends, causes and consequences were no longer distinguishable. Neither he nor she, whether separately or together, could have disentangled and analyzed it all, still less could any outsider, acting for them—and who would have the patience to hear the argument on both sides, to trace the true story and pass sentence? It had taken Pavel Ivanovich a long time to get over his surprise that he had found the willpower to struggle out of the grinder and crawl away to nurse his wounds.

He had seen it often before in their last excruciating years together and again that morning, her wry grimace of pity and grief as she said, "Ah, what does it matter?"—mingling condescending mockery of his inadequacy with hopeless sadness for herself.

Lyoka too had lived all those years, and the three hundred sixty-five days in each of them, as his wedded wife, undivorced but long since a stranger (she always became something of a stranger as soon as she escaped from his influence), and yet he could tell from his dreams that she thought of him almost every day, and perhaps that very day in Kazan she had dreamt a dream that mirrored his own.

For some reason—why?—they had brought into the world and reared and educated a daughter, who was now mired in such a marriage herself (but that was just as it should be) and such a stranger, so remote that it no longer mattered what she said her maiden name had been, Varsonofiev or some other, or who her family were, all that mattered was that she had gone away and severed all contact.

This time of gradual awakening, struggling to haul himself out of nocturnal nonexistence, and to face the dictates of daytime, was also a time for reviewing the memories which rose spontaneously and flitted through his mind.

The nagging power of memory can make the past seem more real than the present.

It had become so difficult to wake up and begin his day! He was after all not so very old, but his inability to jump up and spring into action like a young man slowed down his awakening. It was a mental rather than a physical disability, not so much physical as psychological impotence. His mind, more heavily weighed down into the nocturnal state than ever, was slower to emerge from it, cautiously and reluctantly returning to this world.

In those first minutes of reemergence the world seemed so harsh, so oppressive, that living in it, struggling around in it, was hardship enough. His obligations were so burdensome. And all that he had ever done was botched and flawed.

Gone was the confidence with which he had once met the morning: up with you and get to work quickly! Gone was his former commitment to action, his eagerness for success. He no longer cared.

Nowadays he could think of very little in his past life which should not have been done differently.

Lyoka, for instance. At first he had thought of separation from her as a healing process, and the only way to save his soul. It was only some five or seven or eight years later that Pavel Ivanovich realized the truth: separation from her had ruptured his soul. It was as though he had lost his buoyancy forever and acquired an eternal stoop.

Now he could see it all. It had been a mistake long ago to take up with her, to believe in her. It had been a mistake to live with her for so many years. And it had been a mistake to part from her. Nothing but mistakes all along the line.

In old age the heart begins to feel heavy, and you carry it around like a burden. All the problems of your past life, even those easy to bear in earlier decades, surmounted (or so you thought) successfully, and put behind you long ago, are suddenly found to be still with you, pressing down like so many stone slabs on your chest.

Yet Varsonofiev had almost gotten to like these slow, laborious, lonely awakenings. He could lie for half an hour, or sometimes a whole hour, motionless, having neither the strength nor the will to spring the catch of his watch on the bedside table and look at the time. Busy noises from the outside would sometimes reach his ears, but he was not concerned to interpret them. He lay thinking whatever thoughts came into his head, helped by his scrutiny of the patterns carved in the dark, unwhitewashed ceiling.

As consciousness gradually reached the upper level of his mind, Varsonofiev eased himself up on his pillow. He waited a few more minutes while wakefulness flowed downward to his chest, to his trunk, along his arms and legs, willing his body to obey, readying it to rise and take up its burden.

He heaved a sigh, and lowered his legs to the floor, with no great difficulty. It seemed rather cold in the room. He took his robe from its usual place on the back of a chair heaped with last night's books, put it on, and took a few steps, gradually straightening up.

His thoughts, not his years, had bowed him.

He touched the white tiles of the Dutch stove in passing. It was barely warm. It would have to be stoked higher: seen through the windows the weather was damp, gloomy, dirty, with perhaps a slight drizzle falling.

He went through two other low-ceilinged rooms, past chests and bookcases, a Japanese screen, piles of newspapers on the floor and on chairs, more cupboards, a commode, a wardrobe, all of it from the last century, none of it displaced for fifteen, twenty, thirty years, a wolfskin, more bookshelves crammed with books up to the ceiling, some upright, some lying down, some in old leather bindings, some quite new. Past a stack of firewood—and he was in the mezzanine looking down into the hallway. There was a samovar, big enough to serve twenty, never used. He began descending the creaking stairs.

At the end of the spacious hallway, beyond a large chest, was the front entrance, a double door with a dark glass handle. Pavel Ivanovich sprang the stiff catch and, huddling into his robe as the damp cold hit him, stuck out his head and slid his hand into the oak mailbox. All three newspapers—two from Moscow, one from Petersburg—had arrived, one day late.

Leaving the door off the latch so that the servant could get in, he went back upstairs.

Now that the morning was his own at last, he felt drawn to the occupations in which he was happiest—solitary reflection and paper-work would restore his equilibrium. But although it was now more than five years since Varsonofiev had finally realized that no newspaper could ever clarify his or anyone else's thoughts, but could only make them more simplistic and superficial, or else aggravate a partisan bias, like a habitual smoker or a drunkard he could not fight his craving. By now he was incapable of excluding newspapers completely from his life, he was addicted. As a rule he tried not to pick them up in the morning. That left some of the best hours of the day for thinking, and after lunch, the newspapers, like smoking, were less noxious. But some-times, although he had forbidden himself to do it, he went to get them automatically on rising, ruining his day and perhaps sullying his soul. Today he had gone to get them deliberately, impatient to read about the Duma sessions, or perhaps just to see how few or how many blanks the censorship had notched up.

He could not wait to get to his study, but spread them out on a little table next to the disused samovar and began perusing them. Yes, there were plenty of blank spaces, and they spoke louder and more eloquently than the rest. They were much richer in meaning than any-thing the speaker could actually have said.

He began, of course, by reading Milyukov's speech.

And was staggered by its emptiness. Measured not against the high peaks of human wisdom, but the minor eminence of Milyukov's own. It was not the speech of a statesman, it was a farrago of slanderous gossip. He had never been a powerful speaker, never known how to dominate an assembly, his skill had been in divining the average view of his audience and expressing it in middle-of-the-road terms. Milyu-kov lacked intellectual depth, his thoughts were those of an earth-bound positivist, but it was these very limitations which gave him the energy to be a political leader. He was incapable of giving his party, his parliament, or his country anything more than ephemeral political slogans.

Varsonofiev not only knew him, but had twice been involved in public argument with him, about the symposium *Vekhi*. Nothing was more characteristic of Milyukov than his fury with *Vekhi*, and the way in which he had ranged over Russia seeking to refute a book which had annoyed and provoked him with its profundity.

His sterility as a scholar was equally surprising: inaccuracy in the use of sources, intrusive "conclusions" instead of factual history, jealous concern for his own reputation. And yet he regarded Russia as a country not yet mature enough to appreciate him: just recently, in Oslo, he had complained that "eight generations of civilization in Russia" were insufficient (he was counting of course, from Peter I). He was always full of admiration for himself, and sometimes let slip that he measured himself against Herzen—even though a felicitous style was not among his gifts, indeed he was utterly devoid of talent.

Varsonofiev had set out with the rest of them—Petrunkevich, Shakhovskoy, Vernadsky . . . In 1902 they had even thought of sending him abroad to publish *Osvobozhdenie*. This was thought of at the time as condemnation to exile in perpetuity—shades of Herzen again. But the young Pyotr Struve had volunteered for the job.

No more than ten years ago Varsonofiev had been one of that loud-mouthed, petty-minded crowd, with Rodichev, Vinaver, Milyukov. His fervor as a deputy in the Duma had been perfectly sincere. In the heat of battle he had never once doubted. To him, as to the others, the dissolution of the Duma on 16 June had seemed an act of arbitrary violence unparalleled in history.

This although he was no longer a boy but a man of fifty.

If he had remained as he was then, his name would be in today's newspapers. A startling thought.

Nothing about us is more surprising than our capacity to remain sincere as our lives, and our minds, change completely. Looking back, we are astonished to realize that we were once no less certain of our old views than we are of their replacements.

Varsonofiev had undergone a complete transformation, and by no means a slow one. Why had he fought so passionately before? It had all been a mistake. The smug busybodies of the League of Liberation were like a flock of big stupid birds, all flapping their wings in unison.

Impatiently laboring in vain, trying to change the course of such a vessel, without fully understanding its nature. But its course is beyond our comprehension, and we have no right to anything more than the slightest adjustment of the wheel. With no sudden jerks.

Five decades? Six? Seven? How long should it take to understand that the life of a community cannot be reduced to politics or wholly encompassed by government?

The time in which we live has unfathomable depths beneath it. Our age is a mere film on the surface of time.

[7 4]

Now that he had seen Gurko there was nothing to keep him there. But his train did not leave till the next morning, and after reserving his ticket at the Rail Transport Department he was left with one more free evening in Mogilev. Wondering how best to spend it, and whether there was anyone else he should see, he decided to call at the post office again. There might just be a second letter from Olda, and he would not have liked to miss it! What better way to spend the evening than to sit down and write her a long letter, which would have been impossible yesterday when he was so worked up. Now that his future was decided, now that he was on his way back to Romania, and there was no knowing when they would next meet, he could at least pretend that he was spending the evening with Olda.

The square and Bolshaya Sadovaya Street were unrecognizable under the snow. The sidewalks had been partly cleared, leaving narrow paths between deep drifts. It was too cold for strollers, and the stalls along the monastery wall were closed. Only the larger shops and the pharmacies were as brightly lit as ever. The place which yesterday had seemed so romantic was changed beyond recognition.

But in the post office the same unsmiling clerk stood behind the same polished counter. He flicked through a bundle of envelopes with the same alert efficiency and—yes!—handed over another letter.

Vorotyntsev seized this windfall eagerly and made off. Glancing at the writing as he went, he was at a loss.

He did not realize at first what he was looking at.

He pulled up short.

Strange! It hadn't immediately registered that the letter was from Alina.

The last thing he had expected.

How could he have failed to recognize that bold sprawl, those mannered flourishes, those oval loops above and below.

But her writing was larger than usual. Untidier. Somehow more frightening.

He hadn't been expecting it. He had thought that nothing would happen until he was back with his regiment, that she would not write before that. He had thought that he could put all these unpleasantnessess out of his mind for a while.

How could she have tracked him down? Of course! He had shown her Svechin's telegram. She had seemed to ignore it at the time. But he had deliberately left it on the table.

Now there was this letter.

There was a sort of desperation in that wild scrawl. As on that last morning in Moscow.

Pretend that he hadn't received it? After all, it was only by chance that he had looked in at the post office. He need not have gone there again. Should he postpone this painful business until he reached his regiment? Or at least until he got to Army HQ?

He was reluctant to spoil the happiness he had felt last night—that extraordinarily warm November night with snow in the offing. After parting with Nechvolodov he had walked and walked, back and forth, on the dark Rampart, as the wind gradually got colder, unable to stop walking. His reply to Olda swirled through his mind, but he had collapsed on his bed and fallen asleep without writing a single line.

Now he was abruptly reminded of Alina's existence. It had been dishonest of him to forget her.

He went over to the reading desk, chose a different section this time, and broke the envelope open with one finger, leaving a jagged edge.

No "Dear Georgi." Not even "Georgi." He felt at once as though he had been brutally stripped naked.

"What good to me is a husband for whom I am not the best of women? What good to me is a husband who is not the best of men?"

Jolted by this body blow, Georgi could not force himself to read the words in order, but raced feverishly ahead, expecting to find something dreadful and irreparable.

"I could not reconcile myself to the fact that she exists, not for a single week. I was not created for the 'role' of 'one wife among others'! Do you think that I can go on living in such a hell? Knowing that you may have gone to her at this very moment? It would be many times easier to say farewell to life."

Oh, God!

"But you wouldn't let me commit suicide."

No, no, it couldn't come to that!

But, skipping half a page, as if the most terrifying lines had excited some magnetic force on him, he read: "The price I must pay for taking that path is suicide!"

He remembered the fluttering in her throat. How she had fainted in the guesthouse. The numbness of her arms after her heart attack. All this could have happened again, dozens of times in those last few days, without any suicide attempt. And he had abandoned her, left so lightheartedly, felt such a sense of liberation.

And she had struggled to write as her strength failed her.

"If I am to go on living, the only way out for me is to leave you."

The floor seemed to slip from under him. His legs, his whole body became weightless: she had withdrawn that first dreadful threat and he was airborne with joy, joy that stung like a whiplash! *Free!* Was he free?

This, he saw now, was what he had wanted. Wanted without daring to dream, or give the slightest hint, or even admit it to himself.

He felt again as he had felt the night before, felt like a balloon, soaring . . . felt like shouting for joy. But it was only for a moment. Wounding words dragged him down to earth.

"What sacrifice did you ever make for me? What did you ever go without?"

It was true. He had lived, he had pursued his career . . . for himself, not for her.

"Choose one of us, but not in Petersburg. Go to her if you must! I don't want your charity! I have outgrown that! I have come to my senses!"

Freedom! Freedom! He exulted in spite of himself. How he had longed for this!

But the next lines were a heartrending cry that cut him to the quick.

"You are free! But I too am free again! I may fall. I may become a geisha, but I am still free! You will never need to pity me again!"

No signature either.

Georgi screwed up his eyes. A searing pain seemed to melt them.

He had not experienced this sensation since childhood.

The burning sensation troubled his sleep, and became more and more painful as his sleep became shallower.

Not a figurative burn—a real one as though someone was touching the walls of his heart with a rod dipped in iodine. Burning his heart, not figuratively—his actual heart, to the left of center in his chest, pumping blood, pumping it now irregularly, missing beats because of the burning.

This intolerable burning bored deeper and deeper into his sleep until at last he was prodded out of it, but even after he awoke the burning continued.

He had found no refuge in sleep. And it felt as if the night was still far from its end.

In the prevailing darkness, with no hint of light at the window, this torment gripped him all the more cruelly.

A week ago, it was Alina who had tossed and turned, night after night, while the wall of her heart was seared by pain like this—no, surely worse! Several iodine rods at once! And he, a detached onlooker, had found it almost beautiful. She had become prettier, gentler, and he had imagined that they could amicably, with extraordinary goodwill toward each other . . .

Now it had caught up with him and pierced him to the heart. My poor, weak little girl! What have I brought upon you? I owned up, went away—and left you to eat your heart out!

He was staggered by the agony, the violence of his pity for Alina. He could scarcely hide his tears as he hurried back from the post office to lock himself in his room. In the guesthouse with her he had felt nothing like this overpowering pity.

Alina, her vulnerability showing in her dear gray tear-stained eyes, stood before him, projected from her wounded distance, as clearly visible in the darkness as if illuminated.

What terrible thing had he done? What a disaster! What had he done to her?!

Her love for him was her whole life. What suffering it must have cost her to think of sacrificing herself. To give him his freedom!

This was something that had never occurred to him! He had said nothing to provoke it. Quite the contrary: he had said, "Nothing in the world could make me abandon you!"

Sharing was impossible for her. Her immediate impulse was divorce! She was ready to divorce him! She did not realize what she was suggesting, couldn't see how soon she would come to grief.

He remembered her word "geisha," her heartbroken cry—he could almost hear the sob in her voice. Poor innocent—you really think you could? That catch in her voice—like someone taking on a task beyond her powers, like a little girl trying to sing a grown-up aria. It was so like her! This desperation, this impulse to leap into the abyss, without stopping to think, just to "show" somebody!

Freedom? Before he had even asked for it? Before it had even unfolded its wings in his mind? Suddenly, like a brick on his head . . . freedom.

Alina's sacrifice had robbed Georgi of his buoyancy. He could no longer believe that he had . . . When? Yesterday? Yes, only yesterday evening. Had hurried from the post office to the Rampart, cheerful, light on his feet, young, unaware that the happiness he had won was about to be eclipsed, wrested from him.

But it had happened.

That which in Petersburg he had taken to be the most dazzling success of his life. That which in Moscow still seemed like a fresh torrential stream pouring into his life . . . had suddenly laid him flat on his back in the darkness. A disaster from which there was no escape. A disaster he could not come to terms with, could not live with.

Olda's words, which had rung so clearly the night before, were muffled now by the eddying fog of unhappiness. He could no longer hear them. Her exquisite, intelligent features were obscured as if by a smoke screen, and he could not see her whole face at once, only where the smoke thinned, one sad eye, the fold of anxious disagreement on her brow, a section of her upper lip. Not all of it at once. And no sound at all reached him.

But Alina's agonized shriek shrilled in his ears, lodged there like a needle.

That was her character! Prostrate one moment—soaring aloft the next! With trebled strength! Purse-lipped pride: the decision must be hers! No one must decide for her! And her decision would follow her first impulse! I am not the best of women? So let us part!

But a few hours, or maybe a few minutes later, she would break down . . .

"You will see me in such a brill . . ."

Did she really have any idea what her decision meant? Would she really be able to live without him? Would she ever recover?

No, my poor girl, you'll go to pieces! How can I possibly let that happen? My dear little girl, what have I brought you to? It was not just his heart aching, it was his whole chest, as if shattered.

But . . . Olda? Olda! Olda, of whom he would never have dared to dream! Let me see you! Come from behind your smoke screen! Let me see you and hear you! Help me! You are the clever one, you always know what to do!

No, she would not show herself.

Only in snatches.

In fragmentary memories.

And suddenly her words came into his mind—her very own words: wise human beings make the best of reality, instead of dreaming up substitutes for it.

She had been talking about something quite different, but still . . .

Well, it was his fate. His duty? The burden of age. Forty years old was not twenty. A man's eyes should be opened at twenty.

But General Levachev had misled him, given him bad advice.

Sleep had now ebbed beyond recall.

On his back under that huge mass of darkness he felt particularly helpless, at the mercy of thoughts burning through him like a flame, drilling into him like an auger.

Of course they loved one another. Of course they got on well together. How could they part now?

There was so much that was good . . . he could remember hardly anything that was not good, not touching, not endearing in their ten years together. How patiently she had shared his years as a penniless junior officer, deprived of so many of life's pleasures. She knew that enlightened officers usually abandoned the army, but had put no pressure on him to do so. And he really had loved hearing Chopin and Schumann from the next room.

He was all the more helplessly trapped because he had never expected anything remotely like it.

Why had things taken such a terrifying turn? Surely it need never have come to this?

Just because he had told the truth?

Perhaps he should have kept silent, as others did?

How had it all started? Released from his Transylvanian hole in the ground like an overcharged shell, he had sped, ineffectually, point-lessly, ingloriously over great distances to splash down unexploded into a bog.

He lay there as if paralyzed.

For the first time in his life he was unsure what to do next—and that hurt more than anything. His salvation had always been the cer-tainty that all would turn out well. It was not an assurance born of knowledge or reflection, but an inborn feeling, part of his very being: however bad things are, it's all for the best! Fair weather will always follow foul! The going may be hard, but we shall struggle through to better days! Thinking so, he had always been at peace with himself. However gloomy the news might be, there was always sunlight in his soul. He could not live in any other way. And if ever his optimism was briefly dented, it was as though he had fallen sick.

But now—he had lost this assurance, and was terrified to think that it might be forever.

He had behaved throughout those last few weeks with unblinking confidence and the results were all bad, all was lost.

His throat contracted as if gripped by pincers.

A sudden pang! Wasn't there something about suicide somewhere else in the letter? (She'd mentioned it more than once—the thought must be constantly with her.)

He realized that he hadn't read the letter properly and couldn't remember all that was in it! He had perused it several times, but its message had not sunk into a mind as heavy as lead, and he had sought refuge in sleep. He must read it again at once!

He had forgotten where the light switch was, and started looking for matches. (Extraordinary: he couldn't sleep, had lain eating his heart out in the darkness, and yet had not lit a single cigarette. Hadn't even thought of it.)

He struck a match, switched on the overhead light, and found that he was fully dressed. He had removed only his sword and his boots.

He went over to the table to read the letter again.

How she loved him! "It would be far, far easier to part with life!" And: "This is how you have repaid me for my loyalty, for all my sac-rifices. For never betraying you. For surrendering my youth to you. For taking on the role of meek little wife, and making a comfortable home for you to work in. And, now, in return for all that—you betray me?"

Now he had to smoke. One cigarette, then another.

He walked around the room in his stocking feet.

And read on.

"Come to your senses! Why is it only I who have to fight my feel-ings? Why can't you fight yours?"

True. He was the stronger. He was the one who should be fighting.

Perhaps their love was not what it had been, but he was responsible for Alina, not she for him.

If they could just get over this shock, the hurt would cease to rankle, they could make peace.

But what of Olda? What did she have in mind? What had she said, what had she been thinking back there? He couldn't recall. He hadn't given it a thought.

Now, with the light on, Olda was still harder to see than in the dark.

"To go on living . . ."

Hopelessly trapped! He was dizzy with self-loathing.

There was no way out.

He felt like a murderer.

There was no time to lose! Must hurry, go at once . . . One more flare-up, and she might . . .

She might already have . . . while her letter was on the way . . .

"The price of taking that course . . . would be suicide . . ."

If she suddenly took it into her head . . .

Why should Alina be left to struggle alone?

It was true.

In a moment of desperation . . . you might do anything . . .

That's it! I'll send a telegram to placate her, an affectionate telegram. Make sure she gets it tomorrow morning.

It was still very early, but there was always someone on duty at the telegraph office.

He pulled his boots on quickly.

As he was dressing he caught sight of himself in the wardrobe mirror. He looked old, seedy, lost, bloodshot . . .

He had lapsed into old age overnight. And felt it. His forties were over.

He went down the hotel corridor, treading softly. The others were still sleeping.

It was dark and damp outside, with a hint of snow that made him shiver. Treacherous weather.

No moon, no stars in the sky. Streetlamps still burning on street corners here and there. All windows were dark. No passersby.

He walked on, hunched up. More like a beaten dog than a soldier. It was impossible to believe that the lighthearted cheerfulness of the day before yesterday would ever return.

Alina just took everything too tragically. Hadn't he told her, over and over, that he would never leave her? I would never even think of it. Yet she . . . the very first thing she thought of was to break with him.

No, he wouldn't be her accomplice in that.

Alina, Alina, I do love you, you know! Just remember that . . .

Because he was walking, because he was moving into action, it hurt less. Things began to assume normal dimensions, return to their normal course. (Yes. The old lightheartedness was still there somewhere in the corner of his chest, lingering on.)

Walking by the dark monastery wall, with its incrustation of snowed-in booths, he found himself passing a broad gate, half open, caught a glimpse of warm light and took a step backward, hesitating . . .

The gate was open wide, so were the church doors beyond it, and he could see the inner glass doors. Light shone through them, and he could see candles in tall candlesticks. The service had already begun, or was about to begin.

But from where he was not a sound could be heard within, not a soul could be seen, no priest, no monks, no parishioners.

If a service was in progress it seemed to be conducting itself in the middle of the night.

He hesitated. Should he go in, or shouldn't he?

No, the telegram couldn't wait, he must hurry.

He strode off toward the telegraph office.

All his life, he had been drawn on by a single purpose, always in a hurry—always as now, striding headlong forward.

[7 5]

Darkness.

Silence.

But this is not the grave. You are still alive. For one brief moment you lie there forgetful of your grief. Then you are wide awake.

Half a second at most. Then a stab of pain. Remembering what happened last, what happened yesterday. But not just that—the whole series of events, each one a knife wound. And all the time your head is aching, your breast is aching, leaving you helpless. If only you could lie there, remembering nothing. Just resting, listening to the hush, the profound silence all along Arapovskaya Street, all over Tambov. But no—it all comes back, like a tattoo of hammerblows. Yesterday's letter. A child's grave. Zhenya's grave, the Little Rascal's grave. His last days. You got back too late. From here, from Tambov. The desolate bitterness left by that lovers' meeting, those two blissful days with no thought of disaster. In this very room?

A little grave in a country graveyard. On a damp autumn day.

And now—*he* had another woman!

The searing current ran through her brain, along the same grooves again and again, cauterizing . . . Switch it off! Let go of me!

Why does he write to me like this now?

She fought against it, broke the circuit. Lay there as if in a swoon, a healing sleep, disconnected from the chain of stinging shocks.

But the burning sensation returned. By a roundabout route. As if what she now remembered belonged to another life. Her mother had lain dying, and she had gone into hiding because she was pregnant, and it would be better for mother not to see daughter at all than to see her like that. She had not arrived in time to close her mother's eyes.

Then, from a third life, something now easily borne, so remote that it no longer rankled—Zhenya's father.

At the time it had seemed impossibly complicated, an insoluble problem. How could she persuade him to tell his wife? Left to himself he would never have the courage. But why had it seemed so important? She no longer remembered. She had no thought of stealing him, weak and irresolute as he was. But the indignity of it choked her—the idea of being an invisible appendage, a thief in the night, not a person in her own right. No, there must be clarity.

Such a weak man. But where were the strong ones? Under nervous strain not one of them was strong. Wasn't Fyodor just as weak?

Weak! Blind! Hopelessly muddled! Floating like a bit of wood wherever the current carried him. When you were with him you forgave him, because of his naïveté, his emerald eyes, you found yourself wanting to believe in him, to draw him upward, but when you parted— what was there left? A void. And to cap it all, he writes to say . . . !

Let me go! Switch it off.

She could think of Zhenya's father calmly now. It was a relief, even. Try to concentrate on *him*.

She had once seen him as one of those characters whom Chekhov portrayed so faithfully. They were at large everywhere, nice, amiable people who wouldn't hurt a fly and would never make anything of themselves. Was it angst, or just dreaminess? Eternally seeking—but not striving to find. Satisfied with whatever comes along: life's like that—make the best of it. (Fyodor was just the same!) It was easy to foresee, right from the beginning, how it would end: he would remain in his shell forever, seeking (but not too eagerly), and only Zinaida herself would be shattered. When he was seeing her off to the country to have her child he had promised to come quickly, to come at once, promised faithfully. And afterward to reorganize his life, for his son's sake! And he had not been lying, he had meant every word.

But he had not even come to look at his son.

Men's lives are roomier, easier, they do not even have to try to understand themselves, they feel no need to examine themselves in depth. But a woman's life is narrow, and she must live in depth.

The other woman too? Was it the same for her? Did she live in depth? If she were only half a woman, wouldn't she feel the same hurt?

But the Little Rascal was dead!!! Her little boy! Little Zhenya! Before he had time to learn the first thing about the world, before he could distinguish places, or faces, or even the parts of his own body. He had recognized only his mother, and only vaguely. He had struggled out of nonexistence, slept away three-quarters of his time, and promptly returned there. That old-mannish look with which newborn infants survey this inhospitable world had only just left him. His soft hair had only just begun to grow, his head was just assuming a more human shape, the fold in his neck had disappeared . . . when suddenly his lips turned blue. And he was no more.

"They'll say"—damn them! For herself Zina had never been in the least afraid of what "they'll say." Still, she wasn't going to risk killing her mother. But hadn't she given the sick woman a push in that direction by not going to see her? Shouldn't she at least have gone to the funeral? More "they'll say." She shuddered.

Perhaps it was the same for that other woman. Perhaps she was not so much concerned to hold on to her husband as afraid of what "they'll say." It could be too much for her to take.

Yet for Fyodor's sake she had rushed here, braving the disapproval of her sister and brother-in-law, fearlessly inviting him into their home. And here, in the drawing room of their childhood, the drawing room in which he had once been introduced to her family, and she, a high school girl, had gazed in rapturous awe on this former member of the Duma, who had suffered for his principles (!), and was a writer (!), and had twinkling emerald eyes(!) . . . in that very same drawing room, she had walked around naked at his request while he lay on the sofa lazily looking her over with those same emerald eyes.

It was only three weeks ago, only three weeks, since they had dallied around here shamelessly, while her son was falling sick in Korovainovo!

For six years she had been tantalized, allured, even when she was an unripe girl and far away, by the presentiment that with Fyodor some revelation awaited her. In those two days together with him she had been lost to the world—yet all the time a feeling of emptiness, of disillusionment was growing within her, and as soon as they parted, as soon as she was aboard the train to Kirsanov, it suffused her whole being, all her raptures seemed degrading, all illusion, all dross, and in her revulsion she could not understand why she had ever gone there. She must hurry back to her son! Her anxiety for her abandoned child was excruciating. What if something had happened to him? What if he were ill?

A peasant woman, beside her in the Korovainovo cemetery, had called her own tiny dead child "a piece torn from my womb."

Torn . . .

From my . . .

Womb . . .

Gone . . .

I wish I had gone too.

So—now?

So no one had ever seen her secret infant. Neither his father. Nor his . . . stepfather? There had not been time. It was as though he had never lived, except in his mother's memory. There wasn't even a photograph. Nothing to show anyone, ever.

Was that what she had wanted? To keep him hidden? "Stepfather"! He had scattered and abandoned children of his own, lovelessly—he himself probably didn't know where. He had made only one of them an exception and adopted him. What inferior creatures men were, if they could not even love their own children.

But supposing they had had a child of their own? Surely she would have won him over, endeared it to him?

On the train to Kirsanov she had been desperate: it had only just begun—and it was all over. It could not go on! Over as soon as begun—and nothing left to remember! He was hopelessly coarse-grained, primitive, incapable of understanding higher things. Over the years his letters had been so many cruel lessons to her, he wrote gratuitously about other women, tried to put her off, rapped her fingers to break her hold on him, and she had thought it was all just a rough game, could not believe that he cared nothing for her, that he might write her off at any moment, that he meant every word when he said that as far as women were concerned he did not pick and choose, he was content with those who cost least to woo, he wasted no effort on conquest, but let no opportunity slip . . . And still she remembered his radiant smile, his endearing shyness in literature classes, she had always believed that he had a soul, dormant it was true, but needing only to be cleansed, needing only the help of a woman's hand, and his front-row pupil was perfectly capable of providing that! For six years she had been true as a compass needle amidst his sordid revelations, believed that it was all a pose, that beneath the surface there was some hidden treasure, as yet unmined, known to no one. He was cynically frank because he had never known what it was to be loved.

How her hopes had soared, how she had exulted, when she found that he could rise above jealousy of another man's child!

And then they were alone together, in each other's arms. And . . . and it was as if none of it had ever happened.

In fact, she had always been afraid of getting to know him more closely. Eager to—and afraid to . . .

Before she got back to her son, before she was told about his illness, she was already in despair, already full of revulsion—determined never to meet Fyodor again, perhaps not even to write to him.

EMPTINESS!

Emptiness! Zhenya could have lived, filled her life with his own, but now there was nothing but emptiness! A vacuum never to be filled by any other human being, any other child! *That* being would never exist again on this earth. A life that never was, that would remain a mirage, a life linked with, intersected by, no other.

She had not wanted to write to him anyway. But when Little Rascal vanished everything had gone dark, and she was dumbstruck. What could she write to him? There would be no miracle.

Such treachery: abandoning a helpless little boy, so that by herself she could . . .

But there was a second and worse betrayal: under that very roof, in that same empty house, listening to that very clock striking, to be thinking of him now, burning for him again, when she should be thinking only of Zhenya.

Unexpectedly, and unthinkingly, she had found herself drawn by her son's death to the church. It was a path she had never once taken in her young days. Now, it was as if she had been going there all her life. The peasant women who were her neighbors had stood so unobtrusively around the little coffin. They had carried it to the cemetery.

But to stay on in Korovainovo after the funeral and until the ninth-day service would have been too much for her. She abandoned his lonely grave, lonely forever now, since it was his destiny to remain forever in the Korovainovo cemetery, and rushed off to see her aunt in the Convent of the Ascension at Tambov.

Her aunt had told her to come at any time: if anything goes wrong, come and see me. But all she ever had to offer was the promise of solace in the world to come, none of it had anything to do with the turmoil of life here and now. Zinaida would answer her rudely. Forget it, Auntie, God the Comforter is an absurdity. Why go to such trouble to create a world which was going to need consoling?

Now, though, she had found that it was all very simple, and that this solace was very much needed, like fragrant pitch cooling to fill deep ruts and smooth over sharp stones. It was with her aunt that Zinaida began to recover her balance.

Instead of brooding over the future she could no longer look forward to with her son, she asked herself: Where was he now? That he was nowhere was unthinkable: to have lived only a little while could not be the same as never having been conceived.

My . . . womb . . . torn from . . .

Then she had come across Father Aloni in the church at nearby Utkino—a kindly priest, serious-minded as simple Russian people generally are, broad-shouldered and benevolent. After conducting the ninth-day service he had talked to Zinaida at length, and with serene ease. After which her equilibrium was even more secure.

Zina had of old defended the Church against the "progressives," even when she was an unbeliever. Just to be contrary.

Now that she had recovered her equilibrium and was thinking more calmly Zina had found the strength and the equanimity to write to Fyodor about the death of her son. Perhaps this was how her recovery could begin. But she was not to reach the twice-ninth day without shocks. Yesterday, like a bolt out of the blue, she had received his letter. It had passed hers in the mail—otherwise he would not have written it. You should know, he wrote, that I have someone else, and that it is serious.

Someone else—a third someone, a twentieth . . . Why, then, had he come to her? Why had he not admitted it? Why this blissful reunion (or meaningless farce)? That was what really hurt, that was her hell. Was it for him, was it for this that she had destroyed her little boy?

Was this the man she had wanted to save? To purify?

To think that she had believed in him! Danced to his tune!

Who are you? Tell me.

She was sitting up in bed.

She lit the lamp.

Replaced the glass chimney with a firm hand.

Her childhood home, untidy and deserted now, seemed still gloomier. Dark doorways opened into other dark rooms.

This was where she had displayed herself to him.

She must tear herself away! From this bed, before all her ribs were crushed! From these rooms. This house. Go anywhere. So long as she was not alone!

Alone—she would hang herself, there would be nothing else to do. She would not be able to go on! Life would be impossible! Especially here. She must get away from this vault, this blackness, this silence, in which her mother had lain dying, and in which they had indulged their passion—while in that other place her baby was dying.

Why did you ask me to come? If you hadn't I wouldn't have rushed to join you—and *he* would not have taken sick!

Now she was dressed.

I must go somewhere, anywhere! To somebody, anybody! Fall on someone's breast—I . . . can't go on alone!

The simplest thing would be to go to her aunt. The convent gates would be open by now—the nuns rose before daylight.

But for some reason she could not go to her aunt. It would have been so natural, and so salutary, to run to her immediately after Zhenya's death. But *now* it was impossible.

How have all these troubles piled up? At twenty-two, for other people, life is just beginning. But your path is blocked by a landslide of troubles. Life has no place for you, hang yourself, why don't you!

Yes, hang yourself! This yellow scarf will do. A long, strong scarf.

To have been so pure, to know yourself to be upright, noble even, and then in a single year to wreak such havoc, ruin so many lives, become so hopelessly entangled. That other family—shattered! Mama betrayed! Little Zhenya—betrayed.

He was the only one she hadn't betrayed.

So he had betrayed her.

It wasn't so very early. People were up and around. It was dark because this was November. Anyway, I must get out of here.

She covered her head with her scarf. Can't stay here. Can't be by myself—it'll end badly.

But somehow it seemed absolutely impossible to go to her aunt in the convent.

My hands are trembling. Now I've dropped the key. I won't be able to find it . . . Perhaps it's slipped into that crack on the doorstep . . . Why don't I leave it and just go . . . No, I mustn't, it's my sister's home.

She burst into tears. She had held out as long as she could, but now she was weeping. Where could it be, that piece of iron?

Not a soul to be seen on Arapovskaya Street. If lamps had been lit it was behind shuttered windows. People took their time getting up. Took their time living. Spent an hour over their prayers.

There were streetlamps on the corner of High Street. And one on the corner of Dolevaya Street, but its light did not reach her.

She went back inside for matches. What was her aunt really like? She had been in the convent for a long, long time. Being a saint was easy enough. But understanding a sinful woman was impossible for her. A woman who had not suffered this ordeal could not possibly understand one who had.

She struck match after match, but the wind blew them all out. In the end she found where the key had hidden itself.

She locked the door, and set off.

The way to her aunt would have taken her along Bolshaya Street, past Studenets, as far as Voznesensky Street. For no particular reason she walked toward Dolevaya instead.

It was damp. And dark. Breezy too, along Dolevaya, and she felt the wind through her flimsy head scarf. It was bracing.

She walked on, alone, no one on the street, no one standing at a front gate. She might have spoken to the first person she met, but there was no one. On warm evenings, all Tambov sat on benches, or stood at garden gates. Now the city was deserted.

To whom could she turn? Everything was closed. Everyone was indoors.

She used to think that the worse things were, the more interesting life became; when things got better they settled down into a too peaceful pattern, a humdrum routine. But no. That was all very well until the ice gave way under you. When it did, you would be crying out, "Give me a hand! Give me a hand! Pull me out of here!"

She had loved Fyodor for six years, and little Zhenya for only six months. But to him she had been his whole world. He had known nothing and no one else.

And that was all she had needed. So what was the point of those letters? Why, when she was fulfilled, had she called to *him?* She had held out for so many years, determined not to be importunate, hedging words of affection with irony, rewriting anything that sounded too affectionate. And after all that she had thrown herself at him.

It was not as if he would find happiness with "the other one." Of course not. But then he had no need of love or happiness, or of anyone to share his life. He was mean-spirited and probably beyond salvation.

Her little one would never toddle on his own little feet. Never even say "mama." He had been given time for nothing.

How could she face her aunt after getting that letter yesterday? How could such a trollop ever hold her head up again? It had been bad enough having a child by a married man.

Now she was crossing Dvoryanskaya. The cold wind blew still stronger there, rounding the curved facade of the Gentry Assembly. Two cabs dashed by, one after the other, returning empty from the station, their drivers leaning into the wind.

Zinaida came to a stop, out in the wind, in the middle of the square.

The Utkino church stood there before her. A faint light shone through the elongated windows. A few shadowy figures were making their way there from different directions.

She had not consciously intended to come there. Her legs had brought her unbidden.

But where *could* she go? Not back where she had come from. Not home, to be by herself—anything but that.

The windows were suffused with light, as on a feast day. But a subdued light, soothing to a sick soul.

Since those obligatory services at school she had hardly ever entered a church except for the blessing of the Easter cakes. Though she had sometimes wanted to, by way of protest against the prevailing fashion. True, she had attended a communion service with organ music in a Lutheran church in Moscow, but she had thought of that as a concert.

There too, her thoughts had been of him. Conscious of her own nothingness, in the presence of sublime music she had remembered him, and become so sorry for him: his one thought was to get on, to rise in the world, to achieve something, but he was already in his forties, he had done nothing, he had no niche of his own, he was a failure. And she had yearned to save him.

All by herself?

She passed by two or three beggars in the doorway—she had come out without her purse—and entered the church. There were lamps before all the icons, and a few candles, but just one electric light, over the choir. Not a single chandelier was lit. That explained the subdued half-light.

Zina loved icon lamps. Her mother used to have one at home. In the intimacy of the attic bedroom, the woman and the icon, with a lamp between them. It gave only a little light, but it knew a great deal. What bottomless depths there were in that dialogue. All the things said there, all the blessings asked!

The service was just beginning in the side chapel on the right, the Chapel of Our Lady, where there was an icon, modest in size but renowned throughout the country, of the Tambov Virgin. Almost all the parishioners had congregated. A cantor recited some incomprehensible and interminably dreary rigmarole, while a priest, invisible in the sanctuary, interpolated occasional brief responses.

Zina, almost oblivious of her surroundings, went down the broad, empty middle aisle. She stood near a pillar and looked upward.

The pillar ended in an arch which carried her eyes along its smooth curve until it merged with the vaulted dome.

The dome itself, up above the nave, was like a miniature round heaven. Enough diffused light from icons and lamps reached the heights for her to see that this celestial hemisphere was wholly occupied by a head-and-shoulders representation of God the Father looking down from the clouds. When morning came the dawn light would reach that spot through narrow windows in the dome. The sun's first and last rays would find it. At present it was in semi-darkness but, lit from below, the countenance of the Lord of Hosts, majestic in conception, was half visible and half recognizable. There was no trace of consolatory tenderness in the Creator's tense expression, but nor could vengefulness or menace have any place there. He Himself was the heaven above us all, and we were sustained by Him. This attempt to show the face of God in human lineaments, humanized, had been arrogant presumption on the part of the artist. But from beyond and through what was painted there the unimaginable looked down—a portrayal of the Power that sustains the world. And whoever encountered the gaze of those celestial Eyes, and whoever was privileged to glimpse even momentarily that Brow, understood with a shock not his own nullity but the place which he was designed and privileged to occupy in the general harmony. And that he was called upon not to disrupt that harmony.

There Zinaida stood, and went on standing, with her head thrown back, staring into that immensity, deaf to what was happening in the church, with no thought of praying, no thought of anything. What floated above her could not be conveyed in words, was indeed out of reach of thought. It was a wave of life-giving will, surging also into the human breast. Her vocal cords tightened, heat flooded her swollen neck, her legs were unsteady but she had not the strength to tear herself away. Chilled by what she had seen, she stood shivering like a sacrificial victim awaiting the stroke, stood for as long as her neck could endure the strain, scarcely feeling the floor beneath her, unable to pray, to beseech, to question . . .

A passive receptacle of the Divine Will, she began to feel easier and stronger. Gone was the burning desire she had felt at home to break out, run away, see someone, anyone, talk. Standing there, she felt no urge to run. She stood staring upward, her neck growing numb, but the iron bands that had immobilized her for so many days relaxed, gradually fell away, released her.

She was beginning to feel giddy. She put her hands to her head and with an effort restored it to its normal position. She walked on a little way over the flagstones.

In the side chapel to the right a priest emerged from the sanctuary and bowed to the closed gates, but it was not Father Aloni.

Zinaida found herself, with no one else near her, facing a large icon of Christ, with a big pink lamp burning before it. The icon and its lamp filled her field of vision, shutting out the rest of the church. Somewhere a service was in progress, but she did not catch a single word. She stood gazing on the Saviour's brown-tinted face.

It was a completely human face, though its complexion was not of this world. It had other peculiarities: the hair descended in two straggling locks, the nose was impossibly long and thin, the raised fingers were frozen in a gesture of benediction. The eyes held an enigmatic omniscience . . . knowing all, from the beginning to the end of time, things of which we never dream. A mind at ease might not have responded to these depths. But Zinaida, with her heightened perception, saw that Christ was suffering acutely, suffering yet not complaining. His compassion was for all those who approached him—and so at that moment for her. His eyes could absorb whatever pain there might yet be—all her pain, as they had absorbed many times as much before, and would absorb whatever pain was still to come. He had learned to live with pain as something inevitable. And he could grant release from all pain.

A weight was lifted from her.

The pink glass of the icon lamp, and the light it gave, were also unusual. This was not the pinkness of a dawn sky, or of a blush. It was a pinkness with an otherworldly mauve tint, remote from all earthly colors. And that strange light made the dark brown, all-knowing countenance seem all the more perceptive.

In that ghostly pink light it seemed more impossible than ever to believe that her son was . . . nowhere. She could see now that *somewhere* there was *something*.

The icon and the lamp swam before her eyes.

How fortunate that she had strayed unthinkingly to this place. She had no wish to go elsewhere. No wish to pour her heart out to anyone else, as she had longed to a little while ago. That was now the last thing she needed.

Now she could hear the chant from nearby: "For my iniquities have risen above my head, they have weighed me down like a heavy burden ...I cry out in the torment of my heart: O Lord, all my desires are open to Thee, and my lamentations are not hidden from Thee."

She shuddered. Her whole story had been known here before her coming. They were proclaiming it aloud.

She made no attempt to pray. She scarcely knew how to. But some kind of block, some inhibition had been removed from her mind and her breast, and she found herself thinking again. Thinking not in jerks and jolts, which hurt and burned, but contemplating herself as though she were someone else.

She thought that as the Church defined sin she was a sinner three times over.

No, four.

Five, even. (Her reckoning went unquestioned—it might have concerned someone else.)

She had seduced a married man, and the damage she had done was not merely superficial. By insisting that he should "tell" she had split that family irreparably. She had abandoned her dying mother. She had abandoned her son for her lover. She . . . that made four. What was the fifth? There was a fifth sin somewhere.

"For my soul is overwhelmed with calamities, and my life is close to the bottomless pit."

Her eyes too became clear, and now, at an angle and in front of her, she saw—and her heart leapt to see him—Father Aloni standing sideways to her by the central pulpit, hearing confessions. Matins was still in progress in the side chapel, but he was hearing confessions, soundlessly, it seemed. Standing beside the lectern, head bowed, he listened closely to another bowed head, then covered it with his stole, made the sign of the cross, and dismissed the penitent. There were several of them waiting, and the line was moving slowly.

Zinaida observed this as something which did not concern her. She had no need to confess. She could see into herself clearly enough without that.

When she reviewed her past feelings she knew that she had never been two-faced, never set out to deceive or to damage anyone. She had wanted only to follow her natural, womanly path. Surely she, like any other woman, had a right to do that? She had not succeeded, she had made only false starts, and—oh, God!—how difficult it was to start at all. You emerge from adolescence feeling so free, so light— why did things immediately become so difficult and confused, why were other people, all of them, and their destinies, always in your way, so that at every move you had to step over or else collide with someone else? How could you start again from the beginning?

She had never meant to harm anyone! Why, then, at every turn in her life did she have to tread on someone?

No, she was being unfair to herself. There was one person toward whom she felt no guilt. For him she had always wanted the best—little though he realized it. She had wanted to open his eyes to the talent of which he was unaware, and likely to remain so all his life. Reading his complacent confidences with bated breath she had seen more and more certainly that she and she alone was the one he needed! She alone could enlarge his life and help him to fulfill himself—but largeness and diversity were not in his character. He was base and trivial. And he bore all the blame—because he had weakly let her go her own way, because he had been ready to surrender her to the first taker. It was he who had driven her to it. And then—to behave as he had yesterday, as much as to say be off and take your devotion and your sacrifices somewhere else! Yet even in rejecting her he had been false! If he loved another (if only he could, if only he were mercifully granted the grace to love, but he was incapable of it), if he loved another why had he gone out of his way to Tambov?

Ah, that was it, the fourth sin, or was it the fifth, wrenched from her like something that had become part of her. It was as if her dress had caught fire, and tearing it off and not tearing it off were alike impossible—her fifth sin had stuck to her, merged with her! She had stayed away from her aunt because she knew the answer she would get, and that it was not the one she needed, not the one she would have thought up for herself.

Father Aloni dismissed his last penitent and looked around for others. His eyes swept over the central aisle, he saw her and nodded an invitation, assuming that she had come to see him.

She had not, of course. But he stood waiting. Upright, solid, simple, broad-faced, his thick, wavy hair brushed back from a large, smooth brow, the eyes beneath it bright.

He beckoned, waited.

She had not come there for him!

But still he waited, and called out to her, thinking, of course, that she was still struggling with her fresh grief.

Well, since she was there . . . And he was still waiting. And if not him, who was it she had come to see? Why had she come there?

One step, another, a third—she was walking toward him, unintentionally, surprising herself.

Careful—don't trip on the steps up to the choir stalls. She had eyes only for that broad-browed face, framed by an auburn beard, and for his encouraging gaze.

She bowed her head toward the lectern. Her forehead rested on the tooled cover of the Gospel, and there was a crucifix to her right.

Gospel and crucifix watched over her confession. The lectern—she saw it now—was a steep slope, a rough steep slope—and up that slope she had to drag her whole life, struggling under the burden, and against the friction.

Confession at school had been a joke, a giggle. One wave of the stole over your head and you were absolved. The priest's questions were condescending, meant for infants. You almost expected him to get you a bonbon from the sideboard. "I have sinned, Father, I have sinned"—and off you flitted. She had never been to confession since. Now she waited impatiently for him to question her.

The priest, hovering unseen above her, also waited. She could not raise her head, look into his eyes and speak to him simply, one human being to another, as she had after the requiem. She felt that she must answer to a superior being.

It was good that she was not looking into his eyes.

In fact, she could not see him at all. Nor anyone else. Only the crucifix, as she knelt with her brow pressed to the Gospel.

No questions were asked, no answers demanded. She must struggle through the darkness unaided.

She had not wanted to hear what her aunt or her sister nuns might say, they were all too holy to understand. But could she speak now?

Speak, yes, but not say what hurt most! Let her thoughts come tumbling out—tell everything (but not quite everything)! You know all the things you've done, you've gone over them a hundred and twenty times. Can't you, just this once, wrest them out of their protective covering of complicitous silence, say it all out loud? Impossible. (Everything else—yes—but not that one thing!)

Hopeless. But no more hopeless than sitting at home alone in an empty house. And wherever she might go it would be just as hopeless. How could she haul herself up this steep incline beside the crucifix? Tell another person, a stranger, all that had happened? Without mincing her words, without dissembling? (Easier to do such things than to talk about them! Would she have voice enough, breath enough?) She plunged in without preliminary explanation, throat dry, voice cracked.

"I have seduced a married man."

She was over the first threshold. No—that was all in the past. Why had she done it? That was the question.

"I seduced him without really loving him. In fact . . . when I really loved someone else . . . It was just that . . . I'd reached the age . . . I had to have an outlet for my emotions."

If only some question were asked above her bowed head! An opinion expressed, a condemnation delivered! Or perhaps some murmur of sympathy? But was she even being listened to?

"I made him confess to his wife. And by doing so . . . I suppose . . . I ruined their lives . . . forever."

The second threshold. A life as heavy as lead. How to haul it up the slope? But every time she put something into words a weight seemed to fall away.

She had not yet finished, though. She must punish herself to the full.

"It was all for no purpose . . . all for nothing . . . I am profoundly penitent."

Not true. It had a purpose. Not altogether clear or precise, but . . . I knew beforehand that we should part . . . No, I didn't . . .

"It was for a contemptible purpose . . . To snatch him for myself . . . No, it was simply out of vanity. Because the other man didn't love me."

It had suddenly become so much easier to speak.

"You see, I've loved him . . . the other one . . . all my life."

When you speak of love you should feel that you have wings. But she was struggling up that slope, every sin a stone over which she stumbled and slithered backward, nose to the ground.

"And then I . . . concealed my pregnancy from my mother. I decided to hide myself in the country. My mother fell ill, she was dying, and I didn't get there . . . I let her down . . . for the child's sake."

Untrue. Another equivocation.

"No, it was because I was ashamed. Because of my vanity."

It was like using the grapnel at a wellhead, with three hooks facing different ways—and what you have to do is find down there, in the dark depths of your soul, a hot stone, fish for it, grip it, only the hooks won't take hold, it breaks loose, seventy times over it breaks loose until at last, with delicate movements, as cautiously as if it was your dearest treasure, you latch on to it, draw it upward, raise it carefully, carefully, then seize it. You burn your fingers but you have rid your soul of it.

"I abandoned my child . . . for a lovers' meeting . . . Like a mad thing . . . And while I was away he got sick . . . And because I wasn't there he died . . ."

Another great stone dragged painfully, breathlessly, upward, and tipped onto the surface. Her brow was bathed in cold sweat.

What could the priest think of her now? He had been so full of pity for the grief-stricken young mother.

But it was as if every stone thrown out had ceased to be part of her—forever? or just for the moment?—so that she could look at it objectively instead of dragging it around inside her.

She had not once raised her head to glance at the priest, she wouldn't dare to, and none of the other penitents had done so. But, without hearing a single sound from him, she realized that it was not the priest hovering invisibly over her who was hearing her confession! He was only the necessary witness.

That was what made it so hard—that she was left to herself. But it was also a relief. A relief for how long? Could a word she said aloud outweigh guilt, sin, evil?

Yet strangely, incomprehensibly, as soon as the words were out a weight was lifted from her. If only for the moment.

As for forgiveness—who could forgive such things? How could any other person grant you forgiveness? You must bear the burden alone, labor on alone.

But that means movement. All that is piled up in a living breast cannot lie there inert forever. If it did, we would ourselves be stones.

But what does he mean by it, hovering over me without saying a word? He might help with a question, a sound of some sort, a murmur of encouragement.

But once you have learned how to drag these stones out with your grappling hook—your throat is less dry, speech becomes less hesitant, confession flows faster, until your words tumble over themselves as you hurry to snatch at and identify all your betrayals (your own betrayals! You were blaming *him* a little while ago, but that was a lie!), mention them for the second time (all futile! all rejected!), or perhaps it wasn't the second time? Perhaps this was another betrayal? Yes, I have betrayed you again, sinned not against your life this time, but against the still fresh, still warm memory of you, before your little grave has been smoothed over, that will have to wait till next spring—and who is it I am thinking of again? Of *him*, of *him*, that is why I fled, among flying sparks, like a mad thing swerving so as not to burn myself, at times even leaping through the flames, unable to find the straight path, which anyway did not exist, over the baking-hot earth, the soles of my feet burning, returning to the same place—he rapped my fingers, said keep away, get your claws out of me—for six years I had thought of him, and now I am thinking of him again, I have sacrificed my little son, and before I am out of mourning here it comes again, for the fifth time like a tornado, and now . . . there is no pulling this stone out, it is ablaze! Scorched as I am, desire writhes in me like a fiery serpent—the desire to conceive again! Conceive a child of his! He has never known this joy—with me!

And however much the priest might object, and try to forbid it, whether he forgave her or not, she realized, horrified, that she was fatally tied. Tied to *him*.

Was she doomed, then, yet again, to deprive someone else? To snatch, to steal what was not hers? Was it impossible to walk this earth without trampling others? Simply to walk on the grass-grown earth?

How treacherous the earth's crust was! At every step there was molten lava underfoot! If you tried to run it would cave in under you!

Flinching from the flames, she dropped her hook, staggered back from the well, and—oh, God!—had all the stones crashed back down there? Help me, O God! You see that I want to tear myself away! I want to change! But this is one disaster too many . . .

She had struggled as far as she could up the slope, and now lay prostrate, one temple against the crucifix, her meager strength, that of a single human being, exhausted.

She was silent.

She felt the weight of something woven rest on her head, shutting out the little she could still see. And through the fabric she felt the touch of a hand making the sign of the cross.

And a voice—no ordinary voice, one capable of soaring above a thousand others, of supplication, of suffering, of repentance, now hushed and meant for her alone, but with the same significance as when it reverberated in the dome.

"May the Lord Our God Jesus Christ through His grace and the munificence of His love for mankind . . ."

She had blurted out all she had to say, however horrible it was she had done all she had to do, and now she crouched with her head pressed to the crucifix, breathless.

But another Breath, the Spirit, hovered over her and stole tremulously into her.

". . . forgive you, my child, all your transgressions. And I, an unworthy priest, with the authority vested by Him in me . . ."

He stressed not his authority, but his unworthiness. Grief-stricken witness of her struggle against grief, he testified to her forgiveness.

"I pardon you and absolve you of all your sins . . ."

He pronounced these words as weightily and as meaningfully as if he knew of many details which she had not mentioned and, having weighed them, nonetheless unhesitatingly forgave her.

But Zinaida herself did not feel that all was forgiven, forgotten and over. And that her labor had not been in vain.

She still had a question to ask. Perhaps she had already formulated it when she was jumping about to avoid being burned.

He withdrew his stole, and she quietly raised her uncovered head to look at Father Aloni.

She saw his frank gaze, his honest, firm, guileless, big-browed face. Yes, he had understood her question, and let it be seen that he had.

But, with splayed fingers, he gently but firmly pressed her head down.

She was at a loss until she saw the Gospel there beneath her.

She kissed the ancient dark red cover with its half-effaced embossed pattern.

Still gripping her head with his fingers, he guided it toward the crucifix.

She pressed her lips to its silvery surface.

And again threw back her head with that mute question still in her gaze.

Father Aloni's eyes were moist with unshed tears.

He had said what was required of him, and need say no more. But she waited, head thrown back, for words meant only for her.

His thick lips moved among the dark auburn undergrowth.

"In each of us there is a mystery greater than we realize. And it is in communion with God that we are able to catch a glimpse of it. Learn to pray. Truly, you are capable of it."

But as yet she did not feel herself to be capable of it. For her this was no answer.

His gray eyes gazed on her sorrowfully, compassionately. He saw that she wanted him to continue.

"The world holds no sufferings worse than those caused by family problems. They leave festering sores on the heart itself. For as long as we live this is our earthly lot. You can rarely decide for another that he or she should do or not do this or that. How can anyone forbid you to love when Christ said that there is nothing higher than love? And He made no exceptions, for love of any kind whatsoever."

Index of Names

Adler, Friedrich ("Fritz") (1879–1960) Son of secretary of Austrian Social Democratic Party. Shot Count Stürgkh, Prime Minister of Austria-Hungary, in October 1916.

Adler, Viktor (1852–1918) Austrian socialist leader, prominent in Second International.

Adzhemov, Moisei (1878–?) Deputy in Second, Third, and Fourth Dumas. Prominent member of Kadet Party.

Agou Surname used by Nikolai II in letters to his wife.

Aladin, Aleksei (1873–?) Leader of the Trudovik group in the First Duma.

Aleksandr II (1818–81) The "Tsar Liberator," presided over the emancipation of the serfs, the introduction of the zemstvos, modernization of the judicial system, easing of the burden of military service. Assassinated 13 March 1881 by members of the Narodnaya Volya (People's Will) Party.

Aleksandr III (1845–94) Became heir to the throne on the death of his older brother in 1865. Discontinued and in part reversed his father's program of reform. Played an important part in bringing about the alliance with France.

Aleksandr Mikhailovich ("Sandro") Grand Duke (1866–1933) Friend of Nikolai II in his youth. Married Nikolai's sister Ksenia.

Aleksandr Nevsky (1220–63) Grand Prince of Novgorod. Defeated the Swedes on the Neva (1240), then the Teutonic Knights (1242). Canonized.

Aleksandra Fyodorovna (1872–1918) Empress. Born Princess Alix of Hesse. Married the future Nikolai II in 1894. Murdered together with her husband and children by the Bolsheviks.

Alekseev, Evgeni Ivanovich (1843–1909) Viceroy in the Far East 1903–5.

Alekseev, Mikhail Vasilievich (1857–1918) Infantry general, Chief of Staff, first on the Southwestern, then on the Northwestern Front. From 5 September 1915 Chief of General Staff. On sick leave 21 November 1916 to 7 March 1917. Advised the Tsar to abdicate in March 1917. Commander in Chief till 3 June 1917. After the October Revolution organized first White Army on the Don.

Aleksei Aleksandrovich, Grand Duke (1850–1908) Brother of Aleksandr III. Commander in Chief of the Russian navy during the war with Japan.

Aleksei Mikhailovich (1629–76) The second Romanov Tsar. Father of Peter the Great.

Anna Ivanovna (1693–1740) Daughter of Ivan V (Peter the Great's half brother). Empress of Russia 1730–40.

Arakcheev, Aleksei (1769–1834) Artillery general. Favorite of Paul I and Aleksandr I.

Armand, Inessa (née Steffen) (1874–1920) Bolshevik. French wife of the industrialist Armand, and subsequently of his brother. Close friend and ally of Lenin from 1909.

Artamonov, Leonid (1859–1932) General. Explorer. Court-martialed for abandoning Soldau (East Prussia) in August 1914.

Kurlov, Pavel (1860–1923) Chief of the Okhrana at the time of Stolypin's assassination. Disgraced, but rehabilitated with the help of the Rasputin clique. Vice-Minister of the Interior from December 1916. Arrested by Provisional Government. Emigrated.

Kuropatkin, Aleksei (1848–1925) Commander in Chief during the war with Japan, 1904–5. Commanded an army corps, then the Northern Army Group, until August 1916. Then governor of Turkestan. Author of works on the Balkan and Central Asian campaigns and on the war with Japan.

Lechitsky, Platon (1856–1925) Commander of 9th Army 1914–17.

Ledebour, Georg (1850–1947) German Social Democrat, attended Zimmerwald Conference.

Levashov, Sergei (1857–?) Professor of medicine. Rightist deputy in Fourth Duma.

Liebknecht, Karl (1871–1919) German Social Democrat. Leader with Rosa Luxemburg of the left-wing, antiwar Spartacist faction, assassinated.

Lilina, Zinaida (1882–1929) Bolshevik, abroad 1908–17. Linked with Zinoviev.

Litvinov, Maksim (real name Vallakh) (1876–1951) Social Democrat from 1898, Leninist from 1901. Procured arms from abroad during 1905 Revolution. Briefly Soviet representative in London in 1917. Deputy People's Commissar for Foreign Affairs 1921, Commissar 1930–May 1939.

Lurie, Mikhail (Yuri Larin) (1882–1932) Social Democrat from 1901. Bolshevik from August 1917.

Lutovinov, Yuri (1887–1924) Militant worker. Social Democrat from 1904. After the October Revolution member of the Workers' Opposition with Shlyapnikov and Kollontai. Committed suicide.

Luxemburg, Rosa (1871–1919) Co-founder of the Social Democratic Party of Poland and Lithuania. From 1898 active in German Social Democratic Party. From 1914 leader with Karl Liebknecht of Spartacus League, spent most of the war in prison. Assassinated with Liebknecht during the Spartacus rising.

Lvov, Georgi Evgenievich (1861–1925) Kadet politician. Chairman of the All-Russian Union of Zemstvos. After February Revolution Prime Minister until replaced by Kerensky in July.

Maklakov, Nikolai (1871–1918) Minister of the Interior 1912–15. Shot by the Bolsheviks with Shcheglovitov in reprisal for Fanny Kaplan's attempt on Lenin's life (August 1918).

Maklakov, Vasili (1870–1957) Lawyer, leading member of Kadet Party. Ambassador of Provisional Government to France 1917.

Markov, Nikolai (1876–1943) Deputy in Third and Fourth Dumas, leader of the extreme right. One of the leaders of the Union of the Russian People (Black Hundreds). Called Markov II as the younger of two Markovs in the Duma.

Martov, Yuli Osipovich (real name Tsederbaum) (1873–1923) Social Democrat from 1892. Co-editor with Lenin of *Iskra*, broke with him in 1903, after which he led the Menshevik faction of the Russian Social Democratic Party.

Meller-Zakomelsky, Aleksandr, Baron (1844–1923) General. Played a major part in repressions after the 1905 Revolution.

Meshchersky, Vladimir, Prince (1839–1914) Novelist, right-wing publicist, newspaper proprietor.

Olga Aleksandrovna, Grand Duchess (1882–1960)   Younger sister of Nikolai II. Married Prince Peter of Oldenburg, divorced 1916. Married cavalry officer Nikolai Kulikovsky.

Olminsky, Mikhail (1863–1933)   Bolshevik from 1903. Journalist, collaborated with Lenin on *Pravda* and other publications. After the Revolution historian of the Party.

Osipanov, Vasili (1861–87)   Revolutionary and terrorist, member of the People's Will Party. Executed together with Aleksandr Ulyanov (Lenin's brother).

Pannekoek, Anton (1873–1960)   Dutch Social Democrat, then member of the Communist Party of the Netherlands.

Parvus (nom de guerre of Israel Lazarevich Gelfand [Helfand] (1867–1924))   Played prominent part in 1905 Revolution. Invented theory of "permanent revolution." Successful businessman. Funded revolutionaries (especially Bolsheviks).

Pavel Aleksandrovich, Grand Duke (1860–1919)   Uncle of Nikolai II. Cavalry general. Shot by Bolsheviks without a trial.

Peters, Jacob (1866–1942)   Latvian Bolshevik. Vice president of the Cheka. Purged in the late 1930s.

Petrunkevich, Ivan (1843–1928)   Lawyer. One of the organizers of Zemstvo congresses. Prominent member of Kadet Party.

Philippe, Nizier-Anthelme (1849–1905)   A French "healer" patronized by the imperial couple in 1901–2.

Pyanykh, Ivan (1864–1929)   Peasant. SR (Socialist Revolutionary) deputy in Second Duma. Sentenced to death 1909, sentence commuted to life imprisonment. Freed by Revolution of February 1917.

Pyatakov, Grigori Leonidovich (1890–1937)   Anarchist, then from 1910 Bolshevik. In 1917 chairman of the Kiev Soviet. In 1918 headed the Soviet government of the Ukraine. From 1918 supporter of Trotsky. Chief defendant at the second show trial in 1937. Executed.

Rennenkampf, Paul (1854–1918)   General. Distinguished himself in Boxer War. His inaction in East Prussia was held responsible for the loss of Samsonov's army in August 1914. Equally ineffectual at Lodz in November 1916, he was dismissed. Shot by the Bolsheviks 1918.

Rodichev, Fyodor (1853–1923)   Jurist. Kadet leader, deputy in all four Dumas.

Rodzyanko, Mikhail (1859–1923)   Octobrist. President of the Duma 1911–17.

Roland-Holst, Henrietta (1869–1952)   Dutch Social Democrat. Communist 1918–27.

Romberg, Gisbert von (1866–1939)   German ambassador to Switzerland.

Rubinstein, Dmitri   Financier. Director of the Private Commercial Bank and the Russo-French Bank. Philanthropist. Arrested in the summer of 1916, charged with a fraudulent operation in France, imprisoned at Pskov, freed allegedly after bribing Rasputin to persuade the Empress to intercede for him.

Rukhlov, Sergei   Minister of Communications 1909–15.

Ruzsky, Nikolai (1854–1918)   General, army commander. Shot by the Bolsheviks.

Samarin, Aleksandr (1869–1932)   Procurator of the Holy Synod July–October 1916. Enemy of Rasputin, dismissed on the Empress's insistence. Remained in Russia after the October Revolution. Died in exile at Kostroma.

Vandervelde, Emile (1866–1938)   Belgian Social Democrat, prominent in the Second International.

Varun-Sekret, Sergei (1868–?)   Duma deputy, Octobrist, vice president of the Duma.

Vasilissa   In 1812 Vasilissa Kozhina, wife of a village headman in Smolensk province, led a band of women and young people armed with sickles, forks, and axes who killed or took prisoner a large number of Napoleon's soldiers.

Vertinsky, Aleksandr (1889–1957)   Writer and singer of popular songs. Emigrated in 1919. Returned to the U.S.S.R. in 1943.

Vinaver, Maksim (1863–1926)   Lawyer. One of the founders of the Kadet Party, deputy in the First Duma. Member of the White government in the Crimea 1919.

Vishnevsky, Aleksandr (1862–?)   Extreme right-wing deputy in Third and Fourth Dumas.

Vladimir (Bogoyavlensky) (1848–1918)   Metropolitan of Petrograd, removed to Kiev at Rasputin's behest. Murdered by the Bolsheviks.

Volkonsky, Prince Vladimir (1868–1953)   Right-wing deputy in Third and Fourth Dumas. Vice president of Fourth Duma.

Volodarsky, Vladimir (1891–1918)   Member of Jewish Bund, then a Menshevik. Joined Bolsheviks after the October Revolution. Popular orator. Assassinated by a Socialist Revolutionary.

Vorontsov-Dashkov, Ilarion (1837–1916)   Minister of the Court 1881–97. Viceroy of the Caucasus 1905–15.

Vyrubova, Anna (1884–1954)   Lady-in-waiting to the Empress. For some years her closest friend and intermediary between the imperial couple and Rasputin. Fled to Finland after the Revolution and lived there in obscurity.

Witte, Sergei (1849–1915)   Minister of Finance 1892–1903. Chairman of Council of Ministers October 1905–April 1906 (replaced by Goremykin). Author of important memoirs.

Yakhontov, Arkadi (1876–1938)   Deputy secretary-general to Council of Ministers 1914–15.

Yakubova, A. A. (1870–1917)   Economist. Menshevik. Politically inactive after 1905.

Yanushkevich, Nikolai (1868–1918)   General, expert on "military administration." Chief of General Staff under Grand Duke Nikolai Nikolaevich, then on the Grand Duke's staff in the Caucasus. Assassinated while under arrest.

Yusupov, Feliks (1856–1928)   Governor-general of Moscow, father of Rasputin's assassin.

Zalutsky, Pyotr (1887–1937)   Originally a Socialist Revolutionary, a Bolshevik from 1907. Trotskyist in the 1920s, deported 1934, presumably executed.

Zamyslovsky, Georgi (1872–?)   Extreme right-wing deputy in Third and Fourth Dumas.

Zasulich, Vera (1849–1919)   Populist terrorist, tried in 1873 for an attempt on the life of the governor of St. Petersburg, acquitted, fled abroad, became one of the Menshevik leaders, opponent of the Bolshevik regime.

Zemlyachka, Rosalia (originally Zalkind) (1876–1947)   Bolshevik. *Iskra* agent. A favorite of Stalin during and after the Great Purge of 1935–38.

Zetkin, Klara (1857–1933)   German Social Democrat. Founding member of the Spartacus League, then of the German Communist Party. Reichstag deputy 1920–33.